HENRY JAMES

HENRY JAMES

NOVELS 1886–1890
The Princess Casamassima
The Reverberator
The Tragic Muse

THE LIBRARY OF AMERICA

The paper used in this publication meets the
minimum requirements of the American National Standard for
Information Sciences—Permanence of Paper for Printed
Library Materials, ANSI Z39.48—1984.

Distributed to the trade in the United States
and Canada by the Viking Press.

Library of Congress Catalog Number: 88-82724
For cataloging information, see end of Notes section.
ISBN 0–940450–56–9

First Printing
The Library of America—43

Manufactured in the United States of America

DANIEL MARK FOGEL
WROTE THE NOTES AND SELECTED
THE TEXTS FOR THIS VOLUME

Grateful acknowledgment is made to the National Endowment for the Humanities, the Ford Foundation, and the Andrew W. Mellon Foundation for their generous support of this series.

Contents

THE
PRINCESS CASAMASSIMA

A Novel

I

'OH YES, I daresay I can find the child, if you would like
to see him,' Miss Pynsent said; she had a fluttering wish
to assent to every suggestion made by her visitor, whom she
regarded as a high and rather terrible personage. To look for
the little boy she came out of her small parlour, which she
had been ashamed to exhibit in so untidy a state, with paper
'patterns' lying about on the furniture and snippings of stuff
scattered over the carpet—she came out of this somewhat
stuffy sanctuary, dedicated at once to social intercourse and to
the ingenious art to which her life had been devoted, and,
opening the house door, turned her eyes up and down the
little street. It would presently be tea-time, and she knew that
at that solemn hour Hyacinth narrowed the circle of his wanderings. She was anxious and impatient, and in a fever of
excitement and complacency, not wanting to keep Mrs. Bowerbank waiting, though she sat there, heavily and consideringly, as if she meant to stay; and wondering not a little
whether the object of her quest would have a dirty face. Mrs.
Bowerbank had intimated so definitely that she thought it remarkable on Miss Pynsent's part to have taken care of him
gratuitously for so many years, that the humble dressmaker,
whose imagination took flights about every one but herself,
and who had never been conscious of an exemplary benevolence, suddenly aspired to appear, throughout, as devoted to
the child as she had struck her solemn, substantial guest as
being, and felt how much she should like him to come in
fresh and frank, and looking as pretty as he sometimes did.
Miss Pynsent, who blinked confusedly as she surveyed the
outer prospect, was very much flushed, partly with the agitation of what Mrs. Bowerbank had told her, and partly
because, when she offered that lady a drop of something refreshing, at the end of so long an expedition, she had said she
couldn't think of touching anything unless Miss Pynsent
would keep her company. The cheffonier (as Amanda was
always careful to call it), beside the fireplace, yielded up a

3

small bottle which had formerly contained eau-de-cologne and which now exhibited half a pint of a rich gold-coloured liquid. Miss Pynsent was very delicate; she lived on tea and watercress, and she kept the little bottle in the cheffonier only for great emergencies. She didn't like hot brandy and water, with a lump or two of sugar, but she partook of half a tumbler on the present occasion, which was of a highly exceptional kind. At this time of day the boy was often planted in front of the little sweet-shop on the other side of the street, an establishment where periodical literature, as well as tough toffy and hard lollipops, was dispensed, and where song-books and pictorial sheets were attractively exhibited in the small-paned, dirty window. He used to stand there for half an hour at a time, spelling out the first page of the romances in the *Family Herald* and the *London Journal*, and admiring the obligatory illustration in which the noble characters (they were always of the highest birth) were presented to the carnal eye. When he had a penny he spent only a fraction of it on stale sugar-candy; with the remaining halfpenny he always bought a ballad, with a vivid woodcut at the top. Now, however, he was not at his post of contemplation; nor was he visible anywhere to Miss Pynsent's impatient glance.

'Millicent Henning, tell me quickly, have you seen my child?' These words were addressed by Miss Pynsent to a little girl who sat on the doorstep of the adjacent house, nursing a dingy doll, and who had an extraordinary luxuriance of dark brown hair, surmounted by a torn straw hat. Miss Pynsent pronounced her name Enning.

The child looked up from her dandling and patting, and after a stare of which the blankness was somewhat exaggerated, replied: 'Law no, Miss Pynsent, I never see him.'

'Aren't you always messing about with him, you naughty little girl?' the dressmaker returned, with sharpness. 'Isn't he round the corner, playing marbles, or—or some jumping game?' Miss Pynsent went on, trying to be suggestive.

'I assure *you*, he never plays nothing,' said Millicent Henning, with a mature manner which she bore out by adding, 'And I don't know why I should be called naughty, neither.'

'Well, if you want to be called good, please go and find

him and tell him there's a lady here come on purpose to see him, this very instant.' Miss Pynsent waited a moment, to see if her injunction would be obeyed, but she got no satisfaction beyond another gaze of deliberation, which made her feel that the child's perversity was as great as the beauty, somewhat soiled and dimmed, of her insolent little face. She turned back into the house, with an exclamation of despair, and as soon as she had disappeared Millicent Henning sprang erect and began to race down the street in the direction of another, which crossed it. I take no unfair advantage of the innocence of childhood in saying that the motive of this young lady's flight was not a desire to be agreeable to Miss Pynsent, but an extreme curiosity on the subject of the visitor who wanted to see Hyacinth Robinson. She wished to participate, if only in imagination, in the interview that might take place, and she was moved also by a quick revival of friendly feeling for the boy, from whom she had parted only half an hour before with considerable asperity. She was not a very clinging little creature, and there was no one in her own domestic circle to whom she was much attached; but she liked to kiss Hyacinth when he didn't push her away and tell her she was tiresome. It was in this action and epithet he had indulged half an hour ago; but she had reflected rapidly (while she stared at Miss Pynsent) that this was the worst he had ever done. Millicent Henning was only eight years of age, but she knew there was worse in the world than that.

Mrs. Bowerbank, in a leisurely, roundabout way, wandered off to her sister, Mrs. Chipperfield, whom she had come into that part of the world to see, and the whole history of the dropsical tendencies of whose husband, an undertaker with a business that had been a blessing because you could always count on it, she unfolded to Miss Pynsent between the sips of a second glass. She was a high-shouldered, towering woman, and suggested squareness as well as a pervasion of the upper air, so that Amanda reflected that she must be very difficult to fit, and had a sinking at the idea of the number of pins she would take. Her sister had nine children and she herself had seven, the eldest of whom she left in charge of the others when she went to her service. She was on duty at the prison only during the day; she had to be there at seven in the morning, but she got her evenings at home, quite regular and comfortable. Miss Pynsent thought it wonderful she could talk of comfort in such a life as that, but could easily imagine she should be glad to get away at night, for at that time the place must be much more terrible.

'And aren't you frightened of them—ever?' she inquired, looking up at her visitor with her little heated face.

Mrs. Bowerbank was very slow, and considered her so long before replying, that she felt herself to be, in an alarming degree, in the eye of the law; for who could be more closely connected with the administration of justice than a female turnkey, especially so big and majestic a one? 'I expect they are more frightened of me,' she replied at last; and it was an idea into which Miss Pynsent could easily enter.

'And at night I suppose they rave, quite awful,' the little dressmaker suggested, feeling vaguely that prisons and madhouses came very much to the same.

'Well, if they do, we hush 'em up,' Mrs. Bowerbank remarked, rather portentously; while Miss Pynsent fidgeted to the door again, without results, to see if the child had become visible. She observed to her guest that she couldn't call it anything but contrary that he should not turn up, when he knew so well, most days in the week, when his tea was ready. To which Mrs. Bowerbank rejoined, fixing her companion again with the steady orb of justice, 'And do he have his tea, that way, by himself, like a little gentleman?'

'Well, I try to give it to him tidy-like, at a suitable hour,' said Miss Pynsent, guiltily. 'And there might be some who would say that, for the matter of that, he *is* a little gentleman,' she added, with an effort at mitigation which, as she immediately became conscious, only involved her more deeply.

'There are people silly enough to say anything. If it's your parents that settle your station, the child hasn't much to be thankful for,' Mrs. Bowerbank went on, in the manner of a woman accustomed to looking facts in the face.

Miss Pynsent was very timid, but she adored the aristocracy, and there were elements in the boy's life which she was not prepared to sacrifice even to a person who represented such a possibility of grating bolts and clanking chains. 'I suppose we oughtn't to forget that his father was very high,' she suggested, appealingly, with her hands clasped tightly in her lap.

'His father? Who knows who *he* was? He doesn't set up for having a father, does he?'

'But, surely, wasn't it proved that Lord Frederick——?'

'My dear woman, nothing was proved except that she stabbed his lordship in the back with a very long knife, that he died of the blow, and that she got the full sentence. What does such a piece as that know about fathers? The less said about the poor child's ancestors the better!'

This view of the case caused Miss Pynsent fairly to gasp, for it pushed over with a touch a certain tall imaginative structure which she had been piling up for years. Even as she heard it crash around her she couldn't forbear the attempt to save at least some of the material. 'Really—really,' she panted, 'she never had to do with any one but the nobility!'

Mrs. Bowerbank surveyed her hostess with an expressionless eye. 'My dear young lady, what does a respectable little body like you, that sits all day with her needle and scissors, know about the doings of a wicked low foreigner that carries a knife? I was there when she came in, and I know to what she had sunk. Her conversation was choice, I assure you.'

'Oh, it's very dreadful, and of course I know nothing in particular,' Miss Pynsent quavered. 'But she wasn't low when I worked at the same place with her, and she often told me she would do nothing for any one that wasn't at the very top.'

'She might have talked to you of something that would have done you both more good,' Mrs. Bowerbank remarked, while the dressmaker felt rebuked in the past as well as in the present. 'At the very top, poor thing! Well, she's at the very bottom now. If she wasn't low when she worked, it's a pity she didn't stick to her work; and as for pride of birth, that's an article I recommend your young friend to leave to others. You had better believe what I say, because I'm a woman of the world.'

Indeed she was, as Miss Pynsent felt, to whom all this was very terrible, letting in the cold light of the penal system on a dear, dim little theory. She had cared for the child because maternity was in her nature, and this was the only manner in which fortune had put it in her path to become a mother. She

had as few belongings as the baby, and it had seemed to her
that he would add to her importance in the little world of
Lomax Place (if she kept it a secret how she came by him),
quite in the proportion in which she should contribute to
his maintenance. Her weakness and loneliness went out to
his, and in the course of time this united desolation was
peopled by the dressmaker's romantic mind with a hundred
consoling evocations. The boy proved neither a dunce nor a
reprobate; but what endeared him to her most was her conviction that he belonged, 'by the left hand,' as she had read
in a novel, to an ancient and exalted race, the list of whose
representatives and the record of whose alliances she had
once (when she took home some work and was made to
wait, alone, in a lady's boudoir) had the opportunity of
reading in a fat red book, eagerly and tremblingly consulted.
She bent her head before Mrs. Bowerbank's overwhelming
logic, but she felt in her heart that she shouldn't give the
child up for all that, that she believed in him still, and that
she recognised, as distinctly as she revered, the quality of her
betters. To believe in Hyacinth, for Miss Pynsent, was to believe that he *was* the son of the extremely immoral Lord
Frederick. She had, from his earliest age, made him feel that
there was a grandeur in his past, and as Mrs. Bowerbank
would be sure not to approve of such aberrations Miss
Pynsent prayed she might not question her on that part of
the business. It was not that, when it was necessary, the little
dressmaker had any scruple about using the arts of prevarication; she was a kind and innocent creature, but she told fibs
as freely as she invented trimmings. She had, however, not
yet been questioned by an emissary of the law, and her heart
beat faster when Mrs. Bowerbank said to her, in deep tones,
with an effect of abruptness, 'And pray, Miss Pynsent, does
the child know it?'

'Know about Lord Frederick?' Miss Pynsent palpitated.

'Bother Lord Frederick! Know about his mother.'

'Oh, I can't say that. I have never told him.'

'But has any one else told him?'

To this inquiry Miss Pynsent's answer was more prompt
and more proud; it was with an agreeable sense of having
conducted herself with extraordinary wisdom and propriety

that she replied, 'How could any one know? I have never breathed it to a creature!'

Mrs. Bowerbank gave utterance to no commendation; she only put down her empty glass and wiped her large mouth with much thoroughness and deliberation. Then she said, as if it were as cheerful an idea as, in the premises, she was capable of expressing, 'Ah, well, there'll be plenty, later on, to give him all information!'

'I pray God he may live and die without knowing it!' Miss Pynsent cried, with eagerness.

Her companion gazed at her with a kind of professional patience. 'You don't keep your ideas together. How can he go to her, then, if he's never to know?'

'Oh, did you mean she would tell him?' Miss Pynsent responded, plaintively.

'Tell him! He won't need to be told, once she gets hold of him and gives him—what she told me.'

'What she told you?' Miss Pynsent repeated, open-eyed.

'The kiss her lips have been famished for, for years.'

'Ah, poor desolate woman!' the little dressmaker murmured, with her pity gushing up again. 'Of course he'll see she's fond of him,' she pursued, simply. Then she added, with an inspiration more brilliant, 'We might tell him she's his aunt!'

'You may tell him she's his grandmother, if you like. But it's all in the family.'

'Yes, on that side,' said Miss Pynsent, musingly and irrepressibly. 'And will she speak French?' she inquired. 'In that case he won't understand.'

'Oh, a child will understand its own mother, whatever she speaks,' Mrs. Bowerbank returned, declining to administer a superficial comfort. But she subjoined, opening the door for escape from a prospect which bristled with dangers, 'Of course, it's just according to your own conscience. You needn't bring the child at all, unless you like. There's many a one that wouldn't. There's no compulsion.'

'And would nothing be done to me, if I didn't?' poor Miss Pynsent asked, unable to rid herself of the impression that it was somehow the arm of the law that was stretched out to touch her.

'The only thing that could happen to you would be that *he* might throw it up against you later,' the lady from the prison observed, with a gloomy impartiality.

'Yes, indeed, if he were to know that I had kept him back.'

'Oh, he'd be sure to know, one of these days. We see a great deal of that—the way things come out,' said Mrs. Bowerbank, whose view of life seemed to abound in cheerless contingencies. 'You must remember that it is her dying wish, and that you may have it on your conscience.'

'That's a thing I *never* could abide!' the little dressmaker exclaimed, with great emphasis and a visible shiver; after which she picked up various scattered remnants of muslin and cut paper and began to roll them together with a desperate and mechanical haste. 'It's quite awful, to know what to do— if you are very sure she *is* dying.'

'Do you mean she's shamming? we have plenty of that —but we know how to treat 'em.'

'Lord, I suppose so,' murmured Miss Pynsent; while her visitor went on to say that the unfortunate person on whose behalf she had undertaken this solemn pilgrimage might live a week and might live a fortnight, but if she lived a month, would violate (as Mrs. Bowerbank might express herself) every established law of nature, being reduced to skin and bone, with nothing left of her but the main desire to see her child.

'If you're afraid of her talking, it isn't much she'd be able to say. And we shouldn't allow you more than about eight minutes,' Mrs. Bowerbank pursued, in a tone that seemed to refer itself to an iron discipline.

'I'm sure I shouldn't want more; that would be enough to last me many a year,' said Miss Pynsent, accommodatingly. And then she added, with another illumination, 'Don't you think he might throw it up against me that I *did* take him? People might tell him about her in later years; but if he hadn't seen her he wouldn't be obliged to believe them.'

Mrs. Bowerbank considered this a moment, as if it were rather a super-subtle argument, and then answered, quite in the spirit of her official pessimism, 'There is one thing you may be sure of: whatever you decide to do, as soon as ever he

grows up he will make you wish you had done the opposite.'
Mrs. Bowerbank called it oppo*site*.

'Oh, dear, then, I'm glad it will be a long time.'

'It will be ever so long, if once he gets it into his head! At
any rate, you must do as you think best. Only, if you come,
you mustn't come when it's all over.'

'It's too impossible to decide.'

'It is, indeed,' said Mrs. Bowerbank, with superior consistency. And she seemed more placidly grim than ever when she
remarked, gathering up her loosened shawl, that she was
much obliged to Miss Pynsent for her civility, and had been
quite freshened up: her visit had so completely deprived her
hostess of that sort of calm. Miss Pynsent gave the fullest expression to her perplexity in the supreme exclamation:

'If you could only wait and see the child, I'm sure it would
help you to judge!'

'My dear woman, I don't want to judge—it's none of our
business!' Mrs. Bowerbank exclaimed; and she had no sooner
uttered the words than the door of the room creaked open
and a small boy stood there gazing at her. Her eyes rested on
him a moment, and then, most unexpectedly, she gave an inconsequent cry. 'Is that the child? Oh, Lord o' mercy, don't
take *him*!'

'Now *ain't* he shrinking and sensitive?' demanded Miss
Pynsent, who had pounced upon him, and, holding him an
instant at arm's length, appealed eagerly to her visitor. 'Ain't
he delicate and high-bred, and wouldn't he be thrown into a
state?' Delicate as he might be the little dressmaker shook him
smartly for his naughtiness in being out of the way when he
was wanted, and brought him to the big, square-faced, deep-
voiced lady who took up, as it were, all that side of the room.
But Mrs. Bowerbank laid no hand upon him; she only
dropped her gaze from a tremendous height, and her forbearance seemed a tribute to that fragility of constitution on
which Miss Pynsent desired to insist, just as her continued
gravity was an implication that this scrupulous woman might
well not know what to do.

'Speak to the lady nicely, and tell her you are very sorry to
have kept her waiting.'

The child hesitated a moment, while he reciprocated Mrs. Bowerbank's inspection, and then he said, with a strange, cool, conscious indifference (Miss Pynsent instantly recognised it as his aristocratic manner), 'I don't think she can have been in a very great hurry.'

There was irony in the words, for it is a remarkable fact that even at the age of ten Hyacinth Robinson was ironical; but the subject of his allusion, who was not nimble withal, appeared not to interpret it; so that she rejoined only by remarking, over his head, to Miss Pynsent, 'It's the very face of her over again!'

'Of *her*? But what do you say to Lord Frederick?'

'I *have* seen lords that wasn't so dainty!'

Miss Pynsent had seen very few lords, but she entered, with a passionate thrill, into this generalisation; controlling herself, however, for she remembered the child was tremendously sharp, sufficiently to declare, in an edifying tone, that he would look more like what he ought to if his face were a little cleaner.

'It was probably Millicent Henning dirtied my face when she kissed me,' the boy announced, with slow gravity, looking all the while at Mrs. Bowerbank. He exhibited not a symptom of shyness.

'Millicent Henning is a very bad little girl; she'll come to no good,' said Miss Pynsent, with familiar decision, and also, considering that the young lady in question had been her effective messenger, with marked ingratitude.

Against this qualification the child instantly protested. 'Why is she bad? I don't think she is bad; I like her very much.' It came over him that he had too hastily shifted to her shoulders the responsibility of his unseemly appearance, and he wished to make up to her for that betrayal. He dimly felt that nothing but that particular accusation could have pushed him to it, for he hated people who were not fresh, who had smutches and streaks. Millicent Henning generally had two or three, which she borrowed from her doll, into whom she was always rubbing her nose and whose dinginess was contagious. It was quite inevitable she should have left her mark under his own nose when she claimed her reward for coming to tell him about the lady who wanted him.

Miss Pynsent held the boy against her knee, trying to present him so that Mrs. Bowerbank should agree with her about his having the air of race. He was exceedingly diminutive, even for his years, and though his appearance was not positively sickly it seemed written in his attenuated little person that he would never be either tall or strong. His dark blue eyes were separated by a wide interval, which increased the fairness and sweetness of his face, and his abundant curly hair, which grew thick and long, had the golden brownness predestined to elicit exclamations of delight from ladies when they take the inventory of a child. His features were smooth and pretty; his head was set upon a slim little neck; his expression, grave and clear, showed a quick perception as well as a great credulity; and he was altogether, in his innocent smallness, a refined and interesting figure.

'Yes, he's one that would be sure to remember,' said Mrs. Bowerbank, mentally contrasting him with the undeveloped members of her own brood, who had never been retentive of anything but the halfpence which they occasionally contrived to filch from her. Her eyes descended to the details of his toilet: the careful mending of his short breeches and his long, coloured stockings, which she was in a position to appreciate, as well as the knot of bright ribbon which the dressmaker had passed into his collar, slightly crumpled by Miss Henning's embrace. Of course Miss Pynsent had only one to look after, but her visitor was obliged to recognise that she had the highest standard in respect to buttons. 'And you *do* turn him out so it's a pleasure,' she went on, noting the ingenious patches in the child's shoes, which, to her mind, were repaired for all the world like those of a little nobleman.

'I'm sure you're very civil,' said Miss Pynsent, in a state of severe exaltation. 'There's never a needle but mine has come near him. That's exactly what I think: the impression would go so deep.'

'Do you want to see me only to look at me?' Hyacinth inquired, with a candour which, though unstudied, had again much of the force of satire.

'I'm sure it's very kind of the lady to notice you at all!' cried his protectress, giving him an ineffectual jerk. 'You're no bigger than a flea; there are many that wouldn't spy you out.'

'You'll find he's big enough, I expect, when he begins to go,' Mrs. Bowerbank remarked, tranquilly; and she added that now she saw how he was turned out she couldn't but feel that the other side was to be considered. In her effort to be discreet, on account of his being present (and so precociously attentive), she became slightly enigmatical; but Miss Pynsent gathered her meaning, which was that it was very true the child would take everything in and keep it: but at the same time it was precisely his being so attractive that made it a kind of sin not to gratify the poor woman, who, if she knew what he looked like to-day, wouldn't forgive his adoptive mamma for not producing him. 'Certainly, in her place, I should go off easier if I had seen them curls,' Mrs. Bowerbank declared, with a flight of maternal imagination which brought her to her feet, while Miss Pynsent felt that she was leaving her dreadfully ploughed up, and without any really fertilising seed having been sown. The little dressmaker packed the child upstairs to tidy himself for his tea, and while she accompanied her visitor to the door told her that if she would have a little more patience with her she would think a day or two longer what was best and write to her when she should have decided. Mrs. Bowerbank continued to move in a realm superior to poor Miss Pynsent's vacillations and timidities, and her impartiality gave her hostess a high idea of her respectability; but the way was a little smoothed when, after Amanda had moaned once more, on the threshold, helplessly and irrelevantly, 'Ain't it a pity she's so bad?' the ponderous lady from the prison rejoined, in those tones which seemed meant to resound through corridors of stone, 'I assure you there's a many that's much worse!'

II

MISS PYNSENT, when she found herself alone, felt that she was really quite upside down; for the event that had just occurred had never entered into her calculations: the very nature of the case had seemed to preclude it. All she knew, and all she wished to know, was that in one of the dreadful institutions constructed for such purposes her quondam comrade was serving out the sentence that had been substituted for the other (the unspeakable horror) almost when the halter was already round her neck. As there was no question of *that* concession being stretched any further, poor Florentine seemed only a little more dead than other people, having no decent tombstone to mark the place where she lay. Miss Pynsent had therefore never thought of her dying again; she had no idea to what prison she had been committed on being removed from Newgate (she wished to keep her mind a blank about the matter, in the interest of the child), and it could not occur to her that out of such silence and darkness a second voice would reach her, especially a voice that she should really have to listen to. Miss Pynsent would have said, before Mrs. Bowerbank's visit, that she had no account to render to any one; that she had taken up the child (who might have starved in the gutter) out of charity, and had brought him up, poor and precarious as her own subsistence had been, without a penny's help from another source; that the mother had forfeited every right and title; and that this had been understood between them—if anything, in so dreadful an hour, could have been said to be understood—when she went to see her at Newgate (that terrible episode, nine years before, overshadowed all Miss Pynsent's other memories): went to see her because Florentine had sent for her (a name, face and address coming up out of the still recent but sharply separated past of their working-girl years), as the one friend to whom she could appeal with some chance of a pitying answer. The effect of violent emotion, with Miss Pynsent, was not to make her sit with idle hands or fidget about to no purpose; under its influence, on the contrary, she threw herself into little jobs, as a fugitive takes to by-paths, and clipped and cut, and stitched and basted, as if she were running a race with hysterics. And while her hands, her scissors, her needle flew, an infinite succession of fantastic possibilities trotted through her confused little head; she had a furious imagination, and the act of reflection, in her mind, was always a panorama of figures and scenes. She had had her picture of the future, painted in rather rosy hues, hung up before her now for a good many years; but it seemed to her that Mrs. Bowerbank's heavy hand had suddenly punched a hole in the canvas. It must be added, however, that if Amanda's thoughts were apt to be bewildering visions they sometimes led her to make up her mind, and on this particular September evening she arrived at a momentous decision. What she made up her mind to was to take advice, and in pursuance of this view she rushed downstairs, and, jerking Hyacinth away from his simple but unfinished repast, packed him across the street to tell Mr. Vetch (if he had not yet started for the theatre) that she begged he would come in to see her when he came home that night, as she had something very particular she wished to say to him. It didn't matter if he should be very late, he could come in at any hour—he would see her light in the window—and he would do her a real mercy. Miss Pynsent knew it would be of no use for her to go to bed; she felt as if she should never close her eyes again. Mr. Vetch was her most distinguished friend; she had an immense appreciation of his cleverness and knowledge of the world, as well as of the purity of his taste in matters of conduct and opinion; and she had already consulted him about Hyacinth's education. The boy needed no urging to go on such an errand, for he, too, had his ideas about the little fiddler, the second violin in the orchestra of the Bloomsbury Theatre. Mr. Vetch had once obtained for the pair an order for two seats at a pantomime, and for Hyacinth the impression of that ecstatic evening had consecrated him, placed him for ever in the golden glow of the footlights. There were things in life of which, even at the age of ten, it was a conviction of the boy's that it would be his fate never to see enough, and one of them was the wonder-world illuminated by those playhouse lamps. But there would be chances, perhaps, if one didn't lose sight of Mr. Vetch; he might open the door again; he was a privileged, magical mortal, who went to the play every night.

He came in to see Miss Pynsent about midnight; as soon as she heard the lame tinkle of the bell she went to the door to let him in. He was an original, in the fullest sense of the word: a lonely, disappointed, embittered, cynical little man, whose musical organisation had been sterile, who had the nerves, the sensibilities, of a gentleman, and whose fate had condemned him, for the last ten years, to play a fiddle at a second-rate theatre for a few shillings a week. He had ideas of his own about everything, and they were not always very improving. For Amanda Pynsent he represented art, literature (the literature of the play-bill), and philosophy, and she always felt about him as if he belonged to a higher social sphere, though his earnings were hardly greater than her own and he lived in a single back-room, in a house where she had never seen a window washed. He had, for her, the glamour of reduced gentility and fallen fortunes; she was conscious that he spoke a different language (though she couldn't have said in what the difference consisted) from the other members of her humble, almost suburban circle; and the shape of his hands was distinctly aristocratic. (Miss Pynsent, as I have intimated, was immensely preoccupied with that element in life.) Mr. Vetch displeased her only by one of the facets of his character—his blasphemous republican, radical views, and the contemptuous manner in which he expressed himself about the nobility. On that ground he worried her extremely, though he never seemed to her so clever as when he horrified her most. These dreadful theories (expressed so brilliantly that, really, they might have been dangerous if Miss Pynsent had not known her own place so well) constituted no presumption against his refined origin; they were explained, rather, to a certain extent, by a just resentment at finding himself excluded from his proper place. Mr. Vetch was short, fat and bald, though he was not much older than Miss Pynsent, who was not much older than some people who called themselves forty-five; he always went to the theatre in evening-dress, with a flower in his button-hole, and wore a glass in one eye. He looked placid and genial, and as if he would fidget at the most about the 'get up' of his linen; you would

have thought him finical but superficial, and never have suspected that he was a revolutionist, or even a critic of life.
Sometimes, when he could get away from the theatre early
enough, he went with a pianist, a friend of his, to play dance-
music at small parties; and after such expeditions he was particularly cynical and startling; he indulged in diatribes against
the British middle-class, its Philistinism, its snobbery. He seldom had much conversation with Miss Pynsent without telling her that she had the intellectual outlook of a caterpillar;
but this was his privilege after a friendship now of seven
years' standing, which had begun (the year after he came to
live in Lomax Place) with her going over to nurse him, on
learning from the milk-woman that he was alone at Number
17—laid up with an attack of gastritis. He always compared
her to an insect or a bird, and she didn't mind, because she
knew he liked her, and she herself liked all winged creatures.
How indeed could she complain, after hearing him call the
Queen a superannuated form and the Archbishop of Canterbury a grotesque superstition?

He laid his violin-case on the table, which was covered with
a confusion of fashion-plates and pincushions, and glanced
toward the fire, where a kettle was gently hissing. Miss
Pynsent, who had put it on half an hour before, read his
glance, and reflected with complacency that Mrs. Bowerbank
had not absolutely drained the little bottle in the cheffonier.
She placed it on the table again, this time with a single glass,
and told her visitor that, as a great exception, he might light
his pipe. In fact, she always made the exception, and he always replied to the gracious speech by inquiring whether she
supposed the greengrocers' wives, the butchers' daughters, for
whom she worked, had fine enough noses to smell, in the
garments she sent home, the fumes of his tobacco. He knew
her 'connection' was confined to small shopkeepers, but she
didn't wish others to know it, and would have liked them to
believe it was important that the poor little stuffs she made up
(into very queer fashions, I am afraid) should not surprise the
feminine nostril. But it had always been impossible to impose
on Mr. Vetch; he guessed the truth, the untrimmed truth,
about everything in a moment. She was sure he would do so
now, in regard to this solemn question which had come up

about Hyacinth; he would see that though she was agreeably flurried at finding herself whirled in the last eddies of a case that had been so celebrated in its day, her secret wish was to shirk her duty (if it *was* a duty); to keep the child from ever knowing his mother's unmentionable history, the shame that attached to his origin, the opportunity she had had of letting him see the wretched woman before she died. She knew Mr. Vetch would read her troubled thoughts, but she hoped he would say they were natural and just: she reflected that as he took an interest in Hyacinth he wouldn't desire him to be subjected to a mortification that might rankle for ever and perhaps even crush him to the earth. She related Mrs. Bowerbank's visit, while he sat upon the sofa in the very place where that majestic woman had reposed, and puffed his smoke-wreaths into the dusky little room. He knew the story of the child's birth, had known it years before, so she had no startling revelation to make. He was not in the least agitated at learning that Florentine was dying in prison and had managed to get a message conveyed to Amanda; he thought this so much in the usual course that he said to Miss Pynsent, 'Did you expect her to live on there for ever, working out her terrible sentence, just to spare you the annoyance of a dilemma, or any reminder of her miserable existence, which you have preferred to forget?' That was just the sort of question Mr. Vetch was sure to ask, and he inquired, further, of his dismayed hostess, whether she were sure her friend's message (he called the unhappy creature her friend) had come to her in the regular way. The warders, surely, had no authority to introduce visitors to their captives; and was it a question of her going off to the prison on the sole authority of Mrs. Bowerbank? The little dressmaker explained that this lady had merely come to sound her, Florentine had begged so hard. She had been in Mrs. Bowerbank's ward before her removal to the infirmary, where she now lay ebbing away, and she had communicated her desire to the Catholic chaplain, who had undertaken that some satisfaction—of inquiry, at least— should be given her. He had thought it best to ascertain first whether the person in charge of the child would be willing to bring him, such a course being perfectly optional, and he had some talk with Mrs. Bowerbank on the subject, in which it

was agreed between them that if she would approach Miss
Pynsent and explain to her the situation, leaving her to do
what she thought best, he would answer for it that the consent of the governor of the prison should be given to the
interview. Miss Pynsent had lived for fourteen years in Lomax
Place, and Florentine had never forgotten that this was her
address at the time she came to her at Newgate (before her
dreadful sentence had been commuted), and promised, in an
outgush of pity for one whom she had known in the days of
her honesty and brightness, that she would save the child,
rescue it from the workhouse and the streets, keep it from the
fate that had swallowed up the mother. Mrs. Bowerbank had
a half-holiday, and a sister living also in the north of London, to whom she had been for some time intending a visit;
so that after her domestic duty had been performed it had
been possible for her to drop in on Miss Pynsent in a natural, casual way and put the case before her. It would be just
as she might be disposed to view it. She was to think it over
a day or two, but not long, because the woman was so ill,
and then write to Mrs. Bowerbank, at the prison. If she
should consent, Mrs. Bowerbank would tell the chaplain,
and the chaplain would obtain the order from the governor
and send it to Lomax Place; after which Amanda would immediately set out with her unconscious victim. But should
she—*must* she—consent? That was the terrible, the heart-
shaking question, with which Miss Pynsent's unaided wisdom had been unable to grapple.

'After all, he isn't hers any more—he's mine, mine only,
and mine always. I should like to know if all I have done
for him doesn't make him so!' It was in this manner that
Amanda Pynsent delivered herself, while she plied her needle, faster than ever, in a piece of stuff that was pinned to
her knee.

Mr. Vetch watched her awhile, blowing silently at his pipe,
with his head thrown back on the high, stiff, old-fashioned
sofa, and his little legs crossed under him like a Turk's. 'It's
true you have done a good deal for him. You are a good little
woman, my dear Pinnie, after all.' He said 'after all,' because
that was a part of his tone. In reality he had never had a

moment's doubt that she was the best little woman in the north of London.

'I have done what I could, and I don't want no fuss made about it. Only it does make a difference when you come to look at it—about taking him off to see another woman. And *such* another woman—and in such a place! I think it's hardly right to take an innocent child.'

'I don't know about that; there are people that would tell you it would do him good. If he didn't like the place as a child, he would take more care to keep out of it later.'

'Lord, Mr. Vetch, how can you think? And him such a perfect little gentleman!' Miss Pynsent cried.

'Is it you that have made him one?' the fiddler asked. 'It doesn't run in the family, you'd say.'

'Family? what do you know about that?' she replied, quickly, catching at her dearest, her only hobby.

'Yes, indeed, what does any one know? what did she know herself?' And then Miss Pynsent's visitor added, irrelevantly, 'Why should you have taken him on your back? Why did you want to be so good? No one else thinks it necessary.'

'I didn't want to be good. That is, I do want to, of course, in a general way: but that wasn't the reason then. But I had nothing of my own—I had nothing in the world but my thimble.'

'That would have seemed to most people a reason for not adopting a prostitute's bastard.'

'Well, I went to see him at the place where he was (just where she had left him, with the woman of the house), and I saw what kind of a shop *that* was, and felt it was a shame an innocent child should grow up in such a place.' Miss Pynsent defended herself as earnestly as if her inconsistency had been of a criminal cast. 'And he wouldn't have grown up, neither. *They* wouldn't have troubled themselves long with a helpless baby. *They'd* have played some trick on him, if it was only to send him to the workhouse. Besides, I always was fond of tiny creatures, and I have been fond of this one,' she went on, speaking as if with a consciousness, on her own part, of almost heroic proportions. 'He was in my way the first two or three years, and it was a good deal of a pull to look after the

business and him together. But now he's like the business—
he seems to go of himself.'

'Oh, if he flourishes as the business flourishes, you can just
enjoy your peace of mind,' said the fiddler, still with his manner of making a small dry joke of everything.

'That's all very well, but it doesn't close my eyes to that
poor woman lying there and moaning just for the touch of his
little 'and before she passes away. Mrs. Bowerbank says she
believes I will bring him.'

'Who believes? Mrs. Bowerbank?'

'I wonder if there's anything in life holy enough for you to
take it seriously,' Miss Pynsent rejoined, snapping off a
thread, with temper. 'The day you stop laughing I should like
to be there.'

'So long as you are there, I shall never stop. What is it you
want me to advise you? to take the child, or to leave the
mother to groan herself out?'

'I want you to tell me whether he'll curse me when he
grows older.'

'That depends upon what you do. However, he will probably do it in either case.'

'You don't believe that, because you like him,' said
Amanda, with acuteness.

'Precisely; and he'll curse me too. He'll curse every one. He
won't be happy.'

'I don't know how you think I bring him up,' the little
dressmaker remarked, with dignity.

'You don't bring him up; he brings you up.'

'That's what you have always said; but you don't know. If
you mean that he does as he likes, then he ought to be happy.
It ain't kind of you to say he won't be,' Miss Pynsent added,
reproachfully.

'I would say anything you like, if what I say would help the
matter. He's a thin-skinned, morbid, mooning little beggar,
with a good deal of imagination and not much perseverance,
who will expect a good deal more of life than he will find in
it. That's why he won't be happy.'

Miss Pynsent listened to this description of her *protégé* with
an appearance of criticising it mentally; but in reality she
didn't know what 'morbid' meant, and didn't like to ask. 'He's

the cleverest person I know, except yourself,' she said in a moment; for Mr. Vetch's words had been in the key of what she thought most remarkable in him. What that was she would have been unable to say.

'Thank you very much for putting me first,' the fiddler rejoined, after a series of puffs. 'The youngster is interesting, one sees that he has a mind, and in that respect he is—I won't say unique, but peculiar. I shall watch him with curiosity, to see what he grows into. But I shall always be glad that I am a selfish brute of a bachelor, that I never invested in that class of goods.'

'Well, you *are* comforting. You would spoil him more than I do,' said Amanda.

'Possibly, but it would be in a different way. I wouldn't tell him every three minutes that his father was a duke.'

'A duke I never mentioned!' the little dressmaker cried, with eagerness. 'I never specified any rank, nor said a word about any one in particular. I never so much as insinuated the name of his lordship. But I may have said that if the truth was to be found out, he might be proved to be connected—in the way of cousinship, or something of the kind—with the highest in the land. I should have thought myself wanting if I hadn't given him a glimpse of that. But there is one thing I have always added—that the truth never *is* found out.'

'You are still more comforting than I!' Mr. Vetch exclaimed. He continued to watch her, with his charitable, round-faced smile, and then he said, 'You won't do what I say; so what is the use of my telling you?'

'I assure you I will, if you say you believe it's the only right.'

'Do I often say anything so asinine? Right—right? what have you to do with that? If you want the only right, you are very particular.'

'Please, then, what am I to go by?' the dressmaker asked, bewildered.

'You are to go by this, by what will take the youngster down.'

'Take him down, my poor little pet?'

'Your poor little pet thinks himself the flower of creation. I

don't say there is any harm in that: a fine, blooming, odorif-
erous conceit is a natural appendage of youth and cleverness.
I don't say there is any great harm in it, but if you want a
guide as to how you are to treat the boy, that's as good a
guide as any other.'

'You want me to arrange the interview, then?'

'I don't want you to do anything but give me another sip of
brandy. I just say this: that I think it's a great gain, early in
life, to know the worst; then we don't live in a fool's paradise.
I did that till I was nearly forty; then I woke up and found I
was in Lomax Place.' Whenever Mr. Vetch said anything that
could be construed as a reference to a former position which
had had elements of distinction, Miss Pynsent observed a respectful, a tasteful, silence, and that is why she did not challenge him now, though she wanted very much to say that
Hyacinth was no more 'presumptious' (that was the term she
should have used) than he had reason to be, with his genteel
figure and his wonderful intelligence; and that as for thinking
himself a 'flower' of any kind, he knew but too well that he
lived in a small black-faced house, miles away from the West
End, rented by a poor little woman who took lodgers, and
who, as they were of such a class that they were not always to
be depended upon to settle her weekly account, had a strain
to make two ends meet, in spite of the sign between her
windows—

MISS AMANDA PYNSENT.
Modes et Robes.
DRESSMAKING IN ALL ITS BRANCHES. COURT-DRESSES,
MANTLES AND FASHIONABLE BONNETS.

Singularly enough, her companion, before she had permitted herself to interpose, took up her own thought (in one of
its parts), and remarked that perhaps she would say of the
child that he was, so far as his actual circumstances were concerned, low enough down in the world, without one's wanting him to be any lower. 'But by the time he's twenty, he'll
persuade himself that Lomax Place was a bad dream, that
your lodgers and your dressmaking were as imaginary as they
are vulgar, and that when an old friend came to see you late at

night it was not your amiable practice to make him a glass of brandy and water. He'll teach himself to forget all this: he'll have a way.'

'Do you mean he'll forget *me*, he'll deny me?' cried Miss Pynsent, stopping the movement of her needle, short off, for the first time.

'As the person designated in that attractive blazonry on the outside of your house, decidedly he will; and me, equally, as a bald-headed, pot-bellied fiddler, who regarded you as the most graceful and refined of his acquaintance. I don't mean he'll disown you and pretend he never knew you: I don't think he will ever be such an odious little cad as that; he probably won't be a sneak, and he strikes me as having some love, and possibly even some gratitude, in him. But he will, in his imagination (and that will always persuade him), subject you to some extraordinary metamorphosis; he will dress you up.'

'He'll dress me up!' Amanda ejaculated, quite ceasing to follow the train of Mr. Vetch's demonstration. 'Do you mean that he'll have the property—that his relations will take him up?'

'My dear, delightful, idiotic Pinnie, I am speaking in a figurative manner. I don't pretend to say what his precise position will be when we are relegated; but I affirm that relegation will be our fate. Therefore don't stuff him with any more illusions than are necessary to keep him alive; he will be sure to pick up enough on the way. On the contrary, give him a good stiff dose of the truth at the start.'

'Dear me, dear me, of course you see much further into it than I could ever do,' Pinnie murmured, as she threaded a needle.

Mr. Vetch paused a minute, but apparently not out of deference to this amiable interruption. He went on suddenly, with a ring of feeling in his voice. 'Let him know, because it will be useful to him later, the state of the account between society and himself; he can then conduct himself accordingly. If he is the illegitimate child of a French good-for-naught who murdered one of her numerous lovers, don't shuffle out of sight so important a fact. I regard that as a most valuable origin.'

'Lord, Mr. Vetch, how you talk!' cried Miss Pynsent, staring. 'I don't know what one would think, to hear you.'

'Surely, my dear lady, and for this reason: that those are the people with whom society has to count. It hasn't with you and me.' Miss Pynsent gave a sigh which might have meant either that she was well aware of that, or that Mr. Vetch had a terrible way of enlarging a subject, especially when it was already too big for her; and her philosophic visitor went on: 'Poor little devil, let him see her, let him see her.'

'And if later, when he's twenty, he says to me that if I hadn't meddled in it he need never have known, he need never have had that shame, pray what am I to say to him then? That's what I can't get out of my head.'

'You can say to him that a young man who is sorry for having gone to his mother when, in her last hours, she lay groaning for him on a pallet in a penitentiary, deserves more than the sharpest pang he can possibly feel.' And the little fiddler, getting up, went over to the fireplace and shook out the ashes of his pipe.

'Well, I am sure it's natural he should feel badly,' said Miss Pynsent, folding up her work with the same desperate quickness that had animated her throughout the evening.

'I haven't the least objection to his feeling badly; that's not the worst thing in the world! If a few more people felt badly, in this sodden, stolid, stupid race of ours, the world would wake up to an idea or two, and we should see the beginning of the dance. It's the dull acceptance, the absence of reflection, the impenetrable density.' Here Mr. Vetch stopped short; his hostess stood before him with eyes of entreaty, with clasped hands.

'Now, Anastasius Vetch, don't go off into them dreadful wild theories!' she cried, always ungrammatical when she was strongly moved. 'You always fly away over the house-tops. I thought you liked him better—the dear little unfortunate.'

Anastasius Vetch had pocketed his pipe; he put on his hat with the freedom of old acquaintance and of Lomax Place, and took up his small coffin-like fiddle-case. 'My good Pinnie, I don't think you understand a word I say. It's no use talking—do as you like!'

'Well, I must say I don't think it was worth your coming in

at midnight only to tell me that. I don't like anything—I hate the whole dreadful business!'

He bent over, in his short plumpness, to kiss her hand, as he had seen people do on the stage. 'My dear friend, we have different ideas, and I never shall succeed in driving mine into your head. It's because I *am* fond of him, poor little devil; but you will never understand that. I want him to know everything, and especially the worst—the worst, as I have said. If I were in his position, I shouldn't thank you for trying to make a fool of me!'

'A fool of you? as if I thought of anything but his 'appiness!' Amanda Pynsent exclaimed. She stood looking at him, but following her own reflections; she had given up the attempt to enter into his whims. She remembered, what she had noticed before, in other occurrences, that his reasons were always more extraordinary than his behaviour itself; if you only considered his life you wouldn't have thought him so fanciful. 'Very likely I think too much of that,' she added. 'She wants him and cries for him; that's what keeps coming back to me.' She took up her lamp to light Mr. Vetch to the door (for the dim luminary in the passage had long since been extinguished), and before he left the house he turned, suddenly, stopping short, and said, his composed face taking a strange expression from the quizzical glimmer of his little round eyes—

'What does it matter after all, and why do you worry? What difference can it make what happens—on either side— to such low people?'

III

M RS. BOWERBANK had let her know she would meet her, almost at the threshold of the dreadful place; and this thought had sustained Miss Pynsent in her long and devious journey, performed partly on foot, partly in a succession of omnibuses. She had had ideas about a cab, but she decided to reserve the cab for the return, as then, very likely, she should be so shaken with emotion, so overpoweringly affected, that it would be a comfort to escape from observation. She had no confidence that if once she passed the door of the prison she should ever be restored to liberty and her customers; it seemed to her an adventure as dangerous as it was dismal, and she was immensely touched by the clear-faced eagerness of the child at her side, who strained forward as brightly as he had done on another occasion, still celebrated in Miss Pynsent's industrious annals, a certain sultry Saturday in August, when she had taken him to the Tower. It had been a terrible question with her, when once she made up her mind, what she should tell him about the nature of their errand. She determined to tell him as little as possible, to say only that she was going to see a poor woman who was in prison on account of a crime she had committed years before, and who had sent for her, and caused her to be told at the same time that if there was any child she could see—as children (if they were good) were bright and cheering—it would make her very happy that such a little visitor should come as well. It was very difficult, with Hyacinth, to make reservations or mysteries; he wanted to know everything about everything, and he projected the light of a hundred questions upon Miss Pynsent's incarcerated friend. She had to admit that she had been her friend (for where else was the obligation to go to see her?); but she spoke of the acquaintance as if it were of the slightest (it had survived in the memory of the prisoner only because every one else—the world was so very hard!—had turned away from her), and she congratulated herself on a happy inspiration when she represented the crime for which such a penalty had been exacted as the theft of a gold watch, in a moment of irresistible temptation. The woman had had a wicked husband, who maltreated and deserted her, and she was very poor, almost starving, dreadfully pressed. Hyacinth listened to her history with absorbed attention, and then he said:

'And hadn't she any children—hadn't she a little boy?'

This inquiry seemed to Miss Pynsent a portent of future embarrassments, but she met it as bravely as she could, and replied that she believed the wretched victim of the law had had (once upon a time) a very small baby, but she was afraid she had completely lost sight of it. He must know they didn't allow babies in prisons. To this Hyacinth rejoined that of course they would allow him, because he was—really—big. Miss Pynsent fortified herself with the memory of her other pilgrimage, to Newgate, upwards of ten years before; she had escaped from that ordeal, and had even had the comfort of knowing that in its fruits the interview had been beneficent. The responsibility, however, was much greater now, and, after all, it was not on her own account she was in a nervous tremor, but on that of the urchin over whom the shadow of the house of shame might cast itself.

They made the last part of their approach on foot, having got themselves deposited as near as possible to the river and keeping beside it (according to advice elicited by Miss Pynsent, on the way, in a dozen confidential interviews with policemen, conductors of omnibuses, and small shopkeepers), till they came to a big, dark building with towers, which they would know as soon as they looked at it. They knew it, in fact, soon enough, when they saw it lift its dusky mass from the bank of the Thames, lying there and sprawling over the whole neighbourhood, with brown, bare, windowless walls, ugly, truncated pinnacles, and a character unspeakably sad and stern. It looked very sinister and wicked, to Miss Pynsent's eyes, and she wondered why a prison should have such an evil face if it was erected in the interest of justice and order—an expression of the righteous forces of society. This particular penitentiary struck her as about as bad and wrong as those who were in it; it threw a blight over the whole place and made the river look foul and poisonous, and the opposite bank, with its protrusion of long-necked chimneys, unsightly gasometers and deposits of rubbish, wear the aspect of a region at whose expense the jail had been populated. She

looked up at the dull, closed gates, tightening her grasp of
Hyacinth's small hand; and if it was hard to believe anything
so blind and deaf and closely fastened would relax itself to let
her in, there was a dreadful premonitory sinking of the heart
attached to the idea of its taking the same trouble to let her
out. As she hung back, murmuring vague ejaculations, at the
very goal of her journey, an incident occurred which fanned
all her scruples and reluctances into life again. The child
suddenly jerked his hand out of her own, and placing it behind him, in the clutch of the other, said to her respectfully
but resolutely, while he planted himself at a considerable
distance—

'I don't like this place.'

'Neither do I like it, my darling,' cried the dressmaker, piti-
fully. 'Oh, if you knew how little!'

'Then we will go away. I won't go in.'

She would have embraced this proposition with alacrity if it
had not become very vivid to her while she stood there, in the
midst of her shrinking, that behind those sullen walls the
mother who bore him was even then counting the minutes.
She was alive, in that huge, dark tomb, and it seemed to Miss
Pynsent that they had already entered into relation with her.
They were near her, and she knew it; in a few minutes she
would taste the cup of the only mercy (except the reprieve
from hanging!) she had known since her fall. A few, a very
few minutes would do it, and it seemed to Miss Pynsent that
if she should fail of her charity now the watches of the night,
in Lomax Place, would be haunted with remorse—perhaps
even with something worse. There was something inside that
waited and listened, something that would burst, with an awful sound, a shriek, or a curse, if she were to lead the boy
away. She looked into his pale face for a moment, perfectly
conscious that it would be vain for her to take the tone of
command; besides, that would have seemed to her shocking.
She had another inspiration, and she said to him in a manner
in which she had had occasion to speak before—

'The reason why we have come is only to be kind. If we are
kind we shan't mind its being disagreeable.'

'Why should we be kind, if she's a bad woman?' Hyacinth
inquired. 'She must be very low; I don't want to know her.'

'Hush, hush,' groaned poor Amanda, edging toward him with clasped hands. 'She is not bad now; it has all been washed away—it has been expiated.'

'What's expiated?' asked the child, while she almost kneeled down in the dust, catching him to her bosom.

'It's when you have suffered terribly—suffered so much that it has made you good again.'

'Has *she* suffered very much?'

'For years and years. And now she is dying. It proves she is very good now, that she should want to see us.'

'Do you mean because *we* are good?' Hyacinth went on, probing the matter in a way that made his companion quiver, and gazing away from her, very seriously, across the river, at the dreary waste of Battersea.

'We shall be good if we are pitiful, if we make an effort,' said the dressmaker, seeming to look up at him rather than down.

'But if she is dying? I don't want to see any one die.'

Miss Pynsent was bewildered, but she rejoined, desperately, 'If we go to her, perhaps she won't. Maybe we shall save her.'

He transferred his remarkable little eyes—eyes which always appeared to her to belong to a person older than herself, to her face; and then he inquired, 'Why should I save her, if I don't like her?'

'If she likes you, that will be enough.'

At this Miss Pynsent began to see that he was moved. 'Will she like me very much?'

'More, much more than any one.'

'More than you, now?'

'Oh,' said Amanda quickly, 'I mean more than she likes any one.'

Hyacinth had slipped his hands into the pockets of his scanty knickerbockers, and, with his legs slightly apart, he looked from his companion back to the immense dreary jail. A great deal, to Miss Pynsent's sense, depended on that moment. 'Oh, well,' he said, at last, 'I'll just step in.'

'Deary, deary!' the dressmaker murmured to herself, as they crossed the bare semicircle which separated the gateway from the unfrequented street. She exerted herself to pull the bell, which seemed to her terribly big and stiff, and while she waited, again, for the consequences of this effort, the boy broke out, abruptly:

'How can she like me so much if she doesn't know me?'

Miss Pynsent wished the gate would open before an answer to this question should become imperative, but the people within were a long time arriving, and their delay gave Hyacinth an opportunity to repeat it. So the dressmaker rejoined, seizing the first pretext that came into her head, 'It's because the little baby she had, of old, was also named Hyacinth.'

'That's a queer reason,' the boy murmured, staring across again at the Battersea shore.

A moment afterwards they found themselves in a vast interior dimness, with a grinding of keys and bolts going on behind them. Hereupon Miss Pynsent gave herself up to an overruling providence, and she remembered, later, no circumstance of what happened to her until the great person of Mrs. Bowerbank loomed before her in the narrowness of a strange, dark corridor. She only had a confused impression of being surrounded with high black walls, whose inner face was more dreadful than the other, the one that overlooked the river; of passing through gray, stony courts, in some of which dreadful figures, scarcely female, in hideous brown, misfitting uniforms and perfect frights of hoods, were marching round in a circle; of squeezing up steep, unlighted staircases at the heels of a woman who had taken possession of her at the first stage, and who made incomprehensible remarks to other women, of lumpish aspect, as she saw them erect themselves, suddenly and spectrally, with dowdy untied bonnets, in uncanny corners and recesses of the draughty labyrinth. If the place had seemed cruel to the poor little dressmaker outside, it may be believed that it did not strike her as an abode of mercy while she pursued her tortuous way into the circular shafts of cells, where she had an opportunity of looking at captives through grated peepholes and of edging past others who had temporarily been turned into the corridors—silent women, with fixed eyes, who flattened themselves against the stone walls at the brush of the visitor's dress and whom Miss Pynsent was afraid to glance at. She never had felt so immured, so made sure of; there were walls within walls and galleries on top of galleries; even the daylight lost its colour, and you couldn't imagine what o'clock it was. Mrs. Bowerbank appeared to have failed her, and that made her feel worse; a panic seized her, as she went, in regard to the child. On him, too, the horror of the place would have fallen, and she had a sickening prevision that he would have convulsions after they got home. It was a most improper place to have brought him, no matter who had sent for him and no matter who was dying. The stillness would terrify him, she was sure—the penitential dumbness of the clustered or isolated women. She clasped his hand more tightly, and she felt him keep close to her, without speaking a word. At last, in an open doorway, darkened by her ample person, Mrs. Bowerbank revealed herself, and Miss Pynsent thought it (afterwards) a sign of her place and power that she should not condescend to apologise for not having appeared till that moment, or to explain why she had not met the bewildered pilgrims near the principal entrance, according to her promise. Miss Pynsent could not embrace the state of mind of people who didn't apologise, though she vaguely envied and admired it, she herself spending much of her time in making excuses for obnoxious acts she had not committed. Mrs. Bowerbank, however, was not arrogant, she was only massive and muscular; and after she had taken her timorous friends in tow the dressmaker was able to comfort herself with the reflection that even so masterful a woman couldn't inflict anything gratuitously disagreeable on a person who had made her visit in Lomax Place pass off so pleasantly.

It was on the outskirts of the infirmary that she had been hovering, and it was into certain dismal chambers dedicated to sick criminals, that she presently ushered her companions. These chambers were naked and grated, like all the rest of the place, and caused Miss Pynsent to say to herself that it must be a blessing to be ill in such a hole, because you couldn't possibly pick up again, and then your case was simple. Such simplification, however, had for the moment been offered to very few of Florentine's fellow-sufferers, for only three of the small, stiff beds were occupied—occupied by white-faced women in tight, sordid caps, on whom, in the stale, ugly room, the sallow light itself seemed to rest without pity. Mrs.

Bowerbank discreetly paid no attention whatever to Hyacinth; she only said to Miss Pynsent, with her hoarse distinctness, 'You'll find her very low; she wouldn't have waited
another day.' And she guided them, through a still further
door, to the smallest room of all, where there were but three
beds, placed in a row. Miss Pynsent's frightened eyes rather
faltered than inquired, but she became aware that a woman
was lying on the middle bed, and that her face was turned
toward the door. Mrs. Bowerbank led the way straight up to
her, and, giving a business-like pat to her pillow, looked invitation and encouragement to the visitors, who clung together
not far within the threshold. Their conductress reminded
them that very few minutes were allowed them, and that they
had better not dawdle them away; whereupon, as the boy still
hung back, the little dressmaker advanced alone, looking at
the sick woman with what courage she could muster. It
seemed to her that she was approaching a perfect stranger, so
completely had nine years of prison transformed Florentine.
She felt, immediately, that it was a mercy she hadn't told Hyacinth she was pretty (as she used to be), for there was no
beauty left in the hollow, bloodless mask that presented itself
without a movement. She *had* told him that the poor woman
was good, but she didn't look so, nor, evidently, was he
struck with it as he stared back at her across the interval he
declined to traverse, kept (at the same time) from retreating
by her strange, fixed eyes, the only portion of all her wasted
person in which there was still any appearance of life. She
looked unnatural to Amanda Pynsent, and terribly old; a
speechless, motionless creature, dazed and stupid, whereas
Florentine Vivier, in the obliterated past, had been her idea of
personal, as distinguished from social, brilliancy. Above all
she seemed disfigured and ugly, cruelly misrepresented by her
coarse cap and short, rough hair. Amanda, as she stood beside
her, thought with a sort of scared elation that Hyacinth
would never guess that a person in whom there was so little
trace of smartness—or of cleverness of any kind—was his
mother. At the very most it might occur to him, as Mrs. Bowerbank had suggested, that she was his grandmother. Mrs.
Bowerbank seated herself on the further bed, with folded
hands, like a monumental timekeeper, and remarked, in the

manner of one speaking from a sense of duty, that the poor thing wouldn't get much good of the child unless he showed more confidence. This observation was evidently lost upon the boy; he was too intensely absorbed in watching the prisoner. A chair had been placed at the head of her bed, and Miss Pynsent sat down without her appearing to notice it. In a moment, however, she lifted her hand a little, pushing it out from under the coverlet, and the dressmaker laid her own hand softly upon it. This gesture elicited no response, but after a little, still gazing at the boy, Florentine murmured, in words no one present was in a position to understand—

'Dieu de Dieu, qu'il est beau!'

'She won't speak nothing but French since she has been so bad—you can't get a natural word out of her,' Mrs. Bowerbank said.

'It used to be so pretty when she spoke English—and so very amusing,' Miss Pynsent ventured to announce, with a feeble attempt to brighten up the scene. 'I suppose she has forgotten it all.'

'She may well have forgotten it—she never gave her tongue much exercise. There was little enough trouble to keep *her* from chattering,' Mrs. Bowerbank rejoined, giving a twitch to the prisoner's counterpane. Miss Pynsent settled it a little on the other side and considered, in the same train, that this separation of language was indeed a mercy; for how could it ever come into her small companion's head that he was the offspring of a person who couldn't so much as say good morning to him? She felt, at the same time, that the scene might have been somewhat less painful if they had been able to communicate with the object of their compassion. As it was, they had too much the air of having been brought together simply to look at each other, and there was a grewsome awkwardness in that, considering the delicacy of Florentine's position. Not, indeed, that she looked much at her old comrade; it was as if she were conscious of Miss Pynsent's being there, and would have been glad to thank her for it —glad even to examine her for her own sake, and see what change, for her, too, the horrible years had brought, but felt, more than this, that she had but the thinnest pulse of energy left and that not a moment that could still be of use to her

was too much to take in her child. She took him in with all
the glazed entreaty of her eyes, quite giving up his poor little
protectress, who evidently would have to take her gratitude
for granted. Hyacinth, on his side, after some moments of
embarrassing silence—there was nothing audible but Mrs.
Bowerbank's breathing—had satisfied himself, and he turned
about to look for a place of patience while Miss Pynsent
should finish her business, which as yet made so little show.
He appeared to wish not to leave the room altogether, as that
would be a confession of a vanquished spirit, but to take
some attitude that should express his complete disapproval of
the unpleasant situation. He was not in sympathy, and he
could not have made it more clear than by the way he presently went and placed himself on a low stool, in a corner, near
the door by which they had entered.

'*Est-il possible, mon Dieu, qu'il soit gentil comme ça?*' his
mother moaned, just above her breath.

'We are very glad you should have cared—that they look
after you so well,' said Miss Pynsent, confusedly, at random;
feeling, first, that Hyacinth's coldness was perhaps excessive
and his scepticism too marked, and then that allusions to the
way the poor woman was looked after were not exactly
happy. They didn't matter, however, for she evidently heard
nothing, giving no sign of interest even when Mrs. Bowerbank, in a tone between a desire to make the interview more
lively and an idea of showing that she knew how to treat the
young, referred herself to the little boy.

'Is there nothing the little gentleman would like to say,
now, to the unfortunate? Hasn't he any pleasant remark to
make to her about his coming so far to see her when she's so
sunk? It isn't often that children are shown over the place (as
the little man has been), and there's many that would think
they were lucky if they could see what he has seen.'

'*Mon pauvre joujou, mon pauvre chéri,*' the prisoner went on,
in her tender, tragic whisper.

'He only wants to be very good; he always sits that way at
home,' said Miss Pynsent, alarmed at Mrs. Bowerbank's address and hoping there wouldn't be a scene.

'He might have stayed at home then—with this wretched
person moaning after him,' Mrs. Bowerbank remarked, with

some sternness. She plainly felt that the occasion threatened to be wanting in brilliancy, and wished to intimate that though she was to be trusted for discipline, she thought they were all getting off too easily.

'I came because Pinnie brought me,' Hyacinth declared, from his low perch. 'I thought at first it would be pleasant. But it ain't pleasant—I don't like prisons.' And he placed his little feet on the cross-piece of the stool, as if to touch the institution at as few points as possible.

The woman in bed continued her strange, almost whining plaint. '*Il ne veut pas s'approcher, il a honte de moi.*'

'There's a many that begin like that!' laughed Mrs. Bowerbank, who was irritated by the boy's contempt for one of her Majesty's finest establishments.

Hyacinth's little white face exhibited no confusion; he only turned it to the prisoner again, and Miss Pynsent felt that some extraordinary dumb exchange of meanings was taking place between them. 'She used to be so elegant; she *was* a fine woman,' she observed, gently and helplessly.

'*Il a honte de moi—il a honte, Dieu le pardonne!*' Florentine Vivier went on, never moving her eyes.

'She's asking for something, in her language. I used to know a few words,' said Miss Pynsent, stroking down the bed, very nervously.

'Who is that woman? what does she want?' Hyacinth asked, his small, clear voice ringing over the dreary room.

'She wants you to come near her, she wants to kiss you, sir,' said Mrs. Bowerbank, as if it were more than he deserved.

'I won't kiss her; Pinnie says she stole a watch!' the child answered with resolution.

'Oh, you dreadful—how could you ever?' cried Pinnie, blushing all over and starting out of her chair.

It was partly Amanda's agitation, perhaps, which, by the jolt it administered, gave an impulse to the sick woman, and partly the penetrating and expressive tone in which Hyacinth announced his repugnance: at any rate, Florentine, in the most unexpected and violent manner, jerked herself up from her pillow, and, with dilated eyes and waving hands, shrieked out, '*Ah, quelle infamie!* I never stole a watch, I never stole anything—anything! *Ah, par exemple!*' Then she fell back, sobbing with the passion that had given her a moment's strength.

'I'm sure you needn't put more on her than she has by rights,' said Mrs. Bowerbank, with dignity, to the dressmaker, laying a large red hand upon the patient, to keep her in her place.

'Mercy, more? I thought it so much less!' cried Miss Pynsent, convulsed with confusion and jerking herself, in a wild tremor, from the mother to the child, as if she wished to fling herself upon one for contrition and upon the other for revenge.

'*Il a honte de moi — il a honte de moi!*' Florentine repeated, in the misery of her sobs. '*Dieu de bonté, quelle horreur!*'

Miss Pynsent dropped on her knees beside the bed and, trying to possess herself of Florentine's hand again, protested with a passion almost equal to that of the prisoner (she felt that her nerves had been screwed up to the snapping-point, and now they were all in shreds) that she hadn't meant what she had told the child, that he hadn't understood, that Florentine herself hadn't understood, that she had only said she had been accused and meant that no one had ever believed it. The Frenchwoman paid no attention to her whatever, and Amanda buried her face and her embarrassment in the side of the hard little prison-bed, while, above the sound of their common lamentation, she heard the judicial tones of Mrs. Bowerbank.

'The child is delicate, you might well say! I'm disappointed in the effect — I was in hopes you'd hearten her up. The doctor'll be down on *me*, of course; so we'll just pass out again.'

'I'm very sorry I made you cry. And you must excuse Pinnie — I asked her so many questions.'

These words came from close beside the prostrate dressmaker, who, lifting herself quickly, found the little boy had advanced to her elbow and was taking a nearer view of the mysterious captive. They produced upon the latter an effect even more powerful than his unfortunate speech of a moment before; for she found strength to raise herself, partly, in her bed again, and to hold out her arms to him, with the same thrilling sobs. She was talking still, but she had become quite inarticulate, and Miss Pynsent had but a glimpse of her white, ravaged face, with the hollows of its eyes and the rude crop of her hair. Amanda caught the child with an eagerness almost as great as Florentine's, and drawing him to the head of the bed, pushed him into his mother's arms. 'Kiss her—kiss her, and we'll go home!' she whispered desperately, while they closed about him, and the poor dishonoured head pressed itself against his young cheek. It was a terrible, irresistible embrace, to which Hyacinth submitted with instant patience. Mrs. Bowerbank had tried at first to keep her *protégée* from rising, evidently wishing to abbreviate the scene; then, as the child was enfolded, she accepted the situation and gave judicious support from behind, with an eye to clearing the room as soon as this effort should have spent itself. She propped up her patient with a vigorous arm; Miss Pynsent rose from her knees and turned away, and there was a minute's stillness, during which the boy accommodated himself as he might to his strange ordeal. What thoughts were begotten at that moment in his wondering little mind Miss Pynsent was destined to learn at another time. Before she had faced round to the bed again she was swept out of the room by Mrs. Bowerbank, who had lowered the prisoner, exhausted, with closed eyes, to her pillow, and given Hyacinth a business-like little push, which sent him on in advance. Miss Pynsent went home in a cab—she was so shaken; though she reflected, very nervously, on getting into it, on the opportunities it would give Hyacinth for the exercise of inquisitorial rights. To her surprise, however, he completely neglected them; he sat in silence, looking out of the window, till they re-entered Lomax Place.

IV

WELL, you'll have to guess my name before I'll tell you,' the girl said, with a free laugh, pushing her way into the narrow hall and leaning against the tattered wall-paper, which, representing blocks of marble with beveled edges, in streaks and speckles of black and gray, had not been renewed for years and came back to her out of the past. As Miss Pynsent closed the door, seeing her visitor was so resolute, the light filtered in from the street, through the narrow, dusty glass above it, and then the very smell and sense of the place returned to Millicent; a kind of musty dimness, with the vision of a small, steep staircase at the end, covered with a strip of oilcloth which she recognised, and made a little less dark by a window in the bend (you could see it from the hall), from which you could almost bump your head against the house behind. Nothing was changed except Miss Pynsent, and of course the girl herself. She had noticed, outside, that the sign between the windows had not even been touched up; there was still the same preposterous announcement of 'fashionable bonnets'—as if the poor little dressmaker had the slightest acquaintance with that style of head-dress, of which Miss Henning's own knowledge was now so complete. She could see Miss Pynsent was looking at her hat, which was a wonderful composition of flowers and ribbons; her eyes had travelled up and down Millicent's whole person, but they rested in fascination on this ornament. The girl had forgotten how small the dressmaker was; she barely came up to her shoulder. She had lost her hair, and wore a cap, which Millicent noticed in return, wondering if that were a specimen of what she thought the fashion. Miss Pynsent stared up at her as if she had been six feet high; but she was used to that sort of surprised admiration, being perfectly conscious that she was a magnificent young woman.

'Won't you take me into your shop?' she asked. 'I don't want to order anything; I only want to inquire after your 'ealth; and isn't this rather an awkward place to talk?' She made her way further in, without waiting for permission, seeing that her startled hostess had not yet guessed.

'The show-room is on the right hand,' said Miss Pynsent, with her professional manner, which was intended, evidently, to mark a difference. She spoke as if on the other side, where the horizon was bounded by the partition of the next house, there were labyrinths of apartments. Passing in after her guest she found the young lady already spread out upon the sofa, the everlasting sofa, in the right-hand corner as you faced the window, covered with a light, shrunken shroud of a strange yellow stuff, the tinge of which revealed years of washing, and surmounted by a coloured print of Rebekah at the Well, balancing, in the opposite quarter, with a portrait of the Empress of the French, taken from an illustrated newspaper and framed and glazed in the manner of 1853. Millicent looked about her, asking herself what Miss Pynsent had to show and acting perfectly the part of the most brilliant figure the place had ever contained. The old implements were there on the table: the pincushions and needle-books; the pink measuring-tape with which, as children, she and Hyacinth used to take each other's height; and the same collection of fashion-plates (she could see in a minute), crumpled, sallow and fly-blown. The little dressmaker bristled, as she used to do, with needles and pins (they were stuck all over the front of her dress), but there were no rustling fabrics tossed in heaps about the room—nothing but the skirt of a shabby dress (it might have been her own), which she was evidently repairing and had flung upon the table when she came to the door. Miss Henning speedily arrived at the conclusion that her hostess's business had not increased, and felt a kind of good-humoured, luxurious scorn of a person who knew so little what was to be got out of London. It was Millicent's belief that she herself was already perfectly acquainted with the resources of the metropolis.

'Now tell me, how is Hyacinth? I should like so much to see him,' she remarked, extending a pair of large protrusive feet and supporting herself on the sofa by her hands.

'Hyacinth?' Miss Pynsent repeated, with majestic blankness, as if she had never heard of such a person. She felt that the girl was cruelly, scathingly, well dressed; she couldn't imagine who she was, nor with what design she could have presented herself.

'Perhaps you call him Mr. Robinson, to-day—you always wanted him to hold himself so high. But to his face, at any rate, I'll call him as I used to: you see if I don't!'

'Bless my soul, you must be the little 'Enning!' Miss Pynsent exclaimed, planted before her and going now into every detail.

'Well, I'm glad you have made up your mind. I thought you'd know me directly. I had a call to make in this part, and it came into my 'ead to look you up. I don't like to lose sight of old friends.'

'I never knew you—you've improved so,' Miss Pynsent rejoined, with a candour justified by her age and her consciousness of respectability.

'Well, *you* haven't changed; you were always calling me something horrid.'

'I dare say it doesn't matter to you now, does it?' said the dressmaker, seating herself, but quite unable to take up her work, absorbed as she was in the examination of her visitor.

'Oh, I'm all right now,' Miss Henning replied, with the air of one who had nothing to fear from human judgments.

'You were a pretty child—I never said the contrary to that; but I had no idea you'd turn out like this. You're too tall for a woman,' Miss Pynsent added, much divided between an old prejudice and a new appreciation.

'Well, I enjoy beautiful 'ealth,' said the young lady; 'every one thinks I'm twenty.' She spoke with a certain artless pride in her bigness and her bloom, and as if, to show her development, she would have taken off her jacket or let you feel her upper arm. She was very handsome, with a shining, bold, good-natured eye, a fine, free, facial oval, an abundance of brown hair, and a smile which showed the whiteness of her teeth. Her head was set upon a fair, strong neck, and her tall young figure was rich in feminine curves. Her gloves, covering her wrists insufficiently, showed the redness of those parts, in the interstices of the numerous silver bracelets that encircled them, and Miss Pynsent made the observation that her hands were not more delicate than her feet. She was not graceful, and even the little dressmaker, whose preference for distinguished forms never deserted her, indulged in the mental reflection that she was common, for all her

magnificence; but there was something about her indescribably fresh, successful and satisfying. She was, to her blunt,
expanded fingertips, a daughter of London, of the crowded
streets and hustling traffic of the great city; she had drawn
her health and strength from its dingy courts and foggy
thoroughfares, and peopled its parks and squares and cres-
cents with her ambitions; it had entered into her blood and
her bone, the sound of her voice and the carriage of her
head; she understood it by instinct and loved it with passion; she represented its immense vulgarities and curiosities,
its brutality and its knowingness, its good-nature and its impudence, and might have figured, in an allegorical procession, as a kind of glorified townswoman, a nymph of the
wilderness of Middlesex, a flower of the accumulated par-
ishes, the genius of urban civilisation, the muse of cockneyism. The restrictions under which Miss Pynsent regarded her
would have cost the dressmaker some fewer scruples if she
had guessed the impression she made upon Millicent, and
how the whole place seemed to that prosperous young lady
to smell of poverty and failure. Her childish image of Miss
Pynsent had represented her as delicate and dainty, with
round loops of hair fastened on her temples by combs, and
associations of brilliancy arising from the constant manipulation of precious stuffs—tissues at least which Millicent regarded with envy. But the little woman before her was bald
and white and pinched; she looked shrunken and sickly and
insufficiently nourished; her small eyes were sharp and suspicious, and her hideous cap did not disguise her meagreness.
Miss Henning thanked her stars, as she had often done before, that she had not been obliged to get *her* living by
drudging over needlework year after year in that undiscoverable street, in a dismal little room where nothing had been
changed for ages; the absence of change had such an exasperating effect upon her vigorous young nature. She reflected with complacency upon her good fortune in being
attached to a more exciting, a more dramatic, department of
the dressmaking business, and noticed that though it was already November there was no fire in the neatly-kept grate
beneath the chimney-piece, on which a design, partly architectural, partly botanical, executed in the hair of Miss

Pynsent's parents, was flanked by a pair of vases, under glass, containing muslin flowers.

If she thought Miss Pynsent's eyes suspicious it must be confessed that this lady felt very much upon her guard in the presence of so unexpected and undesired a reminder of one of the least honourable episodes in the annals of Lomax Place. Miss Pynsent esteemed people in proportion to their success in constituting a family circle—in cases, that is, when the ma-terials were under their hand. This success, among the various members of the house of Henning, had been of the scantiest, and the domestic broils in the establishment adjacent to her own, whose vicissitudes she was able to follow, as she sat at her window at work, by simply inclining an ear to the thin partition behind her—these scenes, amid which the crash of crockery and the imprecations of the wounded were fre-quently audible, had long been the scandal of a humble but harmonious neighbourhood. Mr. Henning was supposed to occupy a place of confidence in a brush-factory, while his wife, at home, occupied herself with the washing and mend-ing of a considerable brood, mainly of sons. But economy and sobriety, and indeed a virtue more important still, had never presided at their councils. The freedom and frequency of Mrs. Henning's relations with a stove-polisher in the Euston Road were at least not a secret to a person who lived next door and looked up from her work so often that it was a wonder it was always finished so quickly. The little Hennings, unwashed and unchidden, spent most of their time either in pushing each other into the gutter or in running to the public-house at the corner for a pennyworth of gin, and the borrowing propensi-ties of their elders were a theme for exclamation. There was no object of personal or domestic use which Mrs. Henning had not at one time or another endeavoured to elicit from the dressmaker; beginning with a mattress, on an occasion when she was about to take to her bed for a considerable period, and ending with a flannel petticoat and a pewter teapot. Lo-max Place had, eventually, from its over-peeping windows and doorways, been present at the seizure, by a long-suffering landlord, of the chattels of this interesting family and at the ejectment of the whole insolvent group, who departed in a straggling, jeering, unabashed, cynical manner, carrying with them but little of the sympathy of the street. Millicent, whose childish intimacy with Hyacinth Robinson Miss Pynsent had always viewed with vague anxiety—she thought the girl a 'nasty little thing,' and was afraid she would teach the innocent orphan low ways—Millicent, with her luxuriant tresses, her precocious beauty, her staring, mocking manner on the doorstep, was at this time twelve years of age. She vanished with her vanishing companions; Lomax Place saw them turn the corner, and returned to its occupations with a conviction that they would make shipwreck on the outer reefs. But neither spar nor splinter floated back to their former haunts, and they were engulfed altogether in the fathomless deeps of the town. Miss Pynsent drew a long breath; it was her conviction that none of them would come to any good, and Millicent least of all.

When, therefore, this young lady reappeared, with all the signs of accomplished survival, she could not fail to ask herself whether, under a specious seeming, the phenomenon did not simply represent the triumph of vice. She was alarmed, but she would have given her silver thimble to know the girl's history, and between her alarm and her curiosity she passed an uncomfortable half-hour. She felt that the familiar, mysterious creature was playing with her; revenging herself for former animadversions, for having been snubbed and miscalled by a peering little spinster who now could make no figure beside her. If it was not the triumph of vice it was at least the triumph of impertinence, as well as of youth, health, and a greater acquaintance with the art of dress than Miss Pynsent could boast, for all her ridiculous signboards. She perceived, or she believed she perceived, that Millicent wanted to scare her, to make her think she had come after Hyacinth; that she wished to inveigle, to corrupt him. I should be sorry to impute to Miss Henning any motive more complicated than the desire to amuse herself, of a Saturday afternoon, by a ramble which her vigorous legs had no occasion to deprecate; but it must be confessed that when it occurred to her that Miss Pynsent regarded her as a ravening wolf and her early playmate as an unspotted lamb, she laughed out, in her hostess's anxious face, irrelevantly and good humouredly, without deigning to explain. But what, indeed, had she come for, if she had not come after Hyacinth? It was not for the love of the dressmaker's pretty ways. She remembered the boy and some of their tender passages, and in the wantonness of her full-blown freedom—her attachment, also, to any tolerable pretext for wandering through the streets of London and gazing into shop-windows—she had said to herself that she would dedicate an afternoon to the pleasures of memory, would revisit the scenes of her childhood. She considered that her childhood had ended with the departure of her family from Lomax Place. If the tenants of that obscure locality never learned what their banished fellows went through, Millicent retained a deep impression of those horrible intermediate years. The family, as a family, had gone down-hill, to the very bottom; and in her humbler moments Millicent sometimes wondered what lucky star had checked her own descent, and indeed enabled her to mount the slope again. In her humbler moments, I say, for as a general thing she was provided with an explanation of any good fortune that might befall her. What was more natural than that a girl should do well when she was at once so handsome and so clever? Millicent thought with compassion of the young persons whom a niggardly fate had endowed with only one of these advantages. She was good-natured, but she had no idea of gratifying Miss Pynsent's curiosity; it seemed to her quite a sufficient kindness to stimulate it.

She told the dressmaker that she had a high position at a great haberdasher's in the neighbourhood of Buckingham Palace; she was in the department for jackets and mantles; she put on all these articles to show them off to the customers, and on her person they appeared to such advantage that nothing she took up ever failed to go off. Miss Pynsent could imagine, from this, how highly her services were prized. She had had a splendid offer from another establishment, in Oxford Street, and she was just thinking whether she should accept it. 'We have to be beautifully dressed, but I don't care, because I like to look nice,' she remarked to her hostess, who at the end of half an hour, very grave, behind the clumsy glasses which she had been obliged to wear of late years, seemed still not to know what to make of her. On the subject of her family, of her history during the interval that was to be accounted for, the girl was large and vague, and Miss Pynsent saw that the domestic circle had not even a shadow of sanctity for her. She stood on her own feet, and she stood very firm. Her staying so long, her remaining over the half hour, proved to the dressmaker that she had come for Hyacinth; for poor Amanda gave her as little information as was decent, told her nothing that would encourage or attract. She simply mentioned that Mr. Robinson (she was careful to speak of him in that manner) had given his attention to bookbinding, and had served an apprenticeship at an establishment where they turned out the best work of that kind that was to be found in London.

'A bookbindery? Laws!' said Miss Henning. 'Do you mean they get them up for the shops? Well, I always thought he would have something to do with books.' Then she added, 'But I didn't think he would ever follow a trade.'

'A trade?' cried Miss Pynsent. 'You should hear Mr. Robinson speak of it. He considers it one of the fine arts.'

Millicent smiled, as if she knew how people often considered things, and remarked that very likely it was tidy, comfortable work, but she couldn't believe there was much to be seen in it. 'Perhaps you will say there is more than there is here,' she went on, finding at last an effect of irritation, of reprehension, an implication of aggressive respectability, in the image of the patient dressmaker, sitting for so many years in her close, brown little den, with the foggy familiarities of Lomax Place on the other side of the pane. Millicent liked to think that she herself was strong, and she was not strong enough for that.

This allusion to her shrunken industry seemed to Miss Pynsent very cruel; but she reflected that it was natural one should be insulted if one talked to a vulgar girl. She judged this young lady in the manner of a person who was not vulgar herself, and if there was a difference between them she was right in feeling it to be in her favour. Miss Pynsent's 'cut,' as I have intimated, was not truly fashionable, and in the application of gimp and the distribution of ornament she was not to be trusted; but, morally, she had the best taste in the world. 'I haven't so much work as I used to have, if that's what you mean. My eyes are not so good, and my health has failed with advancing years.'

I know not to what extent Millicent was touched by the dignity of this admission, but she replied, without embarrassment, that what Miss Pynsent wanted was a smart young assistant, some nice girl with a pretty taste, who would brighten up the business and give her new ideas. 'I can see you have got the same old ones, always: I can tell that by the way you have stuck the braid on that dress;' and she directed a poke of her neat little umbrella to the drapery in the dressmaker's lap. She continued to patronise and exasperate her, and to offer her consolation and encouragement with the heaviest hand that had ever been applied to Miss Pynsent's sensitive surface. Poor Amanda ended by gazing at her as if she were a public performer of some kind, a ballad-singer or a conjurer, and went so far as to ask herself whether the hussy could be (in her own mind) the 'nice girl' who was to regild the tarnished sign. Miss Pynsent had had assistants, in the past—she had even, once, for a few months, had a 'forewoman;' and some of these damsels had been precious specimens, whose misdemeanours lived vividly in her memory. Never, all the same, in her worst hour of delusion, had she trusted her interests to such an extravagant baggage as this. She was quickly reassured as to Millicent's own views, perceiving more and more that she was a tremendous highflyer, who required a much larger field of action than the musty bower she now honoured, heaven only knew why, with her presence. Miss Pynsent held her tongue, as she always did, when the sorrow of her life had been touched, the thought of the slow, inexorable decline on which she had entered that day, nearly ten years before, when her hesitations and scruples resolved themselves into a hideous mistake. The deep conviction of error, on that unspeakably important occasion, had ached and throbbed within her ever since like an incurable disease. She had sown in her boy's mind the seeds of shame and rancour; she had made him conscious of his stigma, of his exquisitely vulnerable spot, and condemned him to know that for him the sun would never shine as it shone for most others. By the time he was sixteen years old she had learned—or believed she had learned—the judgment he passed upon her, and at that period she had lived through a series of horrible months, an ordeal in which every element of her old prosperity perished. She cried her eyes out, on coming to a sense of her aberration, blinded and weakened herself with weeping, so that for a moment it seemed as if she should never be able to touch a needle again. She lost all interest in her work, and that artistic imagination which had always been her pride deserted her, together with the reputation of keeping the tidiest lodgings in Lomax Place. A couple of commercial gentlemen and a Welsh plumber, of religious tendencies, who for several years had made her establishment their home, withdrew their patronage on the ground that the airing of her beds was not what it used to be, and disseminated cruelly this injurious legend. She ceased to notice or to care how sleeves were worn, and on the question of flounces and gores her mind was a blank. She fell into a grievous debility, and then into a long, low, languid fever, during which Hyacinth tended her with a devotion which only made the wrong she had done him seem more bitter, and in which, so soon as she was able to hold up her head a little, Mr. Vetch came and sat with her through the dull hours of convalescence. She re-established to a certain extent, after a while, her connection, so far as the letting of her rooms was concerned (from the other department of her activity the tide had ebbed apparently for ever); but nothing was the same again, and she knew it was the beginning of the end. So it had gone on, and she watched the end approach; she felt it was very near indeed when a child she had seen playing in the gutters came to flaunt it over her in silk and lace. She gave a low, inaudible sigh of relief when at last Millicent got up and stood before her, smoothing the glossy cylinder of her umbrella.

'Mind you give my love to Hyacinth,' the girl said, with an assurance which showed all her insensibility to tacit protests. 'I don't care if you do guess that if I have stopped so long it was in the hope he would be dropping in to his tea. You can tell him I sat an hour, on purpose, if you like; there's no shame in my wanting to see my little friend. He may know I call him that!' Millicent continued, with her show-room

laugh, as Miss Pynsent judged it to be; conferring these per-
missions, successively, as if they were great indulgences. 'Do
give him my love, and tell him I hope he'll come and see me.
I see you won't tell him anything. I don't know what you're
afraid of; but I'll leave my card for him, all the same.' She
drew forth a little bright-coloured pocket-book, and it was
with amazement that Miss Pynsent saw her extract from it a
morsel of engraved pasteboard—so monstrous did it seem
that one of the squalid little Hennings should have lived to
display this emblem of social consideration. Millicent enjoyed
the effect she produced as she laid the card on the table, and
gave another ringing peel of merriment at the sight of her
hostess's half-hungry, half-astonished look. 'What *do* you
think I want to do with him? I could swallow him at a single
bite!' she cried.

Poor Amanda gave no second glance at the document on
the table, though she had perceived it contained, in the corner, her visitor's address, which Millicent had amused herself,
ingeniously, with not mentioning: she only got up, laying
down her work with a trembling hand, so that she should be
able to see Miss Henning well out of the house. 'You needn't
think I shall put myself out to keep him in the dark. I shall
certainly tell him you have been here, and exactly how you
strike me.'

'Of course you'll say something nasty—like you used to
when I was a child. You let me 'ave it then, you know!'

'Ah, well,' said Miss Pynsent, nettled at being reminded of
an acerbity which the girl's present development caused to
appear ridiculously ineffectual, 'you are very different now,
when I think what you've come from.'

'What I've come from?' Millicent threw back her head, and
opened her eyes very wide, while all her feathers and ribbons
nodded. 'Did you want me to stick fast in this low place for
the rest of my days? You have had to stay in it yourself, so you
might speak civilly of it.' She coloured, and raised her voice,
and looked magnificent in her scorn. 'And pray what have
you come from yourself, and what has *he* come from—the
mysterious "Mr. Robinson," that used to be such a puzzle to
the whole Place? I thought perhaps I might clear it up, but
you haven't told me that yet!'

Miss Pynsent turned straight away, covering her ears with her hands. 'I have nothing to tell you! Leave my room—leave my house!' she cried, with a trembling voice.

V

IT WAS in this way that the dressmaker failed either to see or to hear the opening of the door of the room, which obeyed a slow, apparently cautious impulse given it from the hall, and revealed the figure of a young man standing there with a short pipe in his teeth. There was something in his face which immediately told Millicent Henning that he had heard, outside, her last resounding tones. He entered as if, young as he was, he knew that when women were squabbling men were not called upon to be headlong, and evidently wondered who the dressmaker's brilliant adversary might be. She recognised on the instant her old playmate, and without reflection, confusion or diplomacy, in the fulness of her vulgarity and sociability, she exclaimed, in no lower pitch, 'Gracious, Hyacinth Robinson, is *that* your form?'

Miss Pynsent turned round, in a flash, but kept silent; then, very white and trembling, took up her work again and seated herself in her window.

Hyacinth Robinson stood staring; then he blushed all over. He knew who she was, but he didn't say so; he only asked, in a voice which struck the girl as quite different from the old one—the one in which he used to tell her she was beastly tiresome—'Is it of me you were speaking just now?'

'When I asked where you had come from? That was because we 'eard you in the 'all,' said Millicent, smiling. 'I suppose you have come from your work.'

'You used to live in the Place—you always wanted to kiss me,' the young man remarked, with an effort not to show all the surprise and agitation that he felt. 'Didn't she live in the Place, Pinnie?'

Pinnie, for all answer, fixed a pair of strange, pleading eyes upon him, and Millicent broke out, with her recurrent laugh, in which the dressmaker had been right in discovering the note of affectation, 'Do you want to know what you look like? You look for all the world like a little Frenchman! Don't he look like a little Frenchman, Miss Pynsent?' she went on, as if she were on the best possible terms with the mistress of the establishment.

Hyacinth exchanged a look with that afflicted woman; he saw something in her face which he knew very well by this time, and the sight of which always gave him an odd, perverse, unholy satisfaction. It seemed to say that she prostrated herself, that she did penance in the dust, that she was his to trample upon, to spit upon. He did neither of these things, but she was constantly offering herself, and her permanent humility, her perpetual abjection, was a sort of counter-irritant to the soreness lodged in his own heart for ever, which had often made him cry with rage at night, in his little room under the roof. Pinnie meant that, to-day, as a matter of course, and she could only especially mean it in the presence of Miss Henning's remark about his looking like a Frenchman. He knew he looked like a Frenchman, he had often been told so before, and a large part of the time he felt like one—like one of those he had read about in Michelet and Carlyle. He had picked up the French tongue with the most extraordinary facility, with the aid of one of his mates, a refugee from Paris, in the workroom, and of a second-hand dog's-eared dictionary, bought for a shilling in the Brompton Road, in one of his interminable, restless, melancholy, moody, yet all-observant strolls through London. He spoke it (as he believed) as if by instinct, caught the accent, the gesture, the movement of eyebrow and shoulder; so that if it should become necessary in certain contingencies that he should pass for a foreigner he had an idea that he might do so triumphantly, once he could borrow a blouse. He had never seen a blouse in his life, but he knew exactly the form and colour of such a garment, and how it was worn. What these contingencies might be which should compel him to assume the disguise of a person of a social station lower still than his own, Hyacinth would not for the world have mentioned to you; but as they were very present to the mind of our imaginative, ingenious youth we shall catch a glimpse of them in the course of a further acquaintance with him. At the present moment, when there was no question of masquerading, it made him blush again that such a note should be struck by a loud, laughing, handsome girl, who came back out of his past. There was more in Pinnie's weak eyes, now, than her usual profession; there was a dumb intimation, almost as pathetic as the other, that if he cared to let her off easily he would not detain their terrible visitor very long. He had no wish to do that; he kept the door open, on purpose; he didn't enjoy talking to girls under Pinnie's eyes, and he could see that this one had every disposition to talk. So without responding to her observation about his appearance he said, not knowing exactly what to say, 'Have you come back to live in the Place?'

'Heaven forbid I should ever do that!' cried Miss Henning, with genuine emotion. 'I have to live near the establishment in which I'm employed.'

'And what establishment is that, now?' the young man asked, gaining confidence and perceiving, in detail, how handsome she was. He hadn't roamed about London for nothing, and he knew that when a girl was as handsome as that, a jocular tone of address, a pleasing freedom, was *de rigueur*; so he added, 'Is it the Bull and Gate, or the Elephant and Castle?'

'A public house! Well, you haven't got the politeness of a Frenchman, at all events!' Her good-nature had come back to her perfectly, and her resentment of his imputation of her looking like a bar-maid—a blowzy beauty who handled pewter—was tempered by her more and more curious consideration of Hyacinth's form. He was exceedingly 'rum,' but this quality took her fancy, and since he remembered so well that she had been fond of kissing him, in their early days she would have liked to say to him that she stood prepared to repeat this graceful attention. But she reminded herself, in time, that her line should be, religiously, the ladylike, and she was content to exclaim, simply, 'I don't care what a man looks like so long as he's clever. That's the form *I* like!'

Miss Pynsent had promised herself the satisfaction of taking no further notice of her brilliant invader; but the temptation was great to expose her to Hyacinth, as a mitigation of her brilliancy, by remarking sarcastically, according to opportunity, 'Miss 'Enning wouldn't live in Lomax Place for the world. She thinks it too abominably low.'

'So it is; it's a beastly hole,' said the young man.

The poor dressmaker's little dart fell to the ground, and

Millicent exclaimed, jovially, 'Right you are!' while she directed to the object of her childhood's admiration a smile that put him more and more at his ease.

'Don't you suppose I'm clever?' he asked, planted before her with his little legs slightly apart, while, with his hands behind him, he made the open door waver to and fro.

'You? Oh, I don't care whether you are or not!' said Millicent Henning; and Hyacinth was at any rate quick-witted enough to see what she meant by that. If she meant he was so good-looking that he might pass on this score alone her judgment was conceivable, though many women would strongly have dissented from it. He was as small as he had threatened—he had never got his growth—and she could easily see that he was not what she, at least, would call strong. His bones were small, his chest was narrow, his complexion pale, his whole figure almost childishly slight; and Millicent perceived afterward that he had a very delicate hand—the hand, as she said to herself, of a gentleman. What she liked was his face, and something jaunty and entertaining, almost theatrical in his whole little person. Miss Henning was not acquainted with any member of the dramatic profession, but she supposed, vaguely, that that was the way an actor would look in private life. Hyacinth's features were perfect; his eyes, large and much divided, had as their usual expression a kind of witty candour, and a small, soft, fair moustache disposed itself upon his upper lip in a way that made him look as if he were smiling even when his heart was heavy. The waves of his dense, fine hair clustered round a forehead which was high enough to suggest remarkable things, and Miss Henning had observed that when he first appeared he wore his little soft circular hat in a way that left these frontal locks very visible. He was dressed in an old brown velveteen jacket, and wore exactly the bright-coloured necktie which Miss Pynsent's quick fingers used of old to shape out of hoarded remnants of silk and muslin. He was shabby and work-stained, but the observant eye would have noted an idea in his dress (his appearance was plainly not a matter of indifference to himself), and a painter (not of the heroic) would have liked to make a sketch of him. There was something exotic about him, and yet, with his sharp young face, destitute of bloom, but not of sweetness, and a certain conscious cockneyism which pervaded him, he was as strikingly as Millicent, in her own degree, a product of the London streets and the London air. He looked both ingenuous and slightly wasted, amused, amusing, and indefinably sad. Women had always found him touching; yet he made them—so they had repeatedly assured him—die of laughing.

'I think you had better shut the door,' said Miss Pynsent, meaning that he had better shut their departing visitor out.

'Did you come here on purpose to see us?' Hyacinth asked, not heeding this injunction, of which he divined the spirit, and wishing the girl would take her leave, so that he might go out again with her. He should like talking with her much better away from Pinnie, who evidently was ready to stick a bodkin into her, for reasons he perfectly understood. He had seen plenty of them before, Pinnie's reasons, even where girls were concerned who were not nearly so good-looking as this one. She was always in a fearful 'funk' about some woman getting hold of him, and persuading him to make a marriage beneath his station. His station!— poor Hyacinth had often asked himself, and Miss Pynsent, what it could possibly be. He had thought of it bitterly enough, and wondered how in the world he could marry 'beneath' it. He would never marry at all—to that his mind was absolutely made up; he would never hand on to another the burden which had made his own young spirit so intolerably sore, the inheritance which had darkened the whole threshold of his manhood. All the more reason why he should have his compensation; why, if the soft society of women was to be enjoyed on other terms, he should cultivate it with a bold, free mind.

'I thought I would just give a look at the old shop; I had an engagement not far off,' Millicent said. 'But I wouldn't have believed any one who had told me I should find you just where I left you.'

'We needed you to look after us!' Miss Pynsent exclaimed, irrepressibly.

'Oh, you're such a swell yourself!' Hyacinth observed, without heeding the dressmaker.

'None of your impudence! I'm as good a girl as there is in London!' And to corroborate this, Miss Henning went on: 'If you were to offer to see me a part of the way home, I should tell you I don't knock about that way with gentlemen.'

'I'll go with you as far as you like,' Hyacinth replied, simply, as if he knew how to treat that sort of speech.

'Well, it's only because I knew you as a baby!' And they went out together, Hyacinth careful not to look at poor Pinnie at all (he felt her glaring whitely and tearfully at him out of her dim corner—it had by this time grown too dusky to work without a lamp), and his companion giving her an outrageously friendly nod of farewell over her shoulder.

It was a long walk from Lomax Place to the quarter of the town in which (to be near the haberdasher's in the Buckingham Palace Road) Miss Henning occupied a modest back-room; but the influences of the hour were such as to make the excursion very agreeable to our young man, who liked the streets at all times, but especially at nightfall, in the autumn, of a Saturday, when, in the vulgar districts, the smaller shops and open-air industries were doubly active, and big, clumsy torches flared and smoked over hand-carts and costermongers' barrows, drawn up in the gutters. Hyacinth had roamed through the great city since he was an urchin, but his imagination had never ceased to be stirred by the preparations for Sunday that went on in the evening among the toilers and spinners, his brothers and sisters, and he lost himself in all the quickened crowding and pushing and staring at lighted windows and chaffering at the stalls of fishmongers and hucksters. He liked the people who looked as if they had got their week's wage and were prepared to lay it out discreetly; and even those whose use of it would plainly be extravagant and intemperate; and, best of all, those who evidently hadn't received it at all and who wandered about, disinterestedly, vaguely, with their hands in empty pockets, watching others make their bargains and fill their satchels, or staring at the striated sides of bacon, at the golden cubes and triangles of cheese, at the graceful festoons of sausage, in the most brilliant of the windows. He liked the reflection of the lamps on the wet pavements, the feeling and smell of the carboniferous London damp; the way the winter fog blurred and suffused

the whole place, made it seem bigger and more crowded, produced halos and dim radiations, trickles and evaporations, on
the plates of glass. He moved in the midst of these impressions this evening, but he enjoyed them in silence, with an
attention taken up mainly by his companion, and pleased to
be already so intimate with a young lady whom people turned
round to look at. She herself affected to speak of the rush and
crush of the week's end with disgust: she said she liked the
streets, but she liked the respectable ones; she couldn't abide
the smell of fish, and the whole place seemed full of it, so that
she hoped they would soon get into the Edgware Road, towards which they tended and which was a proper street for a
lady. To Hyacinth she appeared to have no connection with
the long-haired little girl who, in Lomax Place, years before,
was always hugging a smutty doll and courting his society;
she was like a stranger, a new acquaintance, and he observed
her curiously, wondering by what transitions she had reached
her present pitch.

    She enlightened him but little on this point, though she
talked a great deal on a variety of subjects, and mentioned to
him her habits, her aspirations, her likes and dislikes. The
latter were very numerous. She was tremendously particular,
difficult to please, he could see that; and she assured him
that she never put up with anything a moment after it had
ceased to be agreeable to her. Especially was she particular
about gentlemen's society, and she made it plain that a
young fellow who wanted to have anything to say to her
must be in receipt of wages amounting at the least to fifty
shillings a week. Hyacinth told her that he didn't earn that,
as yet; and she remarked again that she made an exception
for him, because she knew all about him (or if not all, at
least a great deal), and he could see that her good-nature
was equal to her beauty. She made such an exception that
when, after they were moving down the Edgware Road
(which had still the brightness of late closing, but with more
nobleness), he proposed that she should enter a coffee-house
with him and 'take something' (he could hardly tell himself,
afterwards, what brought him to this point), she acceded
without a demur—without a demur even on the ground of
his slender earnings. Slender as they were, Hyacinth had

them in his pocket (they had been destined in some degree for Pinnie), and he felt equal to the occasion. Millicent partook profusely of tea and bread and butter, with a relish of raspberry jam, and thought the place most comfortable, though he himself, after finding himself ensconced, was visited by doubts as to its respectability, suggested, among other things, by photographs, on the walls, of young ladies in tights. Hyacinth himself was hungry, he had not yet had his tea, but he was too excited, too preoccupied, to eat; the situation made him restless and gave him palpitations; it seemed to be the beginning of something new. He had never yet 'stood' even a glass of beer to a girl of Millicent's stamp—a girl who rustled and glittered and smelt of musk—and if she should turn out as jolly a specimen of the sex as she seemed it might make a great difference in his leisure hours, in his evenings, which were often very dull. That it would also make a difference in his savings (he was under a pledge to Pinnie and to Mr. Vetch to put by something every week) it didn't concern him, for the moment, to reflect; and indeed, though he thought it odious and insufferable to be poor, the ways and means of becoming rich had hitherto not greatly occupied him. He knew what Millicent's age must be, but felt, nevertheless, as if she were older, much older, than himself—she appeared to know so much about London and about life; and this made it still more of a sensation to be entertaining her like a young swell. He thought of it, too, in connection with the question of the respectability of the establishment; if this element was deficient she would perceive it as soon as he, and very likely it would be a part of the general initiation she had given him an impression of that she shouldn't mind it so long as the tea was strong and the bread and butter thick. She described to him what had passed between Miss Pynsent and herself (she didn't call her Pinnie, and he was glad, for he wouldn't have liked it) before he came in, and let him know that she should never dare to come to the place again, as his mother would tear her eyes out. Then she checked herself. 'Of course she ain't your mother! How stupid I am! I keep forgetting.'

Hyacinth had long since convinced himself that he had acquired a manner with which he could meet allusions of this kind: he had had, first and last, so many opportunities to practise it. Therefore he looked at his companion very steadily while he said, 'My mother died many years ago; she was a great invalid. But Pinnie has been awfully good to me.'

'My mother's dead too,' Miss Henning remarked. 'She died very suddenly. I daresay you remember her in the Place.' Then, while Hyacinth disengaged from the past the wavering figure of Mrs. Henning, of whom he mainly remembered that she used to strike him as dirty, the girl added, smiling, but with more sentiment, 'But I have had no Pinnie.'

'You look as if you could take care of yourself.'

'Well, I'm very confiding,' said Millicent Henning. Then she asked what had become of Mr. Vetch. 'We used to say that if Miss Pynsent was your mamma, he was your papa. In our family we used to call him Miss Pynsent's young man.'

'He's her young man still,' Hyacinth said. 'He's our best friend—or supposed to be. He got me the place I'm in now. He lives by his fiddle, as he used to do.'

Millicent looked a little at her companion, after which she remarked, 'I should have thought he would have got you a place at his theatre.'

'At his theatre? That would have been no use. I don't play any instrument.'

'I don't mean in the orchestra, you gaby! You would look very nice in a fancy costume.' She had her elbows on the table, and her shoulders lifted, in an attitude of extreme familiarity. He was on the point of replying that he didn't care for fancy costumes, he wished to go through life in his own character; but he checked himself, with the reflection that this was exactly what, apparently, he was destined not to do. His own character? He was to cover that up as carefully as possible; he was to go through life in a mask, in a borrowed mantle; he was to be, every day and every hour, an actor. Suddenly, with the utmost irrelevance, Miss Henning inquired, 'Is Miss Pynsent some relation? What gave her any right over you?'

Hyacinth had an answer ready for this question; he had determined to say, as he had several times said before, 'Miss

Pynsent is an old friend of my family. My mother was very fond of her, and she was very fond of my mother.' He repeated the formula now, looking at Millicent with the same inscrutable calmness (as he fancied), though what he would have liked to say to her would have been that his mother was none of her business. But she was too handsome to talk that way to, and she presented her large fair face to him, across the table, with an air of solicitation to be cosy and comfortable. There were things in his heart and a torment and a hidden passion in his life which he should be glad enough to lay open to some woman. He believed that perhaps this would be the cure ultimately; that in return for something he might drop, syllable by syllable, into a listening feminine ear, certain other words would be spoken to him which would make his pain for ever less sharp. But what woman could he trust, what ear would be safe? The answer was not in this loud, fresh laughing creature, whose sympathy couldn't have the fineness he was looking for, since her curiosity was vulgar. Hyacinth objected to the vulgar as much as Miss Pynsent herself; in this respect she had long since discovered that he was after her own heart. He had not taken up the subject of Mrs. Henning's death; he felt himself incapable of inquiring about that lady, and had no desire for knowledge of Millicent's relationships. Moreover he always suffered, to sickness, when people began to hover about the question of his origin, the reasons why Pinnie had had the care of him from a baby. Mrs. Henning had been untidy, but at least her daughter could speak of her. 'Mr. Vetch has changed his lodgings: he moved out of No. 17, three years ago,' he said, to vary the topic. 'He couldn't stand the other people in the house; there was a man who played the accordeon.'

Millicent, however, was but moderately interested in this anecdote, and she wanted to know why people should like Mr. Vetch's fiddle any better. Then she added, 'And I think that while he was about it he might have put you into something better than a bookbinder's.'

'He wasn't obliged to put me into anything. It's a very good place.'

'All the same, it isn't where I should have looked to find

you,' Millicent declared, not so much in the tone of wishing to pay him a compliment as of resentment at having miscalculated.

'Where should you have looked to find me? In the House of Commons? It's a pity you couldn't have told me in advance what you would have liked me to be.'

She looked at him, over her cup, while she drank, in several sips. 'Do you know what they used to say in the Place? That your father was a lord.'

'Very likely. That's the kind of rot they talk in that precious hole,' the young man said, without blenching.

'Well, perhaps he was,' Millicent ventured.

'He may have been a prince, for all the good it has done me.'

'Fancy your talking as if you didn't know!' said Millicent.

'Finish your tea—don't mind how I talk.'

'Well, you 'ave got a temper!' the girl exclaimed, archly. 'I should have thought you'd be a clerk at a banker's.'

'Do they select them for their tempers?'

'You know what I mean. You used to be too clever to follow a trade.'

'Well, I'm not clever enough to live on air.'

'You might be, really, for all the tea you drink! Why didn't you go in for some high profession?'

'How was I to go in? Who the devil was to help me?' Hyacinth inquired, with a certain vibration.

'Haven't you got any relations?' said Millicent, after a moment.

'What are you doing? Are you trying to make me swagger?'

When he spoke sharply she only laughed, not in the least ruffled, and by the way she looked at him seemed to like it. 'Well, I'm sorry you're only a journeyman,' she went on, pushing away her cup.

'So am I,' Hyacinth rejoined; but he called for the bill as if he had been an employer of labour. Then, while it was being brought, he remarked to his companion that he didn't believe she had an idea of what his work was and how charming it could be. 'Yes, I get up books for the shops,' he said, when she had retorted that she perfectly understood. 'But the art of the binder is an exquisite art.'

'So Miss Pynsent told me. She said you had some samples at home. I should like to see them.'

'You wouldn't know how good they are,' said Hyacinth, smiling.

He expected that she would exclaim, in answer, that he was an impudent wretch, and for a moment she seemed to be on the point of doing so. But the words changed on her lips, and she replied, almost tenderly, 'That's just the way you used to speak to me, years ago in the Plice.'

'I don't care about that. I hate all that time.'

'Oh, so do I, if you come to that,' said Millicent, as if she could rise to any breadth of view. And then she returned to her idea that he had not done himself justice. 'You used always to be reading: I never thought you would work with your 'ands.'

This seemed to irritate him, and, having paid the bill and given threepence, ostentatiously, to the young woman with a languid manner and hair of an unnatural yellow, who had waited on them, he said, 'You may depend upon it I shan't do it an hour longer than I can help.'

'What will you do then?'

'Oh, you'll see, some day.' In the street, after they had begun to walk again, he went on, 'You speak as if I could have my pick. What was an obscure little beggar to do, buried in a squalid corner of London, under a million of idiots? I had no help, no influence, no acquaintance of any kind with professional people, and no means of getting at them. I had to do something; I couldn't go on living on Pinnie. Thank God, I help her now, a little. I took what I could get.' He spoke as if he had been touched by the imputation of having derogated.

Millicent seemed to imply that he defended himself successfully when she said, 'You express yourself like a gentleman'—a speech to which he made no response. But he began to talk again afterwards, and, the evening having definitely set in, his companion took his arm for the rest of the way home. By the time he reached her door he had confided to her that, in secret, he wrote: he had a dream of literary distinction. This appeared to impress her, and she branched off to remark, with an irrelevance that characterised her, that she didn't care anything about a man's family if she liked the man himself; she thought families were played out. Hyacinth wished she would leave his alone; and while they lingered in front of her house, before she went in, he said—

'I have no doubt you're a jolly girl, and I am very happy to have seen you again. But you have awfully little tact.'

'*I* have little tact? You should see me work off an old jacket!'

He was silent a moment, standing before her with his hands in his pockets. 'It's a good job you're so handsome.'

Millicent didn't blush at this compliment, and probably didn't understand all it conveyed, but she looked into his eyes a while, with a smile that showed her teeth, and then said, more inconsequently than ever, 'Come now, who are you?'

'Who am I? I'm a wretched little bookbinder.'

'I didn't think I ever could fancy any one in that line!' Miss Henning exclaimed. Then she let him know that she couldn't ask him in, as she made it a point not to receive gentlemen, but she didn't mind if she took another walk with him and she didn't care if she met him somewhere—if it were handy. As she lived so far from Lomax Place she didn't care if she met him half-way. So, in the dusky by-street in Pimlico, before separating, they took a casual tryst; the most interesting, the young man felt, that had yet been—he could scarcely call it granted him.

VI

ONE DAY, shortly after this, at the bindery, his friend Poupin was absent, and sent no explanation, as was customary in case of illness or domestic accident. There were two or three men employed in the place whose non-appearance, usually following close upon pay-day, was better unexplained, and was an implication of moral feebleness; but as a general thing Mr. Crookenden's establishment was a haunt of punctuality and sobriety. Least of all had Eustache Poupin been in the habit of asking for a margin. Hyacinth knew how little indulgence he had ever craved, and this was part of his admiration for the extraordinary Frenchman, an ardent stoic, a cold conspirator and an exquisite artist, who was by far the most interesting person in the ranks of his acquaintance and whose conversation, in the workshop, helped him sometimes to forget the smell of leather and glue. His conversation! Hyacinth had had plenty of that, and had endeared himself to the passionate refugee—Poupin had come to England after the Commune of 1871, to escape the reprisals of the government of M. Thiers, and had remained there in spite of amnesties and rehabilitations—by the solemnity and candour of his attention. He was a Republican of the old-fashioned sort, of the note of 1848, humanitary and idealistic, infinitely addicted to fraternity and equality, and inexhaustibly surprised and exasperated at finding so little enthusiasm for them in the land of his exile. Poupin had a high claim upon Hyacinth's esteem and gratitude, for he had been his godfather, his protector at the bindery. When Anastasius Vetch found something for Miss Pynsent's *protégé* to do, it was through the Frenchman, with whom he had accidentally formed an acquaintance, that he found it.

When the boy was about fifteen years of age Mr. Vetch made him a present of the essays of Lord Bacon, and the purchase of this volume had important consequences for Hyacinth. Anastasius Vetch was a poor man, and the luxury of giving was for the most part denied him; but when once in a way he tasted it he liked the sensation to be pure. No man knew better the difference between the common and the rare, or was more capable of appreciating a book which opened well—of which the margin was not hideously chopped and of which the lettering on the back was sharp. It was only such a book that he could bring himself to offer even to a poor little devil whom a fifth-rate dressmaker (he knew Pinnie was fifth-rate) had rescued from the workhouse. So when it became a question of fitting the great Elizabethan with a new coat—a coat of full morocco, discreetly, delicately gilt—he went with his little cloth-bound volume, a Pickering, straight to Mr. Crookenden, whom every one that knew anything about the matter knew to be a prince of binders, though they also knew that his work, limited in quantity, was mainly done for a particular bookseller and only through the latter's agency. Anastasius Vetch had no idea of paying the book-seller's commission, and though he could be lavish (for him) when he made a present, he was capable of taking an immense deal of trouble to save sixpence. He made his way into Mr. Crookenden's workshop, which was situated in a small superannuated square in Soho, and where the proposal of so slender a job was received at first with coldness. Mr. Vetch, however, insisted, and explained with irresistible frankness the motive of his errand: the desire to obtain the best possible binding for the least possible money. He made his conception of the best possible binding so vivid, so exemplary, that the master of the shop at last confessed to that disinterested sympathy which, under favouring circumstances, establishes itself between the artist and the connoisseur. Mr. Vetch's little book was put in hand as a particular service to an eccentric gentleman whose visit had been a smile-stirring interlude (for the circle of listening workmen) in a merely mechanical day; and when he went back, three weeks later, to see whether it were done, he had the pleasure of finding that his injunctions, punctually complied with, had even been bettered. The work had been accomplished with a perfection of skill which made him ask whom he was to thank for it (he had been told that one man should do the whole of it), and in this manner he made the acquaintance of the most brilliant craftsman in the establishment, the incorruptible, the imaginative, the unerring Eustache Poupin.

In response to an appreciation which he felt not to be *banal*

M. Poupin remarked that he had at home a small collection of experiments in morocco, Russia, parchment, of fanciful specimens with which, for the love of the art, he had amused his leisure hours and which he should be happy to show his interlocutor if the latter would do him the honour to call upon him at his lodgings in Lisson Grove. Mr. Vetch made a note of the address and, for the love of the art, went one Sunday afternoon to see the binder's esoteric studies. On this occasion he made the acquaintance of Madame Poupin, a small, fat lady with a bristling moustache, the white cap of an *ouvrière*, a knowledge of her husband's craft that was equal to his own, and not a syllable of English save the words, 'What you think, what you think?' which she introduced with startling frequency. He also discovered that his new acquaintance had been a political proscript and that he regarded the iniquitous fabric of Church and State with an eye scarcely more reverent than the fiddler's own. M. Poupin was a socialist, which Anastasius Vetch was not, and a constructive democrat (instead of being a mere scoffer at effete things), and a theorist and an optimist and a visionary; he believed that the day was to come when all the nations of the earth would abolish their frontiers and armies and custom-houses, and embrace on both cheeks, and cover the globe with boulevards, radiating from Paris, where the human family would sit, in groups, at little tables, according to affinities, drinking coffee (not tea, *par exemple!*) and listening to the music of the spheres. Mr. Vetch neither prefigured nor desired this organised felicity; he was fond of his cup of tea, and only wanted to see the British constitution a good deal simplified; he thought it a much overrated system, but his heresies rubbed shoulders, sociably, with those of the little bookbinder, and his friend in Lisson Grove became for him the type of the intelligent foreigner whose conversation completes our culture. Poupin's humanitary zeal was as unlimited as his English vocabulary was the reverse, and the new friends agreed with each other enough, and not too much, to discuss, which was much better than an unspeakable harmony. On several other Sunday afternoons the fiddler went back to Lisson Grove, and having, at his theatre, as a veteran, a faithful servant, an occasional privilege, he was able to carry thither, one day in the autumn, an order for two seats

in the second balcony. Madame Poupin and her husband
passed a lugubrious evening at the English comedy, where
they didn't understand a word that was spoken, and consoled
themselves by gazing at their friend in the orchestra. But this
adventure did not arrest the development of a friendship into
which, eventually, Amanda Pynsent was drawn. Madame
Poupin, among the cold insularies, lacked female society, and
Mr. Vetch proposed to his amiable friend in Lomax Place to
call upon her. The little dressmaker, who in the course of her
life had known no Frenchwoman but the unhappy Florentine
(so favourable a specimen till she began to go wrong),
adopted his suggestion, in the hope that she should get a few
ideas from a lady whose appearance would doubtless exem-
plify (as Florentine's originally had done) the fine taste of her
nation; but she found the bookbinder and his wife a bewildering mixture of the brilliant and the relaxed, and was
haunted, long afterwards, by the memory of the lady's calico
jacket, her uncorseted form and her carpet slippers.

The acquaintance, none the less, was sealed three months
later by a supper, one Sunday night, in Lisson Grove, to
which Mr. Vetch brought his fiddle, at which Amanda presented to her hosts her adoptive son, and which also revealed
to her that Madame Poupin could dress a Michaelmas goose,
if she couldn't dress a fat Frenchwoman. This lady confided to
the fiddler that she thought Miss Pynsent exceedingly *comme
il faut—dans le genre anglais*; and neither Amanda nor Hyacinth had ever passed an evening of such splendour. It took
its place, in the boy's recollection, beside the visit, years before, to Mr. Vetch's theatre. He drank in the conversation
which passed between that gentleman and M. Poupin. M.
Poupin showed him his bindings, the most precious trophies
of his skill, and it seemed to Hyacinth that on the spot he was
initiated into a fascinating mystery. He handled the books for
half an hour; Anastasius Vetch watched him, without giving
any particular sign. When, therefore, presently, Miss Pynsent
consulted her friend for the twentieth time on the subject of
Hyacinth's 'career'—she spoke as if she were hesitating between the diplomatic service, the army and the church—the
fiddler replied with promptitude, 'Make him, if you can, what
the Frenchman is.' At the mention of a handicraft poor Pinnie

always looked very solemn, yet when Mr. Vetch asked her if she were prepared to send the boy to one of the universities, or to pay the premium required for his being articled to a solicitor, or to make favour, on his behalf, with a bank-director or a mighty merchant, or, yet again, to provide him with a comfortable home while he should woo the muse and await the laurels of literature—when, I say, he put the case before her with this cynical, ironical lucidity, she only sighed and said that all the money she had ever saved was ninety pounds, which, as he knew perfectly well, it would cost her his acquaintance for evermore to take out of the bank. The fiddler had, in fact, declared to her in a manner not to be mistaken that if she should divest herself, on the boy's account, of this sole nest-egg of her old age, he would wash his hands of her and her affairs. Her standard of success for Hyacinth was vague, save on one point, as regards which she was passionately, fiercely firm; she was perfectly determined he should never go into a small shop. She would rather see him a bricklayer or a costermonger than dedicated to a retail business, tying up candles at a grocer's, or giving change for a shilling across a counter. She would rather, she declared on one occasion, see him articled to a shoemaker or a tailor.

A stationer in a neighbouring street had affixed to his window a written notice that he was in want of a smart errand-boy, and Pinnie, on hearing of it, had presented Hyacinth to his consideration. The stationer was a dreadful bullying man, with a patch over his eye, who seemed to think the boy would be richly remunerated with three shillings a week; a contemptible measure, as it seemed to the dressmaker, of his rare abilities and acquirements. His schooling had been desultory, precarious, and had had a certain continuity mainly in his early years, while he was under the care of an old lady who combined with the functions of pew-opener at a neighbouring church the manipulation, in the Place itself, where she resided with her sister, a monthly nurse, of such pupils as could be spared (in their families) from the more urgent exercise of holding the baby and fetching the beer. Later, for a twelvemonth, Pinnie had paid five shillings a week for him at an 'Academy' in a genteel part of Islington, where there was an 'instructor in the foreign languages,' a platform for oratory, and a high social standard, but where Hyacinth suffered from the fact that almost all his mates were the sons of dealers in edible articles—pastry-cooks, grocers and fishmongers—and in this capacity subjected him to pangs and ignominious contrasts by bringing to school, for their exclusive consumption, or for exchange and barter, various buns, oranges, spices, and marine animals, which the boy, with his hands in his empty pockets and the sense of a savourless home in his heart, was obliged to see devoured without his participation. Miss Pynsent would not have pretended that he was highly educated, in the technical sense of the word, but she believed that at fifteen he had read almost every book in the world. The limits of his reading were, in fact, only the limits of his opportunity. Mr. Vetch, who talked with him more and more as he grew older, knew this, and lent him every volume he possessed or could pick up for the purpose. Reading was his happiness, and the absence of any direct contact with a library his principal source of discontent; that is, of that part of his discontent which he could speak out. Mr. Vetch knew that he was really clever, and therefore thought it a woful pity that he could not have furtherance in some liberal walk; but he would have thought it a greater pity still that so bright a lad should be condemned to measure tape or cut slices of cheese. He himself had no influence which he could bring into play, no connection with the great world of capital or the market of labour. That is, he touched these mighty institutions at but one very small point—a point which, such as it was, he kept well in mind.

When Pinnie replied to the stationer round the corner, after he had mentioned the 'terms' on which he was prepared to receive applications from errand-boys, that, thank heaven, she hadn't sunk so low as that—so low as to sell her darling into slavery for three shillings a week—he felt that she only gave more florid expression to his own sentiment. Of course, if Hyacinth did not begin by carrying parcels he could not hope to be promoted, through the more refined nimbleness of tying them up, to a position as accountant or bookkeeper; but both the fiddler and his friend—Miss Pynsent, indeed, only in the last resort—resigned themselves to the forfeiture of this prospect. Mr. Vetch saw clearly that a charming handicraft was a finer thing than a vulgar 'business,' and one day, after his acquaintance with Eustache Poupin had gone a considerable length, he inquired of the Frenchman whether there would be a chance of the lad's obtaining a footing, under his own wing, in Mr. Crookenden's workshop. There could be no better place for him to acquire a knowledge of the most delightful of the mechanical arts; and to be received into such an establishment, and at the instance of such an artist, would be a real start in life. M. Poupin meditated, and that evening confided his meditations to the companion who reduplicated all his thoughts and understood him better even than he understood himself. The pair had no children, and had felt the defect; moreover, they had heard from Mr. Vetch the dolorous tale of the boy's entrance into life. He was one of the disinherited, one of the expropriated, one of the exceptionally interesting; and moreover he was one of themselves, a child, as it were, of France, an offshoot of the sacred race. It is not the most authenticated point in this veracious history, but there is strong reason to believe that tears were shed that night, in Lisson Grove, over poor little Hyacinth Robinson. In a day or two M. Poupin replied to the fiddler that he had now been several years in Mr. Crookenden's employ; that during that time he had done work for him that he would have had *bien du mal* to get done by another, and had never asked for an indulgence, an allowance, a remission, an augmentation. It was time, if only for the dignity of the thing, he should ask for something, and he would make their little friend the subject of his demand. '*La société lui doit bien cela,*' he remarked afterwards, when, Mr. Crookenden proving drily hospitable and the arrangement being formally complete, Mr. Vetch thanked him, in his kindly, casual, bashful English way. He was paternal when Hyacinth began to occupy a place in the malodorous chambers in Soho; he took him in hand, made him a disciple, the recipient of a precious tradition, discovered in him a susceptibility to philosophic as well as technic truth. He taught him French and socialism, encouraged him to spend his evenings in Lisson Grove, invited him to regard Madame Poupin as a second, or rather as a third, mother, and in short made a very considerable mark on the boy's mind. He elicited the latent Gallicism of his nature, and by the time he was twenty Hyacinth, who had completely assimilated his influence, regarded him with a mixture of veneration and amusement. M. Poupin was the person who consoled him most when he was miserable; and he was very often miserable.

His staying away from his work was so rare that, in the afternoon, before he went home, Hyacinth walked to Lisson Grove to see what ailed him. He found his friend in bed, with a plaster on his chest, and Madame Poupin making *tisane* over the fire. The Frenchman took his indisposition solemnly but resignedly, like a man who believed that all illness was owing to the imperfect organisation of society, and lay covered up to his chin, with a red cotton handkerchief bound round his head. Near his bed sat a visitor, a young man unknown to Hyacinth. Hyacinth, naturally, had never been to Paris, but he always supposed that the *intérieur* of his friends in Lisson Grove gave rather a vivid idea of that city. The two small rooms which constituted their establishment contained a great many mirrors, as well as little portraits (old-fashioned prints) of revolutionary heroes. The chimney-piece, in the bedroom, was muffled in some red drapery, which appeared to Hyacinth extraordinarily magnificent; the principal ornament of the salon was a group of small and highly-decorated cups, on a tray, accompanied by gilt bottles and glasses, the latter still more diminutive—the whole intended for black coffee and liqueurs. There was no carpet on the floor, but rugs and mats, of various shapes and sizes, disposed themselves at the feet of the chairs and sofas; and in the sitting-room, where there was a wonderful gilt clock, of the Empire, surmounted with a 'subject' representing Virtue receiving a crown of laurel from the hands of Faith, Madame Poupin, with the aid of a tiny stove, a handful of charcoal, and two or three saucepans, carried on a triumphant *cuisine*. In the windows were curtains of white muslin, much fluted and frilled, and tied with pink ribbon.

VII

'I AM suffering extremely, but we must all suffer, so long as the social question is so abominably, so iniquitously neglected,' Poupin remarked, speaking French and rolling toward Hyacinth his salient, excited-looking eyes, which always had the same proclaiming, challenging expression, whatever his occupation or his topic. Hyacinth had seated himself near his friend's pillow, opposite the strange young man, who had been accommodated with a chair at the foot of the bed.

'Ah, yes; with their filthy politics the situation of the *pauvre monde* is the last thing they ever think of!' his wife exclaimed, from the fire. 'There are times when I ask myself how long it will go on.'

'It will go on till the measure of their imbecility, their infamy, is full. It will go on till the day of justice, till the reintegration of the despoiled and disinherited, is ushered in with an irresistible force.'

'Oh, we always see things go on; we never see them change,' said Madame Poupin, making a very cheerful clatter with a big spoon in a saucepan.

'We may not see it, but *they'll* see it,' her husband rejoined. 'But what do I say, my children? I do see it,' he pursued. 'It's before my eyes, in its luminous reality, especially as I lie here—the revendication, the rehabilitation, the rectification.'

Hyacinth ceased to pay attention, not because he had a differing opinion about what M. Poupin called the *avènement* of the disinherited, but, on the contrary, precisely on account of his familiarity with that prospect. It was the constant theme of his French friends, whom he had long since perceived to be in a state of chronic spiritual inflammation. For them the social question was always in order, the political question always abhorrent, the disinherited always present. He wondered at their zeal, their continuity, their vivacity, their incorruptibility; at the abundant supply of conviction and prophecy which they always had on hand. He believed that at bottom he was sorer than they, yet he had deviations and lapses, moments when the social question bored him and he forgot not only his own wrongs, which would have been pardonable, but those of the people at large, of his brothers and sisters in misery. They, however, were perpetually in the breach, and perpetually consistent with themselves and, what is more, with each other. Hyacinth had heard that the institution of marriage in France was rather lightly considered, but he was struck with the closeness and intimacy of the union in Lisson Grove, the passionate identity of interest: especially on the day when M. Poupin informed him, in a moment of extreme but not indiscreet expansion, that the lady was his wife only in a spiritual, transcendental sense. There were hypocritical concessions and debasing superstitions of which this exalted pair wholly disapproved. Hyacinth knew their vocabulary by heart, and could have said everything, in the same words, that on any given occasion M. Poupin was likely to say. He knew that 'they,' in their phraseology, was a comprehensive allusion to every one in the world but the people—though who, exactly, in their length and breadth, the people were was less definitely established. He himself was of this sacred body, for which the future was to have such compensations; and so, of course, were the Frenchman and his consort, and so was Pinnie, and so were most of the inhabitants of Lomax Place and the workmen in old Crookenden's shop. But was old Crookenden himself, who wore an apron rather dirtier than the rest of them and was a master-hand at 'forwarding,' but who, on the other side, was the occupant of a villa almost detached, at Putney, with a wife known to have secret aspirations toward a page in buttons? Above all, was Mr. Vetch, who earned a weekly wage, and not a large one, with his fiddle, but who had mysterious affinities of another sort, reminiscences of a phase in which he smoked cigars, had a hat-box and used cabs—besides visiting Boulogne? Anastasius Vetch had interfered in his life, atrociously, in a terrible crisis; but Hyacinth, who strove to cultivate justice in his own conduct, believed he had acted conscientiously and tried to esteem him, the more so as the fiddler evidently felt that he had something to make up to him and had treated him with marked benevolence for years. He believed, in short, that Mr. Vetch took a sincere interest in him, and if he should meddle again would meddle in a different way: he used to see him sometimes looking at him with the kindest eyes. It would make a difference, therefore, whether he were of the people or not, inasmuch as in the day of the great revenge it would only be the people who should be saved. It was for the people the world was made: whoever was not of them was against them; and all others were cumberers, usurpers, exploiters, *accapareurs*, as M. Poupin used to say. Hyacinth had once put the question directly to Mr. Vetch, who looked at him a while through the fumes of his eternal pipe and then said, 'Do you think I'm an aristocrat?'

'I didn't know but you were a *bourgeois*,' the young man answered.

'No, I'm neither. I'm a Bohemian.'

'With your evening dress, every night?'

'My dear boy,' said the fiddler, 'those are the most confirmed.'

Hyacinth was only half satisfied with this, for it was by no means definite to him that Bohemians were also to be saved; if he could be sure, perhaps he would become one himself. Yet he never suspected Mr. Vetch of being a 'spy,' though Eustache Poupin had told him that there were a great many who looked a good deal like that: not, of course, with any purpose of incriminating the fiddler, whom he had trusted from the first and continued to trust. The middle-class spy became a very familiar type to Hyacinth, and though he had never caught one of the infamous brotherhood in the act, there were plenty of persons to whom, on the very face of the matter, he had no hesitation in attributing the character. There was nothing of the Bohemian, at any rate, about the Poupins, whom Hyacinth had now known long enough not to be surprised at the way they combined the socialistic passion, a red-hot impatience for the general rectification, with an extraordinary decency of life and a worship of proper work. The Frenchman spoke, habitually, as if the great swindle practised upon the people were too impudent to be endured a moment longer, and yet he found patience for the most exquisite 'tooling,' and took a book in hand with the deliberation of one who should believe that everything was immutably constituted. Hyacinth knew what he thought of priests and theologies, but he had the religion of conscientious craftsmanship, and he reduced the boy, on his side, to a kind of prostration before his delicate, wonder-working fingers. 'What will you have? *J'ai la main parisienne,*' M. Poupin would reply modestly, when Hyacinth's admiration broke out; and he was good enough, after he had seen a few specimens of what our hero could do, to inform him that *he* had the same happy conformation. 'There is no reason why you shouldn't be a good workman, *il n'y a que ça;*' and his own life was practically governed by this conviction. He delighted in the use of his hands and his tools and the exercise of his taste, which was faultless, and Hyacinth could easily imagine how it must torment him to spend a day on his back. He ended by perceiving, however, that consolation was, on this occasion, in some degree conveyed by the presence of the young man who sat at the foot of the bed, and with whom M. Poupin exhibited such signs of acquaintance as to make our hero wonder why he had not seen him before, nor even heard of him.

'What do you mean by an irresistible force?' the young man inquired, leaning back in his chair, with raised arms and his interlocked hands behind him, supporting his head. M. Poupin had spoken French, which he always preferred to do, the insular tongue being an immense tribulation to him; but his visitor spoke English, and Hyacinth immediately perceived that there was nothing French about *him*—M. Poupin could never tell him he had *la main parisienne.*

'I mean a force that will make the bourgeois go down into their cellars and hide, pale with fear, behind their barrels of wine and their heaps of gold!' cried M. Poupin, rolling terrible eyes.

'And in this country, I hope in their coal-bins. *Là-là,* we shall find them even there,' his wife remarked.

''89 was an irresistible force,' said M. Poupin. 'I believe you would have thought so if you had been there.'

'And so was the entrance of the Versaillais, which sent you over here, ten years ago,' the young man rejoined. He saw that Hyacinth was watching him, and he met his eyes, smiling a little, in a way that added to our hero's interest.

'*Pardon, pardon,* I resist!' cried Eustache Poupin, glaring, in

his improvised nightcap, out of his sheets; and Madame repeated that they resisted—she believed well that they resisted! The young man burst out laughing; whereupon his
host declared, with a dignity which even his recumbent position did not abate, that it was really frivolous of him to ask
such questions as that, knowing as he did—what he did
know.

'Yes, I know—I know,' said the young man, good-
naturedly, lowering his arms and thrusting his hands into his
pockets, while he stretched his long legs a little. 'But everything is yet to be tried.'

'Oh, the trial will be on a great scale—*soyez tranquille!* It
will be one of those experiments that constitute a proof.'

Hyacinth wondered what they were talking about, and perceived that it must be something important, for the stranger
was not a man who would take an interest in anything else.
Hyacinth was immensely struck with him—he could see that
he was remarkable—and felt slightly aggrieved that he should
be a stranger: that is, that he should be, apparently, a familiar
of Lisson Grove and yet that M. Poupin should not have
thought his young friend from Lomax Place worthy, up to
this time, to be made acquainted with him. I know not to
what degree the visitor in the other chair discovered these
reflections in Hyacinth's face, but after a moment, looking
across at him, he said in a friendly yet just slightly diffident
way, a way our hero liked, 'And do you know, too?'

'Do I know what?' asked Hyacinth, wondering.

'Oh, if you did, you would!' the young man exclaimed,
laughing again. Such a rejoinder, from any one else, would
have irritated our sensitive hero, but it only made Hyacinth
more curious about his interlocutor, whose laugh was loud
and extraordinarily gay.

'*Mon ami*, you ought to present *ces messieurs*,' Madame
Poupin remarked.

'*Ah ça*, is that the way you trifle with state secrets?' her
husband cried out, without heeding her. Then he went on,
in a different tone: 'M. Hyacinthe is a gifted child, *un enfant
très-doué*, in whom I take a tender interest—a child who has
an account to settle. Oh, a thumping big one! Isn't it so,
mon petit?'

This was very well meant, but it made Hyacinth blush, and, without knowing exactly what to say, he murmured shyly, 'Oh, I only want them to let me alone!'

'He is very young,' said Eustache Poupin.

'He is the person we have seen in this country whom we like the best,' his wife added.

'Perhaps you are French,' suggested the strange young man.

The trio seemed to Hyacinth to be waiting for his answer to this; it was as if a listening stillness had fallen upon them. He found it a difficult moment, partly because there was something exciting and embarrassing in the attention of the other visitor, and partly because he had never yet had to decide that important question. He didn't really know whether he were French or English, or which of the two he should prefer to be. His mother's blood, her suffering in an alien land, the unspeakable, irremediable misery that consumed her, in a place, among a people, she must have execrated— all this made him French; yet he was conscious at the same time of qualities that did not mix with it. He had evolved, long ago, a legend about his mother, built it up slowly, adding piece to piece, in passionate musings and broodings, when his cheeks burned and his eyes filled; but there were times when it wavered and faded, when it ceased to console him and he ceased to trust it. He had had a father too, and his father had suffered as well, and had fallen under a blow, and had paid with his life; and him also he felt in his mind and his body, when the effort to think it out did not simply end in darkness and confusion, challenging still even while they baffled, and inevitable freezing horror. At any rate, he seemed rooted in the place where his wretched parents had expiated, and he knew nothing about any other. Moreover, when old Poupin said, 'M. Hyacinthe,' as he had often done before, he didn't altogether enjoy it; he thought it made his name, which he liked well enough in English, sound like the name of a hair-dresser. Our young friend was under a cloud and a stigma, but he was not yet prepared to admit that he was ridiculous. 'Oh, I daresay I ain't anything,' he replied in a moment.

'*En v'là des bêtises!*' cried Madame Poupin. 'Do you mean to say you are not as good as any one in the world? I should like to see!'

'We all have an account to settle, don't you know?' said the strange young man.

He evidently meant this to be encouraging to Hyacinth, whose quick desire to avert M. Poupin's allusions had not been lost upon him; but our hero could see that he himself would be sure to be one of the first to be paid. He would make society bankrupt, but he would be paid. He was tall and fair and good-natured looking, but you couldn't tell—or at least Hyacinth couldn't—whether he were handsome or ugly, with his large head and square forehead, his thick, straight hair, his heavy mouth and rather vulgar nose, his admirably clear, bright eye, light-coloured and set very deep; for though there was a want of fineness in some of its parts, his face had a marked expression of intelligence and resolution, and denoted a kind of joyous moral health. He was dressed like a workman in his Sunday toggery, having evidently put on his best to call in Lisson Grove, where he was to meet a lady, and wearing in particular a necktie which was both cheap and pretentious, and of which Hyacinth, who noticed everything of that kind, observed the crude, false blue. He had very big shoes—the shoes, almost, of a country labourer—and spoke with a provincial accent, which Hyacinth believed to be that of Lancashire. This didn't suggest cleverness, but it didn't prevent Hyacinth from perceiving that he was the reverse of stupid, that he probably, indeed, had a tremendous head. Our little hero had a great desire to know superior people, and he interested himself on the spot in this strong, humorous fellow, who had the complexion of a ploughboy and the glance of a commander-in-chief and who might have been (Hyacinth thought) a distinguished young *savant* in the disguise of an artisan. The disguise would have been very complete, for he had several brown stains on his fingers. Hyacinth's curiosity, on this occasion, was both excited and gratified; for after two or three allusions, which he didn't understand, had been made to a certain place where Poupin and the stranger had met and expected to meet again, Madame Poupin exclaimed that it was a shame not to take in M. Hyacinthe, who, she would answer for it, had in him the making of one of the pure.

'All in good time, in good time, *ma bonne,*' the invalid replied. 'M. Hyacinthe knows that I count upon him, whether or no I make him an *interne* to-day or wait a while longer.'

'What do you mean by an interne?' Hyacinth asked.

'Mon Dieu, what shall I say!' and Eustache Poupin stared at him solemnly, from his pillow. 'You are very sympathetic, but I am afraid you are too young.'

'One is never too young to contribute one's *obole,*' said Madame Poupin.

'Can you keep a secret?' asked the other visitor, smilingly.

'Is it a plot—a conspiracy?' Hyacinth broke out.

'He asks that as if he were asking if it's a plum-pudding,' said M. Poupin. 'It isn't good to eat, and we don't do it for our amusement. It's terribly serious, my child.'

'It's a kind of society, to which he and I and a good many others belong. There is no harm in telling him that,' the young man went on.

'I advise you not to tell it to Mademoiselle; she is quite in the old ideas,' Madame Poupin suggested to Hyacinth, tasting her *tisane.*

Hyacinth sat baffled and wondering, looking from his fellow-labourer in Soho to his new acquaintance opposite. 'If you have some plan, something to which one can give one's self, I think you might have told me,' he remarked, in a moment, to Poupin.

The latter merely gazed at him a while; then he said to the strange young man, 'He is a little jealous of you. But there is no harm in that; it's of his age. You must know him, you must like him. We will tell you his history some other day; it will make you feel that he belongs to us in fact. It is an accident that he hasn't met you here before.'

'How could *ces messieurs* have met, when M. Paul never comes? He doesn't spoil us!' Madame Poupin cried.

'Well, you see I have my little sister at home to take care of, when I ain't at the shop,' M. Paul explained. 'This afternoon

it was just a chance; there was a lady we know came in to sit
with her.'

'A lady—a real lady?'

'Oh yes, every inch,' said M. Paul, laughing.

'Do you like them to thrust themselves into your apartment
like that, because you have the *désagrément* of being poor? It
seems to be the custom in this country, but it wouldn't suit
me at all,' Madame Poupin continued. 'I should like to see
one of *ces dames*—the real ones—coming in to sit with me!'

'Oh, you are not a cripple; you have got the use of your
legs!'

'Yes, and of my arms!' cried the Frenchwoman.

'This lady looks after several others in our court, and she
reads to my sister.'

'Oh, well, you are patient, you English.'

'We shall never do anything without that,' said M. Paul,
with undisturbed good-humour.

'You are perfectly right; you can't say that too often. It will
be a tremendous job, and only the strong will prevail,' his
host murmured, a little wearily, turning his eyes to Madame
Poupin, who approached slowly, holding the *tisane* in a rather
full bowl, and tasting it again and yet again as she came.

Hyacinth had been watching his fellow-visitor with deepening interest; a fact of which M. Paul apparently became aware,
for he said, presently, giving a little nod in the direction of
the bed, 'He says we ought to know each other. I'm sure I
have nothing against it. I like to know folk, when they're
worth it!'

Hyacinth was too pleased with this even to take it up; it
seemed to him, for a moment, that he couldn't touch it gracefully enough. But he said, with sufficient eagerness, 'Will you
tell me all about your plot?'

'Oh, it's no plot. I don't think I care much for plots.' And
with his mild, steady, light-blue English eye, M. Paul certainly
had not much the appearance of a conspirator.

'Isn't it a new era?' asked Hyacinth, rather disappointed.

'Well, I don't know; it's just a little movement.'

'*Ah bien, voilà du propre;* between us we have thrown him
into a fever!' cried Madame Poupin, who had put down her
bowl on a table near her husband's bed and was bending over

him, with her hand on his forehead. Eustache was flushed, he
had closed his eyes, and it was evident there had been more
than enough conversation. Madame Poupin announced as
much, with the addition that if the young men wished to
make acquaintance they must do it outside; the invalid must
be perfectly quiet. They accordingly withdrew, with apologies
and promises to return for further news on the morrow, and
two minutes afterward Hyacinth found himself standing face
to face with his new friend on the pavement in front of M.
Poupin's residence, under a street-lamp which struggled inef-
fectually with the brown winter dusk.

'Is that your name—M. Paul?' he asked, looking up at
him.

'Oh, bless you, no; that's only her Frenchified way of putting it. My name *is* Paul, though—Paul Muniment.'

'And what's your trade?' Hyacinth demanded, with a jump
into familiarity; for his companion seemed to have told him a
great deal more than was usually conveyed in that item of
information.

Paul Muniment looked down at him from above broad
shoulders. 'I work at a wholesale chemist's, at Lambeth.'

'And where do you live?'

'I live over the water, too; in the far south of London.'

'And are you going home now?'

'Oh yes, I am going to toddle.'

'And may I toddle with you?'

Mr. Muniment considered him further; then he gave a
laugh. 'I'll carry you, if you like.'

'Thank you; I expect I can walk as far as you,' said Hyacinth.

'Well, I admire your spirit, and I daresay I shall like your
company.'

There was something in his face, taken in connection with
the idea that he was concerned in a little movement, which
made Hyacinth feel the desire to go with him till he
dropped; and in a moment they started away together and
took the direction Muniment had mentioned. They discoursed as they went, and exchanged a great many opinions
and anecdotes; but they reached the south-westerly court in
which the young chemist lived with his infirm sister before

he had told Hyacinth anything definite about his little movement, or Hyacinth, on his side, had related to him the circumstances connected with his being, according to M. Poupin, one of the disinherited. Hyacinth didn't wish to press him; he would not for the world have appeared to him indiscreet; and, moreover, though he had taken so great a fancy to Muniment, he was not quite prepared, as yet, to be pressed. Therefore it did not become very clear to him how his companion had made Poupin's acquaintance and how long he had enjoyed it. Paul Muniment nevertheless was to a certain extent communicative about himself, and forewarned Hyacinth that he lived in a very poor little corner. He had his sister to keep—she could do nothing for herself; and he paid a low rent because she had to have doctors, and doses, and all sorts of little comforts. He spent a shilling a week for her on flowers. It was better, too, when you got upstairs, and from the back windows you could see the dome of St. Paul's. Audley Court, with its pretty name, which reminded Hyacinth of Tennyson, proved to be a still dingier nook than Lomax Place; and it had the further drawback that you had to pass through a narrow alley, a passage between high, black walls, to enter it. At the door of one of the houses the young men paused, lingering a little, and then Muniment said, 'I say, why shouldn't you come up? I like you well enough for that, and you can see my sister; her name is Rosy.' He spoke as if this would be a great privilege, and added, humorously, that Rosy enjoyed a call from a gentleman, of all things. Hyacinth needed no urging, and he groped his way, at his companion's heels, up a dark staircase, which appeared to him—for they stopped only when they could go no further—the longest and steepest he had ever ascended. At the top Paul Muniment pushed open a door, but exclaimed, 'Hullo, have you gone to roost?' on perceiving that the room on the threshold of which they stood was unlighted.

'Oh, dear, no; we are sitting in the dark,' a small, bright voice instantly replied. 'Lady Aurora is so kind; she's here still.'

The voice came out of a corner so pervaded by gloom that the speaker was indistinguishable. 'Dear me, that's beautiful!'

Paul Muniment rejoined. 'You'll have a party, then, for I have brought some one else. We are poor, you know, but I daresay we can manage a candle.'

At this, in the dim firelight, Hyacinth saw a tall figure erect itself—a figure angular and slim, crowned with a large, vague hat, surmounted, apparently, with a flowing veil. This unknown person gave a singular laugh, and said, 'Oh, I brought some candles; we could have had a light if we had wished it.' Both the tone and the purport of the words announced to Hyacinth that they proceeded from the lips of Lady Aurora.

VIII

PAUL MUNIMENT took a match out of his pocket and lighted it on the sole of his shoe; after which he applied it to a tallow candle which stood in a tin receptacle on the low mantel-shelf. This enabled Hyacinth to perceive a narrow bed in a corner, and a small figure stretched upon it—a figure revealed to him mainly by the bright fixedness of a pair of large eyes, of which the whites were sharply contrasted with the dark pupil, and which gazed at him across a counterpane of gaudy patchwork. The brown room seemed crowded with heterogeneous objects, and had, moreover, for Hyacinth, thanks to a multitude of small prints, both plain and coloured, fastened all over the walls, a highly-decorated appearance. The little person in the corner had the air of having gone to bed in a picture-gallery, and as soon as Hyacinth became aware of this his impression deepened that Paul Muniment and his sister were very remarkable people. Lady Aurora hovered before him with a kind of drooping erectness, laughing a good deal, vaguely and shyly, as if there were something rather awkward in her being found still on the premises. 'Rosy, girl, I've brought you a visitor,' Paul Muniment said. 'This young man has walked all the way from Lisson Grove to make your acquaintance.' Rosy continued to look at Hyacinth from over her counterpane, and he felt slightly embarrassed, for he had never yet been presented to a young lady in her position. 'You mustn't mind her being in bed—she's always in bed,' her brother went on. 'She's in bed just the same as a little trout is in the water.'

'Dear me, if I didn't receive company because I was in bed, there wouldn't be much use, would there, Lady Aurora?'

Rosy made this inquiry in a light, gay tone, darting her brilliant eyes at her companion, who replied instantly, with still greater hilarity, and in a voice which struck Hyacinth as strange and affected, 'Oh, dear, no, it seems quite the natural place!' Then she added, 'And it's such a pretty bed, such a comfortable bed!'

'Indeed it is, when your ladyship makes it up,' said Rosy; while Hyacinth wondered at this strange phenomenon of a peer's daughter (for he knew she must be that) performing the functions of a housemaid.

'I say, now, you haven't been doing that again to-day?' Muniment asked, punching the mattress of the invalid with a vigorous hand.

'Pray, who would, if I didn't?' Lady Aurora inquired. 'It only takes a minute, if one knows how.' Her manner was jocosely apologetic, and she seemed to plead guilty to having been absurd; in the dim light Hyacinth thought he saw her blush, as if she were much embarrassed. In spite of her blushing, her appearance and manner suggested to him a personage in a comedy. She sounded the letter *r* peculiarly.

'I can do it, beautifully. I often do it, when Mrs. Major doesn't come up,' Paul Muniment said, continuing to thump his sister's couch in an appreciative but somewhat subversive manner.

'Oh, I have no doubt whatever!' Lady Aurora exclaimed, quickly. 'Mrs. Major must have so very much to do.'

'Not in the making-up of beds, I'm afraid; there are only two or three, down there, for so many,' Paul Muniment remarked loudly, and with a kind of incongruous cheerfulness.

'Yes, I have thought a great deal about that. But there wouldn't be room for more, you know,' said Lady Aurora, this time in a very serious tone.

'There's not much room for a family of that sort anywhere—thirteen people of all ages and sizes,' the young man rejoined. 'The world's pretty big, but there doesn't seem room.'

'We are also thirteen at home,' said Lady Aurora, laughing again. 'We are also rather crowded.'

'Surely you don't mean at Inglefield?' Rosy inquired eagerly, in her dusky nook.

'I don't know about Inglefield. I am so much in town.' Hyacinth could see that Inglefield was a subject she wished to turn off, and to do so she added, 'We too are of all ages and sizes.'

'Well, it's fortunate you are not all *your* size!' Paul Muniment exclaimed, with a freedom at which Hyacinth was rather shocked, and which led him to suspect that, though his new friend was a very fine fellow, a delicate tact was not his main characteristic. Later he explained this by the fact that he was rural and provincial, and had not had, like himself, the benefit of metropolitan culture; and later still he asked himself what, after all, such a character as that had to do with tact or with compliments, and why its work in the world was not most properly performed by the simple exercise of a rude, manly strength.

At this familiar allusion to her stature Lady Aurora turned hither and thither, a little confusedly; Hyacinth saw her high, lean figure sway to and fro in the dim little room. Her commotion carried her to the door, and with ejaculations of which it was difficult to guess the meaning she was about to depart, when Rosy detained her, having evidently much more social art than Paul. 'Don't you see it's only because her ladyship is standing up that she's so, you gawk? We are not thirteen, at any rate, and we have got all the furniture we want, so that there's a chair for every one. Do be seated again, Lady Aurora, and help me to entertain this gentleman. I don't know your name, sir; perhaps my brother will mention it when he has collected his wits. I am very glad to see you, though I don't see you very well. Why shouldn't we light one of her ladyship's candles? It's very different to that common thing.'

Hyacinth thought Miss Muniment very charming: he had begun to make her out better by this time, and he watched her little wan, pointed face, framed, on the pillow, by thick black hair. She was a diminutive dark person, pale and wasted with a lifelong infirmity; Hyacinth thought her manner denoted high cleverness—he judged it impossible to tell her age. Lady Aurora said she ought to have gone, long since; but she seated herself, nevertheless, on the chair that Paul pushed towards her.

'Here's a go!' this young man exclaimed. 'You told me your name, but I've clean forgotten it.' Then, when Paul had announced it again, he said to his sister, 'That won't tell you much; there are bushels of Robinsons in the north. But you'll like him; he's a very smart little fellow; I met him at the Poupins.' 'Puppin' would represent the sound by which he designated the French bookbinder, and that was the name by which Hyacinth always heard him called at Mr. Crookenden's. Hyacinth knew how much nearer to the right thing he himself came.

'Your name, like mine, represents a flower,' said the little woman in the bed. 'Mine is Rose Muniment, and her ladyship's is Aurora Langrish. That means the morning, or the dawn; it's the most beautiful of all, don't you think so?' Rose Muniment addressed this inquiry to Hyacinth, while Lady Aurora gazed at her shyly and mutely, as if she admired her manner, her self-possession and flow of conversation. Her brother lighted one of the visitor's candles, and the girl went on, without waiting for Hyacinth's response: 'Isn't it right that she should be called the dawn, when she brings light where she goes? The Puppins are the charming foreigners I have told you about,' she explained to her friend.

'Oh, it's so pleasant knowing a few foreigners!' Lady Aurora exclaimed, with a spasm of expression. 'They are often so very fresh.'

'Mr. Robinson's a sort of foreigner, and he's very fresh,' said Paul Muniment. 'He meets Mr. Puppin quite on his own ground. If I had his command of the lingo it would give me a lift.'

'I'm sure I should be very happy to help you with your French. I feel the advantage of knowing it,' Hyacinth remarked, finely, and became conscious that his declaration drew the attention of Lady Aurora towards him; so that he wondered what he could go on to say, to keep at that level. This was the first time he had encountered, socially, a member of that aristocracy to which he had now for a good while known it was Miss Pynsent's theory that he belonged; and the occasion was interesting, in spite of the lady's appearing to have so few of the qualities of her caste. She was about thirty years of age; her nose was large and, in spite of the sudden retreat of her chin, her face was long and lean. She had the manner of extreme near-sightedness; her front teeth projected from her upper gums, which she revealed when she smiled, and her fair hair, in tangled, silky skeins (Rose Muniment thought it too lovely), drooped over her pink cheeks. Her clothes looked as if she had worn them a good deal in the rain, and the note of a certain disrepair in her apparel was given by a hole in one of her black gloves, through which a white finger gleamed. She was plain and diffident, and she might have been poor; but in the fine grain and sloping, shrinking slimness of her whole person, the delicacy of her curious features, and a kind of cultivated quality in her sweet, vague, civil expression, there was a suggestion of race, of long transmission, of an organism highly evolved. She was not a common woman; she was one of the caprices of an aristocracy. Hyacinth did not define her in this manner to himself, but he received from her the impression that, though she was a simple creature (which he learned later she was not), aristocracies were complicated things. Lady Aurora remarked that there were many delightful books in French, and Hyacinth rejoined that it was a torment to know that (as he did, very well), when you didn't see your way to getting hold of them. This led Lady Aurora to say, after a moment's hesitation, that she had a good lot of her own and that if he liked she should be most happy to lend them to him. Hyacinth thanked her —thanked her even too much, and felt both the kindness and the brilliant promise of the offer (he knew the exasperation of having volumes in his hands, for external treatment, which he couldn't take home at night, having tried that system, surreptitiously, during his first weeks at Mr. Crookenden's and come very near losing his place in consequence), while he wondered how it could be put into practice—whether she would expect him to call at her house and wait in the hall till the books were sent out to him. Rose Muniment exclaimed that that was her ladyship all over—always wanting to make up to people for being less fortunate than herself: she would take the shoes off her feet for any one that might take a fancy to them. At this the visitor declared that she would stop coming to see her, if the girl caught her up, that way, for everything; and Rosy, without heeding this remonstrance, explained to Hyacinth that she thought it the least she could do to give what she had. She was so ashamed of being rich that she wondered the lower classes didn't break into Inglefield and take possession of all the treasures in the Italian room. She was a tremendous socialist; she was worse than any one—she was worse, even, than Paul.

'I wonder if she is worse than me,' Hyacinth said, at a venture, not understanding the allusions to Inglefield and the Italian room, which Miss Muniment made as if she knew all about these places. After Hyacinth knew more of the world he remembered this tone of Muniment's sister (he was to have plenty of observation of it on other occasions) as that of a person who was in the habit of visiting the nobility at their country-seats; she talked about Inglefield as if she had stayed there.

'Hullo, I didn't know you were so advanced!' exclaimed Paul Muniment, who had been sitting silent, sidewise, in a chair that was too narrow for him, with his big arm hugging the back. 'Have we been entertaining an angel unawares?'

Hyacinth seemed to see that he was laughing at him, but he knew the way to face that sort of thing was to exaggerate his meaning. 'You didn't know I was advanced? Why, I thought that was the principal thing about me. I think I go about as far as it is possible to go.'

'I thought the principal thing about you was that you knew French,' Paul Muniment said, with an air of derision which showed Hyacinth that he wouldn't put that ridicule upon him unless he liked him, at the same time that it revealed to him that he himself had just been posturing a little.

'Well, I don't know it for nothing. I'll say something very neat and sharp to you, if you don't look out—just the sort of thing they say so much in French.'

'Oh, do say something of that kind; we should enjoy it so much!' cried Rosy, in perfect good faith, clasping her hands in expectation.

The appeal was embarrassing, but Hyacinth was saved from the consequences of it by a remark from Lady Aurora, who quavered out the words after two or three false starts, appearing to address him, now that she spoke to him directly, with a sort of overdone consideration. 'I should like so very much to know—it would be so interesting—if you don't mind—how far exactly you do go.' She threw back her head very far, and thrust her shoulders forward, and if her chin had been more adapted to such a purpose would have appeared to point it at him.

This challenge was hardly less alarming than the other, for

Hyacinth was far from having ascertained the extent of his advance. He replied, however, with an earnestness with which he tried to make up as far as possible for his vagueness: 'Well, I'm very strong indeed. I think I see my way to conclusions, from which even Monsieur and Madame Poupin would shrink. Poupin, at any rate; I'm not so sure about his wife.'

'I should like so much to know Madame,' Lady Aurora murmured, as if politeness demanded that she should content herself with this answer.

'Oh, Puppin isn't strong,' said Muniment; 'you can easily look over his head! He has a sweet assortment of phrases —they are really pretty things to hear, some of them; but he hasn't had a new idea these thirty years. It's the old stock that has been withering in the window. All the same, he warms one up; he has got a spark of the sacred fire. The principal conclusion that Mr. Robinson sees his way to,' he added to Lady Aurora, 'is that your father ought to have his head chopped off and carried on a pike.'

'Ah, yes, the French Revolution.'

'Lord, I don't know anything about your father, my lady!' Hyacinth interposed.

'Didn't you ever hear of the Earl of Inglefield?' cried Rose Muniment.

'He is one of the best,' said Lady Aurora, as if she were pleading for him.

'Very likely, but he is a landlord, and he has an hereditary seat and a park of five thousand acres all to himself, while we are bundled together into this sort of kennel.' Hyacinth admired the young man's consistency until he saw that he was chaffing; after which he still admired the way he mixed up merriment with the tremendous opinions our hero was sure he entertained. In his own imagination Hyacinth associated bitterness with the revolutionary passion; but the young chemist, at the same time that he was planning far ahead, seemed capable of turning revolutionists themselves into ridicule, even for the entertainment of the revolutionised.

'Well, I have told you often enough that I don't go with you at all,' said Rose Muniment, whose recumbency appeared not in the least to interfere with her sense of responsibility. 'You'll make a tremendous mistake if you try to turn everything round. There ought to be differences, and high and low, and there always will be, true as ever I lie here. I think it's against everything, pulling down them that's above.'

'Everything points to great changes in this country, but if once our Rosy's against them, how can you be sure? That's the only thing that makes me doubt,' her brother went on, looking at her with a placidity which showed the habit of indulgence.

'Well, I may be ill, but I ain't buried, and if I'm content with my position—such a position as it is—surely other folk might be with theirs. Her ladyship may think I'm as good as her, if she takes that notion; but she'll have a deal to do to make *me* believe it.'

'I think you are much better than I, and I know very few people so good as you,' Lady Aurora remarked, blushing, not for her opinions, but for her timidity. It was easy to see that, though she was original, she would have liked to be even more original than she was. She was conscious, however, that such a declaration might appear rather gross to persons who didn't see exactly how she meant it; so she added, as quickly as her hesitating manner permitted, to cover it up, 'You know there's one thing you ought to remember, *àpropos* of revolutions and changes and all that sort of thing; I just mention it because we were talking of some of the dreadful things that were done in France. If there were to be a great disturbance in this country—and of course one hopes there won't—it would be my impression that the people would behave in a different way altogether.'

'What people do you mean?' Hyacinth allowed himself to inquire.

'Oh, the upper class, the people that have got all the things.'

'We don't call them the people,' observed Hyacinth, reflecting the next instant that his remark was a little primitive.

'I suppose you call them the wretches, the villains!' Rose Muniment suggested, laughing merrily.

'All the things, but not all the brains,' her brother said.

'No, indeed, aren't they stupid?' exclaimed her ladyship. 'All the same, I don't think they would go abroad.'

'Go abroad?'

'I mean like the French nobles, who emigrated so much. They would stay at home and resist; they would make more of a fight. I think they would fight very hard.'

'I'm delighted to hear it, and I'm sure they would win!' cried Rosy.

'They wouldn't collapse, don't you know,' Lady Aurora continued. 'They would struggle till they were beaten.'

'And you think they would be beaten in the end?' Hyacinth asked.

'Oh dear, yes,' she replied, with a familiar brevity at which he was greatly surprised. 'But of course one hopes it won't happen.'

'I infer from what you say that they talk it over a good deal among themselves, to settle the line they will take,' said Paul Muniment.

But Rosy intruded before Lady Aurora could answer. 'I think it's wicked to talk it over, and I'm sure we haven't any business to talk it over here! When her ladyship says that the aristocracy will make a fine stand, I like to hear her say it, and I think she speaks in a manner that becomes her own position. But there is something else in her tone which, if I may be allowed to say so, I think a great mistake. If her ladyship expects, in case of the lower classes coming up in that odious manner, to be let off easily, for the sake of the concessions she may have made in advance, I would just advise her to save herself the disappointment and the trouble. They won't be a bit the wiser, and they won't either know or care. If they are going to trample over their betters, it isn't on account of her having seemed to give up everything to us here that they will let *her* off. They will trample on her just the same as on the others, and they'll say that she has got to pay for her title and her grand relations and her fine appearance. Therefore I advise her not to waste her good nature in trying to let herself down. When you're up so high as that you've got to stay there; and if Providence has made you a lady, the best thing you can do is to hold up your head. I can promise your ladyship *I* would!'

The close logic of this speech and the quaint self-possession with which the little bedridden speaker delivered it struck

Hyacinth as amazing, and confirmed his idea that the brother and sister were a most extraordinary pair. It had a terrible effect upon poor Lady Aurora, by whom so stern a lesson from so humble a quarter had evidently not been expected, and who sought refuge from her confusion in a series of bewildered laughs, while Paul Muniment, with his humorous density, which was deliberate, and clever too, not seeing, or at any rate not heeding, that she had been sufficiently snubbed by his sister, inflicted a fresh humiliation by saying, 'Rosy's right, my lady. It's no use trying to buy yourself off. You can't do enough; your sacrifices don't count. You spoil your fun now, and you don't get it made up to you later. To all you people nothing will ever be made up. Enjoy your privileges while they last; it may not be for long.'

Lady Aurora listened to him with her eyes on his face; and as they rested there Hyacinth scarcely knew what to make of her expression. Afterwards he thought he could attach a meaning to it. She got up quickly when Muniment had ceased speaking; the movement suggested that she had taken offence, and he would have liked to show her that he thought she had been rather roughly used. But she gave him no chance, not glancing at him for a moment. Then he saw that he was mistaken and that, if she had flushed considerably, it was only with the excitement of pleasure, the enjoyment of such original talk and of seeing her friends at last as free and familiar as she wished them to be. 'You are the most delightful people—I wish every one could know you!' she broke out. 'But I must really be going.' She went to the bed, and bent over Rosy and kissed her.

'Paul will see you as far as you like on your way home,' this young woman remarked.

Lady Aurora protested against this, but Paul, without protesting in return, only took up his hat and looked at her, smiling, as if he knew his duty; upon which her ladyship said, 'Well, you may see me downstairs; I forgot it was so dark.'

'You must take her ladyship's own candle, and you must call a cab,' Rosy directed.

'Oh, I don't go in cabs. I walk.'

'Well, you may go on the top of a 'bus, if you like; you

can't help being superb,' Miss Muniment declared, watching her sympathetically.

'Superb? Oh, mercy!' cried the poor devoted, grotesque lady, leaving the room with Paul, who asked Hyacinth to wait for him a little. She neglected to bid good-night to our young man, and he asked himself what was to be hoped from that sort of people, when even the best of them—those that wished to be agreeable to the *demos*—reverted inevitably to the supercilious. She had said no more about lending him her books.

IX

'S HE LIVES in Belgrave Square; she has ever so many brothers and sisters; one of her sisters is married to Lord Warmington,' Rose Muniment instantly began, not apparently in the least discomposed at being left alone with a strange young man in a room which was now half dark again, thanks to her brother's having carried off the second and more brilliant candle. She was so interested, for the time, in telling Hyacinth the history of Lady Aurora, that she appeared not to remember how little she knew about himself. Her ladyship had dedicated her life and her pocket-money to the poor and sick; she cared nothing for parties, and races, and dances, and picnics, and life in great houses, the usual amusements of the aristocracy; she was like one of the saints of old come to life again out of a legend. She had made their acquaintance, Paul's and hers, about a year before, through a friend of theirs, such a fine, brave, young woman, who was in St. Thomas's Hospital for a surgical operation. She had been laid up there for weeks, during which Lady Aurora, always looking out for those who couldn't help themselves, used to come and talk to her and read to her, till the end of her time in the ward, when the poor girl, parting with her kind friend, told her how she knew of another unfortunate creature (for whom there was no place there, because she was incurable), who would be mighty thankful for any little attention of that sort. She had given Lady Aurora the address in Audley Court, and the very next day her ladyship had knocked at their door. It wasn't because she was poor—though in all conscience they were pinched enough—but because she had so little satisfaction in her limbs. Lady Aurora came very often, for several months, without meeting Paul, because he was always at his work; but one day he came home early, on purpose to find her, to thank her for her goodness, and also to see (Miss Muniment rather shyly intimated) whether she were really so good as his extravagant little sister made her out. Rosy had a triumph after that: Paul had to admit that her ladyship was beyond anything that any one in his waking senses would believe. She seemed to want to give up everything to those

96

who were below her, and never to expect any thanks at all. And she wasn't always preaching and showing you your duty; she wanted to talk to you sociable-like, as if you were just her own sister. And *her* own sisters were the highest in the land, and you might see her name in the newspapers the day they were presented to the Queen. Lady Aurora had been presented too, with feathers in her head and a long tail to her gown; but she had turned her back upon it all with a kind of terror—a sort of shivering, sinking feeling, which she had often described to Miss Muniment. The day she had first seen Paul was the day they became so intimate (the three of them together), if she might apply such a word as that to such a peculiar connection. The little woman, the little girl, as she lay there (Hyacinth scarcely knew how to characterise her), told our young man a very great secret, in which he found himself too much interested to think of criticising so headlong a burst of confidence. The secret was that, of all the people she had ever seen in the world, her ladyship thought Rosy's Paul the very cleverest. And she had seen the greatest, the most famous, the brightest of every kind, for they all came to stay at Inglefield, thirty and forty of them at once. She had talked with them all and heard them say their best (and you could fancy how they would try to give it out at such a place as that, where there was nearly a mile of conservatories and a hundred wax candles were lighted at a time), and at the end of it all she had made the remark to herself—and she had made it to Rosy too—that there was none of them had such a head on his shoulders as the young man in Audley Court. Rosy wouldn't spread such a rumour as that in the court itself, but she wanted every friend of her brother's (and she could see Hyacinth was that, by the way he listened) to know what was thought of him by them that had an experience of talent. She didn't wish to give it out that her ladyship had lowered herself in any manner to a person that earned his bread in a dirty shop (clever as he *might* be), but it was easy to see she minded what he said as if he had been a bishop—or more, indeed, for she didn't think much of bishops, any more than Paul himself, and that was an idea she had got from him. Oh, she took it none so ill if he came back from his work before she had gone; and to-night

Hyacinth could see for himself how she had lingered. This evening, she was sure, her ladyship would let him walk home with her half the way. This announcement gave Hyacinth the prospect of a considerable session with his communicative hostess; but he was very glad to wait, for he was vaguely, strangely excited by her talk, fascinated by the little queer-smelling, high-perched interior, encumbered with relics, treasured and polished, of a poor north-country home, bedecked with penny ornaments and related in so unexpected a manner to Belgrave Square and the great landed estates. He spent half an hour with Paul Muniment's small, odd, crippled, chattering, clever, trenchant sister, who gave him an impression of education and native wit (she expressed herself far better than Pinnie, or than Millicent Henning), and who startled, puzzled, and at the same time rather distressed, him by the manner in which she referred herself to the most abject class—the class that prostrated itself, that was in a fever and flutter in the presence of its betters. That was Pinnie's attitude, of course; but Hyacinth had long ago perceived that his adoptive mother had generations of plebeian patience in her blood, and that though she had a tender soul she had not a great one. He was more entertained than afflicted, however, by Miss Muniment's tone, and he was thrilled by the frequency and familiarity of her allusions to a kind of life he had often wondered about; this was the first time he had heard it described with that degree of authority. By the nature of his mind he was perpetually, almost morbidly, conscious that the circle in which he lived was an infinitesimally small, shallow eddy in the roaring vortex of London, and his imagination plunged again and again into the waves that whirled past it and round it, in the hope of being carried to some brighter, happier vision—the vision of societies in which, in splendid rooms, with smiles and soft voices, distinguished men, with women who were both proud and gentle, talked about art, literature and history. When Rosy had delivered herself to her complete satisfaction on the subject of Lady Aurora, she became more quiet, asking, as yet, however, no questions about Hyacinth, whom she seemed to take very much for granted. He presently remarked that she must let him come very soon again, and he added, to explain this wish, 'You know you seem to me very curious people.'

Miss Muniment did not in the least repudiate the imputation. 'Oh yes, I daresay we seem very curious. I think we are generally thought so; especially me, being so miserable and yet so lively.' And she laughed till her bed creaked again.

'Perhaps it's lucky you are ill; perhaps if you had your health you would be all over the place,' Hyacinth suggested. And he went on, candidly, 'I can't make it out, your being so up in everything.'

'I don't see why you need make it out! But you would, perhaps, if you had known my father and mother.'

'Were they such a rare lot?'

'I think you would say so if you had ever been in the mines. Yes, in the mines, where the filthy coal is dug out. That's where my father came from—he was working in the pit when he was a child of ten. He never had a day's schooling in his life; but he climbed up out of his black hole into daylight and air, and he invented a machine, and he married my mother, who came out of Durham, and (by her people) out of the pits and misery too. My father had no great figure, but *she* was magnificent—the finest woman in the country, and the bravest, and the best. She's in her grave now, and I couldn't go to look at it even if it were in the nearest churchyard. My father was as black as the coal he worked in: I know I'm just his pattern, barring that *he* did have his legs, when the liquor hadn't got into them. But between him and my mother, for grand, high intelligence there wasn't much to choose. But what's the use of brains if you haven't got a backbone? My poor father had even less of that than I, for with me it's only the body that can't stand up, and with him it was the spirit. He discovered a kind of wheel, and he sold it, at Bradford, for fifteen pounds: I mean the whole right of it, and every hope and pride of his family. He was always straying, and my mother was always bringing him back. She had plenty to do, with me a puny, ailing brat from the moment I opened my eyes. Well, one night he strayed so far that he never came back; or only came back a loose, bloody bundle of clothes. He had fallen into a gravel-pit; he didn't know where he was going. That's the reason my brother will never touch so much as you could wet your finger with, and that I only have a drop once a week or so, in the way of a strengthener. I take what her ladyship brings me, but I take no more. If she could have come to us before my mother went, that would have been a saving! I was only nine when my father died, and I'm three years older than Paul. My mother did for us with all her might, and she kept us decent—if such a useless little mess as me can be said to be decent. At any rate, she kept me alive, and that's a proof she was handy. She went to the wash-tub, and she might have been a queen, as she stood there with her bare arms in the foul linen and her long hair braided on her head. She was terrible handsome, but he would have been a bold man that would have taken upon himself to tell her so. And it was from her we got our education—she was determined we should rise above the common. You might have thought, in her position, that she couldn't go into such things; but she was a rare one for keeping you at your book. She could hold to her idea when my poor father couldn't; and her idea, for us, was that Paul should get learning and should look after me. You can see for yourself that that's what has come about. How he got it is more than I can say, as we never had a penny to pay for it; and of course my mother's cleverness wouldn't have been of much use if he hadn't been clever himself. Well, it was all in the family. Paul was a boy that would learn more from a yellow placard pasted on a wall, or a time-table at a railway station, than many a young fellow from a year at college. That was his only college, poor lad—picking up what he could. Mother was taken when she was still needed, nearly five years ago. There was an epidemic of typhoid, and of course it must pass me over, the goose of a thing—only that I'd have made a poor feast—and just lay that gallant creature on her back. Well, she never again made it ache over her soapsuds, straight and broad as it was. Not having seen her, you wouldn't believe,' said Rose Muniment, in conclusion; 'but I just wanted you to understand that our parents had intellect, at least, to give us.'

Hyacinth listened to this recital with the deepest interest, and without being in the least moved to allow for filial exaggeration; inasmuch as his impression of the brother and sister was such as it would have taken a much more marvellous tale to account for. The very way Rose Muniment sounded the word 'intellect' made him feel this; she pronounced it as if she were distributing prizes for a high degree of it. No doubt the tipsy inventor and the regal laundress had been fine specimens, but that didn't diminish the merit of their highly original offspring. The girl's insistence upon her mother's virtues (even now that her age had become more definite to him he thought of her as a girl) touched in his heart a chord that was always ready to throb—the chord of melancholy, bitter, aimless wonder as to the difference it would have made in *his* spirit if there had been some pure, honourable figure like that to shed her influence over it.

'Are you very fond of your brother?' he inquired, after a little.

The eyes of his hostess glittered at him for a moment. 'If you ever quarrel with him, you'll see whose side I'll take.'

'Ah, before that I shall make you like *me*.'

'That's very possible, and you'll see how I'll fling you over!'

'Why, then, do you object so to his views—his ideas about the way the people will come up?'

'Because I think he'll get over them.'

'Never—never!' cried Hyacinth. 'I have only known him an hour or two, but I deny that, with all my strength.'

'Is that the way you are going to make me like you—contradicting me so?' Miss Muniment inquired, with familiar archness.

'What's the use, when you tell me I shall be sacrificed? One might as well perish for a lamb as for a sheep.'

'I don't believe you're a lamb at all. Certainly you are not, if you want all the great people pulled down, and the most dreadful scenes enacted.'

'Don't you believe in human equality? Don't you want anything done for the groaning, toiling millions—those who have been cheated and crushed and bamboozled from the beginning of time?'

Hyacinth asked this question with considerable heat, but the effect of it was to send his companion off into a new fit of laughter. 'You say that just like a man that my brother described to me three days ago; a little man at some club, whose hair stood up—Paul imitated the way he glowered and screamed. I don't mean that you scream, you know; but you use almost the same words that he did.' Hyacinth scarcely knew what to make of this allusion, or of the picture offered to him of Paul Muniment casting ridicule upon those who spoke in the name of the down-trodden. But Rosy went on, before he had time to do more than reflect that there would evidently be a great deal more to learn about her brother: 'I haven't the least objection to seeing the people improved, but I don't want to see the aristocracy lowered an inch. I like so much to look at it up there.'

'You ought to know my aunt Pinnie—she's just such another benighted idolater!' Hyacinth exclaimed.

'Oh, you are making me like you very fast! And pray, who is your aunt Pinnie?'

'She's a dressmaker, and a charming little woman. I should like her to come and see you.'

'I'm afraid I'm not in her line—I never had on a dress in my life. But, as a charming woman, I should be delighted to see her.'

'I will bring her some day,' said Hyacinth. And then he added, rather incongruously, for he was irritated by the girl's optimism, thinking it a shame that her sharpness should be enlisted on the wrong side, 'Don't you want, for yourself, a better place to live in?'

She jerked herself up, and for a moment he thought she would jump out of her bed at him. 'A better place than this? Pray, how could there be a better place? Every one thinks it's lovely; you should see our view by daylight—you should see everything I've got. Perhaps you are used to something very fine, but Lady Aurora says that in all Belgrave Square there isn't such a cosy little room. If you think I'm not perfectly content, you are very much mistaken!'

Such a sentiment as that could only exasperate Hyacinth, and his exasperation made him indifferent to the fact that he had appeared to cast discredit on Miss Muniment's apartment. Pinnie herself, submissive as she was, had spared him that sort of displeasure; she groaned over the dinginess of Lomax Place sufficiently to remind him that she had not been absolutely stultified by misery. 'Don't you sometimes make your brother very angry?' he asked, smiling, of Rose Muniment.

'Angry? I don't know what you take us for! I never saw him lose his temper in his life.'

'He must be a rum customer! Doesn't he really care for —for what we were talking about?'

For a moment Rosy was silent; then she replied, 'What my brother really cares for—well, one of these days, when you know, you'll tell me.'

Hyacinth stared. 'But isn't he tremendously deep in——' He hesitated.

'Deep in what?'

'Well, in what's going on, beneath the surface. Doesn't he belong to things?'

'I'm sure I don't know what he belongs to—you may ask him!' cried Rosy, laughing gaily again, as the opening door readmitted the subject of their conversation. 'You must have crossed the water with her ladyship,' she went on. 'I wonder who enjoyed their walk most.'

'She's a handy old girl, and she has a goodish stride,' said the young man.

'I think she's in love with you, simply, Mr. Muniment.'

'Really, my dear, for an admirer of the aristocracy you allow yourself a license,' Paul murmured, smiling at Hyacinth.

Hyacinth got up, feeling that really he had paid a long visit; his curiosity was far from satisfied, but there was a limit to the time one should spend in a young lady's sleeping apartment. 'Perhaps she is; why not?' he remarked.

'Perhaps she is, then; she's daft enough for anything.'

'There have been fine folks before who have patted the people on the back and pretended to enter into their life,' Hyacinth said. 'Is she only playing with that idea, or is she in earnest?'

'In earnest—in terrible earnest, my dear fellow. I think she must be rather crowded out at home.'

'Crowded out of Inglefield? Why, there's room for three hundred!' Rosy broke in.

'Well, if that's the kind of mob that's in possession, no wonder she prefers Camberwell. We must be kind to the poor lady,' Paul added, in a tone which Hyacinth noticed. He attributed a remarkable meaning to it; it seemed to say that people such as he were now so sure of their game that they could afford to be magnanimous; or else it expressed a prevision of the doom which hung over her ladyship's head. Muniment asked if Hyacinth and Rosy had made friends, and the girl replied that Mr. Robinson had made himself very agreeable. 'Then you must tell me all about him after he goes, for you know I don't know him much myself,' said her brother.

'Oh yes, I'll tell you everything; you know how I like describing.'

Hyacinth was laughing to himself at the young lady's account of his efforts to please her, the fact being that he had only listened to her own eager discourse, without opening his mouth; but Paul, whether or no he guessed the truth, said to him very pertinently, 'It's very wonderful: she can describe things she has never seen. And they are just like the reality.'

'There's nothing I've never seen,' Rosy rejoined. 'That's the advantage of my lying here in such a manner. I see everything in the world.'

'You don't seem to see your brother's meetings—his secret societies and clubs. You put that aside when I asked you.'

'Oh, you mustn't ask her that sort of thing,' said Paul, lowering at Hyacinth with a fierce frown—an expression which he perceived in a moment to be humorously assumed.

'What am I to do, then, since you won't tell me anything definite yourself?'

'It will be definite enough when you get hanged for it!' Rosy exclaimed, mockingly.

'Why do you want to poke your head into black holes?' Muniment asked, laying his hand on Hyacinth's shoulder, and shaking it gently.

'Don't you belong to the party of action?' said Hyacinth, solemnly.

'Look at the way he has picked up all the silly bits of catchwords!' Paul cried, laughing, to his sister. 'You must have got that precious phrase out of the newspapers, out of some drivelling leader. Is that the party you want to belong to?' he went on, with his clear eyes ranging over his diminutive friend.

'If you'll show me the thing itself I shall have no more occasion to mind the newspapers,' Hyacinth pleaded. It was his view of himself, and it was not an unfair one, that his was a character that would never beg for a favour; but now he felt that in any relation he might have with Paul Muniment such a law would be suspended. This man he could entreat, pray to, go on his knees to, without a sense of humiliation.

'What thing do you mean, infatuated, deluded youth?' Paul went on, refusing to be serious.

'Well, you know you do go to places you had far better keep out of, and that often when I lie here and listen to steps on the stairs I'm sure they are coming in to make a search for your papers,' Miss Muniment lucidly interposed.

'The day they find my papers, my dear, will be the day you'll get up and dance.'

'What did you ask me to come home with you for?' Hyacinth demanded, twirling his hat. It was an effort for him, for a moment, to keep the tears out of his eyes; he found himself forced to put such a different construction on his new friend's hospitality. He had had a happy impression that Muniment perceived in him a possible associate, of a high type, in a subterranean crusade against the existing order of things, and now it came over him that the real use he had been put to was to beguile an hour for a pert invalid. That was all very well, and he would sit by Miss Rosy's bedside, were it a part of his service, every day in the week; only in such a case it should be his reward to enjoy the confidence of her brother. This young man, at the present juncture, justified the high estimate that Lady Aurora Langrish had formed of his intelligence: whatever his natural reply to Hyacinth's question would have been, he invented, at the moment, a better one, and said, at random, smiling, and not knowing exactly what his visitor had meant,

'What did I ask you to come with me for? To see if you would be afraid.'

What there was to be afraid of was to Hyacinth a quantity equally vague; but he rejoined, quickly enough, 'I think you have only to try me to see.'

'I'm sure if you introduce him to some of your low, wicked friends, he'll be quite satisfied after he has looked round a bit,' Miss Muniment remarked, irrepressibly.

'Those are just the kind of people I want to know,' said Hyacinth, ingenuously.

His ingenuousness appeared to touch Paul Muniment. 'Well, I see you're a good 'un. Just meet me some night.'

'Where, where?' asked Hyacinth, eagerly.

'Oh, I'll tell you where when we get away from *her*,' said his friend, laughing, but leading him out of the room again.

X

SEVERAL MONTHS after Hyacinth had made the acquaintance of Paul Muniment, Millicent Henning remarked to him that it was high time he should take her to some place of amusement. He proposed the Canterbury Music Hall; whereupon she tossed her head and affirmed that when a young lady had done for a young man what she had done for him, the least he could do was to take her to some theatre in the Strand. Hyacinth would have been a good deal at a loss to say exactly what she had done for him, but it was familiar to him by this time that she regarded him as under great obligations. From the day she came to look him up in Lomax Place she had taken a position, largely, in his life, and he had seen poor Pinnie's wan countenance grow several degrees more blank. Amanda Pynsent's forebodings had been answered to the letter; that bold-faced apparition had become a permanent influence. She never spoke to him about Millicent but once, several weeks after her interview with the girl; and this was not in a tone of rebuke, for she had divested herself for ever of any maternal prerogative. Tearful, tremulous, deferential inquiry was now her only weapon, and nothing could be more humble and circumspect than the manner in which she made use of it. He was never at home of an evening, at present, and he had mysterious ways of spending his Sundays, with which church-going had nothing to do. The time had been when, often, after tea, he sat near the lamp with the dressmaker, and, while her fingers flew, read out to her the works of Dickens and of Scott; happy hours when he appeared to have forgotten the wrong she had done him and she almost forgot it herself. But now he gulped down his tea so fast that he hardly took off his hat while he sat there, and Pinnie, with her quick eye for all matters of costume, noticed that he wore it still more gracefully askew than usual, with a little victorious, exalted air. He hummed to himself; he fingered his moustache; he looked out of the window when there was nothing to look at; he seemed pre-occupied, absorbed in intellectual excursions, half anxious and half delighted. During the whole winter Miss Pynsent explained everything by three words murmured beneath her breath: 'That forward jade!' On the single occasion, however, on which she sought relief from her agitation in an appeal to Hyacinth, she did not trust herself to designate the girl by any epithet or title.

'There is only one thing I want to know,' she said to him, in a manner which might have seemed casual if in her silence, knowing her as well as he did, he had not already perceived the implication of her thought. 'Does she expect you to marry her, dearest?'

'Does who expect me? I should like to see the woman who does!'

'Of course you know who I mean. The one that came after you—and picked you right up—from the other end of London.' And at the remembrance of that insufferable scene poor Pinnie flamed up for a moment. 'Isn't there plenty of young fellows down in that low part where she lives, without her ravaging over here? Why can't she stick to her own beat, I should like to know?' Hyacinth had flushed at this inquiry, and she saw something in his face which made her change her tone. 'Just promise me this, my precious child: that if you get into any sort of mess with that piece you'll immediately confide it to your poor old Pinnie.'

'My poor old Pinnie sometimes makes me quite sick,' Hyacinth remarked, for answer. 'What sort of a mess do you suppose I'll get into?'

'Well, suppose she does come it over you that you promised to marry her?'

'You don't know what you're talking about. She doesn't want to marry any one to-day.'

'Then what does she want to do?'

'Do you imagine I would tell a lady's secrets?' the young man inquired.

'Dear me, if she was a lady, I shouldn't be afraid!' said Pinnie.

'Every woman's a lady when she has placed herself under one's protection,' Hyacinth rejoined, with his little manner of a man of the world.

'Under your protection? Laws!' cried Pinnie, staring. 'And pray, who's to protect you?'

As soon as she had said this she repented, because it seemed just the sort of exclamation that would have made Hyacinth bite her head off. One of the things she loved him for, however, was that he gave you touching surprises in this line, had sudden inconsistencies of temper that were all for your advantage. He was by no means always mild when he ought to have been, but he was sometimes so when there was no obligation. At such moments Pinnie wanted to kiss him, and she had often tried to make Mr. Vetch understand what a fascinating trait of character this was on the part of their young friend. It was rather difficult to describe, and Mr. Vetch never would admit that he understood, or that he had observed anything that seemed to correspond to the dressmaker's somewhat confused psychological sketch. It was a comfort to her in these days, and almost the only one she had, that she was sure Anastasius Vetch understood a good deal more than he felt bound to acknowledge. He was always up to his old game of being a great deal cleverer than cleverness itself required; and it consoled her present weak, pinched feeling to know that, although he still talked of the boy as if it would be a pity to take him too seriously, that wasn't the way he thought of him. He also took him seriously, and he had even a certain sense of duty in regard to him. Miss Pynsent went so far as to say to herself that the fiddler probably had savings, and that no one had ever known of any one else belonging to him. She wouldn't have mentioned it to Hyacinth for the world, for fear of leading up to a disappointment; but she had visions of a foolscap sheet, folded away in some queer little bachelor's box (she couldn't fancy what men kept in such places), on which Hyacinth's name would have been written down, in very big letters, before a solicitor.

'Oh, I'm unprotected, in the nature of things,' he replied, smiling at his too scrupulous companion. Then he added, 'At any rate, it isn't from that girl any danger will come to me.'

'I can't think why you like her,' Pinnie remarked, as if she had spent on the subject treasures of impartiality.

'It's jolly to hear one woman on the subject of another,' Hyacinth said. 'You're kind and good, and yet you're ready——' He gave a philosophic sigh.

'Well, what am I ready to do? I'm not ready to see you gobbled up before my eyes!'

'You needn't be afraid; she won't drag me to the altar.'

'And pray, doesn't she think you good enough—for one of the beautiful Hennings?'

'You don't understand, my poor Pinnie,' said Hyacinth, wearily. 'I sometimes think there isn't a single thing in life that you understand. One of these days she'll marry an alderman.'

'An alderman—that creature?'

'An alderman, or a banker, or a bishop, or some one of that kind. She doesn't want to end her career to-day; she wants to begin it.'

'Well, I wish she would take you later!' the dressmaker exclaimed.

Hyacinth said nothing for a moment; then he broke out: 'What are you afraid of? Look here, we had better clear this up, once for all. Are you afraid of my marrying a girl out of a shop?'

'Oh, you wouldn't, would you?' cried Pinnie, with a kind of conciliatory eagerness. 'That's the way I like to hear you talk!'

'Do you think I would marry any one who would marry me?' Hyacinth went on. 'The kind of girl who would look at me is the kind of girl I wouldn't look at.' He struck Pinnie as having thought it all out; which did not surprise her, as she had been familiar, from his youth, with his way of following things up. But she was always delighted when he made a remark which showed he was conscious of being of fine clay —flashed out an allusion to his not being what he seemed. He was not what he seemed, but even with Pinnie's valuable assistance he had not succeeded in representing to himself, very definitely, what he was. She had placed at his disposal, for this purpose, a passionate idealism which, employed in some case where it could have consequences, might have been termed profligate, and which never cost her a scruple or a compunction.

'I'm sure a princess might look at you and be none the worse!' she declared, in her delight at this assurance, more positive than any she had yet received, that he was safe from the worst danger. This the dressmaker considered to be the chance of his marrying some person like herself. Still it came over her that his taste might be lowered, and before the subject was dropped, on this occasion, she said to him that of course he must be quite aware of all that was wanting to such a girl as Millicent Henning—she pronounced her name at last.

'Oh, I don't bother about what's wanting to her; I'm content with what she has.'

'Content, dearest—how do you mean?' the little dressmaker quavered. 'Content to make an intimate friend of her?'

'It is impossible I should discuss these matters with you,' Hyacinth replied, grandly.

'Of course I see that. But I should think she would bore you sometimes,' Miss Pynsent murmured, cunningly.

'She does, I assure you, to extinction!'

'Then why do you spend every evening with her?'

'Where should you like me to spend my evenings? At some beastly public-house—or at the Italian opera?' His association with Miss Henning was not so close as that, but nevertheless he wouldn't take the trouble to prove to poor Pinnie that he enjoyed her society only two or three times a week; that on other evenings he simply strolled about the streets (this boyish habit clung to him), and that he had even occasionally the resource of going to the Poupins', or of gossiping and smoking a pipe at some open house-door, when the night was not cold, with a fellow-mechanic. Later in the winter, after he had made Paul Muniment's acquaintance, the aspect of his life changed considerably, though Millicent continued to be exceedingly mixed up with it. He hated the taste of liquor and still more the taste of the places where it was sold; besides which the types of misery and vice that one was liable to see collected in them frightened and harrowed him, made him ask himself questions that pierced the deeper because they were met by no answer. It was both a blessing and a drawback to him that the delicate, charming character of the work he did at Mr. Crookenden's, under Eustache Poupin's influence, was a kind of education of the taste, trained him in the finest discriminations, in the perception of beauty and the hatred of ugliness. This made the brutal, garish, stodgy decoration of public-houses, with their deluge of gaslight, their glittering brass and pewter, their lumpish woodwork and false colours, detestable to him; he was still very young when the 'gin-palace' ceased to convey to him an idea of the palatial.

For this unfortunate but remarkably organised youth, every displeasure or gratification of the visual sense coloured his whole mind, and though he lived in Pentonville and worked in Soho, though he was poor and obscure and cramped and full of unattainable desires, it may be said of him that what was most important in life for him was simply his impressions. They came from everything he touched, they kept him thrilling and throbbing during a considerable part of his waking consciousness, and they constituted, as yet, the principal events and stages of his career. Fortunately, they were sometimes very delightful. Everything in the field of observation suggested this or that; everything struck him, penetrated, stirred; he had, in a word, more impressions than he knew what to do with—felt sometimes as if they would consume or asphyxiate him. He liked to talk about them, but it was only a few, here and there, that he could discuss with Millicent Henning. He let Miss Pynsent imagine that his hours of leisure were almost exclusively dedicated to this young lady, because, as he said to himself, if he were to account to her for every evening in the week it would make no difference—she would stick to her suspicion; and he referred this perversity to the general weight of misconception under which (at this crude period of his growth) he held it was his lot to languish. It didn't matter to one whether one were a little more or a little less misunderstood. He might have remembered that it mattered to Pinnie, who, after her first relief at hearing him express himself so properly on the subject of a matrimonial connection with Miss Henning, allowed her faded, kind, weak face, little by little, to lengthen out to its old solemnity. This came as the days went on, for it wasn't much comfort that he didn't want to marry the young woman in Pimlico, when he allowed himself to be held as tight as if he did. For the present, indeed, she simply said, 'Oh, well, if you see her as she is, I don't care what you do'—a sentiment implying a certain moral recklessness on the part of the good little dressmaker. She was irreproachable herself, but she had lived for more than fifty years in a world of wickedness; like an immense number of London women of her class and kind, she had acquired a certain innocent cynicism, and she judged it quite a minor evil that Millicent should be left lamenting, if only Hyacinth might get out of the scrape. Between a forsaken maiden and a premature, lowering marriage for her beloved little boy, she very well knew which she preferred. It should be added that her impression of Millicent's power to take care of herself was such as to make it absurd to pity her in advance. Pinnie thought Hyacinth the cleverest young man in the world, but her state of mind implied somehow that the young lady in Pimlico was cleverer. Her ability, at any rate, was of a kind that precluded the idea of suffering, whereas Hyacinth's was rather associated with it.

By the time he had enjoyed for three months the acquaintance of the brother and sister in Audley Court the whole complexion of his life seemed changed; it was pervaded by an interest, an excitement, which overshadowed, though it by no means supplanted, the brilliant figure of Miss Henning. It was pitched in a higher key, altogether, and appeared to command a view of horizons equally fresh and vast. Millicent, therefore, shared her dominion, without knowing exactly what it was that drew her old playfellow off, and without indeed demanding of him an account which, on her own side, she was not prepared to give. Hyacinth was, in the language of the circle in which she moved, her fancy, and she was content to occupy, as regards himself, the same graceful and somewhat irresponsible position. She had an idea that she was a very beneficent friend: fond of him and careful of him as an elder sister might be; warning him as no one else could do against the dangers of the town; putting that stiff common sense, of which she was convinced that she possessed an extraordinary supply, at the service of his incurable verdancy; and looking after him, generally, as no one, poor child, had ever done. Millicent made light of the little dressmaker, in this view of Hyacinth's past (she thought Pinnie no better than a starved cat), and enjoyed herself immensely in the character of guide and philosopher, while she pushed the young man with a robust elbow or said to him, 'Well, you *are* a sharp one, you are!' Her theory of herself, as we know, was that she was the

sweetest girl in the world, as well as the cleverest and handsomest, and there could be no better proof of her kindness of
heart than her disinterested affection for a snippet of a bookbinder. Her sociability was certainly great, and so were her
vanity, her grossness, her presumption, her appetite for beer,
for buns, for entertainment of every kind. She represented,
for Hyacinth, during this period, the eternal feminine, and his
taste, considering that he was fastidious, will be wondered at;
it will be judged that she did not represent it very favourably.

It may easily be believed that he scrutinised his infatuation
even while he gave himself up to it, and that he often wondered he should care for a girl in whom he found so much to
object to. She was vulgar, clumsy and grotesquely ignorant;
her conceit was proportionate, and she had not a grain of tact
or of quick perception. And yet there was something so fine
about her, to his imagination, and she carried with such an air
the advantages she did possess, that her figure constantly mingled itself even with those bright visions that hovered before
him after Paul Muniment had opened a mysterious window.
She was bold, and free, and generous, and if she was coarse
she was neither false nor cruel. She laughed with the laugh of
the people, and if you hit her hard enough she would cry
with its tears. When Hyacinth was not letting his imagination
wander among the haunts of the aristocracy, and fancying
himself stretched in the shadow of an ancestral beech, reading
the last number of the *Revue des Deux Mondes*, he was occupied with contemplations of a very different kind; he was absorbed in the struggles and sufferings of the millions whose
life flowed in the same current as his, and who, though they
constantly excited his disgust, and made him shrink and turn
away, had the power to chain his sympathy, to make it glow
to a kind of ecstasy, to convince him, for the time at least,
that real success in the world would be to do something with
them and for them. All this, strange to say, was never so vivid
to him as when he was in Millicent's company; which is a
proof of his fantastic, erratic way of seeing things. She had no
such ideas about herself; they were almost the only ideas she
didn't have. She had no theories about redeeming or uplifting
the people; she simply loathed them, because they were so
dirty, with the outspoken violence of one who had known

poverty, and the strange bedfellows it makes, in a very different degree from Hyacinth, brought up, comparatively, with
Pinnie to put sugar in his tea and keep him supplied with
neckties, like a little swell.

Millicent, to hear her talk, only wanted to keep her skirts
clear and marry some respectable tea-merchant. But for our
hero she was magnificently plebeian, in the sense that implied
a kind of loud recklessness of danger and the qualities that
shine forth in a row. She summed up the sociable, humorous,
ignorant chatter of the masses, their capacity for offensive
and defensive passion, their instinctive perception of their
strength on the day they should really exercise it; and as much
as any of this, their ideal of something smug and prosperous,
where washed hands, and plates in rows on dressers, and
stuffed birds under glass, and family photographs, would
symbolise success. She was none the less plucky for being at
bottom a shameless Philistine, ambitious of a front-garden
with rockwork; and she presented the plebeian character in
none the less plastic a form. Having the history of the French
Revolution at his fingers' ends, Hyacinth could easily see her
(if there should ever be barricades in the streets of London),
with a red cap of liberty on her head and her white throat
bared so that she should be able to shout the louder the
Marseillaise of that hour, whatever it might be. If the festival
of the Goddess of Reason should ever be enacted in the British metropolis (and Hyacinth could consider such possibilities
without a smile, so much was it a part of the little religion he
had to remember, always, that there was no knowing what
might happen) — if this solemnity, I say, should be revived in
Hyde Park, who was better designated than Miss Henning to
figure in a grand statuesque manner, as the heroine of the
occasion? It was plain that she had laid her inconsequent admirer under a peculiar spell, since he could associate her with
such scenes as that while she consumed beer and buns at his
expense. If she had a weakness, it was for prawns; and she
had, all winter, a plan for his taking her down to Gravesend,
where this luxury was cheap and abundant, when the fine
long days should arrive. She was never so frank and facetious
as when she dwelt on the details of a project of this kind; and
then Hyacinth was reminded afresh that it was an immense

good fortune for her that she was handsome. If she had been ugly he couldn't have listened to her; but her beauty glorified even her accent, interfused her cockney genius with prismatic hues, gave her a large and constant impunity.

XI

S HE DESIRED at last to raise their common experience to a loftier level, to enjoy what she called a high-class treat. Their conversation was condemned, for the most part, to go forward in the streets, the wintry, dusky, foggy streets, which looked bigger and more numerous in their perpetual obscurity, and in which everything was covered with damp, gritty smut, an odour extremely agreeable to Miss Henning. Happily she shared Hyacinth's relish of vague perambulation, and was still more addicted than he to looking into the windows of shops, before which, in long, contemplative halts, she picked out freely the articles she shouldn't mind calling her own. Hyacinth always pronounced the objects of her selection hideous, and made no scruple to tell her that she had the worst taste of any girl in the place. Nothing that he could say to her affronted her so much, as her pretensions in the way of a cultivated judgment were boundless. Had not, indeed, her natural aptitude been fortified, in the neighbourhood of Buckingham Palace (there was scarcely anything they didn't sell in the great shop of which she was an ornament), by daily contact with the freshest products of modern industry? Hyacinth laughed this establishment to scorn, and told her there was nothing in it, from top to bottom, that a real artist would look at. She inquired, with answering derision, if this were a description of his own few inches; but in reality she was fascinated, as much as she was provoked, by his air of being difficult to please, of seeing indescribable differences among things. She had given herself out, originally, as very knowing, but he could make her feel stupid. When once in a while he pointed out a commodity that he condescended to like (this didn't happen often, because the only shops in which there was a chance of his making such a discovery were closed at nightfall), she stared, bruised him more or less with her elbow, and declared that if any one should give her such a piece of rubbish she would sell it for fourpence. Once or twice she asked him to be so good as to explain to her in what its superiority consisted—she could not rid herself of a suspicion that there might be something in his opinion, and she was angry at not finding herself as positive as any one. But Hyacinth replied that it was no use attempting to tell her; she wouldn't understand, and she had better continue to admire the insipid productions of an age which had lost the sense of quality—a phrase which she remembered, proposing to herself even to make use of it, on some future occasion, but was quite unable to interpret.

When her companion demeaned himself in this manner it was not with a view of strengthening the tie which united him to his childhood's friend; but the effect followed, on Millicent's side, and the girl was proud to think that she was in possession of a young man whose knowledge was of so high an order that it was inexpressible. In spite of her vanity she was not so convinced of her perfection as not to be full of ungratified aspirations; she had an idea that it might be to her advantage some day to exhibit a sample of that learning; and at the same time, when, in consideration, for instance, of a jeweller's gas-lighted display in Great Portland Street, Hyacinth lingered for five minutes in perfect silence, while she delivered herself according to her wont at such junctures, she was a thousand miles from guessing the feelings which made it impossible for him to speak. She could long for things she was not likely to have; envy other people for possessing them, and say it was a regular shame (she called it a *shime*); draw brilliant pictures of what she should do with them if she did have them; and pass immediately, with a mind unencumbered by superfluous inductions, to some other topic, equally intimate and personal. The sense of privation, with her, was often extremely acute; but she could always put her finger on the remedy. With the imaginative, irresponsible little bookbinder the case was very different; the remedy, with him, was terribly vague and impracticable. He was liable to moods in which the sense of exclusion from all that he would have liked most to enjoy in life settled upon him like a pall. They had a bitterness, but they were not invidious—they were not moods of vengeance, of imaginary spoliation: they were simply states of paralysing melancholy, of infinite sad reflection, in which he felt that in this world of effort and suffering life was endurable, the spirit able to expand, only in the best conditions, and that a sordid struggle, in which one should go down to the grave without having tasted them, was not worth the misery it would cost, the dull demoralisation it would entail.

In such hours the great, roaring, indifferent world of London seemed to him a huge organisation for mocking at his poverty, at his inanition; and then its vulgarest ornaments, the windows of third-rate jewellers, the young man in a white tie and a crush-hat who dandled by, on his way to a dinner-party, in a hansom that nearly ran over one — these familiar phenomena became symbolic, insolent, defiant, took upon themselves to make him smart with the sense that *he* was out of it. He felt, moreover, that there was no consolation or refutation in saying to himself that the immense majority of mankind were out of it with him, and appeared to put up well enough with the annoyance. That was their own affair; he knew nothing of their reasons or their resignation, and if they chose neither to rebel nor to compare, he, at least, among the disinherited, would keep up the standard. When these fits were upon the young man, his brothers of the people fared, collectively, badly at his hands; their function then was to represent in massive shape precisely the grovelling interests which attracted one's contempt, and the only acknowledgment one owed them was for the completeness of the illustration. Everything which, in a great city, could touch the sentient faculty of a youth on whom nothing was lost ministered to his conviction that there was no possible good fortune in life of too 'quiet' an order for him to appreciate — no privilege, no opportunity, no luxury, to which he should not do justice. It was not so much that he wished to enjoy as that he wished to know; his desire was not to be pampered, but to be initiated. Sometimes, of a Saturday, in the long evenings of June and July, he made his way into Hyde Park at the hour when the throng of carriages, of riders, of brilliant pedestrians, was thickest; and though lately, on two or three of these occasions, he had been accompanied by Miss Henning, whose criticism of the scene was rich and distinct, a tremendous little drama had taken place, privately, in his soul. He wanted to drive in every carriage, to mount on every horse, to feel on his arm the hand of every pretty woman in the place. In the midst of this his sense was vivid that he belonged to the class whom the upper ten thousand, as they passed, didn't so much as rest their eyes upon for a quarter of a second. They looked at Millicent, who was safe to be looked at anywhere, and was one of the handsomest girls in any company, but they only reminded him of the high human walls, the deep gulfs of tradition, the steep embankments of privilege and dense layers of stupidity, which fenced him off from social recognition.

And this was not the fruit of a morbid vanity on his part, or of a jealousy that could not be intelligent; his personal discomfort was the result of an exquisite admiration for what he had missed. There were individuals whom he followed with his eyes, with his thoughts, sometimes even with his steps; they seemed to tell him what it was to be the flower of a high civilisation. At moments he was aghast when he reflected that the cause he had secretly espoused, the cause from which M. Poupin and Paul Muniment (especially the latter) had within the last few months drawn aside the curtain, proposed to itself to bring about a state of things in which that particular scene would be impossible. It made him even rather faint to think that he must choose; that he couldn't (with any respect for his own consistency) work, underground, for the enthronement of the democracy, and continue to enjoy, in however platonic a manner, a spectacle which rested on a hideous social inequality. He must either suffer with the people, as he had suffered before, or he must apologise to others, as he sometimes came so near doing to himself, for the rich; inasmuch as the day was certainly near when these two mighty forces would come to a death-grapple. Hyacinth thought himself obliged, at present, to have reasons for his feelings; his intimacy with Paul Muniment, which had now grown very great, laid a good deal of that sort of responsibility upon him. Muniment laughed at his reasons, whenever he produced them, but he appeared to expect him, nevertheless, to have them ready, on demand, and Hyacinth had an immense desire to do what he expected. There were times when he said to himself that it might very well be his fate to be divided, to the point of torture, to be split open by sympathies that pulled him in different ways; for hadn't he an extraordinarily mingled current in his blood, and from the time he could remember was there not one half of him that seemed to be always playing tricks on the other, or getting snubs and pinches from it?

That dim, dreadful, confused legend of his mother's history, as regards which what Pinnie had been able to tell him when he first began to question her was at once too much and too little—this stupefying explanation had supplied him, first and last, with a hundred different theories of his identity. What he knew, what he guessed, sickened him, and what he didn't know tormented him; but in his illuminated ignorance he had fashioned forth an article of faith. This had gradually emerged from the depths of darkness in which he found himself plunged as a consequence of the challenge he had addressed to Pinnie—while he was still only a child—on the memorable day which transformed the whole face of his future. It was one January afternoon. He had come in from a walk; she was seated at her lamp, as usual with her work, and she began to tell him of a letter that one of the lodgers had got, describing the manner in which his brother-in-law's shop, at Nottingham, had been rifled by burglars. He listened to her story, standing in front of her, and then, by way of response, he said to her, 'Who was that woman you took me to see ever so long ago?' The expression of her white face, as she looked up at him, her fear of such an attack all dormant, after so many years—her strange, scared, sick glance was a thing he could never forget, any more than the tone, with her breath failing her, in which she had repeated, 'That woman?'

'That woman, in the prison, years ago—how old was I?— who was dying, and who kissed me so—as I have never been kissed, as I never shall be again! Who *was* she, who WAS she?' Poor Pinnie, to do her justice, had made, after she recovered her breath, a gallant fight: it lasted a week; it was to leave her spent and sore for evermore, and before it was over Anastasius Vetch had been called in. At his instance she retracted the falsehoods with which she had tried to put him off, and she made, at last, a confession, a report, which he had reason to believe was as complete as her knowledge. Hyacinth could never have told you why the crisis occurred on such a day, why his question broke out at that particular moment.

The strangeness of the matter to himself was that the germ of his curiosity should have developed so slowly; that the haunting wonder, which now, as he looked back, appeared to fill his whole childhood, should only after so long an interval have crept up to the air. It was only, of course, little by little that he had recovered his bearings in his new and more poignant consciousness; little by little that he reconstructed his antecedents, took the measure, so far as was possible, of his heredity. His having the courage to disinter, in the *Times*, in the reading-room of the British Museum, a report of his mother's trial for the murder of Lord Frederick Purvis, which was very copious, the affair having been quite a *cause célèbre*; his resolution in sitting under that splendid dome, and, with his head bent to hide his hot eyes, going through every syllable of the ghastly record, had been an achievement of comparatively recent years. There were certain things that Pinnie knew which appalled him; and there were others, as to which he would have given his hand to have some light, that it made his heart ache supremely to find she was honestly ignorant of. He scarcely knew what sort of favour Mr. Vetch wished to make with him (as a compensation for the precious part he had played in the business years before), when the fiddler permitted himself to pass judgment on the family of the wretched young nobleman for not having provided in some manner for the infant child of his assassin. Why should they have provided, when it was evident that they refused absolutely to recognise his lordship's responsibility? Pinnie had to admit this, under Hyacinth's terrible cross-questioning; she could not pretend, with any show of evidence, that Lord Whiteroy and the other brothers (there had been no less than seven, most of them still living) had, at the time of the trial, given any symptom of believing Florentine Vivier's asseverations. That was their affair; he had long since made up his mind that his own was very different. One couldn't believe at will, and fortunately, in the case, he had no effort to make; for from the moment he began to consider the established facts (few as they were, and poor and hideous) he regarded himself, irresistibly, as the son of the recreant, sacrificial Lord Frederick.

He had no need to reason about it; all his nerves and pulses pleaded and testified. His mother had been a daughter of the wild French people (all that Pinnie could tell him of her parentage was that Florentine had once mentioned that in her extreme childhood her father had fallen, in the blood-stained streets of Paris, on a barricade, with his gun in his hand); but on the other side it took an English aristocrat—though a poor specimen, apparently, had to suffice—to account for him. This, with its further implications, became Hyacinth's article of faith; the reflection that he was a bastard involved in a remarkable manner the reflection that he was a gentleman. He was conscious that he didn't hate the image of his father, as he might have been expected to do; and he supposed this was because Lord Frederick had paid so tremendous a penalty. It was in the exaction of that penalty that the moral proof, for Hyacinth, resided; his mother would not have armed herself on account of any injury less cruel than the episode of which her miserable baby was the living sign. She had avenged herself because she had been thrown over, and the bitterness of that wrong had been in the fact that he, Hyacinth, lay there in her lap. *He* was the one to have been killed: that remark our young man often made to himself. That his attitude on this whole subject was of a tolerably exalted, transcendent character, and took little account of any refutation that might be based on a vulgar glance at three or four obtrusive items, is proved by the importance that he attached, for instance, to the name by which his mother had told poor Pinnie (when this excellent creature consented to take him) that she wished him to be called. Hyacinth had been the name of her father, a republican clockmaker, the martyr of his opinions, whose memory she professed to worship; and when Lord Frederick insinuated himself into her confidence he had reasons for preferring to be known as plain Mr. Robinson—reasons, however, which, in spite of the light thrown upon them at the trial, it was difficult, after so many years, to enter into.

Hyacinth never knew that Mr. Vetch had said more than once to Pinnie, 'If her contention as regards that dissolute young swell was true, why didn't she make the child bear his

real name, instead of his false one?'—an inquiry which the
dressmaker answered with some ingenuity, by remarking that
she couldn't call him after a man she had murdered, and that
she supposed the unhappy girl didn't wish to publish to every
one the boy's connection with a crime that had been so much
talked about. If Hyacinth had assisted at this little discussion
it is needless to say that he would have sided with Miss
Pynsent; though that his judgment was independently formed
is proved by the fact that Pinnie's fearfully indiscreet attempts
at condolence should not have made him throw up his version in disgust. It was after the complete revelation that he
understood the romantic innuendoes with which his childhood had been surrounded, and of which he had never
caught the meaning; they having seemed but part and parcel
of the habitual and promiscuous divagations of his too constructive companion. When it came over him that, for years,
she had made a fool of him, to himself and to others, he could
have beaten her, for grief and shame; and yet, before he
administered this rebuke he had to remember that she only
chattered (though she professed to have been extraordinarily
dumb) about a matter which he spent nine-tenths of his time
in brooding over. When she tried to console him for the horror of his mother's history by descanting on the glory of the
Purvises, and reminding him that he was related, through
them, to half the aristocracy of England, he felt that she was
turning the tragedy of his life into a monstrous farce; and yet
he none the less continued to cherish the belief that he was a
gentleman born. He allowed her to tell him nothing about
the family in question, and his stoicism on this subject was
one of the reasons of the deep dejection of her later years. If
he had only let her idealise him a little to himself she would
have felt that she was making up, by so much, for her grand
mistake. He sometimes saw the name of his father's relations
in the newspaper, but he always turned away his eyes from it.
He had nothing to ask of them, and he wished to prove to
himself that he could ignore them (who had been willing to
let him die like a rat) as completely as they ignored him. Decidedly, he cried to himself at times, he was with the people,
and every possible vengeance of the people, as against such
shameless egoism as that; but all the same he was happy to

feel that he had blood in his veins which would account for the finest sensibilities.

He had no money to pay for places at a theatre in the Strand; Millicent Henning having made it clear to him that on this occasion she expected something better than the pit. 'Should you like the royal box, or a couple of stalls at ten shillings apiece?' he asked of her, with a frankness of irony which, with this young lady, fortunately, it was perfectly possible to practise. She had answered that she would content herself with a seat in the second balcony, in the very front; and as such a position involved an expenditure which he was still unable to meet, he waited one night upon Mr. Vetch, to whom he had already, more than once, had recourse in moments of pecuniary embarrassment. His relations with the caustic fiddler were peculiar; they were much better in fact than they were in theory. Mr. Vetch had let him know—long before this, and with the purpose of covering Pinnie to the utmost—the part he had played when the question of the child's being taken to Mrs. Bowerbank's institution was so distressingly presented; and Hyacinth, in the face of this information, had inquired, with some sublimity, what the devil the fiddler had to do with his private affairs. Anastasius Vetch had replied that it was not as an affair of his, but as an affair of Pinnie's, that he had considered the matter; and Hyacinth afterwards had let the question drop, though he had never been formally reconciled to his officious neighbour. Of course his feeling about him had been immensely modified by the trouble Mr. Vetch had taken to get him a place with old Crookenden; and at the period of which I write it had long been familiar to him that the fiddler didn't care a straw what he thought of his advice at the famous crisis, and entertained himself with watching the career of a youth put together of such queer pieces. It was impossible to Hyacinth not to perceive that the old man's interest was kindly; and to-day, at any rate, our hero would have declared that nothing could have made up to him for not knowing the truth, horrible as the truth might be. His miserable mother's embrace seemed to furnish him with an inexhaustible fund of motive, and under the circumstances that was a benefit. What he chiefly objected to in Mr. Vetch was a certain air of still regarding him as extremely juvenile; he would have got on with him much better if the fiddler had consented to recognise the degree in which he was already a man of the world. Vetch knew an immense deal about society, and he seemed to know the more because he never swaggered—it was only little by little you discovered it; but that was no reason for his looking as if his chief entertainment resided in a private, diverting commentary on the conversation of his young friend. Hyacinth felt that he himself gave considerable evidence of liking his fellow-resident in Lomax Place when he asked him to lend him half-a-crown. Somehow, circumstances, of old, had tied them together, and though this partly vexed the little bookbinder it also touched him; he had more than once solved the problem of deciding how to behave (when the fiddler exasperated him) by simply asking him some service. The old man had never refused. It was satisfactory to Hyacinth to remember this, as he knocked at his door, very late, after he had allowed him time to come home from the theatre. He knew his habits: Mr. Vetch never went straight to bed, but sat by his fire an hour, smoking his pipe, mixing a grog, and reading some old book. Hyacinth knew when to go up by the light in his window, which he could see from a court behind.

'Oh, I know I haven't been to see you for a long time,' he said, in response to the remark with which the fiddler greeted him; 'and I may as well tell you immediately what has brought me at present—in addition to the desire to ask after your health. I want to take a young lady to the theatre.'

Mr. Vetch was habited in a tattered dressing-gown; his apartment smelt strongly of the liquor he was consuming. Divested of his evening-gear he looked to our hero so plucked and blighted that on the spot Hyacinth ceased to hesitate as to his claims in the event of a social liquidation; he, too, was unmistakably a creditor. 'I'm afraid you find your young lady rather expensive.'

'I find everything expensive,' said Hyacinth, as if to finish that subject.

'Especially, I suppose, your secret societies.'

'What do you mean by that?' the young man asked, staring.

'Why, you told me, in the autumn, that you were just about to join a few.'

'A few? How many do you suppose?' And Hyacinth checked himself. 'Do you suppose if I had been serious I would tell?'

'Oh dear, oh dear,' Mr. Vetch murmured, with a sigh. Then he went on: 'You want to take her to my shop, eh?'

'I'm sorry to say she won't go there. She wants something in the Strand: that's a great point. She wants very much to see the *Pearl of Paraguay*. I don't wish to pay anything, if possible; I am sorry to say I haven't a penny. But as you know people at the other theatres, and I have heard you say that you do each other little favours, from place to place—*à charge de revanche*, as the French say—it occurred to me that you might be able to get me an order. The piece has been running a long time, and most people (except poor devils like me) must have seen it: therefore there probably isn't a rush.'

Mr. Vetch listened in silence, and presently he said, 'Do you want a box?'

'Oh no; something more modest.'

'Why not a box?' asked the fiddler, in a tone which Hyacinth knew.

'Because I haven't got the clothes that people wear in that sort of place, if you must have such a definite reason.'

'And your young lady—has she got the clothes?'

'Oh, I daresay; she seems to have everything.'

'Where does she get them?'

'Oh, I don't know. She belongs to a big shop; she has to be fine.'

'Won't you have a pipe?' Mr. Vetch asked, pushing an old tobacco-pouch across the table to his visitor; and while the young man helped himself he puffed a while in silence. 'What will she do with you?' he inquired at last.

'What will who do with me?'

'Your big beauty—Miss Henning. I know all about her from Pinnie.'

'Then you know what she'll do with me!' Hyacinth returned, with rather a scornful laugh.

'Yes, but, after all, it doesn't very much matter.'

'I don't know what you are talking about,' said Hyacinth.

'Well, now the other matter—the International—are you very deep in that?' the fiddler went on, as if he had not heard him.

'Did Pinnie tell you also about that?' his visitor asked.

'No, our friend Eustace has told me a good deal. He knows you have put your head into something. Besides, I see it,' said Mr. Vetch.

'How do you see it, pray?'

'You have got such a speaking eye. Any one can tell, to look at you, that you have become a nihilist, that you're a member of a secret society. You seem to say to every one, "Slow torture won't induce me to tell where it meets!"'

'You won't get me an order, then?' Hyacinth said, in a moment.

'My dear boy, I offer you a box. I take the greatest interest in you.'

They smoked together a while, and at last Hyacinth remarked, 'It has nothing to do with the International.'

'Is it more terrible—more deadly secret?' his companion inquired, looking at him with extreme seriousness.

'I thought you pretended to be a radical,' answered Hyacinth.

'Well, so I am—of the old-fashioned, constitutional, milk-and-water, jog-trot sort. I'm not an exterminator.'

'We don't know what we may be when the time comes,' Hyacinth rejoined, more sententiously than he intended.

'Is the time coming, then, my dear boy?'

'I don't think I have a right to give you any more of a warning than that,' said our hero, smiling.

'It's very kind of you to do so much, I'm sure, and to rush in here at the small hours for the purpose. Meanwhile, in the few weeks, or months, or years, or whatever they are, that are left, you wish to put in as much enjoyment as you can squeeze, with the young ladies: that's a very natural inclination.' Then, irrelevantly, Mr. Vetch inquired, 'Do you see many foreigners?'

'Yes, I see a good many.'

'And what do you think of them?'

'Oh, all sorts of things. I rather like Englishmen better.'

'Mr. Muniment, for example?'

'I say, what do you know about him?' Hyacinth asked.

'I've seen him at Eustace's. I know that you and he are as thick as thieves.'

'He will distinguish himself some day, very much,' said Hyacinth, who was perfectly willing, and indeed very proud, to be thought a close ally of the chemist's assistant.

'Very likely—very likely. And what will *he* do with you?' the fiddler inquired.

Hyacinth got up; the two men looked at each other for an instant. 'Do get me two good places in the second balcony,' said Hyacinth.

Mr. Vetch replied that he would do what he could, and three days afterwards he gave the coveted order to his young friend. As he placed it in his hands he exclaimed, 'You had better put in all the fun you can, you know!'

BOOK SECOND

XII

HYACINTH and his companion took their seats with extreme promptitude before the curtain rose upon the *Pearl of Paraguay*. Thanks to Millicent's eagerness not to be late they encountered the discomfort which had constituted her main objection to going into the pit: they waited for twenty minutes at the door of the theatre, in a tight, stolid crowd, before the official hour of opening. Millicent, bareheaded and very tightly laced, presented a most splendid appearance and, on Hyacinth's part, gratified a certain youthful, ingenuous pride of possession in every respect save a tendency, while ingress was denied them, to make her neighbours feel her elbows and to comment, loudly and sarcastically, on the situation. It was more clear to him even than it had been before that she was a young lady who in public places might easily need a champion or an apologist. Hyacinth knew there was only one way to apologise for a 'female,' when the female was attached very closely and heavily to one's arm, and was reminded afresh how little constitutional aversion Miss Henning had to a row. He had an idea she might think his own taste ran even too little in that direction, and had visions of violent, confused scenes, in which he should in some way distinguish himself: he scarcely knew in what way, and imagined himself more easily routing some hulking adversary by an exquisite application of the retort courteous than by flying at him with a pair of very small fists.

By the time they had reached their places in the balcony Millicent was rather flushed and a good deal ruffled; but she had composed herself in season for the rising of the curtain upon the farce which preceded the melodrama and which the pair had had no intention of losing. At this stage a more genial agitation took possession of her, and she surrendered her sympathies to the horse-play of the traditional prelude. Hyacinth found it less amusing, but the theatre, in any conditions, was full of sweet deception for him. His imagination pro-

jected itself lovingly across the footlights, gilded and coloured
the shabby canvas and battered accessories, and lost itself so
effectually in the fictive world that the end of the piece, however long, or however short, brought with it a kind of alarm,
like a stoppage of his personal life. It was impossible to be
more friendly to the dramatic illusion. Millicent, as the audience thickened, rejoiced more largely and loudly, held herself
as a lady, surveyed the place as if she knew all about it, leaned
back and leaned forward, fanned herself with majesty, gave
her opinion upon the appearance and coiffure of every
woman within sight, abounded in question and conjecture,
and produced from her pocket, a little paper of peppermint-
drops, of which, under cruel threats, she compelled Hyacinth
to partake. She followed with attention, though not always
with success, the complicated adventures of the Pearl of Paraguay, through scenes luxuriantly tropical, in which the male
characters wore sombreros and stilettos, and the ladies either
danced the cachucha or fled from licentious pursuit; but her
eyes wandered, during considerable periods, to the occupants
of the boxes and stalls, concerning several of whom she had
theories which she imparted to Hyacinth while the play went
on, greatly to his discomfiture, he being unable to conceive
of such levity. She had the pretension of knowing who every
one was; not individually and by name, but as regards their
exact social station, the quarter of London in which they
lived, and the amount of money they were prepared to
spend in the neighbourhood of Buckingham Palace. She had
seen the whole town pass through her establishment there,
and though Hyacinth, from his infancy, had been watching
it from his own point of view, his companion made him feel
that he had missed a thousand characteristic points, so different were most of her interpretations from his, and so very
bold and irreverent. Miss Henning's observation of human
society had not been of a nature to impress her with its high
moral tone, and she had a free off-hand cynicism which imposed itself. She thought most ladies were hypocrites, and
had, in all ways, a low opinion of her own sex, which, more
than once, before this, she had justified to Hyacinth by narrating observations of the most surprising kind, gathered
during her career as a shop-girl. There was a pleasing incon-

sequence, therefore, in her being moved to tears in the third act of the play, when the Pearl of Paraguay, dishevelled and distracted, dragging herself on her knees, implored the stern hidalgo her father, to believe in her innocence in spite of the circumstances which seemed to condemn her—a midnight meeting with the wicked hero in the grove of cocoanuts. It was at this crisis, none the less, that she asked Hyacinth who his friends were in the principal box on the left of the stage, and let him know that a gentleman seated there had been watching him, at intervals, for the past half hour.

'Watching *me*! I like that!' said the young man. 'When I want to be watched I take you with me.'

'Of course he has looked at me,' Millicent answered, as if she had no interest in denying that. 'But you're the one he wants to get hold of.'

'To get hold of!'

'Yes, you ninny: don't hang back. He may make your fortune.'

'Well, if you would like him to come and sit by you I'll go and take a walk in the Strand,' said Hyacinth, entering into the humour of the occasion but not seeing, from where he was placed, any gentleman in the box. Millicent explained that the mysterious observer had just altered his position; he had gone into the back of the box, which had considerable depth. There were other persons in it, out of sight; she and Hyacinth were too much on the same side. One of them was a lady, concealed by the curtain; her arm, bare save for its bracelets, was visible at moments on the cushioned ledge. Hyacinth saw it, in effect, reappear there, and even while the play went on contemplated it with a certain interest; but until the curtain fell at the end of the act there was no further symptom that a gentleman wished to get hold of him.

'Now do you say it's me he's after?' Millicent asked abruptly, giving him a sidelong dig, as the fiddlers in the orchestra began to scrape their instruments for the interlude.

'Of course; I am only the pretext,' Hyacinth replied, after he had looked a moment, in a manner which he flattered himself was a proof of quick self-possession. The gentleman designated by his companion was once more at the front, leaning forward, with his arms on the edge. Hyacinth saw that he was looking straight at him, and our young man returned his gaze—an effort not rendered the more easy by the fact that, after an instant, he recognised him.

'Well, if he knows us he might give some sign, and if he doesn't he might leave us alone,' Millicent declared, abandoning the distinction she had made between herself and her companion. She had no sooner spoken than the gentleman complied with the first mentioned of these conditions; he smiled at Hyacinth across the house—he nodded to him with unmistakable friendliness. Millicent, perceiving this, glanced at the young man from Lomax Place and saw that the demonstration had brought a deep colour to his cheek. He was blushing, flushing; whether with pleasure or embarrassment was not immediately apparent to her. 'I say, I say—is it one of your grand relations?' she promptly exclaimed. 'Well, I can stare as well as him;' and she told Hyacinth it was a 'shime' to bring a young lady to the play when you hadn't so much as an opera-glass for her to look at the company. 'Is he one of those lords your aunt was always talking about in the Plice? Is he your uncle, or your grandfather, or your first or second cousin? No, he's too young for your grandfather. What a pity I can't see if he looks like you!'

At any other time Hyacinth would have thought these inquiries in the worst possible taste, but now he was too much given up to other reflections. It pleased him that the gentleman in the box should recognise and notice him, because even so small a fact as this was an extension of his social existence; but it also surprised and puzzled him, and it produced, generally, in his easily-excited organism, an agitation of which, in spite of his attempted self-control, the appearance he presented to Millicent was the sign. They had met three times, he and his fellow-spectator; but they had met under circumstances which, to Hyacinth's mind, would have made a furtive wink, a mere tremor of the eyelid, a more judicious reference to the fact than so public a salutation. Hyacinth would never have permitted himself to greet him first; and this was not because the gentleman in the box belonged —conspicuously as he did so—to a different walk of society. He was apparently a man of forty, tall and lean and loose-jointed; he fell into lounging, dawdling attitudes, and even at a distance he looked lazy. He had a long, smooth, amused, contented face, unadorned with moustache or whisker, and his brown hair parted itself evenly over his forehead, and came forward on either temple in a rich, well-brushed lock which gave his countenance a certain analogy to portraits of English gentlemen about the year 1820. Millicent Henning had a glance of such range and keenness that she was able to make out the details of his evening-dress, of which she appreciated the 'form'; to observe the character of his large hands; and to note that he appeared to be perpetually smiling, that his eyes were extraordinarily light in colour, and that in spite of the dark, well-marked brows arching over them, his fine skin never had produced, and never would produce, a beard. Our young lady pronounced him mentally a 'swell' of the first magnitude, and wondered more than ever where he had picked up Hyacinth. Her companion seemed to echo her thought when he exclaimed, with a little surprised sigh, almost an exhalation of awe, 'Well, I had no idea he was one of that lot!'

'You might at least tell me his name, so that I shall know what to call him when he comes round to speak to us,' the girl said, provoked at her companion's incommunicativeness.

'Comes round to speak to us—a chap like that!' Hyacinth exclaimed.

'Well, I'm sure if he had been your own brother he couldn't have grinned at you more! He may want to make my acquaintance after all; he won't be the first.'

The gentleman had once more retreated from sight, and there was as much evidence as that of the intention Millicent attributed to him. 'I don't think I'm at all clear that I have a right to tell his name,' he remarked, with sincerity, but with a considerable disposition at the same time to magnify an incident which deepened the brilliancy of the entertainment he had been able to offer Miss Henning. 'I met him in a place where he may not like to have it known that he goes.'

'Do you go to places that people are ashamed of? Is it one of your political clubs, as you call them, where that dirty young man from Camberwell, Mr. Monument (what do you call him?) fills your head with ideas that'll bring you to no good? I'm sure your friend over there doesn't look as if he'd be on *your* side.'

Hyacinth had indulged in this reflection himself; but the only answer he made to Millicent was, 'Well, then, perhaps he'll be on yours!'

'Laws, I hope *she* ain't one of the aristocracy!' Millicent exclaimed, with apparent irrelevance; and following the direction of her eyes Hyacinth saw that the chair his mysterious acquaintance had quitted in the stage-box was now occupied by a lady hitherto invisible—not the one who had given them a glimpse of her shoulder and bare arm. This was an ancient personage, muffled in a voluminous, crumpled white shawl —a stout, odd, foreign-looking woman, whose head apparently was surmounted with a light-coloured wig. She had a placid, patient air and a round, wrinkled face, in which, however, a small, bright eye moved quickly enough. Her rather soiled white gloves were too large for her, and round her head, horizontally arranged, as if to keep her wig in its place, she wore a narrow band of tinsel, decorated, in the middle of the forehead, by a jewel which the rest of her appearance would lead the spectator to suppose false. 'Is the old woman his mother? Where did she dig up her clothes? They look as if she had hired them for the evening. Does *she* come to your wonderful club, too? I daresay she cuts it fine, don't she?' Millicent went on; and when Hyacinth suggested, sportively, that the old lady might be, not the gentleman's mother, but his wife or his 'fancy,' she declared that in that case, if he should come to see them, she wasn't afraid. No wonder he wanted to get out of *that* box! The woman in the wig was sitting there on purpose to look at them, but she couldn't say she was particularly honoured by the notice of such an old guy. Hyacinth pretended that he liked her appearance and thought her very handsome; he offered to bet another paper of peppermints that if they could find out she would be some tremendous old dowager, some one with a handle to her name. To this Millicent replied, with an air of experience, that she had never thought the greatest beauty was in the upper class; and her companion could see that she was covertly looking over her shoulder to watch for his political friend and that she would be disappointed if he did not come. This idea did not make Hyacinth jealous, for his mind was occupied with another side of the business; and if he offered sportive suggestions it was because he was really excited, dazzled, by an incident of which the reader will have failed as yet to perceive the larger relations. What moved him was not the pleasure of being patronised by a rich man; it was simply the prospect of new experience—a sensation for which he was always ready to exchange any present boon; and he was convinced that if the gentleman with whom he had conversed in a small occult back-room in Bloomsbury as Captain Godfrey Sholto—the Captain had given him his card—had more positively than in Millicent's imagination come out of the stage-box to see him, he would bring with him rare influences. This nervous presentiment, lighting on our young man, was so keen that it constituted almost a preparation; therefore, when at the end of a few minutes he became aware that Millicent, with her head turned (her face was in his direction), was taking the measure of some one who had come in behind them, he felt that fate was doing for him, by way of a change, as much as could be expected. He got up in his place, but not too soon to see that Captain Sholto had been standing there a moment in contemplation of Millicent, and that this young lady had performed with deliberation the ceremony of taking his measure. The Captain had his hands in his pockets, and wore a crush-hat, pushed a good deal backward. He laughed at the young couple in the balcony in the friendliest way, as if he had known them both for years, and Millicent could see, on a nearer view, that he was a fine distinguished, easy, genial gentleman, at least six feet high, in spite of a habit, or an affectation, of carrying himself in a casual, relaxed, familiar manner. Hyacinth felt a little, after the first moment, as if he were treating them rather too much as a pair of children whom he had stolen upon, to startle; but this impression was speedily removed by the air with which he said, laying his hand on our hero's shoulder as he stood in the little passage at the end of the bench where the holders of Mr. Vetch's order occupied the first seats, 'My dear fellow, I really thought I must come round and speak to you. My spirits are all gone with this brute of a play. And those boxes are fearfully stuffy, you know,' he added, as if Hyacinth had had at least an equal experience of that part of the theatre.

'It's hot here, too,' Millicent's companion murmured. He had suddenly become much more conscious of the high temperature, of his proximity to the fierce chandelier, and he added that the plot of the play certainly was unnatural, though he thought the piece rather well acted.

'Oh, it's the good old stodgy British tradition. This is the only place where you find it still, and even here it can't last much longer; it can't survive old Baskerville and Mrs. Ruffler. 'Gad, how old they are! I remember her, long past her prime, when I used to be taken to the play, as a boy, in the Christmas holidays. Between them, they must be something like a hundred and eighty, eh? I believe one is supposed to cry a good deal about the middle,' Captain Sholto continued, in the same friendly, familiar, encouraging way, addressing himself to Millicent, upon whom, indeed, his eyes had rested almost uninterruptedly from the first. She sustained his glance with composure, but with just enough of an expression of reserve to intimate (what was perfectly true) that she was not in the habit of conversing with gentlemen with whom she was not acquainted. She turned away her face at this (she had already given the visitor the benefit of a good deal of it), and left him, as in the little passage he leaned against the parapet of the balcony with his back to the stage, confronted with Hyacinth, who was now wondering, with rather more vivid a sense of the relations of things, what he had come for. He wanted to do him honour, in return for his civility, but he did not know what one could talk about, at such short notice, to a person whom he immediately perceived to be, in a most extensive, a really transcendent sense of the term, a man of the world. He instantly saw Captain Sholto did not take the play seriously, so that he felt himself warned off that topic, on which, otherwise, he might have had much to say. On the other hand he could not, in the presence of a third person, allude to the matters they had discussed at the 'Sun and Moon'; nor could he suppose his visitor would expect this, though indeed he impressed him as a man of humours and whims, who was amusing himself with everything, including esoteric socialism and a little bookbinder who had so much more of the gentleman about him than one would expect. Captain Sholto may have been a little embarrassed, now that he was completely launched in his attempt at fraternisation, especially after failing to elicit a smile from Millicent's respectability; but he left to Hyacinth the burden of no initiative, and went on to say that it was just this prospect of the dying-out of the old British tradition that had brought him to-night. He was with a friend, a lady who had lived much abroad, who had never seen anything of the kind, and who liked everything that was characteristic. 'You know the foreign school of acting is a very different affair,' he said again to Millicent, who this time replied, 'Oh yes, of course,' and considering afresh the old lady in the box, reflected that she looked as if there were nothing in the world that she, at least, hadn't seen.

'We have never been abroad,' said Hyacinth, candidly, looking into his friend's curious light-coloured eyes, the palest in tint he had ever encountered.

'Oh, well, there's a lot of nonsense talked about that!' Captain Sholto replied; while Hyacinth remained uncertain as to exactly what he referred to, and Millicent decided to volunteer a remark.

'They are making a tremendous row on the stage. I should think it would be very bad in those boxes.' There was a banging and thumping behind the curtain, the sound of heavy scenery pushed about.

'Oh yes; it's much better here, every way. I think you have the best seats in the house,' said Captain Sholto. 'I should like very much to finish my evening beside you. The trouble is I have ladies—a pair of them,' he went on, as if he were seriously considering this possibility. Then, laying his hand again on Hyacinth's shoulder, he smiled at him a moment and indulged in a still greater burst of frankness. 'My dear fellow, that is just what, as a partial reason, has brought me up here to see you. One of my ladies has a great desire to make your acquaintance!'

'To make my acquaintance?' Hyacinth felt himself turning pale; the first impulse he could have, in connection with such an announcement as that—and it lay far down, in the depths of the unspeakable—was a conjecture that it had something to do with his parentage on his father's side. Captain Sholto's smooth, bright face, irradiating such unexpected advances, seemed for an instant to swim before him. The Captain went on to say that he had told the lady of the talks they had had, that she was immensely interested in such matters—'You know what I mean, she really is'—and that as a consequence of what he had said she had begged him to come and ask his—a—his young friend (Hyacinth saw in a moment that the Captain had forgotten his name) to descend into her box for a little while.

'She has a tremendous desire to talk with some one who looks at the whole business from your standpoint, don't you see? And in her position she scarcely ever has a chance, she doesn't come across them—to her great annoyance. So when I spotted you to-night she immediately said that I must introduce you at any cost. I hope you don't mind, for a quarter of an hour. I ought perhaps to tell you that she is a person who is used to having nothing refused her. "Go up and bring him down," you know, as if it were the simplest thing in the world. She is really very much in earnest: I don't mean about wishing to see you—that goes without saying—but about the whole matter that you and I care for. Then I should add —it doesn't spoil anything—that she is the most charming woman in the world, simply! Honestly, my dear boy, she is perhaps the most remarkable woman in Europe.'

So Captain Sholto delivered himself, with the highest naturalness and plausibility, and Hyacinth, listening, felt that he himself ought perhaps to resent the idea of being served up for the entertainment of imperious triflers, but that somehow he didn't, and that it was more worthy of the part he aspired to play in life to meet such occasions calmly and urbanely than to take the trouble of dodging and going roundabout. Of course the lady in the box couldn't be sincere; she might think she was, though even that was questionable; but you couldn't really care for the cause that was exemplified in the little back room in Bloomsbury if you came to the theatre in that style. It was Captain Sholto's style as well, but it had been by no means clear to Hyacinth hitherto that *he* really cared. All the same, this was no time for going into the

question of the lady's sincerity, and at the end of sixty seconds
our young man had made up his mind that he could afford to
humour her. None the less, I must add, the whole proposal
continued to make things dance, to appear fictive, delusive; so
that it sounded, in comparison, like a note of reality when
Millicent, who had been looking from one of the men to the
other, exclaimed—

'That's all very well, but who is to look after me?' Her assumption of the majestic had broken down, and this was the
cry of nature.

Nothing could have been pleasanter and more indulgent of
her alarm than the manner in which Captain Sholto reassured
her. 'My dear young lady, can you suppose I have been unmindful of that? I have been hoping that after I have taken
down our friend and introduced him you would allow me to
come back and, in his absence, occupy his seat.'

Hyacinth was preoccupied with the idea of meeting the
most remarkable woman in Europe; but at this juncture he
looked at Millicent Henning with some curiosity. She rose to
the situation, and replied, 'I am much obliged to you, but I
don't know who you are.'

'Oh, I'll tell you all about that!' the Captain exclaimed,
benevolently.

'Of course I should introduce you,' said Hyacinth, and he
mentioned to Miss Henning the name of his distinguished
acquaintance.

'In the army?' the young lady inquired, as if she must have
every guarantee of social position.

'Yes—not in the navy! I have left the army, but it always
sticks to one.'

'Mr. Robinson, is it your intention to leave me?' Millicent
asked, in a tone of the highest propriety.

Hyacinth's imagination had taken such a flight that the idea
of what he owed to the beautiful girl who had placed herself
under his care for the evening had somehow effaced itself.
Her words put it before him in a manner that threw him
quickly and consciously back upon his honour; yet there was
something in the way she uttered them that made him look at
her harder still before he replied, 'Oh dear, no, of course it
would never do. I must defer to some other occasion the

honour of making the acquaintance of your friend,' he added, to Captain Sholto.

'Ah, my dear fellow, we might manage it so easily now,' this gentleman murmured, with evident disappointment. 'It is not as if Miss—a—Miss—a—were to be alone.'

It flashed upon Hyacinth that the root of the project might be a desire of Captain Sholto to insinuate himself into Millicent's graces; then he asked himself why the most remarkable woman in Europe should lend herself to that design, consenting even to receive a visit from a little bookbinder for the sake of furthering it. Perhaps, after all, she was not the most remarkable; still, even at a lower estimate, of what advantage could such a complication be to her? To Hyacinth's surprise, Millicent's eye made acknowledgment of his implied renunciation; and she said to Captain Sholto, as if she were considering the matter very impartially, 'Might one know the name of the lady who sent you?'

'The Princess Casamassima.'

'Laws!' cried Millicent Henning. And then, quickly, as if to cover up the crudity of this ejaculation, 'And might one also know what it is, as you say, that she wants to talk to him about?'

'About the lower orders, the rising democracy, the spread of nihilism, and all that.'

'The lower orders? Does she think we belong to them?' the girl demanded, with a strange, provoking laugh.

Captain Sholto was certainly the readiest of men. 'If she could see you, she would think you one of the first ladies in the land.'

'She'll never see me!' Millicent replied, in a manner which made it plain that she, at least, was not to be whistled for.

Being whistled for by a princess presented itself to Hyacinth as an indignity endured gracefully enough by the heroes of several French novels in which he had found a thrilling interest; nevertheless, he said, incorruptibly, to the Captain, who hovered there like a Mephistopheles converted to disinterested charity, 'Having been in the army, you will know that one can't desert one's post.'

The Captain, for the third time, laid his hand on his young friend's shoulder, and for a minute his smile rested, in silence, on Millicent Henning. 'If I tell you simply I want to talk with this young lady, that certainly won't help me, particularly, and there is no reason why it should. Therefore I'll tell you the whole truth: I want to talk with her about *you*!' And he patted Hyacinth in a way which conveyed at once that this idea must surely commend him to the young man's companion and that he himself liked him infinitely.

Hyacinth was conscious of the endearment, but he remarked to Millicent that he would do just as she liked; he was determined not to let a member of the bloated upper class suppose that he held any daughter of the people cheap.

'Oh, I don't care if you go,' said Miss Henning. 'You had better hurry—the curtain's going to rise.'

'That's charming of you! I'll rejoin you in three minutes!' Captain Sholto exclaimed.

He passed his hand into Hyacinth's arm, and as our hero lingered still, a little uneasy and questioning Millicent always with his eyes, the girl went on, with her bright boldness, 'That kind of princess—I should like to hear all about her.'

'Oh, I'll tell you that, too,' the Captain rejoined, with his imperturbable pleasantness, as he led his young friend away. It must be confessed that Hyacinth also rather wondered what kind of princess she was, and his suspense on this point made his heart beat fast when, after traversing steep staircases and winding corridors, they reached the small door of the stage-box.

XIII

HYACINTH'S first consciousness, after his companion had opened it, was of his nearness to the stage, on which the curtain had now risen again. The play was in progress, the actors' voices came straight into the box, and it was impossible to speak without disturbing them. This at least was his inference from the noiseless way his conductor drew him in, and, without announcing or introducing him, simply pointed to a chair and whispered, 'Just drop into that; you'll see and hear beautifully.' He heard the door close behind him, and became aware that Captain Sholto had already retreated. Millicent, at any rate, would not be left to languish in solitude very long. Two ladies were seated in the front of the box, which was so large that there was a considerable space between them; and as he stood there, where Captain Sholto had planted him—they appeared not to have noticed the opening of the door—they turned their heads and looked at him. The one on whom his eyes first rested was the old lady whom he had already contemplated at a distance; she looked queerer still on a closer view, and gave him a little friendly, jolly nod. Her companion was partly overshadowed by the curtain of the box, which she had drawn forward with the intention of shielding herself from the observation of the house; she had still the air of youth, and the simplest way to express the instant effect upon Hyacinth of her fair face of welcome is to say that she was dazzling. He remained as Sholto had left him, staring rather confusedly and not moving an inch; whereupon the younger lady put out her hand—it was her left, the other rested on the ledge of the box—with the expectation, as he perceived, to his extreme mortification, too late, that he would give her his own. She converted the gesture into a sign of invitation, and beckoned him, silently but graciously, to move his chair forward. He did so, and seated himself between the two ladies; then, for ten minutes, stared straight before him, at the stage, not turning his eyes sufficiently even to glance up at Millicent in the balcony. He looked at the play, but he was far from seeing it; he had no sense of anything but the woman who sat there, close to him, on his right, with a fragrance in her garments and a light about her which he seemed to see even while his head was averted. The vision had been only of a moment, but it hung before him, threw a vague white mist over the proceedings on the stage. He was embarrassed, overturned, bewildered, and he knew it; he made a great effort to collect himself, to consider the situation lucidly. He wondered whether he ought to speak, to look at her again, to behave differently, in some way; whether she would take him for a clown, for an idiot; whether she were really as beautiful as she had seemed or it were only a superficial glamour, which a renewed inspection would dissipate. While he asked himself these questions the minutes went on, and neither of his hostesses spoke; they watched the play in perfect stillness, so that Hyacinth divined that this was the proper thing and that he himself must remain dumb until a word should be bestowed upon him. Little by little he recovered himself, took possession of his predicament, and at last transferred his eyes to the Princess. She immediately perceived this, and returned his glance, with a soft smile. She might well be a princess—it was impossible to conform more to the finest evocations of that romantic word. She was fair, brilliant, slender, with a kind of effortless majesty. Her beauty had an air of perfection; it astonished and lifted one up, the sight of it seemed a privilege, reward. If the first impression it had given Hyacinth was to make him feel strangely transported, he need not have been too much agitated, for this was the effect the Princess Casamassima produced upon persons of a wider experience and greater pretensions. Her dark eyes, blue or gray, something that was not brown, were as sweet as they were splendid, and there was an extraordinary light nobleness in the way she held her head. That head, where two or three diamond stars glittered in the thick, delicate hair which defined its shape, suggested to Hyacinth something antique and celebrated, which he had admired of old—the memory was vague—in a statue, in a picture, in a museum. Purity of line and form, of cheek and chin and lip and brow, a colour that seemed to live and glow, a radiance of grace and eminence and success—these things were seated in triumph in the face of the Princess, and Hyacinth, as he held himself in his chair, trembling with the revelation, wondered whether she were not altogether of some different substance from the humanity he had hitherto known. She might be divine, but he could see that she understood human needs—that she wished him to be at his ease and happy; there was something familiar in her smile, as if she had seen him many times before. Her dress was dark and rich; she had pearls round her neck, and an old rococo fan in her hand. Hyacinth took in all these things, and finally said to himself that if she wanted nothing more of him than that, he was content, he would like it to go on; so pleasant was it to sit with fine ladies, in a dusky, spacious receptacle which framed the bright picture of the stage and made one's own situation seem a play within the play. The act was a long one, and the repose in which his companions left him might have been a calculated indulgence, to enable him to get used to them, to see how harmless they were. He looked at Millicent, in the course of time, and saw that Captain Sholto, seated beside her, had not the same standard of propriety, inasmuch as he made a remark to her every few minutes. Like himself, the young lady in the balcony was losing the play, thanks to her eyes being fixed on her friend from Lomax Place, whose position she thus endeavoured to gauge. Hyacinth had quite given up the Paraguayan complications; by the end of the half hour his attention might have come back to them, had he not then been engaged in wondering what the Princess would say to him after the descent of the curtain—or whether she would say anything. The consideration of this problem, as the moment of the solution drew nearer, made his heart again beat faster. He watched the old lady on his left, and supposed it was natural that a princess should have an attendant—he took for granted she was an attendant—as different as possible from herself. This ancient dame was without majesty or grace; huddled together, with her hands folded on her stomach and her lips protruding, she solemnly followed the performance. Several times, however, she turned her head to Hyacinth, and then her expression changed; she repeated the jovial, encouraging, almost motherly nod with which she had greeted him when he had made his bow, and by which she appeared to wish to intimate that, better than the serene beauty on the other side, she could enter into the oddity, the discomfort, of his situation. She seemed to say to him that he must keep his head, and that if the worst should come to the worst she was there to look after him. Even when, at last, the curtain descended, it was some moments before the Princess spoke, though she rested her smile upon Hyacinth as if she were considering what he would best like her to say. He might at that instant have guessed what he discovered later —that among this lady's faults (he was destined to learn that they were numerous), not the least eminent was an exaggerated fear of the commonplace. He expected she would make some remark about the play, but what she said was, very gently and kindly, 'I like to know all sorts of people.'

'I shouldn't think you would find the least difficulty in that,' Hyacinth replied.

'Oh, if one wants anything very much, it's sure to be difficult. Every one isn't as obliging as you.'

Hyacinth could think, immediately, of no proper rejoinder to this; but the old lady saved him the trouble by declaring, with a foreign accent, 'I think you were most extraordinarily good-natured. I had no idea you would come—to two strange women.'

'Yes, we are strange women,' said the Princess, musingly.

'It's not true that she finds things difficult; she makes every one do everything,' her companion went on.

The Princess glanced at her; then remarked to Hyacinth, 'Her name is Madame Grandoni.' Her tone was not familiar, but there was a friendly softness in it, as if he had really taken so much trouble for them that it was only just he should be entertained a little at their expense. It seemed to imply, also, that Madame Grandoni's fitness for supplying such entertainment was obvious.

'But I am not Italian—ah no!' the old lady cried. 'In spite of my name, I am an honest, ugly, unfortunate German. But it doesn't matter. She, also, with such a name, isn't Italian, either. It's an accident; the world is full of accidents. But she isn't German, poor lady, any more.' Madame Grandoni appeared to have entered into the Princess's view, and Hyacinth thought her exceedingly amusing. In a moment she added, 'That was a very charming person you were with.'

'Yes, she is very charming,' Hyacinth replied, not sorry to have a chance to say it.

The Princess made no remark on this subject, and Hyacinth perceived not only that from her position in the box she could have had no glimpse of Millicent, but that she would never take up such an allusion as that. It was as if she had not heard it that she asked, 'Do you consider the play very interesting?'

Hyacinth hesitated a moment, and then told the simple truth. 'I must confess that I have lost the whole of this last act.'

'Ah, poor bothered young man!' cried Madame Grandoni. 'You see—you see!'

'What do I see?' the Princess inquired. 'If you are annoyed at being here now, you will like us later; probably, at least. We take a great interest in the things you care for. We take a great interest in the people,' the Princess went on.

'Oh, allow me, allow me, and speak only for yourself!' the elder lady interposed. 'I take no interest in the people; I don't understand them, and I know nothing about them. An honourable nature, of any class, I always respect it; but I will not pretend to a passion for the ignorant masses, because I have it not. Moreover, that doesn't touch the gentleman.'

The Princess Casamassima had, evidently, a faculty of completely ignoring things of which she wished to take no account; it was not in the least the air of contempt, but a kind of thoughtful, tranquil absence, after which she came back to the point where she wished to be. She made no protest against her companion's speech, but said to Hyacinth, as if she were only vaguely conscious that the old lady had been committing herself in some absurd way, 'She lives with me; she is everything to me; she is the best woman in the world.'

'Yes, fortunately, with many superficial defects, I am very good,' Madame Grandoni remarked.

Hyacinth, by this time, was less embarrassed than when he presented himself to the Princess Casamassima, but he was not less mystified; he wondered afresh whether he were not being practised upon for some inconceivable end; so strange did it seem to him that two such fine ladies should, of their own movement, take the trouble to explain each other to a miserable little bookbinder. This idea made him flush; it was as if it had come over him that he had fallen into a trap. He was conscious that he looked frightened, and he was conscious the moment afterwards that the Princess noticed it. This was, apparently, what made her say, 'If you have lost so much of the play I ought to tell you what has happened.'

'Do you think he would follow that any more?' Madame Grandoni exclaimed.

'If you would tell me—if you would tell me——' And then Hyacinth stopped. He had been going to say, 'If you would tell me what all this means and what you want of me, it would be more to the point!' but the words died on his lips, and he sat staring, for the woman at his right hand was simply too beautiful. She was too beautiful to question, to judge by common logic; and how could he know, moreover, what was natural to a person in that exaltation of grace and splendour? Perhaps it was her habit to send out every evening for some *naïf* stranger, to amuse her; perhaps that was the way the foreign aristocracy lived. There was no sharpness in her face, at the present moment at least; there was nothing but luminous sweetness, yet she looked as if she knew what was going on in his mind. She made no eager attempt to reassure him, but there was a world of delicate consideration in the tone in which she said, 'Do you know, I am afraid I have already forgotten what they have been doing in the play? It's terribly complicated; some one or other was hurled over a precipice.'

'Ah, you're a brilliant pair,' Madame Grandoni remarked, with a laugh of long experience. 'I could describe everything. The person who was hurled over the precipice was the virtuous hero, and you will see, in the next act, that he was only slightly bruised.'

'Don't describe anything; I have so much to ask.' Hyacinth had looked away, in tacit deprecation, at hearing himself 'paired' with the Princess, and he felt that she was watching him. 'What do you think of Captain Sholto?' she went on, suddenly, to his surprise, if anything, in his position, could excite that sentiment more than anything else; and as he hesitated, not knowing what to say, she added, 'Isn't he a very curious type?'

'I know him very little,' Hyacinth replied; and he had no sooner uttered the words than it struck him they were far from brilliant—they were poor and flat, and very little calculated to satisfy the Princess. Indeed, he reflected that he had said nothing at all that could place him in a favourable light; so he continued, at a venture: 'I mean I have never seen him at home.' That sounded still more silly.

'At home? Oh, he is never at home; he is all over the world. To-night he was as likely to have been in Paraguay, for instance, as here. He is what they call a cosmopolite. I don't know whether you know that species; very modern, more and more frequent, and exceedingly tiresome. I prefer the Chinese! He had told me he had had a great deal of interesting talk with you. That was what made me say to him, "Oh, do ask him to come in and see me. A little interesting talk, that would be a change!" '

'She is very complimentary to me!' said Madame Grandoni.

'Ah, my dear, you and I, you know, we never talk: we understand each other without that!' Then the Princess pursued, addressing herself to Hyacinth, 'Do you never admit women?'

'Admit women?'

'Into those *séances*—what do you call them?—those little meetings that Captain Sholto described to me. I should like so much to be present. Why not?'

'I haven't seen any ladies,' Hyacinth said. 'I don't know whether it's a rule, but I have seen nothing but men;' and he added, smiling, though he thought the dereliction rather serious, and couldn't understand the part Captain Sholto was playing, nor, considering the grand company he kept, how he had originally secured admittance into the subversive little circle in Bloomsbury, 'You know I'm not sure Captain Sholto ought to go about reporting our proceedings.'

'I see. Perhaps you think he's a spy, or something of that sort.'

'No,' said Hyacinth, after a moment. 'I think a spy would be more careful—would disguise himself more. Besides, after all, he has heard very little.' And Hyacinth smiled again.

'You mean he hasn't really been behind the scenes?' the Princess asked, bending forward a little, and now covering the young man steadily with her deep, soft eyes, as if by this time he must have got used to her and wouldn't flinch from such attention. 'Of course he hasn't, and he never will be; he knows that, and that it's quite out of his power to tell any real secrets. What he repeated to me was interesting, but of course I could see that there was nothing the authorities, anywhere, could put their hand on. It was mainly the talk he had had with you which struck him so very much, and which struck me, as you see. Perhaps you didn't know how he was drawing you out.'

'I am afraid that's rather easy,' said Hyacinth, with perfect candour, as it came over him that he *had* chattered, with a vengeance, in Bloomsbury, and had thought it natural enough then that his sociable fellow-visitor should offer him cigars and attach importance to the views of a clever and original young artisan.

'I am not sure that I find it so! However, I ought to tell you that you needn't have the least fear of Captain Sholto. He's a perfectly honest man, so far as he goes; and even if you had trusted him much more than you appear to have done, he would be incapable of betraying you. However, don't trust him: not because he's not safe, but because—— No matter, you will see for yourself. He has gone into that sort of thing simply to please me. I should tell you, merely to make you understand, that he would do anything for that. That's his own affair. I wanted to know something, to learn something, to ascertain what really is going on; and for a woman everything of that sort is so difficult, especially for a woman in my position, who is known, and to whom every sort of bad faith is sure to be imputed. So Sholto said he would look into the subject for me; poor man, he has had to look into so many subjects! What I particularly wanted was that he should make friends with some of the leading spirits, really characteristic types.' The Princess's voice was low and rather deep, and her tone very quick; her manner of speaking was altogether new to her listener, for whom the pronunciation of her words and the very punctuation of her sentences were a kind of revelation of 'society.'

'Surely Captain Sholto doesn't suppose that *I* am a leading spirit!' Hyacinth exclaimed, with the determination not to be laughed at any more than he could help.

The Princess hesitated a moment; then she said, 'He told me you were very original.'

'He doesn't know, and—if you will allow me to say so—I don't think you know. How should you? I am one of many thousands of young men of my class—you know, I suppose, what that is—in whose brains certain ideas are fermenting. There is nothing original about me at all. I am very young and very ignorant; it's only a few months since I began to talk of the possibility of a social revolution with men who have considered the whole ground much more than I have done. I'm a mere particle in the immensity of the people. All I pretend to is my good faith, and a great desire that justice shall be done.'

The Princess listened to him intently, and her attitude made him feel how little *he*, in comparison, expressed himself like a person who had the habit of conversation; he seemed to himself to stammer and emit common sounds. For a moment she said nothing, only looking at him with her pure smile. 'I do draw you out!' she exclaimed, at last. 'You are much more interesting to me than if you were an exception.' At these last words Hyacinth flinched a hair's breadth; the movement was shown by his dropping his eyes. We know to what extent he really regarded himself as of the stuff of the common herd. The Princess doubtless guessed it as well, for she quickly added, 'At the same time, I can see that you are remarkable enough.'

'What do you think I am remarkable for?'

'Well, you have general ideas.'

'Every one has them to-day. They have them in Bloomsbury to a terrible degree. I have a friend (who understands the matter much better than I) who has no patience with them: he declares they are our danger and our bane. A few very special ideas—if they are the right ones—are what we want.'

'Who is your friend?' the Princess asked, abruptly.

'Ah, Christina, Christina,' Madame Grandoni murmured from the other side of the box.

Christina took no notice of her, and Hyacinth, not under-standing the warning, and only remembering how personal women always are, replied, 'A young man who lives in Cam-berwell, an assistant at a wholesale chemist's.'

If he had expected that this description of his friend was a bigger dose than his hostess would be able to digest, he was greatly mistaken. She seemed to look tenderly at the picture suggested by his words, and she immediately inquired whether the young man were also clever, and whether she might not hope to know him. Hadn't Captain Sholto seen him; and if so, why hadn't he spoken of him, too? When Hyacinth had replied that Captain Sholto had probably seen him, but that he believed he had had no particular conversa-tion with him, the Princess inquired, with startling frankness, whether her visitor wouldn't bring his friend, some day, to see her.

Hyacinth glanced at Madame Grandoni, but that worthy woman was engaged in a survey of the house, through an old-fashioned eye-glass with a long gilt handle. He had per-ceived, long before this, that the Princess Casamassima had no desire for vain phrases, and he had the good taste to feel that, from himself to such a personage, compliments, even if he had wished to pay them, would have had no suitability. 'I don't know whether he would be willing to come. He's the sort of man that, in such a case, you can't answer for.'

'That makes me want to know him all the more. But you'll come yourself, at all events, eh?'

Poor Hyacinth murmured something about the unexpected honour; for, after all, he had a French heredity, and it was not so easy for him to make unadorned speeches. But Madame Grandoni, laying down her eye-glass, almost took the words out of his mouth, with the cheerful exhortation, 'Go and see her—go and see her once or twice. She will treat you like an angel.'

'You must think me very peculiar,' the Princess remarked, sadly.

'I don't know what I think. It will take a good while.'

'I wish I could make you trust me—inspire you with con-fidence,' she went on. 'I don't mean only you, personally, but others who think as you do. You would find I would go with

you—pretty far. I was answering just now for Captain
Sholto; but who in the world is to answer for me?' And her
sadness merged itself in a smile which appeared to Hyacinth
extraordinarily magnanimous and touching.

'Not I, my dear, I promise you!' her ancient companion
ejaculated, with a laugh which made the people in the stalls
look up at the box.

Her mirth was contagious; it gave Hyacinth the audacity to
say to her, 'I would trust *you*, if you did!' though he felt, the
next minute, that this was even a more familiar speech than if
he had said he wouldn't trust her.

'It comes, then, to the same thing,' the Princess went on.
'She would not show herself with me in public if I were not
respectable. If you knew more about me you would understand what has led me to turn my attention to the great social
question. It is a long story, and the details wouldn't interest
you; but perhaps some day, if we have more talk, you will put
yourself a little in my place. I am very serious, you know; I
am not amusing myself with peeping and running away. I am
convinced that we are living in a fool's paradise, that the
ground is heaving under our feet.'

'It's not the ground, my dear; it's you that are turning
somersaults,' Madame Grandoni interposed.

'Ah, you, my friend, you have the happy faculty of believing what you like to believe. I have to believe what I see.'

'She wishes to throw herself into the revolution, to guide
it, to enlighten it,' Madame Grandoni said to Hyacinth,
speaking now with imperturbable gravity.

'I am sure she could direct it in any sense she would wish!'
the young man responded, in a glow. The pure, high dignity
with which the Princess had just spoken, and which appeared
to cover a suppressed tremor of passion, set Hyacinth's pulses
throbbing, and though he scarcely saw what she meant—her
aspirations seeming so vague—her tone, her voice, her wonderful face, showed that she had a generous soul.

She answered his eager declaration with a serious smile and
a melancholy head-shake. 'I have no such pretensions, and my
good old friend is laughing at me. Of course that is very easy;
for what, in fact, can be more absurd, on the face of it, than
for a woman with a title, with diamonds, with a carriage,

with servants, with a position, as they call it, to sympathise with the upward struggles of those who are below? "Give all that up, and we'll believe you," you have a right to say. I am ready to give them up the moment it will help the cause; I assure you that's the least difficulty. I don't want to teach, I want to learn; and, above all, I want to know *à quoi m'en tenir*. Are we on the eve of great changes, or are we not? Is everything that is gathering force, underground, in the dark, in the night, in little hidden rooms, out of sight of governments and policemen and idiotic "statesmen"—heaven save them!—is all this going to burst forth some fine morning and set the world on fire? Or is it to sputter out and spend itself in vain conspiracies, be dissipated in sterile heroisms and abortive isolated movements? I want to know *à quoi m'en tenir,*' she repeated, fixing her visitor with more brilliant eyes, as if he could tell her on the spot. Then, suddenly, she added in a totally different tone, 'Excuse me, I have an idea you speak French. Didn't Captain Sholto tell me so?'

'I have some little acquaintance with it,' Hyacinth murmured. 'I have French blood in my veins.'

She considered him as if he had proposed to her some kind of problem. 'Yes, I can see that you are not *le premier venu*. Now, your friend, of whom you were speaking, is a chemist; and you, yourself—what is your occupation?'

'I'm just a bookbinder.'

'That must be delightful. I wonder if you would bind some books for me.'

'You would have to bring them to our shop, and I can do there only the work that's given out to me. I might manage it by myself, at home,' Hyacinth added, smiling.

'I should like that better. And what do you call home?'

'The place I live in, in the north of London: a little street you certainly never heard of.'

'What is it called?'

'Lomax Place, at your service,' said Hyacinth, laughing.

She laughed back at him, and he didn't know whether her brightness or her gravity were the more charming. 'No, I don't think I have heard of it. I don't know London very well; I haven't lived here long. I have spent most of my life abroad. My husband is a foreigner, an Italian. We don't live together much. I haven't the manners of this country—not of any class; have I, eh? Oh, this country—there is a great deal to be said about it; and a great deal to be done, as you, of course, understand better than any one. But I want to know London; it interests me more than I can say—the huge, swarming, smoky, human city. I mean real London, the people and all their sufferings and passions; not Park Lane and Bond Street. Perhaps you can help me—it would be a great kindness: that's what I want to know men like you for. You see it isn't idle, my having given you so much trouble to-night.'

'I shall be very glad to show you all I know. But it isn't much, and above all it isn't pretty,' said Hyacinth.

'Whom do you live with, in Lomax Place?' the Princess asked, by way of rejoinder to this.

'Captain Sholto is leaving the young lady—he is coming back here,' Madame Grandoni announced, inspecting the balcony with her instrument. The orchestra had been for some time playing the overture to the following act.

Hyacinth hesitated a moment. 'I live with a dressmaker.'

'With a dressmaker? Do you mean—do you mean——?' And the Princess paused.

'Do you mean she's your wife?' asked Madame Grandoni, humorously.

'Perhaps she gives you rooms,' remarked the Princess.

'How many do you think I have? She gives me everything, or she has done so in the past. She brought me up; she is the best little woman in the world.'

'You had better command a dress!' exclaimed Madame Grandoni.

'And your family, where are they?' the Princess continued.

'I have no family.'

'None at all?'

'None at all. I never had.'

'But the French blood that you speak of, and which I see perfectly in your face—you haven't the English expression, or want of expression—that must have come to you through some one.'

'Yes, through my mother.'

'And she is dead?'

'Long ago.'

'That's a great loss, because French mothers are usually so much to their sons.' The Princess looked at her painted fan a moment, as she opened and closed it; after which she said, 'Well, then, you'll come some day. We'll arrange it.'

Hyacinth felt that the answer to this could be only a silent inclination of his little person; and to make it he rose from his chair. As he stood there, conscious that he had stayed long enough and yet not knowing exactly how to withdraw, the Princess, with her fan closed, resting upright on her knee, and her hands clasped on the end of it, turned up her strange, lovely eyes at him, and said—

'Do you think anything will occur soon?'

'Will occur?'

'That there will be a crisis—that you'll make yourselves felt?'

In this beautiful woman's face there was to Hyacinth's bewildered perception something at once inspiring, tempting and mocking; and the effect of her expression was to make him say, rather clumsily, 'I'll try and ascertain;' as if she had asked him whether her carriage were at the door.

'I don't quite know what you are talking about; but please don't have it for another hour or two. I want to see what becomes of the Pearl!' Madame Grandoni interposed.

'Remember what I told you: I would give up everything —everything!' the Princess went on, looking up at the young man in the same way. Then she held out her hand, and this time he knew sufficiently what he was about to take it.

When he bade good-night to Madame Grandoni the old lady exclaimed to him, with a comical sigh, 'Well, she *is* respectable!' and out in the lobby, when he had closed the door of the box behind him, he found himself echoing these words and repeating mechanically, 'She *is* respectable!' They were on his lips as he stood, suddenly, face to face with Captain Sholto, who laid his hand on his shoulder once more and shook him a little, in that free yet insinuating manner for which this officer appeared to be remarkable.

'My dear fellow, you were born under a lucky star.'

'I never supposed it,' said Hyacinth, changing colour.

'Why, what in the world would you have? You have the faculty, the precious faculty, of inspiring women with an interest—but an interest!'

'Yes, ask them in the box there! I behaved like a cretin,' Hyacinth declared, overwhelmed now with a sense of opportunities missed.

'They won't tell me that. And the lady upstairs?'

'Well,' said Hyacinth gravely, 'what about her?'

The Captain considered him a moment. 'She wouldn't talk to me of anything but you. You may imagine how I liked it!'

'I don't like it, either. But I must go up.'

'Oh yes, she counts the minutes. Such a charming person!' Captain Sholto added, with more propriety of tone. As Hyacinth left him he called after him, 'Don't be afraid—you'll go far.'

When the young man took his place in the balcony beside Millicent this damsel gave him no greeting, nor asked any question about his adventures in the more aristocratic part of the house. She only turned her fine complexion upon him for some minutes, and as he himself was not in the mood to begin to chatter, the silence continued—continued till after the curtain had risen on the last act of the play. Millicent's attention was now, evidently, not at her disposal for the stage, and in the midst of a violent scene, which included pistol-shots and shrieks, she said at last to her companion, 'She's a tidy lot, your Princess, by what I learn.'

'Pray, what do you know about her?'

'I know what that fellow told me.'

'And pray, what was that?'

'Well, she's a bad 'un, as ever was. Her own husband has had to turn her out of the house.'

Hyacinth remembered the allusion the lady herself had made to her matrimonial situation; nevertheless, what he would have liked to reply to Miss Henning was that he didn't believe a word of it. He withheld the doubt, and after a moment remarked quietly, 'I don't care.'

'You don't care? Well, I do, then!' Millicent cried. And as it was impossible, in view of the performance and the jealous attention of their neighbours, to continue the conversation in

this pitch, she contented herself with ejaculating, in a somewhat lower key, at the end of five minutes, during which she
had been watching the stage, 'Gracious, what dreadful common stuff!'

XIV

HYACINTH did not mention to Pinnie or Mr. Vetch that he had been taken up by a great lady; but he mentioned it to Paul Muniment, to whom he now confided a great many things. He had, at first, been in considerable fear of his straight, loud, north-country friend, who showed signs of cultivating logic and criticism to a degree that was hostile to free conversation; but he discovered later that he was a man to whom one could say anything in the world, if one didn't think it of more importance to be sympathised with than to be understood. For a revolutionist, he was strangely good-natured. The sight of all the things he wanted to change had seemingly no power to irritate him, and if he joked about questions that lay very near his heart his pleasantry was not bitter nor invidious; the fault that Hyacinth sometimes found with it, rather, was that it was innocent to puerility. Our hero envied his power of combining a care for the wide misery of mankind with the apparent state of mind of the cheerful and virtuous young workman who, on Sunday morning, has put on a clean shirt, and, not having taken the gilt off his wages the night before, weighs against each other, for a happy day, the respective attractions of Epping Forest and Gravesend. He was never sarcastic about his personal lot and his daily life; it had not seemed to occur to him, for instance, that 'society' was really responsible for the condition of his sister's spinal column, though Eustache Poupin and his wife (who practically, however, were as patient as he), did everything they could to make him say so, believing, evidently, that it would relieve him. Apparently he cared nothing for women, talked of them rarely, and always decently, and had never a sign of a sweetheart, unless Lady Aurora Langrish might pass for one. He never drank a drop of beer nor touched a pipe; he always had a clear tone, a fresh cheek and a smiling eye, and once excited on Hyacinth's part a kind of elder-brotherly indulgence by the open-mouthed glee and credulity with which, when the pair were present, in the sixpenny gallery, at Astley's, at an equestrian pantomime, he followed the tawdry spectacle. He once told the young bookbinder that he was a suggestive little beggar, and Hyacinth's opinion of him, by this time, was so exalted that the remark had almost the value of a patent of nobility. Our hero treated himself to an unlimited belief in him; he had always dreamed of having some grand friendship, and this was the best opening he had ever encountered. No one could entertain a sentiment of that sort better than Hyacinth, or cultivate a greater luxury of confidence. It disappointed him, sometimes, that it was not more richly repaid; that on certain important points of the socialistic programme Muniment would never commit himself; and that he had not yet shown the *fond du sac*, as Eustache Poupin called it, to so ardent an admirer. He answered particular questions freely enough, and answered them occasionally in a manner that made Hyacinth jump, as when, in reply to an inquiry in regard to his view of capital punishment, he said that, so far from wishing it abolished, he should go in for extending it much further—he should impose it on those who habitually lied or got drunk; but his friend had always a feeling that he kept back his best card and that even in the listening circle in Bloomsbury, when only the right men were present, there were unspoken conclusions in his mind which he didn't as yet think any one good enough to be favoured with. So far, therefore, from suspecting him of half-heartedness, Hyacinth was sure that he had extraordinary things in his head; that he was thinking them out to the logical end, wherever it might land him; and that the night he should produce them, with the door of the club-room guarded and the company bound by a tremendous oath, the others would look at each other and turn pale.

'She wants to see you; she asked me to bring you; she was very serious,' Hyacinth said, relating his interview with the ladies in the box at the play; which, however, now that he looked back upon it, seemed as queer as a dream, and not much more likely than that sort of experience to have a continuation in one's waking hours.

'To bring me—to bring me where?' asked Muniment. 'You talk as if I were a sample out of your shop, or a little dog you had for sale. Has she ever seen me? Does she think I'm smaller than you? What does she know about me?'

'Well, principally, that you're a friend of mine—that's enough for her.'

'Do you mean that it ought to be enough for me that she's a friend of yours? I have a notion you'll have some queer ones before you're done; a good many more than I have time to talk to. And how can I go to see a delicate female, with those paws?' Muniment inquired, exhibiting ten work-stained fingers.

'Buy a pair of gloves,' said Hyacinth, who recognised the serious character of this obstacle. But after a moment he added, 'No, you oughtn't to do that; she wants to see dirty hands.'

'That's easy enough; she needn't send for me for the purpose. But isn't she making game of you?'

'It's very possible, but I don't see what good it can do her.'

'You are not obliged to find excuses for the pampered classes. Their bloated luxury begets evil, impudent desires; they are capable of doing harm for the sake of harm. Besides, is she genuine?'

'If she isn't, what becomes of your explanation?' asked Hyacinth.

'Oh, it doesn't matter; at night all cats are gray. Whatever she is, she's an idle, bedizened jade.'

'If you had seen her, you wouldn't talk of her that way.'

'God forbid I should see her, then, if she's going to corrupt me!'

'Do you suppose she'll corrupt *me*?' Hyacinth demanded, with an expression of face and a tone of voice which produced, on his friend's part, an explosion of mirth.

'How can she, after all, when you are already such a little mass of corruption?'

'You don't think that,' said Hyacinth, looking very grave.

'Do you mean that if I did I wouldn't say it? Haven't you noticed that I say what I think?'

'No, you don't, not half of it: you're as close as a fish.'

Paul Muniment looked at his companion a moment, as if he were rather struck with the penetration of that remark; then he said, 'Well, then, if I should give you the other half of my opinion of you, do you think you'd fancy it?'

'I'll save you the trouble. I'm a very clever, conscientious, promising young chap, and any one would be proud to claim me as a friend.'

'Is that what your Princess told you? She must be a precious piece of goods!' Paul Muniment exclaimed. 'Did she pick your pocket meanwhile?'

'Oh yes; a few minutes later I missed a silver cigar-case, engraved with the arms of the Robinsons. Seriously,' Hyacinth continued, 'don't you consider it possible that a woman of that class should want to know what is going on among the like of us?'

'It depends upon what class you mean.'

'Well, a woman with a lot of jewels and the manners of an angel. It's queer of course, but it's conceivable; why not? There may be unselfish natures; there may be disinterested feelings.'

'And there may be fine ladies in an awful funk about their jewels, and even about their manners. Seriously, as you say, it's perfectly conceivable. I am not in the least surprised at the aristocracy being curious to know what we are up to, and wanting very much to look into it; in their place I should be very uneasy, and if I were a woman with angelic manners very likely I too should be glad to get hold of a soft, susceptible little bookbinder, and pump him dry, bless his heart!'

'Are you afraid I'll tell her secrets?' cried Hyacinth, flushing with virtuous indignation.

'Secrets? What secrets could you tell her, my pretty lad?'

Hyacinth stared a moment. 'You don't trust me—you never have.'

'We will, some day—don't be afraid,' said Muniment, who, evidently, had no intention of unkindness, a thing that appeared to be impossible to him. 'And when we do, you'll cry with disappointment.'

'Well, *you* won't,' Hyacinth declared. And then he asked whether his friend thought the Princess Casamassima a spy; and why, if she were in that line, Mr. Sholto was not—inasmuch as it must be supposed he was not, since they had seen fit to let him walk in and out, at that rate, in the place in Bloomsbury. Muniment did not even know whom he meant, not having had any relations with the gentleman; but he summoned a sufficient image when his companion had described the Captain's appearance. He then remarked, with his usual geniality, that he didn't take him for a spy—he took him for an ass; but even if he had edged himself into the place with every intention to betray them, what handle could he possibly get—what use, against them, could he make of anything he had seen or heard? If he had a fancy to dip into workingmen's clubs (Muniment remembered, now, the first night he came; he had been brought by that German cabinetmaker, who had a stiff neck and smoked a pipe with a bowl as big as a stove); if it amused him to put on a bad hat, and inhale foul tobacco, and call his 'inferiors' 'my dear fellow'; if he thought that in doing so he was getting an insight into the people and going half-way to meet them and preparing for what was coming—all this was his own affair, and he was very welcome, though a man must be a flat who would spend his evening in a hole like that when he might enjoy his comfort in one of those flaming big shops, full of armchairs and flunkies, in Pall Mall. And what did he see, after all, in Bloomsbury? Nothing but a 'social gathering,' where there were clay pipes, and a sanded floor, and not half enough gas, and the principal newspapers; and where the men, as any one would know, were advanced radicals, and mostly advanced idiots. He could pat as many of them on the back as he liked, and say the House of Lords wouldn't last till midsummer; but what discoveries would he make? He was simply on the same lay as Hyacinth's Princess; he was nervous and scared, and he thought he would see for himself.

'Oh, he isn't the same sort as the Princess. I'm sure he's in a very different line!' Hyacinth exclaimed.

'Different, of course; she's a handsome woman, I suppose, and he's an ugly man; but I don't think that either of them will save us or spoil us. Their curiosity is natural, but I have got other things to do than to show them over; therefore you can tell her serene highness that I'm much obliged.'

Hyacinth reflected a moment, and then he said, 'You show Lady Aurora over; you seem to wish to give her the information she desires; and what's the difference? If it's right for her to take an interest, why isn't it right for my Princess?'

'If she's already yours, what more can she want?' Muniment asked. 'All I know of Lady Aurora, and all I look at, is that she comes and sits with Rosy, and brings her tea, and waits upon her. If the Princess will do as much I'll tell her she's a woman of genius; but apart from that I shall never take a grain of interest in her interest in the masses—or in this particular mass!' And Paul Muniment, with his discoloured thumb, designated his own substantial person. His tone was disappointing to Hyacinth, who was surprised at his not appearing to think the episode at the theatre more remarkable and romantic. Muniment seemed to regard his explanation of such a proceeding as all-sufficient; but when, a moment later, he made use, in referring to the mysterious lady, of the expression that she was 'quaking,' Hyacinth broke out—'Never in the world; she's not afraid of anything!'

'Ah, my lad, not afraid of you, evidently!'

Hyacinth paid no attention to this coarse sally, but asked in a moment, with a candour that was proof against further ridicule, 'Do you think she can do me a hurt of any kind, if we follow up our acquaintance?'

'Yes, very likely, but you must hit her back! That's your line, you know: to go in for what's going, to live your life, to gratify the women. I'm an ugly, grimy brute, I've got to watch the fires and mind the shop; but you are one of those taking little beggars who ought to run about and see the world; you ought to be an ornament to society, like a young man in an illustrated story-book. Only,' Muniment added in a moment, 'you know, if she should hurt you very much, *then* I would go and see her!'

Hyacinth had been intending for some time to take Pinnie to call on the prostrate damsel in Audley Court, to whom he had promised that his benefactress (he had told Rose Muniment that she was 'a kind of aunt') should pay this civility; but the affair had been delayed by wan hesitations on the part of the dressmaker, for the poor woman had hard work to imagine, to-day, that there were people in London so forlorn that her countenance could be of value to them. Her social curiosities had become very nearly extinct, and she knew that she no longer made the same figure in public as when her command of the fashions enabled her to illustrate them in her own little person, by the aid of a good deal of whalebone. Moreover she felt that Hyacinth had strange friends and still stranger opinions; she suspected that he took an unnatural interest in politics and was somehow not on the right side, little as she knew about parties or causes; and she had a vague conviction that this kind of perversity only multiplied the troubles of the poor, who, according to theories which Pinnie had never reasoned out, but which, in her bosom, were as deep as religion, ought always to be of the same way of thinking as the rich. They were unlike them enough in their poverty, without trying to add other differences. When at last she accompanied Hyacinth to Camberwell, one Saturday evening at midsummer, it was in a sighing, sceptical, second-best manner; but if he had told her he wished it she would have gone with him to a *soirée* at a scavenger's. There was no more danger of Rose Muniment's being out than of one of the bronze couchant lions in Trafalgar Square having walked down Whitehall; but he had let her know in advance, and he perceived, as he opened her door in obedience to a quick, shrill summons, that she had had the happy thought of inviting Lady Aurora to help her to entertain Miss Pynsent. Such, at least, was the inference he drew from seeing her ladyship's memorable figure rise before him for the first time since his own visit. He presented his companion to their reclining hostess, and Rosy immediately repeated her name to the representative of Belgrave Square. Pinnie curtsied down to the ground, as Lady Aurora put out her hand to her, and slipped noiselessly into a chair beside the bed. Lady Aurora laughed and fidgeted, in a friendly, cheerful, yet at the same time rather pointless manner, and Hyacinth gathered that she had no recollection of having met him before. His attention, however, was mainly given to Pinnie: he watched her jealously, to see whether, on this important occasion, she would not put forth a certain stiff, quaint, polished politeness, of which she possessed the secret and which made her resemble a pair of old-fashioned sugar-tongs. Not only for Pinnie's sake, but for his own as well, he wished her to pass for a superior little woman, and he hoped she wouldn't lose her head if Rosy should begin to talk about Inglefield. She was, evidently, much impressed by Rosy, and kept repeating, 'Dear, dear!' under her breath, as the small, strange person in the bed rapidly explained to her that there was nothing in the world she would have liked so much as to follow *her* delightful profession, but that she couldn't sit up to it, and had never had a needle in her hand but once, when at the end of three minutes it had dropped into the sheets and got into the mattress, so that she had always been afraid it would work out again and stick into her; but it hadn't done so yet, and perhaps it never would—she lay so quiet, she didn't push it about much. 'Perhaps you would think it's me that trimmed the little handkerchief I wear round my neck,' Miss Muniment said; 'perhaps you would think I couldn't do less, lying here all day long, with complete command of my time. Not a stitch of it. I'm the finest lady in London; I never lift my finger for myself. It's a present from her ladyship—it's her ladyship's own beautiful needlework. What do you think of that? Have you ever met any one so favoured before? And the work—just look at the work, and tell me what you think of that!' The girl pulled off the bit of muslin from her neck and thrust it at Pinnie, who looked at it confusedly and exclaimed, 'Dear, dear, dear!' partly in sympathy, partly as if, in spite of the consideration she owed every one, those were very strange proceedings.

'It's very badly done; surely you see that,' said Lady Aurora. 'It was only a joke.'

'Oh yes, everything's a joke!' cried the irrepressible invalid—'everything except my state of health; that's admitted to be serious. When her ladyship sends me five shillings' worth of coals it's only a joke; and when she brings me a bottle of the finest port, that's another; and when she climbs up seventy-seven stairs (there are seventy-seven, I know perfectly, though I never go up or down), at the height of the London season, to spend the evening with me, that's the best of all. I know all about the London season, though I never go out, and I appreciate what her ladyship gives up. She is very jocular indeed, but, fortunately, I know how to take it. You can see that it wouldn't do for me to be touchy, can't you, Miss Pynsent?'

'Dear, dear, I should be so glad to make you anything myself; it would be better—it would be better——' Pinnie murmured, hesitating.

'It would be better than my poor work. I don't know how
to do that sort of thing, in the least,' said Lady Aurora.

'I'm sure I didn't mean that, my lady—I only meant it
would be more convenient. Anything in the world she might
fancy,' the dressmaker went on, as if it were a question of the
invalid's appetite.

'Ah, you see I don't wear things—only a flannel jacket, to
be a bit tidy,' Miss Muniment rejoined. 'I go in only for smart
counterpanes, as you can see for yourself;' and she spread her
white hands complacently over her coverlet of brilliant patchwork. 'Now doesn't that look to you, Miss Pynsent, as if it
might be one of her ladyship's jokes?'

'Oh, my good friend, how can you? I never went so far as
that!' Lady Aurora interposed, with visible anxiety.

'Well, you've given me almost everything; I sometimes forget. This only cost me sixpence; so it comes to the same thing
as if it had been a present. Yes, only sixpence, in a raffle in a
bazaar at Hackney, for the benefit of the Wesleyan Chapel,
three years ago. A young man who works with my brother,
and lives in that part, offered him a couple of tickets; and he
took one, and I took one. When I say "I," of course I mean
that he took the two; for how should I find (by which I
mean, of course, how should *he* find) a sixpence in that little
cup on the chimney-piece unless he had put it there first? Of
course my ticket took a prize, and of course, as my bed is my
dwelling-place, the prize was a beautiful counterpane, of every
colour of the rainbow. Oh, there never was such luck as
mine!' Rosy exclaimed, flashing her gay, strange eyes at Hyacinth, as if on purpose to irritate him with her contradictious
optimism.

'It's very lovely; but if you would like another, for a
change, I've got a great many pieces,' Pinnie remarked, with a
generosity which made the young man feel that she was ac-
quitting herself finely.

Rose Muniment laid her little hand on the dressmaker's
arm, and responded, quickly, 'No, not a change, not a change.

How can there be a change when there's already everything? There's everything here—every colour that was ever seen, or composed, or dreamed of, since the world began.' And with her other hand she stroked, affectionately, her variegated quilt. 'You have a great many pieces, but you haven't as many as there are here; and the more you should patch them together the more the whole thing would resemble this dear, dazzling old friend. I have another idea, very, very charming, and perhaps her ladyship can guess what it is.' Rosy kept her fingers on Pinnie's arm, and, smiling, turned her brilliant eyes from one of her female companions to the other, as if she wished to associate them as much as possible in their interest in her. 'In connection with what we were talking about a few minutes ago—couldn't your ladyship just go a little further, in the same line?' Then, as Lady Aurora looked troubled and embarrassed, blushing at being called upon to answer a co-nundrum, as it were, so publicly, her infirm friend came to her assistance. 'It will surprise you at first, but it won't when I have explained it: my idea is just simply a pink dressing-gown!'

'A pink dressing-gown!' Lady Aurora repeated.

'With a neat black trimming! Don't you see the connection with what we were talking of before our good visitors came in?'

'That would be very pretty,' said Pinnie. 'I have made them like that, in my time. Or blue, trimmed with white.'

'No, pink and black, pink and black—to suit my complex-ion. Perhaps you didn't know I have a complexion; but there are very few things I haven't got! Anything at all I should fancy, you were so good as to say. Well now, I fancy that! Your ladyship does see the connection by this time, doesn't she?'

Lady Aurora looked distressed, as if she felt that she cer-tainly ought to see it but was not sure that even yet it didn't escape her, and as if, at the same time, she were struck with the fact that this sudden evocation might result in a strain on the little dressmaker's resources. 'A pink dressing-gown would certainly be very becoming, and Miss Pynsent would be very kind,' she said; while Hyacinth made the mental comment that it was a largeish order, as Pinnie would have, obviously, to furnish the materials as well as the labour. The amiable coolness with which the invalid laid her under contribution was, however, to his sense, quite in character, and he reflected that, after all, when you were stretched on your back like that you had the right to reach out your hands (it wasn't far you could reach at best), and seize what you could get. Pinnie declared that she knew just the article Miss Muniment wanted, and that she would undertake to make a sweet thing of it; and Rosy went on to say that she must explain of what use such an article would be, but for this purpose there must be another guess. She would give it to Miss Pynsent and Hyacinth—as many times as they liked: What *had* she and Lady Aurora been talking about before they came in? She clasped her hands, and her eyes glittered with her eagerness, while she continued to turn them from Lady Aurora to the dressmaker. What would they imagine? What would they think natural, delightful, magnificent—if one could only end, at last, by making out the right place to put it? Hyacinth suggested, successively, a cage of Java sparrows, a music-box and a shower-bath—or perhaps even a full-length portrait of her ladyship; and Pinnie looked at him askance, in a frightened way, as if perchance he were joking too broadly. Rosy at last relieved their suspense and announced, 'A sofa, just a sofa, now! What do you say to that? Do you suppose that's an idea that could have come from any one but her ladyship? She must have all the credit of it; she came out with it in the course of conversation. I believe we were talking of the peculiar feeling that comes just under the shoulder-blades if one never has a change. She mentioned it as she might have mentioned a plaster, or another spoonful of that American stuff. We are thinking it over, and one of these days, if we give plenty of time to the question, we shall find the place, the very nicest and snuggest of all, and no other. I hope *you* see the connection with the pink dressing-gown,' she remarked to Pinnie, 'and I hope you see the importance of the question, Shall anything go? I should like you to look round a bit, and tell me what you would answer if I were to say to you, *Can* anything go?'

XV

I'M SURE there's nothing *I* should like to part with,' Pinnie returned; and while she surveyed the scene Lady Aurora, with delicacy, to lighten Amanda's responsibility, got up and turned to the window, which was open to the summer-evening and admitted still the last rays of the long day. Hyacinth, after a moment, placed himself beside her, looking out with her at the dusky multitude of chimney-pots and the small black houses, roofed with grimy tiles. The thick, warm air of a London July floated beneath them, suffused with the everlasting uproar of the town, which appeared to have sunk into quietness but again became a mighty voice as soon as one listened for it; here and there, in poor windows, glimmered a turbid light, and high above, in a clearer, smokeless zone, a sky still fair and luminous, a faint silver star looked down. The sky was the same that, far away in the country, bent over golden fields and purple hills and gardens where nightingales sang; but from this point of view everything that covered the earth was ugly and sordid, and seemed to express, or to represent, the weariness of toil. In an instant, to Hyacinth's surprise, Lady Aurora said to him, 'You never came, after all, to get the books.'

'Those you kindly offered to lend me? I didn't know it was an understanding.'

Lady Aurora gave an uneasy laugh. 'I have picked them out; they are quite ready.'

'It's very kind of you,' the young man rejoined. 'I will come and get them some day, with pleasure.' He was not very sure that he would; but it was the least he could say.

'She'll tell you where I live, you know,' Lady Aurora went on, with a movement of her head in the direction of the bed, as if she were too shy to mention it herself.

'Oh, I have no doubt she knows the way—she could tell me every street and every turn!' Hyacinth exclaimed.

'She has made me describe to her, very often, how I come and go. I think that few people know more about London than she. She never forgets anything.'

'She's a wonderful little witch—she terrifies me!' said Hyacinth.

Lady Aurora turned her modest eyes upon him. 'Oh, she's so good, she's so patient!'

'Yes, and so wise, and so self-possessed.'

'Oh, she's immensely clever,' said her ladyship. 'Which do you think the cleverest?'

'The cleverest?'

'I mean of the girl and her brother.'

'Oh, I think he, some day, will be prime minister of England.'

'Do you really? I'm so glad!' cried Lady Aurora, with a flush of colour in her face. 'I'm so glad you think that will be possible. You know it ought to be, if things were right.'

Hyacinth had not professed this high faith for the purpose of playing upon her ladyship's feelings, but when he perceived her eager responsiveness he felt almost as if he had been making sport of her. Still, he said no more than he believed when he remarked, in a moment, that he had the greatest expectations of Paul Muniment's future: he was sure that the world would hear of him, that England would feel him, that the public, some day, would acclaim him. It was impossible to associate with him without feeling that he was very strong, that he must play an important part.

'Yes, people wouldn't believe—they wouldn't believe,' Lady Aurora murmured softly, appreciatively. She was evidently very much pleased with what Hyacinth was saying. It was moreover a pleasure to himself to place on record his opinion of his friend; it seemed to make that opinion more clear, to give it the force of an invocation, a prophecy. This was especially the case when he asked why on earth nature had endowed Paul Muniment with such extraordinary powers of mind, and powers of body too—because he was as strong as a horse—if it had not been intended that he should do something great for his fellow-men. Hyacinth confided to her ladyship that he thought the people in his own class generally very stupid—what he should call third-rate minds. He wished it were not so, for heaven knew that he felt kindly to them and only asked to cast his lot with theirs; but he was obliged to confess that centuries of poverty, of ill-paid toil, of bad, insufficient food and wretched homes, had not a favourable effect upon the higher faculties. All the more reason that when there was a splendid exception, like Paul Muniment, it should count for a tremendous force—it had so much to make up for, to act for. And then Hyacinth repeated that in his own low walk of life people had really not the faculty of thought; their minds had been simplified—reduced to two or three elements. He saw that this declaration made his interlocutress very uncomfortable; she turned and twisted herself, vaguely, as if she wished to protest, but she was far too considerate to interrupt him. He had no desire to distress her, but there were times in which it was impossible for him to withstand the perverse satisfaction he took in insisting on his lowliness of station, in turning the knife about in the wound inflicted by such explicit reference, and in letting it be seen that if his place in the world was immeasurably small he at least had no illusions about either himself or his fellows. Lady Aurora replied, as quickly as possible, that she knew a great deal about the poor—not the poor like Rose Muniment, but the terribly, hopelessly poor, with whom she was more familiar than Hyacinth would perhaps believe—and that she was often struck with their great talents, with their quick wit, with their conversation being really much more entertaining, to her at least, than what one usually heard in drawing-rooms. She often found them immensely clever.

Hyacinth smiled at her, and said, 'Ah, when you get to the lowest depths of poverty, they may become very brilliant again. But I'm afraid I haven't gone so far down. In spite of my opportunities, I don't know many absolute paupers.'

'I know a great many.' Lady Aurora hesitated, as if she didn't like to boast, and then she added, 'I daresay I know more than any one.' There was something touching, beautiful, to Hyacinth, in this simple, diffident admission; it confirmed his impression that Lady Aurora was in some mysterious, incongruous, and even slightly ludicrous manner a heroine, a creature of a noble ideal. She perhaps guessed that he was indulging in reflections that might be favourable to her, for she said, precipitately, the next minute, as if there were nothing she dreaded so much as the danger of a compliment, 'I think your aunt's so very attractive—and I'm sure Rose Muniment thinks so.' No sooner had she spoken than she blushed again; it appeared to have occurred to her that he might suppose she wished to contradict him by presenting this case of his aunt as a proof that the baser sort, even in a prosaic upper layer, were not without redeeming points. There was no reason why she should not have had this intention; so without sparing her, Hyacinth replied—

'You mean that she's an exception to what I was saying?'

Lady Aurora stammered a little; then, at last, as if, since he wouldn't spare her, she wouldn't spare him, either, 'Yes, and you're an exception, too; you'll not make me believe you're wanting in intelligence. The Muniments don't think so,' she added.

'No more do I myself; but that doesn't prove that exceptions are not frequent. I have blood in my veins that is not the blood of the people.'

'Oh, I see,' said Lady Aurora, sympathetically. And with a smile she went on: 'Then you're all the more of an exception—in the upper class!'

Her smile was the kindest in the world, but it did not blind Hyacinth to the fact that from his own point of view he had been extraordinarily indiscreet. He believed a moment before that he would have been proof against the strongest temptation to refer to the mysteries of his lineage, inasmuch as, if made in a boastful spirit (and he had no desire as yet to make it an exercise in humility) any such reference would inevitably contain an element of the grotesque. He had never opened his lips to any one about his birth (since the dreadful days when the question was discussed, with Mr. Vetch's assistance, in Lomax Place); never even to Paul Muniment, never to Millicent Henning nor to Eustache Poupin. He had an impression that people had ideas about him, and with some of Miss Henning's he had been made acquainted: they were of such a nature that he sometimes wondered whether the tie which united him to her were not, on her own side, a secret determination to satisfy her utmost curiosity before she had done with him. But he flattered himself that he was impenetrable, and none the less he had begun to swagger, idiotically, the first time a temptation (to call a temptation) presented itself.

He turned crimson as soon as he had spoken, partly at the sudden image of what he had to swagger about, and partly at the absurdity of a challenge having appeared to proceed from the bashful gentlewoman before him. He hoped she didn't particularly regard what he had said (and indeed she gave no sign whatever of being startled by his claim to a pedigree— she had too much quick delicacy for that; she appeared to notice only the symptoms of confusion that followed it), but as soon as possible he gave himself a lesson in humility by remarking, 'I gather that you spend most of your time among the poor, and I am sure you carry blessings with you. But I frankly confess that I don't understand a lady giving herself up to people like us when there is no obligation. Wretched company we must be, when there is so much better to be had.'

'I like it very much—you don't understand.'

'Precisely—that is what I say. Our little friend on the bed is perpetually talking about your house, your family, your splendours, your gardens and green-houses; they must be magnificent, of course——'

'Oh, I wish she wouldn't; really, I wish she wouldn't. It makes one feel dreadfully!' Lady Aurora interposed, with vehemence.

'Ah, you had better give her her way; it's such a pleasure to her.'

'Yes, more than to any of us!' sighed her ladyship, helplessly.

'Well, how can you leave all those beautiful things, to come and breathe this beastly air, surround yourself with hideous images, and associate with people whose smallest fault is that they are ignorant, brutal and dirty? I don't speak of the ladies here present,' Hyacinth added, with the manner which most made Millicent Henning (who at once admired and hated it), wonder where on earth he had got it.

'Oh, I wish I could make you understand!' cried Lady Aurora, looking at him with troubled, appealing eyes, as if he were unexpectedly discouraging.

'After all, I do understand! Charity exists in your nature as a kind of passion.'

'Yes, yes, it's a kind of passion!' her ladyship repeated, eagerly, very thankful for the word. 'I don't know whether it's charity—I don't mean that. But whatever it is, it's a passion —it's my life—it's all I care for.' She hesitated a moment, as if there might be something indecent in the confession, or dangerous in the recipient; and then, evidently, she was mastered by the comfort of being able to justify herself for an eccentricity that had excited notice, as well as by the luxury of discharging her soul of a long accumulation of timid, sacred sentiment. 'Already, when I was fifteen years old, I wanted to sell all I had and give to the poor. And ever since, I have wanted to do something; it has seemed as if my heart would break if I shouldn't be able!'

Hyacinth was struck with a great respect, which, however, did not prevent him (the words sounded patronising, even to himself), from saying in a moment, 'I suppose you are very religious.'

Lady Aurora looked away, into the thickening dusk, at the smutty housetops, the blurred emanation, above the streets, of lamplight. 'I don't know—one has one's ideas—some of them may be strange. I think a great many clergymen do good, but there are others I don't like at all. I daresay we had too many, always, at home; my father likes them so much. I think I have known too many bishops; I have had the church too much on my back. I daresay they wouldn't think at home, you know, that one was quite what one ought to be; but of course they consider me very odd, in every way, as there's no doubt I am. I should tell you that I don't tell them everything; for what's the use, when people don't understand? We are twelve at home, and eight of us are girls; and if you think it's so very splendid, and *she* thinks so, I should like you both to try it for a little! My father isn't rich, and there is only one of us married, and we are not at all handsome, and—oh, there are all kinds of things,' the young woman went on, looking round at him an instant, shyly but excitedly. 'I don't like society; and neither would you if you were to see the kind there is in London—at least in some parts,' Lady Aurora added, considerately. 'I daresay you wouldn't believe all the humbuggery and the tiresomeness that one has to go through. But I've got out of it; I do as I like, though it has been rather a struggle. I have my liberty, and that is the greatest blessing in life, except the reputation of being queer, and even a little mad, which is a greater advantage still. I'm a little mad, you know; you needn't be surprised if you hear it. That's because I stop in town when they go into the country; all the autumn, all the winter, when there's no one here (except three or four millions), and the rain drips, drips, drips, from the trees in the big, dull park, where my people live. I daresay I oughtn't to say such things to you, but, as I tell you, I'm a little mad, and I might as well keep up my character. When one is one of eight daughters, and there's very little money (for any of us, at least), and there's nothing to do but to go out with three or four others in a mackintosh, one can easily go off one's head. Of course there's the village, and it's not at all a nice one, and there are the people to look after, and heaven knows they're in want of it; but one must work with the vicarage, and at the vicarage there are four more daughters, all old maids, and it's dreary, and it's dreadful, and one has too much of it, and they don't understand what one thinks or feels, or a single word one says to them! Besides they *are* stupid, I admit—the country poor; they are very, very dense. I like Camberwell better,' said Lady Aurora, smiling and taking breath, at the end of her nervous, hurried, almost incoherent speech, of which she had delivered herself pantingly, with strange intonations and grotesque movements of her neck, as if she were afraid from one moment to the other that she would repent, not of her confidence, but of her egotism.

It placed her, for Hyacinth, in an unexpected light, and made him feel that her awkward, aristocratic spinsterhood was the cover of tumultuous passions. No one could have less the appearance of being animated by a vengeful irony; but he saw that this delicate, shy, generous, and evidently most tender creature was not a person to spare, wherever she could prick them, the institutions among which she had been brought up and against which she had violently reacted. Hyacinth had always supposed that a reactionary meant a backslider from the liberal faith, but Rosy's devotee gave a new value to the term; she appeared to have been driven to her present excesses by the squire and the parson and the conservative influences of that upper-class British home which our young man had always supposed to be the highest fruit of civilisation. It was clear that her ladyship was an original, and an original with force; but it gave Hyacinth a real pang to hear her make light of Inglefield (especially the park), and of the opportunities that must have abounded in Belgrave Square. It had been his belief that in a world of suffering and injustice these things were, if not the most righteous, at least the most fascinating. If they didn't give one the finest sensations, where were such sensations to be had? He looked at Lady Aurora with a face which was a tribute to her sudden vividness, and said, 'I can easily understand your wanting to do some good in the world, because you're a kind of saint.'

'A very curious kind!' laughed her ladyship.

'But I don't understand your not liking what your position gives you.'

'I don't know anything about my position. I want to live!'

'And do you call *this* life?'

'I'll tell you what my position is, if you want to know: it's the deadness of the grave!'

Hyacinth was startled by her tone, but he nevertheless laughed back at her, 'Ah, as I say, you're a kind of saint!' She made no reply, for at that moment the door opened, and Paul Muniment's tall figure emerged from the blackness of the staircase into the twilight, now very faint, of the room. Lady Aurora's eyes, as they rested upon him, seemed to declare that such a vision as that, at least, was life. Another person, as tall as himself, appeared behind him, and Hyacinth recognised with astonishment their insinuating friend Captain Sholto. Muniment had brought him up for Rosy's entertainment, being ready, and more than ready, always, to usher in any one in the world, from the prime minister to the common hangman, who might give that young lady a sensation. They must have met at the 'Sun and Moon,' and if the Captain, some accident smoothing the way, had made him half as many advances as he had made some other people Hyacinth could see that it wouldn't take long for Paul to lay him under contribution. But what the mischief was the Captain up to? It cannot be said that our young man arrived, this evening, at an answer to that question. The occasion proved highly festal, and the hostess rose to it without lifting her head from the pillow. Her brother introduced Captain Sholto as a gentleman who had a great desire to know extraordinary people, and she made him take possession of the chair at her bedside, out of which Miss Pynsent quickly edged herself, and asked him who he was, and where he came from, and how Paul had made his acquaintance, and whether he had many friends in Camberwell. Sholto had not the same grand air that hovered about him at the theatre; he was shabbily dressed, very much like Hyacinth himself; but his appearance gave our young man an opportunity to wonder what made him so unmistakably a gentleman in spite of his seedy coat and trousers—in spite too, of his rather overdoing the manner of being appreciative even to rapture and thinking everything and every one most charming and curious. He stood out, in poor Rosy's tawdry little room, among her hideous attempts at decoration, and looked to Hyacinth a being from another sphere, playing over the place and company a smile (one couldn't call it false or unpleasant, yet it was distinctly not natural), of which he had got the habit in camps and courts. It became brilliant when it rested on Hyacinth, and the Captain greeted him as he might have done a dear young friend from whom he had been long and painfully separated. He was easy, he was familiar, he was exquisitely benevolent and bland, and altogether incomprehensible.

Rosy was a match for him, however. He evidently didn't puzzle her in the least; she thought his visit the most natural thing in the world. She expressed all the gratitude that decency required, but appeared to assume that people who climbed her stairs would always find themselves repaid. She remarked that her brother must have met him for the first time that day, for the way that he sealed a new acquaintance was usually by bringing the person immediately to call upon her. And when the Captain said that if she didn't like them he supposed the poor wretches were dropped on the spot, she admitted that this would be true if it ever happened that she disapproved; as yet, however, she had not been obliged to draw the line. This was perhaps partly because he had not brought up any of his political friends—people that he knew only for political reasons. Of these people, in general, she had a very small opinion, and she would not conceal from Captain Sholto that she hoped he was not one of them. Rosy spoke as if her brother represented the Camberwell district in the House of Commons and she had discovered that a parliamentary career lowered the moral tone. The Captain, however, entered quite into her views, and told her that it was as common friends of Mr. Hyacinth Robinson that Mr. Muniment and he had come together; they were both so fond of him that this had immediately constituted a kind of tie. On hearing himself commemorated in such a brilliant way Mr. Hyacinth Robinson averted himself; he saw that Captain Sholto might be trusted to make as great an effort for Rosy's entertainment as he gathered that he had made for that of Millicent Henning, that evening at the theatre. There were not chairs enough to go round, and Paul fetched a three-legged stool from his own apartment, after which he undertook to make tea for the company, with the aid of a tin kettle and a spirit-lamp; these implements having been set out, flanked by half a dozen cups, in honour, presumably, of the little dressmaker, who was to come such a distance. The little dressmaker, Hyacinth observed with pleasure, fell into earnest conversation with Lady Aurora, who bent over her, flushed, smiling, stammering, and apparently so nervous that Pinnie, in comparison, was majestic and serene. They communicated presently to Hyacinth a plan they had unanimously evolved, to the effect that Miss Pynsent should go home to Belgrave Square with her ladyship, to settle certain preliminaries in regard to the pink dressing-gown, toward which, if Miss Pynsent assented, her ladyship hoped to be able to contribute sundry morsels of stuff which had proved their quality in honourable service and might be dyed to the proper tint. Pinnie, Hyacinth could see, was in a state of religious exaltation; the visit to Belgrave Square and the idea of co-operating in such a manner with the nobility were privileges she could not take solemnly enough. The latter luxury, indeed, she began to enjoy without delay; Lady Aurora suggesting that Mr. Muniment might be rather awkward about making tea, and that they should take the business off his hands. Paul gave it up to them, with a pretence of compassion for their conceit, remarking that at any rate it took two women to supplant one man; and Hyacinth drew him to the window, to ask where he had encountered Sholto and how he liked him.

They had met in Bloomsbury, as Hyacinth supposed, and
Sholto had made up to him very much as a country curate
might make up to an archbishop. He wanted to know what
he thought of this and that: of the state of the labour market
at the East End, of the terrible case of the old woman who
had starved to death at Walham Green, of the practicability of
more systematic out-of-door agitation, and the prospects of
their getting one of their own men—one of the Bloomsbury
lot—into Parliament. 'He was mighty civil,' Muniment said,
'and I don't find that he has picked my pocket. He looked as
if he would like me to suggest that *he* should stand as one of
our own men, one of the Bloomsbury lot. He asks too many
questions, but he makes up for it by not paying any attention
to the answers. He told me he would give the world to see a
working-man's "interior." I didn't know what he meant at
first: he wanted a favourable specimen, one of the best; he
had seen one or two that he didn't believe to be up to the
average. I suppose he meant Schinkel, the cabinetmaker, and
he wanted to compare. I told him I didn't know what sort of
a specimen my place would be, but that he was welcome to
look round, and that it contained at any rate one or two original features. I expect he has found that's the case—with
Rosy and the noble lady. I wanted to show him off to Rosy;
he's good for that, if he isn't good for anything else. I told
him we expected a little company this evening, so it might be
a good time; and he assured me that to mingle in such an
occasion as that was the dream of his existence. He seemed in
a rare hurry, as if I were going to show him a hidden treasure,
and insisted on driving me over in a hansom. Perhaps his idea
is to introduce the use of cabs among the working-classes;
certainly, I'll vote for him for Parliament, if that's his line. On
our way over he talked to me about you; told me you were an
intimate friend of his.'

'What did he say about me?' Hyacinth inquired, with
promptness.

'Vain little beggar!'

'Did he call me that?' said Hyacinth, ingenuously.

'He said you were simply astonishing.'

'Simply astonishing?' Hyacinth repeated.

'For a person of your low extraction.'

'Well, I may be queer, but he is certainly queerer. Don't you think so, now you know him?'

Paul Muniment looked at his young friend a moment. 'Do you want to know what he is? He's a tout.'

'A tout? What do you mean?'

'Well, a cat's-paw, if you like better.'

Hyacinth stared. 'For whom, pray?'

'Or a fisherman, if you like better still. I give you your choice of comparisons. I made them up as we came along in the hansom. He throws his nets and hauls in the little fishes—the pretty little shining, wriggling fishes. They are all for her; she swallows 'em down.'

'For her? Do you mean the Princess?'

'Who else should I mean? Take care, my tadpole!'

'Why should I take care? The other day you told me not to.'

'Yes, I remember. But now I see more.'

'Did he speak of her? What did he say?' asked Hyacinth, eagerly.

'I can't tell you now what he said, but I'll tell you what I guessed.'

'And what's that?'

They had been talking, of course, in a very low tone, and their voices were covered by Rosy's chatter in the corner, by the liberal laughter with which Captain Sholto accompanied it, and by the much more discreet, though earnest, inter-mingled accents of Lady Aurora and Miss Pynsent. But Paul Muniment spoke more softly still—Hyacinth felt a kind of suspense—as he replied in a moment, 'Why, she's a monster!'

'A monster?' repeated our young man, from whom, this evening, Paul Muniment seemed destined to elicit ejaculations and echoes.

Muniment glanced toward the Captain, who was apparently more and more fascinated by Rosy. 'In him I think there's no great harm. He's only a conscientious fisherman!'

It must be admitted that Captain Sholto justified to a certain extent this definition by the manner in which he baited his hook for such little facts as might help him to a more intimate knowledge of his host and hostess. When the tea was

made, Rose Muniment asked Miss Pynsent to be so good as
to hand it about. They must let her poor ladyship rest a little,
must they not?—and Hyacinth could see that in her innocent
but inveterate self-complacency she wished to reward and encourage the dressmaker, draw her out and present her still
more, by offering her this graceful exercise. Sholto sprang up
at this, and begged Pinnie to let him relieve her, taking a cup
from her hand; and poor Pinnie, who perceived in a moment
that he was some kind of masquerading gentleman, who was
bewildered by the strange mixture of elements that surrounded her and unused to being treated like a duchess (for
the Captain's manner was a triumph of respectful gallantry),
collapsed, on the instant, into a chair, appealing to Lady Aurora with a frightened smile and conscious that, deeply versed
as she might be in the theory of decorum, she had no prece-
dent that could meet such an occasion. 'Now, how many families would there be in such a house as this, and what should
you say about the sanitary arrangements? Would there be
others on this floor—what is it, the third, the fourth?
—beside yourselves, you know, and should you call it a fair
specimen of a tenement of its class?' It was with such inquiries
as this that Captain Sholto beguiled their tea-drinking, while
Hyacinth made the reflection that, though he evidently meant
them very well, they were characterised by a want of fine tact,
by too patronising a curiosity. The Captain requested information as to the position in life, the avocations and habits, of
the other lodgers, the rent they paid, their relations with each
other, both in and out of the family. 'Now, would there be a
good deal of close packing, do you suppose, and any perceptible want of—a—sobriety?'

Paul Muniment, who had swallowed his cup of tea at a
single gulp—there was no offer of a second—gazed out of
the window into the dark, which had now come on, with his
hands in his pockets, whistling, impolitely, no doubt, but
with brilliant animation. He had the manner of having made
over their visitor altogether to Rosy and of thinking that
whatever he said or did it was all so much grist to her inde-
fatigable little mill. Lady Aurora looked distressed and embarrassed, and it is a proof of the degree to which our little hero
had the instincts of a man of the world that he guessed exactly

how vulgar she thought this new acquaintance. She was doubtless rather vexed, also—Hyacinth had learned this evening that Lady Aurora could be vexed—at the alacrity of Rosy's responses; the little person in the bed gave the Captain every satisfaction, considered his questions as a proper tribute to humble respectability, and supplied him, as regards the population of Audley Court, with statistics and anecdotes which she had picked up by mysterious processes of her own. At last Lady Aurora, upon whom Paul Muniment had not been at pains to bestow much conversation, took leave of her, and signified to Hyacinth that for the rest of the evening she would assume the care of Miss Pynsent. Pinnie looked very tense and solemn, now that she was really about to be transported to Belgrave Square, but Hyacinth was sure she would acquit herself only the more honourably; and when he offered to call for her there, later, she reminded him, under her breath, with a little sad smile, of the many years during which, after nightfall, she had carried her work, pinned up in cloth, about London.

Paul Muniment, according to his habit, lighted Lady Aurora downstairs, and Captain Sholto and Hyacinth were alone for some minutes with Rosy; which gave the former, taking up his hat and stick, an opportunity to say to his young friend, 'Which way are you going? Not my way, by chance?' Hyacinth saw that he hoped for his company, and he became conscious that, strangely as Muniment had indulged him and too promiscuously investigating as he had just shown himself, this ingratiating personage was not more easy to resist than he had been the other night at the theatre. The Captain bent over Rosy's bed as if she had been a fine lady on a satin sofa, promising to come back very soon and very often, and the two men went downstairs. On their way they met Paul Muniment coming up, and Hyacinth felt rather ashamed, he could scarcely tell why, that his friend should see him marching off with the 'tout.' After all, if Muniment had brought him to see his sister, might not he at least walk with him? 'I'm coming again, you know, very often. I daresay you'll find me a great bore!' the Captain announced, as he bade good-night to his host. 'Your sister is a most interesting creature, one of the most interesting creatures I have ever seen, and the whole thing, you know, exactly the sort of thing I wanted to get at, only much more—really, much more—original and curious. It has been a great success, a grand success!'

And the Captain felt his way down the dusky shaft, while Paul Muniment, above, gave him the benefit of rather a wavering candlestick, and answered his civil speech with an 'Oh, well, you take us as you find us, you know!' and an outburst of frank but not unfriendly laughter.

Half-an-hour later Hyacinth found himself in Captain Sholto's chambers, seated on a big divan covered with Persian rugs and cushions and smoking the most delectable cigar that had ever touched his lips. As they left Audley Court the Captain had taken his arm, and they had walked along together in a desultory, colloquial manner, till on Westminster Bridge (they had followed the embankment, beneath St. Thomas's Hospital) Sholto said, 'By the way, why shouldn't you come home with me and see my little place? I've got a few things that might amuse you—some pictures, some odds and ends I've picked up, and a few bindings; you might tell me what you think of them.' Hyacinth assented, without hesitation; he had still in his ear the reverberation of the Captain's inquiries in Rose Muniment's room, and he saw no reason why he, on his side, should not embrace an occasion of ascertaining how, as his companion would have said, a man of fashion would live now.

This particular specimen lived in a large, old-fashioned house in Queen Anne Street, of which he occupied the upper floors, and whose high, wainscoted rooms he had filled with the spoils of travel and the ingenuities of modern taste. There was not a country in the world he did not appear to have ransacked, and to Hyacinth his trophies represented a wonderfully long purse. The whole establishment, from the low-voiced, inexpressive valet who, after he had poured brandy into tall tumblers, gave dignity to the popping of soda-water corks, to the quaint little silver receptacle in which he was invited to deposit the ashes of his cigar, was such a revelation for our appreciative hero that he felt himself hushed and made sad, so poignant was the thought that it took thousands of things which he, then, should never possess nor know to make an accomplished man. He had often, in evening-walks, wondered what was behind the walls of certain spacious, bright-windowed houses in the West End, and now he got an idea. The first effect of the idea was to overwhelm him.

'Well, now, tell me what you thought of our friend the Princess,' the Captain said, thrusting out the loose yellow slippers which his servant had helped to exchange for his shoes. He spoke as if he had been waiting impatiently for the proper moment to ask that question, so much might depend on the answer.

'She's beautiful—beautiful,' Hyacinth answered, almost dreamily, with his eyes wandering all over the room.

'She was so interested in all you said to her; she would like so much to see you again. She means to write to you—I suppose she can address to the "Sun and Moon"?—and I hope you'll go to her house, if she proposes a day.'

'I don't know—I don't know. It seems so strange.'

'What seems strange, my dear fellow?'

'Everything! My sitting here with you; my introduction to that lady; the idea of her wanting, as you say, to see me again, and of her writing to me; and this whole place of yours, with all these dim, rich curiosities hanging on the walls and glinting in the light of that rose-coloured lamp. You yourself, too—you are strangest of all.'

The Captain looked at him, in silence, so fixedly for a while, through the fumes of their tobacco, after he had made this last charge, that Hyacinth thought he was perhaps offended; but this impression was presently dissipated by further manifestations of sociability and hospitality, and Sholto took occasion, later, to let him know how important it was, in the days they were living in, not to have too small a measure of the usual, destined as they certainly were—'in the whole matter of the relations of class with class, and all that sort of thing, you know'—to witness some very startling developments. The Captain spoke as if, for his part, he were a child of his age (so that he only wanted to see all it could show him), down to the point of his yellow slippers. Hyacinth felt that he himself had not been very satisfactory about the Princess; but as his nerves began to tremble a little more into tune with the situation he repeated to his host what Millicent Henning had said about her at the theatre—asked if this young lady had correctly understood him in believing that she had been turned out of the house by her husband.

'Yes, he literally pushed her into the street—or into the garden; I believe the scene took place in the country. But perhaps Miss Henning didn't mention, or perhaps I didn't mention, that the Prince would at the present hour give everything he owns in the world to get her back. Fancy such a scene!' said the Captain, laughing in a manner that struck Hyacinth as rather profane.

He stared, with dilated eyes, at this picture, which seemed to evoke a comparison with the only incident of the sort that had come within his experience—the forcible ejection of intoxicated females from public houses. 'That magnificent being—what had she done?'

'Oh, she had made him feel he was an ass!' the Captain answered, promptly. He turned the conversation to Miss Henning; said he was so glad Hyacinth gave him an opportunity to speak of her. He got on with her famously; perhaps she had told him. They became immense friends—*en tout bien tout honneur, s'entend*. Now, *there* was another London type, plebeian but brilliant; and how little justice one usually did it, how magnificent it was! But she, of course, was a wonderful specimen. 'My dear fellow, I have seen many women, and the women of many countries,' the Captain went on, 'and I have seen them intimately, and I know what I am talking about; and when I tell you that that one—that one——' Then he suddenly paused, laughing in his democratic way. 'But perhaps I am going too far: you must always pull me up, you know, when I do. At any rate, I congratulate you; I do, heartily. Have another cigar. Now what sort of—a—salary would she receive at her big shop, you know? I know where it is; I mean to go there and buy some pocket-handkerchiefs.'

Hyacinth knew neither how far Captain Sholto had been going, nor exactly on what he congratulated him; and he pretended, at least, an equal ignorance on the subject of Millicent's salary. He didn't want to talk about her, moreover, nor about his own life; he wanted to talk about the Captain's, and to elicit information that would be in harmony with his romantic chambers, which reminded our hero somehow of Bulwer's novels. His host gratified this desire most liberally, and told him twenty stories of things that had happened to him in Albania, in Madagascar, and even in Paris. Hyacinth induced him easily to talk about Paris (from a different point of view from M. Poupin's), and sat there drinking in enchantments. The only thing that fell below the high level of his entertainment was the bindings of the Captain's books, which he told him frankly, with the conscience of an artist, were not very good. After he left Queen Anne Street he was quite too excited to go straight home; he walked about with his mind full of images and strange speculations, till the gray London streets began to grow clear with the summer dawn.

XVI

THE ASPECT of South Street, Mayfair, on a Sunday afternoon in August, is not enlivening, yet the Prince had
stood for ten minutes gazing out of the window at the genteel
vacancy of the scene; at the closed blinds of the opposite
houses, the lonely policeman on the corner, covering a yawn
with a white cotton hand, the low-pitched light itself, which
seemed conscious of an obligation to observe the decency of
the British Sabbath. The Prince, however, had a talent for
that kind of attitude; it was one of the things by which he had
exasperated his wife; he could remain motionless, with the aid
of some casual support for his high, lean person, considering
serenely and inexpressively any object that might lie before
him and presenting his aristocratic head at a favourable angle,
for periods of extraordinary length. On first coming into the
room he had given some attention to its furniture and deco-
rations, perceiving at a glance that they were rich and varied;
some of the things he recognised as old friends, odds and
ends the Princess was fond of, which had accompanied her in
her remarkable wanderings, while others were unfamiliar, and
suggested vividly that she had not ceased to 'collect.' The
Prince made two reflections: one was that she was living as
expensively as ever; the other that, however this might be, no
one had such a feeling as she for the *mise-en-scène* of life, such
a talent for arranging a room. She had still the most charming
salon in Europe.

It was his impression that she had taken the house in
South Street but for three months; yet, gracious heaven,
what had she not put into it? The Prince asked himself this
question without violence, for that was not to be his line to-
day. He could be angry to a point at which he himself was
often frightened, but he honestly believed that this was only
when he had been baited beyond endurance and that as a
usual thing he was really as mild and accommodating as the
extreme urbanity of his manner appeared to announce. There
was indeed nothing to suggest to the world in general that
he was an impracticable or vindictive nobleman: his features
were not regular, and his complexion had a bilious tone; but

his dark brown eye, which was at once salient and dull, expressed benevolence and melancholy; his head drooped from his long neck in a considerate, attentive style; and his close-cropped black hair, combined with a short, fine, pointed beard, completed his resemblance to some old portrait of a personage of distinction under the Spanish dominion at Naples. To-day, at any rate, he had come in conciliation, almost in humility, and that is why he did not permit himself even to murmur at the long delay to which he was subjected. He knew very well that if his wife should consent to take him back it would be only after a probation to which this little wait in her drawing-room was a trifle. It was a quarter of an hour before the door opened, and even then it was not the Princess who appeared, but only Madame Grandoni.

Their greeting was a very silent one. She came to him with both hands outstretched, and took his own and held them awhile, looking up at him in a kindly, motherly manner. She had elongated her florid, humorous face to a degree that was almost comical, and the pair might have passed, in their speechless solemnity, for acquaintances meeting in a house in which a funeral was about to take place. It was indeed a house on which death had descended, as he very soon learned from Madame Grandoni's expression; something had perished there for ever, and he might proceed to bury it as soon as he liked. His wife's ancient German friend, however, was not a person to keep up a manner of that sort very long, and when, after she had made him sit down on the sofa beside her, she shook her head, slowly and definitely, several times, it was with a face in which a more genial appreciation of the circumstances had already begun to appear.

'Never—never—never?' said the Prince, in a deep, hoarse voice, which was at variance with his aristocratic slimness. He had much of the aspect which, in late-coming members of long-descended races, we qualify to-day as effete; but his speech might have been the speech of some deep-chested fighting ancestor.

'Surely you know your wife as well as I,' she replied, in Italian, which she evidently spoke with facility, though with a strong guttural accent. 'I have been talking with her: that is what has made me keep you. I have urged her to see you.

I have told her that this could do no harm and would pledge her to nothing. But you know your wife,' Madame Grandoni repeated, with a smile which was now distinctly facetious.

Prince Casamassima looked down at his boots. 'How can one ever know a person like that? I hoped she would see me for five minutes.'

'For what purpose? Have you anything to propose?'

'For what purpose? To rest my eyes on her beautiful face.'

'Did you come to England for that?'

'For what else should I have come?' the Prince inquired, turning his blighted gaze to the opposite side of South Street.

'In London, such a day as this, *già*,' said the old lady, sympathetically. 'I am very sorry for you; but if I had known you were coming I would have written to you that you might spare yourself the pain.'

The Prince gave a low, interminable sigh. 'You ask me what I wish to propose. What I wish to propose is that my wife does not kill me inch by inch.'

'She would be much more likely to do that if you lived with her!' Madame Grandoni cried.

'*Cara signora*, she doesn't appear to have killed you,' the melancholy nobleman rejoined.

'Oh, me? I am past killing. I am as hard as a stone. I went through my miseries long ago; I suffered what you have not had to suffer; I wished for death many times, and I survived it all. Our troubles don't kill us, Prince; it is we who must try to kill them. I have buried not a few. Besides Christina is fond of me, God knows why!' Madame Grandoni added.

'And you are so good to her,' said the Prince, laying his hand on her fat, wrinkled fist.

'*Che vuole?* I have known her so long. And she has some such great qualities.'

'Ah, to whom do you say it?' And Prince Casamassima gazed at his boots again, for some moments, in silence. Suddenly he inquired, 'How does she look to-day?'

'She always looks the same: like an angel who came down from heaven yesterday and has been rather disappointed in her first day on earth!'

The Prince was evidently a man of a simple nature, and Madame Grandoni's rather violent metaphor took his fancy. His face lighted up for a moment, and he replied with eagerness, 'Ah, she is the only woman I have ever seen whose beauty never for a moment falls below itself. She has no bad days. She is so handsome when she is angry!'

'She is very handsome to-day, but she is not angry,' said the old lady.

'Not when my name was announced?'

'I was not with her then; but when she sent for me and asked me to see you, it was quite without passion. And even when I argued with her, and tried to persuade her (and she doesn't like that, you know), she was still perfectly quiet.'

'She hates me, she despises me too much, eh?'

'How can I tell, dear Prince, when she never mentions you?'

'Never, never?'

'That's much better than if she railed at you and abused you.'

'You mean it should give me more hope for the future?' the young man asked, quickly.

Madame Grandoni hesitated a moment. 'I mean it's better for me,' she answered, with a laugh of which the friendly ring covered as much as possible her equivocation.

'Ah, you like me enough to care,' he murmured, turning on her his sad, grateful eyes.

'I am very sorry for you. *Ma che vuole?*'

The Prince had, apparently, nothing to suggest, and he only exhaled, in reply, another gloomy groan. Then he inquired whether his wife pleased herself in that country, and whether she intended to pass the summer in London. Would she remain long in England, and—might he take the liberty to ask?—what were her plans? Madame Grandoni explained that the Princess had found the British metropolis much more to her taste than one might have expected, and that as for plans, she had as many, or as few, as she had always had. Had he ever known her to carry out any arrangement, or to do anything, of any kind, she had selected or determined upon? She always, at the last moment, did the other thing, the one that had been out of the question; and it was for this that

Madame Grandoni herself privately made her preparations. Christina, now that everything was over, would leave London from one day to the other; but they should not know where they were going until they arrived. The old lady concluded by asking the Prince if he himself liked England. He thrust forward his thick lips. 'How can I like anything? Besides, I have been here before; I have friends,' he said.

His companion perceived that he had more to say to her, to extract from her, but that he was hesitating nervously, because he feared to incur some warning, some rebuff, with which his dignity—which, in spite of his position of discomfiture, was really very great—might find it difficult to square itself. He looked vaguely round the room, and presently he remarked, 'I wanted to see for myself how she is living.'

'Yes, that is very natural.'

'I have heard—I have heard——' And Prince Casamassima stopped.

'You have heard great rubbish, I have no doubt.' Madame Grandoni watched him, as if she foresaw what was coming.

'She spends a terrible deal of money,' said the young man.

'Indeed she does.' The old lady knew that, careful as he was of his very considerable property, which at one time had required much nursing, his wife's prodigality was not what lay heaviest on his mind. She also knew that expensive and luxurious as Christina might be she had never yet exceeded the income settled upon her by the Prince at the time of their separation—an income determined wholly by himself and his estimate of what was required to maintain the social consequence of his name, for which he had a boundless reverence. 'She thinks she is a model of thrift—that she counts every shilling,' Madame Grandoni continued. 'If there is a virtue she prides herself upon, it's her economy. Indeed, it's the only thing for which she takes any credit.'

'I wonder if she knows that I'—the Prince hesitated a moment, then he went on—'that I spend really nothing. But I would rather live on dry bread than that, in a country like this, in this English society, she should not make a proper appearance.'

'Her appearance is all you could wish. How can it help being proper, with me to set her off?'

'You are the best thing she has, dear lady. So long as you are with her I feel a certain degree of security; and one of the things I came for was to extract from you a promise that you won't leave her.'

'Ah, let us not tangle ourselves up with promises!' Madame Grandoni exclaimed. 'You know the value of any engagement one may take with regard to the Princess; it's like promising you I will stay in the bath when the hot water is turned on. When I begin to be scalded, I have to jump out! I will stay while I can; but I shouldn't stay if she were to do certain things.' Madame Grandoni uttered these last words very gravely, and for a minute she and her companion looked deep into each other's eyes.

'What things do you mean?'

'I can't say what things. It is utterly impossible to predict, on any occasion, what Christina will do. She is capable of giving us great surprises. The things I mean are things I should recognise as soon as I saw them, and they would make me leave the house on the instant.'

'So that if you have not left it yet——?' the Prince asked, in a low tone, with extreme eagerness.

'It is because I have thought I may do some good by staying.'

The young man seemed only half satisfied with this answer; nevertheless he said in a moment—'To me it makes all the difference. And if anything of the kind you speak of should happen, that would be only the greater reason for your stay-ing—that you might interpose, that you might arrest——' He stopped short; Madame Grandoni was laughing, with her Teutonic homeliness, in his face.

'You must have been in Rome, more than once, when the Tiber had overflowed, *è vero?* What would you have thought then if you had heard people telling the poor wretches in the Ghetto, on the Ripetta, up to their knees in liquid mud, that they ought to interpose, to arrest?'

'*Capisco bene,*' said the Prince, dropping his eyes. He ap-peared to have closed them, for some moments, as if a slow spasm of pain were passing through him. 'I can't tell you what torments me most,' he presently went on, 'the thought that sometimes makes my heart rise into my mouth. It's a haunting fear.' And his pale face and disturbed respiration might indeed have been those of a man before whom some horrible spectre had risen.

'You needn't tell me. I know what you mean, my poor friend.'

'Do you think, then, there *is* a danger—that she will drag my name, do what no one has ever dared to do? That I would never forgive,' said the young man, almost under his breath; and the hoarseness of his whisper lent a great effect to the announcement.

Madame Grandoni wondered for a moment whether she had not better tell him (as it would prepare him for the worst), that his wife cared about as much for his name as for any old label on her luggage; but after an instant's reflection she reserved this information for another hour. Besides, as she said to herself, the Prince ought already to know perfectly to what extent Christina attached the idea of an obligation or an interdict to her ill-starred connection with an ignorant and superstitious Italian race whom she despised for their provinciality, their parsimony and their tiresomeness (she thought their talk the climax of puerility), and whose fatuous conception of their importance in the great modern world she had on various public occasions sufficiently covered with her derision. The old lady finally contented herself with remarking, 'Dear Prince, your wife is a very proud woman.'

'Ah, how could my wife be anything else? But her pride is not my pride. And she has such ideas, such opinions! Some of them are monstrous.'

Madame Grandoni smiled. 'She doesn't think it so necessary to have them when you are not there.'

'Why then do you say that you enter into my fears—that you recognise the stories I have heard?'

I know not whether the good lady lost patience with his persistence; at all events, she broke out, with a certain sharpness, 'Understand this—understand this: Christina will never consider you—your name, your illustrious traditions—in any case in which she doesn't consider, much more, herself!'

The Prince appeared to study, for a moment, this somewhat ambiguous yet portentous phrase; then he slowly got up, with his hat in his hand, and walked about the room, softly, solemnly, as if he were suffering from his long thin feet. He stopped before one of the windows, and took another survey of South Street; then, turning, he suddenly inquired, in a voice into which he had evidently endeavoured to infuse a colder curiosity, 'Is she admired in this place? Does she see many people?'

'She is thought very strange, of course. But she sees whom she likes. And they mostly bore her to death!' Madame Grandoni added, with a laugh.

'Why then do you tell me this country pleases her?'

Madame Grandoni left her place. She had promised Christina, who detested the sense of being under the same roof with her husband, that the Prince's visit should be kept within narrow limits; and this movement was intended to signify as kindly as possible that it had better terminate. 'It is the common people that please her,' she replied, with her hands folded on her crumpled satin stomach and her humorous eyes raised to his face. 'It is the lower orders, the *basso popolo*.'

'The *basso popolo*?' The Prince stared, at this fantastic announcement.

'The *povera gente*,' pursued the old lady, laughing at his amazement.

'The London mob—the most horrible, the most brutal——?'

'Oh, she wishes to raise them.'

'After all, something like that is no more than I had heard,' said the Prince gravely.

'*Che vuole?* Don't trouble yourself; it won't be for long!'

Madame Grandoni saw that this comforting assurance was lost upon him; his face was turned to the door of the room, which had been thrown open, and all his attention was given to the person who crossed the threshold. Madame Grandoni transferred her own to the same quarter, and recognised the little artisan whom Christina had, in a manner so extraordinary and so profoundly characteristic, drawn into her box that night at the theatre, and whom she had since told her old friend she had sent for to come and see her.

'Mr. Robinson!' the butler, who had had a lesson, announced in a loud, colourless tone.

'It won't be for long,' Madame Grandoni repeated, for the Prince's benefit; but it was to Mr. Robinson the words had the air of being addressed.

He stood there while Madame Grandoni signalled to the servant to leave the door open and wait, looking from the queer old lady, who was as queer as before, to the tall foreign gentleman (he recognised his foreignness at a glance), whose eyes seemed to challenge him, to devour him; wondering whether he had made some mistake, and needing to remind himself that he had the Princess's note in his pocket, with the day and hour as clear as her magnificent handwriting could make them.

'Good-morning, good-morning. I hope you are well,' said Madame Grandoni, with quick friendliness, but turning her back upon him at the same time, to ask of the Prince, in Italian, as she extended her hand, 'And do you not leave London soon—in a day or two?'

The Prince made no answer; he still scrutinised the little bookbinder from head to foot, as if he were wondering who the deuce he could be. His eyes seemed to Hyacinth to search for the small neat bundle he ought to have had under his arm, and without which he was incomplete. To the reader, however, it may be confided that, dressed more carefully than he had ever been in his life before, stamped with that extraordinary transformation which the British Sunday often operates in the person of the wage-earning cockney, with his handsome head uncovered and suppressed excitement in his brilliant little face, the young man from Lomax Place might have passed for anything rather than a carrier of parcels. 'The Princess wrote to me, madam, to come and see her,' he remarked, as a precaution, in case he should have incurred the reproach of bad taste, or at least of precipitation.

'Oh yes, I daresay.' And Madame Grandoni guided the Prince to the door, with an expression of the hope that he would have a comfortable journey back to Italy.

A faint flush had come into his face; he appeared to have satisfied himself on the subject of Mr. Robinson. 'I must see you once more—I must—it's impossible!'

'Ah, well, not in this house, you know.'

'Will you do me the honour to meet me, then?' And as

the old lady hesitated, he added, with sudden passion, 'Dearest friend, I entreat you on my knees!' After she had agreed that if he would write to her, proposing a day and place, she would see him, he raised her ancient knuckles to his lips and, without further notice of Hyacinth, turned away. Madame Grandoni requested the servant to announce the other visitor to the Princess, and then approached Mr. Robinson, rubbing her hands and smiling, with her head on one side. He smiled back at her, vaguely; he didn't know what she might be going to say. What she said was, to his surprise—

'My poor young man, may I take the liberty of asking your age?'

'Certainly, madam; I am twenty-four.'

'And I hope you are industrious, and sober, and—what do you call it in English?—steady.'

'I don't think I am very wild,' said Hyacinth, smiling still. He thought the old woman patronising, but he forgave her.

'I don't know how one speaks, in this country, to young men like you. Perhaps one is considered meddling, impertinent.'

'I like the way you speak,' Hyacinth interposed.

She stared, and then with a comical affectation of dignity, replied, 'You are very good. I am glad it amuses you. You are evidently intelligent and clever,' she went on, 'and if you are disappointed it will be a pity.'

'How do you mean, if I am disappointed?' Hyacinth looked more grave.

'Well, I daresay you expect great things, when you come into a house like this. You must tell me if I wound you. I am very old-fashioned, and I am not of this country. I speak as one speaks to young men, like you, in other places.'

'I am not so easily wounded!' Hyacinth exclaimed, with a flight of imagination. 'To expect anything, one must know something, one must understand: isn't it so? And I am here without knowing, without understanding. I have come only because a lady who seems to me very beautiful and very kind has done me the honour to send for me.'

Madame Grandoni examined him a moment, as if she were struck by his good looks, by something delicate that was stamped upon him everywhere. 'I can see you are very clever, very intelligent; no, you are not like the young men I mean. All the more reason'—— And she paused, giving a little sigh. 'I want to warn you a little, and I don't know how. If you were a young Roman, it would be different.'

'A young Roman?'

'That's where I live, properly, in Rome. If I hurt you, you can explain in that way. No, you are not like them.'

'You don't hurt me—please believe that; you interest me very much,' said Hyacinth, to whom it did not occur that he himself might appear patronising. 'Of what do you want to warn me?'

'Well—only to advise you a little. Do not give up anything.'

'What can I give up?'

'Do not give up *yourself*. I say that to you in your interest. I think you have some little trade—I forget what; but whatever it may be, remember that to do it well is the best thing—it is better than paying visits, better even than a Princess!'

'Ah yes, I see what you mean!' Hyacinth exclaimed, exaggerating a little. 'I am very fond of my trade, I assure you.'

'I am delighted to hear it. Hold fast to it, then, and be quiet; be diligent, and honest, and good. I gathered the other night that you are one of the young men who want everything changed—I believe there are a great many in Italy, and also in my own dear old Deutschland—and even think it's useful to throw bombs into innocent crowds, and shoot pistols at their rulers, or at any one. I won't go into that. I might seem to be speaking for myself, and the fact is that for myself I don't care; I am so old that I may hope to spend the few days that are left me without receiving a bullet. But before you go any further please think a little whether you are right.'

'It isn't just that you should impute to me ideas which I may not have,' said Hyacinth, turning very red, but taking more and more of a fancy, all the same, to Madame Grandoni. 'You talk at your ease about our ways and means, but if we were only to make use of those that you would like to see'—— And while he blushed, smiling, the young man shook his head two or three times, with great significance.

'I shouldn't like to see any!' the old lady cried. 'I like people to bear their troubles as one has done one's self. And as for injustice, you see how kind I am to you when I say to you again, don't, don't give anything up. I will tell them to send you some tea,' she added, as she took her way out of the room, presenting to him her round, low, aged back, and dragging over the carpet a scanty and lustreless train.

XVII

HYACINTH had been warned by Mr. Vetch as to what brilliant women might do with him (it was only a word on the old fiddler's lips, but the word had had a point), he had been warned by Paul Muniment, and now he was admonished by a person supremely well placed for knowing—a fact that could not fail to deepen the emotion which, any time these three days, had made him draw his breath more quickly. That emotion, however, was now not of a kind to make him fear remote consequences; as he looked over the Princess Casamassima's drawing-room and inhaled an air that seemed to him inexpressibly delicate and sweet, he hoped that his adventure would throw him upon his mettle only half as much as the old lady had wished to intimate. He considered, one after the other, the different chairs, couches and ottomans the room contained—he wished to treat himself to the most sumptuous—and then, for reasons he knew best, sank into a seat covered with rose-coloured brocade, of which the legs and frame appeared to be of pure gold. Here he sat perfectly still, with only his heart beating very sensibly and his eyes coursing again and again from one object to another. The splendours and suggestions of Captain Sholto's apartment were thrown completely into the shade by the scene before him, and as the Princess did not scruple to keep him waiting for twenty minutes (during which the butler came in and set out, on a small table, a glittering tea-service), Hyacinth had time to count over the innumerable *bibelots* (most of which he had never dreamed of), involved in the personality of a woman of high fashion, and to feel that their beauty and oddity revealed not only whole provinces of art, but refinements of choice, on the part of their owner, complications of mind, and—almost—terrible depths of character.

When at last the door opened and the servant, reappearing, threw it far back, as if to make a wide passage for a person of the importance of his mistress, Hyacinth's suspense became very acute; it was much the same feeling with which, at the theatre, he had sometimes awaited the entrance of a celebrated actress. In this case the actress was to perform for him alone. There was still a moment before she came on, and when she did so she was so simply dressed—besides his seeing her now on her feet—that she looked like a different person. She approached him rapidly, and a little stiffly and shyly, but in the manner in which she shook hands with him there was an evident desire to be frank, and even fraternal. She looked like a different person, but that person had a beauty even more radiant; the fairness of her face shone forth at our young man as if to dissipate any doubts that might have crept over him as to the reality of the vision bequeathed to him by his former interview. And in this brightness and richness of her presence he could not have told you whether she struck him as more proud or more kind.

'I have kept you a long time, but it's supposed not, usually, to be a bad place, my salon; there are various things to look at, and perhaps you have noticed them. Over on that side, for instance, there is rather a curious collection of miniatures.' She spoke abruptly, quickly, as if she were conscious that their communion might be awkward and she were trying to strike, instantly (to conjure that element away), the sort of note that would make them both most comfortable. Quickly, too, she sat down before her tea-tray and poured him out a cup, which she handed him without asking whether he would have it. He accepted it with a trembling hand, though he had no desire for it; he was too nervous to swallow the tea, but it would not have occurred to him that it was possible to decline. When he had murmured that he had indeed looked at all her things but that it would take hours to do justice to such treasures, she asked if he were fond of works of art; adding, however immediately, that she was afraid he had not many opportunities of seeing them, though of course there were the public collections, open to all. Hyacinth said, with perfect veracity, that some of the happiest moments of his life had been spent at the British Museum and the National Gallery, and this reply appeared to interest her greatly, so that she immediately begged him to tell her what he thought of certain pictures and antiques. In this way it was that in an incredibly short space of time, as it appeared to him, he found himself discussing the Bacchus and Ariadne and the Elgin marbles with one of the most remarkable women in Europe.

It is true that she herself talked most, passing precipitately from one point to another, asking him questions and not waiting for answers; describing and qualifying things, expressing feelings, by the aid of phrases that he had never heard before but which seemed to him illuminating and happy—as when, for instance, she asked what art was, after all, but a synthesis made in the interest of pleasure, or said that she didn't like England at all, but loved it. It did not occur to him to think these discriminations pedantic. Suddenly she remarked, 'Madame Grandoni told me you saw my husband.'

'Ah, was the gentleman your husband?'

'Unfortunately! What do you think of him?'

'Oh, I can't think——' Hyacinth murmured.

'I wish I couldn't, either! I haven't seen him for nearly three years. He wanted to see me to-day, but I refused.'

'Ah!' said Hyacinth, staring and not knowing how he ought to receive so unexpected a confidence. Then, as the suggestions of inexperience are sometimes the happiest of all, he spoke simply what was in his mind and said, gently, 'It has made you very nervous.' Afterwards, when he had left the house, he wondered how, at that stage, he could have ventured on such a familiar remark.

The Princess took it with a quick, surprised laugh. 'How do you know that?' But before he had time to tell how, she added, 'Your saying that—that way—shows me how right I was to ask you to come to see me. You know, I hesitated. It shows me you have perceptions; I guessed as much the other night at the theatre. If I hadn't, I wouldn't have asked you. I may be wrong, but I like people who understand what one says to them, and also what one doesn't say.'

'Don't think I understand too much. You might easily exaggerate that,' Hyacinth declared, conscientiously.

'You confirm, completely, my first impression,' the Princess returned, smiling in a way that showed him he really amused her. 'We shall discover the limits of your comprehension! I *am* atrociously nervous. But it will pass. How is your friend the dressmaker?' she inquired, abruptly. And when Hyacinth had briefly given some account of poor Pinnie—told her that she was tolerably well for her, but old and tired and sad, and not very successful—she exclaimed, impatiently, 'Ah, well, she's not the only one!' and came back, with irrelevance, to the former question. 'It's not only my husband's visit—absolutely unexpected!—that has made me fidgety, but the idea that now you have been so kind as to come here you may wonder why, after all, I made such a point of it, and even think any explanation I might be able to give you entirely insufficient.'

'I don't want any explanation,' said Hyacinth.

'It's very nice of you to say that, and I shall take you at your word. Explanations usually make things worse. All the same, I don't want you to think (as you might have done so easily the other evening), that I wish only to treat you as a curious animal.'

'I don't care how you treat me!' said Hyacinth, smiling.

There was a considerable silence, after which the Princess remarked, 'All I ask of my husband is to let me alone. But he won't. He won't reciprocate my indifference.'

Hyacinth asked himself what reply he ought to make to such an announcement as that, and it seemed to him that the least civility demanded was that he should say—as he could with such conviction—'It can't be easy to be indifferent to you.'

'Why not, if I am odious? I can be—oh, there is no doubt of that! However, I can honestly say that with the Prince I have been exceedingly reasonable, and that most of the wrongs—the big ones, those that settled the question—have been on his side. You may tell me of course that that's the pretension of every woman who has made a mess of her marriage. But ask Madame Grandoni.'

'She will tell me it's none of my business.'

'Very true—she might!' the Princess admitted, laughing. 'And I don't know, either, why I should talk to you about my domestic affairs; except that I have been wondering what I could do to show confidence in you, in return for your showing so much in me. As this matter of my separation from my husband happens to have been turned uppermost by his sudden descent upon me, I just mention it, though the subject is tiresome enough. Moreover I ought to let you know that I have very little respect for distinctions of class—the sort of thing they make so much of in this country. They are doubt-less convenient in some ways, but when one has a reason—a reason of feeling—for overstepping them, and one allows one's self to be deterred by some dreary superstition about one's place, or some one else's place, then I think it's ignoble. It always belongs to one's place not to be a poor creature. I take it that if you are a socialist you think about this as I do; but lest, by chance, as the sense of those differences is the English religion, it may have rubbed off even on you, though I am more and more impressed with the fact that you are scarcely more British than I am; lest you should, in spite of your theoretic democracy, be shocked at some of the applica-tions that I, who cherish the creed, am capable of making of it, let me assure you without delay that in that case we shouldn't get on together at all, and had better part company before we go further.' She paused, long enough for Hyacinth to declare, with a great deal of emphasis, that he was not easily shocked; and then, restlessly, eagerly, as if it relieved her to talk, and made their queer interview less abnormal that she should talk most, she arrived at the point that she wanted to know the *people*, and know them intimately—the toilers and strugglers and sufferers—because she was convinced they were the most interesting portion of society, and at the in-quiry, 'What could possibly be in worse taste than for me to carry into such an undertaking a pretension of greater delicacy and finer manners? If I must do that,' she continued, 'it's sim-pler to leave them alone. But I can't leave them alone; they press upon me, they haunt me, they fascinate me. There it is (after all, it's very simple): I want to know them, and I want you to help me!'

'I will help you with pleasure, to the best of my humble ability. But you will be awfully disappointed,' Hyacinth said. Very strange it seemed to him that within so few days two ladies of rank should have found occasion to express to him the same mysterious longing. A breeze from a thoroughly un-expected quarter was indeed blowing over the aristocracy. Nevertheless, though there was much of the same accent of passion in the Princess Casamassima's communication that there had been in Lady Aurora's, and though he felt bound to discourage his present interlocutress as he had done the other, the force that pushed her struck him as a very different mixture from the shy, conscientious, anxious heresies of Rose Muniment's friend. The temper varied in the two women as much as the face and the manner, and that perhaps made their curiosity the more significant.

'I haven't the least doubt of it: there is nothing in life in which I have not been awfully disappointed. But disappointment for disappointment I shall like it better than some others. You'll not persuade me, either, that among the people I speak of, characters and passions and motives are not more natural, more complete, more naïf. The upper classes are so insipid! My husband traces his descent from the fifth century, and he's the greatest bore on earth. That is the kind of people I was condemned to live with after my marriage. Oh, if you knew what I have been through, you would allow that intelligent mechanics (of course I don't want to know idiots), would be a pleasant change. I must begin with some one—mustn't I?—so I began, the other night, with you!' As soon as she had uttered these words the Princess added a correction, with the consciousness of her mistake in her face. It made that face, to Hyacinth, more nobly, tenderly pure. 'The only objection to you, individually, is that you have nothing of the people about you—to-day not even the dress.' Her eyes wandered over him from head to foot, and their friendly beauty made him ashamed. 'I wish you had come in the clothes you wear at your work!'

'You see you do regard me as a curious animal,' he answered.

It was perhaps to contradict this that, after a moment, she began to tell him more about her domestic affairs. He ought to know who she was, unless Captain Sholto had told him; and she related her parentage—American on the mother's side, Italian on the father's—and how she had led, in her younger years, a wandering, Bohemian life, in a thousand different places (always in Europe; she had never been in America and knew very little about it, though she wanted greatly to cross the Atlantic), and largely, at one period, in Rome. She had been married by her people, in a mercenary way, for the sake of a fortune and a title, and it had turned out as badly as her worst enemy could wish. Her parents were dead, luckily

for them, and she had no one near her of her own except
Madame Grandoni, who belonged to her only in the sense
that she had known her as a girl; was an association of her
—what should she call them?—her innocent years. Not that
she had ever been very innocent; she had had a horrible education. However, she had known a few good people—people she respected, then; but Madame Grandoni was the only
one who had stuck to her. She, too, was liable to leave her
any day; the Princess appeared to intimate that her destiny
might require her to take some step which would test severely the old lady's adhesive property. It would detain her
too long to make him understand the stages by which she
had arrived at her present state of mind: her disgust with a
thousand social arrangements, her rebellion against the selfishness, the corruption, the iniquity, the cruelty, the imbecility, of the people who, all over Europe, had the upper hand.
If he could have seen her life, the *milieu* in which, for several
years, she had been condemned to move, the evolution of
her opinions (Hyacinth was delighted to hear her use that
term), would strike him as perfectly logical. She had been
humiliated, outraged, tortured; she considered that she too
was one of the numerous class who could be put on a tolerable footing only by a revolution. At any rate, she had some
self-respect left, and there was still more that she wanted to
recover; the only way to arrive at that was to throw herself
into some effort which would make her forget her own affairs and comprehend the troubles and efforts of others. Hyacinth listened to her with a wonderment which, as she went
on, was transformed into fascinated submission; she seemed
so natural, so vivid, so exquisitely generous and sincere. By
the time he had been with her for half an hour she had
made the situation itself appear natural and usual, and a
third person who should have joined them at this moment
would have observed nothing to make him suppose that
friendly social intercourse between little bookbinders and
Neapolitan princesses was not, in London, a matter of daily
occurrence.

Hyacinth had seen plenty of women who chattered about
themselves and their affairs—a vulgar garrulity of confidence
was indeed a leading characteristic of the sex as he had

hitherto learned to know it—but he was quick to perceive that the great lady who now took the trouble to open herself to him was not of a gossiping habit; that she must be, on the contrary, as a general thing, proudly, ironically, reserved, even to the point of passing, with many people, for a model of the unsatisfactory. It was very possible she was capricious; yet the fact that her present sympathies and curiosities might be a caprice wore, in Hyacinth's eyes, no sinister aspect. Why was it not a noble and interesting whim, and why might he not stand, for the hour at any rate, in the silvery moonshine it threw upon his path? It must be added that he was far from understanding everything she said, and some of her allusions and implications were so difficult to seize that they mainly served to reveal to him the limits of his own acquaintance with life. Her words evoked all sorts of shadowy suggestions of things he was condemned not to know, touching him most when he had not the key to them. This was especially the case with her reference to her career in Italy, on her husband's estates, and her relations with his family; who considered that they had done her a great honour in receiving her into their august circle (putting the best face on a bad business), after they had moved heaven and earth to keep her out of it. The position made for her among these people, and what she had had to suffer from their family tone, their opinions and cus- toms (though what these might be remained vague to her listener), had evidently planted in her soul a lasting resent- ment and contempt; and Hyacinth gathered that the force of reaction and revenge might carry her far, make her modern and democratic and heretical à outrance—lead her to swear by Darwin and Spencer as well as by the revolutionary spirit. He surely need not have been so sensible of the weak spots in his comprehension of the Princess, when he could already sur- mise that personal passion had counted for so much in the formation of her views. This induction, however, which had no harshness, did not make her appear to him any the less a creature compounded of the finest elements; brilliant, deli- cate, complicated, but complicated with something divine. It was not until after he had left her that he became conscious she had forced him to talk, as well as talked herself. He drew a long breath as he reflected that he had not made quite such an ass of himself as might very well have happened; he had been saved by his enjoyment and admiration, which had not gone to his head and prompted him to show that he too, in his improbable little way, was remarkable, but had kept him in a state of anxious, delicious tension, as if the occasion had been a great solemnity. He had said, indeed, much more than he had warrant for, when she questioned him about his socialistic affiliations; he had spoken as if the movement were vast and mature, whereas, in fact, so far, at least, as he was as yet concerned with it, and could answer for it from personal knowledge, it was circumscribed by the hideously papered walls of the little club-room at the 'Sun and Moon.' He reproached himself with this laxity, but it had not been engendered by vanity. He was only afraid of disappointing his hostess too much; of making her say, 'Why in the world, then, did you come to see me, if you have nothing more remarkable to relate?'—an inquiry to which, of course, he would have had an answer ready, if it had not been impossible to him to say that he had never asked to come: his coming was her own affair. He wanted too much to come a second time to have the courage to make that speech. Nevertheless, when she exclaimed, changing the subject abruptly, as she always did, from something else they had been talking about, 'I wonder whether I shall ever see you again!' he replied, with perfect sincerity, that it was very difficult for him to believe anything so delightful could be repeated. There were some kinds of happiness that to many people never came at all, and to others could come only once. He added, 'It is very true I had just that feeling after I left you the other night at the theatre. And yet here I am!'

'Yes, there you are,' said the Princess thoughtfully, as if this might be a still graver and more embarrassing fact than she had yet supposed it. 'I take it there is nothing essentially impossible in my seeing you again; but it may very well be that you will never again find it so pleasant. Perhaps that's the happiness that comes but once. At any rate, you know, I am going away.'

'Oh yes, of course; every one leaves town,' Hyacinth commented, sagaciously.

'Do you, Mr. Robinson?' asked the Princess.

'Well, I don't as a general thing. Nevertheless, it is possible that, this year, I may get two or three days at the seaside. I should like to take my old lady. I have done it before.'

'And except for that you shall be always at work?'

'Yes; but you must understand that I like my work. You must understand that it's a great blessing for a young fellow like me to have it.'

'And if you didn't have it, what would you do? Should you starve?'

'Oh, I don't think I should starve,' the young man replied, judicially.

The Princess looked a little chagrined, but after a moment she remarked, 'I wonder whether you would come to see me, in the country, somewhere.'

'Oh, dear!' Hyacinth exclaimed, catching his breath. 'You are so kind, I don't know what to do.'

'Don't be *banal*, please. That's what other people are. What's the use of my looking for something fresh in other walks of life, if you are going to be *banal* too? I ask you, would you come?'

Hyacinth hesitated a moment. 'Yes, I think I would come. I don't know, at all, how I should do it—there would be several obstacles; but wherever you should call for me, I would come.'

'You mean you can't leave your work, like that; you might lose it, if you did, and be in want of money and much embarrassed?'

'Yes, there would be little difficulties of that kind. You see that immediately, in practice, great obstacles come up, when it's a question of a person like you making friends with a person like me.'

'That's the way I like you to talk,' said the Princess, with a pitying gentleness that seemed to her visitor quite sacred. 'After all, I don't know where I shall be. I have got to pay stupid visits, myself, where the only comfort will be that I shall make the people jump. Every one here thinks me exceedingly odd—as there is no doubt I am! I might be ever so much more so if you would only help me a little. Why shouldn't I have my bookbinder, after all? In attendance, you know, it would be awfully *chic*. We might have immense fun, don't you think so? No doubt it will come. At any rate, I shall return to London when I have got through that *corvée*; I shall be here next year. In the meantime, don't forget me,' she went on, rising to her feet. 'Remember, on the contrary, that I expect you to take me into the slums—into very bad places.' Why the idea of these scenes of misery should have lighted up her face is more than may be explained; but she smiled down at Hyacinth—who, even as he stood up, was of slightly smaller stature—with all her strange, radiant sweetness. Then, in a manner almost equally incongruous, she added a reference to what she had said a moment before. 'I recognise perfectly the obstacles, in practice, as you call them; but though I am not, by nature, persevering, and am really very easily put off, I don't consider that they will prove insurmountable. They exist on my side as well, and if you will help me to overcome mine I will do the same for you, with yours.'

These words, repeating themselves again and again in Hyacinth's consciousness, appeared to give him wings, to help him to float and soar, as he turned that afternoon out of South Street. He had at home a copy of Tennyson's poems— a single, comprehensive volume, with a double column on the page, in a tolerably neat condition, though he had handled it much. He took it to pieces that same evening, and during the following week, in his hours of leisure, at home in his little room, with the tools he kept there for private use, and a morsel of delicate, blue-tinted Russia leather, of which he obtained possession at the place in Soho, he devoted himself to the task of binding the book as perfectly as he knew how. He worked with passion, with religion, and produced a masterpiece of firmness and finish, of which his own appreciation was as high as that of M. Poupin, when, at the end of the week, he exhibited the fruit of his toil, and much more freely expressed than that of old Crookenden, who grunted approbation, but was always too long-headed to create precedents. Hyacinth carried the volume to South Street, as an offering to the Princess; hoping she would not yet have left London, in which case he would ask the servant to deliver it to her, along with a little note he had sat up all night to compose. But the majestic butler, in charge of the house, opening the door yet looking down at him as if from a second-storey window, took the life out of his vision and erected himself as an impenetrable medium. The Princess had been absent for some days; the butler was so good as to inform the young man with the parcel that she was on a visit to a 'juke,' in a distant part of the country. He offered however to receive, and even to forward, anything Hyacinth might wish to leave; but our hero felt a sudden indisposition to launch his humble tribute into the vast, the possibly cold, unknown of a ducal circle. He decided to retain his little package for the present; he would give it to her when he should see her again, and he turned away without parting with it. Later, it seemed to create a sort of material link between the Princess and himself, and at the end of three months it almost appeared to him, not that the exquisite book was an intended present from his own hand, but that it had been placed in that hand by the most remarkable woman in Europe. Rare sensations and impressions, moments of acute happiness, almost always, with Hyacinth, in retrospect, became rather mythic and legendary; and the superior piece of work he had done after seeing her last, in the immediate heat of his emotion, turned into a kind of proof and gage, as if a ghost, in vanishing from sight, had left a palpable relic.

XVIII

THE MATTER concerned him only indirectly, but it may concern the reader more closely to know that before the visit to the duke took place Madame Grandoni granted to Prince Casamassima the private interview she had promised him on that sad Sunday afternoon. She crept out of South Street after breakfast—a repast which under the Princess's roof was served at twelve o'clock, in the foreign fashion —crossed the sultry solitude into which, at such a season, that precinct resolves itself, and entered the Park, where the grass was already brown and a warm, smoky haze prevailed, a sort of summer edition of what was most characteristic in the London air. The Prince met her, by appointment, at the gate, and they went and sat down together under the trees beside the drive, amid a wilderness of empty chairs and with nothing to distract their attention from an equestrian or two, left over from the cavalcades of a fortnight before, and whose vain agitation in the saddle the desolate scene seemed to throw into high relief. They remained there for nearly an hour, though Madame Grandoni, in spite of her leaning to friendly interpretations, could not have told herself what comfort it was to the depressed, embarrassed young man at her side. She had nothing to say to him which could better his case, as he bent his mournful gaze on a prospect which was not, after all, perceptibly improved by its not being Sunday, and could only feel that, with her, he must seem to himself to be nearer his wife—to be touching something she had touched. The old lady wished he would resign himself more, but she was willing to minister to that thin illusion, little as she approved of the manner in which he had conducted himself at the time of the last sharp crisis in the remarkable history of his relations with Christina. He had behaved like a spoiled child, with a bad little nature, in a rage; he had been fatally wanting in dignity and wisdom, and had given the Princess an advantage which she took on the spot and would keep for ever. He had acted without manly judgment, had put his uncles upon her (as if she cared for his uncles! though one of them was a powerful prelate), had been suspicious and jealous on exactly the wrong occasions—occasions on which such ideas were a gratuitous injury. He had not been clever enough or strong enough to make good his valid rights, and had transferred the whole quarrel to a ground where his wife was far too accomplished a woman not to obtain the appearance of victory.

There was another reflection that Madame Grandoni made, as her interview with her dejected friend prolonged itself. She could make it the more freely as, besides being naturally quick and appreciative, she had always, during her Roman career, in the dear old days (mingled with bitterness as they had been for her), lived with artists, archæologists, ingenious strangers, people who abounded in good talk, threw out ideas and played with them. It came over her that, really, even if things had not come to that particular crisis, Christina's active, various, ironical mind, with all its audacities and impatiences, could not have tolerated for long the simple dulness of the Prince's company. The old lady had said to him, on meeting him, 'Of course, what you want to know immediately is whether she has sent you a message. No, my poor friend, I must tell you the truth. I asked her for one, but she told me that she had nothing whatever, of any kind, to say to you. She knew I was coming out to see you. I haven't done so *en cachette*. She doesn't like it, but she accepts the necessity for this once, since you have made the mistake, as she considers it, of approaching her again. We talked about you, last night, after your note came to me—for five minutes; that is, I talked, and Christina was good enough to listen. At the end she said this (what I shall tell you), with perfect calmness, and the appearance of being the most reasonable woman in the world. She didn't ask me to repeat it to you, but I do so because it is the only substitute I can offer you for a message. "I try to occupy my life, my mind, to create interests, in the odious position in which I find myself; I endeavour to get out of myself, my small personal disappointments and troubles, by the aid of such poor faculties as I possess. There are things in the world more interesting, after all, and I hope to succeed in giving my attention to them. It appears to me not too much to ask that the Prince, on his side, should make the same conscientious effort—and leave me alone!"

Those were your wife's remarkable words; they are all I have to give you.'

After she had given them Madame Grandoni felt a pang of regret; the Prince turned upon her a face so white, bewildered and wounded. It had seemed to her that they might form a wholesome admonition, but it was now impressed upon her that, as coming from his wife, they were cruel, and she herself felt almost cruel for having repeated them. What they amounted to was an exquisite taunt of his mediocrity—a mediocrity which was, after all, not a crime. How could the Prince occupy himself, what interests could he create, and what faculties, gracious heaven, did he possess? He was as ignorant as a fish, and as narrow as his hat-band. His expression became pitiful; it was as if he dimly measured the insult, felt it more than saw it—felt that he could not plead incapacity without putting the Princess largely in the right. He gazed at Madame Grandoni, his face worked, and for a moment she thought he was going to burst into tears. But he said nothing—perhaps because he was afraid of that—so that suffering silence, during which she gently laid her hand upon his own, remained his only answer. He might doubtless do so much he didn't, that when Christina touched upon this she was unanswerable. The old lady changed the subject: told him what a curious country England was, in so many ways; offered information as to their possible movements during the summer and autumn, which, within a day or two, had become slightly clearer. But at last, abruptly, as if he had not heard her, he inquired, appealingly, who the young man was who had come in the day he called, just as he was going.

Madame Grandoni hesitated a moment. 'He was the Princess's bookbinder.'

'Her bookbinder? Do you mean her lover?'

'Prince, how can you dream she will ever live with you again?' the old lady asked, in reply to this.

'Why, then, does she have him in her drawing-room —announced like an ambassador, carrying a hat in his hand like mine? Where were his books, his bindings? I shouldn't say this to her,' the Prince added, as if the declaration justified him.

'I told you the other day that she is making studies of the people—the lower orders. The young man you saw is a study.' Madame Grandoni could not help laughing out as she gave her explanation this turn; but her mirth elicited no echo from her interlocutor.

'I have thought that over—over and over; but the more I think the less I understand. Would it be your idea that she is quite crazy? I must tell you I don't care if she is!'

'We are all quite crazy, I think,' said Madame Grandoni; 'but the Princess no more than the rest of us. No, she must try everything; at present she is trying democracy and socialism.'

'*Santo Dio!*' murmured the young man. 'And what do they say here when they see her bookbinder?'

'They haven't seen him, and perhaps they won't. But if they do, it won't matter, because here everything is forgiven. That a person should be singular is all they want. A bookbinder will do as well as anything else.'

The Prince mused a while, and then he said, 'How can she bear the dirt, the bad smell?'

'I don't know what you are talking about. If you mean the young man you saw at the house (I may tell you, by the way, that it was only the first time he had been there, and that the Princess had only seen him once)—if you mean the little bookbinder, he isn't dirty, especially what we should call. The people of that kind, here, are not like our dear Romans. Every one has a sponge, as big as your head; you can see them in the shops.'

'They are full of gin; their faces are purple,' said the Prince; after which he immediately asked, 'If she had only seen him once, how could he have come into her drawing-room that way?'

The old lady looked at him with a certain severity. 'Believe, at least, what *I* say, my poor friend! Never forget that this was how you spoiled your affairs most of all—by treating a person (and such a person!) as if, as a matter of course, she lied. Christina has many faults, but she hasn't that one; that's why I can live with her. She will speak the truth always.'

It was plainly not agreeable to the Prince to be reminded so sharply of his greatest mistake, and he flushed a little as

Madame Grandoni spoke. But he did not admit his error, and she doubted whether he even perceived it. At any rate he remarked rather grandly, like a man who has still a good deal to say for himself, 'There are things it is better to conceal.'

'It all depends on whether you are afraid. Christina never is. Oh, I admit that she is very strange, and when the entertainment of watching her, to see how she will carry out some of her inspirations, is not stronger than anything else, I lose all patience with her. When she doesn't fascinate she can only exasperate. But, as regards yourself, since you are here, and as I may not see you again for a long time, or perhaps ever (at my age—I'm a hundred and twenty!) I may as well give you the key of certain parts of your wife's conduct. It may make it seem to you a little less fantastic. At the bottom, then, of much that she does is the fact that she is ashamed of having married you.'

'Less fantastic?' the young man repeated, staring.

'You may say that there can be nothing more eccentric than that. But you know—or, if not, it isn't for want of her having told you—that the Princess considers that in the darkest hour of her life she sold herself for a title and a fortune. She regards her doing so as such a horrible piece of frivolity that she can never, for the rest of her days, be serious enough to make up for it.'

'Yes, I know that she pretends to have been forced. And does she think she's so serious now?'

'The young man you saw the other day thinks so,' said the old woman, smiling. 'Sometimes she calls it by another name: she says she has thrown herself with passion into being "modern." That sums up the greatest number of things that you and your family are not.'

'Yes, we are not, thank God! *Dio mio, Dio mio!*' groaned the Prince. He seemed so exhausted by his reflections that he remained sitting in his chair after his companion, lifting her crumpled corpulence out of her own, had proposed that they should walk about a little. She had no ill-nature, but she had already noticed that whenever she was with Christina's husband the current of conversation made her, as she phrased it, bump against him. After administering these small shocks she always steered away, and now, the Prince having at last got up and offered her his arm, she tried again to talk with him of things he could consider without bitterness. She asked him about the health and habits of his uncles, and he replied, for the moment, with the minuteness which he had been taught that in such a case courtesy demanded; but by the time that, at her request, they had returned to the gate nearest to South Street (she wished him to come no farther) he had prepared a question to which she had not opened the way.

'And who and what, then, is this English captain? About him there is a great deal said.'

'This English captain?'

'Godfrey Gerald Cholto—you see I know a good deal about him,' said the Prince, articulating the English names with difficulty.

They had stopped near the gate, on the edge of Park Lane, and a couple of predatory hansoms dashed at them from opposite quarters. 'I thought that was coming, and at bottom it is he that has occupied you most!' Madame Grandoni exclaimed, with a sigh. 'But in reality he is the last one you need trouble about; he doesn't count.'

'Why doesn't he count?'

'I can't tell you—except that some people don't, you know. He doesn't even think he does.'

'Why not, when she receives him always—lets him go wherever she goes?'

'Perhaps that is just the reason. When people give her a chance to get tired of them she takes it rather easily. At any rate, you needn't be any more jealous of him than you are of me. He's a convenience, a *factotum*, but he works without wages.'

'Isn't he, then, in love with her?'

'Naturally. He has, however, no hope.'

'Ah, poor gentleman!' said the Prince, lugubriously.

'He accepts the situation better than you. He occupies himself—as she has strongly recommended him, in my hearing, to do—with other women.'

'Oh, the brute!' the Prince exclaimed. 'At all events, he sees her.'

'Yes, but she doesn't see him!' laughed Madame Grandoni, as she turned away.

XIX

THE PINK DRESSING-GOWN which Pinnie had engaged to make for Rose Muniment became, in Lomax Place, a conspicuous object, supplying poor Amanda with a constant theme for reference to one of the great occasions of her life —her visit to Belgrave Square with Lady Aurora, after their meeting at Rosy's bedside. She described this episode vividly to her companion, repeating a thousand times that her lady-ship's affability was beyond anything she could have expected. The grandeur of the house in Belgrave Square figured in her recital as something oppressive and fabulous, tempered though it had been by shrouds of brown holland and the nudity of staircases and saloons of which the trappings had been put away. 'If it's so noble when they're out of town, what can it be when they are all there together and everything is out?' she inquired suggestively; and she permitted herself to be restrictive only on two points, one of which was the state of Lady Aurora's gloves and bonnet-strings. If she had not been afraid to appear to notice the disrepair of these objects, she would have been so happy to offer to do any little mending. 'If she would only come to me every week or two, I would keep up her rank for her,' said Pinnie, with visions of a needle that positively flashed in the disinterested service of the aristocracy. She added that her lady-ship got all dragged out with her long expeditions to Camberwell; she might be in tatters, for all they could do to help her at the top of those dreadful stairs, with that strange sick creature (she was too unnatural), thinking only of her own finery and talking about her complexion. If she wanted pink, she should have pink; but to Pinnie there was something almost unholy in it, like decking out a corpse, or the next thing to it. This was the other element that left Miss Pynsent cold; it could not be other than difficult for her to enter into the importance her ladyship appeared to attach to those pushing people. The girl was unfortunate, certainly, stuck up there like a kitten on a shelf, but in her ladyship's place she would have found some topic more in keeping, while they walked about under those tremendous gilded ceilings. Lady Aurora, seeing how she was struck, showed her all over the house, carrying the lamp herself and telling an old woman who was there—a kind of housekeeper, with ribbons in her cap, who would have pushed Pinnie out if you could push with your eyes—that they would do very well without her. If the pink dressing-gown, in its successive stages of development, filled up the little brown parlour (it was terribly long on the stocks), making such a pervasive rose-coloured presence as had not been seen there for many a day, this was evidently because it was associated with Lady Aurora, not because it was dedicated to her humble friend.

One day, when Hyacinth came home from his work, Pinnie announced to him as soon as he entered the room that her ladyship had been there to look at it—to pass judgment before the last touches were conferred. The dressmaker intimated that in such a case as that her judgment was rather wild, and she had made an embarrassing suggestion about pockets. Whatever could poor Miss Muniment want of pockets, and what had she to put in them? But Lady Aurora had evidently found the garment far beyond anything she expected, and she had been more affable than ever, and had wanted to know about every one in the Place; not in a meddling, prying way, either, like some of those upper-class visitors, but quite as if the poor people were the high ones and she was afraid her curiosity might be 'presumptious.' It was in the same discreet spirit that she had invited Amanda to relate her whole history, and had expressed an interest in the career of her young friend.

'She said you had charming manners,' Miss Pynsent hastened to remark; 'but, before heaven, Hyacinth Robinson, I never mentioned a scrap that it could give you pain that any one should talk about.' There was an heroic explicitness in this, on Pinnie's part, for she knew in advance just how Hyacinth would look at her—fixedly, silently, hopelessly, as if she were still capable of tattling horribly (with the idea that her revelations would increase her importance), and putting forward this hollow theory of her supreme discretion to cover it up. His eyes seemed to say, 'How can I believe you, and yet how can I prove you are lying? I am very helpless, for I can't prove that without applying to the person to whom your incorrigible folly has probably led you to brag, to throw out mysterious and tantalising hints. You know, of course, that I would never condescend to that.' Pinnie suffered, acutely, from this imputation; yet she exposed herself to it often, because she could never deny herself the pleasure, keener still than her pain, of letting Hyacinth know that he was appreciated, admired and, for those 'charming manners' commended by Lady Aurora, even wondered at; and this kind of interest always appeared to imply a suspicion of his secret—something which, when he expressed to himself the sense of it, he called, resenting it at once and yet finding a certain softness in it, 'a beastly *attendrissement.*' When Pinnie went on to say to him that Lady Aurora appeared to feel a certain surprise at his never yet having come to Belgrave Square for the famous books, he reflected that he must really wait upon her without more delay, if he wished to keep up his reputation for charming manners; and meanwhile he considered much the extreme oddity of this new phase of his life (it had opened so suddenly, from one day to the other); a phase in which his society should have become indispensable to ladies of high rank and the obscurity of his condition only an attraction the more. They were taking him up then, one after the other, and they were even taking up poor Pinnie, as a means of getting at him; so that he wondered, with humorous bitterness, whether it meant that his destiny was really seeking him out —that the aristocracy, recognising a mysterious affinity (with that fineness of *flair* for which they were remarkable), were coming to him to save him the trouble of coming to them.

It was late in the day (the beginning of an October evening), and Lady Aurora was at home. Hyacinth had made a mental calculation of the time at which she would have risen from dinner; the operation of 'rising from dinner' having always been, in his imagination, for some reason or other, highly characteristic of the nobility. He was ignorant of the fact that Lady Aurora's principal meal consisted of a scrap of fish and a cup of tea, served on a little stand in the dismantled breakfast-parlour. The door was opened for Hyacinth by the invidious old lady whom Pinnie had described, and who listened to his inquiry, conducted him through the house, and ushered him into her ladyship's presence, without the smallest relaxation of a pair of tightly-closed lips. Hyacinth's hostess was seated in the little breakfast-parlour, by the light of a couple of candles, immersed apparently in a collection of tolerably crumpled papers and account-books. She was ciphering, consulting memoranda, taking notes; she had had her head in her hands, and the silky entanglement of her tresses resisted the rapid effort she made to smooth herself down as she saw the little bookbinder come in. The impression of her fingers remained in little rosy streaks on her pink skin. She exclaimed, instantly, 'Oh, you have come about the books—it's so very kind of you;' and she hurried him off to another room, to which, as she explained, she had had them brought down for him to choose from. The effect of this precipitation was to make him suppose at first that she might wish him to execute his errand as quickly as possible and take himself off; but he presently perceived that her nervousness, her shyness, were of an order that would always give false ideas. She wanted him to stay, she wanted to talk with him, and she had rushed with him at the books in order to gain time and composure for exercising some subtler art. Hyacinth stayed half an hour, and became more and more convinced that her ladyship was, as he had ventured to pronounce her on the occasion of their last meeting, a regular saint. He was privately a little disappointed in the books, though he selected three or four, as many as he could carry, and promised to come back for others: they denoted, on Lady Aurora's part, a limited acquaintance with French literature and even a certain puerility of taste. There were several volumes of Lamartine and a set of the spurious memoirs of the Marquise de Créqui; but for the rest the little library consisted mainly of Marmontel and Madame de Genlis, the Récit d'une Sœur and the tales of M. J. T. de Saint-Germain. There were certain members of an intensely modern school, advanced and scientific realists, of whom Hyacinth had heard and on whom he had long desired to put his hand; but, evidently, none of them had ever stumbled into Lady Aurora's candid collection, though she did possess a couple of Balzac's novels, which, by ill-luck, happened to be just those that Hyacinth had read more than once.

There was, nevertheless, something very agreeable to him in the moments he passed in the big, dim, cool, empty house, where, at intervals, monumental pieces of furniture—not crowded and miscellaneous, as he had seen the appurtenances of the Princess—loomed and gleamed, and Lady Aurora's fantastic intonations awakened echoes which gave him a sense of privilege, of rioting, decently, in the absence of jealous influences. She talked again about the poor people in the south of London, and about the Muniments in particular; evidently, the only fault she had to find with these latter was that they were not poor enough—not sufficiently exposed to dangers and privations against which she could step in. Hyacinth liked her for this, even though he wished she would talk of something else—he hardly knew what, unless it was that, like Rose Muniment, he wanted to hear more about Inglefield. He didn't mind, with the poor, going into questions of poverty—it even gave him at times a strange, savage satisfaction—but he saw that in discussing them with the rich the interest must inevitably be less; they could never treat them *à fond*. Their mistakes and illusions, their thinking they had got hold of the sensations of the destitute when they hadn't at all, would always be more or less irritating. It came over Hyacinth that if he found this want of perspective in Lady Aurora's deep conscientiousness, it would be a queer enough business when he should come to go into the detail of such matters with the Princess Casamassima.

His present hostess said not a word to him about Pinnie, and he guessed that she had an instinctive desire to place him on the footing on which people do not express approbation or surprise at the decency or good-breeding of each other's relatives. He saw that she would always treat him as a gentleman, and that even if he should be basely ungrateful she would never call his attention to the fact that she had done so. He should not have occasion to say to her, as he had said to the Princess, that she regarded him as a curious animal; and it gave him immediately that sense, always so delightful to him, of learning more about life, to perceive there were such different ways (which implied still a good many more), of being a lady of rank. The manner in which Lady Aurora appeared to wish to confer with him on the great problems of pauperism might have implied that he was a benevolent nobleman (of the type of Lord Shaftesbury), who had endowed many charities and was noted, in philanthropic schemes, for his practical sense. It was not less present to him that Pinnie might have tattled, put forward his claims to high consanguinity, than it had been when the dressmaker herself descanted on her lady-ship's condescensions; but he remembered now that he too had only just escaped being asinine, when, the other day, he flashed out an allusion to his accursed origin. At all events, he was much touched by the delicacy with which the earl's daughter comported herself, simply assuming that he was 'one of themselves'; and he reflected that if she did know his history (he was sure he might pass twenty years in her society without discovering whether she did or not), this shade of courtesy, this natural tact, coexisting even with extreme awk-wardness, illustrated that 'best breeding' which he had seen alluded to in novels portraying the aristocracy. The only re-mark on Lady Aurora's part that savoured in the least of look-ing down at him from a height was when she said, cheerfully, encouragingly, 'I suppose that one of these days you will be setting up in business for yourself;' and this was not so cruelly patronising that he could not reply, with a smile equally free from any sort of impertinence, 'Oh dear, no, I shall never do that. I should make a great mess of any attempt to carry on a business. I haven't a particle of that kind of aptitude.'

Lady Aurora looked a little surprised; then she said, 'Oh, I see; you don't like—you don't like'—— She hesitated: he saw she was going to say that he didn't like the idea of going in, to that extent, for a trade; but he stopped her in time from attributing to him a sentiment so foolish, and declared that what he meant was simply that the only faculty he possessed was the faculty of doing his little piece of work, whatever it was, of liking to do it skillfully and prettily, and of liking still better to get his money for it when it was done. His concep-tion of 'business,' or of rising in the world, didn't go beyond that. 'Oh yes, I can fancy!' her ladyship exclaimed; but she looked at him a moment with eyes which showed that he puzzled her, that she didn't quite understand his tone. Before he went away she inquired of him, abruptly (nothing had led up to it), what he thought of Captain Sholto, whom she had seen that other evening in Audley Court. Didn't Hya-cinth think he was very odd? Hyacinth confessed to this impression; whereupon Lady Aurora went on anxiously, eagerly: 'Don't you consider that—that—he is decidedly vulgar?'

'How can I know?'

'You can know perfectly—as well as any one!' Then she added, 'I think it's a pity they should—a—form relations with any one of that kind.'

'They,' of course, meant Paul Muniment and his sister. 'With a person that may be vulgar?' Hyacinth asked, regarding this solicitude as exquisite. 'But think of the people they know—think of those they are surrounded with—think of all Audley Court!'

'The poor, the unhappy, the labouring classes? Oh, I don't call *them* vulgar!' cried her ladyship, with radiant eyes. The young man, lying awake a good deal that night, laughed to himself, on his pillow, not unkindly, at her fear that he and his friends would be contaminated by the familiar of a princess. He even wondered whether she would not find the Princess herself rather vulgar.

XX

It must not be supposed that Hyacinth's relations with Millicent Henning had remained unaffected by the remarkable incident she had witnessed at the theatre. It had made a great impression on the young lady from Pimlico; he never saw her, for several weeks afterwards, that she had not an immense deal to say about it; and though it suited her to take the line of being shocked at the crudity of such proceedings, and of denouncing the Princess for a bold-faced foreigner, of a kind to which any one who knew anything of what could go on in London would give a wide berth, it was easy to see that she was pleased at being brought even into roundabout contact with a person so splendid and at finding her own discriminating approval of Hyacinth confirmed in such high quarters. She professed to derive her warrant for her low opinion of the lady in the box from information given her by Captain Sholto as he sat beside her — information of which at different moments she gave a different version; her anecdotes having nothing in common, at least, save that they were alike unflattering to the Princess. Hyacinth had many doubts of the Captain's pouring such confidences into Miss Henning's ear; under the circumstances it would be such a very unnatural thing for him to do. He *was* unnatural — that was true — and he might have told Millicent, who was capable of having plied him with questions, that his distinguished friend was separated from her husband; but, for the rest, it was more probable that the girl had given the rein to a certain inventive faculty which she had already showed him she possessed, when it was a question of exercising her primitive, half-childish, half-plebeian impulse of destruction, the instinct of pulling down what was above her, the reckless energy that would, precisely, make her so effective in revolutionary scenes. Hyacinth (it has been mentioned) did not consider that Millicent was false, and it struck him as a proof of positive candour that she should make up absurd, abusive stories about a person concerning whom she knew nothing at all, save that she disliked her, and could not hope for esteem, or, indeed, for recognition of any kind, in return. When people were really false you didn't know where you stood with them, and on such a point as this Miss Henning could never be accused of leaving you in obscurity. She said little else about the Captain, and did not pretend to repeat the remainder of his conversation; taking it with an air of grand indifference when Hyacinth amused himself with repaying her strictures on his new acquaintance by drawing a sufficiently derisive portrait of hers.

He took the ground that Sholto's admiration for the high-coloured beauty in the second balcony had been at the bottom of the whole episode: he had persuaded the Princess to pretend she was a socialist and should like therefore to confer with Hyacinth, in order that he might slip into the seat of this too easily deluded youth. At the same time, it never occurred to our young man to conceal the fact that the lady in the box had followed him up; he contented himself with saying that this had been no part of the original plot, but a simple result—not unnatural, after all—of his turning out so much more fascinating than one might have supposed. He narrated, with sportive variations, his visit in South Street, and felt that he would never feel the need, with his childhood's friend, of glossing over that sort of experience. She might make him a scene of jealousy and welcome—there were things that would have much more terror for him than that; her jealousy, with its violence, its energy, even a certain inconsequent, dare-devil humour that played through it, entertained him, illustrated the frankness, the passion and pluck, that he admired her for. He should never be on the footing of sparing Miss Henning's susceptibilities; how fond she might really be of him he could not take upon himself to say, but her affection would never take the form of that sort of delicacy, and their intercourse was plainly foredoomed to be an exchange of thumps and concussions, of sarcastic shouts and mutual *défis*. He liked her, at bottom, strangely, absurdly; but after all it was only well enough to torment her—she could bear so much—not well enough to spare her. Of there being any justification of her jealousy of the Princess he never thought; it could not occur to him to weigh against each other the sentiments he might excite in such opposed bosoms or those that the spectacle of either emotion might have kindled in his own. He had, no doubt, his share of fatuity, but he found himself unable to associate, mentally, a great lady and a shop-girl in a contest for a prize which should present analogies with his own personality. How could they have anything in common—even so small a thing as a desire to possess themselves of Hyacinth Robinson? A fact that he did not impart to Millicent, and that he could have no wish to impart to her, was the matter of his pilgrimage to Belgrave Square. He might be in love with the Princess (how could he qualify, as yet, the bewildered emotion she had produced in him?), and he certainly never would conceive a passion for poor Lady Aurora; yet it would have given him pain much greater than any he felt in the other case, to hear the girl make free with the ministering angel of Audley Court. The difference was, perhaps, somehow in that she appeared really not to touch or arrive at the Princess at all, whereas Lady Aurora was within her range and compass.

After paying him that visit at his rooms Hyacinth lost sight of Captain Sholto, who had not again reappeared at the 'Sun and Moon,' the little tavern which presented so common and casual a face to the world and yet, in its unsuspected rear, offered a security as yet unimpugned to machinations going down to the very bottom of things. Nothing was more natural than that the Captain should be engaged at this season in the recreations of his class; and our young man took for granted that if he were not hanging about the Princess, on that queer footing as to which he himself had a secret hope that he should some day have more light, he was probably ploughing through northern seas on a yacht or creeping after stags in the Highlands; our hero's acquaintance with the light literature of his country being such as to assure him that in one or other of these occupations people of leisure, during the autumn, were necessarily immersed. If the Captain were giving his attention to neither, he must have started for Albania, or at least for Paris. Happy Captain, Hyacinth reflected, while his imagination followed him through all kinds of vivid exotic episodes and his restless young feet continued to tread, through the stale, flat weeks of September and October, the familiar pavements of Soho, Islington, and Pentonville, and the shabby sinuous ways which unite these laborious districts.

He had told the Princess that he sometimes had a holiday at this period and that there was a chance of his escorting his respectable companion to the seaside; but as it turned out, at present, the spare cash for such an excursion was wanting. Hyacinth had indeed, for the moment, an exceptionally keen sense of the absence of this article, and was forcibly reminded that it took a good deal of money to cultivate the society of agreeable women. He not only had not a penny, but he was much in debt, and the explanation of his pinched feeling was in a vague, half-remorseful, half-resigned reference to the numerous occasions when he had had to put his hand in his pocket under penalty of disappointing a young lady whose needs were positive, and especially to a certain high crisis (as it might prove to be) in his destiny, when it came over him that one couldn't call on a princess just as one was. So, this year, he did not ask old Crookenden for the week which some of the other men took (Eustache Poupin, who had never quitted London since his arrival, launched himself, precisely that summer, supported by his brave wife, into the British unknown, on the strength of a return ticket to Worthing); simply because he shouldn't know what to do with it. The best way not to spend money, though it was no doubt not the best in the world to make it, was still to take one's daily course to the old familiar, shabby shop, where, as the days shortened and November thickened the air to a livid yellow, the uncovered flame of the gas, burning often from the morning on, lighted up the ugliness amid which the hand of practice endeavoured to disengage a little beauty—the ugliness of a dingy, belittered interior, of battered, dispapered walls, of work-tables stained and hacked, of windows opening into a foul, drizzling street, of the bared arms, the sordid waistcoat-backs, the smeared aprons, the personal odour, the patient, obstinate, irritating shoulders and vulgar, narrow, inevitable faces, of his fellow-labourers. Hyacinth's relations with his comrades would form a chapter by itself, but all that may be said of the matter here is that the clever little operator from Lomax Place had a kind of double identity, and that much as he lived in Mr. Crookenden's establishment he lived out of it still more. In this busy, pasty, sticky, leathery little world, where wages and beer were the main objects of consideration,

he played his part in a manner which caused him to be regarded as a queer lot, but capable of queerness in the line of
good-nature too. He had not made good his place there
without discovering that the British workman, when animated by the spirit of mirth, has rather a heavy hand, and he
tasted of the practical joke in every degree of violence. During his first year he dreamed, with secret passion and suppressed tears, of a day of bliss when at last they would let
him alone—a day which arrived in time, for it is always an
advantage to be clever, if only one is clever enough. Hyacinth was sufficiently so to have invented a *modus vivendi* in
respect to which M. Poupin said to him, *'Enfin vous voilà
ferme!'* (the Frenchman himself, terribly *éprouvé* at the beginning, had always bristled with firmness and opposed to
insular grossness a refined dignity), and under the influence
of which the scenery of Soho figured as a daily, dusky
phantasmagoria, relegated to the mechanical, passive part of
experience and giving no hostages to reality, or at least to
ambition, save an insufficient number of shillings on Saturday night and spasmodic reminiscences of delicate work that
might have been more delicate still, as well as of certain applications of the tool which he flattered himself were unsurpassed, unless by the supreme Eustache.

One evening in November, after discharging himself of a
considerable indebtedness to Pinnie, he had still a sovereign
in his pocket—a sovereign which seemed to spin there at the
opposed solicitation of a dozen exemplary uses. He had come
out for a walk, with a vague intention of pushing as far as
Audley Court; and lurking within this nebulous design, on
which the damp breath of the streets, making objects seem
that night particularly dim and places particularly far, had
blown a certain chill, was a sense that it would be rather nice
to take something to Rose Muniment, who delighted in a
sixpenny present and to whom, for some time, he had not
rendered any such homage. At last, after he had wandered a
while, hesitating between the pilgrimage to Lambeth and the
possibility of still associating his evening in some way or
other with that of Miss Henning, he reflected that if a sovereign was to be pulled to pieces it was a simplification to get it
changed. He had been traversing the region of Mayfair, partly

with the preoccupation of a short cut and partly from an instinct of self-defence; if one was in danger of spending one's money precipitately it was so much gained to plunge into a quarter in which, at that hour especially, there were no shops for little bookbinders. Hyacinth's victory, however, was imperfect when it occurred to him to turn into a public-house in order to convert his gold into convenient silver. When it was a question of entering these establishments he selected in preference the most decent; he never knew what unpleasant people he might find on the other side of the swinging door. Those which glitter, at intervals, amid the residential gloom of Mayfair partake of the general gentility of the neighbourhood, so that Hyacinth was not surprised (he had passed into the compartment marked 'private bar') to see but a single drinker leaning against the counter on which, with his request very civilly enunciated, he put down his sovereign. He was surprised, on the other hand, when, glancing up again, he became aware that this solitary drinker was Captain Godfrey Sholto.

'Why, my dear boy, what a remarkable coincidence!' the Captain exclaimed. 'For once in five years that I come into a place like this!'

'I don't come in often myself. I thought you were in Madagascar,' said Hyacinth.

'Ah, because I have not been at the "Sun and Moon"? Well, I have been constantly out of town, you know. And then—don't you see what I mean?—I want to be tremendously careful. That's the way to get on, isn't it? But I daresay you don't believe in my discretion!' Sholto laughed. 'What shall I do to make you understand? I say, have a brandy and soda,' he continued, as if this might assist Hyacinth's comprehension. He seemed a trifle flurried, and, if it were possible to imagine such a thing of so independent and whimsical a personage, the least bit abashed or uneasy at having been found in such a low place. It was not any lower, after all, than the 'Sun and Moon.' He was dressed on this occasion according to his station, without the pot-hat and the shabby jacket, and Hyacinth looked at him with a sense that a good tailor must really add a charm to life. Our hero was struck more than ever before with his being the type of man whom, as he strolled about, observing people, he had so often regarded with wonder and envy—the sort of man of whom one said to one's self that he was the 'finest white,' feeling that he had the world in his pocket. Sholto requested the bar-maid to please not dawdle in preparing the brandy and soda which Hyacinth had thought to ease off the situation by accepting: this, indeed, was perhaps what the finest white would naturally do. And when the young man had taken the glass from the counter Sholto appeared to encourage him not to linger as he drank it, and smiled down at him very kindly and amusedly, as if the combination of a very small bookbinder and a big tumbler were sufficiently droll. The Captain took time, however, to ask Hyacinth how he had spent his autumn and what was the news in Bloomsbury; he further inquired about those delightful people over the river. 'I can't tell you what an impression they made upon me—that evening, you know.' After this he remarked to Hyacinth, suddenly, irrelevantly, 'And so you are just going to stay on for the winter, quietly?' Our young man stared: he wondered what other project any one could attribute to him; he could not reflect, immediately, that this was the sort of thing the finest whites said to each other when they met, after their fashionable dispersals, and that his friend had only been guilty of a momentary inadvertence. In point of fact the Captain recovered himself. 'Oh, of course you have got your work, and that sort of thing;' and, as Hyacinth did not succeed in swallowing at a gulp the contents of his big tumbler, he asked him presently whether he had heard anything from the Princess. Hyacinth replied that he could have no news except what the Captain might be good enough to give him; but he added that he did go to see her just before she left town.

'Ah, you did go to see her? That's quite right—quite right.'

'I went, because she very kindly wrote to me to come.'

'Ah, she wrote to you to come?' The Captain fixed Hyacinth for a moment with his curious colourless eyes. 'Do you know you are a devilish privileged mortal?'

'Certainly, I know that.' Hyacinth blushed and felt foolish; the bar-maid, who had heard this odd couple talking about a princess, was staring at him too, with her elbows on the counter.

'Do you know there are people who would give their heads that she should write to them to come?'

'I have no doubt of it whatever!' Hyacinth exclaimed, taking refuge in a laugh which did not sound as natural as he would have liked, and wondering whether his interlocutor were not precisely one of these people. In this case the barmaid might well stare; for deeply convinced as our young man might be that he was the son of Lord Frederick Purvis, there was really no end to the oddity of his being preferred— and by a princess—to Captain Sholto. If anything could have reinforced, at that moment, his sense of this anomaly, it would have been the indescribably gentlemanly way, implying all sorts of common initiations, in which his companion went on.

'Ah, well, I see you know how to take it! And if you are in correspondence with her why do you say that you can hear from her only through me? My dear fellow, I am not in correspondence with her. You might think I would naturally be, but I am not.' He subjoined, as Hyacinth had laughed again, in a manner that might have passed for ambiguous, 'So much the worse for me—is that what you mean?' Hyacinth replied that he himself had had the honour of hearing from the Princess only once, and he mentioned that she had told him that her letter-writing came only in fits, when it was sometimes very profuse: there were months together that she didn't touch a pen. 'Oh, I can imagine what she told you!' the Captain exclaimed. 'Look out for the next fit! She is visiting about. It's a great thing to be in the same house with her—an immense comedy.' He remarked that he had heard, now he remembered, that she either had taken, or was thinking of taking, a house in the country for a few months, and he added that if Hyacinth didn't propose to finish his brandy and soda they might as well turn out. Hyacinth's thirst had been very superficial, and as they turned out the Captain observed, by way of explanation of his having been found in a public-house (it was the only attempt of this kind he made), that any friend of his would always know him by his love of curious out-of-the-way nooks. 'You must have noticed that,' he said—'my taste for exploration. If I hadn't explored I never should have known you, should I? That was rather a nice little girl in there; did you twig her figure? It's a pity they always have such beastly hands.' Hyacinth, instinctively, had made a motion to go southward, but Sholto, passing a hand into his arm, led him the other way. The house they had quitted was near a corner, which they rounded, the Captain pushing forward as if there were some reason for haste. His haste was checked, however, by an immediate collision with a young woman who, coming in the opposite direction, turned the angle as briskly as themselves. At this moment the Captain gave Hyacinth a great jerk, but not before he had caught a glimpse of the young woman's face — it seemed to flash upon him out of the dusk — and given quick voice to his surprise.

'Hallo, Millicent!' This was the simple cry that escaped from his lips, while the Captain, still going on, inquired, 'What's the matter? Who's your pretty friend?' Hyacinth declined to go on, and repeated Miss Henning's baptismal name so loudly that the young woman, who had passed them without looking back, was obliged to stop. Then Hyacinth saw that he was not mistaken, though Millicent gave no audible response. She stood looking at him, with her head very high, and he approached her, disengaging himself from Sholto, who however hung back only an instant before joining them. Hyacinth's heart had suddenly begun to beat very fast; there was a sharp shock in the girl's turning up just in that place at that moment. Yet when she began to laugh, abruptly, with violence, and to ask him why he was looking at her as if she were a kicking horse, he recognised that there was nothing so very extraordinary, after all, in a casual meeting between persons who were such frequenters of the London Streets. Millicent had never concealed the fact that she 'trotted about,' on various errands, at night; and once, when he had said to her that the less a respectable young woman took the evening air alone the better for her respectability, she had asked how respectable he thought she pretended to be, and had remarked that if he would make her a present of a brougham, or even call for her three or four times a week in a cab, she would doubtless preserve more of her social purity. She could turn the tables quickly enough, and she exclaimed, now, professing, on her own side, great astonishment—

'What are you prowling about here for? You're after no good, I'll be bound!'

'Good evening, Miss Henning; what a jolly meeting!' said the Captain, removing his hat with a humorous flourish.

'Oh, how d'ye do?' Millicent returned, as if she did not immediately place him.

'Where were you going so fast? What are you doing?' asked Hyacinth, who had looked from one to the other.

'Well, I never did see such a manner—from one that knocks about like *you!*' cried Miss Henning. 'I'm going to see a friend of mine—a lady's-maid in Curzon Street. Have you anything to say to that?'

'Don't tell us—don't tell us!' Sholto interposed, after she had spoken (she had not hesitated an instant). 'I, at least, disavow the indiscretion. Where may not a charming woman be going when she trips with a light foot through the gathering dusk?'

'I say, what are you talking about?' the girl inquired, with dignity, of Hyacinth's companion. She spoke as if with a resentful suspicion that her foot had not really been perceived to be light.

'On what errand of mercy, of secret tenderness?' the Captain went on, laughing.

'Secret yourself!' cried Millicent. 'Do you two always hunt in couples?'

'All right, we'll turn round and go with you as far as your friend's,' Hyacinth said.

'All right,' Millicent replied.

'All right,' the Captain added; and the three took their way together in the direction of Curzon Street. They walked for a few moments in silence, though the Captain whistled, and then Millicent suddenly turned to Hyacinth.

'You haven't told me where *you* were going, yet.'

'We met in that public-house,' the Captain said, 'and we were each so ashamed of being found in such a place by the other that we tumbled out together, without much thinking what we should do with ourselves.'

'When he's out with me he pretends he can't abide them houses,' Miss Henning declared. 'I wish I had looked in that one, to see who was there.'

'Well, she's rather nice,' the Captain went on. 'She told me her name was Georgiana.'

'I went to get a piece of money changed,' Hyacinth said, with a sense that there was a certain dishonesty in the air; glad that he, at least, could afford to speak the truth.

'To get your grandmother's nightcap changed! I recommend you to keep your money together—you've none too much of it!' Millicent exclaimed.

'Is that the reason you are playing me false?' Hyacinth flashed out. He had been thinking, with still intentness, as they walked; at once nursing and wrestling with a kindled suspicion. He was pale with the idea that he was being bamboozled; yet he was able to say to himself that one must allow, in life, for the element of coincidence, and that he might easily put himself immensely in the wrong by making a groundless charge. It was only later that he pieced his impressions together and saw them—as it appeared—justify each other; at present, as soon as he had uttered it, he was almost ashamed of his quick retort to Millicent's taunt. He ought at least to have waited to see what Curzon Street would bring forth.

The girl broke out upon him immediately, repeating 'False, false?' with high derision, and wanting to know whether that was the way to knock a lady about in public. She had stopped short on the edge of a crossing, and she went on, with a voice so uplifted that he was glad they were in a street that was rather empty at such an hour: 'You're a pretty one to talk about falsity, when a woman has only to leer at you out of an opera-box!'

'Don't say anything about *her*,' the young man interposed, trembling.

'And pray why not about "her," I should like to know? You don't pretend she's a decent woman, I suppose?' Millicent's laughter rang through the quiet neighbourhood.

'My dear fellow, you know you *have* been to her,' Captain Sholto remarked, smiling.

Hyacinth turned upon him, staring, at once challenged and baffled by his ambiguous part in an incident it was doubtless possible to magnify but it was not possible to treat as perfectly simple. 'Certainly, I have been to the Princess Casamassima, thanks to you. When you came and begged me, when you dragged me, do you make it a reproach? Who the devil are you, any way, and what do you want of me?' our hero cried—his mind flooded in a moment with everything in the Captain that had puzzled and eluded him. This swelling tide obliterated on the spot everything that had entertained and gratified him.

'My dear fellow, whatever I am, I am not an ass,' this gentleman replied, with imperturbable good-humour. 'I don't reproach you with anything. I only wanted to put in a word as a peacemaker. My good friends—my good friends,' and he laid a hand, in his practised way, on Hyacinth's shoulder, while, with the other pressed to his heart, he bent on the girl a face of gallantry which had something paternal in it, 'I am determined this absurd misunderstanding shall end as lovers' quarrels ought always to end.'

Hyacinth withdrew himself from the Captain's touch and said to Millicent, 'You are not really jealous of—of any one. You pretend that, only to throw dust in my eyes.'

To this sally Miss Henning returned him an answer which promised to be lively, but the Captain swept it away in the profusion of his protests. He pronounced them a dear delightful, abominable young couple; he declared it was most interesting to see how, in people of their sort, the passions lay near the surface; he almost pushed them into each other's arms; and he wound up by proposing that they should all terminate their little differences by proceeding together to the Pavilion music-hall, the nearest place of entertainment in that neighbourhood, leaving the lady's-maid in Curzon Street to dress her mistress's wig in peace. He has been presented to the reader as an accomplished man, and it will doubtless be felt that the picture is justified when I relate that he placed this idea in so attractive a light that his companions finally entered a hansom with him and rattled toward the haunt of pleasure, Hyacinth sandwiched, on the edge of the seat, between the others. Two or three times his ears burned; he felt that if there was an understanding between them they had now, behind him, a rare opportunity for carrying it out. If it was at his expense, the whole evening constituted for them, indeed, an opportunity, and this thought rendered his diversion but scantily absorbing, though at the Pavilion the Captain engaged a private box and ordered ices to be brought in. Hyacinth cared so little for his little pink pyramid that he suffered Millicent to consume it after she had disposed of her own. It was present to him, however, that if he should make a fool of himself the folly would be of a very gross kind, and this is why he withheld a question which rose to his lips repeatedly—a disposition to inquire of his entertainer why the mischief he had hurried him so out of the public-house, if he had not been waiting there, preconcertedly, for Millicent. We know that in Hyacinth's eyes one of this young lady's compensatory merits had been that she was not deceitful, and he asked himself if a girl could change, that way, from one month to the other. This was optimistic, but, all the same, he reflected, before leaving the Pavilion, that he could see quite well what Lady Aurora meant by thinking Captain Sholto vulgar.

XXI

PAUL MUNIMENT had fits of silence, while the others were talking; but on this occasion he had not opened his lips for half an hour. When he talked Hyacinth listened, almost holding his breath; and when he said nothing Hyacinth watched him fixedly, listening to the others only through the medium of his candid countenance. At the 'Sun and Moon' Muniment paid very little attention to his young friend, doing nothing that should cause it to be perceived they were particular pals; and Hyacinth even thought, at moments, that he was bored or irritated by the serious manner in which the bookbinder could not conceal from the world that he regarded him. He wondered whether this were a system, a calculated prudence, on Muniment's part, or only a manifestation of that superior brutality, latent in his composition, which never had an intention of unkindness but was naturally intolerant of palaver. There was plenty of palaver at the 'Sun and Moon'; there were nights when a blast of imbecility seemed to blow over the place, and one felt ashamed to be associated with so much insistent ignorance and flat-faced vanity. Then every one, with two or three exceptions, made an ass of himself, thumping the table and repeating over some inane phrase which appeared for the hour to constitute the whole furniture of his mind. There were men who kept saying, 'Them was my words in the month of February last, and what I say I stick to—what I say I stick to;' and others who perpetually inquired of the company, 'And what the plague am I to do with seventeen shillings—with seventeen shillings? What am I to do with them—will ye tell me that?' an interrogation which, in truth, usually ended by eliciting a ribald reply. There were still others who remarked, to satiety, that if it was not done to-day it would have to be done to-morrow, and several who constantly proclaimed their opinion that the only way was to pull up the Park rails again—just to pluck them straight up. A little shoemaker, with red eyes and a grayish face, whose appearance Hyacinth deplored, scarcely ever expressed himself but in the same form of words: 'Well, are we in earnest, or ain't we in earnest?—that's the thing I

want to know.' He was terribly in earnest himself, but this was almost the only way he had of showing it; and he had much in common (though they were always squabbling) with a large red-faced man, of uncertain attributes and stertorous breathing, who was understood to know a good deal about dogs, had fat hands, and wore on his forefinger a big silver ring, containing some one's hair—Hyacinth believed it to be that of a terrier, snappish in life. He had always the same refrain: 'Well, now, are we just starving, or ain't we just starving? I should like the v'ice of the company on that question.'

When the tone fell as low as this Paul Muniment held his peace, except that he whistled a little, leaning back, with his hands in his pockets and his eyes on the table. Hyacinth often supposed him to be on the point of breaking out and letting the company know what he thought of them—he had a perfectly clear vision of what he must think: but Muniment never compromised his popularity to that degree; he judged it— this he once told Hyacinth—too valuable an instrument, and cultivated the faculty of patience, which had the advantage of showing one more and more that one must do one's thinking for one's self. His popularity, indeed, struck Hyacinth as rather an uncertain quantity, and the only mistake he had seen a symptom of on his friend's part was a tendency to overestimate it. Muniment thought many of their colleagues asinine, but it was Hyacinth's belief that he himself knew still better how asinine they were; and this inadequate conception supported, in some degree, on Paul's part, his theory of his influence—an influence that would be stronger than any other on the day he should choose to exert it. Hyacinth only wished that day would come; it would not be till then, he was sure, that they would all know where they were, and that the good they were striving for, blindly, obstructedly, in a kind of eternal dirty intellectual fog, would pass from the stage of crude discussion and mere sharp, tantalising desirableness into that of irresistible reality. Muniment was listened to unanimously, when he spoke, and was much talked about, usually with a knowing, implicit allusiveness, when he was absent; it was generally admitted that he could see further than most. But it was suspected that he wanted to see further than was necessary; as one of the most inveterate frequenters of the club remarked one evening, if a man could see as far as he could chuck a brick, that was far enough. There was an idea that he had nothing particular to complain of, personally, or that if he had he didn't complain of it—an attitude which perhaps contained the germs of a latent disaffection. Hyacinth could easily see that he himself was exposed to the same imputation, but he couldn't help it; it would have been impossible to him to keep up his character for sincerity by revealing, at the 'Sun and Moon,' the condition of his wardrobe, or announcing that he had not had a pennyworth of bacon for six months. There were members of the club who were apparently always in the enjoyment of involuntary leisure—narrating the vainest peregrinations in search of a job, the cruelest rebuffs, the most vivid anecdotes of the insolence of office. They made Hyacinth uncomfortably conscious, at times, that if *he* should be out of work it would be wholly by his own fault; that he had in his hand a bread-winning tool on which he might absolutely count. He was also aware, however, that his position in this little band of malcontents (it was little only if measured by the numbers that were gathered together on any one occasion; he liked to think it was large in its latent possibilities, its mysterious ramifications and affiliations), was peculiar and distinguished; it would be favourable if he had the kind of energy and assurance that would help him to make use of it. He had an intimate conviction—the proof of it was in the air, in the sensible facility of his footing at the 'Sun and Moon'— that Eustache Poupin had taken upon himself to disseminate the anecdote of his origin, of his mother's disaster; in consequence of which, as the victim of social infamy, of heinous laws, it was conceded to him that he had a larger account to settle even than most. He was *ab ovo* a revolutionist, and that balanced against his smart neckties, a certain suspicious security that was perceived in him as to the *h* (he had had from his earliest years a natural command of it), and the fact that he possessed the sort of hand on which there is always a premium—an accident somehow to be guarded against in a thorough-going system of equality. He never challenged Poupin on the subject, for he owed the Frenchman too much to reproach him with any officious step that was meant in kindness; and moreover his fellow-labourer at old Crook-

enden's had said to him, as if to anticipate such an impugn-
ment of his discretion, 'Remember, my child, that I am
incapable of drawing aside any veil that you may have preferred to drop over your lacerated personality. Your moral
dignity will always be safe with me. But remember at the
same time that among the disinherited there is a mystic language which dispenses with proofs—a freemasonry, a recip-
rocal divination; they understand each other with half a
word.' It was with half a word, then, in Bloomsbury, that
Hyacinth had been understood; but there was a certain delicacy within him that forbade him to push his advantage, to
treat implications of sympathy, none the less definite for being roundabout, as steps in the ladder of success. He had no
wish to be a leader because his mother had murdered her
lover and died in penal servitude: these circumstances recommended intentness but they also suggested modesty. When
the gathering at the 'Sun and Moon' was at its best, and its
temper seemed really an earnest of what was the basis of all its
calculations—that the people was only a sleeping lion, already breathing shorter and beginning to stretch its limbs—
at these hours, some of them thrilling enough, Hyacinth
waited for the voice that should allot to him the particular
part he was to play. His ambition was to play it with brilliancy, to offer an example—an example, even, that might
survive him—of pure youthful, almost juvenile, consecration.
He was conscious of no commission to give the promises, to
assume the responsibilities, of a redeemer, and he had no envy
of the man on whom this burden should rest. Muniment, indeed, might carry it, and it was the first article of his faith that
to help him to carry it the better he himself was ready for any
sacrifice. Then it was—on these nights of intenser vibration—that Hyacinth waited for a sign.

They came oftener, this second winter, for the season was
terribly hard; and as in that lower world one walked with
one's ear nearer the ground, the deep perpetual groan of London misery seemed to swell and swell and form the whole
undertone of life. The filthy air came into the place in the
damp coats of silent men, and hung there till it was brewed to
a nauseous warmth, and ugly, serious faces squared themselves through it, and strong-smelling pipes contributed their

element in a fierce, dogged manner which appeared to say that it now had to stand for everything—for bread and meat and beer, for shoes and blankets and the poor things at the pawnbroker's and the smokeless chimney at home. Hyacinth's colleagues seemed to him wiser then, and more permeated with intentions boding ill to the satisfied classes; and though the note of popularity was still most effectively struck by the man who could demand oftenest, unpractically, 'What the plague am I to do with seventeen shillings?' it was brought home to our hero on more than one occasion that revolution was ripe at last. This was especially the case on the evening I began by referring to, when Eustache Poupin squeezed in and announced, as if it were a great piece of news, that in the east of London, that night, there were forty thousand men out of work. He looked round the circle with his di-lated foreign eye, as he took his place; he seemed to address the company individually as well as collectively, and to make each man responsible for hearing him. He owed his position at the 'Sun and Moon' to the brilliancy with which he repre-sented the political exile, the magnanimous immaculate citi-zen wrenched out of bed at dead of night, torn from his hearthstone, his loved ones and his profession, and hurried across the frontier with only the coat on his back. Poupin had performed in this character now for many years, but he had never lost the bloom of the outraged proscript, and the passionate pictures he had often drawn of the bitterness of exile were moving even to those who knew with what suc-cess he had set up his household gods in Lisson Grove. He was recognised as suffering everything for his opinions; and his hearers in Bloomsbury—who, after all, even in their most concentrated hours, were very good-natured—ap-peared never to have made the subtle reflection, though they made many others, that there was a want of tact in his call-ing upon them to sympathise with him for being one of themselves. He imposed himself by the eloquence of his as-sumption that if one were not in the beautiful France one was nowhere worth speaking of, and ended by producing an impression that that country had an almost supernatural charm. Muniment had once said to Hyacinth that he was sure Poupin would be very sorry if he should be enabled to go home again (as he might, from one week to the other, the Republic being so indulgent and the amnesty to the Communards constantly extended), for over there he couldn't be a refugee; and however this might be he certainly flourished a good deal in London on the basis of this very fact that he was miserable there.

'Why do you tell us that, as if it was so very striking? Don't we know it, and haven't we known it always? But you are right; we behave as if we knew nothing at all,' said Mr. Schinkel, the German cabinet-maker, who had originally introduced Captain Sholto to the 'Sun and Moon.' He had a long, unhealthy, benevolent face and greasy hair, and constantly wore a kind of untidy bandage round his neck, as if for a local ailment. 'You remind us—that is very well; but we shall forget it in half an hour. We are not serious.'

'*Pardon, pardon;* for myself, I do not admit that!' Poupin replied, striking the table with his finger-tips several times, very fast. 'If I am not serious, I am nothing.'

'Oh no, you are something,' said the German, smoking his monumental pipe with a contemplative air. 'We are all something; but I am not sure it is anything very useful.'

'Well, things would be worse without us. I'd rather be in here, in *this* kind of muck, than outside,' remarked the fat man who understood dogs.

'Certainly, it is very pleasant, especially if you have your beer; but not so pleasant in the east, where fifty thousand people starve. It is a very unpleasant night,' the cabinet-maker went on.

'How can it be worse?' Eustache Poupin inquired, looking defiantly at the German, as if to make him responsible for the fat man's reflection. 'It is so bad that the imagination recoils, refuses.'

'Oh, we don't care for the imagination!' the fat man declared. 'We want a compact body, in marching order.'

'What do you call a compact body?' the little gray-faced shoemaker demanded. 'I daresay you don't mean your kind of body.'

'Well, I know what I mean,' said the fat man, severely.

'That's a grand thing. Perhaps one of these days you'll tell us.'

'You'll see it for yourself, perhaps, before that day comes,' the gentleman with the silver ring rejoined. 'Perhaps when you do, you'll remember.'

'Well, you know, Schinkel says we don't,' said the shoe-maker, nodding at the cloud-compelling German.

'I don't care what no man says!' the dog-fancier exclaimed, gazing straight before him.

'They say it's a bad year—the blockheads in the news-papers,' Mr. Schinkel went on, addressing himself to the company at large. 'They say that on purpose—to convey the impression that there are such things as good years. I ask the company, has any gentleman present ever happened to notice that article? The good year is yet to come: it might begin to-night, if we like; it all depends on our being able to be serious for a few hours. But that is too much to expect. Mr. Muniment is very serious; he looks as if he was waiting for the signal; but he doesn't speak—he never speaks, if I want particularly to hear him. He only considers, very deeply, I am sure. But it is almost as bad to think without speaking as to speak without thinking.'

Hyacinth always admired the cool, easy way in which Muniment comported himself when the attention of the public was directed towards him. These manifestations of curiosity, or of hostility, would have put him out immensely, himself. When a lot of people, especially the kind of people who were collected at the 'Sun and Moon,' looked at him, or listened to him, at once, he always blushed and stammered, feeling that if he couldn't have a million of spectators (which would have been inspiring), he should prefer to have but two or three; there was something very embarrassing in twenty.

Muniment smiled, for an instant, good-humouredly; then, after a moment's hesitation, looking across at the German, and the German only, as if his remark were worth noticing, but it didn't matter if the others didn't understand the reply, he said simply, 'Hoffendahl's in London.'

'Hoffendahl? *Gott in Himmel!*' the cabinet-maker ex-claimed, taking the pipe out of his mouth. And the two men exchanged a longish glance. Then Mr. Schinkel remarked, 'That surprises me, *sehr*. Are you very sure?'

Muniment continued, for a moment, to look at him. 'If I keep quiet for half an hour, with so many valuable suggestions flying all round me, you think I say too little. Then if I open my head to give out three words, you appear to think I say too much.'

'Ah, no; on the contrary, I want you to say three more. If you tell me you have seen him I shall be perfectly satisfied.'

'Upon my word, I should hope so! Do you think he's the kind of party a fellow says he has seen?'

'Yes, when he hasn't!' said Eustache Poupin, who had been listening. Every one was listening now.

'It depends on the fellow he says it to. Not even here?' the German asked.

'Oh, here!' Paul Muniment exclaimed, in a peculiar tone, and resumed his muffled whistle again.

'Take care—take care; you will make me think you haven't!' cried Poupin, with his excited expression.

'That's just what I want,' said Muniment.

'*Nun*, I understand,' the cabinetmaker remarked, restoring his pipe to his lips after an interval almost as momentous as the stoppage of a steamer in mid-ocean.

'*'Ere, 'ere?*' repeated the small shoemaker, indignantly. 'I daresay it's as good as the place he came from. He might look in and see what he thinks of it.'

'That's a place you might tell us a little about now,' the fat man suggested, as if he had been waiting for his chance.

Before the shoemaker had time to notice this challenge some one inquired, with a hoarse petulance, who the blazes they were talking about; and Mr. Schinkel took upon himself to reply that they were talking about a man who hadn't done what he had done by simply exchanging abstract ideas, however valuable, with his friends in a respectable pot-house.

'What the devil has he done, then?' some one else demanded; and Muniment replied, quietly, that he had spent twelve years in a Prussian prison, and was consequently still an object of a good deal of interest to the police.

'Well, if you call that very useful, I must say I prefer a pot-house!' cried the shoemaker, appealing to all the company and looking, as it appeared to Hyacinth, particularly hideous.

'*Doch, doch*, it is useful,' the German remarked, philosophically, among his yellow clouds.

'Do you mean to say you are not prepared for that, yourself?' Muniment inquired of the shoemaker.

'Prepared for that? I thought we were going to smash that sort of shop altogether; I thought that was the main part of the job.'

'They will smash best, those who have been inside,' the German declared; 'unless, perhaps, they are broken, enervated. But Hoffendahl is not enervated.'

'Ah, no; no smashing, no smashing,' Muniment went on. 'We want to keep them standing, and even to build a few more; but the difference will be that we shall put the correct sort in.'

'I take your idea—that Griffin is one of the correct sort,' the fat man remarked, indicating the shoemaker.

'I thought we was going to 'ave their 'eads—all that bloomin' lot!' Mr. Griffin declared, protesting; while Eustache Poupin began to enlighten the company as to the great Hoffendahl, one of the purest martyrs of their cause, a man who had been through everything—who had been scarred and branded, tortured, almost flayed, and had never given them the names they wanted to have. Was it possible they didn't remember that great combined attempt, early in the sixties, which took place in four Continental cities at once and which, in spite of every effort to smother it up—there had been editors and journalists transported even for hinting at it—had done more for the social question than anything before or since? 'Through him being served in the manner you describe?' some one asked, with plainness; to which Poupin replied that it was one of those failures that are more glorious than any success. Muniment said that the affair had been only a flash in the pan, but that the great value of it was this—that whereas some forty persons (and of both sexes) had been engaged in it, only one had been seized and had suffered. It had been Hoffendahl himself who was collared. Certainly he had suffered much, he had suffered for every one; but from that point of view—that of the economy of material—the thing had been a rare success.

'Do you know what I call the others? I call 'em bloody

sneaks!' the fat man cried; and Eustache Poupin, turning to Muniment, expressed the hope that he didn't really approve of such a solution—didn't consider that an economy of heroism was an advantage to any cause. He himself esteemed Hoffendahl's attempt because it had shaken, more than any-thing—except, of course, the Commune—had shaken it since the French Revolution, the rotten fabric of the actual social order, and because that very fact of the impunity, the invisibility, of the persons concerned in it had given the pred-atory classes, had given all Europe, a shudder that had not yet subsided; but for his part, he must regret that some of the associates of the devoted victim had not come forward and insisted on sharing with him his tortures and his captivity.

'*C'aurait été d'un bel exemple!*' said the Frenchman, with an impressive moderation of statement which made even those who could not understand him see that he was saying some-thing fine; while the cabinet-maker remarked that in Hoffen-dahl's place any of them would have stood out just the same. He didn't care if they set it down to self-love (Mr. Schinkel called it 'loaf'), but he might say that he himself would have done so if he had been trusted and had been bagged.

'I want to have it all drawn up clear first; then I'll go in,' said the fat man, who seemed to think it was expected of him to be reassuring.

'Well, who the dickens is to draw it up, eh? That's what we happen to be talking about,' returned his antagonist the shoe-maker.

'A fine example, old man? Is that your idea of a fine exam-ple?' Muniment, with his amused face, asked of Poupin. 'A fine example of asininity! Are there capable people, in such plenty, about the place?'

'Capable of greatness of soul, I grant you not.'

'Your greatness of soul is usually greatness of blundering. A man's foremost duty is not to get collared. If you want to show you're capable, that's the way.'

At this Hyacinth suddenly felt himself moved to speak. 'But some one must be caught, always, must he not? Hasn't some one always been?'

'Oh, I daresay you'll be, if you like it!' Muniment replied, without looking at him. 'If they succeed in potting you, do as

Hoffendahl did, and do it as a matter of course; but if they don't, make it your supreme duty, make it your religion, to lie close and keep yourself for another go. The world is full of unclean beasts whom I shall be glad to see shovelled away by the thousand; but when it's a question of honest men and men of courage, I protest against the idea that two should be sacrificed where one will serve.'

'*Trop d'arithmétique—trop d'arithmétique!* That is fearfully English!' Poupin cried.

'No doubt, no doubt; what else should it be? You shall never share my fate, if I have a fate and I can prevent it!' said Muniment, laughing.

Eustache Poupin stared at him and his merriment, as if he thought the English frivolous as well as calculating; then he rejoined, 'If I suffer, I trust it may be for suffering humanity, but I trust it may also be for France.'

'Oh, I hope you ain't going to suffer any more for France,' said Mr. Griffin. 'Hasn't it done that insatiable old country of yours some good, by this time, all you've had to put up with?'

'Well, I want to know what Hoffendahl has come over for; it's very kind of him, I'm sure. What is he going to do for *us*?—that's what *I* want to know,' remarked in a loud, argumentative tone a personage at the end of the table most distant from Muniment's place. His name was Delancey, and he gave himself out as holding a position in a manufactory of soda-water; but Hyacinth had a secret belief that he was really a hairdresser—a belief connected with a high, lustrous curl, or crest, which he wore on the summit of his large head, and the manner in which he thrust over his ear, as if it were a barber's comb, the pencil with which he was careful to take notes of the discussions carried on at the 'Sun and Moon.' His opinions were distinct and frequently expressed; he had a watery (Muniment had once called it a soda-watery) eye, and a personal aversion to a lord. He desired to change everything except religion, of which he approved.

Muniment answered that he was unable to say, as yet, what the German revolutionist had come to England for, but that he hoped to be able to give some information on the matter the next time they should meet. It was very certain Hoffendahl hadn't come for nothing, and he would undertake to declare that they would all feel, within a short time, that he had given a lift to the cause they were interested in. He had had a great experience, and they might very well find it useful to consult. If there was a way for them, then and there, he was sure to know the way. 'I quite agree with the majority of you—as I take it to be,' Muniment went on, with his fresh, cheerful, reasonable manner—'I quite agree with you that the time has come to settle upon it and to follow it. I quite agree with you that the actual state of things is'—he paused a moment, and then went on in the same pleasant tone—'is hellish.'

These remarks were received with a differing demonstration: some of the company declaring that if the Dutchman cared to come round and smoke a pipe they would be glad to see him—perhaps he'd show where the thumb-screws had been put on; others being strongly of the opinion that they didn't want any more advice—they had already had advice enough to turn a donkey's stomach. What they wanted was to put forth their might without any more palaver; to do something, or for some one; to go out somewhere and smash something, on the spot—why not?—that very night. While they sat there and talked, there were about half a million of people in London that didn't know where the h—— the morrow's meal was to come from; what they wanted to do, unless they were just a collection of pettifogging old women, was to show them where to get it, to take it to them with heaped-up hands. Hyacinth listened, with a divided attention, to interlaced iterations, while the talk blew hot and cold; there was a genuine emotion, to-night, in the rear of the 'Sun and Moon,' and he felt the contagion of excited purpose. But he was following a train of his own; he was wondering what Muniment had in reserve (for he was sure he was only playing with the company), and his imagination, quickened by the sense of impending relations with the heroic Hoffendahl and the discussion as to the alternative duty of escaping or of facing one's fate, had launched itself into possible perils—into the idea of how he might, in a given case, settle for himself that question of paying for the lot. The loud, contradictory, vain, unpractical babble went on about him, but he was definitely conscious only that the project of breaking into the bakers' shops was well before the assembly and was receiving a vigorous treatment, and that there was likewise a good deal of reference to the butchers and grocers, and even to the fishmongers. He was in a state of inward exaltation; he was seized by an intense desire to stand face to face with the sublime Hoffendahl, to hear his voice, to touch his mutilated hand. He was ready for anything: he knew that he himself was safe to breakfast and dine, poorly but sufficiently, and that his colleagues were perhaps even more crude and clumsy than usual; but a breath of popular passion had passed over him, and he seemed to see, immensely magnified, the monstrosity of the great ulcers and sores of London—the sick, eternal misery crying, in the darkness, in vain, confronted with granaries and treasure-houses and places of delight where shameless satiety kept guard. In such a mood as this Hyacinth felt that there was no need to consider, to reason: the facts themselves were as imperative as the cry of the drowning; for while pedantry gained time didn't starvation gain it too? He knew that Muniment disapproved of delay, that he held the day had come for a forcible rectification of horrible inequalities. In the last conversation they had had together his chemical friend had given him a more definite warrant than he had ever done before for numbering him in the party of immediate action, though indeed he remarked on this occasion, once more, that that particular formula which the little bookbinder appeared to have taken such a fancy to was mere gibberish. He hated that sort of pretentious label; it was fit only for politicians and amateurs. None the less he had been as plain as possible on the point that their game must be now to frighten society, and frighten it effectually; to make it believe that the swindled classes were at last fairly in league— had really grasped the idea that, closely combined, they would be irresistible. They were not in league, and they hadn't in their totality grasped any idea at all—Muniment was not slow to make that equally plain. All the same, society was scareable, and every great scare was a gain for the people. If Hyacinth had needed warrant to-night for a faith that transcended logic, he would have found it in his recollection of this quiet profession; but his friend's words came back to him mainly to make him wonder what that friend had in his head just now. He took no part in the violence of the talk; he had called Schinkel to come round and sit beside him, and the two appeared to confer together in comfortable absorption, while the brown atmosphere grew denser, the passing to and fro of fire-brands more lively, and the flush of faces more portentous. What Hyacinth would have liked to know most of all was why Muniment had not mentioned to him, first, that Hoffendahl was in London, and that he had seen him; for he *had* seen him, though he had dodged Schinkel's question— of that Hyacinth instantly felt sure. He would ask for more information later; and meanwhile he wished, without resentment, but with a certain helpless, patient longing, that Muniment would treat him with a little more confidence. If there were a secret in regard to Hoffendahl (and there evidently was: Muniment, quite rightly, though he had dropped the announcement of his arrival, for a certain effect, had no notion of sharing the rest of what he knew with that raw roomful), if there were something to be silent and devoted about, Hyacinth ardently hoped that to him a chance would be given to show how he could practise this superiority. He felt hot and nervous; he got up suddenly, and, through the dark, tortuous, greasy passage which communicated with the outer world, he went forth into the street. The air was foul and sleety, but it refreshed him, and he stood in front of the public-house and smoked another pipe. Bedraggled figures passed in and out, and a damp, tattered, wretched man, with a spongy, purple face, who had been thrust suddenly across the threshold, stood and whimpered in the brutal blaze of the row of lamps. The puddles glittered roundabout, and the silent vista of the street, bordered with low black houses, stretched away, in the wintry drizzle, to right and left, losing itself in the huge tragic city, where unmeasured misery lurked beneath the dirty night, ominously, monstrously, still, only howling, in its pain, in the heated human cockpit behind him. Ah, what could he do? What opportunity would rise? The blundering, divided counsels he had been listening to only made the helplessness of every one concerned more abject. If he had a definite wish while he stood there it was that that exalted, deluded company should pour itself forth, with

Muniment at its head, and surge through the sleeping city, gathering the myriad miserable out of their slums and burrows, and roll into the selfish squares, and lift a tremendous hungry voice, and awaken the gorged indifferent to a terror that would bring them down. Hyacinth lingered a quarter of an hour, but this grand spectacle gave no sign of coming off, and he finally returned to the noisy club-room, in a state of tormented wonder as to what better idea than this very bad one (which seemed to our young man to have at the least the merit that it *was* an idea) Muniment could be revolving in that too-comprehensive brain of his.

As he re-entered the place he saw that the meeting was breaking up in disorder, or at all events in confusion, and that, certainly, no organised attempt at the rescue of the proletariat would take place that night. All the men were on their feet and were turning away, amid a shuffling of benches and chairs, a hunching of shaggy shoulders, a frugal lowering of superfluous gas, and a varied vivacity of disgust and resignation. The moment after Hyacinth came in, Mr. Delancey, the supposititious hairdresser, jumped upon a chair at the far end of the room, and shrieked out an accusation which made every one stop and stare at him.

'Well, I want you all to know what strikes me, before we part company. There isn't a man in the blessed lot that isn't afraid of his bloody skin—afraid, afraid, afraid! I'll go anywhere with any one, but there isn't another, by G——, by what I can make out! There isn't a mother's son of you that'll risk his precious bones!'

This little oration affected Hyacinth like a quick blow in the face; it seemed to leap at him personally, as if a three-legged stool, or some hideous hob-nailed boot, had been shied at him. The room surged round, heaving up and down, while he was conscious of a loud explosion of laughter and scorn; of cries of 'Order, order!' of some clear word of Muniment's, 'I say, Delancey, just step down;' of Eustache Poupin shouting out, *'Vous insultez le peuple—vous insultez le peuple!'* of other retorts, not remarkable for refinement. The next moment Hyacinth found that he had sprung up on a chair, opposite to the barber, and that at the sight of so rare a phenomenon the commotion had suddenly checked itself. It was the first time he had asked the ear of the company, and it was given on the spot. He was sure he looked very white, and it was even possible they could see him tremble. He could only hope that this didn't make him ridiculous when he said, 'I don't think it's right of him to say that. There are others, besides him. At all events, I want to speak for myself: it may do some good; I can't help it. I'm not afraid; I'm very sure I'm not. I'm ready to do anything that will do any good; anything, anything—I don't care a rap. In such a cause I should like the idea of danger. I don't consider my bones precious in the least, compared with some other things. If one is sure one isn't afraid, and one is accused, why shouldn't one say so?'

It appeared to Hyacinth that he was talking a long time, and when it was over he scarcely knew what happened. He felt himself, in a moment, down almost under the feet of the other men; stamped upon with intentions of applause, of familiarity; laughed over and jeered over, hustled and poked in the ribs. He felt himself also pressed to the bosom of Eustache Poupin, who apparently was sobbing, while he heard some one say, 'Did ye hear the little beggar, as bold as a lion?' A trial of personal prowess between him and Mr. Delancey was proposed, but somehow it didn't take place, and at the end of five minutes the club-room emptied itself, not, evidently, to be reconstituted, outside, in a revolutionary procession. Paul Muniment had taken hold of Hyacinth, and said, 'I'll trouble you to stay, you little desperado. I'll be blowed if I ever expected to see *you* on the stump!' Muniment remained, and M. Poupin and Mr. Schinkel lingered in their overcoats, beneath a dim, surviving gasburner, in the unventilated medium in which, at each renewed gathering, the Bloomsbury club seemed to recognise itself.

'Upon my word, I believe you're game,' said Muniment, looking down at him with a serious face.

'Of course you think it's swagger, "self-loaf," as Schinkel says. But it isn't.' Then Hyacinth asked, 'In God's name, why don't we do something?'

'Ah, my child, to whom do you say it?' Eustache Poupin exclaimed, folding his arms, despairingly.

'Whom do you mean by "we"?' said Muniment.

'All the lot of us. There are plenty of them ready.'

'Ready for what? There is nothing to be done here.'

Hyacinth stared. 'Then why the deuce do you come?'

'I daresay I shan't come much more. This is a place you have always overestimated.'

'I wonder if I have overestimated you,' Hyacinth murmured, gazing at his friend.

'Don't say that—he's going to introduce us to Hoffendahl!' Schinkel exclaimed, putting away his pipe in a receptacle almost as large as a fiddlecase.

'Should you like to see the genuine article, Robinson?' Muniment asked, with the same unusual absence of jocosity in his tone.

'The genuine article?' Hyacinth looked from one of his companions to the other.

'You have never seen it yet—though you think you have.'

'And why haven't you shown it to me before?'

'Because I had never seen you on the stump.' This time Muniment smiled.

'Bother the stump! I was trusting you.'

'Exactly so. That gave me time.'

'Don't come unless your mind is made up, *mon petit*,' said Poupin.

'Are you going now—to see Hoffendahl?' Hyacinth cried.

'Don't shout it all over the place. He wants a genteel little customer like you,' Muniment went on.

'Is it true? Are we all going?' Hyacinth demanded, eagerly.

'Yes, these two are in it; they are not very artful, but they are safe,' said Muniment, looking at Poupin and Schinkel.

'Are *you* the genuine article, Muniment?' asked Hyacinth, catching this look.

Muniment dropped his eyes on him; then he said, 'Yes, you're the boy he wants. It's at the other end of London; we must have a growler.'

'Be calm, my child; *me voici!*' And Eustache Poupin led Hyacinth out.

They all walked away from the 'Sun and Moon,' and it was not for some five minutes that they encountered the four-wheeled cab which deepened so the solemnity of their expedition. After they were seated in it, Hyacinth learned that

Hoffendahl was in London but for three days, was liable to hurry away on the morrow, and was accustomed to receive visits at all kinds of queer hours. It was getting to be midnight; the drive seemed interminable, to Hyacinth's impatience and curiosity. He sat next to Muniment, who passed his arm round him, as if by way of a tacit expression of indebtedness. They all ended by sitting silent, as the cab jogged along murky miles, and by the time it stopped Hyacinth had wholly lost, in the drizzling gloom, a sense of their whereabouts.

BOOK THIRD

XXII

HYACINTH got up early—an operation attended with very little effort, as he had scarcely closed his eyes all night. What he saw from his window made him dress as rapidly as a young man could do who desired more than ever that his appearance should not give strange ideas about him: an old garden, with parterres in curious figures, and little intervals of lawn which appeared to our hero's cockney vision fantastically green. At one end of the garden was a parapet of mossy brick, which looked down on the other side into a canal, or moat, or quaint old pond; and from the same standpoint there was also a view of a considerable part of the main body of the house (Hyacinth's room appeared to be in a wing commanding the extensive, irregular back), which was richly gray wherever it was not green with ivy and other dense creepers, and everywhere infinitely like a picture, with a high-piled, ancient, russet roof, broken by huge chimneys and queer peep-holes and all manner of odd gables and windows on different lines and antique patches and protrusions, and a particularly fascinating architectural excrescence in which a wonderful clock-face was lodged—a clock-face covered with gilding and blazonry but showing many traces of the years and the weather. Hyacinth had never in his life been in the country—the real country, as he called it, the country which was not the mere raveled fringe of London—and there entered through his open casement the breath of a world enchantingly new and, after his recent feverish hours, inexpressibly refreshing to him; a sense of sweet, sunny air and mingled odours, all strangely pure and agreeable, and a kind of musical silence, the greater part of which seemed to consist of the voices of birds. There were tall, quiet trees near by, and afar off, and everywhere; and the group of objects which greeted Hyacinth's eyes evidently formed only a corner of larger spaces and a more complicated scene. There was a world to be revealed to him: it lay waiting, with the dew upon it, under his windows, and he must go down and take his first steps in it.

The night before, at ten o'clock, when he arrived, he had only got the impression of a mile-long stretch of park, after turning in at a gate; of the cracking of gravel under the wheels of the fly; and of the glow of several windows, suggesting in-door cheer, in a façade that lifted a variety of vague pinnacles into the starlight. It was much of a relief to him then to be informed that the Princess, in consideration of the lateness of the hour, begged to be excused till the morrow; the delay would give him time to recover his balance and look about him. This latter opportunity was offered him first as he sat at supper in a vast dining-room, with the butler, whose acquaintance he had made in South Street, behind his chair. He had not exactly wondered how he should be treated: there was too much vagueness in his conception of the way in which, at a country-house, invidious distinctions might be made and shades of importance illustrated; but it was plain that the best had been ordered for him. He was, at all events, abundantly content with his reception and more and more excited by it. The repast was delicate (though his other senses were so awake that hunger dropped out and he ate, as it were, without eating), and the grave mechanical servant filled his glass with a liquor that reminded him of some lines in Keats—in the 'Ode to a Nightingale.' He wondered whether he should hear a nightingale at Medley (he knew nothing about the seasons of this vocalist), and also whether the butler would attempt to talk to him, had ideas about him, knew or suspected who he was and what; which, after all, there was no reason for his doing, unless it might be the poverty of the luggage that had been transported from Lomax Place. Mr. Withers, however (it was in this manner that Hyacinth heard him addressed by the cabman who conveyed the visitor from the station), gave no further symptom of sociability than to ask him at what time he would be called in the morning; to which our young man replied that he preferred not to be called at all—he would get up by himself. The butler rejoined, 'Very good, sir,' while Hyacinth thought it probable that he puzzled him a good deal, and even considered the question of giving him a glimpse of his identity, lest it should be revealed, later, in a manner less graceful. The object of this anticipatory step, in Hyacinth's mind, was that he should not be oppressed and embarrassed with attentions to which he was unused; but the idea came to nothing, for the simple reason that before he spoke he found that he already *was* inured to being waited upon. His impulse to deprecate attentions departed, and he became conscious that there were none he should care to miss, or was not quite prepared for. He knew he probably thanked Mr. Withers too much, but he couldn't help this—it was an irrepressible tendency and an error he should doubtless always commit.

He lay in a bed constituted in a manner so perfect to insure rest that it was probably responsible in some degree for his restlessness, and in a large, high room, where long dressing-glasses emitted ghostly glances even after the light was extinguished. Suspended on the walls were many prints, mezzotints and old engravings, which Hyacinth supposed, possibly without reason, to be fine and rare. He got up several times in the night, lighted his candle and walked about looking at them. He looked at himself in one of the long glasses, and in a place where everything was on such a scale it seemed to him more than ever that Mademoiselle Vivier's son was a tiny particle. As he came downstairs he encountered housemaids, with dusters and brooms, or perceived them, through open doors, on their knees before fireplaces; and it was his belief that they regarded him more boldly than if he had been a guest of the usual kind. Such a reflection as that, however, ceased to trouble him after he had passed out of doors and begun to roam through the park, into which he let himself loose at first, and then, in narrowing circles, through the nearer grounds. He rambled for an hour, in a state of breathless ecstasy; brushing the dew from the deep fern and bracken and the rich borders of the garden, tasting the fragrant air, and stopping everywhere, in murmuring rapture, at the touch of some exquisite impression. His whole walk was peopled with recognitions; he had been dreaming all his life of just such a place and such objects, such a morning and such a chance. It was the last of April, and everything was fresh and vivid; the great trees, in the early air, were a blur of tender shoots. Round the admirable house he revolved repeatedly; catching every point and tone, feasting on its expression, and wondering whether the Princess would observe his pro-

ceedings from the window, and whether, if she did, they
would be offensive to her. The house was not hers, but only
hired for three months, and it could flatter no princely pride
that he should be struck with it. There was something in the
way the gray walls rose from the green lawn that brought
tears to his eyes; the spectacle of long duration unassociated
with some sordid infirmity or poverty was new to him; he
had lived with people among whom old age meant, for the
most part, a grudged and degraded survival. In the majestic
preservation of Medley there was a kind of serenity of success,
an accumulation of dignity and honour.

A footman sought him out, in the garden, to tell him that
breakfast was ready. He had never thought of breakfast, and
as he walked back to the house, attended by the inscrutable
flunkey, this offer appeared a free, extravagant gift, unexpected and romantic. He found he was to breakfast alone, and
he asked no questions; but when he had finished the butler
came in and informed him that the Princess would see him
after luncheon, but that in the meanwhile she wished him to
understand that the library was entirely at his service. 'After
luncheon'—that threw the hour he had come for very far into
the future, and it caused him some confusion of mind that the
Princess should think it worth while to invite him to stay at
her house from Saturday evening to Monday morning if it
had been her purpose that so much of his visit should elapse
without their meeting. But he felt neither slighted nor impatient; the impressions that had already crowded upon him
were in themselves a sufficient reward, and what could one do
better, precisely, in such a house as that, than wait for a princess? The butler showed him the way to the library, and left
him planted in the middle of it, staring at the treasures that he
instantly perceived it contained. It was an old brown room, of
great extent—even the ceiling was brown, though there were
figures in it dimly gilt—where row upon row of finely-
lettered backs returned his discriminating professional gaze.
A fire of logs crackled in a great chimney, and there were
alcoves with deep window-seats, and arm-chairs such as he
had never seen, luxurious, leather-covered, with an adjust-
ment for holding one's volume; and a vast writing-table, before one of the windows, furnished with a perfect magazine

of paper and pens, inkstands and blotters, seals, stamps, candlesticks, reels of twine, paper-weights, book-knives. Hyacinth had never imagined so many aids to correspondence, and before he turned away he had written a note to Millicent, in a hand even more beautiful than usual—his penmanship was very minute, but at the same time wonderfully free and fair—largely for the pleasure of seeing 'Medley Hall' stamped in crimson, heraldic-looking characters at the top of his paper. In the course of an hour he had ravaged the collection, taken down almost every book, wishing he could keep it a week, and put it back quickly, as his eye caught the next, which appeared even more desirable. He discovered many rare bindings, and gathered several ideas from an inspection of them— ideas which he felt himself perfectly capable of reproducing. Altogether, his vision of true happiness, at that moment, was that, for a month or two, he should be locked into the library at Medley. He forgot the outer world, and the morning waned—the beautiful vernal Sunday—while he lingered there.

He was on the top of a ladder when he heard a voice remark, 'I am afraid they are very dusty; in this house, you know, it is the dust of centuries;' and, looking down, he saw Madame Grandoni stationed in the middle of the room. He instantly prepared to descend, to make her his salutation, when she exclaimed, 'Stay, stay, if you are not giddy; we can talk from here! I only came in to show you we *are* in the house, and to tell you to keep up your patience. The Princess will probably see you in a few hours.'

'I really hope so,' said Hyacinth, from his perch, rather dismayed at the 'probably.'

'*Natürlich,*' the old lady rejoined; 'but people have come, sometimes, and gone away without seeing her. It all depends upon her mood.'

'Do you mean even when she has sent for them?'

'Oh, who can tell whether she has sent for them or not?'

'But she sent for me, you know,' Hyacinth declared, staring down—struck with the odd effect of Madame Grandoni's wig in that bird's-eye view.

'Oh yes, she sent for you, poor young man!' The old lady looked up at him with a smile, and they remained a moment

exchanging a silent scrutiny. Then she added, 'Captain Sholto
has come, like that, more than once; and he has gone away no
better off.'

'Captain Sholto?' Hyacinth repeated.

'Very true, if we talk at this distance I must shut the door.'
She took her way back to it (she had left it open), and pushed
it to; then advanced into the room again, with her superannuated, shuffling step, walking as if her shoes were too big for
her. Hyacinth meanwhile descended the ladder. '*Ecco!* She's a
capricciosa,' said the old lady.

'I don't understand how you speak of her,' Hyacinth remarked, gravely. 'You seem to be her friend, yet you say
things that are not favourable to her.'

'Dear young man, I say much worse to her about herself
than I should ever say to you. I am rude, oh yes—even to
you, to whom, no doubt, I ought to be particularly kind. But
I am not false. It is not our German nature. You will hear me
some day. I *am* the friend of the Princess; it would be well
enough if she never had a worse one! But I should like to be
yours, too—what will you have? Perhaps it is of no use. At
any rate, here you are.'

'Yes, here I am, decidedly!' Hyacinth laughed, uneasily.

'And how long shall you stay? Excuse me if I ask that; it is
part of my rudeness.'

'I shall stay till to-morrow morning. I must be at my work
by noon.'

'That will do very well. Don't you remember, the other
time, how I told you to remain faithful?'

'That was very good advice. But I think you exaggerate my
danger.'

'So much the better,' said Madame Grandoni; 'though now
that I look at you well I doubt it a little. I see you are one of
those types that ladies like. I can be sure of that, because I like
you myself. At my age—a hundred and twenty—can I not
say that? If the Princess were to do so, it would be different;
remember that—that any flattery she may ever offer you will
be on her lips much less discreet. But perhaps she will never
have the chance; you may never come again. There are people
who have come only once. *Vedremo bene.* I must tell you that I
am not in the least against a young man taking a holiday, a

little quiet recreation, once in a while,' Madame Grandoni
continued, in her disconnected, discursive, confidential way.
'In Rome they take it every five days; that is, no doubt, too
often. In Germany, less often. In this country, I cannot understand whether it is an increase of effort: the English Sunday is so difficult! This one will, however, in any case, have
been beautiful for you. Be happy, make yourself comfortable;
but go home to-morrow!' And with this injunction Madame
Grandoni took her way again to the door, while Hyacinth
went to open it for her. 'I can say that, because it is not my
house. I am only here like you. And sometimes I think I also
shall go to-morrow!'

'I imagine you have not, like me, your living to get, every
day. That is reason enough for me,' said Hyacinth.

She paused in the doorway, with her expressive, ugly,
kindly little eyes on his face. 'I believe I am nearly as poor as
you. And I have not, like you, the appearance of nobility. Yet
I am noble,' said the old lady, shaking her wig.

'And I am not!' Hyacinth rejoined, smiling.

'It is better not to be lifted up high, like our friend. It does
not give happiness.'

'Not to one's self, possibly; but to others!' From where
they stood, Hyacinth looked out into the great panelled and
decorated hall, lighted from above and roofed with a far-away
dim fresco, and the reflection of this grandeur came into his
appreciative eyes.

'Do you admire everything here very much—do you receive great pleasure?' asked Madame Grandoni.

'Oh, so much—so much!'

She considered him a moment longer. *Poverino!* she murmured, as she turned away.

A couple of hours later the Princess sent for Hyacinth, and
he was conducted upstairs, through corridors carpeted with
crimson and hung with pictures, and ushered into a kind of
bright drawing-room, which he afterwards learned that his
hostess regarded as her boudoir. The sound of music had
come to him outside the door, so that he was prepared to find
her seated at the piano, if not to see her continue to play after
he appeared. Her face was turned in the direction from which
he entered, and she smiled at him while the servant, as if he

had just arrived, formally pronounced his name, without lifting her hands from the keys. The room, placed in an angle of
the house and lighted from two sides, was large and sunny,
upholstered in fresh, gay chintz, furnished with all sorts of
sofas and low, familiar seats and convenient little tables, most
of them holding great bowls of early flowers, littered over
with books, newspapers, magazines, photographs of celebrities, with their signatures, and full of the marks of luxurious
and rather indolent habitation. Hyacinth stood there, not advancing very far, and the Princess, still playing and smiling,
nodded toward a seat near the piano. 'Put yourself there and
listen to me.' Hyacinth obeyed, and she played a long time
without glancing at him. This left him the more free to rest
his eyes on her own face and person, while she looked about
the room, vaguely, absently, but with an expression of quiet
happiness, as if she were lost in her music, soothed and pacified by it. A window near her was half open, and the soft
clearness of the day and all the odour of the spring diffused
themselves, and made the place cheerful and pure. The Princess struck him as extraordinarily young and fair, and she
seemed so slim and simple, and friendly too, in spite of having neither abandoned her occupation nor offered him her
hand, that he sank back in his seat at last, with the sense that
all his uneasiness, his nervous tension, was leaving him, and
that he was safe in her kindness, in the free, original way with
which she evidently would always treat him. This peculiar
manner—half consideration, half fellowship—seemed to him
already to have the sweetness of familiarity. She played ever
so movingly, with different pieces succeeding each other; he
had never listened to music, nor to a talent, of that order.
Two or three times she turned her eyes upon him, and then
they shone with the wonderful expression which was the essence of her beauty; that profuse, mingled light which seemed
to belong to some everlasting summer, and yet to suggest
seasons that were past and gone, some experience that was
only an exquisite memory. She asked him if he cared for music, and then added, laughing, that she ought to have made
sure of this before; while he answered—he had already told
her so in South Street; she appeared to have forgotten—that
he was awfully fond of it.

The sense of the beauty of women had been given to our young man in a high degree; it was a faculty that made him conscious, to adoration, of every element of loveliness, every delicacy of feature, every shade and tone, that contributed to charm. Even, therefore, if he had appreciated less the deep harmonies the Princess drew from the piano, there would have been no lack of interest in his situation, in such an opportunity to watch her admirable outline and movement, the noble form of her head and face, the gathered-up glories of her hair, the living flower-like freshness which had no need to turn from the light. She was dressed in fair colours, as simply as a young girl. Before she ceased playing she asked Hyacinth what he would like to do in the afternoon: would he have any objection to taking a drive with her? It was very possible he might enjoy the country. She seemed not to attend to his answer, which was covered by the sound of the piano; but if she had done so it would have left her very little doubt as to the reality of his inclination. She remained gazing at the cornice of the room, while her hands wandered to and fro; then suddenly she stopped, got up and came toward her companion. 'It is probable that is the most I shall ever bore you; you know the worst. Would you very kindly close the piano?' He complied with her request, and she went to another part of the room and sank into an arm-chair. When he approached her again she said, 'Is it really true that you have never seen a park, nor a garden, nor any of the beauties of nature, and that sort of thing?' She was alluding to something he had said in his letter, when he answered the note by which she proposed to him to run down to Medley; and after he assured her that it was perfectly true she exclaimed, 'I'm so glad—I'm so glad! I have never been able to show any one anything new, and I have always thought I should like it so—especially to a sensitive nature. Then you *will* come and drive with me?' She asked this as if it would be a great favour.

That was the beginning of the communion—so singular, considering their respective positions—which he had come to Medley to enjoy; and it passed into some very remarkable phases. The Princess had the most extraordinary way of taking things for granted, of ignoring difficulties, of assuming that her preferences might be translated into fact. After Hyacinth had remained with her ten minutes longer—a period mainly occupied with her exclamations of delight at his having seen so little of the sort of thing of which Medley consisted (Where should he have seen it, gracious heaven? he asked himself); after she had rested, thus briefly, from her exertions at the piano, she proposed that they should go out-of-doors together. She was an immense walker—she wanted her walk. She left him for a short time, giving him the last number of the *Revue des Deux Mondes* to entertain himself withal, and calling his attention, in particular, to a story of M. Octave Feuillet (she should be so curious to know what he thought of it); and reappeared with her hat and parasol, drawing on her long gloves and presenting herself to our young man, at that moment, as a sudden incarnation of the heroine of M. Feuillet's novel, in which he had instantly become immersed. On their way downstairs it occurred to her that he had not yet seen the house and that it would be amusing for her to show it to him; so she turned aside and took him through it, up and down and everywhere, even into the vast, old-fashioned kitchen, where there was a small, red-faced man in a white jacket and apron and a white cap (he removed the latter ornament to salute the little bookbinder), with whom his companion spoke Italian, which Hyacinth understood sufficiently to perceive that she addressed her cook in the second person singular, as if he had been a feudal retainer. He remembered that was the way the three Musketeers spoke to their lackeys. The Princess explained that the gentleman in the white cap was a delightful creature (she couldn't endure English servants, though she was obliged to have two or three), who would make her plenty of risottos and polentas—she had quite the palate of a contadina. She showed Hyacinth everything: the queer transmogrified corner that had once been a chapel; the secret stairway which had served in the persecutions of the Catholics (the owners of Medley were, like the Princess herself, of the old persuasion); the musicians' gallery, over the hall; the tapestried room, which people came from a distance to see; and the haunted chamber (the two were sometimes confounded, but they were quite distinct), where a dreadful individual at certain times made his appearance—a dwarfish ghost, with an enormous head, a dispossessed brother, of long ago (the eldest), who had passed for an idiot, which he wasn't, and had somehow been made away with. The Princess offered her visitor the privilege of sleeping in this apartment, declaring, however, that nothing would induce *her* even to enter it alone, she being a benighted creature, consumed with abject superstitions. 'I don't know whether I am religious, and whether, if I were, my religion would be superstitious. But my superstitions are certainly religious.' She made her young friend pass through the drawing-room very cursorily, remarking that they should see it again: it was rather stupid—drawing-rooms in English country-houses were always stupid; indeed, if it would amuse him, they would sit there after dinner. Madame Grandoni and she usually sat upstairs, but they would do anything that he should find more comfortable.

At last they went out of the house together, and as they did so she explained, as if she wished to justify herself against the imputation of extravagance, that, though the place doubtless struck him as absurdly large for a couple of quiet women, and the whole thing was not in the least what she would have preferred, yet it was all far cheaper than he probably imagined; she would never have looked at it if it hadn't been cheap. It must appear to him so preposterous for a woman to associate herself with the great uprising of the poor and yet live in palatial halls—a place with forty or fifty rooms. This was one of only two allusions she made that day to her democratic sympathies; but it fell very happily, for Hyacinth had been reflecting precisely upon the anomaly she mentioned. It had been present to him all day; it added much to the way life practised on his sense of the tragic-comical to think of the Princess's having retired to that magnificent residence in order to concentrate her mind upon the London slums. He listened, therefore, with great attention while she related that she had taken the house only for three months, in any case, because she wanted to rest, after a winter of visiting and living in public (as the English spent their lives, with all their celebrated worship of the 'home'), and yet didn't wish as yet to return to town—though she was obliged to confess that she had still the place in South Street on her hands, thanks to her deciding unexpectedly to go on with it rather than move out her things. But one had to keep one's things somewhere, and why wasn't that as good a receptacle as another? Medley was not what she would have chosen if she had been left to herself; but she had not been left to herself—she never was; she had been bullied into taking it by the owners, whom she had met somewhere and who had made up to her immensely, persuading her that she might really have it for nothing—for no more than she would give for the little honeysuckle cottage, the old parsonage embowered in clematis, which were really what she had been looking for. Besides it was one of those old musty mansions, ever so far from town, which it was always difficult to let, or to get a price for; and then it was a wretched house for living in. Hyacinth, for whom his three hours in the train had been a series of happy throbs, had not been struck with its geographical remoteness, and he asked the Princess what she meant, in such a connection, by using the word 'wretched.' To this she replied that the place was tumbling to pieces, inconvenient in every respect, full of ghosts and bad smells. 'That is the only reason I come to have it. I don't want you to think me more luxurious than I am, or that I throw away money. Never, never!' Hyacinth had no standard by which he could measure the importance his opinion would have for her, and he perceived that though she judged him as a creature still open to every initiation, whose *naïveté* would entertain her, it was also her fancy to treat him as an old friend, a person to whom she might have had the habit of referring her difficulties. Her performance of the part she had undertaken to play was certainly complete, and everything lay before him but the reason she had for playing it.

One of the gardens at Medley took the young man's heart beyond the others; it had high brick walls, on the sunny sides of which was a great training of apricots and plums, and straight walks, bordered with old-fashioned homely flowers, inclosing immense squares where other fruit-trees stood upright and mint and lavender floated in the air. In the southern quarter it overhung a small, disused canal, and here a high embankment had been raised, which was also long and broad and covered with fine turf; so that the top of it, looking down at the canal, made a magnificent grassy terrace, than which, on a summer's day, there could be no more delightful place for strolling up and down with a companion—all the more that, at either end, was a curious pavilion, in the manner of a tea-house, which completed the scene in an old-world sense and offered rest and privacy, a refuge from sun or shower. One of these pavilions was an asylum for gardeners' tools and superfluous flower-pots; the other was covered, inside, with a queer Chinese paper, representing ever so many times over a group of people with faces like blind kittens, having tea while they sat on the floor. It also contained a big, clumsy inlaid cabinet, in which cups and saucers showed themselves through doors of greenish glass, together with a carved co-coanut and a pair of outlandish idols. On a shelf, over a sofa, not very comfortable though it had cushions of faded tapes-try, which looked like samplers, was a row of novels, out of date and out of print—novels that one couldn't have found any more and that were only there. On the chimney-piece was a bowl of dried rose-leaves, mixed with some aromatic spice, and the whole place suggested a certain dampness.

On the terrace Hyacinth paced to and fro with the Princess until she suddenly remembered that he had not had his lun-cheon. He protested that this was the last thing he wished to think of, but she declared that she had not asked him down to Medley to starve him and that he must go back and be fed. They went back, but by a very roundabout way, through the park, so that they really had half an hour's more talk. She explained to him that she herself breakfasted at twelve o'clock, in the foreign fashion, and had tea in the afternoon; as he too was so foreign he might like that better, and in this case, on the morrow, they would breakfast together. He could have coffee, and anything else he wanted, brought to his room when he woke up. When Hyacinth had sufficiently composed himself, in the presence of this latter image—he thought he saw a footman arranging a silver service at his bedside—he mentioned that really, as regarded the morrow, he should have to be back in London. There was a train at nine o'clock; he hoped she didn't mind his taking it. She looked at him a moment, gravely and kindly, as if she were considering an abstract idea, and then she said, 'Oh yes, I mind it very much. Not to-morrow—some other day.' He made no rejoinder, and the Princess spoke of something else; that is, his rejoinder was private, and consisted of the reflection that he *would* leave Medley in the morning, whatever she might say. He simply couldn't afford to stay; he couldn't be out of work. And then Madame Grandoni thought it so important; for though the old lady was obscure she was decidedly impressive. The Princess's protest, however, was to be reckoned with; he felt that it might take a form less cursory than the words she had just uttered, which would make it embarrassing. She was less solemn, less explicit, than Madame Grandoni had been, but there was something in her slight seriousness and the delicate way in which she signified a sort of command that seemed to tell him his liberty was going—the liberty he had managed to keep (till the other day, when he gave Hoffendahl a mortgage on it), and the possession of which had in some degree consoled him for other forms of penury. This made him uneasy; what would become of him if he should add another servitude to the one he had undertaken, at the end of that long, anxious cab-drive in the rain, in that dim back-bedroom of a house as to whose whereabouts he was even now not clear, while Muniment and Poupin and Schinkel, all visibly pale, listened and accepted the vow? Muniment and Poupin and Schinkel—how disconnected, all the same, he felt from them at the present hour; how little he was the young man who had made the pilgrimage in the cab; and how the two latter, at least, if they could have a glimpse of him now, would wonder what he was up to!

As to this, Hyacinth wondered sufficiently himself, while the Princess touched upon the people and places she had seen, the impressions and conclusions she had gathered, since their former meeting. It was to such matters as these that she directed the conversation; she appeared to wish to keep it off his own concerns, and he was surprised at her continued avoidance of the slums and the question of her intended sacrifices. She mentioned none of her friends by name, but she talked of their character, their houses, their manners, taking for granted, as before, that Hyacinth would always follow. So far as he followed he was edified, but he had to admit to himself that half the time he didn't know what she was talking about. At all events, if *he* had been with the dukes (she didn't call her associates dukes, but Hyacinth was sure they were of that order), he would have got more satisfaction from them. She appeared, on the whole, to judge the English world severely; to think poorly of its wit, and even worse of its morals. 'You know people oughtn't to be both corrupt and dull,' she said; and Hyacinth turned this over, feeling that he certainly had not yet caught the point of view of a person for whom the aristocracy was a collection of bores. He had sometimes taken great pleasure in hearing that it was fabulously profligate, but he was rather disappointed in the bad account the Princess gave of it. She remarked that she herself was very corrupt—she ought to have mentioned that before—but she had never been accused of being stupid. Perhaps he would discover it, but most of the people she had had to do with thought her only too lively. The second allusion that she made to their ulterior designs (Hyacinth's and hers) was when she said, 'I determined to see it'—she was speaking still of English society—'to learn for myself what it really is, before we blow it up. I have been here now a year and a half, and, as I tell you, I feel that I have seen. It is the old régime again, the rottenness and extravagance, bristling with every iniquity and every abuse, over which the French Revolution passed like a whirlwind; or perhaps even more a reproduction of Roman society in its decadence, gouty, apoplectic, depraved, gorged and clogged with wealth and spoils, selfishness and scepticism, and waiting for the onset of the barbarians. You and I are the barbarians, you know.' The Princess was pretty general, after all, in her animadversions, and regaled him with no anecdotes (he rather missed them) that would have betrayed the hospitality she had enjoyed. She couldn't treat him absolutely as if he had been an ambassador. By way of defending the aristocracy he said to her that it couldn't be true they were all a bad lot (he used that expression because she had let him know that she liked him to speak in the manner of the people), inasmuch as he had an acquaintance among them—a noble lady—who was one of the purest, kindest, most conscientious human beings it was possible to imagine. At this she stopped short and looked at him; then she asked, 'Whom do you mean—a noble lady?'

'I suppose there is no harm saying. Lady Aurora Langrish.'
'I don't know her. Is she nice?'

'I like her ever so much.'

'Is she pretty, clever?'

'She isn't pretty, but she is very uncommon,' said Hyacinth.

'How did you make her acquaintance?' As he hesitated, she went on, 'Did you bind some books for her?'

'No. I met her in a place called Audley Court.'

'Where is that?'

'In Camberwell.'

'And who lives there?'

'A young woman I was calling on, who is bedridden.'

'And the lady you speak of—what do you call her, Lydia Languish?—goes to see her?'

'Yes, very often.'

The Princess was silent a moment, looking at him. 'Will you take me there?'

'With great pleasure. The young woman I speak of is the sister of the chemist's assistant you will perhaps remember that I mentioned to you.'

'Yes, I remember. It must be one of the first places we go to. I am sorry,' the Princess added, walking on. Hyacinth inquired what she might be sorry for, but she took no notice of his question, and presently remarked, 'Perhaps she goes to see him.'

'Goes to see whom?'

'The chemist's assistant—the brother.' She said this very seriously.

'Perhaps she does,' Hyacinth rejoined, laughing. 'But she is a fine sort of woman.'

The Princess repeated that she was sorry, and he again asked her for what—for Lady Aurora's being of that sort? To which she replied, 'No; I mean for my not being the first—what is it you call them?—noble lady that you have encountered.'

'I don't see what difference that makes. You needn't be afraid you don't make an impression on me.'

'I was not thinking of that. I was thinking that you might be less fresh than I thought.'

'Of course I don't know what you thought,' said Hyacinth, smiling.

'No; how should you?'

XXIII

H E WAS in the library, after luncheon, when word was
brought to him that the carriage was at the door, for
their drive; and when he went into the hall he found Madame
Grandoni, bonneted and cloaked, awaiting the descent of the
Princess. 'You see I go with you. I am always there,' she remarked, jovially. 'The Princess has me with her to take care of
her, and this is how I do it. Besides, I never miss my drive.'

'You are different from me; this will be the first I have ever
had in my life.' He could establish that distinction without
bitterness, because he was too pleased with his prospect to
believe the old lady's presence could spoil it. He had nothing
to say to the Princess that she might not hear. He didn't dislike her for coming, even after she had said to him, in answer
to his own announcement, speaking rather more sententiously
than was her wont, 'It doesn't surprise me that you have not
spent your life in carriages. They have nothing to do with
your trade.'

'Fortunately not,' he answered. 'I should have made a ridiculous coachman.'

The Princess appeared, and they mounted into a great
square barouche, an old-fashioned, high-hung vehicle, with a
green body, a faded hammer-cloth and a rumble where the
footman sat (the Princess mentioned that it had been let with
the house), which rolled ponderously and smoothly along
the winding avenue and through the gilded gates (they were
surmounted with an immense escutcheon) of the park. The
progress of this oddly composed trio had a high respectability, and that is one of the reasons why Hyacinth felt the
occasion to be tremendously memorable. There might still be
greater joys in store for him—he was by this time quite at
sea, and could recognise no shores—but he would never
again in his life be so respectable. The drive was long and
comprehensive, but very little was said while it lasted. 'I shall
show you the whole country: it is exquisitely beautiful; it
speaks to the heart.' Of so much as this his hostess had informed him at the start; and she added, in French, with a
light, allusive nod at the rich, humanised landscape, *Voilà ce*

que j'aime en Angleterre.' For the rest, she sat there opposite to him, in quiet fairness, under her softly-swaying, lace-fringed parasol: moving her eyes to where she noticed that his eyes rested; allowing them, when the carriage passed anything particularly charming, to meet his own; smiling as if she enjoyed the whole affair very nearly as much as he; and now and then calling his attention to some prospect, some picturesque detail, by three words of which the cadence was sociable. Madame Grandoni dozed most of the time, with her chin resting on rather a mangy ermine tippet, in which she had enveloped herself; expanding into consciousness at moments, however, to greet the scenery with comfortable polyglot ejaculations. If Hyacinth was exalted, during these delightful hours, he at least measured his exaltation, and it kept him almost solemnly still, as if with the fear that a wrong movement of any sort would break the charm, cause the curtain to fall upon the play. This was especially the case when his senses oscillated back from the objects that sprang up by the way, every one of which was a rich image of something he had longed for, to the most beautiful woman in England, who sat there, close to him, as completely for his benefit as if he had been a painter engaged to make her portrait. More than once he saw everything through a mist; his eyes were full of tears.

That evening they sat in the drawing-room after dinner, as the Princess had promised, or, as he was inclined to consider it, threatened him. The force of the threat was in his prevision that the ladies would make themselves fine, and that in contrast with the setting and company he should feel dingier than ever; having already on his back the only tolerably decent coat he possessed, and being unable to exchange it for a garment of the pattern that civilised people (so much he knew, if he couldn't emulate them), put on about eight o'clock. The ladies, when they came to dinner, looked festal indeed; but Hyacinth was able to make the reflection that he was more pleased to be dressed as he was dressed, meanly and unsuitably as it was, than he should have been to present such a figure as Madame Grandoni, in whose toggery there was something comical. He was coming more and more round to the sense that if the Princess didn't mind his poorness, in every way, he had no call to mind it himself. His present circumstances were not of his seeking—they had been forced upon him; they were not the fruit of a disposition to push. How little the Princess minded—how much, indeed, she enjoyed the consciousness that in having him about her in that manner she was playing a trick upon society, the false and conventional society she had measured and despised—was manifest from the way she had introduced him to the people they found awaiting them in the hall on the return from their drive: four ladies, a mother and three daughters, who had come over to call, from Broome, a place some five miles off. Broome was also a great house, as he gathered, and Lady Marchant, the mother, was the wife of a county magnate. She explained that they had come in on the persuasion of the butler, who had represented the return of the Princess as imminent, and who then had administered tea without waiting for this event. The evening had drawn in chill; there was a fire in the hall, and they all sat near it, round the tea-table, under the great roof which rose to the top of the house. Hyacinth conversed mainly with one of the daughters, a very fine girl with a straight back and long arms, whose neck was encircled so tightly with a fur boa that, to look a little to one side, she was obliged to move her whole body. She had a handsome, inanimate face, over which the firelight played without making it more lively, a beautiful voice, and the occasional command of a few short words. She asked Hyacinth with what pack he hunted, and whether he went in much for tennis, and she ate three muffins.

Our young man perceived that Lady Marchant and her daughters had already been at Medley, and even guessed that their reception by the Princess, who probably thought them of a tiresome type, had not been enthusiastic; and his imagination projected itself, further still, into the motives which, in spite of this tepidity, must have led them, in consideration of the rarity of princesses in that country, to come a second time. The talk, in the firelight, while Hyacinth laboured, rather recklessly (for the spirit of the occasion, on his hostess's part, was passing into his own blood), with his muffin-eating beauty—the conversation, accompanied with the light click of delicate tea-cups, was as well-bred as could be consistent with an odd, evident *parti-pris* of the Princess's to make poor

Lady Marchant explain everything. With great urbanity of manner, she professed complete inability to understand the sense in which her visitor meant her thin remarks; and Hyacinth was scarcely able to follow her here, he wondered so what interest she could have in trying to appear dense. It was only afterwards he learned that the Marchant family produced a very peculiar, and at moments almost maddening, effect upon her nerves. He asked himself what would happen to that member of it with whom he was engaged if it should be revealed to her that she was conversing (how little soever) with a beggarly London artisan; and though he was rather pleased at her not having discovered his station (for he didn't attribute her brevity to this idea), he entertained a little the question of its being perhaps his duty not to keep it hidden from her, not to flourish in a cowardly disguise. What did she take him for—or, rather, what didn't she take him for—when she asked him if he hunted? Perhaps that was because it was rather dark; if there had been more light in the great vague hall she would have seen he was not one of themselves. Hyacinth felt that by this time he had associated a good deal with swells, but they had always known what he was and had been able to elect how to treat him. This was the first occasion on which a young gentlewoman had not been warned, and, as a consequence, he appeared to pass muster. He determined not to unmask himself, on the simple ground that he should by the same stroke betray the Princess. It was quite open to her to lean over and say to Miss Marchant, 'You know he's a wretched little bookbinder, earning a few shillings a week in a horrid street in Soho. There are all kinds of low things—and I suspect even something very horrible—connected with his birth. It seems to me I ought to mention it.' He almost wished she would mention it, for the sake of the strange, violent sensation of the thing, a curiosity quivering within him to know what Miss Marchant would do at such a pinch, and what chorus of ejaculations—or, what appalled, irremediable silence—would rise to the painted roof. The responsibility, however, was not his; he had entered a phase of his destiny where responsibilities were suspended. Madame Grandoni's tea had waked her up; she came, at every crisis, to the rescue of the conversation, and talked to the visitors about Rome, where they had once spent a winter, describing with much drollery the manner in which the English families she had seen there for nearly half a century (and had met, of an evening, in the Roman world) inspected the ruins and monuments and squeezed into the great ceremonies of the church. Clearly, the four ladies didn't know what to make of the Princess; but, though they perhaps wondered if she were a paid companion, they were on firm ground in the fact that the queer, familiar, fat person had been acquainted with the Millingtons, the Bunburys and the Tripps.

After dinner (during which the Princess allowed herself a considerable license of pleasantry on the subject of her recent visitors, declaring that Hyacinth must positively go with her to return their call, and must see their interior, their manner at home), Madame Grandoni sat down to the piano, at Christina's request, and played to her companions for an hour. The spaces were large in the big drawing-room, and our friends had placed themselves at a distance from each other. The old lady's music trickled forth discreetly into the pleasant dimness of the candlelight; she knew dozens of Italian local airs, which sounded like the forgotten tunes of a people, and she followed them by a series of tender, plaintive German *Lieder*, awaking, without violence, the echoes of the high, pompous apartment. It was the music of an old woman, and seemed to quaver a little, as her singing might have done. The Princess, buried in a deep chair, listened, behind her fan. Hyacinth at least supposed she listened; at any rate, she never moved. At last Madame Grandoni left the piano and came toward the young man. She had taken up, on the way, a French book, in a pink cover, which she nursed in the hollow of her arm, and she stood looking at Hyacinth.

'My poor little friend, I must bid you good-night. I shall not see you again for the present, as, to take your early train, you will have left the house before I put on my wig—and I never show myself to gentlemen without it. I have looked after the Princess pretty well, all day, to keep her from harm, and now I give her up to you, for a little. Take the same care, I beg you. I must put myself into my dressing-gown; at my age, at this hour, it is the only thing. What will you have? I hate to be tight,' pursued Madame Grandoni, who appeared even in her ceremonial garment to have evaded this discomfort successfully enough. 'Do not sit up late,' she added; 'and do not keep him, Christina. Remember that for an active young man like Mr. Robinson, going every day to his work, there is nothing more exhausting than such an unoccupied life as ours. For what do we do, after all? His eyes are very heavy. *Basta!*'

During this little address the Princess, who made no rejoinder to that part of it which concerned herself, remained hidden behind her fan; but after Madame Grandoni had wandered away she lowered this emblazoned shield and rested her eyes for a while on Hyacinth. At last she said, 'Don't sit half a mile off. Come nearer to me. I want to say something to you that I can't shout across the room.' Hyacinth instantly got up, but at the same moment she also rose; so that, approaching each other, they met half-way, before the great marble chimney-piece. She stood a little, opening and closing her fan; then she remarked, 'You must be surprised at my not having yet spoken to you about our great interest.'

'No, indeed, I am not surprised at anything.'

'When you take that tone I feel as if we should never, after all, become friends,' said the Princess.

'I hoped we were, already. Certainly, after the kindness you have shown me, there is no service of friendship that you might ask of me——'

'That you wouldn't gladly perform? I know what you are going to say, and have no doubt you speak truly. But what good would your service do me if, all the while, you think of me as a hollow-headed, hollow-hearted trifler, behaving in the worst possible taste and oppressing you with her attentions? Perhaps you can think of me as—what shall I call it?—as a kind of coquette.'

Hyacinth demurred. 'That would be very conceited.'

'Surely, you have the right to be as conceited as you please, after the advances I have made you! Pray, who has a better one? But you persist in remaining humble, and that is very provoking.'

'It is not I that am provoking; it is life, and society, and all the difficulties that surround us.'

'I am precisely of that opinion—that they are exasperating; that when I appeal to you, frankly, candidly, disinterestedly—simply because I like you, for no other reason in the world—to help me to disregard and surmount these obstructions, to treat them with the contempt they deserve, you drop your eyes, you even blush a little, and make yourself small, and try to edge out of the situation by pleading general devotion and insignificance. Please remember this: you cease to be insignificant from the moment I have anything to do with you. My dear fellow,' the Princess went on, in her free, audacious, fraternising way, to which her beauty and simplicity gave nobleness, 'there are people who would be very glad to enjoy, in your place, that form of obscurity.'

'What do you wish me to do?' Hyacinth asked, as quietly as he could.

If he had had an idea that this question, to which, as coming from his lips, and even as being uttered with perceptible impatience, a certain unexpectedness might attach, would cause her a momentary embarrassment, he was completely out in his calculation. She answered on the instant: 'I want you to give me time! That's all I ask of my friends, in general—all I ever asked of the best I have had. But none of them ever did it; none of them, that is, save the excellent creature who has just left us. She understood me long ago.'

'That's all I, on my side, ask of you,' said Hyacinth, smiling. 'Give me time, give me time,' he murmured, looking up at her splendour.

'Dear Mr. Hyacinth, I have given you months!—months since our first meeting. And at present, haven't I given you the whole day? It has been intentional, my not speaking to you of our plans. Yes, our plans; I know what I am saying. Don't try to look stupid; you will never succeed. I wished to leave you free to amuse yourself.'

'Oh, I have amused myself,' said Hyacinth.

'You would have been very fastidious if you hadn't! However, that is precisely, in the first place, what I wished you to come here for. To observe the impression made by such a place as this on such a nature as yours, introduced to it for the first time, has been, I assure you, quite worth my while. I have already given you a hint of how extraordinary I think it that you should be what you are without having seen—what shall I call them?—beautiful, delightful old things. I have been watching you; I am frank enough to tell you that. I want you to see more—more—more!' the Princess exclaimed, with a sudden flicker of passion. 'And I want to talk with you about this matter, as well as others. That will be for to-morrow.'

'To-morrow?'

'I noticed Madame Grandoni took for granted just now that you are going. But that has nothing to do with the business. She has so little imagination!'

Hyacinth shook his head, smiling. 'I can't stay!' He had an idea his mind was made up.

She returned his smile, but there was something strangely touching—it was so sad, yet, as a rebuke, so gentle—in the tone in which she replied, 'You oughtn't to force me to beg. It isn't nice.'

He had reckoned without that tone; all his reasons suddenly seemed to fall from under him, to liquefy. He remained a moment, looking on the ground; then he said, 'Princess, you have no idea—how should you have?—into the midst of what abject, pitiful preoccupations you thrust yourself. I have no money—I have no clothes.'

'What do you want of money? This isn't an hotel.'

'Every day I stay here I lose a day's wages; and I live on my wages from day to day.'

'Let me, then, give you wages. You will work for me.'

'What do you mean—work for you?'

'You will bind all my books. I have ever so many foreign ones, in paper.'

'You speak as if I had brought my tools!'

'No, I don't imagine that. I will give you the wages now, and you can do the work, at your leisure and convenience, afterwards. Then, if you want anything, you can go over to Bonchester and buy it. There are very good shops; I have used them.' Hyacinth thought of a great many things at this juncture; the Princess had that quickening effect upon him. Among others, he thought of these two: first, that it was in-delicate (though such an opinion was not very strongly held either in Pentonville or in Soho) to accept money from a woman; and second, that it was still more indelicate to make such a woman as that go down on her knees to him. But it took more than a minute for one of these convictions to prevail over the other, and before that he had heard the Princess continue, in the tone of mild, disinterested argument: 'If we believe in the coming democracy, if it seems to us right and just, and we hold that in sweeping over the world the great wave will wash away a myriad iniquities and cruelties, why not make some attempt, with our own poor means—for one must begin somewhere—to carry out the spirit of it in our lives and our manners? I want to do that. I try to do it—in my relations with you, for instance. But you hang back; you are not democratic!'

The Princess accusing him of a patrician offishness was a very fine stroke; nevertheless it left him lucidity enough (though he still hesitated an instant, wondering whether the words would not offend her) to say, with a smile, 'I have been strongly warned against you.'

The offence seemed not to touch her. 'I can easily understand that. Of course my proceedings—though, after all, I have done little enough as yet—must appear most unnatural. *Che vuole?* as Madame Grandoni says.'

A certain knot of light blue ribbon, which formed part of the trimming of her dress, hung down, at her side, in the folds of it. On these glossy loops Hyacinth's eyes happened for a moment to have rested, and he now took one of them up and carried it to his lips. 'I will do all the work for you that you will give me. If you give it on purpose, by way of munificence, that is your own affair. I myself will estimate the price. What decides me is that I shall do it so well; at least it shall be better than any one else can do—so that if you employ me there will have been that reason. I have brought you a book—so you can see. I did it for you last year, and went to South Street to give it to you, but you had already gone.'

'Give it to me to-morrow.' These words appeared to express so exclusively the calmness of relief at finding that he could be reasonable, as well as that of a friendly desire to see the proof of his talent, that he was surprised when she said, in the next breath, irrelevantly, 'Who was it warned you against me?'

He feared she might suppose he meant Madame Grandoni, so he made the plainest answer, having no desire to betray the old lady, and reflecting that, as the likelihood was small that his friend in Camberwell would ever consent to meet the Princess (in spite of her plan of going there), no one would be hurt by it. 'A friend of mine in London—Paul Muniment.'

'Paul Muniment?'

'I think I mentioned him to you the first time we met.'

'The person who said something good? I forget what it was.'

'It was sure to be something good if he said it; he is very wise.'

'That makes his warning very flattering to me! What does he know about me?'

'Oh, nothing, of course, except the little that I could tell him. He only spoke on general grounds.'

'I like his name—Paul Muniment,' the Princess said. 'If he resembles it, I think I should like him.'

'You would like him much better than me.'

'How do you know how much—or how little—I like you? I am determined to keep hold of you, simply for what you can show me.' She paused a moment, with her beautiful, intelligent eyes smiling into his own, and then she continued, 'On general grounds, *bien entendu,* your friend was quite right to warn you. Now those general grounds are just what I have undertaken to make as small as possible. It is to reduce them to nothing that I talk to you, that I conduct myself with regard to you as I have done. What in the world is it I am trying to do but, by every device that my ingenuity suggests, fill up the inconvenient gulf that yawns between my position and yours? You know what I think of "positions"; I told you in London. For Heaven's sake let me feel that I have—a little —succeeded!' Hyacinth satisfied her sufficiently to enable her, five minutes later, apparently to entertain no further doubt on the question of his staying over. On the contrary, she burst into a sudden ebullition of laughter, exchanging her bright, lucid insistence for one of her singular sallies. 'You must absolutely go with me to call on the Marchants; it will be too delightful to see you there!'

As he walked up and down the empty drawing-room it occurred to him to ask himself whether that was mainly what she was keeping him for—so that he might help her to play one of her tricks on the good people at Broome. He paced there, in the still candlelight, for a longer time than he measured; until the butler came and stood in the doorway, looking at him silently and fixedly, as if to let him know that he interfered with the custom of the house. He had told the Princess that what determined him was the thought of the manner in which he might exercise his craft in her service; but this was only half the influence that pressed him into forgetfulness of what he had most said to himself when, in Lomax Place, in an hour of unprecedented introspection, he wrote the letter by which he accepted the invitation to Medley. He would go there (so he said), because a man must be gallant, especially if he be a little bookbinder; but after he should be there he would insist at every step upon knowing what he was in for. The change that had taken place in him now, from one moment to another, was that he had simply ceased to care what he was in for. All warnings, reflections, considerations of verisimilitude, of the delicate, the natural and the possible, of the value of his independence, had become as nothing to him. The cup of an exquisite experience—a week in that enchanted palace, a week of such immunity from Lomax Place and old Crookenden as he had never dreamed of—was at his lips; it was purple with the wine of novelty, of civilisation, and he couldn't push it aside without drinking. He might go home ashamed, but he would have for evermore in his mouth the taste of nectar. He went upstairs, under the eye of the butler, and on his way to his room, at the turning of a corridor, found himself face to face with Madame Grandoni. She had apparently just issued from her own apartment, the door of which stood open, near her; she might have been hovering there in expectation of his footstep. She had donned her dressing-gown, which appeared to give her every facility for respiration, but she had not yet parted with her wig. She still had her pink French book under her arm; and her fat little hands, tightly locked together in front of her, formed the clasp of her generous girdle.

'Do tell me it is positive, Mr. Robinson!' she said, stopping short.

'What is positive, Madame Grandoni?'

'That you take the train in the morning.'

'I can't tell you that, because it wouldn't be true. On the contrary, it has been settled that I shall stay over. I am very sorry if it distresses you—but *che vuole?*' Hyacinth added, smiling.

Madame Grandoni was a humorous woman, but she gave him no smile in return; she only looked at him a moment, and then, shrugging her shoulders silently but expressively, shuffled back to her room.

XXIV

I CAN give you your friend's name—in a single guess. He is Diedrich Hoffendahl!' They had been strolling more and more slowly, the next morning, and as she made this announcement the Princess stopped altogether, standing there under a great beech with her eyes upon Hyacinth's and her hands full of primroses. He had breakfasted at noon, with his hostess and Madame Grandoni, but the old lady had fortunately not joined them when the Princess afterwards proposed that he should accompany her on her walk in the park. She told him that her venerable friend had let her know, while the day was still very young, that she thought it in the worst possible taste of the Princess not to have allowed Mr. Robinson to depart; to which Christina had replied that concerning tastes there was no disputing and that they had disagreed on such matters before without any one being the worse. Hyacinth expressed the hope that they wouldn't dispute about *him*—of all thankless subjects in the world; and the Princess assured him that she never disputed about anything. She held that there were other ways than that of arranging one's relations with people; and Hyacinth guessed that she meant that when a difference became sharp she broke off altogether. On her side, then, there was as little possibility as on his that they should ever quarrel; their acquaintance would be a solid friendship or it would be nothing at all. The Princess gave it from hour to hour more of this quality, and it may be imagined how safe Hyacinth felt by the time he began to tell her that something had happened to him, in London, three months before, one night (or rather in the small hours of the morning), that had altered his life altogether—had, indeed, as he might say, changed the terms on which he held it. He was aware that he didn't know exactly what he meant by this last phrase; but it expressed sufficiently well the new feeling that had come over him since that interminable, tantalising cab-drive in the rain.

The Princess had led to this, almost as soon as they left the house; making up for her avoidance of such topics the day before by saying, suddenly, 'Now tell me what is going

284

on among your friends. I don't mean your worldly acquaintances, but your colleagues, your brothers. *Où en êtes-vous*, at
the present time? Is there anything new, is anything going
to be done; I am afraid you are always simply dawdling and
muddling.' Hyacinth felt as if, of late, he had by no means
either dawdled or muddled; but before he had committed
himself so far as to refute the imputation the Princess exclaimed, in another tone, 'How annoying it is that I can't
ask you anything without giving you the right to say to
yourself, "After all, what do I know? May she not be in the
pay of the police?" '

'Oh, that doesn't occur to me,' said Hyacinth, with a smile.

'It might, at all events; by which I mean it may, at any
moment. Indeed, I think it ought.'

'If you were in the pay of the police you wouldn't trouble
your head about me.'

'I should make you think that, certainly! That would be my
first care. However, if you have no tiresome suspicions so
much the better,' said the Princess; and she pressed him again
for some news from behind the scenes.

In spite of his absence of doubt on the subject of her honesty—he felt that he should never again entertain any such
trumpery idea as that she might be an agent on the wrong
side—he did not open himself immediately; but at the end of
half an hour he let her know that the most important event of
his life had taken place, scarcely more than the other day, in
the most unexpected manner. And to explain in what it had
consisted, he said, 'I pledged myself, by everything that is
sacred.'

'To what did you pledge yourself?'

'I took a vow—a tremendous, terrible vow—in the presence of four witnesses,' Hyacinth went on.

'And what was it about, your vow?'

'I gave my life away,' said Hyacinth, smiling.

She looked at him askance, as if to see how he would make
such an announcement as that; but she wore no smile—her
face was politely grave. They moved together a moment, exchanging a glance, in silence, and then she said, 'Ah, well,
then, I'm all the more glad you stayed!'

'That was one of the reasons.'

'I wish you had waited—till after you had been here,' the Princess remarked.

'Why till after I had been here?'

'Perhaps then you wouldn't have given away your life. You might have seen reasons for keeping it.' And now, at last, she treated the matter gaily, as Hyacinth had done. He replied that he had not the least doubt that, on the whole, her influence was relaxing; but without heeding this remark she went on: 'Be so good as to tell me what you are talking about.'

'I'm not afraid of you, but I'll give you no names,' said Hyacinth; and he related what had happened in the back-room in Bloomsbury, in the course of that evening of which I have given some account. The Princess listened, intently, while they strolled under the budding trees with a more interrupted step. Never had the old oaks and beeches, renewing themselves in the sunshine as they did to-day, or naked in some gray November, witness such an extraordinary series of confidences, since the first pair that sought isolation wandered over the grassy slopes and ferny dells beneath them. Among other things Hyacinth mentioned to his companion that he didn't go to the 'Sun and Moon' any more; he now perceived, what he ought to have perceived long before, that this particular temple of their faith, and everything that pretended to get hatched there, was a hopeless sham. He had been a rare muff, from the first, to take it seriously. He had done so mainly because a friend of his, in whom he had confidence, appeared to set him the example; but now it turned out that this friend (it was Paul Muniment again, by the way) had always thought the men who went there a pack of duffers and was only trying them because he tried everything. There was nobody you could begin to call a first-rate man there, putting aside another friend of his, a Frenchman named Poupin—and Poupin was magnificent, but he wasn't first-rate. Hyacinth had a standard, now that he had seen a man who was the very incarnation of a programme. You felt that *he* was a big chap the very moment you came into his presence.

'Into whose presence, Mr. Robinson?' the Princess inquired.

'I don't know that I ought to tell you, much as I believe in you! I am speaking of the very remarkable individual with whom I entered into that engagement.'

'To give away your life?'

'To do something which in a certain contingency he will require of me. He will require my poor little carcass.'

'Those plans have a way of failing—unfortunately,' the Princess murmured, adding the last word more quickly.

'Is that a consolation, or a lament?' Hyacinth asked. 'This one shall not fail, so far as it depends on me. They wanted an obliging young man—the place was vacant—I stepped in.'

'I have no doubt you are right. We must pay for what we do.' The Princess made that remark calmly and coldly; then she said, 'I think I know the person in whose power you have placed yourself.'

'Possibly, but I doubt it.'

'You can't believe I have already gone so far? Why not? I have given you a certain amount of proof that I don't hang back.'

'Well, if you know my friend, you have gone very far indeed.'

The Princess appeared to be on the point of pronouncing a name; but she checked herself, and asked suddenly, smiling, 'Don't they also want, by chance, an obliging young woman?'

'I happen to know he doesn't think much of women, my first-rate man. He doesn't trust them.'

'Is that why you call him first-rate? You have very nearly betrayed him to me.'

'Do you imagine there is only one of that opinion?' Hyacinth inquired.

'Only one who, having it, still remains a superior man. That's a very difficult opinion to reconcile with others which it is important to have.'

'Schopenhauer did so, successfully,' said Hyacinth.

'How delightful that you should know Schopenhauer!' The Princess exclaimed. 'The gentleman I have in my eye is also German.' Hyacinth let this pass, not challenging her, because he wished not to be challenged in return, and the Princess went on, 'Of course such an engagement as you speak of must make a tremendous difference, in everything.'

'It has made this difference, that I have now a far other sense from any I had before of the reality, the solidity, of what is being prepared. I was hanging about outside, on the steps of the temple, among the loafers and the gossips, but now I have been in the innermost sanctuary—I have seen the holy of holies.'

'And it's very dazzling?'

'Ah, Princess!' sighed the young man.

'Then it *is* real, it *is* solid?' she pursued. 'That's exactly what I have been trying to make up my mind about, for so long.'

'It is more strange than I can say. Nothing of it appears above the surface; but there is an immense underworld, peopled with a thousand forms of revolutionary passion and devotion. The manner in which it is organised is what astonished me; I knew that, or thought I knew it, in a general way, but the reality was a revelation. And on top of it all, society lives! People go and come, and buy and sell, and drink and dance, and make money and make love, and seem to know nothing and suspect nothing and think of nothing; and iniquities flourish, and the misery of half the world is prated about as a 'necessary evil,' and generations rot away and starve, in the midst of it, and day follows day, and everything is for the best in the best of possible worlds. All that is one-half of it; the other half is that everything is doomed! In silence, in darkness, but under the feet of each one of us, the revolution lives and works. It is a wonderful, immeasurable trap, on the lid of which society performs its antics. When once the machinery is complete, there will be a great rehearsal. That rehearsal is what they want me for. The invisible, impalpable wires are everywhere, passing through everything, attaching themselves to objects in which one would never think of looking for them. What could be more strange and incredible, for instance, than that they should exist just here?'

'You make me believe it,' said the Princess, thoughtfully.

'It matters little whether one believes it or not!'

'You have had a vision,' the Princess continued.

'*Parbleu*, I have had a vision! So would you, if you had been there.'

'I wish I had!' she declared, in a tone charged with such ambiguous implications that Hyacinth, catching them a moment after she had spoken, rejoined, with a quick, incongruous laugh—

'No, you would have spoiled everything. He made me see, he made me feel, he made me do, everything he wanted.'

'And why should he have wanted you, in particular?'

'Simply because I struck him as the right person. That's his affair: I can't tell you. When he meets the right person he chalks him. I sat on the bed. (There were only two chairs in the dirty little room, and by way of a curtain his overcoat was hung up before the window.) He didn't sit, himself; he leaned against the wall, straight in front of me, with his hands behind him. He told me certain things, and his manner was extraordinarily quiet. So was mine, I think I may say; and indeed it was only poor Poupin who made a row. It was for my sake, somehow: he didn't think we were all conscious enough; he wanted to call attention to my sublimity. There was no sublimity about it—I simply couldn't help myself. He and the other German had the two chairs, and Muniment sat on a queer old battered, hair-covered trunk, a most foreign-looking article.' Hyacinth had taken no notice of the little ejaculation with which his companion greeted, in this last sentence, the word 'other.'

'And what did Mr. Muniment say?' she presently inquired.

'Oh, he said it was all right. Of course he thought that, from the moment he determined to bring me. He knew what the other fellow was looking for.'

'I see.' Then the Princess remarked, 'We have a curious way of being fond of you.'

'Whom do you mean by "we"?'

'Your friends. Mr. Muniment and I, for instance.'

'I like it as well as any other. But you don't feel alike. I have an idea you are sorry.'

'Sorry for what?'

'That I have put my head in a noose.'

'Ah, you're severe—I thought I concealed it so well!' The Princess exclaimed. He admitted that he had been severe, and begged her pardon, for he was by no means sure that there was not a hint of tears in her voice. She looked away from him for a minute, and it was after this that, stopping short, she remarked, as I have related, 'He is Diedrich Hoffendahl.'

Hyacinth stared for a moment, with parted lips. 'Well, you *are* in it, more than I supposed!'

'You know he doesn't trust women,' his companion smiled.

'Why in the world should you have cared for any light *I* can throw, if you have ever been in relation with him?'

She hesitated a little. 'Oh, you are very different. I like you better,' she added.

'Ah, if it's for that!' murmured Hyacinth.

The Princess coloured, as he had seen her colour before, and in this accident, on her part, there was an unexpectedness, something touching. 'Don't try to fix my inconsistencies on me,' she said, with a humility which matched her blush. 'Of course there are plenty of them, but it will always be kinder of you to let them pass. Besides, in this case they are not so serious as they seem. As a product of the 'people,' and of that strange, fermenting underworld (what you say of it is so true!) you interest me more, and have more to say to me, even than Hoffendahl—wonderful creature as he assuredly is.'

'Would you object to telling me how and where you came to know him?'

'Through a couple of friends of mine in Vienna, two of the affiliated, both passionate revolutionists and clever men. They are Neapolitans, originally *poveretti*, like yourself, who emigrated, years ago, to seek their fortune. One of them is a teacher of singing, the wisest, most accomplished person in his line I have ever known. The other, if you please, is a confectioner! He makes the most delicious *pâtisserie fine*. It would take long to tell you how I made *their* acquaintance, and how they put me into relation with the Maestro, as they called him, of whom they spoke with bated breath. It is not from yesterday—though you don't seem able to believe it—that I have had a care for all this business. I wrote to Hoffendahl, and had several letters from him; the singing-master and the pastry-cook went bail for my sincerity. The next year I had an interview with him at Wiesbaden; but I can't tell you the circumstances of our meeting, in that place, without implicating another person, to whom, at present at least, I have no right to give you a clue. Of course Hoffendahl made an immense impression on me; he seemed to me the Master indeed, the very genius of a new social order, and I fully understand the manner in which you were affected by him. When he was in London, three months ago, I knew it, and I knew where to write to him. I did so, and asked him if he wouldn't see me somewhere. I said I would meet him in any hole he should designate. He answered by a charming letter, which I will show you—there is nothing in the least compromising in it—but he declined my offer, pleading his short stay and a press of engagements. He will write to me, but he won't trust me. However, he shall some day!'

Hyacinth was thrown quite off his balance by this representation of the ground the Princess had already traversed, and the explanation was still but half restorative when, on his asking her why she hadn't exhibited her titles before, she replied, 'Well, I thought my being quiet was the better way to draw you out.' There was but little difficulty in drawing him out now, and before their walk was over he had told her more definitely what Hoffendahl demanded. This was simply that he should hold himself ready, for the next five years, to do, at a given moment, an act which would in all probability cost him his life. The act was as yet indefinite, but one might get an idea of it from the penalty involved, which would certainly be capital. The only thing settled was that it was to be done instantly and absolutely, without a question, a hesitation or a scruple, in the manner that should be prescribed, at the moment, from headquarters. Very likely it would be to kill some one—some humbug in a high place; but whether the individual should deserve it or should not deserve it was not Hyacinth's affair. If he recognised generally Hoffendahl's wisdom—and the other night it had seemed to shine like a northern aurora—it was not in order that he might challenge it in the particular case. He had taken a vow of blind obedience, as the Jesuit fathers did to the head of their order. It was because they had carried out their vows (having, in the first place, great administrators) that their organisation had been mighty, and that sort of mightiness was what people who felt as Hyacinth and the Princess felt should go in for. It was not certain that he should be collared, any more than it was certain that he should bring down his man; but it was much to be looked for, and it was what he counted on and indeed preferred. He should probably take little trouble to escape, and he should never enjoy the idea of hiding (after the fact), or running away. If it were a question of putting a bullet into some one, he himself should naturally deserve what would come to him. If one did that sort of thing there was an indelicacy in not being ready to pay for it; and he, at least, was perfectly willing. He shouldn't judge; he should simply execute. He didn't pretend to say what good his little job might do, or what *portée* it might have; he hadn't the data for appreciating it, and simply took upon himself to believe that at headquarters they knew what they were about. The thing was to be a feature in a very large plan, of which he couldn't measure the scope—something that was to be done simultaneously in a dozen different countries. The effect was to be very much in this immense coincidence. It was to be hoped it wouldn't be spoiled. At any rate, *he* wouldn't hang fire, whatever the other fellows might do. He didn't say it because Hoffendahl had done him the honour of giving him the business to do, but he believed the Master knew how to pick out his men. To be sure, Hoffendahl had known nothing about him in advance; he had only been suggested by those who were looking out, from one day to the other. The fact remained however that when Hyacinth stood before him he recognised him as the sort of little chap that he had in his eye (one who could pass through a small orifice). Humanity, in his scheme, was classified and subdivided with a truly German thoroughness, and altogether of course from the point of view of the revolution, as it might forward or obstruct it. Hyacinth's little job was a very small part of what Hoffendahl had come to England for; he had in his hand innumerable other threads. Hyacinth knew nothing of these, and didn't much want to know, except that it was marvellous, the way Hoffendahl kept them apart. He had exactly the same mastery of them that a great musician—that the Princess herself—had of the keyboard of the piano; he treated all things, persons, institutions, ideas, as so many notes in his great symphonic revolt. The day would come when Hyacinth, far down in the treble, would feel himself touched by the little finger of the composer, would become audible (with a small, sharp crack) for a second.

It was impossible that our young man should not feel, at the end of ten minutes, that he had charmed the Princess into the deepest, most genuine attention; she was listening to him as she had never listened before. He enjoyed having that effect upon her, and his sense of the tenuity of the thread by which his future hung, renewed by his hearing himself talk about it, made him reflect that at present anything in the line of enjoyment was so much gained. The reader may judge whether he had passed through a phase of excitement after finding himself on his new footing of utility in the world; but that had finally spent itself, through a hundred forms of restlessness, of vain conjecture—through an exaltation which alternated with despair and which, equally with the despair, he concealed more successfully than he supposed. He would have detested the idea that his companion might have heard his voice tremble while he told his story; but though to-day he had really grown used to his danger and resigned, as it were, to his consecration, and though it could not fail to be agreeable to him to perceive that he was thrilling, he could still not guess how very remarkable, in such a connection, the Princess thought his composure, his lucidity and good-humour. It is true she tried to hide her wonder, for she owed it to her self-respect to let it still appear that even she was prepared for a personal sacrifice as complete. She had the air—or she endeavoured to have it—of accepting for him everything that he accepted for himself; nevertheless, there was something rather forced in the smile (lovely as it was) with which she covered him, while she said, after a little, 'It's very serious—it's very serious indeed, isn't it?' He replied that the serious part was to come—there was no particular grimness for him (comparatively) in strolling in that sweet park and gossiping with her about the matter; and it occurred to her presently to suggest to him that perhaps Hoffendahl would never give him any sign at all, and he would wait all the while, *sur les dents*, in a false suspense. He admitted that this would be a sell, but declared that either way he would be sold, though differently; and that at any rate he would have conformed to the great religious rule—to live each hour as if it were to be one's last.

'In holiness, you mean—in great *recueillement?*' the Princess asked.

'Oh dear, no; simply in extreme thankfulness for every minute that's added.'

'Ah, well, there will probably be a great many,' she rejoined.

'The more the better—if they are like this.'

'That won't be the case with many of them, in Lomax Place.'

'I assure you that since that night Lomax Place has improved.' Hyacinth stood there, smiling, with his hands in his pockets and his hat pushed back a little.

The Princess appeared to consider this fact with an extreme intellectual curiosity. 'If, after all, then, you are not called, you will have been positively happy.'

'I shall have had some fine moments. Perhaps Hoffendahl's plot is simply for that; Muniment may have put him up to it!'

'Who knows? However, with me you must go on as if nothing were changed.'

'Changed from what?'

'From the time of our first meeting at the theatre.'

'I'll go on in any way you like,' said Hyacinth; 'only the real difference will be there.'

'The real difference?'

'That I shall have ceased to care for what you care about.'

'I don't understand,' said the Princess.

'Isn't it enough, now, to give my life to the beastly cause,' the young man broke out, 'without giving my sympathy?'

'The beastly cause?' the Princess murmured, opening her deep eyes.

'Of course it is really just as holy as ever; only the people I find myself pitying now are the rich, the happy.'

'I see. You are very curious. Perhaps you pity my husband,' the Princess added in a moment.

'Do you call him one of the happy?' Hyacinth inquired, as they walked on again.

In answer to this she only repeated, 'You are very curious!'

I have related the whole of this conversation, because it supplies a highly important chapter of Hyacinth's history, but it will not be possible to trace all the stages through which the friendship of the Princess Casamassima with the young man she had constituted her bookbinder was confirmed. By the end of a week the standard of fitness she had set up in the place of exploded proprieties appeared the model of justice and convenience; and during this period many other things happened. One of them was that Hyacinth drove over to Broome with his hostess, and called on Lady Marchant and her daughters; an episode from which the Princess appeared to derive an exquisite gratification. When they came away he asked her why she hadn't told the ladies who he was. Otherwise, where was the point? And she replied, 'Simply because they wouldn't have believed me. That's your fault!' This was the same note she had struck when, the third day of his stay (the weather had changed for the worse, and a rainy afternoon kept them in-doors), she remarked to him, irrelevantly and abruptly, 'It *is* most extraordinary, your knowing about Schopenhauer!' He answered that she really seemed quite unable to accustom herself to his little talents; and this led to a long talk, longer than the one I have already narrated, in which he took her still further into his confidence. Never had the pleasure of conversation (the greatest he knew), been so largely opened to him. The Princess admitted, frankly, that he would, to her sense, take a great deal of accounting for; she observed that he was, no doubt, pretty well used to himself, but he must give other people time. 'I have watched you, constantly, since you have been here, in every detail of your behaviour, and I am more and more *intriguée*. You haven't a vulgar intonation, you haven't a common gesture, you never make a mistake, you do and say everything exactly in the right way. You come out of the hole you have described to me, and yet you might have stayed in country-houses all your life. You are much better than if you had! *Jugez donc*, from the way I talk to you! I have to make no allowances. I have seen Italians with that sort of natural tact and taste, but I didn't know one ever found it in any Anglo-Saxon in whom it hadn't been cultivated at a vast expense; unless, indeed, in certain little American women.'

'Do you mean I'm a gentleman?' asked Hyacinth, in a peculiar tone, looking out into the wet garden.

She hesitated, and then she said, 'It's I who make the mistakes!' Five minutes later she broke into an exclamation which touched him almost more than anything she had ever done, giving him the highest opinion of her delicacy and sympathy and putting him before himself as vividly as if the words were a little portrait. 'Fancy the strange, the bitter fate: to be constituted as you are constituted, to feel the capacity that you must feel, and yet to look at the good things of life only through the glass of the pastry-cook's window!'

'Every class has its pleasures,' Hyacinth rejoined, with perverse sententiousness, in spite of his emotion; but the remark didn't darken their mutual intelligence, and before they separated that evening he told her the things that had never yet passed his lips—the things to which he had awaked when he made Pinnie explain to him the visit to the prison. He told her, in a word, what he was.

XXV

HYACINTH took several long walks by himself, beyond the gates of the park and through the neighbouring country—walks during which, committed as he was to reflection on the general 'rumness' of his destiny, he had still a delighted attention to spare for the green dimness of leafy lanes, the attraction of meadow-paths that led from stile to stile and seemed a clue to some pastoral happiness, some secret of the fields; the hedges thick with flowers, bewilderingly common, for which he knew no names, the picture-making quality of thatched cottages, the mystery and sweetness of blue distances, the bloom of rural complexions, the quaintness of little girls bobbing curtsies by waysides (a sort of homage he had never prefigured); the soft sense of the turf under feet that had never ached but from paving-stones. One morning, as he had his face turned homeward, after a long stroll, he heard behind him the sound of a horse's hoofs, and, looking back, perceived a gentleman, who would presently pass him, advancing up the road which led to the lodge-gates of Medley. He went his way and, as the horse overtook him, noticed that the rider slackened pace. Then he turned again, and recognised in this personage his brilliant occasional friend Captain Sholto. The Captain pulled up alongside of him, saluting him with a smile and a movement of the whip-handle. Hyacinth stared with surprise, not having heard from the Princess that she was expecting him. He gathered, however, in a moment, that she was not; and meanwhile he received an impression, on Sholto's part, of riding-gear that was 'knowing'—of gaiters and spurs and a curious waistcoat; perceiving that this was a phase of the Captain's varied nature which he had not yet had an opportunity to observe. He struck him as very high in the air, perched on his big, lean chestnut, and Hyacinth noticed that if the horse was heated the rider was cool.

'Good-morning, my dear fellow. I thought I should find you here!' the Captain exclaimed. 'It's a good job I've met you this way, without having to go to the house.'

'Who gave you reason to think I was here?' Hyacinth

asked; partly occupied with the appositeness of this inquiry and partly thinking, as his eyes wandered over his handsome friend, bestriding so handsome a beast, what a jolly thing it would be to know how to ride. He had already, during the few days he had been at Medley, had time to observe that the knowledge of luxury and the extension of one's sensations beget a taste for still newer pleasures.

'Why, I knew the Princess was capable of asking you,' Sholto said; 'and I learned at the "Sun and Moon" that you had not been there for a long time. I knew furthermore that as a general thing you go there a good deal, don't you? So I put this and that together, and judged you were out of town.'

This was very luminous and straightforward, and might have satisfied Hyacinth were it not for that irritating reference to the Princess's being 'capable of asking him.' He knew as well as the Captain that it had been tremendously eccentric in her to do so, but somehow a transformation had lately taken place in him which made it disagreeable for him to receive that view from another, and particularly from a gentleman of whom, on a certain occasion, several months before, he had had strong grounds for thinking unfavourably. He had not seen Sholto since the evening when a queer combination of circumstances caused him, more queerly still, to sit and listen to comic songs in the company of Millicent Henning and this admirer. The Captain did not conceal his admiration; Hyacinth had his own ideas about his taking that line in order to look more innocent. That evening, when he accompanied Millicent to her lodgings (they parted with Sholto on coming out of the Pavilion), the situation was tense between the young lady and her childhood's friend. She let him have it, as she said; she gave him a dressing which she evidently intended should be memorable, for having suspected her, for having insulted her before a military gentleman. The tone she took, and the magnificent audacity with which she took it, reduced him to a kind of gratified helplessness; he watched her at last with something of the excitement with which he would have watched a clever but uncultivated actress, while she worked herself into a passion which he believed to be fictitious. He gave more credence to his jealousy and to the whole air of the case than to her vehement repudiations, enlivened though these were by tremendous head-tossings and skirt-shakings. But he felt baffled and outfaced, and took refuge in sarcasms which after all proved as little as her high gibes; seeking a final solution in one of those beastly little French shrugs, as Millicent called them, with which she had already reproached him with interlarding his conversation.

The air was never cleared, though the subject of their dispute was afterwards dropped, Hyacinth promising himself to watch his playmate as he had never done before. She let him know, as may well be supposed, that she had her eye on *him*, and it must be confessed that as regards the exercise of a right of supervision he had felt himself at a disadvantage ever since the night at the theatre. It mattered little that she had pushed him into the Princess's box (for she herself had not been jealous beforehand; she had wanted too much to know what such a person could be 'up to,' desiring, perhaps, to borrow a hint), and it mattered little, also, that his relations with the great lady were all for the sake of suffering humanity; the atmosphere, none the less, was full of thunder for many weeks, and it scarcely signified from which quarter the flash and the explosion proceeded. Hyacinth was a good deal surprised to find that he should care whether Millicent deceived him or not, and even tried to persuade himself that he didn't; but there was a grain of conviction in his heart that some kind of personal affinity existed between them and that it would torment him more never to see her at all than to see her go into tantrums in order to cover her tracks. An inner sense told him that her mingled beauty and grossness, her vulgar vitality, the spirit of contradiction yet at the same time of attachment that was in her, had ended by making her indispensable to him. She bored him as much as she irritated him; but if she was full of execrable taste she was also full of life, and her rustlings and chatterings, her wonderful stories, her bad grammar and good health, her insatiable thirst, her shrewd perceptions and grotesque opinions, her mistakes and her felicities, were now all part of the familiar human sound of his little world. He could say to himself that she came after him much more than he went after her, and this helped him, a little, to believe, though the logic was but lame, that she was

not making a fool of him. If she were really taking up with a
swell he didn't see why she wished to retain a bookbinder. Of
late, it must be added, he had ceased to devote much consideration to Millicent's ambiguities; for although he was lingering on at Medley for the sake of suffering humanity he was
quite aware that to say so (if she should ask him for a reason)
would have almost as absurd a sound as some of the girl's
own speeches. As regards Sholto, he was in the awkward position of having let him off, as it were, by accepting his hospitality, his bounty; so that he couldn't quarrel with him
except on a fresh pretext. This pretext the Captain had apparently been careful not to give, and Millicent had told him,
after the triple encounter in the street, that he had driven him
out of England, the poor gentleman whom he insulted by his
low insinuations even more (why 'even more' Hyacinth
hardly could think) than he outraged herself. When he asked
her what she knew about the Captain's movements she made
no scruple to announce to him that the latter had come to her
great shop to make a little purchase (it was a pair of silk
braces, if she remembered rightly, and she admitted, perfectly,
the transparency of the pretext), and had asked her with much
concern whether his gifted young friend (that's what he
called him—Hyacinth could see he meant well) was still in a
huff. Millicent had answered that she was afraid he was—
the more shame to him; and then the Captain had said that
it didn't matter, for he himself was on the point of leaving
England for several weeks (Hyacinth—he called him Hyacinth this time—couldn't have ideas about a man in a foreign country, could he?), and he hoped that by the time he
returned the little cloud would have blown over. Sholto had
added that she had better tell him frankly—recommending
her at the same time to be gentle with their morbid friend—
about his visit to the shop. Their candour, their humane precautions, were all very well; but after this, two or three
evenings, Hyacinth passed and repassed the Captain's chambers in Queen Anne Street, to see if, at the window, there
were signs of his being in London. Darkness, however, prevailed, and he was forced to comfort himself a little when, at
last making up his mind to ring at the door and inquire, by
way of a test, for the occupant, he was informed, by the

superior valet whose acquaintance he had already made, and whose air of wearing a jacket left behind by his master confirmed the statement, that the gentleman in question was at Monte Carlo.

'Have you still got your back up a little?' the Captain demanded, without rancour; and in a moment he had swung a long leg over the saddle and dismounted, walking beside his young friend and leading his horse by the bridle. Hyacinth pretended not to know what he meant, for it came over him that after all, even if he had not condoned, at the time, the Captain's suspected treachery, he was in no position, sitting at the feet of the Princess, to sound the note of jealousy in relation to another woman. He reflected that the Princess had originally been, in a manner, Sholto's property, and if he did *en fin de compte* wish to quarrel with him about Millicent he would have to cease to appear to poach on the Captain's preserves. It now occurred to him, for the first time, that the latter had intended a kind of exchange; though it must be added that the Princess, who on a couple of occasions had alluded slightingly to her military friend, had given him no sign of recognising this gentleman's claim. Sholto let him know, at present, that he was staying at Bonchester, seven miles off; he had come down from London and put up at the inn. That morning he had ridden over on a hired horse (Hyacinth had supposed this steed was a very fine animal, but Sholto spoke of it as an infernal screw); he had been taken by the sudden fancy of seeing how his young friend was coming on.

'I'm coming on very well, thank you,' said Hyacinth, with some shortness, not knowing exactly what business it was of the Captain's.

'Of course you understand my interest in you, don't you? I'm responsible for you—I put you forward.'

'There are a great many things in the world that I don't understand, but I think the thing I understand least is your interest in me. Why the devil——' And Hyacinth paused, breathless with the force of his inquiry. Then he went on, 'If I were you, I shouldn't care a filbert for the sort of person that I happen to be.'

'That proves how different my nature is to yours! But I

don't believe it, my boy; you are too generous for that.'
Sholto's imperturbability always appeared to grow with the
irritation it produced, and it was proof even against the just
resentment excited by his want of tact. That want of tact was
sufficiently marked when he went on to say, 'I wanted to see
you here, with my own eyes. I wanted to see how it looked; it
is a rum sight! Of course you know what I mean, though you
are always trying to make a fellow explain. I don't explain
well, in any sense, and that's why I go in only for clever
people, who can do without it. It's very grand, her having
brought you down.'

'Grand, no doubt, but hardly surprising, considering that,
as you say, I was put forward by you.'

'Oh, that's a great thing for me, but it doesn't make any
difference to her!' Sholto exclaimed. 'She may care for certain
things for themselves, but it will never signify a jot to her
what I may have thought about them. One good turn deserves another. I wish you would put *me* forward!'

'I don't understand you, and I don't think I want to,' said
Hyacinth, as his companion strolled beside him.

The latter put a hand on his arm, stopping him, and they
stood face to face a moment. 'I say, my dear Robinson, you're
not spoiled already, at the end of a week—how long is it? It
isn't possible you're jealous!'

'Jealous of whom?' asked Hyacinth, whose failure to comprehend was perfectly genuine.

Sholto looked at him a moment; then, with a laugh, 'I
don't mean Miss Henning.' Hyacinth turned away, and the
Captain resumed his walk, now taking the young man's arm
and passing his own through the bridle of the horse. 'The
courage of it, the insolence, the *crânerie*! There isn't another
woman in Europe who could carry it off.'

Hyacinth was silent a little; after which he remarked, 'This
is nothing, here. You should have seen me the other day over
at Broome, at Lady Marchant's.'

'Gad, did she take you there? I'd have given ten pounds
to see it. There's no one like her!' cried the Captain, gaily,
enthusiastically.

'There's no one like me, I think—for going.'

'Why, didn't you enjoy it?'

'Too much—too much. Such excesses are dangerous.'

'Oh, I'll back you,' said the Captain; then, checking their pace, he inquired, 'Is there any chance of our meeting her? I won't go into the park.'

'You won't go to the house?' Hyacinth demanded, staring.

'Oh dear, no, not while you're there.'

'Well, I shall ask the Princess about you, and have done with it, once for all.'

'Lucky little beggar, with your fireside talks!' the Captain exclaimed. 'Where does she sit now, in the evening? She won't tell you anything except that I'm a nuisance; but even if she were willing to take the trouble to throw some light upon me it wouldn't be of much use, because she doesn't understand me herself.'

'You are the only thing in the world then of which that can be said,' Hyacinth returned.

'I dare say I am, and I am rather proud of it. So far as the head is concerned, the Princess is all there. I told you, when I presented you, that she was the cleverest woman in Europe, and that is still my opinion. But there are some mysteries you can't see into unless you happen to have a little heart. The Princess hasn't, though doubtless just now you think that's her strong point. One of these days you'll see. I don't care a straw, myself, whether she has or not. She has hurt me already so much she can't hurt me any more, and my interest in her is quite independent of that. To watch her, to adore her, to see her lead her life and act out her extraordinary nature, all the while she treats me like a brute, is the only thing I care for to-day. It doesn't do me a scrap of good, but, all the same, it's my principal occupation. You may believe me or not—it doesn't in the least matter; but I'm the most disinterested human being alive. She'll tell you I'm a tremendous ass, and so one is. But that isn't all.'

It was Hyacinth who stopped this time, arrested by something new and natural in the tone of his companion, a simplicity of emotion which he had not hitherto associated with him. He stood there a moment looking up at him, and thinking again what improbable confidences it decidedly appeared to be his lot to receive from gentlefolks. To what quality in himself were they a tribute? The honour was one he could easily dispense with; though as he scrutinised Sholto he found something in his curious light eyes—an expression of cheerfulness not disconnected from veracity—which put him into a less fantastic relation with this jaunty, factitious personage. 'Please go on,' he said, in a moment.

'Well, what I mentioned just now is my real and only motive, in anything. The rest is mere gammon and rubbish, to cover it up—or to give myself the change, as the French say.'

'What do you mean by the rest?' asked Hyacinth, thinking of Millicent Henning.

'Oh, all the straw one chews, to cheat one's appetite; all the rot one dabbles in, because it may lead to something which it never does lead to; all the beastly buncombe (you know) that you and I have heard together in Bloomsbury and that I myself have poured out, damme, with an eloquence worthy of a better cause. Don't you remember what I have said to you— all as my own opinion—about the impending change of the relations of class with class? Impending fiddlesticks! I believe those that are on top the heap are better than those that are under it, that they mean to stay there, and that if they are not a pack of poltroons they will.'

'You don't care for the social question, then?' Hyacinth inquired, with an aspect of which he was conscious of the blankness.

'I only took it up because she did. It hasn't helped me,' Sholto remarked, smiling. 'My dear Robinson,' he went on, 'there is only one thing I care for in life: to have a look at that woman when I can, and when I can't, to approach her in the sort of way I'm doing now.'

'It's a very curious sort of way.'

'Indeed it is; but if it is good enough for me it ought to be good enough for you. What I want you to do is this—to induce her to ask me over to dine.'

'To induce her——?' Hyacinth murmured.

'Tell her I'm staying at Bonchester and it would be an act of common humanity.'

They proceeded till they reached the gates, and in a moment Hyacinth said, 'You took up the social question, then, because she did; but do you happen to know why she took it up?'

'Ah, my dear fellow, you must find that out for yourself. I found you the place, but I can't do your work for you!'

'I see—I see. But perhaps you'll tell me this: if you had free access to the Princess a year ago, taking her to the theatre and that sort of thing, why shouldn't you have it now?'

This time Sholto's white pupils looked strange again. '*You* have it now, my dear fellow, but I'm afraid it doesn't follow that you'll have it a year hence. She was tired of me then, and of course she's still more tired of me now, for the simple reason that I'm more tiresome. She has sent me to Coventry, and I want to come out for a few hours. See how conscientious I am—I won't pass the gates.'

'I'll tell her I met you,' said Hyacinth. Then, irrelevantly, he added, 'Is that what you mean by her having no heart?'

'Her treating me as she treats me? Oh, dear, no; her treating you!'

This had a portentous sound, but it did not prevent Hyacinth from turning round with his visitor (for it was the greatest part of the oddity of the present meeting that the hope of a little conversation with him, if accident were favourable, had been the motive not only of Sholto's riding over to Medley but of his coming down to stay, in the neighbourhood, at a musty inn in a dull market-town), it did not prevent him, I say, from bearing the Captain company for a mile on his backward way. Our young man did not pursue this particular topic much further, but he discovered still another reason or two for admiring the light, free action with which his companion had unmasked himself, and the nature of his interest in the revolutionary idea, after he had asked him, abruptly, what he had had in his head when he travelled over that evening, the summer before (he didn't appear to have come back as often as he promised), to Paul Muniment's place in Camberwell. What was he looking for, whom was he looking for, there?

'I was looking for anything that would turn up, that might take her fancy. Don't you understand that I'm always looking? There was a time when I went in immensely for illuminated missals, and another when I collected horrible ghost-stories (she wanted to cultivate a belief in ghosts), all for her. The day I saw she was turning her attention to the rising democracy I began to collect little democrats. That's how I collected you.'

'Muniment read you exactly, then. And what did you find to your purpose in Audley Court?'

'Well, I think the little woman with the popping eyes—she reminded me of a bedridden grasshopper—will do. And I made a note of the other one, the old virgin with the high nose, the aristocratic sister of mercy. I'm keeping them in reserve for my next propitiatory offering.'

Hyacinth was silent a moment. 'And Muniment himself—can't you do anything with him?'

'Oh, my dear fellow, after you he's poor!'

'That's the first stupid thing you have said. But it doesn't matter, for he dislikes the Princess—what he knows of her—too much ever to consent to see her.'

'That's his line, is it? Then he'll do!' Sholto cried.

XXVI

'OF COURSE he may come, and stay as long as he likes!'
the Princess exclaimed, when Hyacinth, that afternoon,
told her of his encounter, with the sweet, bright surprise her
face always wore when people went through the form (supererogatory she apparently meant to declare it) of asking
her leave. From the manner in which she granted Sholto's
petition—with a geniality that made light of it, as if the
question were not worth talking of, one way or the other—
it might have been supposed that the account he had given
Hyacinth of their relations was an elaborate but none the
less foolish hoax. She sent a messenger with a note over to
Bonchester, and the Captain arrived just in time to dress for
dinner. The Princess was always late, and Hyacinth's
toilet, on these occasions, occupied him considerably (he was
acutely conscious of its deficiencies, and yet tried to persuade
himself that they were positively honourable and that the
only garb of dignity, for him, was the costume, as it were, of
his profession); therefore when the fourth member of the little party descended to the drawing-room Madame Grandoni
was the only person he found there.

'*Santissima Vergine!* I'm glad to see you! What good wind
has sent you?' she exclaimed, as soon as Sholto came into the
room.

'Didn't you know I was coming?' he asked. 'Has the idea of
my arrival produced so little agitation?'

'I know nothing of the affairs of this house. I have given
them up at last, and it was time. I remain in my room.' There
was nothing at present in the old lady's countenance of her
usual spirit of cheer; it expressed anxiety, and even a certain
sternness, and the excellent woman had perhaps at this moment more than she had ever had in her life of the air of a
duenna who took her duties seriously. She looked almost august. 'From the moment you come it's a little better. But it is
very bad.'

'Very bad, dear madam?'

'Perhaps you will be able to tell me where Christina *veut
en venir*. I have always been faithful to her—I have always

been loyal. But to-day I have lost patience. It has no sense.'

'I am not sure I know what you are talking about,' Sholto said; 'but if I understand you I must tell you I think it's magnificent.'

'Yes, I know your tone; you are worse than she, because you are cynical. It passes all bounds. It is very serious. I have been thinking what I should do.'

'Precisely; I know what you would do.'

'Oh, this time I shouldn't come back!' the old lady declared. 'The scandal is too great; it is intolerable. My only fear is to make it worse.'

'Dear Madame Grandoni, you can't make it worse, and you can't make it better,' Sholto rejoined, seating himself on the sofa beside her. 'In point of fact, no idea of scandal can possibly attach itself to our friend. She is above and outside of all such considerations, such dangers. She carries everything off; she heeds so little, she cares so little. Besides, she has one great strength—she does no wrong.'

'Pray, what do you call it when a lady sends for a bookbinder to come and live with her?'

'Why not for a bookbinder as well as for a bishop? It all depends upon who the lady is, and what she is.'

'She had better take care of one thing first,' cried Madame Grandoni—'that she shall not have been separated from her husband!'

'The Princess can carry off even that. It's unusual, it's eccentric, it's fantastic, if you will, but it isn't necessarily wicked. From her own point of view our friend goes straight. Besides, she has her opinions.'

'Her opinions are perversity itself.'

'What does it matter,' asked Sholto, 'if they keep her quiet?'

'Quiet! Do you call this quiet?'

'Surely, if you'll only be so yourself. Putting the case at the worst, moreover, who is to know he's her bookbinder? It's the last thing you'd take him for.'

'Yes, for that she chose him carefully,' the old lady murmured, still with a discontented eyebrow.

'*She* chose him? It was I who chose him, dear lady!' The Captain exclaimed, with a laugh which showed how little he shared her solicitude.

'Yes, I had forgotten; at the theatre,' said Madame Grandoni, gazing at him as if her ideas were confused but a certain repulsion from her interlocutor nevertheless disengaged itself. 'It was a fine turn you did him there, poor young man!'

'Certainly, he will have to be sacrificed. But why was I bound to consider him so much? Haven't I been sacrificed myself?'

'Oh, if he bears it like you!' cried the old lady, with a short laugh.

'How do you know how I bear it? One does what one can,' said the Captain, settling his shirt-front. 'At any rate, remember this: she won't tell people who he is, for his own sake; and he won't tell them, for hers. So, as he looks much more like a poet, or a pianist, or a painter, there won't be that sensation you fear.'

'Even so it's bad enough,' said Madame Grandoni. 'And he's capable of bringing it out, suddenly, himself.'

'Ah, if he doesn't mind it, she won't! But that's his affair.'

'It's too terrible, to spoil him for his station,' the old lady went on. 'How can he ever go back?'

'If you want him kept, then, indefinitely, you are inconsistent. Besides, if he pays for it, he deserves to pay. He's an abominable little conspirator against society.'

Madame Grandoni was silent a moment; then she looked at the Captain with a gravity which might have been impressive to him, had not his accomplished jauntiness suggested an insensibility to that sort of influence. 'What, then, does Christina deserve?' she asked, with solemnity.

'Whatever she may get; whatever, in the future, may make her suffer. But it won't be the loss of her reputation. She is too distinguished.'

'You English are strange. Is it because she's a princess?' Madame Grandoni reflected, audibly.

'Oh, dear, no, her princedom is nothing here. We can easily beat that. But we can't beat——' And Sholto paused a moment.

'What then?' his companion asked.

'Well, the perfection of her indifference to public opinion and the unaffectedness of her originality; the sort of thing by which she has bedeviled me.'

'Oh, *you!*' murmured Madame Grandoni.

'If you think so poorly of me why did you say just now that you were glad to see me?' Sholto demanded, in a moment.

'Because you make another person in the house, and that is more regular; the situation is by so much less—what did you call it?—eccentric. *Nun,*' the old lady went on, in a moment, 'so long as you are here I won't go off.'

'Depend upon it that I shall be here until I'm turned out.'

She rested her small, troubled eyes upon him, but they betrayed no particular enthusiasm at this announcement. 'I don't understand how, for yourself, on such an occasion, you should like it.'

'Dear Madame Grandoni, the heart of man, without being such a hopeless labyrinth as the heart of woman, is still sufficiently complicated. Don't I know what will become of the little beggar?'

'You are very horrible,' said the ancient woman. Then she added, in a different tone, 'He is much too good for his fate.'

'And pray wasn't I, for mine?' the Captain asked.

'By no manner of means!' Madame Grandoni answered, rising and moving away from him.

The Princess had come into the room, accompanied by Hyacinth. As it was now considerably past the dinner-hour the old lady judged that this couple, on their side, had met in the hall and had prolonged their conversation there. Hyacinth watched with extreme interest the way the Princess greeted the Captain—observed that it was very simple, easy and friendly. At dinner she made no stranger of him, including him in everything, as if he had been a useful familiar, like Madame Grandoni, only a little less venerable, yet not giving him any attention that might cause their eyes to meet. She had told Hyacinth that she didn't like his eyes, nor indeed, very much, any part of him. Of course any admiration, from almost any source, could not fail to be in some degree agreeable to a woman, but of any little impression that one might ever have produced the mark she had made on Godfrey

Sholto was the one that ministered least to her vanity. He had been useful, undoubtedly, at times, but at others he had been an intolerable bore. He was so uninteresting in himself, so shallow, so unoccupied and superfluous, and really so frivolous, in spite of his pretension (of which she was unspeakably weary) of being all wrapped up in a single idea. It had never, by itself, been sufficient to interest her in any man, the fact that he was in love with her; but indeed she could honestly say that most of the people who had liked her had had, on their own side, something—something in their character or circumstances—that one could care a little about. Not so far as would do any harm, save perhaps in one or two cases; but still, something.

Sholto was a curious and not particularly edifying English type (as the Princess further described him); one of those strange beings produced by old societies that have run to seed, corrupt, exhausted civilisations. He was a cumberer of the earth, and purely selfish, in spite of his devoted, disinterested airs. He was nothing whatever in himself, and had no character or merit save by tradition, reflection, imitation, superstition. He had a longish pedigree—he came of some musty, mouldy 'county family,' people with a local reputation and an immense lack of general importance; he had taken the greatest care of his little fortune. He had travelled all over the globe several times, 'for the shooting,' in that brutal way of the English. That was a pursuit which was compatible with the greatest stupidity. He had a little taste, a little cleverness, a little reading, a little good furniture, a little French and Italian (he exaggerated these latter quantities), an immense deal of assurance, and complete leisure. That, at bottom, was all he represented—idle, trifling, luxurious, yet at the same time pretentious leisure, the sort of thing that led people to invent false, humbugging duties, because they had no real ones. Sholto's great idea of himself (after his profession of being her slave), was that he was a cosmopolite—exempt from every prejudice. About the prejudices the Princess couldn't say and didn't care; but she had seen him in foreign countries, she had seen him in Italy, and she was bound to say he understood nothing about those people. It was several years before, shortly after her marriage, that she had first encountered him.

He had not begun immediately to take the adoring line, but it had come little by little. It was only after she had separated from her husband that he had begun really to hang about her; since when she had suffered much from him. She would do him one justice, however: he had never, so far as she knew, had the impudence to represent himself as anything but hopeless and helpless. It was on this that he took his stand; he wished to pass for the great model of unrewarded constancy. She couldn't imagine what he was waiting for; perhaps it was for the death of the Prince. But the Prince would never die, nor had she the least desire that he should. She had no wish to be harsh, for of course that sort of thing, from any one, was very flattering; but really, whatever feeling poor Sholto might have, four-fifths of it were purely theatrical. He was not in the least a natural human being, but had a hundred affectations and attitudes, the result of never having been obliged to put his hand to anything; having no serious tastes and yet being born to a little 'position.' The Princess remarked that she was so glad Hyacinth had no position, had been forced to do something else in life but amuse himself; that was the way she liked her friends now. She had said to Sholto again and again, 'There are plenty of others who will be much more pleased; why not go to *them*? It's such a waste of time:' and she was sure he had taken her advice, and was by no means, as regards herself, the absorbed, annihilated creature he endeavoured to appear. He had told her once that he tried to take an interest in other women—though indeed he had added that it was of no use. Of what use did he expect anything he could possibly do to be? Hyacinth did not tell the Princess that he had reason to believe the Captain's effort in this direction had not been absolutely vain; but he made that reflection, privately, with increased confidence. He recognised a further truth even when his companion said, at the end, that, with all she had touched upon, he was a queer combination. Trifler as he was, there was something sinister in him too; and she confessed she had had a vague feeling, at times, that some day he might do her a hurt. Hyacinth, at this, stopped short, on the threshold of the drawing-room, and asked in a low voice, 'Are you afraid of him?'

The Princess looked at him a moment; then smiling, '*Dio mio*, how you say that! Should you like to kill him for me?'

'I shall have to kill some one, you know. Why not him, while I'm about it, if he troubles you?'

'Ah, my friend, if you should begin to kill every one who had troubled me!' the Princess murmured, as they went into the room.

XXVII

HYACINTH knew there was something out of the way as soon as he saw Lady Aurora's face look forth at him, in answer to his tap, while she held the door ajar. What was she doing in Pinnie's bedroom?—a very poor place, into which the dressmaker, with her reverence, would never have admitted a person of that quality unless things were pretty bad. She was solemn, too; she didn't laugh, as usual; she had removed her large hat, with its limp, old-fashioned veil, and she raised her finger to her lips. Hyacinth's first alarm had been immediately after he let himself into the house, with his latch-key, as he always did, and found the little room on the right of the passage, in which Pinnie had lived ever since he remembered, fireless and untenanted. As soon as he had paid the cabman, who put down his portmanteau for him in the hall (he was not used to paying cabmen, and was conscious he gave him too much, but was too impatient, in his sudden anxiety, to care), he hurried up the vile staircase, which seemed viler, even through his preoccupation, than ever, and gave the knock, accompanied by a call the least bit tremulous, immediately answered by Lady Aurora. She drew back into the room a moment, while he stared, in his dismay; then she emerged again, closing the door behind her—all with the air of enjoining him to be terribly quiet. He felt, suddenly, so sick at the idea of having lingered at Medley while there was distress in the wretched little house to which he owed so much, that he scarcely found strength for an articulate question, and obeyed, mechanically, the mute, urgent gesture by which Lady Aurora appealed to him to go downstairs with her. It was only when they stood together in the deserted parlour (it was as if he perceived for the first time what an inelegant odour prevailed there), that he asked, 'Is she dying—is she dead?' That was the least the strained sadness looking out from the face of the noble visitor appeared to announce.

'Dear Mr. Robinson, I'm so sorry for you. I wanted to write, but I promised her I wouldn't. She is very ill—we are very anxious. It began ten days ago, and I suppose I *must* tell

314

you how much she has gone down.' Lady Aurora spoke with
more than all her usual embarrassments and precautions, eagerly, yet as if it cost her much pain: pausing a little after
everything she said, to see how he would take it; then going
on, with a propitiatory rush. He learned presently what was
the matter, what doctor she had sent for, and that if he would
wait a little before going into the room it would be so much
better; the invalid having sunk, within half an hour, into a
doze of a less agitated kind than she had had for some time,
from which it would be an immense pity to run the risk of
waking her. The doctor gave her the right things, as it seemed
to her ladyship, but he admitted that she had very little power
of resistance. He was of course not a very large practitioner,
Mr. Buffery, from round the corner, but he seemed really
clever; and she herself had taken the liberty (as she confessed
to this she threw off one of her odd laughs, and her colour
rose), of sending an elderly, respectable person—a kind of
nurse. She was out just then; she had to go, for an hour, for
the air—'only when I come, of course,' said Lady Aurora.
Dear Miss Pynsent had had a cold hanging about her, and
had not taken care of it. Hyacinth would know how plucky
she was about that sort of thing; she took so little interest in
herself. 'Of course a cold is a cold, whoever has it; isn't it?'
said Lady Aurora. Ten days before, she had taken an addi-
tional chill through falling asleep in her chair, in the evening,
down there, and letting the fire go out. 'It would have been
nothing if she had been like you or me, you know,' her ladyship went on; 'but just as she was then, it made the difference.
The day was horribly damp, and it had struck into the lungs,
and inflammation had set in. Mr. Buffery says she was impov-
erished, just rather low and languid, you know.' The next
morning she had bad pains and a good deal of fever, yet she
had got up. Poor Pinnie's gracious ministrant did not make
clear to Hyacinth what time had elapsed before she came to
her relief, nor by what means she had been notified, and he
saw that she slurred this over from the admirable motive of
wishing him not to feel that the little dressmaker had suffered
by his absence or called for him in vain. This, apparently, had
indeed not been the case, if Pinnie had opposed, successfully,
his being written to. Lady Aurora only said, 'I came in very

soon, it was such a delightful chance. Since then she has had everything; only it's sad to see a person *need* so little. She did want you to stay; she has clung to that idea. I speak the simple truth, Mr. Robinson.'

'I don't know what to say to you—you are so extraordinarily good, so angelic,' Hyacinth replied, bewildered and made weak by a strange, unexpected shame. The episode he had just traversed, the splendour he had been living in and drinking so deep of, the unnatural alliance to which he had given himself up while his wretched little foster-mother struggled alone with her death-stroke—he could see it was that; the presentiment of it, the last stiff horror, was in all the place—the contrast seemed to cut him like a knife, and to make the horrible accident of his absence a perversity of his own. 'I can never blame you, when you are so kind, but I wish to God I had known!' he broke out.

Lady Aurora clasped her hands, begging him to judge her fairly. 'Of course it was a great responsibility for us, but we thought it right to consider what she urged upon us. She went back to it constantly, that your visit should *not* be cut short. When you should come of yourself, it would be time enough. I don't know exactly where you have been, but she said it was such a pleasant house. She kept repeating that it would do you so much good.'

Hyacinth felt his eyes filling with tears. 'She's dying—she's dying! How can she live when she's like that?'

He sank upon the old yellow sofa, the sofa of his lifetime and of so many years before, and buried his head on the shabby, tattered arm. A succession of sobs broke from his lips—sobs in which the accumulated emotion of months and the strange, acute conflict of feeling that had possessed him for the three weeks just past found relief and a kind of solution. Lady Aurora sat down beside him and laid her fingertips gently on his hand. So, for a minute, while his tears flowed and she said nothing, he felt her timid, consoling touch. At the end of the minute he raised his head; it came back to him that she had said 'we' just before, and he asked her whom she meant.

'Oh, Mr. Vetch, don't you know? I have made his acquaintance; it's impossible to be more kind.' Then, while, for an instant, Hyacinth was silent, wincing, pricked with the thought that Pinnie had been beholden to the fiddler while *he* was masquerading in high life, Lady Aurora added, 'He's a charming musician. She asked him once, at first, to bring his violin; she thought it would soothe her.'

'I'm much obliged to him, but now that I'm here we needn't trouble him,' said Hyacinth.

Apparently there was a certain dryness in his tone, which was the cause of her ladyship's venturing to reply, after an hesitation, 'Do let him come, Mr. Robinson; let him be near you! I wonder whether you know that—that he has a great affection for you.'

'The more fool he; I have always treated him like a brute!' Hyacinth exclaimed, colouring.

The way Lady Aurora spoke proved to him, later, that she now definitely did know his secret, or one of them, rather; for at the rate things had been going for the last few months he was making a regular collection. She knew the smaller—not, of course, the greater; she had, decidedly, been illuminated by Pinnie's divagations. At the moment he made that reflection, however, he was almost startled to perceive how completely he had ceased to resent such betrayals and how little it suddenly seemed to signify that the innocent source of them was about to be quenched. The sense of his larger secret swallowed up that particular anxiety, making him ask himself what it mattered, for the time that was left to him, that people should whisper to each other his little mystery. The day came quickly when he believed, and yet didn't care, that it had been universally imparted.

After Lady Aurora left him, promising she would call him the first moment it should seem prudent, he walked up and down the cold, stale parlour, immersed in his meditations. The shock of the danger of losing Pinnie had already passed away; he had achieved so much, of late, in the line of accepting the idea of death that the little dressmaker, in taking her departure, seemed already to benefit by this curious discipline. What was most vivid to him, in the deserted scene of Pinnie's unsuccessful industry, was the changed vision with which he had come back to objects familiar for twenty years. The picture was the same, and all its horrid elements, wearing a kind of greasy gloss in the impure air of Lomax Place, made, through the mean window-panes, a dismal *chiaroscuro*— showed, in their polished misery, the friction of his own little life; but the eyes with which he looked at it had new terms of comparison. He had known the place was hideous and sordid, but its aspect to-day was pitiful to the verge of the sickening; he couldn't believe that for years together he had accepted and even, a little, revered it. He was frightened at the sort of service that his experience of grandeur had rendered him. It was all very well to have assimilated that element with a rapidity which had surprises even for himself; but with sensibilities now so improved what fresh arrangement could one come to with the very humble, which was in its nature uncompromising? Though the spring was far advanced the day was a dark drizzle, and the room had the clamminess of a finished use, an ooze of dampness from the muddy street, where the areas were a narrow slit. No wonder Pinnie had felt it at last, and her small under-fed organism had grown numb and ceased to act. At the thought of her limited, stinted life, the patient, humdrum effort of her needle and scissors, which had ended only in a show-room where there was nothing to show and a pensive reference to the cut of sleeves no longer worn, the tears again rose to his eyes; but he brushed them aside when he heard a cautious tinkle at the house-door, which was presently opened by the little besmirched slavey retained for the service of the solitary lodger—a domestic easily bewildered, who had a squint and distressed Hyacinth by wearing shoes that didn't match, though they were of an equal antiquity and resembled each other in the facility with which they dropped off. Hyacinth had not heard Mr. Vetch's voice in the hall, apparently because he spoke in a whisper; but the young man was not surprised when, taking every precaution not to make the door creak, he came into the parlour. The fiddler said nothing to him at first; the two men only looked at each other for a long minute. Hyacinth saw what he most wanted to know—whether *he* knew the worst about Pinnie; but what was further in his eyes (they had an expression considerably different from any he had hitherto seen in them), defined itself to our hero only little by little.

'Don't you think you might have written me a word?' said
Hyacinth, at last. His anger at having been left in ignorance
had quitted him, but he thought the question fair. None the
less, he expected a sarcastic answer, and was surprised at the
mild reasonableness with which Mr. Vetch replied—

'I assure you, no responsibility, in the course of my life,
ever did more to distress me. There were obvious reasons for
calling you back, and yet I couldn't help wishing you might
finish your visit. I balanced one thing against the other; it was
very difficult.'

'I can imagine nothing more simple. When people's nearest
and dearest are dying, they are usually sent for.'

The fiddler gave a strange, argumentative smile. If Lomax
Place and Miss Pynsent's select lodging-house wore a new
face of vulgarity to Hyacinth, it may be imagined whether the
renunciation of the niceties of the toilet, the resigned seedi-
ness, which marked Mr. Vetch's old age was unlikely to lend
itself to comparison. The glossy butler at Medley had had a
hundred more of the signs of success in life. 'My dear boy,
this case was exceptional,' said the old man. 'Your visit had a
character of importance.'

'I don't know what you know about it. I don't remember
that I told you anything.'

'No, certainly, you have never told me much. But if, as is
probable, you have seen that kind lady who is now upstairs,
you will have learned that Pinnie made a tremendous point of
your not being disturbed. She threatened us with her displeasure if we should hurry you back. You know what Pinnie's
displeasure is!' As, at this, Hyacinth turned away with a gesture of irritation, Mr. Vetch went on, 'No doubt she is absurdly fanciful, poor dear thing; but don't, now, cast any
disrespect upon it. I assure you, if she had been here alone,
suffering, sinking, without a creature to tend her, and nothing before her but to die in a corner, like a starved cat, she
would still have faced that fate rather than cut short by a single hour your experience of novel scenes.'

Hyacinth was silent for a moment. 'Of course I know what
you mean. But she spun her delusion—she always did, all of
them—out of nothing. I can't imagine what she knows about

my "experience" of any kind of scenes. I told her, when I went out of town, very little more than I told you.'

'What she guessed, what she gathered, has been, at any rate, enough. She has made up her mind that you have formed a connection by means of which you will come, somehow or other, into your own. She has done nothing but talk about your grand kindred. To her mind, you know, it's all one, the aristocracy, and nothing is simpler than that the person—very exalted, as she believes—with whom you have been to stay should undertake your business with her friends.'

'Oh, well,' said Hyacinth, 'I'm very glad not to have deprived you of that entertainment.'

'I assure you the spectacle was exquisite.' Then the fiddler added, 'My dear fellow, please leave her the idea.'

'Leave it? I'll do much more!' Hyacinth exclaimed. 'I'll tell her my great relations have adopted me and that I have come back in the character of Lord Robinson.'

'She will need nothing more to die happy,' Mr. Vetch observed.

Five minutes later, after Hyacinth had obtained from his old friend a confirmation of Lady Aurora's account of Miss Pynsent's condition, Mr. Vetch explaining that he came over, like that, to see how she was, half a dozen times a day—five minutes later a silence had descended upon the pair, while Hyacinth waited for some sign from Lady Aurora that he might come upstairs. The fiddler, who had lighted a pipe, looked out of the window, studying intently the physiognomy of Lomax Place; and Hyacinth, making his tread discreet, walked about the room with his hands in his pockets. At last Mr. Vetch observed, without taking his pipe out of his lips or looking round, 'I think you might be a little more frank with me at this time of day and at such a crisis.'

Hyacinth stopped in his walk, wondering for a moment, sincerely, what his companion meant, for he had no consciousness at present of an effort to conceal anything he could possibly tell (there were some things, of course, he couldn't); on the contrary, his life seemed to him particularly open to the public view and exposed to invidious comment. It was at this moment he first observed a certain difference; there was a

tone in Mr. Vetch's voice that he had never perceived before—an absence of that note which had made him say, in
other days, that the impenetrable old man was diverting himself at his expense. It was as if his attitude had changed, become more explicitly considerate, in consequence of some
alteration or promotion on Hyacinth's part, his having grown
older, or more important, or even simply more surpassingly
curious. If the first impression made upon him by Pinnie's old
neighbour, as to whose place in the list of the sacrificial (his
being a gentleman or one of the sovereign people) he formerly was so perplexed; if the sentiment excited by Mr. Vetch
in a mind familiar now for nearly a month with forms of in-
dubitable gentility was not favourable to the idea of fraternisation, this secret impatience on Hyacinth's part was speedily
corrected by one of the sudden reactions or quick conversions
of which the young man was so often the victim. In the light
of the fiddler's appeal, which evidently meant more than it
said, his musty antiquity, his typical look of having had, for
years, a small, definite use and taken all the creases and con-
tractions of it, his visible expression, even, of ultimate parsimony and of having ceased to care for the shape of his
trousers because he cared more for something else—these
things became so many reasons for turning round, going over
to him, touching signs of an invincible fidelity, the humble,
continuous, single-minded practice of daily duties and an art
after all very charming; pursued, moreover, while persons of
the species our restored prodigal had lately been consorting
with fidgeted from one selfish sensation to another and
couldn't even live in the same place for three months together.

'What should you like me to do, to say, to tell you? Do you
want to know what I have been doing in the country? I
should have first to know, myself,' Hyacinth said.

'Have you enjoyed it very much?'

'Yes, certainly, very much—not knowing anything about
Pinnie. I have been in a beautiful house, with a beautiful
woman.'

Mr. Vetch had turned round; he looked very impartial,
through the smoke of his pipe.

'Is she really a princess?'

'I don't know what you mean by "really." I suppose all titles are great rot. But every one seems agreed to call her so.'

'You know I have always liked to enter into your life; and to-day the wish is stronger than ever,' the old man observed, presently, fixing his eyes very steadily on Hyacinth's.

The latter returned his gaze for a moment; then he asked, 'What makes you say that just now?'

The fiddler appeared to deliberate, and at last he replied, 'Because you are in danger of losing the best friend you have ever had.'

'Be sure I feel it. But if I have got you——' Hyacinth added.

'Oh, me! I'm very old, and very tired of life.'

'I suppose that that's what one arrives at. Well, if I can help you in any way you must lean on me, you must make use of me.'

'That's precisely what I was going to say to you,' said Mr. Vetch. 'Should you like any money?'

'Of course I should! But why should you offer it to me?'

'Because in saving it up, little by little, I have had you in mind.'

'Dear Mr. Vetch,' said Hyacinth, 'you have me too much in mind. I'm not worth it, please believe that; for all sorts of reasons. I should make money enough for any uses I have for it, or have any right to have, if I stayed quietly in London and attended to my work. As you know, I can earn a decent living.'

'Yes, I can see that. But if you stayed quietly in London what would become of your princess?'

'Oh, they can always manage, ladies in that position.'

'Hanged if I understand her position!' cried Mr. Vetch, but without laughing. 'You have been for three weeks without work, and yet you look uncommonly smart.'

'You see, my living has cost me nothing. When you stay with great people you don't pay your score,' Hyacinth explained, with great gentleness. 'Moreover, the lady whose hospitality I have been enjoying has made me a very handsome offer of work.'

'What kind of work?'

'The only kind I know. She is going to send me a lot of books, to do up for her.'

'And to pay you fancy prices?'

'Oh, no; I am to fix the prices myself.'

'Are not transactions of that kind rather disagreeable, with a lady whose hospitality one has been enjoying?' Mr. Vetch inquired.

'Exceedingly! That is exactly why I shall do the books and then take no money.'

'Your princess is rather clever!' the fiddler exclaimed, in a moment, smiling.

'Well, she can't force me to take it if I won't,' said Hyacinth.

'No; you must only let *me* do that.'

'You have curious ideas about me,' the young man declared.

Mr. Vetch turned about to the window again, remarking that he had curious ideas about everything. Then he added, after an interval—

'And have you been making love to your great lady?'

He had expected a flash of impatience in reply to this inquiry, and was rather surprised at the manner in which Hyacinth answered: 'How shall I explain? It is not a question of that sort.'

'Has she been making love to you, then?'

'If you should ever see her you would understand how absurd that supposition is.'

'How shall I ever see her?' returned Mr. Vetch. 'In the absence of that privilege I think there is something in my idea.'

'She looks quite over my head,' said Hyacinth, simply. 'It's by no means impossible you may see her. She wants to know my friends, to know the people who live in the Place. And she would take a particular interest in you, on account of your opinions.'

'Ah, I have no opinions now, none any more!' the old man broke out, sadly. 'I only had them to frighten Pinnie.'

'She was easily frightened,' said Hyacinth.

'Yes, and easily reassured. Well, I like to know about your life,' his neighbour sighed, irrelevantly. 'But take care the great lady doesn't lead you too far.'

'How do you mean, too far?'

'Isn't she an anarchist—a nihilist? Doesn't she go in for a general rectification, as Eustace calls it?'

Hyacinth was silent a moment. 'You should see the place—you should see what she wears, what she eats and drinks.'

'Ah, you mean that she is inconsistent with her theories? My dear boy, she would be a droll woman if she were not. At any rate, I'm glad of it.'

'Glad of it?' Hyacinth repeated.

'For you, I mean, when you stay with her; it's more luxurious!' Mr. Vetch exclaimed, turning round and smiling. At this moment a little rap on the floor above, given by Lady Aurora, announced that Hyacinth might at last come up and see Pinnie. Mr. Vetch listened and recognised it, and it led him to say, with considerable force, *'There's* a woman whose theories and conduct do square!'

Hyacinth, on the threshold, leaving the room, stopped long enough to reply, 'Well, when the day comes for my friend to give up—you'll see.'

'Yes, I have no doubt there are things she will bring herself to sacrifice,' the old man remarked; but Hyacinth was already out of hearing.

XXVIII

M R. VETCH waited below till Lady Aurora should come
down and give him the news he was in suspense for.
His mind was pretty well made up about Pinnie. It had
seemed to him, the night before, that death was written in her
face, and he judged it on the whole a very good moment for
her to lay down her earthly burden. He had reasons for believing that the future could not be sweet to her. As regards
Hyacinth, his mind was far from being at ease; for though he
was aware in a general way that he had taken up with strange
company, and though he had flattered himself of old that he
should be pleased to see the boy act out his life and solve the
problem of his queer inheritance, he was worried by the absence of full knowledge. He put out his pipe, in anticipation
of Lady Aurora's reappearance, and without this consoler he
was more accessible still to certain fears that had come to him
in consequence of a recent talk, or rather an attempt at a talk,
with Eustache Poupin. It was through the Frenchman that he
had gathered the little he knew about the occasion of Hyacinth's unprecedented excursion. His ideas on the subject had
been very inferential; for Hyacinth had made a mystery of his
absence to Pinnie, merely letting her know that there was a
lady in the case and that the best luggage he could muster and
the best way his shirts could be done up would still not be
good enough. Poupin had seen Godfrey Sholto at the 'Sun
and Moon,' and it had come to him, through Hyacinth, that
there was a remarkable feminine influence in the Captain's
life, mixed up in some way with his presence in Bloomsbury—an influence, moreover, by which Hyacinth himself,
for good or for evil, was in peril of being touched. Sholto was
the young man's visible link with a society for which Lisson
Grove could have no importance in the scheme of the universe but as a short cut (too disagreeable to be frequently
used) out of Bayswater; therefore if Hyacinth left town with a
new hat and a pair of kid gloves it must have been to move in
the direction of that superior circle and in some degree, at
least, at the solicitation of the before-mentioned feminine influence. So much as this the Frenchman suggested, explicitly

enough, as his manner was, to the old fiddler; but his talk had
a flavour of other references which excited Mr. Vetch's curiosity much more than they satisfied it. They were obscure; they
evidently were painful to the speaker; they were confused and
embarrassed and totally wanting in the luminosity which usually characterised the lightest allusions of M. Poupin. It was
the fiddler's fancy that his friend had something on his mind
which he was not at liberty to impart, and that it related to
Hyacinth and might, for those who took an interest in the
singular lad, constitute a considerable anxiety. Mr. Vetch, on
his own part, nursed this anxiety into a tolerably definite
shape: he persuaded himself that the Frenchman had been
leading the boy too far in the line of social criticism, had
given him a push on some crooked path where a slip would
be a likely accident. When on a subsequent occasion, with
Poupin, he indulged in a hint of this suspicion, the bookbinder flushed a good deal and declared that his conscience
was pure. It was one of his peculiarities that when his colour
rose he looked angry, and Mr. Vetch held that his displeasure
was a proof that in spite of his repudiations he had been un-
wise; though before they parted Eustache gave this sign of
softness, that he shed tears of emotion, of which the reason
was not clear to the fiddler and which appeared in a general
way to be dedicated to Hyacinth. The interview had taken
place in Lisson Grove, where Madame Poupin, however, had
not shown herself.

Altogether the old man was a prey to suppositions which
led him to feel how much he himself had outlived the democratic glow of his prime. He had ended by accepting everything (though, indeed, he couldn't swallow the idea that a
trick should be played upon Hyacinth), and even by taking an
interest in current politics, as to which, of old, he had held
the opinion (the same that the Poupins held to-day), that they
had been invented on purpose to throw dust in the eyes of
disinterested reformers and to circumvent the social solution.
He had given up that problem some time ago; there was no
way to clear it up that didn't seem to make a bigger mess than
the actual muddle of human affairs, which, by the time one
had reached sixty-five, had mostly ceased to exasperate. Mr.
Vetch could still feel a certain sharpness on the subject of the

prayer-book and the bishops; and if at moments he was a little ashamed of having accepted this world he could reflect that at all events he continued to repudiate every other. The idea of great changes, however, took its place among the dreams of his youth; for what was any possible change in the relations of men and women but a new combination of the same elements? If the elements could be made different the thing would be worth thinking of; but it was not only impossible to introduce any new ones—no means had yet been discovered for getting rid of the old. The figures on the chessboard were still the passions and jealousies and superstitions and stupidities of man, and their position with regard to each other, at any given moment, could be of interest only to the grim, invisible fates who played the game—who sat, through the ages, bow-backed over the table. This laxity had come upon the old man with the increase of his measurement round the waist, of the little heap of half-crowns and half-sovereigns that had accumulated in a tin box with a very stiff padlock, which he kept under his bed, and of the interwoven threads of sentiment and custom that united him to the dress-maker and her foster-son. If he was no longer pressing about the demands he felt he should have a right to make of society, as he had been in the days when his conversation scandalised Pinnie, so he was now not pressing for Hyacinth, either; reflecting that though, indeed, the constituted powers might have to 'count' with him, it would be in better taste for him not to be importunate about a settlement. What he had come to fear for him was that he should be precipitated by crude agencies, with results in which the deplorable might not exclude the ridiculous. It may even be said that Mr. Vetch had a secret project of settling a little on his behalf.

Lady Aurora peeped into the room, very noiselessly, nearly half an hour after Hyacinth had left it, and let the fiddler know that she was called to other duties but that the nurse had come back and the doctor had promised to look in at five o'clock. She herself would return in the evening, and meanwhile Hyacinth was with his aunt, who had recognised him, without a protest; indeed seemed intensely happy that he should be near her again, and lay there with closed eyes, very weak and speechless, with his hand in hers. Her restlessness had passed and her fever abated, but she had no pulse to speak of and Lady Aurora did not disguise the fact that, in her opinion, she was rapidly sinking. Mr. Vetch had already accepted it, and after her ladyship had quitted him he lighted another philosophic pipe upon it, lingering on, till the doctor came, in the dressmaker's dismal, forsaken bower, where, in past years, he had indulged in so many sociable droppings-in and hot tumblers. The echo of all her little simple surprises and pointless contradictions, her gasping reception of contemplative paradox, seemed still to float in the air; but the place felt as relinquished and bereaved as if she were already beneath the sod. Pinnie had always been a wonderful hand at 'putting away'; the litter that testified to her most elaborate efforts was often immense, but the reaction in favour of an unspeckled carpet was greater still; and on the present occasion, before taking to her bed, she had found strength to sweep and set in order as daintily as if she had been sure that the room would never again know her care. Even to the old fiddler, who had not Hyacinth's sensibility to the scenery of life, it had the cold propriety of a place arranged for an interment. After the doctor had seen Pinnie, that afternoon, there was no doubt left as to its soon being the stage of dismal preliminaries.

Miss Pynsent, however, resisted her malady for nearly a fortnight more, during which Hyacinth was constantly in her room. He never went back to Mr. Crookenden's, with whose establishment, through violent causes, his relations seemed indefinitely suspended; and in fact, for the rest of the time that Pinnie demanded his care he absented himself but twice from Lomax Place for more than a few minutes. On one of these occasions he travelled over to Audley Court and spent an hour there; on the other he met Millicent Henning, by appointment, and took a walk with her on the Embankment. He tried to find a moment to go and thank Madame Poupin for a sympathetic offering, many times repeated, of *tisane*, concocted after a receipt thought supreme by the couple in Lisson Grove (though little appreciated in the neighbourhood generally); but he was obliged to acknowledge her kindness only by a respectful letter, which he composed with some trouble, though much elation, in the French tongue, peculiarly favourable, as he believed, to little courtesies of this kind. Lady Aurora came again and again to the darkened house, where she diffused her beneficent influence in nightly watches, in the most modern sanative suggestions, in conversations with Hyacinth, directed with more ingenuity than her fluttered embarrassments might have led one to attribute to her, to the purpose of diverting his mind, and in tea-makings (there was a great deal of this liquid consumed on the premises during Pinnie's illness), after a system more enlightened than the usual fashion of Pentonville. She was the bearer of several messages and of a good deal of medical advice from Rose Muniment, whose interest in the dressmaker's case irritated Hyacinth by its fine courage, which even at second-hand was still obtrusive; she appeared very nearly as resigned to the troubles of others as she was to her own.

Hyacinth had been seized, the day after his return from Medley, with a sharp desire to do something enterprising and superior on Pinnie's behalf. He felt the pressure of a sort of angry sense that she was dying of her poor career, of her uneffaced remorse for the trick she had played him in his boyhood (as if he hadn't long ago, and indeed at the time, forgiven it, judging it to have been the highest wisdom!) of something basely helpless in the attitude of her little circle. He wanted to do something which should prove to himself that he had got the best opinion about the invalid that it was possible to have: so he insisted that Mr. Buffery should consult with a West End doctor, if the West End doctor would consent to meet Mr. Buffery. A physician capable of this condescension was discovered through Lady Aurora's agency (she had not brought him of her own movement, because on the one hand she hesitated to impose on the little household in Lomax Place the expense of such a visit, and on the other, with all her narrow personal economies for the sake of her charities, had not the means to meet it herself); and in prevision of the great man's fee Hyacinth applied to Mr. Vetch, as he had applied before, for a loan. The great man came, and was wonderfully civil to Mr. Buffery, whose conduct of the case he pronounced judicious; he remained several minutes in the house, while he gazed at Hyacinth over his spectacles (he seemed rather more occupied with him than with the patient), and almost the whole of the Place turned out to stare at his chariot. After all, he consented to accept no fee. He put the question aside with a gesture full of urbanity—a course disappointing and displeasing to Hyacinth, who felt in a manner cheated of the full effect of the fine thing he had wished to do for Pinnie; though when he said as much (or something like it) to Mr. Vetch, the caustic fiddler greeted the observation with a face of amusement which, considering the situation, verged upon the unseemly.

Hyacinth, at any rate, had done the best he could, and the fashionable doctor had left directions which foreshadowed relations with an expensive chemist in Bond Street—a prospect by which our young man was to some extent consoled. Poor Pinnie's decline, however, was not arrested, and one evening, more than a week after his return from Medley, as he sat with her alone, it seemed to Hyacinth that her spirit must already have passed away. The nurse had gone down to her supper, and from the staircase a perceptible odour of fizzling bacon indicated that a more cheerful state of things prevailed in the lower regions. Hyacinth could not make out whether Miss Pynsent were asleep or awake; he believed she had not lost consciousness, yet for more than an hour she had given no sign of life. At last she put out her hand, as if she knew he was near her and wished to feel for his, and murmured, 'Why did she come? I didn't want to see her.' In a moment, as she went on, he perceived to whom she was alluding: her mind had travelled back, through all the years, to the dreadful day (she had described every incident of it to him), when Mrs. Bowerbank had invaded her quiet life and startled her sensitive conscience with a message from the prison. 'She sat there so long—so long. She was very large, and I was frightened. She moaned, and moaned, and cried—too dreadful. I couldn't help it—I couldn't help it!' Her thought wandered from Mrs. Bowerbank in the discomposed show-room, enthroned on the yellow sofa, to the tragic creature at Milbank, whose accents again, for the hour, lived in her ears; and mixed with this mingled vision was still the haunting sense that she herself might have acted differently. That had been cleared up in the past, so far as Hyacinth's intention was concerned; but what was most alive in Pinnie at the present moment was the passion of repentance, of still further expiation. It sickened Hyacinth that she should believe these things were still necessary, and he leaned over her and talked tenderly, with words of comfort and reassurance. He told her not to think of that dismal, far-off time, which had ceased long ago to have any consequences for either of them; to consider only the future, when she should be quite strong again and he would look after her and keep her all to himself and take care of her better, far better, than he had ever done before. He had thought of many things while he sat with Pinnie, watching the shadows made by the night-lamp—high, imposing shadows of objects low and mean—and among them he had followed, with an imagination that went further in that direction than ever before, the probable consequences of his not having been adopted in his babyhood by the dressmaker. The workhouse and the gutter, ignorance and cold, filth and tatters, nights of huddling under bridges and in doorways, vermin, starvation and blows, possibly even the vigorous efflorescence of an inherited disposition to crime—these things, which he saw with unprecedented vividness, suggested themselves as his natural portion. Intimacies with a princess, visits to fine old country-houses, intelligent consideration, even, of the best means of inflicting a scare on the classes of privilege, would in that case not have been within his compass; and that Pinnie should have rescued him from such a destiny and put these luxuries within his reach was an amelioration which really amounted to success, if he could only have the magnanimity to regard it so.

Her eyes were open and fixed on him, but the sharp ray the little dressmaker used to direct into Lomax Place as she plied her needle at the window had completely left them. 'Not there—what should I do there?' she inquired, very softly. 'Not with the great—the great——' and her voice failed.

'The great what? What do you mean?'

'You know—you know,' she went on, making another effort. 'Haven't you been with them? Haven't they received you?'

'Ah, they won't separate us, Pinnie; they won't come between us as much as that,' said Hyacinth, kneeling by her bed.

'*You* must be separate—that makes me happier. I knew they would find you at last.'

'Poor Pinnie, poor Pinnie,' murmured the young man.

'It was only for that—now I'm going,' she went on.

'If you'll stay with me you needn't fear,' said Hyacinth, smiling at her.

'Oh, what would *they* think?' asked the dressmaker.

'I like you best,' said Hyacinth.

'You have had me always. Now it's their turn; they have waited.'

'Yes, indeed, they have waited!' Hyacinth exclaimed.

'But they will make it up; they will make up everything!' the invalid panted. Then she added, 'I couldn't—couldn't help it!'—which was the last flicker of her strength. She gave no further sign of consciousness, and four days later she ceased to breathe. Hyacinth was with her, and Lady Aurora, but neither of them could recognise the moment.

Hyacinth and Mr. Vetch carried her bier, with the help of Eustache Poupin and Paul Muniment. Lady Aurora was at the funeral, and Madame Poupin as well, and twenty neighbours from Lomax Place; but the most distinguished person (in appearance at least) in the group of mourners was Millicent Henning, the grave yet brilliant beauty of whose countenance, the high propriety of whose demeanour, and the fine taste and general style of whose black 'costume' excited no little attention. Mr. Vetch had his idea; he had been nursing it ever since Hyacinth's return from Medley, and three days after Pinnie had been consigned to the earth he broached it to his young friend. The funeral had been on a Friday, and Hyacinth had mentioned to him that he should return to Mr. Crookenden's on the Monday morning. This was Sunday night, and Hyacinth had been out for a walk, neither with Millicent Henning nor with Paul Muniment, but alone, after the manner of old days. When he came in he found the fiddler waiting for him, and burning a tallow candle, in the blighted show-room. He had three or four little papers in his hand, which exhibited some jottings of his pencil, and Hyacinth guessed, what was the truth but not all the truth, that he had come to speak to him about business. Pinnie had left a little will, of which she had appointed her old friend executor; this fact had already become known to our hero, who thought such an arrangement highly natural. Mr. Vetch informed him of the purport of this simple and judicious document, and mentioned that he had been looking into the dressmaker's 'affairs.' They consisted, poor Pinnie's affairs, of the furniture of the house in Lomax Place, of the obligation to pay the remainder of a quarter's rent, and of a sum of money in the savings-bank. Hyacinth was surprised to learn that Pinnie's economies had produced fruit at this late day (things had gone so ill with her in recent years, and there had been often such a want of money in the house), until Mr. Vetch explained to him, with eager clearness, that he himself had watched over the little hoard, accumulated during the period of her comparative prosperity, with the stiff determination that it should be sacrificed only in case of desperate necessity. Work had become scarce with Pinnie, but she could still do it when it came, and the money was to be kept for the very possible period when she should be helpless. Mercifully enough, she had not lived to see that day, and the sum in the bank had survived her, though diminished by more than half. She had left no debts but the matter of the house and those incurred during her illness. Of course the fiddler had known—he hastened to give his young friend this assurance—that Pinnie, had she become infirm, would have been able to count absolutely upon *him* for the equivalent, in her old age, of the protection she had given him in his youth. But what if an accident had overtaken Hyacinth? What if he had incurred some nasty penalty for his revolutionary dabblings, which, little dangerous as they might be to society, were quite capable, in a country where authority, though good-natured, liked occasionally to make an example, to put him on the wrong side of a prison-wall? At any rate, for better or worse, by pinching and scraping, she had saved a little, and of that little, after everything was paid off, a fraction would still be left. Everything was bequeathed to Hyacinth—everything but a couple of plated candlesticks and the old 'cheffonier,' which had been so handsome in its day; these Pinnie begged Mr. Vetch to accept in recognition of services beyond all price. The furniture, everything he didn't want for his own use, Hyacinth could sell in a lump, and with the proceeds he could wipe out old scores. The sum of money would remain to him; it amounted, in its reduced condition, to about thirty-seven pounds. In mentioning this figure Mr. Vetch appeared to imply that Hyacinth would be master of a very pretty little fortune. Even to the young man himself, in spite of his recent initiations, it seemed far from contemptible; it represented sudden possibilities of still not returning to old Crookenden's. It represented them, that is, till, presently, he remembered the various advances made him by the fiddler, and reflected that by the time these had been repaid there would hardly be twenty pounds left. That, however, was a far larger sum than he had ever had in his pocket at once. He thanked the old man for his information, and remarked—and there was no hypocrisy in the speech—that he was very sorry Pinnie had not given herself the benefit of the whole of the little fund in her lifetime. To this her executor replied that it had yielded her an interest far beyond any other investment; for he was persuaded she believed she should never live to enjoy it, and this faith was rich in pictures, visions of the effect such a windfall would produce in Hyacinth's career.

'What effect did she mean—do you mean?' Hyacinth inquired. As soon as he had spoken he felt that he knew what the old man would say (it would be a reference to Pinnie's belief in his reunion with his 'relations,' and the facilities that thirty-seven pounds would afford him for cutting a figure among them); and for a moment Mr. Vetch looked at him as if exactly that response were on his lips. At the end of the moment, however, he replied, quite differently—

'She hoped you would go abroad and see the world.' The fiddler watched his young friend; then he added, 'She had a particular wish that you should go to Paris.'

Hyacinth had turned pale at this suggestion, and for a moment he said nothing. 'Ah, Paris!' he murmured, at last.

'She would have liked you even to take a little run down to Italy.'

'Doubtless that would be pleasant. But there is a limit to what one can do with twenty pounds.'

'How do you mean, with twenty pounds?' the old man asked, lifting his eyebrows, while the wrinkles in his forehead made deep shadows in the candle-light.

'That's about what will remain, after I have settled my account with you.'

'How do you mean, your account with me? I shall not take any of your money.'

Hyacinth's eyes wandered over his interlocutor's suggestive rustiness. 'I don't want to be ungracious, but suppose *you* should lose your powers.'

'My dear boy, I shall have one of the resources that was open to Pinnie. I shall look to you to be the support of my old age.'

'You may do so with perfect safety, except for that danger you just mentioned, of my being imprisoned or hanged.'

'It's precisely because I think it will be less if you go abroad that I urge you to take this chance. You will see the world, and you will like it better. You will think society, even as it is, has some good points,' said Mr. Vetch.

'I have never liked it better than the last few months.'

'Ah well, wait till you see Paris!'

'Oh, Paris—Paris,' Hyacinth repeated, vaguely, staring into the turbid flame of the candle as if he made out the most brilliant scenes there; an attitude, accent and expression which the fiddler interpreted both as the vibration of a latent hereditary chord and a symptom of the acute sense of opportunity.

BOOK FOURTH

XXIX

THE BOULEVARD was all alive, brilliant with illuminations, with the variety and gaiety of the crowd, the dazzle of shops and cafés seen through uncovered fronts or immense lucid plates, the flamboyant porches of theatres and the flashing lamps of carriages, the far-spreading murmur of talkers and strollers, the uproar of pleasure and prosperity, the general magnificence of Paris on a perfect evening in June. Hyacinth had been walking about all day—he had walked from rising till bed-time every day of the week that had elapsed since his arrival—and now an extraordinary fatigue, which, however, was not without its delight (there was a kind of richness, a sweet satiety, in it), a tremendous lassitude had fallen upon him, and he settled himself in a chair beside a little table in front of Tortoni's, not so much to rest from it as to enjoy it. He had seen so much, felt so much, learned so much, thrilled and throbbed and laughed and sighed so much, during the past several days, that he was conscious at last of the danger of becoming incoherent to himself, of the need of balancing his accounts.

To-night he came to a full stop; he simply sat at the door of the most dandified café in Paris and felt his pulse and took stock of his impressions. He had been intending to visit the Variétés theatre, which blazed through intermediate lights and through the thin foliage of trees not favoured by the asphalt, on the other side of the great avenue. But the impression of Chaumont—he relinquished that, for the present; it added to the luxury of his situation to reflect that he should still have plenty of time to see the *succès du jour*. The same effect proceeded from his determination to order a *marquise*, when the waiter, whose superior shirt-front and whisker emerged from the long white cylinder of an apron, came to take his commands. He knew the decoction was expensive—he had learnt as much at the moment he happened to overhear, for the first time, a mention of it; which had been the night before, in his place in a stall, during an *entr'acte*, at the

Comédie Française. A gentleman beside him, a young man in evening-dress, conversing with an acquaintance in the row behind, recommended the latter to refresh himself with the article in question after the play: there was nothing like it, the speaker remarked, of a hot evening, in the open air, when one was thirsty. The waiter brought Hyacinth a tall glass of champagne, in which a pine-apple ice was in solution, and our hero felt that he had hoped for a sensation no less delicate when he looked for an empty table on Tortoni's terrace. Very few tables were empty, and it was his belief that the others were occupied by high celebrities; at any rate they were just the types he had had a prevision of and had wanted most to meet, when the extraordinary opportunity to come abroad with his pocket full of money (it was more extraordinary, even, than his original meeting with the Princess), became real to him in Lomax Place. He knew about Tortoni's from his study of the French novel, and as he sat there he had a vague sense of fraternising with Balzac and Alfred de Musset; there were echoes and reminiscences of their works in the air, confounding themselves with the indefinable exhalations, the strange composite odour, half agreeable, half impure, of the boulevard. 'Splendid Paris, charming Paris'—that refrain, the fragment of an invocation, a beginning without an end, hummed itself perpetually in Hyacinth's ears; the only articulate words that got themselves uttered in the hymn of praise which his imagination had been offering to the French capital from the first hour of his stay. He recognised, he greeted, with a thousand palpitations, the seat of his maternal ancestors—was proud to be associated with so much of the superb, so many proofs of a civilisation that had no visible rough spots. He had his perplexities, and he had even now and then a revulsion for which he had made no allowance, as when it came over him that the most brilliant city in the world was also the most bloodstained; but the great sense that he understood and sympathised was preponderant, and his comprehension gave him wings—appeared to transport him to still wider fields of knowledge, still higher sensations.

In other days, in London, he had thought again and again of his mother's father, the revolutionary watch-maker who had known the ecstasy of the barricade and had paid for it

with his life, and his reveries had not been sensibly chilled by
the fact that he knew next to nothing about him. He figured
him in his mind, had a conviction that he was very short, like
himself, and had curly hair, an immense talent for his work
and an extraordinary natural eloquence, together with many
of the most attractive qualities of the French character. But he
was reckless, and a little cracked, and probably immoral; he
had difficulties and debts and irrepressible passions; his life
had been an incurable fever and its tragic termination was a
matter of course. None the less it would have been a charm to
hear him talk, to feel the influence of a gaiety which even
political madness could never quench; for his grandson had a
theory that he spoke the French tongue of an earlier time,
delightful and sociable in accent and phrase, exempt from the
commonness of modern slang. This vague yet vivid personage
became Hyacinth's constant companion, from the day of his
arrival; he roamed about with Florentine's boy, hand in hand,
sat opposite to him at dinner, at the small table in the restaurant, finished the bottle with him, made the bill a little longer,
and treated him to innumerable revelations and counsels. He
knew the lad's secret without being told, and looked at him
across the diminutive tablecloth, where the great tube of
bread, pushed aside a little, left room for his elbows (it puzzled Hyacinth that the people of Paris should ever have had
the fierceness of hunger when the loaves were so big), gazed
at him with eyes of deep, kind, glowing comprehension and
with lips which seemed to murmur that when one was to die
to-morrow one was wise to eat and drink to-day. There was
nothing venerable, no constraint of importance or disapproval, in this edifying and impalpable presence; the young
man considered that Hyacinth Vivier was of his own time of
life and could enter into his pleasures as well as his pains.
Wondering, repeatedly, where the barricade on which his
grandfather fell had been erected, he at last satisfied himself
(but I am unable to trace the process of the induction) that it
had bristled across the Rue Saint-Honoré, very near to the
church of Saint-Roch. The pair had now roamed together
through all the museums and gardens, through the principal
churches (the republican martyr was very good-natured about
this), through the passages and arcades, up and down the

great avenues, across all the bridges, and above all, again and again, along the river, where the quays were an endless entertainment to Hyacinth, who lingered by the half-hour beside the boxes of old books on the parapets, stuffing his pockets with five-penny volumes, while the bright industries of the Seine flashed and glittered beneath him, and on the other bank the glorious Louvre stretched either way for a league. Our young man took almost the same sort of satisfaction in the Louvre as if he had erected it; he haunted the museum during all the first days, couldn't look enough at certain pictures, nor sufficiently admire the high polish of the great floors in which the golden, frescoed ceilings repeated themselves. All Paris struck him as tremendously artistic and decorative; he felt as if hitherto he had lived in a dusky, frowsy, Philistine world, in which the taste was the taste of Little Peddlington and the idea of beautiful arrangement had never had an influence. In his ancestral city it had been active from the first, and that was why his quick sensibility responded; and he murmured again his constant refrain, when the fairness of the great monuments arrested him, in the pearly, silvery light, or he saw them take gray-blue, delicate tones at the end of stately vistas. It seemed to him that Paris expressed herself, and did it in the grand style, while London remained vague and blurred, inarticulate, blunt and dim.

Eustache Poupin had given him letters to three or four democratic friends, ardent votaries of the social question, who had by a miracle either escaped the cruelty of exile or suffered the outrage of pardon, and, in spite of republican *mouchards*, no less infamous than the imperial, and the periodical swoops of a despotism which had only changed its buttons and postage-stamps, kept alive the sacred spark which would some day become a consuming flame. Hyacinth, however, had not had the thought of delivering these introductions; he had accepted them because Poupin had had such a solemn glee in writing them, and also because he had not the courage to let the couple in Lisson Grove know that since that terrible night at Hoffendahl's a change had come over the spirit of his dream. He had not grown more concentrated, he had grown more relaxed, and it was inconsistent with relaxation that he should rummage out Poupin's friends—one of whom lived in the Batignolles and the others in the Faubourg Saint-Antoine—and pretend that he cared for what they cared for in the same way as they cared for it. What was supreme in his mind to-day was not the idea of how the society that surrounded him should be destroyed; it was, much more, the sense of the wonderful, precious things it had produced, of the brilliant, impressive fabric it had raised. That destruction was waiting for it there was forcible evidence, known to himself and others, to show; but since this truth had risen before him, in its magnitude he had become conscious of a transfer, partial if not complete, of his sympathies; the same revulsion of which he had given a sign to the Princess in saying that now he pitied the rich, those who were regarded as happy. While the evening passed, therefore, as he kept his place at Tortoni's, the emotion that was last to visit him was a compunction for not having put himself in relation with poor Poupin's friends, for having neglected to make the acquaintance of earnest people.

Who in the world, if one should come to that, was as earnest as he himself, or had given such signal even though secret proofs of it? He could lay that unction to his soul in spite of his having amused himself cynically, spent all his time in theatres, galleries, walks of pleasure. The feeling had not failed him with which he accepted Mr. Vetch's furtherance—the sense that since he was destined to perish in his flower he was right to make a dash at the beautiful, horrible world. That reflection had been natural enough, but what was strange was the fiddler's own impulse, his desire to do something pleasant for him, to beguile him and ship him off. What had been most odd in that was the way Mr. Vetch appeared to overlook the fact that his young friend had already had, that year, such an episode of dissipation as was surely rare in the experience of London artisans. This was one of the many things Hyacinth thought of; he thought of the others in turn and out of turn; it was almost the first time he had sat still long enough (except at the theatre), to collect himself. A hundred confused reverberations of the recent past crowded upon him, and he saw that he had lived more intensely in the previous six months than in all the rest of his existence. The succession of events finally straightened itself, and he tasted some

of the rarest, strangest moments over again. His last week at
Medley, in especial, had already become a kind of fable, the
echo of a song; he could read it over like a story, gaze at it as
he would have gazed at some exquisite picture. His visit there
had been perfect to the end, and even the three days that
Captain Sholto's sojourn lasted had not broken the spell, for
the three more that had elapsed before his own departure (the
Princess herself had given him the signal), were the most important of all. It was then the Princess had made it clear to
him that she was in earnest, was prepared for the last sacrifice.
She was now his standard of comparison, his authority, his
measure, his perpetual reference; and in taking possession of
his mind to this extent she had completely renewed it. She
was altogether a new term, and now that he was in a foreign
country he observed how much her conversation, itself so foreign, had prepared him to understand it. In Paris he saw, of
course, a great many women, and he noticed almost all of
them, especially the actresses; confronting, mentally, their
movement, their speech, their manner of dressing, with that
of his extraordinary friend. He judged that she was beyond
them in every respect, though there were one or two actresses
who had the air of trying to copy her.

The recollection of the last days he had spent with her affected him now like the touch of a tear-washed cheek. She
had shed tears for him, and it was his suspicion that her secret
idea was to frustrate the redemption of his vow to Hoffendahl, to the immeasurable body that Hoffendahl represented.
She pretended to have accepted it, and what she said was
simply that when he should have played his part she would
engage to save him—to fling a cloud about him, as the
goddess-mother of the Trojan hero used, in Virgil's poem, to
escamoter Æneas. What she meant was, in his view, to prevent
him from playing his part at all. She was in earnest for herself,
not for him. The main result of his concentrated intimacy
with her had been to make him feel that he was good enough
for anything. When he had asked her, the last day, if he might
write to her she had said, Yes, but not for two or three weeks.
He had written after Pinnie's death, and again just before
coming abroad, and in doing so had taken account of something else she had said in regard to their correspondence—

that she didn't wish vague phrases, protestations or compliments; she wanted the realities of his life, the smallest,
most personal details. Therefore he had treated her to the
whole business of the break-up in Lomax Place, including the
sale of the rickety furniture. He had told her what that transaction brought—a beggarly sum, but sufficient to help a little
to pay debts; and he had informed her furthermore that one
of the ways Mr. Vetch had taken to hurry him off to Paris was
to offer him a present of thirty pounds out of his curious little
hoard, to add to the sum already inherited from Pinnie—
which, in a manner that none of Hyacinth's friends, of course,
could possibly regard as frugal, or even as respectable, was
now consecrated to a mere excursion. He even mentioned
that he had ended by accepting the thirty pounds, adding that
he feared there was something demoralising in his peculiar
situation (she would know what he meant by that): it disposed one to take what one could get, made one at least very
tolerant of whims that happened to be munificent.

What he did not mention to the Princess was the manner in
which he had been received by Paul Muniment and by Millicent Henning on his return from Medley. Millicent's reception had been the queerest; it had been quite unexpectedly
mild. She made him no scene of violence, and appeared to
have given up the line of throwing a blur of recrimination
over her own nefarious doings. She treated him as if she liked
him for having got in with the swells; she had an appreciation
of success which would lead her to handle him more tenderly
now that he was really successful. She tried to make him describe the style of life that was led in a house where people
were invited to stay like that without having to pay, and she
surprised him almost as much as she gratified him by not indulging in any of her former digs at the Princess. She was
lavish of ejaculations when he answered certain of her questions—ejaculations that savoured of Pimlico, 'Oh, I say!' and
'Oh, my stars!'—and he was more than ever struck with her
detestable habit of saying, 'Aye, that's where it is,' when he
had made some remark to which she wished to give an intelligent and sympathetic assent. But she didn't jeer at the Princess's private character; she stayed her satire, in a case where
there was such an opening for it. Hyacinth reflected that this

was lucky for her: he couldn't have stood it (nervous and anxious as he was about Pinnie), if she had had the bad taste, at such a time as that, to be profane and insulting. In that case he would have broken with her completely—he would have been too disgusted. She displeased him enough, as it was, by her vulgar tricks of speech. There were two or three little recurrent irregularities that aggravated him to a degree quite out of proportion to their importance, as when she said 'full up' for full, 'sold out' for sold, or remarked to him that she supposed he was now going to chuck up his work at old Crookenden's. These phrases had fallen upon his ear many a time before, but now they seemed almost unpardonable enough to quarrel about. Not that he had any wish to quarrel, for if the question had been pushed he would have admitted that to-day his intimacy with the Princess had caused any rights he might have had upon Millicent to lapse. Millicent did not push it, however; she only, it was evident, wished to convey to him that it was better for both parties they should respect each other's liberty. A genial understanding on this subject was what Miss Henning desired, and Hyacinth forbade himself to inquire what use she proposed to make of her freedom. During the month that elapsed between Pinnie's death and his visit to Paris he had seen her several times, for the respect for each other's freedom had somehow not implied cessation of intercourse, and it was only natural she should have been soft to him in his bereaved condition. Hyacinth's sentiment about Pinnie was deep, and Millicent was clever enough to guess it; the consequence of which was that on these occasions she was very soft indeed. She talked to him almost as if she had been his mother and he a convalescent child; called him her dear, and a young rascal, and her old boy; moralised a good deal, abstained from beer (till she learned he had inherited a fortune), and when he remarked once (moralising a little, too), that after the death of a person we have loved we are haunted by the memory of our failures of kindness, of generosity, rejoined, with a dignity that made the words almost a contribution to philosophy, 'Yes, that's where it is!'

Something in her behaviour at this period had even made Hyacinth wonder whether there were not some mystical sign in his appearance, some subtle betrayal in the very expression of his face, of the predicament in which he had been placed by Diedrich Hoffendahl; he began to suspect afresh the operation of that 'beastly *attendrissement*' he had detected of old in people who had the benefit of Miss Pynsent's innuendoes. The compassion Millicent felt for him had never been one of the reasons why he liked her; it had fortunately been corrected, moreover, by his power to make her furious. This evening, on the boulevard, as he watched the interminable successions, one of the ideas that came to him was that it was odd he should like her even yet; for heaven knew he liked the Princess better, and he had hitherto supposed that when a sentiment of this kind had the energy of a possession it made a clean sweep of all minor predilections. But it was clear to him that Millicent still existed for him; that he couldn't feel he had quite done with her, or she with him; and that in spite of his having now so many other things to admire there was still a comfort in the recollection of her robust beauty and her primitive passions. Hyacinth thought of her as some clever young barbarian who in ancient days should have made a pilgrimage to Rome might have thought of a Dacian or Iberian mistress awaiting his return on the rough provincial shore. If Millicent considered his visit at a 'hall' a proof of the sort of success that was to attend him (how he reconciled this with the supposition that she perceived, as a ghostly irradiation, intermingled with his curly hair, the aureola of martyrdom, he would have had some difficulty in explaining), if Miss Henning considered, on his return from Medley, that he had taken his place on the winning side, it was only consistent of her to borrow a grandeur from his further travels; and, indeed, by the time he was ready to start she spoke of the plan as if she had invented it herself and had even contributed materially to the funds required. It had been her theory, from the first, that she only liked people of spirit; and Hyacinth certainly had never had so much spirit as when he launched himself into Continental adventures. He could say to himself, quite without bitterness, that of course she would profit by his absence to put her relations with Sholto on a comfortable footing; yet, somehow, at this moment, as her face came back to him amid the crowd of faces about him, it had not that

gentleman's romantic shadow across it. It was the brilliancy of
Paris, perhaps, that made him see things rosy; at any rate, he
remembered with kindness something that she had said to
him the last time he saw her and that had touched him exceedingly at the moment. He had happened to observe to her,
in a friendly way, that now Miss Pynsent had gone she was,
with the exception of Mr. Vetch, the person in his whole circle who had known him longest. To this Millicent had replied
that Mr. Vetch wouldn't live for ever, and then she should
have the satisfaction of being his very oldest friend. 'Oh, well,
I shan't live for ever, either,' said Hyacinth; which led her to
inquire whether by chance he had a weakness of the chest.
'Not that I know of, but I might get killed in a row;' and
when she broke out into scorn of his silly notion of turning
everything up (as if any one wanted to know what a costermonger would like, or any of that low sort at the East End!)
he amused himself with asking her if she were satisfied with
the condition of society and thought nothing ought to be
done for people who, at the end of a lifetime of starvation-
wages, had only the reward of the hideous workhouse and a
pauper's grave.

'I shouldn't be satisfied with anything, if ever you was to
slip up,' Millicent answered, simply, looking at him with her
beautiful boldness. Then she added, 'There's one thing I can
tell *you*, Mr. Robinson: that if ever any one was to do you a
turn——' And she paused again, tossing back the head she
carried as if it were surmounted by a tiara, while Hyacinth
inquired what would occur in that contingency. 'Well, there'd
be *one* left behind who would take it up!' she announced; and
in the tone of the declaration there was something brave and
genuine. It struck Hyacinth as a strange fate—though not
stranger, after all, than his native circumstances—that one's
memory should come to be represented by a shop-girl over-
laden with bracelets of imitation silver; but he was reminded
that Millicent was a fine specimen of a woman of a type opposed to the whining, and that in her free temperament many
disparities were reconciled.

XXX

O N THE OTHER HAND the brilliancy of Paris had not
much power to transfigure the impression made upon
him by such intercourse with Paul Muniment as he had
enjoyed during the weeks that followed Pinnie's death—an
impression considerably more severe than any idea of
renunciation or oblivion that could connect itself with Millicent. Why it should have had the taste of sadness was not
altogether clear, for Muniment's voice was as distinct as any
in the chorus of approbation excited by the news that Hyacinth was about to cultivate the most characteristic of the
pleasures of gentility—a sympathetic unanimity, of which the
effect was to place his journey to Paris in a light almost ridiculous. What had got into them all, and did they think he was
good for nothing but to amuse himself? Mr. Vetch had been
the most zealous, but the others clapped him on the back in
almost exactly the same manner as he had seen his mates in
Soho bring their palms down on one of their number when it
was disclosed to them that his 'missus' had made him yet once
again a father. That had been Poupin's tone, and his wife's as
well; and even poor Schinkel, with his everlasting bandage,
whom he had met in Lisson Grove, appeared to think it necessary to remark that a little run across the Rhine, while he
was about it, would open his eyes to a great many wonders.
The Poupins shed tears of joy, and the letters which have already been mentioned, and which lay day after day on the
mantel-shelf of the little room our hero occupied in a *hôtel
garni*, tremendously tall and somewhat lopsided, in the Rue
Jacob (that recommendation proceeded also from Lisson
Grove, the garni being kept by a second cousin of Madame
Eustache), these valuable documents had been prepared by
the obliging exile many days before his young friend was
ready to start. It was almost refreshing to Hyacinth when old
Crookenden, the sole outspoken dissentient, told him he was
a blockhead to waste his money on the bloody French. This
worthy employer of labour was evidently disgusted at such an
innovation; if he wanted a little recreation why couldn't he
take it as it had been taken in Soho from the beginning of

time, in the shape of a trip to Hampton Court or two or three
days of alcoholic torpor? Old Crookenden was right. Hyacinth conceded freely that he was a blockhead, and was only a
little uncomfortable that he couldn't explain why he didn't
pretend not to be and had a kind of right to that compensatory luxury.

Paul guessed why, of course, and smiled approval with a
candour which gave Hyacinth a strange, inexpressible heart-
ache. He already knew that his friend's view of him was that
he was ornamental and adapted to the lighter kinds of socialistic utility—constituted to show that the revolution was not
necessarily brutal and illiterate; but in the light of the cheerful
stoicism with which Muniment regarded the sacrifice our
hero was committed to, the latter had found it necessary to
remodel a good deal his original conception of the young
chemist's nature. The result of this process was not that he
admired it less but that he felt almost awe-stricken in the presence of it. There had been an element of that sort in his
appreciation of Muniment from the first, but it had been
infinitely deepened by the spectacle of his sublime consistency. Hyacinth felt that he himself could never have risen to
that point. He was competent to make the promise to Hoffendahl, and he was equally competent to keep it; but he
could not have had the same fortitude for another, could not
have detached himself from personal prejudice so effectually
as to put forward, in that way, for the terrible 'job,' a little
chap he liked. That Muniment liked him it never occurred to
Hyacinth to doubt, and certainly he had all the manner of it
to-day: he had never been more good-humoured, more placidly talkative; he was like an elder brother who knew that the
'youngster' was clever, and was rather proud of it even when
there was no one there to see. That air of suspending their
partnership for the moment, which had usually marked him
at the 'Sun and Moon,' was never visible in other places; in
Audley Court he only chaffed Hyacinth occasionally for taking him too seriously. To-day his young friend hardly knew
just how to take him; the episode of which Hoffendahl was
the central figure had, as far as one could see, made so little
change in his life. As a conspirator he was so extraordinarily
candid, and bitterness and denunciation so rarely sat on his

lips. It was as if he had been ashamed to complain; and indeed, for himself, as the months went on, he had nothing particular to complain of. He had had a rise, at the chemical works, and a plan of getting a larger room for Rosy was under serious consideration. On behalf of others he never sounded the pathetic note—he thought that sort of thing unbusiness-like; and the most that he did in the way of expatiation on the wrongs of humanity was occasionally to mention certain statistics, certain 'returns,' in regard to the remuneration of industries, applications for employment and the discharge of hands. In such matters as these he was deeply versed, and he moved in a dry statistical and scientific air in which it cost Hyacinth an effort of respiration to accompany him. Simple and kindly as he was, and thoughtful of the woes of beasts, attentive and merciful to small insects, and addicted even to kissing dirty babies in Audley Court, he sometimes emitted a short satiric gleam which showed that his esteem for the poor was small and that if he had no illusions about the people who had got everything into their hands he had as few about those who had egregiously failed to do so. He was tremendously reasonable, which was largely why Hyacinth admired him, having a desire to be so himself but finding it terribly difficult.

Muniment's absence of passion, his fresh-coloured coolness, his easy, exact knowledge, the way he kept himself clean (except for the chemical stains on his hands), in circumstances of foul contact, constituted a group of qualities that had always appeared to Hyacinth singularly enviable. Most enviable of all was the force that enabled him to sink personal sentiment where a great public good was to be attempted and yet keep up the form of caring for that minor interest. It seemed to Hyacinth that if *he* had introduced a young fellow to Hoffendahl for his purposes, and Hoffendahl had accepted him on such a recommendation, and everything had been settled, he would have preferred never to look at the young fellow again. That was his weakness, and Muniment carried it off far otherwise. It must be added that he had never made an allusion to their visit to Hoffendahl; so that Hyacinth also, out of pride, held his tongue on the subject. If his friend didn't wish to express any sympathy for him he was not going to beg for it (especially as he didn't want it), by restless references. It had originally been a surprise to him that Muniment should be willing to countenance a possible assassination; but after all none of his ideas were narrow (Hyacinth had a sense that they ripened all the while), and if a pistol-shot would do any good he was not the man to raise pedantic objections. It is true that, as regards his quiet acceptance of the predicament in which Hyacinth might be placed by it, our young man had given him the benefit of a certain amount of doubt; it had occurred to him that perhaps Muniment had his own reasons for believing that the summons from Hoffendahl would never really arrive, so that he might only be treating himself to the entertainment of judging of a little bookbinder's nerve. But in this case, why did he take an interest in the little book-binder's going to Paris? That was a thing he would not have cared for had he held that in fact there was nothing to fear. He despised the sight of idleness, and in spite of the indul-gence he had more than once been good enough to express on the subject of Hyacinth's epicurean tendencies what he would have been most likely to say at present was, 'Go to Paris? Go to the dickens! Haven't you been out at grass long enough for one while, didn't you lark enough in the country there with the noble lady, and hadn't you better take up your tools again before you forget how to handle them?' Rosy had said something of that sort, in her free, familiar way (what-ever her intention, she had been, in effect, only a little less sarcastic than old Crookenden): that Mr. Robinson was going in for a life of leisure, a life of luxury, like herself; she must congratulate him on having the means and the time. Oh, the time—that was the great thing! She could speak with knowl-edge, having always enjoyed these advantages herself. And she intimated—or was she mistaken?—that his good fortune em-ulated hers also in the matter of his having a high-born and beneficent friend (such a blessing, now he had lost dear Miss Pynsent), who covered him with little attentions. Rose Muni-ment, in short, had been more exasperating than ever.

The boulevard became even more brilliant as the evening went on, and Hyacinth wondered whether he had a right to occupy the same table for so many hours. The theatre on the other side discharged its multitude; the crowd thickened on the wide asphalt, on the terrace of the café; gentlemen, accompanied by ladies of whom he knew already how to characterise the type—*des femmes très-chic*—passed into the portals of Tortoni. The nightly emanation of Paris seemed to rise more richly, to float and hang in the air, to mingle with the universal light and the many-voiced sound, to resolve itself into a thousand solicitations and opportunities, addressed however mainly to those in whose pockets the chink of a little loose gold might respond. Hyacinth's retrospections had not made him drowsy, but quite the reverse; he grew restless and excited, and a kind of pleasant terror of the place and hour entered into his blood. But it was nearly midnight, and he got up to walk home, taking the line of the boulevard toward the Madeleine. He passed down the Rue Royale, where comparative stillness reigned; and when he reached the Place de la Concorde, to cross the bridge which faces the Corps Législatif, he found himself almost isolated. He had left the human swarm and the obstructed pavements behind, and the wide spaces of the splendid square lay quiet under the summer stars. The plash of the great fountains was audible, and he could almost hear the wind-stirred murmur of the little wood of the Tuileries on one side, and of the vague expanse of the Champs Elysées on the other. The place itself—the Place Louis Quinze, the Place de la Révolution—had given him a sensible emotion, from the day of his arrival; he had recognised so quickly its tremendously historic character. He had seen, in a rapid vision, the guillotine in the middle, on the site of the inscrutable obelisk, and the tumbrils, with waiting victims, were stationed round the circle now made majestic by the monuments of the cities of France. The great legend of the French Revolution, sanguinary and heroic, was more real to him here than anywhere else; and, strangely, what was most present was not its turpitude and horror, but its magnificent energy, the spirit of life that had been in it, not the spirit of death. That shadow was effaced by the modern fairness of fountain and statue, the stately perspective and composition; and as he lingered, before crossing the Seine, a sudden sense overtook him, making his heart sink with a kind of desolation—a sense of everything that might hold one to the world, of the sweetness of not dying, the fascination of great cities,

the charm of travel and discovery, the generosity of admiration. The tears rose to his eyes, as they had done more than
once in the past six months, and a question, low but poignant, broke from his lips, ending in nothing. 'How could
he—how *could* he——?' It may be explained that 'he' was a
reference to Paul Muniment; for Hyacinth had dreamed of
the religion of friendship.

Three weeks after this he found himself in Venice, whence
he addressed to the Princess Casamassima a letter of which I
reproduce the principal passages.

'This is probably the last time I shall write to you before I
return to London. Of course you have been in this place, and
you will easily understand why here, especially here, the spirit
should move me. Dear Princess, what an enchanted city, what
ineffable impressions, what a revelation of the exquisite! I
have a room in a little *campo* opposite to a small old church,
which has cracked marble slabs let into the front; and in the
cracks grow little wild delicate flowers, of which I don't know
the name. Over the door of the church hangs an old battered
leather curtain, polished and tawny, as thick as a mattress, and
with buttons in it, like a sofa; and it flops to and fro, laboriously, as women and girls, with shawls on their heads and
their feet in little wooden shoes which have nothing but toes,
pass in and out. In the middle of the campo is a fountain,
which looks still older than the church; it has a primitive,
barbaric air, and I have an idea it was put there by the first
settlers—those who came to Venice from the mainland, from
Aquileia. Observe how much historical information I have already absorbed; it won't surprise you, however, for you never
wondered at anything after you discovered I knew something
of Schopenhauer. I assure you, I don't think of that musty
misogynist in the least to-day, for I bend a genial eye on the
women and girls I just spoke of, as they glide, with a small
clatter and with their old copper water-jars, to the fountain.
The Venetian girl-face is wonderfully sweet and the effect is
charming when its pale, sad oval (they all look underfed), is
framed in the old faded shawl. They also have very fascinating
hair, which never has done curling, and they slip along together, in couples or threes, interlinked by the arms and never
meeting one's eye (so that its geniality doesn't matter),

dressed in thin, cheap cotton gowns, whose limp folds make the same delightful line that everything else in Italy makes. The weather is splendid and I roast—but I like it; apparently, I was made to be spitted and "done," and I discover that I have been cold all my life, even when I thought I was warm. I have seen none of the beautiful patricians who sat for the great painters—the gorgeous beings whose golden hair was intertwined with pearls; but I am studying Italian in order to talk with the shuffling, clicking maidens who work in the bead-factories—I am determined to make one or two of them look at me. When they have filled their old water-pots at the fountain it is jolly to see them perch them on their heads and patter away over the polished Venetian stones. It's a charm to be in a country where the women don't wear the hideous British bonnet. Even in my own class (excuse the expression—I remember it used to offend you), I have never known a young female, in London, to put her nose out of the door without it; and if you had frequented such young females as much as I have you would have learned of what degradation that dreary necessity is the source. The floor of my room is composed of little brick tiles, and to freshen the air, in this temperature, one sprinkles it, as you no doubt know, with water. Before long, if I keep on sprinkling, I shall be able to swim about; the green shutters are closed, and the place makes a very good tank. Through the chinks the hot light of the campo comes in. I smoke cigarettes, and in the pauses of this composition recline on a faded magenta divan in the corner. Convenient to my hand, in that attitude, are the works of Leopardi and a second-hand dictionary. I am very happy—happier than I have ever been in my life save at Medley—and I don't care for anything but the present hour. It won't last long, for I am spending all my money. When I have finished this I shall go forth and wander about in the splendid Venetian afternoon; and I shall spend the evening in that enchanted square of St. Mark's, which resembles an immense open-air drawing-room, listening to music and feeling the sea-breeze blow in between those two strange old columns, in the piazzetta, which seem to make a portal for it. I can scarcely believe that it's of myself that I am telling these fine things; I say to myself a dozen times a day that Hyacinth

Robinson is not in it—I pinch my leg to see if I'm not dreaming. But a short time hence, when I have resumed the exercise of my profession, in sweet Soho, I shall have proof enough that it has been my very self: I shall know that by the terrible grind I shall feel my work to be.

'That will mean, no doubt, that I'm deeply demoralised. It won't be for you, however, in this case, to cast the stone at me; for my demoralisation began from the moment I first approached you. Dear Princess, I may have done you good, but you haven't done me much. I trust you will understand what I mean by that speech, and not think it flippant or impertinent. I may have helped you to understand and enter into the misery of the people (though I protest I don't know much about it), but you have led my imagination into quite another train. However, I don't mean to pretend that it's all your fault if I have lost sight of the sacred cause almost altogether in my recent adventures. It is not that it has not been there to see, for that perhaps is the clearest result of extending one's horizon—the sense, increasing as we go, that want and toil and suffering are the constant lot of the immense majority of the human race. I have found them everywhere, but I haven't minded them. Excuse the cynical confession. What has struck me is the great achievements of which man has been capable in spite of them—the splendid accumulations of the happier few, to which, doubtless, the miserable many have also in their degree contributed. The face of Europe appears to be covered with them, and they have had much the greater part of my attention. They seem to me inestimably precious and beautiful, and I have become conscious, more than ever before, of how little I understand what, in the great rectification, you and Poupin propose to do with them. Dear Princess, there are things which I shall be sorry to see you touch, even you with your hands divine; and—shall I tell you *le fond de ma pensée*, as you used to say?—I feel myself capable of fighting for them. You can't call me a traitor, for you know the obligation that I recognise. The monuments and treasures of art, the great palaces and properties, the conquests of learning and taste, the general fabric of civilisation as we know it, based, if you will, upon all the despotisms, the cruelties, the exclusions, the monopolies and the rapacities of the past, but thanks to which, all the same, the world is less impracticable and life more tolerable—our friend Hoffendahl seems to me to hold them too cheap and to wish to substitute for them something in which I can't somehow believe as I do in things with which the aspirations and the tears of generations have been mixed. You know how extraordinary I think our Hoffendahl (to speak only of him); but if there is one thing that is more clear about him than another it is that he wouldn't have the least feeling for this incomparable, abominable old Venice. He would cut up the ceilings of the Veronese into strips, so that every one might have a little piece. I don't want every one to have a little piece of anything, and I have a great horror of that kind of invidious jealousy which is at the bottom of the idea of a redistribution. You will say that I talk of it at my ease, while, in a delicious capital, I smoke cigarettes on a magenta divan; and I give you leave to scoff at me if it turns out that, when I come back to London without a penny in my pocket, I don't hold the same language. I don't know what it comes from, but during the last three months there has crept over me a deep mistrust of that same grudging attitude—the intolerance of positions and fortunes that are higher and brighter than one's own; a fear, moreover, that I may, in the past, have been actuated by such motives, and a devout hope that if I am to pass away while I am yet young it may not be with that odious stain upon my soul.'

XXXI

H YACINTH spent three days, after his return to London, in a process which he supposed to be the quest of a lodging; but in reality he was pulling himself together for the business of his livelihood—an effort he found by no means easy or agreeable. As he had told the Princess, he was demoralised, and the perspective of Mr. Crookenden's dirty staircase had never seemed so steep. He lingered on the brink, before he plunged again into Soho; he wished not to go back to the shop till he should be settled, and he delayed to get settled in order not to go back to the shop. He saw no one during this interval, not even Mr. Vetch; he waited to call upon the fiddler till he should have the appearance of not coming as a beggar or a borrower—have recovered his employment and be able to give an address, as he had heard Captain Sholto say. He went to South Street—not meaning to go in at once but wishing to look at the house—and there he had the surprise of perceiving a bill of sale in the window of the Princess's late residence. He had not expected to find her in town (he had heard from her the last time three weeks before, and then she said nothing about her prospects), but he was puzzled by this indication that she had moved away altogether. There was something in this, however, which he felt that at bottom he had looked for; it appeared a proof of the justice of a certain suspicious, uneasy sentiment from which one could never be quite free, in one's intercourse with the Princess—a vague apprehension that one might suddenly stretch out one's hand and miss her altogether from one's side. Hyacinth decided to ring at the door and ask for news of her; but there was no response to his summons: the stillness of an August afternoon (the year had come round again from his first visit) hung over the place, the blinds were down and the caretaker appeared to be absent. Under these circumstances Hyacinth was much at a loss; unless, indeed, he should address a letter to his wonderful friend at Medley. It would doubtless be forwarded, though her short lease of the country-house had terminated, as he knew, several weeks before. Captain Sholto was of course a possible medium of communication; but nothing would have induced Hyacinth to ask such a service of him.

He turned away from South Street with a curious sinking of the heart; his state of ignorance struck inward, as it were— had the force of a vague, disquieting portent. He went to old Crookenden's only when he had arrived at his last penny. This, however, was very promptly the case. He had disembarked at London Bridge with only seventeen pence in his pocket, and he had lived on that sum for three days. The old fiddler in Lomax Place was having a chop before he went to the theatre, and he invited Hyacinth to share his repast, sending out at the same time for another pot of beer. He took the youth with him to the play, where, as at that season there were very few spectators, he had no difficulty in finding him a place. He seemed to wish to keep hold of him, and looked at him strangely, over his spectacles (Mr. Vetch wore the homely double glass in these latter years), when he learned that Hyacinth had taken a lodging not in their old familiar quarter but in the unexplored purlieus of Westminster. What had determined our young man was the fact that from this part of the town the journey was comparatively a short one to Camberwell; he had suffered so much, before Pinnie's death, from being separated by such a distance from his best friends. There was a pang in his heart connected with the image of Paul Muniment, but none the less the prospect of an evening hour in Audley Court, from time to time, appeared one of his most definite sources of satisfaction in the future. He could have gone straight to Camberwell to live, but that would carry him too far from the scene of his profession; and in Westminster he was much nearer to old Crookenden's than he had been in Lomax Place. He said to Mr. Vetch that if it would give him pleasure he would abandon his lodging and take another in Pentonville. But the old man replied, after a moment, that he should be sorry to put that constraint upon him; if he were to make such an exaction Hyacinth would think he wanted to watch him.

'How do you mean, to watch me?'

Mr. Vetch had begun to tune his fiddle, and he scraped it a little before answering. 'I mean it as I have always meant it. Surely you know that in Lomax Place I had my eyes on you. I

watched you as a child on the edge of a pond watches the
little boat he has constructed and set afloat.'

'You couldn't discover much. You saw, after all, very little
of me,' Hyacinth said.

'I made what I could of that little; it was better than
nothing.'

Hyacinth laid his hand gently on the old man's arm; he had
never felt so kindly to him, not even when he accepted the
thirty pounds, before going abroad, as at this moment. 'Certainly I will come and see you.'

'I was much obliged to you for your letters,' Mr. Vetch
remarked, without heeding these words, and continuing to
scrape. He had always, even into the shabbiness of his old
age, kept that mark of English good-breeding (which is composed of some such odd elements), that there was a shyness,
an aversion to possible phrase-making, in his manner of expressing gratitude for favours, and that in spite of this cursory
tone his acknowledgment had ever the accent of sincerity.

Hyacinth took but little interest in the play, which was an
inanimate revival; he had been at the Théâtre Français and the
tradition of that house was still sufficiently present to him to
make any other style of interpretation appear of the clumsiest.
He sat in one of the front stalls, close to the orchestra; and
while the piece went forward—or backward, ever backward,
as it seemed to him—his thoughts wandered far from the
shabby scene and the dusty boards, revolving round a question which had come up immensely during the last few hours.
The Princess was a *capricciosa*—that, at least, was Madame
Grandoni's account of her: and was that blank, expressionless
house in South Street a sign that an end had come to the
particular caprice in which he had happened to be involved?
He had returned to London with an ache of eagerness to be
with her again on the same terms as at Medley, a throbbing
sense that unless she had been abominably dishonest he might
count upon her. This state of mind was by no means complete security, but it was so sweet that it mattered little
whether it were sound. Circumstances had favoured in an extraordinary degree his visit to her, and it was by no means
clear that they would again be so accommodating or that
what had been possible for a few days should be possible

with continuity, in the midst of the ceremonies and complications of London. Hyacinth felt poorer than he had ever felt
before, inasmuch as he had had money and spent it, whereas
in previous times he had never had it to spend. He never for
an instant regretted his squandered fortune, for he said to
himself that he had made a good bargain and become master
of a precious equivalent. The equivalent was a rich experience—an experience which would become richer still as he
should talk it over, in a low chair, close to hers, with the
all-comprehending, all-suggesting lady of his life. His poverty
would be no obstacle to their intercourse so long as he should
have a pair of legs to carry him to her door; for she liked him
better shabby than when he was furbished up, and she had
given him too many pledges, they had taken together too
many appointments, worked out too many programmes, to
be disconcerted (on either side) by obstacles that were merely
a part of the general conventionality. He was to go with her
into the slums, to introduce her to the worst that London
contained (he should have, precisely, to make acquaintance
with it first), to show her the reality of the horrors of which
she dreamed that the world might be purged. He had ceased,
himself, to care for the slums, and had reasons for not wishing to spend his remnant in the contemplation of foul things;
but he would go through with his part of the engagement.
He might be perfunctory, but any dreariness would have a
gilding that should involve an association with her. What if
she should have changed, have ceased to care? What if, from a
kind of royal insolence which he suspected to lurk somewhere
in the side-scenes of her nature, though he had really not once
seen it peep out, she should toss back her perfect head with a
movement signifying that he was too basely literal and that
she knew him no more? Hyacinth's imagination represented
her this evening in places where a barrier of dazzling light
shut her out from access, or even from any appeal. He saw
her with other people, in splendid rooms, where 'the dukes'
had possession of her, smiling, satisfied, surrounded, covered
with jewels. When this vision grew intense he found a reassurance in reflecting that after all she would be unlikely to
throw him personally over so long as she should remain
mixed up with what was being planned in the dark, and that

it would not be easy for her to liberate herself from that entanglement. She had of course told him more, at Medley, of the manner in which she had already committed herself, and he remembered, with a strange perverse elation, that she had gone very far indeed.

In the intervals of the foolish play Mr. Vetch, who lingered in his place in the orchestra while his mates descended into the little hole under the stage, leaned over the rail and asked his young friend occasional questions, carrying his eyes at the same time up about the dingy house, at whose smoky ceiling and tarnished galleries he had been staring for so many a year. He came back to Hyacinth's letters, and said, 'Of course you know they were clever; they entertained me immensely. But as I read them I thought of poor Pinnie: I wished she could have listened to them; they would have made her so happy.'

'Yes, poor Pinnie,' Hyacinth murmured, while Mr. Vetch went on:

'I was in Paris in 1840; I stayed at a small hotel in the Rue Mogador. I judge everything is changed, from your letters. Does the Rue Mogador still exist? Yes, everything is changed. I daresay it's all much finer, but I liked it very much as it was then. At all events, I am right in supposing—am I not?— that it cheered you up considerably, made you really happy.'

'Why should I have wanted any cheering? I was happy enough,' Hyacinth replied.

The fiddler turned his old white face upon him; it had the unhealthy smoothness which denotes a sedentary occupation, thirty years spent in a close crowd, amid the smoke of lamps and the odour of stage-paint. 'I thought you were sad about Pinnie,' he remarked.

'When I jumped, with that avidity, at your proposal that I should take a tour? Poor old Pinnie!' Hyacinth added.

'Well, I hope you think a little better of the world. We mustn't make up our mind too early in life.'

'Oh, I have made up mine: it's an awfully jolly place.'

'Awfully jolly, no; but I like it as I like an old pair of shoes—I like so much less the idea of putting on the new ones.'

'Why should I complain?' Hyacinth asked. 'What have I known but kindness? People have done such a lot for me.'

'Oh, well, of course, they have liked you. But that's all right,' murmured Mr. Vetch, beginning to scrape again. What remained in Hyacinth's mind from this conversation was the fact that the old man, whom he regarded distinctly as cultivated, had thought his letters clever. He only wished that he had made them cleverer still; he had no doubt of his ability to have done so.

It may be imagined whether the first hours he spent at old Crookenden's, after he took up work again, were altogether to his taste, and what was the nature of the reception given him by his former comrades, whom he found exactly in the same attitudes and the same clothes (he knew and hated every article they wore), and with the same primitive pleasantries on their lips. Our young man's feelings were mingled; the place and the people appeared to him loathsome, but there was something delightful in handling his tools. He gave a little private groan of relief when he discovered that he still liked his work and that the pleasant swarm of his ideas (in the matter of sides and backs), returned to him. They came in still brighter, more suggestive form, and he had the satisfaction of feeling that his taste had improved, that it had been purified by experience, and that the covers of a book might be made to express an astonishing number of high conceptions. Strange enough it was, and a proof, surely, of our little hero's being a genuine artist, that the impressions he had accumulated during the last few months appeared to mingle and confound themselves with the very sources of his craft and to be susceptible of technical representation. He had quite determined, by this time, to carry on his life as if nothing were hanging over him, and he had no intention of remaining a little bookbinder to the end of his days; for that medium, after all, would translate only some of his conceptions. Yet his trade was a resource, an undiminished resource, for the present, and he had a particular as well as a general motive in attempting new flights—the prevision of the exquisite work which he was to do during the coming year for the Princess and which it was very definite to him he owed her. When that debt should have been paid and his other arrears made up he proposed to himself to write something. He was far from having decided as yet what it should be; the only point settled was that it should be very remarkable and should not, at least on the face of it, have anything to do with a fresh deal of the social pack. That was to be his transition—into literature; to bind the book, charming as the process might be, was after all much less fundamental than to write it. It had occurred to Hyacinth more than once that it would be a fine thing to produce a brilliant death-song.

It is not surprising that among such reveries as this he should have been conscious of a narrow range in the tone of his old workfellows. They had only one idea: that he had come into a thousand pounds and had gone to spend them in France with a regular high one. He was aware, in advance, of the diffusion of this legend, and did his best to allow for it, taking the simplest course, which was not to contradict it but to catch the ball as it came and toss it still further, enlarging and embroidering humorously until Grugan and Roker and Hotchkin and all the rest, who struck him as not having washed since he left them, seemed really to begin to understand how it was he could have spent such a rare sum in so short a time. The impressiveness of this achievement helped him greatly to slip into his place; he could see that, though the treatment it received was superficially irreverent, the sense that he was very sharp and that the springs of his sharpness were somehow secret gained a good deal of strength from it. Hyacinth was not incapable of being rather pleased that it *should* be supposed, even by Grugan, Roker and Hotchkin, that he could get rid of a thousand pounds in less than five months, especially as to his own conscience the fact had altogether yet to be proved. He got off, on the whole, easily enough to feel a little ashamed, and he reflected that the men at Crookenden's, at any rate, showed no symptoms of the social jealousy lying at the bottom of the desire for a fresh deal. This was doubtless an accident, and not inherent in the fact that they were highly skilled workmen (old Crookenden had no others), and therefore sure of constant employment; for it was impossible to be more skilled, in one's own line, than Paul Muniment was, and yet he (though not out of jealousy, of course), went in for the great restitution. What struck him most, after he had got used again to the sense of his apron and bent his back a while over his battered table, was the simple, synthetic patience of the others, who had bent *their* backs and felt the rub of that dirty drapery all the while he was lounging in the halls of Medley, dawdling through boulevards and museums, and admiring the purity of the Venetian girl-face. With Poupin, to be sure, his relations were special; but the explanations that he owed the sensitive Frenchman were not such as could make him very unhappy, once he had determined to resist as much as possible the friction of his remaining days. There was moreover more sorrow than anger in Poupin's face when he learned that his young friend and pupil had failed to cultivate, in Paris, the rich opportunities he had offered him. 'You are cooling off, my child; there is something about you! Have you the weakness to flatter yourself that anything has been done, or that humanity suffers a particle less? *Enfin*, it's between you and your conscience.'

'Do you think I want to get out of it?' Hyacinth asked, smiling; Eustache Poupin's phrases about humanity, which used to thrill him so, having grown of late strangely hollow and *rococo*.

'You owe me no explanations; the conscience of the individual is absolute, except, of course, in those classes in which, from the very nature of the infamies on which they are founded, no conscience can exist. Speak to me, however, of my Paris; *she* is always divine,' Poupin went on; but he showed signs of irritation when Hyacinth began to praise to him the magnificent creations of the arch-fiend of December. In the presence of this picture he was in a terrible dilemma: he was gratified as a Parisian and a patriot but he was disconcerted as a lover of liberty; it cost him a pang to admit that anything in the sacred city was defective, yet he saw still less his way to concede that it could owe any charm to the perjured monster of the second Empire, or even to the hypocritical, mendacious republicanism of the régime before which the sacred Commune had gone down in blood and fire. 'Ah, yes, it's very fine, no doubt,' he remarked at last, 'but it will be finer still when it's ours!'—a speech which caused Hyacinth to turn back to his work with a slight feeling of sickness. Everywhere, everywhere, he saw the ulcer of envy—the passion of a party which hung together for the purpose of despoiling another to its advantage. In old Eustache, one of the 'pure,' this was particularly sad.

XXXII

THE LANDING at the top of the stairs in Audley Court was always dark; but it seemed darker than ever to Hyacinth while he fumbled for the door-latch, after he had heard Rose Muniment's penetrating voice bid him come in. During that instant his ear caught the sound—if it could trust itself—of another voice, which prepared him, a little, for the spectacle that offered itself as soon as the door (his attempt to reach the handle, in his sudden agitation, proving fruitless), was opened to him by Paul. His friend stood there, tall and hospitable, saying something loud and jovial, which he didn't distinguish. His eyes had crossed the threshold in a flash, but his step faltered a moment, only to obey, however, the vigour of Muniment's outstretched hand. Hyacinth's glance had gone straight, and though with four persons in it Rosy's little apartment looked crowded, he saw no one but the object of his quick preconception—no one but the Princess Casamassima, seated beside the low sofa (the grand feature introduced during his absence from London), on which, arrayed in the famous pink dressing-gown, Miss Muniment now received her visitors. He wondered afterwards why he should have been so startled; for he had said, often enough, both to himself and to the Princess, that so far as she was concerned he was proof against astonishment; it was so evident that, in her behaviour, the unexpected was the only thing to be looked for. In fact, now that he perceived she had made her way to Camberwell without his assistance, the feeling that took possession of him was a kind of embarrassment; he blushed a little as he entered the circle, the fourth member of which was inevitably Lady Aurora Langrish. Was it that his intimacy with the Princess gave him a certain sense of responsibility for her conduct in respect to people who knew her as yet but a little, and that there was something that required explanation in the confidence with which she had practised a descent upon them? It is true that it came over our young man that by this time, perhaps, they knew her a good deal; and moreover a woman's conduct spoke for itself when she could sit looking, in that fashion, like a radiant angel dressed in a

simple bonnet and mantle and immensely interested in an appealing corner of the earth. It took Hyacinth but an instant
to perceive that her character was in a different phase from any
that had yet been exhibited to him. There had been a brilliant
mildness about her the night he made her acquaintance, and
she had never ceased, at any moment since, to strike him as an
exquisitely human, sentient, pitying organisation; unless it
might be, indeed, in relation to her husband, against whom—
for reasons, after all, doubtless, very sufficient—her heart appeared absolutely steeled. But now her face turned to him
through a sort of glorious charity. She had put off her splendour, but her beauty was unquenchably bright; she had made
herself humble for her pious excursion; she had, beside Rosy
(who, in the pink dressing-gown, looked much the more luxurious of the two), almost the attitude of an hospital nurse;
and it was easy to see, from the meagre line of her garments,
that she was tremendously in earnest. If Hyacinth was flurried
her own countenance expressed no confusion; for her, evidently, this queer little chamber of poverty and pain was a
place in which it was perfectly natural that *he* should turn up.
The sweet, still greeting her eyes offered him might almost
have conveyed to him that she had been waiting for him, that
she knew he would come and that there had been a tacit appointment for that very moment. They said other things beside, in their beautiful friendliness; they said, 'Don't notice
me too much, or make any kind of scene. I have an immense
deal to say to you, but remember that I have the rest of our
life before me to say it in. Consider only what will be easiest
and kindest to these people, these delightful people, whom I
find enchanting (why didn't you ever tell me more—I mean
really more—about them?) It won't be particularly complimentary to them if you have the air of seeing a miracle in my
presence here. I am very glad of your return. The quavering,
fidgety "ladyship" is as fascinating as the others.'

   Hyacinth's reception at the hands of his old friends was
cordial enough quite to obliterate the element of irony that
had lurked, three months before, in their godspeed; their
welcome was not boisterous, but it seemed to express the
idea that the occasion was already so rare and agreeable that
his arrival was all that was needed to make it perfect. By the

time he had been three minutes in the room he was able to
measure the impression produced by the Princess, who, it
was clear, had thrown a spell of adoration over the little
company. This was in the air, in the face of each, in their
excited, smiling eyes and heightened colour; even Rosy's
wan grimace, which was at all times screwed up to ecstasy,
emitted a supererogatory ray. Lady Aurora looked more
than ever dishevelled with interest and wonder; the long
strands of her silky hair floated like gossamer, as, in her extraordinary, religious attention (her hands were raised and
clasped to her bosom, as if she were praying), her respiration
rose and fell. She had never seen any one like the Princess;
but Hyacinth's apprehension, of some months before, had
been groundless—she evidently didn't think her vulgar. She
thought her divine, and a revelation of beauty and benig-
nity; and the illuminated, amplified room could contain no
dissentient opinion. It was her beauty, primarily, that
'fetched' them, Hyacinth could easily see, and it was not hidden from him that the sensation was as active in Paul Muniment as in his companions. It was not in Paul's nature to be
jerkily demonstrative, and he had not lost his head on the
present occasion; but he had already appreciated the difference between one's preconception of a meretricious, factitious fine lady and the actual influence of such a personage.
She was gentler, fairer, wiser, than a chemist's assistant
could have guessed in advance. In short, she held the trio in
her hand (she had reduced Lady Aurora to exactly the same
simplicity as the others), and she performed, admirably, artistically, for their benefit. Almost before Hyacinth had had
time to wonder how she had found the Muniments out (he
had no recollection of giving her specific directions), she
mentioned that Captain Sholto had been so good as to introduce her; doing so as if she owed him that explanation
and were a woman who would be scrupulous in such a case.
It was rather a blow to him to hear that she had been accepting the Captain's mediation, and this was not softened
by her saying that she was too impatient to wait for his own
return; he was apparently so happy on the Continent that
one couldn't be sure it would ever take place. The Princess
might at least have been sure that to see her again very soon

was still more necessary to his happiness than anything the Continent could offer.

It came out in the conversation he had with her, to which the others listened with respectful curiosity, that Captain Sholto had brought her a week before, but then she had seen only Miss Muniment. 'I took the liberty of coming again, by myself, to-day, because I wanted to see the whole family,' the Princess remarked, looking from Paul to Lady Aurora, with a friendly gaiety in her face which purified the observation (as regarded her ladyship), of impertinence. The Princess added, frankly, that she had now been careful to arrive at an hour when she thought Mr. Muniment might be at home. 'When I come to see gentlemen, I like at least to find them,' she continued, and she was so great a lady that there was no small diffidence in her attitude; it was a simple matter for her to call on a chemist's assistant, if she had a reason. Hyacinth could see that the reason had already been brought forward—her immense interest in problems that Mr. Muniment had completely mastered, and in particular their common acquaintance with the extraordinary man whose mission it was to solve them. Hyacinth learned later that she had pronounced the name of Hoffendahl. A part of the lustre in Rosy's eye came no doubt from the explanation she had inevitably been moved to make in respect to any sympathy with wicked theories that might be imputed to *her*; and of course the effect of this intensely individual little protest (such was always its effect), emanating from the sofa and the pink dressing-gown, was to render the Muniment interior still more quaint and original. In that spot Paul always gave the go-by, humorously, to any attempt to draw out his views, and you would have thought, to hear him, that he allowed himself the reputation of having them only in order to get a 'rise' out of his sister and let their visitors see with what wit and spirit she could repudiate them. This, however, would only be a reason the more for the Princess's following up her scent. She would doubtless not expect to get at the bottom of his ideas in Audley Court; the opportunity would occur, rather, in case of his having the civility (on which surely she might count), to come and talk them over with her in her own house.

Hyacinth mentioned to her the disappointment he had had in South Street, and she replied, 'Oh, I have given up that house, and taken quite a different one.' But she didn't say where it was, and in spite of her having given him so much the right to expect she would communicate to him a matter so nearly touching them both as a change of address, he felt a great shyness about asking.

Their companions watched them as if they considered that something rather brilliant, now, would be likely to come off between them; but Hyacinth was too full of regard to the Princess's tacit notification to him that they must not appear too thick, which was after all more flattering than the most pressing inquiries or the most liberal announcements about herself could have been. She never asked him when he had come back; and indeed it was not long before Rose Muniment took that business upon herself. Hyacinth, however, ventured to assure himself whether Madame Grandoni were still with the Princess, and even to remark (when she had replied, 'Oh yes, still, still. The great refusal, as Dante calls it, has not yet come off'), 'You ought to bring her to see Miss Rosy. She is a person Miss Rosy would particularly appreciate.'

'I am sure I should be most happy to receive any friend of the Princess Casamassima,' said this young lady, from the sofa; and when the Princess answered that she certainly would not fail to produce Madame Grandoni some day, Hyacinth (though he doubted whether the presentation would really take place), guessed how much she wished her old friend might have heard the strange bedizened little invalid make that speech.

There were only three other seats, for the introduction of the sofa (a question so profoundly studied in advance), had rendered necessary the elimination of certain articles; so that Muniment, on his feet, hovered round the little circle, with his hands in his pockets, laughing freely and sociably but not looking at the Princess; though, as Hyacinth was sure, he was none the less agitated by her presence.

'You ought to tell us about foreign parts and the grand things you have seen; except that, doubtless, our distinguished visitor knows all about them,' Muniment said to

Hyacinth. Then he added, 'Surely, at any rate, you have seen nothing more worthy of your respect than Camberwell.'

'Is this the worst part?' the Princess asked, looking up with her noble, interested face.

'The worst, madam? What grand ideas you must have! We admire Camberwell immensely.'

'It's my brother's ideas that are grand!' cried Rose Muniment, betraying him conscientiously. 'He does want everything changed, no less than you, Princess; though he is more cunning than you, and won't give one a handle where one can take him up. He thinks all this part most objectionable—as if dirty people won't always make everything dirty where they live! I dare say he thinks there ought to be no dirty people, and it may be so; only if every one was clean, where would be the merit? You would get no credit for keeping yourself tidy. At any rate, if it's a question of soap and water, every one can begin by himself. My brother thinks the whole place ought to be as handsome as Brompton.'

'Ah, yes, that's where the artists and literary people live, isn't it?' asked the Princess, attentively.

'I have never seen it, but it's very well laid out,' Rosy rejoined, with her competent air.

'Oh, I like Camberwell better than that,' said Muniment, hilariously.

The Princess turned to Lady Aurora, and with the air of appealing to her for her opinion gave her a glance which travelled in a flash from the topmost bow of her large, misfitting hat to the crumpled points of her substantial shoes. 'I must get *you* to tell me the truth,' she murmured. 'I want so much to know London—the real London. It seems so difficult!'

Lady Aurora looked a little frightened, but at the same time gratified, and after a moment she responded, 'I believe a great many artists live in St. John's Wood.'

'I don't care about the artists!' the Princess exclaimed, shaking her head, slowly, with the sad smile which sometimes made her beauty so inexpressibly touching.

'Not when they have painted you such beautiful pictures?' Rosy demanded. 'We know about your pictures—we have admired them so much. Mr. Hyacinth has described to us your precious possessions.'

The Princess transferred her smile to Rosy, and rested it on that young lady's shrunken countenance with the same ineffable head-shake. 'You do me too much honour. I have no possessions.'

'Gracious, was it all a make-believe?' Rosy cried, flashing at Hyacinth an eye that was never so eloquent as when it demanded an explanation.

'I have nothing in the world—nothing but the clothes on my back!' the Princess repeated, very gravely, without looking at the young man.

The words struck him as an admonition, so that, though he was much puzzled, he made no attempt, for the moment, to reconcile the contradiction. He only replied, 'I meant the things in the house. Of course I didn't know whom they belonged to.'

'There are no things in my house now,' the Princess went on; and there was a touch of pure, high resignation in the words.

'Laws, I shouldn't like that!' Rose Muniment declared, glancing, with complacency, over her own decorated walls. 'Everything here belongs to me.'

'I shall bring Madame Grandoni to see you,' said the Princess, irrelevantly but kindly.

'Do you think it's not right to have a lot of things about?' Lady Aurora, with sudden courage, queried of her distinguished companion, pointing her chin at her but looking into the upper angle of the room.

'I suppose one must always settle that for one's self. I don't like to be surrounded with objects I don't care for; and I can care only for one thing—that is, for one class of things—at a time. Dear lady,' the Princess went on, 'I fear I must confess to you that my heart is not in *bibelots*. When thousands and tens of thousands haven't bread to put in their mouths, I can dispense with tapestry and old china.' And her fair face, bent charmingly, conciliatingly, on Lady Aurora, appeared to argue that if she was narrow at least she was candid.

Hyacinth wondered, rather vulgarly, what strange turn she had taken, and whether this singular picture of her denuded personality were not one of her famous caprices, a whimsical joke, a nervous perversity. Meanwhile, he heard Lady Aurora urge, anxiously, 'But don't you think we ought to make the world more beautiful?'

'Doesn't the Princess make it so by the mere fact of her existence?' Hyacinth demanded; his perplexity escaping, in a harmless manner, through this graceful hyperbole. He had observed that, though the lady in question could dispense with old china and tapestry, she could not dispense with a pair of immaculate gloves, which fitted her like a charm.

'My people have a mass of things, you know, but I have really nothing myself,' said Lady Aurora, as if she owed this assurance to such a representative of suffering humanity.

'The world will be beautiful enough when it becomes good enough,' the Princess resumed. 'Is there anything so ugly as unjust distinctions, as the privileges of the few contrasted with the degradation of the many? When we want to beautify, we must begin at the right end.'

'Surely there are none of us but what have our privileges!' Rose Muniment exclaimed, with eagerness. 'What do you say to mine, lying here between two members of the aristocracy, and with Mr. Hyacinth thrown in?'

'You are certainly lucky—with Lady Aurora Langrish. I wish she would come and see *me*,' the Princess murmured, getting up.

'Do go, my lady, and tell me if it's so poor!' Rosy went on, gaily.

'I think there can't be too many pictures and statues and works of art,' Hyacinth broke out. 'The more the better, whether people are hungry or not. In the way of ameliorating influences, are not those the most definite?'

'A piece of bread and butter is more to the purpose, if your stomach's empty,' the Princess declared.

'Robinson has been corrupted by foreign influences,' Paul Muniment suggested. 'He doesn't care for bread and butter now; he likes French cookery.'

'Yes, but I don't get it. And have you sent away the little man, the Italian, with the white cap and apron?' Hyacinth asked of the Princess.

She hesitated a moment, and then she replied, laughing, and not in the least offended at his question, though it was an attempt to put her in the wrong from which Hyacinth had

not been able to refrain, in his astonishment at these ascetic
pretensions, 'I have sent him away many times!'

Lady Aurora had also got up; she stood there gazing at her
beautiful fellow-visitor with a timidity which made her wonder only more apparent. 'Your servants must be awfully fond
of you,' she said.

'Oh, my servants!' murmured the Princess, as if it were only
by a stretch of the meaning of the word that she could be said
to enjoy the ministrations of menials. Her manner seemed to
imply that she had a charwoman for an hour a day. Hyacinth
caught the tone, and determined that since she was going, as
it appeared, he would break off his own visit and accompany
her. He had flattered himself, at the end of three weeks of
Medley, that he knew her in every phase, but here was a field
of freshness. She turned to Paul Muniment and put out her
hand to him, and while he took it in his own his face was
visited by the most beautiful eyes that had ever rested there.
'Will you come and see me, one of these days?' she asked,
with a voice as sweet and clear as her glance.

Hyacinth waited for Paul's answer with an emotion that
could only be accounted for by his affectionate sympathy,
the manner in which he had spoken of him to the Princess
and which he wished him to justify, the interest he had in
his appearing, completely, the fine fellow he believed him.
Muniment neither stammered nor blushed; he held himself
straight, and looked back at his interlocutress with an eye almost as crystalline as her own. Then, by way of answer, he
inquired, 'Well, madam, pray what good will it do me?' And
the tone of the words was so humorous and kindly, and so
instinct with a plain manly sense, that though they were not
gallant Hyacinth was not ashamed for him. At the same moment he observed that Lady Aurora was watching their
friend as if she had at least an equal stake in what he might
say.

'Ah, none; only me, perhaps, a little.' With this rejoinder,
and with a wonderful sweet, indulgent dignity, in which there
was none of the stiffness of pride or resentment, the Princess
quitted him and approached Lady Aurora. She asked her if *she*
wouldn't do her the kindness to come. She should like so
much to know her, and she had an idea there was a great deal

they might talk about. Lady Aurora said she should be delighted, and the Princess took one of her cards out of her pocket and gave it to the noble spinster. After she had done so she stood a moment holding her hand, and remarked, 'It has really been such a happiness to me to meet you. Please don't think it's very clumsy if I say I *do* like you so!' Lady Aurora was evidently exceedingly moved and impressed; but Rosy, when the Princess took farewell of her, and the irrepressible invalid had assured her of the pleasure with which she should receive her again, admonished her that in spite of this she could never conscientiously enter into such theories.

'If every one was equal,' she asked, 'where would be the gratification I feel in getting a visit from a grandee? That's what I have often said to her ladyship, and I consider that I've kept her in her place a little. No, no; no equality while *I*'m about the place!'

The company appeared to comprehend that there was a natural fitness in Hyacinth's seeing the great lady on her way, and accordingly no effort was made to detain him. He guided her, with the help of an attendant illumination from Muniment, down the dusky staircase, and at the door of the house there was a renewed brief leave-taking with the young chemist, who, however, showed no signs of relenting or recanting in respect to the Princess's invitation. The warm evening had by this time grown thick, and the population of Audley Court appeared to be passing it, for the most part, in the open air. As Hyacinth assisted his companion to thread her way through groups of sprawling, chattering children, gossiping women with bare heads and babies at the breast, and heavily-planted men smoking very bad pipes, it seemed to him that their project of exploring the slums was already in the way of execution. He said nothing till they had gained the outer street, and then, pausing a moment, he inquired how she would be conveyed. Had she a carriage somewhere, or should he try and get a cab?

'A carriage, my dear fellow? For what do you take me? I won't trouble you about a cab: I walk everywhere now.'

'But if I had not been here?'

'I should have gone alone,' said the Princess, smiling at him through the turbid twilight of Camberwell.

'And where, please, gracious heaven? I may at least have the honour of accompanying you.'

'Certainly, if you can walk so far.'

'So far as what, dear Princess?'

'As Madeira Crescent, Paddington.'

'Madeira Crescent, Paddington?' Hyacinth stared.

'That's what I call it when I'm with people with whom I wish to be fine, like you. I have taken a small house there.'

'Then it's really true that you have given up your beautiful things?'

'I have sold them all, to give to the poor.'

'Ah, Princess!' the young man almost moaned; for the memory of some of her treasures was vivid within him.

She became very grave, even stern, and with an accent of reproach that seemed to show she had been wounded where she was most sensitive, she demanded, 'When I said I was willing to make the last sacrifice, did you then believe I was lying?'

'Haven't you kept *anything*?' Hyacinth went on, without heeding this challenge.

She looked at him a moment. 'I have kept *you*!' Then she took his arm, and they moved forward. He saw what she had done; she was living in a little ugly, bare, middle-class house and wearing simple gowns; and the energy and good faith of her behaviour, with the abruptness of the transformation, took away his breath. 'I thought I should please you so much,' she added, after they had gone a few steps. And before he had time to reply, as they came to a part of the street where there were small shops, those of butchers, greengrocers and pork-pie men, with open fronts, flaring lamps and humble purchasers, she broke out, joyously, 'Ah, this is the way I like to see London!'

XXXIII

THE HOUSE in Madeira Crescent was a low, stucco-fronted edifice, in a shabby, shallow semicircle, and Hyacinth could see, as they approached it, that the window-place in the parlour (which was on a level with the street-door), was ornamented by a glass case containing stuffed birds and surmounted by an alabaster Cupid. He was suffi-ciently versed in his London to know that the descent in the scale of the gentility was almost immeasurable for a person who should have moved into that quarter from the neigh-bourhood of Park Lane. The street was not squalid, and it was strictly residential; but it was mean and meagre and fourth-rate, and had in the highest degree that paltry, paro-chial air, that absence of style and elevation, which is the stamp of whole districts of London and which Hyacinth had already more than once mentally compared with the high-piled, important look of the Parisian perspective. It possessed in combination every quality which should have made it de-testable to the Princess; it was almost as bad as Lomax Place. As they stopped before the narrow, ill-painted door, on which the number of the house was marked with a piece of common porcelain, cut in a fanciful shape, it appeared to Hyacinth that he had felt, in their long walk, the touch of the passion which led his companion to divest herself of her superfluities, but that it would take the romantic out of one's heroism to settle one's self in such a *mesquin*, Philistine row. However, if the Princess had wished to mortify the flesh she had chosen an effective means of doing so, and of mortifying the spirit as well. The long light of the gray sum-mer evening was still in the air, and Madeira Crescent wore a soiled, dusty expression. A hand-organ droned in front of a neighbouring house, and the cart of the local washer-woman, to which a donkey was harnessed, was drawn up opposite. The local children, as well, were dancing on the pavement, to the music of the organ, and the scene was sur-veyed, from one of the windows, by a gentleman in a dirty dressing-gown, smoking a pipe, who made Hyacinth think of Mr. Micawber. The young man gave the Princess a deep look, before they went into the house, and she smiled, as if she understood everything that was passing in his mind.

The long, circuitous walk with her, from the far-away south of London, had been strange and delightful; it reminded Hyacinth, more queerly than he could have expressed, of some of the rambles he had taken on summer evenings with Millicent Henning. It was impossible to resemble this young lady less than the Princess resembled her, but in her enjoyment of her unwonted situation (she had never before, on a summer's evening—to the best of Hyacinth's belief, at least—lost herself in the unfashionable districts on the arm of a seedy artisan), the distinguished personage exhibited certain coincidences with the shop-girl. She stopped, as Millicent had done, to look into the windows of vulgar establishments, and amused herself with picking out abominable objects that she should like to possess; selecting them from a new point of view, that of a reduced fortune and the domestic arrangements of the 'lower middle class,' deriving extreme diversion from the idea that she now belonged to that aggrieved body. She was in a state of light, fresh, sociable exhilaration which Hyacinth had hitherto, in the same degree, not seen in her, and before they reached Madeira Crescent it had become clear to him that her present phase was little more than a brilliant *tour de force*, which he could not imagine her keeping up long, for the simple reason that after the novelty and strangeness of the affair had passed away she would not be able to endure the contact of so much that was common and ugly. For the moment her discoveries in this line diverted her, as all discoveries did, and she pretended to be sounding, in a scientific spirit—that of the social philosopher, the student and critic of manners—the depths of the British Philistia. Hyacinth was struck, more than ever, with the fund of life that was in her, the energy of feeling, the high, free, reckless spirit. These things expressed themselves, as the couple proceeded, in a hundred sallies and droll proposals, kindling the young man's pulses and making him conscious of the joy with which, in any extravagance, he would bear her company to the death. She appeared to him, at this moment, to be playing with life so audaciously and defiantly that the end of it all would inevitably be some violent catastrophe.

She desired exceedingly that Hyacinth should take her to a music-hall or a coffee-tavern; she even professed a curiosity to see the inside of a public-house. As she still had self-possession enough to remember that if she stayed out beyond a certain hour Madame Grandoni would begin to worry about her, they were obliged to content themselves with the minor 'lark,' as the Princess was careful to designate their peep into an establishment, glittering with polished pewter and brass, which bore the name of the 'Happy Land.' Hyacinth had feared that she would be nervous after the narrow, befingered door had swung behind her, or that, at all events, she would be disgusted at what she might see and hear in such a place and would immediately wish to retreat. By good luck, however, there were only two or three convivial spirits in occupancy, and the presence of the softer sex was apparently not so rare as to excite surprise. The softer sex, furthermore, was embodied in a big, hard, red woman, the publican's wife, who looked as if she were in the habit of dealing with all sorts and mainly interested in seeing whether even the finest put down their money before they were served. The Princess pretended to 'have something,' and to admire the ornamentation of the bar; and when Hyacinth asked her in a low tone what disposal they should make, when the great changes came, of such an embarrassing type as that, replied, off-hand, 'Oh, drown her in a barrel of beer!' She professed, when they came out, to have been immensely interested in the 'Happy Land,' and was not content until Hyacinth had fixed an evening on which they might visit a music-hall together. She talked with him largely, by fits and starts, about his adventures abroad and his impressions of France and Italy; breaking off, suddenly, with some irrelevant but almost extravagantly appreciative allusion to Rose Muniment and Lady Aurora; then returning with a question as to what he had seen and done, the answer to which, however, in many cases, she was not at pains to wait for. Yet it implied that she had paid considerable attention to what he told her that she should be able to say, towards the end, with that fraternising frankness which was always touching because it appeared to place her at one's mercy, to show that she counted on one's having an equal loyalty, 'Well, my dear

friend, you have not wasted your time; you know everything, you have missed nothing; there are lots of things you
can tell me, and we shall have some famous talks in the winter evenings.' This last reference was apparently to the coming season, and there was something in the tone of quiet
friendship with which it was uttered, and which seemed to
involve so many delightful things, something that, for Hyacinth, bound them still closer together. To live out of the
world with her that way, lost among the London millions,
in a queer little cockneyfied retreat, was a refinement of intimacy, and better even than the splendid chance he had enjoyed at Medley.

They found Madame Grandoni sitting alone in the twilight,
very patient and peaceful, and having, after all, it was clear,
accepted the situation too completely to fidget at such a trifle
as her companion's not coming home at a ladylike hour. She
had placed herself in the back part of the tawdry little
drawing-room, which looked into a small, smutty garden, and
from the front window, which was open, the sound of the
hurdy-gurdy and the voices of the children, who were romp-
ing to its music, came in to her through the summer dusk.
The influence of London was there, in a kind of mitigated,
far-away hum, and for some reason or other, at that moment,
the place, to Hyacinth, took on the semblance of the home of
an exile—a spot and an hour to be remembered with a throb
of fondness in some danger or sorrow of after years. The old
lady never moved from her chair as she saw the Princess come
in with the little bookbinder, and her eyes rested on Hyacinth
as familiarly as if she had seen him go out with her in the
afternoon. The Princess stood before Madame Grandoni a
moment, smiling. 'I have done a great thing. What do you
think I have done?' she asked, as she drew off her gloves.

'God knows! I have ceased to think!' said the old woman,
staring up, with her fat, empty hands on the arms of her
chair.

'I have come on foot from the far south of London—how
many miles? four or five—and I'm not a particle tired.'

'*Che forza, che forza!*' murmured Madame Grandoni. 'She
will knock you up, completely,' she added, turning to Hyacinth with a kind of customary compassion.

'Poor darling, *she* misses the carriage,' Christina remarked, passing out of the room.

Madame Grandoni followed her with her eyes, and Hyacinth thought he perceived a considerable lassitude, a plaintive bewilderment and *hébétement*, in the old woman's face. 'Don't you like to use cabs—I mean hansoms?' he asked, wishing to say something comforting to her.

'It is not true that I miss anything; my life is only too full,' she replied. 'I lived worse than this—in my bad days.' In a moment she went on: 'It's because you are here—she doesn't like Assunta to come.'

'Assunta—because I am here?' Hyacinth did not immediately catch her meaning.

'You must have seen her Italian maid at Medley. She has kept her, and she's ashamed of it. When we are alone Assunta comes for her bonnet. But she likes you to think she waits on herself.'

'That's a weakness—when she's so strong! And what does Assunta think of it?' Hyacinth asked, looking at the stuffed birds in the window, the alabaster Cupid, the wax flowers on the chimney-piece, the florid antimacassars on the chairs, the sentimental engravings on the walls—in frames of *papier-mâché* and 'composition,' some of them enveloped in pink tissue-paper—and the prismatic glass pendants which seemed attached to everything.

'She says, "What on earth will it matter to-morrow?"'

'Does she mean that to-morrow the Princess will have her luxury back again? Hasn't she sold all her beautiful things?'

Madame Grandoni was silent a moment. 'She has kept a few. They are put away.'

'*A la bonne heure!*' cried Hyacinth, laughing. He sat down with the ironical old woman; he spent nearly half an hour in desultory conversation with her, before candles were brought in, and while Christina was in Assunta's hands. He noticed how resolutely the Princess had withheld herself from any attempt to sweeten the dose she had taken it into her head to swallow, to mitigate the ugliness of her vulgar little house. She had respected its horrible idiosyncrasies, and left, rigidly, in their places the gimcracks which found favour in Madeira Crescent. She had flung no draperies over the pretentious furniture and disposed no rugs upon the staring carpet; and it was plainly her theory that the right way to acquaint one's self with the sensations of the wretched was to suffer the anguish of exasperated taste. Presently a female servant came in—not the sceptical Assunta, but a stunted young woman of the maid-of-all-work type, the same who had opened the door to the pair a short time before—and informed Hyacinth that the Princess wished him to understand that he was expected to remain to tea. He learned from Madame Grandoni that the custom of an early dinner, followed in the evening by the frugal repast of the lower orders, was another of Christina's mortifications; and when, shortly afterwards, he saw the table laid in the back parlour, which was also the dining-room, and observed the nature of the crockery with which it was decorated, he perceived that whether or no her earnestness were durable, it was at any rate, for the time, intense. Madame Grandoni narrated to him, definitely, as the Princess had done only in scraps, the history of the two ladies since his departure from Medley, their relinquishment of that fine house and the sudden arrangements Christina had made to change her mode of life, after they had been only ten days in South Street. At the climax of the London season, in a society which only desired to treat her as one of its brightest ornaments, she had retired to Madeira Crescent, concealing her address (with only partial success, of course), from every one, and inviting a celebrated curiosity-monger to come and look at her *bibelots* and tell her what he would give her for the lot. In this manner she had parted with them at a fearful sacrifice. She had wished to avoid the nine days' wonder of a public sale; for, to do her justice, though she liked to be original she didn't like to be notorious, an occasion of vulgar chatter. What had precipitated her determination was a remonstrance received from her husband, just after she left Medley, on the subject of her excessive expenditure; he had written to her that it was past a joke (as she had appeared to consider it), and that she must really pull up. Nothing could gall her more than an interference on that head (she maintained that she knew the exact figure of the Prince's income, and that her allowance was an insignificant part of it), and she had pulled up with a vengeance, as Hyacinth perceived. The young man divined on this occasion one of the Princess's sharpest anxieties (he had never thought of it before), the danger of Casamassima's really putting the screw on—attempting to make her come back and live with him by withholding supplies altogether. In this case she would find herself in a very tight place, though she had a theory that if she should go to law about the matter the courts would allow her a separate maintenance. This course, however, it would scarcely be in her character to adopt; she would be more likely to waive her right and support herself by lessons in music and the foreign tongues, supplemented by the remnant of property that had come to her from her mother. That she was capable of returning to the Prince some day, through not daring to face the loss of luxury, was an idea that could not occur to Hyacinth, in the midst of her assurances, uttered at various times, that she positively yearned for a sacrifice; and such an apprehension was less present to him than ever as he listened to Madame Grandoni's account of the manner in which her rupture with the fashionable world had been effected. It must be added that the old lady remarked, with a sigh, that she didn't know how it would all end, as some of Christina's economies were very costly; and when Hyacinth pressed her a little she went on to say that it was not at present the question of complications arising from the Prince that troubled her most, but the fear that Christina was seriously compromised by her reckless, senseless correspondences—letters arriving from foreign countries, from God knew whom (Christina never told her, nor did she desire it), all about uprisings and liberations (of so much one could be sure), and other matters that were no concern of honest folk. Hyacinth scarcely knew what Madame Grandoni meant by this allusion, which seemed to show that, during the last few months, the Princess had considerably extended her revolutionary connection: he only thought of Hoffendahl, whose name, however, he was careful not to pronounce, and wondered whether his hostess had been writing to the Master to intercede for *him*, to beg that he might be let off. His cheeks burned at the thought, but he contented himself with remarking to Madame Grandoni that their extraordinary friend enjoyed the sense of danger. The old lady wished to know how she would enjoy the hangman's rope (with which, *du train dont elle allait*, she might easily make acquaintance); and when he expressed the hope that she didn't regard him as a counsellor of imprudence, replied, 'You, my poor child? Oh, I saw into you at Medley. You are a simple *codino!*'

The Princess came in to tea in a very dull gown, with a bunch of keys at her girdle; and nothing could have suggested the thrifty housewife better than the manner in which she superintended the laying of the cloth and the placing on it of a little austere refreshment—a pile of bread and butter, flanked by a pot of marmalade and a morsel of bacon. She filled the teapot out of a little tin canister locked up in a cupboard, of which the key worked with difficulty, and made the tea with her own superb hands; taking pains, however, to explain to Hyacinth that she was far from imposing that régime on Madame Grandoni, who understood that the grocer had a standing order to supply her, for her private consumption, with any delicacy she might desire. For herself, she had never been so well as since she followed a homely diet. On Sundays they had muffins, and sometimes, for a change, a smoked haddock, or even a fried sole. Hyacinth was lost in adoration of the Princess's housewifely ways and of the exquisite figure that she made as a little *bourgeoise*; judging that if her attempt to combine plain living with high thinking were all a comedy, at least it was the most finished entertainment she had yet offered him. She talked to Madame Grandoni about Lady Aurora; described her with much drollery, even to the details of her dress; declared that she was a delightful creature and one of the most interesting persons she had seen for an age; expressed to Hyacinth the conviction that she should like her exceedingly, if Lady Aurora would only believe a little in *her*. 'But I shall like her, whether she does or not,' said the Princess. 'I always know when that's going to happen; it isn't so common. She will begin very well with me, and be "fascinated"—isn't that the way people begin with me?—but she won't understand me at all, or make out in the least what kind of a queer fish I am, though I shall try to show her. When she thinks she does, at last, she will give me up in disgust, and will never know that she has understood me quite wrong. That has been the way with most of the people I have liked; they have run away from me *à toutes jambes*. Oh, I have inspired aversions!' laughed the Princess, handing Hyacinth his cup of tea. He recognised it by the aroma as a mixture not inferior to that of which he had partaken at Medley. 'I have never succeeded in knowing any one who would do me good; for by the time I began to improve, under their influence, they could put up with me no longer.'

'You told me you were going to visit the poor. I don't understand what your Gräfin was doing there,' said Madame Grandoni.

'She had come out of charity—in the same way as I. She evidently goes about immensely over there; I shall entreat her to take me with her.'

'I thought you had promised to let me be your guide, in those explorations,' Hyacinth remarked.

The Princess looked at him a moment. 'Dear Mr. Robinson, Lady Aurora knows more than you.'

'There have been times, surely, when you have complimented me on my knowledge.'

'Oh, I mean more about the lower classes!' the Princess exclaimed; and, oddly enough, there was a sense in which Hyacinth was unable to deny the allegation. He presently returned to something she had said a moment before, declaring that it had not been the way with Madame Grandoni and him to take to their heels, and to this she replied, 'Oh, you'll run away yet; don't be afraid!'

'I think that if I had been capable of quitting you I should have done it by this time; I have neglected such opportunities,' the old lady sighed. Hyacinth now perceived that her eye had quite lost its ancient twinkle; she was troubled about many things.

'It is true that if you didn't leave me when I was rich, it wouldn't look well for you to leave me at present,' the Princess suggested; and before Madame Grandoni could reply to this speech she said to Hyacinth, 'I liked the man, your friend Muniment, so much for saying he wouldn't come to see me. "What good would it do him," poor fellow? What good would it do him, indeed? You were not so difficult: you held off a little and pleaded obstacles, but one could see you would come down,' she continued, covering her guest with her mystifying smile. 'Besides, I was smarter then, more splendid; I had on gewgaws and suggested worldly lures. I must have been more attractive. But I liked him for refusing,' she repeated; and of the many words she uttered that evening it was these that made most impression on Hyacinth. He remained for an hour after tea, for on rising from the table she had gone to the piano (she had not deprived herself of this resource, and had a humble instrument, of the so-called 'cottage' kind), and begun to play in a manner that reminded him of her playing the day of his arrival at Medley. The night had grown close, and as the piano was in the front room he opened, at her request, the window that looked into Madeira Crescent. Beneath it assembled the youth of both sexes, the dingy loiterers who had clustered an hour before around the hurdy-gurdy. But on this occasion they did not caper about; they remained still, leaning against the area-rails and listening to the wondrous music. When Hyacinth told the Princess of the spell she had thrown upon them she declared that it made her singularly happy; she added that she was really glad, almost proud, of her day; she felt as if she had begun to do something for the people. Just before he took leave she encountered some occasion for saying to him that she was certain the man in Audley Court wouldn't come; and Hyacinth forbore to contradict her, because he believed that in fact he wouldn't.

XXXIV

OW RIGHT she had been to say that Lady Aurora would probably be fascinated at first was proved the first time Hyacinth went to Belgrave Square, a visit he was led to pay very promptly, by a deep sense of the obligations under which her ladyship had placed him at the time of Pinnie's death. The circumstances in which he found her were quite the same as those of his visit the year before; she was spending the unfashionable season in her father's empty house, amid a desert of brown holland and the dormant echoes of heavy conversation. He had seen so much of her during Pinnie's illness that he felt (or had felt then) that he knew her almost intimately—that they had become real friends, almost comrades, and might meet henceforth without reserves or ceremonies; yet she was as fluttered and awkward as she had been on the other occasion: not distant, but entangled in new coils of shyness and apparently unmindful of what had happened to draw them closer. Hyacinth, however, always liked extremely to be with her, for she was the person in the world who quietly, delicately, and as a matter of course treated him most like a gentleman. She had never said the handsome, flattering things to him that had fallen from the lips of the Princess, and never explained to him her view of him; but her timid, cursory, receptive manner, which took all sorts of equalities for granted, was a homage to the idea of his refinement. It was in this manner that she now conversed with him on the subject of his foreign travels; he found himself discussing the political indications of Paris and the Ruskinian theories of Venice, in Belgrave Square, quite like one of the cosmopolites bred in that region. It took him, however, but a few minutes to perceive that Lady Aurora's heart was not in these considerations; the deferential smile she bent upon him, while she sat with her head thrust forward and her long hands clasped in her lap, was slightly mechanical, her attitude perfunctory. When he gave her his views of some of the *arrière-pensées* of M. Gambetta (for he had views not altogether, as he thought, deficient in originality), she did not interrupt, for she never interrupted; but she took advantage of his first pause to say, quickly, irrelevantly, 'Will the Princess Casamassima come again to Audley Court?'

'I have no doubt she will come again, if they would like her to.'

'I do hope she will. She is very wonderful,' Lady Aurora continued.

'Oh, yes, she is very wonderful. I think she gave Rosy pleasure,' said Hyacinth.

'Rosy can talk of nothing else. It would really do her great good to see the Princess again. Don't you think she is different from anybody that one has ever seen?' But her ladyship added, before waiting for an answer to this, 'I liked her quite extraordinarily.'

'She liked you just as much. I know it would give her great pleasure if you should go to see her.'

'Fancy!' exclaimed Lady Aurora; but she instantly obtained the Princess's address from Hyacinth, and made a note of it in a small, shabby book. She mentioned that the card the Princess had given her in Camberwell proved to contain no address, and Hyacinth recognised that vagary—the Princess was so off-hand. Then she said, hesitating a little, 'Does she really care for the poor?'

'If she doesn't,' the young man replied, 'I can't imagine what interest she has in pretending to.'

'If she does, she's very remarkable—she deserves great honour.'

'You really care; why is she more remarkable than you?' Hyacinth demanded.

'Oh, it's very different—she's so wonderfully attractive!' Lady Aurora replied, making, recklessly, the only allusion to the oddity of her own appearance in which Hyacinth was destined to hear her indulge. She became conscious of it the moment she had spoken, and said, quickly, to turn it off, 'I should like to talk with her, but I'm rather afraid. She's tremendously clever.'

'Ah, what she is you'll find out when you know her!' Hyacinth sighed, expressively.

His hostess looked at him a little, and then, vaguely, exclaimed, 'How very interesting!' The next moment she continued, 'She might do so many other things; she might charm the world.'

'She does that, whatever she does,' said Hyacinth, smiling. 'It's all by the way; it needn't interfere.'

'That's what I mean, that most other people would be content—beautiful as she is. There's great merit, when you give up something.'

'She has known a great many bad people, and she wants to know some good,' Hyacinth rejoined. 'Therefore be sure to go to her soon.'

'She looks as if she had known nothing bad since she was born,' said Lady Aurora, rapturously. 'I can't imagine her going into all the dreadful places that she would have to.'

'You have gone into them, and it hasn't hurt you,' Hyacinth suggested.

'How do you know that? My family think it has.'

'You make me glad that I haven't a family,' said the young man.

'And the Princess—has she no one?'

'Ah, yes, she has a husband. But she doesn't live with him.'

'Is he one of the bad persons?' asked Lady Aurora, as earnestly as a child listening to a tale.

'Well, I don't like to abuse him, because he is down.'

'If I were a man, I should be in love with her,' said Lady Aurora. Then she pursued, 'I wonder whether we might work together.'

'That's exactly what she hopes.'

'I won't show her the worst places,' said her ladyship, smiling.

To which Hyacinth replied, 'I suspect you will do what every one else has done, namely, exactly what she wants!' Before he took leave he said to her, 'Do you know whether Paul Muniment liked the Princess?'

Lady Aurora meditated a moment, apparently with some intensity. 'I think he considered her extraordinarily beautiful—the most beautiful person he had ever seen.'

'Does he still believe her to be a humbug?'

'Still?' asked Lady Aurora, as if she didn't understand.

'I mean that that was the impression apparently made upon him last winter by my description of her.'

'Oh, I'm sure he thinks her tremendously plucky!' That was all the satisfaction Hyacinth got just then as to Muniment's estimate of the Princess.

A few days afterward he returned to Madeira Crescent, in the evening, the only time he was free, the Princess having given him a general invitation to take tea with her. He felt that he ought to be discreet in acting upon it, though he was not without reasons that would have warranted him in going early and often. He had a peculiar dread of her growing tired of him—boring herself in his society; yet at the same time he had rather a sharp vision of her boring herself without him, in the dull summer evenings, when even Paddington was out of town. He wondered what she did, what visitors dropped in, what pastimes she cultivated, what saved her from the sudden vagary of throwing up the whole of her present game. He remembered that there was a complete side of her life with which he was almost unacquainted (Lady Marchant and her daughters, at Medley, and three or four other persons who had called while he was there, being, in his experience, the only illustrations of it), and knew not to what extent she had, in spite of her transformation, preserved relations with her old friends; but he could easily imagine a day when she should discover that what she found in Madeira Crescent was less striking than what she missed. Going thither a second time Hyacinth perceived that he had done her great injustice; she was full of resources, she had never been so happy, she found time to read, to write, to commune with her piano, and above all to think—a delightful detachment from the invasive, vulgar, gossiping, distracting world she had known hitherto. The only interruption to her felicity was that she received quantities of notes from her former acquaintance, challenging her to give some account of herself, to say what had become of her, to come and stay with them in the country; but with these importunate missives she took a very short way—she simply burned them, without answering. She told Hyacinth immediately that Lady Aurora had called on her, two days before, at an hour when she was not in, and she had straightway addressed her, in return, an invitation to come to tea, any evening, at eight o'clock. That was the way the people in Madeira Crescent entertained each other (the Prin-

cess knew everything about them now, and was eager to impart her knowledge); and the evening, she was sure, would be
much more convenient to Lady Aurora, whose days were
filled with good works, peregrinations of charity. Her ladyship arrived ten minutes after Hyacinth; she told the Princess
that her invitation had been expressed in a manner so irresistible that she was unwilling to wait more than a day to respond. She was introduced to Madame Grandoni, and tea
was immediately served; Hyacinth being gratefully conscious
the while of the supersubtle way in which Lady Aurora forbore to appear bewildered at meeting him in such society.
She knew he frequented it, and she had been witness of his
encounter with the Princess in Audley Court; but it might
have startled her to have ocular evidence of the footing on
which he stood. Everything the Princess did or said, at this
time, had for effect, whatever its purpose, to make her seem
more rare and fine; and she had seldom given him greater
pleasure than by the exquisite art she put forward to win
Lady Aurora's confidence, to place herself under the pure and
elevating influence of the noble spinster. She made herself
small and simple; she spoke of her own little aspirations and
efforts; she appealed and persuaded; she laid her white hand
on Lady Aurora's, gazing at her with an interest which was
evidently deeply sincere, but which, all the same, derived half
its effect from the contrast between the quality of her beauty,
the whole air of her person, and the hard, dreary problems of
misery and crime. It was touching, and Lady Aurora was
touched; that was very evident as they sat together on the
sofa, after tea, and the Princess protested that she only wanted
to know what her new friend was doing—what she had done
for years—in order that she might go and do likewise. She
asked personal questions with a directness that was sometimes
embarrassing to the subject—Hyacinth had seen that habit in
her from the first—and Lady Aurora, though she was
charmed and excited, was not quite comfortable at being so
publicly probed and sounded. The public was formed of
Madame Grandoni and Hyacinth; but the old lady (whose
intercourse with the visitor had consisted almost wholly
of watching her with a quiet, speculative anxiety), presently
shuffled away, and was heard, through the thin partitions that

prevailed in Madeira Crescent, to ascend to her own apartment. It seemed to Hyacinth that he ought also, in delicacy,
to retire, and this was his intention, from one moment to the
other; to him, certainly (and the second time she met him),
Lady Aurora had made as much of her confession as he had
a right to look for. After that one little flash of egotism he
had never again heard her allude to her own feelings or circumstances.

'Do you stay in town, like this, at such a season, on purpose to attend to your work?' the Princess asked; and there
was something archly rueful in the tone in which she made
this inquiry, as if it cost her just a pang to find that in taking
such a line she herself had not been so original as she hoped.
'Mr. Robinson has told me about your big house in Belgrave
Square—you must let me come and see you there. Nothing
would make me so happy as that you should allow me to help
you a little—how little soever. Do you like to be helped, or
do you like to go alone? Are you very independent, or do you
need to look up, to cling, to lean upon some one? Excuse me
if I ask impertinent questions; we speak that way—rather,
you know—in Rome, where I have spent a large part of my
life. That idea of your being there alone in your great dull
house, with all your charities and devotions, makes a kind of
picture in my mind; it's quaint and touching, like something
in some English novel. Englishwomen are so accomplished,
are they not? I am really a foreigner, you know, and though I
have lived here a while it takes one some time to find those
things out *au juste*. Therefore, is your work for the people
only one of your occupations, or is it everything, does it absorb your whole life? That's what I should like it to be for
me! Do your family like you to throw yourself into all this, or
have you had to brave a certain amount of ridicule? I dare say
you have; that's where you English are strong, in braving
ridicule. They have to do it so often, haven't they? I don't
know whether I could do it. I never tried; but with you I
would brave anything. Are your family clever and sympathetic? No? the kind of thing that one's family generally is?
Ah, well, dear lady, we must make a little family together. Are
you encouraged or disgusted? Do you go on doggedly, or
have you any faith, any great idea, that lifts you up? Are you

religious, now, *par exemple*? Do you do your work in connection with any ecclesiasticism, any missions, or priests or sisters? I'm a Catholic, you know—but so little! I shouldn't
mind in the least joining hands with any one who is really
doing anything. I express myself awkwardly, but perhaps you
know what I mean. Possibly you don't know that I am one of
those who believe that a great social cataclysm is destined to
take place, and that it can't make things worse than they are
already. I believe, in a word, in the people doing something
for themselves (the others will never do anything for them),
and I am quite willing to help them. If that shocks you I shall
be immensely disappointed, because there is something in the
impression you make on me that seems to say that you
haven't the usual prejudices, and that if certain things were to
happen you wouldn't be afraid. You are shy, are you not?—
but you are not timorous. I suppose that if you thought the
inequalities and oppressions and miseries which now exist
were a necessary part of life, and were going on for ever, you
wouldn't be interested in those people over the river (the bedridden girl and her brother, I mean); because Mr. Robinson
tells me that they are advanced socialists—or at least the
brother is. Perhaps you'll say that you don't care for him; the
sister, to your mind, being the remarkable one. She is, indeed,
a perfect little *femme du monde*—she talks so much better
than most of the people in society. I hope you don't mind my
saying that, because I have an idea that you are not in society.
You can imagine whether I am! Haven't you judged it, like
me, condemned it, and given it up? Are you not sick of the
egotism, the snobbery, the meanness, the frivolity, the immorality, the hypocrisy? Isn't there a great resemblance in our
situation? I don't mean in our nature, for you are far better
than I shall ever be. Aren't you quite divinely good? When I
see a woman of your sort (not that I often do!) I try to be a
little less bad. You have helped hundreds, thousands, of people; you must help me!'

These remarks, which I have strung together, did not, of
course, fall from the Princess's lips in an uninterrupted
stream; they were arrested and interspersed by frequent inarticulate responses and embarrassed protests. Lady Aurora
shrank from them even while they gratified her, blinking and

fidgeting in the brilliant, direct light of her hostess's attentions. I need not repeat her answers, the more so as they none
of them arrived at completion, but passed away into nervous
laughter and averted looks, the latter directed at the ceiling,
the floor, the windows, and appearing to constitute a kind of
entreaty to some occult or supernatural power that the conversation should become more impersonal. In reply to the
Princess's allusion to the convictions prevailing in the Muniment family, she said that the brother and sister thought differently about public questions, but were of the same mind
with regard to persons of the upper class taking an interest in
the working people, attempting to enter into their life: they
held it was a great mistake. At this information the Princess
looked much disappointed; she wished to know if the Muniments thought it was impossible to do them any good. 'Oh, I
mean a mistake from *our* point of view,' said Lady Aurora.
'They wouldn't do it in our place; they think we had much
better occupy ourselves with our own pleasures.' And as the
Princess stared, not comprehending, she went on: 'Rosy
thinks we have a right to our own pleasures under all circumstances, no matter how badly off the poor may be; and her
brother takes the ground that we will not have them long,
and that in view of what may happen we are great fools not
to make the most of them.'

'I see, I see. That is very strong,' the Princess murmured, in
a tone of high appreciation.

'I dare say. But all the same, whatever is going to come,
one *must* do something.'

'You do think, then, that something is going to come?' said
the Princess.

'Oh, immense changes, I dare say. But I don't belong to
anything, you know.'

The Princess hesitated a moment. 'No more do I. But many
people do. Mr. Robinson, for instance.' And she gave Hyacinth a familiar smile.

'Oh, if the changes depend on me!' the young man exclaimed, blushing.

'They won't set the Thames on fire—I quite agree to that!'

Lady Aurora had the manner of not considering that
she had a warrant for going into the question of Hyacinth's

affiliations; so she stared abstractedly at the piano and in a moment remarked to the Princess, 'I am sure you play awfully well; I should like so much to hear you.'

Hyacinth felt that their hostess thought this *banal*. She had not asked Lady Aurora to spend the evening with her simply that they should fall back on the resources of the vulgar. Nevertheless, she replied with perfect good-nature that she should be delighted to play; only there was a thing she should like much better, namely, that Lady Aurora should narrate her life.

'Oh, don't talk about mine; yours, yours!' her ladyship cried, colouring with eagerness and, for the first time since her arrival, indulging in the free gesture of laying her hand upon that of the Princess.

'With so many narratives in the air, I certainly had better take myself off,' said Hyacinth, and the Princess offered no opposition to his departure. She and Lady Aurora were evidently on the point of striking up a tremendous intimacy, and as he turned this idea over, walking away, it made him sad, for strange, vague reasons, which he could not have expressed.

XXXV

THE SUNDAY following this occasion Hyacinth spent almost entirely with the Muniments, with whom, since his return to his work, he had been able to have no long, fraternising talk, of the kind that had marked their earlier relations. The present, however, was a happy day; it refreshed exceedingly the sentiments with which he now regarded the inscrutable Paul. The warm, bright September weather gilded even the dinginess of Audley Court, and while, in the morning, Rosy's brother and their visitor sat beside her sofa, the trio amused themselves with discussing a dozen different plans for giving a festive turn to the day. There had been moments, in the last six months, when Hyacinth had the sense that he should never again be able to enter into such ideas as that, and these moments had been connected with the strange perversion taking place in his mental image of the man whose hardness (of course he was obliged to be hard), he had never expected to see turned upon a passionate admirer. But now, for the hour at least, the darkness had cleared away, and Paul's company was in itself a comfortable, inspiring influence. He had never been kinder, jollier, safer, as it were; it had never appeared more desirable to hold fast to him and trust him. Less than ever would an observer have guessed there was a reason why the two young men might have winced as they looked at each other. Rosy naturally took part in the question debated between her companions—the question whether they should limit their excursion to a walk in Hyde Park; should embark at Lambeth pier on the penny steamer, which would convey them to Greenwich; or should start presently for Waterloo station and go thence by train to Hampton Court. Miss Muniment had visited none of these places, but she contributed largely to the discussion, for which she seemed perfectly qualified; talked about the crowd on the steamer, and the inconvenience arising from drunken persons on the return, quite as if she had suffered from these drawbacks; said that the view from the hill at Greenwich was terribly smoky, and at that season the fashionable world—half the attraction, of course—was wholly absent from Hyde

Park; and expressed strong views in favour of Wolsey's old palace, with whose history she appeared intimately acquainted. She threw herself into her brother's holiday with eagerness and glee, and Hyacinth marvelled again at the stoicism of the hard, bright creature, polished, as it were, by pain, whose imagination appeared never to concern itself with her own privations, so that she could lie in her close little room the whole golden afternoon, without bursting into sobs as she saw the western sunbeams slant upon the shabby, ugly, familiar paper of her wall and thought of the far-off fields and gardens which she should never see. She talked immensely of the Princess, for whose beauty, grace and benevolence she could find no sufficient praise; declaring that of all the fair faces that had ever hung over her couch (and Rosy spoke as from immense opportunities for comparison), she had far the noblest and most refreshing. She seemed to make a kind of light in the room and to leave it behind her after she had gone. Rosy could call up her image as she could hum a tune she had heard, and she expressed in her quaint, particular way how, as she lay there in the quiet hours, she repeated over to herself the beautiful air. The Princess might be anything, she might be royal or imperial, and Rosy was well aware how little *she* should complain of the dullness of her life when such apparitions as that could pop in any day. She made a difference in the place—it gave it a kind of finish for her to have come there; if it was good enough for a princess, it was good enough for *her*, and she hoped she shouldn't hear again of Paul's wishing her to move out of a room with which she should have henceforth such delightful associations. The Princess had found her way to Audley Court, and perhaps she wouldn't find it to another lodging—they couldn't expect her to follow them about London at their pleasure; and at any rate she had evidently been very much struck with the little room, so that if they were quiet and patient who could say but the fancy would take her to send them a bit of carpet, or a picture, or even a mirror with a gilt frame, to make it a bit more tasteful? Rosy's transitions from pure enthusiasm to the imaginative calculation of benefit were performed with a serenity peculiar to herself. Her chatter had so much spirit and point that it always commanded attention, but to-day

Hyacinth was less tolerant of it than usual, because so long as
it lasted Muniment held his tongue, and what he had been
anxious about was much more Paul's impression of the Princess. Rosy made no remark to him on the monopoly he had
so long enjoyed of this wonderful lady; she had always had
the manner of a kind of indulgent incredulity about Hyacinth's social adventures, and he saw the day might easily
come when she would begin to talk of the Princess as if she
herself had been the first to discover her. She had much to
say, however, about the nature of the acquaintance Lady Aurora had formed with her, and she was mainly occupied with
the glory she had drawn upon herself by bringing two such
exalted persons together. She fancied them alluding, in the
great world, to the occasion on which 'we first met, at Miss
Muniment's, you know;' and she related how Lady Aurora,
who had been in Audley Court the day before, had declared
that she owed her a debt she could never repay. The two
ladies had liked each other more, almost, than they liked any
one; and wasn't it a rare picture to think of them moving
hand in hand, like twin roses, through the bright upper air?
Muniment inquired, in rather a coarse, unsympathetic way,
what the mischief she ever wanted of *her*; which led Hyacinth
to demand in return, 'What do you mean? What does who
want of whom?'

'What does the beauty want of *our* poor lady? She has a
totally different stamp. I don't know much about women, but
I can see that.'

'How do you mean—a different stamp? They both have
the stamp of their rank!' cried Rosy.

'Who can ever tell what women want, at any time?' Hyacinth said, with the off-handedness of a man of the world.

'Well, my boy, if you don't know any more than I, you
disappoint me! Perhaps if we wait long enough she will tell us
some day herself.'

'Tell you what she wants of Lady Aurora?'

'I don't mind about Lady Aurora so much; but what in the
name of long journeys does she want with *us*?'

'Don't you think you're worth a long journey?' Rosy asked,
gaily. 'If you were not my brother, which is handy for seeing
you, and I were not confined to my sofa, I would go from

one end of England to the other to make your acquaintance! He's in love with the Princess,' she went on, to Hyacinth, 'and he asks those senseless questions to cover it up. What does any one want of anything?'

It was decided, at last, that the two young men should go down to Greenwich, and after they had partaken of bread and cheese with Rosy they embarked on a penny-steamer. The boat was densely crowded, and they leaned, rather squeezed together, in the fore part of it, against the rail of the deck, and watched the big black fringe of the yellow stream. The river was always fascinating to Hyacinth. The mystified entertainment which, as a child, he had found in all the aspects of London came back to him from the murky scenery of its banks and the sordid agitation of its bosom: the great arches and pillars of the bridges, where the water rushed, and the funnels tipped, and sounds made an echo, and there seemed an overhanging of interminable processions; the miles of ugly wharves and warehouses; the lean protrusions of chimney, mast, and crane; the painted signs of grimy industries, staring from shore to shore; the strange, flat, obstructive barges, straining and bumping on some business as to which everything was vague but that it was remarkably dirty; the clumsy coasters and colliers, which thickened as one went down; the small, loafing boats, whose occupants, somehow, looking up from their oars at the steamer, as they rocked in the oily undulations of its wake, appeared profane and sarcastic; in short, all the grinding, puffing, smoking, splashing activity of the turbid flood. In the good-natured crowd, amid the fumes of vile tobacco, beneath the shower of sooty particles, and to the accompaniment of a bagpipe of a dingy Highlander, who sketched occasionally a smothered reel, Hyacinth forbore to speak to his companion of what he had most at heart; but later, as they lay on the brown, crushed grass, on one of the slopes of Greenwich Park, and saw the river stretch away and shine beyond the pompous colonnades of the hospital, he asked him whether there was any truth in what Rosy had said about his being sweet on their friend the Princess. He said 'their friend' on purpose, speaking as if, now that she had been twice to Audley Court, Muniment might be regarded as knowing her almost as well as he himself did. He wished to

conjure away the idea that he was jealous of Paul, and if he
desired information on the point I have mentioned this was
because it still made him almost as uncomfortable as it had
done at first that his comrade should take the scoffing view.
He didn't easily see such a fellow as Muniment wheel about
from one day to the other, but he had been present at the
most exquisite exhibition he had ever observed the Princess
make of that divine power of conciliation which was not perhaps in social intercourse the art she chiefly exercised but was
certainly the most wonderful of her secrets, and it would be
remarkable indeed that a sane young man should not have
been affected by it. It was familiar to Hyacinth that Muniment was not easily touched by women, but this might perfectly have been the case without detriment to the Princess's
ability to work a miracle. The companions had wandered
through the great halls and courts of the hospital; had gazed
up at the glories of the famous painted chamber and admired
the long and lurid series of the naval victories of England—
Muniment remarking to his friend that he supposed he had
seen the match to all that in foreign parts, offensive little travelled beggar that he was. They had not ordered a fish-dinner
either at the 'Trafalgar' or the 'Ship' (having a frugal vision of
tea and shrimps with Rosy, on their return), but they had
laboured up and down the steep undulations of the shabby,
charming park; made advances to the tame deer and seen
them amble foolishly away; watched the young of both sexes,
hilarious and red in the face, roll in promiscuous entanglement over the slopes; gazed at the little brick observatory,
perched on one of the knolls, which sets the time of English
history and in which Hyacinth could see that his companion
took a kind of technical interest; wandered out of one of the
upper gates and admired the trimness of the little villas at
Blackheath, where Muniment declared that it was his idea of
supreme social success to be able to live. He pointed out two
or three small, semi-detached houses, faced with stucco, and
with 'Mortimer Lodge' or 'The Sycamores' inscribed upon
the gate-posts, and Hyacinth guessed that these were the sort
of place where he would like to end his days—in high, pure
air, with a genteel window for Rosy's couch and a cheerful
view of suburban excursions. It was when they came back

into the park that, being rather hot and a little satiated, they stretched themselves under a tree and Hyacinth yielded to his curiosity.

'Sweet on her—sweet on her, my boy!' said Muniment. 'I might as well be sweet on the dome of St. Paul's, which I just make out off there.'

'The dome of St. Paul's doesn't come to see you, and doesn't ask you to return the visit.'

'Oh, I don't return visits—I've got a lot of jobs of my own to do. If I don't put myself out for the Princess, isn't that a sufficient answer to your question?'

'I'm by no means sure,' said Hyacinth. 'If you went to see her, simply and civilly, because she asked you, I shouldn't regard it as a proof that you had taken a fancy to her. Your hanging off is more suspicious; it may mean that you don't trust yourself—that you are in danger of falling in love if you go in for a more intimate acquaintance.'

'It's a rum job, your wanting me to make up to her. I shouldn't think it would suit your book,' Muniment rejoined, staring at the sky, with his hands clasped under his head.

'Do you suppose I'm afraid of you?' his companion asked. 'Besides,' Hyacinth added in a moment, 'why the devil should I care, now?'

Muniment, for a little, made no rejoinder; he turned over on his side, and with his arm resting on the ground leaned his head on his hand. Hyacinth felt his eyes on his face, but he also felt himself colouring, and didn't meet them. He had taken a private vow never to indulge, to Muniment, in certain inauspicious references, and the words he had just spoken had slipped out of his mouth too easily. 'What do you mean by that?' Paul demanded, at last; and when Hyacinth looked at him he saw nothing but his companion's strong, fresh, irresponsible face. Muniment, before speaking, had had time to guess what he meant by it.

Suddenly, an impulse that he had never known before, or rather that he had always resisted, took possession of him. There was a mystery which it concerned his happiness to clear up, and he became unconscious of his scruples, of his pride, of the strength that he had believed to be in him—the strength for going through his work and passing away without a look behind. He sat forward on the grass, with his arms round his knees, and bent upon Muniment a face lighted up by his difficulties. For a minute the two men's eyes met with extreme clearness, and then Hyacinth exclaimed, 'What an extraordinary fellow you are!'

'You've hit it there!' said Muniment, smiling.

'I don't want to make a scene, or work on your feelings, but how will you like it when I'm strung up on the gallows?'

'You mean for Hoffendahl's job? That's what you were alluding to just now?' Muniment lay there, in the same attitude, chewing a long blade of dry grass, which he held to his lips with his free hand.

'I didn't mean to speak of it; but after all, why shouldn't it come up? Naturally, I have thought of it a good deal.'

'What good does that do?' Muniment returned. 'I hoped you didn't, and I noticed you never spoke of it. You don't like it; you would rather throw it up,' he added.

There was not in his voice the faintest note of irony or contempt, no sign whatever that he passed judgment on such a tendency. He spoke in a quiet, human, memorising manner, as if it had originally quite entered into his thought to allow for weak regrets. Nevertheless the complete reasonableness of his tone itself cast a chill on his companion's spirit; it was like the touch of a hand at once very firm and very soft, but strangely cold.

'I don't want in the least to throw the business up, but did you suppose I liked it?' Hyacinth asked, with rather a forced laugh.

'My dear fellow, how could I tell? You like a lot of things I don't. You like excitement and emotion and change, you like remarkable sensations, whereas I go in for a holy calm, for sweet repose.'

'If you object, for yourself, to change, and are so fond of still waters, why have you associated yourself with a revolutionary movement?' Hyacinth demanded, with a little air of making rather a good point.

'Just for that reason!' Muniment answered, with a smile. 'Isn't our revolutionary movement as quiet as the grave? Who knows, who suspects, anything like the full extent of it?'

'I see—you take only the quiet parts!'

In speaking these words Hyacinth had had no derisive intention, but a moment later he flushed with the sense that they had a sufficiently petty sound. Muniment, however, appeared to see no offence in them, and it was in the gentlest, most suggestive way, as if he had been thinking over what might comfort his comrade, that he replied, 'There's one thing you ought to remember—that it's quite on the cards it may never come off.'

'I don't desire that reminder,' Hyacinth said; 'and, moreover, you must let me say that, somehow, I don't easily fancy *you* mixed up with things that don't come off. Anything you have to do with will come off, I think.'

Muniment reflected a moment, as if his little companion were charmingly ingenious. 'Surely, I have nothing to do with this idea of Hoffendahl's.'

'With the execution, perhaps not; but how about the conception? You seemed to me to have a great deal to do with it the night you took me to see him.'

Muniment changed his position, raising himself, and in a moment he was seated, Turk-fashion, beside his mate. He put his arm over his shoulder and held him, studying his face; and then, in the kindest manner in the world, he remarked, 'There are three or four definite chances in your favour.'

'I don't want comfort, you know,' said Hyacinth, with his eyes on the distant atmospheric mixture that represented London.

'What the devil *do* you want?' Muniment asked, still holding him, and with perfect good-humour.

'Well, to get inside of *you* a little; to know how a chap feels when he's going to part with his best friend.'

'To part with him?' Muniment repeated.

'I mean, putting it at the worst.'

'I should think you would know by yourself, if you're going to part with me!'

At this Hyacinth prostrated himself, tumbled over on the grass, on his face, which he buried in his arms. He remained in this attitude, saying nothing, for a long time; and while he lay there he thought, with a sudden, quick flood of association, of many strange things. Most of all, he had the sense of the brilliant, charming day; the warm stillness, touched with cries of amusement; the sweetness of loafing there, in an interval of work, with a friend who was a tremendously fine fellow, even if he didn't understand the inexpressible. Muniment also kept silent, and Hyacinth perceived that he was unaffectedly puzzled. He wanted now to relieve him, so that he pulled himself together again and turned round, saying the first thing he could think of, in relation to the general subject of their conversation, that would carry them away from the personal question. 'I have asked you before, and you have told me, but somehow I have never quite grasped it (so I just touch on the matter again), exactly what good you think it will do.'

'This idea of Hoffendahl's? You must remember that as yet we know only very vaguely what it is. It is difficult, therefore, to measure closely the importance it may have, and I don't think I have ever, in talking with you, pretended to fix that importance. I don't suppose it will matter immensely whether your own engagement is carried out or not; but if it is it will have been a detail in a scheme of which the general effect will be decidedly useful. I believe, and you pretend to believe, though I am not sure you do, in the advent of the democracy. It will help the democracy to get possession that the classes that keep them down shall be admonished from time to time that they have a very definite and very determined intention of doing so. An immense deal will depend upon that. Hoffendahl is a capital admonisher.'

Hyacinth listened to this explanation with an expression of interest that was not feigned; and after a moment he rejoined, 'When you say you believe in the democracy, I take for granted you mean you positively wish for their coming into power, as I have always supposed. Now what I really have never understood is this—why you should desire to put forward a lot of people whom you regard, almost without exception, as donkeys.'

'Ah, my dear lad,' laughed Muniment, 'when one undertakes to meddle in human affairs one must deal with human material. The upper classes have the longest ears.'

'I have heard you say that you were working for an equality in human conditions, to abolish the immemorial inequality.

What you want, then, for all mankind is a similar *nuance* of asininity.'

'That's very clever; did you pick it up in France? The low tone of our fellow-mortals is a result of bad conditions; it is the conditions I want to alter. When those that have no start to speak of have a good one, it is but fair to infer that they will go further. I want to try them, you know.'

'But why equality?' Hyacinth asked. 'Somehow, that word doesn't say so much to me as it used to. Inequality—inequality! I don't know whether it's by dint of repeating it over to myself, but *that* doesn't shock me as it used.'

'They didn't put you up to that in France, I'm sure!' Muniment exclaimed. 'Your point of view has changed; you have risen in the world.'

'Risen? Good God, what have I risen to?'

'True enough; you were always a bloated little swell!' And Muniment gave his young friend a sociable slap on the back. There was a momentary bitterness in its being imputed to such a one as Hyacinth, even in joke, that he had taken sides with the fortunate ones of the earth, and he had it on his tongue's end to ask his friend if he had never guessed what his proud titles were—the bastard of a murderess, spawned in a gutter, out of which he had been picked by a sewing-girl. But his life-long reserve on this point was a habit not easily broken, and before such an inquiry could flash through it Muniment had gone on: 'If you've ceased to believe we can do anything, it will be rather awkward, you know.'

'I don't know what I believe, God help me!' Hyacinth remarked, in a tone of an effect so lugubrious that Paul gave one of his longest, most boyish-sounding laughs. And he added, 'I don't want you to think I have ceased to care for the people. What am I but one of the poorest and meanest of them?'

'You, my boy? You're a duke in disguise, and so I thought the first time I ever saw you. That night I took you to Hoffendahl you had a little way with you that made me forget it; I mean that your disguise happened to be better than usual. As regards caring for the people, there's surely no obligation at all,' Muniment continued. 'I wouldn't if I could help it—I promise you that. It all depends on what you see. The way I've used my eyes in this abominable metropolis has led to my seeing that present arrangements won't do. They won't do,' he repeated, placidly.

'Yes, I see that, too,' said Hyacinth, with the same doleful-ness that had marked his tone a moment before—a doleful-ness begotten of the rather helpless sense that, whatever he saw, he saw (and this was always the case), so many other things beside. He saw the immeasurable misery of the people, and yet he saw all that had been, as it were, rescued and re-deemed from it: the treasures, the felicities, the splendours, the successes, of the world. All this took the form, sometimes, to his imagination, of a vast, vague, dazzling presence, an ir-radiation of light from objects undefined, mixed with the at-mosphere of Paris and of Venice. He presently added that a hundred things Muniment had told him about the foul hor-rors of the worst districts of London, pictures of incredible shame and suffering that he had put before him, came back to him now, with the memory of the passion they had kindled at the time.

'Oh, I don't want you to go by what I have told you; I want you to go by what you have seen yourself. I remember there were things you told me that weren't bad in their way.' And at this Paul Muniment sprang to his feet, as if their con-versation had drawn to an end, or they must at all events be thinking of their homeward way. Hyacinth got up, too, while his companion stood there. Muniment was looking off to-ward London, with a face that expressed all the healthy sin-gleness of his vision. Suddenly Paul remarked, as if it occurred to him to complete, or at any rate confirm, the declaration he had made a short time before, 'Yes, I don't believe in the millennium, but I do believe in the democracy.'

The young man, as he spoke these words, struck his com-rade as such a fine embodiment of the spirit of the people; he stood there, in his powerful, sturdy newness, with such an air of having learnt what he had learnt and of good-nature that had purposes in it, that our hero felt the simple inrush of his old, frequent pride at having a person of that promise, a na-ture of that capacity, for a friend. He passed his hand into Muniment's arm and said, with an imperceptible tremor in his voice, 'It's no use your saying I'm not to go by what you tell me. I would go by what you tell me, anywhere. There's no awkwardness to speak of. I don't know that I believe exactly what you believe, but I believe in you, and doesn't that come to the same thing?'

Muniment evidently appreciated the cordiality and candour of this little tribute, and the way he showed it was by a movement of his arm, to check his companion, before they started to leave the spot, and by looking down at him with a certain anxiety of friendliness. 'I should never have taken you to Hoffendahl if I hadn't thought you would jump at the job. It was that flaring little oration of yours, at the club, when you floored Delancey for saying you were afraid, that put me up to it.'

'I did jump at it—upon my word I did; and it was just what I was looking for. That's all correct!' said Hyacinth, cheerfully, as they went forward. There was a strain of heroism in these words—of heroism of which the sense was not conveyed to Muniment by a vibration in their interlocked arms. Hyacinth did not make the reflection that he was infernally literal; he dismissed the sentimental problem that had bothered him; he condoned, excused, admired—he merged himself, resting happy for the time in the consciousness that Paul was a grand fellow, that friendship was a purer feeling than love, and that there was an immense deal of affection between them. He did not even observe at that moment that it was preponderantly on his own side.

XXXVI

A CERTAIN Sunday in November, more than three months after she had gone to live in Madeira Crescent, was so important an occasion for the Princess Casamassima that I must give as complete an account of it as the limits of my space will allow. Early in the afternoon a loud peal from her door-knocker came to her ear; it had a sound of resolution, almost of defiance, which made her look up from her book and listen. She was sitting by the fire, alone, with a volume of a heavy work on Labour and Capital in her hand. It was not yet four o'clock, but she had had candles for an hour; a dense brown fog made the daylight impure, without suggesting an answer to the question whether the scheme of nature had been to veil or to deepen the sabbatical dreariness. She was not tired of Madeira Crescent—such an idea she would indignantly have repudiated; but the prospect of a visitor was rather pleasant to her—the possibility even of his being an ambassador, or a cabinet minister, or another of the eminent personages with whom she had associated before embracing the ascetic life. They had not knocked at her present door hitherto in any great numbers, for more reasons than one; they were out of town, and she had taken pains to diffuse the belief that she had left England. If the impression prevailed, it was exactly the impression she had desired; she forgot this fact whenever she felt a certain surprise, even, it may be, a certain irritation, in perceiving that people were not taking the way to Madeira Crescent. She was making the discovery, in which she had had many predecessors, that in London it is only too possible to hide one's self. It was very much in that fashion that Godfrey Sholto was in the habit of announcing himself, when he reappeared after the intervals she explicitly imposed upon him; there was a kind of artlessness, for so world-worn a personage, in the point he made of showing that he knocked with confidence, that he had as good a right as any other. This afternoon she was ready to accept a visit from him: she was perfectly detached from the shallow, frivolous world in which he lived, but there was still a freshness in her renunciation which coveted reminders and enjoyed comparisons; he would prove to her how right she had been to do exactly what she was doing. It did not occur to her that Hyacinth Robinson might be at her door, for it was understood between them that, except by special appointment, he was to come to see her only in the evening. She heard in the hall, when the servant arrived, a voice that she failed to recognise; but in a moment the door of the room was thrown open and the name of Mr. Muniment was pronounced. It may be said at once that she felt great pleasure in hearing it, for she had both wished to see more of Hyacinth's extraordinary friend and had given him up, so little likely had it begun to appear that he would put himself out for her. She had been glad he wouldn't come, as she had told Hyacinth three months before; but now that he had come she was still more glad.

Presently he was sitting opposite to her, on the other side of the fire, with his big foot crossed over his big knee, his large, gloved hands fumbling with each other, drawing and smoothing the gloves (of very red, new-looking dog-skin) in places, as if they hurt him. So far as the size of his extremities, and even his attitude and movement, went, he might have belonged to her former circle. With the details of his dress remaining vague in the lamp-light, which threw into relief mainly his powerful, important head, he might have been one of the most considerable men she had ever known. The first thing she said to him was that she wondered extremely what had brought him at last to come to see her: the idea, when she proposed it, evidently had so little attraction for him. She had only seen him once since then — the day she met him coming into Audley Court as she was leaving it, after a visit to his sister — and, as he probably remembered, she had not on that occasion repeated her invitation.

'It wouldn't have done any good, at the time, if you had,' Muniment rejoined, with his natural laugh.

'Oh, I felt that; my silence wasn't accidental!' the Princess exclaimed, joining in his merriment.

'I have only come now — since you have asked me the reason — because my sister hammered at me, week after week, dinning it into me that I ought to. Oh, I've been under the lash! If she had left me alone I wouldn't have come.'

The Princess blushed on hearing these words, but not with shame or with pain; rather with the happy excitement of being spoken to in a manner so fresh and original. She had never before had a visitor who practised so racy a frankness, or who, indeed, had so curious a story to tell. She had never before so completely failed, and her failure greatly interested her, especially as it seemed now to be turning a little to success. She had succeeded promptly with every one, and the sign of it was that every one had rendered her a monotony of homage. Even poor little Hyacinth had tried, in the beginning, to say sweet things to her. This very different type of man appeared to have his thoughts fixed on anything but sweetness; she felt the liveliest hope that he would move further and further away from it. 'I remember what you asked me—what good it would do you. I couldn't tell you then; and though I now have had a long time to turn it over, I haven't thought of it yet.'

'Oh, but I hope it will do me some,' said Paul. 'A fellow wants a reward, when he has made a great effort.'

'It does me some,' the Princess remarked, gaily.

'Naturally, the awkward things I say amuse you. But I don't say them for that, but just to give you an idea.'

'You give me a great many ideas. Besides, I know you already a good deal.'

'From little Robinson, I suppose,' said Muniment.

The Princess hesitated. 'More particularly from Lady Aurora.'

'Oh, she doesn't know much about me!' the young man exclaimed.

'It's a pity you say that, because she likes you.'

'Yes, she likes me,' Muniment replied, serenely.

Again the Princess hesitated. 'And I hope you like her.'

'Ay, she's a dear old girl!'

The Princess reflected that her visitor was not a gentleman, like Hyacinth; but this made no difference in her present attitude. The expectation that he would be a gentleman had had nothing to do with her interest in him; that, in fact, had rested largely on the supposition that he had a rich plebeian strain. 'I don't know that there is any one in the world I envy so much,' she remarked; an observation which her visitor received in silence. 'Better than any one I have ever met she has solved the problem—which, if we are wise, we all try to solve, don't we?—of getting out of herself. She has got out of herself more perfectly than any one I have ever known. She has merged herself in the passion of doing something for others. That's why I envy her,' said the Princess, with an explanatory smile, as if perhaps he didn't understand her.

'It's an amusement, like any other,' said Paul Muniment.

'Ah, not like any other! It carries light into dark places; it makes a great many wretched people considerably less wretched.'

'How many, eh?' asked the young man, not exactly as if he wished to dispute, but as if it were always in him to enjoy an argument.

The Princess wondered why he should desire to argue at Lady Aurora's expense. 'Well, one who is very near to you, to begin with.'

'Oh, she's kind, most kind; it's altogether wonderful. But Rosy makes *her* considerably less wretched,' Paul Muniment rejoined.

'Very likely, of course; and so she does me.'

'May I inquire what you are wretched about?' Muniment went on.

'About nothing at all. That's the worst of it. But I am much happier now than I have ever been.'

'Is that also about nothing?'

'No, about a sort of change that has taken place in my life. I have been able to do some little things.'

'For the poor, I suppose you mean. Do you refer to the presents you have made to Rosy?' the young man inquired.

'The presents?' The Princess appeared not to remember. 'Oh, those are trifles. It isn't anything one has been able to give; it's some talks one has had, some convictions one has arrived at.'

'Convictions are a source of very innocent pleasure,' said the young man, smiling at his interlocutress with his bold, pleasant eyes, which seemed to project their glance further than any she had seen.

'Having them is nothing. It's the acting on them,' the Princess replied.

'Yes; that doubtless, too, is good.' He continued to look at her peacefully, as if he liked to consider that this might be what she had asked him to come for. He said nothing more, and she went on:

'It's far better, of course, when one is a man.'

'I don't know. Women do pretty well what they like. My sister and you have managed, between you, to bring me to this.'

'It's more your sister, I suspect, than I. But why, after all, should you have disliked so much to come?'

'Well, since you ask me,' said Paul Muniment, 'I will tell you frankly, though I don't mean it uncivilly, that I don't know what to make of you.'

'Most people don't,' returned the Princess. 'But they usually take the risk.'

'Ah, well, I'm the most prudent of men.'

'I was sure of it; that is one of the reasons why I wanted to know you. I know what some of your ideas are—Hyacinth Robinson has told me; and the source of my interest in them is partly the fact that you consider very carefully what you attempt.'

'That I do—I do,' said Muniment, simply.

The tone in which he said this would have been almost ignoble, as regards a kind of northern canniness which it expressed, had it not been corrected by the character of his face, his youth and strength, and his military eye. The Princess recognised both the shrewdness and the latent audacity as she rejoined, 'To do anything with you would be very safe. It would be sure to succeed.'

'That's what poor Hyacinth thinks,' said Paul Muniment.

The Princess wondered a little that he could allude in that light tone to the faith their young friend had placed in him, considering the consequences such a trustfulness might yet have; but this curious mixture of qualities could only make her visitor, as a tribune of the people, more interesting to her. She abstained for the moment from touching on the subject of Hyacinth's peculiar position, and only said, 'Hasn't he told you about me? Hasn't he explained me a little?'

'Oh, his explanations are grand!' Muniment exclaimed, hilariously. 'He's fine sport when he talks about you.'

'Don't betray him,' said the Princess, gently.

'There's nothing to betray. You would be the first to admire it if you were there. Besides, I don't betray,' the young man added.

'I love him very much,' said the Princess; and it would have been impossible for the most impudent cynic to smile at the manner in which she made the declaration.

Paul accepted it respectfully. 'He's a sweet little lad, and, putting her ladyship aside, quite the light of our home.'

There was a short pause after this exchange of amenities, which the Princess terminated by inquiring, 'Wouldn't some one else do his work quite as well?'

'His work? Why, I'm told he's a master-hand.'

'Oh, I don't mean his bookbinding.' Then the Princess added, 'I don't know whether you know it, but I am in correspondence with Hoffendahl. I am acquainted with many of our most important men.'

'Yes, I know it. Hyacinth has told me. Do you mention it as a guarantee, so that I may know you are genuine?'

'Not exactly; that would be weak, wouldn't it?' the Princess asked. 'My genuineness must be in myself—a matter for you to appreciate as you know me better; not in my references and vouchers.'

'I shall never know you better. What business is it of mine?'

'I want to help you,' said the Princess, and as she made this earnest appeal her face became transfigured; it wore an expression of the most passionate yet the purest longing. 'I want to do something for the cause you represent; for the millions that are rotting under our feet—the millions whose whole life is passed on the brink of starvation, so that the smallest accident pushes them over. Try me, test me; ask me to put my hand to something, to prove that I am as deeply in earnest as those who have already given proof. I know what I am talking about—what one must meet and face and count with, the nature and the immensity of your organisation. I am not playing. No, I am not playing.'

Paul Muniment watched her with his steady smile until this sudden outbreak had spent itself. 'I was afraid you would be like this—that you would turn on the fountains and let off the fireworks.'

'Permit me to believe you thought nothing about it. There is no reason my fireworks should disturb you.'

'I have always had a fear of women.'

'I see—that's a part of your prudence,' said the Princess, reflectively. 'But you are the sort of man who ought to know how to use them.'

Muniment said nothing, immediately, in answer to this; the way he appeared to consider the Princess suggested that he was not following closely what she said, so much as losing himself in certain matters which were beside that question— her beauty, for instance, her grace, her fragrance, the spectacle of a manner and quality so new to him. After a little, however, he remarked, irrelevantly, 'I'm afraid I'm very rude.'

'Of course you are, but it doesn't signify. What I mainly object to is that you don't answer my questions. Would not some one else do Hyacinth Robinson's work quite as well? Is it necessary to take a nature so delicate, so intellectual? Oughtn't we to keep him for something finer?'

'Finer than what?'

'Than what Hoffendahl will call upon him to do.'

'And pray what is that?' the young man demanded. 'You know nothing about it; no more do I,' he added in a moment. 'It will require whatever it will. Besides, if some one else might have done it, no one else volunteered. It happened that Robinson did.'

'Yes, and you nipped him up!' the Princess exclaimed.

At this expression Muniment burst out laughing. 'I have no doubt you can easily keep him, if you want him.'

'I should like to do it in his place—that's what I should like,' said the Princess.

'As I say, you don't even know what it is.'

'It may be nothing,' she went on, with her grave eyes fixed on her visitor. 'I dare say you think that what I wanted to see you for was to beg you to let him off. But it wasn't. Of course it's his own affair, and you can do nothing. But oughtn't it to make some difference, when his opinions have changed?'

'His opinions? He never had any opinions,' Muniment replied. 'He is not like you and me.'

'Well, then, his feelings, his attachments. He hasn't the passion for democracy he had when I first knew him. He's much more tepid.'

'Ah, well, he's quite right.'

The Princess stared. 'Do you mean that *you* are giving up——?'

'A fine stiff conservative is a thing I perfectly understand,' said Paul Muniment. 'If I were on the top, I'd stick there.'

'I see, you are not narrow,' the Princess murmured, appreciatively.

'I beg your pardon, I am. I don't call that wide. One must be narrow to penetrate.'

'Whatever you are, you'll succeed,' said the Princess. 'Hyacinth won't, but you will.'

'It depends upon what you call success!' the young man exclaimed. And in a moment, before she replied, he added, looking about the room, 'You've got a very lovely dwelling.'

'Lovely? My dear sir, it's hideous. That's what I like it for,' the Princess added.

'Well, I like it; but perhaps I don't know the reason. I thought you had given up everything—pitched your goods out of window, for a grand scramble.'

'Well, so I have. You should have seen me before.'

'I should have liked that,' said Muniment, smiling. 'I like to see solid wealth.'

'Ah, you're as bad as Hyacinth. I am the only consistent one!' the Princess sighed.

'You have a great deal left, for a person who has given everything away.'

'These are not mine—these abominations—or I would give them, too!' Paul's hostess rejoined, artlessly.

Muniment got up from his chair, still looking about the room. 'I would give my nose for such a place as this. At any rate, you are not yet reduced to poverty.'

'I have a little left—to help you.'

'I dare say you've a great deal,' said Paul, with his north-country accent.

'I could get money—I could get money,' the Princess continued, gravely. She had also risen, and was standing before him.

These two remarkable persons faced each other, their eyes met again, and they exchanged a long, deep glance of mutual scrutiny. Each seemed to drop a plummet into the other's mind. Then a strange and, to the Princess, unexpected expression passed over the countenance of the young man; his lips compressed themselves, as if he were making a strong effort, his colour rose, and in a moment he stood there blushing like a boy. He dropped his eyes and stared at the carpet, while he observed, 'I don't trust women—I don't trust women!'

'I am sorry, but, after all, I can understand it,' said the Princess; 'therefore I won't insist on the question of your allowing me to work with you. But this appeal I will make to you: help me a little yourself—help me!'

'How do you mean, help you?' Muniment demanded, raising his eyes, which had a new, conscious look.

'Advise me; you will know how. I am in trouble—I have gone very far.'

'I have no doubt of that!' said Paul, laughing.

'I mean with some of those people abroad. I'm not frightened, but I'm perplexed; I want to know what to do.'

'No, you are not frightened,' Muniment rejoined, after a moment.

'I am, however, in a sad entanglement. I think you can straighten it out. I will give you the facts, but not now, for we shall be interrupted; I hear my old lady on the stairs. For this, you must come to see me again.'

At this point the door opened, and Madame Grandoni appeared, cautiously, creepingly, as if she didn't know what might be going on in the parlour. 'Yes, I will come again,' said Paul Muniment, in a low but distinct tone; and he walked away, passing Madame Grandoni on the threshold, without having exchanged the hand-shake of farewell with his hostess. In the hall he paused an instant, feeling she was behind him; and he learned that she had not come to exact from him this omitted observance, but to say once more, dropping her voice, so that her companion, through the open door, might not hear—

'I *could* get money—I could!'

Muniment passed his hand through his hair, and, as if he

had not heard her, remarked, 'I have not given you, after all, half Rosy's messages.'

'Oh, that doesn't matter!' the Princess answered, turning back into the parlour.

Madame Grandoni was in the middle of the room, wrapped in her old shawl, looking vaguely around her, and the two ladies heard the house-door close. 'And pray, who may that be? Isn't it a new face?' the elder one inquired.

'He's the brother of the little person I took you to see over the river—the chattering cripple with the wonderful manners.'

'Ah, she had a brother! That, then, was why you went?'

It was striking, the good-humour with which the Princess received this rather coarse thrust, which could have been drawn from Madame Grandoni only by the petulance and weariness of increasing age, and the antipathy she now felt to Madeira Crescent and everything it produced. Christina bent a calm, charitable smile upon her ancient companion, and replied—

'There could have been no question of our seeing him. He was, of course, at his work.'

'Ah, how do I know, my dear? And is he a successor?'

'A successor?'

'To the little bookbinder.'

'My darling,' said the Princess, 'you will see how absurd that question is when I tell you he's his greatest friend!'

XXXVII

HALF AN HOUR after Paul Muniment's departure the
Princess heard another rat-tat-tat at her door; but this
was a briefer, discreeter peal, and was accompanied by a
faint tintinnabulation. The person who had produced it was
presently ushered in, without, however, causing Madame
Grandoni to look round, or rather to look up, from an arm-
chair as low as a sitz-bath, and of very much the shape of
such a receptacle, in which, near the fire, she had been immersed. She left this care to the Princess, who rose on hearing the name of the visitor pronounced, inadequately, by
her maid. 'Mr. Fetch,' Assunta called it; but the Princess recognised without difficulty the little fat, 'reduced' fiddler of
whom Hyacinth had talked to her, who, as Pinnie's most intimate friend, had been so mixed up with his existence, and
whom she herself had always had a curiosity to see. Hyacinth had not told her he was coming, and the unexpectedness of the apparition added to its interest. Much as she
liked seeing queer types and exploring out-of-the-way social
corners, she never engaged in a fresh encounter, nor formed
a new relation of this kind, without a fit of nervousness, a
fear that she might be awkward and fail to hit the right
tone. She perceived in a moment, however, that Mr. Vetch
would take her as she was and require no special adjust-
ments; he was a gentleman and a man of experience, and she
would only have to leave the tone to him. He stood there
with his large, polished hat in his two hands, a hat of the
fashion of ten years before, with a rusty sheen and an undulating brim—stood there without a salutation or a speech,
but with a little fixed, acute, tentative smile, which seemed
half to inquire and half to explain. What he explained was
that he was clever enough to be trusted, and that if he had
come to see her that way, abruptly, without an invitation, he
had a reason which she would be sure to think good enough
when she should hear it. There was even a certain jauntiness
in this confidence—an insinuation that he knew how to
present himself to a lady; and though it quickly appeared
that he really did, that was the only thing about him that

was inferior—it suggested a long experience of actresses at rehearsal, with whom he had formed habits of advice and compliment.

'I know who you are—I know who you are,' said the Princess, though she could easily see that he knew she did.

'I wonder whether you also know why I have come to see you,' Mr. Vetch replied, presenting the top of his hat to her as if it were a looking-glass.

'No, but it doesn't matter. I am very glad; you might even have come before.' Then the Princess added, with her characteristic honesty, 'Don't you know of the great interest I have taken in your nephew?'

'In my nephew? Yes, my young friend Robinson. It is in regard to him that I have ventured to intrude upon you.'

The Princess had been on the point of pushing a chair toward him, but she stopped in the act, staring, with a smile. 'Ah, I hope you haven't come to ask me to give him up!'

'On the contrary—on the contrary!' the old man rejoined, lifting his hand expressively, and with his head on one side, as if he were holding his violin.

'How do you mean, on the contrary?' the Princess demanded, after he had seated himself and she had sunk into her former place. As if that might sound contradictious, she went on: 'Surely he hasn't any fear that I shall cease to be a good friend to him?'

'I don't know what he fears; I don't know what he hopes,' said Mr. Vetch, looking at her now with a face in which she could see there was something more tonic than old-fashioned politeness. 'It will be difficult to tell you, but at least I must try. Properly speaking, I suppose, it's no business of mine, as I am not a blood-relation to the boy; but I have known him since he was an urchin, and I can't help saying that I thank you for your great kindness to him.'

'All the same, I don't think you like it,' the Princess remarked. 'To me it oughtn't to be difficult to say anything.'

'He has told me very little about you; he doesn't know I have taken this step,' the fiddler said, turning his eyes about the room, and letting them rest on Madame Grandoni.

'Why do you call it a "step"?' the Princess asked. 'That's

what people say when they have to do something disagreeable.'

'I call very seldom on ladies. It's a long time since I have
been in the house of a person like the Princess Casamassima. I
remember the last time,' said the old man. 'It was to get some
money from a lady at whose party I had been playing—for a
dance.'

'You must bring your fiddle, sometime, and play to us. Of
course I don't mean for money,' the Princess rejoined.

'I will do it with pleasure, or anything else that will gratify
you. But my ability is very small. I only know vulgar music—
things that are played at theatres.'

'I don't believe that; there must be things you play for
yourself, in your room, alone.'

For a moment the old man made no reply; then he said,
'Now that I see you, that I hear you, it helps me to understand.'

'I don't think you do see me!' cried the Princess, kindly,
laughing; while the fiddler went on to ask whether there
were any danger of Hyacinth's coming in while he was
there. The Princess replied that he only came, unless by pre-
arrangement, in the evening, and Mr. Vetch made a request
that she would not let their young friend know that he himself had been with her. 'It doesn't matter; he will guess it, he
will know it by instinct, as soon as he comes in. He is terribly subtle,' said the Princess; and she added that she had
never been able to hide anything from him. Perhaps it served
her right, for attempting to make a mystery of things that
were not worth it.

'How well you know him!' Mr. Vetch murmured, with his
eyes wandering again to Madame Grandoni, who paid no attention to him as she sat staring at the fire. He delayed, visibly, to say what he had come for, and his hesitation could
only be connected with the presence of the old lady. He said
to himself that the Princess might have divined this from his
manner; he had an idea that he could trust himself to convey
such an intimation with clearness and yet with delicacy. But
the most she appeared to apprehend was that he desired to be
presented to her companion.

'You must know the most delightful of women. She also takes a particular interest in Mr. Robinson: of a different kind from mine—much more sentimental!' And then she explained to the old lady, who seemed absorbed in other ideas, that Mr. Vetch was a distinguished musician, a person whom she, who had known so many in her day, and was so fond of that kind of thing, would like to talk with. The Princess spoke of 'that kind of thing' quite as if she herself had given it up, though Madame Grandoni heard her by the hour together improvising on the piano revolutionary battle-songs and pæans.

'I think you are laughing at me,' Mr. Vetch said to the Princess, while Madame Grandoni twisted herself slowly round in her chair and considered him. She looked at him leisurely, up and down, and then she observed, with a sigh—

'Strange people—strange people!'

'It is indeed a strange world, madam,' the fiddler replied; after which he inquired of the Princess whether he might have a little conversation with her in private.

She looked about her, embarrassed and smiling. 'My dear sir, I have only this one room to receive in. We live in a very small way.'

'Yes, your excellency *is* laughing at me. Your ideas are very large, too. However, I would gladly come at any other time that might suit you.'

'You impute to me higher spirits than I possess. Why should I be so gay?' the Princess asked. 'I should be delighted to see you again. I am extremely curious as to what you may have to say to me. I would even meet you anywhere—in Kensington Gardens or the British Museum.'

The fiddler looked at her a moment before replying; then, with his white old face flushing a little, he exclaimed, 'Poor dear little Hyacinth!'

Madame Grandoni made an effort to rise from her chair, but she had sunk so low that at first it was not successful. Mr. Vetch gave her his hand, to help her, and she slowly erected herself, keeping hold of him for a moment after she stood there. 'What did she tell me? That you are a great musician?

Isn't that enough for any man? You ought to be content, my dear gentleman. It has sufficed for people whom I don't believe you surpass.'

'I don't surpass any one,' said poor Mr. Vetch. 'I don't know what you take me for.'

'You are not a conspirator, then? You are not an assassin? It surprises me, but so much the better. In this house one can never know. It is not a good house, and if you are a respectable person it is a pity you should come here. Yes, she is very gay, and I am very sad. I don't know how it will end. After me, I hope. The world is not good, certainly; but God alone can make it better.' And as the fiddler expressed the hope that he was not the cause of her leaving the room, she went on, 'Doch, doch, you are the cause; but why not you as well as another? I am always leaving it for some one or for some thing, and I would sooner do so for an honest man, if you *are* one—but, as I say, who can tell?—than for a destroyer. I wander about. I have no rest. I have, however, a very nice room, the best in the house. Me, at least, she does not treat ill. It looks to-day like the end of all things. If you would turn your climate the other side up, the rest would do well enough. Good-night to you, whoever you are.'

The old lady shuffled away, in spite of Mr. Vetch's renewed apologies, and the Princess stood before the fire, watching her companions, while he opened the door. 'She goes away, she comes back; it doesn't matter. She thinks it's a bad house, but she knows it would be worse without her. I remember now,' the Princess added. 'Mr. Robinson told me that you had been a great democrat in old days, but that now you had ceased to care for the people.'

'The people—the people? That is a vague term. Whom do you mean?'

The Princess hesitated. 'Those you used to care for, to plead for; those who are underneath every one, every thing, and have the whole social mass crushing them.'

'I see you think I'm a renegade. The way certain classes arrogate to themselves the title of the people has never pleased me. Why are some human beings the people, and the people only, and others not? I am of the people myself, I have worked all my days like a knife-grinder, and I have really never changed.'

'You must not let me make you angry,' said the Princess, laughing and sitting down again. 'I am sometimes very provoking, but you must stop me off. You wouldn't think it, perhaps, but no one takes a snub better than I.'

Mr. Vetch dropped his eyes a minute; he appeared to wish to show that he regarded such a speech as that as one of the Princess's characteristic humours, and knew that he should be wanting in respect to her if he took it seriously or made a personal application of it. 'What I want is this,' he began, after a moment: 'that you will—that you will——' But he stopped before he had got further. She was watching him, listening to him, and she waited while he paused. It was a long pause, and she said nothing. 'Princess,' the old man broke out at last, 'I would give my own life many times for that boy's!'

'I always told him you must have been fond of him!' she cried, with bright exultation.

'Fond of him? Pray, who can doubt it? I made him, I invented him!'

'He knows it, moreover,' said the Princess, smiling. 'It is an exquisite organisation.' And as the old man gazed at her, not knowing, apparently, what to make of her tone, she continued: 'It is a very interesting opportunity for me to learn certain things. Speak to me of his early years. How was he as a child? When I like people I want to know everything about them.'

'I shouldn't have supposed there was much left for you to learn about our young friend. You have taken possession of his life,' the fiddler added, gravely.

'Yes, but as I understand you, you don't complain of it? Sometimes one does so much more than one has intended. One must use one's influence for good,' said the Princess, with the noble, gentle air of accessibility to reason that sometimes lighted up her face. And then she went on, irrelevantly: 'I know the terrible story of his mother. He told it me himself, when he was staying with me; and in the course of my life I think I have never been more affected.'

'That was my fault, that he ever learned it. I suppose he also told you that.'

'Yes, but I think he understood your idea. If you had the question to determine again, would you judge differently?'

'I thought it would do him good,' said the old man, simply and rather wearily.

'Well, I dare say it has,' the Princess rejoined, with the manner of wishing to encourage him.

'I don't know what was in my head. I wanted him to quarrel with society. Now I want him to be reconciled to it,' Mr. Vetch remarked, earnestly. He appeared to wish the Princess to understand that he made a great point of this.

'Ah, but he is!' she immediately returned. 'We often talk about that; he is not like me, who see all kinds of abominations. He's a tremendous aristocrat. What more would you have?'

'Those are not the opinions that he expresses to me,' said Mr. Vetch, shaking his head sadly. 'I am greatly distressed, and I don't understand. I have not come here with the presumptuous wish to cross-examine you, but I should like very much to know if I *am* wrong in believing that he has gone about with you in the bad quarters—in St. Giles's and Whitechapel.'

'We have certainly inquired and explored together,' the Princess admitted, 'and in the depths of this huge, luxurious, wanton, wasteful city we have seen sights of unspeakable misery and horror. But we have been not only in the slums; we have been to a music hall and a penny-reading.'

The fiddler received this information at first in silence, so that his hostess went on to mention some of the phases of life they had observed; describing with great vividness, but at the same time with a kind of argumentative moderation, several scenes which did little honour to 'our boasted civilisation.' 'What wonder is it, then, that he should tell me that things cannot go on any longer as they are?' he asked, when she had finished. 'He said only the other day that he should regard himself as one of the most contemptible of human beings if he should do nothing to alter them, to better them.'

'What wonder, indeed? But if he said that, he was in one of his bad days. He changes constantly, and his impressions change. The misery of the people is by no means always weighing on his heart. You tell me what he has told you; well, he has told me that the people may perish over and over, rather than the conquests of civilisation shall be sacrificed to them. He declares, at such moments, that they will be sacrificed—sacrificed utterly—if the ignorant masses get the upper hand.'

'He needn't be afraid! That will never happen.'

'I don't know. We can at least try!'

'Try what you like, madam, but, for God's sake, get the boy out of his mess!'

The Princess had suddenly grown excited, in speaking of the cause she believed in, and she gave, for the moment, no heed to this appeal, which broke from Mr. Vetch's lips with a sudden passion of anxiety. Her beautiful head raised itself higher, and the deep expression that was always in her eyes became an extraordinary radiance. 'Do you know what I say to Mr. Robinson when he makes such remarks as that to me? I ask him what he means by civilisation. Let civilisation come a little, first, and then we will talk about it. For the present, face to face with those horrors, I scorn it, I deny it!' And the Princess laughed ineffable things, like some splendid syren of the Revolution.

'The world is very sad and very hideous, and I am happy to say that I soon shall have done with it. But before I go I want to save Hyacinth. If he's a little aristocrat, as you say, there is so much the less fitness in his being ground in your mill. If he doesn't even believe in what he pretends to do, that's a pretty situation! What is he in for, madam? What devilish folly has he undertaken?'

'He is a strange mixture of contradictory impulses,' said the Princess, musingly. Then, as if calling herself back to the old man's question, she continued: 'How can I enter into his affairs with you? How can I tell you his secrets? In the first place, I don't know them, and if I did—fancy me!'

The fiddler gave a long, low sigh, almost a moan, of discouragement and perplexity. He had told the Princess that now he saw her he understood how Hyacinth should have become her slave, but he would not have been able to tell her that he understood her own motives and mysteries, that he embraced the immense anomaly of her behaviour. It came over him that she was incongruous and perverse, a more complicated form of the feminine character than any he had hitherto dealt with, and he felt helpless and baffled, foredoomed to failure. He had come prepared to flatter her without scruple, thinking that would be the clever, the efficacious, method of dealing with her; but he now had a sense that this primitive device had, though it was strange, no application to such a nature, while his embarrassment was increased rather than diminished by the fact that the lady at least made the effort to be accommodating. He had put down his hat on the floor beside him, and his two hands were clasped on the knob of an umbrella which had long since renounced pretensions to compactness; he collapsed a little, and his chin rested on his folded hands. 'Why do you take such a line? Why do you believe such things?' he asked; and he was conscious that his tone was weak and his inquiry beside the question.

'My dear sir, how do you know what I believe? However, I have my reasons, which it would take too long to tell you, and which, after all, would not particularly interest you. One must see life as one can; it comes, no doubt, to each of us in different ways. You think me affected, of course, and my behaviour a fearful *pose*; but I am only trying to be natural. Are you not yourself a little inconsequent?' the Princess went on, with the bright mildness which had the effect of making Mr. Vetch feel that he should not extract any pledge of assistance from her. 'You don't want our young friend to pry into the wretchedness of London, because it excites his sense of justice. It is a strange thing to wish, for a person of whom one is fond and whom one esteems, that his sense of justice shall not be excited.'

'I don't care a fig for his sense of justice—I don't care a fig for the wretchedness of London; and if I were young, and beautiful, and clever, and brilliant, and of a noble position, like you, I should care still less. In that case I should have very little to say to a poor mechanic—a youngster who earns his living with a glue-pot and scraps of old leather.'

'Don't misrepresent him; don't make him out what you know he's not!' the Princess retorted, with her baffling smile. 'You know he's one of the most civilised people possible.'

The fiddler sat breathing unhappily. 'I only want to keep him—to get him free.' Then he added, 'I don't understand you very well. If you like him because he's one of the lower orders, how can you like him because he's a swell?'

The Princess turned her eyes on the fire a moment, as if this little problem might be worth considering, and presently she answered, 'Dear Mr. Vetch, I am very sure you don't mean to be impertinent, but some things you say have that effect. Nothing is more annoying than when one's sincerity is doubted. I am not bound to explain myself to you. I ask of my friends to trust me, and of the others to leave me alone. Moreover, anything not very nice you may have said to me, out of awkwardness, is nothing to the insults I am perfectly prepared to see showered upon me before long. I shall do things which will produce a fine crop of them—oh, I shall do things, my dear sir! But I am determined not to mind them. Come, therefore, pull yourself together. We both take such an interest in young Robinson that I can't see why in the world we should quarrel about him.'

'My dear lady,' the old man pleaded, 'I have indeed not the least intention of failing in respect or courtesy, and you must excuse me if I don't look after my manners. How can I when I am so worried, so haunted? God knows I don't want to quarrel. As I tell you, I only want to get Hyacinth free.'

'Free from what?' the Princess asked.

'From some abominable brotherhood or international league that he belongs to, the thought of which keeps me awake at night. He's just the sort of youngster to be made a catspaw.'

'Your fears seem very vague.'

'I hoped you would give me chapter and verse.'

'On what do your suspicions rest? What grounds have you?' the Princess inquired.

'Well, a great many; none of them very definite, but all contributing something—his appearance, his manner, the way he strikes me. Dear madam, one feels those things, one guesses. Do you know that poor, infatuated phrase-monger, Eustache Poupin, who works at the same place as Hyacinth? He's a very old friend of mine, and he's an honest man, considering everything. But he is always conspiring, and corresponding, and

pulling strings that make a tinkle which he takes for the
death-knell of society. He has nothing in life to complain of,
and he drives a roaring trade. But he wants folks to be equal,
heaven help him; and when he has made them so I suppose
he's going to start a society for making the stars in the sky all
of the same size. He isn't serious, though he thinks that he's
the only human being who never trifles; and his machinations, which I believe are for the most part very innocent, are
a matter of habit and tradition with him, like his theory that
Christopher Columbus, who discovered America, was a
Frenchman, and his hot foot-bath on Saturday nights. He has
not confessed to me that Hyacinth has taken some secret engagement to do something for the cause which may have
nasty consequences, but the way he turns off the idea makes
me almost as uncomfortable as if he had. He and his wife
are very sweet on Hyacinth, but they can't make up their
minds to interfere; perhaps for them, indeed, as for me,
there is no way in which interference can be effective. Only *I*
didn't put him up to those devil's tricks—or, rather, I did
originally! The finer the work, I suppose, the higher the
privilege of doing it; yet the Poupins heave socialistic sighs
over the boy, and their peace of mind evidently isn't all that
it ought to be, if they have given him a noble opportunity. I
have appealed to them, in good round terms, and they have
assured me that every hair of his head is as precious to them
as if he were their own child. That doesn't comfort me
much, however, for the simple reason that I believe the old
woman (whose grandmother, in Paris, in the Revolution,
must certainly have carried bloody heads on a pike), would
be quite capable of chopping up her own child, if it would
do any harm to proprietors. Besides, they say, what influence have they on Hyacinth any more? He is a deplorable
little back-slider; he worships false gods. In short, they will
give me no information, and I dare say they themselves are
tied up by some unholy vow. They may be afraid of a vengeance if they tell tales. It's all sad rubbish, but rubbish may
be a strong motive.'

The Princess listened attentively, following her visitor with
patience. 'Don't speak to me of the French; I have never liked
them.'

'That's awkward, if you're a socialist. You are likely to meet them.'

'Why do you call me a socialist? I hate labels and tickets,' she declared. Then she added, 'What is it you suppose on Mr. Robinson's part?—for you must suppose something.'

'Well, that he may have drawn some accursed lot, to do some idiotic thing—something in which even he himself doesn't believe.'

'I haven't an idea of what sort of thing you mean. But, if he doesn't believe in it he can easily let it alone.'

'Do you think he's a customer who will back out of an engagement?' the fiddler asked.

The Princess hesitated a moment. 'One can never judge of people, in that way, until they are tested.' The next thing, she inquired, 'Haven't you even taken the trouble to question him?'

'What would be the use? He would tell me nothing. It would be like a man giving notice when he is going to fight a duel.'

The Princess sat for some moments in thought; she looked up at Mr. Vetch with a pitying, indulgent smile. 'I am sure you are worrying about a mere shadow; but that never prevents, does it? I still don't see exactly how I can help you.'

'Do you want him to commit some atrocity, some infamy?' the old man murmured.

'My dear sir, I don't want him to do anything in all the wide world. I have not had the smallest connection with any arrangement of any kind, that he may have entered into. Do me the honour to trust me,' the Princess went on, with a certain dryness of tone. 'I don't know what I have done to deprive myself of your confidence. Trust the young man a little, too. He is a gentleman, and he will behave like a gentleman.'

The fiddler rose from his chair, smoothing his hat, silently, with the cuff of his coat. He stood there, whimsical and piteous, as if the sense that he had still something to urge mingled with that of his having received his dismissal, and both of them were tinged with the oddity of another idea. 'That's exactly what I am afraid of!' he exclaimed. Then he added, continuing to look at her, 'But he *must* be very fond of life.'

The Princess took no notice of the insinuation contained in these words, and indeed it was of a sufficiently impalpable character. 'Leave him to me—leave him to me. I am sorry for your anxiety, but it was very good of you to come to see me. That has been interesting, because you have been one of our friend's influences.'

'Unfortunately, yes! If it had not been for me, he would not have known Poupin, and if he hadn't known Poupin he wouldn't have known his chemical friend—what's his name? Muniment.'

'And has that done him harm, do you think?' the Princess asked. She had got up.

'Surely: that fellow has been the main source of his infection.'

'I lose patience with you,' said the Princess, turning away.

And indeed her visitor's persistence was irritating. He went on, lingering, with his head thrust forward and his short arms out at his sides, terminating in his hat and umbrella, which he held grotesquely, as if they were intended for emphasis or illustration: 'I have supposed for a long time that it was either Muniment or you that had got him into his scrape. It was you I suspected most—much the most; but if it isn't you, it must be he.'

'You had better go to him, then!'

'Of course I will go to him. I scarcely know him—I have seen him but once—but I will speak my mind.'

The Princess rang for her maid to usher the fiddler out, but at the moment he laid his hand on the door of the room she checked him with a quick gesture. 'Now that I think of it, don't go to Mr. Muniment. It will be better to leave him quiet. Leave him to me,' she added, smiling.

'Why not, why not?' he pleaded. And as she could not tell him on the instant why not, he asked, 'Doesn't he know?'

'No, he doesn't know; he has nothing to do with it.' She suddenly found herself desiring to protect Paul Muniment from the imputation that was in Mr. Vetch's mind—the imputation of an ugly responsibility; and though she was not a person who took the trouble to tell fibs, this repudiation, on his behalf, issued from her lips before she could check it. It was a result of the same desire, though it was also an incon-

sequence, that she added, 'Don't do that—you'll spoil everything!' She went to him, suddenly eager, and herself opened
the door for him. 'Leave him to me—leave him to me,' she
continued, persuasively, while the fiddler, gazing at her, dazzled and submissive, allowed himself to be wafted away. A
thought that excited her had come to her with a bound, and
after she had heard the house door close behind Mr. Vetch
she walked up and down the room half an hour, restlessly,
under the possession of it.

BOOK FIFTH

XXXVIII

HYACINTH FOUND, this winter, considerable occupation for his odd hours, his evenings and holidays and scraps of leisure, in putting in hand the books which he had promised himself, at Medley, to inclose in covers worthy of the high station and splendour of the lady of his life (these brilliant attributes had not then been shuffled out of sight), and of the confidence and generosity she showed him. He had determined she should receive from him something of value, and took pleasure in thinking that after he was gone they would be passed from hand to hand as specimens of rare work, while connoisseurs bent their heads over them, smiling and murmuring, handling them delicately. His invention stirred itself, and he had a hundred admirable ideas, many of which he sat up late at night to execute. He used all his skill, and by this time his skill was of a very high order. Old Crookenden recognised it by raising the rates at which he was paid; and though it was not among the traditions of the proprietor of the establishment in Soho, who to the end wore the apron with his workmen, to scatter sweet speeches, Hyacinth learned accidentally that several books that he had given him to do had been carried off and placed on a shelf of treasures at the villa, where they were exhibited to the members of the Crookenden circle who came to tea on Sundays. Hyacinth himself, indeed, was included in this company on a great occasion—invited to a musical party where he made the acquaintance of half a dozen Miss Crookendens, an acquaintance which consisted in his standing in a corner, behind several broad-backed old ladies, and watching the rotation, at the piano and the harp, of three or four of his master's thick-fingered daughters. 'You know it's a tremendously musical house,' said one of the old ladies to another (she called it ' 'ouse'); but the principal impression made upon him by the performance of the Miss Crookendens was that it was wonderfully different from the Princess's playing.

He knew that he was the only young man from the shop

who had been invited, not counting the foreman, who was sixty years old and wore a wig which constituted in itself a kind of social position, besides being accompanied by a little frightened, furtive wife, who closed her eyes, as if in the presence of a blinding splendour, when Mrs. Crookenden spoke to her. The Poupins were not there—which, however, was not a surprise to Hyacinth, who knew that (even if they had been asked, which they were not), they had objections of principle to putting their feet *chez les bourgeois*. They were not asked because, in spite of the place Eustache had made for himself in the prosperity of the business, it had come to be known that his wife was somehow not his wife (though she was certainly no one's else); and the evidence of this irregularity was conceived to reside, vaguely, in the fact that she had never been seen save in a camisole. There had doubtless been an apprehension that if she had come to the villa she would not have come with the proper number of hooks and eyes, though Hyacinth, on two or three occasions, notably the night he took the pair to Mr. Vetch's theatre, had been witness of the proportions to which she could reduce her figure when she wished to give the impression of a lawful tie.

It was not clear to him how the distinction conferred upon him became known in Soho, where, however, it excited no sharpness of jealousy—Grugan, Roker and Hotchkin being hardly more likely to envy a person condemned to spend a genteel evening than they were to envy a monkey performing antics on a barrel-organ: both forms of effort indicated an urbanity painfully acquired. But Roker took his young comrade's breath half away with his elbow and remarked that he supposed he saw the old man had spotted him for one of the darlings at home; inquiring, furthermore, what would become in that case of the little thing he took to France, the one to whom he had stood champagne and lobster. This was the first allusion Hyacinth had heard made to the idea that he might some day marry his master's daughter, like the virtuous apprentice of tradition; but the suggestion, somehow, was not inspiring, even when he had thought of an incident or two which gave colour to it. None of the Miss Crookendens spoke to him—they all had large faces and short legs and a comical resemblance to that elderly male with wide nostrils,

their father, and, unlike the Miss Marchants, at Medley, they
knew who he was—but their mother, who had on her head
the plumage of a cockatoo, mingled with a structure of glass
beads, looked at him with an almost awful fixedness and asked
him three distinct times if he would have a glass of negus.

He had much difficulty in getting his books from the Princess; for when he reminded her of the promise she had given
him at Medley to make over to him as many volumes as he
should require, she answered that everything was changed
since then, that she was completely *dépouillée*, that she had
now no pretension to have a library, and that, in fine, he had
much better leave the matter alone. He was welcome to any
books that were in the house, but, as he could see for himself,
these were cheap editions, on which it would be foolish to
expend such work as his. He asked Madame Grandoni to help
him—to tell him, at least, whether there were not some good
volumes among the things the Princess had sent to be ware-
housed; it being known to him, through casual admissions of
her own, that she had allowed her maid to save certain articles
from the wreck and pack them away at the Pantechnicon. This
had all been Assunta's work, the woman had begged so hard
for a few reservations—a loaf of bread for their old days; but
the Princess herself had washed her hands of the business.
'*Chè, chè*, there are boxes, I am sure, in that place, with a little
of everything,' said the old lady, in answer to his inquiry; and
Hyacinth conferred with Assunta, who took a sympathetic,
talkative, Italian interest in his undertaking and promised to
fish out for him whatever worthy volumes should remain. She
came to his lodging, one evening, in a cab, with an armful of
pretty books, and when he asked her where they had come
from waved her forefinger in front of her nose, in a manner
both mysterious and expressive. He brought each volume to
the Princess, as it was finished; but her manner of receiving it
was to shake her head over it with a kind, sad smile. 'It's
beautiful, I am sure, but I have lost my sense for such things.
Besides, you must always remember what you once told me,
that a woman, even the most cultivated, is incapable of feeling
the difference between a bad binding and a good. I remember
your once saying that fine ladies had brought shoemaker's
bindings to your shop, and wished them imitated. Certainly

those are not the differences I most feel. My dear fellow, such things have ceased to speak to me; they are doubtless charming, but they leave me cold. What will you have? One can't serve God and mammon.' Her thoughts were fixed on far other matters than the delight of dainty covers, and she evidently considered that in caring so much for them Hyacinth resembled the mad emperor who fiddled in the flames of Rome. European society, to her mind, was in flames, and no frivolous occupation could give the measure of the emotion with which she watched them. It produced occasionally demonstrations of hilarity, of joy and hope, but these always took some form connected with the life of the people. It was the people she had gone to see, when she accompanied Hyacinth to a music-hall in the Edgeware Road; and all her excursions and pastimes, this winter, were prompted by her interest in the classes on whose behalf the revolution was to be wrought.

To ask himself whether she were in earnest was now an old story to him, and, indeed, the conviction he might arrive at on this head had ceased to have any practical relevancy. It was just as she was, superficial or profound, that she held him, and she was, at any rate, sufficiently animated by a purpose for her doings to have consequences, actual and possible. Some of these might be serious, even if she herself were not, and there were times when Hyacinth was much visited by the apprehension of them. On the Sundays that she had gone with him into the darkest places, the most fetid holes, in London, she had always taken money with her, in considerable quantities, and always left it behind. She said, very naturally, that one couldn't go and stare at people, for an impression, without paying them, and she gave alms right and left, indiscriminately, without inquiry or judgment, as simply as the abbess of some beggar-haunted convent, or a lady-bountiful of the superstitious, unscientific ages who should have hoped to be assisted to heaven by her doles. Hyacinth never said to her, though he sometimes thought it, that since she was so full of the modern spirit her charity should be administered according to the modern lights, the principles of economical science; partly because she was not a woman to be directed and regulated—she could take other people's ideas, but she could never take their way. Besides, what did it matter? To himself, what did it matter to-day whether he were drawn into right methods or into wrong ones, his time being too short for regret or for cheer? The Princess was an embodied passion—she was not a system; and her behaviour, after all, was more addressed to relieving herself than to relieving others. And then misery was sown so thick in her path that wherever her money was dropped it fell into some trembling palm. He wondered that she should still have so much cash to dispose of, until she explained to him that she came by it through putting her personal expenditure on a rigid footing. What she gave away was her savings, the margin she had succeeded in creating; and now that she had tasted of the satisfaction of making little hoards for such a purpose she regarded her other years, with their idleness and waste, their merely personal motives, as a long, stupid sleep of the conscience. To do something for others was not only so much more human, but so much more amusing!

She made strange acquaintances, under Hyacinth's conduct; she listened to extraordinary stories, and formed theories about them, and about the persons who narrated them to her, which were often still more extraordinary. She took romantic fancies to vagabonds of either sex, attempted to establish social relations with them, and was the cause of infinite agitation to the gentleman who lived near her in the Crescent, who was always smoking at the window, and who reminded Hyacinth of Mr. Micawber. She received visits that were a scandal to the Crescent, and Hyacinth neglected his affairs, whatever they were, to see what tatterdemalion would next turn up at her door. This intercourse, it is true, took a more fruitful form as her intimacy with Lady Aurora deepened; her ladyship practised discriminations which she brought the Princess to recognise, and before the winter was over Hyacinth's services in the slums were found unnecessary. He gave way with relief, with delight, to Lady Aurora, for he had not in the least understood his behaviour for the previous four months, nor taken himself seriously as a *cicerone*. He had plunged into a sea of barbarism without having any civilising energy to put forth. He was conscious that the people were miserable—more conscious, it often seemed to him, than

they themselves were; so frequently was he struck with their
brutal insensibility, a grossness impervious to the taste of better things or to any desire for them. He knew it so well that
the repetition of contact could add no vividness to the conviction; it rather smothered and befogged his impression,
peopled it with contradictions and difficulties, a violence of
reaction, a sense of the inevitable and insurmountable. In
these hours the poverty and ignorance of the multitude
seemed so vast and preponderant, and so much the law of life,
that those who had managed to escape from the black gulf
were only the happy few, people of resource as well as children of luck; they inspired in some degree the interest and
sympathy that one should feel for survivors and victors, those
who have come safely out of a shipwreck or a battle. What
was most in Hyacinth's mind was the idea, of which every
pulsation of the general life of his time was a syllable, that the
flood of democracy was rising over the world; that it would
sweep all the traditions of the past before it; that, whatever it
might fail to bring, it would at least carry in its bosom a
magnificent energy; and that it might be trusted to look after
its own. When democracy should have its way everywhere, it
would be its fault (whose else?) if want and suffering and
crime should continue to be ingredients of the human lot.
With his mixed, divided nature, his conflicting sympathies,
his eternal habit of swinging from one view to another, Hyacinth regarded this prospect, in different moods, with different kinds of emotion. In spite of the example Eustache
Poupin gave him of the reconcilement of disparities, he was
afraid the democracy wouldn't care for perfect bindings or for
the finest sort of conversation. The Princess gave up these
things in proportion as she advanced in the direction she had
so audaciously chosen; and if the Princess could give them up
it would take very transcendent natures to stick to them. At
the same time there was joy, exultation, in the thought of
surrendering one's self to the wave of revolt, of floating in the
tremendous tide, of feeling one's self lifted and tossed, carried
higher on the sun-touched crests of billows than one could
ever be by a dry, lonely effort of one's own. That vision could
deepen to a kind of ecstasy; make it indifferent whether one's
ultimate fate, in such a heaving sea, were not almost certainly

to be submerged in bottomless depths or dashed to pieces on resisting cliffs. Hyacinth felt that, whether his personal sympathy should rest finally with the victors or the vanquished, the victorious force was colossal and would require no testimony from the irresolute.

The reader will doubtless smile at his mental debates and oscillations, and not understand why a little bastard bookbinder should attach importance to his conclusions. They were not important for either cause, but they were important for himself, if only because they would rescue him from the torment of his present life, the perpetual laceration of the rebound. There was no peace for him between the two currents that flowed in his nature, the blood of his passionate, plebeian mother and that of his long-descended, supercivilised sire. They continued to toss him from one side to the other; they arrayed him in intolerable defiances and revenges against himself. He had a high ambition: he wanted neither more nor less than to get hold of the truth and wear it in his heart. He believed, with the candour of youth, that it is brilliant and clear-cut, like a royal diamond; but in whatever direction he turned in the effort to find it, he seemed to know that behind him, bent on him in reproach, was a tragic, wounded face. The thought of his mother had filled him, originally, with the vague, clumsy fermentation of his first impulses toward social criticism; but since the problem had become more complex by the fact that many things in the world as it was constituted grew intensely dear to him, he had tried more and more to construct some conceivable and human countenance for his father—some expression of honour, of tenderness and recognition, of unmerited suffering, or at least of adequate expiation. To desert one of these presences for the other—that idea had a kind of shame in it, as an act of treachery would have had; for he could almost hear the voice of his father ask him if it were the conduct of a gentleman to take up the opinions and emulate the crudities of fanatics and cads. He had got over thinking that it would not have become his father to talk of what was proper to gentlemen, and making the mental reflection that from him, at least, the biggest cad in London could not have deserved less consideration. He had worked himself round to allowances, to interpretations, to such hypotheses as the evidence in the *Times*, read in the British Museum on that never-to-be-forgotten afternoon, did not exclude; though they had been frequent enough, and too frequent, his hours of hot resentment against the man who had attached to him the stigma he was to carry for ever, he threw himself, in other conditions, and with a certain success, into the effort to find condonations, excuses, for him. It was comparatively easy for him to accept himself as the son of a terribly light Frenchwoman; there seemed a deeper obloquy even than that in his having for his other parent a nobleman altogether wanting in nobleness. He was too poor to afford it. Sometimes, in his imagination, he sacrificed one to the other, throwing over Lord Frederick much the oftener; sometimes, when the theory failed that his father would have done great things for him if he had lived, or the assumption broke down that he had been Florentine Vivier's only lover, he cursed and disowned them alike; sometimes he arrived at conceptions which presented them side by side, looking at him with eyes infinitely sad but quite unashamed—eyes which seemed to tell him that they had been hideously unfortunate but had not been base. Of course his worst moments now, as they had always been the worst, were those in which his grounds for thinking that Lord Frederick had really been his father perversely fell away from him. It must be added that they always passed, for the mixture that he felt himself so tormentingly, so insolubly, to be could be accounted for in no other manner.

I mention these dim broodings not because they belong in an especial degree to the history of our young man during the winter of the Princess's residence in Madeira Crescent, but because they were a constant element in his moral life and need to be remembered in any view of him at a given time. There were nights of November and December, as he trod the greasy pavements that lay between Westminster and Paddington, groping his way through the baffled lamp-light and tasting the smoke-seasoned fog, when there was more happiness in his heart than he had ever known. The influence of his permeating London had closed over him again; Paris and Milan and Venice had shimmered away into reminiscence and picture; and as the great city which was most his own lay round him under her pall, like an immeasurable breathing

monster, he felt, with a vague excitement, as he had felt before, only now with more knowledge, that it was the richest
expression of the life of man. His horizon had been immensely widened, but it was filled, again, by the expanse that
sent dim night-gleams and strange blurred reflections and em-
anations into a sky without stars. He suspended, as it were,
his small sensibility in the midst of it, and it quivered there
with joy and hope and ambition, as well as with the effort of
renunciation. The Princess's quiet fireside glowed with deeper
assurances, with associations of intimacy, through the dusk
and the immensity; the thought of it was with him always,
and his relations with the mistress of it were more organised
than they had been in his first vision of her. Whether or no it
was better for the cause she cherished that she should have
been reduced to her present simplicity, it was better, at least,
for Hyacinth. It made her more near and him more free; and
if there had been a danger of her nature seeming really to take
the tone of the vulgar things about her, he would only have
had to remember her as she was at Medley to restore the perspective. In truth, her beauty always appeared to have the setting that best became it; her fairness made the element in
which she lived and, among the meanest accessories, constituted a kind of splendour. Nature had multiplied the difficulties in the way of her successfully representing herself as
having properties in common with the horrible populace of
London. Hyacinth used to smile at this pretension in his
night-walks to Paddington, or homeward; the populace of
London were scattered upon his path, and he asked himself
by what wizardry they could ever be raised to high participa-
tions. There were nights when every one he met appeared to
reek with gin and filth, and he found himself elbowed by figures as foul as lepers. Some of the women and girls, in particular, were appalling—saturated with alcohol and vice, brutal,
bedraggled, obscene. 'What remedy but another deluge, what
alchemy but annihilation?' he asked himself, as he went his
way; and he wondered what fate there could be, in the great
scheme of things, for a planet overgrown with such vermin,
what redemption but to be hurled against a ball of consuming
fire. If it was the fault of the rich, as Paul Muniment held, the
selfish, congested rich, who allowed such abominations to

flourish, that made no difference, and only shifted the shame; for the terrestrial globe, a visible failure, produced the cause as well as the effect.

It did not occur to Hyacinth that the Princess had withdrawn her confidence from him because, for the work of investigating still further the condition of the poor, she placed herself in the hands of Lady Aurora. He could have no jealousy of the noble spinster; he had too much respect for her philanthropy, the thoroughness of her knowledge, and her capacity to answer any question it could come into the Princess's extemporising head to ask, and too acute a consciousness of his own desultory and superficial attitude toward the great question. It was enough for him that the little parlour in Madeira Crescent was a spot round which his thoughts could revolve, and toward which his steps could direct themselves, with an unalloyed sense of security and privilege. The picture of it hung before him half the time, in colours to which the feeling of the place gave a rarity that doubtless did not literally characterise the scene. His relations with the Princess had long since ceased to appear to him to belong to the world of fable; they were as natural as anything else (everything in life was queer enough); he had by this time assimilated them, as it were, and they were an indispensable part of the happiness of each. 'Of each'—Hyacinth risked that, for there was no particular vanity now involved in his perceiving that the most remarkable woman in Europe was, simply, very fond of him. The quiet, familiar, fraternal welcome he found on the nasty winter nights was proof enough of that. They sat together like very old friends, whom long pauses, during which they simply looked at each other with kind, acquainted eyes, could not make uncomfortable. Not that the element of silence was the principal part of their conversation, for it interposed only when they had talked a great deal. Hyacinth, on the opposite side of the fire, felt at times almost as if he were married to his hostess, so many things were taken for granted between them. For intercourse of that sort, intimate, easy, humorous, circumscribed by drawn curtains and shaded lamp-light, and interfused with domestic embarrassments and confidences, all turning to the jocular, the Princess was incomparable. It was her theory of her present existence that she was picnicking;

but all the accidents of the business were happy accidents. There was a household quietude in her steps and gestures, in the way she sat, in the way she listened, in the way she played with the cat, or looked after the fire, or folded Madame Grandoni's ubiquitous shawl; above all, in the inveteracy with which she spent her evenings at home, never dining out nor going to parties, ignorant of the dissipations of the town. There was something in the isolation of the room, when the kettle was on the hob and he had given his wet umbrella to the maid and the Princess made him sit in a certain place near the fire, the better to dry his shoes—there was something that evoked the idea of the *vie de province*, as he had read about it in French works. The French term came to him because it represented more the especial note of the Princess's company, the cultivation, the facility, of talk. She expressed herself often in the French tongue itself; she could borrow that convenience, for certain shades of meaning, though she had told Hyacinth that she didn't like the people to whom it was native. Certainly, the quality of her conversation was not provincial; it was singularly free and unrestricted; there was nothing one mightn't say to her or that she was not liable to say herself. She had cast off prejudices and gave no heed to conventional danger-posts. Hyacinth admired the movement—his eyes seemed to see it—with which, in any direction, intellectually, she could fling open her windows. There was an extraordinary charm in this mixture of liberty and humility—in seeing a creature capable, socially, of immeasurable flights sit dove-like, with folded wings.

The young man met Lady Aurora several times in Madeira Crescent (her days, like his own, were filled with work, and she came in the evening), and he knew that her friendship with the Princess had arrived at a rich maturity. The two ladies were a source of almost rapturous interest to each other, and each rejoiced that the other was not a bit different. The Princess prophesied freely that her visitor would give her up—all nice people did, very soon; but to Hyacinth the end of her ladyship's almost breathless enthusiasm was not yet in view. She was bewildered, but she was fascinated; and she thought the Princess not only the most distinguished, the most startling, the most edifying and the most original person in the world, but the most amusing and the most delightful to have tea with. As for the Princess, her sentiment about Lady Aurora was the same that Hyacinth's had been: she thought her a saint, the first she had ever seen, and the purest specimen conceivable; as good in her way as St. Francis of Assisi, as tender and naïve and transparent, of a spirit of charity as sublime. She held that when one met a human flower as fresh as that in the dusty ways of the world one should pluck it and wear it; and she was always inhaling Lady Aurora's fragrance, always kissing her and holding her hand. The spinster was frightened at her generosity, at the way her imagination embroidered; she wanted to convince her (as the Princess did on her own side), that such exaggerations destroyed their unfortunate subject. The Princess delighted in her clothes, in the way she put them on and wore them, in the economies she practised in order to have money for charity and the ingenuity with which these slender resources were made to go far, in the very manner in which she spoke, a kind of startled simplicity. She wished to emulate her in all these particulars; to learn how to economise still more cunningly, to get her bonnets at the same shop, to care as little for the fit of her gloves, to ask, in the same tone, 'Isn't it a bore Susan Crotty's husband has got a ticket-of-leave?' She said Lady Aurora made her feel like a French milliner, and that if there was anything in the world she loathed it was a French milliner. Each of these persons was powerfully affected by the other's idiosyncrasies, and each wanted the other to remain as she was while she herself should be transformed into the image of her friend.

One evening, going to Madeira Crescent a little later than usual, Hyacinth met Lady Aurora on the doorstep, leaving the house. She had a different air from any he had seen in her before; appeared flushed and even a little agitated, as if she had been learning a piece of bad news. She said, 'Oh, how do you do?' with her customary quick, vague laugh; but she went her way, without stopping to talk.

Hyacinth, on going in, mentioned to the Princess that he had encountered her, and this lady replied, 'It's a pity you didn't come a little sooner. You would have assisted at a scene.'

'At a scene?' Hyacinth repeated, not understanding what violence could have taken place between mutual adorers.

'She made me a scene of tears, of earnest remonstrance—perfectly well meant, I needn't tell you. She thinks I am going too far.'

'I imagine you tell her things that you don't tell me,' said Hyacinth.

'Oh, you, my dear fellow!' the Princess murmured. She spoke absent-mindedly, as if she were thinking of what had passed with Lady Aurora, and as if the futility of telling things to Hyacinth had become a commonplace.

There was no annoyance for him in this, his pretension to keep pace with her 'views' being quite extinct. The tone they now, for the most part, took with each other was one of mutual derision, of shrugging commiseration for insanity on the one hand and benightedness on the other. In discussing with her he exaggerated deliberately, went to fantastic lengths in the way of reaction; and it was their habit and their entertainment to hurl all manner of denunciation at each other's head. They had given up serious discussion altogether, and when they were not engaged in bandying, in the spirit of burlesque, the amenities I have mentioned, they talked of matters as to which it could not occur to them to differ. There were evenings when the Princess did nothing but relate her life and all that she had seen of humanity, from her earliest years, in a variety of countries. If the evil side of it appeared mainly to have been presented to her view, this did not diminish the interest and vividness of her reminiscences, nor her power, the greatest Hyacinth had ever encountered, of light pictorial, dramatic evocation. She was irreverent and invidious, but she made him hang on her lips; and when she regaled him with anecdotes of foreign courts (he delighted to know how sovereigns lived and conversed), there was often, for hours together, nothing to indicate that she would have liked to get into a conspiracy and he would have liked to get out of one. Nevertheless, his mind was by no means exempt from wonder as to what she was really doing in the dark and in what queer consequences she might find herself landed. When he questioned her she wished to know by what title, with his sentiments, he pretended to inquire. He did so but little, not being himself altogether convinced of the validity of his warrant; but on one occasion, when she challenged him, he replied, smiling and hesitating, 'Well, I must say, it seems to me that, from what I have told you, it ought to strike you that I have a title.'

'You mean your famous engagement, your vow? Oh, that will never come to anything.'

'Why won't it come to anything?'

'It's too absurd, it's too vague. It's like some silly humbug in a novel.'

'*Vous me rendez la vie!*' said Hyacinth, theatrically.

'You won't have to do it,' the Princess went on.

'I think you mean I won't do it. I have offered, at least; isn't that a title?'

'Well, then, you won't do it,' said the Princess; and they looked at each other a couple of minutes in silence.

'You will, I think, at the pace you are going,' the young man resumed.

'What do you know about the pace? You are not worthy to know!'

He did know, however; that is, he knew that she was in communication with foreign socialists and had, or believed she had, irons on the fire—that she held in her hand some of the strings that are pulled in great movements. She received letters that made Madame Grandoni watch her askance, of which, though she knew nothing of their contents and had only her general suspicions and her scent for disaster, now become constant, the old woman had spoken more than once to Hyacinth. Madame Grandoni had begun to have sombre visions of the interference of the police: she was haunted with the idea of a search for compromising papers; of being dragged, herself, as an accomplice in direful plots, into a court of justice—possibly into a prison. 'If she would only burn—if she would only burn! But she keeps—I know she keeps!' she groaned to Hyacinth, in her helpless gloom. Hyacinth could only guess what it might be that she kept; asking himself whether she were seriously entangled, were being exploited by revolutionary Bohemians, predatory adventurers who counted on her getting frightened at a given moment and offering hush-money to be allowed to slip out (out of a complicity which they, of course, would never have taken seriously); or were merely coquetting with paper schemes, giving herself cheap sensations, discussing preliminaries which, for her, could have no second stage. It would have been easy for Hyacinth to smile at the Princess's impression that she was 'in it,' and to conclude that even the cleverest women do not know when they are superficial, had not the vibration remained which had been imparted to his nerves two years before, of which he had spoken to his hostess at Medley — the sense, vividly kindled and never quenched, that the forces secretly arrayed against the present social order were pervasive and universal, in the air one breathed, in the ground one trod, in the hand of an acquaintance that one might touch, or the eye of a stranger that might rest a moment on one's own. They were above, below, within, without, in every contact and combination of life; and it was no disproof of them to say it was too odd that they should lurk in a particular improbable form. To lurk in improbable forms was precisely their strength, and they would doubtless exhibit much stranger incidents than this of the Princess's being a genuine participant even when she flattered herself that she was.

'You do go too far,' Hyacinth said to her, the evening Lady Aurora had passed him at the door.

To which she answered, 'Of course I do — that's exactly what I mean. How else does one know one has gone far enough? That poor, dear woman! She's an angel, but she isn't in the least in it,' she added, in a moment. She would give him no further satisfaction on the subject; when he pressed her she inquired whether he had brought the copy of Browning that he had promised the last time. If he had, he was to sit down and read it to her. In such a case as this Hyacinth had no disposition to insist; he was glad enough not to talk about the everlasting nightmare. He took *Men and Women* from his pocket, and read aloud for half an hour; but on his making some remark on one of the poems, at the end of this time he perceived the Princess had been paying no attention. When he charged her with this levity she only replied, looking at him musingly, 'How *can* one, after all, go too far? That's a word of cowards.'

'Do you mean her ladyship is a coward?'

'Yes, in not having the courage of her opinions, of her conclusions. The way the English can go half-way to a thing, and then stick in the middle!' the Princess exclaimed, impatiently.

'That's not your fault, certainly!' said Hyacinth. 'But it seems to me that Lady Aurora, for herself, goes pretty far.'

'We are all afraid of some things, and brave about others,' the Princess went on.

'The thing Lady Aurora is most afraid of is the Princess Casamassima,' Hyacinth remarked.

His companion looked at him, but she did not take this up. 'There is one particular in which she would be very brave. She would marry her friend—your friend—Mr. Muniment.'

'Marry him, do you think?'

'What else, pray?' the Princess asked. 'She adores the ground he walks on.'

'And what would Belgrave Square, and Inglefield, and all the rest of it, say?'

'What do they say already, and how much does it make her swerve? She would do it in a moment, and it would be fine to see it, it would be magnificent,' said the Princess, kindling, as she was apt to kindle, at the idea of any great freedom of action.

'That certainly wouldn't be a case of what you call sticking in the middle,' Hyacinth rejoined.

'Ah, it wouldn't be a matter of logic; it would be a matter of passion. When it's a question of that, the English, to do them justice, don't stick!'

This speculation of the Princess's was by no means new to Hyacinth, and he had not thought it heroic, after all, that their high-strung friend should feel herself capable of sacrificing her family, her name, and the few habits of gentility that survived in her life, of making herself a scandal, a fable, and a nine days' wonder, for Muniment's sake; the young chemist's assistant being, to his mind, as we know, exactly the type of man who produced convulsions, made ruptures and renunciations easy. But it was less clear to him what ideas Muniment might have on the subject of a union with a young woman who should have come out of her class for him. He would marry some day, evidently, because he would do all the natural, human, productive things; but for the present he had business on hand which would be likely to pass first. Besides—Hyacinth had seen him give evidence of this—he didn't think people could really come out of their class; he held that the stamp of one's origin is ineffaceable and that the best thing one can do is to wear it and fight for it. Hyacinth could easily imagine how it would put him out to be mixed up, closely, with a person who, like Lady Aurora, was fighting on the wrong side. 'She can't marry him unless he asks her, I suppose—and perhaps he won't,' he reflected.

'Yes, perhaps he won't,' said the Princess, thoughtfully.

XXXIX

O N SATURDAY afternoons Paul Muniment was able to leave his work at four o'clock, and on one of these occasions, some time after his visit to Madeira Crescent, he came into Rosy's room at about five, carefully dressed and brushed, and ruddy with the freshness of an abundant washing. He stood at the foot of her sofa, with a conscious smile, knowing how she chaffed him when his necktie was new; and after a moment, during which she ceased singing to herself as she twisted the strands of her long black hair together and let her eyes travel over his whole person, inspecting every detail, she said to him, 'My dear Mr. Muniment, you are going to see the Princess.'

'Well, have you anything to say against it?' Mr. Muniment asked.

'Not a word; you know I like princesses. But you have.'

'Well, my girl, I'll not speak it to you,' the young man rejoined. 'There's something to be said against everything, if you'll give yourself trouble enough.'

'I should be very sorry if ever anything was said against you.'

'The man's a sneak who is only and always praised,' Muniment remarked. 'If you didn't hope to be finely abused, where would be the encouragement?'

'Ay, but not with reason,' said Rosy, who always brightened to an argument.

'The better the reason, the greater the incentive to expose one's self. However, you won't hear it, if people do heave bricks at me.'

'I won't hear it? Pray, don't I hear everything? I should like any one to keep anything from *me*!' And Miss Muniment gave a toss of her recumbent head.

'There's a good deal I keep from you, my dear,' said Paul, rather dryly.

'You mean there are things I don't want, I don't take any trouble, to know. Indeed and indeed there are: things that I wouldn't know for the world—that no amount of persuasion would induce me, not if you was to go down on your knees.

But if I did—if I did, I promise you that just as I lie here I should have them all in my pocket. Now there are others,' the young woman went on—'there are others that you will just be so good as to tell me. When the Princess asked you to come and see her you refused, and you wanted to know what good it would do. I hoped you would go, then; I should have liked you to go, because I wanted to know how she lived, and whether she had things handsome, or only in the poor way she said. But I didn't push you, because I couldn't have told you what good it *would* do you: that was only the good it would have done me. At present I have heard everything from Lady Aurora, and I know that it's all quite decent and tidy (though not really like a princess a bit), and that she knows how to turn everything about and put it best end foremost, just as I do, like, though *I* oughtn't to say it, no doubt. Well, you have been, and more than once, and I have had nothing to do with it; of which I am very glad now, for reasons that you perfectly know—you're too honest a man to pretend you don't. Therefore, when I see you going again, I just inquire of you, as you inquired of her, what good *does* it do you?'

'I like it—I like it, my dear,' said Paul, with his fresh, unembarrassed smile.

'I dare say you do. So should I, in your place. But it's the first time I have heard you express the idea that we ought to do everything we like.'

'Why not, when it doesn't hurt any one else?'

'Oh, Mr. Muniment, Mr. Muniment!' Rosy exclaimed, with exaggerated solemnity, holding up a straight, attenuated forefinger at him. Then she added, 'No, she doesn't do you good, that beautiful, brilliant woman.'

'Give her time, my dear—give her time,' said Paul, looking at his watch.

'Of course you are impatient, but you *must* hear me. I have no doubt she'll wait for you; you won't lose your turn. Please, what would you do if any one was to break down altogether?'

'My bonny lassie,' the young man rejoined, 'if *you* only keep going, I don't care who fails.'

'Oh, I shall keep going, if it's only to look after my friends and get justice for them,' said Miss Muniment—'the delicate, sensitive creatures who require support and protection. Have you really forgotten that we have such a one as that?'

The young man walked to the window, with his hands in his pockets, and looked out at the fading light. 'Why does she go herself, then, if she doesn't like her?'

Rose Muniment hesitated a moment. 'Well, I'm glad I'm not a man!' she broke out. 'I think a woman on her back is cleverer than a man on his two legs. And you such a wonderful one, too!'

'You are all too clever for me, my dear. If she goes—and twenty times a week, too—why shouldn't I go, once in ever so long? Especially as I like her, and Lady Aurora doesn't.'

'Lady Aurora doesn't? Do you think she'd be guilty of hypocrisy? Lady Aurora delights in her; she won't let me say that she herself is fit to dust the Princess's shoes. I needn't tell *you* how she goes down before them she likes. And I don't believe you care a button; you have got something in your head, some wicked game or other, that you think she can hatch for you.'

At this Paul Muniment turned round and looked at his sister a moment, smiling still and whistling just audibly. 'Why shouldn't I care? Ain't I soft, ain't I susceptible?'

'I never thought I should hear you ask that, after what I have seen these four years. For four years she has come, and it's all for you, as well it might be, and you never showing any more sense of what she'd be willing to do for you than if you had been that woollen cat on the hearth-rug!'

'What would you like me to do? Would you like me to hang round her neck and hold her hand, the same as you do?' Muniment asked.

'Yes, it would do me good, I can tell you. It's better than what I see—the poor lady getting spotted and dim, like a mirror that wants rubbing.'

'You know a good deal, Rosy, but you don't know everything,' Muniment remarked in a moment, with a face that gave no sign of seeing a reason in what she said. 'Your mind is too poetical. There's nothing that I should care for that her ladyship would be willing to do for me.'

'She would marry you at a day's notice—she'd do that.'

'I shouldn't care for that. Besides, if I was to ask her she would never come into the place again. And I shouldn't care for that, for you.'

'Never mind me; I'll take the risk!' cried Rosy, gaily.

'But what's to be gained, if I can have her, for you, without any risk?'

'You won't have her for me, or for any one, when she's dead of a broken heart.'

'Dead of a broken tea-cup!' said the young man. 'And, pray, what should we live on, when you had got us set up?—the three of us, without counting the kids.'

He evidently was arguing from pure good-nature, and not in the least from curiosity; but his sister replied as eagerly as if he would be floored by her answer: 'Hasn't she got two hundred a year of her own? Don't I know every penny of her affairs?'

Paul Muniment gave no sign of any mental criticism he may have made on Rosy's conception of the delicate course, or of a superior policy; perhaps, indeed, for it is perfectly possible, her inquiry did not strike him as having a mixture of motives. He only rejoined, with a little pleasant, patient sigh, 'I don't want the dear old girl's money.'

His sister, in spite of her eagerness, waited twenty seconds; then she flashed at him, 'Pray, do you like the Princess's better?'

'If I did, there would be more of it,' he answered, quietly.

'How can she marry you? Hasn't she got a husband?' Rosy cried.

'Lord, how you give me away!' laughed her brother. 'Daughters of earls, wives of princes—I have only to pick.'

'I don't speak of the Princess, so long as there's a prince. But if you haven't seen that Lady Aurora is a beautiful, wonderful exception, and quite unlike any one else in all the wide world—well, all I can say is that *I* have.'

'I thought it was your opinion,' Paul objected, 'that the swells should remain swells, and the high ones keep their place.'

'And, pray, would she lose hers if she were to marry you?'

'Her place at Inglefield, certainly,' said Paul, as patiently as if his sister could never tire him with any insistence or any minuteness.

'Hasn't she lost that already? Does she ever go there?'

'Surely you appear to think so, from the way you always question her about it,' replied Paul.

'Well, they think her so mad already that they can't think her any madder,' his sister continued. 'They have given her up, and if she were to marry you——'

'If she were to marry me, they wouldn't touch her with a ten-foot pole,' Paul broke in.

Rosy flinched a moment; then she said, serenely, 'Oh, I don't care for that!'

'You ought to, to be consistent, though, possibly, she shouldn't, admitting that she wouldn't. You have more imagination than logic—which of course, for a woman, is quite right. That's what makes you say that her ladyship is in affliction because I go to a place that she herself goes to without the least compulsion.'

'She goes to keep you off,' said Rosy, with decision.

'To keep me off?'

'To interpose, with the Princess; to be nice to her and conciliate her, so that she may not take you.'

'Did she tell you any such rigmarole as that?' Paul inquired, this time staring a little.

'Do I need to be told things, to know them? I am not a fine, strong, superior male; therefore I can discover them for myself,' answered Rosy, with a dauntless little laugh and a light in her eyes which might indeed have made it appear that she was capable of wizardry.

'You make her out at once too passionate and too calculating,' the young man rejoined. 'She has no personal feelings, she wants nothing for herself. She only wants one thing in the world—to make the poor a little less poor.'

'Precisely; and she regards you, a helpless, blundering bachelor, as one of them.'

'She knows I am not helpless so long as you are about the place, and that my blunders don't matter so long as you correct them.'

'She wants to assist me to assist you, then!' the girl exclaimed, with the levity with which her earnestness was always interfused; it was a spirit that seemed, at moments, in argument, to mock at her own contention. 'Besides, isn't that the very thing you want to bring about?' she went on. 'Isn't that what you are plotting and working and waiting for? She wants to throw herself into it—to work with you.'

'My dear girl, she doesn't understand a pennyworth of what I think. She couldn't if she would.'

'And no more do I, I suppose you mean.'

'No more do you; but with you it's different. If you would, you could. However, it matters little who understands and who doesn't, for there's mighty little of it. I'm not doing much, you know.'

Rosy lay there looking up at him. 'It must be pretty thick, when you talk that way. However, I don't care what happens, for I know I shall be looked after.'

'Nothing will happen—nothing will happen,' Paul remarked, simply.

The girl's rejoinder to this was to say in a moment, 'You have a different tone since you have taken up the Princess.'

She spoke with a certain severity, but he broke out, as if he had not heard her, 'I like your idea of the female aristocracy quarrelling over a dirty brute like me.'

'I don't know how dirty you are, but I know you smell of soap,' said Rosy, with serenity. 'They won't quarrel; that's not the way they do it. Yes, you are taking a different tone, for some purpose that I can't discover just yet.'

'What do you mean by that? When did I ever take a tone?' her brother asked.

'Why then do you speak as if you were not remarkable, immensely remarkable—more remarkable than anything any one, male or female, good or bad, of the aristocracy or of the vulgar sort, can ever do for you?'

'What on earth have I ever done to show it?' Paul demanded.

'Oh, I don't know your secrets, and that's one of them. But we're out of the common beyond any one, you and I, and, between ourselves, with the door fastened, we might as well admit it.'

'I admit it for you, with all my heart,' said the young man, laughing.

'Well, then, if I admit it for you, that's all that's required.'

The brother and sister considered each other a while in silence, as if each were tasting, agreeably, the distinction the other conferred; then Muniment said, 'If I'm such an awfully superior chap, why shouldn't I behave in keeping?'

'Oh, you do, you do!'

'All the same, you don't like it.'

'It isn't so much what you do; it's what *she* does.'

'How do you mean, what she does?'

'She makes Lady Aurora suffer.'

'Oh, I can't go into that,' said Paul. 'A man feels like a muff, talking about the women that "suffer" for him.'

'Well, if they do it, I think *you* might bear it!' Rosy exclaimed. 'That's what a man is. When it comes to being sorry, oh, that's too ridiculous!'

'There are plenty of things in the world I'm sorry for,' Paul rejoined, smiling. 'One of them is that you should keep me gossiping here when I want to go out.'

'Oh, I don't care if I worry her a little. Does she do it on purpose?' Rosy continued.

'You ladies must settle all that together,' Muniment answered, rubbing his hat with the cuff of his coat. It was a new one, the bravest he had ever possessed, and in a moment he put it on his head, as if to reinforce his reminder to his sister that it was time she should release him.

'Well, you do look genteel,' she remarked, complacently, gazing up at him. 'No wonder she has lost her head! I mean the Princess,' she explained. 'You never went to any such expense for her ladyship.'

'My dear, the Princess is worth it—she's worth it,' said the young man, speaking seriously now, and reflectively.

'Will she help you very much?' Rosy demanded, with a strange, sudden transition to eagerness.

'Well,' said Paul, 'that's rather what I look for.'

She threw herself forward on her sofa, with a movement that was rare with her, and shaking her clasped hands she exclaimed, 'Then go off, go off quickly!'

He came round and kissed her, as if he were not more struck than usual with her freakish inconsistency. 'It's not bad to have a little person at home who wants a fellow to succeed.'

'Oh, I know they will look after me,' she said, sinking back upon her pillow with an air of agreeable security.

He was aware that whenever she said 'they,' without further elucidation, she meant the populace surging up in his rear, and he rejoined, always hilarious, 'I don't think we'll leave it much to "them."'

'No, it's not much you'll leave to them, I'll be bound.'

He gave a louder laugh at this, and said, 'You're the deepest of the lot, Miss Muniment.'

Her eyes kindled at his praise, and as she rested them on her brother's she murmured, 'Well, I pity the poor Princess, too, you know.'

'Well, now, I'm not conceited, but I don't,' Paul returned, passing in front of the little mirror on the mantel-shelf.

'Yes, you'll succeed, and so shall I—but *she* won't,' Rosy went on.

Muniment stopped a moment, with his hand on the latch of the door, and said, gravely, almost sententiously, 'She is not only beautiful, as beautiful as a picture, but she is uncommon sharp, and she has taking ways, beyond anything that ever was known.'

'I know her ways,' his sister replied. Then, as he left the room, she called after him, 'But I don't care for anything, so long as you become prime minister of England!'

Three quarters of an hour after this Muniment knocked at the door in Madeira Crescent, and was immediately ushered into the parlour, where the Princess, in her bonnet and mantle, sat alone. She made no movement as he came in; she only looked up at him with a smile.

'You are braver than I gave you credit for,' she said, in her rich voice.

'I shall learn to be brave, if I associate a while longer with you. But I shall never cease to be shy,' Muniment added, standing there and looking tall in the middle of the small room. He cast his eyes about him for a place to sit down, but the Princess gave him no help to choose; she only watched him, in silence, from her own place, with her hands quietly folded in her lap. At last, when, without remonstrance from her, he had selected the most uncomfortable chair in the room, she replied—

'That's only another name for desperate courage. I put on my bonnet, on the chance, but I didn't expect you.'

'Well, here I am—that's the great thing,' Muniment said, good-humouredly.

'Yes, no doubt it's a very great thing. But it will be a still greater thing when you are there.'

'I am afraid you hope too much,' the young man observed. 'Where is it? I don't think you told me.'

The Princess drew a small folded letter from her pocket, and, without saying anything, held it out to him. He got up to take it from her, opened it, and, as he read it, remained standing in front of her. Then he went straight to the fire and thrust the paper into it. At this movement she rose quickly, as if to save the document, but the expression of his face, as he turned round to her, made her stop. The smile that came into her own was a little forced. 'What are you afraid of?' she asked. 'I take it the house is known. If we go, I suppose we may admit that we go.'

Muniment's face showed that he had been annoyed, but he answered, quietly enough, 'No writing—no writing.'

'You are terribly careful,' said the Princess.

'Careful of you—yes.'

She sank down upon her sofa again, asking her companion to ring for tea; they would do much better to have some before going out. When the order had been given, she remarked, 'I see I shall have much less keen emotion than when I acted by myself.'

'Is that what you go in for—keen emotion?'

'Surely, Mr. Muniment. Don't you?'

'God forbid! I hope to have as little of it as possible.'

'Of course one doesn't want any vague rodomontade, one wants to do something. But it would be hard if one couldn't have a little pleasure by the way.'

'My pleasure is in quietness,' said Paul Muniment, smiling.

'So is mine. But it depends on how you understand it. Quietness, I mean, in the midst of a tumult.'

'You have rare ideas about tumults. They are not good in themselves.'

The Princess considered this a moment; then she remarked, 'I wonder if you are too prudent. I shouldn't like that. If it is made an accusation against you that you have been—where we are going—shall you deny it?'

'With that prospect it would be simpler not to go at all, wouldn't it?' Muniment inquired.

'Which prospect do you mean? That of being found out, or that of having to lie?'

'I suppose that if you lie you are not found out,' Muniment replied, humorously.

'You won't take me seriously,' said the Princess. She spoke without irritation, without resentment, with a kind of resigned sadness. But there was a certain fineness of reproach in the tone in which she added, 'I don't believe you want to go at all.'

'Why else should I have come, especially if I don't take you seriously?'

'That has never been a reason for a man's not going to see a woman,' said the Princess. 'It's usually a reason in favour of it.'

Muniment turned his smiling eyes over the room, looking from one article of furniture to another: this was a way he had when he was engaged in a discussion, and it suggested not so much that he was reflecting on what his interlocutor said as that his thoughts were pursuing a cheerfully independent course. Presently he observed, 'I don't know that I quite understand what you mean by that question of taking a woman seriously.'

'Ah, you are very perfect,' murmured the Princess. 'Don't you consider that the changes you look for will be also for our benefit?'

'I don't think they will alter your position.'

'If I didn't hope for that, I wouldn't do anything,' said the Princess.

'Oh, I have no doubt you'll do a great deal.'

The young man's companion was silent for some minutes, during which he also was content to say nothing. 'I wonder you can find it in your conscience to work with me,' she observed at last.

'It isn't in my conscience I find it,' said Muniment, laughing.

The maid-servant brought in the tea, and while the Princess was making a place for it on a little table beside her she exclaimed, 'Well, I don't care, for I think I have you in my power!'

'You have every one in your power,' returned Muniment.

'Every one is no one,' the Princess replied, rather dryly; and a moment later she said to him, 'That extraordinary little sister of yours—surely you take *her* seriously?'

'I'm wonderful fond of her, if that's what you mean. But I don't think her position will ever be altered.'

'Are you alluding to her position in bed? If you consider that she will never recover her health,' the Princess said, 'I am very sorry to hear it.'

'Oh, her health will do. I mean that she will continue to be, like all the most amiable women, just a kind of ornament to life.'

The Princess had already perceived that he pronounced amiable 'emiable;' but she had accepted this peculiarity of her visitor in the spirit of imaginative transfigurement in which she had accepted several others. 'To your life, of course. She can hardly be said to be an ornament to her own.'

'Her life and mine are all one.'

'She is certainly magnificent,' said the Princess. While he was drinking his tea she remarked to him that for a revolutionist he was certainly most extraordinary; and he inquired, in answer, whether it were not rather in keeping for revolutionists to be extraordinary. He drank three cups, declaring that his hostess's decoction was fine; it was better, even, than Lady Aurora's. This led him to observe, as he put down his third cup, looking round the room again, lovingly, almost covetously, 'You've got everything so handy, I don't see what interest you can have.'

'How do you mean, what interest?'

'In getting in so uncommon deep.'

On the instant the Princess's expression flashed into pure passion. 'Do you consider that I am in—really far?'

'Up to your neck, ma'am.'

'And do you think that *il y va* of my neck—I mean that it's in danger?' she translated, eagerly.

'Oh, I understand your French. Well, I'll look after you,' Muniment said.

'Remember, then, definitely, that I expect not to lie.'

'Not even for me?' Then Muniment added, in the same familiar tone, which was not rough nor wanting in respect, but only homely and direct, suggestive of growing acquaintance, 'If I was your husband I would come and take you away.'

'Please don't speak of my husband,' said the Princess, gravely. 'You have no qualification for doing so; you know nothing whatever about him.'

'I know what Hyacinth has told me.'

'Oh, Hyacinth!' the Princess murmured, impatiently. There was another silence of some minutes, not disconnected, apparently, from this reference to the little bookbinder; but when Muniment spoke, after the interval, it was not to carry on the allusion.

'Of course you think me very plain, very rude.'

'Certainly, you have not such a nice address as Hyacinth,' the Princess rejoined, not desiring, on her side, to evade the topic. 'But that is given to very few,' she added; 'and I don't know that pretty manners are exactly what we are working for.'

'Ay, it won't be very endearing when we cut down a few allowances,' said Muniment. 'But I want to please you; I want to be as much as possible like Hyacinth,' he went on.

'That is not the way to please me. I don't forgive him; he's very silly.'

'Ah, don't say that; he's a little brick!' Muniment exclaimed.

'He's a dear fellow, with extraordinary qualities, but so deplorably conventional.'

'Yes, talking about taking things seriously—*he* takes them seriously,' remarked Muniment.

'Has he ever told you his life?' asked the Princess.

'He hasn't required to tell me. I've seen a good bit of it.'

'Yes, but I mean before you knew him.'

Muniment reflected a moment. 'His birth, and his poor mother? I think it was Rosy told me about that.'

'And, pray, how did *she* know?'

'Ah, when you come to the way Rosy knows!' said Muniment, laughing. 'She doesn't like people in that predicament. She thinks we ought all to be finely born.'

'Then they agree, for so does poor Hyacinth.' The Princess hesitated an instant; then she said, as if with a quick effort, 'I want to ask you something. Have you had a visit from Mr. Vetch?'

'The old gentleman who fiddles? No, he has never done me that honour.'

'It was because I prevented him, then. I told him to leave it to me.'

'To leave what, now?' Muniment looked at her in placid perplexity.

'He is in great distress about Hyacinth—about the danger he runs. You know what I mean.'

'Yes, I know what you mean,' Muniment replied, slowly. 'But what does *he* know about it? I thought it was supposed to be a deadly secret.'

'So it is. He doesn't know anything; he only suspects.'

'How do you know, then?'

The Princess hesitated again. 'Oh, I'm like Rosy—I find out. Mr. Vetch, as I suppose you are aware, has known Hyacinth all his life; he takes a most affectionate interest in him. He believes there is something hanging over him, and he wants it to be turned off, to be stopped.' The Princess paused at this, but her visitor made no response, and she continued: 'He was going to see you, to beg you to do something, to interfere; he seemed to think that your power, in such a matter, would be very great; but, as I tell you, I requested him, as a particular favour to me, to let you alone.'

'What favour would it be to you?' Muniment asked.

'It would give me the satisfaction of feeling that you were not worried.'

Muniment appeared struck with the curious inadequacy of this explanation, considering what was at stake; he broke into a laugh and remarked, 'That was considerate of you, beyond everything.'

'It was not meant as consideration for you; it was a piece of calculation.' The Princess, having made this announcement, gathered up her gloves and turned away, walking to the chimney-piece, where she stood a moment arranging her bonnet-ribbons in the mirror with which it was decorated. Muniment watched her with evident curiosity; in spite both of his inaccessibility to nervous agitation and of the sceptical theories he entertained about her, he was not proof against her general faculty of creating a feeling of suspense, a tension of interest, on the part of those who associated with her. He followed her movements, but plainly he didn't follow her calculations, so that he could only listen more attentively when she inquired suddenly, 'Do you know why I asked you to come and see me? Do you know why I went to see your sister? It was all a plan,' said the Princess.

'We hoped it was just an ordinary humane, social impulse,' the young man returned.

'It was humane, it was even social, but it was not ordinary. I wanted to save Hyacinth.'

'To save him?'

'I wanted to be able to talk with you just as I am talking now.'

'That was a fine idea!' Muniment exclaimed, ingenuously.

'I have an exceeding, a quite inexpressible, regard for him. I have no patience with some of his opinions, and that is why I permitted myself to say just now that he is silly. But, after all, the opinions of our friends are not what we love them for, and therefore I don't see why they should be what we hate them for. Hyacinth Robinson's nature is singularly generous and his intelligence very fine, though there *are* some things that he muddles up. You just now expressed strongly your own regard for him; therefore we ought to be perfectly agreed. Agreed, I mean, about getting him out of his scrape.'

Muniment had the air of a man who felt that he must consider a little before he assented to these successive propositions; it being a limitation of his intellect that he could not respond without understanding. After a moment he answered, referring to the Princess's last remark, in which the others appeared to culminate, and at the same time shaking his head a little and smiling, 'His scrape isn't important.'

'You thought it was when you got him into it.'

'I thought it would give him pleasure,' said Muniment.

'That's not a reason for letting people do what isn't good for them.'

'I wasn't thinking so much about what would be good for him as about what would be bad for some others. He can do as he likes.'

'That's easy to say. They must be persuaded not to call upon him.'

'Persuade them, then, dear madam.'

'How can I persuade them? If I could, I wouldn't have approached you. I have no influence, and even if I had my motives would be suspected. You are the one to interpose.'

'Shall I tell them he funks it?' Muniment asked.

'He doesn't—he doesn't!' exclaimed the Princess.

'On what ground, then, shall I put it?'

'Tell them he has changed his opinions.'

'Wouldn't that be rather like denouncing him as a traitor, and doing it hypocritically?'

'Tell them then it's simply my wish.'

'That won't do *you* much good,' Muniment said, with his natural laugh.

'Will it put me in danger? That's exactly what I want.'

'Yes; but as I understand you, you want to suffer *for* the people, not by them. You are very fond of Robinson; it couldn't be otherwise,' the young man went on. 'But you ought to remember that, in the line you have chosen, our affections, our natural ties, our timidities, our shrinkings——' His voice had become low and grave, and he paused a little, while the Princess's deep and lovely eyes, attaching themselves to his face, showed that in an instant she was affected by this unwonted adjuration. He spoke now as if he were taking her seriously. 'All those things are as nothing, and must never weigh a feather beside our service.'

The Princess began to draw on her gloves. 'You're a most extraordinary man.'

'That's what Rosy tells me.'

'Why don't you do it yourself?'

'Do Hyacinth's job? Because it's better to do my own.'

'And, pray, what is your own?'

'I don't know,' said Paul Muniment, with perfect serenity and good-nature. 'I expect to be instructed.'

'Have you taken an oath, like Hyacinth?'

'Ah, madam, the oaths *I* take I don't tell,' said the young man, gravely.

'Oh, you . . . !' the Princess murmured, with an ambiguous cadence. She appeared to dismiss the question, but to suggest at the same time that he was very abnormal. This imputation was further conveyed by the next words she uttered: 'And can you see a dear friend whirled away like that?'

At this, for the first time, Paul Muniment exhibited a certain irritation. 'You had better leave my dear friend to me.'

The Princess, with her eyes still fixed upon him, gave a long, soft sigh. 'Well, then, shall we go?'

Muniment took up his hat again, but he made no movement toward the door. 'If you did me the honour to seek my acquaintance, to ask me to come and see you, only in order to say what you have just said about Hyacinth, perhaps we needn't carry out the form of going to the place you proposed. Wasn't this only your pretext?'

'I believe you *are* afraid!' the Princess exclaimed; but in spite of her exclamation the pair presently went out of the house. They quitted the door together, after having stood on the step for a moment, looking up and down, apparently for a cab. So far as the darkness, which was now complete, permitted the prospect to be scanned, there was no such vehicle within hail. They turned to the left, and after a walk of several minutes, during which they were engaged in small, dull by-streets, emerged upon a more populous way, where there were lighted shops and omnibuses and the evident chance of a hansom. Here they paused again, and very soon an empty hansom passed, and, at a sign, pulled up near them. Meanwhile, it should be recorded, they had been followed, at an interval, by a cautious figure, a person who, in Madeira Crescent, when they came out of the house, was stationed on the other side of the street, at a considerable distance. When they appeared he retreated a little, still however keeping them in sight. When they moved away he moved in the same direction, watching them but maintaining his distance. He drew nearer, seemingly because he could not control his eagerness, as they turned into Westbourne Grove, and during the minute they stood there he was exposed to recognition by the Princess if she had happened to turn her head. In the event of her having felt such an impulse she would have discovered, in the lamplight, that her noble husband was hovering in her rear. But the Princess was otherwise occupied; she failed to see that at one moment he came so close as to suggest that he had an intention of addressing himself to the couple. The reader scarcely needs to be informed that his real intention was to satisfy himself as to the kind of person his wife was walking with. The time allowed him for this research was brief, especially as he had perceived, more rapidly than he sometimes perceived things, that they were looking for a vehicle and that with its assistance they would pass out of his range—a reflection which caused him to give half his attention to the business of hailing any second cab which should come that way. There are parts of London in which you may never see a cab at all, but there are none in which you may see only one; in accordance with which fortunate truth Prince Casamassima was able to wave his stick to good purpose as soon as the two objects of his pursuit had rattled away. Behind them now, in the gloom, he had no fear of being seen. In little more than an instant he had jumped into another hansom, the driver of which accompanied the usual exclamation of 'All right, sir!' with a small, amused grunt, which the Prince thought eminently British, after he had hissed at him, over the hood, expressively, and in a manner by no means indicative of that nationality, the injunction, 'Follow, follow, follow!'

XL

A N HOUR after the Princess had left the house with Paul Muniment, Madame Grandoni came down to supper, a meal of which she partook, in gloomy solitude, in the little back parlour. She had pushed away her plate, and sat motionless, staring at the crumpled cloth, with her hands folded on the edge of the table, when she became aware that a gentleman had been ushered into the drawing-room and was standing before the fire in an attitude of discreet expectancy. At the same moment the maid-servant approached the old lady, remarking with bated breath, 'The Prince, the Prince, mum! It's you he 'ave asked for, mum!' Upon this, Madame Grandoni called out to the visitor from her place, addressed him as her poor illustrious friend and bade him come and give her his arm. He obeyed with solemn alacrity, and conducted her into the front room, near the fire. He helped her to arrange herself in her arm-chair and to gather her shawl about her; then he seated himself near her and remained with his dismal eyes bent upon her. After a moment she said, 'Tell me something about Rome. The grass in Villa Borghese must already be thick with flowers.'

'I would have brought you some, if I had thought,' he answered. Then he turned his gaze about the room. 'Yes, you may well ask, in such a black little hole as this. My wife should not live here,' he added.

'Ah, my dear friend, for all that she's your wife!' the old woman exclaimed.

The Prince sprang up in sudden, passionate agitation, and then she saw that the rigid quietness with which he had come into the room and greeted her was only an effort of his good manners. He was really trembling with excitement. 'It is true—it is true! She *has* lovers—she *has* lovers!' he broke out. 'I have seen it with my eyes, and I have come here to know!'

'I don't know what you have seen, but your coming here to know will not have helped you much. Besides, if you have seen, you know for yourself. At any rate, I have ceased to be able to tell you.'

'You are afraid—you are afraid!' cried the visitor, with a wild accusatory gesture.

Madame Grandoni looked up at him with slow speculation. 'Sit down and be tranquil, very tranquil. I have ceased to pay attention—I take no heed.'

'Well, I do, then,' said the Prince, subsiding a little. 'Don't you know she has gone out to a house, in a horrible quarter, with a man?'

'I think it highly probable, dear Prince.'

'And who is he? That's what I want to discover.'

'How can I tell you? I haven't seen him.'

He looked at her a moment, with his distended eyes. 'Dear lady, is that kind to me, when I have counted on you?'

'Oh, I am not kind any more; it's not a question of that. I am angry—as angry, almost, as you.'

'Then why don't you watch her, eh?'

'It's not with her I am angry. It's with myself,' said Madame Grandoni, meditatively.

'For becoming so indifferent, do you mean?'

'On the contrary, for staying in the house.'

'Thank God, you are still here, or I couldn't have come. But what a lodging for the Princess!' the visitor exclaimed. 'She might at least live in a manner befitting.'

'Eh, the last time you were in London you thought it was too costly!' she cried.

He hesitated a moment. 'Whatever she does is wrong. Is it because it's so bad that you must go?' he went on.

'It is foolish—foolish—foolish,' said Madame Grandoni, slowly, impressively.

'Foolish, *chè, chè!* He was in the house nearly an hour, this one.'

'In the house? In what house?'

'Here, where you sit. I saw him go in, and when he came out it was after a long time, with her.'

'And where were you, meanwhile?'

Again Prince Casamassima hesitated. 'I was on the other side of the street. When they came out I followed them. It was more than an hour ago.'

'Was it for that you came to London?'

'Ah, what I came for! To put myself in hell!'

'You had better go back to Rome,' said Madame Grandoni.

'Of course I will go back, but if you will tell me who this one is! How can you be ignorant, dear friend, when he comes freely in and out of the house where I have to watch, at the door, for a moment that I can snatch? He was not the same as the other.'

'As the other?'

'Doubtless there are fifty! I mean the little one whom I met in the other house, that Sunday afternoon.'

'I sit in my room almost always now,' said the old woman. 'I only come down to eat.'

'Dear lady, it would be better if you would sit here,' the Prince remarked.

'Better for whom?'

'I mean that if you did not withdraw yourself you could at least answer my questions.'

'Ah, but I have not the slightest desire to answer them,' Madame Grandoni replied. 'You must remember that I am not here as your spy.'

'No,' said the Prince, in a tone of extreme and simple melancholy. 'If you had given me more information I should not have been obliged to come here myself. I arrived in London only this morning, and this evening I spent two hours walking up and down opposite the house, like a groom waiting for his master to come back from a ride. I wanted a personal impression. It was so that I saw him come in. He is not a gentleman—not even like some of the strange ones here.'

'I think he is Scotch,' remarked Madame Grandoni.

'Ah, then, you *have* seen him?'

'No, but I have heard him. He speaks very loud—the floors of this house are not built as we build in Italy—and his voice is the same that I have heard in the people of that country. Besides, she has told me—some things. He is a chemist's assistant.'

'A chemist's assistant? *Santo Dio!* And the other one, a year ago—more than a year ago—was a bookbinder.'

'Oh, the bookbinder!' murmured Madame Grandoni.

'And does she associate with no people of good? Has she no other society?'

'For me to tell you more, Prince, you must wait till I am free,' said the old lady.

'How do you mean, free?'

'I must choose. I must either go away—and then I can tell you what I have seen—or if I stay here I must hold my tongue.'

'But if you go away you will have seen nothing,' the Prince objected.

'Ah, plenty as it is—more than I ever expected to!'

The Prince clasped his hands together in tremulous suppliance; but at the same time he smiled, as if to conciliate, to corrupt. 'Dearest friend, you torment my curiosity. If you will tell me this, I will never ask you anything more. Where did they go? For the love of God, what is that house?'

'I know nothing of their houses,' she returned, with an impatient shrug.

'Then there are others—there are many?' She made no answer, but sat brooding, with her chin in her protrusive kerchief. Her visitor presently continued, in a soft, earnest tone, with his beautiful Italian distinctness, as if his lips cut and carved the sound, while his fine fingers quivered into quick, emphasising gestures, 'The street is small and black, but it is like all the streets. It has no importance; it is at the end of an endless imbroglio. They drove for twenty minutes; then they stopped their cab and got out. They went together on foot some minutes more. There were many turns; they seemed to know them well. For me it was very difficult—of course I also got out; I had to stay so far behind—close against the houses. Chiffinch Street, N.E.—that was the name,' the Prince continued, pronouncing the word with difficulty; 'and the house is number 32—I looked at that after they went in. It's a very bad house—worse than this; but it has no sign of a chemist, and there are no shops in the street. They rang the bell—only once, though they waited a long time; it seemed to me, at least, that they did not touch it again. It was several minutes before the door was opened; and that was a bad time for me, because as they stood there they looked up and down. Fortunately you know the air of this place! I saw no light in the house—not even after they went in. Who let them enter I couldn't tell. I waited nearly half an hour, to see how long they would stay and what they would do on coming out; then, at last, my impatience brought me here, for to know she was absent made me hope I might see you. While I was there two persons went in—two men, together, smoking, who looked like *artisti* (I didn't see them near), but no one came out. I could see they took their cigars—and you can fancy what tobacco!—into the presence of the Princess. Formerly,' pursued Madame Grandoni's visitor, with a touching attempt at a jocular treatment of this point, 'she never tolerated smoking—never mine, at least. The street is very quiet—very few people pass. Now what is the house? Is it where that man lives?' he asked, almost in a whisper.

He had been encouraged by her consenting, in spite of her first protests, to listen to him—he could see she *was* listening; and he was still more encouraged when, after a moment, she answered his question by a question of her own. 'Did you cross the river to go there? I know that he lives over the water.'

'Ah, no, it was not in that part. I tried to ask the cabman who brought me back to explain to me what it is called; but I couldn't make him understand. They have heavy minds,' the Prince declared. Then he pursued, drawing a little closer to his hostess, 'But what were they doing there? Why did she go with him?'

'They are plotting. There!' said Madame Grandoni.

'You mean a secret society, a band of revolutionists and murderers? *Capisco bene*—that is not new to me. But perhaps they only pretend it's for that,' added the Prince.

'Only pretend? Why should they pretend? That is not Christina's way.'

'There are other possibilities,' the Prince observed.

'Oh, of course, when your wife goes away with strange men, in the dark, to far-away houses, you can think anything you like, and I have nothing to say to your thoughts. I have my own, but they are my own affair, and I shall not undertake to defend Christina, for she is indefensible. When she does the things she does, she provokes, she invites, the worst construction; there let it rest, save for this one remark, which I will content myself with making: if she were a licentious woman she would not behave as she does now, she would not expose herself to irresistible interpretations; the appearance of everything would be good and proper. I simply tell you what I believe. If I believed that what she is doing concerned you alone, I should say nothing about it—at least sitting here. But it concerns others, it concerns every one, so I will open my mouth at last. She has gone to that house to break up society.'

'To break it up, yes, as she has wanted before?'

'Oh, more than before! She is very much entangled. She has relations with people who are watched by the police. She has not told me, but I have perceived it by simply living with her.'

Prince Casamassima stared. 'And is *she* watched by the police?'

'I can't tell you; it is very possible—except that the police here is not like that of other countries.'

'It is more stupid,' said the Prince. He gazed at Madame Grandoni with a flush of shame on his face. 'Will she bring us to *that* scandal? It would be the worst of all.'

'There is one chance—the chance that she will get tired of it,' the old lady remarked. 'Only the scandal may come before that.'

'Dear friend, she is the devil,' said the Prince, solemnly.

'No, she is not the devil, because she wishes to do good.'

'What good did she ever wish to do to me?' the Italian demanded, with glowing eyes.

Madame Grandoni shook her head very sadly. 'You can do no good, of any kind, to each other. Each on your own side, you must be quiet.'

'How can I be quiet when I hear of such infamies?' Prince Casamassima got up, in his violence, and, in a tone which caused his companion to burst into a short, incongruous laugh as soon as she heard the words, exclaimed, 'She shall *not* break up society!'

'No, she will bore herself before the trick is played. Make up your mind to that.'

'That is what I expected to find—that the caprice was over. She has passed through so many follies.'

'Give her time—give her time,' replied Madame Grandoni.

'Time to drag my name into an assize-court? Those people are robbers, incendiaries, murderers!'

'You can say nothing to me about them that I haven't said to her.'

'And how does she defend herself?'

'Defend herself? Did you ever hear Christina do that?' Madame Grandoni asked. 'The only thing she says to me is, "Don't be afraid; I promise you by all that's sacred that you shan't suffer." She speaks as if she had it all in her hands. That is very well. No doubt I'm a selfish old woman, but, after all, one has a heart for others.'

'And so have I, I think I may pretend,' said the Prince. 'You tell me to give her time, and it is certain that she will take it, whether I give it or not. But I can at least stop giving her money. By heaven, it's my duty, as an honest man.'

'She tells me that as it is you don't give her much.'

'Much, dear lady? It depends on what you call so. It's enough to make all these scoundrels flock around her.'

'They are not all scoundrels, any more than she is. That is the strange part of it,' said the old woman, with a weary sigh.

'But this fellow, the chemist—to-night—what do you call him?'

'She has spoken to me of him as a most estimable young man.'

'But she thinks it's estimable to blow us all up,' the Prince returned. 'Doesn't *he* take her money?'

'I don't know what he takes. But there are some things— heaven forbid one should forget them! The misery of London is something fearful.'

'*Che vuole?* There is misery everywhere,' returned the Prince. 'It is the will of God. *Ci vuol' pazienza!* And in this country does no one give alms?'

'Every one, I believe. But it appears that it is not enough.'

The Prince said nothing for a moment; this statement of Madame Grandoni's seemed to present difficulties. The solution, however, soon suggested itself; it was expressed in the inquiry, 'What will you have in a country which has not the true faith?'

'Ah, the true faith is a great thing; but there is suffering even in countries that have it.'

'*Evidentemente*. But it helps suffering to be borne, and, later, it makes it up; whereas here! . . .' said the old lady's visitor, with a melancholy smile. 'If I may speak of myself, it is to me, in my circumstances, a support.'

'That is good,' said Madame Grandoni.

He stood before her, resting his eyes for a moment on the floor. 'And the famous Cholto—Godfrey Gerald—does he come no more?'

'I haven't seen him for months, and know nothing about him.'

'He doesn't like the chemists and the bookbinders, eh?' asked the Prince.

'Ah, it was he who first brought them—to gratify your wife.'

'If they have turned him out, then, that is very well. Now, if only some one could turn *them* out!'

'*Aspetta, aspetta!*' said the old woman.

'That is very good advice, but to follow it isn't amusing.' Then the Prince added, 'You alluded, just now, as to something particular, to *quel giovane*, the young artisan whom I met in the other house. Is he also estimable, or has he paid the penalty of his crimes?'

'He has paid the penalty, but I don't know of what. I have nothing bad to tell you of him, except that I think his star is on the wane.'

'*Poverino!*' the Prince exclaimed.

'That is exactly the manner in which I addressed him the first time I saw him. I didn't know how it would happen, but I felt that it would happen somehow. It has happened through his changing his opinions. He has now the same idea as you—*ci vuol' pazienza.*'

The Prince listened with the same expression of wounded eagerness, the same parted lips and excited eyes, to every added fact that dropped from Madame Grandoni's lips. 'That, at least, is more honest. Then *he* doesn't go to Chiffinch Street?'

'I don't know about Chiffinch Street; but it would be my impression that he doesn't go anywhere that Christina and the other one—the Scotchman—go together. But these are delicate matters,' the old woman pursued.

They seemed much to interest her interlocutor. 'Do you mean that the Scotchman is—what shall I call it?—his successor?'

For a moment Madame Grandoni made no reply. 'I think that this case is different. But I don't understand; it was the other, the little one, who helped her to know the Scotchman.'

'And now they have quarrelled—about my wife? It is all tremendously edifying!' the Prince exclaimed.

'I can't tell you, and shouldn't have attempted it, only that Assunta talks to me.'

'I wish she would talk to me,' said the Prince, wistfully.

'Ah, my friend, if Christina were to find you getting at her servants!'

'How could it be worse for me than it is now? However, I don't know why I speak as if I cared, for I don't care any more. I have given her up. It is finished.'

'I am glad to hear it,' said Madame Grandoni, gravely.

'You yourself made the distinction, perfectly. So long as she endeavoured only to injure *me*, and in my private capacity, I could condone, I could wait, I could hope. But since she has so recklessly thrown herself into the most criminal undertakings, since she lifts her hand with a determined purpose, as you tell me, against the most sacred institutions—it is too much; ah, yes, it is too much! She may go her way; she is no wife of mine. Not another penny of mine shall go into her pocket, and into that of the wretches who prey upon her, who have corrupted her.'

'Dear Prince, I think you are right. And yet I am sorry!' sighed the old woman, extending her hand for assistance to rise from her chair. 'If she becomes really poor, it will be much more difficult for me to leave her. *This* is not poverty, and not even a good imitation of it, as she would like it to be. But what will be said of me if having remained with her through so much of her splendour, I turn away from her the moment she begins to want?'

'Dear lady, do you ask that to make me relent?' the Prince inquired, after an hesitation.

'Not in the least; for whatever is said and whatever you do, there is nothing for me in decency, at present, but to pack my trunk. Judge, by the way I have tattled.'

'If you will stay on, she shall have everything.' The Prince spoke in a very low tone, with a manner that betrayed the shame he felt at his attempt at bribery.

Madame Grandoni gave him an astonished glance and moved away from him. 'What does that mean? I thought you didn't care.'

I know not what explanation of his inconsequence her companion would have given her if at that moment the door of the room had not been pushed open to permit the entrance of Hyacinth Robinson. He stopped short on perceiving that Madame Grandoni had a visitor, but before he had time to say anything the old lady addressed him with a certain curtness. 'Ah, you don't fall well; the Princess isn't at home.'

'That was mentioned to me, but I ventured to come in to see you, as I have done before,' Hyacinth replied. Then he added, as if he were retreating, 'I beg many pardons. I was not told that you were not alone.'

'My visitor is going, but I am going too,' said Madame Grandoni. 'I must take myself to my room—I am all falling to pieces. Therefore kindly excuse me.'

Hyacinth had had time to recognise the Prince, and this nobleman paid him the same compliment, as was proved by his asking of Madame Grandoni, in a rapid aside, in Italian, 'Isn't it the bookbinder?'

'*Sicuro,*' said the old lady; while Hyacinth, murmuring a regret that he should find her indisposed, turned back to the door.

'One moment—one moment, I pray!' the Prince interposed, raising his hand persuasively and looking at him with an unexpected, exaggerated smile. 'Please introduce me to the gentleman,' he added, in English, to Madame Grandoni.

She manifested no surprise at the request—she had none left, apparently, for anything—but pronounced the name of Prince Casamassima, and then added, for Hyacinth's benefit, 'He knows who you are.'

'Will you permit me to keep you a very little minute?' the Prince continued, addressing the other visitor; after which he remarked to Madame Grandoni, 'I will speak with him a little. It is perhaps not necessary that we should incommode you, if you do not wish to stay.'

She had for a moment, as she tossed off a satirical little laugh, a return of her ancient drollery. 'Remember that if you talk long she may come back! Yes, yes, I will go upstairs. *Felicissima notte, signori!*' She took her way to the door, which Hyacinth, considerably bewildered, held open for her.

The reasons for which Prince Casamassima wished to converse with him were mysterious; nevertheless, he was about to close the door behind Madame Grandoni, as a sign that he was at the service of her companion. At this moment the latter extended again a courteous, remonstrant hand. 'After all, as my visit is finished and as yours comes to nothing, might we not go out?'

'Certainly, I will go with you,' said Hyacinth. He spoke with an instinctive stiffness, in spite of the Prince's queer affability, and in spite also of the fact that he felt sorry for the nobleman, to whose countenance Madame Grandoni's last injunction, uttered in English, had brought a deep and painful blush. It is needless to go into the question of what Hyacinth, face to face with an aggrieved husband, may have had on his conscience, but he assumed, naturally enough, that the situation might be grave, though indeed the Prince's manner was, for the moment, incongruously conciliatory. Hyacinth invited his new acquaintance to pass, and in a minute they were in the street together.

'Do you go here—do you go there?' the Prince inquired, as they stood a moment before the house. 'If you will permit, I will take the same direction.' On Hyacinth's answering that it was indifferent to him the Prince said, turning to the right, 'Well, then, here, but slowly, if that pleases you, and only a little way.' His English was far from perfect, but his errors were mainly errors of pronunciation, and Hyacinth was struck with his effort to express himself very distinctly, so that in intercourse with a little representative of the British populace his foreignness should not put him at a disadvantage. Quick as he was to perceive and appreciate, Hyacinth noted how a certain quality of breeding that was in his companion enabled him to compass that coolness, and he mentally applauded his success in a difficult feat. Difficult he judged it because it seemed to him that the purpose for which the Prince wished to speak to him was one which must require a deal of explanation, and it was a sign of training to explain adequately, in a foreign tongue, especially if one were agitated, to a person in a social position very different from one's own. Hyacinth knew what the Prince's estimate of *his* importance must be (he could have no illusions as to the character of the people his wife received); but while he heard him carefully put one word after the other he was able to smile to himself at his needless precautions. Hyacinth reflected that at a pinch he could have encountered him in his own tongue; during his stay at Venice he had picked up an Italian vocabulary. 'With Madame Grandoni I spoke of you,' the Prince announced, dispassionately, as they walked along. 'She told me a thing that interested me,' he added; 'that is why I walk with you.' Hyacinth said nothing, deeming that better by silence than in any other fashion he held himself at the disposal of his interlocutor. 'She told me you have changed—you have no more the same opinions.'

'The same opinions?'

'About the arrangement of society. You desire no more the assassination of the rich.'

'I never desired any such thing!' said Hyacinth, indignantly.

'Oh, if you have changed, you can confess,' the Prince rejoined, in an encouraging tone. 'It is very good for some people to be rich. It would not be right for all to be poor.'

'It would be pleasant if all could be rich,' Hyacinth suggested.

'Yes, but not by stealing and shooting.'

'No, not by stealing and shooting. I never desired that.'

'Ah, no doubt she was mistaken. But to-day you think we must have patience,' the Prince went on, as if he hoped very much that Hyacinth would allow this valuable conviction to be attributed to him. 'That is also my view.'

'Oh, yes, we must have patience,' said Hyacinth, who was now smiling to himself in the dark.

They had by this time reached the end of the little Crescent, where the Prince paused under the street-lamp. He considered Hyacinth's countenance for a moment by its help, and then he pronounced, 'If I am not mistaken, you know very well the Princess.'

Hyacinth hesitated a moment. 'She has been very kind to me.'

'She is my wife—perhaps you know.'

Again Hyacinth hesitated, but after a moment he replied, 'She has told me that she is married.' As soon as he had spoken these words he thought them idiotic.

'You mean you would not know if she had not told you, I suppose. Evidently, there is nothing to show it. You can think if that is agreeable to me.'

'Oh, I can't think, I can't judge,' said Hyacinth.

'You are right—that is impossible.' The Prince stood before his companion, and in the pale gaslight the latter saw more of his face. It had an unnatural expression, a look of wasted anxiety; the eyes seemed to glitter, and Hyacinth conceived the unfortunate nobleman to be feverish and ill. He continued in a moment: 'Of course you think it strange—my conversation. I want you to tell me something.'

'I am afraid you are very unwell,' said Hyacinth.

'Yes, I am unwell; but I shall be better if you will tell me. It is because you have come back to good ideas—that is why I ask you.'

A sense that the situation of the Princess's husband was really pitiful, that at any rate he suffered and was helpless, that he was a gentleman and even a person who would never have done any great harm—a perception of these appealing truths came into Hyacinth's heart, and stirred there a desire to be kind to him, to render him any service that, in reason, he might ask. It appeared to Hyacinth that he must be pretty sick to ask any service at all, but that was his own affair. 'If you would like me to see you safely home, I will do that,' our young man remarked; and even while he spoke he was struck with the oddity of his being already on such friendly terms with a person whom he had hitherto supposed to be the worst enemy of the rarest of women. He found himself unable to consider the Prince with resentment.

This personage acknowledged the civility of his offer with a slight inclination of his high slimness. 'I am very much obliged to you, but I will not go home. I will not go home till I know this—to what house she has gone. Will you tell me that?'

'To what house?' Hyacinth repeated.

'She has gone with a person whom you know. Madame Grandoni told me that. He is a Scotch chemist.'

'A Scotch chemist?' Hyacinth stared.

'I saw them myself—two hours, three hours, ago. Listen, listen; I will be very clear,' said the Prince, laying his fore-finger on the other hand with an explanatory gesture. 'He came to that house—this one, where we have been, I mean—and stayed there a long time. I was here in the street—I have passed my day in the street! They came out together, and I watched them, I followed them.'

Hyacinth had listened with wonder, and even with sus-pense; the Prince's manner gave an air of such importance, such mystery, to what he had to relate. But at this he broke out: 'This is not my business—I can't hear it! *I* don't watch, *I* don't follow.'

The Prince stared a moment, in surprise; then he rejoined, more quickly than he had spoken yet, 'But they went to a house where they conspire, where they prepare horrible acts. How can you like that?'

'How do you know it, sir?' Hyacinth inquired, gravely.

'It is Madame Grandoni who has told me.'

'Why, then, do you ask me?'

'Because I am not sure, I don't think she knows. I want to know more, to be sure of what is done in that house. Does she go there only for the revolution,' the Prince demanded, 'or does she go there to be alone with him?'

'With *him*?' The Prince's tone and his excited eyes infused a kind of vividness into the suggestion.

'With the tall man—the chemist. They got into a hansom together; the house is far away, in the lost quarters.'

Hyacinth drew himself together. 'I know nothing about the matter, and I don't care. If that is all you wish to ask me, we had better separate.'

The Prince's face elongated; it seemed to grow paler. 'Then it is not true that you hate those abominations!'

Hyacinth hesitated a moment. 'How can you know about my opinions? How can they interest you?'

The Prince looked at him with sick eyes; he raised his arms a moment, a certain distance, and then let them drop at his sides. 'I hoped you would help me.'

'When we are in trouble we can't help each other much!' our young man exclaimed. But this austere reflection was lost upon the Prince, who at the moment Hyacinth spoke had already turned to look in the direction from which they had proceeded, the other end of the Crescent, his attention apparently being called thither by the sound of a rapid hansom. The place was still and empty, and the wheels of this vehicle reverberated. The Prince peered at it through the darkness, and in an instant he cried, under his breath, excitedly, 'They have come back—they have come back! Now you can see— yes, the two!' The hansom had slackened pace and pulled up; the house before which it stopped was clearly the house the two men had lately quitted. Hyacinth felt his arm seized by the Prince, who, hastily, by a strong effort, drew him forward several yards. At this moment a part of the agitation that possessed the unhappy Italian seemed to pass into his own blood; a wave of anxiety rushed through him—anxiety as to the relations of the two persons who had descended from the cab; he had, in short, for several instants, a very exact revelation of the state of feeling of a jealous husband. If he had been told, half an hour before, that he was capable of surreptitious peepings, in the interest of such jealousy, he would have resented the insult; yet he allowed himself to be checked by his companion just at the nearest point at which they might safely consider the proceedings of the couple who alighted. It was in fact the Princess, accompanied by Paul Muniment. Hyacinth noticed that the latter paid the cabman, who immediately drove away, from his own pocket. He stood with the Princess for some minutes at the door of the house—minutes during which Hyacinth felt his heart beat insanely, ignobly, he couldn't tell why.

'What does he say? what does *she* say?' hissed the Prince; and when he demanded, the next moment, 'Will he go in again, or will he go away?' our sensitive youth felt that a voice was given to his own most eager thought. The pair were talking together, with rapid sequences, and as the door had not yet been opened it was clear that, to prolong the conversation on the steps, the Princess delayed to ring. 'It will make three, four, hours he has been with her,' moaned the Prince.

'He may be with her fifty hours!' Hyacinth answered, with a laugh, turning away, ashamed of himself.

'He has gone in—*sangue di Dio!*' cried the Prince, catching his companion again by the arm and making him look. All that Hyacinth saw was the door just closing; the Princess and Muniment were on the other side of it. 'Is *that* for the revolution?' the trembling nobleman panted. But Hyacinth made no answer; he only gazed at the closed door an instant, and then, disengaging himself, walked straight away, leaving the Italian, in the darkness, to direct a great helpless, futile shake of his stick at the indifferent house.

XLI

HYACINTH waited a long time, but when at last Millicent came to the door the splendour of her appearance did much to justify her delay. He heard an immense rustling on the staircase, accompanied by a creaking of that inexpensive structure, and then she brushed forward into the narrow, dusky passage where he had been standing for a quarter of an hour. She looked flushed; she exhaled a strong, cheap perfume; and she instantly thrust her muff, a tight, fat, be-ribboned receptacle, at him, to be held while she adjusted her gloves to her large vulgar hands. Hyacinth opened the door—it was so natural an assumption that they would not be able to talk properly in the passage—and they came out to the low steps, lingering there in the yellow Sunday sunshine. A loud ejaculation on the beauty of the day broke from Millicent, though, as we know, she was not addicted to facile admirations. The winter was not over, but the spring had begun, and the smoky London air allowed the baffled citizens, by way of a change, to see through it. The town could refresh its recollections of the sky, and the sky could ascertain the geographical position of the town. The essential dimness of the low perspectives had by no means disappeared, but it had loosened its folds; it lingered as a blur of mist, interwoven with pretty sun-tints and faint transparencies. There was warmth and there was light, and a view of the shutters of shops, and the church bells were ringing. Miss Henning remarked that it was a 'shime' she couldn't have a place to ask a gentleman to sit down; but what were you to do when you had such a grind for your living, and a room, to keep yourself tidy, no bigger than a pill-box? She couldn't, herself, abide waiting outside; she knew something about it when she took things home to ladies to choose (the time they spent was long enough to choose a husband!) and it always made her feel quite miserable. It was something cruel. If she could have what she liked she knew what she would have; and she hinted at a mystic bower where a visitor could sit and enjoy him-self—with the morning paper, or a nice view out of the window, or even a glass of sherry—so that, in an adjacent apartment, she could dress without getting in a fidget, which always made her red in the face.

'I don't know how I 'ave pitched on my things,' she remarked, presenting her magnificence to Hyacinth, who became aware that she had put a small plump book into her muff. He explained that, the day being so fine, he had come to propose to her to take a walk with him, in the manner of ancient times. They might spend an hour or two in the Park and stroll beside the Serpentine, or even paddle about on it, if she liked, and watch the lambkins, or feed the ducks, if she would put a crust in her pocket. The prospect of paddling Miss Henning entirely declined; she had no idea of wetting her flounces, and she left those rough pleasures, especially of a Sunday, to a lower class of young woman. But she didn't mind if she did go for a turn, though he didn't deserve any such favour, after the way he hadn't been near her, if she had died in her garret. She was not one that was to be dropped and taken up at any man's convenience—she didn't keep one of those offices for servants out of place. Millicent expressed the belief that if the day had not been so lovely she would have sent Hyacinth about his business; it was lucky for him that she was always forgiving (such was her sensitive, generous nature), when the sun was out. Only there was one thing—she couldn't abide making no difference for Sunday; it was her personal habit to go to church, and she should have it on her conscience if she gave that up for a lark. Hyacinth had already been impressed, more than once, by the manner in which his blooming friend stickled for the religious observance: of all the queer disparities of her nature, her devotional turn struck him as perhaps the queerest. She held her head erect through the longest and dullest sermon, and came out of the place of worship with her fine face embellished by the publicity of her virtue. She was exasperated by the general secularity of Hyacinth's behaviour, especially taken in conjunction with his general straightness, and was only consoled a little by the fact that if he didn't drink, or fight, or steal, at least he indulged in unlimited wickedness of opinion—theories as bad as anything that people got ten years for. Hyacinth had not yet revealed to her that his theories had somehow lately come to be held with less tension; an instinct of kindness had forbidden him to deprive her of a grievance which ministered so much to sociability. He had not reflected that she would have been more aggrieved, and consequently more delightful, if her condemnation of his godlessness had been deprived of confirmatory indications.

On the present occasion she let him know that she would go for a walk with him if he would first accompany her to church; and it was in vain he represented to her that this proceeding would deprive them of their morning, inasmuch as after church she would have to dine, and in the interval there would be no time left. She replied, with a toss of her head, that she dined when she liked; besides on Sundays she had cold fare—it was left out for her; an argument to which Hyacinth had to assent, his ignorance of her domestic economy being complete, thanks to the maidenly mystery, the vagueness of reference and explanation, in which, in spite of great freedom of complaint, perpetual announcements of intended change, impending promotion and high bids for her services in other quarters, she had always enshrouded her private affairs. Hyacinth walked by her side to the place of worship she preferred—her choice was made apparently from a large experience; and as they went he remarked that it was a good job he wasn't married to her. Lord, how she would bully him, how she would 'squeeze' him, in such a case! The worst of it would be that—such was his amiable, peace-loving nature— he would obey like a showman's poodle. And pray, whom was a man to obey, asked Millicent, if he was not to obey his wife? She sat up in her pew with a majesty that carried out this idea; she seemed to answer, in her proper person, for creeds and communions and sacraments; she was more than devotional, she was almost pontifical. Hyacinth had never felt himself under such distinguished protection; the Princess Casamassima came back to him, in comparison, as a Bohemian, a shabby adventuress. He had come to see her to-day not for the sake of her austerity (he had had too gloomy a week for that), but for that of her genial side; yet now that she treated him to the severer spectacle it struck him for the moment as really grand sport—a kind of magnification of her rich vitality. She had her phases and caprices, like the Princess herself; and if they were not the same as those of the lady of

Madeira Crescent they proved at least that she was as brave a woman. No one but a capital girl could give herself such airs; she would have a consciousness of the large reserve of pliancy required for making up for them. The Princess wished to destroy society and Millicent wished to uphold it; and as Hyacinth, by the side of his childhood's friend, listened to practised intonings, he was obliged to recognise the liberality of a fate which had sometimes appeared invidious. He had been provided with the best opportunities for choosing between the beauty of the original and the beauty of the conventional.

Fortunately, on this particular Sunday, there was no sermon (fortunately, I mean, from the point of view of Hyacinth's heretical impatience), so that after the congregation dispersed there was still plenty of time for a walk in the Park. Our friends traversed that barely-interrupted expanse of irrepressible herbage which stretches from the Birdcage Walk to Hyde Park Corner, and took their way to Kensington Gardens, beside the Serpentine. Once Millicent's religious exercises were over for the day (she as rigidly forbore to repeat them in the afternoon as she made a point of the first service), once she had lifted her voice in prayer and praise, she changed her *allure*; moving to a different measure, uttering her sentiments in a high, free manner, and not minding that it should be perceived that she had on her very best gown and was out, if need be, for the day. She was mainly engaged, for some time, in overhauling Hyacinth for his long absence, demanding, as usual, some account of what he had been 'up to.' He listened to her philosophically, liking and enjoying her chaff, which seemed to him, oddly enough, wholesome and refreshing, and absolutely declining to satisfy her. He remarked, as he had had occasion to do before, that if he asked no explanations of her the least he had a right to expect in return was that she should let him off as easily; and even the indignation with which she received this plea did not make him feel that an *éclaircissement* between them could be a serious thing. There was nothing to explain and nothing to forgive; they were a pair of very fallible individuals, united much more by their weaknesses than by any consistency or fidelity that they might pretend to practise toward each other. It was an old acquaintance—the oldest thing, to-day, except Mr. Vetch's friendship, in Hyacinth's life; and strange as this may appear, it inspired our young man with a kind of indulgent piety. The probability that Millicent 'kept company' with other men had quite ceased to torment his imagination; it was no longer necessary to his happiness to be certain about it in order that he might dismiss her from his mind. He could be as happy without it as with it, and he felt a new modesty in regard to prying into her affairs. He was so little in a position to be stern with her that her assumption that he recognised a right on her own part to chide him seemed to him only a part of her perpetual clumsiness—a clumsiness that was not soothing but was nevertheless, in its rich spontaneity, one of the things he liked her for.

'If you have come to see me only to make jokes at my expense, you had better have stayed away altogether,' she said, with dignity, as they came out of the Green Park. 'In the first place it's rude, in the second place it's silly, and in the third place I see through you.'

'My dear Millicent, the motions you go through, the resentment you profess, are purely perfunctory,' her companion replied. 'But it doesn't matter; go on—say anything you like. I came to see you for recreation, for a little entertainment without effort of my own. I scarcely ventured to hope, however, that you would make me laugh—I have been so dismal for a long time. In fact, I am dismal still. I wish I had your disposition! My mirth is feverish.'

'The first thing I require of any friend is that he should respect me,' Miss Henning announced. 'You lead a bad life. I know what to think about that,' she continued, irrelevantly.

'And is it out of respect for you that you wish me to lead a better one? To-day, then, is so much saved out of my wickedness. Let us get on the grass,' Hyacinth continued; 'it is innocent and pastoral to feel it under one's feet. It's jolly to be with you; you understand everything.'

'I don't understand everything you say, but I understand everything you hide,' the young woman returned, as the great central expanse of Hyde Park, looking intensely green and browsable, stretched away before them.

'Then I shall soon become a mystery to you, for I mean

from this time forth to cease to seek safety in concealment. You'll know nothing about me then, for it will be all under your nose.'

'Well, there's nothing so pretty as nature,' Millicent observed, surveying the smutty sheep who find pasturage in the fields that extend from Knightsbridge to the Bayswater Road. 'What will you do when you're so bad you can't go to the shop?' she added, with a sudden transition. And when he asked why he should ever be so bad as that, she said she could see he *was* in a fever; she hadn't noticed it at first, because he never had had any more complexion than a cheese. Was it something he had caught in some of those back slums, where he went prying about with his wicked ideas? It served him right for taking as little good into such places as ever came out of them. Would his fine friends—a precious lot *they* were, that put it off on him to do all the nasty part!—would they find the doctor, and the port wine, and the money, and all the rest, when he was laid up—perhaps for months—through their putting such rot into his head and his putting it into others that could carry it even less? Millicent stopped on the grass, in the watery sunshine, and bent on her companion an eye in which he perceived, freshly, an awakened curiosity, a friendly, reckless ray, a pledge of substantial comradeship. Suddenly she exclaimed, quitting the tone of exaggerated derision which she had used a moment before, 'You little rascal, you've got something on your heart! Has your Princess given you the sack?'

'My poor girl, your talk is a queer mixture,' Hyacinth murmured. 'But it may well be. It is not queerer than my life.'

'Well, I'm glad you admit that!' the young woman cried, walking on with a flutter of her ribbons.

'Your ideas about my ideas!' Hyacinth continued. 'Yes, you should see me in the back slums. I'm a bigger Philistine than you, Miss Henning.'

'You've got more ridiculous names, if that's what you mean. I don't believe that half the time you know what you do mean, yourself. I don't believe you even know, with all your thinking, what you do think. That's your disease.'

'It's astonishing how you sometimes put your finger on the place,' Hyacinth rejoined. 'I mean to think no more—I mean to give it up. Avoid it yourself, my dear Millicent—avoid it as you would a baleful vice. It confers no true happiness. Let us live in the world of irreflective contemplation—let us live in the present hour.'

'I don't care how I live, nor where I live,' said Millicent, 'so long as I can do as I like. It's them that are over you—it's them that cut it fine! But you never were really satisfactory to me—not as one friend should be to another,' she pursued, reverting irresistibly to the concrete and turning still upon her companion that fine fairness which had no cause to shrink from a daylight exhibition. 'Do you remember that day I came back to Lomax Place ever so long ago, and called on poor dear Miss Pynsent (she couldn't abide me; she didn't like my form), and waited till you came in, and went out for a walk with you, and had tea at a coffee-shop? Well, I don't mind telling you that you weren't satisfactory to me then, and that I consider myself remarkably good-natured, ever since, to have kept you so little up to the mark. You always tried to carry it off as if you were telling one everything, and you never told one nothing at all.'

'What is it you want me to tell, my dear child?' Hyacinth inquired, putting his hand into her arm. 'I'll tell you anything you like.'

'I dare say you'll tell me a lot of trash! Certainly, I tried kindness,' Miss Henning declared.

'Try it again; don't give it up,' said her companion, strolling along with her in close association.

She stopped short, detaching herself, though not with intention. 'Well, then, has she—*has* she chucked you over?'

Hyacinth turned his eyes away; he looked at the green expanse, misty and sunny, dotted with Sunday-keeping figures which made it seem larger; at the wooded boundary of the Park, beyond the grassy moat of Kensington Gardens; at a shining reach of the Serpentine on the one side and the far façades of Bayswater, brightened by the fine weather and the privilege of their view, on the other. 'Well, you know I rather think so,' he replied, in a moment.

'Ah, the nasty brute!' cried Millicent, as they resumed their walk.

Upwards of an hour later they were sitting under the great trees of Kensington Gardens, those scattered over the slope which rises gently from the side of the water most distant from the old red palace. They had taken possession of a couple of the chairs placed there for the convenience of that part of the public for which a penny is not, as the French say, an affair, and Millicent, of whom such speculations were highly characteristic, had devoted considerable conjecture to the question whether the functionary charged with collecting the said penny would omit to come and ask for his fee. Miss Henning liked to enjoy her pleasures *gratis*, as well as to see others do so, and even that of sitting in a penny chair could touch her more deeply in proportion as she might feel that nothing would be paid for it. The man came round, however, and after that her pleasure could only take the form of sitting as long as possible, to recover her money. This question had been settled, and two or three others, of a much weightier kind, had come up. At the moment we again participate in the conversation of the pair Millicent was leaning forward, earnest and attentive, with her hands clasped in her lap and her multitudinous silver bracelets tumbled forward upon her wrists. Her face, with its parted lips and eyes clouded to gentleness, wore an expression which Hyacinth had never seen there before and which caused him to say to her, 'After all, dear Milly, you're a good old fellow!'

'Why did you never tell me before—years ago?' she asked.

'It's always soon enough to commit an imbecility! I don't know why I tell you to-day, sitting here in a charming place, in balmy air, amid pleasing suggestions, without any reason or practical end. The story is hideous, and I have held my tongue for so long! It would have been an effort, an impossible effort, at any time, to do otherwise. Somehow, to-day it hasn't been an effort; and indeed I have spoken just *because* the air is sweet, and the place ornamental, and the day a holiday, and your company exhilarating. All this has had the effect that an object has if you plunge it into a cup of water— the water overflows. Only in my case it's not water, but a very foul liquid indeed. Excuse the bad odour!'

There had been a flush of excitement in Millicent's face

while she listened to what had gone before; it lingered there, and as a colour heightened by emotion is never unbecoming to a handsome woman, it enriched her exceptional expression. 'I wouldn't have been so rough with you,' she presently remarked.

'My dear lass, *this* isn't rough!' her companion exclaimed.

'You're all of a tremble.' She put out her hand and laid it on his own, as if she had been a nurse feeling his pulse.

'Very likely. I'm a nervous little beast,' said Hyacinth.

'Any one would be nervous, to think of anything so awful. And when it's yourself!' And the girl's manner represented the dreadfulness of such a contingency. 'You require sympathy,' she added, in a tone that made Hyacinth smile; the words sounded like a medical prescription.

'A tablespoonful every half-hour,' he rejoined, keeping her hand, which she was about to draw away.

'You would have been nicer, too,' Millicent went on.

'How do you mean, I would have been nicer?'

'Well, I like you now,' said Miss Henning. And this time she drew away her hand, as if, after such a speech, to recover her dignity.

'It's a pity I have always been so terribly under the influence of women,' Hyacinth murmured, folding his arms.

He was surprised at the delicacy with which Millicent replied: 'You must remember that they have a great deal to make up to you.'

'Do you mean for my mother? Ah, *she* would have made it up, if they had let her! But the sex in general have been very nice to me,' he continued. 'It's wonderful the kindness they have shown me, and the amount of pleasure I have derived from their society.'

It would perhaps be inquiring too closely to consider whether this reference to sources of consolation other than those that sprang from her own bosom had an irritating effect on Millicent; at all events after a moment's silence she answered it by asking, 'Does *she* know—your trumpery Princess?'

'Yes, but she doesn't mind it.'

'That's most uncommonly kind of her!' cried the girl, with a scornful laugh.

'It annoys me very much to hear you apply invidious epithets to her. You know nothing about her.'

'How do you know what I know, please?' Millicent asked this question with the habit of her natural pugnacity, but the next instant she dropped her voice, as if she remembered that she was in the presence of a great misfortune. 'Hasn't she treated you most shamefully, and you such a regular dear?'

'Not in the least. It is I that, as you may say, have rounded on her. She made my acquaintance because I was interested in the same things as she was. Her interest has continued, has increased, but mine, for some reason or other, has declined. She has been consistent, and I have been fickle.'

'Your interest has declined, in the Princess?' Millicent questioned, following imperfectly this somewhat complicated statement.

'Oh dear, no. I mean only in some views that I used to have.'

'Ay, when you thought everything should go to the lowest! That's a good job!' Miss Henning exclaimed, with an indulgent laugh, as if, after all, Hyacinth's views and the changes in his views were not what was most important. 'And your grand lady still holds for the costermongers?'

'She wants to take hold of the great question of material misery; she wants to do something to make that misery less. I don't care for her means, I don't like her processes. But when I think of what there is to be done, and of the courage and devotion of those that set themselves to do it, it seems to me sometimes that with my reserves and scruples I'm a very poor creature.'

'You *are* a poor creature—to sit there and put such accusations on yourself!' the girl flashed out. 'If you haven't a spirit for yourself, I promise you I've got one for you! If she hasn't chucked you over why in the name of common sense did you say just now that she has? And why is your dear old face as white as my stocking?'

Hyacinth looked at her awhile without answering, as if he took a placid pleasure in her violence. 'I don't know—I don't understand.'

She put out her hand and took possession of his own; for a minute she held it, as if she wished to check herself, finding some influence in his touch that would help her. They sat in silence, looking at the ornamental water and the landscape-gardening beyond, which was reflected in it; until Millicent turned her eyes again upon her companion and remarked, 'Well, that's the way I'd have served him too!'

It took him a moment to perceive that she was alluding to the vengeance wrought upon Lord Frederick. 'Don't speak of that; you'll never again hear a word about it on my lips. It's all darkness.'

'I always knew you were a gentleman,' the girl went on.

'A queer variety, *cara mia*,' her companion rejoined, not very candidly, as we know the theories he himself had cultivated on this point. 'Of course you had heard poor Pinnie's incurable indiscretions. They used to exasperate me when she was alive, but I forgive her now. It's time I should, when I begin to talk myself. I think I'm breaking up.'

'Oh, it wasn't Miss Pynsent; it was just yourself.'

'Pray, what did I ever say, in those days?'

'It wasn't what you said,' Millicent answered, with refinement. 'I guessed the whole business—except, of course, what she got her time for, and you being taken to that death-bed—that day I came back to the Place. Couldn't you see I was turning it over? And did I ever throw it up at you, whatever high words we might have had? Therefore what I say now is no more than I thought then; it only makes you nicer.'

She was crude, she was common, she even had the vice of unskilful exaggeration, for he himself honestly could not understand how the situation he had described could make him nicer. But when the faculty of affection that was in her rose, as it were, to the surface, it diffused a sense of rest, almost of protection, deepening, at any rate, the luxury of the balmy holiday, the interlude in the grind of the week's work; so that, though neither of them had dined, Hyacinth would have been delighted to sit with her there the whole afternoon. It seemed a pause in something bitter that was happening to him, making it stop awhile or pushing it off to a distance. His thoughts hovered about that with a pertinacity of which they themselves were weary; but they regarded it now with a kind of wounded indifference. It would be too much, no doubt, to say that Millicent's society appeared a compensation, but it seemed at least a resource. She too, evidently, was highly content; she made no proposal to retrace their steps. She interrogated him about his father's family, and whether they were going to let him go on like that always, without ever holding out so much as a little finger to him; and she declared, in a manner that was meant to gratify him by the indignation it conveyed, though the awkwardness of the turn made him smile, that if she were one of them she couldn't 'abear' the thought of a relation of hers being in such a poor way. Hyacinth already knew what Miss Henning thought of his business at old Crookenden's and of the feebleness of a young man of his parts contenting himself with a career which was after all a mere getting of one's living by one's 'ands. He had to do with books; but so had any shop-boy who should carry such articles to the residence of purchasers; and plainly Millicent had never discovered wherein the art he practised differed from that of a plumber, a glazier. He had not forgotten the shock he once administered to her by letting her know that he wore an apron; she looked down on such conditions from the summit of her own intellectual profession, for *she* wore mantles and jackets and shawls, and the long trains of robes exhibited in the window on dummies of wire and taken down to be transferred to her own undulating person, and had never a scrap to do with making them up, but just with talking about them and showing them off, and persuading people of their beauty and cheapness. It had been a source of endless comfort to her, in her arduous evolution, that she herself never worked with her 'ands. Hyacinth answered her inquiries, as she had answered his own of old, by asking her what those people owed to the son of a person who had brought murder and mourning into their bright sublimities, and whether she thought he was very highly recommended to them. His question made her reflect for a moment; after which she returned, with the finest spirit, 'Well, if your position was so miserable, ain't that all the more reason they should give you a lift? Oh, it's something cruel!' she cried; and she added that in his place she would have found a way to bring herself under their notice. *She* wouldn't have drudged out her life in Soho if she had had gentlefolks' blood in her veins! 'If they had noticed you they would have liked

you,' she was so good as to observe; but she immediately
remembered, also, that in that case he would have been carried away quite over her head. She was not prepared to say
that she would have given him up, little good as she had ever
got of him. In that case he would have been thick with real
swells, and she emphasised the 'real' by way of a thrust at the
fine lady of Madeira Crescent—an artifice which was wasted,
however, inasmuch as Hyacinth was sure she had extracted
from Sholto a tolerably detailed history of the personage in
question. Millicent was tender and tenderly sportive, and he
was struck with the fact that his base birth really made little
impression upon her; she accounted it an accident much less
grave than he had been in the habit of doing. She was
touched and moved; but what moved her was his story of his
mother's dreadful revenge, her long imprisonment and his
childish visit to the jail, with the later discovery of his peculiar
footing in the world. These things produced a generous agitation—something the same in kind as the impressions she
had occasionally derived from the perusal of the *Family Herald*. What affected her most, and what she came back to, was
the whole element of Lord Frederick and the mystery of Hyacinth's having got so little good out of his affiliation to that
nobleman. She couldn't get over his friends not having done
something, though her imagination was still vague as to what
they might have done. It was the queerest thing in the world,
to Hyacinth, to find her apparently assuming that if he had
not been so inefficient he might have 'worked' the whole dark
episode as a source of distinction, of glory. *She* wouldn't have
been a nobleman's daughter for nothing! Oh, the left hand
was as good as the right; her respectability, for the moment,
didn't care for that! His long silence was what most astonished her; it put her out of patience, and there was a strange
candour in her wonderment at his not having bragged about
his grand relations. They had become vivid and concrete to
her now, in comparison with the timid shadows that Pinnie
had set into spasmodic circulation. Millicent bumped about in
the hushed past of her companion with the oddest mixture of
sympathy and criticism, and with good intentions which had
the effect of profane voices halloaing for echoes.

'Me only—me and her? Certainly, I ought to be obliged,

even though it is late in the day. The first time you saw her I suppose you told her—that night you went into her box at the theatre, eh? She'd have worse to tell you, I'm sure, if she could ever bring herself to speak the truth. And do you mean to say you never broke it to your big friend in the chemical line?'

'No, we have never talked about it.'

'Men are rare creatures!' Millicent cried. 'You never so much as mentioned it?'

'It wasn't necessary. He knew it otherwise—he knew it through his sister.'

'How do you know that, if he never spoke?'

'Oh, because he was jolly good to me,' said Hyacinth.

'Well, I don't suppose that ruined him,' Miss Henning rejoined. 'And how did his sister know it?'

'Oh, I don't know; she guessed it.'

Millicent stared. 'It was none of her business.' Then she added, 'He *was* jolly good to you? Ain't he good to you now?' She asked this question in her loud, free voice, which rang through the bright stillness of the place.

Hyacinth delayed for a minute to answer her, and when at last he did so it was without looking at her. 'I don't know; I can't make it out.'

'Well, I can, then!' And Millicent jerked him round toward her and inspected him with her big bright eyes. 'You silly baby, has *he* been serving you?' She pressed her question upon him; she asked if that was what disagreed with him. His lips gave her no answer, but apparently, after an instant, she found one in his face. 'Has he been making up to her ladyship—is that his game?' she broke out. 'Do you mean to say she'd look at the likes of him?'

'The likes of him? He's as fine a man as stands!' said Hyacinth. 'They have the same views, they are doing the same work.'

'Oh, he hasn't changed *his* opinions, then—not like you?'

'No, he knows what he wants; he knows what he thinks.'

'Very much the same work, I'll be bound!' cried Millicent, in large derision. 'He knows what he wants, and I dare say he'll get it.'

Hyacinth got up, turning away from her; but she also rose,

and passed her hand into his arm. 'It's their own business; they can do as they please.'

'Oh, don't try to be a saint; you put me out of patience!' the girl responded, with characteristic energy. 'They're a precious pair, and it would do me good to hear you say so.'

'A man shouldn't turn against his friends,' Hyacinth went on, with desperate sententiousness.

'That's for them to remember; there's no danger of *your* forgetting it.' They had begun to walk, but she stopped him; she was suddenly smiling at him, and her face was radiant. She went on, with caressing inconsequence: 'All that you have told me—it *has* made you nicer.'

'I don't see that, but it has certainly made you so. My dear girl, you're a comfort,' Hyacinth added, as they strolled on again.

XLII

H E HAD no intention of going in the evening to Madeira
Crescent, and that is why he asked his companion, before they separated, if he might not see her again, after tea.
The evenings were bitter to him now, and he feared them in
advance. The darkness had become a haunted element; it had
visions for him that passed even before his closed eyes—sharp
doubts and fears and suspicions, suggestions of evil, revelations of suffering. He wanted company, to light up his
gloom, and this had driven him back to Millicent, in a manner not altogether consistent with the respect which it was
still his theory that he owed to his nobler part. He felt no
longer free to drop in at the Crescent, and tried to persuade
himself, in case his mistrust should be overdone, that his reasons were reasons of magnanimity. If Paul Muniment were
seriously occupied with the Princess, if they had work in hand
for which their most earnest attention was required (and Sunday was very likely to be the day they would take: they had
spent so much of the previous Sunday together), it would be
delicate on his part to stay away, to leave his friend a clear
field. There was something inexpressibly representative to him
in the way that friend had abruptly decided to re-enter the
house, after pausing outside with its mistress, at the moment
he himself stood peering through the fog with the Prince.
The movement repeated itself innumerable times, to his moral
perception, suggesting to him things that he couldn't bear to
learn. Hyacinth was afraid of being jealous, even after he had
become so, and to prove to himself that he was not he had
gone to see the Princess one evening in the middle of the
week. Hadn't he wanted Paul to know her, months and
months before, and now was he to entertain a vile feeling at
the first manifestation of an intimacy which rested, in each
party to it, upon aspirations that he respected? The Princess
had not been at home, and he had turned away from the door
without asking for Madame Grandoni; he had not forgotten
that on the occasion of his previous visit she had excused herself from remaining in the drawing-room. After the little maid
in the Crescent had told him the Princess was out he walked

away with a quick curiosity—a curiosity which, if he had listened to it, would have led him to mount upon the first omnibus that travelled in the direction of Camberwell. Was Paul
Muniment, who was such a rare one, in general, for stopping
at home of an evening—was he also out, and would Rosy, in
this case, be in the humour to mention (for of course she
would know), where he had gone? Hyacinth let the omnibus
pass, for he suddenly became aware, with a throb of horror,
that he was in danger of playing the spy. He had not been
near Muniment since, on purpose to leave his curiosity unsat-
isfied. He allowed himself however to notice that the Princess had now not written him a word of consolation, as she
had been so kind as to do once or twice before when he had
knocked at her door without finding her. At present he had
missed her twice in succession, and yet she had given no sign
of regret—regret even on his own behalf. This determined
him to stay away awhile longer; it was such a proof that she
was absorbingly occupied. Hyacinth's glimpse of the Princess
in earnest conversation with Muniment as they returned from
the excursion described by the Prince, his memory of Paul's
relenting figure crossing the threshold once more, could leave
him no doubt as to the degree of that absorption.

Millicent hesitated when Hyacinth proposed to her that
they should finish the day together. She smiled, and her
splendid eyes rested on his with an air of indulgent interrogation; they seemed to ask whether it were worth her while, in
face of his probable incredulity, to mention the *real* reason
why she could not have the pleasure of acceding to his delightful suggestion. Since he would be sure to deride her explanation, would not some trumped-up excuse do as well,
since he could knock that about without hurting her? I know
not exactly in what sense Miss Henning decided; but she confessed at last that there *was* an odious obstacle to their meeting again later—a promise she had made to go and see a
young lady, the forewoman of her department, who was kept
indoors with a bad face, and nothing in life to help her pass
the time. She was under a pledge to spend the evening with
her, and it was not her way to disappoint an expectation. Hyacinth made no comment on this speech; he received it in
silence, looking at the girl gloomily.

'I know what's passing in your mind!' Millicent suddenly broke out. 'Why don't you say it at once, and give me a chance to contradict it? I oughtn't to care, but I do care!'

'Stop, stop—don't let us fight!' Hyacinth spoke in a tone of pleading weariness; she had never heard just that accent before.

Millicent considered a moment. 'I've a mind to play her false. She's a real lady, highly connected, and the best friend I have—I don't count men,' the girl interpolated, smiling—'and there isn't one in the world I'd do such a thing for but you.'

'No, keep your promise; don't play any one false,' said Hyacinth.

'Well, you *are* a gentleman!' Miss Henning murmured, with a sweetness that her voice occasionally took.

'Especially'—Hyacinth began; but he suddenly stopped.

'Especially what? Something impudent, I'll engage! Especially as you don't believe me?'

'Oh, no! Don't let's fight!' he repeated.

'Fight, my darling? I'd fight *for* you!' Miss Henning declared.

Hyacinth offered himself, after tea, the choice between a visit to Lady Aurora and a pilgrimage to Lisson Grove. He was in a little doubt about the former experiment, having an idea that her ladyship's family might have returned to Belgrave Square. He reflected, however, that he could not recognise that as a reason for not going to see her; his relations with her were not clandestine, and she had given him the kindest general invitation. If her august progenitors were at home she was probably at dinner with them; he would take that risk. He had taken it before, without disastrous results. He was determined not to spend the evening alone, and he would keep the Poupins as a more substantial alternative, in case her ladyship should not be able to receive him.

As soon as the great portal in Belgrave Square was drawn open before him, he perceived that the house was occupied and animated—if the latter term might properly be applied to a place which had hitherto given Hyacinth the impression of a magnificent mausoleum. It was pervaded by subdued light and tall domestics; Hyacinth found himself looking down a

kind of colonnade of colossal footmen, an array more imposing even than the retinue of the Princess at Medley. His inquiry died away on his lips, and he stood there struggling
with dumbness. It was manifest to him that some high festival
was taking place, at which his presence could only be deeply
irrelevant; and when a large official, out of livery, bending
over him for a voice that faltered, suggested, not unencourag-
ingly, that it might be Lady Aurora he wished to see, he replied in a low, melancholy accent, 'Yes, yes, but it can't be
possible!' The butler took no pains to controvert this proposition verbally; he merely turned round, with a majestic air of
leading the way, and as at the same moment two of the footmen closed the wings of the door behind the visitor, Hyacinth judged that it was his cue to follow him. In this manner,
after traversing a passage where, in the perfect silence of the
servants, he heard the shorter click of his plebeian shoes upon
a marble floor, he found himself ushered into a small apartment, lighted by a veiled lamp, which, when he had been left
there alone, without further remark on the part of his conductor, he recognised as the scene—only now more amply decorated—of one of his former interviews. Lady Aurora kept
him waiting a few moments, and then fluttered in with an
anxious, incoherent apology. The same transformation had
taken place in her own appearance as in the aspect of her
parental halls: she had on a light-coloured, crumpled-looking,
faintly-rustling dress; her head was adorned with a kind of
languid plume, terminating in little pink tips; and in her hand
she carried a pair of white gloves. All her repressed eagerness
was in her face, and she smiled as if she wished to anticipate
any scruples or embarrassments on the part of her visitor;
frankly recognising the brilliancy of her attire and the startling
implications it might convey. Hyacinth said to her that, no
doubt, on perceiving her family had returned to town, he
ought to have backed out; he knew that must make a difference in her life. But he had been marched in, in spite of himself, and now it was clear that he had interrupted her at
dinner. She answered that no one who asked for her at any
hour was ever turned away; she had managed to arrange that,
and she was very happy in her success. She didn't usually
dine—there were so many of them, and it took so long. Most

of her friends couldn't come at visiting-hours, and it wouldn't be right that she shouldn't ever receive them. On that occasion she *had* been dining, but it was all over; she was only sitting there because she was going to a party. Her parents were dining out, and she was just in the drawing-room with some of her sisters. When they were alone it wasn't so long, though it was rather long afterwards, when they went up again. It wasn't time yet: the carriage wouldn't come for nearly half an hour. She hadn't been to an evening thing for months and months, but—didn't he know?—one sometimes had to do it. Lady Aurora expressed the idea that one ought to be fair all round and that one's duties were not all of the same species; some of them would come up from time to time that were quite different from the others. Of course it wasn't just, unless one did all, and that was why she was in for something to-night. It was nothing of consequence; only the family meeting the family, as they might do of a Sunday, at one of their houses. It was there that papa and mamma were dining. Since they had given her that room for any hour she wanted (it was really tremendously convenient), she had determined to do a party now and then, like a respectable young woman, because it pleased them—though why it should, to see *her* at a place, was more than she could imagine. She supposed it was because it would perhaps keep some people, a little, from thinking she was mad and not safe to be at large— which was of course a sort of thing that people didn't like to have thought of their belongings. Lady Aurora explained and expatiated with a kind of nervous superabundance; she talked more continuously than Hyacinth had ever heard her do before, and the young man saw that she was not in her natural equilibrium. He thought it scarcely probable that she was excited by the simple prospect of again dipping into the great world she had forsworn, and he presently perceived that he himself had an agitating effect upon her. His senses were fine enough to make him feel that he revived certain associations and quickened certain wounds. She suddenly stopped talking, and the two sat there looking at each other, in a kind of occult community of suffering. Hyacinth made several mechanical remarks, explaining, insufficiently, why he had come, and in the course of a very few moments, quite independently of these observations, it seemed to him that there was a deeper, a measurelessly deep, confidence between them. A tacit confession passed and repassed, and each understood the situation of the other. They wouldn't speak of it—it was very definite that they would never do that; for there was something in their common consciousness that was inconsistent with the grossness of accusation. Besides, the grievance of each was an apprehension, an instinct of the soul—not a sharp, definite wrong, supported by proof. It was in the air and in their restless pulses, and not in anything that they could exhibit or complain of. Strange enough it seemed to Hyacinth that the history of each should be the counterpart of that of the other. What had each done but lose that which he or she had never had? Things had gone ill with them; but even if they had gone well, if the Princess had not combined with his friend in that manner which made his heart sink and produced an effect exactly corresponding upon that of Lady Aurora—even in this case what would prosperity, what would success, have amounted to? They would have been very barren. He was sure the singular creature before him would never have had a chance to take the unprecedented social step for the sake of which she was ready to go forth from Belgrave Square for ever; Hyacinth had judged the smallness of Paul Muniment's appetite for that complication sufficiently to have begun really to pity her ladyship long ago. And now, even when he most felt the sweetness of her sympathy, he might wonder what she could have imagined for him in the event of his not having been supplanted—what security, what completer promotion, what honourable, satisfying sequel. They were unhappy because they were unhappy, and they were right not to rail about that.

'Oh, I like to see you—I like to talk with you,' said Lady Aurora, simply. They talked for a quarter of an hour, and he made her such a visit as any gentleman might have made to any lady. They exchanged remarks about the lateness of the spring, about the loan-exhibition at Burlington House—which Hyacinth had paid his shilling to see—about the question of opening the museums on Sunday, about the danger of too much coddling legislation on behalf of the working classes. He declared that it gave him great pleasure to see any sign of her amusing herself; it was unnatural never to do that, and he hoped that now she had taken a turn she would keep it up. At this she looked down, smiling, at her frugal finery, and then she replied, 'I dare say I shall begin to go to balls—who knows?'

'That's what our friends in Audley Court think, you know—that it's the worst mistake you can make, not to drink deep of the cup while you have it.'

'Oh, I'll do it, then—I'll do it for them!' Lady Aurora exclaimed. 'I dare say that, as regards all that, I haven't listened to them enough.' This was the only allusion that passed on the subject of the Muniments.

Hyacinth got up—he had stayed long enough, as she was going out; and as he held out his hand to her she seemed to him a heroine. She would try to cultivate the pleasures of her class if the brother and sister in Camberwell thought it right—try even to be a woman of fashion in order to console herself. Paul Muniment didn't care for her, but she was capable of considering that it might be her duty to regulate her life by the very advice that made an abyss between them. Hyacinth didn't believe in the success of this attempt; there passed before his imagination a picture of the poor lady coming home and pulling off her feathers for ever, after an evening spent in watching the agitation of a ball-room from the outer edge of the circle, with a white, irresponsive face. 'Let us eat and drink, for to-morrow we die,' he said, laughing.

'Oh, I don't mind dying.'

'I think I do,' Hyacinth declared, as he turned away. There had been no mention whatever of the Princess.

It was early enough in the evening for him to risk a visit to Lisson Grove; he calculated that the Poupins would still be sitting up. When he reached their house he found this calculation justified; the brilliancy of the light in the window appeared to announce that Madame was holding a salon. He ascended to this apartment without delay (it was free to a visitor to open the house-door himself), and, having knocked, obeyed the hostess's invitation to enter. Poupin and his wife were seated, with a third person, at a table in the middle of the room, round a staring kerosene lamp adorned with a globe of clear glass, of which the transparency was mitigated only by a circular pattern of bunches of grapes. The third person was his friend Schinkel, who had been a member of the little party that waited upon Hoffendahl. No one said anything as Hyacinth came in; but in their silence the three others got up, looking at him, as he thought, rather strangely.

BOOK SIXTH

XLIII

'M Y CHILD, you are always welcome,' said Eustache Poupin, taking Hyacinth's hand in both his own and holding it for some moments. An impression had come to our young man, immediately, that they were talking about him before he appeared and that they would rather have been left to talk at their ease. He even thought he saw in Poupin's face the kind of consciousness that comes from detection, or at least interruption, in a nefarious act. With Poupin, however, it was difficult to tell; he always looked so heated and exalted, so like a conspirator defying the approach of justice. Hyacinth contemplated the others: they were standing as if they had shuffled something on the table out of sight, as if they had been engaged in the manufacture of counterfeit coin. Poupin kept hold of his hand; the Frenchman's ardent eyes, fixed, unwinking, always expressive of the greatness of the occasion, whatever the occasion was, had never seemed to him to protrude so far from his head. 'Ah, my dear friend, *nous causions justement de vous*,' Eustache remarked, as if this were a very extraordinary fact.

'Oh, *nous causions—nous causions!*' his wife exclaimed, as if to deprecate an indiscreet exaggeration. 'One may mention a friend, I suppose, in the way of conversation, without taking such a liberty.'

'A cat may look at a king, as your English proverb says,' added Schinkel, jocosely. He smiled so hard at his own pleasantry that his eyes closed up and vanished—an effect which Hyacinth, who had observed it before, thought particularly unbecoming to him, appearing as it did to administer the last perfection to his ugliness. He would have consulted his interests by cultivating immobility of feature.

'Oh, a king, a king!' murmured Poupin, shaking his head up and down. 'That's what it's not good to be, *au point où nous en sommes.*'

'I just came in to wish you good-night,' said Hyacinth. 'I'm afraid it's rather late for a call, though Schinkel is here.'

'It's always too late, my very dear, when you come,' the Frenchman rejoined. 'You know if you have a place at our fireside.'

'I esteem it too much to disturb it,' said Hyacinth, smiling and looking round at the three.

'We can easily sit down again; we are a comfortable party. Put yourself beside me.' And the Frenchman drew a chair close to the one, at the table, that he had just quitted.

'He has had a long walk, he is tired—he will certainly accept a little glass,' Madame Poupin announced with decision, moving toward the tray containing the small gilded *liqueur* service.

'We will each accept one, *ma bonne*; it is a very good occasion for a drop of *fine*,' her husband interposed, while Hyacinth seated himself in the chair his host had designated. Schinkel resumed his place, which was opposite; he looked across at Hyacinth without speaking, but his long face continued to flatten itself into a representation of mirth. He had on a green coat, which Hyacinth had seen before; it was a garment of ceremony, such as our young man judged it would have been impossible to procure in London or in any modern time. It was eminently German and of high antiquity, and had a tall, stiff, clumsy collar, which came up to the wearer's ears and almost concealed his perpetual bandage. When Hyacinth had sat down Eustache Poupin did not take possession of his own chair, but stood beside him, resting his hand on his head. At that touch something came over Hyacinth, and his heart sprang into his throat. The idea that occurred to him, conveyed in Poupin's whole manner as well as in the reassuring intention of that caress and in his wife's uneasy, instant offer of refreshment, explained the embarrassment of the circle and reminded our young man of the engagement he had taken with himself to exhibit an extraordinary quietness when a certain crisis in his life should have arrived. It seemed to him that this crisis was in the air, very near—that he should touch it if he made another movement; the pressure of the Frenchman's hand, which was meant as a solvent, only operated as a warning. As he looked across at Schinkel he felt dizzy and a little sick; for a moment, to his senses, the room whirled round. His resolution to be quiet appeared only too easy to keep; he couldn't break it even to the extent of speaking. He knew that his voice would tremble, and that is why he made no answer to Schinkel's rather honeyed words, uttered after an hesitation. '*Also*, my dear Robinson, have you passed your Sunday well—have you had an 'appy day?' Why was every one so endearing? His eyes questioned the table, but encountered nothing but its well-wiped surface, polished for so many years by the gustatory elbows of the Frenchman and his wife, and the lady's dirty pack of cards for 'patience' (she had apparently been engaged in this exercise when Schinkel came in), which indeed gave a little the impression of gamblers surprised, who might have shuffled away the stakes. Madame Poupin, who had dived into a cupboard, came back with a bottle of green chartreuse, an apparition which led the German to exclaim, '*Lieber Gott*, you Vrench, you Vrench, how well you manage! What would you have more?'

The hostess distributed the liquor, but Hyacinth was scarcely able to swallow it, though it was highly appreciated by his companions. His indifference to this luxury excited much discussion and conjecture, the others bandying theories and contradictions, and even ineffectual jokes, about him, over his head, with a volubility which seemed to him unnatural. Poupin and Schinkel professed the belief that there must be something very curious the matter with a man who couldn't smack his lips over a drop of that tap; he must either be in love or have some still more insidious complaint. It was true that Hyacinth was always in love—that was no secret to his friends—and it had never been observed to stop his thirst. The Frenchwoman poured scorn on this view of the case, declaring that the effect of the tender passion was to make one enjoy one's victual (when everything went straight, *bien entendu*; and how could an ear be deaf to the whisperings of such a dear little *bonhomme* as Hyacinth?) in proof of which she deposed that she had never eaten and drunk with such relish as at the time—oh, it was far away now—when she had a soft spot in her heart for her rascal of a husband. For Madame Poupin to allude to her husband as a rascal indicated a high degree of conviviality. Hyacinth sat staring at the empty table with the feeling that he was, somehow, a detached, irresponsible witness of the evolution of his fate. Finally he looked up and said to his friends, collectively, 'What on earth's the matter with you all?' And he followed this inquiry by an invitation that they should tell him what it was they had been saying about him, since they admitted that he had been the subject of their conversation. Madame Poupin answered for them that they had simply been saying how much they loved him, but that they wouldn't love him any more if he became suspicious and *grincheux*. She had been telling Mr. Schinkel's fortune on the cards, and she would tell Hyacinth's if he liked. There was nothing much for Mr. Schinkel, only that he would find something, some day, that he had lost, but would probably lose it again, and serve him right if he did! He objected that he had never had anything to lose, and never expected to have; but that was a vain remark, inasmuch as the time was fast coming when every one would have something—though indeed it was to be hoped that he would keep it when he had got it. Eustache rebuked his wife for her levity, reminded her that their young friend cared nothing for old women's tricks, and said he was sure Hyacinth had come to talk over a very different matter—the question (he was so good as to take an interest in it, as he had done in everything that related to them), of the terms which M. Poupin might owe it to himself, to his dignity, to a just though not exaggerated sentiment of his value, to make in accepting Mr. Crookenden's offer of the foremanship of the establishment in Soho; an offer not yet formally enunciated but visibly in the air and destined—it would seem, at least— to arrive within a day or two. The old foreman was going to set up for himself. The Frenchman intimated that before accepting any such proposal he must have the most substantial guarantees. *'Il me faudrait des conditions très-particulières.'* It was singular to Hyacinth to hear M. Poupin talk so comfortably about these high contingencies, the chasm by which he himself was divided from the future having suddenly doubled its width. His host and hostess sat down on either side of him, and Poupin gave a sketch, in somewhat sombre tints, of the situation in Soho, enumerating certain elements of decomposition which he perceived to be at work there and which he would not undertake to deal with unless he should be given a completely free hand. Did Schinkel understand, and was that what Schinkel was grinning at? Did Schinkel understand that poor Eustache was the victim of an absurd hallucination and that there was not the smallest chance of his being invited to assume a lieutenancy? He had less capacity for tackling the British workman to-day than when he began to rub shoulders with him, and Mr. Crookenden had never in his life made a mistake, at least in the use of his tools. Hyacinth's responses were few and mechanical, and he presently ceased to try to look as if he were entering into the Frenchman's ideas.

'You have some news—you have some news about me,' he remarked, abruptly, to Schinkel. 'You don't like it, you don't like to have to give it to me, and you came to ask our friends here whether they wouldn't help you out with it. But I don't think they will assist you particularly, poor dears! Why do you mind? You oughtn't to mind more than I do. That isn't the way.'

'*Qu'est-ce qu'il dit—qu'est-ce qu'il dit, le pauvre chèri?*' Madame Poupin demanded, eagerly; while Schinkel looked very hard at her husband, as if to ask for direction.

'My dear child, *vous vous faites des idées!*' the latter exclaimed, laying his hand on him remonstrantly.

But Hyacinth pushed away his chair and got up. 'If you have anything to tell me, it is cruel of you to let me see it, as you have done, and yet not satisfy me.'

'Why should I have anything to tell you?' Schinkel asked.

'I don't know that, but I believe you have. I perceive things, I guess things, quickly. That's my nature at all times, and I do it much more now.'

'You do it indeed; it is very wonderful,' said Schinkel.

'Mr. Schinkel, will you do me the pleasure to go away—I don't care where—out of this house?' Madame Poupin broke out, in French.

'Yes, that will be the best thing, and I will go with you,' said Hyacinth.

'If you would retire, my child, I think it would be a service that you would render us,' Poupin returned, appealing to his young friend. 'Won't you do us the justice to believe that you may leave your interests in our hands?'

Hyacinth hesitated a moment; it was now perfectly clear to him that Schinkel had some sort of message for him, and his curiosity as to what it might be had become nearly intolerable. 'I am surprised at your weakness,' he observed, as sternly as he could manage it, to Poupin.

The Frenchman stared at him an instant, and then fell on his neck. 'You are sublime, my young friend—you are sublime!'

'Will you be so good as to tell me what you are going to do with that young man?' demanded Madame Poupin, glaring at Schinkel.

'It's none of your business, my poor lady,' Hyacinth replied, disengaging himself from her husband. 'Schinkel, I wish you would walk away with me.'

'*Calmons-nous, entendons-nous, expliquons-nous!* The situation is very simple,' Poupin went on.

'I will go with you, if it will give you pleasure,' said Schinkel, very obligingly, to Hyacinth.

'Then you will give me that letter first!' Madame Poupin, erecting herself, declared to the German.

'My wife, you are an imbecile!' Poupin groaned, lifting his hands and shoulders and turning away.

'I may be an imbecile, but I won't be a party—no, God help me, not to that!' protested the Frenchwoman, planted before Schinkel as if to prevent his moving.

'If you have a letter for me, you ought to give it to me,' said Hyacinth to Schinkel. 'You have no right to give it to any one else.'

'I will bring it to you in your house, my good friend,' Schinkel replied, with a little wink that seemed to say that Madame Poupin would have to be considered.

'Oh, in his house—I'll go to his house!' cried the lady. 'I regard you, I have always regarded you, as my child,' she declared to Hyacinth, 'and if this isn't an occasion for a mother!'

'It's you that are making it an occasion. I don't know what you are talking about,' said Hyacinth. He had been questioning Schinkel's eye, and he thought he saw there a little twinkle of assurance that he might really depend upon him. 'I have disturbed you, and I think I had better go away.'

Poupin had turned round again; he seized the young man's arm eagerly, as if to prevent his retiring before he had given a certain satisfaction. 'How can you care, when you know everything is changed?'

'What do you mean—everything is changed?'

'Your opinions, your sympathies, your whole attitude. I don't approve of it—*je le constate*. You have withdrawn your confidence from the people; you have said things in this spot, where you stand now, that have given pain to my wife and me.'

'If we didn't love you, we should say that you had betrayed us!' cried Madame Poupin, quickly, taking her husband's idea.

'Oh, I shall never betray you,' said Hyacinth, smiling.

'You will never betray us—of course you think so. But you have no right to act for the people when you have ceased to believe in the people. *Il faut être conséquent, nom de Dieu!*' Poupin went on.

'You will give up all thoughts of acting for me—*je ne permets pas ça!*' exclaimed his wife.

'It is probably not of importance—only a little fraternal greeting,' Schinkel suggested, soothingly.

'We repudiate you, we deny you, we denounce you!' shouted Poupin, more and more excited.

'My poor friends, it is you who have broken down, not I,' said Hyacinth. 'I am much obliged to you for your solicitude, but the inconsequence is yours. At all events, good-night.'

He turned away from them, and was leaving the room, when Madame Poupin threw herself upon him, as her husband had done a moment before, but in silence and with an extraordinary force of passion and distress. Being stout and powerful she quickly got the better of him, and pressed him to her ample bosom in a long, dumb embrace.

'I don't know what you want me to do,' said Hyacinth, as soon as he could speak. 'It's for me to judge of my convictions.'

'We want you to do nothing, because we *know* you have changed,' Poupin replied. 'Doesn't it stick out of you, in every glance of your eye and every breath of your lips? It's only for that, because that alters everything.'

'Does it alter my engagement? There are some things in which one can't change. I didn't promise to believe; I promised to obey.'

'We want you to be sincere—that is the great thing,' said Poupin, edifyingly. 'I will go to see them—I will make them understand.'

'Ah, you should have done that before!' Madame Poupin groaned.

'I don't know whom you are talking about, but I will allow no one to meddle in my affairs.' Hyacinth spoke with sudden vehemence; the scene was cruel to his nerves, which were not in a condition to bear it.

'When it is Hoffendahl, it is no good to meddle,' Schinkel remarked, smiling.

'And pray, who is Hoffendahl, and what authority has he got?' demanded Madame Poupin, who had caught his meaning. 'Who has put him over us all, and is there nothing to do but to lie down in the dust before him? Let him attend to his little affairs himself, and not put them off on innocent children, no matter whether they are with us or against us.'

This protest went so far that, evidently, Poupin felt a little ashamed of his wife. 'He has no authority but what we give him; but you know that we respect him, that he is one of the pure, *ma bonne*. Hyacinth can do exactly as he likes; he knows that as well as we do. He knows there is not a feather's weight of compulsion; he knows that, for my part, I long since ceased to expect anything from him.'

'Certainly, there is no compulsion,' said Schinkel. 'It's to take or to leave. Only *they* keep the books.'

Hyacinth stood there before the three, with his eyes on the floor. 'Of course I can do as I like, and what I like is what I *shall* do. Besides, what are we talking about, with such sudden passion?' he asked, looking up. 'I have no summons, I have no sign. When the call reaches me, it will be time to discuss it. Let it come or not come: it's not my affair.'

'Certainly, it is not your affair,' said Schinkel.

'I can't think why M. Paul has never done anything, all this time, knowing that everything is different now!' Madame Poupin exclaimed.

'Yes, my dear boy, I don't understand our friend,' her husband remarked, watching Hyacinth with suspicious, contentious eyes.

'It's none of his business, any more than ours; it's none of any one's business!' Schinkel declared.

'Muniment walks straight; the best thing you can do is to imitate him,' said Hyacinth, trying to pass Poupin, who had placed himself before the door.

'Promise me only this—not to do anything till I have seen you first,' the Frenchman begged, almost piteously.

'My poor old friend, you are very weak.' And Hyacinth opened the door, in spite of him, and passed out.

'Ah, well, if you *are* with us, that's all I want to know!' the young man heard him say, behind him, at the top of the stairs, in a different voice, a tone of sudden, exaggerated fortitude.

XLIV

HYACINTH hurried down and got out of the house, but he had not the least intention of losing sight of Schinkel. The odd behaviour of the Poupins was a surprise and annoyance, and he had wished to shake himself free from it. He was candidly astonished at the alarm they were so good as to feel for him, for he had never perceived that they had gone round to the hope that the note he had signed (as it were) to Hoffendahl would not be presented. What had he said, what had he done, after all, to give them the right to fasten on him the charge of apostasy? He had always been a free critic of everything, and it was natural that, on certain occasions, in the little parlour in Lisson Grove, he should have spoken in accordance with that freedom; but it was only with the Princess that he had permitted himself really to rail at the democracy and given the full measure of his scepticism. He would have thought it indelicate to express contempt for the opinions of his old foreign friends, to whom associations that made them venerable were attached; and, moreover, for Hyacinth, a change of heart was, in the nature of things, much more an occasion for a hush of publicity and a kind of retrospective reserve; it couldn't prompt one to aggression or jubilation. When one had but lately discovered what could be said on the opposite side one didn't want to boast of one's sharpness—not even when one's new convictions cast shadows that looked like the ghosts of the old.

Hyacinth lingered in the street, a certain distance from the house, watching for Schinkel's exit and prepared to remain there if necessary till the dawn of another day. He had said to his friends, just before, that the manner in which the communication they looked so askance at should reach him was none of his business—it might reach him as it could. This was true enough in theory, but in fact his desire was overwhelming to know what Madame Poupin had meant by her allusion to a letter, destined for him, in Schinkel's possession—an allusion confirmed by Schinkel's own virtual acknowledgment. It was indeed this eagerness that had driven him out of the house, for he had reason to believe that the German would not fail him, and it galled his suspense to see the foolish Poupins try to interpose, to divert the missive from its course. He waited and waited, in the faith that Schinkel was dealing with them in his slow, categorical Teutonic way, and only objurgated the cabinet-maker for having in the first place paltered with his sacred trust. Why hadn't he come straight to him—whatever the mysterious document was—instead of talking it over with French featherheads? Passers were rare, at this hour, in Lisson Grove, and lights were mainly extinguished; there was nothing to look at but the vista of the low black houses, the dim, interspaced street-lamps, the prowling cats who darted occasionally across the road, and the terrible, mysterious, far-off stars, which appeared to him more than ever to see everything and tell nothing. A policeman creaked along on the opposite side of the way, looking across at him as he passed, and stood for some minutes on the corner, as if to keep an eye on him. Hyacinth had leisure to reflect that the day was perhaps not far off when a policeman might have his eye on him for a very good reason—might walk up and down, pass and repass, as he mounted guard over him.

It seemed horribly long before Schinkel came out of the house, but it was probably only half an hour. In the stillness of the street he heard Poupin let his visitor out, and at the sound he stepped back into the recess of a doorway on the same side, so that, in looking out, the Frenchman should not see him waiting. There was another delay, for the two stood talking together interminably and in a low tone on the doorstep. At last, however, Poupin went in again, and then Schinkel came down the street towards Hyacinth, who had calculated that he would proceed in that direction, it being, as Hyacinth happened to know, that of his own lodging. After he had heard Poupin go in he stopped and looked up and down; it was evidently his idea that Hyacinth would be waiting for him. Our hero stepped out of the shallow recess in which he had been flattening himself, and came straight to him, and the two men stood there face to face, in the dusky, empty, sordid street.

'You didn't let them have the letter?'

'Oh no, I retained it,' said Schinkel, with his eyes more than ever like invisible points.

'Then hadn't you better give it to me?'

'We will talk of that—we will talk.' Schinkel made no motion to satisfy his friend; he had his hands in the pockets of his trousers, and his appearance was characterised by an exasperating assumption that they had the whole night before them. He was intolerably methodical.

'Why should we talk? Haven't you talked enough with those people, all the evening? What have they to say about it? What right have you to detain a letter that belongs to me?'

'*Erlauben Sie:* I will light my pipe,' the German remarked. And he proceeded to this business, methodically, while Hyacinth's pale, excited face showed in the glow of the match that he ignited on the rusty railing beside them. 'It is not yours unless I have given it to you,' Schinkel went on, as they walked along. 'Be patient, and I will tell you,' he added, passing his hand into his companion's arm. 'Your way, not so? We will go down toward the Park.' Hyacinth tried to be patient, and he listened with interest when Schinkel said, 'She tried to take it; she attacked me with her hands. But that was not what I went for, to give it up.'

'Is she mad? I don't recognise them,' Hyacinth murmured.

'No, but they lofe you.'

'Why, then, do they try to disgrace me?'

'They think it is no disgrace, if you have changed.'

'That's very well for her; but it's pitiful for him, and I declare it surprises me.'

'Oh, he came round, and he helped me to resist. He pulled his wife off. It was the first shock,' said Schinkel.

'You oughtn't to have shocked them, my dear fellow,' Hyacinth replied.

'I was shocked myself—I couldn't help it.'

'Lord, how shaky you all are!'

'You take it well. I am very sorry. But it is a fine chance,' Schinkel went on, smoking away. His pipe, for the moment, seemed to absorb him, so that after a silence Hyacinth resumed—

'Be so good as to reflect that all this while I don't in the least understand what you are talking about.'

'Well, it was this morning, early,' said the German. 'You know in my country we don't lie in bed late, and what they do in my country I try to do everywhere. I think it is good enough. In winter I get up, of course, long before the sun, and in summer I get up almost at the same time. I should see the fine spectacle of the sunrise, if in London you could see. The first thing I do of a Sunday is to smoke a pipe at my window, which is at the front, you remember, and looks into a little dirty street. At that hour there is nothing to see there—you English are so slow to leave the bed. Not much, however, at any time; it is not important, my little street. But my first pipe is the one I enjoy most. I want nothing else when I have that pleasure. I look out at the new, fresh light— though in London it is not very fresh—and I think it is the beginning of another day. I wonder what such a day will bring; whether it will bring anything good to us poor devils. But I have seen a great many pass, and nothing has come. This morning, however, brought something—something, at least, to you. On the other side of the way I saw a young man, who stood just opposite to my house, looking up at my window. He looked at me straight, without any ceremony, and I smoked my pipe and looked at him. I wondered what he wanted, but he made no sign and spoke no word. He was a very nice young man; he had an umbrella, and he wore spectacles. We remained that way, face to face, perhaps for a quarter of an hour, and at last he took out his watch—he had a watch, too—and held it in his hand, just glancing at it every few minutes, as if to let me know that he would rather not give me the whole day. Then it came over me that he wanted to speak to me! You would have guessed that before, but we good Germans are slow. When we understand, however, we act; so I nodded to him, to let him know I would come down. I put on my coat and my shoes, for I was only in my shirt and stockings (though of course I had on my trousers), and I went down into the street. When he saw me come he walked slowly away, but at the end of a little distance he waited for me. When I came near him I saw that he was a very nice young man indeed—very young, with a very pleas-ant, friendly face. He was also very neat, and he had gloves, and his umbrella was of silk. I liked him very much. He said I should come round the corner, so we went round the corner together. I thought there would be some one there waiting for us; but there was nothing—only the closed shops and the early light and a little spring mist which told that the day would be fine. I didn't know what he wanted; perhaps it was some of our business—that's what I first thought—and perhaps it was only a little game. So I was very careful; I didn't ask him to come into the house. Yet I told him that he must excuse me for not understanding more quickly that he wished to speak with me; and when I said this he said it was not of consequence—he would have waited there, for the chance to see me all day. I told him I was glad I had spared him that, at least, and we had some very polite conversation. He *was* a very nice young man. But what he wanted was simply to put a letter in my hand; as he said himself, he was only a kind of private postman. He gave me the letter—it was not addressed; and when I had taken it I asked him how he knew, and if he wouldn't be sorry if it should turn out that I was not the man for whom the letter was meant. But I didn't give him a start; he told me he knew all it was necessary for him to know—he knew exactly what to do and how to do it. I think he is a valuable member. I asked him if the letter required an answer, and he told me he had nothing to do with that; he was only to put it in my hand. He recommended me to wait till I had gone into the house again to read it. We had a little more talk—always very polite; and he mentioned that he had come so early because he thought I might go out, if he delayed, and because, also, he had a great deal to do and had to take his time when he could. It is true that he looked as if he had plenty to do—as if he was in some very good occupation. I should tell you that he spoke to me always in English, but he is not English; he sounded his words like some kind of foreigner. I suppose he is not German, or he would have spoken to me in German. But there are so many, of all countries! I said if he had so much to do I wouldn't keep him; I would go to my room and open my letter. He said it wasn't important; and then I asked him if he wouldn't come into my room, also, and rest. I told him it wasn't very handsome, my room—because he looked like a young man who would have, for himself, a very neat lodging. Then I found he meant it wasn't important that we should talk any more, and he went away without even offering to shake hands. I don't know if he had other letters to give, but he went away, as I have said, like a postman on his rounds, without giving me any more information.'

It took Schinkel a long time to tell this story—his calm and conscientious thoroughness made no allowance for any painful acuteness of curiosity that Hyacinth might feel. He went from step to step, and treated his different points with friendly explicitness, as if each would have exactly the same interest for his companion. The latter made no attempt to hurry him, and indeed he listened, now, with a kind of intense patience; for he *was* interested, and, moreover, it was clear to him that he was safe with Schinkel; the German would satisfy him in time—wouldn't worry him with attaching conditions to their transaction, in spite of the mistake he had made in going for guidance to Lisson Grove. Hyacinth learned in due course that on returning to his apartment and opening the little packet of which he had been put into possession, Mr. Schinkel had found himself confronted with two separate articles: one a sealed letter superscribed with our young man's name, the other a sheet of paper containing in three lines a request that within two days of receiving it he would hand the letter to the 'young Robinson.' The three lines in question were signed D. H., and the letter was addressed in the same hand. Schinkel professed that he already knew the writing; it was that of Diedrich Hoffendahl. 'Good, good,' he said, exerting a soothing pressure upon Hyacinth's arm. 'I will walk with you to your door, and I will give it to you there; unless you like better that I should keep it till to-morrow morning, so that you may have a quiet sleep—I mean in case it might contain anything that will be disagreeable to you. But it is probably nothing; it is probably only a word to say that you need think no more about your engagement.'

'Why should it be that?' Hyacinth asked.

'Probably he has heard that you repent.'

'That I repent?' Hyacinth stopped him short; they had just reached the top of Park Lane. 'To whom have I given a right to say that?'

'Ah well, if you haven't, so much the better. It may be, then, for some other reason.'

'Don't be an idiot, Schinkel,' Hyacinth returned, as they walked along. And in a moment he went on, 'What the devil did you go and tattle to the Poupins for?'

'Because I thought they would like to know. Besides, I felt my responsibility; I thought I should carry it better if they knew it. And then, I'm like them—I lofe you.'

Hyacinth made no answer to this profession; he asked the next instant, 'Why didn't your young man bring the letter directly to me?'

'Ah, I didn't ask him that! The reason was probably not complicated, but simple—that those who wrote it knew my address and didn't know yours. And wasn't I one of your guarantors?'

'Yes, but not the principal one. The principal one was Muniment. Why was the letter not sent to me through him?'

'My dear Robinson, you want to know too many things. Depend upon it, there are always good reasons. I should have liked it better if it had been Muniment. But if they didn't send to him'—Schinkel interrupted himself; the remainder of his sentence was lost in a cloud of smoke.

'Well, if they didn't send to him,'—Hyacinth persisted.

'You're a great friend of his—how can I tell you?'

At this Hyacinth looked up at his companion askance, and caught an odd glance, accompanied with a smile, which the mild, circumspect German directed toward him. 'If it's anything against him, my being his friend makes me just the man to hear it. I can defend him.'

'Well, it's a possibility that they are not satisfied.'

'How do you mean it—not satisfied?'

'How shall I say it?—that they don't trust him.'

'Don't trust him? And yet they trust me!'

'Ah, my boy, depend upon it, there are reasons,' Schinkel replied; and in a moment he added, 'They know everything—everything. Oh, they go straight!'

The pair pursued the rest of their course for the most part in silence, Hyacinth being considerably struck with something that dropped from his companion in answer to a question he asked as to what Eustache Poupin had said when Schinkel, that evening, first told him what he had come to see him about. '*Il vaut du galme—il vaut du galme:*' that was the Ger-

man's version of the Frenchman's words; and Hyacinth repeated them over to himself several times, almost with the
same accent. They had a certain soothing effect. In fact the
good Schinkel was soothing altogether, as our hero felt when
they stopped at last at the door of his lodging in Westminster
and stood there face to face, while Hyacinth waited—waited.
The sharpness of his impatience had passed away, and he
watched without irritation the loving manner in which the
German shook the ashes out of his big pipe and laid it to rest
in its coffin. It was only after he had gone through this business with his usual attention to every detail of it that he said,
'*Also*, now for the letter,' and, putting his hand inside of his
waistcoat, drew forth the important document. It passed instantly into Hyacinth's grasp, and our young man transferred
it to his own pocket without looking at it. He thought he saw
a shade of disappointment in Schinkel's ugly, kindly face, at
this indication that he should have no present knowledge of
its contents; but he liked that better than his pretending to
say again that it was nothing—that it was only a release.
Schinkel had now the good sense, or the good taste, not to
repeat that remark, and as the letter pressed against his heart
Hyacinth felt still more distinctly that it was something—that
it was a command. What Schinkel did say, in a moment, was
'Now that you have got it, I am very glad. It is more comfortable for me.'

'I should think so!' Hyacinth exclaimed. 'If you hadn't done
your job you would have paid for it.'

Schinkel hesitated a moment while he lingered; then, as
Hyacinth turned away, putting in his door-key, he replied,
'And if you don't do yours, so will you.'

'Yes, as you say, *they* go straight! Good-night.' And our
young man let himself in.

The passage and staircase were never lighted, and the lodgers either groped their way bedward with the infallibility of
practice or scraped the wall with a casual match which, in the
milder gloom of day, was visible in a hundred rich streaks.
Hyacinth's room was on the second floor, behind, and as he
approached it he was startled by seeing a light proceed from
the crevice under the door, the imperfect fitting of which was
in this manner vividly illustrated. He stopped and considered

this mysterious brightness, and his first impulse was to connect it with the incident just ushered in by Schinkel; for what could anything that touched him now be but a part of the same business? It was natural that some punctual emissary should be awaiting him. Then it occurred to him that when he went out to call on Lady Aurora, after tea, he had simply left a tallow candle burning, and that it showed a cynical spirit on the part of his landlady, who could be so close-fisted for herself, not to have gone in and put it out. Lastly, it came over him that he had had a visitor, in his absence, and that the visitor had taken possession of his apartment till his return, seeking sources of comfort, as was perfectly just. When he opened the door he found that this last prevision was the right one, though his visitor was not one of the figures that had risen before him. Mr. Vetch sat there, beside the little table at which Hyacinth did his writing, with his head resting on his hand and his eyes bent on the floor. He looked up when Hyacinth appeared, and said, 'Oh, I didn't hear you; you are very quiet.'

'I come in softly, when I'm late, for the sake of the house—though I am bound to say I am the only lodger who has that refinement. Besides, you have been asleep,' Hyacinth said.

'No, I have not been asleep,' returned the old man. 'I don't sleep much nowadays.'

'Then you have been plunged in meditation.'

'Yes, I have been thinking.' Then Mr. Vetch explained that the woman of the house wouldn't let him come in, at first, till he had given proper assurances that his intentions were pure and that he was moreover the oldest friend Mr. Robinson had in the world. He had been there for an hour; he thought he might find him, coming so late.

Hyacinth answered that he was very glad he had waited and that he was delighted to see him, and expressed regret that he hadn't known in advance of his visit, so that he might have something to offer him. He sat down on his bed, vaguely expectant; he wondered what special purpose had brought the fiddler so far at that unnatural hour. But he only spoke the truth in saying that he was glad to see him. Hyacinth had come up-stairs in a tremor of desire to be alone with the revelation that he carried in his pocket, yet the sight of Anastasius Vetch gave him a sudden relief by postponing solitude. The place where he had put his letter seemed to throb against his side, yet he was thankful to his old friend for forcing him still to leave it so. 'I have been looking at your books,' the fiddler said; 'you have two or three exquisite specimens of your own. Oh yes, I recognise your work when I see it; there are always certain little finer touches. You have a manner, like a master. With such a talent, such a taste, your future leaves nothing to be desired. You will make a fortune and become a great celebrity.'

Mr. Vetch sat forward, to sketch this vision; he rested his hands on his knees and looked very hard at his young friend, as if to challenge him to dispute his flattering views. The effect of what Hyacinth saw in his face was to give him immediately the idea that the fiddler knew something, though it was impossible to guess how he could know it. The Poupins, for instance, had had no time to communicate with him, even granting that they were capable of that baseness; an unwarrantable supposition, in spite of Hyacinth's having seen them, less than an hour before, fall so much below their own standard. With this suspicion there rushed into Hyacinth's mind an intense determination to dissemble before his visitor to the last: he might imagine what he liked, but he should not have a grain of satisfaction—or rather he should have that of being led to believe, if possible, that his suspicions were positively vain and idle. Hyacinth rested his eyes on the books that Mr. Vetch had taken down from the shelf, and admitted that they were very pretty work and that so long as one didn't become blind or maimed the ability to produce that sort of thing was a legitimate source of confidence. Then suddenly, as they continued simply to look at each other, the pressure of the old man's curiosity, the expression of his probing, beseeching eyes, which had become strange and tragic in these latter times and completely changed their character, grew so intolerable that to defend himself Hyacinth took the aggressive and asked him boldly whether it were simply to look at his work, of which he had half a dozen specimens in Lomax Place, that he had made a nocturnal pilgrimage. 'My dear old friend, you have something on your mind—some fantastic fear, some extremely erroneous *idée fixe*. Why has it taken you to-night, in particular? Whatever it is, it has brought you here, at an unnatural hour, you don't know why. I ought of course to be thankful to anything that brings you here; and so I am, in so far as that it makes me happy. But I can't like it if it makes *you* miserable. You're like a nervous mother whose baby's in bed upstairs; she goes up every five minutes to see if he's all right—if he isn't uncovered or hasn't tumbled out of bed. Dear Mr. Vetch, don't, don't worry; the blanket's up to my chin, and I haven't tumbled yet.'

Hyacinth heard himself say these things as if he were listening to another person; the impudence of them, under the circumstances, seemed to him, somehow, so rare. But he believed himself to be on the edge of an episode in which impudence, evidently, must play a considerable part, and he might as well try his hand at it without delay. The way the old man gazed at him might have indicated that he too was able to take the measure of his perversity—that he knew he was false as he sat there declaring that there was nothing the matter, while a brand-new revolutionary commission burned in his pocket. But in a moment Mr. Vetch said, very mildly, as if he had really been reassured, 'It's wonderful how you read my thoughts. I don't trust you; I think there are beastly possibilities. It's not true, at any rate, that I come to look at you every five minutes. You don't know how often I have resisted my fears—how I have forced myself to let you alone.'

'You had better let me come and live with you, as I proposed after Pinnie's death. Then you will have me always under your eyes,' said Hyacinth, smiling.

The old man got up eagerly, and, as Hyacinth did the same, laid his hands upon his shoulders, holding him close. 'Will you now, really, my boy? Will you come to-night?'

'To-night, Mr. Vetch?'

'To-night has worried me more than any other, I don't know why. After my tea I had my pipe and a glass, but I couldn't keep quiet; I was very, very bad. I got to thinking of Pinnie—she seemed to be in the room. I felt as if I could put out my hand and touch her. If I believed in ghosts I should believe I had seen her. She wasn't there for nothing; she was there to add her fears to mine—to talk to me about you. I tried to hush her up, but it was no use—she drove me out of the house. About ten o'clock I took my hat and stick and came down here. You may judge whether I thought it important, as I took a cab.'

'Ah, why do you spend your money so foolishly?' asked Hyacinth, in a tone of the most affectionate remonstrance.

'Will you come to-night?' said the old man, for all rejoinder, holding him still.

'Surely, it would be simpler for you to stay here. I see perfectly that you are ill and nervous. You can take the bed, and I'll spend the night in the chair.'

The fiddler thought a moment. 'No, you'll hate me if I subject you to such discomfort as that; and that's just what I don't want.'

'It won't be a bit different in your room; there, as here, I shall have to sleep in a chair.'

'I'll get another room; we shall be close together,' the fiddler went on.

'Do you mean you'll get another room at this hour of the night, with your little house stuffed full and your people all in bed? My poor Anastasius, you are very bad; your reason totters on its throne,' said Hyacinth, humorously and indulgently.

'Very good, we'll get a room to-morrow. I'll move into another house, where there are two, side by side.' Hyacinth's tone was evidently soothing to him.

'*Comme vous y allez!*' the young man continued. 'Excuse me if I remind you that in case of my leaving this place I have to give a fortnight's notice.'

'Ah, you're backing out!' the old man exclaimed, dropping his hands.

'Pinnie wouldn't have said that,' Hyacinth returned. 'If you are acting, if you are speaking, at the prompting of her pure spirit, you had better act and speak exactly as she would have done. She would have believed me.'

'Believed you? Believed what? What is there to believe? If you'll make me a promise, I will believe that.'

'I'll make you any promise you like,' said Hyacinth.

'Oh, any promise I like—that isn't what I want! I want just one very particular little pledge; and that is really what I came here for to-night. It came over me that I've been an ass, all this time, never to have demanded it of you before. Give it to me now, and I will go home quietly and leave you in peace.' Hyacinth, assenting in advance, requested again that he would formulate his demand, and then the old man said, 'Well, promise me that you will never, under any circumstances whatever, do anything.'

'Do anything?'

'Anything that those people expect of you.'

'Those people?' Hyacinth repeated.

'Ah, don't torment me with pretending not to understand!' the old man begged. 'You know the people I mean. I can't call them by their names, because I don't know them. But you do, and they know you.'

Hyacinth had no desire to torment Mr. Vetch, but he was capable of reflecting that to enter into his thought too easily would be tantamount to betraying himself. 'I suppose I know the people you have in mind,' he said, in a moment; 'but I'm afraid I don't grasp the idea of the promise.'

'Don't they want to make use of you?'

'I see what you mean,' said Hyacinth. 'You think they want me to touch off some train for them. Well, if that's what troubles you, you may sleep sound. I shall never do any of their work.'

A radiant light came into the fiddler's face, and he stared, as if this assurance were too fair for nature. 'Do you take your oath to that? Never anything, anything, anything?'

'Never anything at all.'

'Will you swear it to me by the memory of that good woman of whom we have been speaking and whom we both loved?'

'My dear old Pinnie's memory? Willingly.'

The old man sank down in his chair and buried his face in his hands; the next moment his companion heard him sobbing. Ten minutes later he was content to take his departure, and Hyacinth went out with him to look for another cab. They found an ancient four-wheeler stationed languidly at a crossing of the ways, and before Mr. Vetch got into it he asked his young friend to kiss him. That young friend watched the vehicle get itself into motion and rattle away; he saw it turn a neighbouring corner. Then he approached the nearest gas-lamp and drew from his breast-pocket the letter that Schinkel had given him.

XLV

And Madame Grandoni, then?' asked Hyacinth, reluctant to turn away. He felt pretty sure that he should never knock at that door again, and the desire was strong in him to see once more, for the last time, the ancient, troubled *suivante* of the Princess, whom he had always liked. She had seemed to him ever to be in the slightly ridiculous position of a confidant of tragedy in whom the heroine should have ceased to confide.

'E andata via, caro signorino,' said Assunta, smiling at him as she stood there holding the door open.

'She has gone away? Bless me, when did she go?'

'It is now five days, dear young sir. She has returned to our country.'

'Is it possible?' exclaimed Hyacinth, disappointedly.

'E possibilissimo!' said Assunta. Then she added, 'There were many times when she almost went; but this time—*capisce*——' And without finishing her sentence the Princess's Roman tirewoman indulged in a subtle, suggestive, indefinable play of expression, to which her hands and shoulders contributed, as well as her lips and eyebrows.

Hyacinth looked at her long enough to catch any meaning that she might have wished to convey, but gave no sign of apprehending it. He only remarked, gravely, 'In short she is here no more.'

'And the worst is that she will probably never come back. She didn't go for a long time, but when she decided herself it was finished,' Assunta declared. '*Peccato!*' she added, with a sigh.

'I should have liked to see her again—I should have liked to bid her good-bye.' Hyacinth lingered there in strange, melancholy vagueness; since he had been told the Princess was not at home he had no reason for remaining, save the possibility that she might return before he turned away. This possibility, however, was small, for it was only nine o'clock, the middle of the evening—too early an hour for her to reappear, if, as Assunta said, she had gone out after tea. He looked up and down the Crescent, gently swinging his stick, and became conscious in a moment that Assunta was regarding him with tender interest.

'You should have come back sooner; then perhaps she wouldn't have gone, *povera vecchia*,' she rejoined in a moment. 'It is too many days since you have been here. She liked you—I know that.'

'She liked me, but she didn't like me to come,' said Hyacinth. 'Wasn't that why she went, because we came?'

'Ah, that other one—with the long legs—yes. But you are better.'

'The Princess doesn't think so, and she is the right judge,' Hyacinth replied, smiling.

'Eh, who knows what she thinks? It is not for me to say. But you had better come in and wait. I dare say she won't be long, and it would gratify her to find you.'

Hyacinth hesitated. 'I am not sure of that.' Then he asked, 'Did she go out alone?'

'*Sola, sola*,' said Assunta, smiling. 'Oh, don't be afraid; you were the first!' And she flung open the door of the little drawing-room, with an air of irresistible solicitation and sympathy.

He sat there nearly an hour, in the chair the Princess habitually used, under her shaded lamp, with a dozen objects around him which seemed as much a part of herself as if they had been folds of her dress or even tones of her voice. His thoughts were tremendously active, but his body was too tired for restlessness; he had not been to work, and had been walking about all day, to fill the time; so that he simply reclined there, with his head on one of the Princess's cushions, his feet on one of her little stools—one of the ugly ones, that belonged to the house—and his respiration coming quickly, like that of a man in a state of acute agitation. Hyacinth was agitated now, but it was not because he was waiting for the Princess; a deeper source of emotion had been opened to him, and he had not on the present occasion more sharpness of impatience than had already visited him at certain moments of the past twenty hours. He had not closed his eyes the night before, and the day had not made up for that torment. A fever of reflection had descended upon him, and the range of his imagination had been wide. It whirled him through circles

of immeasurable compass; and this is the reason that, thinking of many things while he sat in the Princess's chair, he
wondered why, after all, he had come to Madeira Crescent,
and what interest he could have in seeing the lady of the
house. He had a very complete sense that everything was over
between them; that the link had snapped which bound them
so closely together for a while. And this was not simply because for a long time now he had received no sign nor communication from her, no invitation to come back, no inquiry
as to why his visits had stopped. It was not because he had
seen her go in and out with Paul Muniment, nor because it
had suited Prince Casamassima to point the moral of her doing so, nor even because, quite independently of the Prince,
he believed her to be more deeply absorbed in her acquaintance with that superior young man than she had ever been in
her relations with himself. The reason, so far as he became
conscious of it in his fitful meditations, could only be a
strange, detached curiosity—strange and detached because
everything else of his past had been engulfed in the abyss that
opened before him as, after Mr. Vetch had left him, he stood
under the lamp in a paltry Westminster street. That had swallowed up all familiar feelings, and yet out of the ruin had
sprung the impulse which brought him to where he sat.

The solution of his difficulty—he flattered himself he had
arrived at it—involved a winding-up of his affairs; and
though, even if no solution had been required, he would have
felt clearly that he had been dropped, yet as even in that case
it would have been sweet to him to bid her good-bye, so, at
present, the desire for some last vision of her own hurrying
fate could still appeal to him. If things had not gone well for
him he was still capable of wondering whether they looked
better for her. It is a singular fact, that there rose in his mind
a sort of incongruous desire to pity her. All these were odd
feelings enough, and by the time half an hour had elapsed
they had throbbed themselves into weariness and into slum-
ber. While he remembered that he was waiting now in a very
different frame from that in which he waited for her in South
Street the first time he went to see her, he closed his eyes and
lost himself. His unconsciousness lasted, he afterwards perceived, nearly half an hour; it terminated in his becoming

aware that the lady of the house was standing before him. Assunta was behind her, and as he opened his eyes she took from her mistress the bonnet and mantle of which the Princess divested herself. 'It's charming of you to have waited,' the latter said, smiling down at him with all her old kindness. 'You are very tired—don't get up; that's the best chair, and you must keep it.' She made him remain where he was; she placed herself near him on a smaller seat; she declared that she was not tired herself, that she didn't know what was the matter with her—nothing tired her now; she exclaimed on the time that had elapsed since he had last called, as if she were reminded of it simply by seeing him again; and she insisted that he should have some tea—he looked so much as if he needed it. She considered him with deeper attention, and wished to know what was the matter with him—what he had done to use himself up; adding that she must begin and look after him again, for while she had the care of him that kind of thing didn't happen. In response to this Hyacinth made a great confession: he admitted that he had stayed away from work and simply amused himself—amused himself by loafing about London all day. This didn't pay—he was beginning to discover it as he grew older; it was doubtless a sign of increasing years when one began to perceive that wanton pleasures were hollow and that to stick to one's tools was not only more profitable but more refreshing. However, he did stick to them, as a general thing; that was no doubt partly why, from the absence of the habit of it, a day off turned out to be rather a grind. When Hyacinth had not seen the Princess for some time he always, on meeting her again, had a renewed, tremendous sense of her beauty, and he had it to-night in an extraordinary degree. Splendid as that beauty had ever been, it seemed clothed at present in transcendant glory, and (if that which was already supremely fine could be capable of greater refinement), to have worked itself free of all earthly grossness and been purified and consecrated by her new life. Her gentleness, when she was in the mood for it, was quite divine (it had always the irresistible charm that it was the humility of a high spirit), and on this occasion she gave herself up to it. Whether it was because he had the consciousness of resting his eyes upon her for the last time, or because she wished to be particularly pleasant to him in order to make up for having, amid other preoccupations, rather dropped him of late (it was probable the effect was a product of both causes), at all events the sight of her loveliness seemed none the less a privilege than it had done the night he went into her box, at the play, and her presence lifted the weight from his soul. He suffered himself to be coddled and absently, even if radiantly, smiled at, and his state of mind was such that it could produce no alteration of his pain to see that on the Princess's part these were inexpensive gifts. She had sent Assunta to bring them tea, and when the tray arrived she gave him cup after cup, with every restorative demonstration; but he had not sat with her a quarter of an hour before he perceived that she scarcely measured a word he said to her or a word that she herself uttered. If she had the best intention of being nice to him, by way of compensation, this compensation was for a wrong that was far from vividly present to her mind. Two points became perfectly clear: one was that she was thinking of something very different from her present, her past, or her future relations with Hyacinth Robinson; the other was that he was superseded indeed. This was so completely the case that it did not even occur to her, it was evident, that the sense of supersession might be cruel to the young man. If she was charming to him it was because she was good-natured and he had been hanging off, and not because she had done him an injury. Perhaps, after all, she hadn't, for he got the impression that it might be no great loss of comfort not to constitute part of her life to-day. It was manifest from her eye, from her smile, from every movement and tone, and indeed from all the irradiation of her beauty, that that life to-day was tremendously wound up. If he had come to Madeira Crescent because he was curious to see how she was getting on, it was sufficiently intimated to him that she was getting on well; that is that she was living more than ever on high hopes and bold plans and far-reaching combinations. These things, from his own point of view, ministered less to happiness, and to be mixed up with them was perhaps not so much greater a sign that one had not lived for nothing, than the grim arrangement which, in the interest of peace, he had just arrived at with himself.

She asked him why he had not been to see her for so long, quite as if this failure were only a vulgar form of social neglect; and she scarcely seemed to notice whether it were a good or a poor excuse when he said he had stayed away because he knew her to be extremely busy. But she did not deny the impeachment; she admitted that she had been busier than ever in her life before. She looked at him as if he would know what that meant, and he remarked that he was very sorry for her.

'Because you think it's all a mistake? Yes, I know that. Perhaps it is; but if it is, it's a magnificent one. If you were scared about me three or four months ago, I don't know what you would think to-day—if you knew! I have risked everything.'

'Fortunately I don't know,' said Hyacinth.

'No, indeed, how should you?'

'And to tell the truth,' he went on, 'that is really the reason I haven't been back here till to-night. I haven't wanted to know—I have feared and hated to know.'

'Then why did you come at last?'

Hyacinth hesitated a moment. 'Out of a kind of inconsistent curiosity.'

'I suppose then you would like me to tell you where I have been to-night, eh?'

'No, my curiosity is satisfied. I have learned something— what I mainly wanted to know—without your telling me.'

She stared an instant. 'Ah, you mean whether Madame Grandoni was gone? I suppose Assunta told you.'

'Yes, Assunta told me, and I was sorry to hear it.'

The Princess looked grave, as if her old friend's departure had been indeed a very serious incident. 'You may imagine how I feel it! It leaves me completely alone; it makes, in the eyes of the world, an immense difference in my position. However, I don't consider the eyes of the world. At any rate, she couldn't put up with me any more—it appears that I am more and more shocking; and it was written!' On Hyacinth's asking what the old lady would do, she replied, 'I suppose she will go and live with my husband.' Five minutes later she inquired of him whether the same reason that he had mentioned just before was the explanation of his absence from

Audley Court. Mr. Muniment had told her that he had not been near him and his sister for more than a month.

'No, it isn't the fear of learning something that would make me uneasy: because, somehow, in the first place it isn't natural to feel uneasy about Paul, and in the second, if it were, he never lets one see anything. It is simply the general sense of real divergence of view. When that divergence becomes sharp, it is better not to pester each other.'

'I see what you mean. But you might go and see his sister.'

'I don't like her,' said Hyacinth, simply.

'Ah, neither do I!' the Princess exclaimed; while her visitor remained conscious of the perfect composure, the absence of false shame, with which she had referred to their common friend. But she was silent after this, and he judged that he had stayed long enough and sufficiently taxed a preoccupied attention. He got up, and was bidding her good-night, when she checked him by saying, suddenly, 'By the way, your not going to see so good a friend as Mr. Muniment, because you disapprove to-day of his work, suggests to me that you will be in an awkward fix, with your disapprovals, the day you are called upon to serve the cause according to your vow.'

'Oh, of course I have thought of that,' said Hyacinth, smiling.

'And would it be indiscreet to ask what you have thought?'

'Ah, so many things, Princess! It would take me a long time to say.'

'I have never talked to you about this, because it seemed to me indelicate, and the whole thing too much a secret of your own breast for even so intimate a friend as I have been to have a right to meddle with it. But I have wondered much— seeing that you cared less and less for the people—how you would reconcile your change of heart with the performance of your engagement. I pity you, my poor friend,' the Princess went on, with a heavenly sweetness, 'for I can imagine nothing more terrible than to find yourself face to face with such an engagement, and to feel at the same time that the spirit which prompted it is dead within you.'

'Terrible, terrible, most terrible,' said Hyacinth, gravely, looking at her.

'But I pray God it may never be your fate!' The Princess hesitated a moment; then she added, 'I see you feel it. Heaven help us all!' She paused, then went on: 'Why shouldn't I tell you, after all? A short time ago I had a visit from Mr. Vetch.'

'It was kind of you to see him,' said Hyacinth.

'He was delightful, I assure you. But do you know what he came for? To beg me, on his knees, to snatch you away.'

'To snatch me away?'

'From the danger that hangs over you. Poor man, he was very pathetic.'

'Oh yes, he has talked to me about it,' Hyacinth said. 'He has picked up the idea, but he knows nothing whatever about it. And how did he expect that you would be able to snatch me?'

'He left that to me; he had only a general conviction of my influence with you.'

'And he thought you would exercise it to make me back out? He does you injustice; you wouldn't!' Hyacinth exclaimed, with a laugh. 'In that case, taking one false position with another, yours would be no better than mine.'

'Oh, speaking seriously, I am perfectly quiet about you and about myself. I know you won't be called,' the Princess returned.

'May I inquire how you know it?'

After a slight hesitation she replied, 'Mr. Muniment tells me so.'

'And how does he know it?'

'We have information. My dear fellow,' the Princess went on, 'you are so much out of it now that if I were to tell you, you wouldn't understand.'

'Yes, no doubt I am out of it; but I still have a right to say, all the same, in contradiction to your imputation of a moment ago, that I care for the people exactly as much as I ever did.'

'My poor Hyacinth, my dear infatuated little aristocrat, was that ever very much?' the Princess asked.

'It was enough, and it is still enough, to make me willing to lay down my life for anything that will really help them.'

'Yes, and of course you must decide for yourself what that is; or, rather, what it's not.'

'I didn't decide when I gave my promise. I agreed to take the decision of others,' Hyacinth said.

'Well, you said just now that in relation to this business of yours you had thought of many things,' the Princess rejoined. 'Have you ever, by chance, thought of anything that *will* help the people?'

'You call me fantastic names, but I'm one of them my-self.'

'I know what you are going to say!' the Princess broke in. 'You are going to say that it will help them to do what you do—to do their work and earn their wages. That's beautiful so far as it goes. But what do you propose for the thousands and thousands for whom no work—on the overcrowded earth, under the pitiless heaven—is to be found? There is less and less work in the world, and there are more and more people to do the little that there is. The old ferocious selfish-nesses *must* come down. They won't come down gracefully, so they must be smashed!'

The tone in which the Princess uttered these words made Hyacinth's heart beat fast, and there was something so inspir-ing in her devoted fairness that the vision of a great heroism flashed up again before him, in all the splendour it had lost—the idea of a tremendous risk and an unregarded sacrifice. Such a woman as that, at such a moment, made every scruple seem a prudence and every compunction a cowardice. 'I wish to God I could see it as you see it!' he exclaimed, after he had looked at her a minute in silent admiration.

'I see simply this: that what we are doing is at least worth trying, and that as none of those who have the power, the place, the means, will try anything else, on *their* head be the responsibility, on *their* head be the blood!'

'Princess,' said Hyacinth, clasping his hands and feeling that he trembled, 'dearest Princess, if anything should happen to *you*'—and his voice fell; the horror of it, a dozen hideous images of her possible perversity and her possible punishment were again before him, as he had already seen them in sinister musings; they seemed to him worse than anything he had imagined for himself.

She threw back her head, looking at him almost in anger. 'To me! And pray why not to me? What title have I to exemption, to security, more than any one else? Why am I so sacrosanct and so precious?'

'Simply because there is no one in the world, and there has never been any one in the world, like you.'

'Oh, thank you!' said the Princess, with a kind of dry impatience, turning away.

The manner in which she spoke put an end to their conversation. It expressed an indifference to what it might interest him to think about her to-day, and even a contempt for it, which brought tears to his eyes. His tears, however, were concealed by the fact that he bent his head over her hand, which he had taken to kiss; after which he left the room without looking at her.

XLVI

'I HAVE received a letter from your husband,' Paul Muniment said to the Princess, the next evening, as soon as he came into the room. He announced this fact with a kind of bald promptitude and with a familiarity of manner which showed that his visit was one of a closely-connected series. The Princess was evidently not a little surprised by it, and immediately asked how in the world the Prince could know his address. 'Couldn't it have been by your old lady?' Muniment inquired. 'He must have met her in Paris. It is from Paris that he writes.'

'What an incorrigible cad!' the Princess exclaimed.

'I don't see that—for writing to me. I have his letter in my pocket, and I will show it to you if you like.'

'Thank you, nothing would induce me to touch anything he has touched,' the Princess replied.

'You touch his money, my dear lady,' Muniment remarked, with the quiet smile of a man who sees things as they are.

The Princess hesitated a little. 'Yes, I make an exception for that, because it hurts him, it makes him suffer.'

'I should think, on the contrary, it would gratify him by showing you in a condition of weakness and dependence.'

'Not when he knows I don't use it for myself. What exasperates him is that it is devoted to ends which he hates almost as much as he hates me and yet which he can't call selfish.'

'He doesn't hate you,' said Muniment, with the tone of pleasant reasonableness that he used when he was most imperturbable. 'His letter satisfies me of that.' The Princess stared, at this, and asked him what he was coming to—whether he were leading up to advising her to go back and live with her husband. 'I don't know that I would go so far as to advise,' he replied; 'when I have so much benefit from seeing you here, on your present footing, that wouldn't sound well. But I'll just make bold to prophesy that you will go before very long.'

'And on what does that extraordinary prediction rest?'

'On this plain fact—that you will have nothing to live upon. You decline to read the Prince's letter, but if you were to look at it it would give you evidence of what I mean. He informs me that I need count upon no more supplies from your hands, as you yourself will receive no more.'

'He addresses you that way, in plain terms?'

'I can't call them very plain, because the letter is written in French, and I naturally have had a certain difficulty in making it out, in spite of my persevering study of the tongue and the fine example set me by poor Robinson. But that appears to be the gist of the matter.'

'And you can repeat such an insult to me without the smallest apparent discomposure? You're the most remarkable man!' the Princess broke out.

'Why is it an insult? It is the simple truth. I do take your money,' said Paul Muniment.

'You take it for a sacred cause; you don't take it for yourself.'

'The Prince isn't obliged to look at that,' Muniment rejoined, laughing.

His companion was silent for a moment; then, 'I didn't know you were on his side,' she replied, gently.

'Oh, you know on what side I am!'

'What does he know? What business has he to address you so?'

'I suppose he knows from Madame Grandoni. She has told him that I have great influence with you.'

'She was welcome to tell him that!' the Princess exclaimed.

'His reasoning, therefore, has been that when I find you have nothing more to give to the cause I will let you go.'

'Nothing more? And does he count me, myself, and every pulse of my being, every capacity of my nature, as nothing?' the Princess cried, with shining eyes.

'Apparently he thinks that I do.'

'Oh, as for that, after all, I have known that you care far more for my money than for me. But it has made no difference to me,' said the Princess.

'Then you see that by your own calculation the Prince is right.'

'My dear sir,' Muniment's hostess replied, 'my interest in you never depended on your interest in me. It depended wholly on a sense of your great destinies. I suppose that what you began to tell me is that he stops my allowance.'

'From the first of next month. He has taken legal advice. It is now clear—so he tells me—that you forfeit your settlements.'

'Can I not take legal advice, too?' the Princess asked. 'Surely I can contest that. I can forfeit my settlements only by an act of my own. The act that led to our separation was *his* act; he turned me out of his house by physical violence.'

'Certainly,' said Muniment, displaying even in this simple discussion his easy aptitude for argument; 'but since then there have been acts of your own——' He stopped a moment, smiling; then he went on: 'Your whole connection with a secret society constitutes an act, and so does your exercise of the pleasure, which you appreciate so highly, of feeding it with money extorted from an old Catholic and princely family. You know how little it is to be desired that these matters should come to light.'

'Why in the world need they come to light? Allegations in plenty, of course, he would have, but not a particle of proof. Even if Madame Grandoni were to testify against me, which is inconceivable, she would not be able to produce a definite fact.'

'She would be able to produce the fact that you had a little bookbinder staying for a month in your house.'

'What has that to do with it?' the Princess demanded. 'If you mean that that is a circumstance which would put me in the wrong as against the Prince, is there not, on the other side, this circumstance, that while our young friend was staying with me Madame Grandoni herself, a person of the highest and most conspicuous respectability, never saw fit to withdraw from me her countenance and protection? Besides, why shouldn't I have my bookbinder, just as I might have (and the Prince should surely appreciate my consideration in not having) my physician and my chaplain?'

'Am I not your chaplain?' said Muniment, with a laugh. 'And does the bookbinder usually dine at the Princess's table?'

'Why not, if he's an artist? In the old times, I know, artists dined with the servants; but not to-day.'

'That would be for the court to appreciate,' Muniment remarked. And in a moment he added, 'Allow me to call your attention to the fact that Madame Grandoni *has* left you—*has* withdrawn her countenance and protection.'

'Ah, but not for Hyacinth!' the Princess returned, in a tone which would have made the fortune of an actress if an actress could have caught it.

'For the bookbinder or for the chaplain, it doesn't matter. But that's only a detail,' said Muniment. 'In any case, I shouldn't in the least care for your going to law.'

The Princess rested her eyes upon him for a while in silence, and at last she replied, 'I was speaking just now of your great destinies, but every now and then you do something, you say something, that makes me doubt of them. It's when you seem afraid. That's terribly against your being a first-rate man.'

'Oh, I know you have thought me a coward from the first of your knowing me. But what does it matter? I haven't the smallest pretension to being a first-rate man.'

'Oh, you are deep, and you are provoking!' murmured the Princess, with a sombre eye.

'Don't you remember,' Muniment continued, without heeding this somewhat passionate ejaculation—'don't you remember how, the other day, you accused me of being not only a coward but a traitor; of playing false; of wanting, as you said, to back out?'

'Most distinctly. How can I help its coming over me, at times, that you have incalculable ulterior views and are only using me—only using us all? But I don't care!'

'No, no; I'm genuine,' said Paul Muniment, simply, yet in a tone which might have implied that the discussion was idle. And he immediately went on, with a transition too abrupt for perfect civility: 'The best reason in the world for your not having a lawsuit with your husband is this: that when you haven't a penny left you will be obliged to go back and live with him.'

'How do you mean, when I haven't a penny left? Haven't I my own property?' the Princess demanded.

'The Prince tells me that you have drawn upon your own property at such a rate that the income to be derived from it amounts, to his positive knowledge, to no more than a thousand francs—forty pounds—a year. Surely, with your habits and tastes, you can't live on forty pounds. I should add that your husband implies that your property, originally, was but a small affair.'

'You have the most extraordinary tone,' observed the Princess, gravely. 'What you appear to wish to express is simply this: that from the moment I have no more money to give you I am of no more value than the skin of an orange.'

Muniment looked down at his shoe awhile. His companion's words had brought a flush into his cheek; he appeared to admit to himself and to her that, at the point at which their conversation had arrived, there was a natural difficulty in his delivering himself. But presently he raised his head, showing a face still slightly embarrassed but none the less bright and frank. 'I have no intention whatever of saying anything harsh or offensive to you, but since you challenge me perhaps it is well that I should let you know that I *do* consider that in giving your money—or, rather, your husband's—to our business you gave the most valuable thing you had to contribute.'

'This is the day of plain truths!' the Princess exclaimed, with a laugh that was not expressive of pleasure. 'You don't count then any devotion, any intelligence, that I may have placed at your service, even rating my faculties modestly?'

'I count your intelligence, but I don't count your devotion, and one is nothing without the other. You are not trusted at headquarters.'

'Not trusted!' the Princess repeated, with her splendid stare. 'Why, I thought I could be hanged to-morrow!'

'They may let you hang, perfectly, without letting you act. You are liable to be weary of us,' Paul Muniment went on; 'and, indeed, I think you are weary of us already.'

'Ah, you *must* be a first-rate man—you are such a brute!' replied the Princess, who noticed, as she had noticed before, that he pronounced 'weary' *weery*.

'I didn't say you were weary of *me*,' said Muniment, blushing again. 'You can never live poor—you don't begin to know the meaning of it.'

'Oh, no, I am not tired of you,' the Princess returned, in a strange tone. 'In a moment you will make me cry with passion, and no man has done that for years. I was very poor when I was a girl,' she added, in a different manner. 'You yourself recognised it just now, in speaking of the insignificant character of my fortune.'

'It had to be a fortune, to be insignificant,' said Muniment, smiling. 'You will go back to your husband!'

To this declaration she made no answer whatever; she only sat looking at him in a sort of desperate calmness. 'I don't see, after all, why they trust you more than they trust me,' she remarked.

'I am not sure that they do,' said Muniment. 'I have heard something this evening which suggests that.'

'And may one know what it is?'

'A communication which I should have expected to be made through me has been made through another person.'

'A communication?'

'To Hyacinth Robinson.'

'To Hyacinth——' The Princess sprang up; she had turned pale in a moment.

'He has got his ticket; but they didn't send it through me.'

'Do you mean his orders? He was here last night,' the Princess said.

'A fellow named Schinkel, a German—whom you don't know, I think, but who was a sort of witness, with me and another, of his undertaking—came to see me this evening. It was through him the summons came, and he put Hyacinth up to it on Sunday night.'

'On Sunday night?' The Princess stared. 'Why, he was here yesterday, and he talked of it, and he told me nothing.'

'That was quite right of him, bless him!' Muniment exclaimed.

The Princess closed her eyes a moment, and when she opened them again Muniment had risen and was standing before her. 'What do they want him to do?' she asked.

'I am like Hyacinth; I think I had better not tell you—at least till it's over.'

'And when will it be over?'

'They give him several days and, I believe, minute instructions,' said Muniment; 'with, however, considerable discretion in respect to seizing his chance. The thing is made remarkably easy for him. All this I know from Schinkel, who himself knew nothing on Sunday, being a mere medium of transmission, but who saw Hyacinth yesterday morning.'

'Schinkel trusts you, then?' the Princess remarked.

Muniment looked at her steadily a moment. 'Yes, but he won't trust you. Hyacinth is to receive a card of invitation to a certain big house,' he went on, 'a card with the name left in blank, so that he may fill it out himself. It is to be good for each of two grand parties which are to be given at a few days' interval. That's why they give him the job—because at a grand party he'll look in his place.'

'He will like that,' said the Princess, musingly—'repaying hospitality with a pistol-shot.'

'If he doesn't like it he needn't do it.'

The Princess made no rejoinder to this, but in a moment she said, 'I can easily find out the place you mean—the big house where two parties are to be given at a few days' interval and where the master is worth your powder.'

'Easily, no doubt. And do you want to warn him?'

'No, I want to do the business first, so that it won't be left for another. If Hyacinth will look in his place at a grand party, should not I look still more in mine? And as I know the individual I should be able to approach him without exciting the smallest suspicion.'

Muniment appeared to consider her suggestion a moment, as if it were practical and interesting; but presently he answered, placidly, 'To fall by your hand would be too good for him.'

'However he falls, will it be useful, valuable?' the Princess asked.

'It's worth trying. He's a very bad institution.'

'And don't you mean to go near Hyacinth?'

'No, I wish to leave him free,' Muniment answered.

'Ah, Paul Muniment,' murmured the Princess, 'you *are* a first-rate man!' She sank down upon the sofa and sat looking up at him. 'In God's name, why have you told me this?' she broke out.

'So that you should not be able to throw it up at me, later, that I had not.'

She threw herself over, burying her face in the cushions, and remained so for some minutes, in silence. Muniment watched her awhile, without speaking; but at last he remarked, 'I don't want to aggravate you, but you *will* go back!' The words failed to cause her even to raise her head, and after a moment he quietly went out.

XLVII

THAT THE PRINCESS had done with him, done with him forever, remained the most vivid impression that Hyacinth had carried away from Madeira Crescent the night before. He went home, and he flung himself on his narrow bed, where the consolation of sleep again descended upon him. But he woke up with the earliest dawn, and the beginning of a new day was a quick revival of pain. He was over-past, he had become vague, he was extinct. The things that Sholto had said to him came back to him, and the compassion of foreknowledge that Madame Grandoni had shown him from the first. Of Paul Muniment he only thought to wonder whether he knew. An insurmountable desire to do justice to him, for the very reason that there might be a temptation to oblique thoughts, forbade him to challenge his friend even in imagination. He vaguely wondered whether *he* would ever be superseded; but this possibility faded away in a stronger light— a kind of dazzling vision of some great tribuneship, which swept before him now and again and in which the figure of the Princess herself seemed merged and extinguished. When full morning came at last, and he got up, it brought with it, in the restlessness which made it impossible to him to remain in his room, a return of that beginning of an answerless question, 'After all—after all——?' which the Princess had planted there the night before when she spoke so bravely in the name of the Revolution. 'After all—after all, since nothing else was tried, or would, apparently, ever be tried——' He had a sense of his mind, which had been made up, falling to pieces again; but that sense in turn lost itself in a shudder which was already familiar—the horror of the public reappearance, on his part, of the imbrued hands of his mother. This loathing of the idea of a *repetition* had not been sharp, strangely enough, till his summons came; in all his previous meditations the growth of his reluctance to act for the 'party of action' had not been the fear of a personal stain, but the simple extension of his observation. Yet now the idea of the personal stain made him horribly sick; it seemed by itself to make service impossible. It rose before him like a kind of

backward accusation of his mother; to suffer it to start out in
the life of her son was in a manner to place her own forgotten, redeemed pollution again in the eye of the world. The
thought that was most of all with him was that he had time—
he had time; he was grateful for that, and saw a kind of delicacy in their having given him a margin—not condemned
him to be pressed by the hours. He had another day, he had
two days, he might take three, he might take several. He
knew he should be terribly weary of them before they were
over; but for that matter they would be over whenever he
liked. Anyhow, he went forth again into the streets, into the
squares, into the parks, solicited by an aimless desire to steep
himself yet once again in the great indifferent city which he
knew and loved and which had had so many of his smiles and
tears and confidences. The day was gray and damp, though
no rain fell, and London had never appeared to him to wear
more proudly and publicly the stamp of her imperial history.
He passed slowly to and fro over Westminster bridge and
watched the black barges drift on the great brown river, and
looked up at the huge fretted palace that rose there as a for-
tress of the social order which he, like the young David, had
been commissioned to attack with a sling and pebble. At last
he made his way to St. James's Park, and he strolled about a
long time. He revolved around it, and he went a considerable
distance up the thoroughfare that communicates with Pimlico. He stopped at a certain point and came back again, and
then he retraced his steps in the former direction. He looked
in the windows of shops, and he looked in particular into the
long, glazed expanse of that establishment in which, at that
hour of the day, Millicent Henning discharged superior functions. Millicent's image had descended upon him after he
came out, and now it moved before him as he went, it clung
to him, it refused to quit him. He made, in truth, no effort to
drive it away; he held fast to it in return, and it murmured
strange things in his ear. She had been so jolly to him on
Sunday; she was such a strong, obvious, simple nature, with
such a generous breast and such a freedom from the sophist-
ries of civilisation. All that he had ever liked in her came back
to him now with a finer air, and there was a moment, during
which he hung over the rail of the bridge that spans the lake

in St. James's Park and mechanically followed the movement of the swans, when he asked himself whether, at bottom, he hadn't liked her better, almost, than any one. He tried to think he had, he wanted to think he had, and he seemed to see the look her eyes would have if he should tell her that he had. Something of that sort had really passed between them on Sunday; only the business that had come up since had superseded it. Now the taste of the vague, primitive comfort that his Sunday had given him came back to him, and he asked himself whether he mightn't know it a second time. After he had thought he couldn't again wish for anything, he found himself wishing that he might believe there was something Millicent could do for him. Mightn't she help him— mightn't she even extricate him? He was looking into a window—not that of her own shop—when a vision rose before him of a quick flight with her, for an undefined purpose, to an undefined spot; and he was glad, at that moment, to have his back turned to the people in the street, because his face suddenly grew red to the tips of his ears. Again and again, all the same, he indulged in the reflection that spontaneous, uncultivated minds often have inventions, inspirations. Moreover, whether Millicent should have any or not, he might at least feel her arms around him. He didn't exactly know what good it would do him or what door it would open; but he should like it. The sensation was not one he could afford to defer, but the nearest moment at which he should be able to enjoy it would be that evening. *He* had thrown over everything, but she would be busy all day; nevertheless, it would be a gain, it would be a kind of foretaste, to see her earlier, to have three words with her. He wrestled with the temptation to go into her haberdasher's, because he knew she didn't like it (he had tried it once, of old); as the visits of gentlemen, even when ostensible purchasers (there were people watching about who could tell who was who), compromised her in the eyes of her employers. This was not an ordinary case, however; and though he hovered about the place a long time, undecided, embarrassed, half ashamed, at last he went in, as by an irresistible necessity. He would just make an appointment with her, and a glance of the eye and a single word would suffice. He remembered his way through the labyrinth of the shop; he knew that her department was on the second floor. He walked through the place, which was crowded, as if he had as good a right as any one else; and as he had entertained himself, on rising, with putting on his holiday garments, in which he made such a distinguished little figure, he was not suspected of any purpose more nefarious than that of looking for some nice thing to give a lady. He ascended the stairs, and found himself in a large room where made-up articles were exhibited and where, though there were twenty people in it, a glance told him he shouldn't find Millicent. She was perhaps in the next one, into which he passed by a wide opening. Here also were numerous purchasers, most of them ladies; the men were but three or four, and the disposal of the wares was in the hands of neat young women attired in black dresses with long trains. At first it appeared to Hyacinth that the young woman he sought was even here not within sight, and he was turning away, to look elsewhere, when suddenly he perceived that a tall gentleman, standing in the middle of the room, was none other than Captain Sholto. It next became plain to him that the person standing upright before the Captain, as still as a lay-figure and with her back turned to Hyacinth, was the object of his own quest. In spite of her averted face he instantly recognised Millicent; he knew her shop-attitude, the dressing of her hair behind, and the long, grand lines of her figure, draped in the last new thing. She was exhibiting this article to the Captain, and he was lost in contemplation. He had been beforehand with Hyacinth as a false purchaser, but he imitated a real one better than our young man, as, with his eyes travelling up and down the front of Millicent's person, he frowned, consideringly, and rubbed his lower lip slowly with his walking-stick. Millicent stood admirably still, and the back-view of the garment she displayed was magnificent. Hyacinth, for a minute, stood as still as she. At the end of that minute he perceived that Sholto saw him, and for an instant he thought he was going to direct Millicent's attention to him. But Sholto only looked at him very hard, for a few seconds, without telling her he was there; to enjoy that satisfaction he would wait till the interloper was gone. Hyacinth gazed back at him for the same length of time—what these two pairs of eyes said to each other requires perhaps no definite mention—and then turned away.

That evening, about nine o'clock, the Princess Casamassima drove in a hansom to Hyacinth's lodgings in Westminster. The door of the house was a little open, and a man stood on the step, smoking his big pipe and looking up and down. The Princess, seeing him while she was still at some distance, had hoped he was Hyacinth, but he proved to be a very different figure indeed from her devoted young friend. He had not a forbidding countenance, but he looked very hard at her as she descended from her hansom and approached the door. She was used to being looked at hard, and she didn't mind this; she supposed he was one of the lodgers in the house. He edged away to let her pass, and watched her while she endeavoured to impart an elasticity of movement to the limp bell-pull beside the door. It gave no audible response, so that she said to him, 'I wish to ask for Mr. Hyacinth Robinson. Perhaps you can tell me——'

'Yes, I too,' the man replied, smiling. 'I have come also for that.'

The Princess hesitated a moment. 'I think you must be Mr. Schinkel. I have heard of you.'

'You know me by my bad English,' her interlocutor remarked, with a sort of benevolent coquetry.

'Your English is remarkably good—I wish I spoke German as well. Only just a hint of an accent, and evidently an excellent vocabulary.'

'I think I have heard, also, of you,' said Schinkel, appreciatively.

'Yes, we know each other, in our circle, don't we? We are all brothers and sisters.' The Princess was anxious, she was in a fever; but she could still relish the romance of standing in a species of back-slum and fraternising with a personage looking like a very tame horse whose collar galled him. 'Then he's at home, I hope; he is coming down to you?' she went on.

'That's what I don't know. I am waiting.'

'Have they gone to call him?'

Schinkel looked at her, while he puffed his pipe. 'I have called him myself, but he will not say.'

'How do you mean—he will not say?'

'His door is locked. I have knocked many times.'

'I suppose he is out,' said the Princess.

'Yes, he may be out,' Schinkel remarked, judicially.

He and the Princess stood a moment looking at each other, and then she asked, 'Have you any doubt of it?'

'Oh, *es kann sein*. Only the woman of the house told me five minutes ago that he came in.'

'Well, then, he probably went out again,' the Princess remarked.

'Yes, but she didn't hear him.'

The Princess reflected, and was conscious that she was flushing. She knew what Schinkel knew about their young friend's actual situation, and she wished to be very clear with him and to induce him to be the same with her. She was rather baffled, however, by the sense that he was cautious, and justly cautious. He was polite and inscrutable, quite like some of the high personages—ambassadors and cabinet-ministers—whom she used to meet in the great world. 'Has the woman been here, in the house, ever since?' she asked in a moment.

'No, she went out for ten minutes, half an hour ago.'

'Surely, then, he may have gone out again in that time!' the Princess exclaimed.

'That is what I have thought. It is also why I have waited here,' said Schinkel. 'I have nothing to do,' he added, serenely.

'Neither have I,' the Princess rejoined. 'We can wait together.'

'It's a pity you haven't got some room,' the German suggested.

'No, indeed; this will do very well. We shall see him the sooner when he comes back.'

'Yes, but perhaps it won't be for long.'

'I don't care for that; I will wait. I hope you don't object to my company,' she went on, smiling.

'It is good, it is good,' Schinkel responded, through his smoke.

'Then I will send away my cab.' She returned to the vehicle and paid the driver, who said, 'Thank you, my lady,' with expression, and drove off.

'You gave him too much,' observed Schinkel, when she came back.

'Oh, he looked like a nice man. I am sure he deserved it.'

'It is very expensive,' Schinkel went on, sociably.

'Yes, and I have no money, but it's done. Was there no one else in the house while the woman was away?' the Princess asked.

'No, the people are out; she only has single men. I asked her that. She has a daughter, but the daughter has gone to see her cousin. The mother went only a hundred yards, round the corner there, to buy a pennyworth of milk. She locked this door, and put the key in her pocket; she stayed at the grocer's, where she got the milk, to have a little conversation with a friend she met there. You know ladies always stop like that—*nicht wahr?* It was half an hour later that I came. She told me that he was at home, and I went up to his room. I got no sound, as I have told you. I came down and spoke to her again, and she told me what I say.'

'Then you determined to wait, as I have done,' said the Princess.

'Oh, yes, I want to see him.'

'So do I, very much.' The Princess said nothing more, for a minute; then she added, 'I think we want to see him for the same reason.'

'Das kann sein—das kann sein.'

The two continued to stand there in the brown evening, and they had some further conversation, of a desultory and irrelevant kind. At the end of ten minutes the Princess broke out, in a low tone, laying her hand on her companion's arm, 'Mr. Schinkel, this won't do. I'm intolerably nervous.'

'Yes, that is the nature of ladies,' the German replied, imperturbably.

'I wish to go up to his room,' the Princess pursued. 'You will be so good as to show me where it is.'

'It will do you no good, if he is not there.'

The Princess hesitated. 'I am not sure he is not there.'

'Well, if he won't speak, it shows he likes better not to have visitors.'

'Oh, he may like to have me better than he does you!' the Princess exclaimed.

'Das kann sein—das kann sein.' But Schinkel made no movement to introduce her into the house.

'There is nothing to-night—you know what I mean,' the Princess remarked, after looking at him for a moment.

'Nothing to-night?'

'At the Duke's. The first party is on Thursday, the other is next Tuesday.'

'*Schön.* I never go to parties,' said Schinkel.

'Neither do I.'

'Except that *this* is a kind of party—you and me,' suggested Schinkel.

'Yes, and the woman of the house doesn't approve of it.' The footstep of the personage in question had been audible in the passage, through the open door, which was presently closed, from within, with a little reprehensive bang. Something in this incident appeared to quicken exceedingly the Princess's impatience and emotion; the menace of exclusion from the house made her wish more even than before to enter it. 'For God's sake, Mr. Schinkel, take me up there. If you won't, I will go alone,' she pleaded.

Her face was white now, and it need hardly be added that it was beautiful. The German considered it a moment in silence; then turned and reopened the door and went in, followed closely by his companion.

There was a light in the lower region, which tempered the gloom of the staircase—as high, that is, as the first floor; the ascent the rest of the way was so dusky that the pair went slowly and Schinkel led the Princess by the hand. She gave a suppressed exclamation as she rounded a sharp turn in the second flight. 'Good God, is that his door, with the light?'

'Yes, you can see under it. There was a light before,' said Schinkel, without confusion.

'And why, in heaven's name, didn't you tell me?'

'Because I thought it would worry you.'

'And doesn't it worry *you?*'

'A little, but I don't mind,' said Schinkel. 'Very likely he may have left it.'

'He doesn't leave candles!' the Princess returned, with vehemence. She hurried up the few remaining steps to the door, and paused there with her ear against it. Her hand grasped the handle, and she turned it, but the door resisted. Then she murmured, pantingly, to her companion, 'We must go in— we must go in!'

'What will you do, when it's locked?' he inquired.

'You must break it down.'

'It is very expensive,' said Schinkel.

'Don't be abject!' cried the Princess. 'In a house like this the fastenings are certainly flimsy; they will easily yield.'

'And if he is not there—if he comes back and finds what we have done?'

She looked at him a moment through the darkness, which was mitigated only by the small glow proceeding from the chink. 'He *is* there! Before God, he is there!'

'Schön, schön,' said her companion, as if he felt the contagion of her own dread but was deliberating and meant to remain calm. The Princess assured him that one or two vigorous thrusts with his shoulder would burst the bolt—it was sure to be some wretched morsel of tin—and she made way for him to come close. He did so, he even leaned against the door, but he gave no violent push, and the Princess waited, with her hand against her heart. Schinkel apparently was still deliberating. At last he gave a low sigh. 'I know they found him the pistol; it is only for that,' he murmured; and the next moment Christina saw him sway sharply to and fro in the gloom. She heard a crack and saw that the lock had yielded. The door collapsed: they were in the light; they were in a small room, which looked full of things. The light was that of a single candle on the mantel; it was so poor that for a moment she made out nothing definite. Before that moment was over, however, her eyes had attached themselves to the small bed. There was something on it—something black, something ambiguous, something outstretched. Schinkel held her back, but only for an instant; she saw everything, and with the very act she flung herself beside the bed, upon her knees. Hyacinth lay there as if he were asleep, but there was a horrible thing, a mess of blood, on the bed, in his side, in his heart. His arm hung limp beside him, downwards, off the narrow couch; his face was white and his eyes were closed. So much Schinkel saw, but only for an instant; a convulsive movement of the Princess, bending over the body while a strange low cry came from her lips, covered it up. He looked about him for the weapon, for the pistol, but the Princess, in her rush at the bed, had pushed it out of sight with her knees. 'It's a pity they found it—if he hadn't had it here!' he exclaimed to her. He had determined to remain calm, so that, on turning round at the quick advent of the little woman of the house, who had hurried up, white, scared, staring, at the sound of the crashing door, he was able to say, very quietly and gravely, 'Mr. Robinson has shot himself through the heart. He must have done it while you were fetching the milk.' The Princess got up, hearing another person in the room, and then Schinkel perceived the small revolver lying just under the bed. He picked it up and carefully placed it on the mantel-shelf, keeping, equally carefully, to himself the reflection that it would certainly have served much better for the Duke.

THE END.

THE REVERBERATOR

I.

"I GUESS my daughter's in here," the old man said, leading the way into the little *salon de lecture*. He was not of the most advanced age, but that is the way George Flack considered him, and indeed he looked older than he was. George Flack had found him sitting in the court of the hotel (he sat a great deal in the court of the hotel), and had gone up to him with characteristic directness and asked him for Miss Francina. Poor Mr. Dosson had with the greatest docility disposed himself to wait upon the young man: he had as a matter of course got up and made his way across the court, to announce to the personage in question that she had a visitor. He looked submissive, almost servile, as he preceded the visitor, thrusting his head forward in his quest; but it was not in Mr. Flack's line to notice that sort of thing. He accepted the old gentleman's good offices as he would have accepted those of a waiter, murmuring no protest for the sake of making it appear that he had come to see him as well. An observer of these two persons would have assured himself that the degree to which Mr. Dosson thought it natural that any one should want to see his daughter was only equalled by the degree to which the young man thought it natural her father should find her for him. There was a superfluous drapery in the doorway of the *salon de lecture*, which Mr. Dosson pushed aside while George Flack stepped in after him.

The reading-room of the Hôtel de l'Univers et de Cheltenham was not of great proportions, and had seemed to Mr. Dosson from the first to consist principally of a bare, highly-polished floor, on which it was easy for a relaxed elderly American to slip. It was composed further, to his perception, of a table with a green velvet cloth, of a fireplace with a great deal of fringe and no fire, of a window with a great deal of curtain and no light, and of the Figaro, which he couldn't read, and the New York Herald, which he had already read. A single person was just now in possession of these conveniences—a young lady who sat with her back to the window, looking straight before her into the conventional room. She was dressed as for the street; her empty hands rested upon the arms of her chair (she had withdrawn her long gloves, which were lying in her lap), and she seemed to be doing nothing as hard as she could. Her face was so much in shadow as to be barely distinguishable; nevertheless as soon as he saw her the young man exclaimed—"Why, it ain't Miss Francie—it's Miss Delia!"

"Well, I guess we can fix that," said Mr. Dosson, wandering further into the room and drawing his feet over the floor without lifting them. Whatever he did he ever seemed to wander: he had a transitory air, an aspect of weary yet patient non-arrival, even when he sat (as he was capable of sitting for hours) in the court of the inn. As he glanced down at the two newspapers in their desert of green velvet he raised a hopeless, uninterested glass to his eye. "Delia, my dear, where is your sister?"

Delia made no movement whatever, nor did any expression, so far as could be perceived, pass over her large young face. She only ejaculated, "Why, Mr. Flack, where did you drop from?"

"Well, this is a good place to meet," her father remarked, as if mildly, and as a mere passing suggestion, to deprecate explanations.

"Any place is good where one meets old friends," said George Flack, looking also at the newspapers. He examined the date of the American sheet and then put it down. "Well, how do you like Paris?" he went on to the young lady.

"We quite enjoy it; but of course we're familiar now."

"Well, I was in hopes I could show you something," Mr. Flack said.

"I guess they've seen most everything," Mr. Dosson observed.

"Well, we've seen more than you!" exclaimed his daughter.

"Well, I've seen a good deal—just sitting there."

A person with a delicate ear might have suspected Mr. Dosson of saying "setting;" but he would pronounce the same word in a different manner at different times.

"Well, in Paris you can see everything," said the young man. "I'm quite enthusiastic about Paris."

"Haven't you been here before?" Miss Delia asked.

"Oh, yes, but it's ever fresh. And how is Miss Francie?"

"She's all right. She has gone up stairs to get something; we are going out again."

"It's very attractive for the young," said Mr. Dosson to the visitor.

"Well, then, I'm one of the young. Do you mind if I go with you?" Mr. Flack continued, to the girl.

"It'll seem like old times, on the deck," she replied. "We're going to the Bon Marché."

"Why don't you go to the Louvre? It's much better."

"We have just come from there: we have had quite a morning."

"Well, it's a good place," the visitor continued.

"It's good for some things but it doesn't come up to my idea for others."

"Oh, they've seen everything," said Mr. Dosson. Then he added, "I guess I'll go and call Francie."

"Well, tell her to hurry," Miss Delia returned, swinging a glove in each hand.

"She knows my pace," Mr. Flack remarked.

"I should think she would, the way you raced!" the girl ejaculated, with memories of the Umbria. "I hope you don't expect to rush round Paris that way."

"I always rush. I live in a rush. That's the way to get through."

"Well, I *am* through, I guess," said Mr. Dosson, philosophically.

"Well, I ain't!" his daughter declared, with decision.

"Well, you must come round often," the old gentleman continued, as a leave-taking.

"Oh, I'll come round! I'll have to rush, but I'll do it."

"I'll send down Francie." And Francie's father crept away.

"And please to give her some more money!" her sister called after him.

"Does she keep the money?" George Flack inquired.

"*Keep* it?" Mr. Dosson stopped as he pushed aside the *portière*. "Oh, you innocent young man!"

"I guess it's the first time you were ever called innocent," Delia remarked, left alone with the visitor.

"Well, I *was*—before I came to Paris."

"Well, I can't see that it has hurt us. We are *not* extravagant."

"Wouldn't you have a right to be?"

"I don't think any one has a right to be."

The young man, who had seated himself, looked at her a moment. "That's the way you used to talk."

"Well, I haven't changed."

"And Miss Francie—has she?"

"Well, you'll see," said Delia Dosson, beginning to draw on her gloves.

Her companion watched her, leaning forward with his elbows on the arms of his chair and his hands interlocked. At last he said, interrogatively: "Bon Marché?"

"No, I got them in a little place I know."

"Well, they're Paris, anyway."

"Of course they're Paris. But you can get gloves anywhere."

"You must show me the little place, anyhow," Mr. Flack continued, sociably. And he observed further, with the same friendliness—"The old gentleman seems all there."

"Oh, he's the dearest of the dear."

"He's a real gentleman—of the old stamp," said George Flack.

"Well, what should you think our father would be?"

"I should think he would be delighted!"

"Well, he is, when we carry out our plans."

"And what are they—your plans?" asked the young man.

"Oh, I never tell them."

"How then does he know whether you carry them out?"

"Well, I guess he'd know it if we didn't," said the girl.

"I remember how secretive you were last year. You kept everything to yourself."

"Well, I know what I want," the young lady pursued.

He watched her button one of her gloves, deftly, with a hairpin which she disengaged from some mysterious function under her bonnet. There was a moment's silence and then they looked up at each other. "I have an idea you don't want me," said George Flack.

"Oh, yes, I do—as a friend."

"Of all the mean ways of trying to get rid of a man, that's the meanest!" he exclaimed.

"Where's the meanness, when I suppose you are not so peculiar as to wish to be anything more!"

"More to your sister, do you mean—or to yourself?"

"My sister *is* myself—I haven't got any other," said Delia Dosson.

"Any other sister?"

"Don't be idiotic. Are you still in the same business?" the girl went on.

"Well, I forget which one I *was* in."

"Why, something to do with that newspaper—don't you remember?"

"Yes, but it isn't that paper any more—it's a different one."

"Do you go round for news—in the same way?"

"Well, I try to get the people what they want. It's hard work," said the young man.

"Well, I suppose if you didn't some one else would. They will have it, won't they?"

"Yes, they will have it." But the wants of the people did not appear at the present moment to interest Mr. Flack as much as his own. He looked at his watch and remarked that the old gentleman didn't seem to have much authority.

"Much authority?" the girl repeated.

"With Miss Francie. She is taking her time, or rather, I mean, she is taking mine."

"Well, if you expect to do anything with her you must give her plenty of that."

"All right: I'll give her all I have." And Miss Dosson's inter-locutor leaned back in his chair with folded arms, as if to let his companion know that she would have to count with his patience. But she sat there in her expressionless placidity, giving no sign of alarm or defeat. He was the first indeed to show a symptom of restlessness: at the end of a few moments he asked the young lady if she didn't suppose her father had told her sister who it was.

"Do you think that's all that's required?" Miss Dosson de-manded. But she added, more graciously—"Probably that's the reason. She's so shy."

"Oh, yes—she used to look it."

"No, that's her peculiarity, that she never looks it, and yet she is intensely so."

"Well, you make it up for her then, Miss Delia," the young man ventured to declare.

"No, for her, I'm not shy—not in the least."

"If it wasn't for you I think I could do something," the young man went on.

"Well, you've got to kill me first!"

"I'll come down on you, somehow, in the Reverberator," said George Flack.

"Oh, that's not what the people want."

"No, unfortunately they don't care anything about *my* affairs."

"Well, we do: we are kinder, Francie and I," said the girl. "But we desire to keep them quite distinct from ours."

"Oh, yours—yours: if I could only discover what they are!" the young journalist exclaimed. And during the rest of the time that they sat there waiting he tried to find out. If an auditor had happened to be present for the quarter of an hour that elapsed and had had any attention to give to these vulgar young persons he would have wondered perhaps at there being so much mystery on one side and so much curiosity on the other—wondered at least at the elaboration of inscrutable projects on the part of a girl who looked to the casual eye as if she were stolidly passive. Fidelia Dosson, whose name had been shortened, was twenty-five years old and had a large white face, with the eyes very far apart. Her forehead was high, but her mouth was small: her hair was light and colourless, and a certain inelegant thickness of figure made her appear shorter than she was. Elegance indeed had not been conferred upon her by Nature, and the Bon Marché and other establishments had to make up for that. To a feminine eye they would scarcely have appeared to have acquitted themselves of their office; but even a woman would not have guessed how little Fidelia cared. She always looked the same; all the contrivances of Paris could not make her look different, and she held them, for herself, in no manner of esteem. It was a plain, blank face, not only without movement, but with a suggestion of obstinacy in its repose; and yet, with its limitations, it was neither stupid nor displeasing. It had an air of intelligent calm—a considering, pondering look that was superior, somehow, to diffidence or anxiety; moreover, the girl had a clear skin and a gentle, dim smile. If she had been a young man (and she had, a little, the head of one) it would probably have been thought of her that she nursed dreams of eminence in some scientific or even political line.

An observer would have gathered, further, that Mr. Flack's acquaintance with Mr. Dosson and his daughters had had its origin in his crossing the Atlantic eastward in their company more than a year before and in some slight association immediately after disembarking; but that each party had come and gone a good deal since then—come and gone however without meeting again. It was to be inferred that in this interval Miss Dosson had led her father and sister back to their native land and had then a second time directed their course to Europe. This was a new departure, said Mr. Flack, or rather a new arrival: he understood that it was not, as he called it, the same old visit. She did not repudiate the accusation, launched by her companion as if it might have been embarrassing, of having spent her time at home in Boston, and even in a suburban portion of it: she confessed that, as Bostonians, they had been capable of that. But now they had come abroad for longer—ever so much: what they had gone home for was to make arrangements for a European sojourn of which the limits were not to be told. So far as this prospect entered into her plans she freely acknowledged it. It appeared to meet with George Flack's approval—he also had a big job on that side and it might take years, so that it would be pleasant to have his friends right there. He knew his way about in Paris—or any place like that—much more than in Boston; if they had been poked away in one of those clever suburbs they would have been lost to him.

"Oh, well, you'll see as much as you want to of us—the way you'll have to take us," Delia Dosson said: which led the young man to inquire what way that was and to remark that he only knew one way to take anything—just as it came. "Oh, well, you'll see," the girl rejoined; and she would give for the present no further explanation of her somewhat chilling speech. In spite of it, however, she professed an interest in Mr. Flack's "job"—an interest which rested apparently upon an interest in the young man himself. The slightly surprised observer whom we have supposed to be present would have perceived that this latter sentiment was founded on a conception of Mr. Flack's intrinsic brilliancy. Would his own impression have justified that?—would he have found such a conception contagious? I forbear to say positively no, for that would charge me with the large responsibility of showing what right our accidental observer might have had to his particular standard. I prefer therefore to note simply that George Flack was quite clever enough to seem a person of importance to Delia Dosson. He was connected (as she supposed) with literature, and was not literature one of the many engaging attributes of her cherished little sister? If Mr. Flack was a writer Francie was a reader: had not a trail of forgotten Tauchnitzes marked the former line of travel of the party of three? The elder sister grabbed them up on leaving hotels and railway-carriages, but usually found that she had brought odd volumes. She considered, however, that as a family they had a sort of superior affinity with the young journalist, and would have been surprised if she had been told that his acquaintance was not a high advantage.

Mr. Flack's appearance was not so much a property of his own as a prejudice on the part of those who looked at him: whoever they might be what they saw mainly in him was that they had seen him before. And, oddly enough, this recognition carried with it in general no ability to remember—that is to recall—him: you could not have evoked him in advance, and it was only when you saw him that you knew you *had* seen him. To carry him in your mind you must have liked him very much, for no other sentiment, not even aversion, would have taught you what distinguished him in his group: aversion in especial would have made you conscious only of what confounded him. He was not a particular person, but a sample or memento—reminding one of certain "goods" for which there is a steady popular demand. You would scarcely have expected him to have a name other than that of his class: a number, like that of the day's newspaper, would have been the most that you would count on, and you would have expected vaguely to find the number high—somewhere up in the millions. As every copy of the newspaper wears the same label, so that of Miss Dosson's visitor would have been "Young commercial American." Let me add that among the accidents of his appearance was that of its sometimes striking other young commercial Americans as fine. He was twenty-seven years of age and had a small square head, a light gray overcoat, and in his right forefinger a curious natural crook which might have served, under pressure, to identify him. But for the convenience of society he ought always to have worn something conspicuous—a green hat or a scarlet necktie. His job was to obtain material in Europe for an American "society-paper."

If it be objected to all this that when Francie Dosson at last came in she addressed him as if she easily placed him, the answer is that she had been notified by her father—more punctually than was indicated by the manner of her response. "Well, the way you *do* turn up," she said, smiling and holding out her left hand to him: in the other hand, or the hollow of her right arm, she had a largeish parcel. Though she had made him wait she was evidently very glad to see him there; and she as evidently required and enjoyed a great deal of that sort of indulgence. Her sister's attitude would have told you so even if her own appearance had not. There was that in her manner to the young man—a perceptible but indefinable shade—which seemed to legitimate the oddity of his having asked in particular for her, as if he wished to see her to the exclusion of her father and sister: a kind of special pleasure which had the air of pointing to a special relation. And yet a spectator, looking from Mr. George Flack to Miss Francie Dosson, would have been much at a loss to guess what special relation could exist between them. The girl was exceedingly, extraordinarily pretty, and without discoverable resemblance to her sister; and there was a brightness in her—a kind of still radiance—which was quite distinct from what is called animation. Rather tall than short, slim, delicate and evidently as light of hand and of foot as it was possible to be, she yet gave no impression of quick movement, of abundant chatter, of excitable nerves and irrepressible life—no hint of being of the most usual (which is perhaps also the most graceful) American type. She was brilliantly but quietly pretty, and your suspicion that she was a little stiff was corrected only by your perception that she was extremely soft. There was nothing in her to confirm the implication that she had rushed about the deck of a Cunarder with a newspaperman. She was as straight as a wand and as fine as a gem; her neck was long and her gray eyes had colour; and from the ripple of her dark brown hair to the curve of her unaffirmative chin every line in her face was happy and pure. She had an unformed voice and very little knowledge.

Delia got up, and they came out of the little reading-room—this young lady remarking to her sister that she hoped she had got all the things. "Well, I had a fiendish hunt for them, we have got so many," Francie replied, with a curious soft drawl. "There were a few dozens of the pocket-handkerchiefs I couldn't find; but I guess I've got most of them, and most of the gloves."

"Well, what are you carting them about for?" George Flack inquired, taking the parcel from her. "You had better let me handle them. Do you buy pocket-handkerchiefs by the hundred?"

"Well, it only makes fifty apiece," said Francie, smiling. "They ain't nice—we're going to change them."

"Oh, I won't be mixed up with that—you can't work that game on these Frenchmen!" the young man exclaimed.

"Oh, with Francie they will take anything back," Delia Dosson declared. "They just love her, all over."

"Well, they're like me then," said Mr. Flack, with friendly hilarity. "I'll take her back, if she'll come."

"Well, I don't think I am ready quite yet," the girl replied. "But I hope very much we shall cross with you again."

"Talk about crossing—it's on these boulevards we want a life-preserver!" Delia remarked. They had passed out of the hotel and the wide vista of the Rue de la Paix stretched up and down. There were many vehicles.

"Won't this thing do? I'll tie it to either of you," George Flack said, holding out his bundle. "I suppose they won't kill you if they love you," he went on, to the younger girl.

"Well, you've got to know me first," she answered, laughing and looking for a chance, while they waited to pass over.

"I didn't know you when I was struck." He applied his disengaged hand to her elbow and propelled her across the street. She took no notice of his observation, and Delia asked her, on the other side, whether their father had given her that money. She replied that he had given her loads—she felt as if he had made his will; which led George Flack to say that he wished the old gentleman was *his* father.

"Why, you don't mean to say you want to be our brother!" Francie exclaimed, as they went down the Rue de la Paix.

"I should like to be Miss Delia's, if you can make that out," said the young man.

"Well, then, suppose you prove it by calling me a cab," Miss Delia returned. "I presume you and Francie don't think this is the deck."

"Don't she feel rich?" George Flack demanded of Francie. "But we do require a cart for our goods;" and he hailed a little yellow carriage, which presently drew up beside the pavement. The three got into it and, still emitting innocent pleasantries, proceeded on their way, while at the Hôtel de l'Univers et de Cheltenham Mr. Dosson wandered down into the court again and took his place in his customary chair.

II.

THE COURT was roofed with glass; the April air was mild; the cry of women selling violets came in from the street and, mingling with the rich hum of Paris, seemed to bring with it faintly the odour of the flowers. There were other odours in the place, warm, succulent and Parisian, which ranged from fried fish to burnt sugar; and there were many things besides: little tables for the post-prandial coffee; piles of luggage inscribed (after the initials, or frequently the name, R. P. Scudamore or D. Jackson Hatch), Philadelphia, Pa., or St. Louis, Mo.; rattles of unregarded bells, flitting of tray-bearing waiters, conversations with the second-floor windows of admonitory landladies, arrivals of young women with coffin-like bandboxes covered with black oilcloth and depending from a strap, sallyings forth of persons staying and arrivals, just afterwards, of other persons to see them; together with vague prostrations on benches of tired heads of American families. It was to this last element that Mr. Dosson himself in some degree contributed, but it must be added that he had not the extremely bereft and exhausted appearance of certain of his fellows. There was an air of meditative patience, of habitual accommodation in him; but you would have guessed that he was enjoying a holiday rather than panting for a truce, and he was not so enfeebled but that he was able to get up from time to time and stroll through the *porte cochère* to have a look at the street.

He gazed up and down for five minutes, with his hands in his pockets, and then came back; that appeared to content him; he asked for very little—had no restlessness that these small excursions would not assuage. He looked at the heaped-up luggage, at the tinkling bells, at the young woman from the *lingère*, at the repudiated visitors, at everything but the other American parents. Something in his breast told him that he knew all about these. It is not upon each other that the animals in the same cage, in a zoological collection, most turn their eyes. There was a silent sociability in him and a superficial fineness of grain that helped to account for his daughter Francie's various delicacies. He was fair and spare and had no figure; you would have seen in a moment that the question of how he should hold himself had never in his life occurred to him. He never held himself at all; providence held him rather (and very loosely), by an invisible string, at the end of which he seemed gently to dangle and waver. His face was so smooth that his thin light whiskers, which grew only far back, scarcely seemed native to his cheeks: they might have been attached there for some harmless purpose of comedy or disguise. He looked for the most part as if he were thinking over, without exactly understanding it, something rather droll which had just occurred; if his eyes wandered his attention rested, and hurried, quite as little. His feet were remarkably small, and his clothes, in which light colours predominated, were visibly the work of a French tailor: he was an American who still held the tradition that it is in Paris a man dresses himself best. His hat would have looked odd in Bond Street or the Fifth Avenue, and his necktie was loose and flowing.

Mr. Dosson, it may further be mentioned, was a man of the simplest composition, a character as cipherable as a sum of two figures. He had a native financial faculty of the finest order, a gift as direct as a beautiful tenor voice, which had enabled him, without the aid of particular strength of will or keenness of ambition, to build up a large fortune while he was still of middle age. He had a genius for happy specula- tion, the quick, unerring instinct of a "good thing;" and as he sat there idle, amused, contented, on the edge of the Parisian street, he might very well have passed for some rare performer who had sung his song or played his trick and had nothing to do till the next call. And he had grown rich not because he was ravenous or hard, but simply because he had an ear, or a nose. He could make out the tune in the discord of the market-place; he could smell success far up the wind. The sec- ond factor in his little addition was that he was an unassum- ing father. He had no tastes, no acquirements nor curiosities, and his daughters represented society for him. He thought much more and much oftener of these young ladies than of his bank-shares and railway-stock; they refreshed much more his sense of ownership, of accumulation. He never compared them with other girls; he only compared his present self to what he would have been without them. His view of them was perfectly simple. Delia had a more unfathomable profundity and Francie a wider acquaintance with literature and art. Mr. Dosson had not perhaps a full perception of his younger daughter's beauty: he would scarcely have pretended to judge of that, more than he would of a valuable picture or vase, but he believed she was cultivated up to the eyes. He had a recollection of tremendous school-bills and, in later days, during their travels, of the way she was always leaving books behind her. Moreover was not her French so good that he could not understand it?

The two girls, at any rate, were the wind in his sail and the only directing, determining force he knew; they converted accident into purpose; without them, as he felt, he would have been the tail without the kite. The wind rose and fell, of course; there were lulls and there were gales; there were intervals during which he simply floated in quiet waters—cast anchor and waited. This appeared to be one of them now; but he could be patient, knowing that he should soon again inhale the brine and feel the dip of his prow. When his daughters were out the determining process gathered force, and their being out with a brilliant young man only deepened the pleasant calm. That belonged to their superior life, and Mr. Dosson never doubted that George M. Flack was brilliant. He represented the newspaper, and the newspaper for this man of genial assumptions represented Mind—it was the great shining presence of our time. To know that Delia and Francie were out with an editor or a correspondent was really to see them dancing in the central glow. This is doubtless why Mr. Dosson had slightly more than usual his air of recovering slowly from a pleasant surprise. The vision to which I allude hung before him, at a convenient distance, and melted into other bright confused aspects: reminiscences of Mr. Flack in other relations—on the ship, on the deck, at the hotel at Liverpool, and in the cars. Whitney Dosson was a loyal father, but he would have thought himself simple had he not had two or three strong convictions: one of which was that the children should never go out with a gentleman they had not seen before. The sense of their having, and his having, seen Mr. Flack before was comfortable to him now: it made it mere placidity for him personally to forego the young man's

society in favour of Delia and Francie. He had not hitherto
been perfectly satisfied that the streets and shops, the general
immensity of Paris, were just the right place for young ladies
alone. But the company of a pleasant gentleman made them
right—a gentleman who was pleasant through being up to
everything, as one connected with that paper (he remembered
its name now, it was celebrated) would have to be. To Mr.
Dosson, in the absence of such happy accidents, his girls
somehow seemed lonely; which was not the way he struck
himself. They were his company but he was scarcely theirs; it
was as if he had them more than they had him.

They were out a long time, but he felt no anxiety, as he
reflected that Mr. Flack's very profession was a prevision of
everything that could possibly happen. The bright French afternoon waned without bringing them back, but Mr. Dosson
still revolved about the court, till he might have been taken
for a *valet de place* hoping to pick up custom. The landlady
smiled at him sometimes, as she passed and re-passed, and
even ventured to remark disinterestedly that it was a pity to
waste such a lovely day indoors—not to take a turn and see
what was going on in Paris. But Mr. Dosson had no sense of
waste: that came to him much more when he was confronted
with historical monuments, or beauties of nature or art,
which he didn't understand nor care for: then he felt a little
ashamed and uncomfortable—but never when he lounged in
that simplifying way in the court. It wanted but a quarter of
an hour to dinner (that he could understand) when Delia and
Francie at last met his view, still accompanied by Mr. Flack
and sauntering in, at a little distance from each other, with a
jaded air which was not in the least a tribute to his possible
solicitude. They dropped into chairs and joked with each
other, with a mixture of sociability and languor, on the subject of what they had seen and done—a question into which
he felt as yet a delicacy as to inquiring. But they had evidently
done a good deal and had a good time: an impression sufficient to rescue Mr. Dosson personally from the consciousness
of failure.

"Won't you just step in and take dinner with us?" he asked
of the young man, with a friendliness begotten of the circumstances.

"Well, that's a handsome offer," George Flack replied, while Delia remarked that they had each eaten about thirty cakes.

"Well, I wondered what you were doing so long. But never mind your cakes. It's twenty minutes past six, and the *table d'hôte* is on time."

"You don't mean to say you dine at the *table d'hôte*!" Mr. Flack ejaculated.

"Why, don't you like that?" Francie drawled sweetly.

"Well, it isn't what you most build on when you come to Paris. Too many flower-pots and chickens' legs."

"Well, would you like one of these restaurants?" asked Mr. Dosson. "I don't care, if you show us a good one."

"Oh, I'll show you a good one—don't you worry."

"Well, you've got to order the dinner then," said Francie.

"Well, you'll see how I could do it!" And the young man looked at her very hard, with an intention of softness.

"He has got an interest in some place," Delia declared. "He has taken us to ever so many stores, and he gets his commission."

"Well, I'd pay you to take them round," said Mr. Dosson; and with much agreeable trifling of this kind it was agreed that they should sally forth for the evening meal under Mr. Flack's guidance.

If he had easily convinced them on this occasion that that was a more original proceeding than worrying those old bones, as he called it, at the hotel, he convinced them of other things besides in the course of the following month and by the aid of repeated visits. What he mainly made clear to them was that it was really most kind of a young man who had so many great public questions on his mind to find sympathy for problems which could fill the telegraph and the press so little as theirs. He came every day to set them in the right path, pointing out its charms to them in a way that made them feel how much they had been in the wrong. He made them feel indeed that they didn't know anything about anything, even about such a matter as ordering shoes—an art in which they vaguely supposed themselves rather strong. He had in fact great knowledge, and it was wonderfully various, and he knew as many people as they knew few. He had appointments—very often with celebrities—for every hour of the day, and memoranda, sometimes in shorthand, on tablets with elastic straps, with which he dazzled the simple folk at the Hôtel de l'Univers et de Cheltenham, whose social life, of narrow range, consisted mainly in reading the lists of Americans who "registered" at the bankers' and at Galignani's. Delia Dosson, in particular, had a way of poring solemnly over these records which exasperated Mr. Flack, who skimmed them and found what he wanted in the flash of an eye: she kept the others waiting while she satisfied herself that Mr. and Mrs. D. S. Rosenheim and Miss Cora Rosenheim and Master Samuel Rosenheim had "left for Brussels."

Mr. Flack was wonderful on all occasions in finding what he wanted (which, as we know, was what he believed the public wanted), and Delia was the only one of the party with whom he was sometimes a little sharp. He had embraced from the first the idea that she was his enemy, and he alluded to it with almost tiresome frequency, though always in a humorous, fearless strain. Even more than by her fashion of hanging over the registers she provoked him by appearing to think that their little party was not sufficient to itself; by wishing, as he expressed it, to work in new stuff. He might have been easy, however, for he had sufficient chance to observe how it was always the fate of the Dossons to miss their friends. They were continually looking out for meetings and combinations that never came off, hearing that people had been in Paris only after they had gone away, or feeling convinced that they were there but not to be found through their not having registered, or wondering whether they should overtake them if they should go to Dresden, and then making up their minds to start for Dresden, only to learn, at the eleventh hour, through some accident, that the elusive party had gone to Biarritz. "We know plenty of people if we could only come across them," Delia had said more than once: she scanned the continent with a wondering, baffled gaze and talked of the unsatisfactory way in which friends at home would "write out" that other friends were "somewhere in Europe." She expressed the wish that such correspondents as that might be in a place that was not at all vague. Two or three times people had called at the hotel when they were out and had left cards for them, without any address, superscribed with a mocking dash of the pencil, "Off to-morrow!" The girl sat looking at these cards, handling them and turning them over for a quarter of an hour at a time; she produced them days afterwards, brooding upon them afresh as if they were a mystic clue. George Flack generally knew where they were, the people who were "somewhere in Europe." Such knowledge came to him by a kind of intuition, by the voices of the air, by indefinable and unteachable processes. But he held his peace on purpose; he didn't want any outsiders; he thought their little party just right. Mr. Dosson's place in the scheme of providence was to go with Delia while he himself went with Francie, and nothing would have induced George Flack to disfigure that equation.

The young man was professionally so occupied with other people's affairs that it should doubtless be mentioned to his praise that he still managed to have affairs—or at least an affair—of his own. That affair was Francie Dosson, and he was pleased to perceive how little *she* cared what had become of Mr. and Mrs. Rosenheim and Master Samuel and Miss Cora. He counted all the things she didn't care about—her soft inadvertent eyes helped him to do that; and they footed up so, as he would have said, that they gave him a pleasant sense of a free field. If she had so few interests there was the greater possibility that a young man of bold conceptions and cheerful manners might become one. She had usually the air of waiting for something, with a sort of amused resignation, while tender, shy, indefinite little fancies hummed in her brain; so that she would perhaps recognise in him the reward of patience. George Flack was aware that he exposed his friends to considerable fatigue; he brought them back pale and taciturn from suburban excursions and from wanderings often rather aimless and casual among the boulevards and avenues of the town. He regarded them at such moments with complacency, however, for these were hours of diminished resistance: he had an idea that he should be able eventually to circumvent Delia if he could only watch for some time when she was tired. He liked to make them all feel helpless and dependent, and this was not difficult with people who were so modest and artless, so unconscious of the boundless power of wealth. Sentiment, in our young man, was not a scruple nor a source of weakness; but he thought it really touching, the little these good people knew of what they could do with their money. They had in their hands a weapon of infinite range and yet they were incapable of firing a shot for themselves. They had a kind of social humility; it appeared never to have occurred to them that, added to their amiability, their money gave them a value. This used to strike George Flack on certain occasions when he came back to find them in the places where he had dropped them while he rushed off to give a turn to one of his screws. They never played him false, never wearied of waiting; always sat patient and submissive, usually at a café to which he had introduced them or in a row of chairs on the boulevard, or in the Tuileries or the Champs Elysées.

He introduced them to many cafés, in different parts of Paris, being careful to choose those which (in his view) young ladies might frequent with propriety, and there were two or three in the neighbourhood of their hotel where they became frequent and familiar figures. As the late spring days grew warmer and brighter they usually sat outside on the "terrace"—the little expanse of small tables at the door of the establishment, where Mr. Flack, on the return, could descry them from afar at their post in exactly the same position to which he had committed them. They complained of no satiety in watching the many-coloured movement of the Parisian streets; and if some of the features in the panorama were base they were only so in a version which the imagination of our friends was incapable of supplying. George Flack considered that he was rendering a positive service to Mr. Dosson: wouldn't the old gentleman have sat all day in the court anyway? and wasn't the boulevard better than the court? It was his theory, too, that he flattered and caressed Miss Francie's father, for there was no one to whom he had furnished more copious details about the affairs, the projects and prospects, of the Reverberator. He had left no doubt in the old gentleman's mind as to the race he himself intended to run, and Mr. Dosson used to say to him every day, the first thing, "Well, where have you got to now?" as if he took a real interest. George Flack narrated his interviews, to which Delia and

Francie gave attention only in case they knew something of the persons on whom the young emissary of the Reverberator had conferred this distinction; whereas Mr. Dosson listened, with his tolerant interposition of "Is that so?" and "Well, that's good," just as submissively when he heard of the celebrity in question for the first time.

In conversation with his daughters Mr. Flack was frequently the theme, though introduced much more by the young ladies than by himself, and especially by Delia, who announced at an early period that she knew what he wanted and that it wasn't in the least what *she* wanted. She amplified this statement very soon—at least as regards her interpretation of Mr. Flack's designs: a certain mystery still hung about her own, which, as she intimated, had much more to recommend them. Delia's vision of the danger as well as the advantage of being a pretty girl was closely connected (and this was natural) with the idea of an "engagement": this idea was in a manner complete in itself—her imagination failed in the oddest way to carry it into the next stage. She wanted her sister to be engaged but she wanted her not at all to be married, and she had not clearly made up her mind as to how Francie was to enjoy both the promotion and the arrest. It was a secret source of humiliation to her that there had as yet to her knowledge been no one with whom her sister had exchanged vows: if her conviction on this subject could have expressed itself intelligibly it would have given you a glimpse of a droll state of mind—a dim theory that a bright girl ought to be able to try successive aspirants. Delia's conception of what such a trial might consist of was strangely innocent: it was made up of calls and walks and buggy-drives and above all of being spoken of as engaged; and it never occurred to her that a repetition of lovers rubs off a young lady's delicacy. She felt herself a born old maid and never dreamed of a lover of her own—he would have been dreadfully in her way; but she dreamed of love as something in its nature very delicate. All the same she discriminated; it did lead to something after all, and she desired that for Francie it should not lead to a union with Mr. Flack. She looked at such a union in the light of that other view which she kept as yet to herself but which she was ready to produce so soon as the right occasion should come up; and she told her sister that she would never speak to her again if she should let this young man suppose—— And here she always paused, plunging again into impressive reticence.

"Suppose what?" Francie asked, as if she were totally unacquainted (which indeed she really was) with the suppositions of young men.

"Well, you'll see, when he begins to say things you won't like." This sounded ominous on Delia's part, but she had in reality very little apprehension; otherwise she would have risen against the custom adopted by Mr. Flack of perpetually coming round: she would have given her attention (though it struggled in general unsuccessfully with all this side of their life) to some prompt means of getting away from Paris. She told her father what in her view the correspondent of the Reverberator was "after"; but it must be added that she did not make him feel very strongly on the matter. This however was not of importance, with her inner sense that Francie would never really do anything—that is would never really like anything—they didn't like.

Her sister's docility was a great comfort to her, especially as it was addressed in the first instance to herself. She liked and disliked certain things much more than the younger girl did either; and Francie was glad to take advantage of her reasons, having so few of her own. They served—Delia's reasons—for Mr. Dosson as well, so that Francie was not guilty of any particular irreverence in regarding her sister rather than her father as the controller of her fate. A fate was rather a cumbersome and formidable possession, which it relieved her that some kind person should undertake the keeping of. Delia had somehow got hold of hers first—before even her father, and ever so much before Mr. Flack; and it lay with Delia to make any change. She could not have accepted any gentleman as a husband without reference to Delia, any more than she could have done up her hair without a glass. The only action taken by Mr. Dosson in consequence of his elder daughter's revelations was to embrace the idea as a subject of daily pleasantry. He was fond, in his intercourse with his children, of some small usual joke, some humorous refrain; and what could have been more in the line of true domestic sport than a little gentle but unintermitted raillery upon Francie's conquest?

Mr. Flack's attributive intentions became a theme of indulgent parental chaff, and the girl was neither dazzled nor annoyed by such familiar references to them. "Well, he *has* told
us about half we know," she used often to reply.

Among the things he told them was that this was the very
best time in the young lady's life to have her portrait painted
and the best place in the world to have it done well; also that
he knew a "lovely artist," a young American of extraordinary
talent, who would be delighted to undertake the work. He
conducted them to this gentleman's studio, where they saw
several pictures by which they were considerably mystified.
Francie protested that she didn't want to be done *that* way,
and Delia declared that she would as soon have her sister
shown up in a magic lantern. They had had the fortune not to
find Mr. Waterlow at home, so that they were free to express
themselves and the pictures were shown them by his servant.
They looked at them as they looked at bonnets and *confections*
when they went to expensive shops; as if it were a question,
among so many specimens, of the style and colour they would
choose. Mr. Waterlow's productions struck them for the most
part in the same manner as those garments which ladies classify as frights, and they went away with a very low opinion of
the young American master. George Flack told them, however, that they couldn't get out of it, inasmuch as he had already written home to the Reverberator that Francie was to
sit. They accepted this somehow as a kind of supernatural
sign that she would have to; for they believed everything that
they heard quoted from a newspaper. Moreover Mr. Flack
explained to them that it would be idiotic to miss such an
opportunity to get something at once precious and cheap; for
it was well known that Impressionism was going to be the art
of the future, and Charles Waterlow was a rising Impression-
ist. It was a new system altogether and the latest improvement
in art. They didn't want to go back, they wanted to go forward, and he would give them an article that would fetch five
times the money in a couple of years. They were not in search
of a bargain, but they allowed themselves to be inoculated
with any reason which they thought would be characteristic
of earnest people; and he even convinced them, after a little,
that when once they had got used to Impressionism they

would never look at anything else. Mr. Waterlow was *the* man, among the young, and he had no interest in praising him, because he was not a personal friend; his reputation was advancing with strides, and any one with any sense would want to secure something before the rush.

III.

THE YOUNG LADIES consented to return to the Avenue de Villiers, and this time they found the celebrity of the future. He was smoking cigarettes with a friend, while coffee was served to the two gentlemen (it was just after luncheon), on a vast divan, covered with scrappy oriental rugs and cushions; it looked, Francie thought, as if the artist had set up a carpet-shop in a corner. She thought him very pleasant; and it may be mentioned without circumlocution that the young lady ushered in by the vulgar American reporter, whom he didn't like and who had already come too often to his studio to pick up "glimpses" (the painter wondered how in the world he had picked *her* up), this charming candidate for portraiture struck Charles Waterlow on the spot as an adorable model. She made, it may further be declared, quite the same impression on the gentleman who was with him and who never took his eyes off her while her own rested, afresh, on several finished and unfinished canvases. This gentleman asked of his friend, at the end of five minutes, the favour of an introduction to her; in consequence of which Francie learned that his name (she thought it singular) was Gaston Probert. Mr. Probert was a kind-eyed, smiling youth, who fingered the points of his moustache; he was represented by Mr. Waterlow as an American, but he pronounced the American language (so at least it seemed to Francie) as if it had been French.

After Francie had quitted the studio with Delia and Mr. Flack (her father, on this occasion, was not of the party), the two young men, falling back upon their divan, broke into expressions of æsthetic rapture, declared that the girl had qualities—oh, but qualities, and a charm of line! They remained there for an hour, contemplating these rare properties in the smoke of their cigarettes. You would have gathered from their conversation (though, as regards much of it, only perhaps with the aid of a grammar and dictionary) that the young lady possessed plastic treasures of the highest order, of which she was evidently quite unconscious. Before this however Mr. Waterlow had come to an understanding with his visitors—it had been settled that Miss Francina should sit for

him at his first hour of leisure. Unfortunately that hour presented itself as still remote and he was unable to make a definite appointment. He had sitters on his hands—he had at
least three portraits to finish before going to Spain. And he
adverted with bitterness to the journey to Spain—a little excursion laid out precisely with his friend Probert for the last
weeks of the spring, the first of the southern summer, the
time of the long days and the real light. Gaston Probert re-
echoed his regrets, for though he had no business with Miss
Francina (he liked her name), he also wanted to see her again.
They half agreed to give up Spain (they had, after all, been
there before), so that Waterlow might take the girl in hand
without delay, the moment he had knocked off his present
work. This amendment did not hold however, for other considerations came up and the artist resigned himself to the arrangement on which the Miss Dossons had quitted him: he
thought it so characteristic of their nationality that they
should settle a matter of that sort for themselves. This was
simply that they should come back in the autumn, when he
should be comparatively free: then there would be a margin
and they might all take their time. At present, before long (by
the time he should be ready), the question of Miss Francina's
leaving Paris for the summer would be sure to come up, and
that would be a tiresome interruption. She liked Paris, she
had no plans for the autumn and only wanted a reason to
come back about the twentieth of September. Mr. Waterlow
remarked humorously that she evidently bossed the shop.
Meanwhile, before starting for Spain, he would see her as
often as possible—his eye would take possession of her.

His companion envied him his eye; he intimated that he
was jealous of his eye. It was perhaps as a step towards establishing his right to be jealous that Mr. Probert left a card
upon the Miss Dossons at the Hôtel de l'Univers et de
Cheltenham, having first ascertained that such a proceeding
would not, by the young American sisters, be regarded as an
unwarrantable liberty. Gaston Probert was an American who
had never been in America, and he was obliged to take counsel on such an emergency as that. He knew that in Paris
young men did not call at hotels on honourable damsels; but
he also knew that honourable damsels did not visit young

men in studios; and he had no guide, no light that he could
trust, save the wisdom of his friend Waterlow, which, however, was for the most part communicated to him in a derisive
and misleading form. Waterlow, who was after all himself an
ornament of the French and the very French school, jeered at
his want of national instinct, at the way he never knew by
which end to take hold of a compatriot. Poor Probert was
obliged to confess that he had had terribly little practice, and
in the great medley of aliens and brothers (and even more of
sisters), he couldn't tell which was which. He would have had
a country and countrymen, to say nothing of countrywomen,
if he could; but that matter had not been settled for him and
there is a difficulty in settling it for one's self. Born in Paris, he
had been brought up altogether on French lines, in a
family which French society had irrecoverably absorbed. His
father, a Carolinian and a Catholic, was a Gallomaniac of the
old American type. His three sisters had married Frenchmen,
and one of them lived in Brittany and the others much of the
time in Touraine. His only brother had fallen, during the terrible year, in defence of their adoptive country. Yet Gaston,
though he had had an old Legitimist marquis for his godfather, was not legally one of its children: his mother had, on
her deathbed, extorted from him the promise that he would
not take service in its armies; she considered, after the death
of her elder son (Gaston, in 1870, was a boy of ten), that the
family had been patriotic enough for courtesy.

The young man therefore, between two stools, had no clear
sitting-place: he wanted to be as American as he could and yet
not less French than he was; he was afraid to give up the little
that he was and find that what he might be was less—he
shrank from a flying leap which might drop him in the middle
of the sea. At the same time he was aware that the only way
to know how it feels to be an American is to try it, and he had
many a purpose of making the westward journey. His family,
however, had been so completely Gallicised that the affairs of
each member of it were the affairs of all the rest, and his
father, his sisters and his brothers-in-law had not yet sufficiently made this scheme their own for him to feel that it was
really his. It was a family in which there was no individual but
only a collective property. Meanwhile he tried, as I say, by

safer enterprises, and especially by going a good deal to see Charles Waterlow in the Avenue de Villiers, whom he believed to be his dearest friend, formed for his affection by Monsieur Carolus. He had an idea that in this manner he kept himself in touch with his countrymen; and he thought he tried especially when he left that card on the Misses Dosson. He was in search of freshness, but he need not have gone far: he need only have turned his lantern upon his own young breast to find a considerable store of it. Like many unoccupied young men at the present hour he gave much attention to art, lived as much as possible in that alternative world, where leisure and vagueness are so mercifully relieved of their crudity. To make up for his want of talent he espoused the talent of others (that is, of several), and was as sensitive and conscientious about them as he might have been about himself. He defended certain of Waterlow's purples and greens as he would have defended his own honour; and in regard to two or three other painters had convictions which belonged almost to the undiscussable part of life. He had not in general a high sense of success, but what kept it down particularly was his indocile hand, the fact that, such as they were, Waterlow's purples and greens, for instance, were far beyond him. If he had not failed there other failures would not have mattered, not even that of not having a country; and it was on the occasion of his friend's agreement to paint that strange, lovely girl, whom he liked so much and whose companions he failed to like, that he felt supremely without a vocation. Freshness was there at least, if he had only had the method. He prayed earnestly, in relation to methods, for a providential reinforcement of Waterlow's sense of this quality. If Waterlow had a fault it was that he was sometimes a little stale.

He avenged himself for the artist's bewildering treatment of his first attempt to approach Miss Francie by indulging, at the end of another week, in a second. He went about six o'clock, when he supposed she would have returned from her day's wanderings, and his prudence was rewarded by the sight of the young lady sitting in the court of the hotel with her father and sister. Mr. Dosson was new to Gaston Probert, but the visitor's intelligence embraced him. The little party was as usual expecting Mr. Flack at any moment, and they had collected down stairs, so that he might pick them up easily. They had, on the first floor, an expensive parlour, decorated in white and gold, with sofas of crimson damask; but there was something lonely in that grandeur and the place had become mainly a receptacle for their tall trunks, with a half-emptied paper of chocolates or *marrons glacés* on every table. After young Probert's first call his name was often on the lips of the simple trio, and Mr. Dosson grew still more jocose, making nothing of a secret of his perception that Francie hit the bull's-eye "every time." Mr. Waterlow had returned their visit, but that was rather a matter of course, because it was they who had gone after him. They had not gone after the other one; it was he who had come after them. When he entered the hotel, as they sat there, this pursuit and its probable motive became startlingly vivid.

Delia had taken the matter much more gravely than her father; she said there was a great deal she wanted to find out. She mused upon these mysteries visibly, but without advancing much, and she appealed for assistance to George Flack, with a candour which he appreciated and returned. If he knew anything he ought to know who Mr. Probert was; and she spoke as if it would be in the natural course that he should elicit the revelation by an interview. Mr. Flack promised to "nose round"; he said the best plan would be that the results should "come back" to her in the Reverberator; he appeared to think that the people could be persuaded that they wanted about a column on Mr. Probert. His researches, however, were fruitless, for in spite of the one fact the girl was able to give him as a starting-point, the fact that their new acquaintance had spent his whole life in Paris, the young journalist couldn't scare up a single person who had even heard of him. He had questioned up and down and all over the place, from the Rue Scribe to the far end of Chaillot, and he knew people who knew others who knew every member of the American colony; that select body which haunted poor Delia's imagination, glittered and re-echoed there in a hundred tormenting roundabout glimpses. That was where she wanted to get Francie, as she said to herself; she wanted to get her right in there. She believed the members of this society to constitute a little kingdom of the blest; and she used to drive through the Avenue Gabriel, the Rue de Marignan and the wide vistas which radiate from the Arch of Triumph and are always changing their names, on purpose to send up wistful glances to the windows (she had learned that all this was the happy quarter) of the enviable but unapproachable colonists. She saw these privileged mortals, as she supposed, in almost every victoria that made a languid lady with a pretty head flash past her, and she had no idea how little honour this theory sometimes did her expatriated countrywomen. Her plan was already made to be on the field again the next winter and take it up seriously, this question of getting Francie in.

When Mr. Flack said to her that young Probert's set couldn't be either the rose or anything near it, since the oldest inhabitant had never heard of them, Delia had a flash of inspiration, an intellectual flight that she herself did not measure at the time. She asked if that did not perhaps prove on the contrary quite the opposite—that they were just *the* cream and beyond all others. Was there not a kind of inner circle, and were they not somewhere about the centre of that? George Flack almost quivered at this pregnant suggestion from so unusual a quarter, for he guessed on the spot that Delia Dosson had divined. "Why, do you mean one of those families that have worked down so far you can't find where they went in?" that was the phrase in which he recognised the truth of the girl's idea. Delia's fixed eyes assented, and after a moment of cogitation George Flack broke out—"That's the kind of family we want a sketch of!"

"Well, perhaps they don't want to be sketched. You had better find out," Delia had rejoined.

The chance to find out might have seemed to present itself when Mr. Probert walked in that confiding way into the hotel; for his arrival was followed, a quarter of an hour later, by that of the representative of the Reverberator. Gaston liked the way they treated him; though demonstrative it was not artificial. Mr. Dosson said they had been hoping he would come round again and Delia remarked that she supposed he had had quite a journey—Paris was so big; and she urged his acceptance of a glass of wine or a cup of tea. She added that that wasn't the place where they usually received (she liked to hear herself talk of "receiving"), and led the party up to her white and gold saloon, where they should be so much more private: she liked also to hear herself talk of privacy. They sat on the red silk chairs and she hoped Mr. Probert would at least taste a sugared chestnut or a chocolate; and when he declined, pleading the imminence of the dinner-hour, she murmured, "Well, I suppose you're so used to them—living so long over here." The allusion to the dinner-hour led Mr. Dosson to express the wish that he would go round and dine with them without ceremony; they were expecting a friend—he generally settled it for them—who was coming to take them round.

"And then we are going to the circus," Francie said, speaking for the first time.

If she had not spoken before she had done something still more to the purpose; she had removed any shade of doubt that might have lingered in the young man's spirit as to her charm of line. He was aware that his Parisian education, acting upon a natural aptitude, had opened him much—rendered him perhaps even morbidly sensitive—to impressions of this order; the society of artists, the talk of studios, the attentive study of beautiful works, the sight of a thousand forms of curious research and experiment, had produced in his mind a new sense, the exercise of which was a conscious enjoyment, and the supreme gratification of which, on several occasions, had given him as many ineffaceable memories. He had once said to his friend Waterlow: "I don't know whether it's a confession of a very poor life, but the most important things that have happened to me in this world have been simply half-a-dozen impressions—impressions of the eye." "Ah, *malheureux*, you're lost!" the painter had exclaimed, in answer to this, and without even taking the trouble to explain his ominous speech. Gaston Probert however had not been frightened by it, and he continued to be thankful for the sensitive plate that nature (with culture added), enabled him to carry in his brain. The impression of the eye was doubtless not everything, but it was so much gained, so much saved, in a world in which other treasures were apt to slip through one's fingers; and above all it had the merit that so many things gave it and that nothing could take it away. He had perceived in a moment that Francie Dosson gave it; and now, seeing her a second time, he felt that she conferred it in a degree which made acquaintance with her one of those "important" facts of which he had spoken to Charles Waterlow. It was in the case of such an accident as this that he felt the value of his Parisian education—his modern sense.

It was therefore not directly the prospect of the circus that induced him to accept Mr. Dosson's invitation; nor was it even the charm exerted by the girl's appearing, in the few words she uttered, to appeal to him for herself. It was his feeling that on the edge of the glittering ring her type would form his entertainment and that if he knew it was rare she herself did not. He liked to be conscious, but he liked others not to be. It seemed to him at this moment, after he had told Mr. Dosson he should be delighted to spend the evening with them, that he was indeed trying hard to discover how it would feel to be an American; he had jumped on the ship, he was pitching away to the west. He had led his sister, Mme. de Brécourt, to expect that he would dine with her (she was having a little party), and if she could see the people to whom, without a scruple, with a quick sense of refreshment and freedom, he now sacrificed her! He knew who was coming to his sister's, in the Place Beauvau: Mme. d'Outreville and M. de Grospré, old M. Courageau, Mme. de Brives, Lord and Lady Trantum, Mlle. de Saintonge; but he was fascinated by the idea of the contrast between what he preferred and what he gave up. His life had long been wanting—painfully wanting—in the element of contrast, and here was a chance to bring it in. He seemed to see it come in powerfully with Mr. Flack, after Miss Dosson had proposed that they should walk off without their initiator. Her father did not favour this suggestion; he said, "We want a double good dinner to-day and Mr. Flack has got to order it." Upon this Delia had asked the visitor if *he* couldn't order—a Frenchman like him; and Francie had interrupted, before he could answer the question—"Well, *are* you a Frenchman? that's just the point, isn't it?" Gaston Probert replied that he had no wish but to be of *her* nationality, and the elder sister asked him if he knew many Americans in Paris. He was obliged to confess that he did not, but he hastened to add that he was eager to go on, now that he had made such a charming beginning.

"Oh, we ain't anything—if you mean that," said the young lady. "If you go on you'll go on beyond us."

"We ain't anything here, my dear, but we are a good deal at home," Mr. Dosson remarked, smiling.

"I think we are very nice anywhere!" Francie exclaimed; upon which Gaston Probert declared that they were as delightful as possible. It was in these amenities that George Flack found them engaged; but there was none the less a certain eagerness in his greeting of the other guest, as if he had it in mind to ask him how soon he could give him half an hour. I hasten to add that, with the turn the occasion presently took, the correspondent of the Reverberator renounced the effort to put Mr. Probert down. They all went out together, and the professional impulse, usually so irresistible in George Flack's mind, suffered a modification. He wanted to put his fellow-visitor down, but in a more human, a more passionate sense. Probert talked very little to Francie, but though Mr. Flack did not know that on a first occasion he would have thought that violent, even rather gross, he knew it was for Francie, and Francie alone, that the fifth member of the party was there. He said to himself suddenly and in perfect sincerity that it was a mean class any way, the people for whom their own country was not good enough. He did not go so far however, when they were seated at the admirable establishment of M. Durand, in the Place de la Madeleine, as to order a bad dinner to spite his competitor; nor did he, to spoil this gentleman's amusement, take uncomfortable seats at the pretty circus in the Champs Elysées to which, at half-past eight o'clock, the company was conveyed (it was a drive of but five minutes) in a couple of cabs. The occasion therefore was superficially smooth, and he could see that the sense of being disagreeable to an American newspaper-man was not needed to make his nondescript rival enjoy it. He hated his accent, he hated his laugh, and he hated above all the lamblike way their companions accepted him. Mr. Flack was quite acute enough to make an important observation: he cherished it and promised himself to bring it to the notice of his gullible friends. Gaston Probert professed a great desire to be of service to the young ladies—to do something which would help them to be happy in Paris; but he gave no hint of an intention to do that which would contribute most to such a result—bring them in contact with the other members, and above all with the female members, of his family. George Flack knew nothing about the matter, but he required for purposes of argument that Mr. Probert's family should have female members, and it was lucky for him that his assumption was just. He thought he foresaw the effect with which he should impress it upon Francie and Delia (but above all upon Delia, who would then herself impress it upon Francie), that it would be time for their French friend to talk when he had brought his mother round. *But he never would*—they might bet their pile on that! He never did, in the sequel, in fact—having, poor young man, no mother to bring. Moreover he was mum (as Delia phrased it to herself) about Mme. de Brécourt and Mme. de Cliché: such, Miss Dosson learned from Charles Waterlow, were the names of his two sisters who had houses in Paris—gathering at the same time the information that one of these ladies was a *marquise* and the other a *comtesse*. She was less exasperated by their nonappearance than Mr. Flack had hoped, and it did not prevent an excursion to dine at Saint-Germain, a week after the evening spent at the circus, which included both of the new admirers. It also as a matter of course included Mr. Flack, for though the party had been proposed in the first instance by Charles Waterlow, who wished to multiply opportunities for studying his future sitter, Mr. Dosson had characteristically constituted himself host and administrator, with the young journalist as his deputy. He liked to invite people and to pay for them, and he disliked to be invited and paid for. He was never inwardly content, on any occasion, unless a great deal of money was spent, and he could be sure enough of the magnitude of the sum only when he himself spent it. He was too simple for conceit or for pride of purse, but he always felt that any arrangements were a little shabby as to which the expenses had not been referred to him. He never told any one how he met them. Moreover Delia had told him that if they should go to Saint-Germain as guests of the artist and his friend Mr. Flack would not be of the company: she was sure those gentlemen would not invite him. In fact she was too acute, for though he liked him little, Charles Waterlow would on this occasion have made a point of expressing by a hospitable attitude his sense of obligation to a man who had brought him such a subject. Delia's hint however was all-sufficient for her father; he would have thought it a gross breach of friendly loyalty to take part in a festival not graced by Mr. Flack's presence. His idea of loyalty was that he should scarcely smoke a cigar unless his friend was there to take another, and he felt rather mean if he went round alone to get shaved. As regards Saint-Germain, he took over the project and George Flack telegraphed for a table on the terrace at the Pavillon Henri Quatre. Mr. Dosson had by this time learned to trust the European manager of the Reverberator to spend his money almost as he himself would.

IV.

DELIA had broken out the evening they took Mr. Probert to the circus; she had apostrophised Francie as they each sat in a red-damask chair after ascending to their apartments. They had bade their companions farewell at the door of the hotel and the two gentlemen had walked off in different directions. But up stairs they had instinctively not separated; they dropped into the first place and sat looking at each other and at the highly-decorated lamps that burned, night after night, in their empty saloon. "Well, I want to know when you're going to stop," Delia said to her sister, speaking as if this remark were a continuation, which it was not, of something they had lately been saying.

"Stop what?" asked Francie, reaching forward for a *marron*.

"Stop carrying on the way you do—with Mr. Flack."

Francie stared, while she consumed her *marron*; then she replied, in her little flat, patient voice, "Why, Delia Dosson, how can you be so foolish?"

"Father, I wish you'd speak to her. Francie, I ain't foolish."

"What do you want me to say to her?" Mr. Dosson inquired. "I guess I've said about all I know."

"Well, that's in fun; I want you to speak to her in earnest."

"I guess there's no one in earnest but you," Francie remarked. "These are not so good as the last."

"No, and there won't be if you don't look out. There's something you can do if you'll just keep quiet. If you can't tell difference of style, well, I can."

"What's the difference of style?" asked Mr. Dosson. But before this question could be answered Francie protested against the charge of carrying on. Quiet? Wasn't she as quiet as a stopped clock? Delia replied that a girl was not quiet so long as she didn't keep others so; and she wanted to know what her sister proposed to do about Mr. Flack. "Why don't you take him and let Francie take the other?" Mr. Dosson continued.

"That's just what I'm after—to make her take the other," said his elder daughter.

"Take him—how do you mean?" Francie inquired.

"Oh, you know how."

"Yes, I guess you know how!" Mr. Dosson laughed, with an absence of prejudice which might have been thought deplorable in a parent.

"Do you want to stay in Europe or not? that's what I want to know," Delia declared to her sister. "If you want to go bang home you're taking the right way to do it."

"What has that got to do with it?" asked Mr. Dosson.

"Should you like so much to reside at that place—where is it?—where his paper is published? That's where you'll have to pull up, sooner or later," Delia pursued.

"Do you want to stay in Europe, father?" Francie said, with her small sweet weariness.

"It depends on what you mean by staying. I want to go home some time."

"Well, then, you've got to go without Mr. Probert," Delia remarked with decision. "If you think he wants to live over there——"

"Why, Delia, he wants dreadfully to go—he told me so himself," Francie argued, with passionless pauses.

"Yes, and when he gets there he'll want to come back. I thought you were so much interested in Paris."

"My poor child, I *am* interested!" smiled Francie. "Ain't I interested, father?"

"Well, I don't know how you could act differently, to show it."

"Well, I do then," said Delia. "And if you don't make Mr. Flack understand I will."

"Oh, I guess he understands—he's so bright," Francie returned.

"Yes, I guess he does—he *is* bright," said Mr. Dosson. "Good-night, chickens," he added; and wandered off to a couch of untroubled repose.

His daughters sat up half an hour later, but not by the wish of the younger girl. She was always passive however, always docile when Delia was, as she said, on the war-path, and though she had none of her sister's insistence she was very courageous in suffering. She thought Delia whipped her up too much, but there was that in her which would have prevented her from ever running away. She could smile and

smile for an hour without irritation, making even pacific answers, though all the while her companion's grossness hurt
something delicate that was in her. She knew that Delia
loved her—not loving herself meanwhile a bit—as no one
else in the world probably ever would; and there was something droll in such plans for her—plans of ambition which
could only involve a loss. The real answer to anything, to
everything Delia might say in her moods of prefigurement
was—"Oh, if you want to make out that people are thinking of me or that they ever will, you ought to remember
that no one can possibly think of me half as much as you
do. Therefore if there is to be any comfort for either of us
we had both much better just go on as we are." She did not
however on this occasion, meet her sister with this syllo-
gism, because there happened to be a certain fascination in
the way Delia set forth the great truth that the star of matrimony, for the American girl, was now shining in the east—
in England and France and Italy. They had only to look
round anywhere to see it: what did they hear of every day in
the week but of the engagement of one of their own com-
peers to some count or some lord? Delia insisted on the fact
that it was in that vast, vague section of the globe to which
she never alluded save as "over here" that the American girl
was now called upon to play, under providence, her part.
When Francie remarked that Mr. Probert was not a count
nor a lord her sister rejoined that she didn't care whether he
was or not. To this Francie replied that she herself didn't
care but that Delia ought to, to be consistent.

"Well, he's a prince compared with Mr. Flack," Delia
declared.

"He hasn't the same ability; not half."

"He has the ability to have three sisters who are just the
sort of people I want you to know."

"What good will they do me?" Francie asked. "They'll hate
me. Before they could turn round I should do something—in
perfect innocence—that they would think monstrous."

"Well, what would that matter if *he* liked you?"

"Oh, but he wouldn't, then! He would hate me too."

"Then all you've got to do is not to do it," Delia said.

"Oh, but I should—every time," her sister went on.

Delia looked at her a moment. "What *are* you talking about?"

"Yes, what am I? It's disgusting!" And Francie sprang up.

"I'm sorry you have such thoughts," said Delia, sententiously.

"It's disgusting to talk about a gentleman—and his sisters and his society and everything else—before he has scarcely looked at you."

"It's disgusting if he isn't just dying; but it isn't if he is."

"Well, I'll make him skip!" Francie went on.

"Oh, you're worse than father!" her sister cried, giving her a push as they went to bed.

They reached Saint-Germain with their companions nearly an hour before the time that had been fixed for dinner; the purpose of this being to enable them to enjoy with what remained of daylight—a stroll on the celebrated terrace and a study of the magnificent view. The evening was splendid and the atmosphere favourable to this entertainment; the grass was vivid on the broad walk beside the parapet, the park and forest were fresh and leafy and the prettiest golden light hung over the curving Seine and the far-spreading city. The hill which forms the terrace stretched down among the vineyards, with the poles delicate yet in their bareness, to the river, and the prospect was spotted here and there with the red legs of the little sauntering soldiers of the garrison. How it came, after Delia's warning in regard to her carrying on (especially as she had not failed to feel the force of her sister's wisdom), Francie could not have told herself: certain it is that before ten minutes had elapsed she perceived, first, that the evening would not pass without Mr. Flack's taking in some way, and for a certain time, peculiar possession of her; and then that he was already doing so, that he had drawn her away from the others, who were stopping behind them to exclaim upon the view, that he made her walk faster, and that he ended by interposing such a distance that she was practically alone with him. This was what he wanted, but it was not all; she felt that he wanted a great many other things. The large perspective of the terrace stretched away before them (Mr. Probert had said it was in the grand style), and he was determined to make her walk to the end. She felt sorry for his determinations; they were an idle exercise of a force intrinsically fine, and she wanted to protest, to let him know that it was really a waste of his great cleverness to count upon her. She was not to be counted on; she was a vague, soft, negative being who had never decided anything and never would, who had not even the merit of coquetry and who only asked to be let alone. She made him stop at last, telling him, while she leaned against the parapet, that he walked too fast; and she looked back at their companions, whom she expected to see, under pressure from Delia, following at the highest speed. But they were not following; they still stood there, only looking, attentively enough, at the absent members of the party. Delia would wave her parasol, beckon her back, send Mr. Waterlow to bring her; Francie looked from one moment to another for some such manifestation as that. But no manifestation came; none at least but the odd spectacle, presently, of the group turning round and, evidently under Delia's direction, retracing its steps. Francie guessed in a moment what was meant by that: it was the most definite signal her sister could have given. It made her feel that Delia counted on her, but to such a different end, just as poor Mr. Flack did, just as Delia wished to persuade her that Mr. Probert did. The girl gave a sigh, looking up at her companion with troubled eyes, at the idea of being made the object of converging policies. Such a thankless, bored, evasive little object as she felt herself! What Delia had said in turning away was—"Yes, I am watching you, and I depend upon you to finish him up. Stay there with him—go off with him (I'll give you half an hour if necessary), only settle him once for all. It is very kind of me to give you this chance; and in return for it I expect you to be able to tell me this evening that he has got his answer. Shut him up!"

Francie did not in the least dislike Mr. Flack. Interested as I am in presenting her favourably to the reader I am yet obliged as a veracious historian to admit that he seemed to her decidedly a brilliant being. In many a girl the sort of appreciation she had of him might easily have been converted by peremptory treatment from outside into something more exalted. I do not misrepresent the perversity of women in saying that our young lady might at this moment have replied to her sister with: "No, I was not in love with him, but somehow since you are so very prohibitive I foresee that I shall be if he asks me." It is doubtless difficult to say more for Francie's simplicity of character than that she felt no need of encouraging Mr. Flack in order to prove to herself that she was not bullied. She didn't care whether she were bullied or not; and she was perfectly capable of letting her sister believe that she had carried mildness to the point of giving up a man she had a secret sentiment for in order to oblige that large-brained young lady. She was not clear herself as to whether it might not be so; her pride, what she had of it, lay in an undistributed, inert form quite at the bottom of her heart and she had never yet invented any consoling theory to cover her want of a high spirit. She felt, as she looked up at Mr. Flack, that she didn't care even if he should think that she sacrificed him to a childish subservience. His bright eyes were hard, as if he could almost guess how cynical she was, and she turned her own again towards her retreating companions. "They are going to dinner; we oughtn't to be dawdling here," she said.

"Well, if they are going to dinner they'll have to eat the napkins. I ordered it and I know when it will be ready," George Flack replied. "Besides they are not going to dinner, they are going to walk in the park. Don't you worry, we sha'n't lose them. I wish we could!" the young man added, smiling.

"You wish we could?"

"I should like to feel that you were under my particular protection."

"Well, I don't know what the dangers are," said Francie, setting herself in motion again. She went after the others, but at the end of a few steps he stopped her again.

"You won't have confidence. I wish you would believe what I tell you."

"You haven't told me anything." And she turned her back to him, looking away at the splendid view. "I admire the scenery," she added in a moment.

"Oh, bother the scenery! I want to tell you something about myself, if I could flatter myself that you would take any interest in it." He had thrust his cane, waist-high, into the low wall of the terrace, and he leaned against it, screwing the point gently round with both hands.

"I'll take an interest if I can understand," said Francie.

"You can understand easy enough, if you'll try. I've got some news from America to-day that has pleased me very much. The Reverberator has taken a jump."

This was not what Francie had expected, but it was better. "Taken a jump?" she repeated.

"It has gone straight up. It's in the second hundred thousand."

"Hundred thousand dollars?" said Francie.

"No, Miss Francie, copies. That's the circulation. But the dollars are footing up, too."

"And do they all come to you?"

"Precious few of them! I wish they did; it's a pleasant property."

"Then it isn't yours?" she asked, turning round to him. It was an impulse of sympathy that made her look at him now, for she already knew how much he had the success of his newspaper at heart. He had once told her he loved the Reverberator as he had loved his first jack-knife.

"Mine? You don't mean to say you suppose I own it!" George Flack exclaimed. The light projected upon her innocence by these words was so strong that the girl blushed, and he went on more tenderly—"It's a pretty sight, the way you and your sister take that sort of thing for granted. Do you think property grows on you, like a moustache? Well, it seems as if it had, on your father. If I owned the Reverberator I shouldn't be stumping round here; I'd give my attention to another branch of the business. That is I would give my attention to all, but I wouldn't go round with the cart. But I'm going to get hold of it, and I want you to help me," the young man went on; "that's just what I wanted to speak to you about. It's a big thing already and I mean to make it bigger: the most universal society-paper the world has seen. That's where the future lies, and the man who sees it first is the man who'll make his pile. It's a field for enlightened enterprise that hasn't yet begun to be worked." He continued, glowing, almost suddenly, with his idea, and one of his eyes half closed itself knowingly, in a way that was habitual with him when he talked consecutively. The effect of this would have been droll to a listener, the note of the prospectus mingling with the accent of passion. But it was not droll to Francie; she only thought it, or supposed it, a proof of the way Mr. Flack saw everything in its largest relations. "There are ten thousand things to do that haven't been done, and I am going to do them. The society-news of every quarter of the globe, furnished by the prominent members themselves (oh, *they* can be fixed—you'll see!) from day to day and from hour to hour and served up at every breakfast-table in the United States—that's what the American people want and that's what the American people are going to have. I wouldn't say it to every one, but I don't mind telling you, that I consider I have about as fine a sense as any one of what's going to be required in future over there. I'm going for the secrets, the *chronique intime*, as they say here; what the people want is just what isn't told, and I'm going to tell it. Oh, they're bound to have the plums! That's about played out, any way, the idea of sticking up a sign of 'private' and thinking you can keep the place to yourself. You can't do it— you can't keep out the light of the Press. Now what I'm going to do is to set up the biggest lamp yet made and to make it shine all over the place. We'll see who's private then! I'll make them crowd in themselves with the information, and as I tell you, Miss Francie, it's a job in which you can give me a lovely push."

"Well, I don't see how," said Francie, candidly. "I haven't got any secrets." She spoke gaily, because she was relieved; she thought she had in reality a glimpse of what he wanted of her. It was something better than she had feared. Since he didn't own the great newspaper (her conception of such matters was of the dimmest), he desired to possess himself of it, and she sufficiently comprehended that money was needed for that. She further seemed to perceive that he presented himself to her as moneyless and that this brought them round by a vague but comfortable transition to a pleasant consciousness that her father was not. The remaining induction, silently made, was quick and happy: she should acquit herself by asking her father for the sum required and just passing it over to Mr. Flack. The greatness of his enterprise and the magnitude of his conceptions appeared to overshadow her as they stood there. This was a delightful

simplification and it did not for a moment strike her as positively unnatural that her companion should have a delicacy
about appealing to Mr. Dosson directly for pecuniary aid,
though indeed she was capable of thinking that odd if she
had meditated upon it. There was nothing simpler to Francie than the idea of putting her hand into her father's
pocket, and she felt that even Delia would be glad to satisfy
the young man by this casual gesture. I must add unfortunately that her alarm came back to her from the way in
which he replied: "Do you mean to say you don't know,
after all I've done?"

"I am sure I don't know what you've done."

"Haven't I tried—all I know—to make you like me?"

"Oh dear, I do like you!" cried Francie; "but how will that
help you?"

"It will help me if you will understand that I love you."

"Well, I don't understand!" replied the girl, walking off.

He followed her; they went on together in silence and then
he said—"Do you mean to say you haven't found that out?"

"Oh, I don't find things out—I ain't an editor!" Francie
laughed.

"You draw me out and then you jibe at me," Mr. Flack
remarked.

"I didn't draw you out. Couldn't you see me just straining
to get away?"

"Don't you sympathise with my ideas?"

"Of course I do, Mr. Flack; I think they're splendid," said
Francie, who did not in the least understand them.

"Well, then, why won't you work with me? Your affection,
your brightness, your faith would be everything to me."

"I'm very sorry—but I can't—I can't," the girl declared.

"You could if you would, quick enough."

"Well, then, I won't!" And as soon as these words were
spoken, as if to mitigate something of their asperity, Francie
paused a moment and said: "You must remember that I never
said I would—nor anything like it. I thought you just wanted
me to speak to my father."

"Of course I supposed you would do that."

"I mean about your paper."

"About my paper?"

"So as he could give you the money—to do what you want."

"Lord, you're too sweet!" George Flack exclaimed, staring. "Do you suppose I would ever touch a cent of your father's money?"—a speech not so hypocritical as it may sound, inasmuch as the young man, who had his own refinements, had never been guilty, and proposed to himself never to be, of the plainness of twitching the purse-strings of his potential father-in-law with his own hand. He had talked to Mr. Dosson by the hour about the interviewing business, but he had never dreamed that this amiable man would give him money as an interesting struggler. The only character in which he could expect it would be that of Francie's husband, and then it would come to Francie—not to him. This reasoning did not diminish his desire to assume such a character, and his love of his profession and his appreciation of the girl at his side ached together in his breast with the same disappointment. She saw that her words had touched him like a lash; they made him blush red for a moment. This caused her own colour to rise— she could scarcely have said why—and she hurried along again. He kept close to her; he argued with her; he besought her to think it over, assured her he was the best fellow in the world. To this she replied that if he didn't leave her alone she would cry—and how would he like that, to bring her back in such a state to the others? He said, "Damn the others!" but that did not help his case, and at last he broke out: "Will you just tell me this, then—is it because you've promised Miss Delia?" Francie answered that she had not promised Miss Delia anything, and her companion went on: "Of course I know what she has got in her head: she wants to get you into the high set—the *grand monde*, as they call it here; but I didn't suppose you'd let her fix your life for you. You were very different before *he* turned up."

"She never fixed anything for me. I haven't got any life and I don't want to have," said Francie. "And I don't know who you are talking about, either!"

"The man without a country. He'll pass you in—that's what your sister wants."

"You oughtn't to abuse him, because it was you that presented him," the girl rejoined.

"I never presented him! I'd like to kick him."

"We should never have seen him if it hadn't been for you."

"That's a fact, but it doesn't make me love him any the better. He's the poorest kind there is."

"I don't care anything about his kind."

"That's a pity, if you're going to marry him. How could I know that when I took you up there?"

"Good-bye, Mr. Flack," said Francie, trying to gain ground from him.

This attempt was of course vain, and after a moment he resumed: "Will you keep me as a friend?"

"Why, Mr. Flack, of course I will!" cried Francie.

"All right," he replied; and they presently rejoined their companions.

V.

GASTON PROBERT made his plan, imparting it to no one but his friend Waterlow, whose help indeed he needed to carry it out. These confidences cost him something, for the clever young painter found his predicament amusing and made no scruple of showing it. Probert was too much in love, however, to be discountenanced by sarcasm. This fact is the more noteworthy as he knew that Waterlow scoffed at him for a purpose—had a theory that that kind of treatment would be salutary. The French taste was in Waterlow's "manner," but it had not yet coloured his view of the relations of a young man of spirit with parents and pastors. He was Gallic to the tip of his finest brush, but the humour of his early American education could not fail to obtrude itself in discussion with a friend in whose life the principle of authority played so large a part. He accused Probert of being afraid of his sisters, which was a crude way (and he knew it) of alluding to the rigidity of the conception of the family among people who had adopted and had even to Waterlow's sense, as the phrase is, improved upon the usages of France. That did injustice (and this the artist also knew), to the delicate nature of the bond which united the different members of the house of Probert, who were each for all and all for each. Family feeling among them was not a tyranny but a religion, and in regard to Mesdames de Brécourt, de Cliché and de Douves what Gaston was most afraid of was seeming to them not to love them. None the less Charles Waterlow, who thought he had charming parts, held that the best way had not been taken to make a man of him, and the spirit in which the painter sometimes endeavoured to repair this mishap was altogether benevolent, though the form was frequently rough. Waterlow combined in an odd manner many of the forms of the Parisian studio with the moral and social ideas of Brooklyn, Long Island, where his first seeds had been implanted.

Gaston Probert desired nothing better than to be a man; what bothered him (and it is perhaps a proof that his instinct was gravely at fault), was a certain vagueness as to the constituents of this personage. He should be made more nearly, as it seemed to him, a brute were he to sacrifice in such an effort the decencies and pieties—holy things all of them—in which he had been reared. It was very well for Waterlow to say that to be a genuine man it was necessary to be a little of a brute; his friend was willing, in theory, to assent even to that. The difficulty was in application, in practice—as to which the painter declared that all that would be simple enough if it only didn't take so much account of the marchioness, the countess and—what was the other one?—the duchess. These young amenities were exchanged between the pair (while Gaston explained, almost as eagerly as if he were scoring a point, that the other one was only a *baronne*), during that brief journey to Spain of which mention has already been made, during the later weeks of the summer, after their return (the young men spent a fortnight together on the coast of Brittany), and above all during the autumn, when they were settled in Paris for the winter, when Mr. Dosson had re-appeared, according to the engagement with his daughters, when the sittings for the portrait had multiplied (the painter was unscrupulous as to the number he demanded), and the work itself, born under a happy star, took on more and more the aspect of a masterpiece. It was at Grenada that Gaston really broke out; there, one balmy night, he communicated to his companion that he would marry Francina Dosson or would never marry any one. The declaration was the more striking as it came after an interval; many days had elapsed since their separation from the young lady and many new and beautiful objects had engaged their attention. It appeared that poor Probert had been thinking of her all the while, and he let his friend know that it was that dinner at Saint Germain that had finished him. What she had been there Waterlow himself had seen: he would not controvert the proposition that she had been irresistible.

In November, in Paris (it was months and weeks before the artist began to please himself), the enamoured youth came very often to the Avenue de Villiers, toward the end of a sitting; and until it was finished, not to disturb the lovely model, he cultivated conversation with the elder sister: Gaston Probert was capable of that. Delia was always there of course, but Mr. Dosson had not once turned up and the newspaper man happily appeared to have taken himself off. The new aspirant learned in fact from Miss Dosson that a crisis in the affairs of his journal had recalled him to the seat of that publication. When the young ladies had gone (and when he did not go with them—he accompanied them not rarely), the visitor was almost lyrical in his appreciation of his friend's work; he had no jealousy of the insight which enabled him to reconstitute the girl on canvas with that perfection. He knew that Waterlow painted her too well to be in love with her and that if he himself could have attacked her in that fashion he would not have wanted to marry her. She bloomed there, on the easel, as brightly as in life, and the artist had caught the sweet essence of her beauty. It was exactly the way in which her lover would have chosen that she should be represented, and yet it had required a perfectly independent hand. Gaston Probert mused on this mystery and somehow felt proud of the picture and responsible for it, though it was as little his property, as yet, as the young lady herself.

When, in December, he told Waterlow of his plan of campaign the latter said, "I will do anything in the world you like—anything you think will help you—but it passes me, my dear fellow why in the world you don't go to them and say, 'I've seen a girl who is as good as cake and pretty as fire, she exactly suits me, I've taken time to think of it and I know what I want: therefore I propose to make her my wife. If you happen to like her so much the better; if you don't be so good as to keep it to yourselves.' That is much the most excellent way. Why, gracious heaven, all these mysteries and machinations?"

"Oh, you don't understand, you don't understand!" sighed Gaston Probert, with many wrinkles on his brow. "One can't break with one's traditions in an hour, especially when there is so much in them that one likes. I shall not love her more if they like her, but I shall love *them* more, and I care about that. You talk as a man who has nothing to consider. I have everything to consider—and I am glad I have. My pleasure in marrying her will be double if my father and my sisters accept her, and I shall greatly enjoy working out the business of bringing them round."

There were moments when Charles Waterlow resented the very terminology of his friend: he hated to hear a man talk about the woman he loved being "accepted." If one accepted her one's self or, rather, were accepted by her, that ended the matter, and the effort to bring round those who gave her the cold shoulder was scarcely consistent with self-respect. Probert explained that of course he knew his relatives would only have to know Francina to like her, to delight in her; but that to know her they would first have to make her acquaintance. This was the delicate point, for social commerce with such people as Mr. Dosson and Delia was not in the least in their usual line and it was impossible to disconnect the poor girl from her appendages. Therefore the whole question must be approached by an oblique movement; it would never do to march straight up to it. The wedge should have a narrow end and Gaston was ready to declare that he had found it. His sister Susan was another name for it; he would break her in first and she would help him to break in the others. She was his favourite relation, his intimate friend—the most modern, the most Parisian and inflammable member of the family. She was not reasonable but she was perceptive; she had imagination and humour and was capable of generosity and enthusiasm and even of infatuation. She had had her own infatuations and ought to allow for those of others. She would not like the Dossons superficially any better than his father or than Margaret or Jane (he called these ladies by their English names, but for themselves, their husbands, their friends and each other they were Suzanne, Marguerite and Jeanne); but there was a considerable chance that he might induce her to take his point of view. She was as fond of beauty and of the arts as he was; this was one of their bonds of union. She appreciated highly Charles Waterlow's talent and there had been a good deal of talk about his painting her portrait. It is true her husband viewed the project with so much colder an eye that it had not been carried out.

According to Gaston's plan she was to come to the Avenue de Villiers to see what the artist had done for Miss Francie; her brother was to have stimulated her curiosity by his rhapsodies, in advance, rhapsodies bearing wholly upon the work itself, the example of Waterlow's powers, and not upon the

young lady, whom he was not to let her know at first that he
had so much as seen. Just at the last, just before her visit, he
was to tell her that he had met the girl (at the studio), and
that she was as remarkable in her way as the picture. Seeing
the picture and hearing this, Mme. de Brécourt, as a disinterested lover of charming impressions, would express a desire
also to enjoy a sight of so rare a creature; upon which Waterlow was to say that that would be easy if she would come in
some day when Miss Francie was sitting. He would give her
two or three dates and Gaston would see that she didn't let
the opportunity pass. She would return alone (this time he
wouldn't go with her), and she would be as much struck as he
hoped. Everything depended on that, but it couldn't fail. The
girl would have to captivate her, but the girl could be trusted,
especially if she didn't know who the demonstrative French
lady was, with her fine plain face, her hair so flaxen as to be
nearly white, her vividly red lips and protuberant, light-
coloured eyes. Waterlow was to do no introducing and to reveal the visitor's identity only after she had gone. This was a
charge he grumbled at; he called the whole business an odious comedy, but his friend knew that if he undertook it he
would acquit himself honourably. After Mme. de Brécourt
had been captivated (the question of whether Francie would
be so received in advance no consideration), her brother
would throw off the mask and convince her that she must
now work with him. Another meeting would be arranged for
her with the girl (in which each would appear in her proper
character), and in short the plot would thicken.

   Gaston Probert's forecast of his difficulties revealed a considerable faculty for analysis, but that was not rare enough in
the French composition of things to make his friend stare. He
brought Suzanne de Brécourt, she was enchanted with the
portrait of the little American, and the rest of the drama
began to follow in its order. Mme. de Brécourt raved, to
Waterlow's face (she had no opinions behind people's backs),
about his mastery of his craft; she could say flattering things
to a man with an assurance altogether her own. She was the
reverse of egotistic and never spoke of herself; her success in
life sprang from a much cleverer selection of her pronouns.
Waterlow, who liked her and wanted to paint her ugliness (it

was so charming, as he would make it), had two opinions about her—one of which was that she knew a hundred times less than she thought (and even than her brother thought), of what she talked about; and the other that she was after all not such a humbug as she seemed. She passed in her family for a rank radical, a bold Bohemian; she picked up expressions out of newspapers, but her hands and feet were celebrated, and her behaviour was not. That of her sisters, as well, had never been effectively exposed.

"But she must be charming, your young lady," she said to Gaston, while she turned her head this way and that as she stood before Francie's image. "She looks like a piece of sculpture—or something cast in silver—of the time of Francis the First; something of Jean Goujon or Germain Pilon." The young men exchanged a glance, for this happened to be a capital comparison, and Gaston replied, in a detached way, that she was well worth seeing.

He went in to have a cup of tea with his sister on the day he knew she would have paid her second visit to the studio, and the first words she greeted him with were—"But she is admirable—*votre petite*—admirable, admirable!" There was a lady calling in the Place Beauvau at the moment—old Mme. d'Outreville, and she naturally asked who was the object of such enthusiasm. Gaston suffered Susan to answer this question; he wanted to hear what she would say. She described the girl almost as well as he would have done, from the point of view of the plastic, with a hundred technical and critical terms, and the old lady listened in silence, solemnly, rather coldly, as if she thought such talk a good deal of a *galimatias*: she belonged to the old-fashioned school and held that a young lady was sufficiently catalogued when it was said that she had a dazzling complexion or the finest eyes in the world.

"*Qu'est-ce que c'est que cette merveille?*" she inquired; to which Mme. de Brécourt replied that it was a little American whom her brother had dug up. "And what do you propose to do with her, may one ask?" Mme. d'Outreville demanded, looking at Gaston Probert with an eye which seemed to read his secret, so that for half a minute he was on the point of breaking out: "I propose to marry her—there!" But he contained himself, only mentioning for the present that he aspired to ascertain to what uses she was adapted; meanwhile, he added, he expected to look at her a good deal, in the measure in which she would allow him. "Ah, that may take you far!" the old lady exclaimed, as she got up to go; and Gaston glanced at his sister, to see if this idea struck her too. But she appeared almost provokingly exempt from alarm: if she had been suspicious it would have been easier to make his confession. When he came back from accompanying Mme. d'Outreville to her carriage he asked her if the girl at the studio had known who she was and if she had been frightened. Mme. de Brécourt stared; she evidently thought that kind of sensibility implied an initiation which a little American, accidentally encountered, could not possibly have. "Why should she be frightened? She wouldn't be even if she had known who I was; much less therefore when I was nothing for her."

"Oh, you were not nothing for her!" Gaston declared; and when his sister rejoined that he was too amiable he brought out his revelation. He had seen the young lady more often than he had told her; he had particularly wished that *she* should see her. Now he wanted his father and Jane and Margaret to do the same, and above all he wanted them to like her, even as she, Susan, liked her. He was delighted that she had been captivated—he had been captivated himself. Mme. de Brécourt protested that she had reserved her independence of judgment, and he answered that if she had thought Miss Dosson repulsive she might have expressed it in another way. When she inquired what he was talking about and what he wanted them all to do with her, he said: "I want you to treat her kindly, tenderly, for such as you see her I am thinking of making her my wife."

"Mercy on us—you haven't asked her?" cried Mme. de Brécourt.

"No, but I have asked her sister what she would say, and she tells me there would be no difficulty."

"Her sister?—the little woman with the big head?"

"Her head is rather out of drawing, but it isn't a part of the affair. She is very inoffensive and she would be devoted to me."

"For heaven's sake then keep quiet. She is as common as a dressmaker's bill."

"Not when you know her. Besides, that has nothing to do with Francie. You couldn't find words enough a moment ago to say that Francie is exquisite, and now you will be so good as to stick to that. Come, be intelligent!"

"Do you call her by her little name, like that?" Mme. de Brécourt asked, giving him another cup of tea.

"Only to you. She is perfectly simple. It is impossible to imagine anything better. And think of the delight of having that charming object before one's eyes—always, always! It makes a different thing of the future."

"My poor child," said Mme. de Brécourt, "you can't pick up a wife like that—the first little American that comes along. You know I hoped you wouldn't marry at all—what a pity I think it—for a man. At any rate, if you expect us to like Miss—what's her name?—Miss Fancy, all I can say is we won't. We can't!"

"I shall marry her then without your approbation."

"Very good. But if she deprives you of that (you have always had it, you are used to it, it's a part of your life), you will hate her at the end of a month."

"I don't care. I shall have had my month."

"And she—poor thing?"

"Poor thing, exactly! You will begin to pity her, and that will make you cultivate her, and that will make you find how adorable she is. Then you'll like her, then you'll love her, then you'll see how discriminating I have been, and we shall all be happy together again."

"But how can you possibly know, with such people, what you have got hold of?"

"By having the sense of delicate things. You pretend to have it, and yet in such a case as this you try to be stupid. Give that up; you might as well first as last, for the girl's an irresistible fact and it will be better to accept her than to let her accept you."

Gaston's sister asked him if Miss Dosson had a fortune, and he said he knew nothing about that. Her father apparently was rich, but he didn't mean to ask for a penny with her. American fortunes moreover were the last things to count upon; they had seen too many examples of that. "Papa will never listen to that," Mme. de Brécourt replied.

"Listen to what?"

"To your not finding out—to your not asking for settlements—*comme cela se fait*."

"Excuse me, papa will find out for himself; and he will know perfectly whether to ask or whether to leave it alone. That's the sort of thing he does know. And he also knows perfectly that I am very difficult to place."

"To place?"

"To find a wife for. I'm neither fish nor flesh. I have no country, no career, no future; I offer nothing; I bring nothing. What position under the sun do I confer? There's a fatuity in our talking as if we could make grand terms. You and the others are well enough: *qui prend mari prend pays*, and you have names which (at least so your husbands say) are tremendously illustrious. But papa and I—I ask you!"

"As a family *nous sommes très-bien*," said Mme. de Brécourt. "You know what we are—it doesn't need any explanation. We are as good as anything there is and have always been thought so. You might do anything you like."

"Well, I shall never take to marry a Frenchwoman."

"Thank you, my dear!" Mme. de Brécourt exclaimed.

"No sister of mine is really French," returned the young man.

"No brother of mine is really mad. Marry whomever you like," Susan went on; "only let her be the best of her kind. Let her be a lady. Trust me, I've studied life. That's the only thing that's safe."

"Francie is the equal of the first lady in the land."

"With that sister—with that hat? Never—never!"

"What's the matter with her hat?"

"The sister's told a story. It was a document—it described them, it classed them. And such a dialect as they speak!"

"My dear, her English is quite as good as yours. You don't even know how bad yours is," said Gaston Probert.

"Well, I don't say 'Parus' and I never asked an Englishman to marry me. You know what our feelings are," his companion pursued; "our convictions, our susceptibilities. We may be wrong—we may be hollow—we may be pretentious; we may not be able to say on what it all rests; but there we are, and the fact is insurmountable. It is simply impossible for us to live with vulgar people. It's a defect, no doubt; it's an immense inconvenience, and in the days we live in it's sadly against one's interest. But we are made like that and we must understand ourselves. It's of the very essence of our nature, and of yours exactly as much as of mine or of that of the others. Don't make a mistake about it—you'll prepare for yourself a bitter future. I know what becomes of us. We suffer, we go through tortures, we die!"

The accent of passionate prophecy was in Mme. de Brécourt's voice, but her brother made her no immediate answer, only indulging restlessly in several turns about the room. At last he observed, taking up his hat: "I shall come to an understanding with her to-morrow, and the next day, about this hour, I shall bring her to see you. Meanwhile please say nothing to any one."

Mme. de Brécourt looked at him a moment; he had his hand on the knob of the door. "What do you mean by her father's appearing rich? That's such a vague term. What do you suppose his means to be?"

"Ah, that's a question *she* would never ask!" cried the young man, passing out.

VI.

THE NEXT MORNING he found himself sitting on one of the red satin sofas beside Mr. Dosson, in this gentleman's private room at the Hôtel de l'Univers et de Cheltenham. Delia and Francie had established their father in the old quarters; they expected to spend the winter in Paris but they had not taken independent apartments, for they had an idea that when you lived that way it was grand but lonely—you didn't meet people on the staircase. The temperature was now such as to deprive the good gentleman of his usual resource of sitting in the court, and he had not yet discovered an effective substitute for this recreation. Without Mr. Flack, at the cafés, he felt too much like a non-consumer. But he was patient and ruminant; Gaston Probert grew to like him and tried to invent amusements for him; took him to see the great markets, the sewers and the Bank of France, and put him in the way of acquiring a beautiful pair of horses (it is perhaps not superfluous to say that this was a perfectly straight proceeding on the young man's part), which Mr. Dosson, little as he resembled a sporting character, found it a welcome pastime on fine afternoons to drive, with a highly scientific hand, from a smart Américaine, in the Bois de Boulogne. There was a reading-room at the banker's, where he spent hours engaged in a manner best known to himself, and he shared the great interest, the constant topic of his daughters—the portrait that was going forward in the Avenue de Villiers. This was the subject round which the thoughts of these young ladies clustered and their activity revolved; it gave a large scope to their faculty for endless repetition, for monotonous insistence, for vague and aimless discussion. On leaving Mme. de Brécourt Francie's lover had written to Delia that he desired half an hour's private conversation with her father on the morrow at half-past eleven; his impatience forbade him to wait for a more canonical hour. He asked her to be so good as to arrange that Mr. Dosson should be there to receive him and to keep Francie out of the way. Delia acquitted herself to the letter.

"Well, sir, what have you got to show?" asked Francie's

father, leaning far back on the sofa and moving nothing but his head, and that very little, toward his interlocutor. Probert was placed sidewise, a hand on each knee, almost facing him, on the edge of the seat.

"To show, sir—what do you mean?"

"What do you do for a living? How do you subsist?"

"Oh, comfortably enough. Of course it would be criminal in you not to satisfy yourself on that point. My income is derived from three sources. First, some property left me by my dear mother. Second, a legacy from my poor brother, who had inherited a small fortune from an old relation of ours who took a great fancy to him (he went to America to see her), and which he divided among the four of us in the will he made at the time of the war."

"The war—what war?" asked Mr. Dosson.

"Why the Franco-German——"

"Oh, *that* old war!" And Mr. Dosson almost laughed. "Well?" he softly continued.

"Then my father is so good as to make me a little allowance; and some day I shall have more—from him."

Mr. Dosson was silent a moment; then he observed, "Why, you seem to have fixed it so you live mostly on other folks."

"I shall never attempt to live on you, sir!" This was spoken with some vivacity by our young man; he felt the next moment that he had said something that might provoke a retort. But his companion only rejoined, mildly, impersonally:

"Well, I guess there won't be any trouble about that. And what does my daughter say?"

"I haven't spoken to her yet."

"Haven't spoken to her?"

"I thought it more orthodox to break ground with you first."

"Well, when I was after Mrs. Dosson I guess I spoke to her quick enough," Francie's father said, humorously. There was an element of reproach in this and Gaston Probert was mystified, for the inquiry about his means a moment before had been in the nature of a challenge. "How will you feel if she won't have you, after you have exposed yourself this way to me?" the old gentleman went on.

"Well, I have a sort of confidence. It may be vain, but God

grant not! I think she likes me personally, but what I am afraid of is that she may consider that she knows too little about me. She has never seen my people—she doesn't know what may be before her."

"Do you mean your family—the folks at home?" said Mr. Dosson. "Don't you believe that. Delia has moused around— *she* has found out. Delia's thorough!"

"Well, we are very simple, kindly, respectable people, as you will see in a day or two for yourself. My father and sisters will do themselves the honour to wait upon you," the young man declared, with a temerity the sense of which made his voice tremble.

"We shall be very happy to see them, sir," Mr. Dosson returned, cheerfully. "Well now, let's see," he added, musing sociably. "Don't you expect to embrace any regular occupation?"

Probert looked at him, smiling. "Have *you* anything of that sort, sir?"

"Well, you have me there!" Mr. Dosson admitted, with a comprehensive sigh. "It doesn't seem as if I required anything, I'm looked after so well. The fact is the girls support me."

"I shall not expect Miss Francie to support me," said Gaston Probert.

"You're prepared to enable her to live in the style to which she's accustomed?" And Mr. Dosson turned a speculative eye upon him.

"Well, I don't think she will miss anything. That is, if she does she will find other things instead."

"I presume she'll miss Delia, and even me, a little."

"Oh, it's easy to prevent that," said Gaston Probert.

"Well, of course we shall be on hand. Continue to reside in Paris?" Mr. Dosson went on.

"I will live anywhere in the world she likes. Of course my people are here—that's a great tie. I am not without hope that it may—with time—become a reason for your daughter."

"Oh, any reason'll do where Paris is concerned. Take some lunch?" Mr. Dosson added, looking at his watch.

They rose to their feet, but before they had gone many steps (the meals of this amiable family were now served in an adjoining room), the young man stopped his companion. "I can't tell you how kind I think it—the way you treat me, and how I am touched by your confidence. You take me just as I am, with no recommendation beyond my own word."

"Well, Mr. Probert, if we didn't like you we wouldn't smile on you. Recommendations in that case wouldn't be any good. And since we do like you there ain't any call for them either. I trust my daughters; if I didn't I'd have stayed at home. And if I trust them, and they trust you, it's the same as if *I* trusted you, ain't it?"

"I guess it is!" said Gaston, smiling.

His companion laid his hand on the door but he paused a moment. "Now are you very sure?"

"I thought I was, but you make me nervous."

"Because there was a gentleman here last year—I'd have put my money on *him*."

"A gentleman—last year?"

"Mr. Flack. You met him surely. A very fine man. I thought she favoured him."

"Seigneur Dieu!" Gaston Probert murmured, under his breath.

Mr. Dosson had opened the door; he made his companion pass into the little dining-room, where the table was spread for the noon-day breakfast. "Where are the chickens?" he inquired, disappointedly. Gaston thought at first that he missed a dish from the board, but he recognised the next moment the old man's usual designation of his daughters. These young ladies presently came in, but Francie looked away from Mr. Probert. The suggestion just dropped by her father had given him a shock (the idea of the girl's "favouring" the newspaperman was inconceivable), but the charming way she avoided his eye convinced him that he had nothing to fear from Mr. Flack.

That night (it had been an exciting day), Delia remarked to her sister that of course she could draw back: upon which Francie repeated the expression, interrogatively, not understanding it. "You can send him a note, saying you won't," Delia explained.

"Won't marry him?"

"Gracious, no! Won't go to see his sister. You can tell him it's her place to come to see you first."

"Oh, I don't care," said Francie, wearily.

Delia looked at her a moment very gravely. "Is that the way you answered him when he asked you?"

"I'm sure I don't know. He could tell you best."

"If you were to speak to me that way I should have said, 'Oh, well, if you don't want it any more than that!'"

"Well, I wish it was you," said Francie.

"That Mr. Probert was me?"

"No; that you were the one he liked."

"Francie Dosson, are you thinking of Mr. Flack?" her sister broke out, suddenly.

"No, not much."

"Well then, what's the matter?"

"You have ideas and opinions; you know whose place it is and what's due and what isn't. You could meet them all."

"Why, how can you say, when that's just what I'm trying to find out!"

"It doesn't matter any way; it will never come off," said Francie.

"What do you mean by that?"

"He'll give me up in a few weeks. I shall do something."

"If you say that again I shall think you do it on purpose!" Delia declared. "*Are* you thinking of George Flack?" she repeated in a moment.

"Oh, do leave him alone!" Francie replied, in one of her rare impatiences.

"Then why are you so queer?"

"Oh, I'm tired!" said Francie, turning away. And this was the simple truth; she was tired of the consideration her sister saw fit to devote to the question of Mr. Probert's not having, since their return to Paris, brought his belongings to see them. She was overdone with Delia's theories on this subject, which varied from day to day, from the assertion that he was keeping his intercourse with his American friends hidden from them because they were uncompromising, in their grandeur, to the doctrine that that grandeur would descend some day upon the Hôtel de l'Univers et de Cheltenham and carry Francie away in a blaze of glory. Sometimes Delia put forth the view that they ought to make certain of Gaston's omissions the ground of a challenge; at other times she opined that they ought to take no notice of them. Francie, in this connection, had no theories, no impulses of her own; and now she was all at once happy and freshly glad and in love and sceptical and frightened and indifferent. Her lover had talked to her but little about his kinsfolk, and she had noticed this circumstance the more because of a remark dropped by Charles Waterlow to the effect that he and his father were great friends: the word seemed to her odd in that application. She knew Gaston saw that gentleman, and the exalted ladies Mr. Probert's daughters, very often, and she therefore took for granted that they knew he saw her. But the most he had done was to say they would come and see her like a shot if once they should believe they could trust her. She had wished to know what he meant by their trusting her, and he had explained that it would appear to them too good to be true— that she should be kind to *him*: something exactly of that sort was what they dreamed of for him. But they had dreamed before and been disappointed, and now they were on their guard. From the moment they should feel they were on solid ground they would join hands and dance round her. Francie's answer to this fanciful statement was that she didn't know what the young man was talking about, and he indulged in no attempt on that occasion to render his meaning more clear; the consequence of which was that he felt he made a poor appearance. His uneasiness had not passed away, for many things in truth were dark to him. He could not see his father fraternising with Mr. Dosson, he could not see Margaret and Jane recognising an alliance in which Delia was one of the allies. He had answered for them because that was the only thing to do; and this only just failed to be criminally reckless. What saved it was the hope he founded upon Mme. de Brécourt and the sense of how well he could answer to the others for Francie. He considered that Susan had, in her first judgment of this young lady, committed herself; she had really comprehended her, and her subsequent protest when she found what was in his heart had been a retractation which he would make her in turn retract. The girl had been revealed to her, and she would come round. A simple interview with Francie would suffice for this result: he promised himself that at the end of half an hour she should be an enthusiastic convert. At the end of an hour she would believe that she herself had invented the match—had discovered the damsel. He would pack her off to the others as the author of the project; she would take it all upon herself, would represent her brother even as a little tepid. *She* would show nothing of that sort, but boast of her wisdom and energy; and she would enjoy the comedy so that she would forget she had opposed him even for a moment. Gaston Probert was a very honourable young man, but his programme involved a good many fibs.

VII.

IT MAY as well be said at once that it was eventually carried out, and that in the course of a fortnight old Mr. Probert and his daughters alighted successively at the Hôtel de l'Univers et de Cheltenham. Francie's visit with her intended to Mme. de Brécourt bore exactly the fruit the young man had foreseen and was followed the very next day by a call from this lady. She took Francie out with her in her carriage and kept her the whole afternoon, driving her over half Paris, chattering with her, kissing her, delighting in her, telling her they were already sisters, paying her compliments which made the girl envy her art of beautiful expression. After she had carried her home the countess rushed off to her father's reflecting with pleasure that at that hour she should probably find her sister Marguerite there. Mme. de Cliché was with the old man in fact (she had three days in the week for coming to the Cours la Reine); she sat near him in the firelight, telling him presumably her troubles; for Maxime de Cliché was not quite the pearl that they originally had supposed. Mme. de Brécourt knew what Marguerite did whenever she took that little ottoman and drew it close to her father's chair: she gave way to her favourite vice, that of dolefulness, which lengthened her long face more; it was unbecoming, if she only knew it. The family was intensely united, as we know; but that did not prevent Mme. de Brécourt's having a certain sympathy for Maxime: he too was one of themselves and she asked herself what *she* would have done if she had been a well-constituted man with a wife whose cheeks were like decks in a high sea. It was the twilight hour in the winter days, before the lamps, that especially brought her out; then she began her plaintive, complicated stories, to which her father listened with such angelic patience. Mme. de Brécourt liked his particular room in the old house in the Cours la Reine; it reminded her of her mother's life and her young days and her dead brother and the feelings connected with her first going into the world. Alphonse and she had had an apartment, by her father's kindness, under that familiar roof, so that she continued to pop in and out, full of her fresh impressions of society, just as she had done when she was a girl. She broke into her sister's confidences now; she announced her *trouvaille* and did battle for it bravely.

Five days later (there had been lively work in the meantime; Gaston turned so pale at moments that she feared it would all result in a mortal illness for him and Marguerite shed gallons of tears), Mr. Probert went to see the Dossons with his son. Mme. de Brécourt paid them another visit, a kind of official affair as she deemed it, accompanied by her husband; and the Baron de Douves and his wife, written to by Gaston, by his father and by Margaret and Susan, came up from the country full of tension and responsibility. M. de Douves was the person who took the family, all round, most seriously and most deprecated anything in the nature of crude and precipitate action. He was a very small black gentleman, with thick eyebrows and high heels (in the country, in the mud, he wore *sabots* with straw in them), who was suspected by his friends of believing that he looked like Louis XIV. It is perhaps a proof that something of the quality of this monarch was really recognised in him that no one had ever ventured to clear up this point by a question. *"La famille c'est moi"* appeared to be his tacit formula, and he carried his umbrella (he had very bad ones), with a kind of sceptral air. Mme. de Brécourt went so far as to believe that his wife, in confirmation of this, took herself in a manner for Mme. de Maintenon: she had lapsed into a provincial existence as she might have harked back to the seventeenth century; the world she lived in seemed about as far away. She was the largest, heaviest member of the family, and in the Vendée she was thought majestic, in spite of old clothes, of which she was fond and which added to her look of having come down from a remote past or reverted to it. She was at bottom an excellent woman, but she wrote *roy* and *foy* like her husband, and the action of her mind was wholly restricted to questions of relationship and alliance. She had an extraordinary patience of research and tenacity of grasp of a clue, and viewed people solely in the light projected upon them by others; that is, not as good or wicked, ugly or handsome, wise or foolish, but as grandsons, nephews, uncles and aunts, brothers and sisters-in-law, cousins and second cousins. There was a certain expectation that she would leave memoirs. In Mme. de Brécourt's eyes this pair were very shabby, they did not *payer de mine*—they fairly smelt of their province; "but for the reality of the thing," she often said to herself, "they are worth all of us. We are diluted and they are pure, and any one with an eye would see it." "The thing" was the legitimist principle, the ancient faith and even, a little, the grand air.

The Marquis de Cliché did his duty with his wife, who mopped the decks, as Susan said, for the occasion, and was entertained in the red satin drawing-room by Mr. Dosson, Delia and Francie. Mr. Dosson wanted to go out when he heard of the approach of Gaston's relations, and the young man had to instruct him that this wouldn't do. The apartment in question had had a various experience, but it had probably never witnessed stranger doings than these laudable social efforts. Gaston was taught to feel that his family made a great sacrifice for him, but in a very few days he said to himself that he was safe, now they knew the worst. They made the sacrifice, they definitely agreed to it, but they judged it well that he should measure the full extent of it. "Gaston must never, never, never be allowed to forget what we have done for him:" Mme. de Brécourt told him that Marguerite de Cliché had expressed herself in that sense, at one of the family conclaves from which he had been absent. These high commissions sat, for several days, with great frequency, and the young man could feel that if there was help for him in discussion his case was promising. He flattered himself that he showed infinite patience and tact, and his expenditure of the latter quality in particular was in itself his only reward, for it was impossible he should tell Francie what arts he had to practise for her. He liked to think however that he practised them successfully; for he held that it was by such arts the civilised man is distinguished from the savage. What they cost him was made up simply in this—that his private irritation produced a kind of cheerful glow in regard to Mr. Dosson and Delia, whom he could not defend nor lucidly explain nor make people like, but whom he had ended, after so many days of familiar intercourse, by liking extremely himself. The way to get on with them—it was an immense simplification—was just to love them; one could do that even if one couldn't talk with them. He succeeded in making Mme. de Brécourt seize this *nuance*; she embraced the idea with her quick inflammability. "Yes," she said, "we must insist on their positive, not on their negative merits: their infinite generosity, their native delicacy. Their native delicacy, above all; we must work that!" And the brother and sister excited each other magnanimously to this undertaking. Sometimes, it must be added, they exchanged a glance which expressed a sudden slightly alarmed sense of the responsibility they had put on.

On the day Mr. Probert called at the Hôtel de l'Univers et de Cheltenham with his son, the pair walked away together, back to the Cours la Reine, without any immediate conversation. All that was said was some words of Mr. Probert's, with Gaston's rejoinder, as they crossed the Place de la Concorde.

"We should have to have them to dinner."

The young man noted his father's conditional, as if his acceptance of the Dossons were not yet complete; but he guessed all the same that the sight of them had not made a difference for the worse: they had let the old gentleman down more easily than was to have been feared. The call had not been noisy—a confusion of sounds; which was very happy, for Mr. Probert was particular in this—he could bear French noise but he could not bear American. As for English, he maintained that there was none. Mr. Dosson had scarcely spoken to him and yet had remained perfectly placid, which was exactly what Gaston would have chosen. Francie's lover knew moreover (though he was a little disappointed that no charmed exclamation should have been dropped as they quitted the hotel), that her spell had worked: it was impossible the old man should not have liked her.

"Ah, do ask them, and let it be very soon," he replied. "They'll like it so much."

"And whom can they meet—who can meet *them*?"

"Only the family—all of us: *au complet*. Other people we can have later."

"All of us, *au complet*—that makes eight. And the three of them," said Mr. Probert. Then he added, "Poor creatures!" This exclamation gave Gaston much pleasure; he passed his hand into his father's arm. It promised well; it denoted a sen-

timent of tenderness for the dear little Dossons, confronted
with a row of fierce French critics, judged by standards that
they had never even heard of. The meeting of the two parents
had not made the problem of their commerce any more clear;
but young Probert was reminded freshly by his father's ejaculation of that characteristic kindness which was really what
he had built upon. The old gentleman, heaven knew, had
prejudices, but if they were numerous, and some of them very
curious, they were not rigid. He had also such nice inconsistent feelings, such irrepressible indulgences, and they would
ease everything off. He was in short an old darling, and with
an old darling, in the long run, one was always safe. When
they reached the house in the Cours la Reine Mr. Probert
said: "I think you told me you are dining out."

"Yes, with our friends."

" 'Our friends?' *Comme vous y allez!* Come in and see me,
then, on your return; but not later than half-past ten."

From this the young man saw that he had swallowed the
dose; if he had made up his mind that it wouldn't do he
would have announced the circumstance without more delay.
This reflection was most agreeable, for Gaston was perfectly
aware of how little he himself would have enjoyed a struggle.
He would have carried it through, but he could not bear to
think of it, and the sense that he was spared it made him feel
at peace with all the world. The dinner at the hotel became a
little banquet in honour of this state of things, especially as
Francie and Delia raved, as they said, about his papa.

"Well, I expected something nice, but he goes far beyond,"
Delia remarked. "That's my idea of a gentleman."

"Ah, for that——!" said Gaston.

"He's so sweet. I'm not a bit afraid of him," Francie
declared.

"Why should you be?"

"Well, I am of you," the girl went on.

"Much you show it!" her lover exclaimed.

"Yes, I am," she insisted, "at the bottom of all."

"Well, that's what a lady should be—of her husband."

"Well, I don't know; I'm more afraid than that. You'll see."

"I wish you were afraid of talking nonsense," said Gaston
Probert.

Mr. Dosson made no observation whatever about their honourable visitor; he listened in genial, unprejudiced silence. It is a sign of his prospective son-in-law's perfect comprehension of him that Gaston knew this silence not to be in any degree restrictive: it did not mean that he had not been pleased. Mr. Dosson had simply nothing to say; he had not, like Gaston, a sensitive plate in his brain, and the important events of his life had never been personal impressions. His mind had had absolutely no history of that sort, and Mr. Probert's appearance had not produced a revolution. If the young man had asked him how he liked his father he would have said, at the most, "Oh, I guess he's all right!" But what was more candid even than this, in Gaston's view (and it was quite touchingly so), was the attitude of the good gentleman and his daughters toward the others, Mesdames de Douves, de Brécourt and de Cliché and their husbands, who had now all filed before them. They believed that the ladies and the gentlemen alike had covered them with endearments, were candidly, gushingly glad to make their acquaintance. They had not in the least seen what was manner, the minimum of decent profession, and what the subtle resignation of old races who have known a long historical discipline and have conventional forms for their feelings—forms resembling singularly little the feelings themselves. Francie took people at their word when they told her that the whole *manière d'être* of her family inspired them with an irresistible sympathy: that was a speech of which Mme. de Cliché had been capable, speaking as if for all the Proberts and for the old noblesse of France. It would not have occurred to the girl that such things need have been said as a mere garniture. Her lover, whose life had been surrounded with garniture and who therefore might have been expected not to notice it, had a fresh sense of it now: he reflected that manner might be a very misleading symbol, might cover pitfalls and bottomless gulfs, when it had attained that perfection and corresponded so little to fact. What he had wanted was that his people should be very civil at the hotel; but with such a high standard of compliment where after all was sincerity? And without sincerity how could people get on together when it came to their settling down to common life? Then the Dossons might have surprises, and the surprises would be painful in proportion as their present innocence was great. As to the high standard itself there was no manner of doubt; it was magnificent in its way.

VIII.

WHEN, on coming home the evening after his father had made the acquaintance of the Dossons, Gaston went into the room in which the old man habitually sat, Mr. Probert said, laying down his book and keeping on his glasses: "Of course you will go on living with me. You must understand that I don't consent to your going away. You will have to occupy the rooms that Susan and Alphonse had."

Gaston observed with pleasure the transition from the conditional to the future and also the circumstance that his father was quietly reading, according to his custom when he sat at home of an evening. This proved he was not too much off the hinge. He read a great deal, and very serious books; works about the origin of things—of man, of institutions, of speech, of religion. This habit he had taken up more particularly since the circle of his social life had grown so much smaller. He sat there alone, turning his pages softly, contentedly, with the lamp-light shining on his refined old head and embroidered dressing-gown. Formerly he was out every night in the week—Gaston was perfectly aware that to many dull people he must even have appeared a little frivolous. He was essentially a social animal, and indeed—except perhaps poor Jane, in her damp old castle in Brittany—they were all social animals. That was doubtless part of the reason why the family had acclimatised itself in France. They had affinities with a society of conversation; they liked general talk and old high *salons*, slightly tarnished and dim, containing precious relics, where there was a circle round the fire and winged words flew about and there was always some clever person before the chimney-piece, holding or challenging the rest. That figure, Gaston knew, especially in the days before he could see for himself, had very often been his father, the lightest and most amiable specimen of the type that liked to take possession of the hearthrug. People left it to him; he was so transparent, like a glass screen, and he never triumphed in argument. His word on most subjects was not felt to be the last (it was usually not more conclusive than a shrugging, inarticulate resignation, an "Ah, you know, what will you have?"); but he had been none the less a part of the essence of some dozen good houses, most of them over the river, in the conservative *faubourg*, and several to-day emptied receptacles, extinguished fires. They made up Mr. Probert's world—a world not too small for him and yet not too large, though some of them supposed themselves to be very great institutions. Gaston knew the succession of events that had helped to make a difference, the most salient of which were the death of his brother, the death of his mother and above all perhaps the extinction of Mme. de Marignac, to whom the old gentleman used still to go three or four evenings out of the seven and sometimes even in the morning besides. Gaston was well aware what a place she had held in his father's life and affection, how they had grown up together (her people had been friends of his grandfather when that fine old Southern worthy came, a widower with a young son and several negroes, to take his pleasure in Paris in the time of Louis Philippe), and how much she had had to do with marrying his sisters. He was not ignorant that her friendship and all its exertions were often mentioned as explaining their position, so remarkable in a society in which they had begun after all as outsiders. But he would have guessed, even if he had not been told, what his father said to that. To offer the Proberts a position was to carry water to the fountain; they had not left their own behind them in Carolina; it had been large enough to stretch across the sea. As to what it was in Carolina there was no need of being explicit. This adoptive Parisian was by nature presupposing, but he was admirably gentle (that was why they let him talk to them before the fire—he was such a sympathising oracle), and after the death of his wife and of Mme. de Marignac, who had been *her* friend too, he was gentler than before. Gaston had been able to see that it made him care less for everything (except indeed the true faith, to which he drew still closer), and this increase of indifference doubtless helped to explain his collapse in relation to common Americans.

"We shall be thankful for any rooms you will give us," the young man said. "We shall fill out the house a little, and won't that be rather an improvement, shrunken as you and I have become?"

"You will fill it out a good deal, I suppose, with Mr. Dosson and the other girl."

"Ah, Francie won't give up her father and sister, certainly; and what should you think of her if she did? But they are not intrusive; they are essentially modest people; they won't put themselves upon us. They have great natural discretion."

"Do you answer for that? Susan does; she is always assuring one of it," Mr. Probert said. "The father has so much that he wouldn't even speak to me."

"He didn't know what to say to you."

"How then shall I know what to say to him?"

"Ah, you always know!" Gaston exclaimed.

"How will that help us if he doesn't know what to answer?"

"You will draw him out—he is full of *bonhomie*."

"Well, I won't quarrel with your *bonhomme* (if he's silent—there are much worse faults), nor even with the fat young lady, though she is evidently vulgar. It is not for ourselves I am afraid; it's for them. They will be very unhappy."

"Never, never!" said Gaston. "They are too simple. They are not morbid. And don't you like Francie? You haven't told me so," he added in a moment.

"She says 'Parus,' my dear boy."

"Ah, to Susan too that seemed the principal obstacle. But she has got over it. I mean Susan has got over the obstacle. We shall make her speak French; she has a capital disposition for it; her French is already almost as good as her English."

"That oughtn't to be difficult. What will you have? Of course she is very pretty and I'm sure she is good. But I won't tell you she is a marvel, because you must remember (you young fellows think your own point of view and your own experience everything), that I have seen beauties without number. I have known the most charming women of our time—women of an order to which Miss Francie, *con rispetto parlando*, will never begin to belong. I'm difficult about women—how can I help it? Therefore when you pick up a little American girl at an inn and bring her to us as a miracle, I feel how standards alter. *J'ai vu mieux que ça, mon cher.* However, I accept everything to-day, as you know;

when once one has lost one's enthusiasm everything is the same, and one might as well perish by the sword as by famine."

"I hoped she would fascinate you on the spot," Gaston remarked, rather ruefully.

"'Fascinate'—the language you fellows use!"

"Well, she will yet."

"She will never know at least that she doesn't: I will promise you that," said Mr. Probert.

"Ah, be sincere with her, father—she's worth it!" his son broke out.

When the old gentleman took that tone, the tone of vast experience and a fastidiousness justified by ineffable recollections, Gaston was more provoked than he could say, though he was also considerably amused, for he had a good while since made up his mind that there was an element of stupidity in it. It was fatuous to square one's self so serenely in the absence of a sense: so far from being fine it was gross not to *feel* Francie Dosson. He thanked God *he* did. He didn't know what old frumps his father might have frequented (the style of 1830, with long curls in front, a vapid simper, a Scotch plaid dress and a body, in a point suggestive of twenty whalebones, coming down to the knees), but he could remember Mme. de Marignac's Tuesdays and Thursdays and Fridays, with Sundays and other days thrown in, and the taste that prevailed in that *milieu*: the books they admired, the verses they read and recited, the pictures, great heaven! they thought good, and the three busts of the lady of the house, in different corners (as a Diana, a Druidess and a *Croyante*: her shoulders were supposed to make up for her head), effigies which to-day—even the least bad, Canova's—would draw down a public castigation upon their authors.

"And what else is she worth?" Mr. Probert asked, after a momentary hesitation.

"How do you mean, what else?"

"Her immense prospects, that's what Susan has been putting forward. Susan's insistence on them was mainly what brought over Jane. Do you mind my speaking of them?"

Gaston was obliged to recognise, privately, the importance of Jane's having been brought over, but he hated to hear it spoken of as if he were under an obligation to it. "To whom, sir?" he asked.

"Oh, only to you."

"You can't do less than Mr. Dosson. As I told you, he waived the question of money and he was superb. We can't be more mercenary than he."

"He waived the question of his own, you mean?" said Mr. Probert.

"Yes, and of yours. But it will be all right." The young man flattered himself that that was as far as he was willing to go, in the way of bribery.

"Well, it's your affair—or your sisters'," his father returned. "It's their idea that it will be all right."

"I should think they would be weary of chattering!" Gaston exclaimed, impatiently.

Mr. Probert looked at him a moment with a vague surprise, but he only said, "I think they are. But the period of discussion is over. We have taken the jump." He added, in a moment, as if from the desire to say something more conciliatory: "Alphonse and Maxime are quite of your opinion."

"Of my opinion?"

"That she is charming."

"Confound them, then, I'm not of theirs!" The form of this rejoinder was childishly perverse, and it made Mr. Probert stare again; but it belonged to one of the reasons for which his children regarded him as an old darling that Gaston could feel after an instant that he comprehended it. The old man said nothing, but took up his book, and his son, who had been standing before the fire, went out of the room. His abstention from protest at Gaston's petulance was the more commendable as he was capable, for his part, of thinking it important that *ces messieurs* should like the little girl at the hotel. Gaston was not, and it would have seemed to him a proof that he was in servitude indeed if he had accepted such an assurance as that as if it mattered. This was especially the case as his father's mention of the approval of two of his brothers-in-law appeared to point to a possible disapproval on the part of the third. Francie's lover cared as little whether she displeased M. de Brécourt as he cared whether she displeased Maxime and Raoul. The old gentleman continued to read, and in a few moments Gaston came back. He had expressed surprise, just before, that his sisters should have found so much to discuss in the idea of his marriage, but he looked at his father now with an air of having more to say—an intimation that the subject must not be considered as exhausted. "It seems rather odd to me that you should all appear to accept the step I am about to take as a sort of disagreeable necessity, when I myself hold that I have been so exceedingly fortunate."

Mr. Probert lowered his book accommodatingly and rested his eyes upon the fire. "You won't be content till we are enthusiastic. She seems a good girl certainly, and in that you are fortunate."

"I don't think you can tell me what would be better—what you would have preferred," said the young man.

"What I would have preferred? In the first place you must remember that I was not madly impatient to see you married."

"I can imagine that, and yet I can't imagine that, as things have turned out, you shouldn't be struck with the felicity. To get something so charming, and to get it of our own species."

"Of our own species? *Tudieu!*" said Mr. Probert looking up.

"Surely it is infinitely fresher and more amusing for me to marry an American. There's a dreariness in the way we have Gallicised."

"Against Americans I have nothing to say; some of them are the best thing the world contains. That's precisely why one can choose. They are far from being all like that."

"Like what, dear father?"

"*Comme ces gens-là.* You know that if they were French, being otherwise what they are, one wouldn't look at them."

"Indeed one would; they would be such curiosities."

"Well, perhaps they are sufficiently so as it is," said Mr. Probert, with a little conclusive sigh.

"Yes, let them pass for that. They will surprise you."

"Not too much, I hope!" cried the old man, opening his volume again.

It will doubtless not startle the reader to learn that the com-

plexity of things among the Proberts was such as to make it
impossible for Gaston to proceed to the celebration of his
nuptials, with all the needful circumstances of material preparation and social support, before some three months should
have expired. He chafed however but moderately at the delay,
for he reflected that it would give Francie time to endear herself to his whole circle. It would also have advantages for the
Dossons; it would enable them to establish by simple but effective arts the *modus vivendi* with that rigid body. It would in
short help every one to get used to everything. Mr. Dosson's
designs and Delia's took no articulate form; what was mainly
clear to Gaston was that his future wife's relatives had as yet
no sense of disconnection. He knew that Mr. Dosson would
do whatever Delia liked and that Delia would like to "start"
her sister. Whether or no she expected to be present at the
finish, she had a definite purpose of seeing the beginning of
the race. Mr. Probert notified Mr. Dosson of what he proposed to "do" for his son, and Mr. Dosson appeared more
amused than anything else at the news. He announced, in
return, no intentions in regard to Francie, and his queer silence was the cause of another convocation of the house of
Probert. Here Mme. de Brécourt's valorous spirit won another victory; she maintained, as she informed her brother,
that there was no possible policy but a policy of confidence.
"Lord help us, is that what they call confidence?" the young
man exclaimed, guessing the way they all looked at each
other; and he wondered how they would look next at poor
Mr. Dosson. Fortunately he could always fall back, for reassurance, upon that revelation of their perfect manners;
though indeed he thoroughly knew that on the day they
should really attempt interference—make a row which might
render him helpless and culminate in a rupture—their courtesy would show its finest flower.

Mr. Probert's property was altogether in the United States:
he resembled various other persons to whom American impressions are mainly acceptable in the form of dividends. The
manner in which he desired to benefit his son on the occasion
of the latter's marriage rendered certain visitations and rein-
vestments necessary in that country. It had long been his conviction that his affairs needed looking into; they had gone on

for years and years without an overhauling. He had thought of going back to see, but now he was too old and too tired and the effort was impossible. There was nothing for it but for Gaston to go, and go quickly, though the moment was rather awkward. The idea was communicated to him and the necessity accepted; then the plan was relinquished: it seemed such a pity he should not wait till after his marriage, when he would be able to take Francie with him. Francie would be such an introducer. This postponement would have taken effect had it not suddenly come out that Mr. Dosson himself wanted to go for a few weeks, in consequence of some news (it was a matter of business), that he had unexpectedly received. It was further revealed that that course presented difficulties, for he could not leave his daughters alone, especially in such a situation. Not only would such a proceeding have given scandal to the Proberts, but Gaston learned, with a good deal of surprise and not a little amusement, that Delia, in consequence of peculiar changes now wrought in her view of things, would have felt herself obliged to protest on the score of propriety. He called her attention to the fact that nothing would be more simple than, in the interval, for Francie to go and stay with Susan or Margaret; Delia herself in that case would be free to accompany her father. But this young lady declared that nothing would induce her to quit the European continent until she had seen her sister through, and Gaston shrank from proposing that she too should spend five weeks in the Place Beauvau or the Rue de Lille. Moreover he was startled, he was a good deal mystified, by the perverse, unsociable way in which Francie asserted that, as yet, she would not lend herself to any staying. *After*, if he liked, but not till then. And she would not at the moment give the reasons of her refusal; it was only very positive and even quite passionate.

All this left her intended no alternative but to say to Mr. Dosson, "I am not such a fool as I look. If you will coach me properly, and trust me, I will rush across and transact your business as well as my father's." Strange as it appeared, Francie could resign herself to this separation from her lover—it would last six or seven weeks—rather than accept the hospitality of his sisters. Mr. Dosson trusted him; he said to him,

"Well, sir, you've got a big brain," at the end of a morning they spent with papers and pencils; upon which Gaston made his preparations to sail. Before he left Paris Francie, to do her justice, confided to him that her objection to going in such an intimate way even to Mme. de Brécourt's had been founded on a fear that in close quarters she would do something that would make them all despise her. Gaston replied, in the first place, that this was gammon and in the second he wanted to know if she expected never to be in close quarters with her new kinsfolk. "Ah, yes, but then it will be safer—we shall be married!" she returned. This little incident occurred three days before the young man started; but what happened just the evening previous was that, stopping for a last word at the Hôtel de l'Univers et de Cheltenham on his way to take the night express to London (he was to sail from Liverpool), he found Mr. George Flack sitting in the red satin saloon. The correspondent of the Reverberator had come back.

IX.

MR. FLACK'S relations with his old friends did not, after his appearance in Paris, take on that familiarity and frequency which had marked their intercourse a year before: he let them know frankly that he could easily see the situation was quite different. They had got into the high set and they didn't care about the past: he alluded to the past as if it had been rich in mutual vows, in pledges now repudiated. "What's the matter? Won't you come round there with us some day?" Mr. Dosson asked; not having perceived for himself any reason why the young journalist should not be a welcome and congruous figure in the Cours la Reine.

Delia wanted to know what Mr. Flack was talking about: didn't he know a lot of people that they didn't know and wasn't it natural they should have their own society? The young man's treatment of the question was humorous, and it was with Delia that the discussion mainly went forward. When he maintained that the Dossons had "shed" him, Mr. Dosson exclaimed, "Well, I guess you'll grow again!" And Francie observed that it was no use for him to pose as a martyr, inasmuch as he knew perfectly well that with all the celebrated people he saw and the way he flew round he had the most enchanting time. She was aware she was a good deal less accessible than she had been the previous spring, for Mesdames de Brécourt and de Cliché (the former much more than the latter) took a considerable number of her hours. In spite of her protest to Gaston against a premature intimacy with his sisters, she spent whole days in their company (they had so much to tell her about what her new life would be, and it was generally very pleasant), and she thought it would be nice if in these intervals he should give himself to her father and even to Delia as he used to do.

But the flaw of a certain insincerity in Mr. Flack's nature seemed to be established by his present tendency to rare visits. He evidently did not care for her father for himself, and though Mr. Dosson was the least querulous of men she divined that he suspected their old companion had fallen away. There were no more wanderings in public places, no more tryings of new cafés. Mr. Dosson used to look sometimes as he had looked of old when George Flack "located" them somewhere; as if he expected to see their sharp cicerone rushing back to them, with his drab overcoat flying in the wind; but this expectation usually died away. He missed Gaston because Gaston this winter had so often ordered his dinner for him, and his society was not sought by the count and the marquis, whose mastery of English was small and their other distractions great. Mr. Probert, it was true, had shown something of a fraternising spirit; he had come twice to the hotel, since his son's departure, and he had said, smiling and reproachful, "You neglect us, you neglect us!" Mr. Dosson had not understood what he meant by this till Delia explained after the visitor withdrew, and even then the remedy for the neglect, administered two or three days later, had not borne any particular fruit. Mr. Dosson called alone, instructed by his daughter, in the Cours la Reine, but Mr. Probert was not at home. He only left a card, on which Delia had superscribed in advance the words "So sorry!" Her father had told her he would give the card if she wanted, but he would have nothing to do with the writing. There was a discussion as to whether Mr. Probert's remark was an allusion to a deficiency of politeness on the article of his sons-in-law. Ought not Mr. Dosson perhaps to call personally, and not simply through the medium of the visits paid by his daughters to their wives, on Messieurs de Brécourt and de Cliché? Once, when this subject came up in George Flack's presence, the old man said he would go round if Mr. Flack would accompany him. "All right!" said Mr. Flack, and this conception became a reality, with the accidental abatement that the objects of the demonstration were absent. "Suppose they get in?" Delia had said lugubriously to her sister.

"Well, what if they do?" Francie asked.

"Why, the count and the marquis won't be interested in Mr. Flack."

"Well then, perhaps he will be interested in them. He can write something about them. They will like that."

"Do you think they would?" Delia demanded, in solemn dubiousness.

"Why, yes, if he should say fine things."

"They do like fine things," said Delia. "They get off so many themselves. Only the way Mr. Flack does it—it's a different style."

"Well, people like to be praised in any style."

"That's so," Delia rejoined, musingly.

One afternoon, coming in about three o'clock, Mr. Flack found Francie alone. She had expressed a wish, after luncheon, for a couple of hours of independence: she intended to write to Gaston, and having accidentally missed a post promised herself that her letter should be of double its usual length. Her companions respected her desire for solitude, Mr. Dosson taking himself off to his daily session in the reading-room of the American bank and Delia (the girls had now a luxurious coach at their command) driving away to the dressmaker's, a frequent errand, to superintend and urge forward the progress of her sister's wedding-clothes. Francie was not skilled in composition; she wrote slowly and in addressing her lover had a painful sense of literary responsibility. Her father and Delia had a theory that when she shut herself up that way she poured forth wonderful pages—it was part of her high cultivation. At any rate, when George Flack was ushered in she was still bending over her blotting-book on one of the gilded tables and there was an inkstain on her pointed forefinger. It was no disloyalty to Gaston but only at the most a sense of weariness in regard to the epistolary form that made her glad to see her visitor. She didn't know how to finish her letter; but Mr. Flack seemed in a manner to terminate it.

"I wouldn't have ventured to propose this, but I guess I can do with it, now it's come," the young man announced.

"What can you do with?" she asked, wiping her pen.

"Well this happy chance. Just you and me together."

"I don't know what it's a chance for."

"Well, for me to be a little less miserable for a quarter of an hour. It makes me so to see you look so happy."

"It makes you miserable?"

"You ought to understand, when I say something magnanimous." And settling himself on the sofa Mr. Flack continued, "Well, how do you get on without Mr. Probert?"

"Very well indeed, thank you."

The tone in which the girl spoke was not an encouragement to free pleasantry, so that if Mr. Flack continued his
inquiries it was in a guarded and respectful manner. He was
eminently capable of reflecting that it was not in his interest
to strike her as indiscreet and profane; he only wanted to appear friendly, worthy of confidence. At the same time he was
not averse to the idea that she should still perceive in him a
certain sense of injury, and that could be indicated only by a
touch of bitterness here and there. The injury, the bitterness
might make her pity him. "Well, you are in the *grand monde*, I
suppose," he resumed at last, not with an air of derision but
resignedly, sympathetically.

"Oh, I'm not in anything; I'm just where I've always been."

"I'm sorry; I hoped you would tell me about it," said Mr.
Flack, gravely.

"You think too much of that. What do you want to know
about it for?"

"Dear Miss Francie, a poor devil of a journalist who has to
get his living by studying up things, he has to think too
much, sometimes, in order to think, or at any rate to do,
enough. We find out what we can—as we can."

Francie listened to this as if it had had the note of pathos.
"What do you want to study up?"

"Everything! I take in everything. It all depends on my opportunity. I try and learn—I try and improve. Every one has
something to tell, and I listen and watch and make my profit
of it. I hoped *you* would have something to tell. I don't believe but what you've seen a good deal of new life. You won't
pretend they haven't roped you in, charming as you are."

"Do you mean if they've been kind to me? They've been
very kind," Francie said. "They want to do even more than
I'll let them."

"Ah, why won't you let them?" George Flack asked, almost
coaxingly.

"Well, I do," the girl went on. "You can't resist them, really; they have such lovely ways."

"I should like to hear you talk about their ways," her companion observed, after a silence.

"Oh, I could talk enough if once I were to begin. But I
don't see why it should interest you."

"Don't I care immensely for everything that concerns you? Didn't I tell you that once?"

"You're foolish if you do, and you would be foolish to say it again," Francie replied.

"Oh, I don't want to say anything, I've had my lesson. But I could listen to you all day." Francie gave an exclamation of impatience and incredulity and Mr. Flack pursued: "Don't you remember what you told me that time we had that talk at Saint-Germain, on the terrace? You said I might remain your friend."

"Well, that's all right," said the girl.

"Then ain't we interested in the development of our friends—in their impressions, their transformations, their adventures? Especially a person like me, who has got to know life—who has got to know the world."

"Do you mean to say I could teach you about life?" Francie demanded.

"About some kinds, certainly. You know a lot of people whom it's difficult to get at unless one takes some extraordinary measures, as you have done."

"What do you mean? What measures have I taken?"

"Well, they have—to get hold of you—and it's the same thing. Pouncing on you, to secure you; I call that energetic, and don't you think I ought to know?" asked Mr. Flack, smiling. "I thought *I* was energetic, but they got ahead of me. They're a society apart, and they must be very curious."

"Yes, they're curious," Francie admitted, with a little sigh. Then she inquired: "Do you want to put them in the paper?"

George Flack hesitated a moment; the air of the question was so candid, suggested so complete an exemption from prejudice. "Oh, I'm very careful about what I put in the paper. I want everything, as I told you: don't you remember the sketch I gave you of my ideals? But I want it in a certain particular way. If I can't get it in the shape I like it I don't want it at all; genuine, first-hand information, straight from the tap, is what I'm after. I don't want to hear what some one or other thinks that some one or other was told that some one or other repeated; and above all I don't want to print it. There's plenty of that flowing in, and the best part of the job is to keep it out. People just yearn to come in; they're dying to, all over the place; there's the biggest crowd at the door. But I say to them: 'You've got to do something first, then I'll see; or at any rate you've got to *be* something!'"

"We sometimes see the Reverberator; you have some fine pieces," Francie replied.

"Sometimes, only? Don't they send it to your father—the weekly edition? I thought I had fixed that," said George Flack.

"I don't know; it's usually lying round. But Delia reads it more than I; she reads pieces aloud. I like to read books; I read as many as I can."

"Well, it's all literature," said Mr. Flack; "it's all the press, the great institution of our time. Some of the finest books have come out first in the papers. It's the history of the age."

"I see you've got the same aspirations," Francie remarked, kindly.

"The same aspirations?"

"Those you told me about that day at Saint-Germain."

"Oh, I keep forgetting that I ever broke out to you that way; everything is so changed."

"Are you the proprietor of the paper now?" the girl went on, determined not to notice this sentimental allusion.

"What do you care? It wouldn't even be delicate in me to tell you; for I *do* remember the way you said you would try and get your father to help me. Don't say you've forgotten it, because you almost made me cry. Any way, that isn't the sort of help I want now and it wasn't the sort of help I meant to ask you for then. I want sympathy and interest; I want some one to whisper once in a while—'Courage, courage; you'll come out all right.' You see I'm a working man and I don't pretend to be anything else," Mr. Flack went on. "I don't live on the accumulations of my ancestors. What I have I earn— what I am I've fought for: I'm a *travailleur*, as they say here. I rejoice in it; but there is one dark spot in it, all the same."

"And what is that?" asked Francie.

"That it makes you ashamed of me."

"Oh, how can you say?" And she got up, as if a sense of oppression, of vague discomfort, had come over her. Her visitor made her fidgety.

"You wouldn't be ashamed to go round with me?"

"Round where?"

"Well, anywhere: just to have one more walk. The very last." George Flack had got up too and he stood there looking at her with his bright eyes, with his hands in the pockets of his overcoat. As she hesitated he continued, "Then I'm not such a friend after all."

Francie rested her eyes for a moment on the carpet; then, raising them—"Where should you like to go?"

"You could render me a service—a real service—without any inconvenience, probably, to yourself. Isn't your portrait finished?"

"Yes, but he won't give it up."

"Who won't give it up?"

"Why, Mr. Waterlow. He wants to keep it near him to look at in case he should take a fancy to change it. But I hope he won't change it—it's so pretty as it is!" Francie declared, smiling.

"I hear it's magnificent, and I want to see it," said George Flack.

"Then why don't you go?"

"I'll go if you'll take me; that's the service you can render me."

"Why, I thought you went everywhere—into the palaces of kings!" Francie cried.

"I go where I'm welcome, not where I'm not. I don't want to push into that studio alone; he doesn't like me. Oh, you needn't protest," the young man went on; "if one is sensitive one is sensitive. I feel those things in the shade of a tone of voice. He doesn't like newspaper-men. Some people don't, you know. I ought to tell you that frankly."

Francie considered again, but looking this time at her visitor. "Why, if it hadn't been for you"—I am afraid she said "hadn't have been"—"I never would have sat to him."

Mr. Flack smiled at her in silence for an instant. "If it hadn't been for me I think you never would have met your future husband."

"Perhaps not," said Francie; and suddenly she blushed red, rather to her companion's surprise.

"I only say that to remind you that after all I have a right to ask you to show me this one little favour. Let me drive with you to-morrow, or next day or any day, to the Avenue de Villiers, and I shall regard myself as amply repaid. With you I sha'n't be afraid to go in, for you have a right to take any one you like to see your picture. It's always done."

"Oh, the day you're afraid, Mr. Flack—!" Francie exclaimed, laughing. She had been much struck by his reminder of what they all owed him; for he truly had been their initiator, the instrument, under providence, that had opened a great new interest to them, and it shocked her generosity, the intimation that he saw himself cast off or disavowed after the prize was gained. Her mind had not lingered on her personal indebtedness to him, for it was not in the nature of her mind to linger; but at present she was glad to spring quickly, at the first word, into the attitude of acknowledgment. It had the effect that simplification always has, it raised her spirits, made her merry.

"Of course I must be quite square with you," the young man said. "If I want to see the picture it's because I want to write about it. The whole thing will go bang into the Reverberator. You must understand that, in advance. I wouldn't write about it without seeing it."

"*J'espère bien!*" said Francie, who was getting on famously with her French. "Of course if you praise him Mr. Waterlow will like it."

"I don't know that he cares for my praise and I don't care much whether *he* likes it or not. If you like it, that's the principal thing."

"Oh, I shall be awfully proud."

"I shall speak of you personally—I shall say you are the prettiest girl that has ever come over."

"You may say what you like," Francie rejoined. "It will be immense fun to be in the newspapers. Come for me at this hour day after to-morrow."

"You're too kind," said George Flack, taking up his hat. He smoothed it down a moment, with his glove; then he said— "I wonder if you will mind our going alone?"

"Alone?"

"I mean just you and me."

"Oh, don't you be afraid! Father and Delia have seen it about thirty times."

"That will be delightful, then. And it will help me to feel, more than anything else could make me do, that we are still old friends. I'll come at 3.15," Mr. Flack went on, but without even yet taking his departure. He asked two or three questions about the hotel, whether it were as good as last year and there were many people in it and they could keep their rooms warm; then, suddenly, in a different order and scarcely waiting for the girl's answer, he said: "And now, for instance, are they very bigoted? That's one of the things I should like to know."

"Very bigoted?"

"Ain't they tremendous Catholics—always talking about the Holy Father, and that sort of thing? I mean Mr. Probert, the old gentleman," Mr. Flack added. "And those ladies, and all the rest of them."

"They are very religious," said Francie. "They are the most religious people I ever saw. They just adore the Holy Father. They know him personally quite well. They are always going down to Rome."

"And do they mean to introduce you to him?"

"How do you mean, to introduce me?"

"Why, to make you a Catholic, to take you also down to Rome."

"Oh, we are going to Rome for our *voyage de noces*!" said Francie, gaily. "Just for a peep."

"And won't you have to have a Catholic marriage? They won't consent to a Protestant one."

"We are going to have a lovely one, just like one that Mme. de Brécourt took me to see at the Madeleine."

"And will it be at the Madeleine too?"

"Yes, unless we have it at Notre Dame."

"And how will your father and sister like that?"

"Our having it at Notre Dame?"

"Yes, or at the Madeleine. Your not having it at the American church."

"Oh, Delia wants it at the best place," said Francie, simply. Then she added: "And you know father ain't much on religion."

"Well now, that's what I call a genuine fact, the sort I was talking about," Mr. Flack replied. Whereupon he at last took himself off, repeating that he would come in two days later, at 3.15 sharp.

Francie gave an account of his visit to her sister, on the return of the latter young lady, and mentioned the agreement they had come to in relation to the drive. Delia, at this, looked grave, asseverating that she didn't know that it was right ("as" it was right, Delia usually said,) that Francie should be so intimate with other gentlemen after she was engaged.

"Intimate? You wouldn't think it's very intimate if you were to see me!" cried Francie, laughing.

"I'm sure I don't want to see you," Delia declared; and her sister, becoming strenuous, authoritative, went on: "Delia Dosson, do you realise that if it hadn't been for Mr. Flack we would never have had that picture, and that if it hadn't been for that picture I should never have got engaged?"

"It would have been better if you hadn't, if that's the way you are going to behave. Nothing would induce me to go with you."

This was what suited Francie; but she was nevertheless struck by Delia's rigidity. "I'm only going to take him to see Mr. Waterlow," she explained.

"Has he become all of a sudden too shy to go alone?"

"Well, you know Mr. Waterlow doesn't like him—and he has made him feel it. You know Gaston told us so."

"He told us *he* couldn't bear him: that's what he told us," said Delia.

"All the more reason I should be kind to him. Why, Delia, do realise," Francie went on.

"That's just what I do," returned the elder girl; "but things that are very different from those you want me to. You have queer reasons."

"I have others too that you may like better. He wants to put a piece in the paper about it."

"About your picture?"

"Yes, and about me. All about the whole thing."

Delia stared a moment. "Well, I hope it will be a good one!" she said with a little sigh of resignation, as if she were accepting the burden of a still larger fate.

X.

WHEN FRANCIE, two days later, passed with Mr. Flack into Charles Waterlow's studio she found Mme. de Cliché before the great canvas. She was pleased by every sign that the Proberts took an interest in her, and this was a considerable symptom, Gaston's second sister's coming all that way (she lived over by the Invalides) to look at the portrait once more. Francie knew she had seen it at an earlier stage; the work had excited curiosity and discussion among the Proberts from the first of their making her acquaintance and they went into considerations about it which had not occurred to the original and her companions—frequently (as we know) as these good people had conversed on the subject. Gaston had told her that opinions differed much in the family as to the merit of the work and that Margaret, precisely, had gone so far as to say that it might be a masterpiece of tone but it didn't make her look like a lady. His father on the other hand had no objection to offer to the character in which it represented her but he didn't think it well painted. *"Regardez-moi ça, et ça, et ça, je vous demande!"* he had exclaimed, making little dashes at the canvas, toward spots that appeared to him eccentric, with his glove, on occasions when the artist was not at hand. The Proberts always fell into French when they spoke on a question of art. "Poor dear papa, he only understands *le vieux jeu!*" Gaston had explained, and he had still further to expound what he meant by the old game. The novelty of Charles Waterlow's game had already been a mystification to Mr. Probert.

Francie remembered now (she had forgotten it) that Margaret de Cliché had told her she meant to come again. She hoped the marquise thought by this time that, on canvas at least, she looked a little more like a lady. Mme. de Cliché smiled at her at any rate and kissed her, as if in fact there could be no mistake. She smiled also at Mr. Flack, on Francie's introducing him, and only looked grave when, after she had asked where the others were—the papa and the *grande-sœur*—the girl replied that she hadn't the least idea: her party consisted only of herself and Mr. Flack. Then Mme. de Cliché became very stern indeed—assumed an aspect that brought back Francie's sense that she was the individual, among all Gaston's belongings, who had pleased her least from the first. Mme. de Douves was superficially more formidable but with her the second impression was most comforting. It was just this second impression of the marquise that was not. There were perhaps others behind it but the girl had not yet arrived at them. Mr. Waterlow might not have been very fond of Mr. Flack, but he was none the less perfectly civil to him, and took much trouble to show him all the work that he had in hand, dragging out canvases, changing lights, taking him off to see things at the other end of the great room. While the two gentlemen were at a distance Mme. de Cliché expressed to Francie the confidence that she would allow her to see her home: on which Francie replied that she was not going home, she was going somewhere else with Mr. Flack. And she explained, as if it simplified the matter, that this gentleman was an editor.

Her interlocutress echoed the term and Francie developed her explanation. He was not the only editor, but one of the many editors, of a great American paper. He was going to publish an article about her picture. Gaston knew him perfectly; it was Mr. Flack who had been the cause of Gaston's being presented to her. Mme. de Cliché looked across at him as if the inadequacy of the cause projected an unfavourable light upon the effect; she inquired whether Francie thought Gaston would like her to drive about Paris alone with an editor. "I'm sure I don't know. I never asked him!" said Francie. "He ought to want me to be polite to a person who did so much for us." Soon after this Mme. de Cliché withdrew, without looking afresh at Mr. Flack, though he stood in her path as she approached the door. She did not kiss our young lady again, and the girl observed that her leave-taking consisted of the simple words, "Adieu, mademoiselle." She had already perceived that in proportion as the Proberts became majestic they had recourse to French.

She and Mr. Flack remained in the studio but a short time longer; and when they were seated in the carriage again, at the door (they had come in Mr. Dosson's open landau), her companion said, "And now where shall we go?" He spoke as if on their way from the hotel he had not touched upon the pleasant vision of a little turn in the Bois. He had insisted then that the day was made on purpose, the air full of spring. At present he seemed to wish to give himself the pleasure of making his companion choose that particular alternative. But she only answered, rather impatiently:

"Wherever you like, wherever you like." And she sat there swaying her parasol, looking about her, giving no order.

"Au Bois," said George Flack to the coachman, leaning back on the soft cushions. For a few moments after the carriage had taken its easy elastic start they were silent; but presently he went on, "Was that lady one of your relations?"

"Do you mean one of Mr. Probert's? She is his sister."

"Is there any particular reason in that why she shouldn't say good-morning to me?"

"She didn't want you to remain with me. She wanted to carry me off."

"What has she got against me?" asked Mr. Flack.

Francie seemed to consider a little. "Oh, it's these French ideas."

"Some of them are very base," said her companion.

The girl made no rejoinder; she only turned her eyes to right and left, admiring the splendid day, the shining city. The great architectural vista was fair: the tall houses, with their polished shop-fronts, their balconies, their signs with accented letters, seemed to make a glitter of gilt and crystal as they rose into the sunny air. The colour of everything was cool and pretty and the sound of everything gay; the sense of a costly spectacle was everywhere. "Well, I like Paris, anyway!" Francie exclaimed at last.

"It's lucky for you, since you've got to live here."

"I haven't got to, there's no obligation. We haven't settled anything about that."

"Hasn't that lady settled it for you?"

"Yes, very likely she has," said Francie, placidly. "I don't like her so well as the others."

"You like the others very much?"

"Of course I do. So would you if they had made so much of you."

"That one at the studio didn't make much of me, certainly."

"Yes, she's the most haughty," said Francie.

"Well, what is it all about?" Mr. Flack inquired. "Who are they, anyway?"

"Oh, it would take me three hours to tell you," the girl replied, laughing. "They go back a thousand years."

"Well, we've got a thousand years—I mean three hours." And George Flack settled himself more on his cushions and inhaled the pleasant air. "I do enjoy this drive, Miss Francie," he went on. "It's many a day since I've been to the Bois. I don't fool around much among the trees."

Francie replied candidly that for her too the occasion was very agreeable, and Mr. Flack pursued, looking round him with a smile, irrelevantly and cheerfully: "Yes, these French ideas! I don't see how you can stand them. Those they have about young ladies are horrid."

"Well, they tell me you like them better after you are married."

"Why, after they are married they're worse—I mean the ideas. Every one knows that."

"Well, they can make you like anything, the way they talk," Francie said.

"And do they talk a great deal?"

"Well, I should think so. They don't do much else, and they talk about the queerest things—things I never heard of."

"Ah, that I'll engage!" George Flack exclaimed.

"Of course I have had most conversation with Mr. Probert."

"The old gentleman?"

"No, very little with him. I mean with Gaston. But it's not he that has told me most—it's Mme. de Brécourt. She relates and relates—it's very interesting. She has told me all their histories, all their troubles and complications."

"Complications?"

"That's what she calls them. It seems very different from America. It's just like a story—they have such strange feelings. But there are things you can see—without being told."

"What sort of things?"

"Well, like Mme. de Cliché's—" But Francie paused, as if for a word.

"Do you mean her complications?"

"Yes, and her husband's. She has terrible ones. That's why one must forgive her if she is rather peculiar. She is very unhappy."

"Do you mean through her husband?"

"Yes, he likes other ladies better. He flirts with Mme. de Brives."

"Mme. de Brives?"

"Yes, she's lovely," said Francie. "She isn't very young, but she's fearfully attractive. And he used to go every day to have tea with Mme. de Villepreux. Mme. de Cliché can't bear Mme. de Villepreux."

"Lord, what a low character he must be!" George Flack exclaimed.

"Oh, his mother was very bad. That was one thing they had against the marriage."

"Who had?—against what marriage?"

"When Maggie Probert became engaged."

"Is that what they call her—Maggie?"

"Her brother does; but every one else calls her Margot. Old Mme. de Cliché had a horrid reputation. Every one hated her."

"Except those, I suppose, who liked her too much. And who is Mme. de Villepreux?"

"She's the daughter of Mme. de Marignac."

"And who is Mme. de Marignac?"

"Oh, she's dead," said Francie. "She used to be a great friend of Mr. Probert—of Gaston's father."

"He used to go to tea with her?"

"Almost every day. Susan says he has never been the same since her death."

"Ah, poor man! And who is Susan?"

"Why, Mme. de Brécourt. Mr. Probert just loved Mme. de Marignac. Mme. de Villepreux isn't so nice as her mother. She was brought up with the Proberts, like a sister, and now she carries on with Maxime."

"With Maxime?"

"That's M. de Cliché."

"Oh, I see—I see!" murmured George Flack, responsively. They had reached the top of the Champs Elysées and were passing below the wondrous arch to which that gentle eminence forms a pedestal and which looks down even on splendid Paris from its immensity and across at the vain mask of the Tuileries and the river-moated Louvre and the twin towers of Notre Dame, painted blue by the distance. The confluence of carriages—a sounding stream, in which our friends become engaged—rolled into the large avenue leading to the Bois de Boulogne. Mr. Flack evidently enjoyed the scene; he gazed about him at their neighbours, at the villas and gardens on either hand; he took in the prospect of the far-stretching brown boskages and smooth alleys of the wood, of the hour that they had yet to spend there, of the rest of Francie's artless prattle, of the place near the lake where they could alight and walk a little; even of the bench where they might sit down. "I see, I see," he repeated with appreciation. "You make me feel quite as if I were in the *grand monde*."

XI.

O NE DAY, at noon, shortly before the time for which Gaston had announced his return, a note was brought to Francie from Mme. de Brécourt. It caused her some agitation, though it contained a clause intended to guard her against vain fears. "Please come to me the moment you have received this—I have sent the carriage. I will explain when you get here what I want to see you about. Nothing has happened to Gaston. We are all here." The coupé from the Place Beauvau was waiting at the door of the hotel and the girl had but a hurried conference with her father and sister; if conference it could be called in which vagueness on one side encountered blankness on the other. "It's for something bad— something bad," Francie said, while she tied her bonnet; though she was unable to think what it could be. Delia, who looked a good deal scared, offered to accompany her; upon which Mr. Dosson made the first remark of a practical character in which he had indulged in relation to his daughter's alliance.

"No you won't—no you won't, my dear. They may whistle for Francie, but let them see that they can't whistle for all of us." It was the first sign he had given of being jealous of the dignity of the Dossons. That question had never troubled him.

"I know what it is," said Delia, while she arranged her sister's garments. "They want to talk about religion. They have got the priests; there's some bishop, or perhaps some cardinal. They want to baptise you."

"You'd better take a waterproof!" Francie's father called after her as she flitted away.

She wondered, rolling toward the Place Beauvau, what they were all there for; that announcement balanced against the reassurance conveyed in the phrase about Gaston. She liked them individually but in their collective form they made her uneasy. In their family parties there was always something of the tribunal. Mme. de Brécourt came out to meet her in the vestibule, drawing her quickly into a small room (not the salon—Francie knew it as her hostess's "own room," a lovely boudoir), in which, considerably to the girl's relief, the rest of the family were not assembled. Yet she guessed in a moment that they were near at hand—they were waiting. Susan looked flushed and strange; she had a queer smile; she kissed her as if she didn't know that she was doing it. She laughed as she greeted her, but her laugh was nervous; she was different every way from anything Francie had hitherto seen. By the time our young lady had perceived these things she was sitting beside her on a sofa and Mme. de Brécourt had her hand, which she held so tight that it almost hurt her. Susan's eyes were in their nature salient, but on this occasion they seemed to have started out of her head.

"We are upside down—terribly agitated. A bomb has fallen into the house."

"What's the matter—what's the matter?" Francie asked, pale, with parted lips. She had a sudden wild idea that Gaston might have found out in America that her father had no money, had lost it all; that it had been stolen during their long absence. But would he cast her off for that?

"You must understand the closeness of our union with you from our sending for you this way—the first, the only person—in a crisis. Our joys are your joys and our indignations are yours."

"What *is* the matter, *please*?" the girl repeated. Their "indignations" opened up a gulf; it flashed upon her, with a shock of mortification that the idea had not come sooner, that something would have come out: a piece in the paper, from Mr. Flack, about her portrait and even (a little) about herself. But that was only more mystifying; for certainly Mr. Flack could only have published something pleasant—something to be proud of. Had he by some incredible perversity or treachery stated that the picture was bad, or even that *she* was? She grew dizzy, remembering how she had refused him and how little he had liked it, that day at Saint-Germain. But they had made that up over and over, especially when they sat so long on a bench together (the time they drove,) in the Bois de Boulogne.

"Oh, the most awful thing; a newspaper sent this morning from America to my father—containing two horrible columns of vulgar lies and scandal about our family, about all of us, about you, about your picture, about poor Marguerite, calling her 'Margot,' about Maxime and Léonie de Villepreux, saying he's her lover, about all our affairs, about Gaston, about your marriage, about your sister and your dresses and your dimples, about our darling father, whose history it professes to relate, in the most ignoble, the most revolting terms. Papa's in the most awful state!" said Mme. de Brécourt, panting to take breath. She had spoken with the volubility of horror and passion. "You are outraged with us and you must suffer with us," she went on. "But who has done it? Who has done it? Who has done it?"

"Why, Mr. Flack—Mr. Flack!" Francie quickly replied. She was appalled, overwhelmed; but her foremost feeling was the wish not to appear to disavow her knowledge.

"Mr. Flack? do you mean that awful person—? He ought to be shot, he ought to be burnt alive. Maxime will kill him, Maxime is in an unspeakable rage. Everything is at end, we have been served up to the rabble, we shall have to leave Paris. How could he know such things? and they are all too infamously false!" The poor woman poured forth her trouble in questions and contradictions and groans; she knew not what to ask first, against what to protest. "Do you mean that person Marguerite saw you with at Mr. Waterlow's? Oh, Francie, what has happened? She had a feeling then, a dreadful foreboding. She saw you afterwards—walking with him—in the Bois."

"Well, I didn't see her," the girl said.

"You were talking with him—you were too absorbed: that's what Margot says. Oh, Francie, Francie!" cried Mme. de Brécourt, catching her breath.

"She tried to interfere at the studio, but I wouldn't let her. He's an old friend—a friend of my father's, and I like him very much. What my father allows, that's not for others to criticise!" Francie continued. She was frightened, extremely frightened, at her companion's air of tragedy and at the dreadful consequences she alluded to, consequences of an act she herself did not know, could not comprehend nor measure yet. But there was an instinct of bravery in her which threw her into defence—defence even of George Flack, though it was a part of her consternation that on her too he should have practised a surprise, a sort of selfish deception.

"Oh, how can you bear with such wretches—how can your father——? What devil has he paid to tattle to him?"

"You scare me awfully—you terrify me," said the girl. "I don't know what you are talking about. I haven't seen it, I don't understand it. Of course I have talked to Mr. Flack."

"Oh, Francie, don't say it—don't *say* it! Dear child, you haven't talked to him in that fashion: vulgar horrors, and such a language!" Mme. de Brécourt came nearer, took both her hands now, drew her closer, seemed to plead with her. "You shall see the paper; they have got it in the other room—the most disgusting sheet. Margot is reading it to her husband; he can't read English, if you can call it English: such a style! Papa tried to translate it to Maxime, but he couldn't, he was too sick. There is a quantity about Mme. de Marignac— imagine only! And a quantity about Jeanne and Raoul and their economies in the country. When they see it in Brittany—heaven preserve us!"

Francie had turned very white; she looked for a minute at the carpet. "And what does it say about me?"

"Some trash about your being the great American beauty, with the most odious details, and your having made a match among the 'rare old exclusives.' And the strangest stuff about your father—his having gone into a 'store' at the age of twelve. And something about your poor sister—heaven help us! And a sketch of our career in Paris, as they call it, and the way that we have got on and our great pretensions. And a passage about Blanche de Douves, Raoul's sister, who had that disease—what do they call it?—that she used to steal things in shops: do you see them reading that? And how did he know such a thing? it's ages ago—it's dead and buried!"

"You told me, you told me yourself," said Francie, quickly. She turned red the instant she had spoken.

"Don't say it's you—don't, don't, my darling!" cried Mme. de Brécourt, who had stared at her a moment. "That's what I want, that's what you must do, that's what I see you this way for, first, alone. I've answered for you, you know; you must repudiate every responsibility. Margot suspects you— she has got that idea—she has given it to the others. I have told them they ought to be ashamed, that it's an outrage to you. I have done everything, for the last hour, to protect you. I'm your godmother, you know, and you mustn't disappoint me. You're incapable, and you must say so, face to face, to my father. Think of Gaston, chérie; *he* will have seen it over there, alone, far from us all. Think of *his* horror and of *his* faith, of what *he* would expect of you." Mme. de Brécourt hurried on, and her companion's bewilderment deepened on seeing that the tears had risen to her eyes and were pouring down her cheeks. "You must say to my father, face to face that you are incapable—you are stainless."

"Stainless?" Francie repeated. "Of course I knew he wanted to write a piece about the picture—and about my marriage."

"About your marriage—of course you knew. Then, wretched girl, you are at the bottom of *all*!" wailed Mme. de Brécourt, flinging herself away from her, falling back on the sofa, covering her face with her hands.

"He told me—he told me when I went with him to the studio!" Francie declared, passionately. "But he has printed more."

"*More?* I should think so!" And Mme. de Brécourt sprang up, standing before her. "And you *let* him—about yourself? You gave him facts?"

"I told him—I told him—I don't know what. It was for his paper—he wants everything. It's a very fine paper."

"A very fine paper?" Mme. de Brécourt stared, with parted lips. "Have you *seen*, have you touched the hideous sheet? Ah, my brother, my brother!" she wailed again, turning away.

"If your brother were here you wouldn't talk to me this way—he would protect me!" cried Francie, on her feet, seizing her little muff and moving to the door.

"Go away, go away or they'll kill you!" Mme. de Brécourt went on, excitedly. "After all I have done for you—after the way I have lied for you!" And she sobbed, trying to repress her sobs.

Francie, at this, broke out into a torrent of tears. "I'll go home. Father, father!" she almost shrieked, reaching the door.

"Oh, your father—he has been a nice father, bringing you up in such ideas!" These words followed her with infinite scorn, but almost as Mme. de Brécourt uttered them, struck by a sound, she sprang after the girl, seized her, drew her back and held her a moment, listening, before she could pass out. "Hush—hush—they are coming in here, they are too anxious! Deny—deny it—say you know nothing! Your sister must have said things—and such things: say it all comes from *her*!"

"Oh, you dreadful—is that what *you* do?" cried Francie, shaking herself free. The door opened as she spoke and Mme. de Brécourt walked quickly to the window, turning her back. Mme. de Cliché was there and Mr. Probert and M. de Brécourt and M. de Cliché. They entered in silence and M. de Brécourt, coming last, closed the door softly behind him. Francie had never been in a court of justice, but if she had had that experience these four persons would have reminded her of the jury filing back into their box with their verdict. They all looked at her hard as she stood in the middle of the room; Mme. de Brécourt gazed out of the window, wiping her eyes; Mme. de Cliché grasped a newspaper, crumpled and partly folded. Francie got a quick impression, moving her eyes from one face to another, that old Mr. Probert was the worst; his mild, ravaged expression was terrible. He was the one who looked at her least; he went to the fireplace and leaned on the mantel, with his head in his hands. He seemed ten years older.

"Ah, mademoiselle, mademoiselle, mademoiselle!" said Maxime de Cliché, slowly, impressively, in a tone of the most respectful but most poignant reproach.

"Have you seen it—have they sent it to you?" his wife asked, thrusting the paper towards her. "It's quite at your service!" But as Francie neither spoke nor took it she tossed it upon the sofa, where, as it opened, falling, the girl read the name of the Reverberator. Mme. de Cliché carried her head very far back.

"She has nothing to do with it—it's just as I told you— she's overwhelmed," said Mme. de Brécourt, remaining at the window.

"You would do well to read it—it's worth the trouble," Alphonse de Brécourt remarked, going over to his wife. Francie saw him kiss her as he perceived her tears. She was angry at her own; she choked and swallowed them; they seemed somehow to put her in the wrong.

"Have you had no idea that any such monstrosity would be perpetrated?" Mme. de Cliché went on, coming nearer to her. She had a manner of forced calmness—as if she wished it to be understood that she was one of those who could be reasonable under any provocation, though she were trembling within—which made Francie draw back. "*C'est pourtant rempli de choses*—which we know you to have been told of—by what folly, great heaven! It's right and left—no one is spared—it's a deluge of insult. My sister perhaps will have told you of the apprehensions I had—I couldn't resist them, though I thought of nothing so awful as this, God knows, the day I met you at Mr. Waterlow's with your journalist."

"I have told her everything—don't you see she's *anéantie*? Let her go, let her go!" exclaimed Mme. de Brécourt, still at the window.

"Ah, your journalist, your journalist, mademoiselle!" said Maxime de Cliché. "I am very sorry to have to say anything in regard to any friend of yours that can give you so little pleasure; but I promise myself the satisfaction of administering him with these hands a dressing he won't forget, if I may trouble you so far as to ask you to let him know it!"

M. de Cliché fingered the points of his moustache; he diffused some powerful scent; his eyes were dreadful to Francie. She wished Mr. Probert would say something kind to her; but she had now determined to be strong. They were ever so many against one; Gaston was far away and she felt heroic. "If you mean Mr. Flack—I don't know what you mean," she said as composedly as possible to M. de Cliché. "Mr. Flack has gone to London."

At this M. de Brécourt gave a free laugh and his brother-in-law replied, "Ah, it's easy to go to London."

"They like such things there; they do them more and more. It's as bad as America!" Mme. de Cliché declared.

"Why have you sent for me—what do you all want me to do? You might explain—I am only an American girl!" said Francie, whose being only an American girl, did not prevent her pretty head from holding itself now as high as Mme. de Cliché's.

Mme. de Brécourt came back to her quickly, laying her hand on her arm. "You are very nervous—you had much better go home. I will explain everything to them—I will make them understand. The carriage is here—it had orders to wait."

"I'm not in the least nervous, but I have made you all so," Francie replied, laughing.

"I defend you, my dear young lady—I insist that you are only a wretched victim, like ourselves," M. de Brécourt remarked, approaching her with a smile. "I see the hand of a woman in it, you know," he went on, to the others; "for there are strokes of a vulgarity that a man doesn't sink to (he can't, his very organisation prevents him) even if he be the greatest cad on earth. But please don't doubt that I have maintained that that woman is not you."

"The way you talk—I don't know how to write," said Francie.

"My poor child, when one knows you as I do!" murmured Mme. de Brécourt, with her arm around her.

"There's a lady who helps him—Mr. Flack has told me so," Francie continued. "She's a literary lady—here in Paris—she writes what he tells her. I think her name is Miss Topping, but she calls herself Florine—or Dorine," Francie added.

"Miss Dosson, you're too rare!" Marguerite de Cliché exclaimed, giving a long moan of pain which ended in an incongruous laugh. "Then you have been three to it," she went on; "that accounts for its perfection!"

Francie disengaged herself again from Mme. de Brécourt and went to Mr. Probert, who stood looking down at the fire, with his back to her. "Mr. Probert, I'm very sorry at what I've done to distress you; I had no idea you would all feel so badly. I didn't mean any harm. I thought you would like it."

The old man turned a little, bending his eyes on her, but without taking her hand as she had hoped. Usually when they met he kissed her. He did not look angry but he looked very ill. A strange inarticulate sound, a kind of exclamation of amazement and mirth, came from the others when she said she thought they would like it; and indeed poor Francie was far from being able to judge of the droll effect of that speech. "Like it—*like it?*" said Mr. Probert, staring at her as if he were a little afraid of her.

"What do you mean? She admits—she admits!" cried Mme. de Cliché to her sister. "Did you arrange it all that day in the Bois—to punish me for having tried to separate you?" she pursued, to the girl, who stood gazing up piteously at the old man.

"I don't know what he has published—I haven't seen it—I don't understand. I thought it was only to be a piece about me."

"About me!" M. de Cliché repeated in English. "*Elle est divine!*" He turned away, raising his shoulders and hands and then letting them fall.

Mme. de Brécourt had picked up the newspaper; she rolled it together, saying to Francie that she must take it home, take it home immediately—then she would see. She only seemed to wish to get her out of the room. But Mr. Probert had fixed the girl with his sick stare. "You gave information for that? You desired it?"

"Why, I didn't desire it, but Mr. Flack did."

"Why do you know such ruffians? Where was your father?" the old man groaned.

"I thought he would just praise my picture and give pleasure to Mr. Waterlow," Francie went on. "I thought he would just speak about my being engaged and give a little account; so many people in America would be interested."

"So many people in America—that's just the dreadful thought, my dear," said Mme. de Brécourt, kindly. "*Voyons,* put it in your muff and tell us what you think of it." And she continued to thrust forward the scandalous journal.

But Francie took no notice of it; she looked round from Mr. Probert at the others. "I told Gaston I should do something you wouldn't like."

"Well, he'll believe it now!" cried Mme. de Cliché.

"My poor child, do you think he will like it any better?" asked Mme. de Brécourt.

Francie fastened her eyes on her a moment. "He'll see it over there—he has seen it now."

"Oh, my dear, you'll have news of him. Don't be afraid!" laughed Mme. de Cliché.

"Did *he* send you the paper?" the girl went on, to Mr. Probert.

"It was not directed in his hand," said M. de Brécourt. "There was some stamp on the band—it came from the office."

"Mr. Flack—is that his hideous name?—must have seen to that," Mme. de Brécourt suggested.

"Or perhaps Florine," M. de Cliché interposed. "I should like to get hold of Florine."

"I did—I did tell him so!" Francie repeated, with her innocent face, alluding to her statement of a moment before and speaking as if she thought the circumstance detracted from the offence.

"So did I—so did we all!" said Mme. de Cliché.

"And will he suffer—as you suffer?" Francie continued, appealing to Mr. Probert.

"Suffer, suffer? He'll die!" cried the old man. "However, I won't answer for him; he'll tell you himself, when he returns."

"He'll die?" asked Francie, with expanded eyes.

"He'll never return—how can he show himself?" said Mme. de Cliché.

"That's not true—he'll come back to stand by me!" the girl flashed out.

"How could you not feel that we were the last—the very last?" asked Mr. Probert, very gently. "How could you not feel that my son was the very last—?"

"*C'est un sens qui lui manque!*" commented Mme. de Cliché.

"Let her go, papa—do let her go home," Mme. de Brécourt pleaded.

"Surely. That's the only place for her to-day!" the elder sister continued.

"Yes, my child—you oughtn't to be here. It's your father—he ought to understand," said Mr. Probert.

"For God's sake don't send for him—let it all stop!" Mme. de Cliché exclaimed.

Francie looked at her; then she said, "Good-bye, Mr. Probert—good-bye, Susan."

"Give her your arm—take her to the carriage," she heard Mme. de Brécourt say to her husband. She got to the door she hardly knew how—she was only conscious that Susan held her once more long enough to kiss her. Poor Susan wanted to comfort her; that showed how bad (feeling as she did) she believed the whole business would yet be. It would be bad because Gaston—Gaston: Francie did not complete that thought, yet only Gaston was in her mind as she hurried to the carriage. M. de Brécourt hurried beside her; she would not take his arm. But he opened the door for her and as she got in she heard him murmur strangely, "You are charming, mademoiselle—charming, charming!"

XII.

H ER ABSENCE had not been long and when she re-
entered the familiar salon at the hotel she found her
father and sister sitting there together as if they were timing
her—a prey to curiosity and suspense. Mr. Dosson however
gave no sign of impatience; he only looked at her in silence
through the smoke of his cigar (he profaned the red satin
splendour with perpetual fumes,) as she burst into the room.
No other word than the one I use expresses the tell-tale character of poor Francie's ingress. She rushed to one of the tables, flinging down her muff and gloves, and the next
moment Delia, who had sprung up as she came in, had
caught her in her arms and was glaring into her face with a
"Francie Dosson—what *have* you been through?" Francie
said nothing at first, only closing her eyes and letting her sister do what she would with her. "She has been crying, father—she *has*," Delia went on, pulling her down upon a sofa
and almost shaking her as she continued. "Will you please
tell? I've been perfectly wild! Yes you have, you dreadful—!"
the elder girl declared, kissing her on the eyes. They opened
at this compassionate pressure and Francie rested them in
their beautiful distress on her father, who had now risen to
his feet and stood with his back to the fire.

"Why, daughter," said Mr. Dosson, "you look as if you had
had quite a worry."

"I told you I should—I told you, I told you!" Francie
broke out, with a trembling voice. "And now it's come!"

"You don't mean to say you've *done* anything?" cried Delia,
very white.

"It's all over—it's all over!" Francie pursued, turning her
eyes to her sister.

"Are you crazy, Francie?" this young lady asked. "I'm sure
you look as if you were."

"Ain't you going to be married, my child?" asked Mr. Dosson, benevolently, coming nearer to her.

Francie sprang up, releasing herself from her sister, and
threw her arms around him. "Will you take me away, father
—will you take me right away?"

"Of course I will, my precious. I'll take you anywhere. I don't want anything—it wasn't *my* idea!" And Mr. Dosson and Delia looked at each other while the girl pressed her face upon his shoulder.

"I never heard such trash—you can't behave that way! Has he got engaged to some one else—in America?" Delia demanded.

"Why, if it's over it's over. I guess it's all right," said Mr. Dosson, kissing his younger daughter. "I'll go back or I'll go on. I'll go anywhere you like!"

"You won't have your daughters insulted, I presume!" Delia cried. "If you don't tell me this moment what has happened I'll drive straight round there and find out."

"*Have* they insulted you, sweetie?" asked the old man, bending over the girl, who simply leaned upon him with her hidden face, with no sound of tears.

Francie raised her head, turning round upon her sister. "Did I ever tell you anything else—did I ever believe in it for an hour?"

"Oh, well, if you've done it on purpose—to triumph over me—we might as well go home, certainly. But I think you had better wait till Gaston comes."

"It will be worse when he comes—if he thinks the same as they do."

"*Have* they insulted you—have they?" Mr. Dosson repeated; while the smoke of his cigar, curling round the question, gave him the air of asking it with placidity.

"They think I've insulted them—they're in an awful state—they're almost dead. Mr. Flack has put it into the paper—everything, I don't know what—and they think it's too fearful. They were all there together—all at me at once, groaning and carrying on. I never saw people so affected."

Delia listened in bewilderment, staring. "So affected?"

"Ah, yes, there's a good deal of that," said Mr. Dosson.

"It's too real—too terrible; you don't understand. It's all printed there—that they're immoral, and everything about them; everything that's private and dreadful."

"Immoral, is that so?" Mr. Dosson asked.

"And about me too, and about Gaston and my marriage, and all sorts of personalities, and all the names, and Mme. de

Villepreux, and everything. It's all printed there and they've read it. It says that one of them steals."

"Will you be so good as to tell me what you are talking about?" Delia inquired, sternly. "Where is it printed and what have we got to do with it?"

"Some one sent it, and I told Mr. Flack."

"Do you mean *his* paper? Oh the horrid brute!" Delia cried, with passion.

"Do they mind so what they see in the papers?" asked Mr. Dosson. "I guess they haven't seen what I've seen. Why, there used to be things about me——!"

"Well, it *is* about us too, about every one. They think it's the same as if I wrote it."

"Well, you know what you *could* do," said Mr. Dosson, smiling at his daughter.

"Do you mean that piece about your picture—that you told me about when you went with him again to see it?" Delia asked.

"Oh, I don't know what piece it is; I haven't seen it."

"Haven't seen it? Didn't they show it to you?"

"Yes—but I couldn't read it. Mme. de Brécourt wanted me to take it—but I left it behind."

"Well, that's like you—like the Tauchnitzes littering up our track. I'll be bound I'd see it," said Delia. "Hasn't it come, doesn't it always come?"

"I guess we haven't had the last—unless it's somewhere round," said Mr. Dosson.

"Father, go out and get it—you can buy it on the boulevard!" Delia continued. "Francie, what *did* you want to tell him?"

"I didn't know; I was just conversing; he seemed to take so much interest."

"Oh, he's a deep one!" groaned Delia.

"Well, if folks are immoral you can't keep it out of the papers—and I don't know as you ought to want to," Mr. Dosson remarked. "If they are I'm glad to know it, lovey." And he gave his younger daughter a glance apparently intended to show that in this case he should know what to do.

But Francie was looking at her sister as if her attention had been arrested. "How do you mean—'a deep one'?"

"Why, he wanted to break it off, the wretch!"

Francie stared; then a deeper flush leapt to her face, in which already there was a look of fever. "To break off my engagement?"

"Yes, just that. But I'll be hanged if he shall! Father, will you allow that?"

"Allow what?"

"Why Mr. Flack's vile interference. You won't let him do as he likes with us, I suppose, will you?"

"It's all done—it's all done!" said Francie. The tears had suddenly started into her eyes again.

"Well, he's so smart that it *is* likely he's too smart," said Mr. Dosson. "But what did they want you to do about it?—that's what I want to know."

"They wanted me to say I knew nothing about it—but I couldn't."

"But you didn't and you don't—if you haven't even read it!" Delia returned.

"Where *is* the d—d thing?" her father asked, looking helplessly about him.

"On the boulevard, at the very first of those kiosks you come to. That old woman has it—the one who speaks English—she always has it. Do go and get it—*do!*" And Delia pushed him, looked for his hat for him.

"I knew he wanted to print something and I can't say I didn't!" Francie said. "I thought he would praise my portrait and that Mr. Waterlow would like that, and Gaston and every one. And he talked to me about the paper—he is always doing that and always was—and I didn't see the harm. But even just knowing him—they think that's vile."

"Well, I should hope we can know whom we like!" Delia declared, jumping in her mystification and alarm from one point of view to another.

Mr. Dosson had put on his hat—he was going out for the paper. "Why, he kept us alive last year," he said.

"Well, he seems to have killed us now!" Delia cried.

"Well, don't give up an old friend," said Mr. Dosson, with

his hand on the door. "And don't back down on anything you've done."

"Lord, what a fuss about an old newspaper!" Delia went on, in her exasperation. "It must be about two weeks old, anyway. Didn't they ever see a society-paper before?"

"They can't have seen much," said Mr. Dosson. He paused, still with his hand on the door. "Don't you worry—Gaston will make it all right."

"Gaston?—it will kill Gaston!"

"Is that what they say?" Delia demanded.

"Gaston will never look at me again."

"Well, then, he'll have to look at *me*," said Mr. Dosson.

"Do you mean that he'll give you up—that he'll be so abject?" Delia went on.

"They say he's just the one who will feel it most. But I'm the one who does that," said Francie, with a strange smile.

"They're stuffing you with lies—because *they* don't like it. He'll be tender and true," answered Delia.

"When *they* hate me?—Never!" And Francie shook her head slowly, still with her touching smile. "That's what he cared for most—to make them like me."

"And isn't he a gentleman, I should like to know?" asked Delia.

"Yes, and that's why I won't marry him—if I've injured him."

"Pshaw! he has seen the papers over there. You wait till he comes," Mr. Dosson enjoined, passing out of the room.

The girls remained there together and after a moment Delia exclaimed: "Well, he has got to fix it—that's one thing I can tell you."

"Who has got to fix it?"

"Why, that villainous man. He has got to publish another piece saying it's all false or all a mistake."

"Yes, you had better make him," said Francie, with a weak laugh. "You had better go after him—down to Nice."

"You don't mean to say he has gone to Nice?"

"Didn't he say he was going there as soon as he came back from London—going right through, without stopping?"

"I don't know but he did," said Delia. Then she added—"The coward!"

"Why do you say that? He can't hide at Nice—they can find him there."

"Are they going after him?"

"They want to shoot him—to stab him, I don't know what—those men."

"Well, I wish they would," said Delia.

"They had better shoot me. I shall defend him. I shall protect him," Francie went on.

"How can you protect him? You shall never speak to him again."

Francie was silent a moment. "I can protect him without speaking to him. I can tell the simple truth—that he didn't print a word but what I told him."

"That can't be so. He fixed it up. They always do, in the papers. Well now, he has got to bring out a piece praising them up—praising them to the skies: that's what he has got to do!" Delia declared, with decision.

"Praising them up? They'll hate that worse," Francie returned, musingly.

Delia stared. "What on earth do they want then?"

Francie had sunk upon the sofa; her eyes were fixed on the carpet. She made no reply to her sister's question but presently she said, "We had better go to-morrow, the first hour that's possible."

"Go where? Do you mean to Nice?"

"I don't care where. Anywhere, to get away."

"Before Gaston comes—without seeing him?"

"I don't want to see him. When they were all ranting and raving at me just now I wished he was there—I told them so. But now I feel differently—I can never see him again."

"I don't suppose you're crazy, are you?" cried Delia.

"I can't tell him it wasn't me—I can't, I can't!" the younger girl pursued.

Delia planted herself in front of her. "Francie Dosson, if you're going to tell him you've done anything wrong you might as well stop before you begin. Didn't you hear what father said?"

"I'm sure I don't know," Francie replied, listlessly.

" 'Don't give up an old friend—there's nothing on earth so mean.' Now isn't Gaston Probert an old friend?"

"It will be very simple—he will give me up."

"Then he'll be a low wretch."

"Not in the least—he'll give me up as he took me. He would never have asked me to marry him if he hadn't been able to get *them* to accept me: he thinks everything in life of *them*. If they cast me off now he'll do just the same. He'll have to choose between us, and when it comes to that he'll never choose me."

"He'll never choose Mr. Flack, if that's what you mean—if you are going to identify yourself so with *him*!"

"Oh, I wish he'd never been born!" Francie suddenly shivered. And then she added that she was sick—she was going to bed, and her sister took her off to her room.

Mr. Dosson, that afternoon, sitting by Francie's bedside, read out from the copy of the Reverberator which he had purchased on the boulevard the dreadful "piece" to his two daughters. It is a remarkable fact that as a family they were rather disappointed in this composition, in which their curiosity found less to repay it than it had expected, their resentment against Mr. Flack less to stimulate it, their imaginative effort to take the point of view of the Proberts less to sustain it, and their acceptance of the promulgation of Francie's innocent remarks as a natural incident of the life of the day less to make them reconsider it. The letter from Paris appeared lively, "chatty," even brilliant, and so far as the personalities contained in it were concerned Mr. Dosson wanted to know if they were not aware over here of the charges brought every day against the most prominent men in Boston. "If there was anything in that style they might talk," he said; and he scanned the effusion afresh with a certain surprise at not finding in it some imputation of pecuniary malversation. The effect of an acquaintance with the text was to depress Delia, who did not exactly see what there was in it to take back or explain away. However, she was aware there were some points they didn't understand, and doubtless these were the scandalous places—the things that had thrown the Proberts into a state. But why should they be in a state if other people didn't understand the allusions—they were peculiar, but peculiarly incomprehensible—any better than she did? The whole thing struck Francie as infinitely less lurid than Mme.

de Brécourt's account of it, and the part about herself and her portrait seemed to make even less of the subject than it easily might have done. It was scanty, it was "skimpy," and if Mr. Waterlow was offended it would not be because they had published too much about him. It was nevertheless clear to her that there were a lot of things that *she* had not told Mr. Flack, as well as a great many that she had: perhaps these were the things that that lady had put in—Florine or Dorine—the one she had mentioned at Mme. de Brécourt's.

All the same, if the communication in the Reverberator gave them at the hotel less of a sensation than had been announced and bristled so much less than was to have been feared with explanations of the anguish of the Proberts, this did not diminish the girl's sense of responsibility nor make the case a whit less grave. It only showed how sensitive and fastidious the Proberts were and therefore with what difficulty they could forgive. Moreover Francie made another reflection as she lay there—for Delia kept her in bed nearly three days, feeling that for the moment at any rate that was an effectual reply to the wish she had signified that they should leave Paris. Perhaps they had got coarse and callous, Francie said to herself; perhaps they had read so many articles like that that they had lost their delicacy, the sense of certain differences and decencies. Then, very weak and vague and passive as she was now, in the bedimmed room, in the soft Parisian bed, and with Delia treating her as much as possible like a sick person, she thought of the lively and chatty letters that they had always seen in the papers and wondered whether they *all* meant a violation of sanctities, a convulsion of homes, a burning of smitten faces, a rupture of girls' engagements. It was present to her as an agreeable negative, I must add, that her father and sister took no strenuous view of her responsibility or of their own: they neither brought the matter up to her as a crime nor made her worse through her feeling that they hovered about in tacit disapproval. There was a pleasant, cheerful helplessness in her father in regard to this as in regard to everything else. There could be no more discussion among them on such a question than there had ever been, for none was needed to illustrate the fact that for these candid minds the newspapers and all they contained were a part of the general fatality of things, of the recurrent freshness of the universe, coming out like the sun in the morning or the stars at night. The thing that worried Francie most while Delia kept her in bed was the apprehension of what her father might do: but this was not a fear of what he might do to Mr. Flack. He would go round perhaps to Mr. Probert's or to Mme. de Brécourt's to reprimand them for having made things so rough for his "chicken." It was true she had scarcely ever seen him reprimand any one for anything; but on the other hand nothing like that had ever happened before to her or to Delia. They had made each other cry once or twice but no one else had ever made them, and no one had ever broken out on them that way and frightened them half to death. Francie wanted her father not to go round; she had a sense that those other people had somehow stores of censure, of superiority in any discussion, which he could not command. She wanted nothing done and no communication to pass—only a proud, unbickering silence on the part of the Dossons. If the Proberts made a noise and they made none it would be they who would have the best appearance. Moreover, now, with each elapsing day she felt that she *did* wish to see Gaston about it. Her desire was to wait, counting the hours, so that she might just explain, saying two or three things. Perhaps these things would not make it better—very likely they would not; but at any rate nothing would have been done in the interval, at least on her part and her father's and Delia's, to make it worse. She told her father that she should not like him to go round, and she was in some degree relieved at perceiving that he did not seem very clear as to what it was open to him to say to the Proberts. He was not afraid but he was vague. His relation to almost everything that had happened to them as a family for a good while back was a sense of the absence of precedents, and precedents were particularly absent now, for he had never before seen a lot of people in a rage about a piece in the paper. Delia also reassured her; she said she would see to it that their father didn't dash off. She communicated to her indeed that he had not the smallest doubt that Gaston, in a few days, would blow them all up much higher than they had blown her and that he was very sorry he had let her go round on that sort of summons to Mme. de Brécourt's. It was for her and the rest to come to Francie and to him, and if they had anything practical to say they would arrive in a body yet. If Mr. Dosson had the sense of his daughter's having been roughly handled he derived some of the consolation of amusement from his persistent humorous view of the Proberts as a "body." If they were consistent with their character or with their complaint they would move *en masse* upon the hotel, and he stayed at home a good deal, as if he were waiting for them. Delia intimated to her sister that this vision cheered them up as they sat, they two, in the red salon while Francie was in bed. Of course it did not exhilarate this young lady, and she even looked for no brighter side now. She knew almost nothing but her sharp little ache of suspense, her presentiment of Gaston's horror, which grew all the while. Delia remarked to her once that he would have seen lots of society-papers over there, he would have become familiar; but this only suggested to the girl (she had strange new moments of quick reasoning at present,) that that really would only prepare him to be disgusted, not to be indifferent. His disgust would be colder than anything she had ever known and would complete her knowledge of him—make her understand him properly for the first time. She would just meet it as briefly as possible; it would finish the business, wind up the episode, and all would be over.

He did not write; that proved it in advance; there had now been two or three posts without a letter. He had seen the paper in Boston or in New York and it had struck him dumb. It was very well for Delia to say that of course he didn't write when he was on the sea: how could they get his letters even if he did? There had been time before—before he sailed; though Delia represented that people never wrote then. They were ever so much too busy at the last and they were going to see their correspondents in a few days anyway. The only missives that came to Francie were a copy of the Reverberator, addressed in Mr. Flack's hand and with a great inkmark on the margin of the fatal letter, and a long note from Mme. de Brécourt, received forty-eight hours after the scene at her house. This lady expressed herself as follows:

"MY DEAR FRANCIE,—I felt very badly after you had gone yesterday morning, and I had twenty minds to go and see you. But we have talked it over conscientiously and it appears to us that we have no right to take any such step till Gaston arrives. The situation is not exclusively ours but belongs to him as well, and we feel that we ought to make it over to him in as simple and compact a form as possible. Therefore, as we regard it, we had better not touch it (it's so delicate, isn't it, my poor child?) but leave it just as it is. They think I even exceed my powers in writing you these simple lines, and that once your participation has been *constatée* (which was the only advantage of that dreadful scene), *everything* should stop. But I have liked you, Francie, I have believed in you, and I don't wish you to be able to say that in spite of the thunderbolt you have drawn down upon us I have not treated you with tenderness. It is a thunderbolt indeed, my poor and innocent but disastrous little friend! We are hearing more of it already—the horrible Republican papers here have *(as we know)* already got hold of the unspeakable sheet and are preparing to reproduce the article: that is such parts of it as they may put forward (with innuendoes and *sous-entendus* to eke out the rest) without exposing themselves to a suit for defamation. Poor Léonie de Villepreux has been with us constantly and Jeanne and her husband have telegraphed that we may expect them day after tomorrow. They are evidently immensely *émotionnés*, for they almost never telegraph. They wish so to receive Gaston. We have determined all the same to be intensely *quiet*, and that will be sure to be his view. Alphonse and Maxime now recognise that it is best to leave Mr. Flack alone, hard as it is to keep one's hands off him. Have you anything to *lui faire dire*—to my precious brother when he arrives? But it is foolish of me to ask you that, for you had much better not answer this. You will no doubt have an opportunity to say to him—whatever, my dear Francie, you *can* say! It will matter comparatively little that you may never be able to say it to your friend, with every allowance,

"SUZANNE DE BRÉCOURT."

Francie looked at this letter and tossed it away without reading it. Delia picked it up, read it to her father, who didn't understand it, and kept it in her possession, poring over it as Mr. Flack had seen her pore over the cards that were left while she was out or over the registers of American travellers. They knew of Gaston's arrival by his telegraphing from Havre (he came back by the French line), and he mentioned the hour—"about dinner-time"—at which he should reach Paris.

Delia, after dinner, made her father take her to the circus, so that Francie should be left alone to receive her intended, who would be sure to hurry round in the course of the evening. The girl herself expressed no preference whatever on this point, and the idea was one of Delia's masterly ones, her flashes of inspiration. There was never any difficulty about imposing such conceptions on her father. But at half-past ten, when they returned, the young man had not appeared, and Francie remained only long enough to say, "I told you so!" with a white face and to march off to her room with her candle. She locked herself in and her sister could not get at her that night. It was another of Delia's inspirations not to try, after she had felt that the door was fast. She forbore, in the exercise of a great discretion, but she herself in the ensuing hours slept not a wink. Nevertheless, the next morning, as early as ten o'clock, she had the energy to drag her father out to the banker's and to keep him out two hours. It would be inconceivable now that Gaston should not turn up before the *déjeûner*. He did turn up; about eleven o'clock he came in and found Francie alone. She perceived, in the strangest way, that he was very pale, at the same time that he was sunburnt; and not for an instant did he smile at her. It was very certain that there was no bright flicker in her own face, and they had the most singular, the most unnatural meeting. As he entered the room he said—"I could not come last evening; they made it impossible; they were all there and we were up till three o'clock this morning." He looked as if he had been through terrible things, and it was not simply the strain of his attention to so much business in America. What passed next she could not remember afterwards; it seemed only a few seconds before he said to her, slowly, holding her hand (before this he had pressed his lips to hers, silently), "Is it true, Francie, what they say (and they swear to it!) that *you* told that blackguard those horrors—that that infamous letter is only a report of *your* talk?"

"I told him everything—it's all me, *me, ME!*" the girl replied, exaltedly, without pretending to hesitate an instant as to what he might mean.

Gaston looked at her with deep eyes; then he walked straight away to the window and remained there in silence.

Francie said nothing more. At last the young man went on, "And I who insisted to them that there was no natural delicacy like yours!"

"Well, you'll never need to insist about anything any more!" she cried. And with this she dashed out of the room by the nearest door. When Delia and Mr. Dosson returned the red salon was empty and Francie was again locked into her room. But this time her sister forced an entrance.

XIII.

M R. DOSSON, as we know, was meditative, and the present occasion could only minister to that side of his nature, especially as, so far at least as the observation of his daughters went, it had not urged him into uncontrollable movement. But the truth is that the intensity, or rather the continuity, of his meditations did engender an act which was not perceived by these young ladies, though its consequences presently became definite enough. While he waited for the Proberts to arrive in a phalanx and noted that they failed to do so he had plenty of time to ask himself—and also to ask Delia—questions about Mr. Flack. So far as they were addressed to his daughter they were promptly answered, for Delia had been ready from the first, as we have seen, to pronounce upon the conduct of the young journalist. Her view of it was clearer every hour; there was a difference however in the course of action which she judged this view to demand. At first he was to be blown up for the mess he had got them into (profitless as the process might be and vain the satisfaction); he was to be visited with the harshest chastisement that the sense of violated confidence could inflict. Now he was simply to be dropped, to be cut, to be let alone to his dying day: the girl quickly recognised that this was a much more distinguished way of showing displeasure. It was in this manner that she characterised it, in her frequent conversations with her father, if that can be called conversation which consisted of his serenely smoking while she poured forth arguments which combined both variety and repetition. The same cause will produce consequences the most diverse: a truth according to which the catastrophe that made Delia express freely the hope that she might never again see so much as the end of Mr. Flack's nose had just the opposite effect upon her father. The one thing he wanted positively to do at present was to let his eyes travel over his young friend's whole person: it seemed to him that that would really make him feel better. If there had been a discussion about this the girl would have kept the field, for she had the advantage of being able to tell her reasons, whereas her father could not have put his into words. Delia had touched on her deepest conviction in saying to Francie that the correspondent of the Reverberator had played them that trick on purpose to get them into such trouble with the Proberts that he might see his own hopes bloom again under cover of their disaster. This had many of the appearances of a strained interpretation, but that did not prevent Delia from placing it before her father several times an hour. It mattered little that he should remark, in return, that he didn't see what good it could do Mr. Flack that Francie—and he and Delia, for all he could guess— should be disgusted with him: to Mr. Dosson's mind that was such a queer way of reasoning. Delia maintained that she understood perfectly, though she couldn't explain—and at any rate she didn't want the manœuvring creature to come flying back from Nice. She didn't want him to know that there had been a scandal, that they had a grievance against him, that any one had so much as heard of his article or cared what he published or didn't publish: above all she didn't want him to know that the Proberts had cooled off. Mixed up with this high rigour on Miss Dosson's part was the oddest secret complacency of reflection that in consequence of what Mr. Flack *had* published the great American community was in a position to know with what fine folks Francie and she were associated. She hoped that some of the people who used to call on them when they were "off to-morrow" would take the lesson to heart.

While she glowed with this consolation as well as with the resentment for which it was required her father quietly addressed a few words, by letter, to George Flack. This communication was not of a minatory order; it expressed on the contrary the loose sociability which was the essence of Mr. Dosson's nature. He wanted to see Mr. Flack, to talk the whole thing over, and the desire to hold him to an account would play but a small part in the interview. It was much more definite to him that the soreness of the Proberts was a kind of unexpected insanity (so little did his experience match it), than that a newspaper-man had misbehaved in trying to turn out an attractive article. As the newspaper-man happened to be the person with whom he had most consorted for some time back he felt drawn to him in the presence of a new problem, and somehow it did not seem to Mr. Dosson to dis-qualify him as a source of comfort that it was just he who had been the fountain of injury. The injury was a sort of ema-nation of the crazy Proberts. Moreover Mr. Dosson could not dislike at such short notice, a man who had smoked so many of his cigars, ordered so many of his dinners and helped him so loyally to spend his money: such acts constituted a bond, and when there was a bond people gave it a little jerk in time of trouble. His letter to Nice was the little jerk.

The morning after Francie had turned her back on Gaston and left him planted in the salon (he had remained ten min-utes, to see if she would reappear, and then had marched out of the hotel), she received by the first post a letter from him, written the evening before. It conveyed his deep regret that their meeting in the morning should have been of so painful, so unnatural a character, and the hope that she did not con-sider, as her strange behaviour had seemed to suggest, that *she* had anything to complain of. There was too much he wanted to say and above all too much he wanted to ask, for him to consent to the indefinite postponement of a necessary inter-view. There were explanations, assurances, *de part et d'autre*, with which it was manifestly impossible that either of them should dispense. He would therefore propose that she should see him, and not be wanting in patience to that end, on the following evening. He did not propose an earlier moment be-cause his hands were terribly full at home. Frankly speaking, the state of things there was of the worst. Jane and her hus-band had just arrived and had made him a violent, an unex-pected scene. Two of the French newspapers had got hold of the article and had given the most perfidious extracts. His father had not stirred out of the house, had not put his foot inside of a club, for more than a week. Marguerite and Max-ime were immediately to start for England, for an indefinite stay. They couldn't face their life in Paris. For himself, he was in the breach, fighting hard and making, on her behalf, assev-erations which it was impossible for him to believe, in spite of the dreadful defiant confession she had appeared to throw at him in the morning, that she would not virtually confirm. He would come in as soon after nine as possible; the morrow, up to that time, would be severe in the Cours la Reine, and he begged her in the meantime not to doubt of his perfect tenderness. So far from his distress having made it less he had never yet felt so much that she had, in his affection, a treasure of indulgence to draw upon.

A couple of hours after this letter arrived Francie lay on one of the satin sofas with her eyes closed and her hand clinched upon it in her pocket. Delia sat near her with a needle in her fingers, certain morsels of silk and ribbon in her lap, several pins in her mouth, and her attention wandering constantly from her work to her sister's face. The weather was now so completely vernal that Mr. Dosson was able to sit in the court, and he had lately resumed this practice, in which he was presumably at the present moment absorbed. Delia had lowered her needle and was watching Francie, to see if she were not asleep—she had been perfectly still for so long— when her glance was drawn to the door, which she heard pushed open. Mr. Flack stood there, looking from one to the other of the young ladies, as if to see which of them would be most agreeably surprised by his visit.

"I saw your father down stairs—he says it's all right," said the journalist, advancing and smiling. "He told me to come straight up—I had quite a talk with him."

"All right—*all right*?" Delia Dosson repeated, springing up. "Yes, indeed, I should say so." Then she checked herself, asking in another manner: "Is that so? father sent you up?" And then, in still another: "Well, have you had a good time at Nice?"

"You'd better all come down and see. It's lovely down there. If you'll come down I'll go right back. I guess you want a change," Mr. Flack went on. He spoke to Delia but he looked at Francie, who showed she had not been asleep by the quick consciousness with which she raised herself on her sofa. She gazed at the visitor with parted lips, but she said nothing. He hesitated a moment, then came toward her, smiling, with his hand out. His bright eyes were brighter than ever, but they had an odd appearance of being smaller, like penetrating points. "Your father has told me all about it. Did you ever hear of anything so ridiculous?"

"All about what?—all about what?" said Delia, whose attempt to represent happy ignorance seemed likely to be spoiled by an intromission of ferocity. She might succeed in appearing ignorant, but she could scarcely succeed in appearing happy. Francie had risen to her feet and had suffered Mr. Flack to possess himself for a moment of her hand, but neither of the girls had asked the young man to sit down. "I thought you were going to stay a month at Nice," Delia continued.

"Well, I was, but your father's letter started me up."

"Father's letter?"

"He wrote me about the row—didn't you know it? Then I broke. You didn't suppose I was going to stay down there when there were such times up here."

"Gracious!" Delia exclaimed.

"Is it pleasant at Nice? Is it very gay? Isn't it very hot now?" Francie asked.

"Oh, it's all right. But I haven't come up here to talk about Nice, have I?"

"Why not, if we want to?" Delia inquired.

Mr. Flack looked at her for a moment very hard, in the whites of the eyes; then he replied, turning back to her sister: "Anything *you* like, Miss Francie. With you one subject is as good as another. Can't we sit down? Can't we be comfortable?" he added.

"Comfortable? Of course we can!" cried Delia, but she remained erect while Francie sank upon the sofa again and their companion took possession of the nearest chair.

"Do you remember what I told you once, that the people *will* have the plums?" George Flack asked of the younger girl.

She looked for an instant as if she were trying to recollect what he had told her; then she said, "*Did* father write to you?"

"Of course he did. That's why I'm here."

"Poor father, sometimes he doesn't know *what* to do!" Delia remarked.

"He told me the Reverberator has made a sensation. I guessed that for myself, when I saw the way the papers here were after it. That thing will go the round you'll see! What brought me was learning from him that they *have* got their backs up."

"What on earth are you talking about?" cried Delia.

Mr. Flack turned his eyes on hers in the same way as a moment before; Francie sat there serious, looking hard at the carpet. "What game are you trying, Miss Delia? It ain't true *you* care what I wrote, is it?" he pursued, addressing himself again to Francie.

She raised her eyes. "Did you write it yourself?"

"What do you care what he wrote—or what does any one care?" Delia broke in.

"It has done the paper more good than anything—every one is so interested," said Mr. Flack, in the tone of reasonable explanation. "And you don't feel that you have anything to complain of, do you?" he added, to Francie, kindly.

"Do you mean because I told you?"

"Why, certainly. Didn't it all spring out of that lovely drive and that walk in the Bois that we had, when you took me to see your portrait? Didn't you understand that I wanted you to know that the public would appreciate a column or two about Mr. Waterlow's new picture, and about you as the subject of it, and about your being engaged to a member of the *grand monde*, and about what was going on in the *grand monde*, which would naturally attract attention through that? Why, Miss Francie, you talked as if you did."

"Did I talk a great deal?" asked Francie.

"Why, most freely—it was too lovely. Don't you remember when we sat there in the Bois?"

"Oh, rubbish!" Delia ejaculated.

"Yes, and Mme. de Cliché passed."

"And you told me she was scandalised. And we laughed—it struck us as idiotic. I said it was affected and pretentious. Your father tells me she is scandalised now—she and all the rest of them—at their names appearing in the Reverberator. I don't hesitate to declare that that's affected and pretentious too. It ain't genuine—and if it is it doesn't count. They pretend to be shocked because it looks exclusive, but in point of fact they like it first-rate."

"Are you talking about that old piece in the paper? Mercy, wasn't that dead and buried days and days ago?" Delia ejaculated. She hovered there in a fever of irritation, fidgeted by the revelation that her father had summoned Mr. Flack to Paris, which struck her almost like a treachery because it seemed to denote a plan. A plan, and an uncommunicated plan, on Mr. Dosson's part was unnatural and alarming; and there was further provocation in his appearing to shirk the responsibility of it by not having come up, at such a moment, with Mr. Flack. Delia was impatient to know what he wanted anyway. Did he want to slide back to a common, though active, young man? Did he want to put Mr. Flack forward with a shallow extemporised optimism as a substitute for the alienated Gaston? If she had not been afraid that something still more complicating than anything that had happened yet might come to pass between her two companions in case of her leaving them together she would have darted down to the court to appease her conjectures, to challenge her father and tell him she should be very much obliged to him if he wouldn't meddle. She felt liberated however, the next moment, for something occurred that struck her as a quick indication of her sister's present emotion.

"Do you know the view I take of the matter, according to what your father has told me?" Mr. Flack inquired. "I don't mean that he suggested the interpretation, but my own knowledge of the world (as the world is constituted over here!) forces it upon my mind. They are scandalised, they are horrified. They never heard anything so dreadful. Miss Francie, that ain't good enough! They know what's in the papers every day of their lives and they know how it got there. They are simply making the thing a pretext to break—because they don't think you're fashionable enough. They're delighted to strike a pretext they can work, and they're all as merry together round there as a lot of boys when school don't keep. That's my view of the business."

"Oh—how can you say such a thing?" drawled Francie, with a tremor in her voice that struck her sister. Her eyes met Delia's at the same moment, and this young woman's heart bounded with the sense that she was safe. Mr. Flack's indelicacy attempted to prove too much (though Miss Dosson had crude notions about the license of the press she felt, even as an untutored woman, what a false step he was now taking), and it seemed to her that Francie, who was revolted (the way she looked at her, in horror, showed that), could be trusted to check his advance.

"What does it matter what he says, my dear?" she cried. "Do make him drop the subject—he's talking very wild. I'm going down to see what father means—I never heard of anything so flat!" At the door she paused a moment to add mutely, with a pressing glance, "Now just wipe him out—mind!" It was the same injunction she had launched at her from afar that day, a year before, they all dined at Saint-Germain, and she could remember how effective it had been then. The next moment she flirted out.

As soon as she had gone Mr. Flack moved nearer to Francie. "Now look here, you are not going back on me, are you?"

"Going back on you—what do you mean?"

"Ain't we together in this thing? Surely we are."

"Together—together?" Francie repeated, looking at him.

"Don't you remember what I said to you—in the clearest terms—before we went to Waterlow's, before our drive? I notified you that I should make use of the whole thing."

"Oh, yes, I understood—it was all for that. I told them so. I never denied it."

"You told them so?"

"When they were crying and going on. I told them I knew it—I told them I gave you the tip, as they say."

She felt Mr. Flack's eyes on her, strangely, as she spoke these words; then he was still nearer to her—he had taken her hand. "Ah, you're too sweet!" She disengaged her hand and in the effort she sprang up; but he, rising too, seemed to press always nearer—she had a sense (it was disagreeable) that he was demonstrative—so that she retreated a little before him. "They were all there roaring and raging, trying to make you believe you have outraged them?"

"All but young Mr. Probert. Certainly they don't like it."

"The cowards!" said George Flack. "And where was young Mr. Probert?"

"He was away—I've told you—in America."

"Ah, yes, your father told me. But now he has come back doesn't he like it either?"

"I don't know, Mr. Flack," Francie replied, impatiently.

"Well, I do, then. He's a coward too—he'll do what his papa tells him—and the countess and the duchess and all the rest: he'll just back down—he'll give you up."

"I can't talk to you about that," said Francie.

"Why not? why is he such a sacred subject, when we *are* together? You can't alter that. It was too lovely, your standing up for me—your not denying me!"

"You put in things I never said. It seems to me it was very different," the girl remarked.

"Everything *is* different when it's printed. What else would be the good of papers? Besides, it wasn't I; it was a lady who helps me here—you've heard me speak of her: Miss Topping. She wants so much to know you—she wants to talk with you."

"And will she publish that?" Francie asked, gravely.

Mr. Flack stared a moment. "Lord, how they have worked on you! And do *you* think it's bad?"

"Do I think what's bad?"

"Why, the letter we are talking about."

"Well—I don't like it."

"Do you think I was dishonourable?"

The girl made no answer to this, but after a moment she said, "Why do you come here this way—why do you ask me such questions?"

He hesitated; then he broke out: "Because I love you—don't you know that?"

"Oh, please don't!" she almost moaned, turning away.

"Why won't you understand it—why won't you understand the rest? Don't you see how it has worked round—the heartless brutes they've turned into, and the way *our* life—yours and mine—is bound to be the same? Don't you see the base way they treat you and that *I* only want to do anything in the world for you?"

Francie made no immediate response to this appeal, but after a moment she began: "Why did you ask so many questions that day?"

"Because I always ask questions—it's my business to ask them. Haven't you always seen me ask you and ask every one all I could? Don't you know they are the very foundation of my work? I thought you sympathised with my work so much—you used to tell me you did."

"Well, I did," said Francie.

"You put it in the past, I see. You don't then any more."

If this remark was on her visitor's part the sign of a rare assurance the girl's gentleness was still unruffled by it. She hesitated, she even smiled; then she replied, "Oh yes, I do— only not so much."

"They *have* worked on you; but I should have thought they would have disgusted you. I don't care—even a little sympathy will do—whatever you've got left." He paused, looking at her, but she remained silent; so he went on: "There was no obligation for you to answer my questions—you might have shut me up, that day, with a word."

"Really?" Francie asked, with all her sweet good faith in her face. "I thought I had to—for fear I should appear ungrateful."

"Ungrateful?"

"Why to you—after what you had done. Don't you remember that it was you that introduced us——?" And she paused, with a kind of weary delicacy.

"Not to those snobs that are screaming like frightened peacocks. I beg your pardon—I haven't *that* on my conscience!"

"Well, you introduced us to Mr. Waterlow and he introduced us to—to his friends," Francie explained, blushing, as if it were a fault, for the inexactness engendered by her magnanimity. "That's why I thought I ought to tell you what you'd like."

"Why, do you suppose if I'd known where that first visit of ours to Waterlow was going to bring you out I'd have taken you within fifty miles——" He stopped suddenly; then in another tone, "Lord, there's no one like you! And you told them it was all *you*?"

"Never mind what I told them."

"Miss Francie," said George Flack, "if you'll marry me I'll never ask a question again. I'll go into some other business."

"Then you didn't do it on purpose?" Francie asked.

"On purpose?"

"To get me into a quarrel with them—so that I might be free again."

"Well, of all the ideas——!" the young man exclaimed, staring. "Your mind never produced that—it was your sister's."

"Wasn't it natural it should occur to me, since if, as you say, you would never consciously have been the means——"

"Ah, but I *was* the means!" Mr. Flack interrupted. "We must go, after all, by what *did* happen."

"Well, I thanked you when I drove with you and let you draw me out. So we're square, aren't we?" The term Francie used was a colloquialism generally associated with levity, but her face, as she spoke, was none the less deeply serious—serious even to pain.

"We're square?" Mr. Flack repeated.

"I don't think you ought to ask for anything more. Good-bye."

"Good-bye? Never!" cried the young man.

He had an air of flushing with disappointment which really showed that he had come with a certain confidence of success.

Something in the way Francie repeated her "Good-bye!" indicated that she perceived this and that in the vision of such a confidence there was little to please her. "Do go away!" she broke out.

"Well, I'll come back very soon," said Mr. Flack, taking his hat.

"Please don't—I don't like it." She had now contrived to put a wide space between them.

"Oh, you tormentress!" he groaned. He went toward the door, but before he reached it he turned round. "Will you tell me this, anyway? *Are* you going to marry Mr. Probert—after this?"

"Do you want to put that in the paper?"

"Of course I do—and say you said it!" Mr. Flack held up his head.

They stood looking at each other across the large room. "Well then—I ain't. There!"

"That's all right," said Mr. Flack, going out.

XIV.

WHEN GASTON PROBERT came in that evening he was received by Mr. Dosson and Delia, and when he asked where Francie was he was told by Delia that she would show herself half an hour later. Francie had instructed her sister that as Gaston would have, first of all, information to give their father about the business he had transacted in America he wouldn't care for a lot of women in the room. When Delia made this speech before Mr. Dosson the old man protested that he was not in any hurry for the business; what he wanted to find out most was whether he had a good time—whether he liked it over there. Gaston might have liked it, but he did not look as if he had had a very good time. His face told of reverses, of suffering; and Delia declared to him that if she had not received his assurance to the contrary she would have believed he was right down sick. He confessed that he had been very sick at sea and was still feeling the effect of it, but insisted that there was nothing the matter with him now. He sat for some time with Mr. Dosson and Delia, and never once alluded to the cloud that hung over their relations. The girl had schooled her father to reticence on this point, and the manner in which she had descended upon him in the morning, after Mr. Flack had come up stairs, was a lesson he was not likely soon to forget. It had been impressed upon him that she was indeed wiser than he could pretend to be, and he was now mindful that he must not speak of the "piece in the paper" unless young Probert should speak of it first. When Delia rushed down to him in the court she began by asking him categorically whom he had wished to do good to by sending Mr. Flack up to their parlour. To Francie or to her? Why, the way they felt then, they detested his very name. To Mr. Flack himself? Why, he had simply exposed him to the biggest snub he had ever got in his life.

"Well, hanged if I understand!" poor Mr. Dosson had said. "I thought you liked the piece—you think it's so queer *they* don't like it." "They," in the parlance of the Dossons, now never meant anything but the Proberts in congress assembled.

"I don't think anything is queer but you!" Delia had retorted; and she had let her father know that she had left Francie in the very act of "handling" Mr. Flack.

"Is that so?" the old gentleman had asked, helplessly.

Francie's visitor came down a few minutes later and passed through the court and out of the hotel without looking at them. Mr. Dosson had been going to call after him, but Delia checked him with a violent pinch. The unsociable manner of the young journalist's departure added to Mr. Dosson's sense of the mystery of things. I think this may be said to have been the only incident in the whole business that gave him a personal pang. He remembered how many of his cigars he had smoked with Mr. Flack and how universal a participant he had made him. This struck him as the failure of friendship, and not the publication of details about the Proberts. Deep in Mr. Dosson's spirit was a sense that if these people had done bad things they ought to be ashamed of themselves and he couldn't pity them, and if they hadn't done them there was no need of making such a rumpus about other people knowing. It was therefore, in spite of the young man's rough exit, still in the tone of American condonation that he had observed to Delia: "He says that's what they like over there and that it stands to reason that if you start a paper you've got to give them what they like. If you want the people with you, you've got to be with the people."

"Well, there are a good many people in the world. I don't think the Proberts are with us much."

"Oh, he doesn't mean them," said Mr. Dosson.

"Well, I do!" cried Delia.

At one of the ormolu tables, near a lamp with a pink shade, Gaston insisted on making at least a partial statement. He did not say that he might never have another chance, but Delia felt with despair that this idea was in his mind. He was very gentle, very polite, but distinctly cold, she thought; he was intensely depressed and for half an hour uttered not the least little pleasantry. There was no particular occasion for that when he talked about "preferred bonds" with her father. This was a language Delia could not translate, though she had heard it from childhood. He had a great many papers to show Mr. Dosson, records of the mission of which he had acquitted himself, but Mr. Dosson pushed them into the drawer of the ormolu table with the remark that he guessed they were all right. Now, after the fact, he appeared to attach but little importance to Gaston's achievements—an attitude which Delia perceived to be slightly disconcerting to the young man. Delia understood it: she had an instinctive sense that her father knew a great deal more than Gaston could tell him even about the work he had committed to him, and also that there was in such punctual settlements an eagerness, a literalism totally foreign to Mr. Dosson's domestic habits. If Gaston had cooled off he wanted at least to be able to say that he had rendered them services in America; but now her father, for the moment at least, scarcely appeared to think his services worth speaking of: a circumstance that left him with more of the responsibility for his cooling. What Mr. Dosson wanted to know was how everything had struck him over there, especially the Pickett Building and the parlour-cars and Niagara and the hotels he had instructed him to go to, giving him an introduction in two or three cases to the gentleman in charge of the office. It was in relation to these themes that Gaston was guilty of a want of spring, as the girl phrased it to herself; that he evinced no superficial joy. He declared however, repeatedly, that it was a most extraordinary country—most extraordinary and far beyond anything he had had any conception of. "Of course I didn't like *everything*," he said, "any more than I like everything anywhere."

"Well, what didn't you like?" Mr. Dosson genially inquired.

Gaston Probert hesitated. "Well, the light for instance."

"The light—the electric?"

"No, the solar! I thought it rather hard, too much like the scratching of a slate-pencil." As Mr. Dosson looked vague at this, as if the reference were to some enterprise (a great lamp-company) of which he had not heard—conveying a suggestion that he was perhaps staying away too long, Gaston immediately added: "I really think Francie might come in. I wrote to her that I wanted particularly to see her."

"I will go and call her—I'll make her come," said Delia, going out. She left her companions together and Gaston returned to the subject of Mr. Munster, Mr. Dosson's former partner, to whom he had taken a letter and who had shown him every sort of civility. Mr. Dosson was pleased at this; nevertheless he broke out, suddenly—

"Look here, you know; if you've got anything to say that you don't think very acceptable you had better say it to *me*." Gaston coloured, but his reply was checked by Delia's quick return. She announced that her sister would be obliged if he would go into the little dining-room—he would find her there. She had something to communicate to him that she could mention only in private. It was very comfortable; there was a lamp and a fire. "Well, I guess she *can* take care of herself!" Mr. Dosson, at this, commented, laughing. "What does she want to say to him?" he demanded, when Gaston had passed out.

"Gracious knows! She won't tell me. But it's too flat, at his age, to live in such terror."

"In such terror?"

"Why, of your father. You've got to choose."

"How, to choose?"

"Why, if there's a person you like and he doesn't like."

"You mean you can't choose your father," said Mr. Dosson, thoughtfully.

"Of course you can't."

"Well then, please don't like any one. But perhaps *I* should like him," added Mr. Dosson, faithful to his cheerful tradition.

"I guess you'd have to!" said Delia.

In the small *salle-à-manger*, when Gaston went in, Francie was standing by the empty table, and as soon as she saw him she said—"You can't say I didn't tell you that I should do something. I did nothing else, from the first. So you were warned again and again; you knew what to expect."

"Ah, don't say that again; if you knew how it acts on my nerves!" the young man groaned. "You speak as if you had done it on purpose—to carry out your absurd threat."

"Well, what does it matter, when it's all over?"

"It's not all over. Would to God it were!"

The girl stared. "Don't you know what I sent for you to come in here for? To bid you good-bye."

"Francie, what has got into you?" he said. "What deviltry, what poison?" It would have been a singular sight to an observer, the opposition of these young figures, so fresh, so candid, so meant for confidence, but now standing apart and looking at each other in a wan defiance which hardened their faces.

"Don't they despise me—don't they hate me? You do yourself! Certainly you'll be glad for me to break off and spare you such a difficulty, such a responsibility."

"I don't understand; it's like some hideous dream!" Gaston Probert cried. "You act as if you were doing something for a wager, and you talk so. I don't believe it—I don't believe a word of it."

"What don't you believe?"

"That you told him—that you told him knowingly. If you'll take that back (it's too monstrous!) if you'll deny it and declare you were practised upon and surprised, everything can still be arranged."

"Do you want me to lie?" asked Francie Dosson. "I thought you would like it."

"Oh, Francie, Francie!" moaned the wretched youth, with tears in his eyes.

"What can be arranged? What do you mean by everything?" she went on.

"Why, they'll accept it; they'll ask for nothing more. It's your participation they can't forgive."

"*They* can't? Why do you talk to me about them? I'm not engaged to them."

"Oh, Francie, *I* am! And it's they who are buried beneath that filthy rubbish!"

She flushed at this characterisation of Mr. Flack's epistle; then she said, in a softer voice: "I'm very sorry—very sorry indeed. But evidently I'm not delicate."

He looked at her, helpless and bitter. "It's not the newspapers, in your country, that would have made you so. Lord, they're too incredible! And the ladies have them on their tables."

"You told me we couldn't here—that the Paris ones are too bad," said Francie.

"Bad they are, God knows; but they have never published anything like that—poured forth such a flood of impudence on decent, quiet people who only want to be left alone."

Francie sank into a chair by the table, as if she were too tired to stand longer, and with her arms spread out on the lamp-lit plush she looked up at him. "Was it there you saw it?"

"Yes, a few days before I sailed. I hated them from the moment I got there—I looked at them very little. But that was a chance. I opened the paper in the hall of an hotel (there was a big marble floor and spittoons!) and my eyes fell upon that horror. It made me ill."

"Did you think it was me?"

"About as soon as I supposed it was my father. But I was too mystified, too tormented."

"Then why didn't you write to me, if you didn't think it was me?"

"Write to you? I wrote to you every three days."

"Not after that."

"Well, I may have omitted a post at the last.—I thought it might be Delia," Gaston added in a moment.

"Oh, she didn't want me to do it—the day I went with him, the day I told him. She tried to prevent me."

"Would to God then she had!"

"Haven't you told them she's delicate too?" Francie asked, in her strange tone.

Gaston made no answer to this; but he broke out—"What power, in heaven's name, has he got over you? What spell has he worked?"

"He's an old friend—he helped us ever so much when we were first in Paris."

"But, my dearest child, what friends—what a man to know!"

"If we hadn't known him we shouldn't have known you. Remember that it was Mr. Flack who brought us that day to Mr. Waterlow's."

"Oh, you would have come some other way," said Gaston.

"Not in the least. We knew nothing about any other way. He helped us in everything—he showed us everything. That was why I told him—when he asked me. I liked him for what he had done."

Gaston, who had now also seated himself, listened to this attentively. "I see. It was a kind of delicacy."

"Oh, a kind!" She smiled.

He remained a little with his eyes on her face. "Was it for me?"

"Of course it was for you."

"Ah, how strange you are!" he exclaimed, tenderly. "Such contradictions—*on s'y perd.* I wish you would say that to *them*, that way. Everything would be right."

"Never, never!" said the girl. "I have wronged them, and nothing will ever be the same again. It was fatal. If I felt as they do I too would loathe the person who should have done such a thing. It doesn't seem to me so bad—the thing in the paper; but you know best. You must go back to them. You know best," she repeated.

"They were the last, the last people in France, to do it to. The sense of excruciation—of pollution," Gaston rejoined, making his reflections audibly.

"Oh, you needn't tell me—I saw them all there!" Francie exclaimed.

"It must have been a dreadful scene. But you *didn't* brave them, did you?"

"Brave them—what are you talking about? To you that idea is incredible!"

"No, it isn't," he said, gently.

"Well, go back to them—go back," she repeated. At this he half threw himself across the table, to seize her hands; but she drew away and, as he came nearer, pushed her chair back, springing up. "You know you didn't come here to tell me you are ready to give them up."

He rose to his feet, slowly. "To give them up? I have been battling with them till I'm ready to drop. You don't know how they feel—how they *must* feel."

"Oh yes, I do. All this has made me older, every hour."

"It has made you more beautiful," said Gaston Probert.

"I don't care. Nothing will induce me to consent to any sacrifice."

"Some sacrifice there must be. Give me time—give me time, I'll manage it. I only wish they hadn't seen you there in the Bois."

"In the Bois?"

"That Marguerite hadn't seen you—with that blackguard. That's the image they can't get over."

"I see you can't either, Gaston. Well, I *was* there and I was very happy. That's all I can say. You must take me as I am."

"Don't—don't; you infuriate me!" he pleaded, frowning.

Francie had seemed to soften, but she was in a sudden flame again. "Of course I do, and I shall do it again. We are too different. Everything makes you so. You can't give them up—ever, ever. Good-bye—good-bye! That's all I wanted to tell you."

"I'll go and throttle him!" Gaston said, lugubriously.

"Very well, go! Good-bye." She had stepped quickly to the door and had already opened it, vanishing as she had done the last time.

"Francie, Francie!" he exclaimed, following her into the passage. The door was not the one that led into the salon; it communicated with the other apartments. The girl had plunged into these—he already heard her locking herself in. Presently he went away, without taking leave of Mr. Dosson and Delia.

"Why, he acts just like Mr. Flack," said the old man, when they discovered that the interview in the dining-room had come to an end.

The next day was a bad day for Charles Waterlow; his work, in the Avenue de Villiers, was terribly interrupted. Gaston Probert invited himself to breakfast with him at noon and remained till the time at which the artist usually went out—an extravagance partly justified by a previous separation of several weeks. During these three or four hours Gaston walked up and down the studio, while Waterlow either sat or stood before his easel. He put his host out vastly and acted on his nerves, but Waterlow was patient with him because he was very sorry for him, feeling the occasion to be a great crisis. His compassion, it is true, was slightly tinged with contempt: nevertheless he looked at the case generously, perceived it to be one in which a friend should be a friend—in which he, in particular, might see the distracted fellow through. Gaston was in a fever; he broke out into passionate arguments which were succeeded by fits of gloomy silence. He roamed about continually, with his hands in his pockets and his hair in a tangle; he could take neither a decision nor a momentary rest. It struck Waterlow more than ever before that he was after all essentially a foreigner; he had the sensibility of one, the sentimental candour, the need for sympathy, the communicative despair. A real young Anglo-Saxon would have buttoned himself up in his embarrassment and been dry and awkward and capable and unconscious of a drama; but Gaston was effusive and appealing and ridiculous and graceful—natural, above all, and egotistical. Indeed, a real young Anglo-Saxon would not have had this particular embarrassment at all for he would not have parted to such an extent with his moral independence. It was this weakness that excited Waterlow's secret scorn: family feeling was all very well, but to see it erected into a superstition affected him very much in the same way as the image of a blackamoor upon his knees before a fetish. He now measured for the first time the root it had taken in Gaston's nature. To act like a man the poor fellow must pull up the root, but the operation was terribly painful—was attended with cries and tears and contortions, with baffling scruples and a sense of sacrilege, the sense of siding with strangers against his own flesh and blood. Every now and then he broke out—"And if you see her—as she looks just now (she's too lovely—too touching!) you would see how right I was originally—when I found in her such a revelation of that type, the French Renaissance, you know, the one we talked about." But he reverted with at least equal frequency to the idea that he seemed unable to throw off, that it was like something done on purpose, with a refinement of cruelty; such an accident to *them*, of all people on earth, the very last, the very last, those who he verily believed would feel it more than any family in the world. When Waterlow asked what made them so exceptionally ticklish he could only say that they just happened to be so; it was his father's influence, his very genius, the worship of privacy and good manners, a hatred of all the new familiarities and profanations. The artist inquired further, at last, rather wearily, what in two words was the practical question his friend desired that he should consider. Whether he should be justified in throwing over Miss Francina—was that it?

"Oh heavens, no! For what sneak do you take me? She made a mistake, but any one might do that. It's whether it strikes you that I should be justified in throwing *them* over."

"It depends upon the sense you attach to justification."

"I mean—should I be miserably unhappy—would it be in their power to make me so?"

"To try—certainly, if they are capable of anything so nasty. The only honourable conduct for them is to let you alone."

"Ah, they won't do that—they like me too much!" Gaston said, ingenuously.

"It's an odd way of liking. The best way to show that would be to let you marry the girl you love."

"Certainly—but they are profoundly convinced that she represents such dangers, such vulgarities, such possibilities of doing other things of the same sort, that it's upon *them* my happiness would be shattered."

"Well, if you yourself have no secret for persuading them of the contrary I'm afraid I can't teach you one."

"Yes, I ought to do it myself," said Gaston, in the candour of his meditations. Then he went on, in his torment of inconsistency—"They never believed in her from the first. My father was perfectly definite about it. At heart they never accepted her; they only pretended to do so because I guaranteed that she was incapable of doing a thing that could ever displease them. Then no sooner was my back turned than she perpetrated that!"

"That was your folly," Waterlow remarked, painting away.

"My folly—to turn my back?"

"No, no—to guarantee."

"My dear fellow—wouldn't you?" Gaston asked, staring.

"Never in the world."

"You would have thought her capable——?"

"*Capabilissima!* and I shouldn't have cared."

"Do you think her then capable of doing it again?"

"I don't care if she is; that's the least of all questions."

"The least——?"

"Ah, don't you see, wretched youth," said Waterlow, pausing from his work and looking up—"don't you see that the question of her possibilities is as nothing compared to that of yours? She's the sweetest young thing I ever saw; but even if she happened not to be I should urge you to marry her, in simple self-preservation."

"In self-preservation?"

"To rescue from destruction the last remnant of your independence. That's a much more important matter even than not treating her shabbily. They are doing their best to kill you morally—to render you incapable of individual life."

"They are—they are!" Gaston declared, with enthusiasm.

"Well then, if you believe it, for heaven's sake go and marry her to-morrow!" Waterlow threw down his implements and added, "And come out of this—into the air."

Gaston however was planted in his path on the way to the door. "And if she does break out again, in the same way?"

"In the same way?"

"In some other manifestation of that terrible order?"

"Well," said Waterlow, "you will at least have got rid of your family."

"Yes, if she does that I shall be glad they are not there! They're right, *pourtant*, they're right," Gaston went on, passing out of the studio with his friend.

"They're right?"

"It was a dreadful thing."

"Yes, thank heaven! It was the finger of providence, to give you your chance." This was ingenious, but, though he could glow for a moment in response to it, Francie's lover—if lover he may in his most infirm aspect be called—looked as if he mistrusted it, thought it slightly sophistical. What really shook him however was his companion's saying to him in the vestibule, when they had taken their hats and sticks and were on the point of going out: "Lord, man, how can you be so impenetrably dense? Don't you see that she's really of the softest, finest material that breathes, that she's a perfect flower of plasticity, that everything you may have an apprehension about will drop away from her like the dead leaves from a rose and that you may make of her any perfect and enchanting thing you yourself have the wit to conceive?"

"Ah, my dear friend!" Gaston Probert murmured, gratefully, panting.

"The limit will be yours, not hers," Waterlow added.

"No, no, I have done with limits," his companion rejoined, ecstatically.

That evening at ten o'clock Gaston went to the Hôtel de l'Univers et de Cheltenham and requested the German waiter to introduce him into the dining-room attached to Mr. Dosson's apartments and then go and tell Miss Francina he was awaiting her there.

"Oh, you'll be better there than in the *zalion*—they have villed it with their luccatch," said the man, who always addressed him in an intention of English and was not ignorant of the tie that united the visitor to the amiable American family, or perhaps even of the modifications it had lately undergone.

"With their luggage?"

"They leave to-morrow morning—oh, I don't think they themselves known for where, sir."

"Please then say to Miss Francina that I have called on very urgent business—that I'm pressed, pressed!"

The eagerness of the sentiment which possessed Gaston at that moment is communicative, but perhaps the vividness with which the waiter placed it before the young lady is better explained by the fact that her lover slipped a five-franc piece into his hand. At any rate she entered the dining-room sooner than Gaston had ventured to hope, though she corrected this promptitude a little by stopping short, drawing back, when she saw how pale he was and how he looked as if he had been crying.

"I have chosen—I have chosen," he said gently, smiling at her in contradiction to these indications.

"You have chosen?"

"I have had to give them up. But I like it so much better than having to give *you* up! I took you first with their assent. That was well enough—it was worth trying for. But now I take you without it. We can live that way too."

"Ah, I'm not worth it. You give up too much!" cried the girl. "We're going away—it's all over." She turned from him quickly, as if to carry out her meaning, but he caught her more quickly still and held her—held her fast and long. She had only freed herself when her father and sister broke in, from the salon, attracted apparently by the audible commotion.

"Oh, I thought you had at least knocked over the lamp!" Delia exclaimed.

"You must take me with you if you are going away, Mr. Dosson," Gaston said. "I will start whenever you like."

"All right—where shall we go?" the old man asked.

"Hadn't you decided that?"

"Well, the girls said they would tell me."

"We were going home," said Francie.

"No we weren't—not a bit!" Delia declared.

"Oh, not there," Gaston murmured, pathetically, looking at Francie.

"Well, when you've fixed it you can take the tickets," Mr. Dosson observed.

"To some place where there are no newspapers," Gaston went on.

"I guess you'll have hard work to find one."

"Dear me, we needn't read them! We wouldn't have read that one if your family hadn't forced us," Delia said to her prospective brother-in-law.

"Well, I shall never be forced—I shall never again in my life look at one," he replied.

"You'll see—you'll have to!" laughed Mr. Dosson.

"No, you'll tell us enough."

Francie had her eyes on the ground; they were all smiling but she. "Won't they forgive me, ever?" she asked, looking up.

"Yes, perfectly, if you can persuade me not to marry you. But in that case what good will their forgiveness do you?"

"Well, perhaps it's better to pay for it."

"To pay for it?"

"By suffering something. For it *was* dreadful."

"Oh, for all you'll suffer——!" Gaston exclaimed, shining down at her.

"It was for you—only for you, as I told you," the girl went on.

"Yes, don't tell me again—I don't like that explanation! I ought to let you know that my father now declines to do anything for me," the young man added, to Mr. Dosson.

"To do anything for you?"

"To give me any money."

"Well, that makes me feel better," said Mr. Dosson.

"There'll be enough for all—especially if we economise in newspapers," Delia declared, jocosely.

"Well, I don't know, after all—the Reverberator came for nothing," her father went on, in the same spirit.

"Don't you be afraid he'll ever send it now!" cried the girl.

"I'm very sorry—because they were lovely," Francie said to Gaston, with sad eyes.

"Let us wait to say that till they come back to us," Gaston returned, somewhat sententiously. He really cared little at this moment whether his relatives were lovely or not.

"I'm sure you won't have to wait long!" Delia remarked, with the same cheerfulness.

" 'Till they come back'?" Mr. Dosson repeated. "Ah, they can't come back now. We won't take them in!" The words fell from his lips with a mild unexpected austerity which imposed itself, producing a momentary silence, and it is a sign of Gaston's complete emancipation that he did not in his heart resent this image of eventual favours denied to his race. The resentment was rather Delia's, but she kept it to herself, for she was capable of reflecting with complacency that the key of the house would after all be hers, so that she could open the door for the Proberts if they should knock. Now that her sister's marriage was really to take place her consciousness that the American people would have been told so was still more agreeable. The party left the Hôtel de l'Univers et de Cheltenham on the morrow, but it appeared to the German waiter, as he accepted another five-franc piece from the happy and now reckless Gaston, that they were even yet not at all clear as to where they were going.

THE END.

THE TRAGIC MUSE

I.

THE PEOPLE of France have made it no secret that those of England, as a general thing, are, to their perception, an inexpressive and speechless race, perpendicular and unsociable, unaddicted to enriching any bareness of contact with verbal or other embroidery. This view might have derived encouragement, a few years ago, in Paris, from the manner in which four persons sat together in silence, one fine day about noon, in the garden, as it is called, of the Palais de l'Industrie—the central court of the great glazed bazaar where, among plants and parterres, gravelled walks and thin fountains, are ranged the figures and groups, the monuments and busts, which form, in the annual exhibition of the Salon, the department of statuary. The spirit of observation is naturally high at the Salon, quickened by a thousand artful or artless appeals, but no particular tension of the visual sense would have been required to embrace the character of the four persons in question. As a solicitation of the eye on definite grounds, they too constituted a successful plastic fact; and even the most superficial observer would have perceived them to be striking products of an insular neighbourhood, representatives of that tweed-and-waterproof class with which, on the recurrent occasions when the English turn out for a holiday—Christmas and Easter, Whitsuntide and the autumn—Paris besprinkles itself at a night's notice. They had about them the indefinable professional look of the British traveller abroad; that air of preparation for exposure, material and moral, which is so oddly combined with the serene revelation of security and of persistence, and which excites, according to individual susceptibility, the ire or the admiration of foreign communities. They were the more unmistakable as they illustrated very favourably the energetic race to which they had the honour to belong. The fresh, diffused light of the Salon made them clear and important; they were finished productions, in their way, and ranged there motionless, on their green bench, they were almost as much on exhibition as if they had been hung on the line.

Three ladies and a young man, they were obviously a family—a mother, two daughters and a son—a circumstance which had the effect at once of making each member of the group doubly typical and of helping to account for their fine taciturnity. They were not, with each other, on terms of ceremony, and moreover they were probably fatigued with their course among the pictures, the rooms on the upper floor. Their attitude, on the part of visitors who had superior features, even if they might appear to some passers-by to have neglected a fine opportunity for completing these features with an expression, was after all a kind of tribute to the state of exhaustion, of bewilderment, to which the genius of France is still capable of reducing the proud.

"*En v'la des abrutis!*" more than one of their fellow-gazers might have been heard to exclaim; and certain it is that there was something depressed and discouraged in this interesting group, who sat looking vaguely before them, not noticing the life of the place, somewhat as if each had a private anxiety. A very close observer would have guessed that though on many questions they were closely united, this present anxiety was not the same for each. If they looked grave, moreover, this was doubtless partly the result of their all being dressed in mourning, as if for a recent bereavement. The eldest of the three ladies had indeed a face of a fine austere mould, which would have been moved to gaiety only by some force more insidious than any she was likely to recognize in Paris. Cold, still and considerably worn, it was neither stupid nor hard, but it was firm, narrow and sharp. This competent matron, acquainted evidently with grief, but not weakened by it, had a high forehead, to which the quality of the skin gave a singular polish—it glittered even when seen at a distance; a nose which achieved a high, free curve; and a tendency to throw back her head and carry it well above her, as if to disengage it from the possible entanglements of the rest of her person. If you had seen her walk you would have perceived that she trod the earth in a manner suggesting that in a world where she had long since discovered that one couldn't have one's own way, one could never tell what annoying aggression might take place, so that it was well, from hour to hour, to save what one could. Lady Agnes saved her head, her white triangular forehead, over which her closely crinkled flaxen hair, reproduced in different shades in her children, made a sort of looped silken canopy, like the marquee at a garden-party. Her daughters were tall, like herself—that was visible even as they sat there—and one of them, the younger evidently, was very pretty: a straight, slender, gray-eyed English girl, with a "good" figure and a fresh complexion. The sister, who was not pretty, was also straight and slender and gray-eyed. But the gray, in this case, was not so pure, nor were the slenderness and the straightness so maidenly. The brother of these young ladies had taken off his hat, as if he felt the air of the summer day heavy in the great pavilion. He was a lean, strong, clear-faced youth, with a straight nose and light-brown hair, which lay continuously and profusely back from his forehead, so that to smooth it from the brow to the neck but a single movement of the hand was required. I cannot describe him better than by saying that he was the sort of young Englishman who looks particularly well abroad, and whose general aspect—his inches, his limbs, his friendly eyes, the modulation of his voice, the cleanness of his flesh-tints and the fashion of his garments—excites on the part of those who encounter him in far countries on the ground of a common speech a delightful sympathy of race. This sympathy is sometimes qualified by an apprehension of undue literalness, but it almost revels as soon as such a danger is dispelled. We shall see quickly enough how accurate a measure it might have taken of Nicholas Dormer. There was food for suspicion, perhaps, in the wandering blankness that sat at moments in his eyes, as if he had no attention at all, not the least in the world, at his command; but it is no more than just to add, without delay, that this discouraging symptom was known, among those who liked him, by the indulgent name of dreaminess. For his mother and sisters, for instance, his dreaminess was notorious. He is the more welcome to the benefit of such an interpretation as there is always held to be something engaging in the combination of the muscular and the musing, the mildness of strength.

After some time—a period during which these good people might have appeared to have come, individually, to the Palais de l'Industrie much less to see the works of art than to think over their domestic affairs—the young man, rousing himself from his reverie, addressed one of the girls.

"I say, Biddy, why should we sit moping here all day? Come and take a turn about with me."

His younger sister, while he got up, leaned forward a little, looking round her, but she gave, for the moment, no further sign of complying with his invitation.

"Where shall we find you, then, if Peter comes?" inquired the other Miss Dormer, making no movement at all.

"I dare say Peter won't come. He'll leave us here to cool our heels."

"Oh, Nick, dear!" Biddy exclaimed in a sweet little voice of protest. It was plainly her theory that Peter would come, and even, a little, her apprehension that she might miss him should she quit that spot.

"We shall come back in a quarter of an hour. Really, I must look at these things," Nick declared, turning his face to a marble group which stood near them, on the right—a man, with the skin of a beast round his loins, tussling with a naked woman in some primitive effort of courtship or capture.

Lady Agnes followed the direction of her son's eyes, and then observed:

"Everything seems very dreadful. I should think Biddy had better sit still. Hasn't she seen enough horrors up above?"

"I dare say that if Peter comes Julia will be with him," the elder girl remarked irrelevantly.

"Well, then, he can take Julia about. That will be more proper," said Lady Agnes.

"Mother, dear, she doesn't care a rap about art. It's a fearful bore looking at fine things with Julia," Nick rejoined.

"Won't you go with him, Grace?" said Biddy, appealing to her sister.

"I think she has awfully good taste!" Grace exclaimed, not answering this inquiry.

"*Don't* say nasty things about her!" Lady Agnes broke out, solemnly, to her son, after resting her eyes on him a moment with an air of reluctant reprobation.

"I say nothing but what she'd say herself," the young man replied. "About some things she has very good taste, but about this kind of thing she has no taste at all."

"That's better, I think," said Lady Agnes, turning her eyes again to the "kind of thing" that her son appeared to designate.

"She's awfully clever—awfully!" Grace went on, with decision.

"Awfully, awfully," her brother repeated, standing in front of her and smiling down at her.

"You *are* nasty, Nick. You know you are," said the young lady, but more in sorrow than in anger.

Biddy got up at this, as if the accusatory tone prompted her to place herself generously at his side. "Mightn't you go and order lunch, in that place, you know?" she asked of her mother. "Then we would come back when it was ready."

"My dear child, I can't order lunch," Lady Agnes replied, with a cold impatience which seemed to intimate that she had problems far more important than those of victualling to contend with.

"I mean Peter, if he comes. I am sure he's up in everything of that sort."

"Oh, hang Peter!" Nick exclaimed. "Leave him out of account, and *do* order lunch, mother; but not cold beef and pickles."

"I must say—about him—you're not nice," Biddy ventured to remark to her brother, hesitating, and even blushing, a little.

"You make up for it, my dear," the young man answered, giving her chin—a very charming, rotund little chin—a friendly whisk with his forefinger.

"I can't imagine what you've got against him," her ladyship murmured, gravely.

"Dear mother, it's a disappointed fondness," Nick argued. "They won't answer one's notes; they won't let one know where they are nor what to expect. 'Hell has no fury like a woman scorned;' nor like a man either."

"Peter has such a tremendous lot to do—it's a very busy time at the Embassy; there are sure to be reasons," Biddy explained, with her pretty eyes.

"Reasons enough, no doubt!" said Lady Agnes, who accompanied these words with an ambiguous sigh, however, as if in Paris even the best reasons would naturally be bad ones.

"Doesn't Julia write to you, doesn't she answer you the very day?" Grace inquired, looking at Nick as if she were the courageous one.

He hesitated a moment, returning her glance with a certain severity. "What do you know about my correspondence? No doubt I ask too much," he went on; "I am so attached to them. Dear old Peter, dear old Julia!"

"She's younger than you, my dear!" cried the elder girl, still resolute.

"Yes, nineteen days."

"I'm glad you know her birthday."

"She knows yours; she always gives you something," Lady Agnes resumed, to her son.

"Her taste is good *then*, isn't it, Nick?" Grace Dormer continued.

"She makes charming presents; but, dear mother, it isn't *her* taste. It's her husband's."

"Her husband's?"

"The beautiful objects of which she disposes so freely are the things he collected, for years, laboriously, devotedly, poor man!"

"She disposes of them to you, but not to others," said Lady Agnes. "But that's all right," she added, as if this might have been taken for a complaint of the limitations of Julia's bounty. "She has to select, among so many, and that's a proof of taste," her ladyship went on.

"You can't say she doesn't choose lovely ones," Grace remarked to her brother, in a tone of some triumph.

"My dear, they are all lovely. George Dallow's judgment was so sure, he was incapable of making a mistake," Nicholas Dormer returned.

"I don't see how you can talk of him; he was dreadful," said Lady Agnes.

"My dear, if he was good enough for Julia to marry, he is good enough for one to talk of."

"She did him a great honour."

"I dare say; but he was not unworthy of it. No such intelligent collection of beautiful objects has been made in England in our time."

"You think too much of beautiful objects," returned her ladyship.

"I thought you were just now implying that I thought too little."

"It's very nice—his having left Julia so well off," Biddy interposed, soothingly, as if she foresaw a tangle.

"He treated her *en grand seigneur*, absolutely," Nick went on.

"He used to look greasy, all the same," Grace Dormer pursued, with a kind of dull irreconcilability. "His name ought to have been Tallow."

"You are not saying what Julia would like, if that's what you are trying to say," her brother remarked.

"Don't be vulgar, Grace," said Lady Agnes.

"I know Peter Sherringham's birthday!" Biddy broke out innocently, as a pacific diversion. She had passed her hand into her brother's arm, to signify her readiness to go with him, while she scanned the remoter portions of the garden as if it had occurred to her that to direct their steps in some such sense might after all be the shorter way to get at Peter.

"He's too much older than you, my dear," Grace rejoined, discouragingly.

"That's why I've noticed it—he's thirty-four. Do you call that too old? I don't care for slobbering infants!" Biddy cried.

"Don't be vulgar," Lady Agnes enjoined again.

"Come, Bid, we'll go and be vulgar together; for that's what we are, I'm afraid," her brother said to her. "We'll go and look at all these low works of art."

"Do you really think it's necessary to the child's development?" Lady Agnes demanded, as the pair turned away. Nicholas Dormer was struck as by a kind of challenge, and he paused, lingering a moment, with his little sister on his arm. "What we've been through this morning in this place, and what you've paraded before our eyes—the murders, the tortures, all kinds of disease and indecency!"

Nick looked at his mother as if this sudden protest surprised him, but as if also there were lurking explanations of it which he quickly guessed. Her resentment had the effect not so much of animating her cold face as of making it colder, less expressive, though visibly prouder. "Ah, dear mother, don't do the British matron!" he exclaimed, good-humouredly.

"British matron is soon said! I don't know what they are coming to."

"How odd that you should have been struck only with the disagreeable things, when, for myself, I have felt it to be the most interesting, the most suggestive morning I have passed for ever so many months!"

"Oh, Nick, Nick!" Lady Agnes murmured, with a strange depth of feeling.

"I like them better in London—they are much less unpleasant," said Grace Dormer.

"They are things you can look at," her ladyship went on. "We certainly make the better show."

"The subject doesn't matter; it's the treatment, the treatment!" Biddy announced, in a voice like the tinkle of a silver bell.

"Poor little Bid!" her brother cried, breaking into a laugh.

"How can I learn to model, mamma dear, if I don't look at things and if I don't study them?" the girl continued.

This inquiry passed unheeded, and Nicholas Dormer said to his mother, more seriously, but with a certain kind explicitness, as if he could make a particular allowance: "This place is an immense stimulus to me; it refreshes me, excites me, it's such an exhibition of artistic life. It's full of ideas, full of refinements; it gives one such an impression of artistic experience. They try everything, they feel everything. While you were looking at the murders, apparently, I observed an immense deal of curious and interesting work. There are too many of them, poor devils; so many who must make their way, who must attract attention. Some of them can only *taper fort*, stand on their heads, turn summersaults or commit deeds of violence, to make people notice them. After that, no doubt, a good many will be quieter. But I don't know; to-day I'm in an appreciative mood—I feel indulgent even to them: they give me an impression of intelligence, of eager observation. All art is one—remember that, Biddy, dear," the young man continued, looking down at his sister with a smile. "It's the same great, many-headed effort, and any ground that's gained by an individual, any spark that's struck in any province, is of use and of suggestion to all the others. We are all in the same boat."

" 'We,' do you say, my dear? Are you really setting up for an artist?" Lady Agnes asked.

Nick hesitated a moment. "I was speaking for Biddy!"

"But you *are* one, Nick—you are!" the girl cried.

Lady Agnes looked for an instant as if she were going to say once more "Don't be vulgar!" But she suppressed these words, if she had intended them, and uttered others, few in number and not completely articulate, to the effect that she hated talking about art. While her son spoke she had watched him as if she failed to follow him; yet something in the tone of her exclamation seemed to denote that she had understood him only too well.

"We are all in the same boat," Biddy repeated, smiling at her.

"Not me, if you please!" Lady Agnes replied. "It's horrid, messy work, your modelling."

"Ah, but look at the results!" said the girl, eagerly, glancing about at the monuments in the garden as if in regard even to them she were, through that unity of art that her brother had just proclaimed, in some degree an effective cause.

"There's a great deal being done here—a real vitality," Nicholas Dormer went on, to his mother, in the same reasonable, informing way. "Some of these fellows go very far."

"They do, indeed!" said Lady Agnes.

"I'm fond of young schools, like this movement in sculpture," Nick remarked, with his slightly provoking serenity.

"They're old enough to know better!"

"Mayn't I look, mamma? It *is* necessary to my development," Biddy declared.

"You may do as you like," said Lady Agnes, with dignity.

"She ought to see good work, you know," the young man went on.

"I leave it to your sense of responsibility." This statement was somewhat majestic, and for a moment, evidently, it tempted Nick, almost provoked him, or at any rate suggested to him an occasion to say something that he had on his mind.

Apparently, however, he judged the occasion on the whole not good enough, and his sister Grace interposed with the inquiry—

"Please, mamma, are we *never* going to lunch?"

"Ah, mother, mother!" the young man murmured, in a troubled way, looking down at Lady Agnes with a deep fold in his forehead.

For her, also, as she returned his look, it seemed an occasion; but with this difference, that she had no hesitation in taking advantage of it. She was encouraged by his slight embarrassment; for ordinarily Nick was not embarrassed. "You used to have so much," she went on; "but sometimes I don't know what has become of it—it seems all, *all* gone!"

"Ah, mother, mother!" he exclaimed again, as if there were so many things to say that it was impossible to choose. But this time he stepped closer, bent over her, and, in spite of the publicity of their situation, gave her a quick, expressive kiss. The foreign observer whom I took for granted in beginning to sketch this scene would have had to admit that the rigid English family had, after all, a capacity for emotion. Grace Dormer, indeed, looked round her to see if at this moment they were noticed. She discovered with satisfaction that they had escaped.

II.

NICK DORMER walked away with Biddy, but he had not gone far before he stopped in front of a clever bust, where his mother, in the distance, saw him playing in the air with his hand, carrying out by this gesture, which presumably was applausive, some critical remark he had made to his sister. Lady Agnes raised her glass to her eyes by the long handle to which rather a clanking chain was attached, perceiving that the bust represented an ugly old man with a bald head; at which her ladyship indefinitely sighed, though it was not apparent in what way such an object could be detrimental to her daughter. Nick passed on, and quickly paused again; this time, his mother discerned, it was before the marble image of a grimacing woman. Presently she lost sight of him; he wandered behind things, looking at them all round.

"I ought to get plenty of ideas for my modelling, oughtn't I, Nick?" his sister inquired of him, after a moment.

"Ah, my poor child, what shall I say?"

"Don't you think I have any capacity for ideas?" the girl continued, ruefully.

"Lots of them, no doubt. But the capacity for applying them, for putting them into practice—how much of that have you?"

"How can I tell till I try?"

"What do you mean by trying, Biddy dear?"

"Why, you know—you've seen me."

"Do you call that trying?" her brother asked, smiling at her.

"Ah, Nick!" murmured the girl, sensitively. Then, with more spirit, she went on: "And please, what do you?"

"Well, this, for instance;" and her companion pointed to another bust—a head of a young man, in terra-cotta, at which they had just arrived; a modern young man, to whom, with his thick neck, his little cap and his wide ring of dense curls, the artist had given the air of a Florentine of the time of Lorenzo.

Biddy looked at the image a moment. "Ah, that's not trying; that's succeeding."

"Not altogether; it's only trying seriously."

"Well, why shouldn't I be serious?"

"Mother wouldn't like it. She has inherited the queer old superstition that art is pardonable only so long as it's bad— so long as it's done at odd hours, for a little distraction, like a game of tennis or of whist. The only thing that can justify it, the effort to carry it as far as one can (which you can't do without time and singleness of purpose), she regards as just the dangerous, the criminal element. It's the oddest hind-part-before view, the drollest immorality."

"She doesn't want one to be professional," Biddy remarked, as if she could do justice to every system.

"Better leave it alone, then: there are duffers enough."

"I don't want to be a duffer," Biddy said. "But I thought you encouraged me."

"So I did, my poor child. It was only to encourage myself."

"With your own work—your painting?"

"With my futile, my ill-starred endeavours. Union is strength; so that we might present a wider front, a larger surface of resistance."

Biddy was silent a moment, while they continued their tour of observation. She noticed how her brother passed over some things quickly, his first glance sufficing to show him whether they were worth another, and recognized in a moment the figures that had something in them. His tone puzzled her, but his certainty of eye impressed her, and she felt what a difference there was yet between them—how much longer, in every case, she would have taken to discriminate. She was aware that she could rarely tell whether a picture was good or bad until she had looked at it for ten minutes; and modest little Biddy was compelled privately to add, "And often not even then." She was mystified, as I say (Nick was often mystifying—it was his only fault), but one thing was definite: her brother was exceedingly clever. It was the consciousness of this that made her remark at last: "I don't so much care whether or no I please mamma, if I please you."

"Oh, don't lean on me. I'm a wretched broken reed. I'm no use *really!*" Nick Dormer exclaimed.

"Do you mean you're a duffer?" Biddy asked, alarmed.

"Frightful, frightful!"

"So that you mean to give up your work—to let it alone, as you advise *me*?"

"It has never been my work, Biddy. If it had, it would be different. I should stick to it."

"And you *won't* stick to it?" the girl exclaimed, standing before him, open-eyed.

Her brother looked into her eyes a moment, and she had a compunction; she feared she was indiscreet and was worrying him. "Your questions are much simpler than the elements out of which my answer should come."

"A great talent—what is simpler than that?"

"One thing, dear Biddy: no talent at all!"

"Well, yours is so real, you can't help it."

"We shall see, we shall see," said Nicholas Dormer. "Let us go look at that big group."

"We shall see if it's real?" Biddy went on, as she accompanied him.

"No; we shall see if I can't help it. What nonsense Paris makes one talk!" the young man added, as they stopped in front of the composition. This was true, perhaps, but not in a sense which he found himself tempted to deplore. The present was far from being his first visit to the French capital: he had often quitted England, and usually made a point of "putting in," as he called it, a few days there on the outward journey to the Continent or on the return; but on this occasion the emotions, for the most part agreeable, attendant upon a change of air and of scene had been more punctual and more acute than for a long time before, and stronger the sense of novelty, refreshment, amusement, of manifold suggestions looking to that quarter of thought to which, on the whole, his attention was apt most frequently, though not most confessedly, to stray. He was fonder of Paris than most of his countrymen, though not so fond, perhaps, as some other captivated aliens: the place had always had the power of quickening sensibly the life of reflection and of observation within him. It was a good while since the reflections engendered by his situation there had been so favourable to the city by the Seine; a good while, at all events, since they had ministered so to excitement, to exhilaration, to ambition, even to a restlessness which was not prevented from being agreeable by the nervous quality in it. Dormer could have given the reason of this unwonted glow; but his preference was very much to keep it to himself. Certainly, to persons not deeply knowing, or at any rate not deeply curious, in relation to the young man's history, the explanation might have seemed to beg the question, consisting as it did of the simple formula that he had at last come to a crisis. Why a crisis—what was it, and why had he not come to it before? The reader shall learn these things in time, if he care enough for them.

For several years Nicholas Dormer had not omitted to see the Salon, which the general voice, this season, pronounced not particularly good. None the less, it was the exhibition of this season that, for some cause connected with his "crisis," made him think fast, produced that effect which he had spoken of to his mother as a sense of artistic life. The precinct of the marbles and bronzes appealed to him especially to-day; the glazed garden, not florally rich, with its new productions alternating with perfunctory plants and its queer damp smell, partly the odour of plastic clay, of the studios of sculptors, spoke to him with the voice of old associations, of other visits, of companionships that were closed—an insinuating eloquence which was at the same time, somehow, identical with the general sharp contagion of Paris. There was youth in the air, and a multitudinous newness, for ever reviving, and the diffusion of a hundred talents, ingenuities, experiments. The summer clouds made shadows on the roof of the great building; the white images, hard in their crudity, spotted the place with provocations; the rattle of plates at the restaurant sounded sociable in the distance, and our young man congratulated himself more than ever that he had not missed the exhibition. He felt that it would help him to settle something. At the moment he made this reflection his eye fell upon a person who appeared—just in the first glimpse—to carry out the idea of help. He uttered a lively ejaculation, which, however, in its want of finish, Biddy failed to understand; so pertinent, so relevant and congruous, was the other party to this encounter.

The girl's attention followed her brother's, resting with his on a young man who faced them without seeing them, engaged as he was in imparting to two persons who were with

him his ideas about one of the works exposed to view. What
Biddy discerned was that this young man was fair and fat and
of the middle stature; he had a round face and a short beard,
and on his crown a mere reminiscence of hair, as the fact that
he carried his hat in his hand permitted it to be observed.
Bridget Dormer, who was quick, estimated him immediately
as a gentleman, but a gentleman unlike any other gentleman
she had ever seen. She would have taken him for a foreigner,
but that the words proceeding from his mouth reached her
ear and imposed themselves as a rare variety of English. It was
not that a foreigner might not have spoken excellent English,
nor yet that the English of this young man was not excellent.
It had, on the contrary, a conspicuous and aggressive perfection, and Biddy was sure that no mere learner would have
ventured to play such tricks with the tongue. He seemed to
draw rich effects and wandering airs from it—to modulate
and manipulate it as he would have done a musical instrument. Her view of the gentleman's companions was less oper-
ative, save that she made the rapid reflection that they were
people whom in any country, from China to Peru, one would
immediately have taken for natives. One of them was an old
lady with a shawl; that was the most salient way in which she
presented herself. The shawl was an ancient, voluminous fabric of embroidered cashmere, such as many ladies wore forty
years ago in their walks abroad, and such as no lady wears
to-day. It had fallen half off the back of the wearer, but at the
moment Biddy permitted herself to consider her she gave it a
violent jerk and brought it up to her shoulders again, where
she continued to arrange and settle it, with a good deal of
jauntiness and elegance, while she listened to the talk of the
gentleman. Biddy guessed that this little transaction took
place very frequently, and she was not unaware that it gave
the old lady a droll, factitious, faded appearance, as if she
were singularly out of step with the age. The other person
was very much younger—she might have been a daughter—
and had a pale face, a low forehead and thick, dark hair. What
she chiefly had, however, Biddy rapidly discovered, was a pair
of largely-gazing eyes. Our young friend was helped to the
discovery by the accident of their resting at this moment, for
a little while—it struck Biddy as very long—on her own.

Both of these ladies were clad in light, thin, scanty gowns, giving an impression of flowered figures and odd transparencies, and in low shoes, which showed a great deal of stocking and were ornamented with large rosettes. Biddy's slightly agitated perception travelled directly to their shoes: they suggested to her vaguely that the wearers were dancers—connected possibly with the old-fashioned exhibition of the shawl-dance. By the time she had taken in so much as this the mellifluous young man had perceived and addressed himself to her brother. He came forward with an extended hand. Nick greeted him and said it was a happy chance—he was uncommonly glad to see him.

"I never come across you—I don't know why," Nick remarked, while the two, smiling, looked each other up and down, like men reunited after a long interval.

"Oh, it seems to me there's reason enough: our paths in life are so different." Nick's friend had a great deal of manner, as was evinced by his fashion of saluting her without knowing her.

"Different, yes, but not so different as that. Don't we both live in London, after all, and in the nineteenth century?"

"Ah, my dear Dormer, excuse me: I don't live in the nineteenth century. *Jamais de la vie!*"

"Nor in London either?"

"Yes—when I'm not in Samarcand! But surely we've diverged since the old days, I adore what you burn; you burn what I adore." While the stranger spoke he looked cheerfully, hospitably, at Biddy; not because it was she, she easily guessed, but because it was in his nature to desire a second auditor—a kind of sympathetic gallery. Her life, somehow, was filled with shy people, and she immediately knew that she had never encountered any one who seemed so to know his part and recognize his cues.

"How do you know what I adore?" Nicholas Dormer inquired.

"I know well enough what you used to."

"That's more than I do myself; there were so many things."

"Yes, there are many things—many, many: that's what makes life so amusing."

"Do you find it amusing?"

"My dear fellow, *c'est à se tordre!* Don't you think so? Ah, it was high time I should meet you—I see. I have an idea you need me."

"Upon my word, I think I do!" Nick said, in a tone which struck his sister and made her wonder still more why, if the gentleman was so important as that, he didn't introduce him.

"There are many gods, and this is one of their temples," the mysterious personage went on. "It's a house of strange idols—isn't it?—and of some curious and unnatural sacrifices."

To Biddy, as much as to her brother, this remark appeared to be offered; but the girl's eyes turned back to the ladies, who, for the moment, had lost their companion. She felt irresponsive and feared she should pass with this familiar cosmopolite for a stiff, scared English girl, which was not the type she aimed at; but there seemed an interdiction even of ocular commerce so long as she had not a sign from Nick. The elder of the strange women had turned her back and was looking at some bronze figure, losing her shawl again as she did so; but the younger stood where their escort had quitted her, giving all her attention to his sudden sociability with others. Her arms hung at her sides, her head was bent, her face lowered, so that she had an odd appearance of raising her eyes from under her brows; and in this attitude she was striking, though her air was unconciliatory, almost dangerous. Did it express resentment at having been abandoned for another girl? Biddy, who began to be frightened—there was a moment when the forsaken one resembled a tigress about to spring—was tempted to cry out that she had no wish whatever to appropriate the gentleman. Then she made the discovery that the young lady had a manner, almost as much as her cicerone, and the rapid induction that it perhaps meant no more than his. She only looked at Biddy from beneath her eyebrows, which were wonderfully arched, but there was a manner in the way she did it. Biddy had a momentary sense of being a figure in a ballet, a dramatic ballet—a subordinate, motionless figure, to be dashed at, to music, or capered up to. It would be a very dramatic ballet indeed if this young person were the heroine. She had magnificent hair, the girl reflected;

and at the same moment she heard Nick say to his interlocutor: "You're not in London—one can't meet you there?"

"I drift, I float," was the answer; "my feelings direct me—if
such a life as mine may be said to have a direction. Where
there's anything to feel I try to be there!" the young man
continued with his confiding laugh.

"I should like to get hold of you," Nick remarked.

"Well, in that case there would be something to feel. Those
are the currents—any sort of personal relation—that govern
my career."

"I don't want to lose you this time," Nick continued, in a
manner that excited Biddy's surprise. A moment before,
when his friend had said that he tried to be where there was
anything to feel, she had wondered how he could endure him.

"Don't lose me, don't lose me!" exclaimed the stranger,
with a countenance and a tone which affected the girl as the
highest expression of irresponsibility that she had ever seen.
"After all, why should you? Let us remain together, unless I
interfere"—and he looked, smiling and interrogative, at
Biddy, who still remained blank, only observing again that
Nick forbore to make them acquainted. This was an anomaly,
since he prized the gentleman so; but there could be no
anomaly of Nick's that would not impose itself upon his
younger sister.

"Certainly, I keep you," said Nick, "unless, on my side, I
deprive those ladies—"

"Charming women, but it's not an indissoluble union. We
meet, we communicate, we part! They are going—I'm seeing
them to the door. I shall come back." With this Nick's friend
rejoined his companions, who moved away with him, the
strange, fine eyes of the girl lingering on Nick, as well as on
Biddy, as they receded.

"Who is he—who are they?" Biddy instantly asked.

"He's a gentleman," Nick replied, unsatisfactorily, and
even, as she thought, with a shade of hesitation. He spoke as
if she might have supposed he was not one; and if he was
really one why didn't he introduce him? But Biddy would not
for the world have put this question to her brother, who now
moved to the nearest bench and dropped upon it, as if to wait
for the other's return. No sooner, however, had his sister

seated herself than he said: "See here, my dear, do you think you had better stay?"

"Do you want me to go back to mother?" the girl asked, with a lengthening visage.

"Well, what do you think?" and Nick smiled down at her.

"Is your conversation to be about—about private affairs?"

"No, I can't say that. But I doubt whether mother would think it the sort of thing that's 'necessary to your development.' "

This assertion appeared to inspire Biddy with the eagerness with which again she broke out: "But who are they—who are they?"

"I know nothing of the ladies. I never saw them before. The man's a fellow I knew very well at Oxford. He was thought immense fun there. We have diverged, as he says, and I had almost lost sight of him, but not so much as he thinks, because I've read him, and read him with interest. He has written a very clever book."

"What kind of a book?"

"A sort of a novel."

"What sort of a novel?"

"Well, I don't know—with a lot of good writing." Biddy listened to this with so much interest that she thought it illogical her brother should add: "I dare say Peter will have come, if you return to mother."

"I don't care if he has. Peter's nothing to me. But I'll go if you wish it."

Nick looked down at her again, and then said: "It doesn't signify. We'll all go."

"All?" Biddy echoed.

"He won't hurt us. On the contrary, he'll do us good."

This was possible, the girl reflected in silence, but none the less the idea struck her as courageous—the idea of their taking the odd young man back to breakfast with them and with the others, especially if Peter should be there. If Peter was nothing to her, it was singular she should have attached such importance to this contingency. The odd young man reappeared, and now that she saw him without his queer female appendages he seemed personally less unusual. He struck her, moreover, as generally a good deal accounted for by the literary character, especially if it were responsible for a lot of good writing. As he took his place on the bench Nick said to him, indicating her, "My sister Bridget," and then mentioned his name, "Mr. Gabriel Nash."

"You enjoy Paris—you are happy here?" Mr. Nash inquired, leaning over his friend to speak to the girl.

Though his words belonged to the situation, it struck her that his tone didn't, and this made her answer him more dryly than she usually spoke. "Oh, yes, it's very nice."

"And French art interests you? You find things here that please?"

"Oh, yes, I like some of them."

Mr. Nash looked at her with kind eyes. "I hoped you would say you like the Academy better."

"She would if she didn't think you expected it," said Nicholas Dormer.

"Oh, Nick!" Biddy protested.

"Miss Dormer is herself an English picture," Gabriel Nash remarked, smiling like a man whose urbanity was a solvent.

"That's a compliment, if you don't like them!" Biddy exclaimed.

"Ah, some of them, some of them; there's a certain sort of thing!" Mr. Nash continued. "We must feel everything, everything that we can. We are here for that."

"You do like English art, then?" Nick demanded, with a slight accent of surprise.

Mr. Nash turned his smile upon him. "My dear Dormer, do you remember the old complaint I used to make of you? You had formulas that were like walking in one's hat. One may see something in a case, and one may not."

"Upon my word," said Nick, "I don't know any one who was fonder of a generalization than you. You turned them off as the man at the street-corner distributes hand-bills."

"They were my wild oats. I've sown them all."

"We shall see that!"

"Oh, they're nothing now—a tame, scanty, homely growth. My only generalizations are my actions."

"We shall see *them*, then."

"Ah, excuse me. You can't see them with the naked eye. Moreover, mine are principally negative. People's actions, I know, are, for the most part, the things they do, but mine are all the things I don't do. There are so many of those, so many, but they don't produce any effect. And then all the rest are shades—extremely fine shades."

"Shades of behaviour?" Nick inquired, with an interest which surprised his sister; Mr. Nash's discourse striking her mainly as the twaddle of the under-world.

"Shades of impression, of appreciation," said the young man, with his explanatory smile. "My only behaviour is my feelings."

"Well, don't you show your feelings? You used to!"

"Wasn't it mainly those of disgust?" Nash asked. "Those operate no longer. I have closed that window."

"Do you mean you like everything?"

"Dear me, no! But I look only at what I do like."

"Do you mean that you have lost the faculty of displeasure?"

"I haven't the least idea. I never try it. My dear fellow," said Gabriel Nash, "we have only one life that we know anything about: fancy taking it up with disagreeable impressions! When, then, shall we go in for the agreeable?"

"What do you mean by the agreeable?" Nick Dormer asked.

"Oh, the happy moments of our consciousness—the multiplication of those moments. We must save as many as possible from the dark gulf."

Nick had excited a certain astonishment on the part of his sister, but it was now Biddy's turn to make him open his eyes a little. She raised her sweet voice and inquired of Mr. Nash—

"Don't you think there are any wrongs in the world—any abuses and sufferings?"

"Oh, so many, so many! That's why one must choose."

"Choose to stop them, to reform them—isn't that the choice?" Biddy asked. "That's Nick's," she added, blushing and looking at this personage.

"Ah, our divergence—yes!" sighed Gabriel Nash. "There are all kinds of machinery for that—very complicated and ingenious. Your formulas, my dear Dormer, your formulas!"

"Hang 'em, I haven't got any!" Nick exclaimed.

"To me, personally, the simplest ways are those that appeal most," Mr. Nash went on. "We pay too much attention to the ugly; we notice it, we magnify it. The great thing is to leave it alone and encourage the beautiful."

"You must be very sure you get hold of the beautiful," said Nick.

"Ah, precisely, and that's just the importance of the faculty of appreciation. We must train our special sense. It is capable of extraordinary extension. Life's none too long for that."

"But what's the good of the extraordinary extension if there is no affirmation of it, if it all goes to the negative, as you say? Where are the fine consequences?" Dormer asked.

"In one's own spirit. One is one's self a fine consequence. That's the most important one we have to do with. I am a fine consequence," said Gabriel Nash.

Biddy rose from the bench at this, and stepped away a little, as if to look at a piece of statuary. But she had not gone far before, pausing and turning, she bent her eyes upon Mr. Nash with a heightened colour, an air of hesitation and the question, after a moment: "Are you an æsthete?"

"Ah, there's one of the formulas! That's walking in one's hat! I've *no* profession, my dear young lady. I've no *état civil*. These things are a part of the complicated, ingenious machinery. As I say, I keep to the simplest way. I find that gives one enough to do. Merely to be is such a *métier*; to live is such an art; to feel is such a career!"

Bridget Dormer turned her back and examined her statue, and her brother said to his old friend: "And to write?"

"To write? Oh, I'll never do it again!"

"You have done it almost well enough to be inconsistent. That book of yours is anything but negative; it's complicated and ingenious."

"My dear fellow, I'm extremely ashamed of it," said Gabriel Nash.

"Ah, call yourself a bloated Buddhist and have done with it!" his companion exclaimed.

"Have done with it? I haven't the least desire for that. And why should one call one's self anything? One only deprives other people of their dearest occupation. Let me add that you don't *begin* to have an insight into the art of life till it ceases to be of the smallest consequence to you what you may be called. That's rudimentary."

"But if you go in for shades, you must also go in for names. You must distinguish," Dormer objected. "The observer is nothing without his categories, his types and varieties."

"Ah, trust him to distinguish!" said Gabriel Nash, sweetly. "That's for his own convenience; he has, privately, a terminology to meet it. That's one's style. But from the moment it's for the convenience of others, the signs have to be grosser, the shades begin to go. That's a deplorable hour! Literature, you see, is for the convenience of others. It requires the most abject concessions. It plays such mischief with one's style that really I have had to give it up."

"And politics?" Nick Dormer asked.

"Well, what about them?" was Mr. Nash's reply, in a peculiar intonation, as he watched his friend's sister, who was still examining her statue. Biddy was divided between irritation and curiosity. She had interposed space, but she had not gone beyond ear-shot. Nick's question made her curiosity throb, especially in its second form, as a rejoinder to their companion's.

"That, no doubt you'll say, is still far more for the convenience of others—is still worse for one's style."

Biddy turned round in time to hear Mr. Nash exclaim: "It has simply nothing in life to do with shades! I can't say worse for it than that."

Biddy stepped nearer at this, and, drawing still further on her courage: "Won't mamma be waiting? Oughtn't we to go to luncheon?" she asked.

Both the young men looked up at her, and Mr. Nash remarked—

"You ought to protest! You ought to save him!"

"To save him?" said Biddy.

"He *had* a style; upon my word he had! But I've seen it go. I've read his speeches."

"You were capable of that?" Dormer demanded.

"For you, yes. But it was like listening to a nightingale in a brass band."

"I think they were beautiful," Biddy declared.

Her brother got up at this tribute, and Mr. Nash, rising too, said, with his bright colloquial air—

"But, Miss Dormer, he had eyes. He was made to see—to see all over, to see everything. There are so few like that."

"I think he still sees," Biddy rejoined, wondering a little why Nick didn't defend himself.

"He sees his side, dear young lady. Poor man, fancy your having a 'side'—you, you—and spending your days and your nights looking at it! I'd as soon pass my life looking at an advertisement on a hoarding."

"You don't see me some day a great statesman?" said Nick.

"My dear fellow, it's exactly what I've a terror of."

"Mercy! don't you admire them?" Biddy cried.

"It's a trade like another, and a method of making one's way which society certainly condones. But when one can be something better!"

"Dear me, what *is* better?" Biddy asked.

The young man hesitated, and Nick, replying for him, said—

"Gabriel Nash is better! You must come and lunch with us. I must keep you—I must!" he added.

"We shall save him yet," Mr. Nash observed genially to Biddy as they went; while the girl wondered still more what her mother would make of him.

III.

AFTER HER companions left her Lady Agnes rested for five minutes in silence with her elder daughter, at the end of which time she observed, "I suppose one must have food, at any rate," and, getting up, quitted the place where they had been sitting. "And where are we to go? I hate eating out-of-doors," she went on.

"Dear me, when one comes to Paris!" Grace rejoined, in a tone which appeared to imply that in so rash an adventure one must be prepared for compromises and concessions. The two ladies wandered to where they saw a large sign of "Buffet" suspended in the air, entering a precinct reserved for little white-clothed tables, straw-covered chairs and long-aproned waiters. One of these functionaries approached them with eagerness and with a *"Mesdames sont seules?"* receiving in return, from her ladyship, the slightly snappish announcement, *"Non; nous sommes beaucoup!"* He introduced them to a table larger than most of the others, and under his protection they took their places at it and began, rather languidly and vaguely, to consider the question of the repast. The waiter had placed a *carte* in Lady Agnes's hands, and she studied it, through her eye-glass, with a failure of interest, while he enumerated, with professional fluency, the resources of the establishment and Grace looked at the people at the other tables. She was hungry and had already broken a morsel from a long glazed roll.

"Not cold beef and pickles, you know," she observed to her mother. Lady Agnes gave no heed to this profane remark, but she dropped her eye-glass and laid down the greasy document. "What does it signify? I dare say it's all nasty," Grace continued; and she added, inconsequently: "If Peter comes he's sure to be particular."

"Let him be particular to come, first!" her ladyship exclaimed, turning a cold eye upon the waiter.

"Poulet chasseur, filets mignons, sauce béarnaise," the man suggested.

"You will give us what I tell you," said Lady Agnes, and she mentioned, with distinctness and authority, the dishes of

727

which she desired that the meal should be composed. He interposed three or four more suggestions, but as they produced absolutely no impression on her he became silent and submissive, doing justice, apparently, to her ideas. For Lady Agnes had ideas; and though it had suited her humour, ten minutes before, to profess herself helpless in such a case, the manner in which she imposed them upon the waiter as original, practical and economical showed the high, executive woman, the mother of children, the daughter of earls, the consort of an official, the dispenser of hospitality, looking back upon a life-time of luncheons. She carried many cares, and the feeding of multitudes (she was honourably conscious of having fed them decently, as she had always done everything) had ever been one of them. "Everything is absurdly dear," she hinted to her daughter, as the waiter went away. To this remark Grace made no answer. She had been used, for a long time back, to hearing that everything was very dear; it was what one always expected. So she found the case herself, but she was silent and inventive about it.

Nothing further passed, in the way of conversation with her mother, while they waited for the latter's orders to be executed, till Lady Agnes reflected, audibly: "He makes me unhappy, the way he talks about Julia."

"Sometimes I think he does it to torment one. One can't mention her!" Grace responded.

"It's better not to mention her, but to leave it alone."

"Yet he never mentions her of himself."

"In some cases that is supposed to show that people like people—though of course something more than that is required," Lady Agnes continued to meditate. "Sometimes I think he's thinking of her; then at others I can't fancy *what* he's thinking of."

"It would be awfully suitable," said Grace, biting her roll.

Her mother was silent a moment, as if she were looking for some higher ground to put it upon. Then she appeared to find this loftier level in the observation: "Of course he must like her; he has known her always."

"Nothing can be plainer than that she likes him," Grace declared.

"Poor Julia!" Lady Agnes exclaimed; and her tone suggested that she knew more about that than she was ready to state.

"It isn't as if she wasn't clever and well read," her daughter went on. "If there were nothing else there would be a reason in her being so interested in politics, in everything that he is."

"Ah, what he is—that's what I sometimes wonder!"

Grace Dormer looked at her mother a moment. "Why, mother, isn't he going to be like papa?" She waited for an answer that didn't come; after which she pursued: "I thought you thought him so like him already."

"Well, I don't," said Lady Agnes, quietly.

"Who is, then? Certainly Percy isn't."

Lady Agnes was silent a moment. "There is no one like your father."

"Dear papa!" Grace exclaimed. Then, with a rapid transition: "It would be so jolly for all of us; she would be so nice to us."

"She is that already, in her way," said Lady Agnes, conscientiously, having followed the return, quick as it was. "Much good does it do her!" And she reproduced the note of her ejaculation of a moment before.

"It does her some, if one looks out for her. I do, and I think she knows it," Grace declared. "One can, at any rate, keep other women off."

"Don't meddle! you're very clumsy," was her mother's not particularly sympathetic rejoinder. "There are other women who are beautiful, and there are others who are clever and rich."

"Yes, but not all in one; that's what's so nice in Julia. Her fortune would be thrown in; he wouldn't appear to have married her for it."

"If he does, he won't," said Lady Agnes, a trifle obscurely.

"Yes, that's what's so charming. And he could do anything then, couldn't he?"

"Well, your father had no fortune, to speak of."

"Yes, but didn't Uncle Percy help him?"

"His wife helped him," said Lady Agnes.

"Dear mamma!" the girl exclaimed. "There's one thing," she added: "that Mr. Carteret will always help Nick."

"What do you mean by 'always'?"

"Why, whether he marries Julia or not."

"Things are not so easy," responded Lady Agnes. "It will all depend on Nick's behaviour. He can stop it to-morrow."

Grace Dormer stared; she evidently thought Mr. Carteret's beneficence a part of the scheme of nature. "How could he stop it?"

"By not being serious. It isn't so hard to prevent people giving you money."

"Serious?" Grace repeated. "Does he want him to be a prig, like Lord Egbert?"

"Yes, he does. And what he'll do for him he'll do for him only if he marries Julia."

"Has he told you?" Grace inquired. And then, before her mother could answer, she exclaimed: "I'm delighted at that!"

"He hasn't told me, but that's the way things happen." Lady Agnes was less optimistic than her daughter, and such optimism as she cultivated was a thin tissue, with a sense of things as they are showing through it. "If Nick becomes rich, Charles Carteret will make him more so. If he doesn't, he won't give him a shilling."

"Oh, mamma!" Grace protested.

"It's all very well to say that in public life money isn't necessary, as it used to be," her ladyship went on, broodingly. "Those who say so don't know anything about it. It's always necessary."

Her daughter was visibly affected by the gloom of her manner, and felt impelled to evoke, as a corrective, a more cheerful idea. "I dare say; but there's the fact—isn't there?—that poor papa had so little."

"Yes, and there's the fact that it killed him!"

These words came out with a strange, quick little flare of passion. They startled Grace Dormer, who jumped in her place and cried, "Oh, mother!" The next instant, however, she added, in a different voice, "Oh, Peter!" for, with an air of eagerness, a gentleman was walking up to them.

"How d'ye do, Cousin Agnes? How d'ye do, little Grace?" Peter Sherringham said, laughing and shaking hands with them; and three minutes later he was settled in his chair at their table, on which the first elements of the repast had been placed. Explanations, on one side and the other, were demanded and produced; from which it appeared that the two parties had been in some degree at cross-purposes. The day before Lady Agnes and her companions travelled to Paris, Sherringham had gone to London for forty-eight hours, on private business of the ambassador's, arriving, on his return by the night-train, only early that morning. There had accordingly been a delay in his receiving Nick Dormer's two notes. If Nick had come to the Embassy in person (he might have done him the honour to call), he would have learned that the second secretary was absent. Lady Agnes was not altogether successful in assigning a motive to her son's neglect of this courteous form; she said: "I expected him, I wanted him, to go; and indeed, not hearing from you, he would have gone immediately—an hour or two hence, on leaving this place. But we are here so quietly, not to go out, not to seem to appeal to the ambassador. He said, 'Oh, mother, we'll keep out of it; a friendly note will do.' I don't know, definitely, what he wanted to keep out of, except it's anything like gaiety. The Embassy isn't gay, I know. But I'm sure his note was friendly, wasn't it? I dare say you'll see for yourself; he's different directly he gets abroad; he doesn't seem to care." Lady Agnes paused a moment, not carrying out this particular elucidation; then she resumed: "He said you would have seen Julia and that you would understand everything from her. And when I asked how she would know, he said, 'Oh, she knows everything!'"

"He never said a word to me about Julia," Peter Sherringham rejoined. Lady Agnes and her daughter exchanged a glance at this; the latter had already asked three times where Julia was, and her ladyship dropped that they had been hoping she would be able to come with Peter. The young man set forth that she was at that moment at an hotel in the Rue de la Paix, but had only been there since that morning: he had seen her before coming to the Champs Elysées. She had come up to Paris by an early train—she had been staying at Versailles, of all places in the world. She had been a week in Paris, on her return from Cannes (her stay *there* had been of nearly a month—fancy!) and then had gone out to Versailles to see Mrs. Billinghurst. Perhaps they would remember her, poor

Dallow's sister. She was staying there to teach her daughters French (she had a dozen or two!) and Julia had spent three days with her. She was to return to England about the 25th. It would make seven weeks that she would have been away from town—a rare thing for her; she usually stuck to it so in summer.

"Three days with Mrs. Billinghurst—how very good-natured of her!" Lady Agnes commented.

"Oh, they're very nice to her," Sherringham said.

"Well, I hope so!" Grace Dormer qualified. "Why didn't you make her come here?"

"I proposed it, but she wouldn't." Another eye-beam, at this, passed between the two ladies, and Peter went on: "She said you must come and see her, at the Hôtel de Hollande."

"Of course we'll do that," Lady Agnes declared. "Nick went to ask about her at the Westminster."

"She gave that up; they wouldn't give her the rooms she wanted, her usual set."

"She's delightfully particular!" Grace murmured. Then she added: "She *does* like pictures, doesn't she?"

Peter Sherringham stared. "Oh, I dare say. But that's not what she has in her head this morning. She has some news from London; she's immensely excited."

"What has she in her head?" Lady Agnes asked.

"What's her news from London?" Grace demanded.

"She wants Nick to stand."

"Nick to stand?" both the ladies cried.

"She undertakes to bring him in for Harsh. Mr. Pinks is dead—the fellow, you know, that got the seat at the general election. He dropped down in London—disease of the heart, or something of that sort. Julia has her telegram, but I see it was in last night's papers."

"Imagine, Nick never mentioned it!" said Lady Agnes.

"Don't you know, mother?—abroad he only reads foreign papers."

"Oh, I know. I've no patience with him," her ladyship continued. "Dear Julia!"

"It's a nasty little place, and Pinks had a tight squeeze—107, or something of that sort; but if it returned a Liberal a year ago, very likely it will do so again. Julia, at any rate, *se fait forte*, as they say here, to put him in."

"I'm sure if she can she will," Grace reflected.

"Dear, dear Julia! And Nick can do something for himself," said the mother of this candidate.

"I have no doubt he can do anything," Peter Sherringham returned, good-naturedly. Then, "Do you mean in expenses?" he inquired.

"Ah, I'm afraid he can't do much in expenses, poor dear boy! And it's dreadful how little we can look to Percy."

"Well, I dare say you may look to Julia. I think that's her idea."

"Delightful Julia!" Lady Agnes ejaculated. "If poor Sir Nicholas could have known! Of course he must go straight home," she added.

"He won't like that," said Grace.

"Then he'll have to go without liking it."

"It will rather spoil *your* little excursion, if you've only just come," Peter suggested; "and the great Biddy's, if she's enjoying Paris."

"We may stay, perhaps—with Julia to protect us," said Lady Agnes.

"Ah, she won't stay; she'll go over for her man."

"Her man?"

"The fellow that stands, whoever he is; especially if he's Nick." These last words caused the eyes of Peter Sherringham's companions to meet again, and he went on: "She'll go straight down to Harsh."

"Wonderful Julia!" Lady Agnes panted. "Of course Nick must go straight there, too."

"Well, I suppose he must see first if they'll have him."

"If they'll have him? Why, how can he tell till he tries?"

"I mean the people at headquarters, the fellows who arrange it."

Lady Agnes coloured a little. "My dear Peter, do you suppose there will be the least doubt of their 'having' the son of his father?"

"Of course it's a great name, Cousin Agnes—a very great name."

"One of the greatest, simply," said Lady Agnes, smiling.

"It's the best name in the world!" Grace Dormer subjoined.

"All the same it didn't prevent his losing his seat."

"By half a dozen votes: it was too odious!" her ladyship cried.

"I remember—I remember. And in such a case as that why didn't they immediately put him in somewhere else?"

"How one sees that you live abroad, Peter! There happens to have been the most extraordinary lack of openings—I never saw anything like it—for a year. They've had their hand on him, keeping him all ready. I dare say they've telegraphed to him."

"And he hasn't told you?"

Lady Agnes hesitated. "He's so odd when he's abroad!"

"At home, too, he lets things go," Grace interposed. "He does so little—takes no trouble." Her mother suffered this statement to pass unchallenged, and she pursued, philosophically: "I suppose it's because he knows he's so clever."

"So he is, dear old boy. But what does he do, what has he been doing, in a positive way?"

"He has been painting."

"Ah, not seriously!" Lady Agnes protested.

"That's the worst way," said Peter Sherringham. "Good things?"

Neither of the ladies made a direct response to this, but Lady Agnes said: "He has spoken repeatedly. They are always calling on him."

"He speaks magnificently," Grace attested.

"That's another of the things I lose, living in far countries. And he's doing the Salon now, with the great Biddy?"

"Just the things in this part. I can't think what keeps them so long," Lady Agnes rejoined. "Did you ever see such a dreadful place?"

Sherringham stared. "Aren't the things good? I had an idea—"

"Good?" cried Lady Agnes. "They're too odious, too wicked."

"Ah," said Peter, laughing, "that's what people fall into, if they live abroad. The French oughtn't to live abroad."

"Here they come," Grace announced, at this point; "but they've got a strange man with them."

"That's a bore, when we want to talk!" Lady Agnes sighed.

Peter got up, in the spirit of welcome, and stood a moment watching the others approach. "There will be no difficulty in talking, to judge by the gentleman," he suggested; and while he remains so conspicuous our eyes may rest on him briefly. He was middling high and was visibly a representative of the nervous rather than of the phlegmatic branch of his race. He had an oval face, fine, firm features and a complexion that tended to the brown. Brown were his eyes, and women thought them soft; dark brown his hair, in which the same critics sometimes regretted the absence of a little undulation. It was perhaps to conceal this plainness that he wore it very short. His teeth were white; his moustache was pointed, and so was the small beard that adorned the extremity of his chin. His face expressed intelligence and was very much alive, and had the further distinction that it often struck superficial observers with a certain foreignness of cast. The deeper sort, however, usually perceived that it was English enough. There was an idea that, having taken up the diplomatic career and gone to live in strange lands, he cultivated the mask of an alien, an Italian or a Spaniard; of an alien in time, even—one of the wonderful ubiquitous diplomatic agents of the sixteenth century. In fact, it would have been impossible to be more modern than Peter Sherringham, and more of one's class and one's country. But this did not prevent a portion of the community—Bridget Dormer, for instance—from admiring the hue of his cheek for its olive richness and his moustache and beard for their resemblance to those of Charles I. At the same time—she rather jumbled her comparisons—she thought he looked like a Titian.

IV.

PETER'S MEETING with Nick was of the friendliest on both sides, involving a great many "dear fellows" and "old boys," and his salutation to the younger of the Miss Dormers consisted of the frankest "Delighted to see you, my dear Bid!" There was no kissing, but there was cousinship in the air, of a conscious, living kind, as Gabriel Nash no doubt quickly perceived, hovering for a moment outside the group. Biddy said nothing to Peter Sherringham, but there was no flatness in a silence which afforded such opportunities for a pretty smile. Nick introduced Gabriel Nash to his mother and to the other two as "a delightful old friend," whom he had just come across, and Sherringham acknowledged the act by saying to Mr. Nash, but as if rather less for his sake than for that of the presenter: "I have seen you very often before."

"Ah, repetition—recurrence: we haven't yet, in the study of how to live, abolished that clumsiness, have we?" Mr. Nash genially inquired. "It's a poverty in the supernumeraries that we don't pass once for all, but come round and cross again, like a procession at the theatre. It's a shabby economy that ought to have been managed better. The right thing would be just *one* appearance, and the procession, regardless of expense, forever and forever different."

The company was occupied in placing itself at table, so that the only disengaged attention, for the moment, was Grace's, to whom, as her eyes rested on him, the young man addressed these last words with a smile. "Alas, it's a very shabby idea, isn't it? The world isn't got up regardless of expense!"

Grace looked quickly away from him, and said to her brother: "Nick, Mr. Pinks is dead."

"Mr. Pinks?" asked Gabriel Nash, appearing to wonder where he should sit.

"The member for Harsh; and Julia wants you to stand," the girl went on.

"Mr. Pinks, the member for Harsh? What names to be sure!" Gabriel mused cheerfully, still unseated.

"Julia wants me? I'm much obliged to her!" observed Nicholas Dormer. "Nash, please sit by my mother, with Peter on her other side."

"My dear, it isn't Julia," Lady Agnes remarked, earnestly, to her son. "Every one wants you. Haven't you heard from your people? Didn't you know the seat was vacant?"

Nick was looking round the table, to see what was on it. "Upon my word I don't remember. What else have you ordered, mother?"

"There's some *bœuf braisé*, my dear, and afterwards some galantine. Here is a dish of eggs with asparagus-tips."

"I advise you to go in for it, Nick," said Peter Sherringham, to whom the preparation in question was presented.

"Into the eggs with asparagus-tips? *Donnez m'en, s'il vous plaît*. My dear fellow, how can I stand? how can I sit? Where's the money to come from?"

"The money? Why, from Jul—" Grace began, but immediately caught her mother's eye.

"Poor Julia, how you do work her!" Nick exclaimed. "Nash, I recommend the asparagus-tips. Mother, he's my best friend; do look after him."

"I have an impression I have breakfasted—I am not sure," Nash observed.

"With those beautiful ladies? Try again; you'll find out."

"The money can be managed; the expenses are very small and the seat is certain," Lady Agnes declared, not, apparently, heeding her son's injunction in respect to Nash.

"Rather—if Julia goes down!" her elder daughter exclaimed.

"Perhaps Julia won't go down!" Nick answered, humorously.

Biddy was seated next to Mr. Nash, so that she could take occasion to ask, "Who are the beautiful ladies?" as if she failed to recognize her brother's allusion. In reality this was an innocent trick: she was more curious than she could have given a suitable reason for about the odd women from whom her neighbour had separated.

"Deluded, misguided, infatuated persons!" Gabriel Nash replied, understanding that she had asked for a description.

"Strange, eccentric, almost romantic types. Predestined victims, simple-minded sacrificial lambs!"

This was copious, yet it was vague, so that Biddy could only respond, "Oh!" But meanwhile Peter Sherringham said to Nick—

"Julia's here, you know. You must go and see her."

Nick looked at him for an instant rather hard, as if to say, "You too?" But Peter's eyes appeared to answer, "No, no, not I;" upon which his cousin rejoined: "Of course I'll go and see her. I'll go immediately. Please to thank her for thinking of me."

"Thinking of you? There are plenty to think of you!" Lady Agnes said. "There are sure to be telegrams at home. We must go back—we must go back!"

"We must go back to England?" Nick Dormer asked; and as his mother made no answer he continued: "Do you mean I must go to Harsh?"

Her ladyship evaded this question, inquiring of Mr. Nash if he would have a morsel of fish; but her gain was small, for this gentleman, struck again by the unhappy name of the bereaved constituency, only broke out: "Ah, what a place to represent! How can you—how can you?"

"It's an excellent place," said Lady Agnes, coldly. "I imagine you have never been there. It's a very good place indeed. It belongs very largely to my cousin, Mrs. Dallow."

Gabriel partook of the fish, listening with interest. "But I thought we had no more pocket-boroughs."

"It's pockets we rather lack, so many of us. There are plenty of Harshes," Nick Dormer observed.

"I don't know what you mean," Lady Agnes said to Gabriel, with considerable majesty.

Peter Sherringham also addressed him with an "Oh, it's all right; they come down on you like a shot!" and the young man continued, ingenuously—

"Do you mean to say you have to pay to get into that place—that it's not *you* that are paid?"

"Into that place?" Lady Agnes repeated, blankly.

"Into the House of Commons. That you don't get a high salary?"

"My dear Nash, you're delightful: don't leave me—don't leave me!" Nick cried; while his mother looked at him with an eye that demanded: "Who is this extraordinary person?"

"What then did you think pocket-boroughs were?" Peter Sherringham asked.

Mr. Nash's facial radiance rested on him. "Why, boroughs that filled your pocket. To do that sort of thing without a bribe—*c'est trop fort!*"

"He lives at Samarcand," Nick Dormer explained to his mother, who coloured perceptibly. "What do you advise me? I'll do whatever you say," he went on to his old acquaintance.

"My dear—my dear!" Lady Agnes pleaded.

"See Julia first, with all respect to Mr. Nash. She's of excellent counsel," said Peter Sherringham.

Gabriel Nash smiled across the table at Dormer. "The lady first—the lady first! I have not a word to suggest as against any idea of hers."

"We must not sit here too long, there will be so much to do," said Lady Agnes, anxiously, perceiving a certain slowness in the service of the *bœuf braisé.*

Biddy had been up to this moment mainly occupied in looking, covertly and at intervals, at Peter Sherringham; as was perfectly lawful in a young lady with a handsome cousin whom she had not seen for more than a year. But her sweet voice now took license to throw in the words: "We know what Mr. Nash thinks of politics: he told us just now he thinks they are dreadful."

"No, not dreadful—only inferior," the personage impugned protested. "Everything is relative."

"Inferior to what?" Lady Agnes demanded.

Mr. Nash appeared to consider a moment. "To anything else that may be in question."

"Nothing else *is* in question!" said her ladyship, in a tone that would have been triumphant if it had not been dry.

"Ah, then!" And her neighbour shook his head sadly. He turned, after this, to Biddy, saying to her: "The ladies whom I was with just now, and in whom you were so good as to express an interest?" Biddy gave a sign of assent, and he went on: "They are persons theatrical; the younger one is trying to go upon the stage."

"And are you assisting her?" Biddy asked, pleased that she had guessed so nearly right.

"Not in the least—I'm rather heading her off. I consider it the lowest of the arts."

"Lower than politics?" asked Peter Sherringham, who was listening to this.

"Dear, no, I won't say that. I think the Théâtre Français a greater institution than the House of Commons."

"I agree with you there!" laughed Sherringham; "all the more that I don't consider the dramatic art a low one. On the contrary, it seems to me to include all the others."

"Yes—that's a view. I think it's the view of my friends."

"Of your friends?"

"Two ladies—old acquaintances—whom I met in Paris a week ago and whom I have just been spending an hour with in this place."

"You should have seen them; they struck me very much," Biddy said to her cousin.

"I should like to see them, if they have really anything to say to the theatre."

"It can easily be managed. Do you believe in the theatre?" asked Gabriel Nash.

"Passionately," Sherringham confessed. "Don't you?"

Before Mr. Nash had had time to answer Biddy had interposed with a sigh: "How I wish I could go—but in Paris I can't!"

"I'll take you, Biddy—I vow I'll take you."

"But the plays, Peter," the girl objected. "Mamma says they're worse than the pictures."

"Oh, we'll arrange that: they shall do one at the Français on purpose for a delightful little English girl."

"Can you make them?"

"I can make them do anything I choose."

"Ah, then, it's the theatre that believes in you," said Gabriel Nash.

"It would be ungrateful if it didn't!" Peter Sherringham laughed.

Lady Agnes had withdrawn herself from between him and

Mr. Nash, and, to signify that she, at least, had finished eating, had gone to sit by her son, whom she held, with some importunity, in conversation. But hearing the theatre talked of, she threw across an impersonal challenge to the paradoxical young man. "Pray, should you think it better for a gentleman to be an actor?"

"Better than being a politician? Ah, comedian for comedian, isn't the actor more honest?"

Lady Agnes turned to her son and exclaimed with spirit: "Think of your great father, Nicholas!"

"He was an honest man; that perhaps is why he couldn't stand it."

Peter Sherringham judged the colloquy to have taken an uncomfortable twist, though not wholly, as it seemed to him, by the act of Nick's queer comrade. To draw it back to safer ground he said to this personage: "May I ask if the ladies you just spoke of are English—Mrs. and Miss Rooth: isn't that the rather odd name?"

"The very same. Only the daughter, according to her kind, desires to be known by some *nom de guerre* before she has even been able to enlist."

"And what does she call herself?" Bridget Dormer asked.

"Maud Vavasour, or Edith Temple, or Gladys Vane—some rubbish of that sort."

"What, then, is her own name?"

"Miriam—Miriam Rooth. It would do very well and would give her the benefit of the prepossessing fact that (to the best of my belief, at least) she is more than half a Jewess."

"It is as good as Rachel Félix," Sherringham said.

"The name's as good, but not the talent. The girl is magnificently stupid."

"And more than half a Jewess? Don't you believe it!" Sherringham exclaimed.

"Don't believe she's a Jewess?" Biddy asked, still more interested in Miriam Rooth.

"No, no—that she's stupid, really. If she is, she'll be the first."

"Ah, you may judge for yourself," Nash rejoined, "if you'll come to-morrow afternoon to Madame Carré, Rue de Constantinople, *à l'entresol*."

"Madame Carré? Why, I've already a note from her—I found it this morning on my return to Paris—asking me to look in at five o'clock and listen to a *jeune Anglaise.*"

"That's my arrangement—I obtained the favour. The ladies want an opinion, and dear old Carré has consented to see them and to give one. Gladys will recite something and the venerable artist will pass judgment."

Sherringham remembered that he had his note in his pocket, and he took it out and looked it over. "She wishes to make her a little audience—she says she'll do better with that—and she asks me because I'm English. I shall make a point of going."

"And bring Dormer if you can: the audience will be better. Will you come, Dormer?" Mr. Nash continued, appealing to his friend,—"will you come with me to see an old French actress and to hear an English amateur recite?"

Nick looked round from his talk with his mother and Grace. "I'll go anywhere with you, so that, as I've told you, I may not lose sight of you, may keep hold of you."

"Poor Mr. Nash, why is he so useful?" Lady Agnes demanded with a laugh.

"He steadies me, mother."

"Oh, I wish you'd take me, Peter," Biddy broke out, wistfully, to her cousin.

"To spend an hour with an old French actress? Do you want to go upon the stage?" the young man inquired.

"No, but I want to see something, to know something."

"Madame Carré is wonderful in her way, but she is hardly company for a little English girl."

"I'm not little, I'm only too big; and *she* goes, the person you speak of."

"For a professional purpose, and with her good mother," smiled Gabriel Nash. "I think Lady Agnes would hardly venture—"

"Oh, I've seen her good mother!" said Biddy, as if she had an impression of what the worth of that protection might be.

"Yes, but you haven't heard her. It's then that you measure her."

Biddy was wistful still. "Is it the famous Honorine Carré, the great celebrity?"

"Honorine in person: the incomparable, the perfect!" said Peter Sherringham. "The first artist of our time, taking her altogether. She and I are old pals; she has been so good as to come and 'say' things, as she does sometimes still *dans le monde* as no one else does, in my rooms."

"Make her come, then; we can go *there!*"

"One of these days!"

"And the young lady—Miriam, Edith, Gladys—make her come too."

Sherringham looked at Nash, and the latter exclaimed: "Oh, you'll have no difficulty; she'll jump at it!"

"Very good; I'll give a little artistic tea, with Julia, too, of course. And you must come, Mr. Nash." This gentleman promised, with an inclination, and Peter continued: "But if, as you say, you're not for helping the young lady, how came you to arrange this interview with the great model?"

"Precisely to stop her. The great model will find her very bad. Her judgments, as you probably know, are Rhadamanthine."

"Poor girl!" said Biddy. "I think you're cruel."

"Never mind; I'll look after them," said Sherringham.

"And how can Madame Carré judge, if the girl recites English?"

"She's so intelligent that she could judge if she recited Chinese," Peter declared.

"That's true, but the *jeune Anglaise* recites also in French," said Gabriel Nash.

"Then she isn't stupid."

"And in Italian, and in several more tongues, for aught I know."

Sherringham was visibly interested. "Very good; we'll put her through them all."

"She must be *most* clever," Biddy went on, yearningly.

"She has spent her life on the Continent; she has wandered about with her mother; she has picked up things."

"And is she a lady?" Biddy asked.

"Oh, tremendous! The great ones of the earth on the

mother's side. On the father's, on the other hand, I imagine, only a Jew stockbroker in the city."

"Then they're rich—or ought to be," Sherringham suggested.

"Ought to be—ah, there's the bitterness! The stockbroker had too short a go—he was carried off in his flower. However, he left his wife a certain property, which she appears to have muddled away, not having the safeguard of being herself a Hebrew. This is what she lived upon till to-day—this and another resource. Her husband, as she has often told me, had the artistic temperament; that's common, as you know, among *ces messieurs*. He made the most of his little opportunities and collected various pictures, tapestries, enamels, porcelains and similar gewgaws. He parted with them also, I gather, at a profit; in short, he carried on a neat little business as a *brocanteur*. It was nipped in the bud, but Mrs. Rooth was left with a certain number of these articles in her hands; indeed they must have constituted the most palpable part of her heritage. She was not a woman of business; she turned them, no doubt, to indifferent account; but she sold them piece by piece, and they kept her going while her daughter grew up. It was to this precarious traffic, conducted with extraordinary mystery and delicacy, that, five years ago, in Florence, I was indebted for my acquaintance with her. In those days I used to collect—Heaven help me!—I used to pick up rubbish which I could ill afford. It was a little phase—we have our little phases, haven't we?" asked Gabriel Nash, with childlike trust—"and I have come out on the other side. Mrs. Rooth had an old green pot, and I heard of her old green pot. To hear of it was to long for it, so that I went to see it, under cover of night. I bought it, and a couple of years ago I overturned it and smashed it. It was the last of the little phase. It was not, however, as you have seen, the last of Mrs. Rooth. I saw her afterwards in London, and I met her a year or two ago in Venice. She appears to be a great wanderer. She had other old pots, of other colours—red, yellow, black, or blue—she could produce them of any complexion you liked. I don't know whether she carried them about with her or whether she had little secret stores in the principal cities of Europe. To-day, at any rate, they seem all gone. On the other hand she has her daughter, who has grown up and who is a precious vase of another kind—less fragile, I hope, than the rest. May she not be overturned and smashed!"

Peter Sherringham and Biddy Dormer listened with attention to this history, and the girl testified to the interest with which she had followed it by saying, when Mr. Nash had ceased speaking: "A Jewish stockbroker, a dealer in curiosities: what an odd person to marry—for a person who was well born! I dare say he was a German."

"His name must have been simply Roth, and the poor lady, to smarten it up, has put in another *o*," Sherringham ingeniously suggested.

"You are both very clever," said Gabriel Nash, "and Rudolf Roth, as I happen to know, was indeed the designation of Maud Vavasour's papa. But, as far as the question of derogation goes, one might as well drown as starve, for what connection is *not* a misalliance when one happens to have the cumbersome, the unaccommodating honour of being a Neville-Nugent of Castle Nugent? Such was the high lineage of Maud's mamma. I seem to have heard it mentioned that Rudolf Roth was very versatile and, like most of his species, not unacquainted with the practice of music. He had been employed to teach the harmonium to Miss Neville-Nugent and she had profited by his lessons. If his daughter is like him—and she is not like her mother—he was darkly and dangerously handsome. So I venture rapidly to reconstruct the situation."

A silence, for the moment, had fallen upon Lady Agnes and her other two children, so that Mr. Nash, with his universal urbanity, practically addressed these last remarks to them as well as to his other auditors. Lady Agnes looked as if she wondered whom he was talking about, and having caught the name of a noble residence she inquired—

"Castle Nugent—where is that?"

"It's a domain of immeasurable extent and almost inconceivable splendour, but I fear it isn't to be found in any prosaic earthly geography!" Lady Agnes rested her eyes on the tablecloth, as if she were not sure a liberty had not been taken with her, and while Mr. Nash continued to abound in descriptive suppositions—"It must be on the banks of the Manzanares or the Guadalquivir"—Peter Sherringham, whose imagination appeared to have been strongly kindled by the sketch of Miriam Rooth, challenging him sociably, reminded him that he had a short time before assigned a low place to the dramatic art and had not yet answered his question as to whether he believed in the theatre. This gave Nash an opportunity to go on:

"I don't know that I understand your question; there are different ways of taking it. Do I think it's important? Is that what you mean? Important, certainly, to managers and stage-carpenters who want to make money, to ladies and gentlemen who want to produce themselves in public by lime-light, and to other ladies and gentlemen who are bored and stupid and don't know what to do with their evening. It's a commercial and social convenience which may be infinitely worked. But important artistically, intellectually? How *can* it be—so poor, so limited a form?"

"Dear me, it strikes me as so rich, so various! Do *you* think it's poor and limited, Nick?" Sherringham added, appealing to his kinsman.

"I think whatever Nash thinks. I have no opinion to-day but his."

This answer of Nick Dormer's drew the eyes of his mother and sisters to him, and caused his friend to exclaim that he was not used to such responsibilities, so few people had ever tested his presence of mind by agreeing with him.

"Oh, I used to be of your way of feeling," Nash said to Sherringham. "I understand you perfectly. It's a phase like another. I've been through it—*j'ai été comme ça.*"

"And you went, then, very often to the Théâtre Français, and it was there I saw you. I place you now."

"I'm afraid I noticed none of the other spectators," Nash explained. "I had no attention but for the great Carré—she was still on the stage. Judge of my infatuation, and how I can allow for yours, when I tell you that I sought her acquaintance, that I couldn't rest till I had told her that I hung upon her lips."

"That's just what *I* told her," returned Sherringham.

"She was very kind to me. She said, '*Vous me rendez des forces.*'"

"That's just what she said to me!"

"And we have remained very good friends."

"So have *we*!" laughed Sherringham. "And such perfect art as hers: do you mean to say you don't consider *that* important—such a rare dramatic intelligence?"

"I'm afraid you read the *feuilletons*. You catch their phrases," Gabriel Nash blandly rejoined. "Dramatic intelligence is never rare; nothing is more common."

"Then why have we so many bad actors?"

"Have we? I thought they were mostly good; succeeding more easily and more completely in that business than in anything else. What could they do—those people, generally—if they didn't do that? And reflect that *that* enables them to succeed! Of course, always, there are numbers of people on the stage who are no actors at all, for it's even easier to our poor humanity to be ineffectively stupid and vulgar than to bring down the house."

"It's not easy, by what I can see, to produce, completely, any artistic effect," Sherringham declared; "and those that the actor produces are among the most moving that we know. You'll not persuade me that to watch such an actress as Madame Carré was not an education of the taste, an enlargement of one's knowledge."

"She did what she could, poor woman, but in what belittling, coarsening conditions! She had to interpret a character in a play, and a character in a play (not to say the whole piece—I speak more particularly of modern pieces) is such a wretchedly small peg to hang anything on! The dramatist shows us so little, is so hampered by his audience, is restricted to so poor an analysis."

"I know the complaint. It's all the fashion now. The *raffinés* despise the theatre," said Peter Sherringham, in the manner of a man abreast with the culture of his age and not to be captured by a surprise. *"Connu, connu!"*

"It will be known better yet, won't it? when the essentially brutal nature of the modern audience is still more perceived, when it has been properly analyzed: the *omnium gatherum* of the population of a big commercial city, at the hour of the day when their taste is at its lowest, flocking out of hideous hotels and restaurants, gorged with food, stultified with buying and selling and with all the other sordid speculations of the day, squeezed together in a sweltering mass, disappointed in their seats, timing the author, timing the actor, wishing to get their money back on the spot, before eleven o'clock. Fancy putting the exquisite before such a tribunal as that! There's not even a question of it. The dramatist wouldn't if he could, and in nine cases out of ten he couldn't if he would. He has to make the basest concessions. One of his principal canons is that he must enable his spectators to catch the suburban trains, which stop at 11.30. What would you think of any other artist—the painter or the novelist—whose governing forces should be the dinner and the suburban trains? The old dramatists didn't defer to them (not so much, at least), and that's why they are less and less actable. If they are touched—the large fellows—it's only to be mutilated and trivialized. Besides, they had a simpler civilization to represent—societies in which the life of man was in action, in passion, in immediate and violent expression. Those things could be put upon the playhouse boards with comparatively little sacrifice of their completeness and their truth. To-day we are so infinitely more reflective and complicated and diffuse that it makes all the difference. What can you do with a character, with an idea, with a feeling, between dinner and the suburban trains? You can give a gross, rough sketch of them, but how little you touch them, how bald you leave them! What crudity compared with what the novelist does!"

"Do you write novels, Mr. Nash?" Peter demanded.

"No, but I read them when they are extraordinarily good, and I don't go to plays. I read Balzac, for instance—I encounter the magnificent portrait of Valérie Marneffe, in 'La Cousine Bette.'"

"And you contrast it with the poverty of Emile Augier's Séraphine in 'Les Lionnes Pauvres'? I was awaiting you there. That's the *cheval de bataille* of you fellows."

"What an extraordinary discussion! What dreadful authors!" Lady Agnes murmured to her son. But he was listening so attentively to the other young men that he made no response, and Peter Sherringham went on:

"I have seen Madame Carré in parts, in the modern repertory, which she has made as vivid to me, caused to abide as

ineffaceably in my memory, as Valérie Marneffe. She is the
Balzac, as one may say, of actresses."

"The miniaturist, as it were, of whitewashers!" Nash rejoined, laughing.

It might have been guessed that Sherringham was irritated,
but the other disputant was so good-humoured that he abundantly recognized his own obligation to appear so.

"You would be magnanimous if you thought the young
lady you have introduced to our old friend would be important."

"She might be much more so than she ever will be."

Lady Agnes got up, to terminate the scene, and even to
signify that enough had been said about people and questions
she had never heard of. Every one else rose, the waiter
brought Nick the receipt of the bill, and Sherringham went
on, to his interlocutor—

"Perhaps she will be more so than you think."

"Perhaps—if *you* take an interest in her!"

"A mystic voice seems to exhort me to do so, to whisper
that, though I have never seen her, I shall find something in
her. What do you say, Biddy, shall I take an interest in her?"

Biddy hesitated a moment, coloured a little, felt a certain
embarrassment in being publicly treated as an oracle.

"If she's not nice I don't advise it."

"And if she *is* nice?"

"You advise it still less!" her brother exclaimed, laughing
and putting his arm round her.

Lady Agnes looked sombre—she might have been saying
to herself: "Dear me, what chance has a girl of mine with a
man who's so agog about actresses?" She was disconcerted
and distressed; a multitude of incongruous things, all the
morning, had been forced upon her attention—displeasing
pictures and still more displeasing theories about them, vague
portents of perversity on the part of Nicholas, and a strange
eagerness on Peter's, learned apparently in Paris, to discuss,
with a person who had a tone she never had been exposed to,
topics irrelevant and uninteresting, the practical effect of
which was to make light of her presence. "Let us leave this—
let us leave this!" she almost moaned. The party moved together toward the door of departure, and her ruffled spirit

was not soothed by hearing her son remark to his terrible friend: "You know you don't leave us—I stick to you!"

At this Lady Agnes broke out and interposed: "Excuse me for reminding you that you are going to call on Julia."

"Well, can't Nash also come to call on Julia? That's just what I want—that she should see him."

Peter Sherringham came humanely to her ladyship's assistance. "A better way, perhaps, will be for them to meet under my auspices, at my 'dramatic tea.' This will enable me to return one favour for another. If Mr. Nash is so good as to introduce me to this aspirant for honours we estimate so differently, I will introduce him to my sister, a much more positive quantity."

"It is easy to see who'll have the best of it!" Grace Dormer exclaimed; and Gabriel Nash stood there serenely, impartially, in a graceful, detached way which seemed characteristic of him, assenting to any decision that relieved him of the grossness of choice, and generally confident that things would turn out well for him. He was cheerfully helpless and sociably indifferent; ready to preside with a smile even at a discussion of his own admissibility.

"Nick will bring you. I have a little corner at the Embassy," Sherringham continued.

"You are very kind. You must bring him, then, to-morrow—Rue de Constantinople."

"At five o'clock—don't be afraid."

"Oh, dear!" said Biddy, as they went on again; and Lady Agnes, seizing his arm, marched off more quickly with her son. When they came out into the Champs Elysées Nick Dormer, looking round, saw that his friend had disappeared. Biddy had attached herself to Peter, and Grace apparently had not encouraged Mr. Nash.

V.

LADY AGNES's idea had been that her son should go straight from the Palais de l'Industrie to the Hôtel de Hollande, with or without his mother and his sisters, as his humour should seem to recommend. Much as she desired to see their brilliant kinswoman and as she knew that her daughters desired it, she was quite ready to postpone their visit, if this sacrifice should contribute to a speedy confrontation for Nick. She was eager that he should talk with Mrs. Dallow, and eager that he should be eager himself; but it presently appeared that he was really not anything that could impartially be called so. His view was that she and the girls should go to the Hôtel de Hollande without delay and should spend the rest of the day with Julia, if they liked. He would go later; he would go in the evening. There were lots of things he wanted to do meanwhile.

This question was discussed with some intensity, though not at length, while the little party stood on the edge of the Place de la Concorde, to which they had proceeded on foot; and Lady Agnes noticed that the "lots of things" to which he proposed to give precedence over an urgent duty, a conference with a person who held out full hands to him, were implied somehow in the friendly glance with which he covered the great square, the opposite bank of the Seine, the steep blue roofs of the quay, the bright immensity of Paris. What in the world could be more important than making sure of his seat?—so quickly did the good lady's imagination travel. And now that idea appealed to him less than a ramble in search of old books and prints, for she was sure this was what he had in his head. Julia would be flattered if she knew it, but of course she must not know it. Lady Agnes was already thinking of the most honourable explanations she could give of the young man's want of precipitation. She would have liked to represent him as tremendously occupied, in his room at their own hotel, in getting off political letters to every one it should concern, and particularly in drawing up his address to the electors of Harsh. Fortunately she was a woman of innumerable discretions, and a part of the worn

look that sat in her face came from her having schooled herself for years, in her relations with her husband and her sons,
not to insist unduly. She would have liked to insist, nature
had formed her to insist, and the self-control had told in more
ways than one. Even now it was powerless to prevent her
suggesting that before doing anything else Nick should at
least repair to the inn and see if there were not some telegrams.

He freely consented to do so much as this, and having
called a cab, that she might go her way with the girls, he
kissed her again, as he had done at the exhibition. This was
an attention that could never displease her, but somehow
when he kissed her often her anxiety was apt to increase: she
had come to recognize it as a sign that he was slipping away
from her. She drove off with a vague sense that at any rate
she and the girls might do something toward keeping the
place warm for him. She had been a little vexed that Peter
had not administered more of a push toward the Hôtel de
Hollande, clear as it had become to her now that there was a
foreignness in Peter which was not to be counted on and
which made him speak of English affairs and even of English
domestic politics as local. Of course they were local, and was
not that the warm human comfort of them? As she left the
two young men standing together in the middle of the Place
de la Concorde, the grand composition of which Nick, as
she looked back, appeared to have paused to admire, (as if
he had not seen it a thousand times!) she wished she might
have thought of Peter's influence with her son as exerted a
little more in favour of localism. She had a sense that he
would not abbreviate the boy's ill-timed *flânerie*. However,
he had been very nice: he had invited them all to dine with
him that evening at a convenient restaurant, promising to
bring Julia and one of his colleagues. So much as this he had
been willing to do to make sure that Nick and his sister
should meet. His want of localism, moreover, was not so
great as that if it should turn out that there *was* anything beneath his manner toward Biddy—! The conclusion of this
reflection is, perhaps, best indicated by the circumstance of
her ladyship's remarking, after a minute, to her younger
daughter, who sat opposite to her in the *voiture de place*, that

it would do no harm if she should get a new hat, and that the article might be purchased that afternoon.

"A French hat, mamma?" said Grace. "Oh, do wait till she gets home!"

"I think they are prettier here, you know," Biddy rejoined; and Lady Agnes said, simply, "I dare say they're cheaper." What was in her mind, in fact, was, "I dare say Peter thinks them becoming." It will be seen that she had plenty of spiritual occupation, the sum of which was not diminished by her learning, when she reached the top of the Rue de la Paix, that Mrs. Dallow had gone out half an hour before and had left no message. She was more disconcerted by this incident than she could have explained or than she thought was right, for she had taken for granted that Julia would be in a manner waiting for them. How did she know that Nick was not coming? When people were in Paris for a few days they didn't mope in the house; but Julia might have waited a little longer or might have left an explanation. Was she then not so much in earnest about Nick's standing? Didn't she recognize the importance of being there to see him about it? Lady Agnes wondered whether Julia's behaviour were a sign that she was already tired of the way this young gentleman treated her. Perhaps she had gone out because an instinct told her that its being important he should see her early would make no difference with him—told her that he wouldn't come. Her heart sank as she glanced at this possibility that Julia was already tired, for she, on her side, had an instinct there were still more tiresome things in store. She had disliked having to tell Mrs. Dallow that Nick wouldn't see her till the evening, but now she disliked still more her not being there to hear it. She even resented a little her kinswoman's not having reasoned that she and the girls would come in any event, and not thought them worth staying in for. It occurred to her that she would perhaps have gone to their hotel, which was a good way up the Rue de Rivoli, near the Palais Royal, and she directed the cabman to drive to that establishment.

As he jogged along she took in some degree the measure of what that might mean, Julia's seeking a little to avoid them. Was she growing to dislike them? Did she think they kept too sharp an eye on her, so that the idea of their standing in a still

closer relation to her would not be enticing? Her conduct up
to this time had not worn such an appearance, unless perhaps a little, just a very little, in the matter of poor Grace.
Lady Agnes knew that she was not particularly fond of poor
Grace, and was even able to guess the reason—the manner
in which Grace betrayed the most that they wanted to make
sure of her. She remembered how long the girl had stayed
the last time she had gone to Harsh. She had gone for an
acceptable week, and she had been in the house a month.
She took a private, heroic vow that Grace should not go
near the place again for a year; that is, not unless Nick and
Julia were married before this. If that were to happen she
shouldn't care. She recognized that it was not absolutely
everything that Julia should be in love with Nick; it was also
better she should dislike his mother and sisters after than before. Lady Agnes did justice to the natural rule in virtue of
which it usually comes to pass that a woman doesn't get on
with her husband's female belongings, and was even willing
to be sacrificed to it in her disciplined degree. But she
desired not to be sacrificed for nothing: if she was to be
objected to as a mother-in-law she wished to be the mother-
in-law first.

   At the hotel in the Rue de Rivoli she had the disappointment of finding that Mrs. Dallow had not called, and also
that no telegrams had come. She went in with the girls for
half an hour, and then she straggled out with them again.
She was undetermined and dissatisfied, and the afternoon
was rather a problem; of the kind moreover that she disliked
most and was least accustomed to: not a choice between different things to do (her life had been full of that), but a
want of anything to do at all. Nick had said to her before
they separated: "You can knock about with the girls, you
know; everything is amusing here." That was easily said,
while he sauntered and gossiped with Peter Sherringham and
perhaps went to see more pictures like those in the Salon.
He was usually, on such occasions, very good-natured about
spending his time with them; but this episode had taken
altogether a perverse, profane form. She had no desire
whatever to knock about, and she was far from finding

everything in Paris amusing. She had no aptitude for aimlessness, and moreover she thought it vulgar. If she had found Julia's card at the hotel (the sign of a hope of catching them just as they came back from the Salon), she would have made a second attempt to see her before the evening; but now certainly they would leave her alone. Lady Agnes wandered joylessly with the girls in the Palais Royal and the Rue de Richelieu, and emerged upon the Boulevard, where they continued their frugal prowl, as Biddy rather irritatingly called it. They went into five shops to buy a hat for Biddy, and her ladyship's presuppositions of cheapness were wofully belied.

"Who in the world is your funny friend?" Peter Sherringham meanwhile asked of his kinsman. He lost no time as they walked together.

"Ah, there's something else you lost by going to Cambridge—you lost Gabriel Nash!"

"He sounds like an Elizabethan dramatist," Sherringham said. "But I haven't lost him, since it appears now that I shall not be able to have you without him."

"Oh, as for that, wait a little. I'm going to try him again, but I don't know how he wears. What I mean is that you have probably lost his freshness. I have an idea he has become conventional, or at any rate serious."

"Bless me, do you call that serious?"

"He used to be so gay. He had a real genius for suggestive paradox. He was a wonderful talker."

"It seems to me he does very well now," said Peter Sherringham.

"Oh, this is nothing. He had great flights of old, very great flights; one saw him rise and rise and turn summersaults in the blue, and wondered how far he could go. He's very intelligent, and I should think it might be interesting to find out what it is that prevents the whole man from being as good as his parts. I mean in case he isn't so good."

"I see you more than suspect that. May it not simply be that he's an ass?"

"That would be the whole—I shall see in time—but it certainly isn't one of the parts. It may be the effect, but it isn't the cause, and it's for the cause that I claim an interest. I imagine you think he's an ass on account of what he said about the theatre, his pronouncing it a coarse art."

"To differ about him that reason will do," said Sherringham. "The only bad one would be one that shouldn't preserve our difference. You needn't tell me you agree with him, for frankly I don't care."

"Then your passion still burns?" Nick Dormer asked.

"My passion?"

"I don't mean for any individual exponent of the contestable art: mark the guilty conscience, mark the rising blush, mark the confusion of mind! I mean the old sign one knew you best by: your permanent stall at the Français, your inveterate attendance at *premières*, the way you 'follow' the young talents and the old."

"Yes, it's still my little hobby: my little folly, if you like. I don't see that I get tired of it. What will you have? Strong predilections are rather a blessing; they are simplifying. I am fond of representation—the representation of life: I like it better, I think, than the real thing. You like it, too, so you have no right to cast the stone. You like it best done one way and I another; and our preference, on either side, has a deep root in us. There is a fascination to me in the way the actor does it, when his talent (ah, he must have that!) has been highly trained (ah, it must *be* that!). The things he can do, in this effort at representation (with the dramatist to give him his lift) seem to me innumerable—he can carry it to a delicacy!—and I take great pleasure in observing them, in recognizing them and comparing them. It's an amusement like another: I don't pretend to call it by any exalted name; but in this vale of friction it will serve. One can lose one's self in it, and it has this recommendation (in common, I suppose, with the study of the other arts), that the further you go in it the more you find. So I go rather far, if you will. But is it the principal sign one knows me by?" Sherringham abruptly asked.

"Don't be ashamed of it, or it will be ashamed of you. I ought to discriminate. You are distinguished among my friends and relations by being a rising young diplomatist; but you know I always want the further distinction, the last analysis. Therefore I surmise that you are conspicuous among rising young diplomatists for the infatuation that you describe in such pretty terms."

"You evidently believe that it will prevent me from rising very high. But pastime for pastime, is it any idler than yours?"

"Than mine?"

"Why, you have half a dozen, while I only allow myself the luxury of one. For the theatre is my sole vice, really. Is this more wanton, say, than to devote weeks to ascertaining in what particular way your friend Mr. Nash may be a twaddler? That's not my ideal of choice recreation, but I would undertake to do it sooner. You're a young statesman (who happens to be *en disponibilité* for the moment), but you spend not a little of your time in besmearing canvas with bright-coloured pigments. The idea of representation fascinates you, but in your case it's representation in oils—or do you practise water-colours too? You even go much further than I, for I study my art of predilection only in the works of others. I don't aspire to leave works of my own. You're a painter, possibly a great one; but I'm not an actor." Nick Dormer declared that he would certainly become one—he was on the way to it; and Sherringham, without heeding this charge, went on: "Let me add that, considering you *are* a painter, your portrait of the complicated Nash is lamentably dim."

"He's not at all complicated; he's only too simple to give an account of. Most people have a lot of attributes and appendages that dress them up and superscribe them, and what I like him for is that he hasn't any at all. It makes him so cool."

"By Jove, you match him there! It's an attribute to be tolerated. How does he manage it?"

"I haven't the least idea—I don't know that he *is* tolerated. I don't think any one has ever detected the process. His means, his profession, his belongings have never anything to do with the question. He doesn't shade off into other people; he's as neat as an outline cut out of paper with scissors. I like him, therefore, because in intercourse with him you know what you've got hold of. With most men you don't: to pick the flower you must break off the whole dusty, thorny, worldly branch; you find you are taking up in your grasp all sorts of other people and things, dangling accidents and conditions. Poor Nash has none of those ramifications; he's the solitary blossom."

"My dear fellow, you would be better for a little of the same pruning!" Sherringham exclaimed; and the young men continued their walk and their gossip, jerking each other this way and that with a sociable roughness consequent on their having been boys together. Intimacy had reigned, of old, between the little Sherringhams and the little Dormers, united by country contiguity and by the circumstance that there was first-cousinship, not neglected, among the parents, Lady Agnes standing in this convertible relation to Lady Windrush, the mother of Peter and Julia as well as of other daughters and of a maturer youth who was to inherit, and who since then had inherited, the ancient barony. Since then many things had altered, but not the deep foundation of sociability. One of our young men had gone to Eton and the other to Harrow (the scattered school on the hill was the tradition of the Dormers), and the divergence had taken its course later, in university years. Bricket, however, had remained accessible to Windrush, and Windrush to Bricket, to which Percival Dormer had now succeeded, terminating the interchange a trifle rudely by letting out that pleasant white house in the midlands (its expropriated inhabitants, Lady Agnes and her daughters, adored it) to an American reputed rich, who, in the first flush of international comparison, considered that for twelve hundred a year he got it at a bargain. Bricket had come to the late Sir Nicholas from his elder brother, who died wifeless and childless. The new baronet, so different from his father (though he recalled at some points the uncle after whom he had been named) that Nick had to make it up by aspirations of resemblance, roamed about the world taking shots which excited the enthusiasm of society, when society heard of them, at the few legitimate creatures of the chase which the British rifle had spared. Lady Agnes, meanwhile, settled with her girls in a gabled, latticed house in a creditable quarter, though it was still a little raw, of the temperate zone of London. It was not into her lap, poor woman, that the revenues of Bricket were poured. There was no dower-house attached to that moderate property, and the allowance with which the estate was charged on her ladyship's behalf was not an incitement to grandeur.

Nick had a room under his mother's roof, which he mainly used to dress for dinner when he dined in Calcutta Gardens, and he had "kept on" his chambers in the Temple; for to a young man in public life an independent address was indispensable. Moreover, he was suspected of having a studio in an out-of-the-way quarter of the town, the indistinguishable parts of South Kensington, incongruous as such a retreat might seem in the case of a member of Parliament. It was an absurd place to see his constituents, unless he wanted to paint their portraits, a kind of representation with which they scarcely would have been satisfied; and in fact the only question of portraiture had been when the wives and daughters of several of them expressed a wish for the picture of their handsome young member. Nick had not offered to paint it himself, and the studio was taken for granted rather than much looked into by the ladies in Calcutta Gardens. Too express a disposition to regard whims of this sort as a pure extravagance was known by them to be open to correction; for they were not oblivious that Mr. Carteret had humours which weighed against them in the shape of convenient cheques nestling between the inside pages of legible letters of advice. Mr. Carteret was Nick's providence, as Nick was looked to, in a general way, to be that of his mother and sisters, especially since it had become so plain that Percy, who was ungracefully selfish, would operate, mainly with a "six-bore," quite out of that sphere. It was not for studios, certainly, that Mr. Carteret sent cheques; but they were an expression of general confidence in Nick, and a little expansion was natural to a young man enjoying such a luxury as that. It was sufficiently felt, in Calcutta Gardens, that Nick could be looked to not to betray such a confidence; for Mr. Carteret's behaviour could have no name at all unless one were prepared to call it encouraging. He had never promised anything, but he was one of the delightful persons with whom the redemption precedes or dispenses with the vow. He had been an early and lifelong friend of the late right honourable gentleman, a political follower, a devoted admirer, a stanch supporter in difficult hours. He had

never married, espousing nothing more reproductive than Sir
Nicholas's views (he used to write letters to the *Times* in favour of them), and had, so far as was known, neither chick
nor child; nothing but an amiable little family of eccentrici-
ties, the flower of which was his odd taste for living in a
small, steep, clean country town, all green gardens and red
walls, with a girdle of hedge-rows, clustering about an immense brown old abbey. When Lady Agnes's imagination
rested upon the future of her second son she liked to remember that Mr. Carteret had nothing to "keep-up:" the inference
seemed so direct that he would keep up Nick.

The most important event in the life of this young man had
been incomparably his victory, under his father's eyes, more
than two years before, in the sharp contest for Crockhurst—a
victory which his consecrated name, his extreme youth, his
ardour in the fray, the general personal sympathy of the party
and the attention excited by the fresh cleverness of his
speeches, tinted with young idealism and yet sticking sufficiently to the question (the burning question, it has since
burnt out), had rendered almost brilliant. There had been
leaders in the newspapers about it, half in compliment to her
husband, who was known to be failing so prematurely (he
was almost as young to die, and to die famous—Lady Agnes
regarded it as famous—as his son had been to stand), which
the boy's mother religiously preserved, cut out and tied together with a ribbon, in the innermost drawer of a favourite
cabinet. But it had been a barren, or almost a barren triumph,
for in the order of importance in Nick's history another incident had run it, as the phrase is, very close: nothing less than
the quick dissolution of the Parliament in which he was so
manifestly destined to give symptoms of a future. He had not
recovered his seat at the general election, for the second contest was even sharper than the first, and the Tories had put
forward a loud, vulgar, rattling, almost bullying man. It was
to a certain extent a comfort that poor Sir Nicholas, who had
been witness of the bright hour, passed away before the darkness. He died, with all his hopes on his second son's head,
unconscious of near disaster, handing on the torch and the
tradition, after a long, supreme interview with Nick, at which
Lady Agnes had not been present but which she knew to have

been a sort of paternal dedication, a solemn communication of ideas on the highest national questions (she had reason to believe he had touched on those of external as well as of domestic and of colonial policy), leaving on the boy's nature and manner from that moment the most unmistakable traces. If his tendency to reverie increased, it was because he had so much to think over in what his pale father had said to him in the hushed, dim chamber, laying upon him the great mission of carrying out the unachieved and reviving a silent voice. It was work cut out for a lifetime, and that "co-ordinating power in relation to detail," which was one of the great characteristics of Sir Nicholas's high distinction (the most analytic of the weekly papers was always talking about it), had enabled him to rescue the prospect from any shade of vagueness or of ambiguity.

Five years before Nick Dormer went up to be questioned by the electors of Crockhurst, Peter Sherringham appeared before a board of examiners who let him off much less easily, though there were also some flattering prejudices in his favour; such influences being a part of the copious, light, unembarrassing baggage with which each of the young men began life. Peter passed, however, passed high, and had his reward in prompt assignment to small, subordinate diplomatic duties in Germany. Since then he had had his professional adventures, which need not arrest us, inasmuch as they had all paled in the light of his appointment, nearly three years previous to the moment of our making his acquaintance, to a secretaryship of embassy in Paris. He had done well and had gone fast, and for the present he was willing enough to rest. It pleased him better to remain in Paris as a subordinate than to go to Honduras as a principal, and Nick Dormer had not put a false colour on the matter in speaking of his stall at the Théâtre Français as a sedative to his ambition. Nick's inferiority in age to his cousin sat on him more lightly than when they had been in their teens; and indeed no one can very well be much older than a young man who has figured for a year, however imperceptibly, in the House of Commons. Separation and diversity had made them strange enough to each other to give a taste to what they shared; they were friends without being particular friends; that further degree could always hang before them as a suitable but not oppressive contingency, and they were both conscious that it was in their interest to keep certain differences to "chaff" each other about—so possible was it that they might have quarrelled if they had only agreed. Peter, as being wide-minded, was a little irritated to find his cousin always so intensely British, while Nick Dormer made him the object of the same compassionate criticism, recognized that he had a rare knack with foreign tongues, but reflected, and even with extravagance declared, that it was a pity to have gone so far from home only to remain so homely. Moreover, Nick had his ideas about the diplomatic mind; it was the moral type of which, on the whole, he thought least favourably. Dry, narrow, barren, poor, he pronounced it in familiar conversation with the clever secretary; wanting in imagination, in generosity, in the finest perceptions and the highest courage. This served as well as anything else to keep the peace between them; it was a necessity of their friendly intercourse that they should scuffle a little, and it scarcely mattered what they scuffled about. Nick Dormer's express enjoyment of Paris, the shop-windows on the quays, the old books on the parapet, the gaiety of the river, the grandeur of the Louvre, all the amusing tints and tones, struck his companion as a sign of insularity; the appreciation of such things having become with Sherringham an unconscious habit, a contented assimilation. If poor Nick, for the hour, was demonstrative and lyrical, it was because he had no other way of sounding the note of farewell to the independent life of which the term seemed now definitely in sight; the sense pressed upon him that these were the last moments of his freedom. He would waste time till half-past seven, because half-past seven meant dinner, and dinner meant his mother, solemnly attended by the strenuous shade of his father and reinforced by Julia.

VI.

WHEN NICK arrived with the three members of his family, Peter Sherringham was seated, in the restaurant at which the tryst had been taken, at a small but immaculate table; but Mrs. Dallow was not yet on the scene, and they had time for a sociable settlement—time to take their places and unfold their napkins, crunch their rolls, breathe the savoury air and watch the door, before the usual raising of heads and suspension of forks, the sort of stir that accompanied most of this lady's movements, announced her entrance. The *dame de comptoir* ducked and re-ducked, the people looked round, Peter and Nick got up, there was a shuffling of chairs—Julia was there. Peter had related how he had stopped at her hotel to bring her with him and had found her, according to her custom, by no means ready; on which, fearing that his guests would come first to the rendezvous and find no proper welcome, he had come off without her, leaving her to follow. He had not brought a friend, as he intended, having divined that Julia would prefer a pure family party, if she wanted to talk about her candidate. Now she stood there, looking down at the table and her expectant kinsfolk, drawing off her gloves, letting her brother draw off her jacket, lifting her hands for some rearrangement of her bonnet. She looked at Nick last, smiling, but only for a moment. She said to Peter, "Are we going to dine here? Oh dear, why didn't you have a private room?"

Nick had not seen her at all for several weeks, and had seen her but little for a year, but her off-hand, cursory manner had not altered in the interval. She spoke remarkably fast, as if speech were not in itself a pleasure—to have it over as soon as possible; and her *brusquerie* was of the kind that friendly critics account for by pleading shyness. Shyness had never appeared to him an ultimate quality or a real explanation of anything; it only explained an effect by another effect, giving a bad fault another name. What he suspected in Julia was that her mind was less graceful than her person; an ugly, a really damnatory idea, which as yet he had only half accepted. It was a case in which she was entitled to the benefit of every

763

doubt and ought not to be judged without a complete trial. Dormer, meanwhile, was afraid of the trial (this was partly why, of late, he had been to see her so little), because he was afraid of the sentence, afraid of anything, happening which should lessen the pleasure it was actually in the power of her beauty to give. There were people who thought her rude, and he hated rude women. If he should fasten on that view, or rather if that view should fasten on him, what could still please and what he admired in her would lose too much of its sweetness. If it be thought odd that he had not yet been able to read the character of a woman he had known since child-hood, the answer is that that character had grown faster than Nick Dormer's observation. The growth was constant, whereas the observation was but occasional, though it had begun early. If he had attempted to phrase the matter to him-self, as he probably had not, he might have said that the effect she produced upon him was too much a compulsion; not the coercion of design, of importunity, nor the vulgar pressure of family expectation, a suspected desire that he should like her enough to marry her, but something that was a mixture of diverse things, of the sense that she was imperious and gener-ous—but probably more the former than the latter—and of a certain prevision of doom, the influence of the idea that he should come to it, that he was predestined.

This had made him shrink from knowing the worst about her; the desire, not to get used to it in time, but what was more characteristic of him, to interpose a temporary illusion. Illusions and realities and hopes and fears, however, fell into confusion whenever he met her after a separation. The sepa-ration, so far as seeing her alone or as continuous talk was concerned, had now been tolerably long; had lasted really ever since his failure to regain his seat. An impression had come to him that she judged that failure rather harshly, had thought he ought to have done better. This was a part of her imperious strain, and a part to which it was not easy to ac-commodate one's self on a present basis. If he were to marry her he should come to an understanding with her: he should give her his own measure as well as take hers. But the under-standing, in the actual case, might suggest too much that he *was* to marry her. You could quarrel with your wife, because there were compensations—for her; but you might not be prepared to offer these compensations as prepayment for the luxury of quarrelling.

It was not that such a luxury would not be considerable, Nick Dormer thought, as Julia Dallow's fine head poised itself before him again; a high spirit was a better thing than a poor one to be mismated with, any day in the year. She had much the same colouring as her brother, but as nothing else in her face was the same the resemblance was not striking. Her hair was of so dark a brown that it was commonly regarded as black, and so abundant that a plain arrangement was required to keep it in discreet relation to the rest of her person. Her eyes were of a gray tint that was sometimes pronounced too light; and they were not sunken in her face, but placed well on the surface. Her nose was perfect, but her mouth was too small; and Nick Dormer, and doubtless other persons as well, had sometimes wondered how, with such a mouth, her face could have expressed decision. Her figure helped it, for she looked tall (being extremely slender), though she was not; and her head took turns and positions which, though they were a matter of but half an inch out of the common, this way or that, somehow contributed to the air of resolution and temper. If it had not been for her extreme delicacy of line and surface she might have been called bold; but as it was she looked refined and quiet—refined by tradition and quiet for a purpose. And altogether she was beautiful, with the pure style of her capable head, her hair like darkness, her eyes like early twilight, her mouth like a rare pink flower.

Peter said that he had not taken a private room because he knew Biddy's tastes; she liked to see the world (she had told him so), the curious people, the coming and going of Paris. "Oh, anything for Biddy!" Julia replied, smiling at the girl and taking her place. Lady Agnes and her elder daughter exchanged one of their looks, and Nick exclaimed jocosely that he didn't see why the whole party should be sacrificed to a presumptuous child. The presumptuous child blushingly protested she had never expressed any such wish to Peter, upon which Nick, with broader humour, revealed that Peter had served them so out of stinginess: he had pitchforked them together in the public room because he wouldn't go to the expense of a *cabinet*. He had brought no guest, no foreigner of distinction nor diplomatic swell, to honour them, and now they would see what a paltry dinner he would give them. Peter stabbed him indignantly with a long roll, and Lady Agnes, who seemed to be waiting for some manifestation on Mrs. Dallow's part which didn't come, concluded, with a certain coldness, that they quite sufficed to themselves for privacy as well as for society. Nick called attention to this fine phrase of his mother's, said it was awfully neat, while Grace and Biddy looked harmoniously at Julia's clothes. Nick felt nervous, and joked a good deal to carry it off—a levity that didn't prevent Julia's saying to him, after a moment: "You might have come to see me to-day, you know. Didn't you get my message from Peter?"

"Scold him, Julia—scold him well. I begged him to go," said Lady Agnes; and to this Grace added her voice with an "Oh, Julia, do give it to him!" These words, however, had not the effect they suggested, for Mrs. Dallow only murmured, with an ejaculation, in her quick, curt way, that that would be making far too much of him. It was one of the things in her which Nick Dormer mentally pronounced ungraceful that a perversity of pride or shyness always made her disappoint you a little if she saw you expected a thing. She was certain to snub effusiveness. This vice, however, was the last thing of which Lady Agnes would have consented to being accused; and Nick, while he replied to Julia that he was certain he shouldn't have found her, was not unable to perceive the operation on his mother of that shade of manner. "He ought to have gone; he owed you that," she went on; "but it's very true he would have had the same luck as we. I went with the girls directly after luncheon. I suppose you got our card."

"He might have come after I came in," said Mrs. Dallow.

"Dear Julia, I'm going to see you to-night. I've been waiting for that," Nick rejoined.

"Of course *we* had no idea when you would come in," said Lady Agnes.

"I'm so sorry. You must come to-morrow. I hate calls at night," Julia remarked.

"Well, then, will you roam with me? Will you wander through Paris on my arm?" Nick asked, smiling. "Will you take a drive with me?"

"Oh, that would be perfection!" cried Grace.

"I thought we were all going somewhere—to the Hippodrome, Peter," said Biddy.

"Oh, not all; just you and me!" laughed Peter.

"I am going home to my bed. I've earned my rest," Lady Agnes sighed.

"Can't Peter take *us*?" asked Grace. "Nick can take you home, mamma, if Julia won't receive him, and I can look perfectly after Peter and Biddy."

"Take them to something amusing; please take them," Mrs. Dallow said to her brother. Her voice was kind, but had the expectation of assent in it, and Nick observed both the indulgence and the pressure. "You're tired, poor dear," she continued to Lady Agnes. "Fancy your being dragged about so! What did you come over for?"

"My mother came because I brought her," Nick said. "It's I who have dragged her about. I brought her for a little change. I thought it would do her good. I wanted to see the Salon."

"It isn't a bad time. I have a carriage, and you must use it; you must use nothing else. It will take you everywhere. I will drive you about to-morrow." Julia dropped these words in the same perfunctory, casual way as any others; but Nick had already noted, and he noted now afresh, with pleasure, that her abruptness was perfectly capable of conveying a benevolence. It was quite sufficiently manifest to him that for the rest of the time she might be near his mother she would do her numberless good turns. She would give things to the girls—he had a private adumbration of that; expensive Parisian, perhaps not perfectly useful things.

Lady Agnes was a woman who measured reciprocities and distances; but she was both too subtle and too just not to recognize the smallest manifestation that might count, either technically or essentially, as a service. "Dear Julia!" she exclaimed, responsively; and her tone made this brevity of acknowledgment sufficient. What Julia had said was all she wanted. "It's so interesting about Harsh," she added. "We're immensely excited."

"Yes, Nick looks it. *Merci, pas de vin.* It's just the thing for you, you know."

"To be sure he knows it. He's immensely grateful. It's really very kind of you."

"You do me a very great honour, Julia," said Nick.

"Don't be tiresome!" exclaimed Mrs. Dallow.

"We'll talk about it later. Of course there are lots of points," Nick pursued. "At present let us be purely convivial. Somehow Harsh is such a false note here. *A tout à l'heure!*"

"My dear fellow, you've caught exactly the tone of Mr. Gabriel Nash," Peter Sherringham observed.

"Who is Mr. Gabriel Nash?" Mrs. Dallow asked.

"Nick, *is* he a gentleman? Biddy says so," Grace Dormer interposed before this inquiry was answered.

"It is to be supposed that any one Nick brings to lunch with us —" Lady Agnes murmured.

"Ah, Grace, with your tremendous standard!" her brother said; while Peter Sherringham replied to Julia that Mr. Nash was Nick's new Mentor or oracle; whom moreover she should see if she would come and have tea with him.

"I haven't the least desire to see him," Julia declared, "any more than I have to talk about Harsh and bore poor Peter."

"Oh, certainly, dear, you would bore me," said Sherringham.

"One thing at a time, then. Let us by all means be convivial. Only you must show me how," Mrs. Dallow went on to Nick. "What does he mean, Cousin Agnes? Does he want us to drain the wine-cup, to flash with repartee?"

"You'll do very well," said Nick. "You are charming, this evening."

"Do go to Peter's, Julia, if you want something exciting. You'll see a marvellous girl," Biddy broke in, with her smile on Peter.

"Marvellous for what?"

"For thinking she can act, when she can't," said the roguish Biddy.

"Dear me, what people you all know! I hate Peter's theatrical people."

"And aren't you going home, Julia?" Lady Agnes inquired. "Home to the hotel?"

"Dear, no, to Harsh, to see about everything."

"I'm in the midst of telegrams. I don't know yet."

"I suppose there's no doubt they'll have him," Lady Agnes decided to pursue.

"Who will have whom?"

"Why, the local people—and the party; those who invite a gentleman to stand. I'm speaking of my son."

"They'll have the person I want them to have, I dare say. There are so many people in it, in one way or another, it's dreadful. I like the way you sit there," Mrs. Dallow added to Nick Dormer.

"So do I," he smiled back at her; and he thought she *was* charming now, because she was gay and easy and willing really, though she might plead incompetence, to understand how jocose a dinner in a pot-house in a foreign town might be. She was in good-humour, or she was going to be, and not grand, nor stiff, nor indifferent, nor haughty, nor any of the things that people who disliked her usually found her and sometimes even a little made him believe her. The spirit of mirth, in some cold natures, manifests itself not altogether happily; their effort of recreation resembles too much the bath of the hippopotamus. But when Mrs. Dallow put her elbows on the table one felt she could be trusted to get them safely off again.

For a family in mourning the dinner was lively; the more so that before it was half over Julia had arranged that her brother, eschewing the inferior spectacle, should take the girls to the Théâtre Français. It was her idea, and Nick had a chance to observe how an idea was apt not to be successfully controverted when it was Julia's. Even the programme appeared to have been pre-arranged to suit it, just the thing for the cheek of the young person—"Il ne Faut Jurer de Rien" and "Mademoiselle de la Seiglière." Peter was all willingness, but it was Julia who settled it, even to sending for the newspaper (her brother, by a rare accident, was unconscious of the evening's bill), and to reassuring Biddy, who was happy but anxious, on the article of their not getting places, their being too late. Peter could always get places: a word from him and the best box was at his disposal. She made him write the word on a card, and saw that a messenger was despatched with it to the Rue de Richelieu; and all this was done without loudness or insistence, parenthetically and authoritatively. The box was bespoken; the carriage, as soon as they had had their coffee, was found to be there; Peter drove off in it with the girls, with the understanding that he was to send it back; Nick sat waiting for it, over the finished repast, with the two ladies, and then his mother was relegated to it and conveyed to her apartments: and all the while it was Julia who governed the succession of events. "Do be nice to her," Lady Agnes murmured to him, as he placed her in the vehicle at the door of the restaurant; and he guessed that it gave her a comfort to have left him sitting there with Mrs. Dallow.

Nick had every disposition to be nice to her; if things went as she liked them it was an acknowledgment of a certain force that was in her—the force of assuming that they would. Julia had her differences—some of them were much for the better; and when she was in a mood like this evening's, liberally dominant, he was ready to encourage her assumptions. While they waited for the return of the carriage, which had rolled away with his mother, she sat opposite to him, with her elbows on the table, playing first with one and then with another of the objects that encumbered it: after five minutes of which she exclaimed, "Oh, I say, we'll go!" and got up abruptly, asking for her jacket. He said something about the carriage's having had orders to come back for them, and she replied: "Well, it can go away again!" She added: "I don't want a carriage; I want to walk;" and in a moment she was out of the place, with the people at the tables turning round again and the *caissière* swaying in her high seat. On the pavement of the boulevard she looked up and down: there were people at little tables, at the door; there were people all over the broad expanse of the asphalt; there was a profusion of light and a pervasion of sound; and everywhere, though the establishment at which they had been dining was not in the thick of the fray, the tokens of a great traffic of pleasure, that night-aspect of Paris which represents it as a huge market for sensations. Beyond the Boulevard des Capucines it flared through the warm evening like a vast bazaar; and opposite the

Café Durand the Madeleine rose theatrical, a high, clever *décor*, before the footlights of the Rue Royale. "Where shall we go, what shall we do?" Mrs. Dallow asked, looking at her companion and somewhat to his surprise, as he had supposed she only wanted to go home.

"Anywhere you like. It's so warm we might drive, instead of going indoors. We might go to the Bois. That would be agreeable."

"Yes, but it wouldn't be walking. However, that doesn't matter. It's mild enough for anything—for sitting out, like all these people. And I've never walked in Paris at night: it would amuse me."

Nick hesitated. "So it might, but it isn't particularly recommended to ladies."

"I don't care, if it happens to suit me."

"Very well, then, we'll walk to the Bastille, if you like."

Julia hesitated, on her side, still looking round her.

"It's too far; I'm tired; we'll sit here." And she dropped beside an empty table, on the "terrace" of M. Durand. "This will do; it's amusing enough, and we can look at the Madeleine; that's respectable. If we must have something we'll have a *madère*; is that respectable? Not particularly? So much the better. What are those people having? *Bocks?* Couldn't we have bocks? Are they very low? Then I shall have one. I've been so wonderfully good—I've been staying at Versailles: *je me dois bien cela.*"

She insisted, but pronounced the thin liquid in the tall glass very disgusting when it was brought. Nick was amazed, reflecting that it was not for such a discussion as this that his mother had left him with such complacency; and indeed he too had, as she would have had, his share of perplexity, observing that nearly half an hour passed without his cousin's saying anything about Harsh.

Mrs. Dallow leaned back against the lighted glass of the café, comfortable and beguiled, watching the passers, the opposite shops, the movement of the square in front of them. She talked about London, about the news written to her in her absence, about Cannes and the people she had seen there, about her poor sister-in-law and her numerous progeny and two or three droll things that had happened at

Versailles. She discoursed considerably about herself, mentioning certain things she meant to do on her return to
town, her plans for the rest of the season. Her carriage came
and stood there, and Nick asked if he should send it away;
to which she said: "No, let it stand a bit." She let it stand a
long time, and then she told him to dismiss it: they would
walk home. She took his arm and they went along the boulevard, on the right hand side, to the Rue de la Paix, saying
little to each other during the transit; and then they passed
into the hotel and up to her rooms. All she had said on the
way was that she was very tired of Paris. There was a shaded
lamp in her *salon*, but the windows were open and the light
of the street, with its undisturbing murmur, as if everything
ran on india-rubber, came up through the interstices of the
balcony and made a vague glow and a flitting of shadows on
the ceiling. Her maid appeared, busying herself a moment;
and when she had gone out Julia said suddenly to her companion: "Should you mind telling me what's the matter with
you?"

"The matter with me?"

"Don't you want to stand?"

"I'll do anything to oblige you."

"Why should you oblige me?"

"Why, isn't that the way people treat you?" asked Nick.

"They treat me best when they are a little serious."

"My dear Julia, it seems to me I'm serious enough. Surely
it isn't an occasion to be so very solemn, the idea of going
down into a stodgy little country town and talking a lot of
rot."

"Why do you call it 'rot'?"

"Because I can think of no other name that, on the whole,
describes it so well. You know the sort of thing. Come! you've
listened to enough of it, first and last. One blushes for it when
one sees it in print, in the local papers. The local papers—ah,
the thought of them makes me want to stay in Paris."

"If you don't speak well it's your own fault: you know how
to, perfectly. And you usually do."

"I always do, and that's what I'm ashamed of. I've got the
cursed humbugging trick of it. I speak beautifully. I can turn
it on, a fine flood of it, at the shortest notice. The better it is

the worse it is, the kind is so inferior. It has nothing to do with the truth or the search for it; nothing to do with intelligence, or candour, or honour. It's an appeal to everything that for one's self one despises," the young man went on—"to stupidity, to ignorance, to density, to the love of names and phrases, the love of hollow, idiotic words, of shutting the eyes tight and making a noise. Do men who respect each other or themselves talk to each other that way? They know they would deserve kicking if they were to attempt it. A man would blush to say to himself in the darkness of the night the things he stands up on a platform in the garish light of day to stuff into the ears of a multitude whose intelligence he pretends that he esteems." Nick Dormer stood at one of the windows, with his hands in his pockets. He had been looking out, but as his words followed each other faster he turned toward Mrs. Dallow, who had dropped upon a sofa with her face to the window. She had given her jacket and gloves to her maid, but had kept on her bonnet; and she leaned forward a little as she sat, with her hands clasped together in her lap and her eyes upon her companion. The lamp, in a corner, was so thickly veiled that the room was in tempered obscurity, lighted almost equally from the street, from the brilliant shop-fronts opposite. "Therefore, why be sapient and solemn about it, like an editorial in a newspaper?" Nick added, with a smile.

She continued to look at him for a moment after he had spoken; then she said: "If you don't want to stand, you have only to say so. You needn't give your reasons."

"It's too kind of you to let me off that! And then I'm a tremendous fellow for reasons; that's my strong point, don't you know? I've a lot more besides those I've mentioned, done up and ready for delivery. The odd thing is that they don't always govern my behaviour. I rather think I do want to stand."

"Then what you said just now was a speech," Mrs. Dallow rejoined.

"A speech?"

"The 'rot,' the humbug of the hustings."

"No, those great truths remain, and a good many others. But an inner voice tells me I'm in for it. And it will be much more graceful to embrace this opportunity, accepting your co-operation, than to wait for some other and forfeit that advantage."

"I shall be very glad to help you anywhere," said Mrs. Dallow.

"Thanks, awfully," murmured the young man, still standing there with his hands in his pockets. "You would do it best in your own place, and I have no right to deny myself such a help."

Julia smiled at him for an instant. "I don't do it badly."

"Ah, you're so political!"

"Of course I am; it's the only decent thing to be. But I can only help you if you'll help yourself. I can do a good deal, but I can't do everything. If you'll work I'll work with you; but if you are going into it with your hands in your pockets I'll have nothing to do with you." Nick instantly changed the position of these members, and sank into a seat with his elbows on his knees. "You're very clever, but you must really take a little trouble. Things don't drop into people's mouths."

"I'll try—I'll try. I have a great incentive," Nick said.

"Of course you have."

"My mother, my poor mother." Mrs. Dallow made a slight exclamation, and he went on: "And of course, always, my father, dear man. My mother's even more political than you."

"I dare say she is, and quite right!" said Mrs. Dallow.

"And she can't tell me a bit more than you can what she thinks, what she believes, what she desires."

"Excuse me, I can tell you perfectly. There's one thing I always desire—to keep out a Tory."

"I see; that's a great philosophy."

"It will do very well. And I desire the good of the country. I'm not ashamed of that."

"And can you give me an idea of what it is—the good of the country?"

"I know perfectly what it isn't. It isn't what the Tories want to do."

"What do they want to do?"

"Oh, it would take me long to tell you. All sorts of trash."

"It would take you long, and it would take them longer! All they want to do is to prevent *us* from doing. On our side, we want to prevent them from preventing us. That's about as clearly as we all see it. So, on one side and the other, it's a beautiful, lucid, inspiring programme."

"I don't believe in you," Mrs. Dallow replied to this, leaning back on her sofa.

"I hope not, Julia, indeed!" He paused a moment, still with his face toward her and his elbows on his knees; then he pursued: "You are a very accomplished woman and a very zealous one; but you haven't an idea, you know—to call an idea. What you mainly want is to be at the head of a political salon; to start one, to keep it up, to make it a success."

"Much you know me!" Julia exclaimed; but he could see through the dimness that she had coloured a little.

"You'll have it, in time, but I won't come to it," Nick went on.

"You can't come less than you do."

"When I say you'll have it, I mean you've already got it. That's why I don't come."

"I don't think you know what you mean," said Mrs. Dallow. "I have an idea that's as good as any of yours, any of those you have treated me to this evening, it seems to me— the simple idea that one ought to do something or other for one's country."

" 'Something or other' certainly covers all the ground. There is one thing one can always do for one's country, which is not to be afraid."

"Afraid of what?"

Nick Dormer hesitated a moment, laughing; then he said: "I'll tell you another time. It's very well to talk so glibly of standing," he added; "but it isn't absolutely foreign to the question that I haven't got the cash."

"What did you do before?" asked Mrs. Dallow.

"The first time, my father paid."

"And the other time?"

"Oh, Mr. Carteret."

"Your expenses won't be at all large; on the contrary," said Julia.

"They sha'n't be; I shall look out sharp for that. I shall have the great Hutchby."

"Of course; but, you know, I want you to do it well." She paused an instant, and then: "Of course you can send the bill to me."

"Thanks, awfully; you're tremendously kind. I shouldn't think of that." Nick Dormer got up as he said these words, and walked to the window again, his companion's eyes resting upon him as he stood for a moment with his back to her. "I shall manage it somehow," he went on.

"Mr. Carteret will be delighted," said Julia.

"I dare say, but I hate taking people's money."

"That's nonsense, when it's for the country. Isn't it for *them*?"

"When they get it back!" Nick replied, turning round and looking for his hat. "It's startlingly late; you must be tired." Mrs. Dallow made no response to this, and he pursued his quest, successful only when he reached a duskier corner of the room, to which the hat had been relegated by his cousin's maid. "Mr. Carteret will expect so much, if he pays. And so would you."

"Yes, I'm bound to say I should!" And Mrs. Dallow emphasized this assertion by the way she rose erect. "If you're only going in to lose, you had better stay out."

"How can I lose, with you?" the young man asked, smiling. She uttered a word, impatiently but indistinguishably, and he continued: "And even if I do, it will have been immense fun."

"It *is* immense fun," said Julia. "But the best fun is to win. If you don't—"

"If I don't?" he repeated, as she hesitated.

"I'll never speak to you again."

"How much you expect, even when you don't pay!"

Mrs. Dallow's rejoinder was a justification of this remark, embodying as it did the fact that if they should receive on the morrow certain information on which she believed herself entitled to count, information tending to show that the Tories meant to fight the seat hard, not to lose it again, she should look to him to be in the field as early as herself. Sunday was a lost day; she should leave Paris on Monday.

"Oh, they'll fight it hard; they'll put up Kingsbury," said Nick, smoothing his hat. "They'll all come down—all that can get away. And Kingsbury has a very handsome wife."

"She is not so handsome as your cousin," Mrs. Dallow hazarded.

"Oh dear, no—a cousin sooner than a wife, any day!" Nick laughed as soon as he had said this, as if the speech had an awkward side; but the reparation, perhaps, scarcely mended it, the exaggerated mock-meekness with which he added: "I'll do any blessed thing you tell me."

"Come here to-morrow, then, as early as ten." She turned round, moving to the door with him; but before they reached it she demanded, abruptly: "Pray, isn't a gentleman to do anything, to be anything?"

"To be anything?"

"If he doesn't aspire to serve the State."

"To make his political fortune, do you mean? Oh, bless me, yes, there are other things."

"What other things, that can compare with that?"

"Well, I, for instance, I'm very fond of the arts."

"Of the arts?"

"Did you never hear of them? I'm awfully fond of painting."

At this Mrs. Dallow stopped short, and her fine gray eyes had for a moment the air of being set further forward in her head. "Don't be odious! Good-night," she said, turning away and leaving him to go.

VII.

PETER SHERRINGHAM, the next day, reminded Nick that
he had promised to be present with him at Madame
Carré's interview with the ladies introduced to her by Gabriel
Nash; and in the afternoon, in accordance with this arrangement, the two men took their way to the Rue de Constantinople. They found Mr. Nash and his friends in the small
beflounced drawing-room of the old actress, who, as they
learned, had sent in a request for ten minutes' grace, having
been detained at a lesson—a rehearsal of a *comédie de salon*,
to be given, for a charity, by a fine lady, at which she had
consented to be present as an adviser. Mrs. Rooth sat on a
black satin sofa, with her daughter beside her, and Gabriel
Nash wandered about the room, looking at the votive offer-
ings which converted the little panelled box, decorated in sallow white and gold, into a theatrical museum: the presents,
the portraits, the wreaths, the diadems, the letters, framed and
glazed, the trophies and tributes and relics collected by Madame Carré during half a century of renown. The profusion
of this testimony was hardly more striking than the confession
of something missed, something hushed, which seemed to
rise from it all and make it melancholy, like a reference to
clappings which, in the nature of things, could now only be
present as a silence: so that if the place was full of history, it
was the form without the fact, or at the most a redundancy of
the one to a pinch of the other—the history of a mask, of a
squeak, a record of movements in the air.

Some of the objects exhibited by the distinguished artist,
her early portraits, in lithograph or miniature, represented the
costume and embodied the manner of a period so remote that
Nick Dormer, as he glanced at them, felt a quickened curiosity to look at the woman who reconciled being alive to-day
with having been alive so long ago. Peter Sherringham already knew how she managed this miracle, but every visit he
paid to her added to his amused, charmed sense that it *was* a
miracle, that his extraordinary old friend had seen things that
he should never, never see. Those were just the things he
wanted to see most, and her duration, her survival, cheated

him agreeably and helped him a little to guess them. His appreciation of the actor's art was so systematic that it had an antiquarian side, and at the risk of representing him as attached to a futility, it must be said that he had as yet hardly known a keener regret for anything than for the loss of that antecedent world, and in particular for his having come too late for the great *comédienne*, the light of the French stage in the early years of the century, of whose example and instruction Madame Carré had had the inestimable benefit. She had often described to him her rare predecessor, straight from whose hands she had received her most celebrated parts, and of whom her own manner was often a religious imitation; but her descriptions troubled him more than they consoled, only confirming his theory, to which so much of his observation had already ministered, that the actor's art, in general, is going down and down, descending a slope with abysses of vulgarity at its foot, after having reached its perfection, more than fifty years ago, in the talent of the lady in question. He would have liked to dwell for an hour beneath the meridian.

Gabriel Nash introduced the new-comers to his companions; but the younger of the two ladies gave no sign of lending herself to this transaction. The girl was very white; she huddled there, silent and rigid, frightened to death, staring, expressionless. If Bridget Dormer had seen her at this moment she might have felt avenged for the discomfiture she had suffered the day before, at the Salon, under the challenging eyes of Maud Vavasour. It was plain at the present hour, that Miss Vavasour would have run away had she not felt that the persons present would prevent her escape. Her aspect made Nick Dormer feel as if the little temple of art in which they were collected had been the waiting-room of a dentist. Sherringham had seen a great many nervous girls trembling before the same ordeal, and he liked to be kind to them, to say things that would help them to do themselves justice. The probability, in a given case, was almost overwhelmingly in favour of their having any other talent one could think of in a higher degree than the dramatic; but he could rarely forbear to interpose, even as against his conscience, to keep the occasion from being too cruel. There were occasions indeed that could scarcely be too cruel to punish properly certain

examples of presumptuous ineptitude. He remembered what
Mr. Nash had said about this blighted maiden, and perceived
that though she might be inept she was now anything but
presumptuous. Gabriel fell to talking with Nick Dormer, and
Peter addressed himself to Mrs. Rooth. There was no use as
yet in saying anything to the girl; she was too scared even to
hear. Mrs. Rooth, with her shawl fluttering about her, nestled
against her daughter, putting out her hand to take one of
Miriam's, soothingly. She had pretty, silly, near-sighted eyes,
a long, thin nose and an upper lip which projected over the
under as an ornamental cornice rests on its support. "So much
depends—really everything!" she said in answer to some sociable observation of Sherringham's. "It's either this," and
she rolled her eyes expressively about the room, "or it's—I
don't know too much what!"

"Perhaps we're too many," Peter hazarded, to her daughter.
"But really, you'll find, after you fairly begin, that you'll do
better with four or five."

Before she answered she turned her head and lifted her fine
eyes. The next instant he saw they were full of tears. The
word she spoke, however, though uttered in a deep, serious
tone, had not the note of sensibility: "Oh, I don't care for
you!" He laughed at this, declared it was very well said and
that if she could give Madame Carré such a specimen as
that—! The actress came in before he had finished his phrase,
and he observed the way the girl slowly got up to meet her,
hanging her head a little and looking at her from under her
brows. There was no sentiment in her face—only a kind of
vacancy of terror which had not even the merit of being fine
of its kind, for it seemed stupid and superstitious. Yet the
head was good, he perceived at the same moment; it was
strong and salient and made to tell at a distance. Madame
Carré scarcely noticed her at first, greeting her only in her
order, with the others, and pointing to seats, composing the
circle with smiles and gestures, as if they were all before the
prompter's box. The old actress presented herself to a casual
glance as a red-faced woman in a wig, with beady eyes, a
hooked nose and pretty hands; but Nick Dormer, who had a
perception of physiognomy, speedily observed that these free
characteristics included a great deal of delicate detail—an

eyebrow, a nostril, a flitting of expressions, as if a multitude of little facial wires were pulled from within. This accomplished artist had in particular a mouth which was visibly a rare instrument, a pair of lips whose curves and fine corners spoke of a lifetime of "points" unerringly made and verses exquisitely spoken, helping to explain the purity of the sound that issued from them. Her whole countenance had the look of long service—of a thing infinitely worn and used, drawn and stretched to excess, with its elasticity overdone and its springs relaxed, yet religiously preserved and kept in repair, like an old valuable time-piece, which might have quivered and rumbled, but could be trusted to strike the hour. At the first words she spoke Gabriel Nash exclaimed, endearingly: *"Ah, la voix de Célimène!"* Célimène, who wore a big red flower on the summit of her dense wig, had a very grand air, a toss of the head and sundry little majesties of manner; in addition to which she was strange, almost grotesque, and to some people would have been even terrifying, capable of re-appearing, with her hard eyes, as a queer vision in the darkness. She excused herself for having made the company wait, and mouthed and mimicked in the drollest way, with intonations as fine as a flute, the performance and the pretensions of the *belles dames* to whom she had just been endeavouring to communicate a few of the rudiments. *"Mais celles-là, c'est une plaisanterie,"* she went on, to Mrs. Rooth; "whereas you and your daughter, *chère madame*—I am sure that you are quite another matter."

The girl had got rid of her tears and was gazing at her, and Mrs. Rooth leaned forward and said insinuatingly: "She knows four languages."

Madame Carré gave one of her histrionic stares, throwing back her head. "That's three too many. The thing is to do something with one of them."

"We're very much in earnest," continued Mrs. Rooth, who spoke excellent French.

"I'm glad to hear it—*il n'y a que ça. La tête est bien*—the head is very good," she said, looking at the girl. "But let us see, my dear child, what you've got in it!" The young lady was still powerless to speak; she opened her lips, but nothing came. With the failure of this effort she turned her deep, sombre eyes upon the three men. "*Un beau regard*—it carries well," Madame Carré hinted. But even as she spoke Miss Rooth's fine gaze was suffused again, and the next moment she had begun to weep. Nick Dormer sprung up; he felt embarrassed and intrusive—there was such an indelicacy in sitting there to watch a poor girl's struggle with timidity. There was a momentary confusion; Mrs. Rooth's tears were seen also to flow; Gabriel Nash began to laugh, addressing however at the same time the friendliest, most familiar encouragement to his companions, and Peter Sherringham offered to retire with Nick on the spot, if their presence was oppressive to the young lady. But the agitation was over in a minute; Madame Carré motioned Mrs. Rooth out of her seat and took her place beside the girl, and Gabriel Nash explained judiciously to the other men that she would be worse if they were to go away. Her mother begged them to remain, "so that there should be at least some English;" she spoke as if the old actress were an army of Frenchwomen. The girl was quickly better, and Madame Carré, on the sofa beside her, held her hand and emitted a perfect music of reassurance. "The nerves, the nerves—they are half of our trade. Have as many as you like, if you've got something else too. *Voyons*—do you know anything?"

"I know some pieces."

"Some pieces of the *répertoire*?"

Miriam Rooth stared as if she didn't understand. "I know some poetry."

"English, French, Italian, German," said her mother.

Madame Carré gave Mrs. Rooth a look which expressed irritation at the recurrence of this announcement. "Does she wish to act in all those tongues? The phrase-book isn't the comedy."

"It is only to show you how she has been educated."

"Ah, chère madame, there is no education that matters! I mean save the right one. Your daughter must have a language, like me, like *ces messieurs*."

"You see if I can speak French," said the girl, smiling dimly at her hostess. She appeared now almost to have collected herself.

"You speak it in perfection."

"And English just as well," said Miss Rooth.

"You oughtn't to be an actress; you ought to be a governess."

"Oh, don't tell us that: it's to escape from that!" pleaded Mrs. Rooth.

"I'm very sure your daughter will escape from that," Peter Sherringham was moved to remark.

"Oh, if *you* could help her!" the lady exclaimed, pathetically.

"She has certainly all the qualities that strike the eye," said Peter.

"You are *most* kind, sir!" Mrs. Rooth declared, elegantly draping herself.

"She knows Célimène; I have heard her do Célimène," Gabriel Nash said to Madame Carré.

"And she knows Juliet, and Lady Macbeth, and Cleopatra," added Mrs. Rooth.

"*Voyons*, my dear child, do you wish to work for the French stage or for the English?" the old actress demanded.

"Ours would have sore need of you, Miss Rooth," Sherringham gallantly interposed.

"Could you speak to any one in London—could you introduce her?" her mother eagerly asked.

"Dear madam, I must hear her first, and hear what Madame Carré says."

"She has a voice of rare beauty, and I understand voices," said Mrs. Rooth.

"Ah, then, if she has intelligence she has every gift."

"She has a most poetic mind," the old lady went on.

"I should like to paint her portrait; she's made for that," Nick Dormer ventured to observe to Mrs. Rooth; partly because he was struck with the girl's capacity as a model, partly to mitigate the crudity of inexpressive spectatorship.

"So all the artists say. I have had three or four heads of her, if you would like to see them: she has been done in several styles. If you were to do her I am sure it would make her celebrated."

"And me too," said Nick, laughing.

"It would indeed, a member of Parliament!" Nash declared.

"Ah, I have the honour—?" murmured Mrs. Rooth, looking gratified and mystified.

Nick explained that she had no honour at all, and meanwhile Madame Carré had been questioning the girl. "Chère madame, I can do nothing with your daughter: she knows too much!" she broke out. "It's a pity, because I like to catch them wild."

"Oh, she's wild enough, if that's all! And that's the very point, the question of where to try," Mrs. Rooth went on. "Into what do I launch her—upon what dangerous, stormy sea? I've thought of it so anxiously."

"Try here—try the French public: they're so much the most serious," said Gabriel Nash.

"Ah, no, try the English: there's such a rare opening!" Sherringham exclaimed, in quick opposition.

"Ah, it isn't the public, dear gentlemen. It's the private side, the other people—it's the life—it's the moral atmosphere."

"*Je ne connais qu'une scène—la nôtre,*" Madame Carré asserted. "I have been informed there is no other."

"And very correctly," said Gabriel Nash. "The theatre in our countries is puerile and barbarous."

"There is something to be done for it, and perhaps mademoiselle is the person to do it," Sherringham suggested, contentiously.

"Ah, but, *en attendant*, what can it do for her?" Madame Carré asked.

"Well, anything that I can help it to do," said Peter Sherringham, who was more and more struck with the girl's rich type. Miriam Rooth sat in silence, while this discussion went on, looking from one speaker to the other with a suspended, literal air.

"Ah, if your part is marked out, I congratulate you, mademoiselle!" said the old actress, underlining the words as she had often underlined such words on the stage. She smiled with large permissiveness on the young aspirant, who appeared not to understand her. Her tone penetrated, however, to certain depths in the mother's nature, adding another stir to agitated waters.

"I feel the responsibility of what she shall find in the life, the standards, of the theatre," Mrs. Rooth explained. "Where is the purest tone—where are the highest standards? that's what I ask," the good lady continued, with a persistent candour which elicited a peal of unceremonious but sociable laughter from Gabriel Nash.

"The purest tone—*qu'est-ce-que-c'est que ça?*" Madame Carré demanded, in the finest manner of modern comedy.

"We are very, *very* respectable," Mrs. Rooth went on, smiling and achieving lightness, too. "What I want to do is to place my daughter where the conduct—and the picture of conduct, in which she should take part—wouldn't be absolutely dreadful. Now, chère madame, how about all that? how about the conduct in the French theatre—the things she should see, the things she should hear?"

"I don't think I know what you are talking about. They are the things she may see and hear everywhere; only they are better done, they are better said. The only conduct that concerns an actress, it seems to me, is her own, and the only way for her to behave herself is not to be a stick. I know no other conduct."

"But there are characters, there are situations, which I don't think I should like to see *her* undertake."

"There are many, no doubt, which she would do well to leave alone!" laughed the Frenchwoman.

"I shouldn't like to see her represent a very bad woman—a *really* bad one," Mrs. Rooth serenely pursued.

"Ah, in England, then, and in your theatre, every one is good? Your plays must be even more ingenious than I supposed."

"We haven't any plays," said Gabriel Nash.

"People will write them for Miss Rooth—it will be a new era," Peter Sherringham rejoined, with wanton, or at any rate combative, optimism.

"Will *you*, sir—will you do something? A sketch of some truly noble female type?" the old lady asked, engagingly.

"Oh, I know what you do with our pieces—to show your

superior virtue!" Madame Carré broke in, before he had time
to reply that he wrote nothing but diplomatic memoranda.
"Bad women? *Je n'ai joué que ça, madame.* 'Really' bad? I
tried to make them real!"

"I can say 'L'Aventurière,'" Miriam interrupted, in a cold
voice which seemed to hint at a want of participation in the
maternal solicitudes.

"Confer on us the pleasure of hearing you, then. Madame
Carré will give you the *réplique*," said Peter Sherringham.

"Certainly, my child; I can say it without the book," Madame Carré responded. "Put yourself there—move that chair
a little away." She patted her young visitor, encouraging her
to rise, settling with her the scene they should take, while the
three men sprang up to arrange a place for the performance.
Miriam left her seat and looked vaguely round her; then, having taken off her hat and given it to her mother, she stood on
the designated spot with her eyes on the ground. Abruptly,
however, instead of beginning the scene, Madame Carré
turned to the elder lady with an air which showed that a rejoinder to this visitor's remarks of a moment before had been
gathering force in her breast.

"You mix things up, chère madame, and I have it on my
heart to tell you so. I believe it's rather the case with you
other English, and I have never been able to learn that either
your morality or your talent is the gainer by it. To be too
respectable to go where things are done best is, in my opinion, to be very vicious indeed; and to do them badly in order
to preserve your virtue is to fall into a grossness more shocking than any other. To do them well is virtue enough, and not
to make a mess of it the only respectability. That's hard
enough to merit Paradise. Everything else is base humbug!
Voilà, chère madame, the answer I have for your scruples!"

"It's admirable—admirable; and I am glad my friend Dormer here has had the great advantage of hearing you utter it!"
Gabriel Nash exclaimed, looking at Nick.

Nick thought it, in effect, a speech denoting an intelligence
of the question, but he rather resented the idea that Nash
should assume that it would strike him as a revelation; and to
show his familiarity with the line of thought it indicated, as
well as to play his part appreciatively in the little circle, he

observed to Mrs. Rooth, as if they might take many things for granted: "In other words, your daughter must find her safeguard in the artistic conscience." But he had no sooner spoken than he was struck with the oddity of their discussing so publicly, and under the poor girl's nose, the conditions which Miss Rooth might find the best for the preservation of her personal integrity. However, the anomaly was light and unoppressive—the echoes of a public discussion of delicate questions seemed to linger so familiarly in the egotistical little room. Moreover the heroine of the occasion evidently was losing her embarrassment; she was the priestess on the tripod, awaiting the afflatus and thinking only of that. Her bared head, of which she had changed the position, holding it erect, while her arms hung at her sides, was admirable; and her eyes gazed straight out of the window, at the houses on the opposite side of the Rue de Constantinople.

Mrs. Rooth had listened to Madame Carré with startled, respectful attention, but Nick, considering her, was very sure that she had not understood her hostess's little lesson. Yet this did not prevent her from exclaiming in answer to him: "Oh, a fine artistic life—what indeed is more beautiful?"

Peter Sherringham had said nothing; he was watching Miriam and her attitude. She wore a black dress, which fell in straight folds; her face, under her mobile brows, was pale and regular, with a strange, strong, tragic beauty. "I don't know what's in her," he said to himself; "nothing, it would seem, from her persistent vacancy. But such a face as that, such a head, is a fortune!" Madame Carré made her commence, giving her the first line of the speech of Clorinde: *"Vous ne me fuyez pas, mon enfant, aujourd'hui."* But still the girl hesitated, and for an instant she appeared to make a vain, convulsive effort. In this effort she frowned portentously; her low forehead overhung her eyes; the eyes themselves, in shadow, stared, splendid and cold, and her hands clinched themselves at her sides. She looked austere and terrible, and during this moment she was an incarnation the vividness of which drew from Sherringham a stifled cry. *"Elle est bien belle—ah, ça!"* murmured the old actress; and in the pause which still preceded the issue of sound from the girl's lips Peter turned to his kinsman and said in a low tone:

"You must paint her just like that."

"Like that?"

"As the Tragic Muse."

She began to speak; a long, strong, colourless voice came quavering from her young throat. She delivered the lines of Clorinde, in the fine interview with Célie, in the third act of the play, with a rude monotony, and then, gaining confidence, with an effort at modulation which was not altogether successful and which evidently she felt not to be so. Madame Carré sent back the ball without raising her hand, repeating the speeches of Célie, which her memory possessed from their having so often been addressed to her, and uttering the verses with soft, communicative art. So they went on through the scene, and when it was over it had not precisely been a triumph for Miriam Rooth. Sherringham forbore to look at Gabriel Nash, and Madame Carré said: "I think you have a voice, *ma fille*, somewhere or other. We must try and put our hand on it." Then she asked her what instruction she had had, and the girl, lifting her eyebrows, looked at her mother, while her mother prompted her.

"Mrs. Delamere, in London; she was once an ornament of the English stage. She gives lessons just to a very few; it's a great favour. Such a very nice person! But above all, Signor Ruggieri—I think he taught us most." Mrs. Rooth explained that this gentleman was an Italian tragedian, in Rome, who instructed Miriam in the proper manner of pronouncing his language, and also in the art of declaiming and gesticulating.

"Gesticulating, I'll warrant," said their hostess. "They mimic as if for the deaf, they emphasize as if for the blind. Mrs. Delamere is doubtless an epitome of all the virtues, but I never heard of her. You travel too much," Madame Carré went on; "that's very amusing, but the way to study is to stay at home, to shut yourself up and hammer at your scales." Mrs. Rooth complained that they had no home to stay at; in rejoinder to which the old actress exclaimed: "Oh, you English, you are *d'une légèreté à faire rougir*. If you haven't a home you must make one. In our profession it's the first requisite."

"But where? That's what I ask!" said Mrs. Rooth.

"Why not here?" Sherringham inquired.

"Oh, here!" And the good lady shook her head, with a world of suggestions.

"Come and live in London, and then I shall be able to paint your daughter," Nick Dormer interposed.

"Is that all that it will take, my dear fellow?" asked Gabriel Nash.

"Ah, London is full of memories," Mrs. Rooth went on. "My father had a great house there—we always came up. But all that's over."

"Study here, and go to London to appear," said Peter Sherringham, feeling frivolous even as he spoke.

"To appear in French?"

"No, in the language of Shakespeare."

"But we can't study that here."

"Monsieur Sherringham means that he will give you lessons," Madame Carré explained. "Let me not fail to say it—he's an excellent critic."

"How do you know that—you who are perfect?" asked Sherringham: an inquiry to which the answer was forestalled by the girl's rousing herself to make it public that she could recite the "Nights" of Alfred de Musset.

"Diable!" said the actress, "that's more than I can! But by all means give us a specimen."

The girl again placed herself in position and rolled out a fragment of one of the splendid conversations of Musset's poet with his muse—rolled it loudly and proudly, tossed it and tumbled it about the room. Madame Carré watched her at first, but after a few moments she shut her eyes, though the best part of the business was to look. Sherringham had supposed Miriam was abashed by the flatness of her first performance, but now he perceived that she could not have been conscious of this; she was rather exhilarated and emboldened. She made a muddle of the divine verses, which, in spite of certain sonorities and cadences, an evident effort to imitate a celebrated actress, a comrade of Madame Carré, whom she had heard declaim them, she produced as if she had but a dim idea of their meaning. When she had finished Madame Carré passed no judgment; she only said, "Perhaps you had better say something English." She suggested some little piece of verse—some fable, if there were fables in English. She

appeared but scantily surprised to hear that there were not—
it was a language of which one expected so little. Mrs. Rooth
said, "She knows her Tennyson by heart. I think he's more
profound than La Fontaine;" and after some deliberation and
delay Miriam broke into "The Lotos-Eaters," from which she
passed directly, almost breathlessly, to "Edward Gray." Sherringham had by this time heard her make four different
attempts, and the only generalization which could be very
present to him was that she uttered these dissimilar compositions in exactly the same tone—a solemn, droning, dragging
measure, adopted with an intention of pathos, a crude idea of
"style." It was funereal, and at the same time it was rough and
childish. Sherringham thought her English performance less
futile than her French, but he could see that Madame Carré
listened to it with even less pleasure. In the way the girl
wailed forth some of her Tennysonian lines he detected a possibility of a thrill. But the further she went, the more violently
she acted on the nerves of Mr. Gabriel Nash: that also he
could discover, from the way this gentleman ended by slipping discreetly to the window and leaning there, with his
head out and his back to the exhibition. He had the art of
mute expression; his attitude said, as clearly as possible: "No,
no, you can't call me either ill-mannered or ill-natured. I'm
the showman of the occasion, moreover, and I avert myself,
leaving you to judge. If there's a thing in life I hate, it's this
idiotic new fashion of the drawing-room recitation, and the
insufferable creatures who practise it, who prevent conversation and whom, as they are beneath it, you can't punish by
criticism. Therefore what I am is only too magnanimous—
bringing these benighted women here, paying with my person, stifling my just repugnance."

At the same time that Sherringham pronounced privately
that the manner in which Miss Rooth had acquitted herself
offered no element of interest, he remained conscious that
something surmounted and survived her failure, something
that would perhaps be worth taking hold of. It was the element of outline and attitude, the way she stood, the way she
turned her eyes, her head, and moved her limbs. These things
held the attention; they had a natural felicity and, in spite of
their suggesting too much the school-girl in the *tableau-*

vivant, a sort of grandeur. Her face, moreover, grew as he watched it; something delicate dawned in it, a dim promise of variety and a touching plea for patience, as if it were conscious of being able to show in time more expressions than the simple and striking gloom which, as yet, had mainly graced it. In short the plastic quality of her person was the only definite sign of a vocation. He almost hated to have to recognize this; he had seen that quality so often when it meant nothing at all that he had come at last to regard it as almost a guarantee of incompetence. He knew Madame Carré valued it, by itself, so little that she counted it out in measuring an histrionic nature; when it was not accompanied with other properties which helped and completed it she was near considering it as a positive hindrance to success—success of the only kind that she esteemed. Far oftener than he, she had sat in judgment on young women for whom hair and eyebrows and a disposition for the statuesque would have worked the miracle of attenuating their stupidity if the miracle were workable. But that particular miracle never was. The qualities she deemed most interesting were not the gifts, but the conquests—the effects the actor had worked hard for, had wrested by unwearying study. Sherringham remembered to have had, in the early part of their acquaintance, a friendly dispute with her on this subject; he having been moved at that time to defend the cause of the gifts. She had gone so far as to say that a serious comedian ought to be ashamed of them—ashamed of resting his case on them; and when Sherringham had cited Mademoiselle Rachel as a great artist whose natural endowment was rich and who had owed her highest triumphs to it, she had declared that Rachel was the very instance that proved her point—a talent embodying one or two primary aids, a voice and an eye, but essentially formed by work, unremitting and ferocious work. "I don't care a straw for your handsome girls," she said; "but bring me the one who is ready to drudge the tenth part of the way Rachel drudged, and I'll forgive her her beauty. Of course, *notez bien*, Rachel wasn't a *bête*: that's a gift, if you like!"

Mrs. Rooth, who was evidently very proud of the figure her daughter had made, appealed to Madame Carré, rashly

and serenely, for a verdict; but fortunately this lady's voluble
bonne came rattling in at the same moment with the tea-tray.
The old actress busied herself in dispensing this refreshment,
an hospitable attention to her English visitors, and under
cover of the diversion thus obtained, while the others talked
together, Sherringham said to his hostess: "Well, is there anything in her?"

"Nothing that I can see. She's loud and coarse."

"She's very much afraid; you must allow for that."

"Afraid of me, immensely, but not a bit afraid of her
authors—nor of you!" added Madame Carré, smiling.

"Aren't you prejudiced by what Mr. Nash has told you?"

"Why prejudiced? He only told me she was very handsome."

"And don't you think she is?"

"Admirable. But I'm not a photographer nor a dressmaker.
I can't do anything with that."

"The head is very noble," said Peter Sherringham. "And the
voice, when she spoke English, had some sweet tones."

"Ah, your English—possibly! All I can say is that I listened
to her conscientiously, and I didn't perceive in what she did a
single *nuance*, a single inflection or intention. But not one,
mon cher. I don't think she's intelligent."

"But don't they often seem stupid at first?"

"Say always!"

"Then don't some succeed—even when they are handsome?"

"When they are handsome they always succeed—in one
way or another."

"You don't understand us English," said Peter Sherringham.

Madame Carré drank her tea; then she replied: "Marry
her, my son, and give her diamonds. Make her an ambassadress; she will look very well."

"She interests you so little that you don't care to do anything for her?"

"To do anything?"

"To give her a few lessons."

The old actress looked at him a moment: after which, rising from her place near the table on which the tea had been

served, she said to Miriam Rooth: "My dear child, I give my voice for the *scène anglaise*. You did the English things best."

"Did I do them well?" asked the girl.

"You have a great deal to learn; but you have force. The principal things *sont encore à dégager*, but they will come. You must work."

"I think she has ideas," said Mrs. Rooth.

"She gets them from you," Madame Carré replied.

"I must say, if it's to be *our* theatre I'm relieved. I think it's safer," the good lady continued.

"Ours is dangerous, no doubt."

"You mean you are more severe," said the girl.

"Your mother is right," the actress smiled; "you have ideas."

"But what shall we do then—how shall we proceed?" Mrs. Rooth inquired.

She made this appeal, plaintively and vaguely, to the three gentlemen; but they had collected a few steps off and were talking together, so that it failed to reach them.

"Work—work—work!" exclaimed the actress.

"In English I can play Shakespeare. I want to play Shakespeare," Miriam remarked.

"That's fortunate, as in English you haven't any one else to play."

"But he's so great—and he's so pure!" said Mrs. Rooth.

"That also seems very fortunate for you," Madame Carré phrased.

"You think me actually pretty bad, don't you?" the girl demanded, with her serious face.

"*Mon Dieu, que vous dirai-je?* Of course you're rough; but so was I, at your age. And if you find your voice it may carry you far. Besides, what does it matter what I think? How can I judge for your English public?"

"How shall I find my voice?" asked Miriam Rooth.

"By trying. Il n'y a que ça. Work like a horse, night and day. Besides, M. Sherringham, as he says, will help you."

Sherringham, hearing his name, turned round, and the girl appealed to him. "Will you help me, really?"

"To find her voice," Madame Carré interposed.

"The voice, when it's worth anything, comes from the heart; so I suppose that's where to look for it," Gabriel Nash suggested.

"Much you know; you haven't got any!" Miriam retorted, with the first scintillation of gaiety she had shown on this occasion.

"Any voice, my child?" Mr. Nash inquired.

"Any heart—or any manners!"

Peter Sherringham made the secret reflection that he liked her better when she was lugubrious; for the note of pertness was not totally absent from her mode of emitting these few words. He was irritated, moreover, for in the brief conference he had just had with the young lady's introducer he had had to face the necessity of saying something optimistic about her, which was not particularly easy. Mr. Nash had said with his bland smile, "And what impression does my young friend make?" to which it appeared to Sherringham that uncomfortable consistency compelled him to reply that there was evidently a good deal in her. He was far from being sure of that. At the same time the young lady, both with the exaggerated "points" of her person and the poverty of her instinct of expression, constituted a kind of challenge—presented herself to him as a subject for inquiry, a problem, a piece of work, an explorable country. She was too bad to jump at, and yet she was too individual to overlook, especially when she rested her tragic eyes on him with the appeal of her deep "Really?" This appeal sounded as if it were in a certain way to his honour, giving him a chance to brave verisimilitude, to brave ridicule even, a little, in order to show, in a special case, what he had always maintained in general, that the direction of a young person's studies for the stage may be an interest of as high an order as any other artistic consideration.

"Mr. Nash has rendered us the great service of introducing us to Madame Carré, and I'm sure we're immensely indebted to him," Mrs. Rooth said to her daughter, with an air affectionately corrective.

"But what good does that do us?" the girl asked, smiling at the actress and gently laying her finger-tips upon her hand. "Madame Carré listens to me with adorable patience and then sends me about my business—in the prettiest way in the world."

"Mademoiselle, you are not so rough; the tone of that is very *juste*. A la bonne heure; work—work!" the actress exclaimed. "There was an inflection there, or very nearly. Practise it till you've got it."

"Come and practise it to me, if your mother will be so kind as to bring you," said Peter Sherringham.

"Do you give lessons—do you understand?" Miriam asked.

"I'm an old playgoer, and I have unbounded belief in my own judgment."

" 'Old,' sir, is too much to say," Mrs. Rooth remonstrated. "My daughter knows your high position, but she is very direct. You will always find her so. Perhaps you'll say there are less honourable faults. We'll come to see you with pleasure. Oh, I've been at the Embassy, when I was her age. Therefore why shouldn't she go to-day? That was in Lord Davenant's time."

"A few people are coming to tea with me to-morrow. Perhaps you will come then, at five o'clock."

"It will remind me of the dear old times," said Mrs. Rooth.

"Thank you; I'll try and do better to-morrow," Miriam remarked, very sweetly.

"You do better every minute!" Sherringham exclaimed, looking at Madame Carré in emphasis of this declaration.

"She is finding her voice," the actress responded.

"She is finding a friend!" cried Mrs. Rooth.

"And don't forget, when you come to London, my hope that you'll come and see *me*," Nick Dormer said to the girl. "To try and paint you—that would do me good!"

"She is finding even two," said Madame Carré.

"It's to make up for one I've lost!" And Miriam looked with very good stage-scorn at Gabriel Nash. "It's he that thinks I'm bad."

"You say that to make me drive you home; you know it will," Nash returned.

"We'll all take you home; why not?" Sherringham asked.

Madame Carré looked at the handsome girl, handsomer than ever at this moment, and at the three young men who had taken their hats and stood ready to accompany her. A deeper expression came for an instant into her hard, bright eyes, while she sighed: "*Ah, la jeunesse!* you'd always have that, my child, if you were the greatest goose on earth!"

VIII.

At Peter Sherringham's, the next day, Miriam Rooth had so evidently come with the expectation of "saying" something that it was impossible such a patron of the drama should forbear to invite her, little as the exhibition at Madame Carré's could have contributed to render the invitation prompt. His curiosity had been more appeased than stimulated, but he felt none the less that he had "taken up" the dark-browed girl and her reminiscential mother and must face the immediate consequences of the act. This responsibility weighed upon him during the twenty-four hours that followed the ultimate dispersal of the little party at the door of the Hôtel de la Garonne.

On quitting Madame Carré's the two ladies had gracefully declined Mr. Nash's offered cab and had taken their way homeward on foot, with the gentlemen in attendance. The streets of Paris at that hour were bright and episodical, and Sherringham trod them good-humouredly enough, and not too fast, leaning a little to talk to the young lady as he went. Their pace was regulated by her mother's, who walked in advance, on the arm of Gabriel Nash (Nick Dormer was on her other side), in refined deprecation. Her sloping back was before them, exempt from retentive stiffness in spite of her rigid principles, with the little drama of her lost and recovered shawl perpetually going on.

Sherringham said nothing to the girl about her performance or her powers; their talk was only of her manner of life with her mother—their travels, their *pensions*, their economies, their want of a home, the many cities she knew well, the foreign tongues and the wide view of the world she had acquired. He guessed easily enough the dolorous type of exile of the two ladies, wanderers in search of Continental cheapness, inured to queer contacts and compromises, "remarkably well connected" in England, but going out for their meals. The girl was but indirectly communicative, not, apparently, from any intention of concealment, but from the habit of associating with people whom she didn't honour with her confidence. She was fragmentary and abrupt, as well as not in the

least shy, subdued to dread of Madame Carré as she had
been for the time. She gave Sherringham a reason for this
fear, and he thought her reason innocently pretentious. "She
admired a great artist more than anything in the world; and
in the presence of art, of *great* art, her heart beat so fast." Her
manners were not perfect, and the friction of a varied experience had rather roughened than smoothed her. She said nothing that showed that she was clever, though he guessed that
this was the intention of two or three of her remarks; but he
parted from her with the suspicion that she was, according to
the contemporary French phrase, a "nature."

The Hôtel de la Garonne was in a small, unrenovated
street, in which the cobble-stones of old Paris still flourished,
lying between the Avenue de l'Opéra and the Place de la
Bourse. Sherringham had occasionally passed through this
dim by-way, but he had never noticed the tall, stale *maison
meublée*, whose aspect, that of a third-rate provincial inn, was
an illustration of Mrs. Rooth's shrunken standard.

"We would ask you to come up, but it's quite at the top
and we haven't a sitting-room," the poor lady bravely explained. "We had to receive Mr. Nash at a café."

Nick Dormer declared that he liked cafés, and Miriam,
looking at his cousin, dropped with a flash of passion the
demand: "Do you wonder that I should want to do something, so that we can stop living like pigs?"

Sherringham recognized eventually, the next day, that
though it might be rather painful to listen to her it was better
to make her recite than to let her do nothing, so effectually
did the presence of his sister and that of Lady Agnes, and
even of Grace and Biddy, appear, by a sort of tacit opposition, to deprive hers, ornamental as it was, of a reason. He
had only to see them all together to perceive that she couldn't
pass for having come to "meet" them—even her mother's
insinuating gentility failed to put the occasion on that footing—and that she must therefore be assumed to have been
brought to show them something. She was not subdued nor
colourless enough to sit there for nothing, or even for conversation (the sort of conversation that was likely to come off),
so that it was inevitable to treat her position as connected
with the principal place on the carpet, with silence and atten-

tion and the pulling together of chairs. Even when so established it struck him at first as precarious, in the light or the
darkness of the inexpressive faces of the other ladies, sitting in
couples and rows on sofas (there were several in addition to
Julia and the Dormers; mainly the wives, with their husbands,
of Sherringham's fellow-secretaries), scarcely one of whom he
felt that he might count upon to say something gushing when
the girl should have finished.

Miss Rooth gave a representation of Juliet drinking her potion, according to the system, as her mother explained, of the
famous Signor Ruggieri—a scene of high, fierce sound, of
many cries and contortions: she shook her hair (which proved
magnificent) half down before the performance was over.
Then she declaimed several short poems by Victor Hugo, selected, among many hundred, by Mrs. Rooth, as the good
lady was careful to make known. After this she jumped to the
American lyre, regaling the company with specimens, both
familiar and fresh, of Longfellow, Lowell, Whittier, Holmes,
and of two or three poetesses revealed to Sherringham on this
occasion. She flowed so copiously, keeping the floor and
rejoicing visibly in her opportunity, that Sherringham was
mainly occupied with wondering how he could make her
leave off. He was surprised at the extent of her repertory,
which, in view of the circumstance that she could never have
received much encouragement—it must have come mainly
from her mother, and he didn't believe in Signor Ruggieri—
denoted a very stiff ambition and a kind of misplaced perseverance. It was her mother who checked her at last, and he
found himself suspecting that Gabriel Nash had intimated to
the old woman that interference was necessary. For himself he
was chiefly glad that Madame Carré was not there. It was
present to him that she would have deemed the exhibition,
with its badness, its assurance, the absence of criticism, almost
indecent.

His only new impression of the girl was that of this same
high assurance—her coolness, her complacency, her eagerness
to go on. She had been deadly afraid of the old actress, but
she was not a bit afraid of a cluster of *femmes du monde*, of
Julia, of Lady Agnes, of the smart women of the Embassy. It
was positively these personages who were rather frightened;

there was certainly a moment when even Julia was scared, for the first time that he had ever seen her. The space was too small; the cries, the rushes of the dishevelled girl were too near. Lady Agnes, much of the time, wore the countenance she might have worn at the theatre during a play in which pistols were fired; and indeed the manner of the young reciter had become more spasmodic, more explosive. It appeared, however, that the company in general thought her very clever and successful; which showed, to Sherringham's sense, how little they understood the matter. Poor Biddy was immensely struck, and grew flushed and absorbed as Miriam, at her best moments, became pale and fatal. It was she who spoke to her first, after it was agreed that they had better not fatigue her any more; she advanced a few steps, happening to be near her, murmuring: "Oh, thank you, thank you so much. I never saw anything so beautiful, so grand."

She looked very red and very pretty as she said this. Peter Sherringham liked her enough to notice and to like her better when she looked prettier than usual. As he turned away he heard Miriam answer, with rather an ungracious irrelevance: "I have seen you before, three days ago, at the Salon, with Mr. Dormer. Yes, I know he's your brother. I have made his acquaintance since. He wants to paint my portrait. Do you think he'll do it well?" He was afraid Miriam was something of a brute, and also somewhat grossly vain. This impression would perhaps have been confirmed if a part of the rest of the short conversation of the two girls had reached his ear. Biddy ventured to remark that she herself had studied modelling a little and that she could understand how any artist would think Miss Rooth a splendid subject. If, indeed, *she* could attempt her head, that would be a chance to do something.

"Thank you," said Miriam, with a laugh. "I think I had rather not *passer par toute la famille!*" Then she added: "If your brother's an artist, I don't understand how he's in Parliament."

"Oh, he isn't in Parliament now; we only hope he will be."

"Oh, I see."

"And he isn't an artist, either," Biddy felt herself conscientiously bound to subjoin.

"Then he isn't anything," said Miss Rooth.

"Well—he's immensely clever."

"Oh, I see," Miss Rooth again replied. "Mr. Nash has puffed him up so."

"I don't know Mr. Nash," said Biddy, guilty of a little dryness, and also of a little misrepresentation, and feeling rather snubbed.

"Well, you needn't wish to."

Biddy stood with her a moment longer, still looking at her and not knowing what to say next, but not finding her any less handsome because she had such odd manners. Biddy had an ingenious little mind, which always tried as much as possible to keep different things separate. It was pervaded now by the observation, made with a certain relief, that if the girl spoke to her with such unexpected familiarity of Nick she said nothing at all about Peter. Two gentlemen came up, two of Peter's friends, and made speeches to Miss Rooth of the kind, Biddy supposed, that people learned to make in Paris. It was also doubtless in Paris, the girl privately reasoned, that they learned to listen to them as this striking performer listened. She received their advances very differently from the way she had received Biddy's. Sherringham noticed his young kinswoman turn away, still blushing, to go and sit near her mother again, leaving Miriam engaged with the two men. It appeared to have come over Biddy that for a moment she had been strangely spontaneous and bold and had paid a little of the penalty. The seat next her mother was occupied by Mrs. Rooth, toward whom Lady Agnes's head had inclined itself with a preoccupied air of benevolence. He had an idea that Mrs. Rooth was telling her about the Neville-Nugents of Castle Nugent, and that Lady Agnes was thinking it odd she never had heard of them. He said to himself that Biddy was generous. She had urged Julia to come, in order that they might see how bad the strange young woman would be; but now that she turned out so dazzling she forgot this calculation and rejoiced in what she innocently supposed to be her triumph. She kept away from Julia, however; she didn't even look at her to invite her also to confess that, in vulgar parlance, they had been sold. He himself spoke to his sister, who was leaning back, in rather a detached way, in the corner of a sofa, saying something which led her to remark in reply: "Ah, I dare say it's extremely fine, but I don't care for tragedy when it treads on one's toes. She's like a cow who has kicked over the milking-pail. She ought to be tied up!"

"My poor Julia, it isn't extremely fine; it isn't fine at all," Sherringham rejoined, with some irritation.

"Excuse me. I thought that was why you invited us."

"I thought she was different," Sherringham said.

"Ah, if you don't care for her, so much the better. It has always seemed to me that you make too much of those people."

"Oh, I do care for her in a way, too. She's interesting." His sister gave him a momentary mystified glance, and he added, "And she's awful!" He felt stupidly annoyed, and he was ashamed of his annoyance, for he could have assigned no reason for it. It didn't make it less, for the moment, to see Gabriel Nash approach Mrs. Dallow, introduced by Nick Dormer. He gave place to the two young men with a certain alacrity, for he had a sense of being put in the wrong, in respect to the heroine of the occasion, by Nash's very presence. He remembered that it had been a part of their bargain, as it were, that he should present that gentleman to his sister. He was not sorry to be relieved of the office by Nick, and he even, tacitly and ironically, wished his cousin's friend joy of a colloquy with Mrs. Dallow. Sherringham's life was spent with people, he was used to people, and both as a host and as a guest he carried them, in general, lightly. He could observe, especially in the former capacity, without uneasiness, take the temperature without anxiety. But at present his company oppressed him; he felt himself nervous, which was the thing in the world that he had always held to be least an honour to a gentleman dedicated to diplomacy. He was vexed with the levity in himself which had made him call them together on so poor a pretext, and yet he was vexed with the stupidity in them which made them think, as they evidently did, that the pretext was sufficient. He inwardly groaned at the precipitancy with which he had saddled himself with the Tragic Muse (a tragic muse who was noisy and pert), and yet he wished his visitors would go away and leave him alone with her.

Nick Dormer said to Mrs. Dallow that he wanted her to know an old friend of his, one of the cleverest men he knew; and he added the hope that she would be gentle and encouraging with him: he was so timid and so easily disconcerted.

Gabriel Nash dropped into a chair by the arm of Julia's sofa, Nick Dormer went away, and Mrs. Dallow turned her glance upon her new acquaintance without a perceptible change of position. Then she emitted, with rapidity, the remark: "It's very awkward when people are told one is clever."

"It's awkward if one isn't," said Mr. Nash, smiling.

"Yes, but so few people are—enough to be talked about."

"Isn't that just the reason why such a matter, such an exception, ought to be mentioned to them?" asked Gabriel Nash. "They mightn't find it out for themselves. Of course, however, as you say, there ought to be a certainty; then they are surer to know it. Dormer's a dear fellow, but he's rash and superficial."

Mrs. Dallow, at this, turned her glance a second time upon her interlocutor; but during the rest of the conversation she rarely repeated the movement. If she liked Nick Dormer extremely (and it may without further delay be communicated to the reader that she did), her liking was of a kind that opposed no difficulty whatever to her not liking (in case of such a complication) a person attached or otherwise belonging to him. It was not in her nature to extend tolerances to others for the sake of an individual she loved: the tolerance was usually consumed in the loving; there was nothing left over. If the affection that isolates and simplifies its object may be distinguished from the affection that seeks communications and contacts for it, Julia Dallow's belonged wholly to the former class. She was not so much jealous as rigidly direct. She desired no experience for the familiar and yet partly mysterious kinsman in whom she took an interest that she would not have desired for herself; and, indeed, the cause of her interest in him was partly the vision of his helping her to the particular emotion that she did desire—the emotion of great affairs and of public action. To have such ambitions for him appeared to her the greatest honour she could do him; her conscience was in it as well as her inclination, and her scheme, in her conception, was noble enough to varnish over any disdain she might feel for forces drawing him another way. She had a prejudice, in general, against his connections, a suspicion of them and a supply of unwrought contempt ready for them. It was a singular circumstance that she was sceptical even when, knowing her as well as he did, he thought them worth recommending to her: the recommendation indeed inveterately confirmed the suspicion.

This was a law from which Gabriel Nash was condemned to suffer, if suffering could on any occasion be predicated of Gabriel Nash. His pretension was, in truth, that he had purged his life of such incongruities, though probably he would have admitted that if a sore spot remained the hand of a woman would be sure to touch it. In dining with her brother and with the Dormers, two evenings before, Mrs. Dallow had been moved to exclaim that Peter and Nick knew the most extraordinary people. As regards Peter the attitudinizing girl and her mother now pointed that moral with sufficient vividness; so that there was little arrogance in taking a similar quality for granted in the conceited man at her elbow, who sat there as if he would be capable, from one moment to another, of leaning over the arm of her sofa. She had not the slightest wish to talk with him about himself, and was afraid, for an instant, that he was on the point of passing from the chapter of his cleverness to that of his timidity. It was a false alarm, however, for instead of this he said something about the pleasures of the monologue, as the distraction that had just been offered was called by the French. He intimated that in his opinion these pleasures were mainly for the performers. They had all, at any rate, given Miss Rooth a charming afternoon; that, of course, was what Miss Dallow's kind brother had mainly intended in arranging the little party. (Mrs. Dallow hated to hear him call her brother "kind"; the term seemed offensively patronizing.) But he himself, he related, was now constantly employed in the same beneficence, listening, two-thirds of his time, to "intonations" and shrieks. She had doubtless observed it herself, how the great current of the age, the adoration of the mime, was almost too strong for any individual; how it swept one along and hurled one against the rocks. As she made no response to this proposition Gabriel Nash asked her if she had not been struck with the main sign of the time, the preponderance of the mountebank, the glory and renown, the personal favour, that he enjoyed. Hadn't she noticed what an immense part of the public attention he held, in London at least? For in Paris society was not so pervaded with him, and the women of the profession, in particular, were not in every drawing-room.

"I don't know what you mean," Mrs. Dallow said. "I know nothing of any such people."

"Aren't they under your feet wherever you turn—their performances, their portraits, their speeches, their autobiographies, their names, their manners, their ugly mugs, as the people say, and their idiotic pretensions?"

"I dare say it depends on the places one goes to. If they're everywhere"—and Mrs. Dallow paused a moment—"I don't go everywhere."

"I don't go anywhere, but they mount on my back, at home, like the Old Man of the Sea. Just observe a little when you return to London," Nash continued, with friendly instructiveness. Mrs. Dallow got up at this—she didn't like receiving directions; but no other corner of the room appeared to offer her any particular reason for crossing to it: she never did such a thing without a great inducement. So she remained standing there, as if she were quitting the place in a moment, which indeed she now determined to do; and her interlocutor, rising also, lingered beside her, unencouraged but unperturbed. He went on to remark that Mr. Sherringham was quite right to offer Miss Rooth an afternoon's sport; she deserved it as a fine, brave, amiable girl. She was highly educated, knew a dozen languages, was of illustrious lineage and was immensely particular.

"Immensely particular?" Mrs. Dallow repeated.

"Perhaps I should say that her mother is, on her behalf. Particular about the sort of people they meet—the tone, the standard. I'm bound to say they're like you: they don't go everywhere. That spirit is meritorious; it should be recognized and rewarded."

Mrs. Dallow said nothing for a moment; she looked vaguely round the room, but not at Miriam Rooth. Nevertheless she presently dropped, in allusion to her, the words: "She's dreadfully vulgar."

"Ah, don't say that to my friend Dormer!" Gabriel Nash exclaimed.

"Are you and he such great friends?" Mrs. Dallow asked, looking at him.

"Great enough to make me hope we shall be greater."

Again, for a moment, she said nothing; then she went on—

"Why shouldn't I say to him that she's vulgar?"

"Because he admires her so much; he wants to paint her."

"To paint her?"

"To paint her portrait."

"Oh, I see. I dare say she'd do for that."

Gabriel Nash laughed gaily. "If that's your opinion of her you are not very complimentary to the art he aspires to practise."

"He aspires to practise?" Mrs. Dallow repeated.

"Haven't you talked with him about it? Ah, you must keep him up to it!"

Julia Dallow was conscious, for a moment, of looking uncomfortable; but it relieved her to demand of her neighbour, in a certain tone, "Are you an artist?"

"I try to be," Nash replied, smiling; "but I work in such a difficult material."

He spoke this with such a clever suggestion of unexpected reference that, in spite of herself, Mrs. Dallow said after him—

"Difficult material?"

"I work in life!"

At this Mrs. Dallow turned away, leaving Nash the impression that she probably misunderstood his speech, thinking he meant that he drew from the living model, or some such platitude: as if there could have been any likelihood that he drew from the dead one. This, indeed, would not fully have explained the abruptness with which she dropped their conversation. Gabriel Nash, however, was used to sudden collapses, and even to sudden ruptures, on the part of his interlocutors, and no man had more the secret of remaining gracefully with his ideas on his hands. He saw Mrs. Dallow approach Nick Dormer, who was talking with one of the ladies of the Embassy, and apparently signify to him that she wished to speak to him. He got up, they had a minute's conversation, and then he turned and took leave of his fellow-visitor. Mrs. Dallow said a word to her brother, Dormer joined her, and then they came together to the door. In this movement they had to pass near Nash, and it gave her an opportunity to nod good-bye to him, which he was by no means sure she would have done if Nick had not been with her. The young man stopped a moment; he said to Nash: "I should like to see you this evening, late; you must meet me somewhere."

"We'll take a walk—I should like that," Nash replied. "I shall smoke a cigar at the café on the corner of the Place de l'Opéra; you'll find me there." Gabriel prepared to compass his own departure, but before doing so he addressed himself to the duty of saying a few words of civility to Lady Agnes. This proved difficult, for on one side she was defended by the wall of the room and on the other rendered inaccessible by Miriam's mother, who clung to her with a quickly-rooted fidelity, showing no symptom of desistance. Gabriel compromised on her daughter Grace, who said to him:

"You were talking with my cousin, Mrs. Dallow."

"*To* her rather than with her," Nash smiled.

"Ah, she's very charming," said Grace.

"She's very beautiful," Nash rejoined.

"And very clever," Miss Dormer continued.

"Very, very intelligent." His conversation with the young lady went little further than this, and he presently took leave of Peter Sherringham; remarking to him, as he shook hands, that he was very sorry for him. But he had courted his fate.

"What do you mean by my fate?" Sherringham asked.

"You've got them for life."

"Why for life, when I now lucidly and courageously recognize that she isn't good?"

"Ah, but she'll become so," said Gabriel Nash.

"Do you think that?" Sherringham inquired, with a candour which made his visitor laugh.

"*You* will—that's more to the purpose!" Gabriel exclaimed, as he went away.

Ten minutes later Lady Agnes substituted a general vague assent to all further particular ones and, with her daughters, withdrew from Mrs. Rooth and from the rest of the company. Peter had had very little talk with Biddy, but the girl kept her disappointment out of her pretty eyes and said to him:

"You told us she didn't know how—but she does!" There was no suggestion of disappointment in this.

Sherringham held her hand a moment. "Ah, it's you who know how, dear Biddy!" he answered; and he was conscious that if the occasion had been more private he would lawfully have kissed her.

Presently three others of his guests departed, and Mr. Nash's assurance that he had them for life recurred to him as he observed that Mrs. Rooth and her daughter quite failed to profit by so many examples. The Lovicks remained—a colleague and his sociable wife—and Peter gave them a hint that they were not to leave him absolutely alone with the two ladies. Miriam quitted Mrs. Lovick, who had attempted, with no great subtlety, to engage her, and came up to Sherringham as if she suspected him of a design of stealing from the room and had the idea of preventing it.

"I want some more tea: will you give me some more? I feel quite faint. You don't seem to suspect how that sort of thing takes it out of you."

Sherringham apologized, extravagantly, for not having seen that she had the proper quantity of refreshment, and took her to the round table, in a corner, on which the little collation had been served. He poured out tea for her and pressed bread-and-butter on her, and *petits fours*, of all which she profusely and methodically partook. It was late; the afternoon had faded and a lamp had been brought in, the wide shade of which shed a fair glow upon the tea-service, the little plates of comestibles. The Lovicks sat with Mrs. Rooth at the other end of the room, and the girl stood at the table drinking her tea and eating her bread-and-butter. She consumed these articles so freely that he wondered if she had been in serious want of food—if they were so poor as to have to count with that sort of privation. This supposition was softening, but still not so much so as to make him ask her to sit down. She appeared indeed to prefer to stand: she looked better so, as if the freedom, the conspicuity of being on her feet and treading a stage were agreeable to her. While Sherringham lingered near her, vaguely, with his hands in his pockets, not knowing exactly what to say and instinctively avoiding, now, the theatrical question (there were moments when he was plentifully tired of it), she broke out, abruptly: "Confess that you think me intolerably bad!"

"Intolerably—no."

"Only tolerably! I think that's worse."

"Every now and then you do something very clever," Sherringham said.

"How many such things did I do to-day?"

"Oh, three or four. I don't know that I counted very carefully."

She raised her cup to her lips, looking at him over the rim of it—a proceeding which gave her eyes a strange expression. "It bores you, and you think it disagreeable," she said in a moment—"a girl always talking about herself." He protested that she could never bore him, and she went on: "Oh, I don't want compliments—I want the truth. An actress has to talk about herself; what else can she talk about, poor vain thing?"

"She can talk sometimes about other actresses."

"That comes to the same thing. You won't be serious. I'm awfully serious." There was something that caught his attention in the way she said this—a longing, half-hopeless, half-argumentative, to be believed in. "If one really wants to do anything one must worry it out; of course everything doesn't come the first day," she pursued. "I can't see everything at once; but I can see a little more—step by step—as I go: can't I?"

"That's the way—that's the way," said Sherringham. "If you see the things to do, the art of doing them will come, if you hammer away. The great point is to see them."

"Yes; and you don't think me clever enough for that."

"Why do you say so, when I've asked you to come here on purpose?"

"You've asked me to come, but I've had no success."

"On the contrary; every one thought you wonderful."

"Oh, they don't know!" said Miriam Rooth. "You've not said a word to me. I don't mind your not having praised me; that would be too *banal*. But if I'm bad—and I know I'm dreadful—I wish you would talk to me about it."

"It's delightful to talk to you," Sherringham said.

"No, it isn't, but it's kind," she answered, looking away from him.

Her voice had a quality, as she uttered these words, which made him exclaim, "Every now and then you say something—!"

She turned her eyes back to him, smiling. "I don't want it to come by accident." Then she added: "If there's any good to be got from trying, from showing one's self, how can it come unless one hears the simple truth, the truth that turns one inside out? It's all for that—to know what one is, if one's a stick!"

"You have great courage, you have rare qualities," said Sherringham. She had begun to touch him, to seem different: he was glad she had not gone.

For a moment she made no response to this, putting down her empty cup and looking vaguely over the table, as if to select something more to eat. Suddenly she raised her head and broke out with vehemence: "I will, I will, I will!"

"You'll do what you want, evidently."

"I will succeed—I will be great. Of course I know too little, I've seen too little. But I've always liked it; I've never liked anything else. I used to learn things, and to do scenes, and to rant about the room, when I was five years old." She went on, communicative, persuasive, familiar, egotistical (as was necessary), and slightly common, or perhaps only natural; with reminiscences, reasons and anecdotes, an unexpected profusion, and with an air of comradeship, of freedom of intercourse, which appeared to plead that she was capable at least of embracing that side of the profession she desired to adopt. He perceived that if she had seen very little, as she said, she had also seen a great deal; but both her experience and her innocence had been accidental and irregular. She had seen very little acting—the theatre was always too expensive. If she could only go often—in Paris, for instance, every night for six months—to see the best, the worst, everything, she would make things out, she would observe and learn what to do, what not to do: it would be a kind of school. But she couldn't, without selling the clothes off her back. It was vile and disgusting to be poor; and if ever she were to know the bliss of having a few francs in her pocket she would make up for it—that she could promise! She had never been acquainted with any one who could tell her anything—if it was good or bad, or right or wrong—except Mrs. Delamere and poor Ruggieri. She supposed they had told her a great deal, but perhaps they hadn't, and she was perfectly willing to give it up if it was bad. Evidently Madame Carré thought so; she thought it was horrid. Wasn't it perfectly divine, the way the old woman had said those verses, those speeches of Célie? If she would only let her come and listen to her once in a while, like that, it was all she would ask. She had got lots of ideas, just from that; she had practised them over, over and over again, the moment she got home. He might ask her mother—he might ask the people next door. If Madame Carré didn't think she could work she might have heard something that would show her. But she didn't think her even good enough to criticize; for that wasn't criticism, telling her her head was good. Of course her head was good; she didn't need travel up to the *quartiers excentriques* to find that out. It was her mother—the way she talked—who gave that idea, that she wanted to be elegant, and very moral, and a *femme du monde*, and all that sort of trash. Of course that put people off, when they were only thinking of the right way. Didn't *she* know, Miriam herself, that that was the only thing to think of? But any one would be kind to her mother who knew what a dear she was. "She doesn't know when it's right or wrong, but she's a perfect saint," said the girl, obscuring considerably her vindication. "She doesn't mind when I say things over by the hour, dinning them into her ears while she sits there and reads. She's a tremendous reader; she's awfully up in literature. She taught me everything herself—I mean all that sort of thing. Of course I'm not so fond of reading; I go in for the book of life." Sherringham wondered whether her mother had not, at any rate, taught her that phrase, and thought it highly probable. "It would give on *my* nerves, the life I lead her," Miriam continued; "but she's really a delicious woman."

The oddity of this epithet made Sherringham laugh, and altogether, in a few minutes, which is perhaps a sign that he abused his right to be a man of moods, the young lady had produced a revolution of curiosity in him, re-awakened his sympathy. Her mixture, as it spread itself before one, was a quickening spectacle: she was intelligent and clumsy—she was underbred and fine. Certainly she was very various, and that was rare; not at all at this moment the heavy-eyed, frightened creature who had pulled herself together with such an effort at Madame Carré's, nor the elated "phenomenon" who had just been declaiming, nor the rather affected and contradictious young person with whom he had walked home from the Rue de Constantinople. Was this succession of phases a sign that she really possessed the celebrated artistic temperament, the nature that made people provoking and interesting? That Sherringham himself was of that shifting complexion is perhaps proved by his odd capacity for being of two different minds at very nearly the same time. Miriam was pretty now, with likeable looks and charming usual eyes. Yes, there were things he could do for her; he had already forgotten the chill of Mr. Nash's irony, of his prophecy. He was even scarcely conscious how much, in general, he detested hints, insinuations, favours asked obliquely and plaintively: that was doubtless also because the girl was so pretty and so fraternizing. Perhaps indeed it was unjust to qualify it as roundabout, the manner in which Miss Rooth conveyed to him that it was open to him not only to pay for lessons for her, but to meet the expense of her nightly attendance, with her mother, at instructive exhibitions of theatrical art. It was a large order, sending the pair to all the plays; but what Sherringham now found himself thinking about was not so much its largeness as that it would be rather interesting to go with them sometimes and point the moral (the technical one), showing her the things he liked, the things he disapproved. She repeated her declaration that she recognized the fallacy of her mother's views about "noble" heroines and about the importance of her looking out for such tremendously proper people. "One must let her talk, but of course it creates a prejudice," she said, with her eyes on Mr. and Mrs. Lovick, who had got up, terminating their communion with Mrs. Rooth. "It's a great muddle, I know, but she can't bear anything coarse—and quite right, too. I shouldn't, either, if I didn't have to. But I don't care where I go if I can act, or who they are if they'll help me. I want to act—that's what I want to do; I don't want to meddle in people's affairs. I can look out for myself—*I'm* all right!" the girl exclaimed, roundly, frankly, with a ring of honesty which made her crude and pure. "As for doing the bad ones, I'm not afraid of that."

"The bad ones?"

"The bad women, in the plays—like Madame Carré. I'll do anything."

"I think you'll do best what you are," remarked Sherringham, laughing. "You're a strange girl."

"*Je crois bien!* Doesn't one have to be, to want to go and exhibit one's self to a loathsome crowd, on a platform, with trumpets and a big drum, for money—to parade one's body and one's soul?"

Sherringham looked at her a moment: her face changed constantly; now there was a little flush and a noble delicacy in it.

"Give it up; you're too good for it," he said, abruptly.

"Never, never—never till I'm pelted!"

"Then stay on here a bit; I'll take you to the theatres."

"Oh, you dear!" Miriam delightedly exclaimed. Mr. and Mrs. Lovick, accompanied by Mrs. Rooth, now crossed the room to them, and the girl went on, in the same tone: "Mamma, dear, he's the best friend we've ever had; he's a great deal nicer than I thought."

"So are you, mademoiselle," said Peter Sherringham.

"Oh, I trust Mr. Sherringham—I trust him infinitely," Mrs. Rooth returned, covering him with her mild, respectable, wheedling eyes. "The kindness of every one has been beyond everything. Mr. and Mrs. Lovick can't say enough. They make the most obliging offers; they want you to know their brother."

"Oh, I say, he's no brother of mine," Mr. Lovick protested, good-naturedly.

"They think he'll be so suggestive, he'll put us up to the right things," Mrs. Rooth went on.

"It's just a little brother of mine—such a dear, clever boy," Mrs. Lovick explained.

"Do you know she has got nine? Upon my honour she has!" said her husband. "This one is the sixth. Fancy if I had to take them over!"

"Yes, it makes it rather awkward," Mrs. Lovick amiably conceded. "He has gone on the stage, poor dear boy; he acts rather well."

"He tried for the diplomatic service, but he didn't precisely dazzle his examiners," Mr. Lovick remarked.

"Edmund's very nasty about him. There are lots of gentlemen on the stage; he's not the first."

"It's such a comfort to hear that," said Mrs. Rooth.

"I'm much obliged to you. Has he got a theatre?" Miriam asked.

"My dear young lady, he hasn't even got an engagement," replied the young man's unsympathizing brother-in-law.

"He hasn't been at it very long, but I'm sure he'll get on. He's immensely in earnest, and he's very good-looking. I just said that if he should come over to see us you might rather like to meet him. He might give you some tips, as my husband says."

"I don't care for his looks, but I *should* like his tips," said Miriam, smiling.

"And *is* he coming over to see you?" asked Sherringham, to whom, while this exchange of remarks, which he had not lost, was going on, Mrs. Rooth had, in lowered accents, addressed herself.

"Not if I can help it, I think!" Mr. Lovick declared, but so jocosely that it was not embarrassing.

"Oh, sir, I'm sure you're fond of him," Mrs. Rooth remonstrated, as the party passed together into the antechamber.

"No, really, I like some of the others—four or five of them; but I don't like Arty."

"We'll make it up to him, then; *we'll* like him," Miriam declared, gaily; and her voice rang in the staircase (Sherringham went a little way with them), with a charm which her host had not perceived in her sportive note the day before.

IX.

NICK DORMER found his friend Nash, that evening, on the spot he had designated, smoking a cigar in the warm, bright night, in front of the café at the corner of the square before the Opera. He sat down with him, but at the end of five minutes he uttered a protest against the crush and confusion, the publicity and vulgarity, of the place, the shuffling procession of the crowd, the jostle of fellow-customers, the perpetual brush of waiters. "Come away. I want to talk to you, and I can't talk here," he said to his companion. "I don't care where we go. It will be pleasant to walk; we'll stroll away to the *quartiers sérieux*. Each time I come to Paris, at the end of three days, I take the boulevard, with its conventional grimace, into greater disfavour. I hate even to cross it, I go half a mile round to avoid it."

The young men took their course together down the Rue de la Paix to the Rue de Rivoli, which they crossed, passing beside the gilded railing of the Tuileries. The beauty of the night—the only defect of which was that the immense illumination of Paris kept it from being quite night enough, made it a sort of bedizened, rejuvenated day—gave a charm to the quieter streets, drew our friends away to the right, to the river and the bridges, the older, duskier city. The pale ghost of the palace that had died by fire hung over them awhile, and, by the passage now open at all times across the garden of the Tuileries, they came out upon the Seine. They kept on and on, moving slowly, smoking, talking, pausing, stopping to look, to emphasize, to compare. They fell into discussion, into confidence, into inquiry, sympathetic or satiric, and into explanation which needed in turn to be explained. The balmy night, the time for talk, the amusement of Paris, the memory of young confabulations gave a quality to the occasion. Nick had already forgotten the little brush he had had with Mrs. Dallow, when they quitted Peter's tea-party together, and that he had been almost disconcerted by the manner in which she characterized the odious man he had taken it into his head to present to her. Impertinent and fatuous she had called him; and when Nick began to explain that he was really neither of these things, though he could imagine his manner might sometimes suggest them, she had declared that she didn't wish to argue about him or even to hear of him again. Nick had not counted on her liking Gabriel Nash, but he had thought it wouldn't matter much if she should dislike him a little. He had given himself the diversion, which he had not dreamed would be cruel to any one concerned, of seeing what she would make of a type she had never encountered before. She had made even less than he expected, and her implication that he had played her a trick had been irritating enough to prevent him from reflecting that the fault might have been in some degree with Nash. But he had recovered from his resentment sufficiently to ask this personage, with every possible circumstance of implied consideration for the lady, what *he*, on his side, had made of his charming cousin.

"Upon my word, my dear fellow, I don't regard that as a fair question," was the answer. "Besides, if you think Mrs. Dallow charming, what on earth need it matter to you what I think? The superiority of one man's opinion over another's is never so great as when the opinion is about a woman."

"It was to help me to find out what I think of yourself," said Nick Dormer.

"Oh, that you'll never do. I shall bother you to the end. The lady with whom you were so good as to make me acquainted is a beautiful specimen of the English garden-flower, the product of high cultivation and much tending; a tall, delicate stem, with the head set upon it in a manner which, as I recall it, is distinctly so much to the good in my day. She's the perfect type of the object *raised*, or bred, and everything about her is homogeneous, from the angle of her elbow to the way she drops that vague, conventional, dry little 'Oh!' which dispenses with all further performance. That sort of completeness is always satisfying. But I didn't satisfy her, and she didn't understand me. I don't think they usually understand."

"She's no worse than I, then."

"Ah, she didn't try."

"No, she doesn't try. But she probably thought you conceited, and she would think so still more if she were to hear you talk about her trying."

"Very likely—very likely," said Gabriel Nash. "I have an idea a good many people think that. It appears to me so droll. I suppose it's a result of my little system."

"Your little system?"

"Oh, it's nothing wonderful. Only the idea of being just the same to every one. People have so bemuddled themselves that the last thing they can conceive is that one should be simple."

"Lord, do you call yourself simple?" Nick ejaculated.

"Absolutely; in the sense of having no interest of my own to push, no nostrum to advertise, no power to conciliate, no axe to grind. I'm not a savage—ah, far from it—but I really think I'm perfectly independent."

"Oh, that's always provoking!" laughed Nick.

"So it would appear, to the great majority of one's fellow-mortals; and I well remember the pang with which I originally made that discovery. It darkened my spirit, at a time when I had no thought of evil. What we like, when we are unregenerate, is that a new-comer should give us a password, come over to our side, join our little camp or religion, get into our little boat, in short, whatever it is, and help us to row it. It's natural enough; we are mostly in different tubs and cockles, paddling for life. Our opinions, our convictions and doctrines and standards, are simply the particular thing that will make the boat go—*our* boat, naturally, for they may very often be just the thing that will sink another. If you won't get in, people generally hate you."

"Your metaphor is very lame," said Nick; "it's the over-crowded boat that goes to the bottom."

"Oh, I'll give it another leg or two! Boats can be big, in the infinite of space, and a doctrine is a raft that floats the better the more passengers it carries. A passenger jumps over from time to time, not so much from fear of sinking as from a want of interest in the course or the company. He swims, he plunges, he dives, he dips down and visits the fishes and the mermaids and the submarine caves; he goes from craft to craft and splashes about, on his own account, in the blue, cool water. The regenerate, as I call them, are the passengers who jump over in search of better fun. I turned my summersault long ago."

"And now, of course, you're at the head of the regenerate; for, in your turn, you all form a select school of porpoises."

"Not a bit, and I know nothing about heads, in the sense you mean. I've grown a tail, if you will; I'm the merman wandering free. It's a delightful trade!"

Before they had gone many steps further Nick Dormer stopped short and said to his companion: "I say, my dear fellow, do you mind mentioning to me whether you are the greatest humbug and charlatan on earth, or a genuine intelligence, one that has sifted things for itself?"

"I do puzzle you—I'm so sorry," Nash replied, benignly. "But I'm very sincere. And I *have* tried to straighten out things a bit for myself."

"Then why do you give people such a handle?"

"Such a handle?"

"For thinking you're an—for thinking you're not wise."

"I dare say it's my manner; they're so unused to candour."

"Why don't you try another?" Nick inquired.

"One has the manner that one can; and mine, moreover, is a part of my little system."

"Ah, if you've got a little system you're no better than any one else," said Nick, going on.

"I don't pretend to be better, for we are all miserable sinners; I only pretend to be bad in a pleasanter, brighter way, by what I can see. It's the simplest thing in the world; I just take for granted a certain brightness in life, a certain frankness. What is essentially kinder than that, what is more harmless? But the tradition of dreariness, of stodginess, of dull, dense, literal prose, has so sealed people's eyes that they have ended by thinking the most normal thing in the world the most fantastic. Why be dreary, in our little day? No one can tell me why, and almost every one calls me names for simply asking the question. But I keep on, for I believe one can do a little good by it. I want so much to do a little good," Gabriel Nash continued, taking his companion's arm. "My persistence is systematic: don't you see what I mean? I won't be dreary—no, no, no; and I won't recognize the necessity, or even, if there is any way out of it, the accident of dreariness in the life that surrounds me. That's enough to make people stare: they're so stupid!"

"They think you're impertinent," Dormer remarked.

At this his companion stopped him short, with an ejaculation of pain, and, turning his eyes, Nick saw under the lamps of the quay that he had brought a vivid blush into Nash's face. "I don't strike *you* that way?" Gabriel asked, reproachfully.

"Oh, me! Wasn't it just admitted that I don't in the least make you out?"

"That's the last thing!" Nash murmured, as if he were thinking the idea over, with an air of genuine distress. "But with a little patience we'll clear it up together, if you care enough about it," he added, more cheerfully. He let his friend go on again and he continued: "Heaven help us all! what do people mean by impertinence? There are many, I think, who don't understand its nature or its limits; and upon my word I have literally seen mere quickness of intelligence or of perception, the jump of a step or two, a little whirr of the wings of talk, mistaken for it. Yes, I have encountered men and women who thought you were impertinent if you were not so stupid as they. The only impertinence is aggression, and I indignantly protest that I am never guilty of *that* clumsiness. Ah, for what do they take one, with *their* presumptions? Even to defend myself, sometimes, I have to make believe to myself that I care. I always feel as if I didn't successfully make others think so. Perhaps they see an impertinence in that. But I dare say the offence is in the things that I take, as I say, for granted; for if one tries to be pleased one passes, perhaps inevitably, for being pleased above all with one's self. That's really not my case, for I find my capacity for pleasure deplorably below the mark I've set. That's why, as I have told you, I cultivate it, I try to bring it up. And I am actuated by positive benevolence; I have that pretension. That's what I mean by being the same to every one, by having only one manner. If one is conscious and ingenious to that end, what's the harm, when one's motives are so pure? By never, *never* making the concession, one may end by becoming a perceptible force for good."

"What concession are you talking about?" asked Nick Dormer.

"Why, that we are only here for dreariness. It's impossible to grant it sometimes, if you wish to withhold it ever."

"And what do you mean by dreariness? That's modern slang, and it's terribly vague. Many good things are dreary—virtue and decency and charity and perseverance and courage and honour."

"Say at once that life is dreary, my dear fellow!" Gabriel Nash exclaimed.

"That's on the whole my most usual impression."

"*C'est là que je vous attends!* I'm precisely engaged in trying what can be done in taking it the other way. It's my little personal experiment. Life consists of the personal experiments of each of us, and the point of an experiment is that it shall succeed. What we contribute is our treatment of the material, our rendering of the text, our style. A sense of the qualities of a style is so rare that many persons should doubtless be forgiven for not being able to read, or at all events to enjoy us; but is that a reason for giving it up—for not being, in this other sphere, if one possibly can, a Macaulay, a Ruskin, a Renan? Ah, we must write our best; it's the great thing we can do in the world, on the right side. One has one's form, *que diable*, and a mighty good thing that one has. I'm not afraid of putting all life into mine, without unduly squeezing it. I'm not afraid of putting in honour and courage and charity, without spoiling them: on the contrary, I'll only do them good. People may not read you at sight, may not like you, but there's a chance they'll come round; and the only way to court the chance is to keep it up—always to keep it up. That's what I do, my dear fellow, if you don't think I've perseverance. If some one likes it here and there, if you give a little impression of solidity, that's your reward; besides, of course, the pleasure for yourself."

"Don't you think your style is a little affected?" Nick asked, laughing, as they proceeded.

"That's always the charge against a personal manner; if you have any at all people think you have too much. Perhaps, perhaps—who can say? Of course one isn't perfect; but that's the delightful thing about art, that there is always more to learn and more to do; one can polish and polish and refine and refine. No doubt I'm rough still, but I'm in the right direction: I make it my business to take for granted an interest in the beautiful."

"Ah, the beautiful—there it stands, over there!" said Nick Dormer. "I am not so sure about yours—I don't know what I've got hold of. But Notre Dame *is* solid; Notre Dame *is* wise; on Notre Dame the distracted mind can rest. Come over and look at her!"

They had come abreast of the low island from which the great cathedral, disengaged to-day from her old contacts and adhesions, rises high and fair, with her front of beauty and her majestic mass, darkened at that hour, or at least simplified, under the stars, but only more serene and sublime for her happy union, far aloft, with the cool distance and the night. Our young men, gossiping as profitably as I leave the reader to estimate, crossed the wide, short bridge which made them face toward the monuments of old Paris—the Palais de Justice, the Conciergerie, the holy chapel of Saint Louis. They came out before the church, which looks down on a square where the past, once so thick in the very heart of Paris, has been made rather a blank, pervaded, however, by the everlasting freshness of the great cathedral-face. It greeted Nick Dormer and Gabriel Nash with a kindness which the centuries had done nothing to dim. The lamplight of the great city washed its foundations, but the towers and buttresses, the arches, the galleries, the statues, the vast rose-window, the large, full composition, seemed to grow clearer as they climbed higher, as if they had a conscious benevolent answer for the upward gaze of men.

"How it straightens things out and blows away one's vapours—anything that's *done*!" said Nick; while his companion exclaimed, blandly and affectionately:

"The dear old thing!"

"The great point is to do something, instead of standing muddling and questioning; and, by Jove, it makes me want to!"

"Want to build a cathedral?" Nash inquired.

"Yes, just that."

"It's you who puzzle *me*, then, my dear fellow. You can't build them out of words."

"What is it the great poets do?" asked Nick.

"*Their* words are ideas—their words are images, enchanting collocations and unforgettable signs. But the verbiage of parliamentary speeches!"

"Well," said Nick, with a candid, reflective sigh, "you can rear a great structure of many things—not only of stones and timbers and painted glass." They walked round Notre Dame, pausing, criticizing, admiring and discussing; mingling the grave with the gay and paradox with contemplation. Behind and at the sides the huge dusky vessel of the church seemed to dip into the Seine, or rise out of it, floating expansively—a ship of stone, with its flying buttresses thrown forth like an array of mighty oars. Nick Dormer lingered near it with joy, with a certain soothing content; as if it had been the temple of a faith so dear to him that there was peace and security in its precinct. And there was comfort too, and consolation of the same sort, in the company, at this moment, of Nash's equal response, of his appreciation, exhibited by his own signs, of the great effect. He felt it so freely and uttered his impression with such vividness that Nick was reminded of the luminosity his boyish admiration had found in him of old, the natural intelligence of everything of that kind. "Everything of that kind" was, in Nick's mind, the description of a wide and bright domain.

They crossed to the further side of the river, where the influence of the Gothic monument threw a distinction even over the Parisian smartnesses—the municipal rule and measure, the importunate symmetries, the "handsomeness" of everything, the extravagance of gaslight, the perpetual click on the neat bridges. In front of a quiet little café on the right bank Gabriel Nash said, "Let's sit down"—he was always ready to sit down. It was a friendly establishment and an unfashionable quarter, far away from the Grand Hôtel; there were the usual little tables and chairs on the quay, the muslin curtains behind the glazed front, the general sense of sawdust and of drippings of watery beer. The place was subdued to stillness, but not extinguished, by the lateness of the hour; no vehicles passed, but only now and then a light Parisian foot. Beyond the parapet they could hear the flow of the Seine. Nick Dormer said it made him think of the old Paris, of the great Revolution, of Madame Roland, *quoi!* Gabriel Nash said they could have watery beer but were not obliged to drink it. They sat a long time; they talked a great deal, and the more they said the more the unsaid came up. Presently Nash found occasion to remark: "I go about my business, like any good citizen—that's all."

"And what *is* your business?"

"The spectacle of the world."

Nick laughed out. "And what do you do with that?"

"What does any one do with a spectacle? I look at it."

"You are full of contradictions and inconsistencies. You described yourself to me half an hour ago as an apostle of beauty."

"Where is the inconsistency? I do it in the broad light of day, whatever I do: that's virtually what I meant. If I look at the spectacle of the world I look in preference at what is charming in it. Sometimes I have to go far to find it—very likely; but that's just what I do. I go far—as far as my means permit me. Last year I heard of such a delightful little spot: a place where a wild fig-tree grows in the south wall, the outer side, of an old Spanish city. I was told it was a deliciously brown corner, with the sun making it warm in winter! As soon as I could I went there."

"And what did you do?"

"I lay on the first green grass—I liked it."

"If that sort of thing is all you accomplish you are not encouraging."

"I accomplish my happiness—it seems to me that's something. I have feelings, I have sensations: let me tell you that's not so common. It's rare to have them; and if you chance to have them it's rare not to be ashamed of them. I go after them—when I judge they won't hurt any one."

"You're lucky to have money for your travelling-expenses," said Nick.

"No doubt, no doubt; but I do it very cheap. I take my stand on my nature, on my disposition. I'm not ashamed of it, I don't think it's so horrible, my disposition. But we've befogged and befouled so the whole question of liberty, of spontaneity, of good-humour and inclination and enjoyment, that there's nothing that makes people stare so as to see one natural."

"You are always thinking too much of 'people.' "

"They say I think too little," Gabriel smiled.

"Well, I've agreed to stand for Harsh," said Nick, with a roundabout transition.

"It's you then who are lucky to have money."

"I haven't," Nick replied. "My expenses are to be paid."

"Then you too must think of 'people.' "

Nick made no answer to this, but after a moment he said: "I wish very much you had more to show for it."

"To show for what?"

"Your little system—the æsthetic life."

Nash hesitated, tolerantly, gaily, as he often did, with an air of being embarrassed to choose between several answers, any one of them would be so right. "Oh, having something to show is such a poor business. It's a kind of confession of failure."

"Yes, you're more affected than anything else," said Nick, impatiently.

"No, my dear boy, I'm more good-natured: don't I prove it? I'm rather disappointed to find that you are not worthy of the esoteric doctrine. But there is, I confess, another plane of intelligence, honourable, and very honourable in its way, from which it *may* legitimately appear important to have something to show. If you *must* confine yourself to that plane I won't refuse you my sympathy. After all, that's what *I* have to show! But the degree of my sympathy must of course depend on the nature of the manifestation that you wish to make."

"You know it very well—you've guessed it," Nick rejoined, looking before him in a conscious, modest way which, if he had been a few years younger, would have been called sheepish.

"Ah, you've broken the scent with telling me you are going to return to the House of Commons," said Nash.

"No wonder you don't make it out! My situation is certainly absurd enough. What I really want to do is to be a painter. That's the abject, crude, ridiculous fact. In this out-of-the-way corner, at the dead of night, in lowered tones, I venture to disclose it to you. Isn't that the æsthetic life?"

"Do you know how to paint?" asked Nash.

"Not in the least. No element of burlesque is therefore wanting to my position."

"That makes no difference. I'm so glad!"

"So glad I don't know how?"

"So glad of it all. Yes, that only makes it better. You're a delightful case, and I like delightful cases. We must see it through. I rejoice that I met you."

"Do you think I can do anything?" Nick inquired.

"Paint good pictures? How can I tell till I've seen some of your work? Doesn't it come back to me that at Oxford you used to sketch very prettily? But that's the last thing that matters."

"What does matter, then?" Nick demanded, turning his eyes on his companion.

"To be on the right side—on the side of beauty."

"There will be precious little beauty if I produce nothing but daubs."

"Ah, you cling to the old false measure of success. I must cure you of that. There will be the beauty of having been disinterested and independent; of having taken the world in the free, brave, personal way."

"I shall nevertheless paint decently if I can," Nick declared.

"I'm almost sorry! It will make your case less clear, your example less grand."

"My example will be grand enough, with the fight I shall have to make."

"The fight—with whom?"

"With myself, first of all. I'm awfully against it."

"Ah, but you'll have me on the other side," smiled Nash.

"Well, you'll have more than a handful to meet—everything, every one that belongs to me, that touches me, near or far: my family, my blood, my heredity, my traditions, my promises, my circumstances, my prejudices; my little past, such as it is; my great future, such as it has been supposed it may be."

"I see, I see; it's admirable!" Nash exclaimed. "And Mrs. Dallow into the bargain," he added.

"Yes, Mrs. Dallow, if you like."

"Are you in love with her?"

"Not in the least."

"Well, she is with you—so I perceived."

"Don't say that," said Nick Dormer, with sudden sternness.

"Ah, you are, you are!" his companion rejoined, judging apparently from this accent.

"I don't know what I am—heaven help me!" Nick broke out, tossing his hat down on his little tin table with vehemence. "I'm a freak of nature and a sport of the mocking gods! Why should they go out of their way to worry me? Why should they do anything so inconsequent, so improbable, so preposterous? It's the vulgarest practical joke. There has never been anything of the sort among us; we are all Philistines to the core, with about as much æsthetic sense as that hat. It's excellent soil—I don't complain of it—but not a soil to grow that flower. From where the devil, then, has the seed been dropped? I look back from generation to generation; I scour our annals without finding the least little sketching grandmother, any sign of a building, or versifying, or collecting, or even tulip-raising ancestor. They were all as blind as bats and none the less happy for that. I'm a wanton variation, an unaccountable monster. My dear father, rest his soul, went through life without a suspicion that there is anything in it that can't be boiled into blue-books; and he became, in that conviction, a very distinguished person. He brought me up in the same simplicity and in the hope of the same eminence. It would have been better if I had remained so. I think it's partly your fault that I haven't," Nick went on. "At Oxford you were very bad company for me, my evil genius; you opened my eyes, you communicated the poison. Since then, little by little, it has been working within me; vaguely, covertly, insensibly at first, but during the last year or two with violence, pertinacity, cruelty. I have taken every antidote in life; but it's no use—I'm stricken. It tears me to pieces, as I may say."

"I see, I follow you," said Nash, who had listened to this

recital with radiant interest and curiosity. "And that's why you are going to stand."

"Precisely—it's an antidote. And, at present, you're another."

"Another?"

"That's why I jumped at you. A bigger dose of you may disagree with me to that extent that I shall either die or get better."

"I shall control the dilution," said Nash. "Poor fellow—if you're elected!" he added.

"Poor fellow either way. You don't know the atmosphere in which I live, the horror, the scandal that my apostasy would inspire, the injury and suffering that it would inflict. I believe it would kill my mother. She thinks my father is watching me from the skies."

"Jolly to make him jump!" Nash exclaimed.

"He would jump indeed; he would come straight down on top of me. And then the grotesqueness of it—to *begin*, all of a sudden, at my age."

"It's perfect indeed; it's a magnificent case," Nash went on.

"Think how it sounds—a paragraph in the London papers: 'Mr. Nicholas Dormer, M.P. for Harsh and son of the late Right Honourable, and so forth and so forth, is about to give up his seat and withdraw from public life in order to devote himself to the practice of portrait-painting. Orders respectfully solicited.' "

"The nineteenth century is better than I thought," said Nash. "It's the portrait that preoccupies you?"

"I wish you could see; you must come immediately to my place in London."

"You wretch, you're capable of having talent!" cried Nash.

"No, I'm too old, too old. It's too late to go through the mill."

"You make *me* young! Don't miss your election, at your peril. Think of the edification."

"The edification?"

"Of your throwing it all up the next moment."

"That would be pleasant for Mr. Carteret," Nick observed.

"Mr. Carteret?"

"A dear old fellow who will wish to pay my agent's bill."

"Serve him right, for such depraved tastes."

"You do me good," said Nick, getting up and turning away.

"Don't call me useless then."

"Ah, but not in the way you mean. It's only if I don't get in that I shall perhaps console myself with the brush," Nick continued, as they retraced their steps.

"In the name of all the muses, then, don't stand. For you *will* get in."

"Very likely. At any rate I've promised."

"You've promised Mrs. Dallow?"

"It's her place; she'll put me in," Nick said.

"Baleful woman! But I'll pull you out!"

X.

FOR SEVERAL DAYS Peter Sherringham had business in hand which left him neither time nor freedom of mind to occupy himself actively with the ladies of the Hôtel de la Garonne. There were moments when they brushed across his memory, but their passage was rapid and not lighted up with any particular complacency of attention; for he shrank considerably from bringing it to the proof—the question of whether Miriam would be an interest or only a bore. She had left him, after their second meeting, with a quickened expectation, but in the course of a few hours that flame had burned dim. Like many other men Sherringham was a mixture of impulse and reflection; but he was peculiar in this, that thinking things over almost always made him think less well of them. He found illusions necessary, so that in order to keep an adequate number going he often earnestly forbade himself that exercise. Mrs. Rooth and her daughter were there and could certainly be trusted to make themselves felt. He was conscious of their anxiety, their calculations, as of a kind of oppression; he knew that, whatever results might ensue, he should have to do something positive for them. An idea of tenacity, of worrying feminine duration, associated itself with their presence; he would have assented with a silent nod to the proposition (enunciated by Gabriel Nash) that he was saddled with them. Remedies hovered before him, but they figured also at the same time as complications; ranging vaguely from the expenditure of money to the discovery that he was in love. This latter accident would be particularly tedious; he had a full perception of the arts by which the girl's mother might succeed in making it so. It would not be a compensation for trouble, but a trouble which in itself would require compensation. Would that balm spring from the spectacle of the young lady's genius? The genius would have to be very great to justify a rising young diplomatist in making a fool of himself.

With the excuse of pressing work he put off his young pupil from day to day, and from day to day he expected to hear her knock at his door. It would be time enough when they came after him; and he was unable to see how, after all, he could serve them even then. He had proposed impetuously a course of theatres; but that would be a considerable personal effort, now that the summer was about to begin, with bad air, stale pieces, tired actors. When, however, more than a week had elapsed without a reminder of his neglected promise, it came over him that he must himself in honour give a sign. There was a delicacy in such discretion—he was touched by being let alone. The flurry of work at the Embassy was over, and he had time to ask himself what, in especial, he should do. He wished to have something definite to suggest before communicating with the Hôtel de la Garonne.

As a consequence of this speculation he went back to Madame Carré, to ask her to reconsider her unfavourable judgment and give the young English lady—to oblige him—a dozen lessons of the sort that she knew how to give. He was aware that this request scarcely stood on its feet; for in the first place Madame Carré never reconsidered, when once she had got her impression, and in the second she never wasted herself on subjects whom nature had not formed to do her honour. He knew that his asking her to strain a point to please him would give her a false idea (for that matter, she had it already) of his relations, actual or prospective, with the girl; but he reflected that he needn't care for that, as Miriam herself probably wouldn't care. What he had mainly in mind was to say to the old actress that she had been mistaken—the *jeune Anglaise* was not such a duffer. This would take some courage, but it would also add to the amusement of his visit.

He found her at home, but as soon as he had expressed the conviction I have mentioned she exclaimed: "Oh, your *jeune Anglaise*, I know a great deal more about her than you! She has been back to see me twice; she doesn't go the longest way round. She charges me like a grenadier, and she asks me to give her—guess a little what!—private recitations, all to herself. If she doesn't succeed it won't be for want of knowing how to thump at doors. The other day, when I came in, she was waiting for me; she had been there for an hour. My private recitations—have you an idea what people pay for them?"

"Between artists, you know, there are easier conditions," Sherringham laughed.

"How do I know if she's an artist? She won't open her mouth to me; what she wants is to make me say things to her. She does make me—I don't know how—and she sits there gaping at me with her big eyes. They look like open pockets!"

"I dare say she'll profit by it," said Sherringham.

"I dare say *you* will! Her face is stupid while she watches me, and when she has tired me out she simply walks away. However, as she comes back—" Madame Carré paused a moment, listened, and then exclaimed: "Didn't I tell you?"

Sherringham heard a parley of voices in the little antechamber, and the next moment the door was pushed open and Miriam Rooth bounded into the room. She was flushed and breathless, without a smile, very direct.

"Will you hear me to-day? I know four things," she immediately began. Then, perceiving Sherringham, she added in the same brisk, earnest tone, as if the matter were of the highest importance: "Oh, how d'ye do? I'm very glad you are here." She said nothing else to him than this, appealed to him in no way, made no allusion to his having neglected her, but addressed herself entirely to Madame Carré, as if he had not been there; making no excuses and using no flattery; taking rather a tone of equal authority, as if she considered that the celebrated artist had a sacred duty toward her. This was another variation, Sherringham thought; it differed from each of the attitudes in which he had previously seen her. It came over him suddenly that so far from there being any question of her having the histrionic nature, she simply had it in such perfection that she was always acting; that her existence was a series of parts assumed for the moment, each changed for the next, before the perpetual mirror of some curiosity or admiration or wonder—some spectatorship that she perceived or imagined in the people about her. Interested as he had ever been in the profession of which she was potentially an ornament, this idea startled him by its novelty and even lent, on the spot, a formidable, a really appalling character to Miriam

Rooth. It struck him abruptly that a woman whose only being was to "make believe," to make believe that she had any
and every being that you liked, that would serve a purpose,
produce a certain effect, and whose identity resided in the
continuity of her personations, so that she had no moral privacy, as he phrased it to himself, but lived in a high wind of
exhibition, of figuration—such a woman was a kind of monster, in whom of necessity there would be nothing to like,
because there would be nothing to take hold of. He felt for a
moment that he had been very simple not before to have
achieved that analysis of the actress. The girl's very face made
it vivid to him now—the discovery that she positively had no
countenance of her own, but only the countenance of the occasion, a sequence, a variety (capable possibly of becoming
immense), of representative movements. She was always trying them, practising them for her amusement or profit, jumping from one to the other and extending her range; and this
would doubtless be her occupation more and more as she acquired ease and confidence. The expression that came nearest
to belonging to her, as it were, was the one that came nearest
to being a blank—an air of inanity when she forgot herself,
watching something. Then her eye was heavy and her mouth
rather common; though it was perhaps just at such a moment
that the fine line of her head told most. She had looked
slightly *bête* even when Sherringham, on their first meeting at
Madame Carré's, said to Nick Dormer that she was the image of the Tragic Muse.

Now, at any rate, he had the apprehension that she might
do what she liked with her face. It was an elastic substance, an
element of gutta-percha, like the flexibility of the gymnast, the
lady who, at a music-hall, is shot from the mouth of a can-
non. He coloured a little at this quickened view of the actress;
he had always looked more poetically, somehow, at that
priestess of art. But what was she, the priestess, when one
came to think of it, but a female gymnast, a mountebank at
higher wages? She didn't literally hang by her heels from a
trapeze, holding a fat man in her teeth, but she made the
same use of her tongue, of her eyes, of the imitative trick, that
her muscular sister made of leg and jaw. It was an odd circumstance that Miriam Rooth's face seemed to him to-day a

finer instrument than old Madame Carré's. It was doubtless that the girl's was fresh and strong, with a future in it, while poor Madame Carré's was worn and weary, with only a past.

The old woman said something, half in jest, half in real resentment, about the brutality of youth, as Miriam went to a mirror and quickly took off her hat, patting and arranging her hair as a preliminary to making herself heard. Sherringham saw with surprise and amusement that the clever French-woman, who had in her long life exhausted every adroitness, was in a manner helpless, condemned, both protesting and consenting. Miriam had taken but a few days and a couple of visits to become a successful force; she had imposed herself, and Madame Carré, while she laughed (yet looked terrible too, with artifices of eye and gesture), was reduced to the last line of defence—that of declaring her coarse and clumsy, say-ing she might knock her down, but that proved nothing. She spoke jestingly enough not to offend Miriam, but her manner betrayed the irritation of an intelligent woman who, at an advanced age, found herself for the first time failing to under-stand. What she didn't understand was the kind of social product that had been presented to her by Gabriel Nash; and this suggested to Sherringham that the *jeune Anglaise* was perhaps indeed rare, a new type, as Madame Carré must have seen innumerable varieties. He guessed that the girl was per-fectly prepared to be abused and that her indifference to what might be thought of her discretion was a proof of life, health and spirit, the insolence of conscious power.

When she had given herself a touch at the glass she turned round, with a rapid *"Ecoutez maintenant!"* and stood leaning a moment, slightly lowered and inclined backward, with her hands behind her and supporting her, on the table in front of the mirror. She waited an instant, turning her eyes from one of her companions to the other as if she were taking posses-sion of them (an eminently conscious, intentional proceeding, which made Sherringham ask himself what had become of her former terror and whether that and her tears had all been a comedy): after which, abruptly straightening herself, she be-gan to repeat a short French poem, a composition modern and delicate, one of the things she had induced Madame Carré to say over to her. She had learned it, practised it, rehearsed it to her mother, and now she had been childishly eager to show what she could do with it. What she mainly did was to reproduce with a crude fidelity, but with extraordinary memory, the intonations, the personal quavers and cadences of her model.

"How bad you make me seem to myself, and if I were you how much better I should say it!" was Madame Carré's first criticism.

Miriam allowed her little time to develop this idea, for she broke out, at the shortest intervals, with the five other specimens of verse to which the old actress had handed her the key. They were all delicate lyrics, of tender or pathetic intention, by contemporary poets—all things demanding perfect taste and art, a mastery of tone, of insinuation, in the interpreter. Miriam had gobbled them up, and she gave them forth in the same way as the first, with close, rude, audacious mimicry. There was a moment when Sherringham was afraid Madame Carré would think she was making fun of her manner, her celebrated simpers and grimaces, so extravagant did the girl's performance cause these refinements to appear.

When she had finished, the old woman said: "Should you like now to hear how *you* do it?" and, without waiting for an answer, phrased and trilled the last of the pieces, from beginning to end, exactly as Miriam had done, making this imitation of an imitation the drollest thing conceivable. If she had been annoyed it was a perfect revenge. Miriam had dropped on a sofa, exhausted, and she stared at first, looking flushed and wild; then she gave way to merriment, laughing with a high sense of comedy. She said afterwards, to defend herself, that the verses in question, and indeed all those she had recited, were of the most difficult sort: you had to do them; they didn't do themselves—they were things in which the *gros moyens* were of no avail. "Ah, my poor child, your means are all gros moyens; you appear to have no others," Madame Carré replied. "You do what you can, but there are people like that; it's the way they are made. They can never come nearer to the delicate; shades don't exist for them, they don't see certain differences. It was to show you a difference that I repeated that thing as you repeat it, as you represent my doing it. If you are struck with the little the two ways have in common, so much the better. But you seem to me to coarsen everything you touch."

Sherringham thought this judgment harsh to cruelty, and perceived that Miss Rooth had the power to set the teeth of her instructress on edge. She acted on her nerves; she was made of a thick, rough substance which the old woman was not accustomed to manipulate. This exasperation, however, was a kind of flattery; it was neither indifference nor simple contempt; it acknowledged a mystifying reality in the girl and even a degree of importance. Miriam remarked, serenely enough, that the things she wanted most to do were just those that were not for the gros moyens, the vulgar obvious dodges, the starts and shouts that any one could think of and that the *gros public* liked. She wanted to do what was most difficult and to plunge into it from the first; and she explained, as if it were a discovery of her own, that there were two kinds of scenes and speeches: those which acted themselves, of which the treatment was plain, the only way, so that you had just to take it; and those which were open to interpretation, with which you had to fight every step, rendering, arranging, doing it according to your idea. Some of the most effective things, and the most celebrated and admired, like the frenzy of Juliet with her potion, were of the former sort; but it was the others she liked best.

Madame Carré received this revelation good-naturedly enough, considering its want of freshness, and only laughed at the young lady for looking so nobly patronizing while she gave it. It was clear that her laughter was partly dedicated to the good faith with which Miriam described herself as preponderantly interested in the subtler problems of her art. Sherringham was charmed with the girl's pluck—if it was pluck and not mere density—the brightness with which she submitted, for a purpose, to the old woman's rough usage. He wanted to take her away, to give her a friendly caution, to advise her not to become a bore, not to expose herself. But she held up her beautiful head in a way that showed she didn't care at present how she exposed herself, and that (it was half coarseness—Madame Carré was so far right—and half fortitude) she had no intention of coming away so long as there was anything to be picked up. She sat, and still she sat, challenging her hostess with every sort of question—some reasonable, some ingenious, some strangely futile and some highly indiscreet; but all with the effect that, contrary to Sherringham's expectation, Madame Carré warmed to the work of answering and explaining, became interested, was content to keep her and to talk. Yet she took her ease; she relieved herself, with the rare cynicism of the artist, all the crudity, the irony and intensity of a discussion of esoteric things, of personal mysteries, of methods and secrets. It was the oddest hour Sherringham had ever spent, even in the course of investigation which had often led him into the *cuisine*, as the French called it, the distillery or back-shop of the admired profession. He got up several times to come away; then he remained, partly in order not to leave Miriam alone with her terrible initiatress, partly because he was both amused and edified, and partly because Madame Carré held him by the appeal of her sharp, confidential old eyes, addressing her talk to him, with Miriam as a subject, a vile illustration. She undressed this young lady, as it were, from head to foot, turned her inside out, weighed and measured and sounded her: it was all, for Sherringham, a new revelation of the point to which, in her profession and nation, a ferocious analysis had been carried, with an intelligence of the business and a special vocabulary. What struck him above all was the way she knew her reasons and everything was sharp and clear in her mind and lay under her hand. If she had rare perceptions she had traced them to their source; she could give an account of what she did; she knew perfectly why; she could explain it, defend it, amplify it, fight for it: and all this was an intellectual joy to her, allowing her a chance to abound and insist and be clever. There was a kind of cruelty, or at least of hardness in it all, to Sherringham's English sense, that sense which can never really reconcile itself to the question of execution and has extraneous sentiments to placate with compromises and superficialities, frivolities that have often a pleasant moral fragrance. In theory there was nothing that he valued more than just such a logical passion as Madame Carré's; but in fact, when he found himself in close quarters with it, it was apt to seem to him an ado about nothing.

If the old woman was hard, it was not that many of her present conclusions, as regards Miriam, were not indulgent, but that she had a vision of the great manner, of right and wrong, of the just and the false, so high and religious that the individual was nothing before it—a prompt and easy sacrifice. It made Sherringham uncomfortable, as he had been made uncomfortable by certain *feuilletons*, reviews of the theatres in the Paris newspapers, which he was committed to thinking important, but of which, when they were very good, he was rather ashamed. When they were very good, that is when they were very thorough, they were very personal, as was inevitable in dealing with the most personal of the arts: they went into details; they put the dots on the *i*'s; they discussed impartially the qualities of appearance, the physical gifts of the actor or actress, finding them in some cases reprehensibly inadequate. Sherringham could not rid himself of a prejudice against these pronouncements; in the case of the actresses especially they appeared to him brutal and indelicate—unmanly as coming from a critic sitting smoking in his chair. At the same time he was aware of the dilemma (he hated it; it made him blush still more) in which his objection lodged him. If one was right in liking the actor's art one ought to have been interested in every candid criticism of it, which, given the peculiar conditions, would be legitimate in proportion as it should be minute. If the criticism that recognized frankly these conditions seemed an inferior or an offensive thing, then what was to be said for the art itself? What an implication, if the criticism was tolerable only so long as it was worthless—so long as it remained vague and timid! This was a knot which Sherringham had never straightened out: he contented himself with saying that there was no reason a theatrical critic shouldn't be a gentleman, at the same time that he often remarked that it was an odious trade, which no gentleman could possibly follow. The best of the fraternity, so conspicuous in Paris, were those who didn't follow it—those who, while pretending to write about the stage, wrote about everything else.

It was as if Madame Carré, in pursuance of her inflamed sense that the art was everything and the individual nothing, save as he happened to serve it, had said: "Well, if she *will* have it she shall; she shall know what she is in for, what I went through, battered and broken in as we all have been— all who are worthy, who have had the honour. She shall know the real point of view." It was as if she were still haunted with Mrs. Rooth's nonsense, her hypocrisy, her scruples—something she felt a need to belabour, to trample on. Miriam took it all as a bath, a baptism, with passive exhilaration and gleeful shivers; staring, wondering, sometimes blushing and failing to follow, but not shrinking nor wounded; laughing, when it was necessary, at her own expense, and feeling evidently that this at last was the air of the profession, an initiation which nothing could undo. Sherringham said to her that he would see her home—that he wanted to talk to her and she must walk away with him. "And it's understood, then, she may come back," he added to Madame Carré. "It's my affair, of course. You'll take an interest in her for a month or two; she will sit at your feet."

"Oh, I'll knock her about; she seems stout enough!" said the old actress.

XI.

WHEN SHE had descended into the street with Sherringham Miriam informed him that she was thirsty, dying to drink something: upon which he asked her if she would have any objection to going with him to a café.

"Objection? I have spent my life in cafés!" she exclaimed. "They are warm in winter and they are full of gaslight. Mamma and I have sat in them for hours, many a time, with a *consommation* of three sous, to save fire and candles at home. We have lived in places we couldn't sit in, if you want to know—where there was only really room if we were in bed. Mamma's money is sent out from England, and sometimes it didn't come. Once it didn't come for months—for months and months. I don't know how we lived. There wasn't any to come; there wasn't any to get home. That isn't amusing when you're away, in a foreign town, without any friends. Mamma used to borrow, but people wouldn't always lend. You needn't be afraid—she won't borrow from you. We are rather better now. Something has been done in England; I don't understand what. It's only fivepence a year, but it has been settled; it comes regularly; it used to come only when we had written and begged and waited. But it made no difference; mamma was always up to her ears in books. They served her for food and drink. When she had nothing to eat she began a novel in ten volumes—the old-fashioned ones; they lasted longest. She knows every *cabinet de lecture* in every town; the little cheap, shabby ones, I mean, in the back streets, where they have odd volumes and only ask a sou, and the books are so old that they smell bad. She takes them to the cafés—the little cheap, shabby cafés, too—and she reads there all the evening. That's very well for her, but it doesn't feed me. I don't like a diet of dirty old novels. I sit there beside her, with nothing to do, not even a stocking to mend; she doesn't think that's *comme il faut*. I don't know what the people take me for. However, we have never been spoken to: any one can see mamma's a lady. As for me, I dare say I might be anything. If you're going to be an actress you must get used to being looked at. There were people in England who used to ask us

to stay; some of them were our cousins—or mamma says
they were. I have never been very clear about our cousins, and
I don't think they were at all clear about us. Some of them are
dead; the others don't ask us any more. You should hear
mamma on the subject of our visits in England. It's very convenient when your cousins are dead, because that explains everything. Mamma has delightful phrases: 'My family is almost
extinct.' Then your family may have been anything you like.
Ours, of course, was magnificent. We did stay in a place once
where there was a deer-park, and also private theatricals. I
played in them; I was only fifteen years old, but I was very
big and I thought I was in heaven. I will go anywhere you
like; you needn't be afraid; we have been in places! I have
learned a great deal that way; sitting beside mamma and
watching people, their faces, their types, their movements.
There's a great deal goes on in cafés: people come to them to
talk things over, their private affairs, their complications; they
have important meetings. Oh, I've observed scenes, between
men and women—very quiet, terribly quiet, but tragic! Once
I saw a woman do something that I'm going to do some day,
when I'm great—if I can get the situation. I'll tell you what it
is some day; I'll do it for you. Oh, it *is* the book of life!"

So Miriam discoursed, familiarly, disconnectedly, as the
pair went their way down the Rue de Constantinople; and
she continued to abound in anecdote and remark after they
were seated face to face at a little marble table in an establishment which Sherringham selected carefully and he had caused
her, at her request, to be accommodated with *sirop d'orgeat*. "I
know what it will come to: Madame Carré will want to keep
me." This was one of the announcements she presently made.

"To keep you?"

"For the French stage. She won't want to let you have me."
She said things of that kind, astounding in self-complacency,
the assumption of quick success. She was in earnest, evidently
prepared to work, but her imagination flew over preliminaries
and probations, took no account of the steps in the process,
especially the first tiresome ones, the test of patience. Sherringham had done nothing for her as yet, given no substantial
pledge of interest; yet she was already talking as if his protection were assured and jealous. Certainly, however, she seemed

to belong to him very much indeed, as she sat facing him in
the Paris café, in her youth, her beauty and her talkative confidence. This degree of possession was highly agreeable to
him, and he asked nothing more than to make it last and go
further. The impulse to draw her out was irresistible, to encourage her to show herself to the end; for if he was really
destined to take her career in hand he counted on some pleasant equivalent—such, for instance, as that she should at least
amuse him.

"It's very singular; I know nothing like it," he said—"your
equal mastery of two languages."

"Say of half a dozen," Miriam smiled.

"Oh, I don't believe in the others to the same degree. I
don't imagine that, with all deference to your undeniable
facility, you would be judged fit to address a German or
an Italian audience in their own tongue. But you might a
French, perfectly, and they are the most particular of all; for
their idiom is supersensitive and they are incapable of endur-
ing the *baragouinage* of foreigners, to which we listen with
such complacency. In fact, your French is better than your
English—it's more conventional; there are little queernesses
and impurities in your English, as if you had lived abroad too
much. Ah, you must work that."

"I'll work it with you. I like the way you speak."

"You must speak beautifully; you must do something for
the standard."

"For the standard?"

"There isn't any, after all; it has gone to the dogs."

"Oh, I'll bring it back. I know what you mean."

"No one knows, no one cares; the sense is gone—it isn't in
the public," Sherringham continued, ventilating a grievance
he was rarely able to forget, the vision of which now suddenly
made a mission full of sanctity for Miriam Rooth. "Purity of
speech, on our stage, doesn't exist. Every one speaks as he
likes, and audiences never notice; it's the last thing they think
of. The place is given up to abominable dialects and individual tricks, any vulgarity flourishes, and on the top of it all the
Americans, with every conceivable crudity, come in to make
confusion worse confounded. And when one laments it people stare; they don't know what one means."

"Do you mean the grand manner, certain pompous pro-
nunciations, the style of the Kembles?"

"I mean any style that *is* a style, that is a system, an art, that
contributes a positive beauty to utterance. When I pay ten
shillings to hear you speak, I want you to know how, *que
diable!* Say that to people and they are mostly lost in stupor;
only a few, the very intelligent ones, exclaim: 'Then do you
want actors to be affected?'"

"And *do* you?" asked Miriam, full of interest.

"My poor child, what else, under the sun, should they be?
Isn't their whole art the affectation *par excellence*? The public
won't stand that to-day, so one hears it said. If that be true, it
simply means that the theatre, as I care for it, that is as a
personal art, is at an end."

"Never, never, never!" the girl cried, in a voice that made a
dozen people look round.

"I sometimes think it—that the personal art *is* at an end,
and that henceforth we shall have only the arts—capable, no
doubt, of immense development in their way (indeed they
have already reached it)—of the stage-carpenter and the cos-
tumer. In London the drama is already smothered in scenery;
the interpretation scrambles off as it can. To get the old personal impression, which used to be everything, you must go
to the poor countries, and most of all to Italy."

"Oh, I've had it; it's very personal!" said Miriam, knowingly.

"You've seen the nudity of the stage, the poor painted, tattered screen behind, and in the empty space the histrionic
figure, doing everything it knows how, in complete possession. The personality isn't our English personality, and it may
not always carry us with it; but the direction is right, and it
has the superiority that it's a human exhibition, not a mechanical one."

"I can act just like an Italian," said Miriam, eagerly.

"I would rather you acted like an Englishwoman, if an Englishwoman would only act."

"Oh, I'll show you!"

"But you're not English," said Sherringham, sociably, with
his arms on the table.

"I beg your pardon; you should hear mamma about our 'race.'"

"You're a Jewess—I'm sure of that," Sherringham went on.

She jumped at this, as he was destined to see, later, that she would jump at anything that would make her more interesting or striking; even at things which, grotesquely, contradicted or excluded each other. "That's always possible, if one's clever. I'm very willing, because I want to be the English Rachel."

"Then you must leave Madame Carré, as soon as you have got from her what she can give."

"Oh, you needn't fear; you sha'n't lose me," the girl replied, with gross, charming fatuity. "My name is Jewish," she went on, "but it was that of my grandmother, my father's mother. She was a baroness, in Germany. That is she was the daughter of a baron."

Sherringham accepted this statement with reservations, but he replied: "Put all that together, and it makes you very sufficiently of Rachel's tribe."

"I don't care, if I'm of her tribe artistically. I'm of the family of the artists; *je me fiche* of any other! I'm in the same style as that woman; I know it."

"You speak as if you had seen her," said Sherringham, amused at the way she talked of "that woman."

"Oh, I know all about her; I know all about all the great actors. But that won't prevent me from speaking divine English."

"You must learn lots of verse; you must repeat it to me," Sherringham went on. "You must break yourself in till you can say anything. You must learn passages of Milton, passages of Wordsworth."

"Did *they* write plays?"

"Oh, it isn't only a matter of plays! You can't speak a part properly till you can speak everything else, anything that comes up, especially in proportion as it's difficult. That gives you authority."

"Oh, yes, I'm going in for authority. There's more chance in English," the girl added, in the next breath. "There are not so many others—the terrible competition. There are so many here—not that I'm afraid," she chattered on. "But we've got America, and they haven't. America's a great place."

"You talk like a theatrical agent. They're lucky not to have it as we have it. Some of them do go, and it ruins them."

"Why, it fills their pockets!" Miriam cried.

"Yes, but see what they pay. It's the death of an actor to play to big populations that don't understand his language. It's nothing then but the *gros moyens*; all his delicacy perishes. However, they'll understand *you*."

"Perhaps I shall be too affected," said Miriam.

"You won't be more so than Garrick or Mrs. Siddons or John Kemble or Edmund Kean. They understood Edmund Kean. All reflection is affectation, and all acting is reflection."

"I don't know; mine is instinct," Miriam replied.

"My dear young lady, you talk of 'yours'; but don't be offended if I tell you that yours doesn't exist. Some day it will, if it comes off. Madame Carré's does, because she has reflected. The talent, the desire, the energy are an instinct; but by the time these things become a performance they are an instinct put in its place."

"Madame Carré is very philosophic. I shall never be like her."

"Of course you won't; you'll be original. But you'll have your own ideas."

"I dare say I shall have a good many of yours," said Miriam, smiling across the table.

They sat a moment looking at each other.

"Don't go in for coquetry; it's a waste of time."

"Well, that's civil!" the girl cried.

"Oh, I don't mean for me; I mean for yourself. I want you to be so concentrated. I am bound to give you good advice. You don't strike me as flirtatious and that sort of thing, and that's in your favour."

"In my favour!"

"It does save time."

"Perhaps it saves too much. Don't you think the artist ought to have passions?"

Sherringham hesitated a moment: he thought an examination of this question premature. "Flirtations are not passions," he replied. "No, you are simple—at least I suspect you are; for of course, with a woman, one would be clever to know." She asked why he pronounced her simple, but he judged it best, and more consonant with fair play, to defer even a treatment of this branch of the question; so that, to change the subject, he said: "Be sure you don't betray me to your friend Mr. Nash."

"Betray you? Do you mean about your recommending affectation?"

"Dear me, no; he recommends it himself. That is he practises it, and on a scale!"

"But he makes one hate it."

"He proves what I mean," said Sherringham: "that the great comedian is the one who raises it to a science. If we paid ten shillings to listen to Mr. Nash, we should think him very fine. But we want to know what it's supposed to be."

"It's too odious, the way he talks about *us*!" Miriam cried, assentingly.

"About 'us'?"

"Us poor actors."

"It's the competition he dislikes," said Sherringham, laughing.

"However, he is very good-natured; he lent mamma thirty pounds," the girl added, honestly. Sherringham, at this information, was not able to repress a certain small twinge which his companion perceived and of which she appeared to mistake the meaning. "Of course he'll get it back," she went on, while Sherringham looked at her in silence for a minute. Fortune had not supplied him profusely with money, but his emotion was not caused by the apprehension that he too would probably have to put his hand in his pocket for Mrs. Rooth. It was simply the instinctive recoil of a fastidious nature from the idea of familiar intimacy with people who lived from hand to mouth, and a sense that that intimacy would have to be defined if it was to go much further. He would wish to know what it was supposed to be, like Gabriel Nash's histrionics. After a moment Miriam mistook his thought still more completely, and in doing so gave him a flash of foreknowledge of the way it was in her to strike from time to time a note exasperatingly, almost consciously vulgar, which one would hate for the reason, among others, that by that time one would be in love with her. "Well, then, he won't—if you don't believe it!" she exclaimed, with a laugh. He was saying to himself that the only possible form was that they should borrow only from him. "You're a funny man: I make you blush," Miriam persisted.

"I must reply with the *tu quoque*, though I have not that effect on you."

"I don't understand," said the girl.

"You're an extraordinary young lady."

"You mean I'm horrid. Well, I dare say I am. But I'm better when you know me."

Sherringham made no direct rejoinder to this, but after a moment he said: "Your mother must repay that money. I'll give it to her."

"You had better give it to him!" cried Miriam. "If once *we* have it—" She interrupted herself, and with another and a softer tone, one of her professional transitions, she remarked: "I suppose you have never known any one that's poor."

"I'm poor myself. That is I'm very far from rich. But why receive favours—?" And here he, in turn, checked himself, with the sense that he was indeed taking a great deal on his back if he pretended already (he had not seen the pair three times) to regulate their intercourse with the rest of the world. But Miriam instantly carried out his thought and more than his thought.

"Favours from Mr. Nash? Oh, he doesn't count!"

The way she dropped these words (they would have been admirable on the stage) made him laugh and say immediately: "What I meant just now was that you are not to tell him, after all my swagger, that I consider that you and I are really required to save our theatre."

"Oh, if we can save it, he shall know it!" Then Miriam added that she must positively get home; her mother would be in a state: she had really scarcely ever been out alone. He mightn't think it, but so it was. Her mother's ideas, those awfully proper ones, were not all talk. She *did* keep her! Sherringham accepted this—he had an adequate, and indeed an analytic vision of Mrs. Rooth's conservatism; but he observed at the same time that his companion made no motion to rise. He made none, either; he only said—

"We are very frivolous, the way we chatter. What you want to do, to get your foot in the stirrup, is supremely difficult. There is everything to overcome. You have neither an engagement nor the prospect of an engagement."

"Oh, you'll get me one!" Miriam's manner expressed that this was so certain that it was not worth dilating upon; so instead of dilating she inquired abruptly, a second time: "Why do you think I'm so simple?"

"I don't then. Didn't I tell you just now that you were extraordinary? That's the term moreover that you applied to yourself when you came to see me—when you said a girl had to be, to wish to go on the stage. It remains the right one, and your simplicity doesn't mitigate it. What's rare in you is that you have—as I suspect, at least—no nature of your own." Miriam listened to this as if she were preparing to argue with it or not, only as it should strike her as being a pleasing picture; but as yet, naturally, she failed to understand. "You are always playing something; there are no intervals. It's the absence of intervals, of a *fond* or background, that I don't comprehend. You're an embroidery without a canvas."

"Yes, perhaps," the girl replied, with her head on one side, as if she were looking at the pattern. "But I'm very honest."

"You can't be everything, a consummate actress and a flower of the field. You've got to choose."

She looked at him a moment. "I'm glad you think I'm so wonderful."

"Your feigning may be honest, in the sense that your only feeling *is* your feigned one," Sherringham went on. "That's what I mean by the absence of a ground or of intervals. It's a kind of thing that's a labyrinth!"

"I know what I am," said Miriam, sententiously.

But her companion continued, following his own train: "Were you really so frightened, the first day you went to Madame Carré's?"

She stared a moment, and then with a flush, throwing back her head: "Do you think I was pretending?"

"I think you always are. However, your vanity (if you had any!) would be natural."

"I have plenty of that—I am not ashamed to own it."

"You would be capable of pretending that you have. But excuse the audacity and the crudity of my speculations—it only proves my interest. What is it that you know you are?"

"Why, an artist. Isn't that a canvas?"

"Yes, an intellectual one, but not a moral."

"Oh yes, it is, too. And I'm a good girl: won't that do?"

"It remains to be seen," Sherringham laughed. "A creature who is *all* an artist—I am curious to see that."

"Surely it has been seen, in lots of painters, lots of musicians."

"Yes, but those arts are not personal, like yours. I mean not so much so. There's something left for—what shall I call it?—for character."

Miriam stared again, with her tragic light. "And do you think I've got no character?" As he hesitated she pushed back her chair, rising rapidly.

He looked up at her an instant—she seemed so "plastic"; and then, rising too, he answered: "Delightful being, you've got a hundred!"

XII.

THE SUMMER arrived and the dense air of the Paris theatres became in fact a still more complicated mixture; yet the occasions were not few on which Peter Sherringham, having placed a box, near the stage (most often a stuffy, dusky *baignoire*), at the disposal of Mrs. Rooth and her daughter, found time to look in, as he said, to spend a part of the evening with them and point the moral of the performance. The pieces, the successes of the winter, had entered the automatic phase: they went on by the force of the impetus acquired, deriving little fresh life from the interpretation, and in ordinary conditions their strong points, as rendered by the actors, would have been as wearisome to Sherringham as an importunate repetition of a good story. But it was not long before he became aware that the conditions could not be regarded as ordinary. There was a new infusion in his consciousness—an element in his life which altered the relations of things. He was not easy till he had found the right name for it—a name the more satisfactory that it was simple, comprehensive and plausible. A new "distraction," in the French sense, was what he flattered himself he had discovered; he could recognize that as freely as possible without being obliged to classify the agreeable resource as a new entanglement. He was neither too much nor too little diverted; he had all his usual attention to give to his work: he had only an employment for his odd hours, which, without being imperative, had over various others the advantage of a certain continuity.

And yet, I hasten to add, he was not so well pleased with it but that, among his friends, he maintained for the present a considerable reserve in regard to it. He had no irresistible impulse to tell people that he had disinterred a strange, handsome girl whom he was bringing up for the theatre. She had been seen by several of his associates at his rooms, but she was not soon to be seen there again. Sherringham's reserve might by the ill-natured have been termed dissimulation, inasmuch as when asked by the ladies of the Embassy what had become of the young person who amused them that day so cleverly, he gave it out that her whereabouts was uncertain and her destiny probably obscure; he let it be supposed in a word that his benevolence had scarcely survived an accidental, charitable occasion. As he went about his customary business, and perhaps even put a little more conscience into the transaction of it, there was nothing to suggest to his companions that he was engaged in a private speculation of a singular kind. It was perhaps his weakness that he carried the apprehension of ridicule too far; but his excuse may be said to be that he held it unpardonable for a man publicly enrolled in the service of his country to be ridiculous. It was of course not out of all order that such functionaries, their private situation permitting, should enjoy a personal acquaintance with stars of the dramatic, the lyric or even the choregraphic stage: high diplomatists had indeed not rarely and not invisibly cultivated this privilege without its proving the sepulchre of their reputation. That a gentleman who was not a fool should consent a little to become one for the sake of a celebrated actress or singer—*cela s'était vu*, though it was not perhaps to be recommended. It was not a tendency that was fostered at headquarters, where even the most rising young men were not encouraged to believe they could never fall. Still, it might pass if it were kept in its place; and there were ancient worthies yet in the profession (not those, however, whom the tradition had helped to go furthest) who held that something of the sort was a graceful ornament of the diplomatic character. Sherringham was aware he was very "rising"; but Miriam Rooth was not yet a celebrated actress. She was only a youthful artist, in conscientious process of formation, encumbered with a mother still more conscientious than herself. She was a young English lady, very earnest about artistic, about remunerative problems. He had accepted the position of a formative influence, and that was precisely what might provoke derision. He was a ministering angel—his patience and good-nature really entitled him to the epithet, and his rewards would doubtless some day define themselves; but meanwhile other promotions were in contingent prospect, for the failure of which these would not, even in their abundance, be a compensation. He kept an unembarrassed eye upon Downing Street; and while it may frankly be said for him that he was neither a pedant nor a prig, he remembered that the last impression he ought to wish to produce there was that of volatility.

He felt not particularly volatile, however, when he sat behind Miriam at the play and looked over her shoulder at the stage: her observation being so keen and her comments so unexpected in their vivacity that his curiosity was refreshed and his attention stretched beyond its wont. If the spectacle before the footlights had now lost much of its annual brilliancy, the fashion in which Miriam followed it came near being spectacle enough. Moreover, in most cases the attendance of the little party was at the Théâtre Français; and it has been sufficiently indicated that Sherringham, though the child of a sceptical age and the votary of a cynical science, was still candid enough to take the serious, the religious view of that establishment—the view of M. Sarcey and of the unregenerate provincial mind. "In the trade that I follow we see things too much in the hard light of reason, of calculation," he once remarked to his young *protégée*; "but it's good for the mind to keep up a superstition or two: it leaves a margin, like having a second horse to your brougham for night-work. The arts, the amusements, the æsthetic part of life are nightwork, if I may say so without suggesting the nefarious. At any rate you want your second horse—your superstition that stays at home when the sun is high—to go your rounds with. The Théâtre Français is my second horse."

Miriam's appetite for this pleasure showed him vividly enough how rarely, in the past, it had been within her reach; and she pleased him at first by liking everything, seeing almost no differences and taking her deep draught undiluted. She leaned on the edge of the box with bright voracity, tasting to the core yet relishing the surface; watching each movement of each actor, attending to the way each thing was said or done as if it were the most important thing, and emitting from time to time applausive or restrictive sounds. It was a very pretty exhibition of enthusiasm, if enthusiasm be ever critical. Sherringham had his wonder about it, as it was a part of the attraction exerted by this young lady that she caused him to have his wonder about everything she did. Was it in fact an exhibition, a line taken for effect, so that at the comedy her own comedy was the most successful of all? That question danced attendance on the liberal intercourse of these young people and fortunately, as yet, did little to embitter Sherringham's share of it. His general sense that she was personating had its especial moments of suspense and perplexity and added variety and even occasionally a degree of excitement to their conversation. At the theatre, for the most part, she was really flushed with eagerness; and with the spectators who turned an admiring eye into the dim compartment of which she pervaded the front, she might have passed for a romantic, or at any rate an insatiable young woman from the country.

Mrs. Rooth took a more placid view, but attended immensely to the story, in respect to which she manifested a patient good faith which had its surprises and its comicalities for Sherringham. She found no play too tedious, no entr'acte too long, no baignoire too hot, no tissue of incidents too complicated, no situation too unnatural and no sentiments too sublime. She gave Sherringham the measure of her power to sit and sit—an accomplishment to which she owed, in the struggle for existence, such superiority as she might be said to have achieved. She could outsit every one, everything else; looking as if she had acquired the practice in repeated years of small frugality combined with large leisure—periods when she had nothing but time to spend and had learned to calculate, in any situation, how long she could stay. "Staying" was so often a saving—a saving of candles, of fire and even (for it sometimes implied a vision of light refreshment) of food. Sherringham perceived soon enough that she was complete in her way, and if he had been addicted to studying the human mixture in its different combinations he would have found in her an interesting compendium of some of the infatuations that survive a hard discipline. He made indeed without difficulty the reflection that her life might have taught her the reality of things, at the same time that he could scarcely help thinking it clever of her to have so persistently declined the lesson. She appeared to have put it by with a deprecating, ladylike smile—a plea of being too soft and bland for experience.

She took the refined, sentimental, tender view of the universe, beginning with her own history and feelings. She believed in everything high and pure, disinterested and orthodox, and even at the Hôtel de la Garonne was unconscious of the shabby or the ugly side of the world. She never despaired: otherwise what would have been the use of being a Neville-Nugent? Only not to have been one—that would have been discouraging. She delighted in novels, poems, perversions, misrepresentations and evasions, and had a capacity for smooth, superfluous falsification which made Sherringham think her sometimes an amusing and sometimes a tedious inventor. But she was not dangerous even if you believed her; she was not even a warning if you didn't. It was harsh to call her a hypocrite, because you never could have resolved her back into her character: there was no reverse to her blazonry. She built in the air and was not less amiable than she pretended: only that was a pretence too. She moved altogether in a world of genteel fable and fancy, and Sherringham had to live in it with her, for Miriam's sake, in sociable, vulgar assent, in spite of his feeling that it was rather a low neighbourhood. He was at a loss how to take what she said—she talked sweetly and discursively of so many things—until he simply perceived that he could only take it always for untrue. When Miriam laughed at her he was rather disagreeably affected: "dear mamma's fine stories" was a sufficiently cynical reference to the immemorial infirmity of a parent. But when the girl backed her up, as he phrased it to himself, he liked that even less.

Mrs. Rooth was very fond of a moral and had never lost her taste for edification. She delighted in a beautiful character and was gratified to find so many represented in the contemporary French drama. She never failed to direct Miriam's attention to them and to remind her that there is nothing in life so precious as the ideal. Sherringham noted the difference between the mother and the daughter and thought it singularly marked—the way that one took everything for the sense, or behaved as if she did, caring above all for the subject and the romance, the triumph or defeat of virtue and the moral comfort of it all, and that the other was especially hungry for the

manner and the art of it, the presentation and the vividness.
Mrs. Rooth abounded in impressive evocations, and yet he
saw no link between her facile genius and that of which Miriam gave symptoms. The poor lady never could have been
accused of successful deceit, whereas success in this line was
exactly what her clever child went in for. She made even the
true seem fictive, while Miriam's effort was to make the fictive
true. Sherringham thought it an odd, unpromising stock (that
of the Neville-Nugents) for a dramatic talent to have sprung
from, till he reflected that the evolution was after all natural:
the figurative impulse in the mother had become conscious,
and therefore higher, through finding an aim, which was
beauty, in the daughter. Likely enough the Hebraic Mr.
Rooth, with his love of old pots and Christian altar-cloths,
had supplied, in the girl's composition, the æsthetic element,
the sense of form. In their visits to the theatre there was nothing that Mrs. Rooth more insisted upon than the unprofit-
ableness of deceit, as shown by the most distinguished
authors—the folly and degradation, the corrosive effect upon
the spirit, of tortuous ways. Sherringham very soon gave up
the futile task of piecing together her incongruous references
to her early life and her family in England. He renounced
even the doctrine that there was a residuum of truth in her
claim of great relationships, for, existent or not, he cared
equally little for her ramifications. The principle of this indifference was at bottom a certain desire to disconnect Miriam;
for it was disagreeable not to be independent in dealing with
her, and he could be fully so only if *she* were.

The early weeks of that summer (they went on indeed into
August) were destined to establish themselves in his memory
as a season of pleasant things. The ambassador went away,
and Sherringham had to wait for his own holiday, which he
did, during the hot days, contentedly enough, in spacious
halls, with a dim, bird-haunted garden. The official world,
and most other worlds withdrew from Paris, and the Place de
la Concorde, a larger, whiter desert than ever, became, by a
reversal of custom, explorable with safety. The Champs Elysées were dusty and rural, with little creaking booths and exhibitions which made a noise like grasshoppers; the Arc de
Triomphe threw its cool, sharp shadow for a mile; the Palais

de l'Industrie glittered in the light of the long days; the cabmen, in their red waistcoats, dozed in their boxes; and Sherringham permitted himself a "pot" hat and rarely met a
friend. Thus was Miriam still more disconnected, and thus
was it possible to deal with her still more independently. The
theatres on the boulevard closed, for the most part, but the
great temple of the Rue de Richelieu, with an æsthetic responsibility, continued imperturbably to dispense examples of
style. Madame Carré was going to Vichy, but she had not yet
taken flight, which was a great advantage for Miriam, who
could now solicit her attention with the consciousness that
she had no engagements *en ville*.

"I make her listen to me—I make her tell me," said the
ardent girl, who was always climbing the slope of the Rue de
Constantinople, on the shady side, where in the July mornings there was a smell of violets from the moist flower-stands
of fat, white-capped *bouquetières*, in the angles of doorways.
Miriam liked the Paris of the summer mornings, the clever
freshness of all the little trades and the open-air life, the cries,
the talk from door to door, which reminded her of the south,
where, in the multiplicity of her habitations, she had lived;
and most of all the great amusement, or nearly, of her walk,
the enviable baskets of the laundress, piled up with frilled and
fluted whiteness—the certain luxury, she felt as she passed,
with quick prevision, of her own dawn of glory. The greatest
amusement perhaps was to recognize the pretty sentiment of
earliness, the particular congruity with the hour, in the studied, selected dress of the little tripping women who were taking the day, for important advantages, while it was tender. At
any rate she always brought with her from her passage
through the town good-humour enough (with the penny
bunch of violets that she stuck in the front of her dress) for
whatever awaited her at Madame Carré's. She told Sherringham that her dear mistress was terribly severe, giving her
the most difficult, the most exhausting exercises—showing a
kind of rage for breaking her in.

"So much the better," Sherringham answered; but he asked
no questions and was glad to let the preceptress and the pupil
fight it out together. He wanted, for the moment, to know as
little as possible about them: he had been overdosed with

knowledge that second day he saw them together. He would send Madame Carré her money (she was really most obliging), and in the meantime he was conscious that Miriam could take care of herself. Sometimes he remarked to her that she needn't always talk "shop" to him: there were times when he was very tired of shop—of hers. Moreover he frankly admitted that he was tired of his own, so that the restriction was not brutal. When she replied, staring: "Why, I thought you considered it as such a beautiful, interesting art!" he had no rejoinder more philosophic than "Well, I do; but there are moments when I'm sick of it, all the same." At other times he said to her: "Oh, yes, the results, the finished thing, the dish perfectly seasoned and served: not the mess of preparation —at least not always—not the experiments that spoil the material."

"I thought you thought just these questions of study, of the artistic education, as you have called it to me, so fascinating," the girl persisted. Sometimes she was very lucid.

"Well, after all I'm not an actor myself," Sherringham answered, laughing.

"You might be one if you were serious," said Miriam. To this her friend replied that Mr. Gabriel Nash ought to hear that; which made her exclaim, with a certain grimness, that she would settle *him* and his theories some day. Not to seem too inconsistent—for it was cruel to bewilder her when he had taken her up to enlighten—Sherringham repeated over that for a man like himself the interest of the whole thing depended on its being considered in a large, liberal way, with an intelligence that lifted it out of the question of the little tricks of the trade, gave it beauty and elevation. Miriam let him know that Madame Carré held that there were no *little* tricks; that everything had its importance as a means to a great end; and that if you were not willing to try to *approfondir* the reason why in a given situation you should scratch your nose with your left hand rather than with your right, you were not worthy to tread any stage that respected itself.

"That's very well; but if I must go into details read me a little Shelley," said the young man, in the spirit of a high *raffiné*.

"You are worse than Madame Carré; you don't know what

to invent: between you you'll kill me!" the girl declared. "I think there's a secret league between you to spoil my voice, or at least to weaken my wind, before I get it. But *à la guerre comme à la guerre!* How can I read Shelley, however, when I don't understand him?"

"That's just what I want to make you do. It's a part of your general training. You may do without that, of course — without culture and taste and perception; but in that case you'll be nothing but a vulgar *cabotine*, and nothing will be of any consequence." Sherringham had a theory that the great lyric poets (he induced her to read and recite as well long passages of Wordsworth and of Swinburne) would teach her many of the secrets of competent utterance, the mysteries of rhythm, the communicableness of style, the latent music of the language and the art of "composing" copious speeches and of keeping her wind in hand. He held in perfect sincerity that there was an indirect enlightenment which would be of the highest importance to her and to which it was precisely, by good fortune, in his power to contribute. She would do better in proportion as she had more knowledge — even knowledge that might appear to have but a remote connection with her business. The actor's talent was essentially a gift, a thing by itself, implanted, instinctive, accidental, equally unconnected with intellect and with virtue — Sherringham was completely of that opinion; but it seemed to him no contradiction to consider at the same time that intellect (leaving virtue, for the moment, out of the question) might be brought into fruitful relation with it. It would be a larger thing if a better mind were projected upon it — without sacrificing the mind. So he lent Miriam books which she never read (she was on almost irreconcilable terms with the printed page), and in the long summer days, when he had leisure, took her to the Louvre to admire the great works of painting and sculpture. Here, as on all occasions, he was struck with the queer jumble of her taste, her mixture of intelligence and puerility. He saw that she never read what he gave her, though she sometimes would have liked him to suppose so; but in the presence of famous pictures and statues she had remarkable flashes of perception. She felt these things, she liked them, though it was always because she had an idea she could use them. The idea was often fantastic, but it showed what an eye she had to her business. "I could look just like that, if I tried." "That's the dress I mean to wear when I do Portia." Such were the observations that were apt to drop from her under the suggestion of antique marbles or when she stood before a Titian or a Bronzino.

When she uttered them, and many others besides, the effect was sometimes irritating to Sherringham, who had to reflect a little to remember that she was no more egotistical than the histrionic conscience demanded. He wondered if there were necessarily something vulgar in the histrionic conscience— something condemned to feel only the tricky personal question. Wasn't it better to be perfectly stupid than to have only one eye open and wear forever, in the great face of the world, the expression of a knowing wink? At the theatre, on the numerous July evenings when the Comédie Française played the repertory, with exponents determined the more sparse and provincial audience should thrill and gape with the tradition, her appreciation was tremendously technical and showed it was not for nothing she was now in and out of Madame Carré's innermost counsels. But there were moments when even her very acuteness seemed to him to drag the matter down, to see it in a small and superficial sense. What he flattered himself that he was trying to do for her (and through her for the stage of his time, since she was the instrument, and incontestably a fine one, that had come to his hand) was precisely to lift it up, make it rare, keep it in the region of distinction and breadth. However, she was doubtless right and he was wrong, he eventually reasoned: you could afford to be vague only if you hadn't a responsibility. He had fine ideas, but she was to do the acting, that is the application of them, and not he; and application was always of necessity a sort of vulgarization, a smaller thing than theory. If some day she should exhibit the great art that it was not purely fanciful to forecast for her, the subject would doubtless be sufficiently lifted up and it wouldn't matter that some of the onward steps should have been lame.

This was clear to him on several occasions when she repeated or acted something for him better than usual: then she quite carried him away, making him wish to ask no more questions but only let her disembroil herself in her own fashion. In these hours she gave him fitfully but forcibly that impression of beauty which was to be her justification. It was too soon for any general estimate of her progress; Madame Carré had at last given her an intelligent understanding, as well as a sore personal sense, of how bad she was. She had therefore begun on a new basis; she had returned to the alphabet and the drill. It was a phase of awkwardness, like the splashing of a young swimmer, but buoyancy would certainly come out of it. For the present there was for the most part no great alteration of the fact that when she did things according to her own idea they were not as yet, and seriously judged, worth the devil, as Madame Carré said; and when she did them according to that of her instructress they were too apt to be a gross parody of that lady's intention. None the less she gave glimpses, and her glimpses made him feel not only that she was not a fool (that was a small relief), but that *he* was not.

He made her stick to her English and read Shakespeare aloud to him. Mrs. Rooth had recognized the importance of an apartment in which they should be able to receive so beneficent a visitor, and was now mistress of a small salon with a balcony and a rickety flower-stand (to say nothing of a view of many roofs and chimneys), a crooked waxed floor, an empire clock, an *armoire à glace* (highly convenient for Miriam's posturings), and several cupboard doors, covered over, allowing for treacherous gaps, with the faded magenta paper of the wall. The thing had been easily done, for Sherringham had said: "Oh, we must have a sitting-room for our studies, you know. I'll settle it with the landlady." Mrs. Rooth had liked his "we" (indeed she liked everything about him), and he saw in this way that she had no insuperable objection to being under a pecuniary obligation so long as it was distinctly understood to be temporary. That he should have his money back with interest as soon as Miriam was launched was a comfort so deeply implied that it only added to intimacy. The window stood open on the little balcony, and when the sun had left it Sherringham and Miriam could linger there, leaning on the rail and talking, above the great hum of Paris, with nothing but the neighbouring tiles and tall tubes to take account of. Mrs. Rooth, in limp garments, much ungirdled, was on the sofa with a novel, making good her frequent assertion that she could put up with any life that would yield her these two articles. There were romantic works that Sherringham had never read, and as to which he had vaguely wondered to what class they were addressed—the earlier productions of M. Eugène Sue, the once-fashionable compositions of Madame Sophie Gay—with which Mrs. Rooth was familiar and which she was ready to peruse once more if she could get nothing fresher. She had always a greasy volume tucked under her while her nose was bent upon the pages in hand. She scarcely looked up even when Miriam lifted her voice to show Sherringham what she could do. These tragic or pathetic notes all went out of the window and mingled with the undecipherable concert of Paris, so that no neighbour was disturbed by them. The girl shrieked and wailed when the occasion required it, and Mrs. Rooth only turned her page, showing in this way a great æsthetic as well as a great personal trust.

She rather annoyed Sherringham by the serenity of her confidence (for a reason that he fully understood only later), save when Miriam caught an effect or a tone so well that she made him, in the pleasure of it, forget her parent was there. He continued to object to the girl's English, with the foreign patches which might pass in prose but were offensive in the recitation of verse, and he wanted to know why she could not speak like her mother. He had to do Mrs. Rooth the justice of recognizing the charm of her voice and accent, which gave a certain richness even to the foolish things she said. They were of an excellent insular tradition, full both of natural and of cultivated sweetness, and they puzzled him when other indications seemed to betray her—to relegate her to the class of the simple dreary. They were like the reverberation of far-off drawing-rooms.

The connection between the development of Miriam's genius and the necessity of an occasional excursion to the country—the charming country that lies in so many directions beyond the Parisian *banlieue*—would not have been immediately apparent to a merely superficial observer; but a day, and then another, at Versailles, a day at Fontainebleau and a trip, particularly harmonious and happy, to Rambouillet, took their place in Sherringham's programme as a part of the legit-imate indirect culture, an agency in the formation of taste. Intimations of the grand style, for instance, would proceed in abundance from the symmetrical palace and gardens of Louis XIV. Sherringham was very fond of Versailles, and went there more than once with the ladies of the Hôtel de la Garonne. They chose quiet hours, when the fountains were dry; and Mrs. Rooth took an armful of novels and sat on a bench in the park, flanked by clipped hedges and old statues, while her young companions strolled away, walked to the Trianon, ex-plored the long, straight vistas of the woods. Rambouillet was vague and pleasant and idle; they had an idea that they found suggestive associations there; and indeed there was an old white château which contained nothing else. They found, at any rate, luncheon and, in the landscape, a charming sense of summer and of little brushed French pictures.

I have said that in these days Sherringham wondered a good deal, and by the time his leave of absence was granted him this practice had engendered a particular speculation. He was surprised that he was not in love with Miriam Rooth, and he considered in moments of leisure the causes of his exemption. He had perceived from the first that she was a "nature," and each time she met his eyes the more vividly it appeared to him that her beauty was rare. You had to get the view of her face, but when you did so it was a splendid mobile mask. And the possessor of this high advantage had frankness and courage and variety and the unusual and the unexpected. She had qualities that seldom went together— impulses and shynesses, audacities and lapses, something coarse, popular and strong, all intermingled with disdains and languors and nerves. And then, above all, she was there, she was accessible, she almost belonged to him. He reflected inge-niously that he owed his escape to a peculiar cause—the fact that they had together a positive outside object. Objective, as it were, was all their communion; not personal and selfish, but a matter of art and business and discussion. Discussion had saved him and would save him further; for they would always have something to quarrel about. Sherringham, who was not a diplomatist for nothing; who had his reasons for steering straight and wished neither to deprive the British public of a rising star nor to change his actual situation for that of a conjugal *impresario*, blessed the beneficence, the salubrity, the pure exorcism of art. At the same time, rather inconsistently and feeling that he had a completer vision than before of the odd animal the artist who happened to have been born a woman, he felt himself warned against a serious connection (he made a great point of the "serious,") with so slippery and ticklish a creature. The two ladies had only to stay in Paris, save their candle-ends and, as Madame Carré had enjoined, practise their scales: there were apparently no autumn visits to English country-houses in prospect for Mrs. Rooth.

Sherringham parted with them on the understanding that in London he would look as thoroughly as possible into the question of an engagement for Miriam. The day before he began his holiday he went to see Madame Carré, who said to him: *"Vous devriez bien nous la laisser."*

"She has got something, then?"

"She has got most things. She'll go far. It is the first time I ever was mistaken. But don't tell her so—I don't flatter her; she'll be too puffed up."

"Is she very conceited?" Sherringham asked.

"Mauvais sujet!" said Madame Carré.

It was on the journey to London that he indulged in some of those questionings of his state which I have mentioned; but I must add that by the time he reached Charing Cross (he smoked a cigar, deferred till after the Channel, in a compartment by himself) it suddenly came over him that they were futile. Now that he had left the girl, a subversive, unpremeditated heart-beat told him—it made him hold his breath a minute in the carriage—that he had after all *not* escaped. He *was* in love with her: he had been in love with her from the first hour.

XIII.

THE DRIVE from Harsh to the Place, as it was called there-abouts, could be achieved by swift horses in less than ten minutes; and if Mrs. Dallow's ponies were capital trotters the general high pitch of the occasion made it congruous that they should show their speed. The occasion was the polling-day, the hour after the battle. The ponies had worked, with all the rest, for the week before, passing and repassing the neat windows of the flat little town (Mrs. Dallow had the compla-cent belief that there was none in the kingdom in which the flower-stands looked more respectable between the stiff mus-lin curtains), with their mistress behind them in her low, smart trap. Very often she was accompanied by the Liberal candidate, but even when she was not the equipage seemed scarcely less to represent his pleasant sociable confidence. It moved in a radiance of ribbons and handbills and hand-shakes and smiles; of quickened intercourse and sudden intimacy; of sympathy which assumed without presuming and gratitude which promised without soliciting. But, under Julia's guid-ance the ponies pattered now, with no indication of a loss of freshness, along the firm, wide avenue which wound and curved, to make up in picturesque effect for not undulating, from the gates opening straight into the town to the Palladian mansion, high, square, gray and clean, which stood, among parterres and fountains, in the centre of the park. A generous steed had been sacrificed to bring the good news from Ghent to Aix, but no such extravagance was after all necessary for communicating with Lady Agnes.

She had remained at the house, not going to the Wheat-sheaf, the Liberal inn, with the others; preferring to await in privacy, and indeed in solitude, the momentous result of the poll. She had come down to Harsh with the two girls in the course of the proceedings. Julia had not thought they would do much good, but she was expansive and indulgent now and she had liberally asked them. Lady Agnes had not a nice can-vassing manner, effective as she might have been in the char-acter of the high, benignant, affable mother—looking sweet participation but not interfering—of the young and hand-

863

some, the shining, convincing, wonderfully clever and certainly irresistible aspirant. Grace Dormer had zeal without art, and Lady Agnes, who during her husband's lifetime had seen their affairs follow the satisfactory principle of a tendency to defer to supreme merit, had never really learned the lesson that voting goes by favour. However, she could pray God if she couldn't flatter the cheesemonger, and Nick felt that she had stayed at home to pray for him. I must add that Julia Dallow was too happy now, flicking her whip in the bright summer air, to say anything so ungracious even to herself as that her companion had been returned in spite of his nearest female relatives. Besides, Biddy *had* been a rosy help: she had looked persuasively pretty, in white and pink, on platforms and in recurrent carriages, out of which she had tossed, blushing and making people remember her eyes, several words that were telling for their very simplicity.

Mrs. Dallow was really too glad for any definite reflection, even for personal exultation, the vanity of recognizing her own large share of the work. Nick was in and he was beside her, tired, silent, vague, beflowered and beribboned, and he had been splendid from beginning to end, delightfully good-humoured and at the same time delightfully clever—still cleverer than she had supposed he could be. The sense that she had helped his cleverness and that she had been repaid by it, or by his gratitude (it came to the same thing), in a way she appreciated, was not triumphant and jealous; for the break of the long tension soothed her, it was as pleasant as an untied ligature. So nothing passed between them on their way to the house; there was no sound in the park but the happy rustle of summer (it seemed an applausive murmur) and the swift progress of the vehicle.

Lady Agnes already knew, for as soon as the result was declared Nick had despatched a man on horseback to her, carrying the figures on a scrawled card. He had been far from getting away at once, having to respond to the hubbub of acclamation, to speak yet again, to thank his electors individually and collectively, to chaff the Tories, to be carried hither and yon, and above all to pretend that the interest of the business was now greater for him than ever. If he said never a word after he put himself in Julia's hands to go home, perhaps it was partly because the consciousness began to glimmer within him that that interest had on the contrary now suddenly diminished. He wanted to see his mother because he knew she wanted to see him, to fold him close in her arms. They had been open there for that purpose for the last half-hour, and her expectancy, now no longer an ache of suspense, was the reason of Julia's round pace. Yet this very expectancy somehow made Nick wince a little. Meeting his mother was like being elected over again.

The others had not come back yet—Lady Agnes was alone in the large bright drawing-room. When Nick went in with Mrs. Dallow he saw her at the further end; she had evidently been walking to and fro, the whole length of it, and her tall, upright black figure seemed in possession of the fair vastness like an exclamation-point at the bottom of a blank page. The room, rich and simple, was a place of perfection as well as of splendour in delicate tints, with precious specimens of French furniture of the last century ranged against walls of pale brocade and here and there a small, almost priceless picture. George Dallow had made it, caring for these things and liking to talk about them (scarcely about anything else); so that it appeared to represent him still, what was best in his kindly, uniform nature—a friendly, competent, tiresome insistence upon purity and homogeneity. Nick Dormer could hear him yet, and could see him, too, fat and with a congenital thickness in his speech, lounging there in loose clothes with his eternal cigarette. "Now, my dear fellow, *that's* what I call form: I don't know what you call it"—that was the way he used to begin. The room was full of flowers in rare vases, but it looked like a place of which the beauty would have had a sweet odour even without them.

Lady Agnes had taken a white rose from one of the clusters and was holding it to her face, which was turned to the door as Nick crossed the threshold. The expression of her figure instantly told him (he saw the creased card that he had sent her lying on one of the beautiful bare tables) how she had been sailing up and down in a majesty of satisfaction. The inflation of her long, plain dress, the brightened dimness of her proud face were still in the air. In a moment he had kissed her and was being kissed, not in quick repetition, but in tender prolongation, with which the perfume of the white rose was mixed. But there was something else too—her sweet, smothered words in his ear: "Oh, my boy, my boy—oh, your father, your father!" Neither the sense of pleasure nor that of pain, with Lady Agnes (and indeed with most of the persons with whom this history is concerned), was a liberation of chatter; so that for a minute all she said again was: "I think of Sir Nicholas. I wish he were here;" addressing the words to Julia, who had wandered forward without looking at the mother and son.

"Poor Sir Nicholas!" said Mrs. Dallow, vaguely.

"Did you make another speech?" Lady Agnes asked.

"I don't know; did I?" Nick inquired.

"I don't know!" Mrs. Dallow replied, with her back turned, doing something to her hat before the glass.

"Oh, I can fancy the confusion, the bewilderment!" said Lady Agnes, in a tone rich in political reminiscence.

"It was really immense fun!" exclaimed Mrs. Dallow.

"Dear Julia!" Lady Agnes went on. Then she added: "It was you who made it sure."

"There are a lot of people coming to dinner," said Julia.

"Perhaps you'll have to speak again," Lady Agnes smiled at her son.

"Thank you; I like the way you talk about it!" cried Nick. "I'm like Iago: 'from this time forth I never will speak word!' "

"Don't say that, Nick," said his mother, gravely.

"Don't be afraid: he'll jabber like a magpie!" And Mrs. Dallow went out of the room.

Nick had flung himself upon a sofa with an air of weariness, though not of completely vanished cheer; and Lady Agnes stood before him fingering her rose and looking down at him. His eyes looked away from hers: they seemed fixed on something she couldn't see. "I hope you've thanked Julia," Lady Agnes dropped.

"Why, of course, mother."

"She has done as much as if you hadn't been sure."

"I wasn't in the least sure—and she has done everything."

"She has been too good—but we've done something. I

hope you don't leave out your father," Lady Agnes amplified, as Nick's glance appeared for a moment to question her "we."

"Never, never!" Nick uttered these words perhaps a little mechanically, but the next minute he continued, as if he had suddenly been moved to think what he could say that would give his mother most pleasure: "Of course his name has worked for me. Gone as he is, he is still a living force." He felt a good deal of a hypocrite, but one didn't win a seat every day in the year. Probably indeed he should never win another.

"He hears you, he watches you, he rejoices in you," Lady Agnes declared.

This idea was oppressive to Nick—that of the rejoicing almost as much as of the watching. He had made his concession, but, with a certain impulse to divert his mother from following up her advantage, he broke out: "Julia's a tremendously effective woman."

"Of course she is!" answered Lady Agnes, knowingly.

"Her charming appearance is half the battle," said Nick, explaining a little coldly what he meant. But he felt that his coldness was an inadequate protection to him when he heard his mother observe, with something of the same sapience—

"A woman is always effective when she likes a person."

It discomposed him to be described as a person liked, and by a woman; and he asked abruptly: "When are you going away?"

"The first moment that's civil—to-morrow morning. *You*'ll stay here, I hope."

"Stay? What shall I stay for?"

"Why, you might stay to thank her."

"I have everything to do."

"I thought everything was done," said Lady Agnes.

"Well, that's why," her son replied, not very lucidly. "I want to do other things—quite other things. I should like to take the next train." And Nick looked at his watch.

"When there are people coming to dinner to meet you?"

"They'll meet *you*—that's better."

"I'm sorry any one is coming," Lady Agnes said, in a tone unencouraging to a deviation from the intensity of things. "I wish we were alone—just as a family. It would please Julia to-day to feel that we *are* one. Do stay with her to-morrow."

"How will that do, when she's alone?"

"She won't be alone, with Mrs. Gresham."

"Mrs. Gresham doesn't count."

"That's precisely why I want you to stop. And her cousin, almost her brother: what an idea that it won't do! Haven't you stayed here before, when there has been no one?"

"I have never stayed much, and there have always been people. At any rate, now it's different."

"It's just because it is different. Besides, it isn't different, and it never was," said Lady Agnes, more incoherent, in her earnestness, than it often happened to her to be. "She always liked you, and she likes you now more than ever, if you call *that* different!" Nick got up at this and, without meeting her eyes, walked to one of the windows, where he stood with his back turned, looking out on the great greenness. She watched him a moment and she might well have been wishing, while he remained gazing there, as it appeared, that it would come to him with the same force as it had come to herself (very often before, but during these last days more than ever), that the level lands of Harsh, stretching away before the window, the French garden, with its symmetry, its screens and its statues, and a great many more things, of which these were the superficial token, were Julia's very own, to do with exactly as she liked. No word of appreciation or envy, however, dropped from the young man's lips, and his mother presently went on: "What could be more natural than that after your triumphant contest you and she should have lots to settle and to talk about—no end of practical questions, no end of business. Aren't you her member, and can't her member pass a day with her, and she a great proprietor?"

Nick turned round at this, with an odd expression. "*Her* member—am I hers?"

Lady Agnes hesitated a moment; she felt that she had need of all her tact. "Well, if the place is hers, and you represent the place—" she began. But she went no further, for Nick interrupted her with a laugh.

"What a droll thing to 'represent,' when one thinks of it! And what does *it* represent, poor torpid little borough, with

its smell of meal and its curiously fat-faced inhabitants? Did
you ever see such a collection of fat faces, turned up at the
hustings? They looked like an enormous sofa, with the cheeks
for the gathers and the eyes for the buttons."

"Oh, well, the next time you shall have a great town," Lady
Agnes replied, smiling and feeling that she *was* tactful.

"It will only be a bigger sofa! I'm joking, of course," Nick
went on, "and I ought to be ashamed of myself. They have
done me the honour to elect me, and I shall never say a word
that's not civil about them, poor dears. But even a new member may joke with his mother."

"I wish you'd be serious with your mother," said Lady
Agnes, going nearer to him.

"The difficulty is that I'm two men; it's the strangest thing
that ever was," Nick pursued, bending his bright face upon
her. "I'm two quite distinct human beings, who have scarcely
a point in common; not even the memory, on the part of one,
of the achievements or the adventures of the other. One man
wins the seat—but it's the other fellow who sits in it."

"Oh, Nick, don't spoil your victory by your perversity!"
Lady Agnes cried, clasping her hands to him.

"I went through it with great glee—I won't deny that: it
excited me, it interested me, it amused me. When once I was
in it I liked it. But now that I'm out of it again—"

"Out of it?" His mother stared. "Isn't the whole point that
you're in?"

"Ah, now I'm only in the House of Commons."

For an instant Lady Agnes seemed not to understand and
to be on the point of laying her finger quickly to her lips with
a "Hush!" as if the late Sir Nicholas might have heard the
"only." Then, as if a comprehension of the young man's
words promptly superseded that impulse, she replied with
force: "You will be in the Lords the day you determine to get
there."

This futile remark made Nick laugh afresh, and not only
laugh but kiss her, which was always an intenser form of mystification for poor Lady Agnes, and apparently the one he
liked best to practise; after which he said: "The odd thing is,
you know, that Harsh has no wants. At least it's not sharply,
not eloquently conscious of them. We all talked them over

together, and I promised to carry them in my heart of hearts. But upon my word I can't remember one of them. Julia says the wants of Harsh are simply the national wants—rather a pretty phrase for Julia. She means *she* does everything for the place; *she's* really their member, and this house in which we stand is their legislative chamber. Therefore the *lacunæ* that I have undertaken to fill up are the national wants. It will be rather a job to rectify some of them, won't it? I don't represent the appetites of Harsh—Harsh is gorged. I represent the ideas of my party. That's what Julia says."

"Oh, never mind what Julia says!" Lady Agnes broke out, impatiently. This impatience made it singular that the very next words she uttered should be: "My dearest son, I wish to heaven you'd marry her. It would be so fitting now!" she added.

"Why now?" asked Nick, frowning.

"She has shown you such sympathy, such devotion."

"Is it for that she has shown it?"

"Ah, you might *feel*—I can't tell you!" said Lady Agnes, reproachfully.

Nick blushed at this, as if what he did feel was the reproach. "Must I marry her because you like her?"

"I? Why, we are *all* as fond of her as we can be."

"Dear mother, I hope that any woman I ever may marry will be a person agreeable not only to you, but also, since you make a point of it, to Grace and Biddy. But I must tell you this—that I shall marry no woman I am not unmistakably in love with."

"And why are you not in love with Julia—charming, clever, generous as she is?" Lady Agnes laid her hands on him—she held him tight. "My darling Nick, if you care anything in the world to make me happy, you'll stay over here to-morrow and be nice to her."

"Be nice to her? Do you mean propose to her?"

"With a single word, with the glance of an eye, the movement of your little finger"—and Lady Agnes paused, looking intensely, imploringly up into Nick's face—"in less time than it takes me to say what I say now, you may have it all." As he made no answer, only returning her look, she added insistently, "You know she's a fine creature—you know she is!"

"Dearest mother, what I seem to know better than anything else in the world is that I love my freedom. I set it far above everything."

"Your freedom? What freedom is there in being poor? Talk of that when Julia puts everything that she possesses at your feet!"

"I can't talk of it, mother—it's too terrible an idea. And I can't talk of *her*, nor of what I think of her. You must leave that to me. I do her perfect justice."

"You don't, or you'd marry her to-morrow. You would feel that the opportunity is exquisitely rare, with everything in the world to make it perfect. Your father would have valued it for you beyond everything. Think a little what would have given *him* pleasure. That's what I meant when I spoke just now of us all. It wasn't of Grace and Biddy I was thinking—fancy!—it was of him. He's with you always; he takes with you, at your side, every step that you take yourself. He would bless devoutly your marriage to Julia; he would feel what it would be for you and for us all. I ask for no sacrifice, and he would ask for none. We only ask that you don't commit the crime—"

Nick Dormer stopped her with another kiss; he murmured: "Mother, mother, mother!" as he bent over her.

He wished her not to go on, to let him off; but the deep deprecation in his voice did not prevent her saying: "You know it—you know it perfectly. All, and more than all that I can tell you, you know."

He drew her closer, kissed her again, held her there as he would have held a child in a paroxysm, soothing her silently till it should pass away. Her emotion had brought the tears to her eyes; she dried them as she disengaged herself. The next moment, however, she resumed, attacking him again:

"For a public man she would be the ideal companion. She's made for public life; she's made to shine, to be concerned in great things, to occupy a high position and to help him on. She would help you in everything as she has helped you in this. Together there is nothing you couldn't do. You can have the first house in England—yes, the first! What freedom *is* there in being poor? How can you do anything without money, and what money can you make for yourself—what money will ever come to you? That's the crime—to throw away such an instrument of power, such a blessed instrument of good."

"It isn't everything to be rich, mother," said Nick, looking at the floor in a certain patient way, with a provisional docility and his hands in his pockets. "And it isn't so fearful to be poor."

"It's vile—it's abject. Don't I know?"

"Are you in such acute want?" Nick asked, smiling.

"Ah, don't make me explain what you have only to look at to see!" his mother returned, as if with a richness of allusion to dark elements in her fate.

"Besides," Nick went on, "there's other money in the world than Julia's. I might come by some of that."

"Do you mean Mr. Carteret's?" The question made him laugh, as her feeble reference, five minutes before, to the House of Lords had done. But she pursued, too full of her idea to take account of such a poor substitute for an answer: "Let me tell you one thing, for I have known Charles Carteret much longer than you, and I understand him better. There's nothing you could do that would do you more good with him than to marry Julia. I know the way he looks at things and I know exactly how that would strike him. It would please him, it would charm him; it would be the thing that would most prove to him that you're in earnest. You need to do something of that sort."

"Haven't I come in for Harsh?" asked Nick.

"Oh, he's very canny. He likes to see people rich. *Then* he believes in them—then he's likely to believe more. He's kind to you because you're your father's son; but I'm sure your being poor takes just so much off."

"He can remedy that so easily," said Nick, smiling still. "Is being kept by Julia what you call making an effort for myself?"

Lady Agnes hesitated; then: "You needn't insult Julia!" she replied.

"Moreover, if I've *her* money, I sha'n't want his," Nick hinted.

Again his mother waited an instant before answering; after

which she produced: "And pray wouldn't you wish to be independent?"

"You're delightful, dear mother—you're very delightful! I
particularly like your conception of independence. Doesn't it
occur to you that at a pinch I might improve my fortune by
some other means than by making a mercenary marriage or
by currying favour with a rich old gentleman? Doesn't it
occur to you that I might work?"

"Work at politics? How does that make money, honourably?"

"I don't mean at politics."

"What do you mean, then?" Lady Agnes demanded, looking at him as if she challenged him to phrase it if he dared.
Her eye appeared to have a certain effect upon him, for he
remained silent, and she continued: "Are you elected or not?"

"It seems a dream," said Nick.

"If you are, act accordingly and don't mix up things that
are as wide asunder as the poles!" She spoke with sternness,
and his silence might have been an admission that her sternness was wholesome to him. Possibly she was touched by it;
at any rate, after a few moments, during which nothing more
passed between them, she appealed to him in a gentler and
more anxious key, which had this virtue to touch him, that he
knew it was absolutely the first time in her life Lady Agnes
had begged for anything. She had never been obliged to beg;
she had got on without it and most things had come to her.
He might judge therefore in what a light she regarded this
boon for which, in her old age, she humbled herself to be a
suitor. There was such a pride in her that he could feel what it
cost her to go on her knees even to her son. He did judge
how it was in his power to gratify her; and as he was generous and imaginative he was stirred and shaken as it came over
him in a wave of figurative suggestion that he might make up
to her for many things. He scarcely needed to hear her ask,
with a pleading wail that was almost tragic: "Don't you see
how things have turned out for us; don't you know how unhappy I am—don't you know what a bitterness—?" She
stopped for a moment, with a sob in her voice, and he recognized vividly this last tribulation, the unhealed wound of her
bereavement and the way she had sunken from eminence to

flatness. "You know what Percival is and the comfort I have from him. You know the property and what he is doing with it and what comfort I get from *that*! Everything's dreary but what you can do for us. Everything's odious, down to living in a hole with one's girls who don't marry. Grace is impossible—I don't know what's the matter with her; no one will look at her, and she's so conceited with it—sometimes I feel as if I could beat her! And Biddy will never marry, and we are three dismal women in a filthy house. What are three dismal women, more or less, in London?"

So, with an unexpected rage of self-exposure, Lady Agnes talked of her disappointments and troubles, tore away the veil from her sadness and soreness. It almost frightened Nick to perceive how she hated her life, though at another time it might have amused him to note how she despised her garden-less house. Of course it was not a country-house, and Lady Agnes could not get used to that. Better than he could do—for it was the sort of thing into which, in any case, a woman enters more than a man—she felt what a lift into brighter air, what a regilding of his sisters' possibilities, his marriage to Julia would effect for them. He couldn't trace the difference, but his mother saw it all as a shining picture. She made the vision shine before him now, somehow, as she stood there like a poor woman crying for a kindness. What was filial in him, all the piety that he owed, especially to the revived spirit of his father, more than ever present on a day of such public pledges, was capable from one moment to the other of trembling into sympathetic response. He had the gift, so embarrassing when it is a question of consistent action, of seeing in an imaginative, interesting light anything that illustrated forcibly the life of another: such things effected a union with something in *his* life, and the recognition of them was ready to become a form of enthusiasm in which there was no consciousness of sacrifice—none scarcely of merit.

Rapidly, at present, this change of scene took place before his spiritual eye. He found himself believing, because his mother communicated the belief, that it was in his option to transform the social outlook of the three women who clung to him and who declared themselves dismal. This was not the highest kind of inspiration, but it was moving, and it associated itself with dim confusions of figures in the past—figures of authority and expectancy. Julia's wide kingdom opened out around him, making the future almost a dazzle of happy power. His mother and sisters floated in the rosy element with beaming faces, in transfigured safety. "The first house in England," she had called it; but it might be the first house in Europe, the first house in the world, by the fine air and the high humanities that should fill it. Everything that was beautiful in the place where he stood took on a more delicate charm; the house rose over his head like a museum of exquisite rewards, and the image of poor George Dallow hovered there obsequious, as if to confess that he had only been the modest, tasteful forerunner, appointed to set it all in order and punctually retire. Lady Agnes's tone penetrated further into Nick's spirit than it had done yet, as she syllabled to him, supremely: "Don't desert us—don't desert us."

"Don't desert you?"

"Be great—be great," said his mother. "I'm old, I've lived, I've seen. Go in for a great material position. That will simplify everything else."

"I will do what I can for you—anything, everything I can. Trust me—leave me alone," said Nick Dormer.

"And you'll stay over—you'll spend the day with her?"

"I'll stay till she turns me out!"

His mother had hold of his hand again now; she raised it to her lips and kissed it. "My dearest son, my only joy!" Then, "I don't see how you can resist her," she added.

"No more do I!"

Lady Agnes looked round the great room with a soft exhalation of gratitude and hope. "If you're so fond of art, what art is equal to all this? The joy of living in the midst of it—of seeing the finest works every day! You'll have everything the world can give."

"That's exactly what was just passing in my own mind. It's too much."

"Don't be selfish!"

"Selfish?" Nick repeated.

"Don't be unselfish, then. You'll share it with us."

"And with Julia a little, I hope," said Nick.

"God bless you!" cried his mother, looking up at him. Her

eyes were detained by the sudden perception of something in his own that was not clear to her; but before she had time to ask for an explanation of it Nick inquired, abruptly—

"Why do you talk so of poor Biddy? Why won't she marry?"

"You had better ask Peter Sherringham," said Lady Agnes.

"What has he got to do with it?"

"How odd of you to ask, when it's so plain how she thinks of him that it's a matter of common chaff!"

"Yes, we've made it so, and she takes it like an angel. But Peter likes her."

"Does he? Then it's the more shame to him to behave as he does. He had better leave his actresses alone. That's the love of art, too!" mocked Lady Agnes.

"Biddy's so charming—she'll marry some one else."

"Never, if she loves him. But Julia will bring it about—Julia will help her," said Lady Agnes, more cheerfully. "That's what you'll do for us—that *she'll* do everything!"

"Why then more than now?" Nick asked.

"Because we shall be yours."

"You are mine already."

"Yes, but *she* isn't. However, she's as good!" exulted Lady Agnes.

"She'll turn me out of the house," said Nick.

"Come and tell me when she does! But there she is—go to her!" And she gave him a push toward one of the windows that stood open to the terrace. Mrs. Dallow had become visible outside; she passed slowly along the terrace, with her long shadow. "Go to her," Lady Agnes repeated—"she's waiting for you."

Nick went out with the air of a man who was as ready to pass that way as any other, and at the same moment his two sisters, freshly restored from the excitements of the town, came into the room from another quarter.

"We go home to-morrow, but Nick will stay a day or two," their mother said to them.

"Dear old Nick!" Grace ejaculated, looking at Lady Agnes.

"He's going to speak," the latter went on. "But don't mention it."

"Don't mention it?" said Biddy, staring. "Hasn't he spoken enough, poor fellow?"

"I mean to Julia," Lady Agnes replied.

"Don't you understand, you goose?" Grace exclaimed to her sister.

XIV.

THE NEXT MORNING brought Nick Dormer many letters and telegrams, and his coffee was placed beside him in his room, where he remained until noon answering these communications. When he came out he learned that his mother and sisters had left the house. This information was given him by Mrs. Gresham, whom he found dealing with her own voluminous budget at one of the tables in the library. She was a lady who received thirty letters a day, the subject-matter of which, as well as of her punctual answers, in a hand that would have been "ladylike" in a manageress, was a puzzle to those who observed her.

She told Nick that Lady Agnes had not been willing to disturb him at his work to say good-bye, knowing she should see him in a day or two in town. Nick was amused at the way his mother had stolen off; as if she feared that further conversation might weaken the spell she believed herself to have wrought. The place was cleared, moreover, of its other visitors, so that, as Mrs. Gresham said, the fun was at an end. This lady expressed the idea that the fun was after all rather heavy. At any rate now they could rest, Mrs. Dallow and Nick and she, and she was glad Nick was going to stay for a little quiet. She liked Harsh best when it was not *en fête*: then one could see what a sympathetic old place it was. She hoped Nick was not dreadfully tired; she feared Julia was completely done up. Mrs. Dallow, however, had transported her exhaustion to the grounds—she was wandering about somewhere. She thought more people would be coming to the house, people from the town, people from the country, and had gone out so as not to have to see them. She had not gone far—Nick could easily find her. Nick intimated that he himself was not eager for more people, whereupon Mrs. Gresham said, rather archly smiling:

"And of course you hate *me* for being here!" He made some protest, and she added: "But I'm almost a part of the house, you know—I'm one of the chairs or tables." Nick declared that he had never seen a house so well furnished, and Mrs. Gresham said: "I believe there *are* to be some people to

878

dinner: rather an interference, isn't it? Julia lives so in public. But it's all for you." And after a moment she added: "It's a wonderful constitution." Nick at first failed to seize her allusion—he thought it a retarded political reference, a sudden tribute to the great unwritten instrument by which they were all governed. He was on the point of saying: "The British? Wonderful!" when he perceived that the intention of his interlocutress was to praise Mrs. Dallow's fine robustness. "The surface so delicate, the action so easy, yet the frame of steel."

Nick left Mrs. Gresham to her correspondence and went out of the house; wondering as he walked whether she wanted him to do the same thing that his mother wanted, so that her words had been intended for a prick—whether even the two ladies had talked over their desire together. Mrs. Gresham was a married woman who was usually taken for a widow; mainly because she was perpetually "sent for" by her friends, and her friends never sent for Mr. Gresham. She came in every case and had the air of being *répandue* at the expense of dingier belongings. Her figure was admired—that is it was sometimes mentioned—and she dressed as if it was expected of her to be smart, like a young woman in a shop or a servant much in view. She slipped in and out, accompanied at the piano, talked to the neglected visitors, walked in the rain and, after the arrival of the post, usually had conferences with her hostess, during which she stroked her chin and looked familiarly responsible. It was her peculiarity that people were always saying things to her in a lowered voice. She had all sorts of acquaintances and in small establishments she sometimes wrote the *menus*. Great ones, on the other hand, had no terrors for her: she had seen too many. No one had ever discovered whether any one else paid her.

If Lady Agnes, in a lowered tone, had discussed with her the propriety of a union between the mistress of Harsh and the hope of the Dormers our young man could take the circumstance for granted without irritation and even with cursory indulgence: for he was not unhappy now and his spirit was light and clear. The summer day was splendid and the world, as he looked at it from the terrace, offered no more worrying ambiguity than a vault of airy blue arching over a lap of solid green. The wide, still trees in the park appeared to

be waiting for some daily inspection, and the rich fields, with
their official frill of hedges, to rejoice in the light which approved them as named and numbered acres. The place looked
happy to Nick, and he was struck with its having a charm to
which he had perhaps not hitherto done justice; something of
the impression that he had received, when he was younger,
from showy "views" of fine country-seats, as if they had been
brighter and more established than life. There were a couple
of peacocks on the terrace, and his eye was caught by the
gleam of the swans on a distant lake, where there was also a
little temple on an island; and these objects fell in with his
humour, which at another time might have been ruffled by
them as representing the Philistine in ornament.

It was certainly a proof of youth and health on his part that
his spirits had risen as the tumult rose and that after he had
taken his jump into the turbid waters of a contested election
he had been able to tumble and splash, not only with a sense
of awkwardness but with a considerable capacity for the
frolic. Tepid as we saw him in Paris he had found his relation
to his opportunity surprisingly altered by his little journey
across the Channel. He saw things in a new perspective and
he breathed an air that excited him unexpectedly. There was
something in it that went to his head—an element that his
mother and his sisters, his father from beyond the grave, Julia
Dallow, the Liberal party and a hundred friends were both
secretly and overtly occupied in pumping into it. If he was
vague about success he liked the fray, and he had a general
rule that when one was in a muddle there was refreshment in
action. The embarrassment, that is the revival of scepticism,
which might produce an inconsistency shameful to exhibit
and yet very difficult to conceal, was safe enough to come
later: indeed at the risk of making our young man appear a
purely whimsical personage I may hint that some such sickly
glow had even now begun to colour one quarter of his mental
horizon.

I am afraid moreover that I have no better excuse for him
than the one he had touched on in the momentous conversation with his mother which I have thought it useful to reproduce in full. He was conscious of a double nature; there were
two men in him, quite separate, whose leading features had

little in common and each of whom insisted on having an independent turn at life. Meanwhile if he was adequately aware that the bed of his moral existence would need a good deal of making over if he was to lie upon it without unseemly tossing, he was also alive to the propriety of not parading his inconsistencies, not letting his unrectified interests become a spectacle to the vulgar. He had none of that wish to appear complicated which is at the bottom of most forms of fatuity; he was perfectly willing to pass as simple; he only aspired to be continuous. If you were not really simple this presented difficulties; but he would have assented to the proposition that you must be as final as you can and that it contributes much to finality to consume the smoke of your inner fire. The fire was the great thing and not the chimney. He had no view of life which counted out the need of learning; it was teaching rather as to which he was conscious of no particular mission. He liked life, liked it immensely, and was willing to study the ways and means of it with a certain patience. He cherished the usual wise monitions, such as that one was not to make a fool of one's self and that one should not carry on one's technical experiments in public. It was because as yet he liked life in general better than it was clear to him that he liked any particular branch of it, that on the occasion of a constituency's holding out a cordial hand to him, while it extended another in a different direction, a certain bloom of boyhood that was on him had not resisted the idea of a match.

He rose to it as he had risen to matches at school, for his boyishness could take a pleasure in an inconsiderate show of agility. He could meet electors and conciliate bores and compliment women and answer questions and roll off speeches and chaff adversaries, because it was amusing and slightly dangerous, like playing football or ascending an Alp—pastimes for which nature had conferred on him an aptitude not so very different in kind from a gallant readiness on platforms. There were two voices which told him that all this was not really action at all, but only a pusillanimous imitation of it: one of them made itself fitfully audible in the depths of his own spirit and the other spoke, in the equivocal accents of a very crabbed hand, from a letter of four pages by Gabriel Nash. However, Nick acted as much as possible under the circumstances, and that was rectifying—it brought with it enjoyment and a working faith. He had not gone counter to the axiom that in a case of doubt one was to hold off; for that applied to choice, and he had not at present the slightest pretension to choosing. He knew he was lifted along, that what he was doing was not first-rate, that nothing was settled by it and that if there was essentially a problem in his life it would only grow tougher with keeping. But if doing one's sum to-morrow instead of to-day does not make the sum easier it at least makes to-day so.

Sometimes in the course of the following fortnight it seemed to him that he had gone in for Harsh because he was sure he should lose; sometimes he foresaw that he should win precisely to punish him for having tried and for his want of candour; and when presently he did win he was almost frightened at his success. Then it appeared to him that he had done something even worse than not choose—he had let others choose for him. The beauty of it was that they had chosen with only their own object in their eye: for what did they know about his strange alternative? He was rattled about so for a fortnight (Julia took care of that) that he had no time to think save when he tried to remember a quotation or an American story, and all his life became an overflow of verbiage. Thought retreated before increase of sound, which had to be pleasant and eloquent, and even superficially coherent, without its aid. Nick himself was surprised at the airs he could play; and often when the last thing at night he shut the door of his room he mentally exclaimed that he had had no idea he was such a mountebank.

I must add that if this reflection did not occupy him long, and if no meditation, after his return from Paris, held him for many moments, there was a reason better even than that he was tired or busy or excited by the agreeable combination of hits and hurrahs. That reason was simply Mrs. Dallow, who had suddenly become a still larger fact in his consciousness than active politics. She *was*, indeed, active politics; that is, if the politics were his, how little soever, the activity was hers. She had ways of showing she was a clever woman that were better than saying clever things, which only prove at the most that one would be clever if one could. The accomplished fact itself was the demonstration that Mrs. Dallow could; and when Nick came to his senses after the proclamation of the victor and the cessation of the noise her figure was, of all the queer phantasmagoria, the most substantial thing that survived. She had been always there, passing, repassing, before him, beside him, behind him. She had made the business infinitely prettier than it would have been without her, added music and flowers and ices, a charm, and converted it into a social game that had a strain of the heroic. It was a garden-party with something at stake, or to celebrate something in advance, with the people let in. The concluded affair had bequeathed him not only a seat in the House of Commons, but a perception of what women may do in high embodiments, and an abyss of intimacy with one woman in particular.

She had wrapped him up in something, he didn't know what—a sense of facility, an overpowering fragrance—and they had moved together in an immense fraternity. There had been no love-making, no contact that was only personal, no vulgarity of flirtation: the hurry of the days and the sharpness with which they both tended to an outside object had made all that irrelevant. It was as if she had been too near for him to see her separate from himself; but none the less, when he now drew breath and looked back, what had happened met his eyes as a composed picture—a picture of which the subject was inveterately Julia and her ponies: Julia wonderfully fair and fine, holding her head more than ever in the manner characteristic of her, brilliant, benignant, waving her whip, cleaving the crowd, thanking people with her smile, carrying him beside her, carrying him to his doom. He had not supposed that in so few days he had driven about with her so much; but the image of it was there, in his consulted conscience, as well as in a personal glow not yet chilled: it looked large as it rose before him. The things his mother had said to him made a rich enough frame for it, and the whole impression, that night, had kept him much awake.

I.

WHILE, after leaving Mrs. Gresham, he was hesitating which way to go and was on the point of hailing a gardener to ask if Mrs. Dallow had been seen, he noticed, as a spot of colour in an expanse of shrubbery, a far-away parasol moving in the direction of the lake. He took his course that way, across the park, and as the bearer of the parasol was strolling slowly it was not five minutes before he had joined her. He went to her soundlessly over the grass (he had been whistling at first, but as he got nearer he stopped), and it was not till he was close to her that she looked round. He had watched her moving as if she were turning things over in her mind, brushing the smooth walks and the clean turf with her dress, slowly making her parasol revolve on her shoulder and carrying in the hand which hung beside her a book which he perceived to be a monthly review.

"I came out to get away," she remarked when he had begun to walk with her.

"Away from me?"

"Ah, that's impossible," said Mrs. Dallow. Then she added: "The day is so nice."

"Lovely weather," Nick dropped. "You want to get away from Mrs. Gresham, I suppose."

Mrs. Dallow was silent a moment. "From everything!"

"Well, I want to get away too."

"It has been such a racket. Listen to the dear birds."

"Yes, our noise isn't so good as theirs," said Nick. "I feel as if I had been married and had shoes and rice thrown after me," he went on. "But not to you, Julia—nothing so good as that."

Mrs. Dallow made no answer to this; she only turned her eyes on the ornamental water which stretched away at their right. In a moment she exclaimed: "How nasty the lake looks!" and Nick recognized in the tone of the words a man-ifestation of that odd shyness—a perverse stiffness at a mo-ment when she probably only wanted to be soft—which, taken in combination with her other qualities, was so far from being displeasing to him that it represented her nearest approach to extreme charm. *He* was not shy now, for he considered, this morning, that he saw things very straight and in a sense altogether superior and delightful. This enabled him to be generously sorry for his companion, if he were the reason of her being in any degree uncomfortable, and yet left him to enjoy the prettiness of some of the signs by which her discomfort was revealed. He would not insist on anything yet: so he observed that his cousin's standard in lakes was too high, and then talked a little about his mother and the girls, their having gone home, his not having seen them that morning, Lady Agnes's deep satisfaction in his victory and the fact that she would be obliged to "do something" for the autumn—take a house or something.

"I'll lend her a house," said Mrs. Dallow.

"Oh, Julia, Julia!" Nick exclaimed.

But Mrs. Dallow paid no attention to his exclamation; she only held up her review and said: "See what I have brought with me to read—Mr. Hoppus's article."

"That's right; then *I* sha'n't have to. You'll tell me about it." He uttered this without believing that she had meant or wished to read the article, which was entitled "The Revision of the British Constitution," in spite of her having encumbered herself with the stiff, fresh magazine. He was conscious that she was not in want of such mental occupation as periodical literature could supply. They walked along and then he added: "But *is* that what we are in for—reading Mr. Hoppus? Is that the sort of thing our constituents expect? Or even worse, pretending to have read him when one hasn't? Oh, what a tangled web we weave!"

"People are talking about it. One has to know. It's the article of the month."

Nick looked at his companion askance a moment. "You say things every now and then for which I could kill you. 'The article of the month,' for instance: I could kill you for that."

"Well, kill me!" Mrs. Dallow exclaimed.

"Let me carry your book," Nick rejoined, irrelevantly. The hand in which she held it was on the side of her on which he was walking, and he put out his own hand to take it. But for a couple of minutes she forbore to give it up, and they held it together, swinging it a little. Before she surrendered it he inquired where she was going.

"To the island," she answered.

"Well, I'll go with you—I'll kill you there."

"The things I say are the right things," said Mrs. Dallow.

"It's just the right things that are wrong. It's because you're so political," Nick went on. "It's your horrible ambition. The woman who has a salon should have read the article of the month. See how one dreadful thing leads to another."

"There are some things that lead to nothing."

"No doubt—no doubt. And how are you going to get over to your island?"

"I don't know."

"Isn't there a boat?"

"I don't know."

Nick had paused a moment, to look round for the boat, but Mrs. Dallow walked on without turning her head. "Can you row?" her companion asked.

"Don't you know I can do everything?"

"Yes, to be sure. That's why I want to kill you. There's the boat."

"Shall you drown me?"

"Oh, let me perish with you!" Nick answered with a sigh. The boat had been hidden from them by the bole of a great tree, which rose from the grass at the water's-edge. It was moored to a small place of embarkation and was large enough to hold as many persons as were likely to wish to visit at once the little temple in the middle of the lake, which Nick liked because it was absurd and Mrs. Dallow had never had a particular esteem for. The lake, fed by a natural spring, was a liberal sheet of water, measured by the scale of park scenery; and though its principal merit was that, taken at a distance, it gave a gleam of abstraction to the concrete verdure, doing the office of an open eye in a dull face, it could also be approached without derision on a sweet summer morning, when it made a lapping sound and reflected candidly various things that were probably finer than itself—the sky, the great trees, the flight of birds.

A man of taste, a hundred years before, coming back from Rome, had caused a small ornamental structure to be erected, on artificial foundations, on its bosom, and had endeavoured to make this architectural pleasantry as nearly as possible a reminiscence of the small ruined rotunda which stands on the bank of the Tiber and is declared by *ciceroni* to have been dedicated to Vesta. It was circular, it was roofed with old tiles, it was surrounded by white columns and it was considerably dilapidated. George Dallow had taken an interest in it (it reminded him not in the least of Rome, but of other things that he liked), and had amused himself with restoring it.

"Give me your hand; sit there, and I'll ferry you," Nick Dormer said.

Mrs. Dallow complied, placing herself opposite to him in the boat; but as he took up the paddles she declared that she preferred to remain on the water—there was too much malice prepense in the temple. He asked her what she meant by that, and she said it was ridiculous to withdraw to an island a few feet square on purpose to meditate. She had nothing to meditate about which required so much attitude.

"On the contrary, it would be just to change the *pose*. It's what we have been doing for a week that's attitude; and to be for half an hour where nobody's looking and one hasn't to keep it up is just what I wanted to put in an idle, irresponsible day for. I am not keeping it up now—I suppose you've noticed," Nick went on, as they floated and he scarcely dipped the oars.

"I don't understand you," said Mrs. Dallow, leaning back in the boat.

Nick gave no further explanation than to ask in a minute: "Have you people to dinner to-night?"

"I believe there are three or four, but I'll put them off if you like."

"Must you *always* live in public, Julia?" Nick continued.

She looked at him a moment, and he could see that she coloured slightly. "We'll go home—I'll put them off."

"Ah no, don't go home; it's too jolly here. Let them come—let them come, poor wretches!"

"How little you know me, when, ever so many times, I have lived here for months without a creature."

"Except Mrs. Gresham, I suppose."

"I have had to have the house going, I admit."

"You are perfect, you are admirable, and I don't criticize you."

"I don't understand you!" she tossed back.

"That only adds to the generosity of what you have done for me," Nick returned, beginning to pull faster. He bent over the oars and sent the boat forward, keeping this up for ten minutes, during which they both remained silent. His companion, in her place, motionless, reclining (the seat in the stern was very comfortable), looked only at the water, the sky, the trees. At last Nick headed for the little temple, saying first however: "Sha'n't we visit the ruin?"

"If you like. I don't mind seeing how they keep it."

They reached the white steps which led up to it. Nick held the boat and Mrs. Dallow got out. He fastened the boat and they went up the steps together, passing through the open door.

"They keep it very well," Nick said, looking round. "It's a capital place to give up everything."

"It might do for you to explain what you mean," said Julia, sitting down.

"I mean to pretend for half an hour that I don't represent the burgesses of Harsh. It's charming—it's very delicate work. Surely it has been retouched."

The interior of the pavilion, lighted by windows which the circle of columns was supposed, outside and at a distance, to conceal, had a vaulted ceiling and was occupied by a few pieces of last-century furniture, spare and faded, of which the colours matched with the decoration of the walls. These and the ceiling, tinted and not exempt from indications of damp, were covered with fine mouldings and medallions. It was a very elegant little tea-house.

Mrs. Dallow sat on the edge of a sofa, rolling her parasol and remarking: "You ought to read Mr. Hoppus's article to me."

"Why, is *this* your salon?" asked Nick, smiling.

"Why are you always talking of that? It's an invention of your own."

"But isn't it the idea you care most about?"

Suddenly, nervously, Mrs. Dallow put up her parasol and sat under it, as if she were not quite sensible of what she was doing. "How much you know me! I don't care about any-thing—that you will ever guess."

Nick Dormer wandered about the room, looking at various things it contained—the odd volumes on the tables, the bits of quaint china on the shelves. "They keep it very well; you've got charming things."

"They're supposed to come over every day and look after them."

"They must come over in force."

"Oh, no one knows."

"It's spick and span. How well you have everything done!"

"I think you've some reason to say so," said Mrs. Dallow. Her parasol was down and she was again rolling it tight.

"But you're right about my not knowing you. Why were you so ready to do so much for me?"

He stopped in front of her and she looked up at him. Her eyes rested on his a minute; then she broke out: "Why do you hate me so?"

"Was it because you like me personally?" Nick asked. "You may think that an odd, or even an odious question; but isn't it natural, my wanting to know?"

"Oh, if you don't know!" Mrs. Dallow exclaimed.

"It's a question of being sure."

"Well, then, if you're not sure—"

"Was it done for me as a friend, as a man?"

"You're not a man; you're a child," said his hostess, with a face that was cold, though she had been smiling the moment before.

"After all, I was a good candidate," Nick went on.

"What do I care for candidates?"

"You're the most delightful woman, Julia," said Nick, sit-ting down beside her, "and I can't imagine what you mean by my hating you."

"If you haven't discovered that I like you, you might as well."

"Might as well discover it?"

Mrs. Dallow was grave; he had never seen her so pale and

never so beautiful. She had stopped rolling her parasol now: her hands were folded in her lap and her eyes were bent on them. Nick sat looking at them too, a trifle awkwardly. "Might as well have hated me," said Mrs. Dallow.

"We have got on so beautifully together, all these days: why shouldn't we get on as well forever and ever?" Mrs. Dallow made no answer, and suddenly Nick said to her: "Ah, Julia, I don't know what you have done to me, but you've done it. You've done it by strange ways, but it will serve. Yes, I hate you," he added, in a different tone, with his face nearer to hers.

"Dear Nick—dear Nick—" she began. But she stopped, for she suddenly felt that he was altogether nearer, nearer than he had ever been to her before, that his arm was round her, that he was in possession of her. She closed her eyes but she heard him ask: "Why shouldn't it be forever, forever?" in a voice that had, for her ear, such a vibration as no voice had ever had.

"You've done it—you've done it," Nick repeated.

"What do you want of me?" she demanded.

"To stay with me, this way, always."

"Ah, not this way," she answered, softly, but as if in pain, and making an effort, with a certain force, to detach herself.

"This way, then—or this!" He took such insistent advantage of her that he had quickly kissed her. She rose as quickly, but he held her yet, and while he did so he said to her in the same tender tone: "If you'll marry me, why shouldn't it be so simple, so good?" He drew her closer again, too close for her to answer. But her struggle ceased and she rested upon him for a minute, she buried her face on his breast.

"You're hard, and it's cruel!" she then exclaimed, breaking away.

"Hard—cruel?"

"You do it with so little!" And with this, unexpectedly to Nick, Mrs. Dallow burst straight into tears. Before he could stop her she was at the door of the pavilion, as if she wished to quit it immediately. There, however, he stopped her, bending over her while she sobbed, unspeakably gentle with her.

"So little? It's with everything—with everything I have."

"I have done it, you say? What do you accuse me of doing?" Her tears were already over.

"Of making me yours; of being so precious, Julia, so exactly what a man wants, as it seems to me. I didn't know you could," he went on, smiling down at her. "I didn't—no, I didn't."

"It's what I say—that you've always hated me."

"I'll make it up to you."

She leaned on the doorway with her head against the lintel. "You don't even deny it."

"Contradict you *now*? I'll admit it, though it's rubbish, on purpose to live it down."

"It doesn't matter," she said, slowly; "for however much you might have liked me, you would never have done so half as much as I have cared for you."

"Oh, I'm so poor!" Nick murmured, cheerfully.

She looked at him, smiling, and slowly shook her head. Then she declared: "You never can."

"I like that! Haven't I asked you to marry me? When did you ever ask me?"

"Every day of my life! As I say, it's hard—for a proud woman."

"Yes, you're too proud even to answer me."

"We must think of it, we must talk of it."

"Think of it? I've thought of it ever so much."

"I mean together. There are things to be said."

"The principal thing is to give me your word."

Mrs. Dallow looked at him in silence; then she exclaimed: "I wish I didn't adore you!" She went straight down the steps.

"You don't, if you leave me now. Why do you go? It's so charming here, and we are so delightfully alone."

"Detach the boat; we'll go on the water," said Mrs. Dallow.

Nick was at the top of the steps, looking down at her. "Ah, stay a little—*do* stay!" he pleaded.

"I'll get in myself, I'll put off," she answered.

At this Nick came down and he bent a little to undo the rope. He was close to her, and as he raised his head he felt it caught; she had seized it in her hands and she pressed her lips to the first place they encountered. The next instant she was in the boat.

This time he dipped the oars very slowly indeed; and while, for a period that was longer than it seemed to them, they floated vaguely, they mainly sat and glowed at each other, as if everything had been settled. There were reasons enough why Nick should be happy; but it is a singular fact that the leading one was the sense of having escaped from a great mistake. The final result of his mother's appeal to him the day before had been the idea that he must act with unimpeachable honour. He was capable of taking it as an assurance that Julia had placed him under an obligation which a gentleman could regard only in one way. If *she* had understood it so, putting the vision, or at any rate the appreciation, of a closer tie into everything she had done for him, the case was conspicuously simple and his course unmistakably plain. That is why he had been gay when he came out of the house to look for her: he could be gay when his course was plain. He could be all the gayer, naturally, I must add, that in turning things over, as he had done half the night, what he had turned up oftenest was the recognition that Julia now had a new personal power over him. It was not for nothing that she had thrown herself personally into his life. She had by her act made him live twice as much, and such a service, if a man had accepted and deeply tasted it, was certainly a thing to put him on his honour. Nick gladly recognized that there was nothing he could do in preference that would not be spoiled for him by any deflection from that point. His mother had made him uncomfortable by intimating to him that Julia was in love with him (he didn't like, in general, to be told such things); but the responsibility seemed easier to carry and he was less shy about it when once he was away from other eyes, with only Julia's own to express that truth and with indifferent nature all around. Besides, what discovery had he made this morning but that he also was in love?

"You must be a very great man," she said to him, in the middle of the lake. "I don't know what you mean about my salon; but I *am* ambitious."

"We must look at life in a large, bold way," Nick replied, resting his oars.

"That's what I mean. If I didn't think you could I wouldn't look at you."

"I could what?"

"Do everything you ought—everything I imagine, I dream of. You *are* clever: you can never make me believe the contrary, after your speech on Tuesday. Don't speak to me! I've seen, I've heard and I know what's in you. I shall hold you to it. You are everything that you pretend not to be."

Nick sat looking at the water while she talked. "Will it always be so amusing?" he asked.

"Will what always be?"

"Why, my career."

"Sha'n't I make it so?"

"It will be yours; it won't be mine," said Nick.

"Ah, don't say that: don't make me out that sort of woman! If they should say it's me, I'd drown myself."

"If they should say what's you?"

"Why, your getting on. If they should say I push you, that I do things for you."

"Well, won't you do them? It's just what I count on."

"Don't be dreadful," said Mrs. Dallow. "It would be loathsome if I were said to be cleverer than you. That's not the sort of man I want to marry."

"Oh, I shall make you work, my dear!"

"Ah, that!" exclaimed Mrs. Dallow, in a tone that might come back to a man in after years.

"You will do the great thing, you will make my life delightful," Nick declared, as if he fully perceived the sweetness of it. "I dare say that will keep me in heart."

"In heart? Why shouldn't you be in heart?" Julia's eyes, lingering on him, searching him, seemed to question him still more than her lips.

"Oh, it will be all right!" cried Nick.

"You'll like success, as well as any one else. Don't tell me—you're not so ethereal!"

"Yes, I shall like success."

"So shall I! And of course I am glad that you'll be able to

do things," Mrs. Dallow went on. "I'm glad you'll have things. I'm glad I'm not poor."

"Ah, don't speak of that," Nick murmured. "Only be nice to my mother: we shall make her supremely happy."

"I'm glad I like your people," Mrs. Dallow dropped. "Leave them to me!"

"You're generous—you're noble," stammered Nick.

"Your mother must live at Broadwood; she must have it for life. It's not at all bad."

"Ah, Julia," her companion replied, "it's well I love you!"

"Why shouldn't you?" laughed Julia; and after this there was nothing said between them till the boat touched the shore. When she had got out Mrs. Dallow remarked that it was time for luncheon; but they took no action in consequence, strolling in a direction which was not that of the house. There was a vista that drew them on, a grassy path skirting the foundations of scattered beeches and leading to a stile from which the charmed wanderer might drop into another division of Mrs. Dallow's property. This lady said something about their going as far as the stile; then the next instant she exclaimed: "How stupid of you—you've forgotten Mr. Hoppus!"

"We left him in the temple of Vesta. Darling, I had other things to think of there."

"I'll send for him," said Mrs. Dallow.

"Lord, can you think of him now?" Nick asked.

"Of course I can—more than ever."

"Shall we go back for him?" Nick inquired, pausing.

Mrs. Dallow made no answer; she continued to walk, saying they would go as far as the stile. "Of course I know you're fearfully vague," she presently resumed.

"I wasn't vague at all. But you were in such a hurry to get away."

"It doesn't signify. I have another one at home."

"Another summer-house?" suggested Nick.

"A copy of Mr. Hoppus."

"Mercy, how you go in for him! Fancy having two!"

"He sent me the number of the magazine; and the other is the one that comes every month."

"Every month—I see," said Nick, in a manner justifying

considerably Mrs. Dallow's charge of vagueness. They had reached the stile and he leaned over it, looking at a great mild meadow and at the browsing beasts in the distance.

"Did you suppose they come every day?" asked Mrs. Dallow.

"Dear no, thank God!" They remained there a little; he continued to look at the animals and before long he added: "Delightful English pastoral scene. Why do they say it won't paint?"

"Who says it won't?"

"I don't know—some of them. It will in France; but somehow it won't here."

"What are you talking about?" Mrs. Dallow demanded.

Nick appeared unable to satisfy her on this point; at any rate instead of answering her directly he said: "Is Broadwood very charming?"

"Have you never been there? It shows how you've treated me. We used to go there in August. George had ideas about it," added Mrs. Dallow. She had never affected not to speak of her late husband, especially with Nick, whose kinsman in a manner he had been and who had liked him better than some others did.

"George had ideas about a great many things."

Julia Dallow appeared to be conscious that it would be rather odd on such an occasion to take this up. It was even odd in Nick to have said it. "Broadwood is just right," she rejoined at last. "It's neither too small nor too big, and it takes care of itself. There's nothing to be done: you can't spend a penny."

"And don't you want to use it?"

"We can go and stay with *them*," said Mrs. Dallow.

"They'll think I bring them an angel." And Nick covered her hand, which was resting on the stile, with his own large one.

"As they regard you yourself as an angel they will take it as natural of you to associate with your kind."

"Oh, *my* kind!" murmured Nick, looking at the cows.

Mrs. Dallow turned away from him as if she were starting homeward, and he began to retrace his steps with her. Suddenly she said: "What did you mean that night in Paris?"

"That night?"

"When you came to the hotel with me, after we had all dined at that place with Peter."

"What did I mean?"

"About your caring so much for the fine arts. You seemed to want to frighten me."

"Why should you have been frightened? I can't imagine what I had in my head: not now."

"You *are* vague," said Julia, with a little flush.

"Not about the great thing."

"The great thing?"

"That I owe you everything an honest man has to offer. How can I care about the fine arts now?"

Mrs. Dallow stopped, looking at him. "Is it because you think you *owe* it—" and she paused, still with the heightened colour in her cheek; then she went on—"that you have spoken to me as you did there?" She tossed her head toward the lake.

"I think I spoke to you because I couldn't help it."

"You *are* vague." And Mrs. Dallow walked on again.

"You affect me differently from any other woman."

"Oh, other women! Why shouldn't you care about the fine arts now?" she added.

"There will be no time. All my days and my years will be none too much to do what you expect of me."

"I don't expect you to give up anything. I only expect you to do more."

"To do more I must do less. I have no talent."

"No talent?"

"I mean for painting."

Mrs. Dallow stopped again. "That's odious! You *have*—you must."

Nick burst out laughing. "You're altogether delightful. But how little you know about it—about the honourable practice of any art!"

"What do you call practice? You'll have all our things—you'll live in the midst of them."

"Certainly I shall enjoy looking at them, being so near them."

"Don't say I've taken you away then."

"Taken me away?"

"From the love of art. I like them myself now, poor George's treasures. I didn't, of old, so much, because it seemed to me he made too much of them—he was always talking."

"Well, I won't talk," said Nick.

"You may do as you like—they're yours."

"Give them to the nation," Nick went on.

"I like that! When we have done with them."

"We shall have done with them when your Vandykes and Moronis have cured me of the delusion that I may be of *their* family. Surely that won't take long."

"You shall paint *me*," said Julia.

"Never, never, never!" Nick uttered these words in a tone that made his companion stare; and he appeared slightly embarrassed at this result of his emphasis. To relieve himself he said, as they had come back to the place beside the lake where the boat was moored: "Sha'n't we really go and fetch Mr. Hoppus?"

She hesitated. "You may go; I won't, please."

"That's not what I want."

"Oblige me by going. I'll wait here." With which Mrs. Dallow sat down on the bench attached to the little landing.

Nick, at this, got into the boat and put off; he smiled at her as she sat there watching him. He made his short journey, disembarked and went into the pavilion; but when he came out with the object of his errand he saw that Mrs. Dallow had quitted her station—she had returned to the house without him. He rowed back quickly, sprang ashore and followed her with long steps. Apparently she had gone fast; she had almost reached the door when he overtook her.

"Why did you basely desert me?" he asked, stopping her there.

"I don't know. Because I'm so happy."

"May I tell mother?"

"You may tell her she shall have Broadwood."

II.

NICK LOST no time in going down to see Mr. Carteret, to whom he had written immediately after the election and who had answered him in twelve revised pages of historical parallel. He used often to envy Mr. Carteret's leisure, a sense of which came to him now afresh, in the summer evening, as he walked up the hill toward the quiet house where enjoyment, for him, had ever been mingled with a vague oppression. He was a little boy again, under Mr. Carteret's roof—a little boy on whom it had been duly impressed that in the wide, plain, peaceful rooms he was not to "touch." When he paid a visit to his father's old friend there were in fact many things—many topics—from which he instinctively kept his hands. Even Mr. Chayter, the immemorial blank butler, who was so like his master that he might have been a twin brother, helped to remind him that he must be good. Mr. Carteret seemed to Nick a very grave person, but he had the sense that Chayter thought him rather frivolous.

Our young man always came on foot from the station, leaving his portmanteau to be carried: the direct way was steep and he liked the slow approach, which gave him a chance to look about the place and smell the new-mown hay. At this season the air was full of it—the fields were so near that it was in the small, empty streets. Nick would never have thought of rattling up to Mr. Carteret's door. It had an old brass plate with his name, as if he had been the principal surgeon. The house was in the high part, and the neat roofs of other houses, lower down the hill, made an immediate prospect for it, scarcely counting however, for the green country was just below these, familiar and interpenetrating, in the shape of small but thick-tufted gardens. There was something growing in all the intervals, and the only disorder of the place was that there were sometimes oats on the pavements. A crooked lane, very clean, with cobblestones, opened opposite to Mr. Carteret's house and wandered towards the old abbey: for the abbey was the secondary fact of Beauclere, after Mr. Carteret. Mr. Carteret sometimes went away and the abbey never did; yet somehow it was most of the essence of the place that it possessed the proprietor of the squarest of the square red houses, with the finest of the arched hall-windows, in three divisions, over the widest of the last-century door-ways. You saw the great abbey from the doorstep, beyond the gardens of course, and in the stillness you could hear the flut-ter of the birds that circled round its huge, short towers. The towers had never been finished, save as time finishes things, by perpetuating their incompleteness. There is something right in old monuments that have been wrong for centuries: some such moral as that was usually in Nick's mind as an emanation of Beauclere, when he looked at the magnificent line of the roof, riding the sky and unsurpassed for length.

When the door with the brass plate was opened and Mr. Chayter appeared in the middle distance (he always advanced just to the same spot, like a prime minister receiving an ambassador), Nick saw anew that he would be wonderfully like Mr. Carteret if he had had an expression. He did not permit himself this freedom; never giving a sign of recogni-tion, often as the young man had been at the house. He was most attentive to the visitor's wants, but apparently feared that if he allowed a familiarity it might go too far. There was always the same question to be asked—had Mr. Carteret fin-ished his nap? He usually had not finished it, and this left Nick what he liked—time to smoke a cigarette in the garden or even, before dinner, to take a turn about the place. He observed now, every time he came, that Mr. Carteret's nap lasted a little longer. There was each year a little more strength to be gathered for the ceremony of dinner: this was the principal symptom—almost the only one—that the clear-cheeked old gentleman gave of not being so fresh as of yore. He was still wonderful for his age. To-day he was particularly careful: Chayter went so far as to mention to Nick that four gentlemen were expected to dinner—an effusiveness perhaps partly explained by the circumstance that Lord Bottomley was one of them.

The prospect of Lord Bottomley was somehow not stir-ring; it only made the young man say to himself with a quick, thin sigh: "This time I *am* in for it!" And he immediately had the unpolitical sense again that there was nothing so pleasant as the way the quiet bachelor house had its best rooms on the big garden, which seemed to advance into them through their wide windows and ruralize their dullness.

"I expect it will be a latish eight, sir," said Mr. Chayter, superintending in the library the production of tea on a large scale. Everything at Mr. Carteret's appeared to Nick to be on a larger scale than anywhere else—the tea-cups, the knives and forks, the door-handles, the chair-backs, the legs of mutton, the candles and the lumps of coal: they represented and apparently exhausted the master's sense of pleasing effect, for the house was not otherwise decorated. Nick thought it really hideous, but he was capable at the same time of extracting a degree of amusement from anything that was strongly characteristic, and Mr. Carteret's interior expressed a whole view of life. Our young man was generous enough to find a hundred instructive intimations in it even at the time it came over him (as it always did at Beauclere) that this was the view he himself was expected to take. Nowhere were the boiled eggs at breakfast so big or in such big receptacles; his own shoes, arranged in his room, looked to him vaster there than at home. He went out into the garden and remembered what enormous strawberries they should have for dinner. In the house there was a great deal of Landseer, of oilcloth, of woodwork painted and "grained."

Finding that he should have time before the evening meal, or before Mr. Carteret would be able to see him, he quitted the house and took a stroll toward the abbey. It covered acres of ground on the summit of the hill, and there were aspects in which its vast bulk reminded him of the ark left high and dry upon Ararat. At least it was the image of a great wreck, of the indestructible vessel of a faith, washed up there by a storm centuries before. The injury of time added to this appearance—the infirmities around which, as he knew, the battle of restoration had begun to be fought. The cry had been raised to save the splendid pile, and the counter-cry by the purists, the sentimentalists, whatever they were, to save it from being saved. They were all exchanging compliments in the morning papers.

Nick sauntered round the church—it took a good while; he leaned against low things and looked up at it while he smoked another cigarette. It struck him as a great pity it should be touched: so much of the past was buried there that it was like desecrating, like digging up a grave. And the years seemed to be letting it down so gently: why jostle the elbow of slow-fingering time? The fading afternoon was exquisitely pure; the place was empty; he heard nothing but the cries of several children, which sounded sweet, who were playing on the flatness of the very old tombs. He knew that this would inevitably be one of the topics at dinner, the restoration of the abbey; it would give rise to a considerable deal of orderly debate. Lord Bottomley, oddly enough, would probably oppose the expensive project, but on grounds that would be characteristic of him even if the attitude were not. Nick's nerves, on this spot, always knew what it was to be soothed; but he shifted his position with a slight impatience as the vision came over him of Lord Bottomley's treating a question of æsthetics. It was enough to make one want to take the other side, the idea of having the same taste as his lordship: one would have it for such different reasons.

Dear Mr. Carteret would be deliberate and fair all round, and would, like his noble friend, exhibit much more architectural knowledge than he, Nick, possessed: which would not make it a whit less droll to our young man that an artistic idea, so little really assimilated, should be broached at that table and in that air. It would remain so outside of their minds and their minds would remain so outside of it. It would be dropped at last however, after half an hour's gentle worrying, and the conversation would incline itself to public affairs. Mr. Carteret would find his natural level—the production of anecdote in regard to the formation of early ministries. He knew more than any one else about the personages of whom certain cabinets would have consisted if they had not consisted of others. His favourite exercise was to illustrate how different everything might have been from what it was, and how the reason of the difference had always been somebody's inability to "see his way" to accept the view of somebody else—a view usually, at the time, discussed, in strict confidence, with Mr. Carteret, who surrounded his actual violation of that confidence, thirty years later, with many precautions against scandal. In this retrospective vein, at the head of his table, the old gentleman always enjoyed an audience or at any rate commanded a silence, often profound. Every one left it to some one else to ask another question; and when by chance some one else did so every one was struck with admiration at any one's being able to say anything. Nick knew the moment when he himself would take a glass of a particular port and, surreptitiously looking at his watch, perceive it was ten o'clock. It might as well be 1830.

All this would be a part of the suggestion of leisure that invariably descended upon him at Beauclere—the image of a sloping shore where the tide of time broke with a ripple too faint to be a warning. But there was another admonition that was almost equally sure to descend upon his spirit in a summer hour, in a stroll about the grand abbey; to sink into it as the light lingered on the rough red walls and the local accent of the children sounded soft in the churchyard. It was simply the sense of England—a sort of apprehended revelation of his country. The dim annals of the place appeared to be in the air (foundations bafflingly early, a great monastic life, wars of the Roses, with battles and blood in the streets, and then the long quietude of the respectable centuries, all corn-fields and magistrates and vicars), and these things were connected with an emotion that arose from the green country, the rich land so infinitely lived in, and laid on him a hand that was too ghostly to press and yet somehow too urgent to be light. It produced a throb that he could not have spoken of, it was so deep, and that was half imagination and half responsibility. These impressions melted together and made a general appeal, of which, with his new honours as a legislator, he was the sentient subject. If he had a love for this particular scene of life, might it not have a love for him and expect something of him? What fate could be so high as to grow old in a national affection? What a grand kind of reciprocity, making mere soreness of all the balms of indifference!

The great church was still open, and he turned into it and wandered a little in the twilight, which had gathered earlier there. The whole structure, with its immensity of height and distance, seemed to rest on tremendous facts—facts of achievement and endurance—and the huge Norman pillars to loom through the dimness like the ghosts of heroes. Nick was more struck with its human than with its divine significance, and he felt the oppression of his conscience as he walked slowly about. It was in his mind that nothing in life was really clear, all things were mingled and charged, and that patriotism might be an uplifting passion even if it had to allow for Lord Bottomley and for Mr. Carteret's blindness on certain sides. Presently he perceived it was nearly half-past seven, and as he went back to his old friend's he could not have told you whether he was in a state of gladness or of gloom.

"Mr. Carteret will be in the drawing-room at a quarter to eight, sir," Chayter said; and Nick, as he went to his chamber, asked himself what was the use of being a member of Parliament if one was still sensitive to an intimation on the part of such a functionary that one ought already to have begun to dress. Chayter's words meant that Mr. Carteret would expect to have a little comfortable conversation with him before dinner. Nick's usual rapidity in dressing was however quite adequate to the occasion, and his host had not appeared when he went down. There were flowers in the unfeminine saloon, which contained several paintings, in addition to the engravings of pictures of animals; but nothing could prevent its reminding Nick of a comfortable committee-room.

Mr. Carteret presently came in, with his gold-headed stick, a laugh like a series of little warning coughs and the air of embarrassment that our young man always perceived in him at first. He was nearly eighty, but he was still shy—he laughed a great deal, faintly and vaguely, at nothing, as if to make up for the seriousness with which he took some jokes. He always began by looking away from his interlocutor, and it was only little by little that his eyes came round; after which their limpid and benevolent blue made you wonder why they should ever be circumspect. He was clean shaven and had a long upper lip. When he had seated himself he talked of "majorities" and showed a disposition to converse on the general subject of the fluctuation of Liberal gains. He had an extraordinary memory for facts of this sort and could mention the figures relating to elections in innumerable places in particular years. To many of these facts he attached great importance, in his simple, kindly, presupposing way; returning five minutes later and correcting himself if he had said that some one, in 1857, had had 6014 instead of 6004.

Nick always felt a great hypocrite as he listened to him, in spite of the old man's courtesy—a thing so charming in it-self that it would have been grossness to speak of him as a bore. The difficulty was that he took for granted all kinds of positive assent, and Nick, in his company, found himself im-mersed in an atmosphere of tacit pledges which constituted the very medium of intercourse and yet made him draw his breath a little in pain when, for a moment, he measured them. There would have been no hypocrisy at all if he could have regarded Mr. Carteret as a mere sweet spectacle, the last or almost the last illustration of a departing tradition of manners. But he represented something more than manners; he represented what he believed to be morals and ideas—ideas as regards which he took your personal deference (not discovering how natural that was) for participation. Nick liked to think that his father, though ten years younger, had found it congruous to make his best friend of the owner of so nice a nature: it gave a softness to his feeling for that memory to be reminded that Sir Nicholas had been of the same general type—a type so pure, so disinterested, so anx-ious about the public good. Just so it endeared Mr. Carteret to him to perceive that he considered his father had done a definite work, prematurely interrupted, which had been an absolute benefit to the people of England. The oddity was however that though both Mr. Carteret's aspect and his ap-preciation were still so fresh, this relation of his to his late distinguished friend made the latter appear to Nick even more irrecoverably dead. The good old man had almost a vocabulary of his own, made up of old-fashioned political phrases and quite untainted with the new terms, mostly bor-rowed from America; indeed, his language and his tone made those of almost any one who might be talking with him appear by contrast rather American. He was, at least nowadays, never severe or denunciatory; but sometimes in telling an anecdote he dropped such an expression as "the rascal said to me," or such an epithet as "the vulgar dog."

Nick was always struck with the rare simplicity (it came out in his countenance) of one who had lived so long and seen so much of affairs that draw forth the passions and perversities of men. It often made him say to himself that Mr. Carteret must have been very remarkable to achieve with his means so many things requiring cleverness. It was as if experience, though coming to him in abundance, had dealt with him with such clean hands as to leave no stain and had never provoked him to any general reflection. He had never proceeded in any ironic way from the particular to the general; certainly he had never made a reflection upon anything so unparliamentary as Life. He would have questioned the taste of such an excrescence, and if he had encountered it on the part of another would have regarded it as a kind of French toy, with the uses of which he was unacquainted. Life, for him, was a purely practical function, not a question of phrasing. It must be added that he had, to Nick's perception, his variations—his back windows opening into grounds more private. That was visible from the way his eye grew cold and his whole polite face rather austere when he listened to something that he didn't agree with or perhaps even understand; as if his modesty did not in strictness forbid the suspicion that a thing he didn't understand would have a probability against it. At such times there was something a little deadly in the silence in which he simply waited, with a lapse in his face, without helping his interlocutor out. Nick would have been very sorry to attempt to communicate to him a matter which he probably would not understand. This cut off of course a multitude of subjects.

The evening passed exactly as Nick had foreseen, even to the rather early dispersal of the guests, two of whom were "local" men, earnest and distinct, though not particularly distinguished. The third was a young, slim, uninitiated gentleman whom Lord Bottomley brought with him and concerning whom Nick was informed beforehand that he was engaged to be married to the Honourable Jane, his lordship's second daughter. There were recurrent allusions to Nick's victory, as to which he had the fear that he might appear to exhibit less interest in it than the company did. He took energetic precautions against this and felt repeatedly a little spent with them, for the subject always came up once more. Yet it was not as his but as theirs that they liked the triumph. Mr.

Carteret took leave of him for the night directly after the other guests had gone, using at this moment the words that he had often used before—

"You may sit up to any hour you like. I only ask that you don't read in bed."

III.

Nick's little visit was to terminate immediately after luncheon the following day: much as the old man enjoyed his being there he would not have dreamed of asking for more of his time now that it had such great public uses. He liked infinitely better that his young friend should be occupied with parliamentary work than only occupied in talking about it with him. Talk about it however was the next best thing, as on the morrow after breakfast Mr. Carteret showed Nick that he considered. They sat in the garden, the morning being warm, and the old man had a table beside him, covered with the letters and newspapers that the post had brought. He was proud of his correspondence, which was altogether on public affairs, and proud in a manner of the fact that he now dictated almost everything. That had more in it of the statesman in retirement, a character indeed not consciously assumed by Mr. Carteret, but always tacitly attributed to him by Nick, who took it rather from the pictorial point of view: remembering on each occasion only afterwards that though he was in retirement he had not exactly been a statesman. A young man, a very sharp, handy young man, came every morning at ten o'clock and wrote for him till lunch-time. The young man had a holiday to-day, in honour of Nick's visit— a fact the mention of which led Nick to make some not particularly sincere speech about *his* being ready to write anything if Mr. Carteret were at all pressed.

"Ah, but your own budget: what will become of that?" the old gentleman objected, glancing at Nick's pockets as if he was rather surprised not to see them stuffed out with documents in split envelopes. His visitor had to confess that he had not directed his letters to meet him at Beauclere: he should find them in town that afternoon. This led to a little homily from Mr. Carteret which made him feel rather guilty; there was such an implication of neglected duty in the way the old man said: "You won't do them justice—you won't do them justice." He talked for ten minutes, in his rich, simple, urbane way, about the fatal consequences of getting behind. It was his favourite doctrine that one should always be a little before; and his own eminently regular respiration seemed to illustrate the idea. A man was certainly before who had so much in his rear.

This led to the bestowal of a good deal of general advice as to the mistakes to avoid at the beginning of a parliamentary career; as to which Mr. Carteret spoke with the experience of one who had sat for fifty years in the House of Commons. Nick was amused, but also mystified and even a little irritated by his talk: it was founded on the idea of observation and yet Nick was unable to regard Mr. Carteret as an observer. "He doesn't observe *me*," he said to himself; "if he did he would see, he wouldn't think—" And the end of this private cogitation was a vague impatience of all the things his venerable host took for granted. He didn't see any of the things that Nick saw. Some of these latter were the light touches of the summer morning scattered through the sweet old garden. The time passed there a good deal as if it were sitting still, with a plaid under its feet, while Mr. Carteret distilled a little more of the wisdom that he had drawn from his fifty years. This immense term had something fabulous and monstrous for Nick, who wondered whether it were the sort of thing his companion supposed *he* had gone in for. It was not strange Mr. Carteret should be different; he might originally have been more—to himself Nick was not obliged to phrase it: what our young man meant was more of what it was perceptible to him that his host was not. Should even he, Nick, be like that at the end of fifty years? What Mr. Carteret was so good as to expect for him was that he should be much more distinguished; and wouldn't this exactly mean much more like that? Of course Nick heard some things that he had heard before; as for instance the circumstances that had originally led the old man to settle at Beauclere. He had been returned for that locality (it was his second seat), in years far remote, and had come to live there because he then had a conscientious conviction (modified indeed by later experience) that a member should be constantly resident. He spoke of this now, smiling rosily, as he might have spoken of some wild aberration of his youth; yet he called Nick's attention to the fact that he still so far clung to his conviction as to hold (though of what might be urged on the other side he was perfectly aware), that a representative should at least be as resident as possible. This gave Nick an opening for saying something that had been on and off his lips all the morning.

"According to that I ought to take up my abode at Harsh."

"In the measure of the convenient I should not be sorry to see you do it."

"It ought to be rather convenient," Nick replied, smiling. "I've got a piece of news for you which I've kept, as one keeps that sort of thing (for it's very good), till the last." He waited a little, to see if Mr. Carteret would guess, and at first he thought nothing would come of this. But after resting his young-looking eyes on him for a moment the old man said—

"I should indeed be very happy to hear that you have arranged to take a wife."

"Mrs. Dallow has been so good as to say that she will marry me," Nick went on.

"That is very suitable. I should think it would answer."

"It's very jolly," said Nick. It was well that Mr. Carteret was not what his guest called observant, or he might have thought there was less gaiety in the sound of this sentence than in the sense.

"Your dear father would have liked it."

"So my mother says."

"And *she* must be delighted."

"Mrs. Dallow, do you mean?" Nick asked.

"I was thinking of your mother. But I don't exclude the charming lady. I remember her as a little girl. I must have seen her at Windrush. Now I understand the zeal and amiability with which she threw herself into your canvass."

"It was her they elected," said Nick.

"I don't know that I have ever been an enthusiast for political women, but there is no doubt that, in approaching the mass of electors, a graceful, affable manner, the manner of the real English lady, is a force not to be despised."

"Mrs. Dallow is a real English lady, and at the same time she's a very political woman," Nick remarked.

"Isn't it rather in the family? I remember once going to see her mother in town and finding the leaders of both parties sitting with her."

"My principal friend, of the others, is her brother Peter. I don't think he troubles himself much about that sort of thing."

"What does he trouble himself about?" Mr. Carteret inquired, with a certain gravity.

"He's in the diplomatic service; he's a secretary in Paris."

"That may be serious," said the old man.

"He takes a great interest in the theatre; I suppose you'll say that may be serious too," Nick added, laughing.

"Oh!" exclaimed Mr. Carteret, looking as if he scarcely understood. Then he continued: "Well, it can't hurt you."

"It can't hurt me?"

"If Mrs. Dallow takes an interest in your interests."

"When a man's in my situation he feels as if nothing could hurt him."

"I'm very glad you're happy," said Mr. Carteret. He rested his mild eyes on our young man, who had a sense of seeing in them for a moment the faint ghost of an old story, the dim revival of a sentiment that had become the memory of a memory. This glimmer of wonder and envy, the revelation of a life intensely celibate, was for an instant infinitely touching. Nick had always had a theory, suggested by a vague allusion from his father, who had been discreet, that their benevolent friend had had in his youth an unhappy love-affair which had led him to forswear for ever the commerce of woman. What remained in him of conscious renunciation gave a throb as he looked at his bright companion, who proposed to take the matter so much the other way. "It's good to marry, and I think it's right. I've not done right, I know it. If she's a good woman it's the best thing," Mr. Carteret went on. "It's what I've been hoping for you. Sometimes I've thought of speaking to you."

"She's a very good woman," said Nick.

"And I hope she's not poor." Mr. Carteret spoke with exactly the same blandness.

"No, indeed, she's rich. Her husband, whom I knew and liked, left her a large fortune."

"And on what terms does she enjoy it?"

"I haven't the least idea," said Nick.

Mr. Carteret was silent a moment. "I see. It doesn't concern you. It needn't concern you," he added in a moment.

Nick thought of his mother, at this, but he remarked: "I dare say she can do what she likes with her money."

"So can I, my dear young friend," said Mr. Carteret.

Nick tried not to look conscious, for he felt a significance in the old man's face. He turned his own everywhere but towards it, thinking again of his mother. "That must be very pleasant, if one has any."

"I wish you had a little more."

"I don't particularly care," said Nick.

"Your marriage will assist you; you can't help that," Mr. Carteret went on. "But I should like you to be under obligations not quite so heavy."

"Oh, I'm so obliged to her for caring for me!"

"That the rest doesn't count? Certainly it's nice of her to like you. But why shouldn't she? Other people do."

"Some of them make me feel as if I abused it," said Nick, looking at his host. "That is, they don't make me, but I feel it," he added, correcting himself.

"I have no son," said Mr. Carteret. "Sha'n't you be very kind to her?" he pursued. "You'll gratify her ambition."

"Oh, she thinks me cleverer than I am."

"That's because she's in love," hinted the old gentleman, as if this were very subtle. "However, you must be as clever as we think you. If you don't prove so—" And he paused, with his folded hands.

"Well, if I don't?" asked Nick.

"Oh, it won't do—it won't do," said Mr. Carteret, in a tone his companion was destined to remember afterwards. "I say I have no son," he continued; "but if I had had one he should have risen high."

"It's well for me such a person doesn't exist. I shouldn't easily have found a wife."

"He should have gone to the altar with a little money in his pocket."

"That would have been the least of his advantages, sir."

"When are you to be married?" Mr. Carteret asked.

"Ah, that's the question. Mrs. Dallow won't say."

"Well, you may consider that when it comes off I will make you a settlement."

"I feel your kindness more than I can say," Nick replied; "but that will probably be the moment when I shall be least conscious of wanting anything."

"You'll appreciate it later—you'll appreciate it very soon. I shall like you to appreciate it," Mr. Carteret went on, as if he had a just vision of the way a young man of a proper spirit should feel. Then he added: "Your father would have liked you to appreciate it."

"Poor father!" Nick exclaimed vaguely, rather embarrassed, reflecting on the oddity of a position in which the ground for holding up his head as the husband of a rich woman would be that he had accepted a present of money from another source. It was plain that he was not fated to go in for independence; the most that he could treat himself to would be dependence that was duly grateful. "How much you expect of me!" he pursued, with a grave face.

"It's only what your father did. He so often spoke of you, I remember, at the last, just after you had been with him alone—you know I saw him then. He was greatly moved by his interview with you, and so was I by what he told me of it. He said he should live on in you—he should work in you. It has always given me a very peculiar feeling, if I may use the expression, about you."

"The feelings are indeed peculiar, dear Mr. Carteret, which take so munificent a form. But you do—oh, you do—expect too much."

"I expect you to repay me!" said the old man gaily. "As for the form, I have it in my mind."

"The form of repayment?"

"No, no—of settlement."

"Ah, don't talk of it now," said Nick, "for, you see, nothing else is settled. No one has been told except my mother. She has only consented to my telling you."

"Lady Agnes, do you mean?"

"Ah, no; dear mother would like to publish it on the house-tops. She's so glad—she wants us to have it over to-morrow. But Julia wishes to wait. Therefore kindly mention it for the present to no one."

"My dear boy, at this rate there is nothing to mention. What does Julia want to wait for?"

"Till I like her better—that's what she says."

"It's the way to make you like her worse. Hasn't she your affection?"

"So much so that her delay makes me exceedingly unhappy."

Mr. Carteret looked at his young friend as if he didn't strike him as very unhappy; but he demanded: "Then what more does she want?" Nick laughed out at this, but he perceived his host had not meant it as an epigram; while the latter went on: "I don't understand. You're engaged or you're not engaged."

"She is, but I am not. That's what she says about it. The trouble is she doesn't believe in me."

"Doesn't she love you then?"

"That's what I ask her. Her answer is that she loves me only too well. She's so afraid of being a burden to me that she gives me my freedom till I've taken another year to think."

"I like the way you talk about other years!" Mr. Carteret exclaimed. "You had better do it while I'm here to bless you."

"She thinks I proposed to her because she got me in for Harsh," said Nick.

"Well, I'm sure it would be a very pretty return."

"Ah, she doesn't believe in me," Nick murmured.

"Then I don't believe in her."

"Don't say that—don't say that. She's a very rare creature. But she's proud, shy, suspicious."

"Suspicious of what?"

"Of everything. She thinks I'm not persistent."

"Persistent?"

"She can't believe I shall arrive at true eminence."

"A good wife should believe what her husband believes," said Mr. Carteret.

"Ah, unfortunately I don't believe it either."

Mr. Carteret looked serious. "Your dear father did."

"I think of that—I think of that," Nick replied. "Certainly it will help me. If I say we're engaged," he went on, "it's because I consider it so. She gives me my liberty, but I don't take it."

"Does she expect you to take back your word?"

"That's what I ask her. *She* never will. Therefore we're as good as tied."

"I don't like it," said Mr. Carteret, after a moment. "I don't like ambiguous, uncertain situations. They please me much better when they are definite and clear." The retreat of expression had been sounded in his face—the aspect it wore when he wished not to be encouraging. But after an instant he added in a tone softer than this: "Don't disappoint me, my dear boy."

"Disappoint you?"

"I've told you what I want to do for you. See that the conditions come about promptly in which I *may* do it. Are you sure that you do everything to satisfy Mrs. Dallow?" Mr. Carteret continued.

"I think I'm very nice to her," Nick protested. "But she's so ambitious. Frankly speaking, it's a pity—for her—that she likes me."

"She can't help that."

"Possibly. But isn't it a reason for taking me as I am? What she wants to do is to take me as I may be a year hence."

"I don't understand if, as you say, even then she won't take back her word," said Mr. Carteret.

"If she doesn't marry me I think she'll never marry again at all."

"What then does she gain by delay?"

"Simply this, as I make it out—that she'll feel she has been very magnanimous. She won't have to reproach herself with not having given me a chance to change."

"To change? What does she think you liable to do?"

Nick was silent a minute. "I don't know!" he said, not at all candidly.

"Everything has altered: young people in my day looked at these questions more naturally," Mr. Carteret declared. "A woman in love has no need to be magnanimous. If she is, she isn't in love," he added shrewdly.

"Oh, Mrs. Dallow's safe—she's safe," Nick smiled.

"If it were a question between you and another gentleman one might comprehend. But what does it mean, between you and nothing?"

"I'm much obliged to you, sir," Nick returned. "The trouble is that she doesn't know what she has got hold of."

"Ah, if you can't make it clear to her!"

"I'm such a humbug," said the young man. His companion stared, and he continued: "I deceive people without in the least intending it."

"What on earth do you mean? Are you deceiving me?"

"I don't know—it depends on what you think."

"I think you're flighty," said Mr. Carteret, with the nearest approach to sternness that Nick had ever observed in him. "I never thought so before."

"Forgive me; it's all right. I'm not frivolous; that I affirm I'm not."

"You *have* deceived me if you are."

"It's all right," Nick stammered, with a blush.

"Remember your name—carry it high."

"I will—as high as possible."

"You've no excuse. Don't tell me, after your speeches at Harsh!" Nick was on the point of declaring again that he was a humbug, so vivid was his inner sense of what *he* thought of his factitious public utterances, which had the cursed property of creating dreadful responsibilities and importunate credulities for him. If *he* was "clever," what fools many other people were! He repressed his impulse, and Mr. Carteret pursued: "If, as you express it, Mrs. Dallow doesn't know what she has got hold of, won't it clear the matter up a little if you inform her that the day before your marriage is definitely settled to take place you will come into something comfortable?"

A quick vision of what Mr. Carteret would be likely to regard as something comfortable flitted before Nick, but it did not prevent him from replying: "Oh, I'm afraid that won't do any good. It would make her like you better, but it wouldn't make her like me. I'm afraid she won't care for any benefit that comes to me from another hand than hers. Her affection is a very jealous sentiment."

"It's a very peculiar one!" sighed Mr. Carteret. "Mine's a jealous sentiment too. However, if she takes it that way don't tell her."

"I'll let you know as soon as she comes round," said Nick.

"And you'll tell your mother," said Mr. Carteret. "I shall like her to know."

"It will be delightful news to her. But she's keen enough already."

"I know that. I may mention now that she has written to me," the old man added.

"So I suspected."

"We have corresponded on the subject," Mr. Carteret continued to confess. "My view of the advantageous character of such an alliance has entirely coincided with hers."

"It was very good-natured of you to leave me to speak first," said Nick.

"I should have been disappointed if you hadn't. I don't like all you have told me. But don't disappoint me now."

"Dear Mr. Carteret!" Nick exclaimed.

"I won't disappoint *you*," the old man went on, looking at his big, old-fashioned watch.

IV.

At first Peter Sherringham thought of asking to be transferred to another post and went so far, in London, as to take what he believed to be good advice on the subject. The advice perhaps struck him as the better for consisting of a strong recommendation to do nothing so foolish. Two or three reasons were mentioned to him why such a request would not, in the particular circumstances, raise him in the esteem of his superiors, and he promptly recognized their force. It next appeared to him that it might help him (not with his superiors, but with himself,) to apply for an extension of leave; but on further reflection he remained convinced that though there are some dangers before which it is perfectly consistent with honour to flee, it was better for every one concerned that he should fight this especial battle on the spot. During his holiday his plan of campaign gave him plenty of occupation. He refurbished his arms, rubbed up his strategy, laid out his lines of defence.

There was only one thing in life that his mind had been very much made up to, but on this question he had never wavered: he would get on to the utmost in his profession. It was a point on which it was perfectly lawful to be unamiable to others—to be vigilant, eager, suspicious, selfish. He had not in fact been unamiable to others, for his affairs had not required it: he had got on well enough without hardening his heart. Fortune had been kind to him and he had passed so many competitors on the way that he could forswear jealousy and be generous. But he had always flattered himself that his hand would not falter on the day he should find it necessary to drop bitterness into his cup. This day would be sure to dawn, for no career was all clear water to the end; and then the sacrifice would find him ready. His mind was familiar with the thought of a sacrifice: it is true that nothing could be plain in advance about the occasion, the object, the victim. All that was tolerably definite was that the propitiatory offering would have to be some cherished enjoyment. Very likely indeed this enjoyment would be associated with the charms of another person—a probability pregnant with the idea that such charms would have to be dashed out of sight. At any rate it never had occurred to Sherringham that he himself might be the sacrifice. You had to pay to get on; but at least you borrowed from others to do it. When you couldn't borrow you didn't get on: for what was the situation in life in which you met the whole requisition yourself?

Least of all had it occurred to our friend that the wrench might come through his interest in that branch of art on which Nick Dormer had rallied him. The beauty of a love of the theatre was precisely that it was a passion exercised on the easiest terms. This was not the region of responsibility. It had the discredit of being sniffed at by the austere; but if it was not, as they said, a serious field, was not the compensation just that you could not be seriously entangled in it? Sherringham's great advantage, as he regarded the matter, was that he had always kept his taste for the drama quite in its place. His facetious cousin was free to pretend that it sprawled through his life; but this was nonsense, as any unprejudiced observer of that life would unhesitatingly attest. There had not been the least sprawling, and his fancy for the art of Garrick had never worn the proportions of an eccentricity. It had never drawn down from above anything approaching a reprimand, a remonstrance, a remark. Sherringham was positively proud of his discretion; for he was a little proud of what he did know about the stage. Trifling for trifling there were plenty of his fellows who had in their lives private infatuations much sillier and less confessable. Had he not known men who collected old invitation-cards (hungry for those of the last century), and others who had a secret passion for shuffleboard? His little weaknesses were intellectual—they were a part of the life of the mind. All the same on the day they showed a symptom of interfering they should be plucked off with a turn of the wrist.

Sherringham scented interference now, and interference in rather an invidious form. It might be a bore, from the point of view of the profession, to find one's self, as a critic of the stage, in love with a *coquine*; but it was a much greater bore to find one's self in love with a young woman whose character remained to be estimated. Miriam Rooth was neither fish nor flesh: one had with her neither the guarantees of one's own class nor the immunities of hers. What was hers, if one came to that? A certain puzzlement about this very point was part of the fascination which she had ended by throwing over him. Poor Sherringham's scheme for getting on had contained no proviso against falling in love, but it had embodied an important clause on the subject of surprises. It was always a surprise to fall in love, especially if one were looking out for it; so this contingency had not been worth official paper. But it became a man who respected the service he had undertaken for the State to be on his guard against predicaments from which the only issue was the rigour of matrimony. An ambitious diplomatist would probably be wise to marry, but only with his eyes very much open. That was the fatal surprise—to be led to the altar in a dream. Sherringham's view of the proprieties attached to such a step was high and strict; and if he held that a man in his position was, especially as the position improved, essentially a representative of the greatness of his country, he considered that the wife of such a personage would exercise in her degree (for instance, at a foreign court) a function no less symbolic. She would always be, in short, a very important quantity, and the scene was strewn with illustrations of this general truth. She might be such a help and she might be such a blight that common prudence required that one should test her in advance. Sherringham had seen women in the career who were stupid or vulgar make a mess of things—it was enough to wring your heart. Then he had his positive idea of the perfect ambassadress, the full-blown lily of the future; and with this idea Miriam Rooth presented no analogy whatever.

The girl had described herself with characteristic directness as "all right"; and so she might be, so she assuredly was: only all right for what? He had divined that she was not sentimental—that whatever capacity she might have for responding to a devotion or for desiring it was at any rate not in the direction of vague philandering. With him certainly she had no disposition to philander. Sherringham was almost afraid to think of this, lest it should beget in him a rage convertible mainly into caring for her more. Rage or no rage, it would be charming to be in love with her if there were no complications; but the complications were in advance just what was clearest in the business. He was perhaps cold-blooded to think of them; but it must be remembered that they were the particular thing which his training had equipped him for dealing with. He was at all events not too cold-blooded to have, for the two months of his holiday, very little inner vision of anything more abstract than Miriam's face. The desire to see it again was as pressing as thirst; but he tried to teach himself the endurance of the traveller in the desert. He kept the Channel between them, but his spirit moved every day an inch nearer to her, until (and it was not long) there were no more inches left. The last thing he expected the future ambassadress to have been was a *fille de théâtre*. The answer to this objection was of course that Miriam was not yet so much of one but that he could easily head her off. Then came worrying retorts to that, chief among which was the sense that to his artistic conscience heading her off would be simple shallowness. The poor girl had a right to her chance, and he should not really alter anything by taking it away from her; for was she not the artist to the tips of her tresses (the ambassadress never in the world), and would she not take it out in something else if one were to make her deviate? So certain was that irrepressible deviltry to insist ever on its own.

Besides, *could* one make her deviate? If she had no disposition to philander, what was his warrant for supposing that she could be corrupted into respectability? How could the career (*his* career) speak to a nature which had glimpses, as vivid as they were crude, of such a different range, and for which success meant quite another sauce to the dish? Would the brilliancy of marrying Peter Sherringham be such a bribe to relinquishment? How could he think so without fatuity— how could he regard himself as a high prize? Relinquishment of the opportunity to exercise a rare talent was not, in the nature of things, an easy effort to a young lady who was conceited as well as ambitious. Besides, she might eat her cake and have it—might make her fortune both on the stage and in the world. Successful actresses had ended by marrying dukes, and was not that better than remaining obscure and marrying a commoner? There were moments when Sherringham tried to think that Miriam's talent was not a force to reckon with; there was so little to show for it as yet that the caprice of believing in it would perhaps suddenly leave her.

But his suspicion that it was real was too uneasy to make such an experiment peaceful, and he came back moreover to his deepest impression—that of her being of the turn of mind for which the only consistency is talent. Had not Madame Carré said at the last that she could "do anything"? It was true that if Madame Carré had been mistaken in the first place she might also be mistaken in the second. But in this latter case she would be mistaken with him, and such an error would be too like a truth.

I ought possibly to hesitate to say how much Sherringham felt the discomfort, for him, of the advantage that Miriam had of him—the advantage of her presenting herself in a light which rendered any passion that he might entertain an implication of duty as well as of pleasure. Why there should be this implication was more than he could say; sometimes he declared to himself that he was superstitious for seeing it. He didn't know, he could scarcely conceive of another case of the same general type in which he would have seen it. In foreign countries there were very few ladies of Miss Rooth's intended profession who would not have regarded it as too strong an order that to console them for not being admitted into drawing-rooms they should have no offset but the exercise of a virtue in which no one would believe. Because in foreign countries actresses were not admitted into drawing-rooms: that was a pure English drollery, ministering equally little to histrionics and to the tone of these resorts. Did the sanctity which to his imagination made it a burden to have to reckon with Miriam come from her being English? Sherringham could remember cases in which that privilege operated as little as possible as a restriction. It came a great deal from Mrs. Rooth, in whom he apprehended depths of calculation as to what she might achieve for her daughter by "working" the idea of a blameless life. Her romantic turn of mind would not in the least prevent her from regarding that idea as a substantial capital, to be laid out to the best worldly advantage. Miriam's essential irreverence was capable, on a pretext, of making mince-meat of it—that he was sure of; for the only capital she recognized was the talent which some day managers and agents would outbid each other in paying for. But she was a good-natured creature; she was fond of her mother, would do anything to oblige (that might work in all sorts of ways), and would probably like the loose slippers of blamelessness quite as well as the high standards of the opposite camp.

Sherringham, I may add, had no desire that she should indulge a different preference: it was foreign to him to compute the probabilities of a young lady's misbehaving for his advantage (that seemed to him definitely base), and he would have thought himself a blackguard if, professing a tenderness for Miriam, he had not wished the thing that was best for her. The thing that was best for her would no doubt be to become the wife of the man to whose suit she should incline her ear. That this would be the best thing for the gentleman in question was however a very different matter, and Sherringham's final conviction was that it would never do for him to act the part of that hypothetic personage. He asked for no removal and no extension of leave, and he proved to himself how well he knew what he was about by never addressing a line, during his absence, to the Hôtel de la Garonne. He would simply go straight and inflict as little injury upon Peter Sherringham as upon any one else. He remained away to the last hour of his privilege and continued to act lucidly in having nothing to do with the mother and daughter for several days after his return to Paris.

It was when this discipline came to an end, one afternoon after a week had passed, that he felt most the force of the reference that has just been made to Mrs. Rooth's private reckonings. He found her at home alone, writing a letter under the lamp, and as soon as he came in she cried out that he was the very person to whom the letter was addressed. She could bear it no longer; she had permitted herself to reproach him with his terrible silence—to ask why he had quite forsaken them. It was an illustration of the way in which her visitor had come to regard her that he rather disbelieved than believed this description of the crumpled papers lying on the table. He was not sure even that he believed that Miriam had just gone out. He told her mother how busy he had been all the while he was away and how much time in particular he had had to give, in London, to seeing on her daughter's behalf the people connected with the theatres.

"Ah, if you pity me, tell me that you've got her an engagement!" Mrs. Rooth cried, clasping her hands.

"I took a great deal of trouble; I wrote ever so many notes, sought introductions, talked with people—such impossible people some of them. In short I knocked at every door, I went into the question exhaustively." And he enumerated the things he had done, imparted some of the knowledge he had gathered. The difficulties were serious, and even with the influence he could command (such as it was) there was very little to be achieved in face of them. Still he had gained ground: there were two or three fellows, men with small theatres, who had listened to him better than the others, and there was one in particular whom he had a hope he might really have interested. From him he had extracted certain merciful assurances: he would see Miriam, he would listen to her, he would do for her what he could. The trouble was that no one would lift a finger for a girl unless she were known, and yet that she never could become known until innumerable fingers were lifted. You couldn't go into the water unless you could swim, and you couldn't swim until you had been in the water.

"But new performers appear; they get theatres, they get audiences, they get notices in the newspapers," Mrs. Rooth objected. "I know of these things only what Miriam tells me. It's no knowledge that I was born to."

"It's perfectly true; it's all done with money."

"And how do they come by money?" Mrs. Rooth asked, candidly.

"When they're women people give it to them."

"Well, what people, now?"

"People who believe in them."

"As you believe in Miriam?"

Sherringham was silent a moment. "No, rather differently. A poor man doesn't believe anything in the same way that a rich man does."

"Ah, don't call yourself poor!" groaned Mrs. Rooth.

"What good would it do me to be rich?"

"Why, you could take a theatre; you could do it all yourself."

"And what good would that do me?"

"Why, don't you delight in her genius?" demanded Mrs. Rooth.

"I delight in her mother. You think me more disinterested than I am," Sherringham added, with a certain soreness of irritation.

"I know why you didn't write!" Mrs. Rooth declared, archly.

"You must go to London," Peter said, without heeding this remark.

"Ah, if we could only get there it would be a relief. I should draw a long breath. There at least I know where I am, and what people are. But here one lives on hollow ground!"

"The sooner you get away the better," Sherringham went on.

"I know why you say that."

"It's just what I'm explaining."

"I couldn't have held out if I hadn't been so sure of Miriam," said Mrs. Rooth.

"Well, you needn't hold out any longer."

"Don't *you* trust her?" asked Sherringham's hostess.

"Trust her?"

"You don't trust yourself. That's why you were silent, why we might have thought you were dead, why we might have perished ourselves."

"I don't think I understand you; I don't know what you're talking about," Sherringham said. "But it doesn't matter."

"Doesn't it? Let yourself go: why should you struggle?" the old woman inquired.

Her unexpected insistence annoyed her visitor, and he was silent again, looking at her, on the point of telling her that he didn't like her tone. But he had his tongue under such control that he was able presently to say, instead of this—and it was a relief for him to give audible voice to the reflection: "It's a great mistake, either way, for a man to be in love with an actress. Either it means nothing serious, and what's the use of that? or it means everything, and that's still more delusive."

"Delusive?"

"Idle, unprofitable."

"Surely a pure affection is its own reward," Mrs. Rooth rejoined, with soft reasonableness.

"In such a case how can it be pure?"

"I thought you were talking of an English gentleman," said Mrs. Rooth.

"Call the poor fellow whatever you like: a man with his life to lead, his way to make, his work, his duties, his career to attend to. If it means nothing, as I say, the thing it means least of all is marriage."

"Oh, my own Miriam!" murmured Mrs. Rooth.

"On the other hand fancy the complication if such a man marries a woman who's on the stage."

Mrs. Rooth looked as if she were trying to follow. "Miriam isn't on the stage yet."

"Go to London and she soon will be."

"Yes, and then you'll have your excuse."

"My excuse?"

"For deserting us altogether."

Sherringham broke into laughter at this, the tone was so droll. Then he rejoined: "Show me some good acting and I won't desert you."

"Good acting? Ah, what is the best acting compared with the position of an English lady? If you'll take her as she is you may have her," Mrs. Rooth suddenly added.

"As she is, with all her ambitions unassuaged?"

"To marry *you*—might not that be an ambition?"

"A very paltry one. Don't answer for her, don't attempt that," said Sherringham. "You can do much better."

"Do you think *you* can?" smiled Mrs. Rooth.

"I don't want to; I only want to let it alone. She's an artist; you must give her her head," Peter went on. "You must always give an artist his head."

"But I have known great ladies who were artists. In English society there is always a field."

"Don't talk to me of English society! Thank heaven, in the first place, I don't live in it. Do you want her to give up her genius?"

"I thought you didn't care for it."

"She'd say 'No, I thank you, dear mamma.' "

"My gifted child!" Mrs. Rooth murmured.

"Have you ever proposed it to her?"

"Proposed it?"

"That she should give up trying."

Mrs. Rooth hesitated, looking down. "Not for the reason you mean. We don't talk about love," she simpered.

"Then it's so much less time wasted. Don't stretch out your hand to the worse when it may some day grasp the better," Sherringham pursued. Mrs. Rooth raised her eyes at him as if she recognized the force there might be in that, and he added: "Let her blaze out, let her look about her. Then you may talk to me if you like."

"It's very puzzling," the old woman remarked, artlessly.

Sherringham laughed again; then he said: "Now don't tell me I'm not a good friend."

"You are indeed—you're a very noble gentleman. That's just why a quiet life with you—"

"It wouldn't be quiet for me!" Sherringham broke in. "And that's not what Miriam was made for."

"Don't say that, for my precious one!" Mrs. Rooth quavered.

"Go to London—go to London," her visitor repeated.

Thoughtfully, after an instant, she extended her hand and took from the table the letter on the composition of which he had found her engaged. Then with a quick movement she tore it up. "That's what Mr. Dashwood says."

"Mr. Dashwood?"

"I forgot you don't know him. He's the brother of that lady we met the day you were so good as to receive us; the one who was so kind to us—Mrs. Lovick."

"I never heard of him."

"Don't you remember that she spoke of him and Mr. Lovick didn't seem very kind about him? She told us that if he were to meet us—and she was so good as to insinuate that it would be a pleasure to him to do so—he might give us, as she said, a tip."

Sherringham indulged in a visible effort to recollect. "Yes, he comes back to me. He's an actor."

"He's a gentleman too," said Mrs. Rooth.

"And you've met him and he *has* given you a tip?"

"As I say, he wants us to go to London."

"I see, but even I can tell you that."

"Oh, yes," said Mrs. Rooth; "but *he* says he can help us."

"Keep hold of him then, if he's in the business."

"He's a perfect gentleman," said Mrs. Rooth. "He's immensely struck with Miriam."

"Better and better. Keep hold of him."

"Well, I'm glad you don't object," Mrs. Rooth smiled.

"Why should I object?"

"You don't consider us as *all* your own?"

"My own? Why, I regard you as the public's—the world's."

Mrs. Rooth gave a little shudder. "There's a sort of chill in that. It's grand, but it's cold. However, I needn't hesitate then to tell you that it's with Mr. Dashwood that Miriam has gone out."

"Why hesitate, gracious heaven?" But in the next breath Sherringham asked: "Where has she gone?"

"You don't like it!" laughed Mrs. Rooth.

"Why should it be a thing to be enthusiastic about?"

"Well, he's charming, and *I* trust him."

"So do I," said Sherringham.

"They've gone to see Madame Carré."

"She has come back then?"

"She was expected back last week. Miriam wants to show her how she has improved."

"And *has* she improved?"

"How can I tell—with my mother's heart?" asked Mrs. Rooth. "I don't judge; I only wait and pray. But Mr. Dashwood thinks she's wonderful."

"That's a blessing. And when did he turn up?"

"About a fortnight ago. We met Mrs. Lovick at the English church, and she was so good as to recognize us and speak to us. She said she had been away with her children, or she would have come to see us. She had just returned to Paris."

"Yes, I've not yet seen her," said Sherringham. "I see Lovick, but he doesn't talk of his brother-in-law."

"I didn't, that day, like his tone about him," Mrs. Rooth observed. "We walked a little way with Mrs. Lovick and she asked Miriam about her prospects and if she were working. Miriam said she had no prospects."

"That was not very nice to *me*," Sherringham interrupted.

"But when you had left us in black darkness, where *were* our prospects?"

"I see; it's all right. Go on."

"Then Mrs. Lovick said her brother was to be in Paris a few days and she would tell him to come and see us. He arrived, she told him and he came. *Voilà!*" said Mrs. Rooth.

"So that now (so far as *he* is concerned) Miss Rooth has prospects?"

"He isn't a manager unfortunately."

"Where does he act?"

"He isn't acting just now; he has been abroad. He has been to Italy, I believe, and he is just stopping here on his way to London."

"I see; he *is* a perfect gentleman," said Sherringham.

"Ah, you're jealous of him."

"No, but you're trying to make me so. The more competitors there are for the glory of bringing her out, the better for her."

"Mr. Dashwood wants to take a theatre," said Mrs. Rooth.

"Then perhaps he's our man."

"Oh, if you'd help him!" cried Mrs. Rooth.

"Help him?"

"Help him to help us."

"We'll all work together; it will be very jolly," said Sherringham gaily. "It's a sacred cause, the love of art, and we shall be a happy band. Dashwood's his name?" he added in a moment. "Mrs. Lovick wasn't a Dashwood."

"It's his *nom de théâtre*—Basil Dashwood. Do you like it?" Mrs. Rooth inquired.

"You say that as Miriam might do: her talent is catching."

"She's always practising—always saying things over and over, to seize the tone. I have her voice in my ears. He wants *her* not to have any."

"Not to have any?"

"Any *nom de théâtre*. He wants her to use her own; he likes it so much. He says it will do so well—you can't better it."

"He's a capital adviser," said Sherringham, getting up. "I'll come back to-morrow."

"I won't ask you to wait till they return, they may be so long," Mrs. Rooth replied.

"Will he come back with her?" Sherringham inquired, smoothing his hat.

"I hope so, at this hour. With my child in the streets I tremble. We don't live in cabs, as you may easily suppose."

"Did they go on foot?" Sherringham continued.

"Oh yes; they started in high spirits."

"And is Mr. Basil Dashwood acquainted with Madame Carré?"

"Oh no, but he longed to be introduced to her; he implored Miriam to take him. Naturally she wishes to oblige him. She's very nice to him—if he can do anything."

"Quite right; that's the way."

"And she also wanted him to see what she can do for the great critic," Mrs. Rooth added.

"The great critic?"

"I mean that terrible old woman in the red wig."

"That's what I should like to see too," said Sherringham.

"Oh, she has gone ahead; she is pleased with herself. 'Work, work, work,' said Madame Carré. Well, she has worked, worked, worked. That's what Mr. Dashwood is pleased with even more than with other things."

"What do you mean by other things?"

"Oh, her genius and her fine appearance."

"He approves of her fine appearance? I ask because you think he knows what will take."

"I know why you ask," said Mrs. Rooth. "He says it will be worth hundreds of thousands to her."

"That's the sort of thing I like to hear," Sherringham rejoined. "I'll come in to-morrow," he repeated.

"And shall you mind if Mr. Dashwood's here?"

"Does he come every day?"

"Oh, they're always at it."

"Always at it?"

"Why, she acts to him—every sort of thing—and he says if it will do."

"How many days has he been here then?"

Mrs. Rooth reflected. "Oh, I don't know. Since he turned up they've passed so quickly."

"So far from 'minding' it I'm eager to see him," Sher-ringham declared; "and I can imagine nothing better than what you describe—if he isn't an ass."

"Dear me, if he isn't clever you must tell us: we can't afford to be deceived!" Mrs. Rooth exclaimed, innocently and plain-tively. "What do we know—how can we judge?" she added.

Sherringham hesitated, with his hand on the latch. "Oh, I'll tell you what I think of him!"

V.

WHEN HE GOT into the street he looked about him for a cab, but he was obliged to walk some distance before encountering one. In this little interval he saw no reason to modify the determination he had formed in descending the steep staircase of the Hôtel de la Garonne; indeed the desire which prompted it only quickened his pace. He had an hour to spare and he too would go to see Madame Carré. If Miriam and her companion had proceeded to the Rue de Constantinople on foot he would probably reach the house as soon as they. It was all quite logical: he was eager to see Miriam—that was natural enough; and he had admitted to Mrs. Rooth that he was keen on the subject of Mrs. Lovick's theatrical brother, in whom such effective aid might perhaps reside. To catch Miriam really revealing herself to the old actress (since that was her errand), with the jump she believed herself to have taken, would be a very happy stroke, the thought of which made her benefactor impatient. He presently found his cab and, as he bounded in, bade the coachman drive fast. He learned from Madame Carré's portress that her illustrious *locataire* was at home and that a lady and a gentleman had gone up some time before.

In the little antechamber, after he was admitted, he heard a high voice issue from the salon, and, stopping a moment to listen, perceived that Miriam was already launched in a recitation. He was able to make out the words, all the more that before he could prevent the movement the maid-servant who had let him in had already opened the door of the room (one of the wings of it, there being, as in most French doors, two pieces), before which, within, a heavy curtain was suspended. Miriam was in the act of rolling out some speech from the English poetic drama—

"For I am sick and capable of fears,
  Oppressed with wrongs and therefore full of fears."

He recognized one of the great tirades of Shakespeare's Constance and saw she had just begun the magnificent scene at the beginning of the third act of *King John*, in which the

passionate, injured mother and widow sweeps in wild organ-
tones up and down the scale of her irony and wrath. The
curtain concealed him and he lurked there for three minutes
after he had motioned to the *femme de chambre* to retire on
tiptoe. The trio in the salon, absorbed in the performance,
had apparently not heard his entrance or the opening of the
door, which was covered by the girl's splendid declamation.
Sherringham listened intently, he was so arrested by the spirit
with which she attacked her formidable verses. He had
needed to hear her utter but half a dozen of them to comprehend the long stride she had taken in his absence; they told
him that she had leaped into possession of her means. He
remained where he was till she arrived at—

> "Then speak again; not all thy former tale,
>   But this one word, whether thy tale be true."

This apostrophe, being briefly responded to in another voice,
gave him time quickly to raise the curtain and show himself,
passing into the room with a "Go on, go on!" and a gesture
earnestly deprecating a stop.

Miriam, in the full swing of her part, paused but for an
instant and let herself ring out again, while Peter sank into
the nearest chair and she fixed him with her illumined eyes,
or rather with those of the raving Constance. Madame
Carré, buried in a chair, kissed her hand to him, and a
young man who stood near the girl giving her the cue stared
at him over the top of a little book. "Admirable—magnificent; go on," Sherringham repeated—"go on to the end of
the scene—do it all!" Miriam flushed a little, but he immediately discovered that she had no personal emotion in seeing him again; the cold passion of art had perched on her
banner and she listened to herself with an ear as vigilant as if
she had been a Paganini drawing a fiddle-bow. This effect
deepened as she went on, rising and rising to the great occasion, moving with extraordinary ease and in the largest,
clearest style on the dizzy ridge of her idea. That she had an
idea was visible enough and that the whole thing was very
different from all that Sherringham had hitherto heard her
attempt. It belonged quite to another class of effort; she
seemed now like the finished statue lifted from the ground

to its pedestal. It was as if the sun of her talent had risen above the hills and she knew that she was moving, that she would always move, in its guiding light. This conviction was the one artless thing that glimmered like a young joy through the tragic mask of Constance, and Sherringham's heart beat faster as he caught it in her face. It only made her appear more intelligent; and yet there had been a time when he had thought her stupid! Intelligent was the whole spirit in which she carried the scene, making him cry to himself from point to point: "How she feels it—how she sees it—how she creates it!"

He looked at moments at Madame Carré and perceived that she had an open book in her lap, apparently a French prose version, brought by her visitors, of the play; but she never either glanced at him or at the volume; she only sat screwing into the girl her hard bright eyes, polished by experience like fine old brasses. The young man uttering the lines of the other speakers was attentive in another degree; he followed Miriam in his own copy of the play, to be sure not to miss the cue; but he was elated and expressive, was evidently even surprised; he coloured and smiled, and when he extended his hand to assist Constance to rise, after Miriam, acting out her text, had seated herself grandly on "the huge, firm earth," he bowed over her as obsequiously as if she had been his veritable sovereign. He was a very good-looking young man, tall, well-proportioned, straight-featured and fair, of whom manifestly the first thing to be said on any occasion was that he looked remarkably like a gentleman. He carried this appearance, which proved inveterate and importunate, to a point that was almost a negation of its spirit; that is it might have been a question whether it could be in good taste to wear any character, even that particular one, so much on one's sleeve. It was literally on his sleeve that this young man partly wore his own; for it resided considerably in his attire and especially in a certain close-fitting dark blue frock-coat (a miracle of a fit), which moulded his young form just enough and not too much and constituted (as Sherringham was destined to perceive later) his perpetual uniform or badge. It was not till later that Sherringham began to feel exasperated by Basil Dashwood's "type" (the young stranger was of course Basil

Dashwood), and even by his blue frock-coat, the recurrent, unvarying, imperturbable "good form" of his aspect. This un-professional air ended by striking the observer as the profes-sion that he had adopted, and was indeed (so far as had as yet been indicated) his theatrical capital, his main qualification for the stage.

The powerful, ample manner in which Miriam handled her scene produced its full impression, the art with which she sur-mounted its difficulties, the liberality with which she met its great demand upon the voice, and the variety of expression that she threw into a torrent of objurgation. It was a real composition, studded with passages that called a suppressed "Brava!" to the lips and seeming to show that a talent capable of such an exhibition was capable of anything.

> "But thou art fair, and at thy birth, dear boy,
>   Nature and Fortune join'd to make thee great:
>   Of Nature's gifts thou mayst with lilies boast,
>   And with the half-blown rose."

As Miriam turned to her imagined child with this exquisite apostrophe (she addressed Mr. Dashwood as if he were play-ing Arthur, and he lowered his book, dropped his head and his eyes and looked handsome and ingenuous), she opened at a stroke to Sherringham's vision a prospect that they would yet see her express tenderness better even than anything else. Her voice was enchanting in these lines, and the beauty of her performance was that while she uttered the full fury of the part she missed none of its poetry.

"Where did she get hold of that—where did she get hold of that?" Sherringham wondered while his whole sense vi-brated. "She hadn't got hold of it when I went away." And the assurance flowed over him again that she had found the key to her box of treasures. In the summer, during their weeks of frequent meeting, she had only fumbled with the lock. One October day, while he was away, the key had slipped in, had fitted, or her finger at last had touched the right spring, and the capricious casket had flown open.

It was during the present solemnity that Sherringham, ex-cited by the way she came out and with a hundred startled ideas about her wheeling through his mind, was for the first time and most vividly visited by a perception that ended by becoming frequent with him—that of the perfect presence of mind, unconfused, unhurried by emotion, that any artistic performance requires and that all, whatever the instrument, require in exactly the same degree: the application, in other words, clear and calculated, crystal-firm as it were, of the idea conceived in the glow of experience, of suffering, of joy. Sherringham afterwards often talked of this with Miriam, who however was not able to present him with a neat theory of the subject. She had no knowledge that it was publicly discussed; she was just practically on the side of those who hold that at the moment of production the artist cannot have his wits too much about him. When Peter told her there were people who maintained that in such a crisis he must lose himself in the flurry she stared with surprise and then broke out: "Ah, the idiots!" She eventually became in her judgments, in impatience and the expression of contempt, very free and absolutely irreverent.

"What a splendid scolding!" Sherringham exclaimed when, on the entrance of the Pope's legate, her companion closed the book upon the scene. Peter pressed his lips to Madame Carré's finger-tips; the old actress got up and held out her arms to Miriam. The girl never took her eyes off Sherringham while she passed into Madame Carré's embrace and remained there. They were full of their usual sombre fire, and it was always the case that they expressed too much anything that they expressed at all; but they were not defiant nor even triumphant now—they were only deeply explicative; they seemed to say: "That's the sort of thing I meant; that's what I had in mind when I asked you to try to do something for me." Madame Carré folded her pupil to her bosom, holding her there as the old marquise in a *comédie de mœurs* might, in the last scene, have held her goddaughter the *ingénue*.

"Have you got me an engagement?" Miriam asked of Sherringham. "Yes, he has done something splendid for me," she went on to Madame Carré, resting her hand caressingly on one of the actress's while the old woman discoursed with Mr. Dashwood, who was telling her in very pretty French that he was tremendously excited about Miss Rooth. Madame Carré looked at him as if she wondered how he appeared when he was calm and how, as a dramatic artist, he expressed that condition.

"Yes, yes, something splendid, for a beginning," Sherringham answered, radiantly, recklessly; feeling now only that he would say anything, do anything, to please her. He spent on the spot, in imagination, his last penny.

"It's such a pity you couldn't follow it; you would have liked it so much better," Mr. Dashwood observed to his hostess.

"Couldn't follow it? Do you take me for *une sotte*?" the celebrated artist cried. "I suspect I followed it *de plus près que vous, monsieur!*"

"Ah, you see the language is so awfully fine," Basil Dashwood replied, looking at his shoes.

"The language? Why, she rails like a fish-wife. Is that what you call language? Ours is another business."

"If you understood—if you understood you would see the greatness of it," Miriam declared. And then, in another tone, "Such delicious expressions!"

"*On dit que c'est très fort*. But who can tell if you really say it?" Madame Carré demanded.

"Ah, *par exemple*, I can!" Sherringham exclaimed.

"Oh, you—you're a Frenchman."

"Couldn't he tell if he were not?" asked Basil Dashwood.

The old woman shrugged her shoulders. "He wouldn't know."

"That's flattering to me."

"Oh, you—don't you pretend to complain," Madame Carré said. "I prefer *our* imprecations—those of Camille," she went on. "They have the beauty *des plus belles choses*."

"I can say them too," Miriam broke in.

"*Insolente!*" smiled Madame Carré. "Camille doesn't squat down on the floor in the middle of them."

> "For grief is proud and makes his owner stoop.
> To me and to the state of my great grief
> Let kings assemble,"

Miriam quickly declaimed. "Ah, if you don't feel the way she makes a throne of it!"

"It's really tremendously fine, *chère madame*," Sherringham said. "There's nothing like it."

"*Vous êtes insupportables,*" the old woman answered. "Stay with us. I'll teach you Phèdre."

"Ah, Phædra—Phædra!" Basil Dashwood vaguely ejaculated, looking more gentlemanly than ever.

"You have learned all I have taught you, but where the devil have you learned what I haven't taught you?" Madame Carré went on.

"I've worked—I have; you'd call it work—all through the bright, late summer, all through the hot, dull, empty days. I've battered down the door—I did hear it crash one day. But I'm not so very good yet: I'm only in the right direction."

"*Malicieuse!*" murmured Madame Carré.

"Oh, I can beat that," the girl went on.

"Did you wake up one morning and find you had grown a pair of wings?" Sherringham asked. "Because that's what the difference amounts to—you really soar. Moreover you're an angel," he added, charmed with her unexpectedness, the good-nature of her forbearance to reproach him for not having written to her. And it seemed to him privately that she *was* angelic when in answer to this she said ever so blandly:

"You know you read *King John* with me before you went away. I thought over constantly what you said. I didn't understand it much at the time—I was so stupid. But it all came to me later."

"I wish you could see yourself," Sherringham answered.

"My dear fellow, I do. What do you take me for? I didn't miss a vibration of my voice, a fold of my robe."

"I didn't see you looking," Sherringham returned.

"No one ever will. Do you think I would show it?"

"*Ars celare artem,*" Basil Dashwood jocosely dropped.

"You must first have the art to hide," said Sherringham, wondering a little why Miriam didn't introduce her young friend to him. She was, however, both then and later, perfectly neglectful of such cares, never thinking or heeding how other people got on together. When she found they didn't get on she laughed at them: that was the nearest she came to arranging for them. Sherringham observed, from the moment she felt her strength, the immense increase of her good-humoured inattention to detail—all detail save that of her work, to which she was ready to sacrifice holocausts of feel-ings, when the feelings were other people's. This conferred on her a kind of profanity, an absence of ceremony in her social relations, which was both amusing, because it suggested that she would take what she gave, and formidable, because it was inconvenient and you might not care to give what she would take.

"If you haven't got any art it's not quite the same as if you didn't hide it, is it?" asked Basil Dashwood.

"That's right—say one of your clever things!" murmured Miriam, sweetly, to the young man.

"You're always acting," he answered, in English, with a laugh, while Sherringham remained struck with his expressing just what he himself had felt weeks before.

"And when you have shown them your fish-wife, to your public *de là-bas*, what will you do next?" asked Madame Carré.

"I'll do Juliet—I'll do Cleopatra."

"Rather a big bill, isn't it?" Mr. Dashwood volunteered to Sherringham, in a friendly, discriminating manner.

"Constance and Juliet—take care you don't mix them," said Sherringham.

"I want to be various. You once told me I had a hundred characters," Miriam replied.

"Ah, *vous-en-êtes là?*" cried the old actress. "You may have a hundred characters, but you have only three plays. I'm told that's all there are in English."

Miriam appealed to Sherringham. "What arrangements have you made? What do the people want?"

"The people at the theatre?"

"I'm afraid they don't want King John, and I don't believe they hunger for Antony and Cleopatra," Basil Dashwood sug-gested. "Ships and sieges and armies and pyramids, you know: we mustn't be too heavy."

"Oh, I hate scenery!" sighed Miriam.

"*Elle est superbe,*" said Madame Carré. "You must put those pieces on the stage: how will you do it?"

"Oh, we know how to get up a play in London, Madame

Carré," Basil Dashwood responded, genially. "They put money on it, you know."

"On it? But what do they put *in* it? Who will interpret them? Who will manage a style like that—the style of which the verses she just repeated are a specimen? Whom have you got that one has ever heard of?"

"Oh, you'll hear of a good deal when once she gets started," Basil Dashwood contended, cheerfully.

Madame Carré looked at him a moment; then, "You'll become very bad," she said to Miriam. "I'm glad I sha'n't see it."

"People will do things for me—I'll make them," the girl declared. "I'll stir them up so that they'll have ideas."

"What people, pray?"

"Ah, terrible woman!" Sherringham moaned, theatrically.

"We translate your pieces—there will be plenty of parts," Basil Dashwood said.

"Why then go out of the door to come in at the window?—especially if you smash it! An English arrangement of a French piece is a pretty woman with her back turned."

"Do you really want to keep her?" Sherringham asked of Madame Carré, as if he were thinking for a moment that this after all might be possible.

She bent her strange eyes on him. "No, you are all too queer together; we couldn't be bothered with you, and you're not worth it."

"I'm glad it's together; we can console each other."

"If you only would; but you don't seem to! In short, I don't understand you—I give you up. But it doesn't matter," said the old woman, wearily, "for the theatre is dead and even you, *ma toute-belle*, won't bring it to life. Everything is going from bad to worse, and I don't care what becomes of you. You wouldn't understand us here and they won't understand you there, and everything is impossible, and no one is a whit the wiser, and it's not of the least consequence. Only when you raise your arms lift them just a little higher," Madame Carré added.

"My mother will be happier *chez nous*," said Miriam, throwing her arms straight up with a noble tragic movement.

"You won't be in the least in the right path till your mother's in despair."

"Well, perhaps we can bring that about even in London," Sherringham suggested, laughing.

"Dear Mrs. Rooth—she's great fun," Mr. Dashwood dropped.

Miriam transferred the gloomy beauty of her gaze to him, as if she were practising. "*You* won't upset her, at any rate." Then she stood with her fatal mask before Madame Carré. "I want to do the modern too. I want to do *le drame*, with realistic effects."

"And do you want to look like the portico of the Madeleine when it's draped for a funeral?" her instructress mocked. "Never, never. I don't believe you're various: that's not the way I see you. You're pure tragedy, with *de grands effets de voix*, in the great style, or you're nothing."

"Be beautiful—be only that," Sherringham advised. "Be only what you can be so well—something that one may turn to for a glimpse of perfection, to lift one out of all the vulgarities of the day."

Thus apostrophized, the girl broke out with one of the speeches of Racine's Phædra, hushing her companions on the instant. "You'll be the English Rachel," said Basil Dashwood when she stopped.

"Acting in French!" Madame Carré exclaimed. "I don't believe in an English Rachel."

"I shall have to work it out, what I shall be," Miriam responded with a rich, pensive effect.

"You're in wonderfully good form to-day," Sherringham said to her; his appreciation revealing a personal subjection which he was unable to conceal from his companions, much as he wished it.

"I really mean to do everything."

"Very well; after all, Garrick did."

"Well, I shall be the Garrick of my sex."

"There's a very clever author doing something for me; I should like you to see it," said Basil Dashwood, addressing himself equally to Miriam and to her diplomatic friend.

"Ah, if you have very clever authors!" Madame Carré spun the sound to the finest satiric thread.

"I shall be very happy to see it," said Sherringham.

This response was so benevolent that Basil Dashwood

presently began: "May I ask you at what theatre you have made arrangements?"

Sherringham looked at him a moment. "Come and see me at the Embassy and I'll tell you." Then he added: "I know your sister, Mrs. Lovick."

"So I supposed: that's why I took the liberty of asking such a question."

"It's no liberty; but Mr. Sherringham doesn't appear to be able to tell you," said Miriam.

"Well, you know it's a very curious world, all those theatrical people over there," Sherringham said.

"Ah, don't say anything against them, when I'm one of them," Basil Dashwood laughed.

"I might plead the absence of information, as Miss Rooth has neglected to make us acquainted."

Miriam smiled: "I know you both so little." But she presented them, with a great stately air, to each other, and the two men shook hands while Madame Carré observed them.

"*Tiens!* you gentlemen meet here for the first time? You do right to become friends—that's the best thing. Live together in peace and mutual confidence. *C'est de beaucoup le plus sage.*"

"Certainly, for yoke-fellows," said Sherringham.

He began the next moment to repeat to his new acquaintance some of the things he had been told in London; but their hostess stopped him off, waving the talk away with charming overdone stage-horror and the young hands of the heroines of Marivaux. "Ah, wait till you go, for that! Do you suppose I care for news of your mountebanks' booths?"

VI.

As many people know, there are not, in the famous
Théâtre Français, more than a dozen good seats accessible to ladies. The stalls are forbidden them, the boxes are
a quarter of a mile from the stage and the balcony is a delusion save for a few chairs at either end of its vast horseshoe.
But there are two excellent *baignoires d'avant-scène*, which indeed are by no means always to be had. It was however into
one of them that, immediately after his return to Paris, Sherringham ushered Mrs. Rooth and her daughter, with the further escort of Basil Dashwood. He had chosen the evening of
the reappearance of the celebrated Mademoiselle Voisin (she
had been enjoying a *congé* of three months), an actress whom
Miriam had seen several times before and for whose method
she professed a high though somewhat critical esteem. It was
only for the return of this charming performer that Sherringham had been waiting to respond to Miriam's most ardent wish—that of spending an hour in the *foyer des artistes*
of the great theatre. She was the person whom he knew best
in the house of Molière; he could count upon her to do them
the honours some night when she was in the "bill," and make
the occasion sociable. Miriam had been impatient for it—she
was so convinced that her eyes would be opened in the holy
of holies; but wishing particularly, as he did, to participate in
her impression he had made her promise that she would not
taste of this experience without him—not let Madame Carré,
for instance, take her in his absence. There were questions the
girl wished to put to Mademoiselle Voisin—questions which,
having admired her from the balcony, she felt she was exactly
the person to answer. She was more "in it" now, after all,
than Madame Carré, in spite of her slenderer talent: she was
younger, fresher, more modern and (Miriam found the word)
less academic. Sherringham perfectly foresaw the day when
his young friend would make indulgent allowances for poor
Madame Carré, patronizing her as an old woman of good
intentions.

The play, to-night, was six months old, a large, serious,
successful comedy, by the most distinguished of authors, with

a thesis, a chorus, embodied in one character, a *scène à faire* and a part full of opportunities for Mademoiselle Voisin. There were things to be said about this artist, strictures to be dropped as to the general quality of her art, and Miriam leaned back now, making her comments as if they cost her less; but the actress had knowledge and distinction and pathos, and our young lady repeated several times: "How quiet she is, how wonderfully quiet! Scarcely anything moves but her face and her voice. *Le geste rare*, but really expressive when it comes. I like that economy; it's the only way to make the gesture significant."

"I don't admire the way she holds her arms," Basil Dashwood said: "like a *demoiselle de magasin* trying on a jacket."

"Well, she holds them, at any rate. I dare say it's more than you do with yours."

"Oh, yes, she holds them; there's no mistake about that. 'I hold them, I hope, *hein*?' she seems to say to all the house." The young English professional laughed good-humouredly, and Sherringham was struck with the pleasant familiarity he had established with their brave companion. He was knowing and ready, and he said, in the first entr'acte (they were waiting for the second to go behind), amusing, perceptive things. "They teach them to be ladylike, and Voisin is always trying to show that. 'See how I walk, see how I sit, see how quiet I am and how I have le geste rare. Now can you say I ain't a lady?' She does it all as if she had a class."

"Well, to-night I'm her class," said Miriam.

"Oh, I don't mean of actresses, but of *femmes du monde*. She shows them how to act in society."

"You had better take a few lessons," Miriam retorted.

"You should see Voisin in society," Sherringham interposed.

"Does she go into it?" Mrs. Rooth demanded, with interest.

Sherringham hesitated. "She receives a great many people."

"Why shouldn't they, when they're nice?" Mrs. Rooth continued.

"When the people are nice?" Miriam asked.

"Now don't tell me *she's* not what one would wish," said Mrs. Rooth to Sherringham.

"It depends upon what that is," he answered, smiling.

"What I should wish if she were my daughter," the old woman rejoined, blandly.

"Ah, wish your daughter to act as well as that, and you'll do the handsome thing for her!"

"Well, she *seems* to feel what she says," Mrs. Rooth murmured, piously.

"She has some stiff things to say. I mean about her past," Basil Dashwood remarked. "The past—the dreadful past—on the stage!"

"Wait till the end, to see how she comes out. We must all be merciful!" sighed Mrs. Rooth.

"We've seen it before; you know what happens," Miriam observed to her mother.

"I've seen so many, I get them mixed."

"Yes, they're all in queer predicaments. Poor old mother—what we show you!" laughed the girl.

"Ah, it will be what *you* show me: something noble and wise!"

"I want to do this; it's a magnificent part," said Miriam.

"You couldn't put it on in London; they wouldn't swallow it," Basil Dashwood declared.

"Aren't there things they do there, to get over the difficulties?"

"You can't get over what *she* did," the young man replied.

"Yes, we must pay, we must expiate!" Mrs. Rooth moaned, as the curtain rose again.

When the second act was over our friends passed out of their baignoire into those corridors of tribulation where the bristling *ouvreuse*, like a pawnbroker driving a roaring trade, mounts guard upon piles of heterogeneous clothing, and, gaining the top of the fine staircase which forms the state entrance and connects the statued vestibule of the basement with the grand tier of boxes, opened an ambiguous door, composed of little mirrors, and found themselves in the society of the initiated. The janitors were courteous folk who greeted Sherringham as an acquaintance, and he had no difficulty in marshalling his little troop toward the foyer. They traversed a low, curving lobby, hung with pictures and furnished with velvet-covered benches, where several unrecognized persons, of both sexes, looked at them without hostility, and arrived at an opening on the right from which by a short flight of steps there was a descent to one of the wings of the stage. Here Miriam paused in silent excitement, like a young warrior arrested by a glimpse of the battle-field. Her vision was carried off through a lane of light to the point of vantage from which the actor held the house; but there was a hushed guard over the place, and curiosity could only glance and pass.

Then she came with her companions to a sort of parlour with a polished floor, not large and rather vacant, where her attention flew delightedly to a coat-tree, in a corner, from which three or four dresses were suspended—dresses that she immediately perceived to be costumes in that night's play—accompanied by a saucer of something and a much-worn powder-puff casually left upon a sofa. This was a familiar note in a general impression (it had begun at the threshold) of high decorum—a sense of majesty in the place. Miriam rushed at the powder-puff (there was no one in the room), snatched it up and gazed at it with droll veneration; then stood rapt a moment before the charming petticoats ("That's Dunoyer's first under-skirt," she said to her mother), while Sherringham explained that in this apartment an actress traditionally changed her gown, when the transaction was simple enough, to save the long ascent to her *loge*. He felt like a cicerone showing a church to a party of provincials; and indeed there was a grave hospitality in the air, mingled with something academic and important, the tone of an institution, a temple, which made them all, out of respect and delicacy, hold their breath a little and tread the shining floors with discretion.

These precautions increased (Mrs. Rooth crept in like a friendly but undomesticated cat), after they entered the foyer itself, a square spacious saloon, covered with pictures and relics and draped in official green velvet, where the *genius loci* holds a reception every night in the year. The effect was freshly charming to Sherringham; he was fond of the place, always saw it again with pleasure, enjoyed its honourable look and the way, among the portraits and scrolls, the records of a splendid history, the green velvet and the waxed floors, the genius loci seemed to be "at home" in the quiet lamp-light. At the end of the room, in an ample chimney, blazed a fire of logs. Miriam said nothing; they looked about, noting that most of the portraits and pictures were "old-fashioned," and Basil Dashwood expressed disappointment at the absence of all the people they wanted most to see. Three or four gentlemen in evening dress circulated slowly, looking, like themselves, at the pictures, and another gentleman stood before a lady, with whom he was in conversation, seated against the wall. The foyer, in these conditions, resembled a ball-room cleared for the dance, before the guests or the music had arrived.

"Oh, it's enough to see *this*; it makes my heart beat," said Miriam. "It's full of the vanished past, it makes me cry. I feel them here, the great artists I shall never see. Think of Rachel (look at her grand portrait there!) and how she stood on these very boards and trailed over them the robes of Hermione and Phèdre!" The girl broke out theatrically, as on the spot was right, not a bit afraid of her voice as soon as it rolled through the room; appealing to her companions as they stood under the chandelier and making the other persons present, who had already given her some attention, turn round to stare at so unusual a specimen of the English miss. She laughed musically when she noticed this, and her mother, scandalized, begged her to lower her tone. "It's all right. I produce an effect," said Miriam: "it sha'n't be said that I too haven't had my little success in the maison de Molière." And Sherringham repeated that it was all right—the place was familiar with mirth and passion, there was often wonderful talk there, and it was only the setting that was still and solemn. It happened that this evening—there was no knowing in advance—the scene was not characteristically brilliant; but to confirm his assertion, at the moment he spoke, Mademoiselle Dunoyer, who was also in the play, came into the room attended by a pair of gentlemen.

She was the celebrated, the perpetual, the necessary *ingénue*, who with all her talent could not have represented a woman of her actual age. She had the gliding, hopping movement of a small bird, the same air of having nothing to do with time, and the clear, sure, piercing note, a miracle of exact vocalization. She chaffed her companions, she chaffed the room; she seemed to be a very clever little girl trying to personate a more innocent big one. She scattered her amiability about (showing Miriam how much the children of Molière took their ease), and it quickly placed her in the friendliest communication with Peter Sherringham, who already enjoyed her acquaintance and who now extended it to his companions and in particular to the young lady *sur le point d'entrer au théâtre*.

"You deserve a happier lot," said the actress, looking up at Miriam brightly, as if to a great height, and taking her in; upon which Sherringham left them together a little and led Mrs. Rooth and young Dashwood to consider further some of the pictures.

"Most delightful, most curious," the old woman murmured, about everything; while Basil Dashwood exclaimed, in the presence of most of the portraits: "But their ugliness—their ugliness: did you ever see such a collection of hideous people? And those who were supposed to be good-looking—the beauties of the past—they are worse than the others. Ah, you may say what you will, *nous sommes mieux que ça!*" Sherringham suspected him of irritation, of not liking the theatre of the great rival nation to be thrust down his throat. They returned to Miriam and Mademoiselle Dunoyer, and Sherringham asked the actress a question about one of the portraits, to which there was no name attached. She replied, like a child who had only played about the room, that she was *toute honteuse* not to be able to tell him the original: she had forgotten, she had never asked— "*Vous allez me trouver bien légère!*" She appealed to the other persons present, who formed a gallery for her, and laughed in delightful ripples at their suggestions, which she covered with ridicule. She bestirred herself; she declared she would ascertain, she should not be happy till she did, and swam out of the room, with the prettiest paddles, to obtain the information, leaving behind her a perfume of delicate kindness and gaiety. She seemed above all things obliging, and Sherringham said that she was almost as natural off the stage as on. She didn't come back.

VII.

WHETHER Sherringham had prearranged it is more than
I can say, but Mademoiselle Voisin delayed so long to
show herself that Mrs. Rooth, who wished to see the rest of
the play, though she had sat it out on another occasion, expressed a returning relish for her corner of the baignoire and
gave her conductor the best pretext he could have desired for
asking Basil Dashwood to be so good as to escort her back.
When the young actor, of whose personal preference Sherringham was quite aware, had led Mrs. Rooth away with an
absence of moroseness which showed that his striking analogy
with a gentleman was not kept for the footlights, the two
others sat on a divan in the part of the room furthest from the
entrance, so that it gave them a degree of privacy, and Miriam
watched the coming and going of their fellow-visitors and the
indefinite people, attached to the theatre, hanging about,
while her companion gave a name to some of the figures,
Parisian celebrities.

"Fancy poor Dashwood, cooped up there with mamma!"
the girl exclaimed, whimsically.

"You're awfully cruel to him; but that's of course," said
Sherringham.

"It seems to me I'm as kind as you: you sent him off."

"That was for your mother: she was tired."

"Oh, gammon! And why, if I *were* cruel, should it be of
course?"

"Because you must destroy and torment and consume—
that's your nature. But you can't help your type, can you?"

"My type?" the girl repeated.

"It's bad, perverse, dangerous. It's essentially insolent."

"And pray what is yours, when you talk like that? Would
you say such things if you didn't know the depths of my
good-nature?"

"Your good-nature all comes back to that," said Sherringham. "It's an abyss of ruin—for others. You have no respect. I'm speaking of the artistic character, in the direction
and in the plenitude in which you have it. It's unscrupulous,
nervous, capricious, wanton."

"I don't know about respect: one can be good," Miriam reasoned.

"It doesn't matter, so long as one is powerful," answered Sherringham. "We can't have everything, and surely we ought to understand that we must pay for things. A splendid organization for a special end, like yours, is so rare and rich and fine that we oughtn't to grudge it its conditions."

"What do you call its conditions?" Miriam demanded, turning and looking at him.

"Oh, the need to take its ease, to take up space, to make itself at home in the world, to square its elbows and knock others about. That's large and free; it's the good-nature you speak of. You must forage and ravage and leave a track behind you; you must live upon the country you occupy. And you give such delight that, after all, you are welcome—you are infinitely welcome!"

"I don't know what you mean. I only care for the idea," Miriam said.

"That's exactly what I pretend; and we must all help you to it. You use us, you push us about, you break us up. We are your tables and chairs, the simple furniture of your life."

"Whom do you mean by 'we'?"

Sherringham gave a laugh. "Oh, don't be afraid—there will be plenty of others."

Miriam made no rejoinder to this, but after a moment she broke out again: "Poor Dashwood, immured with mamma—he's like a lame chair that one has put into the corner."

"Don't break him up before he has served. I really believe that something will come out of him," her companion went on. "However, you'll break me up first," he added, "and him probably never at all."

"And why shall I honour you so much more?"

"Because I'm a better article, and you'll feel that."

"You have the superiority of modesty—I see."

"I'm better than a young mountebank—I've vanity enough to say that."

She turned upon him with a flush in her cheek and a splendid dramatic face. "How you hate us! Yes, at bottom, below your little taste, you *hate* us!" she repeated.

He coloured too, met her eyes, looked into them a minute,

seemed to accept the imputation, and then said quickly: "Give it up; come away with me."

"Come away with you?"

"Leave this place: give it up."

"You brought me here, you insisted it should be only you, and now you must stay," she declared, with a head-shake and a laugh. "You should know what you want, dear Mr. Sherringham."

"I do—I know now. Come away, before she comes."

"Before she comes?"

"She's success—this wonderful Voisin—she's triumph, she's full accomplishment: the hard, brilliant realization of what I want to avert for you." Miriam looked at him in silence, the angry light still in her face, and he repeated: "Give it up—give it up."

Her eyes softened after a moment; she smiled and then she said: "Yes, you're better than poor Dashwood."

"Give it up and we'll live for ourselves, *in* ourselves, in something that can have a sanctity."

"All the same, you do hate us," the girl went on.

"I don't want to be conceited, but I mean that I'm sufficiently fine and complicated to tempt you. I'm an expensive modern watch, with a wonderful escapement—therefore you'll smash me if you can."

"Never—never!" said the girl, getting up. "You tell me the hour too well." She quitted her companion and stood looking at Gérôme's fine portrait of the pale Rachel, invested with the antique attributes of tragedy. The rise of the curtain had drawn away most of the company. Sherringham, from his bench, watched Miriam a little, turning his eye from her to the vivid image of the dead actress and thinking that his companion suffered little by the juxtaposition. Presently he came over and joined her again, and she said to him: "I wonder if that is what your cousin had in his mind."

"My cousin?"

"What was his name? Mr. Dormer; that first day at Madame Carré's. He offered to paint my portrait."

"I remember. I put him up to it."

"Was he thinking of this?"

"I don't think he has ever seen it. I dare say I was."

"Well, when we go to London he must do it," said Miriam.

"Oh, there's no hurry," Sherringham replied.

"Don't you want my picture?" asked the girl, with one of her successful touches.

"I'm not sure I want it from you. I don't know quite what he'd make of you."

"He looked so clever—I liked him. I saw him again at your party."

"He's a dear fellow; but what is one to say of a painter who goes for his inspiration to the House of Commons?"

"To the House of Commons?"

"He has lately got himself elected."

"Dear me, what a pity! I wanted to sit for him; but perhaps he won't have me, as I'm not a member of Parliament."

"It's my sister, rather, who has got him in."

"Your sister who was at your house that day? What has she to do with it?"

"Why, she's his cousin, just as I am. And in addition," Sherringham went on, "she's to be married to him."

"Married—really? So he paints *her*, I suppose?"

"Not much, probably. His talent in that line isn't what she esteems in him most."

"It isn't great, then?"

"I haven't the least idea."

"And in the political line?"

"I scarcely can tell. He's very clever."

"He does paint then?"

"I dare say."

Miriam looked at Gérôme's picture again. "Fancy his going into the House of Commons! And your sister put him there?"

"She worked, she canvassed."

"Ah, you're a queer family!" the girl exclaimed, turning round at the sound of a step.

"We're lost—here's Mademoiselle Voisin," said Sherringham.

This celebrity presented herself smiling and addressing Miriam. "I acted for *you* to-night—I did my best."

"What a pleasure to speak to you, to thank you!" the girl murmured, admiringly. She was startled and dazzled.

"I couldn't come to you before, but now I've got a rest—for half an hour," the actress went on. Gracious and passive, as if she were a little tired, she let Sherringham, without looking at him, take her hand and raise it to his lips. "I'm sorry I make you lose the others—they are so good in this act," she added.

"We have seen them before, and there's nothing so good as you," Miriam replied.

"I like my part," said Mademoiselle Voisin, gently, smiling still at our young lady with clear, charming eyes. "One is always better in that case."

"She's so bad sometimes, you know!" Sherringham jested, to Miriam; leading the actress to glance at him kindly and vaguely, with a little silence which, with her, you could not call embarrassment, but which was still less affectation.

"And it's so interesting to be here—*so* interesting!" Miriam declared.

"Ah, you like our old house? Yes, we are very proud of it." And Mademoiselle Voisin smiled again at Sherringham, good-humouredly, as if to say: "Well, here I am, and what do you want of me? Don't ask me to invent it myself, but if you'll tell me I'll do it." Miriam admired the note of discreet interrogation in her voice—the slight suggestion of surprise at their "old house" being liked. The actress was already an astonishment to her, from her seeming still more perfect on a nearer view; which was not, she had an idea, what actresses usually did. This was very encouraging to her; it widened the programme of a young lady about to embrace the scenic career. To have so much to show before the footlights and yet to have so much left when you came off—that was really wonderful. Mademoiselle Voisin's eyes, as one looked into them, were still more agreeable than the distant spectator would have supposed; and there was in her appearance an extreme finish which instantly suggested to Miriam that she herself, in comparison, was big and rough and coarse.

"You're lovely to-night—you're particularly lovely," said Sherringham, very frankly, translating Miriam's own impression and at the same time giving her an illustration of the way that, in Paris at least, gentlemen expressed themselves to the stars of the drama. She thought she knew her companion very well and had been witness of the degree to which, under these circumstances, his familiarity could increase; but his address to the slim, distinguished, harmonious woman before them had a different quality, the note of a special usage. If Miriam had had any apprehension that such directness might be taken as excessive, it was removed by the manner in which Mademoiselle Voisin returned—

"Oh, one is always well enough when one is made up; one is always exactly the same." That served as an example of the good taste with which a star of the drama could receive homage that was wanting in originality. Miriam determined on the spot that this should be the way *she* would receive it. The grace of her new acquaintance was the greater as the becoming bloom which she alluded to as artificial was the result of a science so consummate that it had none of the grossness of a mask. The perception of all this was exciting to our young aspirant, and her excitement relieved itself in the inquiry, which struck her as rude as soon as she had uttered it—

"You acted for *me*? How did you know? What am I to you?"

"Monsieur Sherringham has told me about you. He says we are nothing beside you; that you are to be the great star of the future. I'm proud that you've seen me."

"That of course is what I tell every one," Sherringham said, a trifle awkwardly, to Miriam.

"I can believe it when I see you. *Je vous ai bien observée*," the actress continued, in her sweet, conciliatory tone.

Miriam looked from one of her interlocutors to the other, as if there was a joy to her in this report of Sherringham's remarks, accompanied however, and partly mitigated, by a quicker vision of what might have passed between a secretary of embassy and a creature so exquisite as Mademoiselle Voisin. "Ah, you're wonderful people—a most interesting impression!" she sighed.

"I was looking for you; he had prepared me. We are such old friends!" said the actress, in a tone courteously exempt from intention: upon which Sherringham again took her hand and raised it to his lips, with a tenderness which her whole appearance seemed to bespeak for her, a sort of practical consideration and carefulness of touch, as if she were an object precious and frail, an instrument for producing rare sounds, to be handled, like a legendary violin, with a recognition of its value.

"Your dressing-room is so pretty—show her your dressing-room," said Sherringham.

"Willingly, if she'll come up. *Vous savez, c'est une montée.*"

"It's a shame to inflict it on *you*," Miriam objected.

"*Comment donc?* If it will interest you in the least!" They exchanged civilities, almost caresses, trying which could have the nicest manner to the other. It was the actress's manner that struck Miriam most; it denoted such a training, so much taste, expressed such a ripe conception of urbanity.

"No wonder she acts well when she has that tact—feels, perceives, is so remarkable, *mon Dieu, mon Dieu!*" Miriam said to herself as they followed their conductress into another corridor and up a wide, plain staircase. The staircase was spacious and long, and this part of the establishment was sombre and still, with the gravity of a college or a convent. They reached another passage, lined with little doors, on each of which the name of a comedian was painted; and here the aspect became still more monastic, like that of a row of solitary cells. Mademoiselle Voisin led the way to her own door, obligingly, as if she wished to be hospitable, dropping little subdued, friendly attempts at explanation on the way. At her threshold the monasticism stopped. Miriam found herself in a wonderfully upholstered nook, a nest of lamplight and delicate cretonne. Save for its pair of long glasses it looked like a tiny boudoir, with a water-colour drawing of value in each panel of stretched stuff, its crackling fire, its charming order. It was intensely bright and extremely hot, singularly pretty and exempt from litter. Nothing was lying about, but a small draped doorway led into an inner sanctuary. To Miriam it seemed royal; it immediately made the art of the comedian the most distinguished thing in the world. It was just such a place as they *should* have, in the intervals, if they were expected to be great artists. It was a result of the same evolution as Mademoiselle Voisin herself—not that our young lady found this particular term to her hand, to express her idea. But her mind was flooded with an impression of style, of refinement, of the long continuity of a tradition. The actress said, *"Voilà, c'est tout!"* as if it were little enough and there were even something clumsy in her having brought them so far for nothing and in their all sitting there waiting and looking at each other till it was time for her to change her dress. But to Miriam it was occupation enough to note what she did and said: these things and her whole person and carriage struck her as exquisite in their adaptation to the particular occasion. She had had an idea that foreign actresses were rather of the *cabotin* order; but her hostess suggested to her much more a princess than a cabotine. She would do things as she liked, and straight off: Miriam couldn't fancy her in the gropings and humiliations of rehearsal. Everything in her had been sifted and formed, her tone was perfect, her amiability complete, and she might have been the charming young wife of a secretary of state receiving a pair of strangers of distinction. Miriam observed all her movements. And then, as Sherringham had said, she was particularly lovely.

Suddenly she told Sherringham that she must put him *à la porte*—she wanted to change her dress. He retired and returned to the foyer, where Miriam was to rejoin him after remaining the few minutes more with Mademoiselle Voisin and coming down with her. He waited for his companion, walking up and down and making up his mind; and when she presently came in he said to her:

"Please don't go back for the rest of the play. Stay here." They now had the foyer virtually to themselves.

"I want to stay here. I like it better." She moved back to the chimney-piece, from above which the cold portrait of Rachel looked down, and as he accompanied her he said:

"I meant what I said just now."

"What you said to Voisin?"

"No, no; to you. Give it up and live with *me*."

"Give it up?" And she turned her stage face upon him.

"Give it up and I'll marry you to-morrow."

"This is a happy time to ask it!" she mocked. "And this is a good place."

"Very good indeed, and that's why I speak: it's a place to make one choose—it puts it all before one."

"To make *you* choose, you mean. I'm much obliged, but that's not my choice," laughed Miriam.

"You shall be anything you like—except this."

"Except what I most want to be? I *am* much obliged."

"Don't you care for me? Haven't you any gratitude?" Sherringham asked.

"Gratitude for kindly removing the blessed cup from my lips? I want to be what *she* is—I want it more than ever."

"Ah, what she is!" he replied impatiently.

"Do you mean I can't? We'll see if I can't. Tell me more about her—tell me everything."

"Haven't you seen for yourself, and can't you judge?"

"She's strange, she's mysterious," Miriam declared, looking at the fire. "She showed us nothing—nothing of her real self."

"So much the better, all things considered."

"Are there all sorts of other things in her life? That's what I believe," Miriam went on, raising her eyes to him.

"I can't tell you what there is in the life of such a woman."

"Imagine—when she's so perfect!" the girl exclaimed, thoughtfully. "Ah, she kept me off—she kept me off! Her charming manner is in itself a kind of contempt. It's an abyss—it's the wall of China. She has a hard polish, an inimitable surface, like some wonderful porcelain that costs more than you'd think."

"Do you want to become like that?" Sherringham asked.

"If I could I should be enchanted. One can always try."

"You must act better than she," said Sherringham.

"Better? I thought you wanted me to give it up."

"Ah, I don't know what I want, and you torment me and turn me inside out! What I want is you yourself."

"Oh, don't worry," said Miriam, kindly. Then she added that Mademoiselle Voisin had asked her to come to see her; to which Sherringham replied, with a certain dryness, that she would probably not find that necessary. This made Miriam stare, and she asked, "Do you mean it won't do, on account of mamma's prejudices?"

"Say, this time, on account of mine."

"Do you mean because she has lovers?"

"Her lovers are none of our business."

"None of mine, I see. So you have been one of them?"

"No such luck."

"What a pity! I should have liked to see that. One must see everything, to be able to do everything." And as he inquired what she had wished to see she replied: "The way a woman like that receives one of the old ones."

Sherringham gave a groan at this, which was at the same time partly a laugh, and, turning away and dropping upon a bench, ejaculated: "You'll do—you'll do!"

He sat there some minutes with his elbows on his knees and his face in his hands. Miriam remained looking at the portrait of Rachel; after which she demanded: "Doesn't such a woman as that receive—receive every one?"

"Every one who goes to see her, no doubt."

"And who goes?"

"Lots of men—clever men, eminent men."

"Ah, what a charming life! Then doesn't she go out?"

"Not what we Philistines mean by that—not into society, never. She never enters a lady's drawing-room."

"How strange, when one's as distinguished as that; except that she must escape a lot of stupidities and *corvées*. Then where does she learn such manners?"

"She teaches manners, *à ses heures*: she doesn't need to learn them."

"Oh, she has given me ideas! But in London actresses go into society," Miriam continued.

"Oh, in London *nous mêlons les genres!*"

"And sha'n't *I* go—I mean if I want?"

"You'll have every facility to bore yourself. Don't doubt of it."

"And doesn't she feel excluded?" Miriam asked.

"Excluded from what? She has the fullest life."

"The fullest?"

"An intense artistic life. The cleverest men in Paris talk over her work with her; the principal authors of plays discuss with her subjects and characters and questions of treatment. She lives in the world of art."

"Ah, the world of art—how I envy her! And you offer me Dashwood!"

Sherringham rose in his emotion. "I offer you—?"

Miriam burst out laughing. "You look so droll! You offer me yourself then, instead of all these things."

"My child, I also am a very clever man," he said, smiling, though conscious that for a moment he had stood gaping.

"You are—you are; I delight in you. No ladies at all—*no femmes comme il faut?*" Miriam began again.

"Ah, what do *they* matter? Your business is the artistic life!" he broke out with inconsequence and with a little irritation at hearing her sound that trivial note again.

"You're a dear—your charming good sense comes back to you! What do you want of me then?"

"I want you for myself—not for others; and now, in time, before anything's done."

"Why then did you bring me here? Everything's done; I feel it to-night."

"I know the way you should look at it—if you do look at it at all," Sherringham conceded.

"That's so easy! I thought you liked the stage so," Miriam said, artfully.

"Don't you want me to be a great swell?"

"And don't you want *me* to be?"

"You will be—you'll share my glory."

"So will you share mine."

"The husband of an actress? Yes, I see that!" Sherringham cried, with a frank ring of disgust.

"It's a silly position, no doubt. But if you're too good for it why talk about it? Don't you think I'm important?" Miriam inquired. Her companion stood looking at her, and she suddenly said in a different tone: "Ah, why should we quarrel, when you have been so kind, so generous? Can't we always be friends—the solidest friends?"

Her voice sank to the sweetest cadence and her eyes were grateful and good as they rested on him. She sometimes said things with such perfection that they seemed dishonest, but in this case Sherringham was stirred to an expressive response. Just as he was making it, however, he was moved to utter other words—"Take care, here's Dashwood!" Mrs. Rooth's companion was in the doorway. He had come back to say that they really must relieve him.

VIII.

M RS. DALLOW came up to London soon after the meeting of Parliament; she made no secret of the fact that
she was fond of the place, and naturally in present conditions
it would not have become less attractive to her. But she prepared to withdraw from it again for the Easter vacation, not
to return to Harsh, but to pay a couple of country visits. She
did not however leave town with the crowd—she never did
anything with the crowd—but waited till the Monday after
Parliament rose; facing with composure, in Great Stanhope
Street, the horrors, as she had been taught to consider them,
of a Sunday out of the session. She had done what she could
to mitigate them by asking a handful of "stray men" to dine
with her that evening. Several members of this disconsolate
class sought comfort in Great Stanhope Street in the afternoon, and them for the most part she also invited to come
back at eight o'clock. There were therefore almost too many
people at dinner—there were even a couple of wives. Nick
Dormer came to dinner, but he was not present in the afternoon. Each of the persons who were had said on coming in:
"So you've not gone—I'm awfully glad." Mrs. Dallow had
replied, "No, I've not gone," but she had in no case added
that she was glad, nor had she offered an explanation. She
never offered explanations: she always assumed that no one
could invent them so well as those who had the florid taste to
desire them.

And in this case she was right, for it is probable that few
of her visitors failed to say to themselves that her not having
gone would have had something to do with Dormer. That
could pass for an explanation with many of Mrs. Dallow's
visitors, who as a general thing were not morbidly analytic;
especially with those who met Nick as a matter of course at
the dinner. His being present at this lady's entertainments,
being in her house whenever, as the phrase was, a candle
was lighted, was taken as a sign that there was something
rather particular between them. Nick had said to her more
than once that people would wonder why they didn't marry;
but he was wrong in this, inasmuch as there were many of

their friends to whom it would not have occurred that his position could be improved by it. That they were cousins was a fact not so evident to others as to themselves, in consequence of which they appeared remarkably intimate. The person seeing clearest in the matter was Mrs. Gresham, who lived so much in the world that being alone had become her idea of true sociability. She knew very well that if she had been privately engaged to a young man as amiable as Nick Dormer she would have managed that publicity should not play such a part in their intercourse; and she had her secret scorn for the stupidity of people whose conception of Nick's relation to Julia Dallow rested on the fact that he was always included in her parties. "If he never was there they might talk," she said to herself. But Mrs. Gresham was supersubtle. To her it would have appeared natural that Julia should celebrate the parliamentary recess by going down to Harsh and securing Nick's company there for a fortnight; she recognized Mrs. Dallow's actual plan as a comparatively poor substitute—the project of spending the holidays in other people's houses, to which Nick had also promised to come. Mrs. Gresham was romantic; she wondered what was the good of mere snippets and snatches, the chances that any one might have, when large, still days *à deux* were open to you—chances of which half the sanctity was in what they excluded. However, there were more unsettled matters between Mrs. Dallow and her queer kinsman than even Mrs. Gresham's fine insight could embrace. She was not present on the Sunday before Easter at the dinner in Great Stanhope Street; but if she had been Julia's singular indifference to observation would have stopped short of encouraging her to remain in the drawing-room with Nick after the others had gone. I may add that Mrs. Gresham's extreme curiosity would have emboldened her as little to do so. She would have taken for granted that the pair wished to be alone together, though she would have regarded this only as a snippet.

The guests stayed late and it was nearly twelve o'clock when Nick, standing before the fire in the room they had quitted, broke out to his companion:

"See here, Julia, how long do you really expect me to endure this kind of thing?" Mrs. Dallow made him no answer; she only leaned back in her chair with her eyes upon his. He met her gaze for a moment; then he turned round to the fire and for another moment looked into it. After this he faced Mrs. Dallow again with the exclamation: "It's so foolish—it's so damnably foolish!"

She still said nothing, but at the end of a minute she spoke without answering him. "I shall expect you on Tuesday, and I hope you'll come by a decent train."

"What do you mean by a decent train?"

"I mean I hope you'll not leave it till the last thing before dinner, so that we can have a little walk or something."

"What's a little walk or something? Why, if you make such a point of my coming to Griffin, do you want me to come at all?"

Mrs. Dallow hesitated an instant; then she exclaimed: "I knew you hated it!"

"You provoke me so," said Nick. "You try to, I think."

"And Severals still worse. You'll get out of that if you can," Mrs. Dallow went on.

"If I can? What's to prevent me?"

"You promised Lady Whiteroy. But of course that's nothing."

"I don't care a straw for Lady Whiteroy."

"And you promised me. But that's less still."

"It *is* foolish—it's quite idiotic," said Nick, with his hands in his pockets and his eyes on the ceiling.

There was another silence, at the end of which Mrs. Dallow remarked: "You might have answered Mr. Macgeorge when he spoke to you."

"Mr. Macgeorge—what has he to do with it?"

"He has to do with your getting on a little. If you think that's the way!"

Nick broke into a laugh. "I like lessons in getting on—in other words I suppose you mean in urbanity—from you, Julia!"

"Why not from me?"

"Because you can do nothing base. You're incapable of

putting on a flattering manner, to get something by it: therefore why should you expect me to? You're unflattering—that is you're austere—in proportion as there may be something to be got."

Mrs. Dallow sprang up from her chair, coming towards him. "There is only one thing I want in the world—you know very well."

"Yes, you want it so much that you won't even take it when it's pressed upon you. How long do you seriously expect me to bear it?" Nick repeated.

"I never asked you to do anything base," she said, standing in front of him. "If I'm not clever about throwing myself into things, it's all the more reason you should be."

"If you're not clever, my dear Julia?" Nick, standing close to her, placed his hands on her shoulders and shook her a little with a mixture of tenderness and passion. "You're clever enough to make me furious, sometimes!"

She opened and closed her fan, looking down at it while she submitted to this attenuated violence. "All I want is that when a man like Mr. Macgeorge talks to you, you shouldn't appear to be bored to death. You used to be so charming in that sort of way. And now you appear to take no interest in anything. At dinner to-night you scarcely opened your lips; you treated them all as if you only wished they'd go."

"I did wish they'd go. Haven't I told you a hundred times what I think of your salon?"

"How then do you want me to live?" Mrs. Dallow asked. "Am I not to have a creature in the house?"

"As many creatures as you like. Your freedom is complete, and as far as I am concerned always will be. Only when you challenge me and overhaul me—not justly I think—I must confess the simple truth, that there are many of your friends I don't delight in."

"Oh, *your* idea of pleasant people!" Julia exclaimed. "I should like once for all to know what it really is."

"I can tell you what it really isn't: it isn't Mr. Macgeorge. He's a being almost grotesquely limited."

"He'll be where you'll never be—unless you change."

"To be where Mr. Macgeorge is not would be very much my desire. Therefore why should I change?" Nick demanded.

"However, I hadn't the least intention of being rude to him, and I don't think I was," he went on. "To the best of my ability I assume a virtue if I have it not; but apparently I'm not enough of a comedian."

"If you have it not? It's when you say things like that that you're so dreadfully tiresome. As if there were anything that you haven't or mightn't have!"

Nick turned away from his hostess; he took a few impatient steps in the room, looking at the carpet, with his hands in his pockets again. Then he came back to the fire with the observation: "It's rather hard to be found so wanting when one has tried to play one's part so beautifully." He paused, with his eyes on Mrs. Dallow's; then continued, with a vibration in his voice: "I've imperilled my immortal soul, or at least I've bemuddled my intelligence, by all the things I don't care for that I've tried to do, and all the things I detest that I've tried to be, and all the things I never can be that I've tried to look as if I were—all the appearances and imitations, the pretences and hypocrisies in which I've steeped myself to the eyes; and at the end of it (it serves me right!) my reward is simply to learn that I'm still not half humbug enough!"

Mrs. Dallow looked away from him as soon as he had spoken these words; she attached her eyes to the clock which stood behind him and observed irrelevantly:

"I'm very sorry, but I think you had better go. I don't like you to stay after midnight."

"Ah, what you like and what you don't like, and where one begins and the other ends—all that's an impenetrable mystery!" the young man declared. But he took no further notice of her allusion to his departure, adding in a different tone: " 'A man like Mr. Macgeorge!' When you say a thing of that sort, in a certain particular way, I should rather like to suffer you to perish."

Mrs. Dallow stared; it might have seemed for an instant that she was trying to look stupid. "How can I help it if a few years hence he is certain to be at the head of any Liberal government?"

"We can't help it, of course, but we can help talking about it," Nick smiled. "If we don't mention it, it may not be noticed."

"You're trying to make me angry. You're in one of your vicious moods," observed Mrs. Dallow, blowing out, on the chimney-piece, a guttering candle.

"That I'm exasperated I have already had the honour very positively to inform you. All the same I maintain that I was irreproachable at dinner. I don't want you to think I shall always be so good as that."

"You looked so out of it; you were as gloomy as if every earthly hope had left you, and you didn't make a single contribution to any discussion that took place. Don't you think I observe you?" Mrs. Dallow asked, with an irony tempered by a tenderness that was unsuccessfully concealed.

"Ah, my darling, what you observe!" Nick exclaimed, laughing and stopping. But he added the next moment, more seriously, as if his tone had been disrespectful: "You probe me to the bottom, no doubt."

"You needn't come either to Griffin or to Severals if you don't want to."

"Give them up yourself; stay here with me!"

She coloured quickly, as he said this, and broke out: "Lord! how you hate political houses!"

"How can you say that, when from February to August I spend every blessed night in one?"

"Yes, and hate that worst of all."

"So do half the people who are in it. You must have so many things, so many people, so much *mise-en-scène* and such a perpetual spectacle to live," Nick went on. "Perpetual motion, perpetual visits, perpetual crowds! If you go into the country you'll see forty people every day and be mixed up with them all day. The idea of a quiet fortnight in town, when by a happy if idiotic superstition everybody goes out of it, disconcerts and frightens you. It's the very time, it's the very place, to do a little work and possess one's soul."

This vehement allocution found Mrs. Dallow evidently somewhat unprepared; but she was sagacious enough, instead of attempting for the moment a general rejoinder, to seize on a single phrase and say: "Work? What work can you do in London at such a moment as this?"

Nick hesitated a little. "I might tell you that I wanted to get up a lot of subjects, to sit at home and read blue-books; but that wouldn't be quite what I mean."

"Do you mean you want to paint?"

"Yes, that's it, since you drag it out of me."

"Why do you make such a mystery about it? You're at perfect liberty," said Mrs. Dallow.

She extended her hand, to rest it on the mantel-shelf, but her companion took it on the way and held it in both his own. "You're delightful, Julia, when you speak in that tone—then I know why it is I love you; but I can't do anything if I go to Griffin, if I go to Severals."

"I see—I see," said Julia, reflectively and kindly.

"I've scarcely been inside of my studio for months and I feel quite homesick for it. The idea of putting in a few quiet days there has taken hold of me: I rather cling to it."

"It seems so odd, your having a studio!" Julia dropped, speaking so quickly that the words were almost incomprehensible.

"Doesn't it sound absurd, for all the good it does me, or I do in it? Of course one can produce nothing but rubbish on such terms—without continuity or persistence, with just a few days here and there. I ought to be ashamed of myself, no doubt; but even my rubbish interests me. *'Guenille si l'on veut, ma guenille m'est chère.'* But I'll go down to Harsh with you in a moment, Julia," Nick pursued: "that would do as well, if we could be quiet there, without people, without a creature; and I should really be perfectly content. You'd sit for me; it would be the occasion we've so often wanted and never found."

Mrs. Dallow shook her head slowly, with a smile that had a meaning for Nick. "Thank you, my dear; nothing would induce me to go to Harsh with you."

The young man looked at her. "What's the matter, whenever it's a question of anything of that sort? Are you afraid of me?" She pulled her hand quickly out of his, turning away from him; but he went on: "Stay with me here then, when everything is so right for it. We shall do beautifully—have the whole place, have the whole day to ourselves. Hang your engagements! Telegraph you won't come. We'll live at the studio—you'll sit to me every day. Now or never is our chance—when shall we have so good a one? Think how charming it will be! I'll make you wish awfully that I shall do something."

"I can't get out of Griffin—it's impossible," returned Mrs. Dallow, moving further away, with her back presented to him.

"Then you *are* afraid of me—simply?"

She turned quickly round, very pale. "Of course I am; you are welcome to know it."

He went toward her, and for a moment she seemed to make another slight movement of retreat. This however was scarcely perceptible, and there was nothing to alarm in the tone of reasonable entreaty in which Nick said to her as he went toward her: "Put an end, Julia, to our absurd situation—it really can't go on: you have no right to expect a man to be happy or comfortable in so false a position. We're talked of odiously—of that we may be sure; and yet what good have we of it?"

"Talked of? Do I care for that?"

"Do you mean you're indifferent because there are no grounds? That's just why I hate it."

"I don't know what you're talking about," exclaimed Mrs. Dallow, with quick disdain.

"Be my wife to-morrow—be my wife next week. Let us have done with this fantastic probation and be happy."

"Leave me now—come back to-morrow. I'll write to you." She had the air of pleading with him at present as he pleaded with her.

"You can't resign yourself to the idea of one's looking 'out of it'!" laughed Nick.

"Come to-morrow, before lunch," Mrs. Dallow continued.

"To be told I must wait six months more and then be sent about my business? Ah, Julia, Julia!" murmured the young man.

Something in this simple exclamation—it sounded natural and perfectly unstudied—evidently on the instant made a great impression on his companion. "You shall wait no longer," she said after a short silence.

"What do you mean by no longer?"

"Give me about five weeks—say till the Whitsuntide recess."

"Five weeks are a great deal," smiled Nick.

"There are things to be done—you ought to understand."

"I only understand how I love you."

"Dearest Nick!" said Mrs. Dallow; upon which he caught her in his arms.

"I have your promise then for five weeks hence, to a day?" he demanded, as she released herself.

"We'll settle that—the exact day: there are things to consider and to arrange. Come to luncheon to-morrow."

"I'll come early—I'll come at one," Nick said; and for a moment they stood smiling at each other.

"Do you think I *want* to wait, any more than you?" Mrs. Dallow asked.

"I don't feel so much out of it now!" he exclaimed, by way of answer. "You'll stay, of course, now—you'll give up your visits?"

She had hold of the lappet of his coat; she had kept it in her hand even while she detached herself from his embrace. There was a white flower in his buttonhole which she looked at and played with a moment before she said: "I have a better idea—you needn't come to Griffin. Stay in your studio—do as you like—paint dozens of pictures."

"Dozens? Barbarian!" Nick ejaculated.

The epithet apparently had an endearing suggestion to Mrs. Dallow; at any rate it led her to allow him to kiss her on her forehead—led her to say: "What on earth do I want but that you should do absolutely as you please and be as happy as you can?"

Nick kissed her again, in another place, at this; but he inquired: "What dreadful proposition is coming now?"

"I'll go off and do up my visits and come back."

"And leave me alone?"

"Don't be affected!" said Mrs. Dallow. "You know you'll work much better without me. You'll live in your studio—I shall be well out of the way."

"That's not what one wants of a sitter. How can I paint you?"

"You can paint me all the rest of your life. I shall be a perpetual sitter."

"I believe I could paint you without looking at you," said Nick, smiling down at her. "You do excuse me, then, from those dreary places?"

"How can I insist, after what you said about the pleasure of keeping these days?" Mrs. Dallow asked sweetly.

"You're the best woman on earth; though it does seem odd you should rush away as soon as our little business is settled."

"We shall make it up. I know what I'm about. And now go!" Mrs. Dallow terminated, almost pushing her visitor out of the room.

IX.

IT WAS CERTAINLY singular under the circumstances that on sitting down in his studio after Julia had left town Nick Dormer should not, as regards the effort to reproduce some beautiful form, have felt more chilled by the absence of a friend who was such an embodiment of beauty. She was away and he longed for her, and yet without her the place was more filled with what he wanted to find in it. He turned into it with confused feelings, the most definite of which was a sense of release and recreation. It looked blighted and lonely and dusty, and his old studies, as he rummaged them out, struck him as even clumsier than the last time he had ventured to drop his eyes on them. But amid this neglected litter, in the colourless and obstructed light of a high north window which needed washing, he tasted more sharply the possibility of positive happiness: it appeared to him that, as he had said to Julia, he was more in possession of his soul. It was frivolity and folly, it was puerility to spend valuable hours pottering over the vain implements of an art he had relinquished; and a certain shame that he had felt in presenting his plea to Julia Dallow that Sunday night arose from the sense not of what he clung to, but of what he had given up. He had turned his back upon serious work, so that pottering was now all he could aspire to. It couldn't be fruitful, it couldn't be anything but ridiculous, almost ignoble; but it soothed his nerves, it was in the nature of a secret dissipation. He had never suspected that he should ever have on his own part nerves to count with; but this possibility had been revealed to him on the day it became clear that he was letting something precious go. He was glad he had not to justify himself to the critical, for this might have been a delicate business. The critical were mostly absent; and besides, shut up all day in his studio, how should he ever meet them? It was the place in the world where he felt furthest away from his constituents. That was a part of the pleasure—the consciousness that for the hour the coast was clear and his mind was free. His mother and his sister had gone to Broadwood: Lady Agnes (the phrase sounds brutal, but it represents his state of mind) was well out of the way. He had written to her as soon as Julia left town—he had apprised her of the fact that his wedding-day was fixed: a relief, for poor Lady Agnes, to a period of intolerable mystification, of taciturn wondering and watching. She had said her say the day of the poll at Harsh; she was too proud to ask and too discreet to "nag": so she could only wait for something that didn't arrive. The unconditioned loan of Broadwood had of course been something of a bribe to patience: she had at first felt that on the day she should take possession of that capital house Julia would indeed seem to have come into the family. But the gift had confirmed expectations just enough to make disappointment more bitter; and the discomfort was greater in proportion as Lady Agnes failed to discover what was the matter. Her daughter Grace was much occupied with this question and brought it up in conversation in a manner irritating to her ladyship, who had a high theory of being silent about it, but who however, in the long run, was more unhappy when, in consequence of a reprimand, the girl suggested no reasons at all than when she suggested stupid ones. It eased Lady Agnes a little to discuss the mystery when she could have the air of not having begun.

The letter Nick received from her the first day of Passion Week in reply to his important communication was the only one he read at that moment; not counting of course several notes that Mrs. Dallow addressed to him from Griffin. There were letters piled up, as he knew, in Calcutta Gardens, which his servant had strict orders not to bring to the studio. Nick slept now in the bedroom attached to this retreat; got things as he wanted them from Calcutta Gardens; and dined at his club, where a stray surviving friend or two, seeing him prowl about the library in the evening, was free to suppose that such eccentricity had a crafty political basis. When he thought of his neglected letters he remembered Mr. Carteret's convictions on the subject of not "getting behind"; they made him laugh, in the slightly sonorous painting-room, as he bent over one of the old canvases that he had ventured to turn to the light. He was fully determined however to master his correspondence before going down, the last thing before Parliament should re-assemble, to spend another day at Beauclere. Mastering his correspondence meant in Nick's mind breaking open envelopes; writing answers was scarcely involved in the idea. But Mr. Carteret would never guess that. Nick was not moved even to write to him that the affair with Mrs. Dallow was on the point of taking the form he had been so good as to desire: he reserved the pleasure of this announcement for a personal interview.

The day before Good Friday, in the morning, his stillness was broken by a rat-tat-tat on the outer door of his studio, administered apparently by the knob of a walking-stick. His servant was out and he went to the door, wondering who his visitor could be at such a time, especially of the familiar class. The class was indicated by the visitor's failure to look for the bell; for there was a bell, though it required a little research. In a moment the mystery was solved: the gentleman who stood smiling at him from the threshold could only be Gabriel Nash. Dormer had not seen this whimsical personage for several months and had had no news of him beyond the general intimation that he was abroad. His old friend had sufficiently prepared him at the time of their reunion in Paris for the idea of the fitful in intercourse: and he had not been ignorant on his return from Paris that he should have had an opportunity to miss him if he had not been too busy to take advantage of it. In London, after the episode at Harsh, Gabriel had not reappeared: he had redeemed none of the pledges given the night they walked together to Notre Dame and conversed on important matters. He was to have interposed in Nick's destiny, but he had not interposed; he was to have dragged him in the opposite sense from Mrs. Dallow, but there had been no dragging; he was to have saved him, as he called it, and yet Nick was lost. This circumstance indeed constituted his excuse: the member for Harsh had rushed so to perdition. Nick had for the hour seriously wished to keep hold of him: he valued him as a salutary influence. Yet when he came to his senses after his election our young man had recognized that Nash might very well have reflected on the thanklessness of such a slippery subject—might have considered that he was released from his vows. Of course it had been particularly in the event of a Liberal triumph that he had threatened to make himself felt; the effect of a brand plucked from the burning would be so much greater if the flames were already high. Yet Nick had not held him to the letter of this pledge, and had so fully admitted the right of a properly-constituted æsthete to lose patience with him that he was now far from greeting his visitor with a reproach. He felt much more thrown on his defence.

Gabriel did not attack him however. He brought in only blandness and benevolence and a great content at having obeyed the mystic voice—it was really a remarkable case of second sight—which had whispered to him that the recreant comrade of his prime was in town. He had just come back from Sicily, after a southern winter, according to a custom frequent with him, and had been moved by a miraculous pre-science, unfavourable as the moment might seem, to go and ask for Nick in Calcutta Gardens, where he had extracted from his friend's servant an address not known to all the world. He showed Nick what a mistake it had been to fear a reproach from Gabriel Nash, and how he habitually ignored all lapses and kept up the standard only by taking a hundred fine things for granted. He also abounded more than ever in his own sense, reminding his friend how no recollection of him, no evocation of him in absence could do him justice. You couldn't recall him without seeming to exaggerate him, and then recognized when you saw him that your exaggeration had fallen short. He emerged out of vagueness (his Sicily might have been the Sicily of "A Winter's Tale"), and would evidently be reabsorbed in it; but his presence was positive and pervasive enough. He was very lively while he lasted. His connections were with beauty, urbanity and conversation, as usual, but it was a circle you couldn't find in the *Court Guide*. Nick had a sense that he knew "a lot of æsthetic people," but he dealt in ideas much more than in names and addresses. He was genial and jocose, sunburnt and romantically allusive. Nick gathered that he had been living for many days in a Saracenic tower, where his principal occupation was to watch for the flushing of the west. He had retained all the serenity of his opinions, and made light, with a candour of which the only defect was apparently that it was not quite enough a conscious virtue, of many of the objects of common esteem. When Nick asked him what he had been doing he replied: "Oh, living, you know;" and the tone of the words seemed to offer them as a record of magnificent success. He made a long visit, staying to luncheon and after luncheon, so that the little studio heard all at once more conversation, and of a wider scope, than in the several previous years of its history. With much of our story left to tell, it is a pity that so little of this rich colloquy may be transcribed here; because, as affairs took their course, it marked really (if it be a question of noting the exact point) a turn of the tide in Nick Dormer's personal situation. He was destined to remember the accent with which Nash exclaimed, on his drawing forth sundry specimens of amateurish earnestness: "I say—I say—I say!"

Nick glanced round with a heightened colour. "They're pretty bad, eh?"

"Oh, you're a deep one!" Nash went on.

"What's the matter?"

"Do you call your conduct that of a man of honour?"

"Scarcely, perhaps. But when no one has seen them!"

"That's your villainy. *C'est de l'exquis, du pur exquis.* Come, my dear fellow, this is very serious—it's a bad business," said Gabriel Nash. Then he added, almost with austerity: "You'll be so good as to place before me every patch of paint, every sketch and scrap that this room contains."

Nick complied, in great good-humour. He turned out his boxes and drawers, shovelled forth the contents of bulging portfolios, mounted on chairs to unhook old canvases that had been severely "skied." He was modest and docile and patient and amused, and above all quite thrilled—thrilled with the idea of eliciting a note of appreciation so late in the day. It was the oddest thing how at present in fact he found himself attributing value to Gabriel Nash—attributing to him, among attributions more confused, the dignity of judgment, the authority of intelligence. Nash was an ambiguous being, but he was an excellent touchstone. The two said very little for a while, and they had almost half an hour's silence, during which, after Nick had hastily improvised a little exhibition, there was only a puffing of cigarettes. The visitor walked about, looking at this and that, taking up rough studies and laying them down, asking a question of fact, fishing with his umbrella, on the floor, amid a pile of unarranged sketches. Nick accepted jocosely the attitude of suspense, but there was even more of it in his heart than in his face. So few people had seen his young work—almost no one who really counted. He had been ashamed of it, never showing it to bring on a conclusion, inasmuch as it was precisely of a conclusion that he was afraid. He whistled now while he let his companion take time. He rubbed old panels with his sleeve and dabbed wet sponges on surfaces that had sunk. It was a long time since he had felt so gay, strange as such an assertion sounds in regard to a young man whose bridal day had at his urgent solicitation lately been fixed. He had stayed in town to be alone with his imagination, and suddenly, paradoxically, the sense of that result had arrived with Gabriel Nash.

"Nicholas Dormer," this personage remarked at last, "for grossness of immorality I think I have never seen your equal."

"That sounds so well that I hesitate to risk spoiling it by wishing it explained."

"Don't you recognize in *any* degree the elevated idea of duty?"

"If I don't grasp it with a certain firmness I'm a great failure, for I was quite brought up in it," Nick said.

"Then you are the wretchedest failure I know. Life *is* ugly, after all."

"Do I gather that you yourself recognize obligations of the order you allude to?" asked Nick.

"Do you 'gather'?" Nash stared. "Why, aren't they the very flame of my faith, the burden of my song?"

"My dear fellow, duty is doing, and I inferred that you think rather poorly of doing—that it spoils one's style."

"Doing wrong, assuredly."

"But what do you call right? What's your canon of certainty there?"

"The conscience that's in us—that charming, conversible, infinite thing, the intensest thing we know. But you must treat the oracle civilly if you wish to make it speak. You mustn't stride into the temple in muddy jack-boots, with your hat on your head, as the Puritan troopers tramped into the dear old abbeys. One must do one's best to find out the right, and your criminality appears to be that you have not taken common trouble."

"I hadn't you to ask," smiled Nick. "But duty strikes me as doing *something*. If you are too afraid it may be the wrong thing, you may let everything go."

"Being is doing, and if doing is duty, being is duty. Do you follow?"

"At a great distance."

"To be what one *may* be, really and efficaciously," Nash went on, "to feel it and understand it, to accept it, adopt it, embrace it—that's conduct, that's life."

"And suppose one's a brute or an ass, where's the efficacy?"

"In one's very want of intelligence. In such cases one is out of it—the question doesn't exist; one simply becomes a part of the duty of others. The brute, the ass, neither feels, nor understands, nor accepts, nor adopts. Those fine processes in themselves classify us. They educate, they exalt, they preserve; so that, to profit by them, we must be as perceptive as we can. We must recognize our particular form, the instrument that each of us—each of us who carries anything—carries in his being. Mastering this instrument, learning to play it in perfection—that's what I call duty, what I call conduct, what I call success."

Nick listened with friendly attention and the air of general assent was in his face as he said: "Every one has it then, this individual pipe?"

" 'Every one,' my dear fellow, is too much to say, for the world is full of the crudest *remplissage*. The book of life is padded, ah but padded—a deplorable want of editing. I speak of every one that is any one. Of course there are pipes and pipes—little quavering flutes for the concerted movements and big *cornets-à-piston* for the great solos."

"I see, I see. And what might your instrument be?"

Nash hesitated not a moment; his answer was radiantly ready. "To speak to people just as I am speaking to you. To prevent for instance a great wrong being done."

"A great wrong?"

"Yes—to the human race. I talk—I talk; I say the things that other people don't, that they can't, that they won't," Gabriel continued, with his inimitable candour.

"If it's a question of mastery and perfection, you certainly have them," his companion replied.

"And you haven't, alas; that's the pity of it, that's the scandal. That's the wrong I want to set right, before it becomes too public a shame. I called you just now grossly immoral, on account of the spectacle you present—a spectacle to be hidden from the eye of ingenuous youth: that of a man neglecting his own fiddle to blunder away on that of one of his fellows. We can't afford such mistakes, we can't tolerate such license."

"You think then I *have* a fiddle?" asked Nick.

"A regular Stradivarius! All these things you have shown me are singularly interesting. You have a talent of a wonderfully pure strain."

"I say—I say—I say!" Nick exclaimed, standing in front of his visitor with his hands in his pockets and a blush on his smiling face, and repeating with a change of accent Nash's exclamation of half an hour before.

"I like it, your talent; I measure it, I appreciate it, I insist upon it," Nash went on, between the whiffs of his cigarette. "I have to be accomplished to do so, but fortunately I am. In such a case that's my duty. I shall make you my business for a while. Therefore," Nash added, piously, "don't say I'm unconscious of the moral law."

"A Stradivarius?" said Nick, interrogatively, with his eyes wide open and the thought in his mind of how different this was from having gone to Griffin.

X.

GABRIEL NASH had plenty of further opportunity to elucidate this and other figurative remarks, for he not only spent several of the middle hours of the day with his friend, but came back with him in the evening (they dined together at a little foreign pot-house in Soho, revealed to Nick on this occasion) and discussed the great question far into the night. The great question was whether, on the showing of those examples of his ability with which the room in which they sat was now densely bestrewn, Nick Dormer would be justified in "really going in" for the practice of pictorial art. This may strike many of my readers as a limited and even trivial inquiry, with little of the heroic or the romantic in it; but it was none the less carried to a very fine point by our clever young men. Nick suspected Nash of exaggerating his encouragement in order to play a malign trick on the political world, at whose expense it was his fancy to divert himself (without making that organization bankrupt assuredly), and reminded him that his present accusation of immorality was strangely inconsistent with the wanton hope expressed by him in Paris—the hope that the Liberal candidate at Harsh would be returned. Nash replied first: "Oh, I hadn't been in this place then!" but he defended himself more effectually in saying that it was not of Nick's having got elected that he complained: it was of his visible hesitancy to throw up his seat. Nick requested that he wouldn't speak of this, and his gallantry failed to render him incapable of saying: "The fact is I haven't the nerve for it." They talked then for a while of what he could do, not of what he couldn't; of the mysteries and miracles of reproduction and representation; of the strong, sane joys of the artistic life. Nick made afresh, with more fullness, his great confession, that his private ideal of happiness was the life of a great painter of portraits. He uttered his thought about this so copiously and lucidly that Nash's own abundance was stilled, and he listened almost as if he had been listening to something new, difficult as it was to suppose that there could be a point of view in relation to such a matter with which he was unacquainted.

"There it is," said Nick at last—"there's the naked, preposterous truth: that if I were to do exactly as I liked I should spend my years copying the more or less vacuous countenances of my fellow-mortals. I should find peace and pleasure and wisdom and worth, I should find fascination and a measure of success in it: out of the din and the dust and the scramble, the world of party labels, party cries, party bargains and party treacheries—of humbuggery, hypocrisy and cant. The cleanness and quietness of it, the independent effort to do something, to leave something which shall give joy to man long after the howling has died away to the last ghost of an echo—such a vision solicits me at certain hours with an almost irresistible force."

As he dropped these remarks Nick lolled on a big divan, with one of his long legs folded up; and his visitor stopped in front of him, after moving about the room vaguely and softly, almost on tiptoe, not to interrupt him. "You speak with the eloquence that rises to a man's lips on a very particular occasion; when he has practically, whatever his theory may be, renounced the right and dropped hideously into the wrong. Then his regret for the right, a certain exquisite appreciation of it, takes on an accent which I know well how to recognize."

Nick looked up at him a moment. "You've hit it, if you mean by that that I haven't resigned my seat and that I don't intend to."

"I thought you took it only to give it up. Don't you remember our talk in Paris?"

"I like to be a part of the spectacle that amuses you, but I could scarcely have taken so much trouble as that for it."

"But isn't it an absurd comedy, the life you lead?"

"Comedy or tragedy—I don't know which; whatever it is I appear to be capable of it to please two or three people."

"Then you *can* take trouble," said Nash.

"Yes, for the woman I'm to marry."

"Ah, you're to marry?"

"That's what has come on since we met in Paris, and it makes just the difference."

"Ah, my poor friend," smiled Gabriel, standing there, "no wonder you have an eloquence, an accent!"

"It's a pity I have them in the wrong place. I'm expected to have them in the House of Commons."

"You will when you make your farewell speech there—to announce that you chuck it up. And may I venture to ask who's to be your wife?" Gabriel went on.

"Mrs. Dallow has kindly consented. I think you saw her in Paris."

"Ah, yes: you spoke of her to me. I remember asking you if you were in love with her."

"I wasn't then."

Nash hesitated a moment. "And are you now?"

"Oh dear, yes," said Nick.

"That would be better if it wasn't worse."

"Nothing could be better; it's the best thing that can happen to me."

"Well," said Nash, "you must let me very respectfully approach her. You must let me bring her round."

"Bring her round?"

"Talk her over."

"Over to what?" Nick repeated his companion's words, a little as if it were to gain time, remembering the effect Gabriel Nash had produced upon Julia—an effect which scantily ministered to the idea of another meeting. Julia had had no occasion to allude again to Nick's imperturbable friend; he had passed out of her life at once and forever; but there flickered up a vivid recollection of the contempt he had led her to express, together with a sense of how odd she would think it that her intended should have thrown over two pleasant visits to cultivate such company.

"Over to a proper pride in what you may do—what you may do above all if she will help you."

"I scarcely see how she can help me," said Nick, with an air of thinking.

"She's extremely handsome, as I remember her: you could do great things with her."

"Ah, there's the rub," Nick went on. "I wanted her to sit for me this week, but she wouldn't."

"*Elle a bien tort.* You should do some fine strong type. Is Mrs. Dallow in London?" Nash inquired.

"For what do you take her? She's paying visits."

"Then I have a model for you."

"Then you have—?" Nick stared. "What has that to do with Mrs. Dallow's being away?"

"Doesn't it give you more time?"

"Oh, the time flies!" sighed Nick, in a manner that caused his companion to break into a laugh—a laugh in which for a moment he himself joined, blushing a little.

"Does she like you to paint?" Nash continued, with one of his candid intonations.

"So she says."

"Well, do something fine to show her."

"I'd rather show it to you," Nick confessed.

"My dear fellow, I see it from here, if you do your duty. Do you remember the Tragic Muse?" Nash pursued, explicatively.

"The Tragic Muse?"

"That girl in Paris, whom we heard at the old actress's and whom we afterwards met at the charming entertainment given by your cousin (isn't he?) the secretary of embassy."

"Oh, Peter's girl: of course I remember her."

"Don't call her Peter's; call her rather mine," Nash said, with good-humoured dissuasiveness. "I invented her, I introduced her, I revealed her."

"I thought on the contrary you ridiculed and repudiated her."

"As an individual, surely not; I seem to myself to have been all the while rendering her services. I said I disliked tea-party ranters, and so I do; but if my estimate of her powers was below the mark she has more than punished me."

"What has she done?" asked Nick.

"She has become interesting, as I suppose you know."

"How should I know?"

"You must see her, you must paint her," said Nash. "She tells me that something was said about it that day at Madame Carré's."

"Oh, I remember—said by Peter."

"Then it will please Mr. Sherringham—you'll be glad to do that. I suppose you know all he has done for Miriam?"

"Not a bit. I know nothing about Peter's affairs, unless it be in general that he goes in for mountebanks and mimes and

that it occurs to me I have heard one of my sisters mention—
the rumour had come to her—that he has been backing Miss
Rooth."

"Miss Rooth delights to talk of his kindness: she's charming when she speaks of it. It's to his good offices that she
owes her appearance here."

"Here? Is she in London?" Nick inquired.

"*D'où tombez-vous?* I thought you people read the papers."

"What should I read, when I sit (sometimes!) through the
stuff they put into them?"

"Of course I see that—that your engagement at your own
theatre keeps you from going to others. Learn then," said
Gabriel Nash, "that you have a great competitor and that you
are distinctly not, much as you may suppose it, *the* rising
comedian. The Tragic Muse is the great modern personage.
Haven't you heard people speak of her, haven't you been
taken to see her?"

"I dare say I've heard of her; but with a good many other
things on my mind I had forgotten it."

"Certainly I can imagine what has been on your mind. She
remembers you at any rate; she repays neglect with sympathy.
She wants to come and see you."

"To see me?"

"To be seen by you—it comes to the same thing. She's
worth seeing: you must let me bring her; you'll find her very
suggestive. That idea that you should paint her—she appears
to consider it a sort of bargain."

"A bargain? What will she give me?" Nick asked.

"A splendid model. She *is* splendid."

"Oh, then bring her," said Nick.

XI.

NASH BROUGHT HER, the great modern personage as he had described her, the very next day, and it took Nick Dormer but a short time to appreciate his declaration that Miriam Rooth was splendid. She had made an impression upon him ten months before, but it had haunted him only for a day, immediately overlaid with other images. Yet after Nash had spoken of her a few moments he evoked her again; some of her attitudes, some of her tones began to hover before him. He was pleased in advance with the idea of painting her. When she stood there in fact however it seemed to him that he had remembered her wrong: the brilliant young lady who instantly filled his studio with a presence that it had never known was exempt from the curious clumsiness which had interfused his former admiration of her with a certain pity. Miriam Rooth was light and bright and straight to-day—straight without being stiff and bright without being garish. To Nick's perhaps inadequately sophisticated mind the model, the actress were figures with a vulgar setting; but it would have been impossible to show that taint less than his present extremely natural yet extremely distinguished visitor. She was more natural even than Gabriel Nash ("nature" was still Nick's formula for his old friend), and beside her he appeared almost commonplace.

Nash recognized her superiority with a frankness that was honourable to both of them, testifying in this manner to his sense that they were all three serious beings, worthy to deal with realities. She attracted crowds to her theatre, but to his appreciation of such a fact as that, important doubtless in its way, there were limits which he had already expressed. What he now felt bound in all integrity to express was his perception that she had, in general and quite apart from the question of the box-office, a remarkable, a very remarkable artistic nature. He confessed that she had surprised him there; knowing of her in other days mainly that she was hungry to adopt an overrated profession, he had not imputed to her the normal measure of intelligence. Now he saw—he had had some talks with her—that she *was* intelligent; so much so that he was sorry for the embarrassment it would be to her. Nick could imagine the discomfort of having that sort of commodity to dispose of in such conditions. "She's a distinguished woman—really a distinguished woman," Nash explained, kindly and lucidly, almost paternally; "and the head you can see for yourself."

Miriam, smiling, as she sat on an old Venetian chair, held aloft, with the noblest effect, that portion of her person to which this patronage was extended, and remarked to Nick that, strange as it might appear, she had got quite to like poor Mr. Nash: she could make him go about with her; it was a relief to her mother.

"When I take him she has perfect peace," the girl said; "then she can stay at home and see the interviewers. She delights in that and I hate it, so our friend here is a great comfort. Of course a *femme de théâtre* is supposed to be able to go out alone, but there's a kind of appearance, an added *chic*, in having some one. People think he's my companion; I'm sure they fancy I pay him. I would pay him rather than give him up, for it doesn't matter that he's not a lady. He *is* one in tact and sympathy, as you see. And base as he thinks the sort of thing I do, he can't keep away from the theatre. When you're celebrated, people will look at you who before could never find out for themselves *why* they should."

"When you're celebrated you become handsomer; at least that's what has happened to you, though you were pretty too of old," Gabriel argued. "I go to the theatre to look at your head; it gives me the greatest pleasure. I take up anything of that sort as soon as I find it; one never knows how long it may last."

"Are you speaking of my appearance?" Miriam asked.

"Dear no, of my own pleasure, the first freshness," Nash went on. "Dormer at least, let me tell you in justice to him, hasn't waited till you were celebrated to want to see you again (he stands there open-eyed); for the simple reason that he hadn't the least idea of your renown. I had to announce it to him."

"Haven't you seen me act?" Miriam asked, without reproach, of her host.

"I'll go to-night," said Nick.

"You have your Parliament, haven't you? What do they call it—the demands of public life?" Miriam continued: to which Gabriel Nash rejoined that he had the demands of private as well, inasmuch as he was in love—he was on the point of being married. Miriam listened to this with participation; then she said: "Ah, then, do bring your—what do they call her in English? I'm always afraid of saying something improper—your *future*. I'll send you a box, under the circumstances; you'd like that better." She added that if he were to paint her he would have to see her often on the stage, wouldn't he? to profit by the *optique de la scène* (what did they call *that* in English?) studying her and fixing his impression. Before he had time to respond to this proposition she asked him if it disgusted him to hear her speak like that, as if she were always posing and thinking about herself, living only to be looked at, thrusting forward her person. She often got sick of doing so, already; but *à la guerre comme à la guerre*.

"That's the fine artistic nature, you see—a sort of divine disgust breaking out in her," Nash expounded.

"If you want to paint me at all, of course. I'm struck with the way I'm taking that for granted," Miriam continued. "When Mr. Nash spoke of it to me I jumped at the idea. I remembered our meeting in Paris and the kind things you said to me. But no doubt one oughtn't to jump at ideas when they represent serious sacrifices on the part of others."

"Doesn't she speak well!" Nash exclaimed to Nick. "Oh, she'll go far!"

"It's a great privilege to me to paint you; what title in the world have I to pretend to such a model?" Nick replied to Miriam. "The sacrifice is yours—a sacrifice of time and good-nature and credulity. You come in your beauty and your genius to this shabby place where I've nothing to show, not a guarantee to offer you; and I wonder what I've done to deserve such a gift of the gods."

"Doesn't *he* speak well?" Nash demanded, smiling, of Miriam.

She took no notice of him, but she repeated to Nick that she hadn't forgotten his friendly attitude in Paris; and when he answered that he surely had done very little she broke out, first resting her eyes on him a moment with a deep, reasonable smile and then springing up quickly: "Ah, well, if I must justify myself, I liked you!"

"Fancy my appearing to challenge you!" laughed Nick. "To see you again is to want tremendously to try something; but you must have an infinite patience, because I'm an awful duffer."

Miriam looked round the walls. "I see what you have done—*bien des choses.*"

"She understands—she understands," Gabriel dropped. And he added to Miriam: "Imagine, when he might do something, his choosing a life of shams! At bottom he's like you— a wonderful artistic nature."

"I'll have patience," said the girl, smiling at Nick.

"Then, my children, I leave you—the peace of the Lord be with you." With these words Nash took his departure.

The others chose a position for Miriam's sitting, after she had placed herself in many different attitudes and different lights; but an hour had elapsed before Nick got to work— began, on a large canvas, to knock her in, as he called it. He was hindered a little even by a certain nervousness, the emotion of finding himself, out of a clear sky, confronted with such a sitter and launched in such a task. The situation was incongruous, just after he had formally renounced all manner of "art"—the renunciation taking effect not a bit the less from the whim that he had consciously treated himself to *as* a whim (the last he should ever indulge), the freak of relapsing for a fortnight into a fingering of old sketches, for the purpose, as he might have said, of burning them up, of clearing out his studio and terminating his lease. There were both embarrassment and inspiration in the strange chance of snatching back for an hour a relinquished joy: the jump with which he found he could still rise to such an occasion took away his breath a little, at the same time that the idea—the idea of what one might make of such material—touched him with an irresistible wand. On the spot, to his inner vision, Miriam became a magnificent result, drawing a hundred formative instincts out of their troubled sleep, defying him where he privately felt strongest and imposing herself triumphantly in her own strength. He had the good fortune to see her, as a subject, without striking matches, in a vivid light, and his quick attempt was as exciting as a sudden gallop—it was almost the sense of riding a runaway horse.

She was in her way so fine that he could only think how to "do" her: that hard calculation soon flattened out the consciousness, lively in him at first, that she was a beautiful woman who had sought him out in his retirement. At the end of their first sitting her having sought him out appeared the most natural thing in the world: he had a perfect right to entertain her there—explanations and complications were engulfed in the productive mood. The business of "knocking her in" held up a lamp to her beauty, showed him how much there was of it and that she was infinitely interesting. He didn't want to fall in love with her (*that* would be a sell! as he said to himself), and she promptly became much too interesting for that. Nick might have reflected, for simplification's sake, as his cousin Peter had done, but with more validity, that he was engaged with Miss Rooth in an undertaking that didn't in the least refer to themselves, that they were working together seriously and that work was a suspension of sensibility. But after her first sitting (she came, poor girl, but twice), the need of such exorcisms passed from his spirit: he had so thoroughly, practically taken her up. As to whether Miriam had the same bright, still sense of co-operation to a definite end, the sense of the distinctively technical nature of the answer to every question to which the occasion might give birth, that mystery would be cleared up only if it were open to us to regard this young lady through some other medium than the mind of her friends. We have chosen, as it happens, for some of the advantages it carries with it, the indirect vision; and it fails as yet to tell us (what Nick of course wondered about before he ceased to care, as indeed he intimated to his visitor) why a young person crowned with success should have taken it into her head that there was something for her in so blighted a spot. She should have gone to one of the regular people, the great people: they would have welcomed her with open arms. When Nick asked her if some of the R. A.'s hadn't expressed a desire to have a crack at her she said: "Oh, dear, no, only the tiresome photographers; and fancy *them*, in the future! If mamma could only do *that* for me!" And she added, with the charming fellowship for which she was conspicuous on this occasion: "You know I don't think any one yet has been quite so much struck with me as you."

"Not even Peter Sherringham?" asked Nick, laughing and stepping back to judge of the effect of a line.

"Oh, Mr. Sherringham's different. You're an artist."

"For heaven's sake, don't say that!" cried Nick. "And as regards your art I thought Peter knew more than any one."

"Ah, you're severe," said Miriam.

"Severe?"

"Because that's what he thinks. But he does know a lot—he has been a providence to me."

"And why hasn't he come here to see you act?"

Miriam hesitated a moment. "How do you know he hasn't come?"

"Because I take for granted he would have called on me if he had."

"Does he like you very much?" asked Miriam.

"I don't know. I like him."

"He's a gentleman—*pour cela*," said Miriam.

"Oh, yes, for that!" Nick went on absently, sketching hard.

"But he's afraid of me—afraid to see me."

"Doesn't he think you're good enough?"

"On the contrary—he believes I shall carry him away and he's in a terror of my doing it."

"He ought to like that," said Nick.

"That's what I mean when I say he's not an artist. However, he declares he does like it, only it appears it is not the right thing for him. Oh, the right thing—he's bent upon getting that. But it's not for me to blame him, for I am too. He's coming some night, however: he shall have a dose!"

"Poor Peter!" Nick exclaimed, with a compassion none the less real because it was mirthful: the girl's tone was so expressive of good-humoured, unscrupulous power.

"He's such a curious mixture," Miriam went on; "sometimes I lose patience with him. It isn't exactly trying to serve both God and Mammon, but it's muddling up the stage and the world. The world be hanged; the stage, or anything of that sort (I mean one's faith), comes first."

"Brava, brava, you do me good," Nick murmured, still hilarious and at his work. "But it's very kind of you, when I was in this absurd state of ignorance, to attribute to me the honour of having been more struck with you than any one else," he continued, after a moment.

"Yes, I confess I don't quite see—when the shops were full of my photographs."

"Oh, I'm so poor—I don't go into shops," returned Nick.

"Are you very poor?"

"I live on alms."

"And don't they pay you—the government, the ministry?"

"Dear young lady, for what?—for shutting myself up with beautiful women?"

"Ah, you have others, then?" asked Miriam.

"They are not so kind as you, I confess."

"I'll buy it from you—what you're doing: I'll pay you well when it's done," said the girl. "I've got money now; I make it, you know—a good lot of it. It's too delightful, after scraping and starving. Try it and you'll see. Give up the base, bad world."

"But isn't it supposed to be the base, bad world that pays?"

"Precisely; make it pay, without mercy—squeeze it dry. That's what it's meant for—to pay for art. Ah, if it wasn't for that! I'll bring you a quantity of photographs, to-morrow—you must let me come back to-morrow: it's so amusing to have them, by the hundred, all for nothing, to give away. That's what takes mamma most: she can't get over it. That's luxury and glory; even at Castle Nugent they didn't do that. People used to sketch me, but not so much as mamma *veut bien le dire*; and in all my life I never had but one poor little carte-de-visite, when I was sixteen, in a plaid frock, with the banks of a river, at three francs the dozen."

XII.

IT WAS SUCCESS, Nick felt, that had made Miriam finer—
the full possession of her talent and the sense of the recognition of it. There was an intimation in her presence (if he
had given his mind to it) that for him too the same cause
would produce the same effect—that is would show him that
there is nothing like being launched in the practice of an art
to learn what it may do for one. Nick felt clumsy beside a
person who manifestly now had such an extraordinary familiarity with the point of view. He remembered too the inferiority that had been in his visitor—something clumsy and
shabby, of quite another quality from her actual smartness, as
London people would call it, her well-appointedness and her
evident command of more than one manner. Handsome as
she had been the year before, she had suggested provincial
lodgings, bread-and-butter, heavy tragedy and tears; and if
then she was an ill-dressed girl with thick hair who wanted to
be an actress, she was already in a few weeks an actress who
could act even at not acting. She showed what a light hand
she could have, forbore to startle and looked as well for un-
professional life as Julia: which was only the perfection of her
professional character.

This function came out much in her talk, for there were
many little bursts of confidence as well as many familiar
pauses as she sat there; and she was ready to tell Nick the
whole history of her début—the chance that had suddenly
turned up and that she had caught with a jump as it passed.
He missed some of the details, in his attention to his own
task, and some of them he failed to understand, attached as
they were to the name of Mr. Basil Dashwood, which he
heard for the first time. It was through Mr. Dashwood's extraordinary exertions that a hearing—a morning performance
at a London theatre—had been obtained for her. That had
been the great step, for it had led to the putting on at night of
the play at the same theatre, in place of a wretched thing they
were trying (it was no use) to keep on its feet, and to her
engagement for the principal part. She had made a hit in it
(she couldn't pretend not to know that); but she was already

tired of it, there were so many other things she wanted to do; and when she thought it would probably run a month or two more she was in the humour to curse the odious conditions of artistic production in such an age. The play was a simplified version of a new French piece, a thing that had taken in Paris, at a third-rate theatre, and had now, in London, proved itself good enough for houses mainly made up of ten-shilling stalls. It was Dashwood who had said it would go, if they could get the rights and a fellow to make some changes: he had discovered it at a nasty little theatre she had never been to, over the Seine. They had got the rights and the fellow who had made the changes was practically Dashwood himself; there was another man, in London, Mr. Gushmore—Miriam didn't know whether Nick would ever have heard of him (Nick hadn't), who had done some of it. It had been awfully chopped down, to a mere bone, with the meat all gone; but that was what people in London seemed to like. They were very innocent, like little dogs amusing themselves with a bone. At any rate, she had made something, she had made a figure of the woman (a dreadful idiot, really, especially in what Dashwood had muddled her into); and Miriam added, in the complacency of her young expansion: "Oh, give me fifty words, any time, and the ghost of a situation, and I'll set you up a figure. Besides, I mustn't abuse poor Yolande—she has saved us," she said.

"Yolande?"

"Our ridiculous play. That's the name of the impossible woman. She has put bread into our mouths and she's a loaf on the shelf for the future. The rights are mine."

"You're lucky to have them," said Nick, a little vaguely, troubled about his sitter's nose, which was somehow Jewish without the convex arch.

"Indeed I am. He gave them to me. Wasn't it charming?"

"He gave them—Mr. Dashwood?"

"Dear me, no; where should poor Dashwood have got them? He hasn't a penny in the world. Besides, if he had got them he would have kept them. I mean your blessed cousin."

"I see—they're a present from Peter."

"Like many other things. Isn't he a dear? If it hadn't been for him the shelf would have remained bare. He bought the play for this country and America for four hundred pounds, and on the chance: fancy! There was no rush for it, and how could he tell? And then he gracefully handed it to me. So I have my little capital. Isn't he a duck? You have nice cousins."

Nick assented to the proposition, only putting in an amendment to the effect that surely Peter had nice cousins also, and making, as he went on with his work, a tacit pre-occupied reflection or two; such as that it must be pleasant to render little services like that to youth, beauty and genius (he rather wondered how Peter could afford them), and that, "duck" as he was, Miss Rooth's benefactor was rather taken for granted. *Sic vos non vobis* faintly murmured itself in Nick's brain. This community of interests, or at least of relations, quickened the flight of time, so that he was still fresh when the sitting came to an end. It was settled that Miriam should come back on the morrow, to enable her portrayer to make the most of the few days of the parliamentary recess; and just before she left she asked—

"Then you *will* come to-night?"

"Without fail. I hate to lose an hour of you."

"Then I'll place you. It will be my affair."

"You're very kind," he responded. "Isn't it a simple matter for me to take a stall? This week I suppose they're to be had."

"I'll send you a box," said Miriam. "You shall do it well. There are plenty now."

"Why should I be lost, all alone, in the grandeur of a box?"

"Can't you bring your friend?"

"My friend?"

"The lady you are engaged to."

"Unfortunately she's out of town."

Miriam looked at him with a grand profundity. "Does she leave you alone like that?"

"She thought I should like it—I should be more free to paint. You see I am."

"Yes, perhaps it's good for *me*. Have you got her portrait?" Miriam asked.

"She doesn't like me to paint her."

"Really? Perhaps then she won't like you to paint me."

"That's why I want to be quick," laughed Nick.

"Before she knows it?"

"She'll know it to-morrow. I shall write to her."

Miriam gave him another of her special looks; then she said: "I see; you're afraid of her." And she added, "Mention my name: they'll give you the box at the theatre."

Whether or no Nick were afraid of Mrs. Dallow, he still protested against receiving this bounty from the hands of Miss Rooth—repeated that he would rather take a stall according to his wont and pay for it. This led her to declare with a sudden flicker of passion that if he didn't do as she wished she would never sit to him again.

"Ah then, you have me," returned Nick. "Only I *don't* see why you should give me so many things."

"What in the world have I given you?"

"Why, an idea." And Nick looked at his picture a little ruefully. "I don't mean to say I haven't let it fall and smashed it."

"Ah, an idea—that *is* a great thing for people in our line. But you'll see me much better from the box, and I'll send you Gabriel Nash," Miriam added, getting into the hansom which her host's servant had fetched for her. As Nick turned back into his studio after watching her drive away he laughed at the conception that they were in the same "line."

Nick shared his box at the theatre with Gabriel Nash, who talked during the entr'actes not in the least about the performance or the performer, but about the possible greatness of the art of the portraitist—its reach, its range, its fascination, the magnificent examples it had left us in the past: windows open into history, into psychology, things that were among the most precious possessions of the human race. He insisted, above all, on the interest, the richness arising from this great peculiarity of it: that, unlike most other forms, it was a revelation of two realities, the man whom it was the artist's conscious effort to reveal and the man (the interpreter) expressed in the very quality and temper of that effort. It offered a double vision, the strongest dose of life that art could give, the strongest dose of art that life could give. Nick Dormer had already become aware that he had two states of mind in listening to Gabriel Nash: one of them in which he laughed, doubted, sometimes even reprobated, and at any rate failed to follow or to accept; the other in which this contemplative genius seemed to take the words out of his mouth, to utter for him, better and more completely, the very things he was on the point of saying. Nash's saying them at such moments appeared to make them true, to set them up in the world, and to-night he said a good many, especially as to the happiness of cultivating one's own garden; growing there in stillness and freedom certain strong, pure flowers that would bloom forever, long after the rank weeds of the hour were withered and blown away.

It was to keep Miriam Rooth in his eye for his object that Nick had come to the play; and she dwelt there all the evening, being constantly on the stage. He was so occupied in watching her face (for he now saw pretty clearly what he should attempt to make of it) that he was conscious only in a secondary degree of the story she illustrated, and in regard to her acting in particular had mainly a surprised sense that she was extraordinarily quiet. He remembered her loudness, her violence in Paris, at Peter Sherringham's, her wild wails, the first time, at Madame Carré's; compared with which her present manner was eminently temperate and modern. Nick Dormer was not critical at the theatre; he believed what he saw and had a pleasant sense of the inevitable; therefore he would not have guessed what Gabriel Nash had to tell him— that for Miriam, with her tragic cast and her peculiar attributes, her present performance, full of actuality, of light, fine indications and, in parts, of pointed touches of comedy, was a rare *tour de force*. It went on altogether in a register that he had not supposed her to possess; in which, as he said, she didn't touch her capital, doing it wholly with her little savings. It gave him the idea that she was capable of almost anything.

In one of the intervals they went round to see her; but for Nick this purpose was partly defeated by the wonderful amiability with which he was challenged by Mrs. Rooth, whom they found sitting with her daughter and who attacked him with a hundred questions about his dear mother and his charming sisters. She maintained that that day in Paris they had shown her a kindness she should never forget. She abounded also in gracious expressions in regard to the portrait he had so cleverly begun, declaring that she was so eager to see it, however little he might as yet have accomplished, that she should do herself the honour to wait upon him in the morning, when Miriam came to sit.

"I'm acting for *you* to-night," the girl said to Nick, before he returned to his place.

"No, that's exactly what you are not doing," Nash interposed, with one of his intellectual superiorities. "You have stopped acting, you have reduced it to the least that will do, you simply *are*—you are just the visible image, the picture on the wall. It keeps you wonderfully in focus. I have never seen you so beautiful."

Miriam stared at this; then it could be seen that she coloured. "What a luxury in life to have everything explained! He's the great explainer," she said, turning to Nick.

He shook hands with her for good-night. "Well then, we must give him lots to do."

She came to his studio in the morning, but unaccompanied by her mother; in allusion to whom she simply said: "Mamma wished to come, but I wouldn't let her." They proceeded promptly to business. The girl divested herself of her hat and coat, taking the position already established for her. After they had worked for more than an hour, with much less talk than the day before, Nick being extremely absorbed and Miriam wearing in silence the kindest, most religious air of consideration for the sharp tension she imposed upon him—at the end of this period of patience, pervaded by a holy calm, our young lady suddenly got up and exclaimed, "I say, I *must* see it!" with which, quickly, she stepped down from her place and came round to the canvas. She had, at Nick's request, not looked at his work the day before. He fell back, glad to rest, and put down his palette and brushes.

"*Ah bien, c'est tapé!*" Miriam cried, as she stood before the easel. Nick was pleased with her ejaculation, he was even pleased with what he had done; he had had a long, happy spurt and felt excited and sanctioned. Miriam, retreating also a little, sank into a high-backed, old-fashioned chair that stood two or three yards from the picture, and reclined in it, with her head on one side, looking at the rough resemblance. She made a remark or two about it, to which Nick replied standing behind her and after a moment leaning on the top of the chair. He was away from his work and his eyes searched it with a kind of fondness of hope. They rose, however, as he presently became conscious that the door of the large room opposite to him had opened without making a sound and that some one stood upon the threshold. The person on the threshold was Julia Dallow.

As soon as he perceived her Nick wished he had posted a letter to her the night before. He had written only that morning. Nevertheless there was genuine joy in the words with which he bounded towards her—"Ah, my dear Julia, what a jolly surprise!"—for her unannounced descent spoke to him above all of an irresistible desire to see him again sooner than they had arranged. She had taken a step forward, but she had done no more, stopping short at the sight of the strange woman, so divested of visiting-gear that she looked half undressed, who lounged familiarly in the middle of the room and over whom Nick had been still more familiarly hanging. Julia's eyes rested on this embodied unexpectedness, and as they did so she grew pale—so pale that Nick, observing it, instinctively looked back to see what Miriam had done to produce such an effect. She had done nothing at all, which was precisely what was embarrassing; only staring at the intruder, motionless and superb. She seemed, somehow, in indolent possession of the place, and even in that instant Nick noted how handsome she looked; so that he exclaimed somewhere, inaudibly, in a region beneath his other emotions: "How I should like to paint her *that* way!" Mrs. Dallow transferred her eyes for a single moment to Nick's; then they turned away—away from Miriam, ranging over the room.

"I've got a sitter, but you mustn't mind that; we're taking a rest. I'm delighted to see you," said Nick. He closed the door of the studio behind her; his servant was still at the outer door, which was open and through which he saw Julia's carriage drawn up. This made her advance a little further, but still she said nothing; she dropped no answer even when Nick went on, with a sense of awkwardness: "When did you come back? I hope nothing has gone wrong. You come at a very interesting moment," he continued, thinking as soon as he had spoken that they were such words as might have made her laugh. She was far from laughing; she only managed to look neither at him nor at Miriam and to say, after a little, when he had repeated his question about her return:

"I came back this morning—I came straight here."

"And nothing's wrong, I hope?"

"Oh, no—everything's all right," she replied very quickly and without expression. She vouchsafed no explanation of her premature return and took no notice of the seat Nick offered her; neither did she appear to hear him when he begged her not to look yet at the work on the easel—it was in such a dreadful state. He was conscious, as he phrased it, that his request gave to Miriam's position directly in front of his canvas an air of privilege which her neglect to recognize in any way Mrs. Dallow's entrance or her importance did nothing to correct. But that mattered less if the appeal failed to reach Julia's intelligence, as he judged, seeing presently how deeply she was agitated. Nothing mattered in face of the sense of danger which took possession of him after she had been in the room a few moments. He wanted to say: "What's the difficulty? Has anything happened?" but he felt that she would not like him to utter words so intimate in presence of the person she had been rudely startled to find between them. He pronounced Miriam's name to Mrs. Dallow and Mrs. Dallow's to Miriam, but Julia's recognition of the ceremony was so slight as to be scarcely perceptible. Miriam had the air of waiting for something more before she herself made a sign; and as nothing more came she continued to be silent and not to budge. Nick added a remark to the effect that Mrs. Dallow would remember to have had the pleasure of meeting Miss Rooth the year before—in Paris, that day, at her brother Peter's; to which Mrs. Dallow rejoined, "Ah, yes," without any qualification, while she looked down at some rather rusty studies, on panels, which were ranged along the floor, resting against the base of the wall. Her agitation was evidently a pain to herself; she had had a shock of extreme violence, and Nick saw that as Miriam showed no symptom of offering to give up her sitting her stay would be of the briefest. He wished Miriam would do something—say she would go, get up, move about; as it was she had the appearance of watching from her point of vantage Mrs. Dallow's discomfiture. He made a series of inquiries about Julia's doings in the country, to two or three of which she gave answers monosyllabic and scarcely comprehensible, while she turned her eyes round and round the room as if she were looking for something she couldn't find—for an escape, for something that was not Miriam. At last she said—it was at the end of a very few minutes:

"I didn't come to stay—when you're so busy. I only looked in to see if you were here. Good-bye."

"It's charming of you to have come. I'm so glad you've seen for yourself how well I'm occupied," Nick replied, not unaware that he was very red. This made Mrs. Dallow look at him, while Miriam considered them both. Julia's eyes had something in them that he had never seen before—a flash of fright by which he was himself frightened. "Of course I'll see you later," he added, laughing awkwardly, while she reached the door, while she opened it herself and got off without a good-day to Miriam. "I wrote to you this morning—you've missed my letter," he repeated behind her, having already given her this information. The door of the studio was very near that of the house, but before Mrs. Dallow had reached the street the visitors' bell was set ringing. The passage was narrow and she kept in advance of Nick, anticipating his motion to open the street-door. The bell was tinkling still when, by the action of her own hand, a gentleman on the step stood revealed.

"Ah my dear, don't go!" Nick heard pronounced in quick, soft dissuasion and in the now familiar accents of Gabriel Nash. The rectification followed more quickly still, if that were a rectification which scarcely improved the matter: "I beg a thousand pardons. I thought you were Miriam."

Gabriel gave way, and Mrs. Dallow dashed out of the house. Her carriage, a victoria with a pair of horses who had got hot, had taken a turn up the street, but the coachman had already perceived his mistress and was rapidly coming back. He drew near; not so fast however but that Gabriel Nash had time to accompany Mrs. Dallow to the edge of the pavement with an apology for the freedom into which he had blundered. Nick was at her other hand, waiting to put her into her carriage and freshly disconcerted by the encounter with Nash, who somehow, as he stood making Julia an explanation that she didn't listen to, looked less eminent than usual, though not more conscious of difficulties. Nick coloured deeper and watched the footman spring down as the victoria drove up; he heard Nash say something about the honour of having met Mrs. Dallow in Paris. Nick wanted him to go into the house; he damned inwardly his want of delicacy. He desired a word with Julia alone—as much alone as the two inconvenient servants would allow. But Nash was not too much discouraged to say: "You came for a glimpse of the great model? *Doesn't* she sit? That's what I wanted too, this morning—just a look, for a blessing on the day. Ah, but *you*, madam—"

Julia had sprung into the carriage while he was still speaking and had flashed out to the coachman a "Home!" which of itself set the vehicle in motion. The carriage went a few yards, but while Gabriel, with a magnificent bow, turned away, Nick Dormer, with his hand on the edge of the hood, moved with it.

"You don't like it, but I'll explain," he said, laughing and in a low tone.

"Explain what?" Mrs. Dallow asked, still very pale and grave, but showing nothing in her voice. She was thinking of the servants. She could think of them even then.

"Oh, it's all right. I'll come in at five," Nick returned, gallantly jocular, while the carriage rolled away.

Gabriel had gone into the studio and Nick found him standing in admiration before Miriam, who had resumed the position in which she was sitting.

"Lord, she's good to-day! Isn't she good to-day?" Nash broke out, seizing Nick by the arm to give him a certain view. Miriam looked indeed still handsomer than before, and she had taken up her attitude again with a splendid sphinx-like air of being capable of keeping it forever. Nick said nothing, but he went back to work with a tingle of confusion, which proved in fact, when he resumed his palette, to be a sharp and, after a moment, a delightful stimulus. Miriam spoke never a word, but she was doubly grand, and for more than an hour, till Nick, exhausted, declared he must stop, the industrious silence was broken only by the desultory discourse of Gabriel Nash.

XIII.

NICK DORMER went to Great Stanhope Street at five o'clock and learned, rather to his surprise, that Mrs. Dallow was not at home—to his surprise because he had told her he would come at that hour, and he attributed to her, with a certain simplicity, an eager state of mind in regard to his explanation. Apparently she was not eager; the eagerness was his own—he was eager to explain. He recognized, not without a certain consciousness of magnanimity in doing so, that there had been some reason for her quick withdrawal from his studio, or at any rate for her extreme discomposure there. He had a few days before put in a plea for a snatch of worship in that sanctuary, and she had accepted and approved it; but the worship, when the curtain happened to blow back, proved to be that of a magnificent young woman, an actress with disordered hair, who wore in a singular degree the aspect of a person settled to spend the day. The explanation was easy: it resided in the circumstance that when one was painting, even very badly and only for a moment, one had to have models. Nick was impatient to give it, with frank, affectionate lips and a full, jocose admission that it was natural Julia should have been startled; and he was the more impatient that, though he would not in the least have expected her to like finding a strange woman domesticated for the hour under his roof, she had disliked it even more than would have seemed probable. That was because, not having heard from him about the matter, the impression was for the moment irresistible with her that a trick had been played her. But three minutes with him alone would make the difference.

They would indeed have a considerable difference to make, Nick reflected, as minutes much more numerous elapsed without bringing Mrs. Dallow home. For he had said to the butler that he would come in and wait (though it was odd she should not have left a message for him): she would doubtless return from one moment to the other. Nick had of course full license to wait, anywhere he preferred; and he was ushered into Julia's particular sitting-room and supplied with tea and the evening papers. After a quarter of an hour however he

gave little attention to these beguilements, owing to the increase of his idea that it was odd that when she definitely
knew he was coming she should not have taken more pains to
be at home. He walked up and down and looked out of the
window, took up her books and dropped them again, and
then, as half an hour had elapsed, began to feel rather angry.
What could she be about when, at a moment when London
was utterly empty, she could not be paying visits? A footman
came in to attend to the fire; whereupon Nick questioned him
as to the manner in which Mrs. Dallow was probably engaged. The man revealed the fact that his mistress had gone
out only a quarter of an hour before Nick arrived, and, as if
he appreciated the opportunity for a little decorous conversation, gave him still more information than he asked for. From
this it appeared that, as Nick knew or could surmise, she had
the evening previous, in the country, telegraphed for the victoria to meet her in the morning at Paddington and had gone
straight from the station to the studio, while her maid, with
her luggage, proceeded in a cab to Great Stanhope Street. On
leaving the studio however she had not come directly home;
she had chosen this unusual season for an hour's drive in the
Park. She had finally re-entered her house, but had remained
up-stairs all day, seeing no one and not coming down to luncheon. At four o'clock she had ordered the brougham for four
forty-five, and had got into it punctually, saying "To the
Park!" as she did so.

Nick, after the footman had left him, felt himself much
mystified by Julia's sudden passion for the banks of the Serpentine, forsaken and foggy now, inasmuch as the afternoon
had come on gray and the light was waning. She usually
hated the Park and she hated a closed carriage. He had a discomfortable vision of her, shrunken into a corner of her
brougham and veiled as if she had been crying, revolving
round the solitude of the Drive. She had of course been
deeply disconcerted, and she was nervous and upset: the motion of the carriage soothed her and made her fidget less. Nick
remembered that in the morning, at his door, she had appeared to be going home; so she had turned into the Park on
second thoughts, as she passed. He lingered another half
hour, walked up and down the room many times and thought

of many things. Had she misunderstood him when he said he would come at five? Couldn't she be sure, even if she had, that he would come early rather than late, and might she not have left a message for him on the chance? Going out that way a few minutes before he was to come had even a little the air of a thing done on purpose to offend him; as if she had been so displeased that she had taken the nearest occasion of giving him a sign that she meant to break. But were these the things that Julia did and was that the way she did them—his fine, proud, delicate, generous Julia?

When six o'clock came poor Nick felt distinctly resentful; but he stayed ten minutes longer, on the possibility that Mrs. Dallow would in the morning have understood him to mention that hour. The April dusk began to gather and the unsociability of her behaviour, especially if she were still rumbling about the Park, became absurd. Anecdotes came back to Nick, vaguely remembered, heard he couldn't have said when or where, of poor artists for whom life had been rendered difficult by wives who wouldn't allow them the use of the living female model and who made scenes if, on the staircase, they encountered such sources of inspiration. These ladies struck him as vulgar and odious persons, with whom it seemed grotesque that Julia should have anything in common. Of course she was not his wife yet, and of course if she were he should have washed his hands of every form of activity requiring the services of the sitter; but even these qualifications left him with a capacity to shudder at the way Julia just escaped ranking herself with the heavy-handed.

At a quarter-past six he rang a bell and told the servant who answered it that he was going and that Mrs. Dallow was to be informed as soon as she came in that he had expected to find her and had waited an hour and a quarter for her. But he had just reached the doorstep, on his departure, when her brougham, emerging from the evening mist, stopped in front of the house. Nick stood at the door, hanging back till she got out, allowing the servants to help her. She saw him—she was not veiled, like his mental image of her; but this did not prevent her from pausing to give an order to the coachman, a matter apparently requiring some discussion. When she came to the door Nick remarked to her that he had been waiting an eternity for her; to which she replied that he must not make a grievance to her of that—she was too unwell to do justice to it. He immediately professed regret and sympathy, adding, however, that in that case she had much better not have gone out. She made no answer to this—there were three servants in the hall who looked as if they might understand at least what was *not* said to them: only when he followed her in she asked if his idea had been to stay longer.

"Certainly, if you're not too ill to see me."

"Come in, then," Julia said, turning back after having gone to the foot of the stairs.

This struck him immediately as a further restriction of his visit: she would not readmit him to the drawing-room or to her boudoir; she would receive him in an impersonal apartment down-stairs, in which she saw people on business. What did she want to do to him? He was prepared by this time for a scene of jealousy; for he was sure he had learned to read her character justly in feeling that if she had the appearance of a cold woman she had also on certain occasions a liability to extreme emotion. She was very still, but every now and then she would fire off a pistol. As soon as Nick had closed the door she said, without sitting down:

"I dare say you saw I didn't like that at all."

"My having a sitter, that way? I was very much annoyed at it myself," Nick answered.

"Why were you annoyed? She's very handsome," said Mrs. Dallow, perversely.

"I didn't know you looked at her!" Nick laughed.

Julia hesitated a moment. "Was I very rude?"

"Oh, it was all right. It was only awkward for me, because you didn't know," Nick replied.

"I did know; that's why I came."

"How do you mean? My letter couldn't have reached you."

"I don't know anything about your letter," said Mrs. Dallow, casting about her for a chair and then seating herself on the edge of a sofa, with her eyes on the floor.

"She sat to me yesterday; she was there all the morning; but I didn't write to tell you. I went at her with great energy and, absurd as it may seem to you, found myself very tired afterwards. Besides, in the evening I went to see her act."

"Does she act?" asked Mrs. Dallow.

"She's an actress; it's her profession. Don't you remember her that day at Peter's, in Paris? She's already a celebrity; she has great talent; she's engaged at a theatre here and is making a sensation. As I tell you, I saw her last night."

"You needn't tell me," Mrs. Dallow replied, looking up at him with a face of which the intense, the tragic sadness startled him.

He had been standing before her, but at this he instantly sat down beside her, taking her passive hand. "I want to, please; otherwise it must seem so odd to you. I knew she was coming when I wrote to you the day before yesterday. But I didn't tell you then, because I didn't know how it would turn out and I didn't want to exult in advance over a poor little attempt that might come to nothing. Moreover it was no use speaking of the matter at all unless I told you exactly how it came about," Nick went on, explaining kindly, copiously. "It was the result of a visit unexpectedly paid me by Gabriel Nash."

"That man—the man who spoke to me?" Julia asked, startled into a shuddering memory.

"He did what he thought would please you, but I dare say it didn't. You met him in Paris and didn't like him; so I thought it best to hold my tongue about him."

"Do *you* like him?"

"Very much."

"Great heaven!" Julia ejaculated, almost under her breath.

"The reason I was annoyed was because, somehow, when you came in, I suddenly had the air of having got out of those visits and shut myself up in town to do something that I had kept from you. And I have been very unhappy till I could explain."

"You don't explain—you can't explain," Mrs. Dallow declared, turning on her companion eyes which, in spite of her studied stillness, expressed deep excitement. "I knew it—I knew everything; that's why I came."

"It was a sort of second-sight—what they call a brain-wave," Nick smiled.

"I felt uneasy, I felt a kind of call; it came suddenly, yesterday. It was irresistible; nothing could have kept me this morning."

"That's very serious, but it's still more delightful. You mustn't go away again," said Nick. "We must stick together —forever and ever."

He put his arm round her, but she detached herself as soon as she felt its pressure. She rose quickly, moving away, while, mystified, he sat looking up at her as she had looked a few moments before at him. "I've thought it all over; I've been thinking of it all day," she began. "That's why I didn't come in."

"Don't think of it too much; it isn't worth it."

"You like it more than anything else. You do—you can't deny it," she went on.

"My dear child, what are you talking about?" Nick asked, gently.

"That's what you like—doing what you were this morning; with women lolling, with their things off, to be painted, and people like that man."

Nick slowly got up, hesitating. "My dear Julia, apart from the surprise, this morning, do you object to the living model?"

"Not a bit, for you."

"What's the inconvenience, then, since in my studio they are only for me?"

"You love it, you revel in it; that's what you want, and that's the only thing you want!" Julia broke out.

"To have models, lolling women, do you mean?"

"That's what I felt, what I knew, what came over me and haunted me yesterday, so that I couldn't throw it off. It seemed to me that if I could see it with my eyes and have the perfect proof I should feel better, I should be quiet. And now I *am*—after a struggle of some hours, I confess. I *have* seen; the whole thing's clear and I'm satisfied."

"I'm not, and to me the whole thing isn't clear. What exactly are you talking about?" Nick demanded.

"About what you were doing this morning. That's your innermost preference, that's your secret passion."

"A little go at something serious? Yes, it was almost serious," said Nick. "But it was an accident, this morning and yesterday: I got on better than I intended."

"I'm sure you have immense talent," Mrs. Dallow remarked, with a joylessness that was almost droll.

"No, no, I might have had. I've plucked it up: it's too late for it to flower. My dear Julia, I'm perfectly incompetent and perfectly resigned."

"Yes, you looked so this morning, when you hung over her. Oh, she'll bring back your talent!"

"She's an obliging and even an intelligent creature, and I've no doubt she would if she could. But I've received from *you* all the help that any woman is destined to give me. No one can do for me again what you have done."

"I shouldn't try it again; I acted in ignorance. Oh, I've thought it all out!" Julia declared. Then, with a strange face of anguish resting on his, she said: "Before it's too late—before it's too late!"

"Too late for what?"

"For you to be free—for you to be free. And for me—for me to be free too. You hate everything I like!" she exclaimed, with a trembling voice. "Don't pretend, don't pretend!" she went on, as a sound of protest broke from him.

"I thought you wanted me to paint," protested Nick, flushed and staring.

"I do—I do. That's why you must be free, why we must part."

"Why we must part?"

"Oh, I've turned it over. I've faced the truth. It wouldn't do at all," said Mrs. Dallow.

"I like the way you talk of it, as if it were a trimming for your dress!" Nick rejoined, with bitterness. "Won't it do for you to be loved and cherished as well as any woman in England?"

Mrs. Dallow turned away from him, closing her eyes as if not to see something that would be dangerous to her. "You mustn't give anything up for me. I should feel it all the while and I should hate it. I'm not afraid of the truth, but you are."

"The truth, dear Julia? I only want to know it," said Nick. "It seems to me I've got hold of it. When two persons are united by the tenderest affection and are sane and generous and just, no difficulties that occur in the union their life makes for them are insurmountable, no problems are insoluble."

Mrs. Dallow appeared for a moment to reflect upon this; it was spoken in a tone that might have touched her. At any rate at the end of the moment, lifting her eyes, she announced: "I hate art, as you call it. I thought I did, I knew I did; but till this morning I didn't know how much."

"Bless your soul, *that* wasn't art," pleaded Nick. "The real thing will be a thousand miles away from us; it will never come into the house, *soyez tranquille.* Why then should you worry?"

"Because I want to understand, I want to know what I'm doing. You're an artist: you are, you are!" Mrs. Dallow cried, accusing him passionately.

"My poor Julia, it isn't so easy as that, nor a character one can take on from one day to the other. There are all sorts of things; one must be caught young and put through the mill and see things as they are. There would be sacrifices I never can make."

"Well then, there are sacrifices for both of us, and I can't make them either. I dare say it's all right for you, but for me it would be a terrible mistake. When I think I'm doing something I mustn't do just the opposite," Julia went on, as if she wished to explain and be clear. "There are things I've thought of, the things I like best; and they are not what you mean. It would be a great deception, and it's not the way I see my life, and it would be misery if we don't understand."

Nick looked at her in hard perplexity, for she did not succeed in explaining as well as she wished. "If we don't understand what?"

"That we are awfully different—that you are doing it all for me."

"And is that an objection to me—what I do for you?" asked Nick.

"You do too much. You're awfully good, you're generous, you're a dear fellow; but I don't believe in it. I didn't, at bottom, from the first—that's why I made you wait, why I gave you your freedom. Oh, I've suspected you! I had my ideas. It's all right for you, but it won't do for me: I'm different altogether. Why should it always be put upon me, when I hate it? What have I done? I was drenched with it, before." These last words, as they broke forth, were accompanied, even as the speaker uttered them, with a quick blush; so that Nick could as quickly discern in them the uncalculated betrayal of an old irritation, an old shame almost—her late husband's flat, inglorious taste for pretty things, his indifference to every chance to play a public part. This had been the mortification of her youth, and it was indeed a perversity of fate that a new alliance should contain for her even an oblique demand for the same spirit of accommodation, impose on her the secret bitterness of the same concessions. As Nick stood there before her, struggling sincerely with the force that he now felt to be strong in her, the intense resolution to break with him, a force matured in a few hours, he read a riddle that hitherto had baffled him, saw a great mystery become simple. A personal passion for him had all but thrown her into his arms (the sort of thing that even a vain man—and Nick was not especially vain—might hesitate to recognize the strength of); held in check, with a tension of the cord at moments of which he could still feel the vibration, by her deep, her rare ambition, and arrested at the last only just in time to save her calculations. His present glimpse of the immense extent of these calculations did not make him think her cold or poor; there was in fact a positive strange heat in them and they struck him rather as grand and high. The fact that she could drop him even while she longed for him—drop him because it was now fixed in her mind that he would not after all serve her determination to be associated, so far as a woman could, with great affairs; that she could postpone, and postpone to an uncertainty, the satisfaction of a gnawing tenderness and judge for the long run—this exhibition of will and courage, of the large plan that possessed her, commanded his admiration on the spot. He paid the heavy penalty of being a man of imagination; he was capable of far excursions of the spirit, disloyalties to habit and even to faith, and open to wondrous communications. He ached for the moment to convince her that he would achieve what he wouldn't, for the vision of his future that she had tried to entertain shone before him as a bribe and a challenge. It seemed to him there was nothing he couldn't fancy enough, to be so fancied by her. Presently he said:

"You want to be sure the man you marry will be prime minister of England. But how can you be sure, with any one?"

"I can be sure some men won't," Mrs. Dallow replied.

"The only safe thing, perhaps, would be to marry Mr. Macgeorge," Nick suggested.

"Possibly not even him."

"You're a prime minister yourself," Nick answered. "To hold fast to you as I hold, to be determined to be of your party—isn't that political enough, since you are the incarnation of politics?"

"Ah, how you hate them!" Julia moaned. "I saw that when I saw you this morning. The whole place reeked of it."

"My dear child, the greatest statesmen have had their distractions. What do you make of my hereditary talent? That's a tremendous force."

"It wouldn't carry you far." Then Mrs. Dallow added: "You must be a great artist." Nick gave a laugh at the involuntary contempt of this, but she went on: "It's beautiful of you to want to give up anything, and I like you for it. I shall always like you. We shall be friends, and I shall always take an interest—"

He stopped her at this, made a movement which interrupted her phrase, and she suffered him to hold her hand as if she were not afraid of him now. "It isn't only for you," he argued gently; "you're a great deal, but you're not everything. Innumerable vows and pledges repose upon my head. I'm inextricably committed and dedicated. I was brought up in the temple; my father was a high priest and I'm a child of the Lord. And then the life itself—when *you* speak of it I feel stirred to my depths: it's like a herald's trumpet. Fight *with* me, Julia—not against me! Be on my side, and we shall do everything. It *is* fascinating, to be a great man before the people—to be loved by them, to be followed by them. An artist isn't—never, never. Why *should* he be? Don't forget how clever I am."

"Oh, if it wasn't for that!" she rejoined, flushed with the effort to resist his tone. She asked abruptly: "Do you pretend that if I were to die to-morrow you would stay in the House?"

"If you were to die? God knows! But you do singularly little justice to my incentives," Nick continued. "My political career is everything to my mother."

Julia hesitated a moment; then she inquired: "Are you afraid of your mother?"

"Yes, particularly; for she represents infinite possibilities of disappointment and distress. She represents all my father's as well as all her own; and in them my father tragically lives again. On the other hand I see him in bliss, as I see my mother, over our marriage and our life of common aspirations; though of course that's not a consideration that I can expect to have power with you."

Mrs. Dallow shook her head slowly, even smiling a little with an air of recovered calmness and lucidity. "You'll never hold high office."

"But why not take me as I am?"

"Because I'm abominably keen about that sort of thing; I must recognize it. I must face the ugly truth. I've been through the worst; it's all settled."

"The worst, I suppose, was when you found me this morning."

"Oh, that was all right—for you."

"You're magnanimous, Julia; but evidently what's good enough for me isn't good enough for you." Nick spoke with bitterness.

"I don't like you enough—that's the obstacle," said Mrs. Dallow bravely.

"You did a year ago; you confessed to it."

"Well, a year ago was a year ago. Things are changed to-day."

"You're very fortunate—to be able to throw away a devotion," Nick replied.

Julia had her pocket-handkerchief in her hand, and at this

she quickly pressed it to her lips, as if to check an exclamation. Then for an instant she appeared to be listening as if for a sound from outside. Nick interpreted her movement as an honourable impulse to repress the words: "Do you mean the devotion that I was witness of this morning?" But immediately afterwards she said something very different: "I thought I heard a ring. I've telegraphed for Mrs. Gresham."

"Why did you do that?" asked Nick.

"Oh, I want her."

He walked to the window, where the curtains had not been drawn, and saw in the dusk a cab at the door. When he turned back he said: "Why won't you trust me to make you like me, as you call it, better? If I make you like me as well as I like you, it will be about enough, I think."

"Oh, I like you enough for *your* happiness. And I don't throw away a devotion," Mrs. Dallow continued. "I shall be constantly kind to you. I shall be beautiful to you."

"You'll make me lose a fortune," declared Nick.

Julia stared, then she coloured. "Ah, you may have all the money you want."

"I don't mean yours," he answered, flushing in his turn. He had determined on the instant, since it might serve, to tell her what he had never spoken of to her before. "Mr. Carteret last year promised me a pot of money on the day I should stand up with you. He has set his heart on our marriage."

"I'm sorry to disappoint Mr. Carteret," said Julia. "I'll go and see him. I'll make it all right," she went on. "Besides, you'll make a fortune by your portraits. The great men get a thousand, just for a head."

"I'm only joking," Nick returned, with sombre eyes that contradicted this profession. "But what things you deserve I should do!"

"Do you mean striking likenesses?"

"You do hate it! Pushed to that point, it's curious," the young man audibly mused.

"Do you mean you're joking about Mr. Carteret's promise?"

"No, the promise is real; but I don't seriously offer it as a reason."

"I shall go to Beauclere," said Mrs. Dallow. "You're an

hour late," she added in a different tone; for at that moment the door of the room was thrown open and Mrs. Gresham, the butler pronouncing her name, was ushered in.

"Ah, don't impugn my punctuality; it's my character!" the useful lady exclaimed, putting a sixpence from the cabman into her purse. Nick went off, at this, with a simplified farewell—went off foreseeing exactly what he found the next day, that Mrs. Gresham would have received orders not to budge from her hostess's side. He called on the morrow, late in the afternoon, and Julia saw him liberally, in pursuance of her assertion that she would be "beautiful" to him, that she had not thrown away his devotion; but Mrs. Gresham remained immutably a spectator of her liberality. Julia looked at him kindly, but her companion was more benignant still; so that what Nick did with his own eyes was not to appeal to Mrs. Dallow to see him for a moment alone, but to solicit, in the name of this luxury, the second occupant of the drawing-room. Mrs. Gresham seemed to say, while Julia said very little: "I understand, my poor friend, I know everything (she has told me only *her* side, but I'm so competent that I know yours too), and I enter into the whole thing deeply. But it would be as much as my place is worth to accommodate you." Still, she did not go so far as to give him an inkling of what he learned on the third day and what he had not gone so far as to suspect—that the two ladies had made rapid arrangements for a scheme of foreign travel. These arrangements had already been carried out when, at the door of the house in Great Stanhope Street, the fact was imparted to Nick that Mrs. Dallow and her friend had started that morning for Paris.

XIV.

ON THEIR WAY to Florence, Julia Dallow and Mrs. Gresham spent three days in Paris, where Peter Sherringham had as much conversation with his sister as it often befell one member of that family to have with another. That is on two different occasions he enjoyed half an hour's gossip with her in her sitting-room at the hotel. On one of these occasions he took the liberty of asking her whether or no definitely, she meant to marry Nick Dormer. Julia expressed to him that she was much obliged for his interest, but that Nick and she were nothing more than relations and good friends. "He wants to marry you, tremendously," Peter remarked; to which Mrs. Dallow simply made answer: "Well, then, he may want!"

After this they sat silent for some moments, as if the subject had been quite threshed out between them. Peter felt no impulse to penetrate further, for it was not a habit of the Sherringhams to talk with each other of their love-affairs; and he was conscious of the particular deterrent that he and Julia had in general so different a way of feeling that they could never go far together in discussion. He liked her and was sorry for her, thought her life lonely and wondered she didn't make a "great" marriage. Moreover he pitied her for being without the interests and consolations that he had found substantial: those of the intellectual, the studious order he considered these to be, not knowing how much she supposed that she reflected and studied or what an education she had found in her political aspirations, regarded by him as scarcely more a personal part of her than the livery of her servants or the jewels George Dallow's money had bought. Her relations with Nick were unfathomable to him; but they were not his affair. No affair of Julia's was sufficiently his to justify him in an attempt to understand it. That there should have been any question of her marrying Nick was the anomaly to him, rather than that the question should have been dropped. He liked his clever cousin very well as he was—enough to have a vague sense that he might be spoiled by being altered into a brother-in-law. Moreover, though he was not perhaps dis-

tinctly conscious of this, Peter pressed lightly on Julia's doings
from a tacit understanding that in this case she would let him
off as easily. He could not have said exactly what it was that
he judged it pertinent to be let off from: perhaps from irritating inquiry as to whether he had given any more tea-parties
for young ladies connected with the theatre.

Peter's forbearance however did not bring him all the security he prefigured. After an interval he indeed went so far as
to ask Julia if Nick had been wanting in respect to her; but
this was a question intended for sympathy, not for control.
She answered: "Dear, no—though he's very provoking."
Thus Peter guessed that they had had a quarrel in which it
didn't concern him to interpose: he added the epithet and her
flight from England together and they made up, to his perception, one of the little magnified embroilments which do
duty for the real in superficial lives. It was worse to provoke
Julia than not, and Peter thought Nick's doing so not particularly characteristic of his versatility for good. He might wonder why she didn't marry the member for Harsh if the subject
had come up; but he wondered still more why Nick didn't
marry her. Julia said nothing, again, as if to give him a chance
to make some inquiry which would save her from gushing;
but as his idea appeared to be to change the subject, and as
he changed it only by silence, she was reduced to resuming
presently:

"I should have thought you would have come over to see
your friend the actress."

"Which of my friends? I know so many actresses," Peter
rejoined.

"The woman you inflicted on us in this place a year ago—
the one who is in London now."

"Oh, Miriam Rooth! I should have liked to come over, but
I've been tied fast. Have you seen her?"

"Yes, I've seen her."

"Do you like her?"

"Not at all."

"She has a lovely voice," Peter hazarded, after a moment.

"I don't know anything about her voice—I haven't heard
it."

"But she doesn't act in pantomime, does she?"

"I don't know anything about her acting. I saw her in private—in Nick Dormer's studio."

"In Nick Dormer's studio? What was she doing there?"

"She was sprawling over the room and staring at me."

If Mrs. Dallow had wished to "draw" her brother it is probable that at this point she suspected she had succeeded, in spite of the care he took to divest his tone of everything like emotion in uttering the words: "Why, does he know her so well? I didn't know."

"She's sitting to him for her portrait; at least she was then."

"Oh, yes, I remember: I put him up to that. I'm greatly interested. Is the portrait good?"

"I haven't the least idea—I didn't look at it. I dare say it's clever," Julia added.

"How in the world does Nick find time to paint?"

"I don't know. That horrid man brought her."

"What horrid man?" Peter demanded.

"The one Nick thinks so clever—the vulgar little man who was at your place that day and tried to talk to me. I remember he abused theatrical people to me—as if I cared anything about them. But he has apparently something to do with this girl."

"Oh, I recollect him—I had a discussion with him," Peter said.

"How could you? I must go and dress," Julia went on.

"He *was* clever, remarkably. Miss Rooth and her mother were old friends of his, and he was the first person to speak of them to me."

"What a distinction! I thought him disgusting!" exclaimed Mrs. Dallow, who was pressed for time and who had now got up.

"Oh, you're severe," said Peter; but as they separated she had given him something to think of.

That Nick was painting a beautiful actress was no doubt in part at least the reason why he was provoking and why his most intimate female friend had come abroad. The fact did not render him provoking to Peter Sherringham: on the contrary Peter had been quite sincere when he qualified it as interesting. It became indeed on reflection so interesting that it had perhaps almost as much to do with Sherringham's rush over to London as it had to do with Julia's coming away. Reflection taught Peter further that the matter was altogether a delicate one, and suggested that it was odd he should be mixed up with it in fact, when, as Julia's business, he had wished only to keep out of it. It was his own business a little too: there was somehow a still more pointed implication of that in his sister's saying to him the next day that she wished immensely he would take a fancy to Biddy Dormer. She said more: she said there had been a time when she believed he *had* done so—believed too that the poor child herself had believed the same. Biddy was far away the nicest girl she knew—the dearest, sweetest, cleverest, *best*, and one of the prettiest creatures in England, which never spoiled anything. She would make as charming a wife as ever a man had, suited to any position, however high, and (Julia didn't mind mentioning it, since Peter would believe it whether she mentioned it or no) was so predisposed in his favour that he would have no trouble at all. In short she herself would see him through—she would answer for it that he would only have to speak. Biddy's life at home was horrid; she was very sorry for her—the child was worthy of a better fate. Peter wondered what constituted the horridness of Biddy's life, and perceived that it mainly arose from the fact that Julia disliked Lady Agnes and Grace; profiting comfortably by the freedom to do so conferred upon her by her having given them a house of which she had perhaps not felt the want till they were in possession of it. He knew she had always liked Biddy, but he asked himself (this was the rest of his wonder) why she had taken to liking her so extraordinarily just now. He liked her himself—he even liked to be talked to about her and he could believe everything Julia said: the only thing that mystified him was her motive for suddenly saying it. He assured her that he was infinitely indebted to her for her expenditure of imagination on his behalf, but that he was sorry if he had put it into any one's head (most of all into the girl's own) that he had looked at Biddy with a covetous eye. He knew not whether she would make a good wife, but he liked her quite too much to wish to put such a ticklish matter to the test. She was surely not intended for cruel experiments. As it happened he was not thinking of marrying any one—he had ever so many reasons against it. Of course one was never safe against accidents, but one could at least take precautions, and he didn't mind telling her that there were several he *had* taken.

"I don't know what you mean, but it seems to me quite the best precaution would be to care for a charming, steady girl like Biddy," Mrs. Dallow replied. "Then you would be quite in shelter, you would know the worst that can happen to you, and it wouldn't be bad." The objection Peter had made to this argument is not important, especially as it was not remarkably candid; it need only be mentioned that before he and Julia parted she said to him, still in reference to Bridget Dormer: "Do go and see her and be nice to her: she'll save you disappointments."

These last words reverberated in Sherringham's mind; there was a shade of the portentous in them and they seemed to proceed from a larger knowledge of the subject than he himself as yet possessed. They were not absent from his memory when, in the beginning of May, availing himself, to save time, of the night-service, he crossed from Paris to London. He arrived before the breakfast-hour and went to his sister's house in Great Stanhope Street, where he always found quarters whether she were in town or not. If she were at home she welcomed him, and if she were not the relaxed servants hailed him for the chance he gave them to recover their "form." In either case his allowance of space was large and his independence complete. He had obtained permission this year to take in fractions instead of as a single draught the leave of absence to which he was entitled; and there was moreover a question of his being transferred to another Embassy, in which event he believed that he might count upon a month or two in England before proceeding to his new post.

He waited after breakfast but a very few minutes before jumping into a hansom and rattling away to the north. A part of his waiting indeed consisted of a fidgety walk up Bond Street, during which he looked at his watch three or four times while he paused at shop-windows for fear of being a little early. In the cab, as he rolled along, after having given an address—Balaklava Place, St. John's Wood—the fear that he should be too early took curiously at moments the form of a fear that he should be too late: a symbol of the inconsistencies of which his spirit at present was full. Peter Sherringham was nervous, too nervous for a diplomatist, and haunted with inclinations, and indeed with purposes, which contradicted each other. He wanted to be out of it and yet he dreaded not to be in it, and on this particular occasion the sense of exclusion made him sore. At the same time he was not unconscious of the impulse to stop his cab and make it turn round and drive due south. He saw himself launched in the breezy fact while, morally speaking, he was hauled up on the hot sand of the principle, and he had the intelligence to perceive how little these two faces of the same idea had in common. However, as the sense of movement encouraged him to reflect, a principle was a poor affair if it remained mere inaction. Yet from the moment it turned to action it manifestly could only be the particular action in which he was engaged; so that he was in the absurd position of thinking his behaviour more consummate for the reason that it was directly opposed to his intentions.

He had kept away from London ever since Miriam Rooth came over; resisting curiosity, sympathy, importunate haunting passion and considering that his resistance, founded, to be salutary, on a general scheme of life, was the greatest success he had yet achieved. He was deeply occupied with plucking up the feeling that attached him to her, and he had already, by various little ingenuities, loosened some of its roots. He suffered her to make her first appearance on any stage without the comfort of his voice or the applause of his hand; saying to himself that the man who could do the more could do the less and that such an act of fortitude was a proof he should keep straight. It was not exactly keeping straight to run over to London three months later and, the hour he arrived, scramble off to Balaklava Place; but after all he pretended only to be human and aimed in behaviour only at the heroic, not at the monstrous. The highest heroism was three parts tact. He had not written to Miriam that he was coming to England and would call upon her at eleven o'clock in the morning, because it was his secret pride that he had ceased to correspond with her. Sherringham took his prudence where he could find it, and in doing so was rather like a drunkard who should flatter

himself that he had forsworn liquor because he didn't touch
lemonade.

It is an example of how much he was drawn in different
directions at once that when, on reaching Balaklava Place and
alighting at the door of a small much-ivied house which resembled a gate-lodge bereft of its park, he learned that Miss
Rooth had only a quarter of an hour before quitted the spot
with her mother (they had gone to the theatre, to rehearsal,
said the maid who answered the bell he had set tinkling behind a dingy plastered wall): when at the end of his pilgrimage he was greeted by a disappointment he suddenly found
himself relieved and for the moment even saved. Providence
was after all taking care of him and he submitted to Providence. He would still be watched over doubtless, even if he
should follow the two ladies to the theatre, send in his card
and obtain admission to the histrionic workshop. All his old
technical interest in the girl's development flamed up again,
and he wondered what she was rehearsing, what she was to
do next. He got back into his hansom and drove down the
Edgware Road. By the time he reached the Marble Arch he
had changed his mind again—he had determined to let Miriam alone for that day. The day would be over at eight o'clock
in the evening (he hardly played fair), and then he should
consider himself free. Instead of going to the theatre he drove
to a shop in Bond Street, to take a place for the play. On first
coming out he had tried, at one of those establishments
strangely denominated "libraries," to get a stall, but the people to whom he applied were unable to accommodate him—
they had not a single seat left. His second attempt, at another
"library," was more successful: he was unable to obtain a stall,
but by a miracle he might have a box. There was a certain
wantonness in paying for a box to see a play on which he had
already expended four hundred pounds; but while he was
mentally measuring this abyss an idea came into his head
which flushed the extravagance with a slight rose-tint.

Peter came out of the shop with the voucher for the box in
his pocket, turned into Piccadilly, noted that the day was
growing warm and fine, felt glad that this time he had no
business, unless it were business to leave a card or two on
official people, and asked himself where he should go if he

didn't go after Miriam. Then it was that it struck him as most acutely desirable, and even most important, that he should see Nick Dormer's portrait of her. He wondered which would be the natural place at that hour of the day to look for the artist. The House of Commons was perhaps the nearest one, but Nick, incongruous as his proceedings certainly were, probably didn't keep the picture there; and moreover it was not generally characteristic of him to be in the natural place. The end of Peter's debate was that he again entered a hansom and drove to Calcutta Gardens. The hour was early for calling, but cousins with whom one's intercourse was mainly a conversational scuffle would accept it as a practical illustration of that method. And if Julia wanted him to be nice to Biddy (which was exactly, though with a different view, what he wanted himself), what could be nicer than to pay his visit to Lady Agnes (he would have in decency to go to see her some time) at a friendly, fraternizing hour, when they would all be likely to be at home?

Unfortunately, as it turned out, they were not at home, so that Peter had to fall back on neutrality and the butler, who was however, more luckily, an old friend. Her ladyship and Miss Dormer were absent from town, paying a visit; and Mr. Dormer was also away, or was on the point of going away for the day. Miss Bridget was in London, but was out: Peter's informant mentioned with earnest vagueness that he thought she had gone somewhere to take a lesson. On Peter's asking what sort of a lesson he meant, he replied, "Oh, I think the a-sculpture, you know, sir." Peter knew, but Biddy's lesson in a-sculpture (it sounded on the butler's lips like a fashionable new art) struck him a little as a mockery of the benevolent spirit in which he had come to look her up. The man had an air of participating respectfully in his disappointment and, to make up for it, added that he might perhaps find Mr. Dormer at his other address. He had gone out early and had directed his servant to come to Rosedale Road in an hour or two with a portmanteau: he was going down to Beauclere in the course of the day, Mr. Carteret being ill— perhaps Mr. Sherringham didn't know it. Perhaps too Mr. Sherringham would catch him in Rosedale Road before he took his train—he was to have been busy there for an hour.

This was worth trying, and Peter immediately drove to Rosedale Road; where, in answer to his ring, the door was opened to him by Biddy Dormer.

XV.

WHEN BIDDY saw him her cheek exhibited the prettiest pleased, surprised red that he had ever observed there, though he was not unacquainted with its fluctuations, and she stood still, smiling at him with the outer dazzle in her eyes, making no motion for him to enter. She only said: "Oh, Peter!" And then: "I'm all alone."

"So much the better, dear Biddy. Is that any reason I shouldn't come in?"

"Dear, no—do come in. You've just missed Nick; he has gone to the country—half an hour ago." She had on a large apron, and in her hand she carried a small stick, besmeared, as his quick eye saw, with modelling-clay. She dropped the door and fled back before him into the studio, where, when he followed her, she was in the act of flinging a cloth over a rough head, in clay, which, in the middle of the room, was supported on a high wooden stand. The effort to hide what she had been doing before he caught a glimpse of it made her redder still and led to her smiling more, to her laughing with a charming confusion of shyness and gladness. She rubbed her hands on her apron, she pulled it off, she looked delightfully awkward, not meeting Peter's eye, and she said: "I'm just scraping here a little—you mustn't mind me. What I do is awful, you know. Peter, please don't look. I've been coming here lately to make my little mess, because mamma doesn't particularly like it at home. I've had a lesson from a lady who exhibits; but you wouldn't suppose it, to see what I do. Nick's so kind; he lets me come here; he uses the studio so little; I do what I please. What a pity he's gone—he would have been so glad. I'm really alone—I hope you don't mind. Peter, *please* don't look."

Peter was not bent upon looking; his eyes had occupation enough in Biddy's own agreeable aspect, which was full of an unusual element of domestication and responsibility. Though she had taken possession, by exception, of her brother's quarters, she struck her visitor as more at home and more herself than he had ever seen her. It was the first time she had been to his vision so separate from her mother and sister. She

seemed to know this herself and to be a little frightened by
it—just enough to make him wish to be reassuring. At the
same time Peter also on this occasion found himself touched
with diffidence, especially after he had gone back and closed
the door and settled down to a regular visit; for he became
acutely conscious of what Julia had said to him in Paris and
was unable to rid himself of the suspicion that it had been
said with Biddy's knowledge. It was not that he supposed his
sister had told the girl that she meant to do what she could to
make him propose to her: that would have been cruel to her
(if she liked him enough to consent), in Julia's uncertainty.
But Biddy participated by imagination, by divination, by a
clever girl's secret tremulous instincts, in her good friend's
views about her, and this probability constituted for Sherringham a sort of embarrassing publicity. He had impressions, possibly gross and unjust, in regard to the way women
move constantly together amid such considerations and subtly
intercommunicate, when they do not still more subtly dissemble, the hopes or fears of which persons of the opposite sex
form the subject. Therefore poor Biddy would know that if
she failed to strike him in the right light it would not be for
want of his attention's having been called to her claims. She
would have been tacitly rejected, virtually condemned. Peter
could not, without a slight sense of fatuity, endeavour to
make up for this to her by kindness; he was aware that if any
one knew it a man would be ridiculous who should take so
much as that for granted. But no one would know it: oddly
enough, in this calculation of security he left Biddy herself
out. It did not occur to him that she might have a secret small
irony to spare for his ingenious and magnanimous impulse to
show her how much he liked her in order to make her forgive
him for not liking her more. This magnanimity at any rate
coloured the whole of Sherringham's visit to Rosedale Road,
the whole of the pleasant, prolonged chat that kept him there
for more than an hour. He begged the girl to go on with her
work and not to let him interrupt it; and she obliged him at
last, taking the cloth off the lump of clay and giving him a
chance to be delightful by guessing that the shapeless mass
was intended, or would be intended after a while, for Nick.
He saw that she was more comfortable when she began to

smooth it and scrape it with her little stick again, to manipulate it with an ineffectual air of knowing how; for this gave
her something to do, relieved her nervousness and permitted
her to turn away from him when she talked.

Peter walked about the room and sat down; got up and
looked at Nick's things; watched her at moments in silence
(which made her always say in a minute that he was not to
look at her so or she could do nothing); observed how her
position, before her high stand, her lifted arms, her turns of
the head, considering her work this way and that, all helped
her to be pretty. She repeated again and again that it was an
immense pity about Nick, till he was obliged to say he didn't
care a straw for Nick: he was perfectly content with the company he found. This was not the sort of thing he thought it
right, under the circumstances, to say; but then even the circumstances did not require him to pretend he liked her less
than he did. After all she was his cousin; she would cease to
be so if she should become his wife; but one advantage of her
not entering into that relation was precisely that she would
remain his cousin. It was very pleasant to find a young,
bright, slim, rose-coloured kinswoman all ready to recognize
consanguinity when one came back from cousinless foreign
lands. Peter talked about family matters; he didn't know, in
his exile, where no one took an interest in them, what a fund
of latent curiosity about them was in him. It was in him to
gossip about them and to enjoy the sense that he and Biddy
had indefeasible properties in common—ever so many things
as to which they would understand each other *à demi-mot*.
He smoked a cigarette, because she begged him to, said that
people always smoked in studios—it made her feel so much
more like an artist. She apologized for the badness of her
work on the ground that Nick was so busy he could scarcely
ever give her a sitting; so that she had to do the head from
photographs and occasional glimpses. They had hoped to be
able to put in an hour that morning, but news had suddenly
come that Mr. Carteret was worse, and Nick had hurried
down to Beauclere. Mr. Carteret was very ill, poor old dear,
and Nick and he were immense friends. Nick had always been
charming to him. Peter and Biddy took the concerns of the
houses of Dormer and Sherringham in order, and the young

man felt after a little as if they were as wise as a French *conseil de famille*, settling what was best for every one. He heard all about Lady Agnes and manifested an interest in the detail of her existence that he had not supposed himself to possess, though indeed Biddy threw out intimations which excited his curiosity, presenting her mother in a light that might call upon his sympathy.

"I don't think she has been very happy or very pleased, of late," the girl said. "I think she has had some disappointments, poor dear mamma; and Grace has made her go out of town for three or four days, for a little change. They have gone down to see an old lady, Lady St. Dunstans, who never comes to London now, and who, you know—she's tremendously old—was papa's godmother. It's not very lively for Grace, but Grace is such a dear she'll do anything for mamma. Mamma will go anywhere to see people she can talk with about papa."

Biddy added, in reply to a further inquiry from Peter, that what her mother was disappointed about was—well, themselves, her children and all their affairs; and she explained that Lady Agnes wanted all kinds of things for them that didn't come to them, that they didn't get or seem likely to get, so that their life appeared altogether a failure. She wanted a great deal, Biddy admitted; she really wanted everything and she had thought in her happier days that everything was to be hers. She loved them all so much, and then she was proud: she couldn't get over the thought of their not being successful. Sherringham was unwilling to press, at this point, for he suspected one of the things that Lady Agnes wanted; but Biddy relieved him a little by saying that one of these things was that Grace should get married.

"That's too unselfish of her," rejoined Peter, who didn't care for Grace. "Cousin Agnes ought to keep her near her always, if Grace is so obliging and devoted."

"Oh, mamma would give up anything of that sort for our good; she wouldn't sacrifice us that way!" Biddy exclaimed. "Besides, I'm the one to stay with mamma; not that I can manage and look after her and do everything so well as Grace. But, you know, I want to," said Biddy, with a liquid note in her voice, giving her lump of clay a little stab.

"But doesn't your mother want the rest of you to get married—Percival and Nick and you?" Peter asked.

"Oh, she has given up Percy. I don't suppose she thinks it would do. Dear Nick, of course—that's just what she does want."

Sherringham hesitated. "And you, Biddy?"

"Oh, I dare say; but that doesn't signify—I never shall."

Peter got up, at this; the tone of it set him in motion and he took a turn round the room. He said something to her about her being too proud; to which she replied that that was the only thing for a girl to be, to get on.

"What do you mean by getting on?" Peter demanded, stopping, with his hands in his pockets, on the other side of the studio.

"I mean crying one's eyes out!" Biddy unexpectedly exclaimed; but she drowned the effect of this pathetic paradox in a foolish laugh and in the quick declaration: "Of course it's about Nick that poor mother's really broken-hearted."

"What's the matter with Nick?" Sherringham asked, diplomatically.

"Oh, Peter, what's the matter with Julia?" Biddy quavered softly, back to him, with eyes suddenly frank and mournful. "I dare say you know what we all hoped—what we all supposed, from what they told us. And now they won't!" said Biddy.

"Yes, Biddy, I know. I had the brightest prospect of becoming your brother-in-law: wouldn't that have been it—or something like that? But it is indeed visibly clouded. What's the matter with them? May I have another cigarette?" Peter came back to the wide, cushioned bench where he had been lounging: this was the way they took up the subject he wanted most to look into. "Don't they know how to love?" he went on, as he seated himself again.

"It seems a kind of fatality!" sighed Biddy.

Peter said nothing for some moments, at the end of which he inquired whether his companion were to be quite alone during her mother's absence. She replied that her mother was very droll about that—she would never leave her alone: she thought something dreadful would happen to her. She had therefore arranged that Florence Tressilian should come and stay in Calcutta Gardens for the next few days, to look after her and see she did no wrong. Peter asked who Florence Tressilian might be: he greatly hoped, for the success of Lady Agnes's precautions, that she was not a flighty young genius like Biddy. She was described to him as tremendously nice and tremendously clever, but also tremendously old and tremendously safe; with the addition that Biddy was tremendously fond of her and that while she remained in Calcutta Gardens they expected to enjoy themselves tremendously. She was to come that afternoon, before dinner.

"And are you to dine at home?" said Peter.

"Certainly; where else?"

"And just you two, alone? Do you call that enjoying yourselves tremendously?"

"It will do for me. No doubt I oughtn't, in modesty, to speak for poor Florence."

"It isn't fair to her; you ought to invite some one to meet her."

"Do you mean you, Peter?" the girl asked, turning to him quickly, with a look that vanished the instant he caught it.

"Try me; I'll come like a shot."

"That's kind," said Biddy, dropping her hands and now resting her eyes on him gratefully. She remained in this position a moment, as if she were under a charm; then she jerked herself back to her work with the remark: "Florence will like that immensely."

"I'm delighted to please Florence, your description of her is so attractive!" Sherringham laughed. And when the girl asked him if he minded if there were not a great feast, because when her mother went away she allowed her a fixed amount for that sort of thing and, as he might imagine, it wasn't millions— when Biddy, with the frankness of their pleasant kinship, touched anxiously on this economical point (illustrating, as Peter saw, the lucidity with which Lady Agnes had had in her old age to learn to recognize the occasions when she could be conveniently frugal), he answered that the shortest dinners were the best, especially when one was going to the theatre. That was his case to-night, and did Biddy think he might look to Miss Tressilian to go with him? They would have to dine early; he wanted not to miss a moment.

"The theatre—Miss Tressilian?" Biddy stared, interrupted and in suspense again.

"Would it incommode you very much to dine say at 7.15 and accept a place in my box? The finger of Providence was in it when I took a box an hour ago. I particularly like your being free to go—if you are free."

Biddy became fairly incoherent with pleasure. "Dear Peter, how good you are! They'll have it at any hour. Florence will be so glad."

"And has Florence seen Miss Rooth?"

"Miss Rooth?" the girl repeated, redder than before. He perceived in a moment that she had heard that he had devoted much time and attention to that young lady. It was as if she were conscious that he would be conscious in speaking of her, and there was a sweetness in her allowance for him on that score. But Biddy was more confused for him than he was for himself. He guessed in a moment how much she had thought over what she had heard; this was indicated by her saying vaguely: "No, no, I've not seen her." Then she became aware that she was answering a question he had not asked her, and she went on: "We shall be too delighted. I saw her— perhaps you remember—in your rooms in Paris. I thought her so wonderful then! Every one is talking of her here. But we don't go to the theatre much, you know: we don't have boxes offered us except when *you* come. Poor Nick is too much taken up in the evening. I've wanted awfully to see her. They say she's magnificent."

"I don't know," said Peter. "I haven't seen her."

"You haven't seen her?"

"Never, Biddy. I mean on the stage. In private, often— yes," Sherringham added, conscientiously.

"Oh!" Biddy exclaimed, bending her face on Nick's bust again. She asked him no question about the new star, and he offered her no further information. There were things in his mind that pulled him different ways, so that for some minutes silence was the result of the conflict. At last he said, after an hesitation caused by the possibility that she was ignorant of the fact he had lately elicited from Julia, though it was more probable she might have learned it from the same source:

"Am I perhaps indiscreet in alluding to the circumstance that Nick has been painting Miss Rooth's portrait?"

"You are not indiscreet in alluding to it to me, because I know it."

"Then there's no secret nor mystery about it?"

Biddy considered a moment. "I don't think mamma knows it."

"You mean you have been keeping it from her because she wouldn't like it?"

"We're afraid she may think that papa wouldn't have liked it."

This was said with an absence of humour which for an instant moved Sherringham to mirth; but he quickly recovered himself, repenting of any apparent failure of respect to the high memory of his late celebrated relative. He rejoined quickly, but rather vaguely: "Ah, yes, I remember that great man's ideas;" and then he went on: "May I ask if you know it, the fact that we are talking of, through Julia or through Nick?"

"I know it from both of them."

"Then, if you're in their confidence, may I further ask whether this undertaking of Nick's is the reason why things seem to be at an end between them?"

"Oh, I don't think she likes it," returned Biddy.

"Isn't it good?"

"Oh, I don't mean the picture—she hasn't seen it; but his having done it."

"Does she dislike it so much that that's why she won't marry him?"

Biddy gave up her work, moving away from it to look at it. She came and sat down on the long bench on which Sherringham had placed himself. Then she broke out: "Oh, Peter, it's a great trouble—it's a very great trouble; and I can't tell you, for I don't understand it."

"If I ask you, it's not to pry into what doesn't concern me; but Julia is my sister, and I can't, after all, help taking some interest in her life. But she tells me very little. She doesn't think me worthy."

"Ah, poor Julia!" Biddy murmured, defensively. Her tone recalled to him that Julia had thought him worthy to unite himself to Bridget Dormer, and inevitably betrayed that the girl was thinking of that also. While they both thought of it they sat looking into each other's eyes.

"Nick, I'm sure, doesn't treat *you* that way. I'm sure he confides in you; he talks to you about his occupations, his ambitions," Peter continued. "And you understand him, you enter into them, you are nice to him, you help him."

"Oh, Nick's life—it's very dear to me," said Biddy.

"That must be jolly for him."

"It makes *me* very happy."

Peter uttered a low, ambiguous groan; then he exclaimed, with irritation: "What the deuce is the matter with them then? Why can't they hit it off and be quiet and rational and do what every one wants them to do?"

"Oh, Peter, it's awfully complicated," said Biddy, with sagacity.

"Do you mean that Nick's in love with her?"

"In love with Julia?"

"No, no, with Miriam Rooth."

Biddy shook her head slowly; then with a smile which struck him as one of the sweetest things he had ever seen (it conveyed, at the expense of her own prospects, such a shy, generous little mercy of reassurance): "He isn't, Peter," she declared. "Julia thinks it's trifling—all that sort of thing," she added. "She wants him to go in for different honours."

"Julia's the oddest woman. I thought she loved him," Sherringham remarked. "And when you love a person—" He continued to reflect, leaving his sentence impatiently unfinished, while Biddy, with lowered eyes, sat waiting (it interested her) to learn what you did when you loved a person. "I can't conceive her giving him up. He has great ability, besides being such a good fellow."

"It's for his happiness, Peter—that's the way she reasons," Biddy explained. "She does it for an idea; she has told me a great deal about it, and I see the way she feels."

"You try to, Biddy, because you are such a dear good-natured girl, but I don't believe you do in the least. It's too little the way you yourself would feel. Julia's idea, as you call it, must be curious."

"Well, it is, Peter," Biddy mournfully admitted. "She won't risk not coming out at the top."

"At the top of what?"

"Oh, of everything." Biddy's tone showed a trace of awe of such high views.

"Surely one's at the top of everything when one's in love."

"I don't know," said the girl.

"Do you doubt it?" Sherringham demanded.

"I've never been in love and I never shall be."

"You're as perverse in your way as Julia. But I confess I don't understand Nick's attitude any better. He seems to me, if I may say so, neither fish nor flesh."

"Oh, his attitude is very noble, Peter; his state of mind is wonderfully interesting," Biddy pleaded. "Surely *you* must be in favour of art," she said.

Sherringham looked at her a moment. "Dear Biddy, your little digs are as soft as zephyrs."

She coloured, but she protested. "My little digs? What do you mean? Are you not in favour of art?"

"The question is delightfully simple. I don't know what you're talking about. Everything has its place. A parliamentary life scarcely seems to me the situation for portrait-painting."

"That's just what Nick says."

"You talk of it together a great deal?"

"Yes, Nick's very good to me."

"Clever Nick! And what do you advise him?"

"Oh, to *do* something."

"That's valuable," Peter laughed. "Not to give up his sweetheart for the sake of a paint-pot, I hope?"

"Never, never, Peter! It's not a question of his giving up, for Julia has herself drawn back. I think she never really felt safe; she loved him, but she was afraid of him. Now she's only afraid—she has lost the confidence she tried to have. Nick has tried to hold her, but she has jerked herself away.

Do you know what she said to me? She said: 'My confidence has gone forever.' "

"I didn't know she was such a prig!" Sherringham exclaimed. "They're queer people, verily, with water in their veins instead of blood. You and I wouldn't be like that, should we? though you *have* taken up such a discouraging position about caring for a fellow."

"I care for art," poor Biddy returned.

"You do, to some purpose," said Peter, glancing at the bust.

"To that of making you laugh at me."

"Would you give a good man up for that?"

"A good man? What man?"

"Well, say me—if I wanted to marry you."

Biddy hesitated a little. "Of course I would, in a moment. At any rate, I'd give up the House of Commons. That's what Nick's going to do now—only you mustn't tell any one."

Sherringham stared. "He's going to chuck up his seat?"

"I think his mind is made up to it. He has talked me over—we have had some deep discussions. Yes, I'm on the side of art!" said Biddy, ardently.

"Do you mean in order to paint—to paint Miss Rooth?" Peter went on.

"To paint every one—that's what he wants. By keeping his seat he hasn't kept Julia, and she was the thing he cared most for, in public life. When he has got out of the whole thing his attitude, as he says, will be at least clear. He's tremendously interesting about it, Peter; he has talked to me wonderfully; he *has* won me over. Mamma's heart-broken; telling her will be the hardest part."

"If she doesn't know, why is she heart-broken?"

"Oh, at the marriage not coming off—she knows that. That's what she wanted. She thought it perfection. She blames Nick fearfully. She thinks he held the whole thing in his hand and that he has thrown away a magnificent opportunity."

"And what does Nick say to her?"

"He says, 'Dear old mummy!' "

"That's good," said Sherringham.

"I don't know what will become of her when this other blow arrives," Biddy pursued. "Poor Nick wants to please

her—he does, he does. But, as he says, you can't please every
one, and you must, before you die, please yourself a little."

Peter Sherringham sat looking at the floor; the colour had
risen to his face while he listened to the girl. Then he sprang
up and took another turn about the room. His companion's
artless but vivid recital had set his blood in motion. He had
taken Nick Dormer's political prospects very much for
granted, thought of them as definite and brilliant and seduc-
tive. To learn there was something for which he was ready to
renounce such honours, and to recognize the nature of that
bribe, affected Sherringham powerfully and strangely. He felt
as if he had heard the sudden blare of a trumpet, and he felt at
the same time as if he had received a sudden slap in the face.
Nick's bribe was "art"—the strange temptress with whom he
himself had been wrestling and over whom he had finally ventured to believe that wisdom and training had won a victory.
There was something in the conduct of his old friend and
playfellow that made all his reasonings small. Nick's unexpected choice acted on him as a reproach and a challenge. He
felt ashamed at having placed himself so unromantically on
his guard, rapidly saying to himself that if Nick could afford
to allow so much for "art" he might surely exhibit some of
the same confidence. There had never been the least avowed
competition between the cousins—their lines lay too far apart
for that; but nevertheless they rode in sight of each other, and
Sherringham had at present the sensation of suddenly seeing
Nick Dormer give his horse the spur, bound forward and fly
over a wall. He was put on his mettle and he had not to look
long to spy an obstacle that he too might ride at. High rose
his curiosity to see what warrant his kinsman might have for
such risks—how he was mounted for such exploits. He really
knew little about Nick's talent—so little as to feel no right to
exclaim "What an ass!" when Biddy gave him the news which
only the existence of real talent could redeem from absurdity.
All his eagerness to ascertain what Nick had been able to
make of such a subject as Miriam Rooth came back to him;
though it was what mainly had brought him to Rosedale
Road he had forgotten it in the happy accident of his encounter with Biddy. He was conscious that if the surprise of a
revelation of power were in store for him Nick would be

justified more than he himself would feel reinstated in his self-respect. For the courage of renouncing the forum for the studio hovered before him as greater than the courage of marrying an actress whom one was in love with: the reward in the latter case was so much more immediate. Peter asked Biddy what Nick had done with his portrait of Miriam. He hadn't seen it anywhere in rummaging about the room.

"I think it's here somewhere, but I don't know," Biddy replied, getting up and looking vaguely round her.

"Haven't you seen it? Hasn't he shown it to you?"

The girl rested her eyes on him strangely a moment; then she turned them away from him with a mechanical air of seeking for the picture. "I think it's in the room, put away with its face to the wall."

"One of those dozen canvases with their backs to us?"

"One of those perhaps."

"Haven't you tried to see?"

"I haven't touched them," said Biddy, colouring.

"Hasn't Nick had it out to show you?"

"He says it's in too bad a state—it isn't finished—it won't do."

"And haven't you had the curiosity to turn it round for yourself?"

The embarrassed look in poor Biddy's face deepened, and it seemed to Sherringham that her eyes pleaded with him a moment, that there was a menace of tears in them, a gleam of anguish. "I've had an idea he wouldn't like it."

Her visitor's own desire however had become too lively for easy forbearance. He laid his hand on two or three canvases which proved, as he extricated them, to be either blank or covered with rudimentary forms. "Dear Biddy, are you as docile, as obliging as that?" he asked, pulling out something else.

The inquiry was meant in familiar kindness, for Peter was struck, even to admiration, with the girl's having a sense of honour which all girls have not. She must in this particular case have longed for a sight of Nick's work—the work which had brought about such a crisis in his life. But she had passed hours in his studio alone, without permitting herself a stolen peep; she was capable of that if she believed it would please

him. Sherringham liked a charming girl's being capable of
that (he had known charming girls who would not have
been), and his question was really an expression of respect.
Biddy, however, apparently discovered some light mockery in
it, and she broke out incongruously:

"I haven't wanted so much to see it. I don't care for her so
much as that."

"So much as that?"

"I don't care for his actress—for that vulgar creature. I
don't like her!" said Biddy, unexpectedly.

Peter stared. "I thought you hadn't seen her."

"I saw her in Paris—twice. She was wonderfully clever, but
she didn't charm me."

Sherringham quickly considered, and then he said benevolently: "I won't inflict the picture upon you then; we'll leave it
alone for the present." Biddy made no reply to this at first,
but after a moment she went straight over to the row of
stacked canvases and exposed several of them to the light.
"Why did you say you wished to go to the theatre to-night?"
her companion continued.

Still the girl was silent; then she exclaimed, with her back
turned to him and a little tremor in her voice, while she drew
forth one of her brother's studies after the other: "For the
sake of your company, Peter! Here it is, I think," she added,
moving a large canvas with some effort. "No, no, I'll hold it
for you. Is that the light?"

She wouldn't let him take it; she bade him stand off and
allow her to place it in the right position. In this position she
carefully presented it, supporting it, at the proper angle, from
behind and showing her head and shoulders above it. From
the moment his eyes rested on the picture Sherringham accepted this service without protest. Unfinished, simplified and
in some portions merely suggested, it was strong, brilliant
and vivid and had already the look of life and the air of an
original thing. Sherringham was startled, he was strangely affected—he had no idea Nick moved with that stride. Miriam
was represented in three-quarters, seated, almost down to her
feet. She leaned forward, with one of her legs crossed over the
other, her arms extended and foreshortened, her hands locked
together round her knee. Her beautiful head was bent a little,

broodingly, and her splendid face seemed to look down at life. She had a grand appearance of being raised aloft, with a wide regard, from a height of intelligence, for the great field of the artist, all the figures and passions he may represent. Peter wondered where his kinsman had learned to paint like that. He almost gasped at the composition of the thing, at the drawing of the moulded arms. Biddy Dormer abstained from looking round the corner of the canvas as she held it; she only watched, in Peter's eyes, for *his* impression of it. This she easily caught, and he could see that she had done so when after a few minutes he went to relieve her. She let him lift the thing out of her grasp; he moved it and rested it, so that they could still see it, against the high back of a chair.

"It's tremendously good," he said.

"Dear, dear Nick," Biddy murmured, looking at it now.

"Poor, poor Julia!" Sherringham was prompted to exclaim, in a different tone. His companion made no rejoinder to this, and they stood another minute or two side by side in silence, gazing at the portrait. Then Sherringham took up his hat— he had no more time, he must go. "Will you come to-night all the same?" he asked, with a laugh that was somewhat awkward, putting out his hand to Biddy.

"All the same?"

"Why, you say she's a terrible creature," Peter went on with his eyes on the painted face.

"Oh, anything for art!" said Biddy, smiling.

"Well, at seven o'clock then." And Sherringham went away immediately, leaving the girl alone with the Tragic Muse and feeling again, with a quickened rush, a sense of the beauty of Miriam, as well as a new comprehension of the talent of Nick.

XVI.

IT WAS NOT till noon, or rather later, the next day, that Sherringham saw Miriam Rooth. He wrote her a note that evening, to be delivered to her at the theatre, and during the performance she sent round to him a card with "All right—come to luncheon to-morrow," scrawled upon it in pencil.

When he presented himself in Balaklava Place he learned that the two ladies had not come in—they had gone again, early, to rehearsal; but they had left word that he was to be pleased to wait—they would come in from one moment to the other. It was further mentioned to him, as he was ushered into the drawing-room, that Mr. Dashwood was on the ground. This circumstance however Sherringham barely noted: he had been soaring so high for the past twelve hours that he had almost lost consciousness of the minor differences of earthly things. He had taken Biddy Dormer and her friend Miss Tressilian home from the play, and after leaving them he had walked about the streets, he had roamed back to his sister's house, in a state of exaltation intensified by the fact that all the evening he had contained himself, thinking it more decorous and considerate, less invidious not to "rave." Sitting there in the shade of the box with his companions, he had watched Miriam in attentive but inexpressive silence, glowing and vibrating inwardly, but, for these fine, deep reasons, not committing himself to the spoken rapture. Delicacy, it appeared to him, should rule the hour; and indeed he had never had a pleasure more delicate than this little period of still observation and repressed ecstasy. Miriam's art lost nothing by it, and Biddy's mild nearness only gained. This young lady was silent also—wonderingly, dauntedly, as if she too were conscious in relation to the actress of various other things beside her mastery of her art. To this mastery Biddy's attitude was a candid and liberal tribute: the poor girl sat quenched and pale, as if in the blinding light of a comparison by which it would be presumptuous even to be annihilated. Her subjection however was a gratified, a charmed subjection: there was a beneficence in such beauty—the beauty of the figure that moved before the footlights and spoke in music—even if it deprived one of hope. Peter didn't say to her, in vulgar elation and in reference to her whimsical profession of dislike at the studio: "Well, do you find this performer so disagreeable now?" and she was grateful to him for his forbearance, for the tacit kindness of which the idea seemed to be: "My poor child, I would prefer you if I could; but—judge for yourself —how can I? Expect of me only the possible. Expect that certainly, but only that." In the same degree Peter liked Biddy's sweet, hushed air of judging for herself, of recognizing his discretion and letting him off, while she was lost in the illusion, in the convincing picture of the stage. Miss Tressilian did most of the criticism: she broke out cheerfully and sonorously from time to time, in reference to the actress: "Most striking, certainly," or, "She *is* clever, isn't she?" It was a manner to which her companions found it impossible to respond. Miss Tressilian was disappointed in nothing but their enjoyment: they didn't seem to think the exhibition as amusing as she.

Walking away through the ordered void of Lady Agnes's quarter, with the four acts of the play glowing again before him in the smokeless London night, Sherringham found the liveliest thing in his impression the certitude that if he had never seen Miriam before and she had had for him none of the advantages of association, he would still have recognized in her performance the most interesting thing that the theatre had ever offered him. He floated in a sense of the felicity of it, in the general encouragement of a thing perfectly done, in the almost aggressive bravery of still larger claims for an art which could so triumphantly, so exquisitely render life. "Render it?" Peter said to himself. "Create it and reveal it, rather; give us something new and large and of the first order!" He had *seen* Miriam now; he had never seen her before; he had never seen her till he saw her in her conditions. Oh, her conditions— there were many things to be said about them; they were paltry enough as yet, inferior, inadequate, obstructive, as compared with the right, full, finished setting of such a talent; but the essence of them was now irremovably in Sherringham's eye, the vision of how the uplifted stage and the listening house transformed her. That idea of her having no character of her own came back to him with a force that made him laugh in the empty street: this was a disadvantage she was so exempt from that he appeared to himself not to have known her till to-night. Her character was simply to hold you by the particular spell; any other—the good-nature of home, the relation to her mother, her friends, her lovers, her debts, the practice of virtues or industries or vices—was not worth speaking of. These things were the fictions and shadows; the representation was the deep substance.

Sherringham had, as he went, an intense vision (he had often had it before) of the conditions which were still absent, the great and complete ones, those which would give the girl's talent a superior, glorious stage. More than ever he desired them, mentally invoked them, filled them out in imagination, cheated himself with the idea that they were possible. He saw them in a momentary illusion and confusion: a great academic, artistic theatre, subsidized and unburdened with money-getting, rich in its repertory, rich in the high quality and the wide array of its servants, and above all in the authority of an impossible administrator—a manager personally disinterested, not an actor with an eye to the main chance, pouring forth a continuity of tradition, striving for perfection, laying a splendid literature under contribution. He saw the heroine of a hundred "situations," variously dramatic and vividly real; he saw comedy and drama and passion and character and English life; he saw all humanity and history and poetry, and perpetually, in the midst of them, shining out in the high relief of some great moment, an image as fresh as an unveiled statue. He was not unconscious that he was taking all sorts of impossibilities and miracles for granted; but it really seemed to him for the time that the woman he had been watching three hours, the incarnation of the serious drama, would be a new and vivifying force. The world was just then so bright to him that Basil Dashwood struck him at first as an harmonious minister of that force.

It must be added that before Miriam arrived the breeze that filled Sherringham's sail began to sink a little. He passed out of the eminently "let" drawing-room, where twenty large photographs of the young actress bloomed in the desert; he went into the garden by a glass-door that stood open, and found Mr. Dashwood reclining on a bench and smoking cigarettes. This young man's conversation was a different music—it took him down, as he felt; showed him, very sensibly and intelligibly, it must be confessed, the actual theatre, the one they were all concerned with, the one they would have to make the miserable best of. It was fortunate for Sherringham that he kept his intoxication mainly to himself: the Englishman's habit of not being effusive still prevailed with him, even after his years of exposure to the foreign infection. Nothing could have been less exclamatory than the meeting of the two men, with its question or two, its remark or two about Sherringham's arrival in London; its offhand "I noticed you last night—I was glad you turned up at last," on one side, and its attenuated "Oh, yes, it was the first time—I was very much interested," on the other. Basil Dashwood played a part in "Yolande," and Sherringham had had the satisfaction of taking the measure of his aptitude. He judged it to be of the small order, as indeed the part, which was neither that of the virtuous nor that of the villainous hero, restricted him to two or three inconspicuous effects and three or four changes of dress. He represented an ardent but respectful young lover whom the distracted heroine found time to pity a little and even to rail at; but it was impressed upon Sherringham that he scarcely represented young love. He looked very well, but Peter had heard him already in a hundred contemporary pieces; he never got out of rehearsal. He uttered sentiments and breathed vows with a nice voice, with a shy, boyish tremor in it, but as if he were afraid of being chaffed for it afterwards; giving the spectator in the stalls the feeling of holding the prompt-book and listening to a recitation. He made one think of country-houses and lawn-tennis and private theatricals; than which there could not be, to Sherringham's sense, an association more disconnected with the actor's art.

Dashwood knew all about the new thing, the piece in rehearsal; he knew all about everything—receipts and salaries and expenses and newspaper articles, and what old Baskerville said and what Mrs. Ruffler thought: matters of superficial concern to Sherringham, who wondered, before Miriam appeared, whether she talked with her "walking-gentleman" about them by the hour, deep in them and finding them not vulgar and boring, but the natural air of her life and the essence of her profession. Of course she did—she naturally would; it was all in the day's work and he might feel sure she wouldn't turn up her nose at the shop. He had to remind himself that he didn't care if she didn't—that he would think worse of her if she should. She certainly had much confabulation with her competent playfellow, talking shop by the hour: Sherringham could see that from the familiar, customary way Dashwood sat there with his cigarette, as if he were in possession and on his own ground. He divined a great intimacy between the two young artists, but asked himself at the same time what he, Peter Sherringham, had to say about it. He didn't pretend to control Miriam's intimacies, it was to be supposed; and if he had encouraged her to adopt a profession which abounded in opportunities for comradeship it was not for him to cry out because she had taken to it kindly. He had already descried a fund of utility in Mrs. Lovick's light brother; but it irritated him all the same, after a while, to hear Basil Dashwood represent himself as almost indispensable. He was practical—there was no doubt of that; and this idea added to Sherringham's paradoxical sense that as regards the matters actually in question he himself had not this virtue. Dashwood had got Mrs. Rooth the house; it happened by a lucky chance that Laura Lumley, to whom it belonged (Sherringham would know Laura Lumley?) wanted to get rid, for a mere song, of the remainder of a lease. She was going to Australia with a troupe of her own. They just stepped into it; it was good air—the best sort of air to live in, to sleep in, in London, for people in their line. Sherringham wondered what Miriam's personal relations with this deucedly knowing gentleman might be, and was again able to assure himself that they might be anything in the world she liked, for any stake he, Peter, had in them. Dashwood told him of all the smart people who had tried to take up the new star—the way the London world had already held out its hand; and perhaps it was Sherringham's irritation, the crushed sentiment I just mentioned, that gave a little heave in the exclamation: "Oh, that—that's all rubbish; the less of that the better!" At this Basil Dashwood stared; he evidently felt snubbed; he had expected his interlocutor to be pleased with the names of the eager ladies who had "called"—which proved to Sherringham that he took a low view of his art. The secretary of embassy explained, it is to be hoped not pedantically, that this art was serious work and that society was humbug and imbecility; also that of old the great comedians wouldn't have known such people. Garrick had essentially his own circle.

"No, I suppose they didn't call, in the old narrow-minded time," said Basil Dashwood.

"Your profession didn't call. They had better company—that of the romantic, gallant characters they represented. They lived with *them*, and it was better all round." And Peter asked himself—for the young man looked as if that struck him as a dreary period—if *he* only, for Miriam, in her new life, or among the futilities of those who tried to find her accessible, expressed the artistic idea. This at least, Sherringham reflected, was a situation that could be improved.

He learned from Dashwood that the new play, the thing they were rehearsing, was an old play, a romantic drama of thirty years before, covered, from infinite queer handling, with a sort of dirty glaze. Dashwood had a part in it, but there was an act in which he didn't appear, and that was the act they were doing that morning. "Yolande" had done all "Yolande" could do: Sherringham was mistaken if he supposed "Yolande" was such a tremendous hit. It had done very well, it had run three months, but they were by no means coining money with it. It wouldn't take them to the end of the season; they had seen for a month past that they would have to put on something else. Miss Rooth moreover wanted a new part; she was impatient to show what a range she was capable of. She had grand ideas; she thought herself very good-natured to repeat the same thing for three months. Basil Dashwood lighted another cigarette and described to his companion some of Miss Rooth's ideas. He gave Sherringham a great deal of information about her—about her character, her temper, her peculiarities, her little ways, her manner of producing some of her effects. He spoke with familiarity and confidence, as if he knew more about her than any one else—as if he had invented or discovered her, were in a sense her proprietor or guarantor. It was the talk of the shop, with a perceptible shrewdness in it and a touching young candour; the expansiveness of the commercial spirit when it relaxes and generalizes, is conscious it is safe with another member of the guild.

Sherringham could not help protesting against the lame old war-horse whom it was proposed to bring into action, who had been ridden to death and had saved a thousand desperate fields; and he exclaimed on the strange passion of the good British public for sitting again and again through expected situations, watching for speeches they had heard and surprises that struck the hour. Dashwood defended the taste of London, praised it as loyal, constant, faithful; to which Sherringham retorted with some vivacity that it was faithful to rubbish. He justified this sally by declaring that the play in rehearsal *was* rubbish, clumsy mediocrity which had outlived its convenience, and that the fault was the want of life in the critical sense of the public, which was ignobly docile, opening its mouth for its dose, like the pupils of Dotheboys Hall; not insisting on something different, on a fresh preparation. Dashwood asked him if he then wished Miss Rooth to go on playing for ever a part she had repeated more than eighty nights on end: he thought the modern "run" was just what he had heard him denounce, in Paris, as the disease the theatre was dying of. This imputation Sherringham gainsaid; he wanted to know if she couldn't change to something less stale than the piece in question. Dashwood opined that Miss Rooth must have a strong part and that there happened to be one for her in the before-mentioned venerable novelty. She had to take what she could get; she wasn't a girl to cry for the moon. This was a stop-gap—she would try other things later; she would have to look round her: you couldn't have a new piece left at your door every day with the milk. On one point Sherringham's mind might be at rest: Miss Rooth was a woman who would do every blessed thing there was to do. Give her time and she would walk straight through the repertory. She was a woman who would do this—she was a woman who would do that: Basil Dashwood employed this phrase so often that Sherringham, nervous, got up and threw an unsmoked cigarette away. Of course she was a woman: there was no need of Dashwood's saying it a hundred times!

As for the repertory, the young man went on, the most

beautiful girl in the world could give but what she had. He explained, after Sherringham sat down again, that the noise made by Miss Rooth was not exactly what this admirer appeared to suppose. Sherringham had seen the house the night before; would recognize that, though good, it was very far from great. She had done very well, very well indeed, but she had never gone above a point which Dashwood expressed in pounds sterling, to the edification of his companion, who vaguely thought the figure high. Sherringham remembered that he had been unable to get a stall, but Dashwood insisted that the girl had not leaped into commanding fame: that was a thing that never happened in fact—it happened only in pretentious works of fiction. She had attracted notice, unusual notice for a woman whose name the day before had never been heard of: she was recognized as having, for a novice, extraordinary cleverness and confidence—in addition to her looks of course, which were the thing that had really fetched the crowd. But she hadn't been the talk of London; she had only been the talk of Gabriel Nash. He wasn't London, more was the pity. He knew the æsthetic people—the worldly, semi-smart ones, not the frumpy, sickly lot who wore dirty drapery; and the æsthetic people had run after her. Basil Dashwood instructed Sherringham sketchily as to the different sects in the great religion of beauty, and was able to give him the particular "note" of the critical clique to which Miriam had begun so quickly to owe it that she had a vogue. The information made the secretary of embassy feel very ignorant of the world, very uninitiated and buried in his little professional hole. Dashwood warned him that it would be a long time before the general public would wake up to Miss Rooth, even after she had waked up to herself: she would have to do some really big thing first. *They* knew it was in her, the big thing—Sherringham and he, and even poor Nash—because they had seen her as no one else had; but London never took any one on trust—it had to be cash down. It would take their young lady two or three years to pay out her cash and get her equivalent. But of course the equivalent would be simply a gold-mine. Within its limits however, her success was already quite a fairy-tale: there was magic in the way she had concealed, from the first, her want of experience. She absolutely made you think she had a lot of it, more than any one else. Mr. Dashwood repeated several times that she was a cool hand—a deucedly cool hand; and that he watched her himself, saw ideas come to her, saw her try different dodges on different nights. She was always alive—she liked it herself. She gave *him* ideas, long as he had been on the stage. Naturally she had a great deal to learn—a tremendous lot to learn: a cosmopolite like Sherringham would understand that a girl of that age, who had never had a friend but her mother—her mother was greater fun than ever now—naturally *would* have. Sherringham winced at being called a "cosmopolite" by his young companion, just as he had winced a moment before at hearing himself lumped, in esoteric knowledge, with Dashwood and Gabriel Nash; but the former of these gentlemen took no account of his sensibility while he enumerated a few of the things that the young actress had to learn. Dashwood was a mixture of acuteness and innocent fatuity; and Sherringham had to recognize that he had some of the elements of criticism in him when he said that the wonderful thing in the girl was that she learned so fast—learned something every night, learned from the same old piece a lot more than any one else would have learned from twenty. "That's what it is to be a genius," Sherringham remarked. "Genius is only the art of getting your experience fast, of stealing it, as it were; and in this sense Miss Rooth's a regular brigand." Dashwood assented good-humouredly; then he added, "Oh, she'll do!" It was exactly in these simple words, in speaking to her, that Sherringham had phrased the same truth; yet he didn't enjoy hearing them on his neighbour's lips: they had a profane, patronizing sound, suggestive of displeasing equalities.

The two men sat in silence for some minutes, watching a fat robin hop about on the little seedy lawn; at the end of which they heard a vehicle stop on the other side of the garden wall and the voices of people descending from it. "Here they come, the dear creatures," said Basil Dashwood, without moving; and from where they sat Sherringham saw the small door in the wall pushed open. The dear creatures were three in number, for a gentleman had added himself to Mrs. Rooth and her daughter. As soon as Miriam's eyes fell upon her Parisian friend she stopped short, in a large, droll theatrical attitude, and, seizing her mother's arm, exclaimed passionately: "Look where he sits, the author of all my woes—cold, cynical, cruel!" She was evidently in the highest spirits; of which Mrs. Rooth partook as she cried indulgently, giving her a slap: "Oh, get along, you gipsy!"

"She's always up to something," Basil Dashwood commented, as Miriam, radiant and with a conscious stage tread, glided towards Sherringham as if she were coming to the footlights. He rose slowly from his seat, looking at her and struck with her beauty; he had been impatient to see her, yet in the act his impatience had had a disconcerting check.

Sherringham had had time to perceive that the man who had come in with her was Gabriel Nash, and this recognition brought a low sigh to his lips as he held out his hand to her—a sigh expressive of the sudden sense that his interest in her now could only be a gross community. Of course that didn't matter, since he had set it, at the most, such rigid limits; but none the less he stood vividly reminded that it would be public and notorious, that inferior people would be inveterately mixed up with it, that she had crossed the line and sold herself to the vulgar, making him indeed only one of an equalized multitude. The way Gabriel Nash turned up there just when he didn't want to see him made Peter feel that it was a complicated thing to have a friendship with an actress so clearly destined to be famous. He quite forgot that Nash had known Miriam long before his own introduction to her and had been present at their first meeting, which he had in fact in a measure brought about. Had Sherringham not been so cut out to make trouble of this particular joy he might have found some adequate assurance that she distinguished him in the way in which, taking his hand in both of hers, she looked up at him and murmured, "Dear old master!" Then, as if this were not acknowledgment enough, she raised her head still higher and, whimsically, gratefully, charmingly, almost nobly, she kissed him on the lips, before the other men, before the good mother whose "Oh, you honest creature!" made everything regular.

XVII.

IF PETER SHERRINGHAM was ruffled by some of Miriam's circumstances there was comfort and consolation to be drawn from others, beside the essential fascination (there was no doubt about that now) of the young lady's own society. He spent the afternoon, they all spent the afternoon, and the occasion reminded him of a scene in "Wilhelm Meister." Mrs. Rooth had little resemblance to Mignon, but Miriam was remarkably like Philina. Luncheon was delayed two or three hours; but the long wait was a positive source of gaiety, for they all smoked cigarettes in the garden and Miriam gave striking illustrations of the parts she was studying. Sherringham was in the state of a man whose toothache has suddenly stopped—he was exhilarated by the cessation of pain. The pain had been the effort to remain in Paris after Miriam came to London, and the balm of seeing her now was the measure of the previous soreness.

Gabriel Nash had, as usual, plenty to say, and he talked of Nick Dormer's picture so long that Sherringham wondered whether he did it on purpose to vex him. They went in and out of the house; they made excursions to see how lunch was coming on; and Sherringham got half an hour alone, or virtually alone, with the object of his unsanctioned passion— drawing her publicly away from the others and making her sit with him in the most sequestered part of the little gravelled grounds. There was summer enough in the trees to shut out the adjacent villas, and Basil Dashwood and Gabriel Nash lounged together at a convenient distance, while Nick's whimsical friend tried experiments upon the histrionic mind. Miriam confessed that, like all comedians, they ate at queer hours; she sent Dashwood in for biscuits and sherry—she proposed sending him round to the grocer's in the Circus Road for superior wine. Sherringham judged him to be the factotum of the little household: he knew where the biscuits were kept and the state of the grocer's account. When Peter congratulated the young actress on having so useful an associate she said genially, but as if the words disposed of him: "Oh, he's awfully handy!" To this she added: "You're not, you know;" resting the kindest, most pitying eyes on him. The sensation they gave him was as sweet as if she had stroked his cheek, and her manner was responsive even to tenderness. She called him "Dear master" again, and sometimes "Cher maître," and appeared to express gratitude and reverence by every intonation.

"You're doing the humble dependent now," he said: "you do it beautifully, as you do everything." She replied that she didn't make it humble enough—she couldn't; she was too proud, too insolent in her triumph. She liked that, the triumph, too much, and she didn't mind telling him that she was perfectly happy. Of course as yet the triumph was very limited; but success was success, whatever its quantity; the dish was a small one, but it had the right taste. Her imagination had already bounded beyond the first phase, unexpectedly brilliant as this had been: her position struck her as modest compared with a future that was now vivid to her. Sherringham had never seen her so soft and sympathetic; she had insisted, in Paris, that her personal character was that of the good girl (she used the term in a fine loose way), and it was impossible to be a better girl than she showed herself this pleasant afternoon. She was full of gossip and anecdote and drollery; she had exactly the air that he would have liked her to have—that of thinking of no end of things to tell him. It was as if she had just returned from a long journey, had had strange adventures and made wonderful discoveries. She began to speak of this and that, and broke off to speak of something else; she talked of the theatre, of the newspapers and then of London, of the people she had met and the extraordinary things they said to her, of the parts she was going to take up, of lots of new ideas that had come to her about the art of comedy. She wanted to do comedy now—to do the comedy of London life. She was delighted to find that seeing more of the world suggested things to her; they came straight from the fact, from nature, if you could call it nature: so that she was convinced more than ever that the artist ought to *live*, to get on with his business, gather ideas, lights from experience—ought to welcome any experience that would give him lights. But work, of course, *was* experience, and everything in one's life that was good was work. That was the jolly thing in the actor's trade—it made up for other elements that were odious: if you only kept your eyes open nothing could happen to you that wouldn't be food for observation and grist to your mill, showing you how people looked and moved and spoke—cried and grimaced, or writhed and dissimulated, in given situations. She saw all round her things she wanted to "do"—London was full of them, if you had eyes to see. Miriam demanded imperiously why people didn't take them up, put them into plays and parts, give one a chance with them: she expressed her sharp impatience of the general literary stupidity. She had never been chary of this particular displeasure, and there were moments (it was an old story and a subject of frank raillery to Sherringham) when to hear her you might have thought there was no cleverness anywhere but in her disdainful mind. She wanted tremendous things done, that she might use them, but she didn't pretend to say exactly what they were to be, nor even approximately how they were to be handled: her ground was rather that if *she* only had a pen—it was exasperating to have to explain! She mainly contented herself with declaring that nothing had really been touched: she felt that more and more as she saw more of people's goings-on.

Sherringham went to her theatre again that evening and he made no scruple of going every night for a week. Rather, perhaps I should say, he made a scruple; but it was a part of the pleasure of his life during these arbitrary days to overcome it. The only way to prove to himself that he could overcome it was to go; and he was satisfied, after he had been seven times, not only with the spectacle on the stage but with his own powers of demonstration. There was no satiety however with the spectacle on the stage, inasmuch as that only produced a further curiosity. Miriam's performance was a living thing, with a power to change, to grow, to develop, to beget new forms of the same life. Peter Sherringham contributed to it in his amateurish way, watching with solicitude the fate of his contributions. He talked it over in Balaklava Place, suggested modifications, variations worth trying. Miriam professed herself thankful for any refreshment that could be administered to her interest in "Yolande," and, with an effectiveness that showed large resource, touched up her part and drew several new airs from it. Sherringham's suggestions bore upon her way of uttering certain speeches, the intonations that would have more beauty or make the words mean more. Miriam had her ideas, or rather she had her instincts, which she defended and illustrated, with a vividness superior to argument, by a happy pictorial phrase or a snatch of mimicry; but she was always for trying; she liked experiments and caught at them, and she was especially thankful when some one gave her a showy reason, a plausible formula, in a case where she only stood upon an intuition. She pretended to despise reasons and to like and dislike at her sovereign pleasure; but she always honoured the exotic gift, so that Sherringham was amused with the liberal way she produced it, as if she had been a naked islander rejoicing in a present of crimson cloth.

Day after day he spent most of his time in her society, and Miss Laura Lumley's recent habitation became the place in London to which his thoughts were most attached. He was highly conscious that he was not now carrying out that principle of abstention which he had brought to such maturity before leaving Paris; but he contented himself with a much cruder justification of this inconsequence than he would have thought adequate in advance. It consisted simply in the idea that to be identified with the first public steps of a young genius was a delightful experience. What was the harm of it, if the genius were real? Sherringham's main security was now that his relations with Miriam had been frankly placed under the protection of the idea of legitimate extravagance. In this department they made a very creditable figure and required much less watching and pruning than when it was his effort to fit them into a worldly plan. Sherringham had a sense of real wisdom when he said to himself that it surely should be enough that this momentary intellectual participation in the girl's dawning fame was a charming thing. Charming things, in a busy man's life, were not frequent enough to be kicked out of the way. Balaklava Place, looked at in this philosophic way, became almost idyllic: it gave Peter the pleasantest impression he had ever had of London.

The season happened to be remarkably fine; the temperature was high, but not so high as to keep people from the theatre. Miriam's "business" visibly increased, so that the question of putting on the second play underwent some reconsideration. The girl insisted, showing in her insistence a temper of which Sherringham had already caught some splendid gleams. It was very evident that through her career it would be her expectation to carry things with a high hand. Her managers and agents would not find her an easy victim or a calculable force: but the public would adore her, surround her with the popularity that attaches to a humorous, good-natured princess, and her comrades would have a kindness for her because she wouldn't be selfish. They too would form in a manner a portion of her affectionate public. This was the way Sherringham read the signs, liking her whimsical tolerance of some of her vulgar playfellows almost well enough to forgive their presence in Balaklava Place, where they were a sore trial to her mother, who wanted her to multiply her points of contact only with the higher orders. There were hours when Sherringham thought he foresaw that her principal relation to the proper world would be to have, within two or three years, a grand battle with it, making it take her, if she let it have her at all, absolutely on her own terms: a picture which led our young man to ask himself, with a helplessness that was not exempt, as he perfectly knew, from absurdity, what part *he* should find himself playing in such a contest and if it would be reserved to him to be the more ridiculous as a peacemaker or as a heavy auxiliary.

"She might know any one she would, and the only person she appears to take any pleasure in is that dreadful Miss Rover," Mrs. Rooth whimpered, more than once, to Sherringham, who recognized in the young lady so designated the principal complication of Balaklava Place.

Miss Rover was a little actress who played at Miriam's theatre, combining with an unusual aptitude for delicate comedy a less exceptional absence of rigour in private life. She was pretty and quick and clever, and had a fineness that Miriam professed herself already in a position to estimate as rare. She had no control of her inclinations; yet sometimes they were wholly laudable, like the devotion she had formed for her beautiful colleague, whom she admired not only as an ornament of the profession but as a being of a more fortunate

essence. She had had an idea that real ladies were "nasty"; but
Miriam was not nasty, and who could gainsay that Miriam
was a real lady? The girl justified herself to Sherringham, who
had found no fault with her; she knew how much her mother
feared that the proper world wouldn't come in if they knew
that the improper, in the person of pretty Miss Rover, was on
the ground. What did she care who came and who didn't, and
what was to be gained by receiving half the snobs in London?
People would have to take her exactly as they found her—
that they would have to learn; and they would be much mistaken if they thought her capable of becoming a snob too for
the sake of their sweet company. She didn't pretend to be
anything but what she meant to be, the best general actress of
her time; and what had that to do with her seeing or not
seeing a poor ignorant girl who had lov— Well, she needn't
say what Fanny had. She had met her in the way of business—she didn't say she would have run after her. She had
liked her because she wasn't a stick, and when Fanny Rover
had asked her quite wistfully if she mightn't come and see her,
she hadn't bristled with scandalized virtue. Miss Rover was
not a bit more stupid or more ill-natured than any one else: it
would be time enough to shut the door when she should become so.

Sherringham commended even to extravagance the liberality of such comradeship; said that of course a woman didn't
go into that profession to see how little she could swallow.
She was right to live with the others so long as they were at
all possible, and it was for her, and only for her, to judge how
long that might be. This was rather heroic on Peter's part, for
his assumed detachment from the girl's personal life still left
him a margin for some forms of uneasiness. It would have
made, in his spirit, a great difference for the worse that the
woman he loved, and for whom he wished no baser lover
than himself, should have embraced the prospect of consorting only with the cheaper kind. It was all very well, but Fanny
Rover was simply a *cabotine*, and that sort of association was
an odd training for a young woman who was to have been
good enough (he couldn't forget that—he kept remembering
it as if it might still have a future use) to be his wife. Certainly
he ought to have thought of such things before he permitted

himself to become so interested in a theatrical nature. His heroism did him service however for the hour: it helped him by the end of the week to feel tremendously broken in to Miriam's little circle. What helped him most indeed was to reflect that she would get tired of a good many of its members herself in time; for it was not that they were shocking (very few of them shone with that intense light), but that they could be trusted in the long run to bore you.

There was a lovely Sunday in particular that he spent almost wholly in Balaklava Place—he arrived so early—when, in the afternoon, all sorts of odd people dropped in. Miriam held a reception in the little garden and insisted on almost all the company's staying to supper. Her mother shed tears to Sherringham, in the desecrated house, because they had accepted, Miriam and she, an invitation—and in Cromwell Road too—for the evening. Miriam decreed that they shouldn't go: they would have much better fun with their good friends at home. She sent off a message—it was a terrible distance—by a cabman, and Sherringham had the privilege of paying the messenger. Basil Dashwood, in another vehicle, proceeded to an hotel that he knew, a mile away, for supplementary provisions, and came back with a cold ham and a dozen of champagne. It was all very Bohemian and journalistic and picturesque, very supposedly droll and enviable to outsiders; and Miriam told anecdotes and gave imitations of the people she would have met if she had gone out: so no one had a sense of loss—the two occasions were fantastically united. Mrs. Rooth drank champagne for consolation; though the consolation was imperfect when she remembered that she might have drunk it (not quite so much indeed) in Cromwell Road.

Taken in connection with the evening before, the day formed for Sherringham the most complete exhibition he had had of Miriam Rooth. He had been at the theatre, to which the Saturday night happened to have brought the fullest house she had yet played to, and he came early to Balaklava Place, to tell her once again (he had told her half a dozen times the evening before) that, with the excitement of her biggest audience, she had surpassed herself, acted with remarkable intensity. It pleased her to hear it, and the spirit with which she interpreted the signs of the future and, during an hour he spent alone with her, Mrs. Rooth being up-stairs and Basil Dashwood not arrived, treated him to specimens of fictive emotion of various kinds, was beyond any natural abundance that he had yet seen in a woman. The impression could scarcely have been other if she had been playing wild snatches to him at the piano: the bright, up-darting flame of her talk rose and fell like an improvisation on the keys. Later, all the rest of the day, he was fascinated by the good grace with which she fraternized with her visitors, finding the right words for each, the solvent of incongruities, the right ideas to keep vanity quiet and make humility gay. It was a wonderful expenditure of generous, nervous life. But what Sherringham read in it above all was the sense of success in youth, with the future large, and the action of that force upon all the faculties. Miriam's limited past had yet pinched her enough to make emancipation sweet, and the emancipation had come at last in an hour. She had stepped into her magic shoes, divined and appropriated everything they could give her, become in a day a really original contemporary. Sherringham was of course not less conscious of that than Nick Dormer had been when, in the cold light of his studio, he saw how she had altered.

But the great thing, to his mind and, these first days, the irresistible seduction of the theatre, was that she was a rare incarnation of beauty. Beauty was the principle of everything she did and of the way, unerringly, she did it—an exquisite harmony of line and motion and attitude and tone, what was most general and most characteristic in her performance. Accidents and instincts played together to this end and constituted something which was independent of her talent or of her merit, in a given case, and which in its influence, to Sherringham's imagination, was far superior to any merit and to any talent. It was a supreme infallible felicity, a source of importance, a stamp of absolute value. To see it in operation, to sit within its radius and feel it shift and revolve and change and never fail, was a corrective to the depression, the humiliation, the bewilderment of life. It transported Sherringham from the vulgar hour and the ugly fact; drew him to something which had no reason but its sweetness, no name nor place save as the pure, the distant, the antique. It was what

most made him say to himself: "Oh, hang it, what does it
matter?" when he reflected that an *homme sérieux* (as they said
in Paris) rather gave himself away (as they said in America) by
going every night to the same theatre for all the world to
stare. It was what kept him from doing anything but hover
round Miriam—kept him from paying any other visits, from
attending to any business, from going back to Calcutta Gardens. It was a spell which he shrank intensely from breaking,
and the cause of a hundred postponements, confusions and
incoherences. It made of the crooked little stucco villa in St.
John's Wood a place in the upper air, commanding the prospect; a nest of winged liberties and ironies, hanging far aloft
above the huddled town. One should live at altitudes when
one could—they braced and simplified; and for a happy interval Sherringham never touched the earth.

It was not that there were no influences tending at moments to drag him down—an abasement from which he escaped only because he was up so high. We have seen that Basil
Dashwood could affect him at times like a piece of wood tied
to his ankle, through the circumstance that he made Miriam's
famous conditions—those of the public exhibition of her genius—seem small and prosaic; so that Sherringham had to
remind himself that perhaps this smallness was involved in
their being at all. She carried his imagination off into infinite
spaces, whereas she carried Dashwood's only into the box-
office and the revival of plays that were barbarously bad. The
worst was that it was open to him to believe that a sharp
young man who was in the business might know better than
he. Another possessor of superior knowledge (he talked, that
is, as if he knew better than any one) was Gabriel Nash, who
appeared to have abundant leisure to haunt Balaklava Place,
or in other words appeared to enjoy the same command of his
time as Peter Sherringham. Our young diplomatist regarded
him with mingled feelings, for he had not forgotten the contentious character of their first meeting or the degree to
which he had been moved to urge upon Nick Dormer's consideration that his talkative friend was probably an ass. This
personage turned up now as an admirer of the charming creature he had scoffed at, and there was something exasperating
in the quietude of his inconsistency, of which he had not the

least embarrassing consciousness. Indeed he had such arbitrary and desultory ways of looking at any question that it was difficult, in vulgar parlance, to have him; his sympathies hummed about like bees in a garden, with no visible plan, no economy in their flight. He thought meanly of the modern theatre and yet he had discovered a fund of satisfaction in the most promising of its exponents; so that Sherringham more than once said to him that he should really, to keep his opinions at all in hand, attach more value to the stage or less to the interesting actress. Miriam made infinitely merry at his expense and treated him as the most abject of her slaves: all of which was worth seeing as an exhibition, on Nash's part, of the imperturbable. When Sherringham mentally pronounced him impudent he felt guilty of an injustice—Nash had so little the air of a man with something to gain. Nevertheless he felt a certain itching in his boot-toe when his fellow-visitor exclaimed, explicatively (in general to Miriam herself), in answer to a charge of tergiversation: "Oh, it's all right: it's the voice, you know—the enchanting voice!" He meant by this, as indeed he more fully set forth, that he came to the theatre, or to the villa in St. John's Wood, simply to treat his ear to the sound (the richest then to be heard on earth, as he maintained) issuing from Miriam's lips. Its richness was quite independent of the words she might pronounce or the poor fable they might subserve, and if the pleasure of hearing her in public was the greater by reason of the larger volume of her utterance, it was still highly agreeable to see her at home, for it was there that the artistic nature that he freely conceded to her came out most. He spoke as if she had been formed by the bounty of nature to be his particular recreation, and as if, being an expert in innocent joys, he took his pleasure wherever he found it.

He was perpetually in the field, sociable, amiable, communicative, inveterately contradicted but never confounded, ready to talk to any one about anything and making disagreement (of which he left the responsibility wholly to others) a basis of intimacy. Every one knew what he thought of the theatrical profession, and yet it could not be said that he did not regard its members as the exponents of comedy, inasmuch as he often elicited their foibles in a way that made even Sher-

ringham laugh, notwithstanding his attitude of reserve where
Nash was concerned. At any rate, though he had committed
himself on the subject of the general fallacy of their attempt,
he put up with their company, for the sake of Miriam's
accents, with a practical philosophy that was all his own.
Miriam pretended that he was her supreme, her incorrigible
adorer, masquerading as a critic to save his vanity and tolerated for his secret constancy in spite of being a bore. To Sherringham he was not a bore, and the secretary of embassy felt a
certain displeasure at not being able to regard him as one. He
had seen too many strange countries and curious things, observed and explored too much to be void of illustration. Peter
had a suspicion that if he himself was in the *grandes espaces*
Gabriel Nash probably had a still wider range. If among Miriam's associates Basil Dashwood dragged him down, Gabriel
challenged him rather to higher and more fantastic flights. If
he saw the girl in larger relations than the young actor, who
mainly saw her in ill-written parts, Nash went a step further
and regarded her, irresponsibly and sublimely, as a priestess of
harmony, with whom the vulgar ideas of success and failure
had nothing to do. He laughed at her "parts," holding that
without them she would be great. Sherringham envied him
his power to content himself with the pleasures he could get:
he had a shrewd impression that contentment was not destined to be the sweetener of his own repast.

Above all Nash held his attention by a constant element of
unstudied reference to Nick Dormer, who, as we know, had
suddenly become much more interesting to his cousin. Sherringham found food for observation, and in some measure for
perplexity, in the relations of all these clever people with each
other. He knew why his sister, who had a personal impatience
of unapplied ideas, had not been agreeably affected by Mr.
Nash and had not viewed with complacency a predilection for
him in the man she was to marry. This was a side by which he
had no desire to resemble Julia Dallow, for he needed no
teaching to divine that Gabriel had not set her intelligence in
motion. He, Peter, would have been sorry to have to confess
that he could not understand him. He understood furthermore that Miriam, in Nick's studio, might very well have appeared to Julia a formidable power. She was younger, but she

had quite as much her own form and she was beautiful enough to have made Nick compare her with Mrs. Dallow even if he had been in love with that lady—a pretension as to which Peter had private ideas.

Sherringham for many days saw nothing of the member for Harsh, though it might have been said that, by implication, he participated in the life of Balaklava Place. Had Nick given Julia tangible grounds, and was his unexpectedly fine rendering of Miriam an act of virtual infidelity? In that case in what degree was Miriam to be regarded as an accomplice in his defection, and what was the real nature of this young lady's esteem for her new and (as he might be called) distinguished ally? These questions would have given Peter still more to think about if he had not flattered himself that he had made up his mind that they concerned Nick and Miriam infinitely more than they concerned him. Miriam was personally before him, so that he had no need to consult for his pleasure his fresh recollection of the portrait. But he thought of this striking production each time he thought of his enterprising kinsman. And that happened often, for in his hearing Miriam often discussed the happy artist and his possibilities with Gabriel Nash, and Gabriel broke out about them to Miriam. The girl's tone on the subject was frank and simple: she only said, with an iteration that was slightly irritating, that Mr. Dormer had been tremendously kind to her. She never mentioned Julia's irruption to Julia's brother; she only referred to the portrait, with inscrutable amenity, as a direct consequence of Peter's fortunate suggestion that first day at Madame Carré's. Gabriel Nash, however, showed such a disposition to expatiate sociably and luminously on the peculiarly interesting character of what he called Dormer's predicament and on the fine suspense which it was fitted to kindle in the breast of discerning friends, that Peter wondered, as I have already hinted, if this insistence were not a subtle perversity, a devilish little invention to torment a man whose jealousy was presumable. Yet on the whole Nash struck him as but scantily devilish and as still less occupied with the prefigurement of *his* emotions. Indeed, he threw a glamour of romance over Nick; tossed off such illuminating yet mystifying references to him that Sherringham found himself capable of a magnanimous curiosity, a desire to follow out the chain of events. He learned from Gabriel that Nick was still away, and he felt as if he could almost submit to instruction, to initiation. The rare charm of these unregulated days was troubled—it ceased to be idyllic— when, late on the evening of the second Sunday, he walked away with Gabriel southward from St. John's Wood. For then something came out.

XVIII.

IT MATTERED not so much what the doctors thought (and Sir Matthew Hope, the greatest of them all, had been down twice in one week) as that Mr. Chayter, the omniscient butler, declared with all the authority of his position and his experience that Mr. Carteret was very bad indeed. Nick Dormer had a long talk with him (it lasted six minutes) the day he hurried to Beauclere in response to a telegram. It was Mr. Chayter who had taken upon himself to telegraph, in spite of the presence in the house of Mr. Carteret's nearest relation and only surviving sister, Mrs. Lendon. This lady, a large, mild, healthy woman, with a heavy tread, who liked early breakfasts, uncomfortable chairs and the advertisement-sheet of the *Times*, had arrived the week before and was awaiting the turn of events. She was a widow and lived in Cornwall, in a house nine miles from a station, which had, to make up for this inconvenience, as she had once told Nick, a delightful old herbaceous garden. She was extremely fond of an herbaceous garden; her principal interest was in that direction. Nick had often seen her—she came to Beauclere once or twice a year. Her sojourn there made no great difference; she was only an "Urania dear," for Mr. Carteret to look across the table at when, on the close of dinner, it was time for her to retire. She went out of the room always as if it were after some one else; and on the gentlemen "joining" her later (the junction was not very close) she received them with an air of gratified surprise.

Chayter honoured Nick Dormer with a regard which approached, without improperly competing with it, the affection his master had placed on the same young head, and Chayter knew a good many things. Among them he knew his place; but it was wonderful how little that knowledge had rendered him inaccessible to other kinds. He took upon himself to send for Nick without speaking to Mrs. Lendon, whose influence was now a good deal like that of a large occasional piece of furniture which had been introduced in case it should be required. She was one of the solid conveniences that a comfortable house would have; but you couldn't talk with a mahogany sofa or a folding-screen. Chayter knew how much she had "had" from her brother, and how much her two daughters had each received on marriage; and he was of the opinion that it was quite enough, especially considering the society in which they (you could scarcely call it) moved. He knew beyond this that they would all have more, and that was why he hesitated little about communicating with Nick. If Mrs. Lendon should be ruffled at the intrusion of a young man who neither was the child of a cousin nor had been formally adopted, Chayter was parliamentary enough to see that the forms of debate were observed. He had indeed a slightly compassionate sense that Mrs. Lendon was not easily ruffled. She was always down an extraordinary time before breakfast (Chayter refused to take it as in the least admonitory), but she usually went straight into the garden (as if to see that none of the plants had been stolen in the night), and had in the end to be looked for by the footman in some out-of-the-way spot behind the shrubbery, where, plumped upon the ground, she was doing something "rum" to a flower.

Mr. Carteret himself had expressed no wishes. He slept most of the time (his failure at the last had been sudden, but he was rheumatic and seventy-seven), and the situation was in Chayter's hands. Sir Matthew Hope had opined, even on his second visit, that he would rally and go on, in rudimentary comfort, some time longer; but Chayter took a different and a still more intimate view. Nick was embarrassed: he scarcely knew what he was there for from the moment he could give his good old friend no conscious satisfaction. The doctors, the nurses, the servants, Mrs. Lendon, and above all the settled equilibrium of the square, thick house, where an immutable order appeared to slant through the polished windows and tinkle in the quieter bells, all represented best the kind of supreme solace to which the master was most accessible.

For the first day it was judged better that Nick should not be introduced into the darkened chamber. This was the decision of the two decorous nurses, of whom the visitor had had a glimpse and who, with their black uniforms and fresh faces of business, suggested a combination of the barmaid and the nun. He was depressed, yet restless, felt himself in a false position and thought it lucky Mrs. Lendon had powers of placid acceptance. They were old acquaintances: she treated him with a certain ceremony, but it was not the rigour of mistrust. It was much more an expression of remote Cornish respect for young abilities and distinguished connections, inasmuch as she asked him a great deal about Lady Agnes and about Lady Flora and Lady Elizabeth. He knew she was kind and ungrudging, and his principal chagrin was the sense of meagre information and of responding poorly in regard to his uninteresting aunts. He sat in the garden with newspapers and looked at the lowered blinds in Mr. Carteret's windows; he wandered around the abbey with cigarettes and lightened his tread and felt grave, wishing that everything were over. He would have liked much to see Mr. Carteret again, but he had no desire that Mr. Carteret should see him. In the evening he dined with Mrs. Lendon, and she talked to him, at his request and as much as she could, about her brother's early years, his beginnings of life. She was so much younger that they appeared to have been rather a tradition of her own youth; but her talk made Nick feel how tremendously different Mr. Carteret had been at that period from what he, Nick, was to-day. He had published at the age of thirty a little volume (it was thought wonderfully clever) called "The Incidence of Rates"; but Nick had not yet collected the material for any such treatise. After dinner Mrs. Lendon, who was in full dress, retired to the drawing-room, where at the end of ten minutes she was followed by Nick, who had remained behind only because he thought Chayter would expect it. Mrs. Lendon almost shook hands with him again, and then Chayter brought in coffee. Almost in no time afterwards he brought in tea, and the occupants of the drawing-room sat for a slow half-hour, during which the lady looked round at the apartment with a sigh and said: "Don't you think poor Charles had exquisite taste?"

Fortunately at this moment the "local man" was ushered in. He had been up-stairs and he entered, smiling, with the remark: "It's quite wonderful—it's quite wonderful." What was wonderful was a marked improvement in the breathing, a distinct indication of revival. The doctor had some tea and he chatted for a quarter of an hour in a way that showed what a "good" manner and how large an experience a local man

could have. When he went away Nick walked out with him.
The doctor's house was near by and he had come on foot. He
left Nick with the assurance that in all probability Mr. Carteret, who was certainly picking up, would be able to see him
on the morrow. Our young man turned his steps again to the
abbey and took a stroll about it in the starlight. It never
looked so huge as when it reared itself in the night, and Nick
had never felt more fond of it than on this occasion, more
comforted and confirmed by its beauty. When he came back
he was readmitted by Chayter, who surveyed him in respectful deprecation of the frivolity which had led him to attempt
to help himself through such an evening in such a way.

Nick went to bed early and slept badly, which was unusual
with him; but it was a pleasure to him to be told almost as
soon as he came out of his room that Mr. Carteret had asked
for him. He went in to see him and was struck with the
change in his appearance. He had however spent a day with
him just after the New Year, and another at the beginning of
March, so that he had perceived the first symptoms of mortal
alteration. A week after Julia Dallow's departure for the Continent Nick had devoted several hours to Beauclere and to the
intention of telling his old friend how the happy event had
been brought to naught—the advantage that he had been so
good as to desire for him and to make the condition of a
splendid gift. Before this, for a few days, Nick had been keeping back, to announce it personally, the good news that Julia
had at last set their situation in order: he wanted to enjoy the
old man's pleasure—so sore a trial had her arbitrary behaviour been for a year. Mrs. Dallow had offered Mr. Carteret a
conciliatory visit before Christmas—had come down from
London one day to lunch with him, but only with the effect
of making him subsequently exhibit to poor Nick, as the victim of her whimsical hardness, a great deal of earnest commiseration in a jocose form. Upon his honour, as he said, she was
as clever and "specious" a woman (this was the odd expression he used) as he had ever seen in his life. The merit of her
behaviour on this occasion, as Nick knew, was that she had
not been specious at her lover's expense: she had breathed no
doubt of his public purpose and had had the feminine courage to say that in truth she was older than he, so that it was

only fair to give his affections time to mature. But when Nick saw their sympathizing host after the rupture that I lately narrated he found him in no state to encounter a disappointment: he was seriously ailing, it was the beginning of worse things and no time for trying on a sensation. After this excursion Nick went back to town saddened by Mr. Carteret's now unmistakably settled decline, but rather relieved that he had not been forced to make his confession. It had even occurred to him that the need for making it might not come up if the ebb of his old friend's strength should continue unchecked. He might pass away in the persuasion that everything would happen as he wished it, though indeed without enriching Nick on his wedding-day to the tune that he had promised. Very likely he had made legal arrangements in virtue of which his bounty would take effect in the right conditions and in them alone. At present Nick had a larger confession to treat him to—the last three days had made the difference; but, oddly enough, though his responsibility had increased his reluctance to speak had vanished: he was positively eager to clear up a situation over which it was not consistent with his honour to leave a shade.

The doctor had been right when he came in after dinner; it was clear in the morning that they had not seen the last of Mr. Carteret's power of picking up. Chayter, who had been in to see him, refused austerely to change his opinion with every change in his master's temperature; but the nurses took the cheering view that it would do their patient good for Mr. Dormer to sit with him a little. One of them remained in the room, in the deep window-seat, and Nick spent twenty minutes by the bedside. It was not a case for much conversation, but Mr. Carteret seemed to like to look at him. There was life in his kind old eyes, which would express itself yet in some further wise provision. He laid his liberal hand on Nick's with a confidence which showed it was not yet disabled. He said very little, and the nurse had recommended that the visitor himself should not overflow in speech; but from time to time he murmured with a faint smile: "To-night's division, you know—you mustn't miss it." There was to be no division that night, as it happened, but even Mr. Carteret's aberrations were parliamentary. Before Nick left him he had been able to assure him that he was rapidly getting better, that such valuable hours must not be wasted. "Come back on Friday, if they come to the second reading." These were the words with which Nick was dismissed, and at noon the doctor said the invalid was doing very well, but that Nick had better leave him alone for that day. Our young man accordingly determined to go up to town for the night and even, if he should receive no summons, for the next day. He arranged with Chayter that he should be telegraphed to if Mr. Carteret were either better or worse.

"Oh, he can't very well be worse, sir," Chayter replied, inexorably; but he relaxed so far as to remark that of course it wouldn't do for Nick to neglect the House.

"Oh, the House!" Nick sighed, ambiguously, avoiding the butler's eye. It would be easy enough to tell Mr. Carteret, but nothing would have sustained him in the effort to make a clean breast to Chayter.

He might be ambiguous about the House, but he had the sense of things to be done awaiting him in London. He telegraphed to his servant and spent that night in Rosedale Road. The things to be done were apparently to be done in his studio: his servant met him there with a large bundle of letters. He failed that evening to stray within two miles of Westminster, and the legislature of his country reassembled without his support. The next morning he received a telegram from Chayter, to whom he had given Rosedale Road as an address. This missive simply informed him that Mr. Carteret wished to see him, and it seemed to imply that he was better, though Chayter wouldn't say so. Nick again took his place in the train to Beauclere. He had been there very often, but it was present to him that now, after a little, he should go only once more, for a particular dismal occasion. All that was over—everything that belonged to it was over. He learned on his arrival—he saw Mrs. Lendon immediately—that his old friend had continued to pick up. He had expressed a strong and a perfectly rational desire to talk with Nick, and the doctor had said that if it was about anything important it was much better not to oppose him. "He says it's about something very important," Mrs. Lendon remarked, resting shy eyes on him while she added that *she* was looking after her brother for the hour. She had sent those wonderful young ladies out to see the abbey. Nick paused with her outside of Mr. Carteret's door. He wanted to say something comfortable to her in return for her homely charity—give her a hint, which she was far from looking for, that practically he had now no interest in her brother's estate. This was impossible of course. Her absence of irony gave him no pretext, and such an allusion would be an insult to her simple discretion. She was either not thinking of his interest at all, or she was thinking of it with the tolerance of a mind trained to a hundred decent submissions. Nick looked for an instant into her mild, uninvestigating eyes, and it came over him supremely that the goodness of these people was singularly pure: they were a part of what was cleanest and sanest and dullest in humanity. There had been just a little mocking inflection in Mrs. Lendon's pleasant voice; but it was dedicated to the young ladies in the black uniforms (she could perhaps be satirical about *them*), and not to the theory of the "importance" of Nick's interview with her brother. Nick's arrested desire to let her know he was not dangerous translated itself into a vague friendliness and into the abrupt, rather bewildering words: "I can't tell you half the good I think of you." As he passed into Mr. Carteret's room it occurred to him that she would perhaps interpret this speech as an acknowledgment of obligation—of her good-nature in not keeping him away from the rich old man.

I.

M R. CARTERET was propped up on pillows, and in this
attitude, beneath the high, spare canopy of his bed,
presented himself to Nick's picture-seeking vision as a figure
in a clever composition or a novel. He had gathered
strength, though this strength was not much in his voice; it
was mainly in his brighter eye and his air of being pleased
with himself. He put out his hand and said: "I dare say you
know why I sent for you;" upon which Nick sank into the
seat he had occupied the day before, replying that he had
been delighted to come, whatever the reason. Mr. Carteret
said nothing more about the division or the second reading;
he only murmured that they were keeping the newspapers
for him. "I'm rather behind—I'm rather behind," he went
on; "but two or three quiet mornings will make it all right.
You can go back to-night, you know—you can easily go
back." This was the only thing not quite straight that Nick
saw in him—his making light of his young friend's flying to
and fro. Nick sat looking at him with a sense that was half
compunction and half the idea of the rare beauty of his face,
to which, strangely, the waste of illness now seemed to have
restored some of its youth. Mr. Carteret was evidently conscious that this morning he should not be able to go on
long, so that he must be practical and concise. "I dare say
you know—you have only to remember," he continued.

"You know what a pleasure it is to me to see you—there
can be no better reason than that."

"Hasn't the year come round—the year of that foolish arrangement?"

Nick thought a little, asking himself if it were really necessary to disturb his companion's earnest faith. Then the consciousness of the falsity of his own position surged over him
again, and he replied: "Do you mean the period for which
Mrs. Dallow insisted on keeping me dangling? Oh, that's
over."

"And are you married—has it come off?" the old man asked, eagerly. "How long have I been ill?"

"We are uncomfortable, unreasonable people, not deserving of your interest. We are not married," Nick said.

"Then I haven't been ill so long," Mr. Carteret sighed, with vague relief.

"Not very long—but things *are* different," Nick continued. The old man's eyes rested on his, and Nick noted how much larger they appeared. "You mean the arrangements are made—the day is at hand?"

"There are no arrangements," Nick smiled: "but why should it trouble you?"

"What then will you do—without arrangements?" Mr. Carteret's inquiry was plaintive and childlike.

"We shall do nothing—there is nothing to be done. We are not to be married—it's all off," said Nick. Then he added: "Mrs. Dallow has gone abroad."

The old man, motionless among his pillows, gave a long groan. "Ah, I don't like that."

"No more do I, sir."

"What's the matter? It was so good—so good."

"It wasn't good enough for her," Nick Dormer declared.

"For her? Is she so great as that? She told me she had the greatest regard for you. You're good enough for the best, my dear boy," Mr. Carteret went on.

"You don't know me; I *am* disappointing. Mrs. Dallow had, I believe, a great regard for me; but I have forfeited her regard."

The old man stared at this cynical announcement: he searched his companion's face for some attenuation of the words. But Nick apparently struck him as unashamed; and a faint colour coming into his withered cheek indicated his mystification and alarm. "Have you been unfaithful to her?" he demanded, considerately.

"She thinks so—it comes to the same thing. As I told you a year ago, she doesn't believe in me."

"You ought to have made her—you ought to have made her," said Mr. Carteret. Nick was about to utter some rejoinder when he continued: "Do you remember what I told you I would give you if you did? Do you remember what I told you I would give you on your wedding-day?"

"You expressed the most generous intentions; and I remember them as much as a man may do who has no wish to remind you of them."

"The money is there—I have put it aside."

"I haven't earned it—I haven't earned a penny of it. Give it to those who deserve it more."

"I don't understand—I don't understand," Mr. Carteret murmured, with the tears of weakness coming into his eyes. His face flushed and he added: "I'm not good for much discussion; I'm very much disappointed."

"I think I may say it's not my fault—I have done what I can," returned Nick.

"But when people are in love they do more than that."

"Oh, it's all over!" Nick exclaimed; not caring much now, for the moment, how disconcerted his companion might be, so long as he disabused him of the idea that they were partners to a bargain. "We've tormented each other and we've tormented you; and that is all that has come of it."

"Don't you care for what I would have done for you—shouldn't you have liked it?"

"Of course one likes kindness—one likes money. But it's all over," Nick repeated. Then he added: "I fatigue you, I knock you up, with telling you these uncomfortable things. I only do so because it seems to me right you should know. But don't be worried—everything will be all right."

He patted his companion's hand reassuringly, he leaned over him affectionately; but Mr. Carteret was not easily soothed. He had practised lucidity all his life, he had expected it of others and he had never given his assent to an indistinct proposition. He was weak, but he was not too weak to perceive that he had formed a calculation which was now vitiated by a wrong factor—put his name to a contract of which the other side had not been carried out. More than fifty years of conscious success pressed him to try to understand; he had never muddled his affairs and he couldn't muddle them now. At the same time he was aware of the necessity of economizing his effort, and he evidently gathered himself, within, patiently and almost cunningly, for the right question and the

right induction. He was still able to make his agitation reflective, and it could still consort with his high hopes of Nick
that he should find himself regarding the declaration that
everything would be all right as an inadequate guarantee. So,
after he had looked a moment into his companion's eyes, he
inquired:

"Have you done anything bad?"

"Nothing worse than usual," laughed Nick.

"Everything should have been better than usual."

"Ah, well, it hasn't been that—that I must say."

"Do you sometimes think of your father?" Mr. Carteret
continued.

Nick hesitated a moment. "*You* make me think of him—
you have always that pleasant effect."

"His name would have lived—it mustn't be lost."

"Yes, but the competition to-day is terrible," Nick replied.

Mr. Carteret considered this a moment, as if he found a
serious flaw in it; after which he began again: "I never supposed you were a trifler."

"I'm determined not to be."

"I thought her charming. Don't you love her?" Mr. Carteret asked.

"Don't ask me that to-day, for I feel sore and resentful. I
don't think she has treated me well."

"You should have held her—you shouldn't have let her
go," the old man returned, with unexpected fire.

His companion flushed at this, so strange it seemed to him
to receive a lesson in energy from a dying octogenarian. Yet
after an instant Nick answered modestly enough: "I haven't
been clever enough, no doubt."

"Don't say that—don't say that," Mr. Carteret murmured,
looking almost frightened. "Don't think I can allow you any
mitigation of that sort. I know how well you've done. You're
taking your place. Several gentlemen have told me. Hasn't she
felt a scruple, knowing my settlement on you was contingent?" he pursued.

"Oh, she hasn't known—hasn't known anything about it."

"I don't understand; though I think you explained somewhat, a year ago," Mr. Carteret said, with discouragement. "I
think she wanted to speak to me—of any intentions I might

have in regard to you—the day she was here. Very nicely, very properly she would have done it, I'm sure. I think her idea was that I ought to make any settlement quite independent of your marrying her or not marrying her. But I tried to convey to her—I don't know whether she understood me—that I liked her too much for that, I wanted too much to make sure of her."

"To make sure of me, you mean," said Nick. "And now, after all, you see you haven't."

"Well, perhaps it was that," sighed the old man, confusedly.

"All this is very bad for you—we'll talk again," Nick rejoined.

"No, no—let us finish it now. I like to know what I'm doing. I shall rest better when I do know. There are great things to be done; the future will be full—the future will be fine," Mr. Carteret wandered.

"Let me say this for Julia: that if we hadn't been sundered her generosity to me would have been complete, she would have put her great fortune absolutely at my disposal," Nick said, after a moment. "Her consciousness of all that naturally carries her over any particular distress in regard to what won't come to me now from another source."

"Ah, don't lose it," pleaded the old man, painfully.

"It's in your hands, sir," reasoned Nick.

"I mean Mrs. Dallow's fortune. It will be of the highest utility. That was what your father missed."

"I shall miss more than my father did," said Nick.

"She'll come back to you—I can't look at you and doubt that."

Nick shook his head slowly, smiling. "Never, never, never! You look at me, my grand old friend, but you don't see me. I'm not what you think."

"What is it—what is it? *Have* you been bad?" Mr. Carteret panted.

"No, no; I'm not bad. But I'm different."

"Different?"

"Different from my father—different from Mrs. Dallow—different from you."

"Ah, why do you perplex me?" moaned the old man. "You've done something."

"I don't want to perplex you, but I *have* done something," said Nick, getting up.

He had heard the door open softly behind him and Mrs. Lendon come forward with precautions. "What has he done—what has he done?" quavered Mr. Carteret to his sister. She however, after a glance at the patient, motioned Nick away and, bending over the bed, replied, in a voice expressive at that moment of a sharply contrasted plenitude of vital comfort:

"He has only excited you, I'm afraid, a little more than is good for you. Isn't your dear old head a little too high?" Nick regarded himself as justly banished and he quitted the room with a ready acquiescence in any power to carry on the scene of which Mrs. Lendon might find herself possessed. He felt distinctly brutal as he heard his host emit a soft, troubled exhalation of assent to some change of position. But he would have reproached himself more if he had wished less to guard against the acceptance of an equivalent for duties unperformed. Mr. Carteret had had in his mind, characteristically, the idea of an enlightened agreement, and there was something more to be said about that.

Nick went out of the house and stayed away for two or three hours, quite ready to consider that the place was quieter and safer without him. He haunted the abbey, as usual, and sat a long time in its simplifying stillness, turning over many things. He came into the house again at the luncheon-hour, through the garden, and heard, somewhat to his surprise and greatly to his relief, that Mr. Carteret had composed himself promptly enough after their agitating interview. Mrs. Lendon talked at luncheon much as if she expected her brother to be, as she said, really quite fit again. She asked Nick no embarrassing question; which was uncommonly good of her, he thought, considering that she might have said: "What in the world were you trying to get out of him?" She only told our young man that the invalid had very little doubt he should be able to see him again, about half-past seven, for a *very* short time: this timid emphasis was Mrs. Lendon's single tribute to the critical spirit. Nick divined that Mr. Carteret's desire for further explanations was really strong and had been capable of sustaining him through a bad morning—capable even of helping him (it would be a secret and wonderful momentary victory over his weakness) to pass it off for a good one. He wished he might make a sketch of him from the life, as he had seen him after breakfast; he had a conviction he could make a strong one, and it would be a precious memento. But he shrank from proposing this—Mr. Carteret might think it un-parliamentary. The doctor had called while Nick was out, and he came again at five o'clock, without our young man's seeing him. Nick was busy in his room at that hour: he wrote a short letter which took him a long time. But apparently there had been no veto on a resumption of talk, for at half-past seven the old man sent for him. The nurse, at the door, said: "Only a moment, I hope, sir?" but she took him in and then with-drew.

The prolonged daylight was in the room, and Mr. Carteret was again established on his pile of pillows, but with his head a little lower. Nick sat down by him and began to express the hope that he had not upset him in the morning; but the old man, with fixed, expanded eyes, took up their conversation exactly where they had left it.

"What have you done—what have you done? Have you associated yourself with some other woman?"

"No, no; I don't think she can accuse me of that."

"Well, then, she'll come back to you, if you take the right way with her."

It might have been droll to hear Mr. Carteret, in his situa-tion, giving his views on the right way with women; but Nick was not moved to enjoy that diversion. "I've taken the wrong way. I've done something which will spoil my prospects in that direction for ever. I've written a letter," Nick went on; but his companion had already interrupted him.

"You've written a letter?"

"To my constituents, informing them of my determination to resign my seat."

"To resign your seat?"

"I've made up my mind, after no end of reflection, dear Mr. Carteret, to work in a different line. I have a project of becoming a painter. So I've given up the idea of a political life."

"A painter?" Mr. Carteret seemed to turn whiter.

"I'm going in for the portrait in oils: it sounds absurd, I know, and I only mention it to show you that I don't in the least expect you to count upon me." Mr. Carteret had continued to stare, at first; then his eyes slowly closed and he lay motionless and blank. "Don't let it trouble you now; it's a long story and rather a poor one; when you get better I'll tell you all about it. We'll talk it over amicably, and I'll bring you to my side," Nick went on hypocritically. He had laid his hand on Mr. Carteret's again: it felt cold, and as the old man remained silent he had a moment of exaggerated fear.

"This is dreadful news," said Mr. Carteret, opening his eyes.

"Certainly it must seem so to you, for I've always kept from you (I was ashamed, and my present confusion is a just chastisement) the great interest I have always taken in the"— Nick hesitated, and then added, with an intention of humour and a sense of foolishness—"in the pencil and the brush." He spoke of his present confusion; but it must be confessed that his manner showed it but little. He was surprised at his own serenity, and had to recognize that at the point things had come to now he was profoundly obstinate and quiet.

"The pencil—the brush? They're not the weapons of a gentleman," said Mr. Carteret.

"I was sure that would be your view. I repeat that I mention them only because you once said you intended to do something for me, as the phrase is, and I thought you oughtn't to do it in ignorance."

"My ignorance was better. Such knowledge isn't good for me."

"Forgive me, my dear old friend. When you're better you'll see it differently."

"I shall never be better now."

"Ah, no," pleaded Nick, "it will do you good after a little. Think it over quietly and you'll be glad I've stopped being a humbug."

"I loved you—I loved you as my son," moaned the old man.

Nick sank on his knee beside the bed and leaned over him tenderly. "Get better, get better, and I'll be your son for the rest of your life."

"Poor Dormer—poor Dormer!" Mr. Carteret softly wailed.

"I admit that if he had lived I probably shouldn't have done it," said Nick. "I dare say I should have deferred to his prejudices, even if I thought them narrow."

"Do you turn against your father?" Mr. Carteret asked, making, to disengage his arm from the young man's touch, an effort in which Nick recognized the irritation of conscious weakness. Nick got up, at this, and stood a moment looking down at him, while Mr. Carteret went on: "Do you give up your name, do you give up your country?"

"If I do something good my country may like it," Nick contended.

"Do you regard them as equal, the two glories?"

"Here comes your nurse, to blow me up and turn me out," said Nick.

The nurse had come in, but Mr. Carteret managed to direct to her an audible, dry, courteous "Be so good as to wait till I send for you," which arrested her, in the large room, at some distance from the bed, and then had the effect of making her turn on her heel with a professional laugh. She appeared to think that an old gentleman with the fine manner of his prime might still be trusted to take care of himself. When she had gone Mr. Carteret went on, addressing Nick, with the inquiry for which his deep displeasure lent him strength: "Do you pretend there is a nobler life than a high political career?"

"I think the noble life is doing one's work well. One can do it very ill and be very base and mean in what you call a high political career. I haven't been in the House so many months without finding that out. It contains some very small souls."

"You should stand against them—you should expose them!" stammered Mr. Carteret.

"Stand against them—against one's own party?"

The old man looked bewildered a moment at this; then he broke out: "God forgive you, are you a Tory—are you a Tory?"

"How little you understand me!" laughed Nick, with a ring of bitterness.

"Little enough—little enough, my boy. Have you sent your electors your dreadful letter?"

"Not yet; but it's ready, and I sha'n't change my mind."

"You will—you will; you'll think better of it, you'll see your duty," said the old man, almost coaxingly.

"That seems very improbable, for my determination, crudely and abruptly as, to my great regret, it comes to you here, is the fruit of a long and painful struggle. The difficulty is that I see my duty just in this other effort."

"An effort? Do you call it an effort to fall away, to sink far down, to give up *every* effort? What does your mother say, heaven help her?" Mr. Carteret pursued, before Nick could answer the other question.

"I haven't told her yet."

"You're ashamed, you're ashamed!" Nick only looked out of the western window at this; he felt himself growing red. "Tell her it would have been sixty thousand; I had the money all ready."

"I sha'n't tell her that," said Nick, redder still.

"Poor woman—poor dear woman!" Mr. Carteret whimpered.

"Yes, indeed; she won't like it."

"Think it all over again; don't throw away a splendid future!" These words were uttered with a recovering flicker of passion. Nick Dormer had never heard such an accent on his old friend's lips. But the next instant Mr. Carteret began to murmur: "I'm tired—I'm very tired," and sank back with a groan and with closed lips.

Nick assured him tenderly that he had only too much cause to be exhausted, but that the worst was over now. He smoothed his pillows for him and said he must leave him, he would send in the nurse.

"Come back—come back," Mr. Carteret pleaded before he quitted him; "come back and tell me it's a horrible dream."

Nick did go back, very late that evening; Mr. Carteret had sent a message to his room. But one of the nurses was on the ground this time and she remained there with her watch in her hand. The invalid's chamber was shrouded and darkened; the shaded candle left the bed in gloom. Nick's interview with his venerable host was the affair of but a moment; the nurse interposed, impatient and not understanding. She heard Nick tell Mr. Carteret that he had posted his letter now, and Mr. Carteret flashed out, with an acerbity which savoured still of the sordid associations of a world he had not done with: "Then of course my settlement doesn't take effect!"

"Oh, that's all right," Nick answered, kindly; and he went off the next morning by the early train—his injured host was still sleeping. Mrs. Lendon's habits made it easy for her to be present in matutinal bloom at the young man's hasty breakfast, and she sent a particular remembrance to Lady Agnes and (when Nick should see them) to the Ladies Flora and Elizabeth. Nick had a prevision of the spirit in which his mother at least would now receive hollow compliments from Beauclere.

The night before, as soon as he had quitted Mr. Carteret, the old man said to the nurse that he wished her to tell Mr. Chayter that, the first thing in the morning, he must go and fetch Mr. Mitton. Mr. Mitton was the first solicitor at Beauclere.

II.

THE REALLY formidable thing for Nick was to tell his mother: a truth of which he was so conscious that he had the matter out with her the very morning he returned from Beauclere. She and Grace had come back the afternoon before from Lady St. Dunstans', and knowing this (she had written him her intention from the country), he drove straight from the station to Calcutta Gardens. There was a little room there, on the right of the house-door, which was known as his own room, but in which of a morning, when he was not at home, Lady Agnes sometimes wrote her letters. These were always numerous, and when she heard our young man's cab she happened to be engaged with them at the big brass-mounted bureau which had belonged to his father, where, behind an embankment of works of political reference, she seemed to herself to make public affairs feel the point of her elbow.

She came into the hall to meet her son and to hear about Mr. Carteret, and Nick went straight back into the room with her and closed the door. It would be in the evening paper and she would see it, and he had no right to allow her to wait for that. It proved indeed a terrible hour; and when, ten minutes later, Grace, who learned up-stairs that her brother had come back, went down for further news of him she heard from the hall a sound of voices which made her first pause and then retrace her steps on tiptoe. She mounted to the drawing-room and crept about there, palpitating, looking at moments into the dull street and wondering what on earth was going on. She had no one to express her wonder to, for Florence Tressilian had departed and Biddy, after breakfast, had betaken herself, in accordance with a custom now inveterate, to Rosedale Road. Her mother was crying passionately—a circumstance tremendous in its significance, for Lady Agnes had not often been brought so low. Nick had seen her cry, but this almost awful spectacle had seldom been given to Grace; and it forced her to believe at present that some dreadful thing had happened.

That was of course in order, after Nick's mysterious quarrel with Julia, which had made his mother so ill and which now apparently had been followed up with new horrors. The row, as Grace mentally phrased it, had had something to do with this incident, some deeper depth of disappointment had opened up. Grace asked herself if they were talking about Broadwood; if Nick had demanded that, in the conditions so unpleasantly altered, Lady Agnes should restore that pretty property to its owner. This was very possible, but why should he so suddenly have broken out about it? And moreover their mother, though sore to bleeding about the whole business—for Broadwood, in its fresh comfort, was too delightful—would not have met this pretension with tears, inasmuch as she had already declared that they couldn't decently continue to make use of the place. Julia had said of course they must go on, but Lady Agnes was prepared with an effective rejoinder to this. It didn't consist of words—it was to be austerely practical, was to consist of letting Julia see, at the moment she should least expect it, that they quite wouldn't go on. Lady Agnes was ostensibly waiting for that moment—the moment when her renunciation would be most impressive.

Grace was conscious of how, for many days, her mother and she had been moving in darkness, deeply stricken by Nick's culpable (oh, he was culpable!) loss of his prize, but feeling there was an element in the matter they didn't grasp, an undiscovered explanation which would perhaps make it still worse, though it might make *them* a little better. Nick had explained nothing; he had simply said: "Dear mother, we don't hit it off, after all; it's an awful bore, but we don't," as if that were, under the circumstances, an adequate balm for two aching hearts. From Julia, naturally, satisfying attenuations were not to be looked for; and though Julia very often did the thing you wouldn't suppose she was not unexpectedly apologetic in this case. Grace recognized that in such a position it would savour of apology for her to impart to Lady Agnes her grounds for letting Nick off; and she would not have liked to be the person to suggest to Julia that any one looked for anything from her. Neither of the disunited pair blamed the other or cast an aspersion, and it was all very magnanimous and superior and impenetrable and exasperating. With all this Grace had a suspicion that

Biddy knew something more, that for Biddy the tormenting curtain had been lifted.

Biddy came and went in these days with a perceptible air of detachment from the tribulations of home. It made her fortunately very pretty — still prettier than usual; it sometimes happened that at moments when Grace was most angry she had a faint, sweet smile which might have been drawn from a source of private consolation. It was perhaps in some degree connected with Peter Sherringham's visit, as to which the girl was not silent. When Grace asked her if she had secret information and if it pointed to the idea that everything would be all right in the end, she pretended to know nothing (What should she know? she asked, with the loveliest candour), and begged her sister not to let Lady Agnes believe that she was any better off than they. She contributed nothing to their gropings toward the light save a better patience than theirs, but she went with noticeable regularity, on the pretext of her foolish modelling, to Rosedale Road. She was frankly on Nick's side; not going so far as to say he had been right, but saying distinctly that she was sure that, whatever had happened, he couldn't help it. This was striking, because, as Grace knew, the younger of the sisters had been much favoured by Julia and would not have sacrificed her easily. It associated itself in the irritated mind of the elder with Biddy's frequent visits to the studio and made Miss Dormer ask herself whether the crisis in Nick's and Julia's business had not somehow been linked to that unnatural spot.

She had gone there two or three times while Biddy was working, to pick up any clue to the mystery that might peep out. But she had put her hand upon nothing, save once on the personality of Gabriel Nash. She found this strange creature, to her surprise, paying a visit to her sister — he had come for Nick, who was absent: she remembered how they had met him in Paris and how he had frightened her. When she asked Biddy afterwards how she could receive him that way Biddy replied that even she, Grace, would have some charity for him if she could hear how fond he was of poor Nick. He talked to her only of Nick — of nothing else. Grace observed how she spoke of Nick as injured, and noted the implication that some one else had ceased to be fond of him and was thereby condemned in Biddy's eyes. It seemed to Grace that some one else had at least a right not to like some of his friends. The studio struck her as mean and horrid; and so far from suggesting to her that it could have played a part in making Nick and Julia fall out, she only felt how little its dusty want of consequence could count one way or the other for Julia. Grace, who had opinions on art, saw no merit whatever in those "impressions" on canvas, from Nick's hand, with which the place was bestrewn. She didn't wish her brother to have talent in that direction; yet it was secretly humiliating to her that he had not more.

Nick felt a pang of almost horrified penitence, in the little room on the right of the hall, the moment after he had made his mother really understand that he had thrown up his seat and it would probably be in the evening papers. That she would take it badly was an idea that had pressed upon him hard enough; but she took it even worse than he had feared. He measured, in the look that she gave him when the full truth loomed upon her, the mortal cruelty of her discomfiture: her face was like that of a passenger on a ship who sees the huge bows of another vessel towering close out of the fog. There are visions of dismay before which the best conscience recoils; and though Nick had made his choice on all the grounds there were a few minutes in which he would gladly have admitted that his wisdom was a dark mistake. His heart was in his throat, he had gone too far; he had been ready to disappoint his mother—he had not been ready to destroy her.

Lady Agnes, I hasten to add, was not destroyed; she made, after her first drowning gasp, a tremendous scene of opposition, in the face of which Nick speedily fell back upon his intrenchments. She must know the worst, he had thought; so he told her everything, including the little story of the forfeiture of his "expectations" from Mr. Carteret. He showed her this time not only the face of the matter but what lay below it; narrated briefly the incident in his studio which had led to Julia Dallow's deciding that she couldn't after all put up with him. This was wholly new to Lady Agnes; she had had no clue to it, and he could instantly see how it made the case worse for her, adding a hideous positive to an abominable negative. He perceived now that, distressed and distracted as she had been by his rupture with Julia, she had still held to the faith that their engagement would come on again; believing evidently that he had a personal empire over the mistress of Harsh which would bring her back. Lady Agnes was forced to recognize that empire as precarious, to forswear the hope of a blessed renewal, from the moment it was a question of base infatuations on his own part. Nick confessed to an infatuation but did his best to show her it was not base; that it was not (since Julia had had faith in his loyalty) for the person of the young lady who had been discovered posturing to him and whom he had seen but half a dozen times in his life. He endeavoured to give his mother a notion of who this young lady was and to remind her of the occasion, in Paris, when they all had seen her together. But Lady Agnes's mind and memory were a blank on the subject of Miss Miriam Rooth, and she wanted to know nothing whatever about her: it was enough that she was the cause of their ruin, that she was mixed up with his unspeakable folly. Her ladyship needed to know nothing of Miss Rooth to allude to her as if it were superfluous to give a definite name to the class to which she belonged.

But she gave a name to the group in which Nick had now taken his place, and it made him feel, after the lapse of years, like a small blamed, sorry boy again; for it was so far away he could scarcely remember it (besides there having been but a moment or two of that sort in his happy childhood), the time when his mother had slapped him and called him a little fool. He was a big fool now—a huge, immeasurable one; she repeated the term over and over, with high-pitched passion. The most painful thing in this painful hour was perhaps his glimpse of the strange feminine cynicism that lurked in her fine sense of injury. Where there was such a complexity of revolt it would have been difficult to pick out particular complaints; but Nick could see that to Lady Agnes's imagination he was most a fool for not having kept his relations with the actress, whatever they were, better from Julia's knowledge. He remained indeed freshly surprised at the ardour with which she had rested her hopes on Julia. Julia was certainly a combination—she was fascinating, she was a sort of leading woman and she was rich; but after all (putting aside what she might be to a man in love with her), she was not the keystone of the universe. Yet the form in which the consequences of his apostasy appeared most to come home to Lady Agnes was the loss, for the Dormer family, of the advantages attached to the possession of Mrs. Dallow. The larger mortification would round itself later; for the hour the damning thing was that Nick had really made Julia a present of an unforgivable grievance. He had clinched their separation by his letter to his electors; and that above all was the wickedness of the letter. Julia would have got over the other woman, but she would never get over his becoming a nobody.

Lady Agnes challenged him upon this low prospect exactly as if he had embraced it with the malignant purpose of making Julia's return impossible. She contradicted her premises and lost her way in her wrath. What had made him suddenly turn round if he had been in good faith before? He had never been in good faith — never, never; he had had from his earliest childhood the nastiest hankerings after a vulgar little daubing, trash-talking life; they were not in him, the grander, nobler aspirations — they never had been — and he had been anything but honest to lead her on, to lead them all on, to think he would do something: the fall and the shame would have been less for them if they had come earlier. Moreover, what need under heaven had he to tell Charles Carteret of his cruel folly on his very death-bed? — as if he mightn't have let it all alone and accepted the benefit the old man was so delighted to confer. No wonder the old man would keep his money for his heirs, if that was the way Nick proposed to repay him; but where was the common sense, where was the common charity, where was the common decency, of tormenting him with such vile news in his last hours? Was he trying what he could invent that would break her heart, that would send her in sorrow down to her grave? Weren't they all miserable enough, and hadn't he a ray of pity for his wretched sisters?

The relation of effect and cause, in regard to his sisters' wretchedness, was but dimly discernible to Nick, who however easily perceived that his mother genuinely considered that his action had disconnected them all, still more than she

held they were already disconnected, from the good things of
life. Julia was money, Mr. Carteret was money, and everything else was poverty. If these precious people had been primarily money for Nick, it was after all a gracious tribute to
his distributive power to have taken for granted that for the
rest of the family too the difference would have been so great.
For days, for weeks and months afterward the little room on
the right of the hall seemed to our young man to vibrate, as if
the very walls and window-panes still suffered, with the most
disagreeable ordeal he had ever been through.

III.

THAT EVENING—the evening of his return from Beauclere—Nick was conscious of a keen desire to get away,
to go abroad, to leave behind him the little chatter his resignation would be sure to produce in an age of publicity which
never discriminated as to the quality of events. Then he felt it
was better to stay, to see the business through on the spot.
Besides, he would have to meet his constituents (would a
parcel of cheese-eating burgesses ever have been "met" on so
queer an occasion?) and when that was over the worst would
be over. Nick had an idea that he knew in advance how it
would feel to be pointed at as a person who had given up a
considerable chance of eventual "office" to take likenesses at
so much a head. He wouldn't attempt, down at Harsh, to
touch on the question of motive; for, given the nature of the
public mind of Harsh, that would be a strain on his faculty of
expression. But as regards the chaff of the political world and
of society he had an idea he should find chaff enough for
answers. It was true that when his mother chaffed him in her
own effective way he had felt rather flattened out; but then
one's mother might have a heavier hand than any one else.

He had not thrown up the House of Commons to amuse
himself; he had thrown it up to work, to sit quietly down and
bend over his task. If he should go abroad his mother might
think he had some weak-minded view of joining Julia Dallow
and trying, with however little hope, to win her back—an
illusion it would be singularly pernicious to encourage. His
desire for Julia's society had succumbed, for the present at any
rate, to an irresistible interruption—he had become more and
more conscious that they spoke a different language. Nick felt
like a young man who has gone to the Rhineland to "get up"
his German for an examination—committed to talk, to read,
to dream only in the new idiom. Now that he had taken his
jump everything was simplified, at the same time that everything was pitched in a higher, more excited key; and he
wondered how in the absence of a common dialect he had
conversed on the whole so happily with Julia. Then he had
after-tastes of understandings tolerably independent of words.

He was excited because every fresh responsibility is exciting, and there was no manner of doubt that he had accepted one. No one knew what it was but himself (Gabriel Nash scarcely counted—his whole attitude on the question of responsibility was so wanton), and he would have to ask his dearest friends to take him on trust. Rather, he would ask nothing of any one, but would cultivate independence, mulishness and gaiety and fix his thoughts on a bright if distant morrow. It was disagreeable to have to remember that his task would not be sweetened by a sense of heroism; for if it might be heroic to give up the muses for the strife of great affairs, no romantic glamour worth speaking of would ever gather round an Englishman who in the prime of his strength had given up great or even small affairs for the muses. Such an original might himself privately, perversely regard certain phases of this inferior commerce as a great affair; but who would give him the benefit of that sort of confidence—except indeed a faithful, clever, excited little sister Biddy, if he should have the good luck to have one? Biddy was in fact all ready for heroic flights and eager to think she might fight the battle of the beautiful by her brother's side; so that Nick had really to moderate her and remind her that his actual job was not a crusade, with bugles and banners, but a gray, sedentary grind, whose charm was all at the core. You might have an emotion about it, and an emotion that would be a help, but this was not the sort of thing you could show—the end in view would seem ridiculously small for it. Nick asked Biddy how one could talk to people about the "responsibility" of what she would see him pottering at in his studio.

Nick therefore didn't talk any more than he was forced to, having moreover a sense that that side of the situation would be plentifully looked after by Gabriel Nash. He left the burden of explanation to others, meeting them on the ground of inexhaustible satire. He saw that he should live for months in a thick cloud of irony, not the finest air of the season, and he adopted the weapon to which a person whose use of tobacco is only occasional resorts when every one else produces a cigar—he puffed the empirical, defensive cigarette. He accepted the idea of a mystery in his behaviour and abounded so in that sense that his critics were themselves bewildered.

Some of them felt that they got, as the phrase is, little out of him—he rose in his good-humour so much higher than the "rise" they had looked for—on his very first encounter with the world after his scrimmage with his mother. He went to a dinner-party (he had accepted the invitation many days before), having seen his resignation, in the form of a telegram from Harsh, announced in the evening papers. The people he found there had seen it as well, and the most imaginative of them wanted to know what he was going to do. Even the least imaginative asked if it were true he had changed his politics. He gave different answers to different persons, but left most of them under the impression that he had remarkable conscientious scruples. This however was not a formidable occasion, for there happened to be no one present he was particularly fond of. There were old friends whom it would not be so easy to satisfy—Nick was almost sorry, for an hour, that he had so many old friends. If he had had more enemies the case would have been simpler; and he was fully aware that the hardest thing of all would be to be let off too easily. Then he would appear to himself to have been put on his generosity, and his deviation would wear its ugliest face.

When he left the place at which he had been dining he betook himself to Rosedale Road: he saw no reason why he should go down to the House, though he knew he had not done with that yet. He had a dread of behaving as if he supposed he should be expected to make a farewell speech, and was thankful his eminence was not of a nature to create on such an occasion a demand for his oratory. He had in fact nothing whatever to say in public—not a word, not a syllable. Though the hour was late he found Gabriel Nash established in his studio, drawn thither by the fine exhilaration of having seen an evening paper. Trying it late, on the chance, he had been told by Nick's servant that Nick would sleep there that night, and he had come in to wait, he was so eager to congratulate him. Nick submitted with a good grace to his society—he was tired enough to go to bed, but he was restless too—in spite of feeling now, oddly enough, that Nash's congratulations could add little to his fortitude. He had felt a good deal, before, as if he were in Nash's hands; but now that he had made his final choice he seemed to himself to be altogether in his own. Gabriel was wonderful, but no Gabriel could assist him much henceforth.

Gabriel was indeed more wonderful than ever, while he lolled on a divan and emitted a series of reflections which were even more ingenious than opportune. Nick walked up and down the room, and it might have been supposed from his manner that he was impatient for his visitor to withdraw. This idea would have been contradicted however by the fact that subsequently, after Nash had taken leave, he continued to perambulate. He had grown used to Nash—had a sense that he had heard all he had to say. That was one's penalty with persons whose main gift was for talk, however irrigating; talk engendered a sense of sameness much sooner than action. The things a man did were necessarily more different from each other than the things he said, even if he went in for surprising you. Nick felt Nash could never surprise him any more save by doing something.

He talked of his host's future, he talked of Miriam Rooth and of Peter Sherringham, whom he had seen at Miriam Rooth's and whom he described as in a predicament delightful to behold. Nick asked a question or two about Peter's predicament and learned rather to his disappointment that it consisted only of the fact that he was in love with Miriam. He requested his visitor to do better than this; whereupon Nash added the touch that Sherringham wouldn't be able to have her. "Oh, they have ideas!" he said, when Nick asked him why.

"What ideas? So has he, I suppose."

"Yes, but they're not the same."

"Oh well, they'll arrange something," said Nick.

"You'll have to help them a bit. She's in love with another man," Nash returned.

"Do you mean with you?"

"Oh, I'm never another man," said Nash; "I'm more the wrong one than the man himself. It's you she's after." And upon Nick's asking him what he meant by this he added: "While you were engaged in transferring her image to your sensorium you stamped your own upon hers."

Nick stopped in his walk, staring. "Ah, what a bore!"

"A bore? Don't you think she's agreeable?"

Nick hesitated. "I wanted to go on with her—now I can't."

"My dear fellow, it only makes her handsomer: I wondered what was the matter with her."

"Oh, that's twaddle," said Nick, turning away. "Besides, has she told you?"

"No, but her mother has."

"Has she told her mother?"

"Mrs. Rooth says not. But I have known Mrs. Rooth to say that which isn't."

"Apply that rule then to the information you speak of."

"Well, since you press me, I know more," said Nash. "Miriam knows you are engaged to a certain lady; she told me as much, told me she had seen her here. That was enough to set Miriam off—she likes forbidden fruit."

"I'm not engaged to any lady. I was, but we've altered our minds."

"Ah, what a pity!" sighed Nash.

"Mephistopheles!" Nick rejoined, stopping again and looking at his visitor gravely.

"Pray, whom do you call Margaret? May I ask if your failure of interest in the political situation is the cause of this change in your personal one?" Nash went on. Nick signified to him that he might not; whereupon Gabriel added: "I am not in the least devilish—I only mean it's a pity you've altered your minds, because now perhaps Miriam will alter hers. She goes from one thing to another. However, I won't tell her."

"I will, then," said Nick, between jest and earnest.

"Would that really be prudent?" Nash asked, with an intonation that made hilarity prevail.

"At any rate," Nick resumed, "nothing would induce me to interfere with Peter Sherringham. That sounds fatuous, but to you I don't mind appearing an ass."

"The thing would be to get Sherringham—out of spite—to entangle himself with another woman."

"What good would that do?"

"Oh, Miriam would begin to fancy him then."

"Spite surely isn't a conceivable motive—for a healthy man."

"Ah, Sherringham isn't a healthy man. He's too much in love."

"Then he won't care for another woman."

"He would try to, and that would produce its effect—its effect on Miriam."

"You talk like an American novel. Let him try, and God keep us all straight." Nick thought, in extreme silence, of his poor little Biddy and hoped—he would have to see to it a little—that Peter wouldn't "try" on her. He changed the subject and before Nash went away took occasion to remark to him—the occasion was offered by some new allusion of the visitor's to the sport he hoped to extract from seeing Nick carry out everything to which he stood committed—that the great comedy would fall very flat, the great incident would pass unnoticed.

"Oh, if you'll simply do your part I'll take care of the rest," said Nash.

"If you mean by doing my part working like a beaver, it's all right," Nick replied.

"Ah, you reprobate, you'll become a fashionable painter, a P. R. A.!" his companion groaned, getting up to go.

When he had gone Nick threw himself back on the cushions of the divan and, with his hands locked above his head, sat a long time lost in thought. He had sent his servant to bed; he was unmolested. He gazed before him into the gloom produced by the unheeded burning out of the last candle. The vague outer light came in through the tall studio window, and the painted images, ranged about, looked confused in the dusk. If his mother had seen him she might have thought he was staring at his father's ghost.

IV.

THE NIGHT Peter Sherringham walked away from Bala-klava Place with Gabriel Nash the talk of the two men directed itself, as was natural under the circumstances, to the question of Miriam's future renown and the pace, as Nash called it, at which she would go. Critical spirits as they both were, and one of them as dissimulative in passion as the other was paradoxical in the absence of it, they yet took this renown for granted as completely as the simple-minded, a pair of hot spectators in the pit, might have done, and exchanged observations on the assumption that the only uncertain element would be the pace. This was a proof of general subjugation. Peter wished not to show, but he wished to know; and in the restlessness of his anxiety he was ready even to risk exposure, great as the sacrifice might be of the imperturbable, urbane scepticism most appropriate to a secretary of embassy. He was unable to rid himself of the sense that Gabriel Nash had got up earlier than he, had had opportunities in days already distant, the days of Mrs. Rooth's hungry foreign rambles. Something of authority and privilege stuck to him from this, and it made Sherringham still more uncomfortable when he was most conscious that at the best even the trained diplomatic mind would never get a grasp of Miriam as a whole. She was constructed to revolve like the terrestrial globe; some part or other of her was always out of sight or in shadow.

Sherringham talked to conceal his feelings and, like every man doing a thing from that sort of intention, did it perhaps too much. They agreed that, putting strange accidents aside, Miriam would go further than any one had gone, in England at least and within the memory of man; and that it was a pity, as regards marking the comparison, that for so long no one had gone any distance worth speaking of. They further agreed that it would naturally seem absurd to any one who didn't know, their prophesying such big things on such small evidence; and they agreed lastly that the absurdity quite vanished as soon as the prophets knew as *they* knew. Their knowledge (they quite recognized this) was simply confidence raised to a high point—the communication of the girl's own confidence.

The conditions were enormously to make, but it was of the very essence of Miriam's confidence that she would make them. The parts, the plays, the theatres, the "support," the audiences, the critics, the money were all to be found, but she cast a spell which prevented that from seeming a serious hitch. One might not see from one day to the other what she would do or how she would do it, but she would none the less go on. She would have to construct her own road, as it were, but at the worst there would only be delays in making it. These delays would depend on the hardness of the stones she had to break.

As Sherringham had perceived, you never knew where to "have" Gabriel Nash; a truth exemplified in his unexpected delight at the prospect of Miriam's drawing forth the modernness of the age. You might have thought he would loathe that modernness; but he had a brilliant, amused, amusing vision of it, saw it as something huge and ornamentally vulgar. Its vulgarity would rise to the grand style, like that of a London railway station, and Miriam's publicity would be as big as the globe itself. All the machinery was ready, the platform laid; the facilities, the wires and bells and trumpets, the colossal, deafening newspaperism of the period—its most distinctive sign—were waiting for her, their predestined mistress, to press her foot on the spring and set them all in motion. Gabriel brushed in a large bright picture of her progress through the time and round the world, round it and round it again, from continent to continent and clime to clime; with populations and deputations, reporters and photographers, placards and interviews and banquets, steamers, railways, dollars, diamonds, speeches and artistic ruin all jumbled into her train. Regardless of expense the spectacle would be and thrilling, though somewhat monotonous, the drama—a drama more bustling than any she would put on the stage and a spectacle that would beat everything for scenery. In the end her divine voice would crack, screaming to foreign ears and antipodal barbarians, and her clever manner would lose all quality, simplified to a few unmistakable knock-down dodges. Then she would be at the fine climax of life and glory, still young and insatiate, but already coarse, hard and raddled, with nothing left to do and nothing left to do it with, the remaining years all before her and the *raison d'être* all behind. It would be curious and magnificent and grotesque.

"Oh, she'll have some good years—they'll be worth having," Sherringham insisted, as they went. "Besides, you see her too much as a humbug and too little as a real producer. She has ideas—great ones; she loves the thing for itself. That may keep a woman serious."

"Her greatest idea must always be to show herself; and fortunately she has a splendid self to show. I think of her absolutely as a real producer, but as a producer whose production is her own person. No 'person,' even as fine a one as hers, will stand that for more than an hour, so that humbuggery has very soon to lend a hand. However," Nash continued, "if she's a fine humbug it will do as well, and perfectly suit the time. We can all be saved by vulgarity; that's the solvent of all difficulties and the blessing of this delightful age. Let no man despair; a new hope has dawned."

"She'll do her work like any other worker, with the advantage over many that her talent is rare," Peter replied. "Compared with the life of many women, that's security and sanity of the highest order. Then she can't help her beauty. You can't vulgarize that."

"Oh, can't you?" exclaimed Gabriel Nash.

"It will abide with her till the day of her death. It isn't a mere superficial freshness. She's very noble."

"Yes, that's the pity of it," said Nash. "She's a capital girl, and I quite admit that she'll do for a while a lot of good. She will have brightened up the world for a great many people; she will have brought the ideal nearer to them, held it fast for an hour, with its feet on earth and its great wings trembling. That's always something, for blessed is he who has dropped even the smallest coin into the little iron box that contains the precious savings of mankind. Miriam will doubtless have dropped a big gold piece. It will be found, in the general scramble, on the day the race goes bankrupt. And then, for herself, she will have had a great go at life."

"Oh, yes, she'll have got out of her hole; she won't have vegetated," said Sherringham. "That makes her touching to me; it adds to the many good reasons for which one may want to help her. She's tackling a big job, and tackling it by herself; throwing herself upon the world, in good faith, and dealing with it as she can; meeting alone, in her youth, her beauty and her generosity all the embarrassments of notoriety and all the difficulties of a profession of which, if one half is what's called brilliant, the other half is odious."

"She has great courage, but should you speak of her as solitary, with such a lot of us all round her?" Gabriel asked.

"She's a great thing for you and me, but we're a small thing for her."

"Well, a good many small things may make up a considerable one," Nash returned. "There must always be the man; he's the indispensable element in such a life, and he'll be the last thing she'll ever want for."

"What man are you talking about?" Sherringham asked, rather confusedly.

"The man of the hour, whoever he is. She'll inspire innumerable devotions."

"Of course she will, and they will be precisely a part of the insufferable side of her life."

"Insufferable to whom?" Nash inquired. "Don't forget that the insufferable side of her life will be just the side she'll thrive on. You can't eat your cake and have it, and you can't make omelettes without breaking eggs. You can't at once sit by the fire and fly about the world, and you can't go round and round the globe without having adventures. You can't be a great actress without quivering nerves. If you haven't them you'll only be a small one. If you have them, your friends will be pretty sure to hear of them. Your nerves and your adventures, your eggs and your cake, are part of the cost of the most expensive of professions. If you do your business at all you should do it handsomely, so that the costs may run up tremendously. You play with human passions, with exaltations and ecstasies and terrors, and if you trade on the fury of the elements you must know how to ride the storm."

"Those are the fine old commonplaces about the artistic temperament, but I usually find the artist a very meek, decent little person," said Sherringham.

"You never find the artist—you only find his work, and that's all you need find. When the artist's a woman and the woman's an actress, meekness and decency will doubtless be there in the right proportions," Nash went on. "Miriam will represent them for you, if you give her her starting-point, with the utmost charm."

"Of course she'll have devotions—that's all right," said Sherringham, impatiently.

"And—don't you see?—they'll mitigate her solitude, they'll even enliven it," Nash remarked.

"She'll probably box a good many ears: that'll be lively," Peter rejoined, with some grimness.

"Oh, magnificent! it will be a merry life. Yet with its tragic passages, its distracted or its pathetic hours," Nash continued. "In short a little of everything."

The two men walked on without further speech, till at last Sherringham said: "The best thing for a woman in her situation is to marry some good fellow."

"Oh, I dare say she'll do that too!" Nash laughed; a remark in consequence of which Peter again lapsed into silence. Gabriel left him to enjoy his silence for some minutes; after which he added: "There's a good fellow she'd marry to-morrow."

Peter hesitated. "Do you mean her friend Dashwood?"

"No, no, I mean Nick Dormer."

"She'd marry him?" Sherringham asked.

"I mean her head's full of him. But she'll hardly get the chance."

"Does she like him so much as that?" Sherringham went on.

"I don't know quite how much you mean, but enough for all practical ends."

"Marrying a fashionable actress—that's hardly a practical end."

"Certainly not, but I'm not speaking from his point of view. Moreover I thought you just now said it would be such a good thing for her."

"To marry Nick Dormer?"

"You said a good fellow, and he's the very best."

"I wasn't thinking of the man, but of the marriage. It would protect her, make things safe and comfortable for her and keep a lot of cads and blackguards away."

"She ought to marry the prompter or the box-keeper," said Nash. "Then it would be all right. I think indeed they generally do, don't they?"

Sherringham felt for a moment a strong disposition to drop his companion on the spot—to cross to the other side of the street and walk away without him. But there was a different impulse which struggled with this one and, after a minute, overcame it—the impulse which led to his saying presently: "Has she told you that—that she's in love with Nick?"

"No, no—that's not the way I know it."

"Has Nick told you, then?"

"On the contrary, I've told him."

"You've rendered him a questionable service if you've no proof," said Peter.

"My proof is only that I've seen her with him. She's charming, poor thing."

"But surely she isn't in love with every man she's charming to."

"I mean she's charming to me," Nash replied. "I see her that way. But judge for yourself—the first time you get a chance."

"When shall I get a chance? Nick doesn't come near her."

"Oh, he'll come, he'll come; his picture isn't finished."

"You mean *he'll* be the box-keeper then?"

"My dear fellow, I shall never allow it," said Gabriel Nash. "It would be idiotic and quite unnecessary. He's beautifully arranged, in quite a different line. Fancy his taking that sort of job on his hands! Besides, she would never expect it; she's not such a goose. They're very good friends—it will go on that way. She's an excellent sort of woman for him to know; she'll give him lots of ideas of the plastic kind. He would have been up there before this, but he has been absorbed in this delightful squabble with his constituents. That of course is pure amusement; but when once it's well launched he'll get back to business and his business will be a very different matter from Miriam's. Imagine him writing her advertisements, living on her money, adding up her profits, having rows and recriminations with her agent, carrying her shawl, spending his days in her rouge-pot. The right man for that, if she must have one, will turn up. *'Pour le mariage, non.'* Miriam isn't an idiot; she really, for a woman, quite sees things as they are."

As Sherringham had not crossed the street and left Gabriel planted, he was obliged to brave the torment of this suggestive flow. But descrying in the dusky vista of the Edgware Road a vague and vigilant hansom, he waved his stick with eagerness and with the abrupt declaration that he was tired, must drive the rest of the way. He offered Nash, as he entered the vehicle, no seat, but this coldness was not reflected in the lucidity with which that master of every subject went on to affirm that there was, of course, a danger—the danger that in given circumstances Miriam would leave the stage.

"Leave it you mean for some man?"

"For the man we're talking about."

"For Nick Dormer?" Peter asked from his place in the cab, his paleness lighted by its lamps.

"If he should make it a condition. But why should he— why should he make *any* conditions? He's not an ass either. You see it would be a bore," Nash continued while the hansom waited, "because if she were to do anything of that sort she would make him pay for the sacrifice."

"Oh yes, she'd make him pay for the sacrifice," Sherringham repeated.

"And then, when he had paid, she'd go back to her foot-lights," Gabriel added, explicatively, from the curbstone, as Sherringham closed the apron of the cab.

"I see—she'd go back—good-night," Peter replied. "*Please* go on!" he cried to the driver through the hole in the roof. And when the vehicle rolled away he subjoined to himself: "Of course she would—and quite right!"

V.

"JUDGE FOR YOURSELF when you get a chance," Nash had said; and as it turned out Sherringham was able to judge two days later, for he found his cousin in Balaklava Place on the Tuesday following his walk with Gabriel. He had not only stayed away from the theatre on the Monday evening (he regarded this as an achievement of some importance), but had not been near Miriam during the day. He had meant to absent himself from her company on Tuesday as well; a determination confirmed by the fact that the afternoon turned out wet. But when, at ten minutes to five o'clock, he jumped into a hansom and directed its course to St. John's Wood, it was precisely upon the weather that he shifted the responsibility of his behaviour.

Miriam had dined when he reached the villa, but she was lying down—she was tired—before going to the theatre. Mrs. Rooth was however in the drawing-room with three gentlemen, in two of whom the fourth visitor was not startled to recognize Basil Dashwood and Gabriel Nash. Dashwood appeared to have become Miriam's brother-in-arms and a second child—a fonder one—to Mrs. Rooth; it had come to Sherringham's knowledge the last time he was in Balaklava Place that the young actor had finally moved his lodgings into the quarter, making himself a near neighbour for all sorts of convenience. "Hang his convenience!" Peter thought, perceiving that Mrs. Lovick's "Arty" was now altogether one of the family. Oh, the family—it was a queer one to be connected with; that consciousness was acute in Sherringham's breast to-day as he entered Mrs. Rooth's little circle. The room was filled with cigarette-smoke and there was a messy coffee-service on the piano, whose keys Basil Dashwood lightly touched for his own diversion. Nash, addressing the room, of course, was at one end of a little sofa, with his nose in the air, and Nick Dormer was at the other end, seated much at his ease, with a certain privileged appearance of having been there often before, though Sherringham knew he had not. He looked uncritical and very young, as rosy as a school-boy on a half-holiday. It was past five o'clock in the day, but Mrs. Rooth was not dressed; there was however no want of finish in her elegant attitude—the same relaxed grandeur (she seemed to let you understand) for which she used to be distinguished at Castle Nugent when the house was full. She toyed incongruously, in her unbuttoned wrapper, with a large tinsel fan which resembled a theatrical property.

It was one of the discomforts of Sherringham's situation that many of those minor matters which are, superficially at least, most characteristic of the histrionic life had power to displease him, so that he was obliged to make the effort of indulgence. He disliked besmoked drawing-rooms and irregular meals and untidy arrangements; he could suffer from the vulgarity of Mrs. Rooth's apartments, the importunate photographs (they gave on his nerves), the barbarous absence of signs of an orderly domestic life, the odd volumes from the circulating library (you could see what they were—the very covers told you—at a glance) tumbled about with cups or glasses on them. He had not waited till now to make the reflection that it was a strange thing fate should have goaded *him* into that sort of contact; but as he stood before Mrs. Rooth and her companions he made it perhaps more pointedly than ever. Her companions, somehow, who were not responsible, didn't keep him from making it; which was particularly odd, as they were not, superficially, in the least of Bohemian type. Almost the first thing that struck him, as it happened, in coming into the room, was the essential good looks of his cousin, who was a gentleman to the eye in a different degree from the high-collared Dashwood. Peter didn't hate him for being such a pleasant young Englishman; his consciousness was traversed rather by a fresh wave of annoyance at Julia's failure to get on with him on that substantial basis.

It was Sherringham's first encounter with Nick since his arrival in London: they had been, on one side and the other, so much taken up with their own affairs. Since their last meeting Nick had, as we know, to his kinsman's perception, really taken on a new character: he had done a fine stroke of business in a quiet way. This made him a figure to be counted with, and in just the sense in which Peter desired

least to count with him. Poor Sherringham, after his summersault in the blue, was much troubled these last days; he
was ravaged by contending passions; he paid, every hour, in
a torment of unrest, for what was false in his position, the
impossibility of being consistent, the opposition of interest
and desire. Nick, his junior and a lighter weight, had settled
his problem and showed no wounds: there was something
impertinent and mystifying in it. He looked too innocently
young and happy there, and too careless and modest and
amateurish for a rival or for the genius that he was apparently going to try to be—the genius that, the other day in
the studio with Biddy, Peter had got a startled glimpse of his
capacity for being. Sherringham would have liked to feel
that he had grounds of resentment, that Julia had been badly
treated or that Nick was fatuous, for in that case he might
have regarded him as offensive. But where was the offence
of his merely being liked by a woman in respect to whom
Peter had definitely denied himself the luxury of pretensions,
especially if the offender had taken no action in the matter?
It could scarcely be called culpable action to call, casually, on
an afternoon when the lady was invisible. Peter, at any rate,
was distinctly glad Miriam was invisible; and he proposed to
himself to suggest to Nick after a little that they should
adjourn together—they had such interesting things to talk
about. Meanwhile Nick greeted him with candid tones and
pleasant eyes, in which he could read neither confusion nor
defiance. Sherringham was reassured against a danger he believed he didn't recognize and puzzled by a mystery he flattered himself he didn't mind. And he was still more ashamed
of being reassured than of being puzzled.

It must be recorded that Miriam remained invisible only a
few minutes longer. Nick, as Sherringham gathered, had
been about a quarter of an hour in the house, which would
have given the girl, aroused from her repose, about time to
array herself to come down to him. At all events she was in
the room, prepared apparently to go to the theatre, very
shortly after Sherringham had become sensible of how glad
he was she was out of it. Familiarity had never yet cured
him of a certain tremor of expectation and even of suspense
in regard to her entrances; a flutter caused by the simple

circumstance of her infinite variety. To say she was always acting suggests too much that she was often fatiguing; for her changing face affected this particular admirer at least not as a series of masks, but as a response to perceived differences, an intensity of sensibility, or still more as something cleverly constructive, like the shifting of the scene in a play or a room with many windows. Her incarnations were incalculable, but if her present denied her past and declined responsibility for her future, it made a good thing of the hour and kept the actual very actual. This time the actual was a bright, gentle, graceful, smiling young woman in a new dress, eager to go out, drawing on fresh gloves, who looked as if she were about to step into a carriage and (it was Gabriel Nash who thus formulated her physiognomy) do a lot of London things.

The young woman had time to spare however, and she sat down and talked and laughed and presently gave, as it seemed to Sherringham, a finer character to the tawdry little room. It was honourable enough if it belonged to her. She described herself as in a state of nervous bewilderment—exhausted, stupefied, blinded with the rehearsals of the forthcoming piece (the first night was close at hand and it was going to be *d'un mauvais*—they would all see!), but there was no correspondence between this account of the matter and her present kindly gaiety. She sent her mother away—to "put on some clothes or something"—and, left alone with the visitors, went to a long glass between the windows, talking always to Nick Dormer, and revised and rearranged a little her own attire. She talked to Nick over her shoulder, and to Nick only, as if he were the guest to recognize and the others didn't count. She broke out immediately about his having thrown up his seat, wished to know if the strange story told her by Mr. Nash were true—that he had knocked all the hopes of his party into pie.

Nick took it in this way and gave a jocular picture of his party's ruin, the critical condition of public affairs: evidently as yet he remained inaccessible to shame or repentance. Sherringham, before Miriam's entrance, had not, in shaking hands with Nick, made even a roundabout allusion to his odd "game:" there seemed a sort of muddled good taste in being silent about it. He winced a little on seeing how his scruples had been wasted, and was struck with the fine, jocose, direct turn of his kinsman's conversation with the young actress. It was a part of her unexpectedness that she took the heavy literal view of Nick's behaviour; declared frankly, though without ill-nature, that she had no patience with his folly. She was horribly disappointed—she had set her heart on his being a great statesman, one of the rulers of the people and the glories of England. What was so useful, what was so noble?—how it belittled everything else! She had expected him to wear a cordon and a star some day (and to get them very soon), and to come and see her in her *loge*: it would look so well. She talked like a lovely Philistine, except perhaps when she expressed surprise at hearing—she heard it from Gabriel Nash—that in England gentlemen accoutred with those emblems of their sovereign's esteem didn't so far forget themselves as to stray into the dressing-rooms of actresses. She admitted, after a moment, that they were quite right—the dressing-rooms of actresses were nasty places; but she was sorry, for that was the sort of thing she had always figured, in a corner—a distinguished man, slightly bald, in evening dress, with orders, admiring the smallness of a satin shoe and saying witty things. Gabriel Nash was convulsed with hilarity at this—such a vision of the British political hero. Coming back from the glass and making him give her his place on the sofa, she seated herself near Nick and continued to express her regret at his perversity.

"They all say that—all the charming women, but I shouldn't have looked for it from you," Nick replied. "I've given you such an example of what I can do in another line."

"Do you mean my portrait? Oh, I've got it, with your name and 'M.P.' in the corner, and that's precisely why I'm content. 'M.P.' in the corner of a picture is delightful, but I want to break the mould: I don't in the least insist on your giving specimens to others. And the artistic life, when you can lead another—if you have any alternative, however modest—is a very poor business. It comes last in dignity—after everything else. Ain't I up to my eyes in it and don't I know?"

"You talk like my broken-hearted mother," said Nick.

"Does she hate it so intensely?"

"She has the darkest ideas about it—the wildest theories. I can't imagine where she gets them; partly, I think, from a general conviction that the 'æsthetic'—a horrible insidious foreign disease—is eating the healthy core out of English life (dear old English life!) and partly from the charming drawings in *Punch* and the clever satirical articles, pointing at mysterious depths of contamination, in the other weekly papers. She believes there's a dreadful coterie of uncannily clever and desperately refined people, who wear a kind of loose, faded uniform and worship only beauty—which is a fearful thing—that Nash has introduced me to it, that I now spend all my time in it, and that for its sweet sake I have repudiated the most sacred engagements. Poor Nash, who, so far as I can make out, isn't in any sort of society, however bad!"

"But I'm uncannily clever," Nash interposed, "and though I can't afford the uniform (I believe you get it best somewhere in South Audley Street), I do worship beauty. I really think it's me the weekly paper means."

"Oh, I've read the articles—I know the sort!" said Basil Dashwood.

Miriam looked at him. "Go and see if the brougham's there—I ordered it early."

Dashwood, without moving, consulted his watch. "It isn't time yet—I know more about the brougham than you. I've made a rattling good arrangement for her—it really costs her nothing," the young actor continued confidentially to Sherringham, near whom he had placed himself.

"Your mother's quite right to be broken-hearted," Miriam declared, "and I can imagine exactly what she has been through. I should like to talk with her—I should like to see her." Nick broke into ringing laughter, reminding her that she had talked to him, while she sat for her portrait, in directly the opposite sense, most suggestively and inspiringly; and Nash explained that she was studying the part of a political duchess and wished to take observations for it, to work herself into the character. Miriam might in fact have been a political duchess as she sat with her head erect and her gloved hands folded, smiling with aristocratic dimness at Nick. She shook her head with stately sadness; she might have been representing Mary Stuart in Schiller's play. "I've changed since that. I want you to be the grandest thing there is—the counsellor of kings."

Peter Sherringham wondered if possibly it were not since she had met his sister in Nick's studio that she had changed, if perhaps it had not occurred to her that it would give Julia the sense of being more effectually routed to know that the woman who had thrown the bomb was one who also tried to keep Nick in the straight path. This indeed would involve an assumption that Julia might know, whereas it was perfectly possible that she mightn't and more than possible that if she should she wouldn't care. Miriam's essential fondness for trying different ways was always there as an adequate reason for any particular way; a truth which however sometimes only half prevented the particular way from being vexatious to Sherringham.

"Yet after all who is more æsthetic than you and who goes in more for the beautiful?" Nick asked. "You're never so beautiful as when you pitch into it."

"Oh, I'm an inferior creature, of an inferior sex, and I have to earn my bread as I can. I'd give it all up in a moment, my odious trade—for an inducement."

"And pray what do you mean by an inducement?" Nick demanded.

"My dear fellow, she means you—if you'll give her a permanent engagement to sit for you!" exclaimed Gabriel Nash. "What crude questions you ask!"

"I like the way she talks," Basil Dashwood broke in, "when I gave up the most brilliant prospects, of very much the same kind as Mr. Dormer's, expressly to go on the stage."

"You're an inferior creature too," said Miriam.

"Miss Rooth is very hard to satisfy," Sherringham observed. "A man of distinction, slightly bald, in evening dress, with orders, in the corner of her *loge*—she has such a personage ready made to her hand and she doesn't so much as look at him. Am I not an inducement? Have I not offered you a permanent engagement?"

"Your orders—where are your orders?" Miriam inquired with a sweet smile, getting up.

"I shall be a minister next year and an ambassador before you know it. Then I shall stick on everything that can be had."

"And they call *us* mountebanks!" cried the girl. "I've been so glad to see you again—do you want another sitting?" she went on, to Nick, as if to take leave of him.

"As many as you'll give me—I shall be grateful for all," Nick answered. "I should like to do you as you are at present. You're totally different from the woman I painted—you're wonderful."

"The Comic Muse!" laughed Miriam. "Well, you must wait till our first nights are over—I'm *sur les dents* till then. There's everything to do, and I have to do it all. That fellow's good for nothing—for nothing but domestic life," and she glanced at Basil Dashwood. "He hasn't an idea—not one that you'd willingly tell of him, though he's rather useful for the stables. We've got stables now—or we try to look as if we had: Dashwood's ideas are *de cette force*. In ten days I shall have more time."

"The Comic Muse? Never, never," Sherringham protested. "You're not to go smirking through the age and down to posterity—I'd rather see you as Medusa crowned with serpents. That's what you look like when you look best."

"That's consoling—when I've just bought a new bonnet! I forgot to tell you just now that when you're an ambassador you may propose anything you like," Miriam went on. "But excuse me if I make that condition. Seriously speaking, come to me glittering with orders and I shall probably succumb. I can't resist stars and garters. Only you must, as you say, have them all. I *don't* like to hear Mr. Dormer talk the slang of the studio—like that phrase just now: it *is* a fall to a lower state. However, when one is low one must crawl, and I'm crawling down to the Strand. Dashwood, see if mamma's ready. If she isn't I decline to wait; you must bring her in a hansom. I'll take Mr. Dormer in the brougham; I want to talk with Mr. Dormer; he must drive with me to the theatre. His situation is full of interest." Miriam led the way out of the room as she continued to chatter, and when she reached the house-door, with the four men in her train, the carriage had just drawn up at the garden-gate. It appeared that Mrs. Rooth was not ready, and the girl, in spite of a remonstrance from Nick, who had the sense of usurping the old lady's place, repeated her injunction that she should be brought on in a cab. Miriam's companions accompanied her to the gate, and she insisted upon Nick's taking his seat in the brougham and taking it first. Before she entered she put out her hand to Sherringham and, looking up at him, held his own kindly. "Dear old master, aren't you coming to-night? I miss you when you're not there."

"Don't go—don't go—it's too much," Nash interposed.

"She *is* wonderful," said Basil Dashwood, regarding her admiringly; "she *has* gone into the rehearsals, tooth and nail. But nothing takes it out of her."

"Nothing puts it into you, my dear!" Miriam returned. Then she went on, to Sherringham: "You're the faithful one—you're the one I count on." He was not looking at her; his eyes travelled into the carriage, where they rested on Nick Dormer, established on the further seat with his face turned toward the further window. He was the one, faithful or no, counted on or no, whom a charming woman had preferred to carry off, and there was a certain triumph for him in that fact; but it pleased Sherringham to imagine that his attitude was a little foolish. Miriam discovered something of this sort in Sherringham's eyes; for she exclaimed abruptly: "Don't kill him—he doesn't care for me!" With this she passed into the carriage, which rolled away.

Sherringham stood watching it a moment, till he heard Basil Dashwood again beside him. "You wouldn't believe what I made him do it for—a little fellow I know."

"Good-bye; take good care of Mrs. Rooth," said Gabriel Nash, waving a cheerful farewell to the young actor. He gave a smiling survey of the heavens and remarked to Sherringham that the rain had stopped. Was he walking, was he driving, should they be going in the same direction? Sherringham cared little about his direction and had little account of it to give; he simply moved away in silence, with Gabriel at his side. Gabriel was partly an affliction to him; indeed the fact that he had assumed a baleful fascination made him only a deeper affliction. Sherringham moreover did him the justice to observe that he could hold his peace occasionally: he had for instance this afternoon taken little part in the conversation in Balaklava Place. Peter greatly disliked to talk to him of Miriam, but he liked Nash to talk of her and he even liked him to say such things as he might contradict. He was not however moved to contradict an assertion dropped by his companion, disconnectedly, at the end of a few minutes, to the effect that she was after all the most good-natured creature alive. All the same, Nash added, it wouldn't do for her to take possession of an organization like Nick's; and he repeated that for his part he would never allow it. It would be on his conscience to interfere. To which Sherringham replied disingenuously that they might all do as they liked—it didn't matter a button to *him*. And with an effort to carry off that comedy he changed the subject.

VI.

PETER SHERRINGHAM would not for a moment have admitted that he was jealous of Nick Dormer, but he would
almost have liked to be accused of it; for this would have
given him an opportunity to declare with plausibility that so
uncomfortable a passion had no application to his case. How
could a man be jealous when he was not a suitor? how could
he pretend to guard a property which was neither his own
nor destined to become his own? There could be no question
of loss when one had nothing at stake and no question of
envy when the responsibility of possession was exactly what
one prayed to be delivered from. The measure of one's susceptibility was one's pretensions, and Peter was not only ready
to declare over and over again that, thank God, he had none:
his spiritual detachment was still more complete—he literally
suffered from the fact that the declaration was but little elicited. He connected an idea of virtue and honour with his attitude; for surely it was a high example of conduct to have
quenched a personal passion for the sake of the public service.
He had gone over the whole question at odd, irrepressible
hours; he had returned, spiritually speaking, the buffet administered to him in a moment, that day in Rosedale Road,
by the spectacle of the *crânerie* with which Nick could let
worldly glories slide. Resolution for resolution he preferred
after all another sort, and his own crânerie would be shown
in the way he should stick to his profession and stand up for
British interests. If Nick had leaped over a wall he would leap
over a river. The course of his river was already traced and his
loins were already girded. Thus he was justified in holding
that the measure of a man's susceptibility was a man's attitude: that was the only thing he was bound to give an account of.

He was perpetually giving an account of it to his own soul,
in default of other listeners. He was quite angry at having
tasted a sweetness in Miriam's assurance, at the carriage door,
bestowed indeed with very little solemnity, that Nick didn't
care for her. Wherein did it concern him that Nick cared for
her or that Nick didn't? Wherein did it signify to him that

Gabriel Nash should have taken upon himself to disapprove
of a union between the young actress and the young painter
and to frustrate an accident that might perhaps be happy? For
those had also been cooling words at the hour, though Peter
blushed on the morrow to think that he had perceived
in them anything but Nash's personal sublimity. He was
ashamed of having been refreshed, and refreshed by so sickly
a draught, because it was his theory that he was not in a fever.
As for keeping an eye on Nick, it would soon become clear to
that young man and that young man's charming friend that
he had quite other uses for his sharpness. Nick and Miriam
and Gabriel Nash could straighten out their complications
according to their light. He would never speak to Nick of
Miriam; he felt indeed just now as if he should never speak
to Nick of anything. He had traced the course of his river,
as I say, and the real proof would be the way he should fly
through the air. It was a case for action—for vigorous, unmistakable action. He had done very little since his arrival in
London but moon round a *fille de théâtre* who was taken up
partly, though she bluffed it off, with another man and partly
with arranging new petticoats for a beastly old "poetic
drama;" but this little waste of time should instantly be made
up. He had given himself a certain rope and he had danced to
the end of his rope, and now he would dance back. That was
all right—so right that Sherringham could only express to
himself how right it was by whistling gaily.

He whistled as he went to dine with a great personage, the
day after his meeting with Nick in Balaklava Place; a great
personage to whom he had originally paid his respects—it
was high time—the day before that meeting, the Monday
previous. The sense of omissions to repair, of a superior line
to take, perhaps made him study with more intensity to please
the personage, who gave him ten minutes and asked him five
questions. A great many doors were successively opened before any palpitating pilgrim who was about to enter the presence of this distinguished man; but they were discreetly
closed again behind Sherringham, and I must ask the reader
to pause with me at the nearer end of the momentary vista.
This particular pilgrim fortunately felt that he could count
upon being recognized not only as a faithful if obscure official

in the great hierarchy, but as a clever young man who happened to be connected by blood with people his lordship had
intimately known. No doubt it was simply as the clever young
man that Peter received the next morning from the dispenser
of his lordship's hospitality a note asking him to dine on the
morrow. He had received such cards before and he always
responded to the invitation: he did so however on the present
occasion with a sense of unusual intention. In due course his
intention was translated into words: before the gentlemen left
the dining-room he took the liberty of asking his noble host if
during the next few days there would be three minutes more
that he might, in his extreme benevolence, bestow upon him.

"What is it you want? Tell me now," the master of his fate
replied, motioning to the rest of the company to pass out and
detaining Peter in the dining-room.

Peter's excellent training covered every contingency: he
could be concise or diffuse, as the occasion required. Even he
himself however was surprised at the quick felicity of the
terms in which he was conscious of conveying that if it were
compatible with higher conveniences he should peculiarly like
to be transferred to duties in a more distant quarter of the
globe. Indeed though Sherringham was fond of thinking of
himself as a man of emotions controlled by training, it is not
impossible that there was a greater candour than he knew in
the expression of his face and even the slight tremor of his
voice as he presented this petition. He had wished extremely
that his manner should be good in doing so, but perhaps the
best part of it for his interlocutor was just the part in which it
failed—in which it confessed a secret that the highest diplomacy would not have confessed. Sherringham remarked to
the minister that he didn't care in the least where the place
might be, nor how little coveted a post; the further away the
better and the climate didn't matter. He would only prefer of
course that there should be really something to do, although
he would make the best of it even if there were not. He
stopped in time, or at least he thought he did, not to appear
to suggest that he covertly sought relief from the misery of a
hindered passion in a flight to latitudes unfavourable to human life. His august patron gave him a sharp look which, for
a moment, seemed the precursor of a sharper question; but

the moment elapsed and the question did not come. This considerate omission, characteristic of a true man of the world and representing quick guesses and still quicker indifferences, made Sherringham from that moment his lordship's ardent partisan. What did come was a good-natured laugh and the exclamation: "You know there are plenty of swamps and jungles, if you want that sort of thing." Sherringham replied that it was very much that sort of thing he did want; whereupon his interlocutor continued: "I'll see—I'll see; if anything turns up, you shall hear."

Something turned up the very next day: our young man, taken at his word, found himself indebted to the post for a large, stiff, engraved official letter, in which the high position of minister to the smallest of Central American republics was offered to him. The republic, though small, was big enough to be "shaky," and the position, though high, was not so exalted that there were not much greater altitudes above it to which it was a stepping-stone. Sherringham took one thing with another, rejoiced at his easy triumph, reflected that he must have been even more noticed at headquarters than he had hoped, and, on the spot, consulting nobody and waiting for nothing, signified his unqualified acceptance of the place. Nobody with a grain of sense would have advised him to do anything else. It made him happier than he had supposed he should ever be again; it made him feel professionally in the train, as they said in Paris; it was serious, it was interesting, it was exciting, and Sherringham's imagination, letting itself loose into the future, began once more to scale the crowning heights. It was very simple to hold one's course if one really tried, and he blessed shaky republics. A further communication informed him that he would be expected to return to Paris for a short interval a week later and that he would before that time be advised of the date at which he was to proceed to his remoter duties.

VII.

THE FIRST THING Peter now did was to go and see Lady Agnes Dormer; it is not unworthy of note that he took on the other hand no step to make his promotion known to Miriam Rooth. To render it more probable he should find her he went at the luncheon-hour; and she was indeed on the point of sitting down to that repast with Grace. Biddy was not at home—Biddy was never at home now, her mother said: she was always at Nick's place, she spent her life there, she ate and drank there, she almost slept there. What she found to do there in so many hours, or what was the irresistible spell, Lady Agnes could not pretend that she had succeeded in discovering. She spoke of this baleful resort only as "Nick's place," and she spoke of it at first as little as possible. She thought it very probable however that Biddy would come in early that afternoon: there was something or other, some common social duty, that she had condescended to promise she would perform with Grace. Poor Lady Agnes, whom Sherringham found in a very grim yet very tremulous condition (she assured her visitor her nerves were all gone), almost abused her younger daughter for two minutes, having evidently a deep-seated need of abusing some one. I must add however that she didn't wait to meet Grace's eye before recovering, by a rapid gyration, her view of the possibilities of things—those possibilities from which she still might squeeze, as a mother, the drop that would sweeten her cup. "Dear child," she had the presence of mind to add, "her only fault is after all that she adores her brother. She has a capacity for adoration and must always take her gospel from some one."

Grace declared to Peter that her sister would have stayed at home if she had dreamed he was coming, and Lady Agnes let him know that she had heard all about the hour he had spent with the poor child at Nick's place and about his extraordinary good-nature in taking the two girls to the play. Peter lunched in Calcutta Gardens, spending an hour there which proved at first unexpectedly and, as it seemed to him, unfairly dismal. He knew from his own general perceptions,

from what Biddy had told him and from what he had heard
Nick say in Balaklava Place, that Lady Agnes would have
been wounded by her son's apostasy; but it was not till he
saw her that he appreciated the dark difference this young
man's behaviour had made in the outlook of his family. Evidently that behavior had, as he phrased it, pulled the bottom
out of innumerable private calculations. These were things
that no outsider could measure and they were none of an
outsider's business; it was enough that Lady Agnes struck
him really as a woman who had received her death-blow. She
looked ten years older; she was white and haggard and
tragic. Her eyes burned with a strange intermittent fire
which made him say to himself that her children had better
look out for her. When they were not filled with this unnatural flame they were suffused with comfortless tears; and altogether the afflicted lady was very bad—very bad indeed. It
was because he had known she would be very bad that he
had in his kindness called upon her in exactly this manner;
but he recognized that to undertake to be kind to her in
proportion to her need might carry one very far. He was
glad he himself had not a wronged, mad mother, and he
wondered how Nick Dormer could endure the home he had
ruined. Apparently he didn't endure it very much, but had
taken definitive and highly convenient refuge in Rosedale
Road.

Peter's judgment of his young kinsman was considerably
confused, and a sensible element in it was the consciousness
that he was perhaps just now not in the best state of mind
for judging him at all. At the same time, though he held in
general that an intelligent man has a legible warrant for doing the particular thing he prefers, he could scarcely help
asking himself whether in the exercise of a virile freedom it
had been absolutely indispensable that Nick should work
such domestic woe. He admitted indeed that this was an
anomalous vision of Nick, as the worker of domestic woe.
Then he saw that Lady Agnes's grievance (there came a moment, later, when she asserted as much) was not quite what
Nick, in Balaklava Place, had represented it—with questionable taste perhaps—to a mocking actress; was not a mere
shocked quarrel with his adoption of a "low" career, or a

horror, the old-fashioned horror, of the strange licenses taken by artists under pretext of being conscientious: the day for this was past and English society thought the brush and the fiddle as good as anything else, with two or three exceptions. It was not what he had taken up but what he had put down that made the sorry difference, and the tragedy would have been equally great if he had become a wine-merchant or a horse-dealer. Peter had gathered at first that Lady Agnes would not trust herself to speak directly of her trouble, and he obeyed what he supposed to be the best discretion in making no allusion to it. But a few minutes before they rose from luncheon she broke out, and when he attempted to utter a word of mitigation there was something that went to his heart in the way she returned: "Oh, you don't know— you don't know!"

He perceived Grace's eyes fixed upon him at this instant with a look of supplication, and he was uncertain as to what she wanted—that he should say something more to console her mother or should hurry away from the subject. Grace looked old and plain and (he had thought, on coming in) rather cross, but she evidently wanted something. "You don't know," Lady Agnes repeated, with a trembling voice—"you don't know." She had pushed her chair a little away from the table; she held her pocket-handkerchief pressed hard to her mouth, almost stuffed into it, and her eyes were fixed on the floor. She made him feel as if he did know—knew what towering piles of confidence and hope had been dashed to the earth. Then Lady Agnes finished her sentence unexpectedly: "You don't know what my life with my husband was." Here, on the other hand, Peter was slightly at fault—he didn't exactly see what her life with her husband had to do with it. What was clear to him however was that they literally had looked for the very greatest things from Nick. It was not quite easy to see why this had been the case—it had not been precisely Sherringham's own pre-figurement. Nick appeared to have had the faculty of com-municating that sort of faith to women; he had originally given Julia a tremendous dose of it, though she had since shaken off the effects.

"Do you really think he would have done such great things,

politically speaking?" Peter inquired. "Do you consider that
the root of the matter was in him?"

Lady Agnes hesitated a moment, looking rather hard at
her visitor. "I only think what all his friends—all his father's
friends—have thought. He was his father's son, after all.
No young man ever had a finer training, and he gave, from
the first, repeated proof of having the highest sort of ability,
the highest sort of ambition. See how he got in everywhere. Look at his first seat—look at his second," Lady
Agnes continued. "Look at what every one says at this
moment."

"Look at all the papers!" said Grace. "Did you ever hear
him speak?" she asked. And when Peter reminded her that he
had spent his life in foreign lands she went on: "Well, you lost
something."

"It was very charming," said Lady Agnes quietly.

"Of course he's charming, whatever he does," Peter conceded. "He'll be a charming artist."

"Oh, heaven!" groaned Lady Agnes, rising quickly.

"He won't—that's the worst," Grace amended. "It isn't as
if he'd do things people would like. I've been to his place and
I never saw such a horrid lot of things—not at all clever or
pretty."

"You know nothing whatever about the matter!" Lady
Agnes exclaimed, with unexpected asperity. Then she added,
to Peter, that, as it happened, her children did have a good
deal of artistic taste: Grace was the only one who was totally
deficient in it. Biddy was very clever—Biddy really might
learn to do pretty things. And anything the poor child could
learn was now no more than her duty—there was so little
knowing what the future had in store for them all.

"You think too much of the future—you take terribly
gloomy views," said Peter, looking for his hat.

"What other views can one take, when one's son has deliberately thrown away a fortune?"

"Thrown one away? Do you mean through not marrying—?"

"I mean through killing by his perversity the best friend he
ever had."

Sherringham stared a moment; then with laughter: "Ah, but Julia isn't dead of it!"

"I'm not talking of Julia," said Lady Agnes, with a good deal of majesty. "Nick isn't mercenary, and I'm not complaining of that."

"She means Mr. Carteret," Grace explained. "He would have done anything if Nick had stayed in the House."

"But he's not dead?"

"Charles Carteret is dying," said Lady Agnes—"his end is very, very near. He has been a sort of providence to us—he was Sir Nicholas's second self. But he won't stand such nonsense, and that chapter's closed."

"You mean he has dropped Nick out of his will?"

"Cut him off utterly. He has given him notice."

"The old scoundrel! But Nick will work the better for that—he'll depend on himself."

"Yes, and whom shall *we* depend on?" Grace demanded.

"Don't be vulgar, for God's sake!" her mother ejaculated with a certain inconsequence.

"Oh, leave Nick alone—he'll make a lot of money," Peter declared cheerfully, following his two companions into the hall.

"I don't in the least care whether he does or not," said Lady Agnes. "You must come up-stairs again—I've lots to say to you yet," she went on, seeing that Peter had taken his hat. "You must arrange to come and dine with us immediately; it's only because I've been so steeped in misery that I didn't write to you the other day—directly after you called. We don't give parties, as you may imagine, but if you'll come just as we are, for old acquaintance' sake—"

"Just with Nick—if Nick will come—and dear Biddy," Grace interposed.

"Nick must certainly come, as well as dear Biddy, whom I hoped so much to find," Peter rejoined. "Because I'm going away—I don't know when I shall see them again."

"Wait with mamma. Biddy will come in at any moment," Grace urged.

"You're going away?" asked Lady Agnes, pausing at the foot of the stairs and turning her white face upon him. Something in the tone of her voice showed that she had been struck by his own tone.

"I have had promotion, and you must congratulate me. They are sending me out as minister to a little hot hole in Central America—five thousand miles away. I shall have to go rather soon."

"Oh, I'm so glad!" Lady Agnes breathed. Still she paused at the foot of the stair and still she gazed.

"How very delightful, because it will lead, straight off, to all sorts of other good things!" Grace exclaimed.

"Oh, I'm crawling up, and I'm an excellency," Peter laughed.

"Then if you dine with us your excellency must have great people to meet you."

"Nick and Biddy—they're great enough."

"Come up-stairs—come up-stairs," said Lady Agnes, turning quickly and beginning to ascend.

"Wait for Biddy—I'm going out," Grace continued, extending her hand to her kinsman. "I shall see you again—not that you care; but good-bye now. Wait for Biddy," the girl repeated in a lower tone, fastening her eyes on his with the same urgent, mystifying gleam that he thought he had perceived in them at luncheon.

"Oh, I'll go and see her in Rosedale Road," he answered.

"Do you mean to-day—now?"

"I don't know about to-day, but before I leave England."

"Well, she'll be in immediately," said Grace. "Good-bye to your excellency."

"Come up, Peter—*please* come up," called Lady Agnes, from the top of the stairs.

He mounted, and when he found himself in the drawing-room with her, with the door closed, she told him that she was exceedingly interested in his fine prospects, that she wished to hear all about his new position. She rang for coffee and indicated the seat he would find most comfortable: he had for a moment an apprehension that she would tell him he might if he liked light a cigar. For Peter Sherringham had suddenly become restless—too restless to occupy a comfortable chair; he seated himself in it only to jump up again, and he went to the window—while he communicated to his hostess the very little that he knew about his prospective post —on hearing a vehicle drive up to the door. A strong light had just been thrown into his mind, and it seemed to grow stronger when, looking out of the window, he saw Grace Dormer issue from the house in a bonnet and jacket which had all the air of having been assumed with extraordinary speed. Her jacket was unbuttoned, her gloves were dangling from her hand and she was tying her bonnet-strings. The vehicle into which she hastily sprang was a hansom-cab which had been summoned by the butler from the doorstep and which rolled away with her after she had given the cabman an address.

"Where is Grace going in such a hurry?" he asked of Lady Agnes; to which she replied that she had not the least idea— her children, at the pass they had all come to, knocked about as they liked.

Peter sat down again; he stayed a quarter of an hour and then he stayed longer, and during this time his appreciation of what Lady Agnes had in her mind gathered force. She showed him clearly enough what she had in her mind, although she showed it by no clumsy nor reprehensible overtures. It looked out of her sombre, conscious eyes and quavered in her preoccupied, perfunctory tones. She manifested an extravagant interest in his future proceedings, the probable succession of events in his career, the different honours he would be likely to come in for, the salary attached to his actual appointment, the salary attached to the appointments that would follow—they would be sure to, wouldn't they?—and what he might reasonably expect to save. Oh, he must save—Lady Agnes was an advocate of saving; and he must take tremendous pains and get on and be clever and ambitious: he must make himself indispensable and rise to the top. She was urgent and suggestive and sympathetic; she threw herself into the vision of his achievements and emoluments as if to satisfy a little the sore hunger with which Nick's treachery had left her. This was touching to Peter Sherringham, and he did not remain unmoved even at those more importunate moments when, as she fell into silence, fidgeting feverishly with a morsel of fancy-work that she had plucked from a table, her whole presence became an intense repressed appeal to him. What that appeal would have been had it been uttered was: "Oh, Peter, take little Biddy; oh, my dear young friend, understand your interests at the same time that you understand mine; be kind and reasonable and clever; save me all further anxiety and tribulation and accept my lovely, faultless child from my hands."

That was what Lady Agnes had always meant, more or less, that was what Grace had meant, and they meant it with singular lucidity on the present occasion. Lady Agnes meant it so much that from one moment to another Peter scarcely knew what she might do; and Grace meant it so much that she had rushed away in a hansom to fetch her sister from the studio. Grace, however, was a fool, for Biddy certainly wouldn't come. The news of his promotion had set them off, adding brightness to their idea of his being an excellent match; bringing home to them sharply the sense that if he were going away to strange countries he must take Biddy with him—that something at all events must be settled about Biddy before he went. They had suddenly began to throb with the conviction that they had no time to lose.

Strangely enough, the perception of all this had not the effect of throwing Peter on the defensive, or at least of making him wish to bolt. When once he had discovered what was in the air he recognized a propriety, a real felicity in it; could not deny that he was in certain ways a good match, since it was quite probable he would go far; and was even generous enough (as he had no fear of being dragged to the altar) to enter into the conception that he might offer some balm to a mother who had had a horrid disappointment. The feasibility of marrying Biddy was not exactly augmented by the idea that his doing so would be a great offset to what Nick had made Lady Agnes suffer; but at any rate Peter did not dislike his strenuous companion so much as to wish to punish her for being strenuous. He was not afraid of her, whatever she might do; and though he was unable to grasp the practical relevancy of Biddy's being produced on the instant he was willing to linger for half an hour on the chance of her turning up.

There was a certain contagion in Lady Agnes's appeal—it made him appeal sensibly to himself. For indeed, as it is time to say, the glass of our young man's spirit had been polished for that reflection. It was only at this moment that he became really candid with himself. When he made up his mind that his only safety was in flight and took the strong measure of asking for assistance to flee, he was very conscious that another and probably still more effectual safeguard (especially if the two should be conjoined) lay in the hollow of his hand. Julia Dallow's words in Paris had come back to him and had seemed much wiser than when they were spoken: "She'll save you disappointments; you would know the worst that can happen to you, and it wouldn't be bad." Julia had put it into a nutshell—Biddy would probably save him disappointments. And then she was—well, she was Biddy. Peter knew better what that was since the hour he had spent with her in Rosedale Road. But he had brushed away the sense of it, though he was aware that in doing so he took only half measures, was even guilty of a sort of fraud upon himself. If he was sincere in wishing to put a gulf between his future and that portion of his past and present which was associated with Miriam Rooth, there was a very simple way to do so. He had dodged that way, dishonestly fixing upon another which, taken alone, was far from being so good; but Lady Agnes brought him back to it. She held him in magnanimous contemplation of it, during which the safety, as Julia had called it, of the remedy became fascinating to his mind, especially as that safety appeared not to exclude a concomitant sweetness. It would be simple and it would swallow up his problems; it would put an end to all alternatives, which, as alternatives were otherwise putting an end to him, would be an excellent thing. It would settle the whole question of his future, and it was high time this should be settled.

Peter took two cups of coffee while he made out his future with Lady Agnes, but though he drank them slowly he had finished them before Biddy turned up. He stayed three-quarters of an hour, saying to himself that she wouldn't come—why should she come? Lady Agnes said nothing about this; she really, in vulgar vocables, said nothing about any part of the business. But she made him fix the next day but one for coming to dinner, and her repeated declaration that there would be no one else, not another creature but themselves, had almost the force of a legal paper. In giving his word that he would come without fail and not write the next day to throw them over for some function that he should choose to dub obligatory, Peter felt quite as if he were putting his name to such a document. He went away at half-past three; Biddy of course hadn't come, and he had been certain she wouldn't. He couldn't imagine what Grace's idea had been, nor what pretext she had put forward to her sister. Whatever it had been, Biddy had seen through it and hated such machinations. Peter could only like her the better for that.

VIII.

L ADY AGNES would doubtless have done better, in her own interest or in that of her child, to have made sure of Peter's company for the very next evening. This she had indeed attempted, but the application of the idea had failed. Peter had a theory that he was inextricably engaged; moreover her ladyship could not take upon herself to answer for Nick. Of course they must have Nick, though, to tell the truth, the hideous truth, she and her son were scarcely upon terms. Peter insisted on Nick, he wished particularly to see him and he gave his hostess notice that he would make each of them forgive everything to the other. Lady Agnes declared that all her son had to forgive was her loving him more than her life, and she would have challenged Peter, had he allowed it, on the general ground of the comparative dignity of the two arts of painting portraits and governing nations. Peter declined the challenge; the most he did was to intimate that he perhaps saw Nick more vividly as a painter than as a governor. Later he remembered vaguely something Lady Agnes had said about their being a governing family.

He was going, by what he could ascertain, to a very queer climate, and he had many preparations to make. He gave his best attention to these, and for a couple of hours after leaving Lady Agnes he rummaged London for books from which he might extract information about his new habitat. It made apparently no great figure in literature, so that Peter could reflect that he was perhaps destined to find a salutary distraction in filling the void with a volume of impressions. After he had gathered that there were no books he went into the Park. He treated himself to an afternoon or two there when he happened to drop upon London in the summer: it refreshed his sense of the British interests he would have to stand up for. Moreover, he had been hiding more or less, and now all that was changed and this was the simplest way not to hide. He met a host of friends, made his situation as public as possible and accepted on the spot a great many invitations, subject to the mental reservation that he should allow none of them to interfere with his being present the first night of Miriam's new venture. He was going to the equator to get away from her, but to break with the past with some decency of form he must show an affected interest, if he could muster none other, in an occasion that meant so much for her. The least intimate of her associates would do that, and Peter remembered that, at the expense of good manners, he had stayed away from her first appearance on any stage. He would have been shocked if he had found himself obliged to go back to Paris without giving her his personal countenance at the imminent crisis, so good a right had she to expect it.

It was nearly eight o'clock when he went to Great Stanhope Street to dress for dinner and learn that a note which he found on the hall table, and which bore the marks of hasty despatch, had come in three or four hours before. It exhibited the signature of Miriam Rooth and informed him that she positively expected him at the theatre at eleven o'clock the next morning, for which hour a dress-rehearsal of the revived play had been hurriedly determined upon, the first night being now definitely fixed for the impending Saturday. She counted upon his attendance at both ceremonies, but she had particular reasons for wishing to see him at the rehearsal. "I want you to see and judge and tell me," she said, "for my mind's like a flogged horse—it won't give another kick." It was for the Saturday he had made Lady Agnes his promise; he had thought of the possibility of the play in doing so, but had rested in the faith that, from valid symptoms, this complication would not occur till the following week. He decided nothing on the spot in relation to the conflict—it was enough to dash off three words to Miriam to the effect that he would sooner perish than fail her on the morrow.

He went to the theatre in the morning, and the episode proved curious and instructive. Though there were twenty people in the stalls it bore little resemblance to those *répétitions générales* to which, in Paris, his love of the drama had often attracted him and which, taking place at night in the theatre closed to the public, are virtually first performances with invited spectators. They were, to his sense, always settled and stately and were rehearsals of the *première* even more than rehearsals of the play. The present occasion was less august; it was not so much a concert as a confusion of sounds, and it took audible and at times disputatious counsel with itself. It was rough and frank and spasmodic, but it was vivid and strong and, in spite of the serious character of the piece, often exceedingly droll; while it gave Sherringham, oddly enough, a livelier sense than he had ever had of bending over the hissing, smoking, sputtering caldron in which a palatable performance is stewed. He looked into the gross darkness that may result from excess of light; that is he understood how knocked up, on the eve of production, every one concerned in the preparation of a play might be, with nerves overstretched and glasses blurred, awaiting the test and the response, the echo to be given back by the big, receptive, artless, stupid, delightful public. Sherringham's interest had been great in advance, and as Miriam, since his arrival, had taken him much into her confidence he knew what she intended to do and had discussed a hundred points with her. They had differed about some of them and she had always said: "Ah, but wait till you see how I shall do it at the time!" That was usually her principal reason and her most convincing argument. She had made some changes at the last hour—she was going to do several things in another way. But she wanted a touchstone, she wanted a fresh ear and, as she told Sherringham when he went behind after the first act, that was why she had insisted on this private performance, to which a few fresh ears were to be admitted. They didn't want to let her have it—they were a parcel of donkeys; but as to what she meant in general to have she had given them a hint which she flattered herself they wouldn't soon forget.

Miriam spoke as if she had had a great battle with her fellow-workers and had routed them utterly. It was not the first time Sherringham had heard her talk as if such a life as hers could only be a fighting life, so that she frankly recognized the fine uses of a faculty for making a row. She rejoiced that she had this faculty, for she knew what to do with it; and though there might be a certain swagger in taking such a stand in advance, when one had done the infinitely little that she had done, yet she trusted to the future to show how right she should have been in believing that a pack of idiots would never hold out against her, would know that they couldn't afford to. Her assumption of course was that she fought for

the light and the right, for the good way and the thorough,
for doing a thing properly if one did it at all. What she had
really wanted was the theatre closed for a night and the dress-
rehearsal, put on for a few people, given instead of "Yolande."
That she had not got, but she would have it the next time.
She spoke as if her triumphs behind the scenes as well as
before would go by leaps and bounds, and Sherringham
perfectly believed, for the time, that she would drive her
coadjutors in front of her like sheep. Her tone was the sort of
thing that would have struck one as preposterous if one didn't
believe in her; but if one did believe in her it only seemed
thrown in with the other gifts. How was she going to act that
night, and what could be said for such a hateful way of doing
things? She asked Sherringham questions that he was quite
unable to answer; she abounded in superlatives and tremendously strong objections. He had a sharper vision than usual
of the queer fate, for a peaceable man, of being involved in a
life of so violent a rhythm: one might as well be hooked to a
Catharine-wheel and whiz round in flame and smoke.

It was only for five minutes, in the wing, amid jostling and
shuffling and shoving, that they held this conference. Miriam,
splendid in a brocaded anachronism, a false dress of the beginning of the century, and excited and appealing, imperious
and reckless and good-natured, full of exaggerated propositions, supreme determinations and comical irrelevancies,
showed as radiant a young head as the stage had ever seen.
Other people quickly surrounded her, and Sherringham saw
that though she wanted a fresh ear and a fresh eye she was
liable to tell those who possessed these advantages that they
didn't know what they were talking about. It was rather hard
with her (Basil Dashwood let him into this, wonderfully
painted and in a dress even more beautiful than Miriam's —
that of a young dandy of the ages of silk): if you were not in
the business you were one kind of donkey and if you *were* in
the business you were another kind. Sherringham noted with
a certain displeasure that Gabriel Nash was not there; he preferred to believe that it was from this observation that his
annoyance happened to come when Miriam, after the remark
just quoted from Dashwood, laughing and saying that at any
rate the thing would do because it would just have to do,

thrust vindictively but familiarly into the young actor's face a magnificent feather fan. "Isn't he too lovely," she asked, "and doesn't he know how to do it?" Basil Dashwood had the sense of costume even more than Sherringham supposed, inasmuch as it now appeared that he had gone profoundly into the question of what his clever comrade was to wear. He had drawn patterns and hunted up stuffs, had helped her to try on her clothes, had bristled with ideas and pins. It is not perfectly easy to explain why Sherringham grudged Gabriel Nash the cynicism of his absence; it may even be thought singular that he should have missed him. At any rate he flushed a little when Miriam, of whom he inquired whether she hadn't invited her oldest and dearest friend, exclaimed: "Oh, he says he doesn't like the kitchen fire—he only wants the pudding!" It would have taken the kitchen fire to account at that moment for the red of Sherringham's cheek; and he was indeed uncomfortably heated by helping to handle, as he phrased it, the saucepans.

This he felt so much after he had returned to his seat, which he forbore to quit again till the curtain had fallen on the last act, that in spite of the high beauty of that part of the performance of which Miriam carried the weight there was a moment when his emancipation led him to give a suppressed gasp of relief, as if he were scrambling up the bank of a torrent after an immersion. The girl herself, at any rate, as was wholly right, was of the incorruptible faith: she had been saturated to good purpose with the great spirit of Madame Carré. That was conspicuous as the play went on and she watched over the detail with weary piety and passion. Sherringham had never liked the piece itself; he thought that as clumsy in form and false in feeling it did little honour to the British theatre; he hated many of the speeches, pitied Miriam for having to utter them and considered that, lighted by that sort of candle, the path of fame might very well lead nowhere.

When the rehearsal was over he went behind again, and in the rose-coloured satin of the *dénoûment* the heroine of the occasion said to him: "Fancy my having to drag through that other stuff to-night—the brutes!" He was vague about the persons designated in this allusion, but he let it pass: he had at the moment a kind of detached foreboding of the way any gentleman familiarly connected with Miriam in the future would probably form the habit of letting objurgations and some other things pass. This had become indeed, now, a frequent state of mind with him; the instant he was before her, near her, next her, he found himself a helpless subject of the spell which, so far at least as he was concerned, she put forth by contact and of which the potency was punctual and absolute: the fit came on, as he said, exactly as some esteemed express-train on a great line bangs at a given moment into the station. At a distance he partly recovered himself—that was the encouragement for going to the shaky republic; but as soon as he entered her presence his life struck him as a thing disconnected from his will. It was as if *he* had been one thing and his behaviour another; he had glimpses of pictures of this difference, drawn, as they might be, from the coming years—little illustrative scenes in which he saw himself in strange attitudes of resignation, always rather sad and still, with a slightly bent head. Such images should not have been inspiring, but it is a fact that they were decidedly fascinating. The gentleman with the bent head had evidently given up something that was dear to him, but it was exactly because he had got his price that he was there. "Come and see me three or four hours hence," Miriam said—"come, that is, about six. I shall rest till then, but I want particularly to talk with you. There will be no one else—not the end of any one's nose. You'll do me good." So of course Peter drove up to Balaklava Place about six.

IX.

I DON'T KNOW—I haven't the least idea—I don't care—
don't ask me," he broke out immediately, in answer to
some question that she put to him, with little delay, about his
sense of the way she had done certain things at the theatre.
Had she not frankly better give up that way and return to
their first idea, the one they had talked over so much? Sherringham declared that it was no idea of his; that at any rate he
should never have another as long as he lived; and that, so
help him heaven, they had talked such things over more than
enough.

"You're tired of me—yes, already," said Miriam, sadly and
kindly. They were alone, her mother had not peeped out, and
she had prepared herself to return to the theatre. "However,
it doesn't matter, and of course your head is full of other
things. You must think me ravenously selfish—perpetually
chattering about my little shop. What will you have, when
one's a shop-girl? You used to like it, but then you weren't a
minister."

"What do you know about my being a minister?" Sherringham asked, leaning back in his chair and gazing at her
from sombre eyes. Sometimes he thought she looked better
on the stage than she did off it, and sometimes he thought the
exact contrary. The former of these convictions had held his
mind in the morning, and it was now punctually followed by
the other. As soon as she stepped on the boards a great and
special alteration usually took place in her—she was in focus
and in her frame; yet there were hours too in which she wore
her world's face before the audience, just as there were hours
when she wore her stage face in the world. She took up either
mask as it suited her humour. To-day Sherringham was seeing
each in its order, and he thought each the best.

"I should know very little if I waited for you to tell me—
that's very certain," Miriam answered. "It's in the papers that
you've got a high appointment, but I don't read the papers
unless there's something in them about myself. Next week I
shall devour them and think them drivelling too, no doubt. It
was Basil Dashwood told me, this afternoon, of your pro-

motion—he has seen it announced somewhere. I'm delighted if it gives you more money and more advantages, but don't expect me to be glad that you're going away to some distant, disgusting country."

"The matter has only just been settled and we have each been busy with our own affairs. Even if you hadn't given me these opportunities," Sherringham went on, "I should have tried to see you to-day, to tell you my news and take leave of you."

"Take leave? Aren't you coming to-morrow?"

"Oh, yes, I shall see you through that. But I shall rush away the very moment it's over."

"I shall be much better then—really I shall," the girl said.

"The better you are the worse you are."

Miriam returned his gaze with a beautiful charity. "If it would do you any good I would be bad."

"The worse you are the better you are!" laughed Sherringham. "You're a kind of devouring demon."

"Not a bit! It's you."

"It's I? I like that."

"It's you who make trouble, who are sore and suspicious and supersubtle, not taking things as they come and for what they are, but twisting them into misery and falsity. Oh, I've watched you enough, my dear friend, and I've been sorry for you—and sorry for myself; for I'm not so taken up with myself as you think. I'm not such a low creature. I'm capable of gratitude, I'm capable of affection. One may live in paint and tinsel, but one isn't absolutely without a soul. Yes, I've got one," the girl went on, "though I do paint my face and practise my intonations. If what you are going to do is good for you I'm very glad. If it leads to good things, to honour and fortune and greatness, I'm enchanted. If it means your being away always, forever and ever, of course that's serious. You know it—I needn't tell you—I regard you as I really don't regard any one else. I have a confidence in you—ah, it's a luxury. You're a gentleman, *mon bon*—ah, you're a gentleman! It's just that. And then you see, you understand, and that's a luxury too. You're a luxury altogether, Mr. Sherringham. Your being where I shall never see you is not a thing I shall enjoy; I know that from the separation of these last months—after our beautiful life in Paris, the best thing that ever happened to me or that ever will. But if it's your career, if it's your happiness, I can miss you and hold my tongue. I *can* be disinterested—I can!"

"What did you desire me to come for?" Sherringham asked, attentive and motionless. The same impression, the old impression was with him again; the sense that if she was sincere it was sincerity of execution, if she was genuine it was the genuineness of doing it well. She did it so well now that this very fact was charming and touching. When she asked him at the theatre to grant her the hour in the afternoon, she wanted candidly (the more as she had not seen him at home for several days) to go over with him once again, on the eve of the great night (it would be for her second attempt the critics would lie so in wait—the first success might have been a fluke), some of her recurrent doubts: knowing from experience what good ideas he often had, how he could give a worrying alternative its quietus at the last. Then she had heard from Dashwood of the change in his situation, and that had really from one moment to the other made her think sympathetically of his preoccupations—led her open-handedly to drop her own. She was sorry to lose him and eager to let him know how good a friend she was conscious that he had been to her. But the expression of this was already, at the end of a minute, a strange bedevilment: she began to listen to herself, to speak dramatically, to represent. She uttered the things she felt as if they were snatches of old play-books, and really felt them the more because they sounded so well. This however didn't prevent them from being as good feelings as those of anybody else, and at the moment Sherringham, to still a rising emotion—which he knew he shouldn't still—articulated the challenge I have just recorded, she seemed to him to have at any rate the truth of gentleness and generosity.

"There's something the matter with you—you're jealous," said Miriam. "You're jealous of Mr. Dormer. That's an example of the way you tangle everything up. Lord, he won't hurt you, nor me either!"

"He can't hurt me, my dear, and neither can you; for I have a nice little heart of stone and a smart new breast-plate of iron. The interest I take in you is something quite extraordinary;

but the most extraordinary thing in it is that it's perfectly prepared to tolerate the interest of others."

"The interest of others needn't trouble it much!" Miriam declared. "If Mr. Dormer had broken off his marriage to such an awfully fine woman (for she is that, your swell of a sister), it isn't for a loud wretch like me. He's kind to me because that's his nature, and he notices me because that's his business; but he's away up in the clouds—a thousand miles over my head. He has got something 'on,' as they say; he's in love with an idea. I think it's a shocking bad one, but that's his own affair. He's quite *exalté*; living on nectar and ambrosia—what he has to spare for us poor crawling things on earth is only a few dry crumbs. I didn't even ask him to come to rehearsal. Besides, he thinks you're in love with me and that it wouldn't be honourable to cut in. He's capable of that—isn't it charming?"

"If he were to relent and give up his scruples, would you marry him?" asked Sherringham.

"Mercy, how you chatter about marrying!" the girl laughed. "You've all got it on the brain."

"Why, I put it that way to please you, because you complained to me last year precisely that this was not what seemed generally to be wanted."

"Oh, last year!" Miriam murmured. Then, differently: "Yes, it's very tiresome!" she exclaimed.

"You told me moreover in Paris, more than once, that you wouldn't listen to anything but that."

"Well, I won't, but I shall wait till I find a husband who's bad enough. One who'll beat me and swindle me and spend my money on other women—that's the sort of man for me. Mr. Dormer, delightful as he is, doesn't come up to that."

"You'll marry Basil Dashwood," Sherringham replied.

"Oh, marry?—call it marry, if you like. That's what poor mother says—she lives in dread of it."

"To this hour," said Sherringham, "I haven't managed to make out what your mother wants. She has so many ideas, as Madame Carré said."

"She wants me to be a tremendous sort of creature—all her ideas are reducible to that. What makes the muddle is that she isn't clear about the kind of creature she wants most. A great actress or a great lady—sometimes she inclines for one and sometimes for the other; but on the whole she persuades herself that a great actress, if she'll cultivate the right people, may *be* a great lady. When I tell her that won't do and that a great actress can never be anything but a great vagabond, then the dear old thing has tantrums and we have scenes—the most grotesque: they'd make the fortune, for a subject, of some play-writing fellow, if he had the wit to guess them; which, luckily for us perhaps, he never will. She usually winds up by protesting—*devinez un peu quoi!*" Miriam added. And as her companion professed his complete inability to divine: "By declaring that rather than take it that way I must marry *you*."

"She's shrewder than I thought. It's the last of vanities to talk about it, but I may mention in passing that if you would marry me you should be the greatest of all possible ladies."

"Heavens, my dear fellow, what natural capacity have I for that?"

"You're artist enough for anything. I shall be a great diplomatist: my resolution is firmly taken. I'm infinitely cleverer than you have the least idea of, and you shall be a great diplomatist's wife."

"And the demon, the devil, the devourer and destroyer, that you are so fond of talking about: what, in such a position, do you do with that element of my nature? *Où le fourrez-vous?*"

"I'll look after it, I'll keep it under. Rather perhaps I should say I'll bribe it and lull it—I'll gorge it with earthly grandeurs."

"That's better," said Miriam; "for a demon that's kept under is a shabby little demon. Don't let us be shabby." Then she added: "Do you really go away the beginning of next week?"

"Monday night, if possible."

"That's to Paris. Before you go to your new post they must give you an interval here."

"I shan't take it—I'm so tremendously keen for my duties. I shall insist on going sooner. Oh, I shall be concentrated now."

"I'll come and act there," said Miriam, with her handsome smile. "I've already forgotten what it was I wanted to discuss with you: it was some trumpery stuff. What I want to say now is only one thing: that it's not in the least true that because my life pitches me in every direction and mixes me up with all sorts of people—or rather with one sort mainly, poor dears!—I haven't a decent character, I haven't common honesty. Your sympathy, your generosity, your patience, your precious suggestions, our dear, sweet days last summer in Paris, I shall never forget. You're the best—you're different from all the others. Think of me as you please and make profane jokes about my matrimonial prospects—I shall think of *you* only in one way. I have a great respect for you. With all my heart I hope you'll be a great diplomatist. God bless you!"

Miriam got up as she spoke and in so doing she glanced at the clock—a movement which somehow only added to the noble gravity of her discourse: it was as if she were considering his time, not her own. Sherringham, at this, rising too, took out his watch and stood a moment with his eyes bent upon it, though without in the least perceiving what the needles marked.

"You'll have to go, to reach the theatre at your usual hour, won't you? Let me not keep you. That is, let me keep you only long enough just to say this, once for all, as I shall never speak of it again. I'm going away to save myself," Sherringham went on deliberately, standing before her and soliciting her eyes with his own. "I ought to go, no doubt, in silence, in decorum, in virtuous submission to hard necessity—without asking for credit or sympathy, without provoking any sort of scene or calling attention to my fortitude. But I can't—upon my soul I can't. I can go, I can see it through, but I can't hold my tongue. I want you to know all about it, so that over there, when I'm bored to death, I shall at least have the exasperatingly vain consolation of feeling that you do know—and that it does neither you nor me any good!"

He paused a moment, upon which Miriam asked: "That I do know what?"

"That I have a consuming passion for you and that it's impossible."

"Ah, impossible, my friend!" she sighed, but with a quickness in her assent.

"Very good; it interferes, the gratification of it would interfere fatally, with the ambition of each of us. Our ambitions are odious, but we are tied fast to them."

"Ah, why ain't we simple?" Miriam quavered. "Why ain't we of the people—*comme tout le monde*—just a man and a girl liking each other?"

Sherringham hesitated a moment; she was so tenderly mocking, so sweetly ambiguous, as she said this. "Because we are precious asses! However, I'm simple enough, after all, to care for you as I have never cared for any human creature. You have, as it happens, a personal charm for me that no one has ever approached, and from the top of your splendid head to the sole of your theatrical shoe (I could go down on my face—there, abjectly—and kiss it!) every inch of you is dear and delightful to me. Therefore good-bye."

Miriam stared, at this, with wider eyes: he had put the matter in a way that struck her. For a moment, all the same, he was afraid she would reply as if she had often heard that sort of thing before. But she was too much moved—the pure colour that had risen to her face showed it—to have recourse to this particular facility. She was moved even to the glimmer of tears, though she gave him her hand with a smile. "I'm so glad you've said all that; for from you I know what it means. Certainly it's better for you to go away. Of course it's all wrong, isn't it?—but that's the only thing it can be: therefore it's all right, isn't it? Some day when we're great people we'll talk these things over; then we shall be quiet, we shall be at peace—let us hope so at least—and better friends than people will know." She paused a moment, smiling still; then she said while he held her hand: "Don't, *don't* come to-morrow night."

With this she attempted to draw her hand away, as if everything were settled and over; but the effect of her movement was that, as he held her hand tight, he was simply drawn toward her and close to her. The effect of this, in turn, was that, releasing her only to possess her more, he seized her in his arms and breathing deeply "I love you!" clasped her in a long embrace. It was so long that it gave the door of the room time to open before either of them had taken notice. Mrs. Rooth, who had not peeped in before, peeped in now, becoming in this matter witness of an incident she could scarcely have expected. The unexpected indeed, for Mrs. Rooth, had never been an insuperable element in things; it was her system, in general, to be too much in harmony to be surprised. As the others turned round they saw her standing there and smiling at them, and heard her ejaculate with wise indulgence:

"Oh, you extravagant children!"

Miriam brushed off her tears, quickly but unconfusedly. "He's going away—he's bidding us farewell."

Sherringham—it was perhaps a result of his general agitation—laughed out at the "us" (he had already laughed at the charge of puerility), and Mrs. Rooth returned: "Going away? Ah, then I must have one too!" And she held out both her hands. Sherringham stepped forward and, taking them, kissed her respectfully on each cheek, in the foreign manner, while she continued: "Our dear old friend—our kind, gallant gentleman!"

"The gallant gentleman has been promoted to a great post—the proper reward of his gallantry," Miriam said. "He's going out as minister to some impossible place—where is it?"

"As minister—how very charming! We *are* getting on." And the old woman gave him a curious little upward interrogative leer.

"Oh, well enough. One must take what one can get," he answered.

"You'll get everything now, I'm sure, sha'n't you?" Mrs. Rooth asked, with an inflection that called back to him, comically (the source was so different), the very vibrations he had noted the day before in Lady Agnes's voice.

"He's going to glory and he'll forget all about us—forget that he has ever known such people. So we shall never see him again, and it's better so. Good-bye, good-bye," Miriam repeated; "the brougham must be there, but I won't take you. I want to talk to mother about you, and we shall say things not fit for you to hear. Oh, I'll let you know what we lose— don't be afraid," she added to Mrs. Rooth. "He's the rising star of diplomacy."

"I knew it from the first—I know how things turn out for such people as you!" cried the old woman, gazing fondly at

Sherringham. "But you don't mean to say you're not coming to-morrow night?"

"Don't—don't; it's great folly," Miriam interposed; "and it's quite needless, since you saw me to-day."

Sherringham stood looking from the mother to the daughter, the former of whom broke out to the latter: "Oh, you dear rogue, to say one has *seen* you yet! You know how you'll come up to it; you'll be transcendent."

"Yes, I shall be there—certainly," said Sherringham, at the door, to Mrs. Rooth.

"Oh, you dreadful goose!" Miriam called after him. But he went out without looking round at her.

X.

NICK DORMER had for the hour quite taken up his abode at his studio, where Biddy usually arrived after breakfast to give him news of the state of affairs in Calcutta Gardens and where many letters and telegrams were now addressed to him. Among such missives, on the morning of the Saturday on which Peter Sherringham had promised to dine at the other house, was a note from Miriam Rooth, informing Nick that if he should not telegraph to put her off she would turn up about half-past eleven, probably with her mother, for just one more sitting. She added that it was a nervous day for her and that she couldn't keep still, so that it would really be very kind to let her come to him as a refuge. She wished to stay away from the theatre, where everything was now settled (or so much the worse for the others if it wasn't), till the evening, but if she were left to herself should be sure to go there. It would keep her quiet and soothe her to sit—he could keep her quiet (he was such a blessing that way!) at any time. Therefore she would give him two or three hours—or rather she would ask him for them—if he didn't positively turn her from the door.

It had not been definite to Nick that he wanted another sitting at all for the slight work, as he held it to be, that Miriam had already helped him to achieve. He regarded this work as a kind of pictorial *obiter dictum*: he had made what he could of it and would have been at a loss to see how he could make more. If it was not finished, this was because it was not finishable; at any rate he had said all he had to say in that particular phrase. Nick Dormer, as it happened, was not just now in the highest spirits; his imagination had within two or three days become conscious of a check which he tried to explain by the idea of a natural reaction. Any important change, any new selection in one's life was exciting, and exaggerate that importance and one's own as little as one would, there was an inevitable strong emotion in renouncing, in the face of considerable opposition, one sort of responsibility for another sort. That made life not perhaps necessarily joyous, but decidedly thrilling, for the hour; and it was all very well till the thrill abated. When this occurred, as it inevitably would, the romance and the poetry of the thing would be exchanged for the flatness and the prose. It was to these latter elements that Nick Dormer had waked up pretty wide on this particular morning; and the prospect was not appreciably more blooming from the fact that he had warned himself in advance that it would be dull. He had known how dull it would be, but now he would have time to learn that even better. A reaction was a reaction, but it was not after all a catastrophe. A part of its privilege would be to make him ask himself if he had not committed a great mistake; that privilege would doubtless even remain within the limits of its nature in leading him to reply to this question in the affirmative. But he would live to withdraw such a concession—this was the first thing to bear in mind.

He was occupied, even while he dressed, in the effort to get forward mentally with some such retractation when, by the first post, Miriam's note arrived. At first it did little to help him in his effort, for it made him contrast her eagerness with his own want of alacrity and ask himself what the deuce he should do with her. Ambition, with her, was always on the charge, and she was not a person to conceive that others might in bad moments listen for the trumpet in vain. It would never have occurred to her that only the day before he had spent a portion of the afternoon quite at the bottom of the hill. He had in fact turned into the National Gallery and had wandered about there for more than one hour, and it was just while he did so that the immitigable recoil had begun perversely to set in. And the perversity was all the greater from the circumstance that if the experience was depressing it was not because he had been discouraged beyond measure by the sight of the grand things that had been done—things so much grander than any that would ever bear his signature. That variation he was duly acquainted with and should taste in abundance again. What had happened to him, as he passed on this occasion from Titian to Rubens and from Gainsborough to Rembrandt, was that he found himself calling the whole art literally into question. What was it after all, at the best, and why had people given it so high a place? Its weakness, its narrowness appeared to him; tacitly blaspheming he looked at several world-famous performances with a lustreless eye. That is he blasphemed if it were blasphemy to say to himself that, with all respect, they were a poor business, only well enough in their small way. The force that produced them was not one of the greatest forces in human affairs; their place was inferior and their connection with the life of man casual and slight. They represented so inadequately the idea, and it was the idea that won the race, that in the long run came in first. He had incontestably been in much closer relation to the idea a few months before than he was to-day: it made up a great deal for the bad side of politics that they were after all a clumsy system for applying and propagating the idea. The love of it had really been at certain hours at the bottom of his disposition to follow them up; though this had not been what he used to talk of most with his political comrades or even with Julia. Certainly, political as Julia was, he had not conferred with her much about the idea. However, this might have been his own fault quite as much as hers, and she probably took such an enthusiasm for granted—she took such a tremendous lot of things for granted. On the other hand he had put this enthusiasm forward frequently in his many discussions with Gabriel Nash, with the effect, it is true, of making that worthy scoff transcendentally at what he was pleased to term his hypocrisy. Gabriel maintained precisely that there were more ideas, more of those that man lived by, in a single room of the National Gallery than in all the statutes of Parliament. Nick had replied to this more than once that the determination of what man did live by was required; to which Nash had retorted (and it was very rarely that he quoted Scripture) that it was at any rate not by bread-and-butter alone. The statutes of Parliament gave him bread-and-butter *tout au plus*.

Nick Dormer at present had no pretension of trying this question over again; he reminded himself that his ambiguity was subjective, as the philosophers said; the result of a mood which in due course would be at the mercy of another mood. It made him curse, and cursing, as a finality, was shaky; so he would throw out a platform beyond it. The time far beyond others to do one's work was when it didn't seem worth doing, for then one gave it a brilliant chance, that of resisting the stiffest test of all—the test of striking one as very bad. To

do the most when there would be the least to be got by it was
to be most in the true spirit of production. One thing at any
rate was very certain, Nick reflected: nothing on earth would
induce him to change back again; not even if this twilight of
the soul should last for the rest of his days. He hardened himself in his posture with a good conscience which, had they
had a glimpse of it, would have made him still more diverting
to those who already thought him so; but now by good fortune Miriam suddenly knocked together the little bridge that
was wanted to carry him over to more elastic ground. If he
had made his sketch it was a proof that he had done her, and
that he had done her flashed upon him as a sign that she
would be still more feasible. He found his platform, as I have
called it, and for a moment in his relief he danced upon it. He
sent out a telegram to Balaklava Place requesting his beautiful
sitter by no manner of means to fail him. When his servant
came back it was to usher into the studio Peter Sherringham,
whom the man had apparently found at the door.

The hour was so early for social intercourse that Nick immediately guessed his visitor had come on some rare errand;
but this inference was instantly followed by the reflection that
Peter might after all only wish to make up by present zeal for
not having been near him before. He forgot that, as he had
subsequently learned from Biddy, their foreign or all but foreign cousin had spent an hour in Rosedale Road, missing him
there but pulling out Miriam's portrait, the day of his own
hurried visit to Beauclere. These young men were not on a
ceremonious footing and it was not in Nick's nature to keep a
record of civilities rendered or omitted; nevertheless he had
been vaguely conscious that during a stay in London, on
Peter's part, which apparently was stretching itself out, he and
his kinsman had foregathered less than of yore. It was indeed
an absorbing moment in the career of each, but at the same
time that he recognized this truth Nick remembered that it
was not impossible Peter might have taken upon himself to
resent some supposititious failure of consideration for Julia;
though this would have been stupid, and the newly-appointed
minister (to he had forgotten where) cultivated a finer habit.
Nick held that as he had treated Julia with studious generosity
she had nothing whatever to reproach him with; so her

brother had therefore still less. It was at any rate none of her
brother's business. There were only two things that would
have made Nick lukewarm about disposing in a few frank
words of all this: one of them his general hatred of talking of
his private affairs (a reluctance in which he and Peter were
well matched); and the other a particular sentiment which
would have involved more of a confession and which could
not be otherwise described than as a perception that the most
definite and even most pleasant consequence of the collapse of
his engagement was, as it happened, an extreme consciousness
of freedom. Nick Dormer's observation was of a different
sort from his cousin's; he noted much less the signs of the
hour and kept altogether a looser register of life. Nevertheless, just as one of our young men had during these days in
London found the air peopled with personal influences, the
concussion of human atoms, so the other, though only asking
to live without too many questions and work without too
many disasters, to be glad and sorry in short on easy terms,
had become aware of a certain social tightness, of the fact that
life is crowded and passion is restless, accident frequent and
community inevitable. Everybody with whom one had relations had other relations too, and even optimism was a mixture and peace an embroilment. The only chance was to let
everything be embroiled but one's temper and everything
spoiled but one's work. It must be added that Nick sometimes
took precautions against irritation which were in excess of the
danger, as departing travellers, about to whiz through foreign
countries, study phrase-books for combinations of words they
will never use. He was at home in the brightness of things—
his longest excursions across the border were short. He had a
dim sense that Peter considered that he made him uncomfortable and might have come now to tell him so; in which case
he should be sorry for Peter in various ways. But as soon as
his visitor began to speak Nick felt suspicion fade into old
friendliness, and this in spite of the fact that Peter's speech
had a slightly exaggerated promptitude, like the promptitude
of business, which might have denoted self-consciousness. To
Nick it quickly appeared better to be glad than to be sorry:
this simple argument was more than sufficient to make him
glad Peter was there.

"My dear Nick, it's an unpardonable hour, isn't it? I wasn't even sure you'd be up, and yet I had to risk it because my hours are numbered. I'm going away to-morrow," Peter went on; "I've a thousand things to do. I've had no talk with you this time such as we used to have of old (it's an irreparable loss, but it's your fault, you know), and as I've got to rush about all day I thought I'd just catch you before any one else does."

"Some one has already caught me, but there's plenty of time," Nick returned.

Peter stared a moment, as if he were going to ask a question; then he thought better of this and said: "I see, I see. I'm sorry to say I've only a few minutes at best."

"Man of crushing responsibilities, you've come to humiliate me!" Nick exclaimed. "I know all about it."

"It's more than I do then. That's not what I've come for, but I shall be delighted if I humiliate you a little by the way. I've two things in mind, and I'll mention the most difficult first. I came here the other day—the day after my arrival in town."

"Ah, yes, so you did; it was very good of you," Nick interrupted, as if he remembered. "I ought to have returned your visit, or left a card or written my name or something, in Great Stanhope Street, oughtn't I? You hadn't got this new thing then, or I would have done so."

Peter eyed him a moment. "I say, what's the matter with you? Am I really unforgivable for having taken that liberty?"

"What liberty?" Nick looked now as if there were nothing whatever the matter with him, and indeed his visitor's allusion was not clear to him. He was thinking only for the instant of Biddy, of whom and whose secret inclinations Grace had insisted on talking to him. They were none of his business, and if he would not for the world have let the girl herself suspect that he had violent lights on what was most screened and curtained in her, much less would he have made Peter a clumsy present of this knowledge. Grace had a queer theory that Peter treated Biddy badly—treated them all, somehow, badly; but Grace's zeal (she had plenty of it, though she affected all sorts of fine indifference) almost always took the form of being wrong. Nick wanted to do only what Biddy would thank him for, and he knew very well what she wouldn't. She wished him and Peter to be great friends, and the only obstacle to this was that Peter was too much of a diplomatist. Peter made him for an instant think of her and of the hour they had lately spent together in the studio in his absence—an hour of which Biddy had given him a history full of detail and of omissions; and this in turn brought Nick's imagination back to his visitor's own side of the matter. That complexity of things of which the sense had lately increased with him, and to which it was owing that any thread one might take hold of would probably lead one to something discomfortable, was illustrated by the fact that while poor Biddy was thinking of Peter it was ten to one that poor Peter was thinking of Miriam Rooth. All this danced before Nick's intellectual vision for a space briefer than my too numerous words.

"I pitched into your treasures—I rummaged among your canvases," Peter said. "Biddy had nothing whatever to do with it—she maintained an attitude of irreproachable reserve. It has been on my conscience all these days, and I ought to have done penance before. I have been putting it off partly because I am so ashamed of my indiscretion. *Que voulez-vous*, my dear Nick? My provocation was great. I heard you had been painting Miss Rooth, so that I couldn't restrain my curiosity. I simply went into that corner and struck out there—a trifle wildly, no doubt. I dragged the young lady to the light—your sister turned pale as she saw me. It was a good deal like breaking open one of your letters, wasn't it? However, I assure you it's all right, for I congratulate you both on your style and on your correspondent."

"You're as clever, as witty, as humorous as ever, old boy," Nick rejoined, going himself into the corner designated by his companion and laying his hands on the same canvas. "Your curiosity is the highest possible tribute to my little attempt, and your sympathy sets me right with myself. There is she again," Nick went on, thrusting the picture into an empty frame; "you shall see her whether you wish to or not."

"Right with yourself? You don't mean to say you've been wrong!" Sherringham returned, standing opposite the portrait.

"Oh, I don't know; I've been kicking up such a row; anything is better than a row."

"She's awfully good—she's awfully true," said Sherringham. "You've done more to it, since the other day; you've put in several things."

"Yes, but I've worked distractedly. I've not altogether conformed to the celebrated recommendation about being off with the old love."

"With the old love?" Sherringham repeated, looking hard at the picture.

"Before you are on with the new!" Nick had no sooner uttered these words than he coloured; it occurred to him that Peter would probably think he was alluding to Julia. He therefore added quickly: "It isn't so easy to cease to represent an affectionate constituency. Really, most of my time for a fortnight has been given up to letter-writing. They've all been unexpectedly charming. I should have thought they would have loathed and despised me. But not a bit of it; they cling to me fondly—they struggle with me tenderly. I've been down to talk with them about it, and we've passed the most sociable, delightful hours. I've designated my successor; I've felt a good deal like the Emperor Charles the Fifth when about to retire to the monastery of Yuste. The more I've seen of them in this way the more I've liked them, and they declare it has been the same with themselves as regards me. We spend our time in assuring each other that we haven't begun to know each other till now. In short, it's all wonderfully jolly, but it isn't business. *C'est magnifique, mais ce n'est pas la guerre.*"

"They're not so charming as they might be if they don't offer to keep you and let you paint."

"They do, almost; it's fantastic," said Nick. "Remember they haven't seen any of my painting yet."

"Well, I'm sorry for you; we live in too enlightened an age," Peter declared. "You can't suffer for art. Your experience is interesting; it seems to show that, at the tremendous pitch of civilization we've reached, you can't suffer from anything but hunger."

"I shall doubtless do that in abundance."

"Never, never, when you paint as well as this."

"Oh, come, you're too good to be true," Nick replied. "But where did you learn that one's larder is full in proportion as one's work is fine?"

Peter gave him no satisfaction on this curious point—he only continued to look at the picture; after which, in a moment, he said: "I'll give you your price for it on the spot."

"Dear boy, you're so magnanimous that you shall have it for nothing!" Nick exclaimed, passing his arm into his companion's.

Peter was silent at first. "Why do you call me magnanimous?"

"Oh, bless my soul, it's hers—I forget!" laughed Nick, failing in his turn to answer the other's inquiry. "But you shall have another."

"Another? Are you going to do another?"

"This very morning. That is I shall begin it. I've heard from her; she's coming to sit—a short time hence."

Peter turned away a little at this, releasing himself, and, as if the movement had been an effect of Nick's words, looked at his watch earnestly, to dissipate that appearance. He fell back, to consider the picture from further off. "The more you do her the better; she has all the qualities of a great model. From that point of view it's a pity she has another trade: she might make so good a thing of this one. But how shall you do her again?" Sherringham continued, ingenuously.

"Oh, I can scarcely say; we'll arrange something; we'll talk it over. It's extraordinary how well she enters into what one wants: she knows more than one does one's self. She isn't the first comer. However, you know all about that, since you invented her, didn't you? That's what she says; she's awfully sweet on you," Nick pursued. "What I ought to do is to try something as different as possible from that thing; not the sibyl, the muse, the tremendous creature, but the charming woman, the person one knows, in different gear, as she appears *en ville*, as she calls it. I'll do something really serious and send it to you out there with my respects. It will remind you of home, and perhaps a little even of me. If she knows it's for you she'll throw herself into it in the right spirit.

Leave it to us, my dear fellow; we'll turn out something good."

"It's jolly to hear you; but I shall send you a cheque," said Peter.

"I suppose it's all right in your position, but you're too proud," his kinsman answered.

"What do you mean by my position?"

"Your exaltation, your high connection with the country, your treating with sovereign powers as the representative of a sovereign power. Isn't that what they call 'em?"

Sherringham, who had turned again toward his companion, listened to this with his eyes fixed on Nick's face, while at the same time he once more drew forth his watch. "Brute!" he exclaimed familiarly, at the same time dropping his eyes on the watch. "At what time did you say you expected your sitter?"

"Oh, we've plenty of time; don't be afraid of letting me see you agitated by her presence."

"Brute!" Sherringham again ejaculated.

This friendly personal note cleared the air, made the communication between the two men closer. "Stay with me and talk to me," said Nick; "I dare say it's good for me. Heaven knows when I shall see you so independently again."

"Have you got something more to show me, then—some other work?" Sherringham asked.

"Must I bribe you by setting my signboards in a row? You know what I've done; by which I mean of course you know what I haven't done. My work, as you are so good as to call it, has hitherto been horrible rot. I've had no time, no opportunity, no continuity. I must go and sit down in a corner and learn my alphabet. That thing isn't good; what I shall do for you won't be good. Don't protest, my dear fellow; nothing will be fit to look at for a long time. And think of my ridiculous age. As the populace say (or don't they say it?) it's a rum go. It won't be amusing."

"Oh, you're so clever you'll get on fast," Sherringham replied, trying to think how he could most directly disobey his companion's injunction not to protest.

"I mean it won't be amusing for others," said Nick, unperturbed by this violation. "They want results, and small blame to them."

"Well, whatever you do, don't talk like Mr. Gabriel Nash," Peter went on. "Sometimes I think you're just going to."

Nick stared a moment. "Why, he never would have said that. 'They want results, the damned fools'—that would have been more in his key."

"It's the difference of a *nuance*. And are you extraordinarily happy?" Peter added, as Nick now obliged him by arranging half a dozen canvases so that he could look at them.

"Not so much so, doubtless, as the artistic life ought to make one; because all one's people are not so infatuated as one's electors. But little by little I'm learning the beauty of obstinacy."

"Your mother's very bad; I lunched with her the day before yesterday."

"Yes, I know—I know," said Nick hastily; "but it's too late—it's too late. I must just peg away here and not mind. I've after all a great advantage in my life."

Sherringham hesitated. "And that would be—?"

"Oh, I mean knowing what I want to do: that's everything, you know."

"It's an advantage however that you've only just come in for, isn't it?"

"Yes, but having waited only makes me prize it the more. I've got it now; and it makes up, for the present, for the absence of some other things."

Again Sherringham was silent awhile. "That sounds a little flat," he remarked at last.

"It depends upon what you compare it with. It's rather more pointed than the House of Commons."

"Oh, I never thought I should like that."

There was another pause, during which Nick moved about the room, turning up old sketches to see if he had anything more to show his visitor, while Sherringham continued to look at the unfinished and in some cases, as it seemed to him, unpromising productions already submitted to his attention. They were much less interesting than the portrait of Miriam Rooth and, it would have appeared, much less significant of ability. For that particular effort Nick's talent had taken an unprecedented spring. This was the reflection that Peter made, as he had made it intensely before; but the words he presently uttered had no visible connection with it. They only consisted of the abrupt inquiry: "Have you heard anything from Julia?"

"Not a syllable. Have you?"

"Dear, no; she never writes to me."

"But won't she on the occasion of your promotion?"

"I dare say not," said Peter: and this was the only reference to Mrs. Dallow that passed between her brother and her late intended. It left a slight agitation of the atmosphere, which Sherringham proceeded to allay by an allusion comparatively speaking more relevant. He expressed disappointment that Biddy should not have come in; having had an idea that she was always in Rosedale Road of a morning. That was the other moiety of his present errand—the wish to see her and give her a message for Lady Agnes, upon whom at so early an hour he had not presumed to intrude in Calcutta Gardens. Nick replied that Biddy did in point of fact almost always turn up, and for the most part early; she came to wish him good morning and start him for the day. She was a devoted Electra, laying a cool, healing hand on a distracted Orestes. He reminded Peter however that he would have a chance of seeing her that evening, and of seeing Lady Agnes; for wasn't he to do them the honour of dining in Calcutta Gardens? Biddy, the day before, had arrived full of that excitement. Peter explained that this was exactly the sad subject of his actual *démarche*: the project of the dinner in Calcutta Gardens had, to his exceeding regret, fallen to pieces. The fact was (didn't Nick know it?) the night had been suddenly and perversely fixed for Miriam's *première*, and he was under a definite engagement with her not to stay away from it. To add to the bore of the thing he was obliged to return to Paris the very next morning. He was quite awfully sorry, for he had promised Lady Agnes: he didn't understand then about Miriam's affair, in regard to which he had given a previous pledge. He was more sorry than he could say, but he could never fail Miss Rooth: he had professed from the first an interest in her which he must live up to a little more. This was his last chance—he hadn't been near her at the trying time she first produced herself. And the second night of the play wouldn't do—it must be the first or nothing. Besides, he couldn't wait over till Monday.

While Peter enumerated these complications his companion was occupied in polishing with a cloth a palette that he had just been scraping. "I see what you mean—I'm very sorry too," said Nick. "I'm sorry you can't give my mother this joy—I give her so little."

"My dear fellow, you might give her a little more. It's rather too much to expect *me* to make up for your omissions!"

Nick looked at Peter with a moment's fixedness while he rubbed his palette; and for that moment he felt the temptation to reply: "There's a way you could do that, to a considerable extent—I think you guess it!—which wouldn't be intrinsically disagreeable." But the impulse passed, without expressing itself in speech, and he simply answered: "You can make this all clear to Biddy when she comes, and she'll make it clear to my mother."

"Poor little Biddy!" Sherringham mentally exclaimed, thinking of the girl with that job before her; but what he articulated was that this was exactly why he had come to the studio. He had inflicted his company on Lady Agnes on Thursday and had partaken of a meal with her, but he had not seen Biddy, though he had waited for her, hoping she would come in. Now he would wait for her again—she was thoroughly worth it.

"Patience, patience, you've always me," said Nick; to which he subjoined: "If it's a question of going to the play I scarcely see why you shouldn't dine at my mother's all the same. People go to the play after dinner."

"Yes, but it wouldn't be fair, it wouldn't be decent: it's a case when I must be in my seat from the rise of the curtain. I should force your mother to dine an hour earlier than usual, and then, in return for this courtesy, go off to my entertainment at eight o'clock, leaving her and Grace and Biddy languishing there. I wish I had proposed in time that they should go with me," Peter continued, not very ingenuously.

"You might do that still," Nick suggested.

"Oh, at this time of day it would be impossible to get a box."

"I'll speak to Miss Rooth about it, if you like, when she comes," smiled Nick.

"No, it wouldn't do," said Peter, turning away and looking once more at his watch. He made tacitly the addition that still less than asking Lady Agnes, for his convenience, to dine early, would *this* be decent, would it be fair. His taking Biddy the night he dined with her and with Miss Tressilian had been something very like a violation of those proprieties. He couldn't say this to Nick, who remarked in a moment that it was all right, for Peter's action left him his own freedom.

"Your own freedom?" Peter echoed interrogatively, turning round.

"Why, you see now I can go to the theatre myself."

"Certainly; I hadn't thought of that. You would have been going."

"I gave it up for the prospect of your company."

"Upon my word, you're too good—I don't deserve such sacrifices," said Sherringham, who saw from Nick's face that this was not a figure of speech but the absolute truth. "Didn't it however occur to you that, as it would turn out, I might—that I even naturally would—myself be going?" he added.

Nick broke into a laugh. "It would have occurred to me if I understood a little better—" And he paused, still laughing.

"If you understood a little better what?" Peter demanded.

"Your situation, simply."

Peter looked at him a moment. "Dine with me to-night independently; we'll go to the theatre together, and then you'll understand it."

"With pleasure, with pleasure: we'll have a jolly evening," said Nick.

"Call it jolly if you like. When did you say she was coming?" Peter asked.

"Biddy? Oh, probably, as I tell you, at any moment."

"I mean the great Miriam," Peter replied.

"The great Miriam, if she's punctual, will be here in about forty minutes."

"And will she be likely to find your sister?"

"My dear fellow, that will depend on whether my sister remains to see her."

"Exactly; but the point is whether you'll allow her to remain, isn't it?"

Nick looked slightly mystified. "Why shouldn't she do as she likes?"

"In that case she'll probably go."

"Yes, unless she stays."

"Don't let her," Peter dropped; "send her away." And to explain this he added: "It doesn't seem exactly the right sort of thing, young girls meeting actresses." His explanation in turn struck him as requiring another clause; so he went on: "At least it isn't thought the right sort of thing abroad, and even in England my foreign ideas stick to me."

Even with this amplification however his proposition evidently still appeared to his companion to have a flaw; which, after he had considered it a moment, Nick exposed in the simple words: "Why, you originally introduced them, in Paris—Biddy and Miss Rooth. Didn't they meet at your rooms and fraternize, and wasn't that much more abroad than this?"

"So they did, but she didn't like it," Peter answered, suspecting that for a diplomatist he looked foolish.

"Miss Rooth didn't like it?" Nick persisted.

"That I confess I've forgotten. Besides, she was not an actress then. What I remember is that Biddy wasn't particularly pleased with her."

"Why, she thought her wonderful—praised her to the skies. I remember too."

"She didn't like her as a woman; she praised her as an actress."

"I thought you said she wasn't an actress then," Nick rejoined.

Peter hesitated. "Oh, Biddy thought so. She has seen her since, moreover. I took her the other night, and her curiosity's satisfied."

"It's not of any consequence, and if there's a reason for it I'll bundle her off directly. But the great Miriam seems such a kind, good woman."

"So she is, charming—charming," said Peter, looking hard at Nick.

"Here comes Biddy now," this young man went on. "I hear her at the door; you can warn her yourself."

"It isn't a question of 'warning'—that's not in the least my idea. But I'll take Biddy away," said Peter.

"That will be still more energetic."

"Oh, it's simply selfish—I like her company." Peter had turned as if to go to the door to meet the girl; but he quickly checked himself, lingering in the middle of the room, and the next instant Biddy had come in. When she saw him there she also stopped.

XI.

"A RRIVE, ARRIVE, my child," said Nick. "Peter's weary of waiting for you."

"Ah, he's come to say he won't dine with us to-night!" Biddy stood with her hand on the latch.

"I leave town to-morrow; I've everything to do; I'm broken-hearted; it's impossible," Peter pleaded. "Please make my peace with your mother; I'm ashamed of not having written to her last night."

Biddy closed the door and came in, while her brother said to her: "How in the world did you guess it?"

"I saw it in the *Morning Post*," Biddy answered, looking at Peter.

"In the *Morning Post*?" her cousin repeated.

"I saw there's to be a first night at that theatre, the one you took us to. So I said: 'Oh, he'll go there.'"

"Yes, I've got to do that too," Peter admitted.

"She's going to sit to me again this morning, the wonderful actress of that theatre—she has made an appointment: so you see I'm getting on," Nick announced to Biddy.

"Oh, I'm so glad—she's so splendid!" The girl looked away from Peter now, but not, though it seemed to fill the place, at the triumphant portrait of Miriam Rooth.

"I'm delighted you've come in. I *have* waited for you," Peter hastened to declare to Biddy, though he was conscious that this was under the circumstances meagre.

"Aren't you coming to see us again?"

"I'm in despair, but I shall really not have time. Therefore it's a blessing not to have missed you here."

"I'm very glad," said Biddy. Then she added: "And you're going to America—to stay a long time?"

"Till I'm sent to some better place."

"And will that better place be as far away?"

"Oh Biddy, it wouldn't be better then," said Peter.

"Do you mean they'll give you something to do at home?"

"Hardly that. But I've got a tremendous lot to do at home to-day." For the twentieth time Peter referred to his watch.

Biddy turned to her brother, who murmured to her: "You

might bid me good morning." She kissed him, and he asked what the news might be in Calcutta Gardens; to which she replied:

"The only news is, of course, that, poor dears! they're making great preparations for Peter. Mamma thinks you must have had such a nasty dinner the other day," the girl continued, to the guest of that romantic occasion.

"Faithless Peter!" said Nick, beginning to whistle and to arrange a canvas in anticipation of Miriam's arrival.

"Dear Biddy, thank your stars you are not in my horrid profession," protested the personage thus designated. "One is bowled about like a cricket-ball, unable to answer for one's freedom or one's comfort from one moment to another."

"Oh, ours is the true profession—Biddy's and mine," Nick broke out, setting up his canvas; "the career of liberty and peace, of charming long mornings, spent in a still north light in the contemplation, and I may even say in the company, of the amiable and the beautiful."

"That certainly is the case when Biddy comes to see you," Peter returned.

Biddy smiled at him. "I come every day. *Anch' io son pittore!* I encourage Nick awfully."

"It's a pity I'm not a martyr; she would bravely perish with me," Nick said.

"You are—you are a martyr—when people say such odious things!" the girl cried. "They do say them. I've heard many more than I've repeated to you."

"It's you yourself then, indignant and sympathetic, who are the martyr," observed Peter, who wanted greatly to be kind to her.

"Oh, I don't care!" she answered, colouring in response to this; and she continued, to Peter: "Don't you think one can do as much good by painting great works of art as by—as by what papa used to do? Don't you think art is necessary to the happiness, to the greatness of a people? Don't you think it's manly and honourable? Do you think a passion for it is a thing to be ashamed of? Don't you think the artist—the conscientious, the serious one—is as distinguished a member of society as any one else?"

Peter and Nick looked at each other and laughed at the way

she had got up her subject, and Nick asked his visitor if she
didn't express it all in perfection. "I delight in general in artists, but I delight still more in their defenders," Peter jested,
to Biddy.

"Ah, don't attack me, if you are wise," Nick said.

"One is tempted to, when it makes Biddy so fine."

"Well, that's the way she encourages me; it's meat and
drink to me," Nick went on. "At the same time I'm bound to
say there is a little whistling in the dark in it."

"In the dark?" his sister demanded.

"The obscurity, my dear child, of your own aspirations,
your mysterious ambitions and plastic visions. Aren't there
some heavyish shadows there?"

"Why, I never cared for politics."

"No, but you cared for life, you cared for society, and you
have chosen the path of solitude and concentration."

"You horrid boy!" said Biddy.

"Give it up, that arduous steep—give it up and come out
with me," Peter interposed.

"Come out with you?"

"Let us walk a little, or even drive a little. Let us at any rate
talk a little."

"I thought you had so much to do," Biddy candidly objected.

"So I have, but why shouldn't you do a part of it with me?
Would there be any harm? I'm going to some tiresome
shops—you'll cheer the economical hour."

The girl hesitated; then she turned to Nick. "Would there
be any harm?"

"Oh, it's none of *his* business!" Peter protested.

"He had better take you home to your mother."

"I'm going home—I sha'n't stay here to-day," said Biddy.
Then to Peter: "I came in a hansom, but I shall walk back.
Come that way with me."

"With singular pleasure. But I shall not be able to go in,"
Sherringham added.

"Oh, that's no matter," said Biddy. "Good-bye, Nick."

"You understand then that we dine together—at seven
sharp. Wouldn't a club be best?" Peter, before going, inquired of Nick. He suggested further which club it should

be; and his words led Biddy, who had directed her steps toward the door, to turn a moment, as if she were on the point of asking reproachfully whether it was for this Peter had given up Calcutta Gardens. But this impulse, if impulse it was, had no sequel except so far as it was a sequel that Peter spontaneously explained to her, after Nick had assented to his conditions, that her brother too had a desire to go to Miss Rooth's first night and had already promised to accompany him.

"Oh, that's perfect; it will be so good for him—won't it? if he's going to paint her again," Biddy responded.

"I think there's nothing so good for him as that he happens to have such a sister as you," Peter observed as they went out. As he spoke he heard outside the sound of a carriage stopping; and before Biddy, who was in front of him, opened the door of the house he had time to say to himself: "What a bore—there's Miriam!" The opened door showed him that he was right—this young lady was in the act of alighting from the brougham provided by Basil Dashwood's thrifty zeal. Her mother followed her, and both the new visitors exclaimed and rejoiced, in their demonstrative way, as their eyes fell upon their valued friend. The door had closed behind Peter, but he instantly and violently rang, so that they should be admitted with as little delay as possible, while he remained slightly disconcerted by the prompt occurrence of an encounter he had sought to avert. It ministered moreover a little to this particular sensation that Miriam appeared to have come somewhat before her time. The incident promised however to pass off in the happiest way. Before he knew it both the ladies had taken possession of Biddy, who looked at them with comparative coldness, tempered indeed by a faint glow of apprehension, and Miriam had broken out:

"We know you, we know you; we saw you in Paris, and you came to my theatre a short time ago with Mr. Sherringham."

"We know your mother, Lady Agnes Dormer. I hope her ladyship is very well," said Mrs. Rooth, who had never struck Sherringham as a more objectionable old woman.

"You offered to do a head of me, or something or other: didn't you tell me you work in clay? I dare say you've forgotten all about it, but I should be delighted," Miriam pursued, with the richest urbanity.

Peter was not concerned with her mother's pervasiveness, though he didn't like Biddy to see even that; but he hoped his companion would take the overcharged benevolence of the young actress in the spirit in which, rather to his surprise, it evidently was offered.

"I've sat to your clever brother many times," said Miriam; "I'm going to sit again. I dare say you've seen what we've done—he's too delightful. *Si vous saviez comme cela me repose!*" she added, turning for a moment to Sherringham. Then she continued, smiling, to Biddy: "Only he oughtn't to have thrown up such prospects, you know. I have an idea I wasn't nice to you that day in Paris—I was nervous and scared and perverse. I remember perfectly; I *was* odious. But I'm better now—you'd see if you were to know me. I'm not a bad girl—really I'm not. But you must have your own friends. Happy they—you look so charming! Immensely like Mr. Dormer, especially about the eyes; isn't she, mamma?"

"She comes of a beautiful Norman race—the finest, purest strain," the old woman simpered. "Mr. Dormer is sometimes so good as to come and see us—we are always at home on Sunday; and if some day you were so venturesome as to come with him you might perhaps find it pleasant, though very different of course from the circle in which you habitually move."

Biddy murmured a vague recognition of these wonderful civilities, and Miriam commented: "Different, yes; but we're all right, you know. Do come," she added. Then turning to Sherringham: "Remember what I told you—I don't expect you to-night."

"Oh, I understand; I shall come," Peter answered, growing red.

"It will be idiotic. Keep him, keep him away—don't let him," Miriam went on, to Biddy; with which, as Nick's portals now were gaping, she drew her mother away.

Peter at this walked off briskly with Biddy, dropping as he did so: "She's too fantastic!"

"Yes, but so tremendously good-looking. I shall ask Nick to take me there," the girl continued after a moment.

"Well, she'll do you no harm. They're all right, as she says. It's the world of art—you were standing up so for art just now."

"Oh, I wasn't thinking so much of that kind," said Biddy.

"There's only one kind—it's all the same thing. If one sort's good the other is."

Biddy walked along a moment. "Is she serious? Is she conscientious?"

"Oh, she has the makings of a great artist," said Peter.

"I'm glad to hear you think a woman can be one."

"In that line there has never been any doubt about it."

"And only in that line?"

"I mean on the stage in general, dramatic or lyric. It's as the actress that the woman produces the most complete and satisfactory artistic results."

"And only as the actress?"

"Yes, there's another art in which she's not bad."

"Which one do you mean?" asked Biddy.

"That of being charming and good and indispensable to man."

"Oh, that isn't an art."

"Then you leave her only the stage. Take it if you like in the widest sense."

Biddy appeared to reflect a moment, as if to see what sense this might be. But she found none that was wide enough, for she cried the next minute: "Do you mean to say there's nothing for a woman but to be an actress?"

"Never in my life. I only say that that's the best thing for a woman to be who finds herself irresistibly carried into the practice of the arts; for there her capacity for them has most application and her incapacity for them least. But at the same time I strongly recommend her not to be an artist if she can possibly help it. It's a devil of a life."

"Oh, I know; men want women not to be anything."

"It's a poor little refuge they try to take from the overwhelming consciousness that you are in fact everything."

"Everything? That's the kind of thing you say to keep us quiet."

"Dear Biddy, you see how well we succeed!" laughed Sherringham; to which the girl responded by inquiring irrelevantly:

"Why is it so necessary for you to go to the theatre tonight, if Miss Rooth doesn't want you to?"

"My dear child, she does. But that has nothing to do with it."

"Why then did she say that she doesn't?"

"Oh, because she meant just the contrary."

"Is she so false then—is she so vulgar?"

"She speaks a special language; practically it isn't false, because it renders her thought, and those who know her understand it."

"But she doesn't use it only to those who know her, since she asked me, who have so little the honour of her acquaintance, to keep you away to-night. How am I to know that she meant by that that I'm to urge you on to go?"

Sherringham was on the point of replying: "Because you have my word for it;" but he shrank in fact from giving his word—he had some fine scruples—and endeavoured to get out of his embarrassment by a general tribute. "Dear Biddy, you're delightfully acute: you're quite as clever as Miss Rooth." He felt however that this was scarcely adequate, and he continued: "The truth is, its being important for me to go is a matter quite independent of that young lady's wishing it or not wishing it. There happens to be a definite, intrinsic propriety in it which determines the matter and which it would take me long to explain."

"I see. But fancy your 'explaining' to me: you make me feel so indiscreet!" the girl cried quickly—an exclamation which touched him because he was not aware that, quick as it had been, Biddy had still had time to be struck first (though she wouldn't for the world have expressed it) with the oddity of such a duty at such a time. In fact that oddity, during a silence of some minutes, came back to Peter himself: the note had been forced—it sounded almost ignobly frivolous for a man on the eve of proceeding to a high diplomatic post. The effect of this however was not to make him break out with: "Hang it, I *will* keep my engagement to your mother!" but to fill him with the wish that he could shorten his actual excursion by taking Biddy the rest of the way in a cab. He was uncomfortable, and there were hansoms about which he looked at wistfully. While he was so occupied his companion took up the talk by an abrupt interrogation.

"Why did she say that Nick oughtn't to have resigned his seat?"

"Oh, I don't know; it struck her so. It doesn't matter much."

"If she's an artist herself why doesn't she like people to go in for art, especially when Nick has given his time to painting her so beautifully? Why does she come there so often if she disapproves of what he has done?"

"Oh, Miriam's disapproval—it doesn't count; it's a manner of speaking."

"Of speaking untruths, do you mean? Does she think just the reverse—is that the way she talks about everything?"

"We always admire most what we can do least," Peter replied; "and Miriam of course isn't political. She ranks painters more or less with her own profession, about which already, new as she is to it, she has no illusions. They're all artists; it's the same general sort of thing. She prefers men of the world—men of action."

"Is that the reason she likes you?" Biddy mocked.

"Ah, she doesn't like me—couldn't you see it?"

Biddy said nothing for a moment; then she asked: "Is that why she lets you call her 'Miriam'?"

"Oh, I don't, to her face."

"Ah, only to mine!" laughed Biddy.

"One says that as one says 'Rachel' of her great predecessor."

"Except that she isn't so great quite yet, is she?"

"Far from it; she's the freshest of novices—she has scarcely been four months on the stage. But no novice has ever been such an adept. She'll go very fast, and I dare say that before long she'll be magnificent."

"What a pity you'll not see that!" Biddy remarked, after a short interval.

"Not see it?"

"If you're thousands of miles away."

"It *is* a pity," Peter said; "and since you mention it I don't mind frankly telling you—throwing myself on your mercy, as it were—that that's why I make such a point of a rare occasion like to-night. I've a weakness for the drama that, as you perhaps know, I've never concealed, and this impression will probably have to last me, in some barren spot, for many, many years."

"I understand—I understand. I hope therefore it will be charming." And Biddy walked faster.

"Just as some other charming impressions will have to last," Peter added, conscious of a certain effort that he was obliged to make to keep up with her. She seemed almost to be running away from him, a circumstance which led him to suggest, after they had proceeded a little further without more words, that if she were in a hurry they had perhaps better take a cab. Her face was strange and touching to him as she turned it to reply quickly:

"Oh, I'm not in the least in a hurry, and I think, really, I had better walk."

"We'll walk then, by all means!" Peter declared, with slightly exaggerated gaiety; in pursuance of which they went on a hundred yards. Biddy kept the same pace; yet it was scarcely a surprise to Sherringham that she should suddenly stop with the exclamation:

"After all, though I'm not in a hurry I'm tired! I had better have a cab; please call that one," she added, looking about her.

They were in a straight, black, ugly street, where the small, cheap, gray-faced houses had no expression save that of a rueful, inconsolable consciousness of its want of identity. They would have constituted a "terrace" if they could, but they had given it up. Even a hansom which loitered across the end of the vista turned a sceptical back upon it, so that Sherringham had to lift his voice in a loud appeal. He stood with Biddy watching the cab approach them. "This is one of the charming things you'll remember," she said, turning her eyes to the general dreariness from the particular figure of the vehicle, which was antiquated and clumsy. Before he could reply she had lightly stepped into the cab; but as he answered: "Most assuredly it is," and prepared to follow her she quickly closed the apron.

"I must go alone; you've lots of things to do—it's all

right;" and through the aperture in the roof she gave the driver her address. She had spoken with decision, and Peter recognized that she wished to get away from him. Her eyes betrayed it as well as her voice, in a look—not a hard one however—which as he stood there with his hand on the cab he had time to take from her. "Good-bye, Peter," she smiled; and as the cab began to rumble away he uttered the same tepid, ridiculous farewell.

XII.

WHEN MIRIAM and her mother went into the studio Nick Dormer had stopped whistling, but he was still gay enough to receive them with every demonstration of sociability. He thought his studio a poor place, ungarnished, untapestried, a mere seat of rude industry, with all its revelations and honours still to come. But both his visitors smiled upon it a good deal in the same way in which they had smiled on Bridget Dormer when they met her at the door: Mrs. Rooth because vague, prudent approbation was the habit of her foolish little face—it was ever the least danger; and Miriam because apparently she was genuinely glad to find herself within the walls which she spoke of now as her asylum. She broke out in this strain to her host almost as soon as she had crossed the threshold, commending his circumstances, his conditions of work as infinitely happier than her own. He was quiet, independent, absolute, free to do what he liked as he liked it, shut up in his little temple with his altar and his divinity; not hustled about in a mob of people, having to posture and grin to pit and gallery, to square himself at every step with insufferable conventions and with the ignorance and vanity of others. He was blissfully alone.

"Mercy, how you do abuse your fine profession! I'm sure I never urged you to adopt it!" Mrs. Rooth cried, in real bewilderment, to her daughter.

"She was abusing mine still more, the other day," joked Nick—"telling me I ought to be ashamed of it and of myself."

"Oh, I never know from one moment to the other—I live with my heart in my mouth," sighed the old woman.

"Aren't you quiet about the great thing—about my behaviour?" Miriam smiled. "My only extravagances are intellectual."

"I don't know what you call your behaviour."

"You would very soon if it were not what it is."

"And I don't know what you call intellectual," grumbled Mrs. Rooth.

"Yes, but I don't see very well how I could make you understand that. At any rate," Miriam went on, looking at Nick,

"I retract what I said the other day about Mr. Dormer. I've no wish to quarrel with him about the way he has determined to dispose of his life, because after all it does suit me very well. It rests me, this little devoted corner; oh, it rests me. It's out of the tussle and the heat, it's deliciously still, and they can't get at me. Ah, when art's like this, *à la bonne heure!*" And she looked round on such a presentment of "art" with a splendid air that made Nick burst out laughing at its contrast with the humble fact. Miriam smiled at him as if she liked to be the cause of his mirth, and went on appealing to him: "You'll always let me come here for an hour, won't you, to take breath—to let the whirlwind pass? You needn't trouble yourself about me; I don't mean to impose on you in the least the necessity of painting me, though if that's a manner of helping you to get on you may be sure it will always be open to you. Do what you like with me in that respect; only let me sit here on a high stool, keeping well out of your way, and see what you happen to be doing. I'll tell you my own adventures when you want to hear them."

"The fewer adventures you have to tell, the better, my dear," said Mrs. Rooth; "and if Mr. Dormer keeps you quiet he will add ten years to my life."

"This is an interesting comment on Mr. Dormer's own quietus, on his independence and sweet solitude," Nick observed. "Miss Rooth has to work with others, which is after all only what Mr. Dormer has to do when he works with Miss Rooth. What do you make of the inevitable sitter?"

"Oh," answered Miriam, "you can say to the sitter: 'Hold your tongue, you brute!'"

"Isn't it a good deal in that manner that I've heard you address your comrades at the theatre?" asked Mrs. Rooth. "That's why my heart's in my mouth."

"Yes, but they hit me back; they reply to me—*comme de raison*—as I should never think of replying to Mr. Dormer. It's a great advantage to him that when he's peremptory with his model it only makes her better, adds to her expression of gloomy grandeur."

"We did the gloomy grandeur in the other picture; suppose therefore we try something different in this," suggested Nick.

"It *is* serious, it *is* grand," murmured Mrs. Rooth, who had taken up a rapt attitude before the portrait of her daughter. "It makes one wonder what she's thinking of. Beautiful, commendable things—that's what it seems to say."

"What can I be thinking of but the tremendous wisdom of my mother?" Miriam inquired. "I brought her this morning to see that thing—she had only seen it in its earliest stage—and not to presume to advise you about anything else you may be so good as to embark on. She wanted, or she professed that she wanted, terribly to know what you had finally arrived at. She was too impatient to wait till you should send it home."

"Ah, send it home—send it home; let us have it always with us!" Mrs. Rooth urged. "It will hold us up; it will keep us on the heights, near the stars—be always for us a symbol and a reminder!"

"You see I was right," Miriam went on; "for she appreciates thoroughly, in her own way, and understands. But if she worries or distracts you I'll send her directly home—I've kept the carriage there on purpose. I must add that I don't feel quite safe to-day in letting her out of my sight. She's liable to make dashes at the theatre and play unconscionable tricks there. I shall never again accuse mamma of a want of interest in my profession. Her interest to-day exceeds even my own. She's all over the place and she has ideas; ah, but ideas! She's capable of turning up at the theatre at five o'clock this afternoon and demanding that the scenery of the third act be repainted. For myself, I've not a word more to say on the subject—I've accepted the situation. Everything is no doubt wrong; but nothing can possibly be right. Let us eat and drink, for to-night we die. If you like, mamma shall go and sit in the carriage, and as there's no means of fastening the doors (is there?) your servant shall keep guard over her."

"Just as you are now—be so good as to remain so; sitting just that way—leaning back, with a smile in your eyes and one hand on the sofa beside you, supporting you a little. I shall stick a flower into the other hand—let it lie in your lap, just as it is. Keep that thing on your head—it's admirably uncovered: do you call the construction a bonnet?—and let your head fall back a little. There it is—it's found. This time I shall really do something, and it will be as different as you like from that crazy job. *Pazienza!*" It was in these irrelevant but earnest words that Nick responded to his sitter's uttered vagaries, of which her charming tone and countenance diminished the superficial acerbity. He held up his hands a moment, to fix her in her limits, and a few minutes afterwards had a happy sense of having begun to work.

"The smile in her eyes—don't forget the smile in her eyes!" Mrs. Rooth exclaimed softly, turning away and creeping about the room. "That will make it so different from the other picture and show the two sides of her genius, with the wonderful range between them. It will be a magnificent pendant; and though I dare say I shall strike you as greedy, you must let me hope you will send it home too."

Mrs. Rooth explored the place discreetly, on tiptoe, gossiping as she went and bending her head and her eyeglass over various objects with an air of imperfect comprehension which did not prevent Nick from being reminded of the story of her underhand commercial habits told by Gabriel Nash at the exhibition in Paris, the first time her name had fallen on his ear. A queer old woman from whom, if you approached her in the right way, you could buy old pots—it was in this character that she had originally been introduced to him. He had lost sight of it afterwards, but it revived again as his observant eyes, at the same time that they followed his active hand, became aware of her instinctive appraising gestures. There was a moment when he laughed out gaily—there was so little in his poor studio to appraise. Mrs. Rooth's vague, polite, disappointed bent back and head made a subject, the subject of a sketch, in an instant: they gave such a sudden pictorial glimpse of the element of race. He found himself seeing the immemorial Jewess in her, holding up a candle in a crammed back-shop. There was no candle indeed, and his studio was not crammed, and it had never occurred to him before that she was of Hebrew strain, except on the general theory, held with pertinacity by several clever people, that most of us are more or less so. The late Rudolf Roth had been, and his daughter was visibly her father's child; so that, flanked by such a pair, good Semitic reasons were surely not wanting to the mother. Receiving Miriam's little satiric shower without shaking her shoulders, she might at any rate have been the descendant of a tribe long persecuted. Her blandness was imperturbable—she professed that she would be as still as a mouse. Miriam, on the other side of the room, in the tranquil beauty of her attitude (it was "found" indeed, as Nick had said), watched her a little and then exclaimed that she wished she had locked her up at home. Putting aside her humorous account of the dangers to which she was exposed from her mother, it was not whimsical to imagine that, within the limits of that repose from which the Neville-Nugents never wholly departed, Mrs. Rooth might indeed be a trifle fidgety and have something on her mind. Nick presently mentioned that it would not be possible for him to "send home" this second performance; and he added, in the exuberance of having already got a little into relation with his work, that perhaps that didn't matter, inasmuch as—if Miriam would give him his time, to say nothing of her own—a third masterpiece might also some day very well come off. His model rose to this without conditions, assuring him that he might count upon her till she grew too old and too ugly and that nothing would make her so happy as that he should paint her as often as Romney had painted the celebrated Lady Hamilton. "Ah, Lady Hamilton!" deprecated Mrs. Rooth; while Miriam, who had on occasion the candour of a fine acquisitiveness, inquired what particular reason there might be for his not letting them have the picture he was now beginning.

"Why, I've promised it to Peter Sherringham—he has offered me money for it," Nick replied. "However, he's welcome to it for nothing, poor fellow, and I shall be delighted to do the best I can for him."

Mrs. Rooth, still prowling, stopped in the middle of the room at this, and Miriam exclaimed: "He offered you money—just as we came in?"

"You met him, then, at the door, with my sister? I supposed you had—he's taking her home," said Nick.

"Your sister's a lovely girl—such an aristocratic type!" breathed Mrs. Rooth. Then she added: "I've a tremendous confession to make to you."

"Mamma's confessions have to be tremendous to correspond with her crimes," said Miriam. "She asked Miss Dormer to come and see us—suggested even that you might bring her some Sunday. I don't like the way mamma does such things—too much humility, too many *simagrées*, after all; but I also said what I could to be nice to her. Your sister *is* charming—awfully pretty and modest. If you were to press me I should tell you frankly that it seems to me rather a social muddle, this rubbing shoulders of 'nice girls' and *filles de théâtre*; I shouldn't think it would do your young ladies much good. However, it's their own affair, and no doubt there's no more need of their thinking we're worse than we are than of their thinking we're better. The people they live with don't seem to know the difference—I sometimes make my reflections about the public one works for."

"Ah, if you go in for the public's knowing differences you're far too particular," Nick laughed. "*D'où tombez-vous?* as you affected French people say. If you have anything at stake on that, you had simply better not play."

"Dear Mr. Dormer, don't encourage her to be so dreadful; for it *is* dreadful, the way she talks," Mrs. Rooth broke in. "One would think we were not respectable—one would think I had never known what I have known and been what I have been."

"What one would think, beloved mother, is that you are a still greater humbug than you are. It's you, on the contrary, who go down on your knees, who pour forth apologies about our being vagabonds."

"Vagabonds—listen to her!—after the education I've given her and our magnificent prospects!" wailed Mrs. Rooth, sinking, with clasped hands, upon the nearest ottoman.

"Not after our prospects, if prospects they are: a good deal before them. Yes, you've taught me tongues, and I'm greatly obliged to you—they no doubt impart variety, as well as incoherency, to my conversation; and that of people in our line is for the most part notoriously monotonous and shoppy. The gift of tongues is in general the sign of your genuine adventurer. Dear mamma, I've no low standard—that's the last thing," Miriam went on. "My weakness is my exalted conception of respectability. Ah, *parlez-moi de ça* and of the way I understand it! Oh, if I were to go in for being respectable you'd see something fine. I'm awfully conservative and I know what respectability is, even when I meet people of society on the accidental middle ground of glowering or smirking. I know also what it isn't—it isn't the sweet union of little girls and actresses. I should carry it much further than any of these people: I should never look at the likes of us! Every hour I live I see that the wisdom of the ages was in the experience of dear old Madame Carré—was in a hundred things she told me. She's founded a rock. After that," Miriam went on, to her host, "I can assure you that if you were so good as to bring Miss Dormer to see us we should be angelically careful of her and surround her with every attention and precaution."

"The likes of us—the likes of us!" Mrs. Rooth repeated plaintively, with ineffectual, theoretical resentment. "I don't know what you are talking about, and I decline to be turned upside down. I have my ideas as well as you, and I repudiate the charge of false humility. I've been through too many troubles to be proud, and a pleasant, polite manner was the rule of my life even in the days when, God knows, I had everything. I've never changed, and if, with God's help, I had a civil tongue then, I have a civil tongue now. It's more than you always have, my poor perverse and passionate child. Once a lady always a lady—all the footlights in the world, turn them up as high as you will, won't make a difference. And I think people know it, people who know anything (if I may use such an expression), and it's because they know it that I'm not afraid to address them courteously. And I must say—and I call Mr. Dormer to witness, for if he could reason with you a bit about it he might render several people a service—your conduct to Mr. Sherringham simply breaks my heart," Mrs. Rooth concluded, with a jump of several steps in the fine modern avenue of her argument.

Nick was appealed to, but he hesitated a moment, and while he hesitated Miriam remarked: "Mother is good—mother is very good; but it is only little by little that you discover how good she is." This seemed to leave Nick free to ask Mrs. Rooth, with the preliminary intimation that what she had just said was very striking, what she meant by her daughter's conduct to Peter Sherringham. Before Mrs. Rooth could answer this question, however, Miriam interposed irrelevantly with one of her own. "Do you mind telling me if you made your sister go off with Mr. Sherringham because you knew it was about time for me to turn up? Poor Mr. Dormer, I get you into trouble, don't I?" she added sympathetically.

"Into trouble?" echoed Nick, looking at her head but not at her eyes.

"Well, we won't talk about that!" Miriam exclaimed, with a rich laugh.

Nick now hastened to say that he had nothing to do with his sister's leaving the studio—she had only come, as it happened, for a moment. She had walked away with Peter Sherringham because they were cousins and old friends: he was to leave England immediately, for a long time, and he had offered her his company going home. Mrs. Rooth shook her head very knowingly over the "long time" that Mr. Sherringham would be absent—she plainly had her ideas about that; and she conscientiously related that in the course of the short conversation they had all had at the door of the house her daughter had reminded Miss Dormer of something that had passed between them in Paris in regard to the charming young lady's modelling her head.

"I did it to make the question of our meeting less absurd—to put it on the footing of our both being artists. I don't ask you if she has talent," said Miriam.

"Then I needn't tell you," answered Nick.

"I'm sure she has talent and a very refined inspiration. I see something in that corner, covered with a mysterious veil," Mrs. Rooth insinuated; which led Miriam to ask immediately:

"Has she been trying her hand at Mr. Sherringham?"

"When should she try her hand, poor dear young lady? He's always sitting with us," said Mrs. Rooth.

"Dear mamma, you exaggerate. He has his moments, when he seems to say his prayers to me; but we've had some success in cutting them down. *Il s'est bien détaché ces-jours-ci*, and I'm very happy for him. Of course it's an impertinent allusion for me to make; but I should be so delighted if I could think of him as a little in love with Miss Dormer," the girl pursued, addressing Nick.

"He is, I think, just a little—just a tiny bit," said Nick, working away; while Mrs. Rooth ejaculated, to her daughter, simultaneously:

"How can you ask such fantastic questions when you know that he's dying for you?"

"Oh, dying!—he's dying very hard!" cried Miriam. "Mr. Sherringham's a man of whom I can't speak with too much esteem and affection, who may be destined to perish by some horrid fever (which God forbid!) in the unpleasant country he's going to. But he won't have caught his fever from your humble servant."

"You may kill him even while you remain in perfect health yourself," said Nick; "and since we're talking of the matter I don't see the harm in my confessing that he strikes me as bad—oh, as very bad indeed."

"And yet he's in love with your sister? —*je n'y suis plus*."

"He tries to be, for he sees that as regards you there are difficulties. He would like to put his hand on some nice girl who would be an antidote to his poison."

"Difficulties are a mild name for them; poison even is a mild name for the ill he suffers from. The principal difficulty is that he doesn't know what he wants. The next is that I don't either—or what I want myself. I only know what I don't want," said Miriam brightly, as if she were uttering some happy, beneficent truth. "I don't want a person who takes things even less simply than I do myself. Mr. Sherringham, poor man, must be very uncomfortable, for one side of him is perpetually fighting against the other side. He's trying to serve God and Mammon, and I don't know how God will come off. What I like in you is that you have definitely let Mammon go—it's the only way. That's my earnest conviction, and yet they call us people light. Poor Mr. Sherringham has tremendous ambitions—tremendous *riguardi*, as we used to say in Italy. He wants to enjoy every comfort and to save every appearance, and all without making a sacrifice. He expects others—me, for instance—to make all the sacrifices. *Merci*, much as I esteem him and much as I owe him! I don't know how he ever came to stray at all into our bold, bad Bohemia: it was a cruel trick for fortune to play him. He can't keep out of it, he's perpetually making dashes across the border, and yet he's not in the least at home there. There's another in whose position (if I were in it) I wouldn't look at the likes of us!"

"I don't know much about the matter, but I have an idea Peter thinks he has made, or at least is making, sacrifices."

"So much the better—you must encourage him, you must help him."

"I don't know what my daughter's talking about—she's much too clever for me," Mrs. Rooth put in. "But there's one way you can encourage Mr. Sherringham—there's one way you can help him; and perhaps it won't make it any worse for a gentleman of your good-nature that it will help me at the same time. Can't I look to you, dear Mr. Dormer, to see that he does come to the theatre to-night—that he doesn't feel himself obliged to stay away?"

"What danger is there of his staying away?" Nick asked.

"If he's bent on sacrifices, that's a very good one to begin with," Miriam observed.

"That's the mad, bad way she talks to him—she has forbidden the dear unhappy gentleman the house!" her mother cried. "She brought it up to him just now, at the door, before Miss Dormer: such very odd form! She pretends to impose her commands upon him."

"Oh, he'll be there—we're going to dine together," said Nick. And when Miriam asked him what that had to do with it he went on: "Why, we've arranged it; I'm going, and he won't let me go alone."

"You're going? I sent you no places," Miriam objected.

"Yes, but I've got one. Why didn't you, after all I've done for you?"

She hesitated a moment. "Because I'm so good. No matter," she added: "if Mr. Sherringham comes I won't act."

"Won't you act for me?"

"She'll act like an angel," Mrs. Rooth protested. "She might do, she might be anything in the world; but she won't take common pains."

"Of one thing there's no doubt," said Miriam: "that compared with the rest of us—poor passionless creatures—mamma does know what she wants."

"And what is that?" inquired Nick, chalking away.

"She wants everything."

"Never, never—I'm much more humble," retorted the old woman; upon which her daughter requested her to give then to Mr. Dormer, who was a reasonable man and an excellent judge, a general idea of the scope of her desires.

As however, Mrs. Rooth, sighing and deprecating, was not quick to comply with the injunction, the girl attempted a short cut to the truth with the abrupt inquiry: "Do you believe for a single moment he'd marry me?"

"Why he has proposed to you—you've told me yourself—a dozen times."

"Proposed what to me? I've told you that neither a dozen times nor once, because I've never understood. He has made wonderful speeches, but he has never been serious."

"You told me he had been in the seventh heaven of devotion, especially that night we went to the foyer of the Français," Mrs. Rooth insisted.

"Do you call the seventh heaven of devotion serious? He's in love with me—*je veux bien*; he's so poisoned, as Mr. Dormer vividly says, as to require an antidote; but he has never spoken to me as if he really expected me to listen to him, and he's the more of a gentleman from that fact. He knows we haven't a common ground—that a grasshopper can't mate with a fish. So he has taken care to say to me only more than he can possibly mean. That makes it just nothing."

"Did he say more than he can possibly mean when he took formal leave of you yesterday—forever and ever?"

"Pray don't you call that a sacrifice?" Nick asked.

"Oh, he took it all back, his sacrifice, before he left the house."

"Then has *that* no meaning?" demanded Mrs. Rooth.

"None that I can make out."

"Oh, I've no patience with you: you can be stupid when you will as well as clever when you will!" the old woman groaned.

"What mamma wishes me to understand and to practise is the particular way to be clever with Mr. Sherringham," said Miriam. "There are doubtless depths of wisdom and virtue in it. But I can only see one way; namely, to be perfectly honest."

"I like to hear you talk—it makes you live, brings you out," Nick mentioned. "And you sit beautifully still. All I want to

say is, please continue to do so; remain exactly as you are—
it's rather important—for the next ten minutes."

"We're washing our dirty linen before you, but it's all
right," Miriam answered, "because it shows you what sort of
people we are, and that's what you need to know. Don't
make me vague and arranged and fine, in this new thing," she
continued: "make me characteristic and real; make life, with
all its horrid facts and truths, stick out of me. I wish you
could put mother in too; make us live there side by side and
tell our little story. 'The wonderful actress and her still more
wonderful mamma'—don't you think that's an awfully good
subject?"

Mrs. Rooth, at this, cried shame on her daughter's wanton
humours, professing that she herself would never accept so
much from Nick's good-nature, and Miriam settled it that at
any rate he was some day and in some way to do her mother
and sail very near the wind.

"She doesn't believe he wants to marry me, any more than
you do," the girl, taking up her dispute again after a moment,
represented to Nick; "but she believes—how indeed can I tell
you what she believes?—that I can work it (that's about it),
so that in the fullness of time I shall hold him in a vise. I'm to
keep him along for the present, but not to listen to him, for if
I listen to him I shall lose him. It's ingenious, it's complicated; but I dare say you follow me."

"Don't move—don't move," said Nick. "Excuse a be-
ginner."

"No, I shall explain quietly. Somehow (here it's *very* complicated and you mustn't lose the thread), I shall be an actress
and make a tremendous lot of money, and somehow, too (I
suppose a little later), I shall become an ambassadress and be
the favourite of courts. So you see it will all be delightful.
Only I shall have to go straight! Mamma reminds me of a
story I once heard about the mother of a young lady who was
in receipt of much civility from the pretender to a crown,
which indeed he, and the young lady too, afterwards more or
less wore. The old countess watched the course of events and
gave her daughter the cleverest advice: '*Tiens bon, ma fille*, and
you shall sit upon a throne.' Mamma wishes me to *tenir bon*

(she apparently thinks there's a danger I may not), so that if I don't sit upon a throne I shall at least parade at the foot of one. And if before that for ten years I pile up the money they'll forgive me the way I've made it. I should hope so, if I've *tenu bon*! Only ten years is a good while to hold out, isn't it? If it isn't Mr. Sherringham it will be some one else. Mr. Sherringham has the great merit of being a bird in the hand. I'm to keep him along, I'm to be still more diplomatic than even he can be."

Mrs. Rooth listened to her daughter with an air of assumed reprobation which melted, before the girl had done, into a diverted, complacent smile—the gratification of finding herself the proprietress of so much wit and irony and grace. Miriam's account of her mother's views was a scene of comedy, and there was instinctive art in the way she added touch to touch and made point upon point. She was so quiet, to oblige her painter, that only her fine lips moved—all her expression was in their charming utterance. Mrs. Rooth, after the first flutter of a less cynical spirit, consented to be sacrificed to an effect of an order she had now been educated to recognize; so that she hesitated only for a moment, when Miriam had ceased speaking, before she broke out endearingly with a little titter and *"Comédienne!"* She looked at Nick Dormer as if to say: "Ain't she fascinating? That's the way she does for you!"

"It's rather cruel, isn't it," said Miriam, "to deprive people of the luxury of calling one an actress as they'd call one a liar? I represent, but I represent truly."

"Mr. Sherringham would marry you to-morrow—there's no question of ten years!" cried Mrs. Rooth, with a comicality of plainness.

Miriam smiled at Nick, appealing for a sort of pity for her mother. "Isn't it droll, the way she can't get it out of her head?" Then turning almost coaxingly to the old woman: *"Voyons,* look about you: they don't marry us like that."

"But they do—*cela se voit tous les jours*. Ask Mr. Dormer."

"Oh, never!" said Miriam: "it would be as if I asked him to give us a practical illustration."

"I shall never give any illustration of matrimony; for me that question's over," said Nick.

Miriam rested kind eyes on him. "Dear me, how you must hate me!" And before he had time to reply she went on, to her mother: "People marry them to make them leave the stage; which proves exactly what I say."

"Ah, they offer them the finest positions," reasoned Mrs. Rooth.

"Do you want me to leave it then?"

"Oh, you can manage if you will!"

"The only managing I know anything about is to do my work. If I manage that, I shall pull through."

"But, dearest, may our work not be of many sorts?"

"I only know one," said Miriam.

At this Mrs. Rooth got up with a sigh. "I see you do wish to drive me into the street."

"Mamma's bewildered—there are so many paths she wants to follow, there are so many bundles of hay. As I told you, she wishes to gobble them all," Miriam went on. Then she added: "Yes, go and take the carriage; take a turn round the Park—you always delight in that—and come back for me in an hour."

"I'm too vexed with you; the air will do me good," said Mrs. Rooth. But before she went she added, to Nick: "I have your assurance that you will bring him then to-night?"

"Bring Peter? I don't think I shall have to drag him," said Nick. "But you must do me the justice to remember that if I should resort to force I should do something that's not particularly in my interest—I should be magnanimous."

"We must always be that, mustn't we?" moralized Mrs. Rooth.

"How could it affect your interest?" Miriam inquired, less abstractly, of Nick.

"Yes, as you say," her mother reminded him, "the question of marriage has ceased to exist for you."

"Mamma goes straight at it!" laughed the girl, getting up while Nick rubbed his canvas before answering. Miriam went to Mrs. Rooth and settled her bonnet and mantle in preparation for her drive; then stood for a moment with a filial arm about her, as if they were waiting for their host's explanation. This however when it came halted visibly.

"Why, you said awhile ago that if Peter was there you wouldn't act."

"I'll act for *him*," smiled Miriam, encircling her mother.

"It doesn't matter whom it's for!" Mrs. Rooth declared sagaciously.

"Take your drive and relax your mind," said the girl, kissing her. "Come for me in an hour; not later, but not sooner." She went with her to the door, bundled her out, closed it behind her and came back to the position she had quitted. "*This* is the peace I want!" she exclaimed, with relief, as she settled into it.

XIII.

PETER SHERRINGHAM said so little during the performance that his companion was struck by his dumbness, especially as Miriam's acting seemed to Nick Dormer magnificent. He held his breath while she was on the stage—she gave the whole thing, including the spectator's emotion, such a lift. She had not carried out her fantastic menace of not exerting herself, and, as Mrs. Rooth had said, it little mattered for whom she acted. Nick was conscious as he watched her that she went through it all for herself, for the idea that possessed her and that she rendered with extraordinary breadth. She could not open the door a part of the way to it and let it simply peep in; if it entered at all it must enter in full procession and occupy the premises in state.

This was what had happened on an occasion which, as Nick noted in his stall, grew larger with each throb of the responsive house; till by the time the play was half over it appeared to stretch out wide arms to the future. Nick had often heard more applause but he had never heard more attention; for they were all charmed and hushed together and success seemed to be sitting down with them. There had been of course plenty of announcement—the newspapers had abounded and the arts of the manager had taken the freest license; but it was easy to feel a fine universal consensus and to recognize the intrinsic buoyancy of the evening. People snatched their eyes from the stage for an instant to look at each other, and a sense of intelligence deepened and spread. It was a part of the impression that the actress was only now really showing, for this time she had verse to deal with and she made it unexpectedly exquisite. She was beauty, she was music, she was truth; she was passion and persuasion and tenderness. She caught up the obstreperous play in soothing, entwining arms and carried it into the high places of poetry, of style. And she had such tones of nature, such concealments of art, such effusions of life, that the whole scene glowed with the colour she communicated, and the house, as if pervaded with rosy fire, glowed back at the scene. Nick looked round in the intervals; he felt excited and flushed—the night had turned into a feast of fraternity and he expected to see people embrace each other. The crowd, the flutter, the triumph, the surprise, the signals and rumours, the heated air, his associates, near him, pointing out other figures, who presumably were celebrated but whom he had never heard of, all amused him and banished every impulse of criticism. Miriam was as satisfactory as some right sensation—she would feed the memory with the ineffaceable.

One of the things that amused Nick, or at least helped to fill his attention, was Peter's attitude, which apparently did not exclude criticism; rather indeed mainly implied it. Sherringham never took his eyes off the actress, but he made no remark about her and he never stirred out of his chair. Nick had from the first a plan of going round to speak to her, but as his companion evidently meant not to move he felt a delicacy in regard to being more forward. During their brief dinner together (they made a rigid point of not being late), Peter had been silent and irremediably serious, but also, his kinsman judged, full of the wish to make it plain that he was calm. In his seat he was calmer than ever; had an air even of trying to suggest to Nick that his attendance, preoccupied as he was with deeper solemnities, was slightly mechanical, the result of a conception of duty, a habit of courtesy. When during a scene in the second act—a scene from which Miriam was absent—Nick observed to him that from his inexpressiveness one might gather he was not pleased, he replied after a moment: "I've been looking for her mistakes." And when Nick rejoined to this that he certainly wouldn't find them he said again, in an odd tone: "No, I sha'n't find them—I sh'a'nt find them." It might have seemed that since the girl's performance was a dazzling success he regarded his evening as rather a failure.

After the third act Nick said candidly: "My dear fellow, how can you sit here? Aren't you going to speak to her?"

To which Peter replied inscrutably: "Lord, no, never again; I bade her good-bye yesterday. She knows what I think of her form. It's very good, but she carries it a little too far. Besides, she didn't want me to come, and it's therefore more discreet to keep away from her."

"Surely it isn't an hour for discretion!" cried Nick. "Excuse me, at any rate, for five minutes."

He went behind and reappeared only as the curtain was rising on the fourth act; and in the interval between the fourth and the fifth he went again for a shorter time. Peter was personally detached, but he consented to listen to his companion's vivid account of the state of things on the stage, where the elation of victory had made every one merry. The strain was over, the ship was in port, and they were all wiping their faces and grinning. Miriam—yes, positively—was grinning too, and she hadn't asked a question about Peter nor sent him a message. They were kissing all round and dancing for joy. They were on the eve, worse luck, of a tremendous run. Peter groaned, irrepressibly, at this; it was, save for a slight manifestation a moment later, the only sign of emotion that Nick's report elicited from him. There was but one voice of regret that they hadn't put on the piece earlier, as the end of the season would interrupt the run. There was but one voice too about the fourth act—it was believed that all London would rush to see the fourth act. There was a wonderful lot of people, and Miriam was charming; she was receiving there, in the ugly place, like a kind of royalty, with a smile and a word for each. She was like a young queen on her accession. When she saw him, Nick, she had kissed her hand to him over the heads of the courtiers. Nick's artless comment on this was that she had such pretty manners. It made Sherringham laugh, apparently at his companion's conception of the manners of a young queen. Mrs. Rooth, with a dozen shawls on her arm, was as red as a turkey; but you couldn't tell whether Miriam was red or pale: she was so cleverly, awfully cleverly, painted—perhaps a little too much. Dashwood of course was greatly to the fore, but you didn't have to mention his own performance to him: he was magnanimous and would use nothing but the feminine pronoun. He didn't say much, indeed, but he evidently had ideas; he nodded significant things and whistled inimitable sounds—"heuh, heuh!" He was perfectly satisfied; moreover he looked further ahead than any one.

It was on coming back to his place after the fourth act that Nick put in, for Sherringham's benefit, most of these touches in his sketch of the situation. If Peter had continued to look for Miriam's mistakes he had not yet found them: the fourth act, bristling with dangers, putting a premium on every sort of cheap effect, had rounded itself without a flaw. Sitting there alone while Nick was away he had leisure to meditate on the wonder of this—on the art with which the girl had separated passion from violence, filling the whole place and never screaming; for it had seemed to him in London sometimes of old that the yell of theatrical emotion rang through the shrinking night like a fatal warning. Miriam had never been more present to him than at this hour; but she was inextricably transmuted—present essentially as the romantic heroine she represented. His state of mind was of the strangest, and he was conscious of its strangeness; just as he was conscious, in his person, of a cessation of resistance which identified itself absurdly with liberation. He felt weak at the same time that he felt excited, and he felt excited at the same time that he knew or believed he knew that his face was a blank. He saw things as a shining confusion, and yet somehow something monstrously definite kept surging out of them. Miriam was a beautiful, actual, fictive, impossible young woman, of a past age and undiscoverable country, who spoke in blank verse and overflowed with metaphor, who was exalted and heroic beyond all human convenience, and who yet was irresistibly real and related to one's own affairs. But that reality was a part of her spectator's joy, and she was not changed back to the common by his perception of the magnificent trick of art with which it was connected. Before Nick Dormer rejoined him Sherringham, taking a visiting-card from his pocket, wrote on it in pencil a few words in a foreign tongue; but as at that moment he saw Nick coming in he immediately put it out of view.

The last thing before the curtain rose on the fifth act Nick mentioned that he had brought him a message from Basil Dashwood, who hoped they both, on leaving the theatre, would come to supper with him, in company with Miriam and her mother and several others: he had prepared a little informal banquet in honour of so famous a night. At this, while the curtain was rising, Peter immediately took out his card again and added something—he wrote the finest small hand you could see. Nick asked him what he was doing, and after an hesitation he replied:

"It's a word to say I can't come."

"To Dashwood? Oh, I shall go," said Nick.

"Well, I hope you'll enjoy it!" his companion replied in a tone which came back to him afterwards.

When the curtain fell on the last act the people stayed, standing up in their places for the most part. The applause shook the house—the recall became a clamour, the relief from a long tension. This was a moment, in any performance, that Sherringham detested, but he stood for an instant beside Nick, who clapped like a school-boy. There was a veritable roar and the curtain drew back at the side most removed from them. Sherringham could see that Basil Dashwood was holding it, making a passage for the male "juvenile lead," who had Miriam in tow. Nick redoubled his efforts; heard the plaudits swell; saw the bows of the leading gentleman, who was hot and fat; saw Miriam, personally conducted and closer to the footlights, grow brighter and bigger and more swaying; and then became aware that Sherringham had with extreme agility slipped out of the stalls. Nick had already lost sight of him— he had apparently taken but a minute to escape from the house. Nick wondered at his quitting him without a farewell, if he was to leave England on the morrow and they were not to meet at the hospitable Dashwood's. He wondered even what Peter was "up to," since, as he had assured him, there was no question of his going round to Miriam. He waited to see this young lady reappear three times, dragging Dashwood behind her at the second with a friendly arm, to whom, in turn, was hooked Miss Fanny Rover, the actress entrusted, in the piece, with the inevitable comic relief. He went out slowly, with the crowd, and at the door looked again for Peter, who struck him as deficient for once in finish. He couldn't know that, in another direction and while he was helping the house to "rise" at Miriam, his kinsman had been particularly explicit.

On reaching the lobby Sherringham had pounced upon a small boy in buttons, who appeared to be superfluously connected with a desolate refreshment-room and was peeping, on tiptoe, at the stage, through the glazed hole in the door of a box. Into one of the child's hands he thrust the card he had drawn again from his waistcoat, and into the other the largest silver coin he could find in the same receptacle, while he bent over him with words of adjuration—words which the little page tried to help himself to apprehend by instantly attempting to peruse the other words written on the card.

"That's no use—it's Italian," said Peter; "only carry it round to Miss Rooth without a minute's delay. Place it in her hand and she'll give you some object—a bracelet, a glove or a flower—to bring me back as a sign that she has received it. I shall be outside; bring me there what she gives you and you shall have another shilling—only fly!"

Sherringham's small messenger sounded him a moment with the sharp face of London wage-earning, and still more of London tip-earning, infancy, and vanished as swiftly as a slave of the Arabian Nights. While his patron waited in the lobby the audience began to pour out, and before the urchin had come back to him Peter was clapped on the shoulder by Nick Dormer.

"I'm glad I haven't lost you," said Nick; "but why didn't you stay to give her a hand?"

"Give her a hand? I hated it."

"My dear fellow, I don't follow you," Nick rejoined. "If you won't come to Dashwood's supper I fear our ways don't lie together."

"Thank him very much; say I have to get up at an unnatural hour." To this Peter added: "I think I ought to tell you she may not be there."

"Miss Rooth? Why, it's for her."

"I'm waiting for a word from her—she may change her mind."

Nick stared at his companion. "For you? Why, what have you proposed?"

"I've proposed marriage," said Peter in a strange voice.

"I say—!" Nick broke out; and at the same moment Peter's messenger squeezed through the press and stood before him.

"She has given me nothing, sir," the boy announced; "but she says I'm to say 'All right!'"

Nick marvelled a moment. "You've proposed through *him*?"

"Ay, and she accepts. Good-night!" Peter exclaimed; and, turning away, he bounded into a hansom. He said something to the driver through the roof, and Nick's eyes followed the cab as it started off. Nick was mystified, was even amused; especially when the youth in buttons, planted there and wondering too, remarked to him:

"Please, sir, he told me he'd give me a shilling, and he've forgot it."

"Oh, I can't pay you for *that*!" Nick laughed. He was vexed about the supper.

XIV.

Peter Sherringham rolled away through the summer night to St. John's Wood. He had put the pressure of strong words upon Miriam, entreating her to drive home immediately, without any one, without even her mother. He wished to see her alone, for a purpose that he would fully and satisfactorily explain—couldn't she trust him? He implored her to remember his own situation and throw over her supper, throw over everything. He would wait for her with unspeakable impatience in Balaklava Place.

He did so when he got there, but it took half an hour. Interminable seemed his lonely vigil in Miss Lumley's drawing-room, where the character of the original proprietress came out to him more than before in a kind of afterglow of old sociabilities, a vulgar ghostly vibration. The numerous candles had been lighted for him, and Mrs. Rooth's familiar fictions were lying about; but his nerves forbade him the solace of taking a chair and a book. He walked up and down, thinking and listening, and as the long window, the balmy air permitting, stood open into the garden he passed several times in and out. A carriage appeared to stop at the gate—then there was nothing; he heard the rare rattle of wheels and the far-off hum of London. His impatience was unreasonable, and though he knew this it persisted; it would have been no easy matter for Miriam to break away from the flock of her felicitators. Still less simple was it doubtless for her to leave poor Dashwood with his supper on his hands. Perhaps she would bring Dashwood with her to time her; she was capable of playing him—that is playing Sherringham—or even playing them both, that trick. Perhaps the little wretch in buttons (Peter remembered now the omitted shilling) had only pretended to go round with his card, had come back with an invented answer. But how could he know, since presumably he couldn't read Italian, that his answer would fit the message? Peter was sorry now that he himself had not gone round, not snatched Miriam bodily away, made sure of her and of what he wanted of her.

When half an hour had elapsed he regarded it as proved

that she wouldn't come, and, asking himself what he should do, determined to drive off again and seize her at Basil Dashwood's feast. Then he remembered Nick had mentioned that this entertainment was not to be held at the young actor's lodgings, but at some tavern or restaurant, the name of which he had not heeded. Suddenly however Sherringham became aware with joy that this name didn't matter, for there was something at the garden-door at last. He rushed out before Miriam had had time to ring, and saw as she stepped out of the carriage that she was alone. Now that she was there, that he had this evidence she had listened to him and trusted him, all his impatience and exasperation melted away and a flood of pleading tenderness came out in the first words he spoke to her. It was far "dearer" of her than he had any right to dream, but she was the best and kindest creature—this showed it— as well as the most wonderful. He was really not off his head with his contradictory ways; no, before heaven, he wasn't, and he would explain, he would make everything clear. Everything was changed.

Miriam stopped short, in the little dusky garden, looking at him in the light of the open window. Then she called back to the coachman—they had left the garden-door open: "Wait for me, mind; I shall want you again."

"What's the matter—won't you stay?" Peter asked. "Are you going out again at this absurd hour? I won't hurt you," he urged gently. And he went back and closed the garden-door. He wanted to say to the coachman: "It's no matter; please drive away." At the same time he wouldn't for the world have done anything offensive to Miriam.

"I've come because I thought it better to-night, as things have turned out, to do the thing you ask me, whatever it may be. That's probably what you calculated I would think, eh? What this evening has been you've seen, and I must allow that your hand's in it. That you know for yourself—that you doubtless felt as you sat there. But I confess I don't imagine what you want of me here, now," Miriam added. She had remained standing in the path.

Peter felt the irony of her "now," and how it made a fool of him, but he had been prepared for it and for much worse. He had begged her not to think him a fool, but in truth at present he cared little if she did. Very likely he was, in spite of his plea that everything was changed—he cared little even himself. However, he spoke in the tone of intense reason and of the fullest disposition to satisfy her. This lucidity only took still more from the dignity of his tergiversation: his separation from her the day before had had such pretensions to being lucid. But the explanation, the justification, were in the very fact, and the fact had complete possession of him. He named it when he replied to Miriam: "I've simply overrated my strength."

"Oh, I knew—I knew! That's why I entreated you not to come!" she groaned. She turned away impatiently, and for a moment he thought she would retreat to her carriage. But he passed his hand into her arm, to draw her forward, and after an instant he felt her yield.

"The fact is we must have this thing out," he said. Then he added, as he made her go into the house, bending over her: "The failure of my strength—that was just the reason of my coming."

She burst out laughing at these words, as she entered the drawing-room, and her laugh made them sound pompous in their false wisdom. She flung off, as a good-natured tribute to the image of their having the thing out, a white shawl that had been wrapped round her. She was still painted and bedizened, in the splendid dress of her fifth act, so that she seemed protected and alienated by the character she had been representing. "Whatever it is you want (when I understand), you'll be very brief, won't you? Do you know I've given up a charming supper for you? Mamma has gone there. I've promised to go back to them."

"You're an angel not to have let her come with you. I'm sure she wanted to," said Sherringham.

"Oh, she's all right, but she's nervous," Miriam rejoined. Then she added quickly: "Couldn't she keep you away after all?"

"Whom are you talking about?" Biddy Dormer was as absent from Sherringham's mind as if she had never existed.

"The charming girl you were with this morning. Is she so afraid of obliging me? Oh, she'd be so good for you!"

"Don't speak of that," said Peter, gravely. "I was in perfect good faith yesterday when I took leave of you. I was—I was. But I can't—I can't: you are too unutterably dear to me."

"Oh, don't—please don't," moaned Miriam. She stood before the fireless chimney-piece with one of her hands upon it. "If it's only to say that, don't you know, what's the use?"

"It isn't only to say that. I've a plan, a perfect plan: the whole thing lies clear before me."

"And what is the whole thing?"

He hesitated a moment. "You say your mother's nervous. Ah, if you knew how nervous I am!"

"Well, I'm not. Go on."

"Give it up—give it up!" stammered Sherringham.

"Give it up?" Miriam fixed him like a mild Medusa.

"I'll marry you to-morrow if you'll renounce; and in return for the sacrifice you make for me I'll do more for you than ever was done for a woman before."

"Renounce, after to-night? Do you call that a plan?" asked Miriam. "Those are old words and very foolish ones: you wanted something of the sort a year ago."

"Oh, I fluttered round the idea then; we were talking in the air. I didn't really believe I could make you see it then, and certainly you didn't see it. My own future moreover wasn't definite to me. I didn't know what I could offer you. But these last months have made a difference, and I do know now. Now what I say is deliberate, it's deeply meditated. I simply can't live without you, and I hold that together we may do great things."

"What sort of things?" Miriam inquired.

"The things of my profession—of my life—the things one does for one's country, the responsibility and the honour of great affairs; deeply fascinating when one's immersed in them, and more exciting than the excitements of the theatre. Care for me only a little and you'll see what they are, they'll take hold of you. Believe me, believe me," Sherringham pleaded, "every fibre of my being trembles in what I say to you."

"You admitted yesterday it wouldn't do," said Miriam. "Where were the fibres of your being then?"

"They trembled even more than now, and I was trying, like an ass, not to feel them. Where was this evening, yesterday—where were the maddening hours I've just spent? Ah, you're the perfection of perfections, and as I sat there to-night you taught me what I really want."

"The perfection of perfections?" the girl repeated interrogatively, with the strangest smile.

"I needn't try to tell you: you must have felt to-night, with such rapture, what you are, what you can do. How can I give that up?" Sherringham asked.

"How can *I*, my poor friend? I like your plans and your responsibilities and your great affairs, as you call them. *Voyons*, they're infantile. I've just shown that I'm a perfection of perfections: therefore it's just the moment to renounce, as you gracefully say? Oh, I was sure, I was sure!" And Miriam paused, resting solicitous, pitying eyes upon her visitor, as if she were trying to think of some arrangement that would help him out of his absurdity. "I was sure, I mean, that if you did come your poor dear doating brain would be quite addled," she presently went on. "I can't be a muff in public just for you, *pourtant*. Dear me, why do you like us so much?"

"Like you? I loathe you!"

"*Je le vois parbleu bien!* I mean, why do you feel us, judge us, understand us so well? I please you because you see, because you know; and because I please you, you must adapt me to your convenience, you must take me over, as they say. You admire me as an artist and therefore you wish to put me into a box in which the artist will breathe her last. Ah, be reasonable; you must let her live!"

"Let her live? As if I could prevent her living!" Peter cried, with unmistakable conviction. "Even if I wanted, how could I prevent a spirit like yours from expressing itself? Don't talk about my putting you in a box, for, dearest child, I'm taking you out of one. The artist is irrepressible, eternal; she'll be in everything you are and in everything you do, and you'll go about with her triumphantly, exerting your powers, charming the world, carrying everything before you."

Miriam's colour rose, through her paint, at this vivid picture, and she asked whimsically: "Shall you like that?"

"Like my wife to be the most brilliant woman in Europe? I think I can do with it."

"Aren't you afraid of me?"

"Not a bit."

"Bravely said. How little you know me after all!" sighed the girl.

"I tell the truth," Peter went on; "and you must do me the justice to admit that I have taken the time to dig deep into my feelings. I'm not an infatuated boy; I've lived, I've had experience, I've observed; in short I know what I'm about. It isn't a thing to reason about; it's simply a need that consumes me. I've put it on starvation diet, but it's no use—really it's no use, Miriam," poor Sherringham pursued, with a soft quaver that betrayed all his sincerity. "It isn't a question of my trusting you; it's simply a question of your trusting me. You're all right, as I've heard you say yourself; you're frank, spontaneous, generous; you're a magnificent creature. Just quietly marry me, and I'll manage you."

"Manage me?" The girl's inflection was droll; it made Sherringham change colour.

"I mean I'll give you a larger life than the largest you can get in any other way. The stage is great, no doubt, but the world is greater. It's a bigger theatre than any of those places in the Strand. We'll go in for realities instead of fables, and you'll do them far better than you do the fables."

Miriam had listened to him attentively, but her face showed her despair at his perverted ingenuity. "Excuse me for saying so, after your delightful tributes to my worth," she returned in a moment, "but I've never listened to such a flood of determined sophistry. You think so well of me that humility itself ought to keep me silent; nevertheless I *must* utter a few shabby words of sense. I'm a magnificent creature on the stage—well and good; it's what I want to be and it's charming to see such evidence that I succeed. But off the stage—come, come: I should lose all my advantages. The fact is so patent that it seems to me I'm very good-natured even to discuss it with you."

"Are you on the stage now, pray? Ah, Miriam, if it were not for the respect I owe you!" her companion murmured.

"If it were not for that I shouldn't have come here to meet

you. My talent is the thing that takes you: could there be a better proof than that it's to-night's exhibition of it that has settled you? It's indeed a misfortune that you're so sensitive to this particular kind of talent, since it plays such tricks with your power to see things as they are. Without it I should be a dull, ignorant, third-rate woman, and yet that's the fate you ask me to face and insanely pretend you are ready to face yourself."

"Without it—without it?" Sherringham cried. "Your own sophistry is infinitely worse than mine. I should like to see you without it for the fiftieth part of a second. What I ask you to give up is the dusty boards of the playhouse and the flaring footlights, but not the very essence of your being. Your talent is yourself, and it's because it's yourself that I yearn for you. If it had been a thing you could leave behind by the easy dodge of stepping off the stage I would never have looked at you a second time. Don't talk to me as if I were a simpleton, with your false simplifications! You were made to charm and console, to represent beauty and harmony and variety to miserable human beings; and the daily life of man is the theatre for that—not a vulgar shop with a turnstile, that's open only once in the twenty-four hours. Without it, verily?" Sherringham went on, with rising scorn and exasperated passion. "Please let me know the first time you're without your face, without your voice, your step, your exquisite spirit, the turn of your head and the wonder of your eye!"

Miriam, at this, moved away from him with a port that resembled what she sometimes showed on the stage when she turned her young back upon the footlights and then, after a few steps, grandly swept round again. This evolution she performed (it was over in an instant) on the present occasion; even to stopping short with her eyes upon him and her head erect. "Surely it's strange," she said, "the way the other solution never occurs to you."

"The other solution?"

"That *you* should stay on the stage."

"I don't understand you," Sherringham confessed.

"Stay on *my* stage; come off your own."

Sherringham hesitated a moment. "You mean that if I'll do that you'll have me?"

"I mean that if it were to occur to you to offer me a little sacrifice on your own side, it might place the matter in a slightly more attractive light."

"Continue to let you act—as my wife?" Sherringham demanded. "Is it a real condition? Am I to understand that those are your terms?"

"I may say so without fear, because you'll never accept them."

"Would *you* accept them, from me—accept the sacrifice, see me throw up my work, my prospects (of course I should have to do that), and simply become your appendage?"

"My dear fellow, you invite me with the best conscience in the world to become yours."

"The cases are not equal. You would make of me the husband of an actress. I should make of you the wife of an ambassador."

"The husband of an actress, *c'est bientôt dit*, in that tone of scorn! If you're consistent," said Miriam, "it ought to be a proud position for you."

"What do you mean, if I'm consistent?"

"Haven't you always insisted on the beauty and interest of our art and the greatness of our mission? Haven't you almost come to blows with poor Gabriel Nash about it? What did all that mean if you won't face the first consequences of your theory? Either it was an enlightened conviction or it was an empty pretence. If it was heartless humbug I'm glad to know it," Miriam rolled out, with a darkening eye. "The better the cause, it seems to me, the better the deed; and if the theatre *is* important to the 'human spirit,' as you used to say so charmingly, and if into the bargain you have the pull of being so fond of me, I don't see why it should be monstrous to give us your services in an intelligent indirect way. Of course if you're not serious we needn't talk at all; but if you are, with your conception of what the actor can do, why is it so base to come to the actor's aid, taking one devotion with another? If I'm so fine I'm worth looking after a bit, and the place where I'm finest is the place to look after me!"

"You were never finer than at this minute, in the deepest domesticity of private life," Sherringham returned. "I have no conception whatever of what the actor can do, and no theory whatever about the importance of the theatre. Any infatuation of that sort has completely quitted me, and for all I care the theatre may go to the dogs."

"You're dishonest, you're ungrateful, you're false!" Miriam flashed. "It was the theatre that brought you here; if it hadn't been for the theatre I never would have looked at you. It was in the name of the theatre you first made love to me; it is to the theatre that you owe every advantage that, so far as I'm concerned, you possess."

"I seem to possess a great many!" groaned Sherringham.

"You might certainly make more of those you have! You make me angry, but I want to be fair," said the glowing girl, "and I can't be unless you will. You are not fair, nor candid, nor honourable, when you swallow your words and abjure your faith, when you throw over old friends and old memories for a selfish purpose."

" 'Selfish purpose' is in your own convenient idiom, *bientôt dit*," Sherringham answered. "I suppose you consider that if I truly esteemed you I should be ashamed to deprive the world of the light of your genius. Perhaps my esteem isn't of the right quality: there are different kinds, aren't there? At any rate I've explained that I propose to deprive the world of nothing at all. You shall be celebrated, *allez*!"

"Rubbish—rubbish!" Miriam mocked, turning away again. "I know of course," she added quickly, "that to befool yourself with such platitudes you must be pretty bad."

"Yes, I'm pretty bad," Sherringham admitted, looking at her dismally. "What do you do with the declaration you made me the other day—the day I found my cousin here—that you'd take me if I should come to you as one who had risen high?"

Miriam reflected a moment. "I remember—the chaff about the orders, the stars and garters. My poor dear friend, don't be so painfully literal. Don't you know a joke when you see it? It was to worry your cousin, wasn't it? But it didn't in the least succeed."

"Why should you wish to worry my cousin?"

"Because he's so provoking. And surely I had my freedom no less than I have it now. Pray, what explanations should I have owed you and in what fear of you should I have gone?

However, that has nothing to do with it. Say I did tell you that we might arrange it on the day that you should come to me covered with glory in the shape of little tinkling medals: why should you anticipate that transaction by so many years and knock me down such a long time in advance? Where is the glory, please, and where are the medals?"

"Dearest girl, am I not going to America (a capital promotion) next month," Sherringham argued, "and can't you trust me enough to believe that I speak with a real appreciation of the facts—that I'm not lying to you, in short—when I tell you that I've my foot in the stirrup? The glory's dawning. *I'm* all right too."

"What you propose to me then is to accompany you *tout bonnement* to your new post."

"You put it in a nutshell," smiled Sherringham.

"You're touching; it has its charm. But you can't get anything in America, you know. I'm assured there are no medals to be picked up there. That's why the diplomatic body hate it."

"It's on the way—it's on the way," Sherringham hammered, feverishly. "They don't keep us long in disagreeable places unless we want to stay. There's one thing you can get anywhere if you're clever, and nowhere if you're not, and in the disagreeable places generally more than in the others: and that (since it's the element of the question we're discussing) is simply success. It's odious to be put on one's swagger, but I protest against being treated as if I had nothing to offer—to offer to a person who has such glories of her own. I'm not a little presumptuous ass; I'm a man accomplished and determined, and the omens are on my side." Peter faltered a moment, and then with a queer expression he went on: "Remember, after all, that, strictly speaking, your glories are also still in the future." An exclamation, at these words, burst from Miriam's lips, but her companion resumed quickly: "Ask my official superiors, ask any of my colleagues if they consider that I've nothing to offer."

Peter Sherringham had an idea, as he ceased speaking, that Miriam was on the point of breaking out with some strong word of resentment at his allusion to the contingent nature of her prospects. But it only twisted the weapon in his wound to hear her saying with extraordinary mildness: "It's perfectly true that my glories are still to come, that I may fizzle out and that my little success of to-day is perhaps a mere flash in the pan. Stranger things have been—something of that sort happens every day. But don't we talk too much of that part of it?" she asked, with a weary tolerance that was noble in its effect. "Surely it's vulgar to consider only the noise one's going to make; especially when one remembers how unintelligent nine-tenths of it will be. It isn't to my glories that I cling; it's simply to my idea, even if it's destined to sink me into obscurity. I like it better than anything else—a thousand times better (I'm sorry to have to put it in such a way) than tossing up my head as the fine lady of a little coterie."

"A little coterie? I don't know what you're talking about!" Peter retorted, with considerable heat.

"A big coterie, then! It's only that, at the best. A nasty, prim 'official' woman, who is perched on her little local pedestal and thinks she's a queen for ever because she's ridiculous for an hour! Oh, you needn't tell me. I've seen them abroad, I could imitate them here. I could do one for you on the spot if I were not so tired. It's scarcely worth mentioning perhaps, but I'm ready to drop." Miriam picked up the white mantle she had tossed off, flinging it round her with her usual amplitude of gesture. "They're waiting for me, and I confess I'm hungry. If I don't hurry they'll eat up all the nice things. Don't say I haven't been obliging, and come back when you're better. Good-night."

"I quite agree with you that we've talked too much about the vulgar side of our question," Peter responded, walking round to get between her and the French window, by which she apparently had a view of leaving the room. "That's because I've wanted to bribe you. Bribery is almost always vulgar."

"Yes, you should do better. *Merci!* There's a cab; some of them have come for me. I must go," Miriam added, listening for a sound that reached her from the road.

Sherringham listened too, making out no cab. "Believe me, it isn't wise to turn your back on such an affection as mine and on such a confidence," he went on, speaking almost in a warning tone (there was a touch of superior sternness in it, as of a rebuke for real folly, but it was meant to be tender), and stopping her within a few feet of the window. "Such things are the most precious that life has to give us," he added, all but didactically.

Miriam had listened again for a moment; then she appeared to give up the idea of the cab. The reader need hardly be told, at this stage of her youthful history, that the right way for her lover to soothe her was not to represent himself as acting for her highest good. "I like your calling it confidence," she presently said; and the deep note of the few words had something of the distant mutter of thunder.

"What is it, then, when I offer you everything I am, everything I have, everything I shall achieve?"

She seemed to measure him for a moment, as if she were thinking whether she should try to pass him. But she remained where she was and she returned: "I'm sorry for you, yes, but I'm also rather ashamed of you."

"Ashamed of me?"

"A brave offer to see me through—that's what I should call confidence. You say to-day that you hate the theatre; and do you know what has made you do it? The fact that it has too large a place in your mind to let you repudiate it and throw it over with a good conscience. It has a deep fascination for you, and yet you're not strong enough to make the concession of taking up with it publicly, in my person. You're ashamed of yourself for that, as all your constant high claims for it are on record; so you blaspheme against it, to try and cover your retreat and your treachery and straighten out your personal situation. But it won't do, my dear fellow—it won't do at all," Miriam proceeded, with a triumphant, almost judicial lucidity which made her companion stare; "you haven't the smallest excuse of stupidity, and your perversity is no excuse at all. Leave her alone altogether—a poor girl who's making her way—or else come frankly to help her, to give her the benefit of your wisdom. Don't lock her up for life under the pretence of doing her good. What does one most good is to see a little honesty. You're the best judge, the best critic, the best observer, the best *believer*, that I've ever come across; you're committed to it by everything you've said to me for a twelvemonth, by the whole turn of your mind, by the way you've followed up this business of ours. If an art is noble and beneficent, one shouldn't be afraid to offer it one's arm. Your cousin isn't: he can make sacrifices."

"My cousin?" shouted Peter. "Why, wasn't it only the other day that you were throwing his sacrifices in his teeth?"

Under this imputation upon her consistency Miriam flinched but for an instant. "I did that to worry *you*," she smiled.

"Why should you wish to worry me if you care so little about me?"

"Care little about you? Haven't I told you often, didn't I tell you yesterday, how much I care? Ain't I showing it now by spending half the night here with you (giving myself away to all those cynics), taking all this trouble to persuade you to hold up your head and have the courage of your opinions?"

"You invent my opinions for your convenience," said Peter. "As long ago as the night I introduced you, in Paris, to Mademoiselle Voisin, you accused me of looking down on those who practise your art. I remember you almost scratched my eyes out because I didn't kootoo enough to your friend Dashwood. Perhaps I didn't; but if already at that time I was so wide of the mark you can scarcely accuse me of treachery now."

"I don't remember, but I dare say you're right," Miriam meditated. "What I accused you of then was probably simply what I reproach you with now: the germ at least of your deplorable weakness. You consider that we do awfully valuable work, and yet you wouldn't for the world let people suppose that you really take our side. If your position was even at that time so false, so much the worse for you, that's all. Oh, it's refreshing," the girl exclaimed, after a pause during which Sherringham seemed to himself to taste the full bitterness of despair, so baffled and derided he felt—"oh, it's refreshing to see a man burn his ships in a cause that appeals to him, give up something for it and break with hideous timidities and snobberies! It's the most beautiful sight in the world."

Sherringham, sore as he was and angry and exasperated, nevertheless burst out laughing at this. "You're magnificent, you give me at this moment the finest possible illustration of what you mean by burning one's ships. Verily, verily, there's no one like you: talk of timidity, talk of refreshment! If I had any talent for it I'd go on the stage to-morrow, to spend my life with you the better."

"If you'll do that I'll be your wife the day after your first appearance. That would be really respectable," said Miriam.

"Unfortunately I've no talent."

"That would only make it the more respectable."

"You're just like Nick," Peter rejoined: "you've taken to imitating Gabriel Nash. Don't you see that it's only if it were a question of my going on the stage myself that there would be a certain fitness in your contrasting me invidiously with Nick Dormer and in my giving up one career for another? But simply to stand in the wing and hold your shawl and your smelling-bottle!" Peter concluded mournfully, as if he had ceased to debate.

"Holding my shawl and my smelling-bottle is a mere detail, representing a very small part of the various precious services, the protection and encouragement for which a woman in my position might be indebted to a man interested in her work and accomplished and determined, as you very justly describe yourself."

"And would it be your idea that such a man should live on the money earned by an exhibition of the person of his still more accomplished and still more determined wife?"

"Why not, if they work together—if there's something of his spirit and his support in everything she does?" Miriam demanded. "*Je vous attendais*, with the famous 'person;' of course that's the great stick they beat us with. Yes, we show it for money, those of us who have anything to show, and some no doubt who haven't, which is the real scandal. What will you have? It's only the envelope of the idea, it's only our machinery, which ought to be conceded to us; and in proportion as the idea takes hold of us do we become unconscious of the clumsy body. Poor old 'person'—if you knew what *we* think of it! If you don't forget it, that's your own affair: it shows that you're dense before the idea."

"That I'm dense?"

"I mean the public is—the public who pays us. After all, they expect us to look at them too, who are not half so well worth it. If you should see some of the creatures who have the face to plant themselves there in the stalls, before one, for three mortal hours! I dare say it would be simpler to have no bodies, but we're all in the same box, and it would be a great injustice to the idea, and we're all showing ourselves all the while; only some of us are not worth paying."

"You're extraordinarily droll, but somehow I can't laugh at you," said Peter, his handsome face lengthened to a point that sufficiently attested the fact. "Do you remember the second time I ever saw you—the day you recited at my place?" he abruptly inquired, a good deal as if he were drawing from his quiver an arrow which, if it was the last, was also one of the most pointed.

"Perfectly, and what an idiot I was, though it was only yesterday!"

"You expressed to me then a deep detestation of the sort of self-exposure to which the profession you were seeking to enter would commit you. If you compared yourself to a contortionist at a country fair I'm only taking my cue from you."

"I don't know what I may have said then," replied Miriam, whose steady flight was not arrested by this ineffectual bolt; "I was, no doubt, already wonderful for talking of things I know nothing about. I was only on the brink of the stream and I perhaps thought the water colder than it is. One warms it a bit one's self, when once one is in. Of course I'm a contortionist and of course there's a hateful side; but don't you see how that very fact puts a price on every compensation, on the help of those who are ready to insist on the *other* side, the grand one, and especially on the sympathy of the person who is ready to insist most and to keep before us the great thing, the element that makes up for everything?"

"The element?" Peter questioned, with a vagueness which was pardonably exaggerated. "Do you mean your success?"

"I mean what you've so often been eloquent about," the girl returned, with an indulgent shrug—"the way we simply stir people's souls. Ah, there's where life can help us," she broke out, with a change of tone, "there's where human relations and affections can help us; love and faith and joy and suffering and experience—I don't know what to call 'em! They suggest things, they light them up and sanctify them, as you may say; they make them appear worth doing." She became radiant for a moment, as if with a splendid vision; then melting into still another accent, which seemed all nature and harmony, she proceeded: "I must tell you that in the matter of what we can do for each other I have a tremendously high ideal. I go in for closeness of union, for identity of interest. A true marriage, as they call it, must do one a lot of good!"

Sherringham stood there looking at her a minute, during which her eyes sustained the rummage of his gaze without a relenting gleam of the sense of cruelty or of paradox. With a passionate but inarticulate ejaculation he turned away from her and remained, on the edge of the window, his hands in his pockets, gazing defeatedly, doggedly, into the featureless night, into the little black garden which had nothing to give him but a familiar smell of damp. The warm darkness had no relief for him, and Miriam's histrionic hardness flung him back against a fifth-rate world, against a bedimmed, star-punctured nature which had no consolation—the bleared, ir-responsive eyes of the London heaven. For the brief space that he glared at these things he dumbly and helplessly raged. What he wanted was something that was not in *that* thick prospect. What was the meaning of this sudden offensive im-portunity of "art," this senseless mocking catch, like some irritating chorus of conspirators in a bad opera, in which Miriam's voice was so incongruously conjoined with Nick's and in which Biddy's sweet little pipe had not scrupled still more bewilderingly to mingle? Art be damned: what commis-sion, after all, had he ever given it to better him or bother him? If the pointless groan in which Peter exhaled a part of his humiliation had been translated into words, these words would have been as heavily charged with the genuine British mistrust of the bothersome principle as if the poor fellow speaking them had never quitted his island. Several acquired perceptions had struck a deep root in him, but there was an immemorial compact formation which lay deeper still. He tried at the present hour to rest upon it spiritually, but found it inelastic; and at the very moment when he was most con-scious of this absence of the rebound or of any tolerable ease his vision was solicited by an object which, as he immediately guessed, could only add to the complication of things.

An undefined shape hovered before him in the garden, half-way between the gate and the house; it remained outside of

the broad shaft of lamplight projected from the window. It
wavered for a moment after it had become aware of Peter's
observation, and then whisked round the corner of the little
villa. This characteristic movement so effectually dispelled the
mystery (it could only be Mrs. Rooth who resorted to such
conspicuous secrecies) that, to feel that the game was up and
his interview over, Sherringham had no need of seeing the
figure reappear on second thoughts and dodge about in the
dusk with a vexatious sportive imbecility. Evidently Miriam's
warning of a few minutes before had been founded: a cab had
deposited her anxious mother at the garden-door. Mrs.
Rooth had entered with precautions; she had approached the
house and retreated; she had effaced herself—had peered and
waited and listened. Maternal solicitude and muddled calculations had drawn her away from a festival as yet only imperfectly commemorative. The heroine of the occasion of course
had been intolerably missed, so that the old woman had both
obliged the company and quieted her own nerves by jumping
insistently into a hansom and rattling up to St. John's Wood
to reclaim the absentee. But if she had wished to be in time
she had also desired not to be abrupt; she would have been
still more embarrassed to say what she aspired to promote
than to phrase what she had proposed to hinder. She wanted
to abstain tastefully, to interfere felicitously, and, more generally and justifiably (the small hours had come), to see what
her young charges were doing. She would probably have
gathered that they were quarrelling, and she appeared now to
be telegraphing to Sherringham to know if it were over. He
took no notice of her signals, if signals they were; he only felt
that before he made way for the odious old woman there was
one faint little spark he might strike from Miriam's flint.

Without letting her guess that her mother was on the premises he turned again to his companion, half expecting that
she would have taken her chance to regard their discussion as
more than terminated and by the other egress flit away from
him in silence. But she was still there; she was in the act of
approaching him with a manifest intention of kindness, and
she looked indeed, to his surprise, like an angel of mercy.

"Don't let us part so disagreeably," she said, "with your
trying to make me feel as if I were merely disobliging. It's no

use talking—we only hurt each other. Let us hold our tongues like decent people and go about our business. It isn't as if you hadn't any cure—when you have such a capital one. Try it, try it, my dear friend—you'll see! I wish you the highest promotion and the quickest—every success and every reward. When you've got them all, some day, and I've become a great swell too, we'll meet on that solid basis and you'll be glad I've been nasty now."

"Surely before I leave you I've a right to ask you this," Sherringham answered, holding fast in both his own the cool hand of farewell that she had finally tormented him with. "Are you ready to follow up by a definite promise your implied assurance that I have a remedy?"

"A definite promise?" Miriam benignly gazed, with the perfection of evasion. "I don't 'imply' that you have a remedy. I declare it on the housetops. That delightful girl—"

"I'm not talking of any delightful girl but you!" Peter broke in with a voice which, as he afterwards learned, struck Mrs. Rooth's ears, in the garden, with affright. "I simply hold you, under pain of being convicted of the grossest prevarication, to the strict sense of what you said a quarter of an hour ago."

"Ah, I've said so many things; one has to do that to get rid of you. You rather hurt my hand," she added, jerking it away in a manner that showed that if she was an angel of mercy her mercy was partly for herself.

"As I understand you, then, I may have some hope if I do renounce my profession?" Peter pursued. "If I break with everything, my prospects, my studies, my training, my emoluments, my past and my future, the service of my country and the ambition of my life, and engage to take up instead the business of watching your interests so far as I may learn how and ministering to your triumphs so far as may in me lie—if after further reflection I decide to go through these preliminaries, have I your word that I may definitely look to you to reward me with your precious hand?"

"I don't think you have any right to put the question to me now," said Miriam, with a promptitude partly produced perhaps by the clear-cut form Peter's solemn speech had given (it was a charm to hear it) to each item of his enumeration. "The case is so very contingent, so dependent on what you ingeniously call your further reflection. While you reserve yourself you ask me to commit myself. If it's a question of further reflection, why did you drag me up here? And then," she added, "I'm so far from wishing you to take any such monstrous step."

"Monstrous, you call it? Just now you said it would be sublime."

"Sublime if it's done with spontaneity, with passion; ridiculous if it's done after further reflection. As you said perfectly a while ago, it isn't a thing to reason about."

"Ah, what a help you'd be to me in diplomacy!" Sherringham cried. "Will you give me a year to consider?"

"Would you trust me for a year?"

"Why not, if I'm ready to trust you for life?"

"Oh, I shouldn't be free then, worse luck. And how much you seem to take for granted one must like you!"

"Remember that you've made a great point of your liking me. Wouldn't you do so still more if I were heroic?"

Miriam looked at him a moment. "I think I should pity you, in such a cause. Give it all to *her*; don't throw away a real happiness!"

"Ah, you can't back out of your position with a few vague and even rather impertinent words!" Sherringham declared. "You accuse me of swallowing my protestations, but you swallow yours. You've painted in heavenly colours the sacrifice I'm talking of, and now you must take the consequences."

"The consequences?"

"Why, my coming back in a year to square you."

"Ah, you're tiresome!" cried Miriam. "Come back when you like. I don't wonder you've grown desperate, but fancy *me* then!" she added, looking past him at a new interlocutor.

"Yes, but if he'll square you!" Peter heard Mrs. Rooth's voice respond conciliatingly behind him. She had stolen up to the window now, she had passed the threshold, she was in the room, but her daughter had not been startled. "What is it he wants to do, dear?" she continued, to Miriam.

"To induce me to marry him if he'll go upon the stage. He'll practise over there, where he's going, and then he'll come back and appear. Isn't it too dreadful? Talk him out of it, stay with him, soothe him!" the girl hurried on. "You'll find some *bibite* and some biscuits in the cupboard—keep him with you, pacify him, give him *his* little supper. Meanwhile I'll go to mine; I'll take the brougham; don't follow!"

With these words Miriam bounded into the garden, and her white drapery shone for an instant in the darkness before she disappeared. Peter looked about him, to pick up his hat, and while he did so he heard the bang of the gate and the quick carriage getting into motion. Mrs. Rooth appeared to sway excitedly for a moment in opposed directions: that of the impulse to rush after Miriam and that of the extraordinary possibility to which the young lady had alluded. She seemed in doubt, but at a venture, detaining him with a maternal touch, she twinkled up at their visitor like an insinuating glow-worm.

"I'm so glad you came."

"I'm not. I've got nothing by it," he said, finding his hat.

"Oh, it was so beautiful!" she coaxed.

"The play—yes, wonderful. I'm afraid it's too late for me to avail myself of the privilege your daughter offers me. Good-night."

"Oh, it's a pity; won't you take *anything*?" asked Mrs. Rooth. "When I heard your voice so high I was scared and I hung back." But before he could reply she added: "Are you really thinking of the stage?"

"It comes to the same thing."

"Do you mean you've proposed?"

"Oh, unmistakably."

"And what does she say?"

"Why, you heard: she says I'm an ass."

"Ah, the little rascal!" laughed Mrs. Rooth. "Leave her to me. I'll help you. But you *are* mad. Give up nothing—least of all your advantages."

"I won't give up your daughter," said Peter, reflecting that if this was cheap it was at any rate good enough for Mrs. Rooth. He mended it a little indeed by adding darkly: "But you can't make her take me."

"I can prevent her taking any one else."

"Oh, can you!" Peter ejaculated, with more scepticism than ceremony.

"You'll see—you'll see." He passed into the garden, but, after she had blown out the candles and drawn the window to, Mrs. Rooth went with him. "All you've got to do is to be yourself—to be true to your fine position," she explained as they proceeded. "Trust me with the rest—trust me and be quiet."

"How can one be quiet after this magnificent evening?"

"Yes, but it's just that!" panted the eager old woman. "It has launched her so, on this sea of dangers, that to make up for the loss of the old security (don't you know?) we must take a still firmer hold."

"Ay, of what?" asked Sherringham, as Mrs. Rooth's comfort became vague while she stopped with him at the garden-door.

"Ah, you know: of the *real* life, of the true anchor!" Her hansom was waiting for her, and she added: "I kept it, you see; but a little extravagance, on the night one's fortune has come!"

Peter stared. Yes, there were people whose fortune had come; but he managed to stammer: "Are you following her again?"

"For you—for you!" And Mrs. Rooth clambered into the vehicle. From the seat, enticingly, she offered him the place beside her. "Won't you come too? I know he asked you." Peter declined with a quick gesture, and as he turned away he heard her call after him, to cheer him on his lonely walk: "I shall keep this up; I shall never lose sight of her!"

XV.

WHEN MRS. DALLOW returned to London, just before London broke up, the fact was immediately known in Calcutta Gardens and was promptly communicated to Nick Dormer by his sister Bridget. He had learnt it in no other way—he had had no correspondence with Julia during her absence. He gathered that his mother and sisters were not ignorant of her whereabouts (he never mentioned her name to them); but as to this he was not sure whether the source of their information was the *Morning Post* or a casual letter received by the inscrutable Biddy. He knew that Biddy had some epistolary commerce with Julia, and he had an impression that Grace occasionally exchanged letters with Mrs. Gresham. Biddy, however, who, as he was well aware, was always studying what he would like, forbore to talk to him about the absent mistress of Harsh, beyond once dropping the remark that she had gone from Florence to Venice and was enjoying gondolas and sunsets too much to leave them. Nick's comment on this was that she was a happy woman to have such a go at Titian and Tintoret: as he spoke and for some time afterwards the sense of how he himself should enjoy a similar "go" made him ache with ineffectual longing.

He had forbidden himself for the present to think of absence, not only because it would be inconvenient and expensive, but because it would be a kind of retreat from the enemy, a concession to difficulty. The enemy was no particular person and no particular body of persons: not his mother; not Mr. Carteret, who, as Nick heard from the doctor at Beauclere, lingered on, sinking and sinking till his vitality appeared to have the vertical depth of a gold-mine; not his pacified constituents, who had found a healthy diversion in returning another Liberal, wholly without Mrs. Dallow's aid (she had not participated even to the extent of a responsive telegram in the election); not his late colleagues in the House, nor the biting satirists of the newspapers, nor the brilliant women he took down at dinner-parties (there was only one sense in which he ever took them down), nor his friends, nor his foes, nor his private thoughts, nor the periodical phantom

of his shocked father: it was simply the general awkwardness
of his situation. This awkwardness was connected with the
sense of responsibility that Gabriel Nash so greatly deprecated—ceasing to roam, of late, on purpose to miss as few
scenes as possible of the drama, rapidly growing dull, alas, of
his friend's destiny; but that compromising relation scarcely
drew the soreness from it. The public flurry produced by
Nick's collapse had only been large enough to mark the flatness of his position when it was over. To have had a few jokes
cracked audibly at one's expense was not an ordeal worth talking of; the hardest thing about it was merely that there had
not been enough of them to yield a proportion of good ones.
Nick had felt, in short, the benefit of living in an age and in a
society where number and pressure have, for the individual
figure, especially when it's a zero, compensations almost
equal to their cruelties.

No, the pinch, for our young man's conscience, after a few
weeks had passed, was simply an acute mistrust of the super-
ficiality of performance into which the desire to justify himself
might hurry him. That desire was passionate as regards Julia
Dallow; it was ardent also as regards his mother; and, to
make it absolutely uncomfortable it was complicated with the
conviction that neither of them would recognize his justification even when they should see it. They probably couldn't if
they would, and very likely they wouldn't if they could. He
assured himself however that this limitation wouldn't matter;
it was their affair—his own was simply to have the right sort
of thing to show. The work he was now attempting was not
the right sort of thing; though doubtless Julia for instance
would dislike it almost as much as if it were. The two portraits of Miriam, after the first exhilaration of his finding himself at large, filled him with no private glee: they were not in
the direction in which for the present he wished really to
move. There were moments when he felt almost angry,
though of course he held his tongue, when by the few
persons who saw them they were pronounced wonderfully
clever. That they were wonderfully clever was just the detestable thing in them, so active had that cleverness been in making them seem better than they were. There were people to
whom he would have been ashamed to show them, and these

were the people whom it would give him most pleasure some day to please. Not only had he many an hour of disgust with his actual work, but he thought he saw, as in an ugly revelation, that nature had cursed him with an odious facility and that the lesson of his life, the sternest and wholesomest, would be to keep out of the trap it had laid for him. He had fallen into this trap on the threshold and he had only scrambled out with his honour. He had a talent for appearance, and that was the fatal thing; he had a damnable suppleness and a gift of immediate response, a readiness to oblige, that made him seem to take up causes which he really left lying, enabled him to learn enough about them in an hour to have all the air of having made them his own. Many people call them their own who had taken them in much less. He was too clever by half, since this pernicious overflow had been at the bottom of deep disappointments and heart-burnings. He had assumed a virtue and enjoyed assuming it, and the assumption had cheated his father and his mother and his affianced wife and his rich benefactor and the candid burgesses of Harsh and the cynical reporters of the newspapers. His enthusiasms had been but young curiosity, his speeches had been young agility, his professions and adhesions had been like postage-stamps without glue: the head was all right, but they wouldn't stick. He stood ready now to wring the neck of the irrepressible vice which certainly would like nothing better than to get him into further trouble. His only real justification would be to turn patience (his own, of course) inside out; yet if there should be a way to misread that recipe his humbugging genius could be trusted infallibly to discover it. Cheap and easy results would dangle before him, little amateurish conspicuities, helped by his history, at exhibitions; putting it in his power to triumph with a quick "What do you say to that?" over those he had wounded. The fear of this danger was corrosive; it poisoned even legitimate joys. If he should have a striking picture at the Academy next year it wouldn't be a crime: yet he couldn't help suspecting any conditions that would enable him to be striking so soon. In this way he felt quite enough how Gabriel Nash "had" him whenever he railed at his fever for proof, and how inferior as a productive force the desire to win over the ill-disposed might be to the

principle of quiet growth. Nash had a foreign manner of lifting up his finger and waving it before him, as if to put an end
to everything, whenever it became, in conversation or discussion, to any extent a question whether any one would like
anything.

It was presumably, in some degree at least, a due respect
for the principle of quiet growth that kept Nick on the spot at
present, made him stick fast to Rosedale Road and Calcutta
Gardens and deny himself the simplifications of absence. Do
what he would he could not despoil himself of the impression
that the disagreeable was somehow connected with the salutary and the "quiet" with the disagreeable, when stubbornly
borne; so he resisted a hundred impulses to run away to Paris
or to Florence and the temptation to persuade himself by material motion that he was launched. He stayed in London because it seemed to him that he was more conscious of what he
had undertaken, and he had a horror of shirking that consciousness. One element in it indeed was the perception that
he would have found no great convenience in a foreign journey, even had his judgment approved such a subterfuge. The
stoppage of his supplies from Beauclere had now become an
historic fact, with something of the majesty of its class about
it: he had had time to see what a difference this would make
in his life. His means were small and he had several old debts,
the number of which, as he believed, loomed large to his
mother's imagination. He could never tell her that she exaggerated, because he told her nothing of that sort now: they
had no intimate talk, for an impenetrable partition, a tall bristling hedge of untrimmed misconceptions had sprung up between them. Poor Biddy had made a hole in it, through which
she squeezed, from side to side, to keep up communications,
at the cost of many rents and scratches; but Lady Agnes
walked straight and stiff, never turning her head, never stopping to pluck the least little daisy of consolation. It was in this
manner she wished to signify that she had accepted her
wrongs. She draped herself in them as in a kind of Roman
mantle, and she had never looked so proud and wasted and
handsome as now that her eyes rested only upon ruins.

Nick was extremely sorry for her, though he thought there
was a dreadful want of grace in her never setting a foot in

Rosedale Road (she mentioned his studio no more than if it had been a private gambling house, or something worse); sorry because he was well aware that for the hour everything must appear to her to have crumbled. The luxury of Broadwood would have to crumble: his mind was very clear about that. Biddy's prospects had withered to the finest, dreariest dust, and Biddy indeed, taking a lesson from her brother's perversities, seemed little disposed to better a bad business. She professed the most peacemaking sentiments, but when it came really to doing something to brighten up the scene she showed herself portentously corrupted. After Peter Sherringham's heartless flight she had wantonly slighted an excellent opportunity to repair her misfortune. Lady Agnes had reason to know, about the end of June, that young Mr. Grindon, the only son (the other children were girls) of an immensely rich industrial and political baronet in the north, was literally waiting for the faintest sign. This reason she promptly imparted to her younger daughter, whose intelligence had to take it in but who had shown it no other consideration. Biddy had set her charming face as a stone; she would have nothing to do with signs, and she, practically speaking, wilfully, wickedly refused a magnificent offer, so that the young man carried his noble expectations elsewhere. How much in earnest he had been was proved by the fact that before Goodwood had come and gone he was captured by Lady Muriel Macpherson. It was superfluous to insist on the frantic determination to get married revealed by such an accident as that. Nick knew of this episode only through Grace, and he deplored its having occurred in the midst of other disasters.

He knew or he suspected something more as well—something about his brother Percival which, if it should come to light, no season would be genial enough to gloss over. It had usually been supposed that Percy's store of comfort against the ills of life was confined to the infallibility of his rifle. He was not sensitive, but he had always the consolation of killing something. It had suddenly come to Nick's ears however that he had another resource as well, in the person of a robust countrywoman, housed in an ivied corner of Warwickshire, in whom he had long been interested and whom, without any flourish of magnanimity, he had ended by making his wife.

The situation of the latest born of the pledges of this affection, a blooming boy (there had been two or three previously), was therefore perfectly regular and of a nature to make a difference in the worldly position, as the phrase is, of his moneyless uncle. If there be degrees in the absolute and Percy had an heir (others, moreover, would supposably come), Nick would have to regard himself as still more moneyless than before. His brother's last step was doubtless, under the circumstances, to be commended; but such discoveries were enlivening only when they were made in other families, and Lady Agnes would scarcely enjoy learning to what tune she had become a grandmother.

Nick forbore from delicacy to intimate to Biddy that he thought it a pity she couldn't care for Mr. Grindon; but he had a private sense that if she had been capable of such an achievement it would have lightened a little the weight he himself had to carry. He bore her a slight grudge, which lasted until Julia Dallow came back; when the circumstance of the girl's being summoned immediately down to Harsh created a diversion that was perhaps after all only fanciful. Biddy, as we know, entertained a theory, which Nick had found occasion to combat, that Mrs. Dallow had not treated him perfectly well; therefore in going to Harsh the very first time Julia held out a hand to her, so jealous a little sister must have recognized a special inducement. The inducement might have been that Julia had comfort for her, that she was acting by the direct advice of this acute lady, that they were still in close communion on the question of the offers Biddy was not to accept, that in short Peter Sherringham's sister had taken upon herself to see that Biddy should remain free until the day of the fugitive's inevitable return. Once or twice indeed Nick wondered whether Mrs. Dallow herself was visited, in a larger sense, by the thought of retracing her steps—whether she wished to draw out her young friend's opinion as to how she might do so gracefully. During the few days she was in town Nick had seen her twice, in Great Stanhope Street, but not alone. She had said to him on one of these occasions, in her odd, explosive way: "I should have thought you'd have gone away somewhere—it must be such a bore." Of course she firmly believed he was staying for Miriam, which he really was not; and probably she had written this false impression off to Peter, who still more probably would prefer to regard it as just. Nick was staying for Miriam only in the sense that he should be very glad of the money he might receive for the portrait he was engaged in painting. That money would be a great convenience to him, in spite of the obstructive ground Miriam had taken in pretending (she had blown half a gale about it) that he had had no right to dispose of such a production without her consent. His answer to this was simply that the purchaser was so little of a stranger that it didn't go, as it were, out of the family, out of hers. It didn't matter that Miriam should protest that if Mr. Sherringham had formerly been no stranger he was now utterly one, so that there could be nothing less soothing to him than to see her hated image on his wall. He would back out of the bargain, and Nick would be left with his work on his hands. Nick jeered at this shallow theory and, when she came to sit, the question served as well as another to sprinkle their familiar silences with chaff. Nick already knew something, as we have seen, of the conditions in which his distracted kinsman had left England; and this connected itself in casual meditation with some of the calculations that he attributed to Julia and Biddy. There had naturally been a sequel to the queer behaviour in which Peter had indulged, at the theatre, on the eve of his departure—a sequel embodied in a remark dropped by Miriam in the course of the first sitting she gave Nick after her great night. "Fancy"—so this observation ran—"fancy the dear man finding time, in the press of all his last duties, to ask me to marry him!"

"He told me you had found time, in the press of all yours, to say you would," Nick replied. And this was pretty much all that had passed on the subject between them, save, of course, that Miriam immediately made it clear that Peter had grossly misinformed him. What had happened was that she had said she would do nothing of the sort. She professed a desire not to be confronted again with this trying theme, and Nick easily fell in with it, from a definite preference he now had not to handle that kind of subject with her. If Julia had false ideas about him, and if Peter had them too, his part of the business was to take the simplest course to establish that falsity. There were difficulties indeed attached even to the simplest course, but there would be a difficulty the less if, in conversation, one should forbear to meddle with the general suggestive topic of intimate unions. It is certain that in these days Nick cultivated the practice of forbearances for which he did not receive, for which perhaps he never would receive, due credit.

He had been convinced for some time that one of the next things he should hear would be that Mrs. Dallow had arranged to marry Mr. Macgeorge or some such leader of multitudes. He could think of that now, he found—think of it with resignation, even when Julia was before his eyes, looking so handsomely forgetful that her air had to be taken as referring still more to their original intimacy than to his comparatively superficial offence. What made this accomplishment of his own remarkable was that there was something else he thought of quite as much—the fact that he had only to see her again to feel by how great a charm she had in the old days taken possession of him. This charm operated apparently in a very direct, primitive way: her presence diffused it and fully established it, but her absence left comparatively little of it behind. It dwelt in the very facts of her person—it was something that she happened physically to be; yet (considering that the question was of something very like loveliness) its envelope of associations, of memories and recurrences, had no great density. She packed it up and took it away with her, as if she had been a woman who had come to sell a set of laces. The laces were as wonderful as ever when they were taken out of the box, but to get another look at them you had to send for the woman. What was above all remarkable was that Miriam Rooth was much less irresistible to our young man than Mrs. Dallow could be when Mrs. Dallow was on the spot. He could paint Miriam, day after day, without any agitating blur of vision; in fact the more he saw of her the clearer grew the atmosphere through which she blazed, the more her richness became one with that of the flowering picture. There are reciprocities and special sympathies in such relations; mysterious affinities they used to be called, divinations of private congruity. Nick had an unexpressed conviction that if, as he had often wanted and proposed, he had embarked with Mrs. Dallow in this particular quest of a great prize, disaster would have overtaken them on the deep waters. Even with the limited risk, indeed, disaster had come; but it was of a different kind and it had the advantage for him that now she couldn't reproach and accuse him as the cause of it—couldn't do so at least on any ground he was obliged to recognize. She would never know how much he had cared for her, how much he cared for her still; inasmuch as the conclusive proof, for himself, was his conscious reluctance to care for another woman, which she positively misread. Some day he would doubtless try to do that; but such a day seemed as yet far off, and he had no spite, no vindictive impulse to help him. The soreness that was mingled with his liberation, the sense of indignity even, as of a full cup suddenly dashed by a blundering hand from his lips, demanded certainly a balm; but it found it for a time in another passion, not in a rancorous exercise of the same—a passion strong enough to make him forget what a pity it was that he was not made to care for two women at once.

As soon as Mrs. Dallow returned to England he broke ground to his mother on the subject of her making Julia understand that she and the girls now regarded their occupancy of Broadwood as absolutely terminated. He had already, several weeks before, picked a little at this arid tract, but in the interval the soil appeared to have formed again. It was disagreeable to him to impose such a renunciation on Lady Agnes, and it was especially disagreeable to have to phrase it and discuss it and perhaps insist upon it. He would have liked the whole business to be tacit—a little triumph of silent delicacy. But he found reasons to suspect that what in fact would be most tacit was Julia's certain endurance of any chance *in*delicacy. Lady Agnes had a theory that they had virtually— "practically," as she said—given up the place, so that there was no need of making a splash about it; but Nick discovered, in the course of a conversation with Biddy more rigorous perhaps than any to which he had ever subjected her, that none of their property had been removed from her delightful house—none of the things (there were ever so many things) that Lady Agnes had caused to be conveyed there when they took possession. Her ladyship was the proprietor of innumerable articles of furniture, relics and survivals of her former

greatness, and moved about the world with a train of heterogeneous baggage; so that her quiet overflow into the spa-
ciousness of Broadwood had had all the luxury of a final
subsidence. What Nick had to propose to her now was a
dreadful combination, a relapse into all the things she most
hated—seaside lodgings, bald storehouses in the Marylebone
Road, little London rooms crammed with things that caught
the dirt and made them stuffy. He was afraid he should really
finish her, and he himself was surprised in a degree at his
insistence. He wouldn't have supposed that he should have
cared so much, but he found he did care intensely. He cared
enough—it says everything—to explain to his mother that
practically her retention of Broadwood would be the violation
of an agreement. Julia had given them the place on the understanding that he was to marry her, and since he was not to
marry her they had no right to keep the place. "Yes, you make
the mess and *we* pay the penalty!" Lady Agnes flashed out;
but this was the only overt protest that she made, except indeed to contend that their withdrawal would be an act ungracious and offensive to Julia. She looked as she had looked
during the months that succeeded his father's death, but she
gave a general grim assent to the proposition that, let Julia
take it as she would, their own duty was unmistakably clear.

It was Grace who was the principal representative of the
idea that Julia would be outraged by such a step; she never
ceased to repeat that she had never heard of anything so
"nasty." Nick would have expected this of Grace, but he felt
rather deserted and betrayed when Biddy murmured to him
that *she* knew—that there was really no need of their sacrificing their mother's comfort to a mere fancy. She intimated
that if Nick would only consent to their going on with
Broadwood as if nothing had happened (or rather as if everything had happened), she would answer for Julia. For almost
the first time in his life Nick disliked what Biddy said to him,
and he gave her a sharp rejoinder, embodying the general
opinion that they all had enough to do to answer for themselves. He remembered afterwards the way she looked at him,
startled, even frightened, with rising tears, before turning
away. He held that it would be time enough to judge how
Julia would take it after they had thrown up the place; and he

made it his duty to see that his mother should address to Mrs. Dallow by letter a formal notification of their retirement. Mrs. Dallow could protest then if she liked. Nick was aware that in general he was not practical; he could imagine why, from his early years, people should have joked him about it. But this time he was determined that his behaviour should be founded on a rigid view of things as they were. He didn't see his mother's letter to Julia, but he knew that it went. He thought she would have been more loyal if she had shown it to him, though of course there could be but little question of loyalty now. That it had really been written however, very much on the lines he dictated, was clear to him from the subsequent surprise which Lady Agnes's blankness did not prevent him from divining.

Julia answered her letter, but in unexpected terms: she had apparently neither resisted nor protested; she had simply been very glad to get her house back again and had not accused any of them of nastiness. Nick saw no more of her letter than he had seen of his mother's, but he was able to say to Grace (to Lady Agnes he was studiously mute): "My poor child, you see, after all, that we haven't kicked up such a row." Grace shook her head and looked gloomy and deeply wise, replying that he had no cause to triumph—they were so far from having seen the end of it yet. Then he guessed that his mother had complied with his wish on the calculation that it would be a mere form, that Julia would entreat them not to be so fantastic, and that he would then, in the presence of her wounded surprise, consent to a quiet continuance, so much in the interest (the air of Broadwood had a purity!) of the health of all of them. But since Julia jumped at their relinquishment he had no chance to be mollified: he had only to persist in having been right.

At bottom, probably, he himself was a little surprised at her eagerness. Literally speaking, it was not perfectly graceful. He was sorry his mother had been so deceived, but he was sorrier still for Biddy's mistake—it showed she might be mistaken about other things. Nothing was left now but for Lady Agnes to say, as she did, substantially, whenever she saw him: "We are to prepare to spend the autumn at Worthing then, or some other horrible place? I don't know their names: it's the

only thing we can afford." There was an implication in this
that if he expected her to drag her girls about to country-
houses, in a continuance of the fidgety effort to work them
off, he must understand at once that she was now too weary
and too sad and too sick. She had done her best for them, and
it had all been vain and cruel, and now the poor creatures
must look out for themselves. To the grossness of Biddy's
misconduct she needn't refer, nor to the golden opportunity
this young lady had forfeited by her odious treatment of Mr.
Grindon. It was clear that this time Lady Agnes was incurably
discouraged; so much so as to fail to glean the dimmest light
from the fact that the girl was really making a long stay at
Harsh. Biddy went to and fro two or three times and then, in
August, fairly settled there; and what her mother mainly saw
in her absence was the desire to keep out of the way of household reminders of her depravity. In fact, as it turned out,
Lady Agnes and Grace, in the first days of August, gathered
themselves together for another visit to the old lady who had
been Sir Nicholas's godmother; after which they went somewhere else, so that the question of Worthing had not to be
immediately faced.

Nick stayed on in London with a passion of work fairly
humming in his ears; he was conscious with joy that for three
or four months, in the empty Babylon, he would have generous days. But toward the end of August he got a letter from
Grace in which she spoke of her situation, and her mother's,
in a manner that made him feel he ought to do something
tactful. They were paying a third visit (he knew that in Calcutta Gardens lady's-maids had been to and fro with boxes,
replenishments of wardrobes), and yet somehow the outlook
for the autumn was dark. Grace didn't say it in so many
words, but what he read between the lines was that they had
no more invitations. What therefore was to become of them?
People liked them well enough when Biddy was with them,
but they didn't care for her mother and her, *tout pur*, and
Biddy was cooped up indefinitely with Julia. This was not the
manner in which Grace used to allude to her sister's happy
visits to Mrs. Dallow, and the change of tone made Nick
wince with a sense of all that had collapsed. Biddy was a little
fish worth landing, in short, scantily as she seemed disposed

to bite, and Grace's rude probity could admit that she herself was not.

Nick had an inspiration: by way of doing something tactful he went down to Brighton and took lodgings for the three ladies, for several weeks, the quietest and sunniest he could find. This he intended as a kindly surprise, a reminder of how he had his mother's comfort at heart, how he could exert himself and save her trouble. But he had no sooner concluded his bargain (it was a more costly one than he had at first calculated) than he was bewildered, as he privately phrased it quite "stumped," at learning that the three ladies were to pass the autumn at Broadwood with Julia. Mrs. Dallow had taken the place into familiar use again and she was now correcting their former surprise at her crude concurrence (this was infinitely characteristic of Julia) by inviting them to share it with her. Nick wondered vaguely what she was "up to;" but when his mother treated herself to the fine irony of addressing him an elaborately humble inquiry as to whether he would consent to their accepting the merciful refuge (she repeated this expression three times), he replied that she might do exactly as she liked: he would only mention that he should not feel himself at liberty to come and see her at Broadwood. This condition proved, apparently, to Lady Agnes's mind, no hindrance, and she and her daughters were presently reinstalled in the very apartments they had learned to love. This time it was even better than before; they had still fewer expenses. The expenses were Nick's: he had to pay a forfeit to the landlady at Brighton for backing out of his contract. He said nothing to his mother about this bungled business—he was literally afraid; but an event that befell at the same moment reminded him afresh that it was not the time to choose to squander money. Mr. Carteret drew his last breath; quite painlessly it seemed, as the closing scene was described at Beauclere when our young man went down to the funeral. Two or three weeks afterwards the contents of his will were made public in the *Illustrated London News*, where it definitely appeared that he had left a very large fortune, not a penny of which was to go to Nick. The provision for Mr. Chayter's declining years was very handsome.

XVI.

MIRIAM had mounted at a bound, in her new part, several steps in the ladder of fame, and at the climax of the London season this fact was brought home to her from hour to hour. It produced a thousand solicitations and entanglements, so that she rapidly learned that to be celebrated takes up almost as much of one's own time as of other people's. Even though, as she boasted, she had reduced to a science the practice of "working" her mother (she made use of the good lady socially to the utmost, pushing her perpetually into the breach), there were many occasions on which it was represented to her that she could not be disobliging without damaging her cause. She made almost an income out of the photographers (their appreciation of her as a subject knew no bounds), and she supplied the newspapers with columns of irreducible copy. To the gentlemen who sought speech of her on behalf of these organs she poured forth, vindictively, floods of unscrupulous romance; she told them all different tales, and as her mother told them others yet more marvellous publicity was cleverly caught by rival versions, surpassing each other in authenticity. The whole case was remarkable, was unique; for if the girl was advertised by the bewilderment of her readers, she seemed to every sceptic, when he went to see her, as fine as if he had discovered her for himself. She was still accommodating enough however, from time to time, to find an hour to come and sit to Nick Dormer, and he helped himself further by going to her theatre whenever he could. He was conscious that Julia Dallow would probably hear of that and triumph with a fresh sense of how right she had been; but this reflection only made him sigh resignedly, so true it struck him as being that there are some things explanation can never better, can never touch.

Miriam brought Basil Dashwood once to see her portrait, and Basil, who commended it in general, directed his criticism mainly to two points—its not yet being finished and its not having gone into that year's Academy. The young actor was visibly fidgety: he felt the contagion of Miriam's rapid pace, the quick beat of her success, and, looking at everything now

from the standpoint of that speculation, could scarcely contain his impatience at the painter's clumsy slowness. He
thought the second picture much better than the other one,
but somehow it ought by that time to be before the public.
Having a great deal of familiar proverbial wisdom, he put
forth with vehemence the idea that in every great crisis there
is nothing like striking while the iron is hot. He even betrayed a sort of impression that with a little good-will Nick
might wind up the job and still get the Academy people to
take him in. Basil knew some of them; he all but offered to
speak to them—the case was so exceptional; he had no doubt
he could get something done. Against the appropriation of
the work by Peter Sherringham he explicitly and loudly protested, in spite of the homeliest recommendations of silence
from Miriam; and it was indeed easy to guess how such an
arrangement would interfere with his own conception of the
eventual right place for the two portraits—the vestibule of
the theatre, where every one going in and out would see
them, suspended face to face and surrounded by photographs,
artistically disposed, of the young actress in a variety of characters. Dashwood showed a largeness of view in the way he
jumped to the conviction that in this position the pictures
would really help to draw. Considering the virtue he attributed to Miriam the idea was exempt from narrow prejudice.

Moreover, though a trifle feverish, he was really genial; he
repeated more than once: "Yes, my dear sir, you've done it
this time." This was a favourite formula with him; when some
allusion was made to the girl's success he greeted it also with
a comfortable "This time she *has* done it." There was a hint of
knowledge and far calculation in his tone. It appeared before
he went that this time even he himself had done it—he had
taken up something that would really answer. He told Nick
more about Miriam, more about her affairs at that moment at
least, than she herself had communicated, contributing
strongly to our young man's impression that one by one every
element of a great destiny was being dropped into her cup.
Nick himself tasted of success vicariously for the hour. Miriam let Dashwood talk only to contradict him, and contradicted him only to show how indifferently she could do it.
She treated him as if she had nothing more to learn about his

folly, but as if it had taken intimate friendship to reveal to her the full extent of it. Nick didn't mind her intimate friendships, but he ended by disliking Dashwood, who irritated him—a circumstance in which poor Julia, if it had come to her knowledge, would doubtless have found a damning eloquence. Miriam was more pleased with herself than ever: she now made no scruple of admitting that she enjoyed all her advantages. She was beginning to have a fuller vision of how successful success could be; she took everything as it came—dined out every Sunday, and even went into the country till the Monday morning; she had a hundred distinguished names on her lips and wonderful tales about the people who were making up to her. She struck Nick as less serious than she had been hitherto, as making even an aggressive show of frivolity; but he was conscious of no obligation to reprehend her for it—the less as he had a dim vision that some effect of that sort, some irritation of his curiosity, was what she desired to produce. She would perhaps have liked, for reasons best known to herself, to look as if she were throwing herself away, not being able to do anything else. He couldn't talk to her as if he took an immense interest in her career, because in fact he didn't; she remained to him primarily and essentially a pictorial subject, with the nature of whose vicissitudes he was concerned (putting common charity and his personal good-nature of course aside) only so far as they had something to say in her face. How could he know in advance what twist of her life would say most? so possible was it even that complete failure or some incalculable perversion would only make her, for his particular purpose, more magnificent.

After she had left him, at any rate, the day she came with Basil Dashwood, and still more on a later occasion, as he turned back to his work when he had put her into her carriage, the last time, for that year, that he saw her—after she had left him it occurred to him, in the light of her quick distinction, that there were mighty differences in the famous artistic life. Miriam was already in the glow of a glory which moreover was probably but a faint spark in relation to the blaze to come; and as he closed the door upon her and took up his palette to rub it with a dirty cloth the little room in which his own battle was practically to be fought looked wofully cold and gray and mean. It was lonely, and yet it peopled with unfriendly shadows (so thick he saw them gathering in winter twilights to come) the duller conditions, the longer patiences, the less immediate and less personal joys. His late beginning was there, and his wasted youth, the mistakes that would still bring forth children after their image, the sedentary solitude, the clumsy obscurity, the poor explanations, the foolishness that he foresaw in having to ask people to wait, and wait longer, and wait again, for a fruition which, to their sense at least, would be an anti-climax. He cared enough for it, whatever it would be, to feel that his pertinacity might enter into comparison even with such a productive force as Miriam's. This was, after all, in his bare studio, the most collective dim presence, the one that was most sociable to him as he sat there and that made it the right place however wrong it was—the sense that it was to the thing in itself he was attached. This was Miriam's case, but the contrast, which she showed him she also felt, was in the number of other things that she got with the thing in itself.

I hasten to add that our young man had hours when this fine substance struck him as requiring, for a complete appeal, no adjunct whatever—as being in its own splendour a summary of all adjuncts and apologies. I have related that the great collections, the National Gallery and the Museum were sometimes rather a series of dead surfaces to him; but the sketch I have attempted of him will have been inadequate if it fails to suggest that there were other days when, as he strolled through them, he plucked right and left perfect nosegays of reassurance. Bent as he was on working in the modern, which spoke to him with a thousand voices, he judged it better, for long periods, not to haunt the earlier masters, whose conditions had been so different (later he came to see that it didn't matter much, especially if one didn't go); but he was liable to accidental deflections from this theory—liable in particular to want to take a look at one of the great portraits of the past. These were the things that were the most inspiring, in the sense that they were the things that, while generations, while worlds had come and gone, seemed most to survive and testify. As he stood before them sometimes the perfection of their survival struck him as the supreme eloquence, the reason that included all others, thanks to the language of art, the richest and most universal. Empires and systems and conquests had rolled over the globe and every kind of greatness had risen and passed away; but the beauty of the great pictures had known nothing of death or change, and the ages had only sweetened their freshness. The same faces, the same figures looked out at different centuries, knowing a deal the century didn't, and when they joined hands they made the indestructible thread on which the pearls of history were strung.

Miriam notified her artist that her theatre was to close on the 10th of August, immediately after which she was to start, with the company, on a tremendous tour of the provinces. They were to make a lot of money, but they were to have no holiday and she didn't want one; she only wanted to keep at it and make the most of her limited opportunities for practice; inasmuch as, at that rate, playing but two parts a year (and such parts—she despised them!) she shouldn't have mastered the rudiments of her trade before decrepitude would compel her to lay it by. The first time she came to the studio after her visit with Dashwood she sprang up abruptly, at the end of half an hour, saying she could sit no more—she had had enough of it. She was visibly restless and preoccupied, and though Nick had not waited till now to discover that she had more moods than he had tints on his palette, he had never yet seen her fitfulness at this particular angle. It was a trifle unbecoming and he was ready to let her go. She looked round the place as if she were suddenly tired of it, and then she said mechanically, in a heartless London way, while she smoothed down her gloves: "So you're just going to stay on?" After he had confessed that this was his dark purpose she continued in the same casual, talk-making manner: "I dare say it's the best thing for you. You're just going to grind, eh?"

"I see before me an eternity of grinding."

"All alone, by yourself, in this dull little hole? You *will* be conscientious, you *will* be virtuous."

"Oh, my solitude will be mitigated—I shall have models and people."

"What people—what models?" Miriam asked, before the glass, arranging her hat.

"Well, no one so good as you."

"That's a prospect!" the girl laughed; "for all the good you've got out of me!"

"You're no judge of that quantity," said Nick, "and even I can't measure it just yet. Have I been rather a brute? I can easily believe it; I haven't talked to you—I haven't amused you as I might. The truth is, painting people is a very absorbing, exclusive occupation. You can't do much to them besides."

"Yes, it's a cruel honour."

"Cruel—that's too much," Nick objected.

"I mean it's one you shouldn't confer on people you like, for when it's over it's over: it kills your interest in them and after you've finished them you don't like them any more."

"Surely I like you," Nick returned, sitting tilted back, before his picture, with his hands in his pockets.

"We've done very well: it's something not to have quarrelled," said Miriam, smiling at him now and seeming more in it. "I wouldn't have had you slight your work—I wouldn't have had you do it badly. But there's no fear of that for you," she went on. "You're the real thing and the rare bird. I haven't lived with you this way without seeing that: you're the sincere artist so much more than I. No, no, don't protest," she added, with one of her sudden fine transitions to a deeper tone. "You'll do things that will hand on your name when my screeching is happily over. Only you do seem to me, I confess, rather high and dry here—I speak from the point of view of your comfort and of my personal interest in you. You strike me as kind of lonely, as the Americans say—rather cut off and isolated in your grandeur. Haven't you any confrères—fellow-artists and people of that sort? Don't they come near you?"

"I don't know them much, I've always been afraid of them, and how can they take me seriously?"

"Well, I've got confrères, and sometimes I wish I hadn't! But does your sister never come near you any more, or is it only the fear of meeting me?"

Nick was aware that his mother had a theory that Biddy was constantly bundled home from Rosedale Road at the approach of improper persons: she was as angry at this as if she wouldn't have been more so if the child had been suffered to stay; but the explanation he gave his present visitor was nearer the truth. He reminded Miriam that he had already told her (he had been careful to do this, so as not to let it appear she was avoided) that her sister was now most of the time in the country, staying with an hospitable relation.

"Oh yes," the girl rejoined to this, "with Mr. Sherringham's sister, Mrs.——what's her name? I always forget it." And when Nick had pronounced the word with a reluctance he doubtless failed sufficiently to conceal (he hated to talk about Mrs. Dallow; he didn't know what business Miriam had with her), she exclaimed: "That's the one—the beauty, the wonderful beauty. I shall never forget how handsome she looked the day she found me here. I don't in the least resemble her, but I should like to have a try at that type, some day, in a comedy of manners. But who will write me a comedy of manners? There it is! The trouble would be, no doubt, that I should push her *à la charge*."

Nick listened to these remarks in silence, saying to himself that if Miriam should have the bad taste (she seemed trembling on the brink of it) to make an allusion to what had passed between the lady in question and himself, he should dislike her utterly. It would show him she was a coarse creature after all. Her good genius interposed however, as against this hard penalty, and she quickly, for the moment at least, whisked away from the topic, demanding, àpropos of comrades and visitors, what had become of Gabriel Nash, whom she had not encountered for so many days.

"I think he's tired of me," said Nick; "he hasn't been near me, either. But, after all, it's natural—he has seen me through."

"Seen you through? Why, you've only just begun."

"Precisely, and at bottom he doesn't like to see me begin. He's afraid I'll do something."

"Do you mean he's jealous?"

"Not in the least, for from the moment one does anything one ceases to compete with him. It leaves him the field more clear. But that's just the discomfort, for him—he feels, as you said just now, kind of lonely; he feels rather abandoned and even, I think, a little betrayed. So far from being jealous he yearns for me and regrets me. The only thing he really takes seriously is to speculate and understand, to talk about the reasons and the essence of things: the people who do that are the highest. The applications, the consequences, the vulgar little effects belong to a lower plane, to which one must doubtless be tolerant and indulgent, but which is after all an affair of comparative accidents and trifles. Indeed he'll probably tell me frankly, the next time I see him, that he can't but feel that to come down to the little questions of action—the little prudences and compromises and simplifications of practice—is for the superior person a really fatal descent. One may be inoffensive and even commendable after it, but one can scarcely pretend to be interesting. *Il en faut comme ça*, but one doesn't haunt them. He'll do his best for me; he'll come back again, but he'll come back sad, and finally he'll fade away altogether. He'll go off to Granada, or somewhere."

"The simplifications of practice?" cried Miriam. "Why, they are just precisely the most blessed things on earth. What should we do without them?"

"What indeed?" Nick echoed. "But if we need them it's because we're not superior persons. We're awful Philistines."

"I'll be one with *you*," the girl smiled. "Poor Nash isn't worth talking about. What was it but a little question of action when he preached to you, as I know he did, to give up your seat?"

"Yes, he has a weakness for giving up—he'll go with you as far as that. But I'm not giving up any more, you see. I'm pegging away, and that's gross."

"He's an idiot—*n'en parlons plus!*" Miriam dropped, gathering up her parasol, but lingering.

"Ah, never for me! He helped me at a difficult time."

"You ought to be ashamed to confess it."

"Oh, you *are* a Philistine," said Nick.

"Certainly I am," Miriam returned going toward the door, "if it makes me one to be sorry, awfully sorry and even rather angry, that I haven't before me a period of the same sort of unsociable pegging away that you have. For want of it I shall never really be good. However, if you don't tell people I've said so, they'll never know. Your conditions are far better than mine and far more respectable: you can do as many things as you like, in patient obscurity, while I'm pitchforked into the *mêlée*, and into the most improbable fame, upon the back of a solitary *cheval de bataille*, a poor broken-winded screw. I foresee that I shall be condemned for the greater part of the rest of my days (do you see that?) to play the stuff I'm acting now. I'm studying Juliet and I want awfully to do her, but really I'm mortally afraid lest, if I should succeed, I should find myself in such a box. Perhaps they'd want Juliet for ever, instead of my present part. You see amid what delightful alternatives one moves. What I want most I never shall have had—five quiet years of hard, all-round work, in a perfect company, with a manager more perfect still, playing five hundred parts and never being heard of. I may be too particular, but that's what I should have liked. I think I'm disgusting, with my successful crudities. It's discouraging; it makes one not care much what happens. What's the use, in such an age, of being good?"

"Good? Your haughty claim is that you're bad."

"I mean *good*, you know—there are other ways. Don't be stupid." And Nick's visitor tapped him—he was at the door with her—with her parasol.

"I scarcely know what to say to you, for certainly it's your fault if you get on so fast."

"I'm too clever—I'm a humbug."

"That's the way I used to be," said Nick.

Miriam rested her wonderful eyes on him; then she turned them over the room, slowly, after which she attached them again, kindly, musingly, on his own. "Ah, the pride of that—the sense of purification! He 'used' to be, forsooth! Poor me! Of course you'll say: 'Look at the sort of thing I've undertaken to produce, compared with what you have.' So it's all right. Become great in the proper way and don't expose me." She glanced back once more into the studio, as if she were leaving it for ever, and gave another last look at the unfinished canvas on the easel. She shook her head sadly. "Poor Mr. Sherringham—with *that*!" she murmured.

"Oh, I'll finish it—it will be very decent," said Nick.

"Finish it by yourself?"

"Not necessarily. You'll come back and sit when you return to London."

"Never, never, never again."

Nick stared. "Why, you've made me the most profuse offers and promises."

"Yes, but they were made in ignorance, and I've backed out of them. I'm capricious too—*faites la part de ça*. I see it wouldn't do—I didn't know it then. We're too far apart—I *am*, as you say, a Philistine." And as Nick protested with vehemence against this unscrupulous bad faith, she added: "You'll find other models; paint Gabriel Nash."

"Gabriel Nash—as a substitute for you?"

"It will be a good way to get rid of him. Paint Mrs. Dallow too," Miriam went on as she passed out of the door which Nick had opened for her—"paint Mrs. Dallow if you wish to eradicate the last possibility of a throb."

It was strange that since only a moment before Nick had been in a state of mind to which the superfluity of this reference would have been the clearest thing about it, he should now have been moved to receive it, quickly, naturally, irreflectively, with the question: "The last possibility? Do you mean in her or in me?"

"Oh, in you. I don't know anything about her."

"But that wouldn't be the effect," rejoined Nick, with the same supervening candour. "I believe that if she were to sit to me the usual law would be reversed."

"The usual law?"

"Which you cited awhile since and of which I recognize the general truth. In the case you speak of I should probably make a frightful picture."

"And fall in love with her again? Then, for God's sake, risk the daub!" Miriam laughed out, floating away to her victoria.

XVII.

Miriam had guessed happily in saying to Nick that to offer to paint Gabriel Nash would be the way to get rid of him. It was with no such invidious purpose indeed that our young man proposed to his intermittent friend to sit; rather, as August was dusty in the London streets, he had too little hope that Nash would remain in town at such a time to oblige him. Nick had no wish to get rid of his private philosopher; he liked his philosophy, and though of course premeditated paradox was the light to read him by, yet he had frequently, in detail, an inspired unexpectedness. He remained, in Rosedale Road, the man in the world who had most the quality of company. All the other men of Nick's acquaintance, all his political friends, represented, often very communicatively, their own affairs, and their own affairs alone; which, when they did it well, was the most their host could ask them. But Nash had the rare distinction that he seemed somehow to stand for *his* affairs, the said host's, with an interest in them unaffected by the ordinary social limitations of capacity. This relegated him to the class of high luxuries, and Nick was well aware that we hold our luxuries by a fitful and precarious tenure. If a friend without personal eagerness was one of the greatest of these it would be evident to the simplest mind that by the law of distribution of earthly boons such a convenience should be expected to forfeit in duration what it displayed in intensity. He had never been without a suspicion that Nash was too good to last, though for that matter nothing had happened to confirm a vague apprehension that the particular way he would break up, or break down, would be by wishing to put Nick in relation with his other disciples.

That would practically amount to a catastrophe, Nick felt; for it was odd that one could both have a great kindness for him and not in the least, when it came to the point, yearn for a view of his belongings. His originality had always been that he appeared to have none; and if in the first instance he had introduced Nick to Miriam and her mother, that was an exception for which Peter Sherringham's interference had been in a great measure responsible. All the same however it was some time before Nick ceased to think it might eventually very well happen that to complete his education, as it were, Gabriel would wish him to foregather a little with minds formed by the same mystical influence. Nick had an instinct, in which there was no consciousness of detriment to Nash, that the pupils, perhaps even the imitators of such a genius would be, as he mentally phrased it, something awful. He could be sure, even Gabriel himself could be sure, of his own reservations, but how could either of them be sure of those of others? Imitation is a fortunate homage only in proportion as it is delicate, and there was an indefinable something in Nash's doctrine that would have been discredited by exaggeration or by zeal. Providence happily appeared to have spared it this probation; so that, after months, Nick had to remind himself that his friend had never pressed upon his attention the least little group of fellow-mystics, nor offered to produce them for his edification. It scarcely mattered now that he was just the man to whom the superficial would attribute that sort of tail; it would probably have been hard, for example, to persuade Lady Agnes, or Julia Dallow, or Peter Sherringham, that he was not most at home in some dusky, untidy, dimly-imagined suburb of "culture," peopled by unpleasant phrase-mongers who thought him a gentleman and who had no human use but to be held up in the comic press, which was probably restrained by decorum from touching upon the worst of their aberrations.

Nick, at any rate, never discovered his academy, nor the suburb in question; never caught, from the impenetrable background of his life, the least reverberation of flitting or flirting, the smallest æsthetic ululation. There were moments when he was even moved to a degree of pity by the silence that poor Gabriel's own faculty of sound made around him—when at least it qualified with thinness the mystery he could never wholly dissociate from him, the sense of the transient and occasional, the likeness to vapour or murmuring wind or shifting light. It was for instance a symbol of this unclassified condition, the lack of all position as a name in well-kept books, that Nick in point of fact had no idea where he lived, would not have known how to go and see him or send him a doctor if he had heard he was ill. He had never walked with him to any door of Gabriel's own, even to pause at the threshold, though indeed Nash had a club, the Anonymous, in some improbable square, of which Nick suspected him of being the only member—he had never heard of another— where it was vaguely understood that letters would some day or other find him. Fortunately it was not necessary to worry about him, so comfortably his whole aspect seemed to imply that he could never be ill. And this was not perhaps because his bloom was healthy, but because it was morbid, as if he had been universally inoculated.

He turned up in Rosedale Road one day after Miriam had left London; he had just come back from a fortnight in Brittany, where he had drawn unusual refreshment from the subtle sadness of the landscape. He was on his way somewhere else; he was going abroad for the autumn, but he was not particular what he did, professing that he had returned to London on purpose to take one last superintending look at Nick. "It's very nice, it's very nice; yes, yes, I see," he remarked, giving a little general assenting sigh as his eyes wandered over the simple scene—a sigh which, to a suspicious ear, would have testified to an insidious reaction.

Nick's ear, as we know, was already suspicious; a fact which would sufficiently account for the expectant smile (it indicated the pleasant apprehension of a theory confirmed) with which he inquired: "Do you mean my pictures are nice?"

"Yes, yes, your pictures and the whole thing."

"The whole thing?"

"Your existence here, in this little remote independent corner of the great city. The disinterestedness of your attitude, the persistence of your effort, the piety, the beauty, in short the example, of the whole spectacle."

Nick broke into a laugh. "How near to having had enough of me you must be when you talk of my example!" Nash changed colour slightly at this; it was the first time in Nick's remembrance that he had given a sign of embarrassment. "*Vous allez me lâcher*, I see it coming; and who can blame you?—for I've ceased to be in the least spectacular. I had my little hour; it was a great deal, for some people don't even have that. I've given you your curious case and I've been generous; I made the drama last for you as long as I could. You'll 'slope,' my dear fellow—you'll quietly slope; and it will be all right and inevitable, though I shall miss you greatly at first. Who knows whether, without you, I shouldn't still have been representing Harsh, heaven help me? You rescued me; you converted me from a representative into an example— that's a shade better. But don't I know where you must be when you're reduced to praising my piety?"

"Don't turn me away," said Nash plaintively; "give me a cigarette."

"I shall never dream of turning you away; I shall cherish you till the latest possible hour. I'm only trying to keep myself in tune with the logic of things. The proof of how I cling is that, precisely, I want you to sit to me."

"To sit to you?" Nick thought his visitor looked a little blank.

"Certainly, for after all it isn't much to ask. Here we are, and the hour is peculiarly propitious—long light days, with no one coming near me, so that I have plenty of time. I had a hope I should have some orders: my younger sister, whom you know and who is a great optimist, plied me with that vision. In fact we invented together a charming sordid little theory that there might be rather a 'run' on me, from the chatter (such as it was) produced by my taking up this line. My sister struck out the idea that a good many of the pretty ladies would think me interesting, would want to be done. Perhaps they do, but they've controlled themselves, for I can't say the run has commenced. They haven't even come to look, but I dare say they don't yet quite take it in. Of course it's a bad time, with every one out of town; though you know they might send for me to come and do them at home. Perhaps they will, when they settle down. A portrait-tour of a dozen country-houses, for the autumn and winter—what do you say to that for a superior programme? I know I excruciate you," Nick added, "but don't you see how it's my interest to try how much you'll still stand?"

Gabriel puffed his cigarette with a serenity so perfect that it might have been assumed to falsify Nick's words. "Mrs. Dallow will send for you—*vous allez voir ça*," he said in a moment, brushing aside all vagueness.

"She'll send for me?"

"To paint her portrait; she'll recapture you on that basis. She'll get you down to one of the country-houses, and it will all go off as charmingly—with sketching in the morning, on days you can't hunt, and anything you like in the afternoon, and fifteen courses in the evening; there'll be bishops and ambassadors staying—as if you were a 'well-known' awfully clever amateur. Take care, take care, for, fickle as you may think me, I can read the future: don't imagine you've come to the end of me yet. Mrs. Dallow and your sister, of both of whom I speak with the greatest respect, are capable of hatching together the most conscientious, delightful plan for you. Your differences with the beautiful lady will be patched up, and you'll each come round a little and meet the other half-way. Mrs. Dallow will swallow your profession if you'll swallow hers. She'll put up with the palette if you'll put up with the country-house. It will be a very unusual one in which you won't find a good north room where you can paint. You'll go about with her and do all her friends, all the bishops and ambassadors, and you'll eat your cake and have it, and every one, beginning with your wife, will forget there is anything queer about you, and everything will be for the best in the best of worlds; so that, together—you and she—you'll become a great social institution, and every one will think she has a delightful husband; to say nothing of course of your having a delightful wife. Ah, my dear fellow, you turn pale, and with reason!" Nash went on: "that's to pay you for having tried to make me let you have it. You have it, then, there! I may be a bore"—the emphasis of this, though a mere shade, testified to the first personal resentment Nick had ever heard his visitor express—"I may be a bore, but once in a while I strike a light, I make things out. Then I venture to repeat, 'Take care, take care.' If, as I say, I respect those ladies infinitely, it is because they will be acting according to the highest wisdom of their sex. That's the sort of thing women invent when they're exceptionally good and clever. When they're not, they don't do so well; but it's not for want of trying. There's only one thing in the world that's better than their charm: it's their conscience. That indeed is a part of their charm. And when they club together, when they earnestly consider, as in the case we're supposing," Nash continued, "then the whole thing takes a lift; for it's no longer the conscience of the individual, it's that of the sex."

"You're so remarkable that, more than ever, I must paint you," Nick returned, "though I'm so agitated by your prophetic words that my hand trembles and I shall doubtless scarcely be able to hold my brush. Look how I rattle my easel trying to put it into position. I see it all there, just as you say it. Yes, it will be a droll day, and more modern than anything yet, when the conscience of women perceives objections to men's being in love with them. You talk of their goodness and cleverness, and it's much to the point. I don't know what else they themselves might do with these things, but I don't see what men can do with them but be fond of them."

"Oh, you'll do it—you'll do it!" cried Nash, brightly jubilant.

"What is it I shall do?"

"Exactly what I just said; if not next year, then the year after, or the year after that. You'll go half-way to meet her, and she'll drag you about and pass you off. You'll paint the bishops and become a social institution. That is, you will if you don't take great care."

"I shall, no doubt, and that's why I cling to you. You must still look after me; don't melt away into a mere improbable reminiscence, a delightful symbolic fable—don't, if you can possibly help it. The trouble is, you see, that you can't really keep hold very tight, because at bottom it will amuse you much more to see me in another pickle than to find me simply jogging down the vista of the years on the straight course. Let me at any rate have some sort of sketch of you, as a kind of feather from the angel's wing, or a photograph of the ghost, to prove to me in the future that you were once a solid, sociable fact, that I didn't utterly fabricate you. Of course I shall be able to say to myself that you can't have been a fable—otherwise you would have had a moral; but that won't be enough, because I'm not sure you won't have had one. Some day you'll peep in here languidly and find me in such an attitude of piety—presenting my bent back to you as I niggle over some interminable botch—that I shall give cruelly on your nerves, and you'll draw away, closing the door softly (for you'll be gentle and considerate about it and spare me—you won't even make me look round), and steal off on tiptoe, never, never to return."

Gabriel consented to sit; he professed he should enjoy it and be glad to give up for it his immediate Continental projects, so vague to Nick, so definite apparently to himself; and he came back three times for the purpose. Nick promised himself a great deal of interest from this experiment; for from the first hour he began to feel that really, as yet, compared to the scrutiny to which he now subjected him, he had never with any intensity looked at his friend. His impression had been that Nash had a head quite fine enough to be a challenge, and that as he sat there, day by day, all sorts of pleasant and paintable things would come out in his face. This impression was not falsified, but the whole problem became more complicated. It struck our young man that he had never *seen* his subject before, and yet somehow this revelation was not produced by the sense of actually seeing it. What was revealed was the difficulty—what he saw was the indefinite and the elusive. He had taken things for granted which literally were not there, and he found things there (except that he couldn't catch them) which he had not hitherto counted in. This baffling effect, being eminently in Nash's line, might have been the result of his whimsical volition, had it not appeared to Nick, after a few hours of the job, that his sitter was not the one who enjoyed it most. He was uncomfortable, at first vaguely and then definitely so—silent, restless, gloomy, dim, as if, when it came to the test, it proved less of a pleasure to him than he could have had an idea of in advance to be infinitely examined and handled, sounded and sifted. He had been willing to try it, in good faith; but frankly he didn't like it. He was not cross, but he was clearly unhappy, and Nick had never heard him say so little, seen him give so little.

Nick felt, accordingly, as if he had laid a trap for him: he asked himself if it were really fair. At the same time there was something fascinating in the oddity of such a relation between the subject and the artist, and Nick was disposed to go on until he should have to stop for very pity. He caught eventually a glimmer of the truth that lay at the bottom of this anomaly; guessed that what made his friend uncomfortable was simply the reversal, in such a combination, of his usual terms of intercourse. He was so accustomed to living upon irony and the interpretation of things that it was strange to him to be himself interpreted, and (as a gentleman who sits for his portrait is always liable to be) interpreted ironically. From being outside of the universe he was suddenly brought into it, and from the position of a free commentator and critic, a sort of amateurish editor of the whole affair, reduced to that of humble ingredient and contributor. It occurred afterwards to Nick that he had perhaps brought on a catastrophe by having happened to say to his companion, in the course of their disjointed pauses, and not only without any cruel intention but with an impulse of genuine solicitude: "But, my dear fellow, what will you do when you're old?"

"Old? What do you call old?" Nash had replied bravely enough, but with another perceptible tinge of irritation. "Must I really inform you, at this time of day, that that term has no application to such a condition as mine? It only belongs to you wretched people who have the incurable superstition of 'doing:' it's the ignoble collapse you prepare for yourselves when you cease to be able to do. For me there'll be no collapse, no transition, no clumsy readjustment of attitude; for I shall only *be*, more and more, with all the accumulations of experience, the longer I live."

"Oh, I'm not particular about the term," said Nick. "If you don't call it old, the ultimate state, call it weary—call it exhausted. The accumulations of experience are practically accumulative of fatigue."

"I don't know anything about weariness. I live easily—it doesn't fatigue me."

"Then you need never die," rejoined Nick.

"Certainly; I dare say I'm eternal."

Nick laughed out at this—it would be such fine news to some people. But it was uttered with perfect gravity, and it might very well have been in the spirit of that gravity that Nash failed to observe his agreement to sit again the next day. The next, and the next, and the next passed, but he never came back.

True enough, punctuality was not important for a man who felt that he had the command of all time. Nevertheless, his disappearance, "without a trace," like a personage in a fairy-tale or a melodrama, made a considerable impression on his friend, as the months went on; so that, though he had never before had the least difficulty about entering into the play of Gabriel's humour, Nick now recalled with a certain fanciful awe the unusual seriousness with which he had ranked himself among imperishable things. He wondered a little whether he had at last gone quite mad. He had never before had such a literal air, and he would have had to be mad to be so commonplace. Perhaps indeed he was acting only more than usual in his customary spirit—thoughtfully contributing, for Nick's enlivenment, a mystery to an horizon now grown unromantic. The mystery at any rate remained; another too came near being added to it. Nick had the prospect, for the future, of the harmless excitement of waiting to see when Nash would turn up, if ever, and the further diversion (it almost consoled him for the annoyance of being left with a second unfinished portrait on his hands) of imagining that the picture he had begun had a singular air of gradually fading from the canvas. He couldn't catch it in the act, but he could have a suspicion, when he glanced at it, that the hand of time was rubbing it away little by little (for all the world as in some delicate Hawthorne tale), making the surface indistinct and bare—bare of all resemblance to the model. Of course the moral of the Hawthorne tale would be that this personage would come back on the day when the last adumbration should have vanished.

XVIII.

ONE DAY, toward the end of March of the following year, or in other words more than six months after the incident I have last had occasion to narrate, Bridget Dormer came into her brother's studio and greeted him with the effusion that accompanies a return from an absence. She had been staying at Broadwood—she had been staying at Harsh. She had various things to tell him about these episodes, about his mother, about Grace, about herself, and about Percy's having come, just before, over to Broadwood for two days; the longest visit with which, almost since they could remember, the head of the family had honoured Lady Agnes. Nick noted however that it had apparently been taken as a great favour, and Biddy loyally testified to the fact that her elder brother was awfully jolly and that his presence had been a pretext for tremendous fun. Nick asked her what had passed about his marriage—what their mother had said to him.

"Oh, nothing," Biddy replied; and he had said nothing to Lady Agnes and not a word to herself. This partly explained, for Nick, the awful jollity and the tremendous fun—none but cheerful topics had been produced; but he questioned his sister further, to a point which led her to say: "Oh, I dare say that before long she'll write to her."

"Who will write to whom?"

"Mamma 'll write to his wife. I'm sure he'd like it. Of course we shall end by going to see her. He was awfully disappointed at what he found in Spain—he didn't find anything."

Biddy spoke of his disappointment almost with commiseration, for she was evidently inclined this morning to a fresh and kindly view of things. Nick could share her feeling only so far as was permitted by a recognition merely general of what his brother must have looked for. It might have been snipe and it might have been bristling boars. Biddy was indeed brief, at first, about everything, in spite of the two months that had intervened since their last meeting; for he saw in a few minutes that she had something behind—something that made her gay and that she wanted to come

1237

to quickly. Nick was vaguely vexed at her being, fresh from Broadwood, so gay as that; for (it was impossible to shut one's eyes to it) what had come to pass, in practice, in regard to that rural retreat, was exactly what he had desired to avert. All winter, while it had been taken for granted that his mother and sisters were doing what he wished, they had been doing the precise contrary. He held Biddy perhaps least responsible, and there was no one he could exclusively blame. He washed his hands of the matter and succeeded fairly well for the most part in forgetting that he was not pleased. Julia Dallow herself in fact appeared to have been the most active member of the little group united to make light of his scruples. There had been a formal restitution of the place, but the three ladies were there more than ever, with the slight difference that they were mainly there with its mistress. Mahomet had declined to go any more to the mountain, so the mountain had virtually come to Mahomet.

After their long visit in the autumn Lady Agnes and her girls had come back to town; but they had gone down again for Christmas, and Julia had taken this occasion to write to Nick that she hoped very much he wouldn't refuse them all his own company for just a little scrap of the supremely sociable time. Nick, after reflection, judged it best not to refuse, and he spent three days under Mrs. Dallow's roof. The "all" proved a great many people, for she had taken care to fill the house. She was a magnificent entertainer, and Nick had never seen her so splendid, so free-handed, so gracefully practical. She was a perfect mistress of the revels; she had organized something festive for every day and for every night. The Dormers were so much in it, as the phrase was, that after all their discomfiture their fortune seemed in an hour to have come back. There had been a moment when, in extemporized charades, Lady Agnes, an elderly figure being required, appeared on the point of undertaking the part of the housekeeper at a castle, who, dropping her *h*'s, showed sheeplike tourists about; but she waived the opportunity in favour of her daughter Grace. Even Grace had a great success. Nick of course was in the charades and in everything, but Julia was not; she only invented, directed, led the applause. When nothing else was going on Nick "sketched" the whole company: they followed him about, they waylaid him on staircases, clamouring to be allowed to sit. He obliged them, so far as he could, all save Julia, who didn't clamour; and, growing rather red, he thought of Gabriel Nash while he bent over the paper. Early in the new year he went abroad for six weeks, but only as far as Paris. It was a new Paris for him then: a Paris of the Rue Bonaparte and three or four professional friends (he had more of these there than in London); a Paris of studios and studies and models, of researches and revelations, comparisons and contrasts, of strong impressions and long discussions and rather uncomfortable economies, small cafés and bad fires and the general sense of being twenty again.

While he was away his mother and sisters (Lady Agnes now sometimes wrote to him) returned to London for a month, and before he was again established in Rosedale Road they went back for a third period to Broadwood. After they had been there five days—and this was the salt of the whole dish—Julia took herself off to Harsh, leaving them in undisturbed possession. They had remained so; they would not come up to town till after Easter. The trick was played, and Biddy, as I have mentioned, was now very content. Her brother presently learned however that the reason of this was not wholly the success of the trick; unless indeed her further ground was only a continuation of it. She was not in London as a forerunner of her mother; she was not even as yet in Calcutta Gardens. She had come to spend a week with Florence Tressilian, who had lately taken the dearest little flat in a charming new place, just put up, on the other side of the Park, with all kinds of lifts and tubes and electricities. Florence had been awfully nice to her—she had been with them ever so long at Broadwood, while the flat was being painted and prepared—and mamma had then let her, let Biddy, promise to come to her, when everything was ready, so that they might have a kind of old maids' house-warming together. If Florence could do without a chaperon now (she had two latch-keys and went alone on the top of omnibuses, and her name was in the Red Book), she was enough of a duenna for another girl. Biddy alluded, with sweet and cynical eyes, to the fine, happy stride she had thus taken in the direction of enlightened spinsterhood; and Nick hung his head, somewhat abashed and humiliated, for, modern as he had supposed himself, there were evidently currents more modern yet.

It so happened on this particular morning Nick had drawn out of a corner his interrupted study of Gabriel Nash; for no purpose more definite (he had only been looking round the room in a rummaging spirit) than to see curiously how much or how little of it remained. It had become to his apprehension such a shadowy affair (he was sure of this, and it made him laugh) that it didn't seem worth putting away, and he left it leaning against a table, as if it had been a blank canvas or a "preparation" to be painted over. In this attitude it attracted Biddy's attention, for to her, on a second glance, it had distinguishable features. She had not seen it before and she asked whom it might represent, remarking also that she could almost guess, but not quite: she had known the original, but she couldn't name him.

"Six months ago, for a few days, it represented Gabriel Nash," Nick replied. "But it doesn't represent anybody or anything now."

"Six months ago? What's the matter with it and why don't you go on?"

"What's the matter with it is more than I can tell you. But I can't go on, because I've lost my model."

Biddy stared an instant. "Is he dead?"

Her brother laughed out at the candid cheerfulness, hopefulness almost, with which this inquiry broke from her. "He's only dead to me. He has gone away."

"Where has he gone?"

"I haven't the least idea."

"Why, have you quarrelled?" Biddy asked.

"Quarrelled? For what do you take us? Does the nightingale quarrel with the moon?"

"I needn't ask which of you is the moon," said Biddy.

"Of course I'm the nightingale. But, more literally," Nick continued, "Nash has melted back into the elements—he is part of the ambient air." Then, as even with this literalness he saw that his sister was mystified, he added: "I have a notion he has gone to India, and at the present moment is reclining on a bank of flowers in the vale of Cashmere."

Biddy was silent a minute, after which she dropped: "Julia will be glad—she dislikes him so."

"If she dislikes him, why should she be glad he's in such a delightful situation?"

"I mean about his going away; she'll be glad of that."

"My poor child, what has Julia to do with it?"

"She has more to do with things than you think," Biddy replied, with some eagerness; but she had no sooner uttered the words than she perceptibly blushed. Hereupon, to attenuate the foolishness of her blush (only it had the opposite effect), she added: "She thinks he has been a bad element in your life."

Nick shook his head, smiling. "She thinks, perhaps, but she doesn't think enough; otherwise, she would arrive at this thought—that she knows nothing whatever about my life."

"Ah, Nick," the girl pleaded, with solemn eyes, "you don't imagine what an interest she takes in it. She has told me, many times—she has talked lots to me about it." Biddy paused and then went on, with an anxious little smile shining through her gravity, as if she were trying cautiously how much her brother would take: "She has a conviction that it was Mr. Nash who made trouble between you."

"My dear Biddy," Nick rejoined, "those are thoroughly second-rate ideas, the result of a perfectly superficial view. Excuse my possibly priggish tone, but they really attribute to Nash a part he's quite incapable of playing. He can neither make trouble nor take trouble; no trouble could ever either have come out of him or have gone into him. Moreover," our young man continued, "if Julia has talked to you so much about the matter, there's no harm in my talking to you a little. When she threw me over in an hour, it was on a perfectly definite occasion. That occasion was the presence in my studio of a dishevelled actress."

"Oh Nick, she has not thrown you over!" Biddy protested. "She has not—I have the proof."

Nick felt, at this direct denial, a certain stir of indignation, and he looked at his sister with momentary sternness. "Has she sent you here to tell me this? What do you mean by the proof?"

Biddy's eyes, at these questions, met her brother's with a strange expression, and for a few seconds, while she looked entreatingly into his own, she wavered there, with parted lips, vaguely stretching out her hands. The next minute she had burst into tears—she was sobbing on his breast. He said "Hallo!" and soothed her; but it was very quickly over. Then she told him what she meant by her "proof," and what she had had on her mind ever since she came into the room. It was a message from Julia, but not to say—not to say what he had asked her just before if she meant; though indeed Biddy, more familiar now, since her brother had had his arm round her, boldly expressed the hope that it might in the end come to the same thing. Julia simply wanted to know (she had instructed Biddy to sound him discreetly) if Nick would undertake her portrait; and the girl wound up this experiment in "sounding" by the statement that their beautiful kinswoman was dying to sit.

"Dying to sit?" repeated Nick, whose turn it was, this time, to feel his colour rise.

"Any time you like after Easter, when she comes up to town. She wants a full-length, and your very best, your most splendid work."

Nick stared, not caring that he had blushed. "Is she serious?"

"Ah, Nick—serious!" Biddy reasoned tenderly. She came nearer to him, and he thought she was going to weep again. He took her by the shoulders, looking into her eyes.

"It's all right, if she knows I am. But why doesn't she come like any one else? I don't refuse people!"

"Nick, dearest Nick!" she went on, with her eyes conscious and pleading. He looked into them intently—as well as she, he could play at sounding—and for a moment, between these young persons, the air was lighted by the glimmer of mutual searchings and suppressed confessions. Nick read deep, and then, suddenly releasing his sister, he turned away. She didn't see his face in that movement, but an observer to whom it had been presented might have fancied that it denoted a foreboding which was not exactly a dread, yet was not exclusively a joy.

The first thing Nick made out in the room, when he could distinguish, was Gabriel Nash's portrait, which immediately filled him with an unreasoning resentment. He seized it and turned it about; he jammed it back into its corner, with its face against the wall. This bustling transaction might have served to carry off the embarrassment with which he had finally averted himself from Biddy. The embarrassment however was all his own; none of it was reflected in the way Biddy resumed, after a silence in which she had followed his disposal of the picture:

"If she's so eager to come here (for it's here that she wants to sit, not in Great Stanhope Street—never!) how can she prove better that she doesn't care a bit if she meets Miss Rooth?"

"She won't meet Miss Rooth," Nick replied, rather dryly.

"Oh, I'm sorry!" said Biddy. She was as frank as if she had achieved a sort of victory over her companion; and she seemed to regret the loss of a chance for Mrs. Dallow to show magnanimity. Her tone made her brother laugh, but she went on, with confidence: "She thought it was Mr. Nash who made Miss Rooth come."

"So he did, by the way," said Nick.

"Well, then, wasn't that making trouble?"

"I thought you admitted there was no harm in her being here."

"Yes, but he hoped there would be."

"Poor Nash's hopes!" Nick laughed. "My dear child, it would take a cleverer head than you or me, or even Julia, who must have invented that wise theory, to say what they were. However, let us agree, that even if they were perfectly devilish my good sense has been a match for them."

"Oh, Nick, that's delightful!" chanted Biddy. Then she added, "Do you mean she doesn't come any more?"

"The dishevelled actress? She hasn't been near me for months."

"But she's in London—she's always acting? I've been away

so much I've scarcely observed," Biddy explained, with a slight change of note.

"The same part, poor creature, for nearly a year. It appears that that's success, in her profession. I saw her in the character several times last summer, but I haven't set foot in her theatre since."

Biddy was silent a moment; then she suggested: "Peter wouldn't have liked that."

"Oh, Peter's likes!" sighed Nick, at his easel, beginning to work.

"I mean her acting the same part for a year."

"I'm sure I don't know; he has never written me a word."

"Nor me either," Biddy returned.

There was another short silence, during which Nick brushed at a panel. It was terminated by his presently saying: "There's one thing, certainly, Peter *would* like—that is simply to be here to-night. It's a great night—another great night—for the dishevelled one. She's to act Juliet for the first time."

"Ah, how I should like to see her!" the girl cried.

Nick glanced at her; she sat watching him. "She has sent me a stall; I wish she had sent me two. I should have been delighted to take you."

"Don't you think you could get another?" asked Biddy.

"They must be in tremendous demand. But who knows, after all?" Nick added, at the same moment, looking round. "Here's a chance—here's a quite extraordinary chance!"

His servant had opened the door and was ushering in a lady whose identity was indeed justly indicated in those words. "Miss Rooth!" the man announced; but he was caught up by a gentleman who came next and who exclaimed, laughing and with a gesture gracefully corrective: "No, no—no longer Miss Rooth!"

Miriam entered the place with her charming familiar grandeur, as she might have appeared, as she appeared every night, early in her first act, at the back of the stage, by the immemorial central door, presenting herself to the house, taking easy possession, repeating old movements, looking from one to the other of the actors before the footlights. The rich "Good morning" that she threw into the air, holding out her hand to Biddy Dormer and then giving her left to Nick (as she might have given it to her own brother), had nothing to tell of intervals or alienations. She struck Biddy as still more terrible, in her splendid practice, than when she had seen her before—the practice and the splendour had now something almost royal. The girl had had occasion to make her courtesy to majesties and highnesses, but the flutter those effigies produced was nothing to the way in which, at the approach of this young lady, the agitated air seemed to recognize something supreme. So the deep, mild eyes that she bent upon Biddy were not soothing, though they were evidently intended to soothe. The girl wondered that Nick could have got so used to her (he joked at her as she came), and later in the day, still under the great impression of this incident, she even wondered that Peter could. It was true that Peter apparently hadn't.

"You never came—you never came," said Miriam to Biddy, kindly, sadly; and Biddy recognizing the allusion, the invitation to visit the actress at home, had to explain how much she had been absent from London, and then even that her brother hadn't proposed to take her. "Very true—he hasn't come himself. What is he doing now?" Miriam asked, standing near Biddy, but looking at Nick, who had immediately engaged in conversation with his other visitor, a gentleman whose face came back to the girl. She had seen this gentleman on the stage with Miss Rooth—that was it, the night Peter took her to the theatre with Florence Tressilian. Oh, that Nick would only do something of that sort now! This desire, quickened by the presence of the strange, expressive woman, by the way she scattered sweet syllables as if she were touching the piano-keys, combined with other things to make Biddy's head swim—other things too mingled to name, admiration and fear and dim divination and purposeless pride and curiosity and resistance, the impulse to go away and the determination not to go. The actress courted her with her voice (what was the matter with her and what did she want?) and Biddy tried in return to give an idea of what Nick was doing. Not succeeding very well she was going to appeal to her brother, but Miriam stopped her, saying it didn't matter; besides, Dashwood was telling Nick something—something they wanted him to know. "We're in a great excitement—he has taken a theatre," Miriam added.

"Taken a theatre?" Biddy was vague.

"We're going to set up for ourselves. He's going to do for me altogether. It has all been arranged only within a day or two. It remains to be seen how it will answer," Miriam smiled. Biddy murmured some friendly hope, and her interlocutress went on: "Do you know why I've broken in here to-day, after a long absence—interrupting your poor brother, taking up his precious time! It's because I'm so nervous."

"About your first night?" Biddy risked.

"Do you know about that—are you coming?" Miriam asked, quickly.

"No, I'm not coming—I haven't a place."

"Will you come if I send you one?"

"Oh, but really, it's too beautiful of you," stammered the girl.

"You shall have a box; your brother shall bring you. You can't squeeze in a pin, I'm told; but I've kept a box, I'll manage it. Only, if I do, you know, mind you come!" Miriam exclaimed, in suppliance, resting her hand on Biddy's.

"Don't be afraid! And may I bring a friend—the friend with whom I'm staying?"

Miriam looked at her. "Do you mean Mrs. Dallow?"

"No, no—Miss Tressilian. She puts me up, she has got a flat. Did you ever see a flat?" asked Biddy, expansively. "My cousin's not in London." Miriam replied that she might bring whom she liked, and Biddy broke out, to her brother: "Fancy what kindness, Nick: we're to have a box to-night, and you're to take me!"

Nick turned to her, smiling, with an expression in his face which struck her even at the time as odd, but which she understood when the sense of it recurred to her later. Mr. Dashwood interposed with the remark that it was all very well to talk about boxes, but that he didn't see where at that time of day any such luxury was to come from.

"You haven't kept one, as I told you?" Miriam demanded.

"As you told me, my dear? Tell the lamb to keep its tender mutton from the wolves!"

"You shall have one: we'll arrange it," Miriam went on, to Biddy.

"Let me qualify that statement a little, Miss Dormer," said Basil Dashwood. "We'll arrange if it's humanly possible."

"We'll arrange it even if it's inhumanly impossible—that's just the point," Miriam declared, to the girl. "Don't talk about trouble—what's he meant for but to take it? *Cela s'annonce bien*, you see," she continued, to Nick: "doesn't it look as if we should pull beautifully together?" And as he replied that he heartily congratulated her—he was immensely interested in what he had been told—she exclaimed, after resting her eyes on him a moment: "What will you have? It seemed simpler! It was clear there had to be some one." She explained further to Nick what had led her to come in at that moment, while Dashwood approached Biddy with civil assurances that they would see, they would leave no stone unturned, though he would not have taken it upon himself to promise.

Miriam reminded Nick of the blessing he had been to her nearly a year before, on her other first night, when she was fidgety and impatient: how he had let her come and sit there for hours—helped her to possess her soul till the evening and keep out of harm's way. The case was the same at present, with the aggravation indeed that he would understand—Dashwood's nerves as well as her own: they were a great deal worse than hers. Everything was ready for Juliet; they had been rehearsing for five months (it had kept her from going mad, with the eternity of the other piece), and *he* had occurred to her again in the last intolerable hours as the friend in need, the salutary stop-gap, no matter how much she bothered him. She shouldn't be turned out? Biddy broke away from Basil Dashwood: she must go, she must hurry off to Miss Tressilian with her news. Florence might make some stupid engagement for the evening: she must be warned in time. The girl took a flushed, excited leave, after having received a renewal of Miriam's pledge and even heard her say to Nick that he must now give back the stall that had been sent him—they would be sure to have another use for it.

XIX.

T HAT NIGHT, at the theatre, in the box (the miracle had
been wrought, the treasure was found), Nick Dormer
pointed out to his two companions the stall he had relinquished, which was close in front—noting how oddly, during the whole of the first act, it remained vacant. The house
was magnificent, the actress was magnificent, everything was
magnificent. To describe again so famous an occasion (it has
been described repeatedly by other reporters) is not in the
compass of the closing words of a history already too sustained. It is enough to say that this great night marked an era
in contemporary art, and that for those who had a spectator's
share in it the word "triumph" acquired a new illustration.
Miriam's Juliet was an exquisite image of young passion and
young despair, expressed in the divinest, truest music that had
ever poured from tragic lips. The great childish audience,
gaping at her points, expanded there before her like a lap to
catch flowers.

During the first interval our three friends in the box had
plenty to talk about, and they were so occupied with it that
for some time they failed to observe that a gentleman had at
last come into the empty stall near the front. This discovery
was presently formulated by Miss Tressilian, in the cheerful
exclamation: "Only fancy—there's Mr. Sherringham!" This
of course immediately became a high wonder—a wonder for
Nick and Biddy, who had not heard of his return; and the
marvel was increased by the fact that he gave no sign of
looking for them, or even at them. Having taken possession
of his place he sat very still in it, staring straight before him
at the curtain. His abrupt reappearance contained mystifying
elements both for Biddy and for Nick, so that it was mainly
Miss Tressilian who had freedom of mind to throw off the
theory that he had come back that very hour—had arrived
from a long journey. Couldn't they see how strange he was
and how brown, how burnt and how red, how tired and
how worn? They all inspected him, though Biddy declined
Miss Tressilian's glass; but he was evidently unconscious of
observation, and finally Biddy, leaning back in her chair,

dropped the fantastic words: "He has come home to marry Juliet."

Nick glanced at her; then he replied: "What a disaster—to make such a journey as that and to be late for the fair!"

"Late for the fair?"

"Why, she's married—these three days. They did it very quietly; Miriam says because her mother hated it and hopes it won't be much known. All the same she's Basil Dashwood's wedded wife—he has come in just in time to take the receipts for Juliet. It's a good thing, no doubt, for there are at least two fortunes to be made out of her, and he'll give up the stage." Nick explained to Miss Tressilian, who had inquired, that the gentleman in question was the actor who was play-ing Mercutio, and he asked Biddy if she had not known that this was what they were telling him in Rosedale Road in the morning. She replied that she had not understood, and she sank considerably behind the drapery of the box. From this cover she was able to launch creditably enough the ex-clamation—

"Poor Peter!"

Nick got up and stood looking at poor Peter. "He ought to come round and speak to us, but if he doesn't see us I suppose he doesn't." Nick quitted the box as if to go to the restored exile. I may add that as soon as he had done so Florence Tressilian bounded over to the dusky corner in which Biddy had nestled. What passed immediately between these young ladies need not concern us: it is sufficient to men-tion that two minutes later Miss Tressilian broke out—

"Look at him, dearest; he's turning his head this way!"

"Thank you, I don't care to look at him," said Biddy; and she doubtless demeaned herself in the high spirit of these words. It nevertheless happened that directly afterwards she became aware that he had glanced at his watch, as if to judge how soon the curtain would rise again, and then had jumped up and passed quickly out of his place. The curtain had risen again without his coming back and without Nick's reappear-ing in the box. Indeed by the time Nick slipped in a good deal of the third act was over; and even then, even when the curtain descended, Peter Sherringham had not returned. Nick sat down in silence, to watch the stage, to which the breathless attention of his companions seemed to be attached, though Biddy after a moment threw back at him a single quick look. At the end of the act they were all occupied with the recalls, the applause and the responsive loveliness of Juliet as she was led out (Mercutio had to give her up to Romeo), and even for a few minutes after the uproar had subsided nothing was said among the three. At last Nick began:

"It's quite true, he has just arrived; he's in Great Stanhope Street. They've given him several weeks, to make up for the uncomfortable way they bundled him off (to arrive in time for some special business that had suddenly to be gone into) when he first went out: he tells me they promised that at the time. He got into Southampton only a few hours ago, rushed up by the first train he could catch and came off here without any dinner."

"Fancy!" said Miss Tressilian; while Biddy asked if Peter might be in good health and had been happy. Nick replied that he said it was a beastly place, but he appeared all right. He was to be in England probably a month, he was awfully brown, he sent his love to Biddy. Miss Tressilian looked at his empty stall and was of the opinion that it would be more to the point for him to come in to see her.

"Oh, he'll turn up; we had a goodish talk in the lobby, where he met me. I think he went out somewhere."

"How odd to come so many thousand miles for this, and then not to stay!" Biddy reflected.

"Did he come on purpose for this?" Miss Tressilian asked.

"Perhaps he's gone out to get his dinner!" joked Biddy.

Her friend suggested that he might be behind the scenes, but Nick expressed a doubt of this; and Biddy asked her brother if he himself were not going round. At this moment the curtain rose: Nick said he would go in the next interval. As soon as it came he quitted the box, remaining absent while it lasted.

All this time, in the house, there was no sign of Peter. Nick reappeared only as the fourth act was beginning, and uttered no word to his companions till it was over. Then, after a further delay produced by renewed evidences of the actress's victory, he described his visit to the stage and the wonderful spectacle of Miriam on the field of battle. Miss Tressilian inquired if he had found Mr. Sherringham with her; to which he replied that, save across the footlights, she had not seen him. At this a soft exclamation broke from Biddy:

"Poor Peter! Where is he, then?"

Nick hesitated a moment. "He's walking the streets."

"Walking the streets?"

"I don't know—I give it up!" Nick replied; and his tone, for some minutes, reduced his companions to silence. But a little later Biddy said:

"Was it for him, this morning, she wanted that place, when she asked you to give yours back?"

"For him, exactly. It's very odd that she just managed to keep it, for all the use he makes of it! She told me just now that she heard from him, at his post, a short time ago, to the effect that he had seen in a newspaper a statement she was going to do Juliet and that he firmly intended, though the ways and means were not clear to him (his leave of absence hadn't yet come out, and he couldn't be sure when it would come), to be present on her first night: therefore she must do him the service to keep a seat for him. She thought this a speech rather in the air, so that in the midst of all her cares she took no particular pains about the matter. She had an idea she had really done with him for a long time. But this afternoon what does he do but telegraph her from Southampton that he keeps his appointment and counts upon her for a stall? Unless she had got back mine she wouldn't have been able to accommodate him. When she was in Rosedale Road this morning she hadn't received his telegram; but his promise, his threat, whatever it was, came back to her; she had a sort of foreboding and thought that, on the chance, she had better have something ready. When she got home she found his telegram, and she told me that he was the first person she saw in the house, through her fright, when she came on in the second act. It appears she was terrified this time, and it lasted half through the play."

"She must be rather annoyed at his having gone away," Miss Tressilian observed.

"Annoyed? I'm not so sure!" laughed Nick.

"Ah, here he comes back!" cried Biddy, behind her fan, as the absentee edged into his seat in time for the fifth act. He stood there a moment, first looking round the theatre; then he turned his eyes upon the box occupied by his relatives, smiling and waving his hand.

"After that he'll surely come and see you," said Miss Tressilian.

"We shall see him as we go out," Biddy replied: "he must lose no more time."

Nick looked at him with a glass; then he exclaimed: "Well, I'm glad he has pulled himself together!"

"Why, what's the matter with him, since he wasn't disappointed in his seat?" Miss Tressilian demanded.

"The matter with him is that a couple of hours ago he had a great shock."

"A great shock?"

"I may as well mention it at last," Nick went on. "I had to say something to him in the lobby there, when we met—something I was pretty sure he couldn't like. I let him have it full in the face—it seemed to me better and wiser. I told him Juliet's married."

"Didn't he know it?" asked Biddy, who, with her face raised, had listened in deep stillness to every word that fell from her brother.

"How should he have known it? It has only just happened, and they've been so clever, for reasons of their own (those people move among a lot of considerations that are absolutely foreign to us), about keeping it out of the papers. They put in a lot of lies, and they leave out the real things."

"You don't mean to say Mr. Sherringham wanted to *marry* her!" Miss Tressilian ejaculated.

"Don't ask me what he wanted—I dare say we shall never know. One thing is very certain: that he didn't like my news and that I sha'n't soon forget the look in his face as he turned away from me, slipping out into the street. He was too much upset—he couldn't trust himself to come back; he had to walk about—he tried to walk it off."

"Let us hope he *has* walked it off!"

"Ah, poor fellow—he couldn't hold out to the end; he has had to come back and look at her once more. He knows she'll be sublime in these last scenes."

"Is he so much in love with her as that? What difference

does it make, with an actress, if she *is* mar—?" But in this rash inquiry Miss Tressilian suddenly checked herself.

"We shall probably never know how much he has been in love with her nor what difference it makes. We shall never know exactly what he came back for, nor why he couldn't stand it out there any longer without relief, nor why he scrambled down here all but straight from the station, nor why, after all, for the last two hours, he has been roaming the streets. And it doesn't matter, for it's none of our business. But I'm sorry for him—she *is* going to be sublime," Nick added. The curtain was rising on the tragic climax of the play.

Miriam Rooth was sublime; yet it may be confided to the reader that during these supreme scenes Bridget Dormer directed her eyes less to the inspired actress than to a figure in the stalls who sat with his own gaze fastened to the stage. It may further be intimated that Peter Sherringham, though he saw but a fragment of the performance, read clear at the last, in the intense light of genius that this fragment shed, that even so, after all, he had been rewarded for his formidable journey. The great trouble of his infatuation subsided, leaving behind it something tolerably deep and pure. This assuagement was far from being immediate, but it was helped on, unexpectedly to him, it began to dawn at least, the very next night he saw the play, when he sat through the whole of it. Then he felt somehow recalled to reality by the very perfection of the representation. He began to come back to it from a period of miserable madness. He had been baffled, he had got his answer; it must last him—that was plain. He didn't fully accept it the first week or the second; but he accepted it sooner than he would have supposed had he known what it was to be when he paced at night, under the southern stars, the deck of the ship that was bringing him to England.

It had been, as we know, Miss Tressilian's view, and even Biddy's, that evening, that Peter Sherringham would join them as they left the theatre. This view however was not confirmed by the event, for the gentleman in question vanished utterly (disappointingly crude behaviour on the part of a young diplomatist who had distinguished himself), before any one could put a hand on him. And he failed to make up for his crudity by coming to see any one the next day, or even the next. Indeed many days elapsed, and very little would have been known about him had it not been that, in the country, Mrs. Dallow knew. What Mrs. Dallow knew was eventually known to Biddy Dormer; and in this way it could be established in his favour that he had remained some extraordinarily small number of days in London, had almost directly gone over to Paris to see his old chief. He came back from Paris—Biddy knew this not from Mrs. Dallow, but in a much more immediate way: she knew it by his pressing the little electric button at the door of Florence Tressilian's flat, one day when the good Florence was out and she herself was at home. He made on this occasion a very long visit. The good Florence knew it not much later, you may be sure (and how he had got their address from Nick), and she took an extravagant satisfaction in it. Mr. Sherringham had never been to see her—the like of her—in his life: therefore it was clear what had made him begin. When he had once begun he kept it up, and Miss Tressilian's satisfaction increased.

Good as she was she could remember without the slightest relenting what Nick Dormer had repeated to them at the theatre about Peter's present post's being a beastly place. However, she was not bound to make a stand at this if persons more nearly concerned, Lady Agnes and the girl herself, didn't mind it. How little *they* minded it, and Grace, and Julia Dallow, and even Nick, was proved in the course of a meeting that took place at Harsh during the Easter holidays. Mrs. Dallow had a small and intimate party to celebrate her brother's betrothal. The two ladies came over from Broadwood; even Nick, for two days, went back to his old hunting-ground, and Miss Tressilian relinquished for as long a time the delights of her newly-arranged flat. Peter Sherringham obtained an extension of leave, so that he might go back to his legation with a wife. Fortunately, as it turned out, Biddy's ordeal, in the more or less torrid zone, was not cruelly prolonged, for the pair have already received a superior appointment. It is Lady Agnes's proud opinion that her daughter is even now shaping their destiny. I say "even now," for these facts bring me very close to contemporary history. During those two days at Harsh Nick arranged with Julia Dallow the conditions, as they might be called, under which she should sit to him; and every one will remember in how recent an exhibition general attention was attracted, as the newspapers said in describing the private view, to the noble portrait of a lady which was the final outcome of that arrangement. Gabriel Nash had been at many a private view, but he was not at that one.

These matters are highly recent however, as I say; so that in glancing about the little circle of the interests I have tried to evoke I am suddenly warned by a sharp sense of modernness. This renders it difficult for me, for example, in taking leave of our wonderful Miriam, to do much more than allude to the general impression that her remarkable career is even yet only in its early prime. Basil Dashwood has got his theatre, and his wife (people know now she *is* his wife) has added three or four new parts to her repertory; but every one is agreed that both in public and in private she has a great deal more to show. This is equally true of Nick Dormer, in regard to whom I may finally say that his friend Nash's predictions about his reunion with Mrs. Dallow have not up to this time been justified. On the other hand, I must not omit to add, this lady has not, at the latest accounts, married Mr. Macgeorge. It is very true there has been a rumour that Mr. Macgeorge is worried about her—has even ceased to believe in her.

THE END.

Chronology

1843   Born April 15 at 21 Washington Place, New York City, the second child (after William, born January 11, 1842, N.Y.C.) of Henry James of Albany and Mary Robertson Walsh of New York. Father lives on inheritance of $10,000 a year, his share of litigated $3,000,000 fortune of his Albany father, William James, an Irish immigrant who came to the U.S. immediately after the Revolution.

1843–45   Accompanied by mother's sister, Catharine Walsh, and servants, the James parents take infant children to England and later to France. Reside at Windsor, where father has nervous collapse ("vastation") and experiences spiritual illumination. He becomes a Swedenborgian (May 1844), devoting his time to lecturing and religious-philosophical writings. James later claimed his earliest memory was a glimpse, during his second year, of the Place Vendôme in Paris with its Napoleonic column.

1845–47   Family returns to New York. Garth Wilkinson James (Wilky) born July 21, 1845. Family moves to Albany at 50 N. Pearl St., a few doors from grandmother Catharine Barber James. Robertson James (Bob or Rob) born August 29, 1846.

1847–55   Family moves to a large house at 58 W. 14th St., New York. Alice James born August 7, 1848. Relatives and father's friends and acquaintances — Horace Greeley, George Ripley, Charles Anderson Dana, William Cullen Bryant, Bronson Alcott, and Ralph Waldo Emerson ("I knew he was great, greater than any of our friends")— are frequent visitors. Thackeray calls during his lecture tour on the English humorists. Summers at New Brighton on Staten Island and Fort Hamilton on Long Island's south shore. On steamboat to Fort Hamilton August 1850, hears Washington Irving tell his father of Margaret Fuller's drowning in shipwreck off Fire Island. Frequently visits Barnum's American Museum on free days. Taken to art shows and theaters; writes and draws stage scenes. Described by father as "a devourer of libraries." Taught in assorted private schools and by tutors in lower Broadway and Greenwich Village. But father claims in 1848 that American schooling fails to provide "sensuous education" for his children and plans to take them to Europe.

1855–58   Family (with Aunt Kate) sails for Liverpool, June 27. James is intermittently sick with malarial fever as they travel to Paris, Lyon, and Geneva. After Swiss summer, leaves for London where Robert Thomson (later Robert Louis Stevenson's tutor) is engaged. Early summer 1856, family moves to Paris. Another tutor engaged and children attend experimental Fourierist school. Acquires fluency in French. Family goes to Boulogne-sur-mer in summer, where James contracts typhoid. Spends late October in Paris, but American crash of 1857 returns family to Boulogne where they can live more cheaply. Attends public school (fellow classmate is Coquelin, the future French actor).

1858–59   Family returns to America and settles in Newport, Rhode Island. Goes boating, fishing, and riding. Attends Reverend W. C. Leverett's Berkeley Institute, and forms friendship with classmate Thomas Sergeant Perry. Takes long walks and sketches with the painter John La Farge.

1859–60   Father, still dissatisfied with American education, returns family to Geneva in October. James attends a pre-engineering school, Institution Rochette, because parents, with "a flattering misconception of my aptitudes," feel he might benefit from less reading and more mathematics. After a few months withdraws from all classes except French, German, and Latin, and joins William as a special student at the Academy (later the University of Geneva) where he attends lectures on literary subjects. Studies German in Bonn during summer 1860.

1860–62   Family returns to Newport in September where William studies with William Morris Hunt, and James sits in on his classes. La Farge introduces him to works of Balzac, Merimée, Musset, and Browning. Wilky and Bob attend Frank Sanborn's experimental school in Concord with children of Hawthorne and Emerson and John Brown's daughter. Early in 1861, orphaned Temple cousins come to live in Newport. Develops close friendship with cousin

Mary (Minnie) Temple. Goes on a week's walking tour in July in New Hampshire with Perry. William abandons art in autumn 1861 and enters Lawrence Scientific School at Harvard. James suffers back injury in a stable fire while serving as a volunteer fireman. Reads Hawthorne ("an American could be an artist, one of the finest").

1862–63   Enters Harvard Law School (Dane Hall). Wilky enlists in the Massachusetts 44th Regiment, and later in Colonel Robert Gould Shaw's 54th, the first black regiment. Summer 1863, Bob joins the Massachusetts 55th, another black regiment, under Colonel Hollowell. James withdraws from law studies to try writing. Sends unsigned stories to magazines. Wilky is badly wounded and brought home to Newport in August.

1864   Family moves from Newport to 13 Ashburton Place, Boston. First tale, "A Tragedy of Error" (unsigned), published in *Continental Monthly* (Feb. 1864). Stays in Northampton, Massachusetts, early August–November. Begins writing book reviews for *North American Review* and forms friendship with its editor, Charles Eliot Norton, and his family, including his sister Grace (with whom he maintains a long-lasting correspondence). Wilky returns to his regiment.

1865   First signed tale, "The Story of a Year," published in *Atlantic Monthly* (March 1865). Begins to write reviews for the newly founded *Nation* and publishes anonymously in it during next fifteen years. William sails on a scientific expedition with Louis Agassiz to the Amazon. During summer James vacations in the White Mountains with Minnie Temple and her family; joined by Oliver Wendell Holmes Jr. and John Chipman Gray, both recently demobilized. Father subsidizes plantation for Wilky and Bob in Florida with black hired workers. (The idealistic but impractical venture fails in 1870.)

1866–68   Continues to publish reviews and tales in Boston and New York journals. William returns from Brazil and resumes medical education. James has recurrence of back ailment and spends summer in Swampscott, Massachusetts. Begins friendship with William Dean Howells. Family moves to 20 Quincy St., Cambridge. William, suffering from nervous ailments, goes to Germany in spring 1867. "Poor Richard," James's longest story to date, published in *Atlantic Monthly* (June–Aug. 1867). William begins intermittent criticism of Henry's story-telling and style (which will continue throughout their careers). Momentary meeting with Charles Dickens at Norton's house. Vacations in Jefferson, New Hampshire, summer 1868. William returns from Europe.

1869–70   Sails in February for European tour. Visits English towns and cathedrals. Through Nortons meets Leslie Stephen, William Morris, Dante Gabriel Rossetti, Edward Burne-Jones, John Ruskin, Charles Darwin, and George Eliot (the "one marvel" of his stay in London). Goes to Paris in May, then travels in Switzerland in summer and hikes into Italy in autumn, where he stays in Milan, Venice (Sept.), Florence, and Rome (Oct. 30–Dec. 28). Returns to England to drink the waters at Malvern health spa in Worcestershire because of digestive troubles. Stays in Paris en route and has first experience of Comédie Française. Learns that his beloved cousin, Minnie Temple, has died of tuberculosis.

1870–72   Returns to Cambridge in May. Travels to Rhode Island, Vermont, and New York to write travel sketches for *The Nation*. Spends a few days with Emerson in Concord. Meets Bret Harte at Howells' home April 1871. *Watch and Ward*, his first novel, published in *Atlantic Monthly* (Aug.–Dec. 1871). Serves as occasional art reviewer for the *Atlantic* January–March 1872.

1872–74   Accompanies Aunt Kate and sister Alice on tour of England, France, Switzerland, Italy, Austria, and Germany from May through October. Writes travel sketches for *The Nation*. Spends autumn in Paris, becoming friends with James Russell Lowell. Escorts Emerson through the Louvre. (Later, on Emerson's return from Egypt, will show him the Vatican.) Goes to Florence in December and from there to Rome, where he becomes friends with actress Fanny Kemble, her daughter Sarah Butler Wister, and William Wetmore Story and his family. In Italy sees old family friend Francis Boott and his daughter Elizabeth (Lizzie), expatriates who have lived for many years in Florentine villa on Bellosguardo. Takes up horseback riding on the Campagna. Encounters Matthew Arnold in April 1873 at Story's. Moves from Rome hotel to rooms of his own. Continues writing and now earns enough to support himself. Leaves Rome in June, spends summer in Bad Homburg. In October goes to Florence, where William joins him. They also visit Rome, William returning to America in March. In Baden-Baden June–August and returns to America September 4, with *Roderick Hudson* all but finished.

1875   *Roderick Hudson* serialized in *Atlantic Monthly* from January (published by Osgood at the end of the year). First book, *A Passionate Pilgrim and Other Tales*, published January 31. Tries living and writing in New York, in rooms at 111 E. 25th Street. Earns $200 a month from novel installments and continued reviewing, but finds New York too expensive. *Transatlantic Sketches*, published in April, sells almost 1,000 copies in three months. In Cambridge in July decides to return to Europe; arranges with John Hay, assistant to the publisher, to write Paris letters for the *New York Tribune*.

1875–76   Arriving in Paris in November, he takes rooms at 29 Rue de Luxembourg (since renamed Cambon). Becomes friend of Ivan Turgenev and is introduced by him to Gustave Flaubert's Sunday parties. Meets Edmond de Goncourt, Émile Zola, G. Charpentier (the publisher), Catulle Mendès, Alphonse Daudet, Guy de Maupassant, Ernest Renan, Gustave Doré. Makes friends with Charles Sanders Peirce, who is in Paris. Reviews (unfavorably) the early Impressionists at the Durand-Ruel gallery. By midsummer has received $400 for *Tribune* pieces, but editor asks for more Parisian gossip and James resigns. Travels in France during July, visiting Normandy and the Midi, and in September crosses to San Sebastian, Spain, to see a bullfight ("I thought the bull, in any case, a finer fellow than any of his tormentors"). Moves to London in December, taking rooms at 3 Bolton Street, Piccadilly, where he will live for the next decade.

1877   *The American* published. Meets Robert Browning and George du Maurier. Leaves London in midsummer for visit to Paris and then goes to Italy. In Rome rides again in Campagna and hears of an episode that inspires "Daisy

Miller." Back in England, spends Christmas at Stratford
with Fanny Kemble.

1878   Publishes first book in England, *French Poets and Novelists*
        (Macmillan). Appearance of "Daisy Miller" in *Cornhill
        Magazine*, edited by Leslie Stephen, is international suc-
        cess, but by publishing it abroad loses American copyright
        and story is pirated in U.S. *Cornhill* also prints "An Inter-
        national Episode." *The Europeans* is serialized in *Atlantic*.
        Now a celebrity, he dines out often, visits country houses,
        gains weight, takes long walks, fences, and does weight-
        lifting to reduce. Elected to Reform Club. Meets Tenny-
        son, George Meredith, and James McNeill Whistler. Wil-
        liam marries Alice Howe Gibbens.

1879   Immersed in London society (". . . dined out during the
        past winter 107 times!"). Meets Edmund Gosse and
        Robert Louis Stevenson, who will later become his close
        friends. Sees much of Henry Adams and his wife, Marian
        (Clover), in London and later in Paris. Takes rooms in
        Paris, September–December. *Confidence* is serialized in
        Scribner's and published by Chatto & Windus. *Hawthorne*
        appears in Macmillan's "English Men of Letters" series.

1880–81 Stays in Florence March–May to work on *The Portrait of
        a Lady*. Meets Constance Fenimore Woolson, American
        novelist and grandniece of James Fenimore Cooper. Re-
        turns to Bolton Street in June, where William visits him.
        Washington Square serialized in *Cornhill Magazine* and
        published in U.S. by Harper & Brothers (Dec. 1880). *The
        Portrait of a Lady* serialized in *Macmillan's Magazine* (Oct.
        1880–Nov. 1881) and *Atlantic Monthly*; published by Mac-
        millan and Houghton, Mifflin (Nov. 1881). Publication
        both in United States and in England yields him the then-
        large income of $500 a month, though book sales are dis-
        appointing. Leaves London in February for Paris, the
        south of France, the Italian Riviera, and Venice, and re-
        turns home in July. Sister Alice comes to London with
        her friend Katharine Loring. James goes to Scotland in
        September.

1881–83 In November revisits America after absence of six years.
        Lionized in New York. Returns to Quincy Street for
        Christmas and sees ailing brother Wilky for the first time

in ten years. In January visits Washington and the Henry
Adamses and meets President Chester A. Arthur. Summoned to Cambridge by mother's death January 29 ("the
sweetest, gentlest, most beneficent human being I have
ever known"). All four brothers are together for the first
time in fifteen years at her funeral. Alice and father move
from Cambridge to Boston. Prepares a stage version of
"Daisy Miller" and returns to England in May. William,
now a Harvard professor, comes to Europe in September.
Proposed by Leslie Stephen, James becomes member,
without the usual red tape, of the Atheneum Club. Travels
in France in October to write *A Little Tour in France*
(published 1884) and has last visit with Turgenev, who is
dying. Returns to England in December and learns of
father's illness. Sails for America but Henry James Sr. dies
December 18, 1882, before his arrival. Made executor of
father's will. Visits brothers Wilky and Bob in Milwaukee
in January. Quarrels with William over division of property—James wants to restore Wilky's share. Macmillan
publishes a collected pocket edition of James's novels and
tales in fourteen volumes. *Siege of London* and *Portraits of
Places* published. Returns to Bolton Street in September.
Wilky dies in November. Constance Fenimore Woolson
comes to London for the winter.

1884–86   Goes to Paris in February and visits Daudet, Zola, and
Goncourt. Again impressed with their intense concern
with "art, form, manner" but calls them "mandarins."
Misses Turgenev, who had died a few months before.
Meets John Singer Sargent and persuades him to settle in
London. Returns to Bolton Street. Sargent introduces
him to young Paul Bourget. During country visits encounters many British political and social figures, including W. E. Gladstone, John Bright, and Charles Dilke.
Alice, suffering from nervous ailment, arrives in England
for visit in November but is too ill to travel and settles
near her brother. *Tales of Three Cities* ("The Impressions
of a Cousin," "Lady Barbarina," "A New England Winter") and "The Art of Fiction" published 1884. Alice goes
to Bournemouth in late January. James joins her in May
and becomes an intimate of Robert Louis Stevenson, who
resides nearby. Spends August at Dover and is visited by
Paul Bourget. Stays in Paris for the next two months.
Moves into a flat at 34 De Vere Gardens in Kensington

early in March 1886. Alice takes rooms in London. *The Bostonians* serialized in *Century* (Feb. 1885– Feb. 1886; published 1886), *The Princess Casamassima* serialized in *Atlantic Monthly* (Sept. 1885–Oct. 1886; published 1886).

1886–87   Leaves for Italy in December for extended stay, mainly in Florence and Venice. Sees much of Constance Fenimore Woolson and stays in her villa. Writes "The Aspern Papers" and other tales. Returns to De Vere Gardens in July and begins work on *The Tragic Muse*. Pays several country visits. Dines out less often ("I know it all—all that one sees by 'going out'—today, as if I had made it. But if I had, I would have made it better!").

1888   *The Reverberator*, *The Aspern Papers*, *Louisa Pallant*, *The Modern Warning*, and *Partial Portraits* published. Elizabeth Boott Duveneck dies. Robert Louis Stevenson leaves for the South Seas. Engages fencing teacher to combat "symptoms of a portentous corpulence." Goes abroad in October to Geneva (where he visits Miss Woolson), Genoa, Monte Carlo, and Paris.

1889–90   Catharine Walsh (Aunt Kate) dies March 1889. William comes to England to visit Alice in August. James goes to Dover in September and then to Paris for five weeks. Writes account of Robert Browning's funeral in Westminster Abbey. Dramatizes *The American* for the Compton Comedy Company. Meets and becomes close friends with American journalist William Morton Fullerton and young American publisher Wolcott Balestier. Goes to Italy for the summer, staying in Venice and Florence, and takes a brief walking tour in Tuscany with W. W. Baldwin, an American physician practicing in Florence. Miss Woolson moves to Cheltenham, England, to be near James. *Atlantic Monthly* rejects his story "The Pupil," but it appears in England. Writes series of drawing-room comedies for theater. Meets Rudyard Kipling. *The Tragic Muse* serialized in *Atlantic Monthly* (Jan. 1889–May 1890; published 1890). *A London Life* (including "The Patagonia," "The Liar," "Mrs. Temperly") published 1889.

1891   *The American* produced at Southport is a success during road tour. After residence in Leamington, Alice returns to London, cared for by Katharine Loring. Doctors discover she has breast cancer. James circulates comedies (*Mrs. Vibert*, later called *Tenants*, and *Mrs. Jasper*, later named *Disengaged*) among theater managers who are cool to his work. Unimpressed at first by Ibsen, writes an appreciative review after seeing a performance of *Hedda Gabler* with Elizabeth Robins, a young Kentucky actress; persuades her to take the part of Mme. de Cintré in the London production of *The American*. Recuperates from flu in Ireland. James Russell Lowell dies. *The American* opens in London, September 26, and runs for seventy nights. Wolcott Balestier dies, and James attends his funeral in Dresden in December.

1892   Alice James dies March 6. James travels to Siena to be near the Paul Bourgets, and Venice, June–July, to visit the Daniel Curtises, then to Lausanne to meet William and his family, who have come abroad for sabbatical. Attends funeral of Tennyson at Westminster Abbey. Augustin Daly agrees to produce *Mrs. Jasper*. *The American* continues to be performed on the road by the Compton Company. *The Lesson of the Master* (with a collection of stories including "The Marriages," "The Pupil," "Brooksmith," "The Solution," and "Sir Edmund Orme") published.

1893   Fanny Kemble dies in January. Continues to write unproduced plays. In March goes to Paris for two months. Sends Edward Compton first act and scenario for *Guy Domville*. Meets William and family in Lucerne and stays a month, returning to London in June. Spends July completing *Guy Domville* in Ramsgate. George Alexander, actor-manager, agrees to produce the play. Daly stages first reading of *Mrs. Jasper*, and James withdraws it, calling the rehearsal a mockery. *The Real Thing and Other Tales* (including "The Wheel of Time," "Lord Beaupré," "The Visit") published.

1894   Constance Fenimore Woolson dies in Venice, January. Shocked and upset, James prepares to attend funeral in Rome but changes his mind on learning she is a suicide. Goes to Venice in April to help her family settle her affairs. Receives one of four copies, privately printed by Miss Loring, of Alice's diary. Finds it impressive but is concerned that so much gossip he told Alice in private has been included (later burns his copy). Robert Louis Ste-

venson dies in the South Pacific. *Guy Domville* goes into
rehearsal. *Theatricals: Two Comedies* and *Theatricals: Second
Series* published.

1895   *Guy Domville* opens January 5 at St. James's Theatre. At
play's end James is greeted by a fifteen-minute roar of
boos, catcalls, and applause. Horrified and depressed, abandons the theater. Play earns him $1,300 after five-week run.
Feels he can salvage something useful from playwriting for
his fiction ("a key that, working in the same *general* way
fits the complicated chambers of *both* the dramatic and the
narrative lock"). Writes scenario for *The Spoils of Poynton*.
Visits Lord Wolseley and Lord Houghton in Ireland. In
the summer goes to Torquay in Devonshire and stays until
November while electricity is being installed in De Vere
Gardens flat. Friendship with W. E. Norris, who resides
at Torquay. Writes a one-act play ("Mrs. Gracedew") at
request of Ellen Terry. *Terminations* (containing "The
Death of the Lion," "The Coxon Fund," "The Middle
Years," "The Altar of the Dead") published.

1896–97   Finishes *The Spoils of Poynton* (serialized in *Atlantic
Monthly* April–Oct. 1896 as *The Old Things*; published
1897). *Embarrassments* ("The Figure in the Carpet,"
"Glasses," "The Next Time," "The Way It Came") published. Takes a house on Point Hill, Playden, opposite the
old town of Rye, Sussex, August–September. Ford Madox Hueffer (later Ford Madox Ford) visits him. Converts
play *The Other House* into novel and works on *What
Maisie Knew* (published Sept. 1897). George du Maurier
dies early in October. Because of increasing pain in wrist,
hires stenographer William MacAlpine in February and
then purchases a typewriter; soon begins direct dictation
to MacAlpine at the machine. Invites Joseph Conrad to
lunch at De Vere Gardens and begins their friendship.
Goes to Bournemouth in July. Serves on jury in London
before going to Dunwich, Suffolk, to spend time with
Temple-Emmet cousins. In late September 1897 signs a
twenty-one-year lease for Lamb House in Rye for £70 a
year ($350). Takes on extra work to pay for setting up his
house—the life of William Wetmore Story ($1,250 ad-
vance) and will furnish an "American Letter" for new
magazine *Literature* (precursor of *Times Literary Supple-
ment*) for $200 a month. Howells visits.

1898   "The Turn of the Screw" (serialized in *Collier's* Jan.–April; published with "Covering End" under the title *The Two Magics*) proves his most popular work since "Daisy Miller." Sleeps in Lamb House for first time June 28. Soon after is visited by William's son, Henry James Jr. (Harry), followed by a stream of visitors: future Justice Oliver Wendell Holmes, Mrs. J. T. Fields, Sarah Orne Jewett, the Paul Bourgets, the Edward Warrens, the Daniel Curtises, the Edmund Gosses, and Howard Sturgis. His witty friend Jonathan Sturges, a young, crippled New Yorker, stays for two months during autumn. *In the Cage* published. Meets neighbors Stephen Crane and H. G. Wells.

1899   Finishes *The Awkward Age* and plans trip to the Continent. Fire in Lamb House delays departure. To Paris in March and then visits the Paul Bourgets at Hyères. Stays with the Curtises in their Venice palazzo, where he meets and becomes friends with Jessie Allen. In Rome meets young American-Norwegian sculptor Hendrik C. Andersen; buys one of his busts. Returns to England in July and Andersen comes for three days in August. William, his wife, Alice, and daughter, Peggy, arrive at Lamb House in October. First meeting of brothers in six years. William now has confirmed heart condition. James B. Pinker becomes literary agent and for first time James's professional relations are systematically organized; he reviews copyrights, finds new publishers, and obtains better prices for work ("the germ of a new career"). Purchases Lamb House for $10,000 with an easy mortgage.

1900   Unhappy at whiteness of beard which he has worn since the Civil War, he shaves if off. Alternates between Rye and London. Works on *The Sacred Fount*. Works on and then sets aside *The Sense of the Past* (never finished). Begins *The Ambassadors*. *The Soft Side*, a collection of twelve tales, published. Niece Peggy comes to Lamb House for Christmas.

1901   Obtains permanent room at the Reform Club for London visits and spends eight weeks in town. Sees funeral of Queen Victoria. Decides to employ a woman typist, Mary Weld, to replace the more expensive overqualified shorthand stenographer, MacAlpine. Completes *The Ambassadors* and begins *The Wings of the Dove*. *The Sacred Fount* published. Has meeting with George Gissing. William James, much improved, returns home after two years in Europe. Young Cambridge admirer Percy Lubbock visits. Discharges his alcoholic servants of sixteen years (the Smiths). Mrs. Paddington is new housekeeper.

1902   In London for the winter but gout and stomach disorder force him home earlier. Finishes *The Wings of the Dove* (published in August). William James Jr. (Billy) visits in October and becomes a favorite nephew. Writes "The Beast in the Jungle" and "The Birthplace."

1903   *The Ambassadors, The Better Sort* (a collection of twelve tales), and *William Wetmore Story and His Friends* published. After another spell in town, returns to Lamb House in May and begins work on *The Golden Bowl.* Meets and establishes close friendship with Dudley Jocelyn Persse, a nephew of Lady Gregory. First meeting with Edith Wharton in December.

1904–05 Completes *The Golden Bowl* (published Nov. 1904). Rents Lamb House for six months, and sails in August for America after twenty years absence. Sees new Manhattan skyline from New Jersey on arrival and stays with Colonel George Harvey, president of Harper's, in Jersey shore house with Mark Twain as fellow guest. Goes to William's country house at Chocorua in the White Mountains, New Hampshire. Re-explores Cambridge, Boston, Salem, Newport, and Concord, where he visits brother Bob. In October stays with Edith Wharton in the Berkshires and motors with her through Massachusetts and New York. Later visits New York, Philadelphia (where he delivers lecture "The Lesson of Balzac"), and then Washington, D.C., as a guest in Henry Adams' house. Meets (and is critical of) President Theodore Roosevelt. Returns to Philadelphia to lecture at Bryn Mawr. Travels to Richmond, Charleston, Jacksonville, Palm Beach, and St. Augustine. Then lectures in St. Louis, Chicago, South Bend, Indianapolis, Los Angeles (with a short vacation at Coronado Beach near San Diego), San Francisco, Portland, and Seattle. Returns to explore New York City ("the terrible town"), May–June. Lectures on "The Question of Our Speech" at Bryn Mawr commencement. Elected to newly founded American Academy of Arts and Letters

(William declines). Returns to England in July; lectures had more than covered expenses of his trip. Begins revision of novels for the New York Edition.

1906–08 Writes "The Jolly Corner" and *The American Scene* (published 1907). Writes eighteen prefaces for the New York Edition (twenty-four volumes published 1907–09). Visits Paris and Edith Wharton in spring 1907 and motors with her in Midi. Travels to Italy for the last time, visiting Hendrik Andersen in Rome, and goes on to Florence and Venice. Engages Theodora Bosanquet as his typist in autumn. Again visits Mrs. Wharton in Paris, spring 1908. William comes to England to give a series of lectures at Oxford and receives an honorary Doctor of Science degree. James goes to Edinburgh in March to see a tryout by the Forbes-Robertsons of his play *The High Bid*, a rewrite in three acts of the one-act play originally written for Ellen Terry (revised earlier as the story "Covering End"). Play gets only five special matinees in London. Shocked by slim royalties from sales of the New York Edition.

1909 Growing acquaintance with young writers and artists of Bloomsbury, including Virginia and Vanessa Stephen and others. Meets and befriends young Hugh Walpole in February. Goes to Cambridge in June as guest of admiring dons and undergraduates and meets John Maynard Keynes. Feels unwell and sees doctors about what he believes may be heart trouble. They reassure him. Late in year burns forty years of his letters and papers at Rye. Suffers severe attacks of gout. *Italian Hours* published.

1910 Very ill in January ("food-loathing") and spends much time in bed. Nephew Harry comes to be with him in February. In March is examined by Sir William Osler, who finds nothing physically wrong. James begins to realize that he has had "a sort of nervous breakdown." William, in spite of now severe heart trouble, and his wife, Alice, come to England to give him support. Brothers and Alice go to Bad Nauheim for cure, then travel to Zurich, Lucerne, and Geneva, where they learn Robertson (Bob) James has died in America of heart attack. James's health begins to improve but William is failing. Sails with William and Alice for America in August. William dies at Chocorua soon after arrival, and James remains with the family for the winter. *The Finer Grain* and *The Outcry* published.

1911   Honorary degree from Harvard in spring. Visits with Howells and Grace Norton. Sails for England July 30. On return to Lamb House, decides he will be too lonely there and starts search for a London flat. Theodora Bosanquet obtains two work rooms adjoining her flat in Chelsea and he begins autobiography, *A Small Boy and Others*. Continues to reside at the Reform Club.

1912   Delivers "The Novel in *The Ring and the Book*," on the 100th anniversary of Browning's birth, to the Royal Society of Literature. Honorary Doctor of Letters from Oxford University June 26. Spends summer at Lamb House. Sees much of Edith Wharton ("the Firebird"), who spends summer in England. (She secretly arranges to have Scribner's put $8,000 into James's account.) Takes 21 Carlyle Mansions, in Cheyne Walk, Chelsea, as London quarters. Writes a long admiring letter for William Dean Howells' seventy-fifth birthday. Meets André Gide. Contracts bad case of shingles and is ill four months, much of the time not able to leave bed.

1913   Moves into Cheyne Walk flat. Two hundred and seventy friends and admirers subscribe for seventieth birthday portrait by Sargent and present also a silver-gilt Charles II porringer and dish ("golden bowl"). Sargent turns over his payment to young sculptor Derwent Wood, who does a bust of James. Autobiography *A Small Boy and Others* published. Goes with niece Peggy to Lamb House for the summer.

1914   *Notes of a Son and Brother* published. Works on "The Ivory Tower." Returns to Lamb House in July. Niece Peggy joins him. Horrified by the war ("this crash of our civilisation," "a nightmare from which there is no waking"). In London in September participates in Belgian Relief, visits wounded in St. Bartholomew's and other hospitals; feels less "finished and useless and doddering" and recalls Walt Whitman and his Civil War hospital visits. Accepts chairmanship of American Volunteer Motor Ambulance Corps in France. *Notes on Novelists* (essays on Balzac, Flaubert, Zola) published.

1915–16   Continues work with the wounded and war relief. Has
           occasional lunches with Prime Minister Asquith and fam-
           ily, and meets Winston Churchill and other war leaders.
           Discovers that he is considered an alien and has to report
           to police before going to coastal Rye. Decides to become
           a British national and asks Asquith to be one of his spon-
           sors. Receives Certificate of Naturalization on July 26.
           H. G. Wells satirizes him in *Boon* ("leviathan retrieving
           pebbles") and James, in the correspondence that follows,
           writes: "Art *makes* life, makes interest, makes importance."
           Burns more papers and photographs at Lamb House in
           autumn. Has a stroke December 2 in his flat, followed by
           another two days later. Develops pneumonia and during
           delirium gives his last confused dictation (dealing with the
           Napoleonic legend) to Theodora Bosanquet, who types it
           on the familiar typewriter. Mrs. William James arrives De-
           cember 13 to care for him. On New Year's Day, George V
           confers the Order of Merit. Dies February 28. Funeral ser-
           vices held at the Chelsea Old Church. The body is cre-
           mated and the ashes are buried in Cambridge Cemetery
           family plot.

Note on the Texts

This volume prints the texts of the three novels published in book form by Henry James between 1886 and 1890: *The Princess Casamassima* (1886), *The Reverberator* (1888), and *The Tragic Muse* (1890). Each was first published serially and then appeared in book form almost simultaneously in England and the United States. James later included these novels in the 1907–09 New York Edition of his collected works, extensively revised to reflect his later style.

When Thomas Bailey Aldrich, editor of *The Atlantic Monthly*, asked James if he had a new novel that could be serialized in the magazine beginning in January 1885, James replied on February 13, 1884, that he "had for a year or two, a very good *sujet de roman* of which I should make use," and that he had tentatively decided to call it *The Princess Casamassima*. He added that he would need twelve installments of about 25 pages each, but that the first installment would not be available for publication before the July 1885 issue. Aldrich agreed to this schedule and offered to pay James $15 a page. At this time James still thought that *The Bostonians*, scheduled to begin serialization in *The Century* in February 1885, would need only six installments for completion. By December 30, 1884, after he had finished writing several installments, he realized that *The Bostonians* would be much longer and asked Aldrich for a two-month extension. Problems over the publication of *The Bostonians* caused James further to delay beginning *The Princess Casamassima*. After completing the second installment of *The Princess Casamassima*, he recorded in his notebook on August 10, 1885, that he had "never yet become engaged in a novel in which, after I had begun to write and send off my MS., the details had remained so vague. This is partly—or indeed wholly—owing to the fact that I have been so terribly preoccupied—up to so lately with the unhappy *Bostonians*." *The Princess Casamassima*, which also ran longer in serial form than originally planned, appeared in fourteen installments between September 1885 and October 1886. James completed each installment only a few months before its publication in *The Atlantic Monthly*; the last one was sent early in July 1886.

James made arrangements with Macmillan and Co. to publish the novel in both England and America, receiving £400 (just under $2,000) as an advance against a royalty of 15%. Because James was then living in England, he was unable to read the magazine proofs of the installments, but instead had to wait for their appearance in *The Atlantic Monthly* before revising and correcting them in preparation for book publication.

Collation of the serial text with that of the Macmillan edition reveals many differences between the two. The American periodical had changed James's English spelling to American spelling (for example, "parlour" to "parlor"); the English spelling is restored in the book. *The Atlantic Monthly* editors also inserted commas into James's text, many of which he removed when revising the magazine copy. (The manuscript of *The Princess Casamassima*, missing only the final installment, is one of the few manuscripts of a novel by James known to be extant; it is in the Aldrich papers in the Houghton Library at Harvard University.) He also made numerous stylistic revisions throughout the novel, sometimes simply changing one word or phrase to another, such as "twitching" to "patting" (4.30), "afraid" to "frightened" (6.13), "a good deal of" to "much of" (267.6). Other revisions were more extensive, such as the expansion of "She had told him so, from the earliest age," to "She had, from his earliest age, made him feel that there was a grandeur in his past" (8.22), or the recasting of "backs looked down upon the discerning youth whose trade was the handling of books, challenging him in every direction" to "backs returned his discriminating professorial gaze" (259.35). James did not revise the book again until he prepared it for the 1907–09 New York Edition of his collected works.

The Princess Casamassima was printed for Macmillan and Co. by the respected Edinburgh firm of R. & R. Clark. At this time English publishers often brought out their books in at least two different forms. A three-volume printing, intended for libraries and affluent readers, would appear first, to be followed by a less expensive single-volume version (and sometimes an even cheaper version would be issued later). Usually the three-volume version would be set in type and printed first; then the spaces between the lines of standing type would be reduced and a larger number of copies of a single-volume version printed. This procedure was reversed in the case of *The Princess Casamassima*. In order to obtain copyright protection it appeared necessary to publish the novel in America nearly simultaneously with its publication in England, so the single-volume copies were printed first in a press run of 3,000, most of which were meant for America, and the others, with a title page bearing the date of 1887, for later distribution in England. Spacing was then added between the lines and 750 three-volume copies were printed for sale in England. Pagination and chapter numbers were changed in the three-volume form: there are fewer lines per page and each volume begins with chapter one, page one. In this process a few lines were adjusted to improve the appearance of the page, some errors were corrected, and more new ones were introduced, but the basic setting of both forms is the same. Publication dates do not reflect the order of printings: the English three-volume printing was officially published October 22, 1886; the American single-volume printing was published November 2, 1886; and the single-volume English version (part of the same printing) was published August 1887. The present volume prints the text of the first single-volume printing of *The Princess Casamassima*.

James began writing *The Reverberator* very soon after he had sketched the story in a notebook entry on November 17, 1887. He sold the story two weeks later for serialization in *Macmillan's Magazine* at $12 a page (£2 10s.; the total amounted to almost $1,000). The novel ran in the magazine from February through July 1888. James was in England during this time and probably read proofs of the serial version before publication.

Macmillan contracted to publish the novel in both America and England. (James received £125, a little over $600, as an advance against a royalty of 15% for both *The Reverberator* and *Partial Portraits*, a collection of essays that Macmillan also published at this time.) Richard Clay and Sons, London and Bungay, set and printed the book. Two separate editions were printed, a one-volume edition of 3,000 copies for export to America, and a two-volume edition of 500 copies for the English market. It is likely that the American edition was printed first in order to be shipped in time for copyright registration. Macmillan's official date for publication of the English edition was June 5, 1888; the American edition was copyrighted June 14, 1888.

Collation of the two editions against the serial version shows that James made fewer revisions in preparing *The Reverberator* for book publication than he had made in *The Princess Casamassima* (perhaps because he had read magazine proofs). Occasional verbal revisions were made in both editions, such as the change from "she seemed engaged in vague contemplation" to "she seemed to be doing nothing as hard as she could" (558.3–4), and the alteration of the description of Mr. Flack from "—moderately tall, moderately short, moderately everything, moderately definite" to "—reminding one of certain 'goods' for which there is a steady popular demand" (564.32–33). Most of James's revisions were in punctuation, particularly the removal of commas. Both book editions retain James's English spelling and have fewer commas than the serial version, but the American edition seems to have been revised more carefully. It also contains fewer typographical errors. James did not revise the book again until he prepared it for his 1907–09 New York Edition. This volume prints the text of the first American edition of *The Reverberator*.

James began thinking about *The Tragic Muse* before he started work on *The Reverberator*. As early as June 19, 1884, he recorded in his notebook that Mrs. Humphry Ward had mentioned to him an idea of hers for a story about an actress, which he thought "might be made interesting—as a study of the histrionic character." In a July 23, 1887, letter to his friend Grace Norton, dated before his notebook entry on *The Reverberator*, he wrote: "I am beginning a novel about half as long (thank God!) as the *Princess*—and which will probably appear, at no very great distant day, as a volume, without preliminary publication in a magazine. It will be called (probably) *The Tragic Muse*." How long James worked on *The Tragic Muse* at this time has not been determined. He apparently changed his mind about "preliminary publication" and offered *The Tragic Muse* to Aldrich for *The Atlantic Monthly*, but Aldrich asked if James could provide a longer serial. James accepted the proposal, replying on March 3, 1888, that he would "probably run two stories (i.e. two subjects I have had in my head) together, interweaving their threads. . . . the thing will bear the name I gave you: 'The Tragic Muse.'" He also later agreed to have Houghton, Mifflin and Company publish the book in America on the condition that he would receive his $15-a-page payment immediately on receipt of each installment rather than after its publication in the magazine. The serial was to begin in January 1889 and run through the year. In October 1888, after James had sent in the first installment, Aldrich wrote to suggest further lengthening the novel to fourteen or fifteen installments so that it could be published in book form in spring 1890, a more favorable time than after Christmas 1889. James readily assented. The projected fifteen installments expanded to seventeen, and the serial ran from January 1889 through May 1890, making it the longest novel James had written so far. His earnings from *The Atlantic Monthly* amounted to almost $5,000.

James gave the corrected copy of the novel to Macmillan on March 25, 1890, for possible publication in England, but was dissatisfied with their offer of two-thirds of the profit with no advance. When Macmillan then offered him £70 against profits he again refused, writing that "in spite of what you tell me of the poor success of my recent books, I still do desire to get a larger sum, and have determined to take what steps I can in this direction." He had earlier decided to employ the literary agent A. P. Watt to handle the serial publication of his work in England, and though not much seems to have come of this arrangement, he now placed the novel with him. Watt quickly arranged to lease the novel for five years to Macmillan for £250. *The Tragic Muse* was published in Boston by Houghton, Mifflin on June 7, 1890, in a two-volume edition of 1,000 copies, printed at the Riverside Press, Cambridge, Massachusetts. Macmillan published the novel in a three-volume edition of 500 copies, printed by Richard Clay and Sons, on June 28, 1890. Both publishers brought out later printings, Macmillan bringing out a one-volume version for its domestic market (reducing the spaces between the lines of the three-volume version), but James made no revisions in these later printings.

Because he had not been able to see magazine proofs earlier, James followed his usual practice of revising many passages in the serial version of *The Tragic Muse* for book publication. He changed phrasing and emphasis, cut authorial explanation, and refined colloquial dialogue. For example, in the first sentence of the first chapter, James revised his description of the way the French view the English from "unaddicted to modifying the bareness of juxtaposition by verbal or other concessions" to "unaddicted to enriching any bareness of contact with verbal or other embroidery" (703.6–7). An example of James's elimination of authorial intrusion comes a little later in the chapter. After the sentence "The sister, who was not pretty, was also straight and slender and gray-eyed," the periodical version had read "Therefore it would be difficult to say why, with so much similarity of cause, there was such difference of effect. Perhaps, after all, she may have had her admirers, and the safest form of my assertion would be that she was not so pretty as the other. Her eyes were dull, and for a part of the impression of length that she produced, her face, in which the cheeks were flat, was excessively responsible." Both book versions were changed, but not exactly in the same way. The passage in the Macmillan edition became: "But the grey, in this case, was not so pure, nor were the slenderness and the straightness so maidenly" (705.11–13); in the Houghton, Mifflin version "straightness" and "slenderness" are transposed. As James had corrected two sets of periodical proofs, it is probable that his corrections were not uniform. He also had time to make further revisions in the English proofs after sending the American proofs back to Houghton, Mifflin. Most of the substantive revisions were made in both the American and English editions, but there remain many differences between the two, in addition to those between English and American spelling. (James's own spelling preference at this time is known to have been English.) The punctuation, particularly the use of commas, is heaviest in *The Atlantic Monthly*; many commas are removed from the Houghton, Mifflin edition, and still more from the Macmillan edition. (James's manuscript of *The Princess Casa-*

massima shows that he used commas sparingly, suggesting that the Macmillan edition is closest to James's own style during this period.) James made no further revisions in the text until he prepared it for the 1907–09 New York Edition of his collected works. The text of the three-volume Macmillan edition of *The Tragic Muse* is printed here.

This volume presents the texts of the original editions chosen for inclusion here but does not attempt to reproduce features of their typographic design, such as the display capitalization of chapter openings. The texts are printed without change except for the correction of typographical errors. Spelling, punctuation, and capitalization are often expressive features, and they are not altered, even when inconsistent or irregular. The following is a list of typographical errors corrected, cited by page and line number: 79.4, know?; 82.22, live?; 111.37, Eustace; 164.17, lad; 193.17, given; 197.17, though; 223.10, if he; 248.18, Mr; 252.18, superflous; 261.32, you you; 266.8, superstitious,; 322.40, What; 363.2, Eustace; 384.24, forebore; 387.14, you,; 389.10–11, forebore; 391.7, cataclyism; 413.22, scramble.; 420.33, Those; 425.19, him.; 457.15, altered.; 469.30, quiet.; 471.32, 'The; 490.11, A; 493.17, 'Millicent; 506.10, Mr; 506.11, Mr; 506.26, Mr; 517.18, Mr; 518.23, 'At; 522.4–5, if makes; 531.23, I; 531.27, 'She; 538.4, Surely; 548.17, Mr; 548.18, me——"; 548.21, Mr; 550.34, is.; 557.13, submissive; 605.20, family,; 615.25, door,; 622.33, much"; 637.11, solicitude; 649.4, husband's; 664.14, do"; 666.12, *me*,; 669.5, If; 719.39, ballad; 756.25, that!); 786.30, respectability; 794.38–39, a the actres s; 797.20, by their; 820.29, he; 824.27, which *may*; 848.11, arts not; 855.22, walk; 910.12, It; 910.14, When; 911.10, more.; 928.22, him?; 940.17, for glimpse; 944.30, trade; 955.35, This a; 1011.4, character?; 1022.13, intincts; 1036.30, wonderingly; 1104.29, say'; 1115.2, it?; 1039.23, as as; 1143.16, giving; 1144.35, geor; 1202.28, consequences.; 1222.14, to were; 1233.3, sex.'; 1246.8, interclocurtess.

Notes

In the notes below, the reference numbers denote page and line of the present volume (the line count includes chapter headings). No note is made for material included in a standard desk-reference book. For the prefaces to the New York Edition of these novels, see: Henry James, *Literary Criticism: French Writers, Other European Writers, The Prefaces to the New York Edition* (New York: The Library of America, 1984).

THE PRINCESS CASAMASSIMA

3.36 cheffonier] Chiffonier, a high, narrow chest of drawers, often surmounted by a mirror.

15.16 Newgate] Newgate Prison, which then housed prisoners awaiting trial, stood opposite the Old Bailey Central Criminal Court at the western end of Newgate Street. It was razed in 1907.

29.25 a big . . . towers] Millbank, a model prison erected according to plans drawn by Jeremy Bentham in 1799, and demolished in 1893. The site is now occupied, in part, by the Tate Gallery.

35.12 *Dieu . . . beau!*] God almighty, how handsome he is!

36.16 *Est-il . . . ça?*] Is it possible, my God, that he should be as pretty (or noble) as that?

36.34 *Mon . . . chéri,*] My poor toy, my poor dear.

37.11 *Il ne . . . de moi.*] He doesn't want to draw near, he is ashamed of me.

37.20 *Dieu le pardonne!*] God forgive him!

38.13 *Dieu . . . horreur!*] Good God, how horrible!

65.19 Commune of 1871] In March 1871 a coalition of radical factions came to power in Paris in the aftermath of France's defeat in the Franco-Prussian War. The conservative national government, under Adolphe Thiers (1797–1877), suppressed the commune in May 1871, at the cost of 20,000–25,000 lives, most of whom were summarily executed after the fighting ended.

65.22–23 Republican . . . 1848] The February Revolution of 1848 in France overthrew the monarchy of Louis Philippe, established the Second Republic, and set off revolutions throughout Europe.

66.9 Pickering] One of the fine editions brought out by London publisher William Pickering (1796–1854).

67.10 *ouvrière*] Worker.

68.25–26 *comme . . . anglais*] Proper, in the English style.

71.24 *bien du mal*] Plenty of difficulty.

71.28 *La société . . . cela,*] The company certainly owes him that.

73.25 revendication] Reclamation.

73.28 *avènement*] Advent; accession, as to a throne; the coming of the Messiah.

75.7–8 *accapareurs*] Monopolists.

76.4 *J'ai . . . parisienne*] I have a Parisian hand, i.e., touch.

76.9 *il n'y a que ça*] There is nothing but that; that's the only (worthwhile) thing.

76.34 '89] 1789, the beginning of the French Revolution.

76.36 entrance . . . Versaillais] Troops of the Thiers government, which was based in Versailles, entered Paris on May 21, 1871, and suppressed the Commune. See note to page 65.19.

77.12 *soyez tranquille*] Rest assured.

79.1 *En . . . bêtises!*] Look at the absurdities in that! (*V'là* is a contraction of *voila*.)

81.6 *désagrément*] Discomfort.

81.38 *Ah . . . propre*] Well, there's a dirty trick.

112.8 Soho] For centuries a foreign quarter, Soho included some of the worst slums in the city, but was also the site of popular restaurants and theaters.

114.26 *Revue . . . Mondes*] *The Review of Two Worlds*, a leading French journal of literature, politics, science, and the fine arts, founded in 1829.

115.25 Goddess of Reason] Festival briefly instituted in revolutionary France by Pierre Gaspard Chaumet (1763–94) and Jacques René Hébert (1757–94). The first ceremony was held in Notre Dame on November 10, 1793.

119.25 a youth . . . lost] Cf. James's advice to aspiring novelists in "The Art of Fiction" (1884): "Try to be one of the people on whom nothing is lost!"

127.10 *Pearl of Paraguay*] A number of *Pearl of . . .* dramas were popular in the late 19th century, such as the French opera *La Perle du Brésil* (*The Pearl of Brazil*) that first played in 1851, and was revived in 1858 and again in 1883.

127.13–14 *à . . . revanche*] Provided that I can do as much for you.

128.2   the International] James changed this to "the Subterranean" in the New York Edition (1909).

130.26–27   retort courteous] The mildest of seven possible responses to an insult enumerated by Touchstone in *As You Like It* (V, iv, 70–72), only one of which, the Lie Direct, need lead to an actual duel, though even that could be avoided with an "if."

154.6–7   *à . . . tenir*] What to believe.

154.22   *le premier venu*] The first comer, i.e., just anyone.

155.7–8   Park . . . Street] Streets bounding the fashionable district of Mayfair; Park Lane was distinguished by its opulent residences, and Bond Street by its exclusive, expensive shops.

159.37   Astley's] An amphitheater (founded 1774) on Westminster Bridge Road that featured shows of horsemanship as well as theatricals.

160.11   *fond du sac*] Bottom of the bag.

163.17   flat] Greenhorn; dupe.

163.19–20   those . . . Mall] The many exclusive men's clubs on Pall Mall.

166.34   London season] The social season, beginning in February and continuing through July.

186.19–20   *en tout . . . s'entend*] With honorable intentions, to be sure.

190.33   *Che vuole?*] What do you expect?

193.32   *è vero?*] Isn't that true?

193.34   the Ripetta] A street in Rome branching off the Piazza del Popolo and running close to and parallel with the Tiber River.

201.34–40   British . . . marbles] Titian's painting of Bacchus and Ariadne (1523) was displayed in the National Gallery; the Elgin Marbles, including the Parthenon frieze by Phidias, were exhibited in the British Museum.

213.23–24   *en cachette*] Secretly.

220.12   *attendrissement*] Tenderness; compassion; pity.

221.28–29   spurious . . . Créqui] The memoirs attributed to Renée Caroline de Froullay, Marquise de Créqui (1714–1803), were written by Courchamps.

221.30–31   Madame de Genlis] Stéphanie-Félicité du Crest, countess of Genlis (1746–1830), French novelist.

221.31   Récit d'une Sœur] *The Nun's Story.*

222.17–18   *à fond*] Thoroughly.

226.33   *défis*]   Challenges.

229.12–13   *Enfin . . .ferme!*]   There you are, resolute at last!

229.13   *éprouvé*]   Tested; sorely tried.

238.34   to pull . . . again]   During the Reform Riot of 1866, the railings of Hyde Park were pulled up for a quarter of a mile and 250 policemen were injured battling demonstrators for political reform.

245.19   *Nun*]   Now; well, now.

246.1   *Doch*]   After all; well, still.

247.14   *C'aurait . . . exemple!*]   That would be a fine example!

248.8   *Trop d'arithmétique*]   Too much arithmetic.

254.34   growler]   A closed one-horse cab with seats inside for four, the driver riding outside.

254.35   *me voici*]   Here I am.

261.39   *Vedremo bene.*]   We'll see now.

265.31   contadina]   Peasant.

271.11–12   Lydia Languish]   The heroine in Richard Sheridan's first play, *The Rivals* (1775).

272.23   hammer-cloth]   An ornamental cloth, hung over a coachman's seat.

272.38–273.1   *Voilà . . . Angleterre.*]   That is what I love about England.

285.2   *Où en êtes-vous*]   Where are you in it? i.e., What terms are you on? At what stage are you?

288.39   *Parbleu*]   Egad; a mild oath deriving from *par Dieu* (by God).

292.11   *portée*]   Importance; consequences.

293.39   *sur les dents*]   On the teeth; i.e., all tired out; on edge.

294.4   *recueillement*]   Peaceful contemplation; reflection; meditation.

295.35   *Jugez donc*]   Judge, then; you can tell.

301.15   *en . . . compte*]   Finally.

302.31   *crânerie*]   Daring; swaggering.

304.8   to give . . . change]   From the French idiom *donner le change*, i.e., to put myself on the wrong scent, the wrong track.

307.37–38   *veut en venir*]   Wants to get to; is getting at.

325.31–34   Lisson . . . Bayswater]   Lisson Grove is in Marylebone, the London district to the east of Bayswater.

328.33–34   the Embankment] Victoria Embankment, running east along the north bank of the Thames from Westminster Bridge to Blackfriars Bridge.

330.36   Milbank] Millbank; see note to page 29.25.

334.2–3   thirty-seven pounds] At that time, $179. Today's equivalent would of course be much higher.

336.3   BOULEVARD] Boulevard des Italiens.

336.25–28   Variétés . . . Chaumont] The Variétés, on the Boulevard Montmartre, was devoted to vaudevilles, farces, and operettas. The actress Céline Chaumont began to establish a major reputation there in 1871.

337.1   Comédie Française] The French national theater, on the Rue de Richelieu, dedicated to the repertoire of classic French drama; also called the Théâtre Français.

339.15–16   Little Peddlington] Imaginary village of quackery, egotism, and humbug invented by playwright John Poole (1786?–1872).

339.28   *mouchards*] Police spies; informers.

340.1–2   Batignolles . . . Saint-Antoine] The Batignolles, a quarter north of the Parc Monceaux, was a favorite residential area of artists; the Faubourg Saint-Antoine was an industrial suburb on the right bank of the Seine.

341.32   *escamoter*] Make away with, whisk away. Cf. Virgil's *Aeneid*, Book One, lines 563–67, and Book Ten, lines 109–11; also, Homer's *Iliad*, Book Five.

346.27–28   *hôtel garni*] Furnished lodgings.

347.1   Hampton Court] Hampton Court Palace (original construction begun in 1515 for Cardinal Wolsey) and Garden, along the Thames, southwest of London.

350.14   Madeleine] A church constructed in the form of a Roman temple.

350.16–17   Corps Législatif] The Palais-Bourbon, used by the Chamber of Deputies.

350.23–28   place . . . obelisk] Called the Place de la Concorde since 1795, the largest square in Paris was originally named for Louis XV, during whose reign it was laid out. In 1792, when the square became known as the Place de la Révolution, an equestrian statue of the king (erected 1763) was replaced by a statue of Liberty, and a guillotine, the instrument of more than 3,000 executions by 1795, was set up. The obelisk of Luxor, built under Ramses II of Egypt (reigned 1304–1237 B.C.), was erected in 1836 in place of the earlier monuments, a few yards from where the guillotine stood.

351.28   Aquileia] Ancient town in northeast Italy.

352.35   square of St. Mark's]   The Piazza San Marco, the central square in
Venice.

352.37–38   two . . . piazzetta]   Granite columns, surmounted by a bronze
lion and by a statue of St. Theodore, standing toward the edge of the Piazzetta (little square) where the Piazza San Marco opens on the Grand Canal.

353.34   *le fond . . . pensée*]   The essence (heart, bottom) of my thought.

356.19   Westminster]   The principal metropolitan borough of London
which, though the center of empire (the site of Houses of Parliament and
Westminster Abbey), contained areas notorious for squalid poverty and vice.

362.28–36   magnificent . . . December]   Louis Napoleon overthrew the
Second Republic in December 1851, and was proclaimed Napoleon III after a
plebiscite in December 1852, establishing the Second Empire. Under his direction, Baron Haussmann supervised a massive program of city planning, including the building of the parks and great boulevards of modern Paris. See
also note to page 76.36.

368.19   the great . . . calls it]   *The Inferno*, Canto III; referring to the
resignation from the papacy of Celestine V in 1294.

369.33   St. John's Wood]   A district to the northwest of Regent's Park,
famed, unlike Brompton, as a residential area favored by artists, writers, and
intellectuals.

375.26   *mesquin*]   Shabby; poor.

375.38   Mr. Micawber]   Wilkens Micawber, in Charles Dickens' *David
Copperfield* (1849–50), though improvident lives in expectation of an upturn in
his fortunes.

378.38   *Che forza*]   What strength!

379.5   *hébétement*]   Dull, animal look.

382.1   *du train . . . allait*]   At the rate she was going.

382.5   *codino*]   Reactionary.

383.1–2   *à toutes jambes*]   At full speed.

383.9   Gräfin]   Countess.

385.36   *arrière-pensées*]   Hidden motives; underlying designs.

385.36–37   M. Gambetta]   Léon Gambetta (1838–82), French statesman
and orator who took a moderate line between radical republicans and monar-
chists in the politics of the Third Republic.

397.35   hospital]   Begun in 1664, the palace at Greenwich was a hospital
for disabled seamen from 1765 to 1869 before becoming the home of the
Royal Naval College in 1873.

398.17–18   famous . . . England] The paintings on the walls and ceiling of the Painted Hall in the southwest block are the work of Sir James Thornhill (1676–1734).

432.10   *dépouillée*] Stripped; divested of her possessions.

440.12   *vie de province*] Life in the provinces; country life.

443.11   *Vous . . . vie!*] You restore life to me!

458.4   *il y va*] It's a question.

470.31   *Ci vuol' pazienza!*] It requires patience!

471.17   *Aspetta*] Wait; go slowly.

471.20   *quel giovane*] That youth.

479.7   *sangue di Dio!*] God's blood!

481.9   Serpentine] The artificial lake in Hyde Park, formed by the interconnection of a string of small ponds, that extends into Kensington Gardens.

484.17   Green Park] Adjacent to Buckingham Palace and catercorner from Hyde Park Corner across Piccadilly.

487.4   old red palace] Kensington Palace, on the western border of Kensington Gardens.

500.36   Burlington House] Old Burlington House, off Piccadilly, from 1866 the home of the Royal Academy of Arts; from 1869 on, its galleries were the site of the annual Exhibition of the Royal Academy.

503.19–20   *nous . . . vous*] It was precisely you of whom we were talking.

503.34–35   *au point . . . sommes*] At the point to which we have come; at this stage of the game.

506.9   *grincheux*] Peevish.

506.32   *Il me . . . très-particulières.*] I must have express guarantees.

507.19   *Qu'est-ce . . . chèri?*] What's he saying, the poor dear?

507.22   *vous . . . idées*] You're giving yourself ideas.

508.15   *Calmons-nous . . . expliquons-nous!*] Let's be calm, let's listen, let's explain!

509.9   *je le constate*] I'm sure of it.

509.18   *Il faut . . . Dieu!*] One must be consistent, in God's name!

509.20–21   *je . . . ça!*] I forbid that!

514.10   *Erlauben Sie*] By your leave; allow me.

518.40   *Il . . . galme*] One must be calm.

523.27   *Comme . . . allez!*]   How you do go on about that!

526.5   *suivante*]   Maid, attendant; i.e., companion.

526.10   *E andata . . . signorino*]   She's gone away, my dear young man.

526.19   tirewoman]   A lady's maid.

526.28   *Peccato!*]   A pity; what a shame.

527.4   *povera vecchia*]   Poor old woman.

545.20   the huge . . . palace]   The Houses of Parliament, also known as the New Palace of Westminster, built (1840–60) to replace the original palace buildings, most of which were destroyed by fire in 1834.

549.6   *es kann sein*]   It may be.

551.8   *Schön*]   Fine; all right.

THE REVERBERATOR

557.33   Figaro]   French political and literary daily newspaper, first published in 1826.

559.9   Bon Marché]   The first, and the most important, modern department store in France, established c. 1860.

559.22   Umbria]   Launched in 1884, the *Umbria* was one of the first trans-Atlantic express liners, named, like all the Cunard liners of the day, for one of the provinces of ancient Italy. It weighed 8,120 tons and had a top speed of 19.5 knots.

564.13   Tauchnitzes]   Inexpensive volumes in a series generally titled "Collection of British and American Authors," published in English by Tauchnitz (Leipzig, Germany) beginning in 1841.

568.32   *lingère*]   Laundry.

571.17   *valet de place*]   A manservant who is available for short periods of time, especially to travelers.

573.6   Galignani's]   Giovanni Antonio Galignani (1757–1821) founded an English-language newspaper, lending library, and bookstore in Paris. To register at Galignani's establishment was to list oneself as a resident of Paris, with a hotel address.

580.2–3   Avenue de Villiers]   A major street in the Batignolles, a district of Paris known as the residence of many artists.

582.19–20   terrible year]   1870, when France was defeated in the Franco-Prussian War.

607.29   *galimatias*]   Pompous nonsense; balderdash.

607.33   *Qu'est-ce . . . merveille?*]   What is this marvel?

610.3   *comme . . . fait*] According to good form.

610.13   *qui . . . pays*] Who takes a husband takes a country.

610.16   *nous . . . très-bien*] We are very good.

612.22   Américaine] A light carriage with a hood over one of the two interchangeable seats.

620.3   *trouvaille*] Discovery, lucky find.

620.21   *La famille c'est moi*] I am the family. A play on the statement of Louis XIV: "*L'etat, c'est moi*" (I am the state).

620.33   *roy* and *foy*] Archaic spellings of *roi* (king), and *foi* (faith or creed).

621.2   *payer de mine*] Look nearly as good as they were.

623.16   *Comme vous y allez!*] How you go on.

624.25   *manière d'être*] Way or style of being.

628.35–36   *con rispetto parlando*] With all due respect.

628.39–40   *J'ai . . . cher.*] I've seen better than that, my dear.

629.29   *Croyante*] A believer.

631.23   *Tudieu!*] Egad! (Thou God).

631.32   *Comme ces gens-là*] Like those people.

640.33   *travailleur*] Worker.

642.22   *J'espère bien!*] I should hope so!

643.24   *voyage de noces*] Wedding trip.

645.7   the Invalides] The celebrated Paris landmark, on the south bank of the Seine, built (1671–76) as a home for disabled veterans, was by the late 19th century primarily a military museum. Napoleon I was interred there in 1840.

645.20–21   *Regardez-moi . . . demande!*] Look at that and that . . . I ask you!

645.37–38   *grandesœur*] Big sister.

657.8–9   *C'est . . . choses*] It is nevertheless full of things.

657.16   *anéantie*] Dumbfounded.

660.29   *C'est . . . manque!*] It's an awareness that she lacks.

672.10   *constatée*] Verified; proved undeniably.

672.19   *sous-entendus*] Implications.

672.28   *lui faire dire*] To say to him.

677.21   *de part et d'autre*]   On both sides.

688.16–17   Pickett Building]   One of the first of the big department stores, erected in 1853 by the merchant-tailor C. B. Pickett at 300–408 Washington Street, Boston.

692.6   *on s'y perd*]   One is lost, bewildered.

696.19   *pourtant*]   However.

THE TRAGIC MUSE

703.10–11   Palais de l'Industrie]   An exhibition hall on the Champs Élyseés, created in 1855 for the first Great Exhibition of Paris and demolished in 1897.

703.14   annual . . . Salon]   The official annual exhibit of the Academy of Art.

704.16   *En . . . abrutis!*]   Look at those dullards!

710.33–34   *taper fort*]   Slap the paint on.

718.23   *Jamais . . . vie!*]   Not on your life!

719.2   *c'est . . . tordre*]   It convulses one with laughter.

722.14   the Academy]   The Royal Academy of Arts.

724.22   *état civil*]   Civil status, profession, or calling.

727.15   *Mesdames sont seules?*]   The ladies are alone?

727.17   *Non . . . beaucoup!*]   No; we are a large party.

727.35   *Poulet chasseur*]   Chicken, hunter-style.

731.33–34   Rue de la Paix]   A major street, notable for attractive shops, running south from the Place de l'Opéra.

732.17   Westminster]   Another large hotel, just down the Rue de la Paix from the Hôtel de Hollande.

733.1–2   *se fait forte*]   Feels confident of being able.

737.15–16   *Donnez . . . plaît.*]   Please give me some of them.

739.8   *c'est trop fort!*]   It's too bad!

740.9   Théâtre Français]   See note to 337.1.

742.3   *jeune Anglaise*]   Young Englishwoman.

743.6–7   *dans le monde*]   In society.

744.16   *brocanteur*]   Secondhand dealer.

746.29   *j'ai . . . ça*]   I've been like that.

746.39–40   *Vous . . . forces.*]   You give me the power.

747.32   *raffinés*]   Persons of highly refined taste.

747.34   *Connu*]   That's an old story!

752.30   *flânerie*]   Aimless stroll.

752.40   *voiture de place*]   Hackney coach.

757.13   *en disponibilité*]   Unattached, free, available.

758.16   Eton . . . Harrow]   Two of the oldest and most prestigious public (i.e., not tuition-free) schools in England.

759.5   the Temple]   One of the four Inns of Court (societies for the study of law), located on the south side of Fleet Street.

759.27   "six-bore"]   A heavy hunting rifle used for large game.

763.10–11   *dame de comptoir*]   Barmaid.

767.5–6   Hippodrome]   The Hippodrome de Longchamp, the principal racecourse for flat races near Paris.

768.3   *Merci . . . vin*]   Thanks, no wine.

768.11   *A . . . l'heure!*]   Later!

769.34   "*Il . . . Rien*"]   *One Never Can Tell*, a comedy (1836) by Alfred de Musset (1810–57).

769.35   "Mademoiselle de la Seiglière"]   A dramatic adaptation (1851) of the 1848 novel of the same title by Jules Sandeau (1811–83).

770.31   *caissière*]   Cashier.

771.7   the Bois]   The Bois de Boulogne, a large, wooded park in Paris.

771.26   *je . . . cela*]   I owe myself that.

779.7   the great *comédienne*]   Mlle. Rachel.

781.14   *la voix de Célimène!*]   The voice of Célimène. Célimène was a young coquette in Molière's *Le Misanthrope* (1666).

781.24–25   *Mais . . . plaisanaterie*]   But them (those ones), it's a joke.

781.36   *il . . . bien*]   That's all that counts. The head is good.

784.21   *Je . . .nôtre*]   I know only one theater—ours.

784.28   *en attendant*]   In the meantime.

785.9   *qu'est . . . ça?*]   What is that?

786.3   *Je . . . ça*]   I played only that.

786.5   'L'Aventurière,']   A play (1848) by Émile Augier (1820–89).

787.29–30   *Vous . . . aujourd'hui.*]   You do not shrink away from me to-day, my child.

787.37–38   *Elle . . . ça!*]   She is very beautiful—ah, just so!

788.36   *d'une . . . rougir*]   Of a simplicity to make one blush.

791.38   *bête*]   Blockhead, fool.

793.6   *sont . . . dégager*]   Are yet to come.

793.31   *Mon . . . dirai-je?*]   My God, what shall I tell you?

793.36   Il . . . ça.]   That's the only thing; that's all there is to it.

796.2   *Ah, la jeunesse!*]   Ah, youth!

798.16–17   *maison meublée*]   Furnished house.

800.33   *passer . . . famille*]   Go through the whole family.

805.17   Old . . . Sea]   In the *Arabian Nights Entertainments* tale "Sindbad the Sailor," the Old Man clings to Sindbad's back for days and cannot be dislodged.

811.19   *quartiers excentriques*]   Outlying districts.

813.12   *Je crois bien!*]   I know that well!

815.12   *quartiers sérieux*]   Serious neighborhoods.

820.12   *C'est . . . attends!*]   I've got you there!

821.20   Conciergerie]   A prison occupying the lower part of the Palais de Justice adjoining the Seine; political prisoners of the French Revolution, including Marie Antoinette, were confined here.

821.20   holy . . . Louis]   St. Louis-en-l'Ile.

833.29   *Ecoutez maintenant!*]   Listen now!

839.34   *comme il faut*]   Proper.

840.28   *sirop d'orgeat*]   Sweetened orange and almond drink.

843.21   *je me fiche*]   I don't give a darn.

845.22–23   thirty pounds] $145 in 1886.

846.6   *tu quoque*]   You, too; so are you.

849.6   *baignoire*]   Ground-floor box.

850.19   *cela s'était vu*]   That happened.

855.17   bouquetières]   Flower-girls, i.e., flower merchants.

856.33–34   *approfondir*]   Go deeper or delve into.

857.3–4   *à . . . guerre!*]   In war as in war, i.e., one must take things as they come.

857.9   *cabotine*]   Second-rate actress.

860.38   *banlieue*]   Suburbs.

861.1   Rambouillet]   A small town 28 miles southwest of Paris; the château there was constructed between the 14th and 18th centuries.

862.18   *Vous . . . laisser*]   You certainly ought to leave her to us.

862.24   *Mauvais sujet!*]   A bad lot!

863.25–27   A generous . . . Aix]   Cf. Robert Browning, "How They Brought the Good News from Ghent to Aix" in *Dramatic Romances* (1848).

866.26–27   Iago . . . word!*]   *Othello*, V, ii, 304.

879.18   *répandue*]   Around and about.

918.37   *coquine*]   Hussy, jade.

931.21   *locataire*]   Tenant.

936.11   *une sotte*]   A fool; an ass.

936.12–13   *de . . . vous*]   More closely than you.

936.21   *On . . . fort*]   They say that it's very powerful.

936.30   Camille]   A character in Pierre Corneille's tragedy *Horace* (1640); making her debut in this role, Mlle. Rachel took Paris by storm.

936.31   *de . . . choses*]   One of the most beautiful things.

937.3   *Vous êtes insupportables*]   You are insufferable.

937.4   Phèdre]   In Jean Racine's *Phèdre* (1677).

938.18   *de là-bas*]   Over there.

938.27   *vous-en-êtes là?*]   Are you into that?

939.37   *chez nous*]   At home.

940.13–14   *des . . . voix*]   Some majestic vocal effects.

941.19   *Tiens!*]   Really! You don't say so!

941.21   *C'est . . . sage.*]   It's by far the most sensible thing.

942.7   *baignoires d'avant-scène*]   Ground-floor boxes in front of the stage.

943.13   *desmoiselle de magasin*]   Shopgirl.

946.17   Hermione]   In Racine's *Andromaque* (1667).

946.27   maison de Molière]   The house of Molière, i.e., the Comédie Française.

947.21–22   *nous . . . ça!*]   We are better than that!

947.28   *toute honteuse*]   Thoroughly ashamed.

947.30   *Vous . . . légère!*]   You are going to find me very light!

953.26   *Je . . . observée*]   I observed you well.

954.6   *Vous . . . montée*]   You know, it's a climb.

954.8   *Comment donc?*]   How then? What of it?

955.1   *Voilà, c'est tout!*]   There, that's all; that's it!

955.18–19   *à la porte*]   At the door, i.e., throw him out.

957.21   *à ses heures*]   When she feels like it.

957.25   *nous . . . genres*]   We jumble up social types.

958.4   femmes . . . faut]   Proper ladies.

959.10–11   Great Stanhope Street]   A fashionable Mayfair address just off Hyde Park.

965.24–25   *'Guenille . . . chère.'*]   "Rags and tatters, maybe: but I am fond of my rags and tatters." From Moliére's *Les Femmes Savantes* (*The Learned Ladies*), II, vii.

973.18   *C'est . . . exquis.*]   It's exquisite, downright exquisite.

975.26   *remplissage*]   Padding.

979.38   *Elle . . . tort.*]   She's very wrong.

981.8   *D'où tombez-vous?*]   Where have you fallen from?

984.11   *optique de la scène*]   Stage illusion.

985.8   *bien de choses*]   Plenty of things.

988.29–30   *veut . . . dire*]   Would have it.

991.12   *Sic . . . vobis*]   Virgil, "Thus do ye, but not for yourselves." This incomplete line was originally written as a challenge to the poet Bathyllus, who had claimed to be the author of a couplet written by Virgil.

994.31   *Ah . . . tapé!*]   Good, it's painted in a free, bold style!

1000.28–29   Serpentine]   See note to 481.9.

1016.39   St. John's Wood]   See note to 369.33.

1023.28   *à demi-mot*]   At a hint.

1042.17   dose . . . Hall]   In Dickens' *Nicholas Nickleby* (1838–39), the brutalized pupils at Dotheboys Hall are forced to take a nightly dose of brimstone and treacle.

1046.7–9   "Wilhelm . . . Philina]   Philine is a mediocre but spirited actress and Mignon an ethereal girl garbed as a boy in Goethe's *Wilhelm Meister's Apprenticeship* (1795–96).

1052.15–16   Cromwell Road]   A street of spacious residences in fashionable South Kensington.

1059.3   Sir Matthew Hope]   This fictitious London physician also appears in James's *The Portrait of a Lady* (1881).

1075.14   sixty thousand]   Just under $300,000, a fortune in the late 19th century.

1089.21   P. R. A.]   President of the Royal Academy (of Arts).

1100.22–23   *d'un mauvais*]   Bad.

1102.6   *Punch*]   Or *The London Charivari*, a satirical magazine founded in 1841.

1102.17   South Audley Street]   Running south from Grosvenor Square to Curzon Street in the fashionable Mayfair district.

1104.12   *sur les dents*]   All tired out.

1104.33   the Strand]   This major street was the site of many West End theaters.

1107.23   *crânerie*]   Daring.

1131.10   *devinez . . . quoi!*]   Divine a little!

1131.24–25   *Où le fourrez-vous?*]   Where do you put that?

1133.5   *comme tout le monde*]   Like all the world; like everybody.

1138.31   *tout au plus*]   At the most.

1142.22   *Que voulez-vous*]   What do you want?

1143.28–29   *C'est . . . guerre*]   "It's magnificent, but it is not war." This battlefield comment on the charge of the Light Brigade at Balaclava (October 25, 1854) was made by French General Pierre Bosquet.

1144.36   *en ville*]   Out on the town.

1153.21   *Anch' io son pittore!*]   "I, too, am a painter." Antonio Corregio (1494–1534) on seeing Raphael's *Saint Cecelia* at Bologna, c. 1525.

1156.10–11   *Si . . . repose!*]   If you knew how that refreshes me!

1163.33–34   *comme de raison*]   With reason.

1167.2   *simagrées*]   Affectations.

1167.37   *parlez-moi de ça*]   Speak to me of that.

1169.33   *Il . . . ces-jours-ci*]   He is quite detached these days.

1170.13   *je . . . plus*]   I don't get it.

1170.30   *riguardi*]   Considerations.

1172.16   *je veux bien*]   I'm willing; okay.

1173.38   *Tiens . . . fille*]   Hold fast, my girl.

1174.36   *cela . . . jours*]   That is seen all the time.

1188.24   *Je . . . bien!*]   I see that perfectly, by heaven!

1191.17   *c'est bientôt dit*]   That's sooner said (than done).

1193.13–14   *tout bonnement*]   Quite frankly.

1197.26   *Je vous attendais*]   I'm waiting for you.

1203.2   *bibite*]   Beverage.

1209.24   Goodwood]   Fashionable races held at the racecourse at Good-wood Park, near Chichester, throughout the week of the last Tuesday in July.

1216.35   *tout pur*]   Unadulterated.

1224.18   *à la charge*]   Into caricature.

1225.13   *Il . . . ça*]   It works that way.

1225.29   *n'en parlons plus*]   Let's speak no more of him.

1227.5   *faites . . . ça*]   Make allowance for that.

1230.37   *Vous . . . lâcher*]   You're going to drop me.

1231.39   *vous . . . ça*]   You'll see.

1239.7   Rue Bonaparte]   Location of the École des Beaux-Arts (founded 1648), a national institution providing art instruction, and also known for its extensive and valuable collection of copies of sculptures and paintings.

1239.38   Red Book]   *Burke's Peerage.*

1247.7–8   *Cela . . . bien*]   That is promising.

CATALOGING INFORMATION

James, Henry, 1843–1916.
    Novels 1886–1890.
    Edited by Daniel Mark Fogel.

    (The Library of America ; 43)
    Contents: The Princess Casamassima—The Reverberator—The
tragic muse.
    I. Title: The Princess Casamassima. II. Title: The Reverberator.
III. Title: The tragic muse. IV. Series.
PS2112   1989   813'.4   88–82724
ISBN 0–940450–56–9

For a list of titles in the Library of America, write:
The Library of America
14 East 60th Street
New York, New York 10022

*This book is set in 10 point Linotron Galliard,
a face designed for photocomposition by Matthew Carter
and based on the sixteenth-century face Granjon. The paper
is acid-free Ecusta Nyalite and meets the requirements for permanence of the American National Standards Institute. The binding
material is Brillianta, a 100% woven rayon cloth made by
Van Heek-Scholco Textielfabrieken, Holland. The composition is by Haddon Craftsmen, Inc., and The
Clarinda Company. Printing and binding
by R. R. Donnelley & Sons Company.
Designed by Bruce Campbell.*

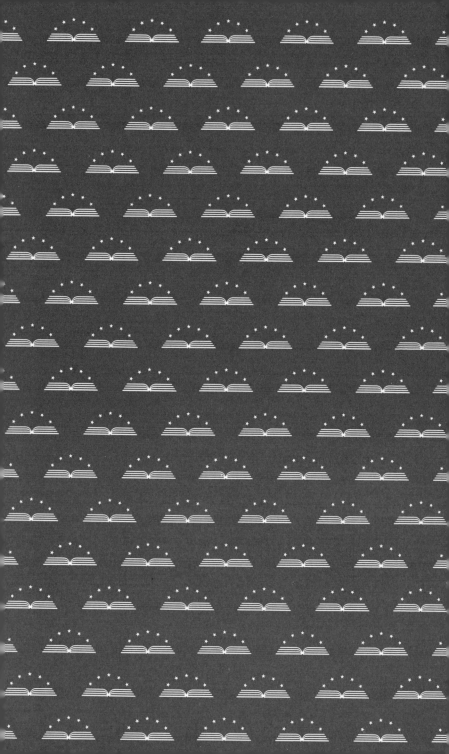